THE ADVENTURES OF AMIR HAMZA

Ghalib Lakhnavi
The
Amir

APR 30 2010

"This _____ lassic
of ep_____ in-
vent_____ For
the _____ za has impor-
tance
—*The New York Times Book Review*

"A true marvel of literary and intellectual engineering, *The Adventures of Amir Hamza* marks the passage of oral narrative into print and synthesizes translation, varying editions and genres into one coherent work."
—*The Washington Post Book World*

"Non-Urdu-speaking readers can at last appreciate an epic 'on par with anything in the Western canon.' And, with luck, the classical pantheon populated by indomitable Achilles, cunning Odysseus and righteous King Arthur will now be joined by a new beloved hero: mercurial, mighty Amir Hamza, astride his winged demon steed, soaring to the heavens."
—*Time International*

"I was also bowled over by a remarkable new translation of *The Adventures of Amir Hamza*, the *Iliad* and *Odyssey* of the medieval Persian world: a rollicking, magic-filled heroic saga, full of myth and imagination. It is the first time it has been translated into English and it is as close as is now possible to the world of the Mughal campfire—those night gatherings of soldiers, Sufis, musicians and camp followers one sees in Mughal miniatures—a storyteller beginning his tale in the clearing of a forest as the embers of the blaze glow red and eager, firelit faces crowd around."
—*New Statesman*, "Books of the Year 2007"

"How wonderful that English-speaking readers now have access to one of the great classical narratives of popular Persian and Islamic culture. The universal appeal of *The Adventures of Amir Hamza* lies in its colorful, playful, and simply beautiful rendition of a world that is both fabulous and greatly entertaining."
—AZAR NAFISI, author of *Reading Lolita in Tehran*

"Extraordinary. Farooqi has translated into English what most of us thought was untranslatable. The adventures of Hamza have beguiled readers in many languages for centuries. This translation from Urdu should interest all students of Eastern literatures."
—C. M. NAIM, professor emeritus of
Urdu Studies, University of Chicago

"Possibly one of the most important fantasy events of the year . . . Farooqi's energetic and stylish translation . . . captures brilliantly the insouciant delights of the storyteller's voice, and gives us a highly readable version of a major work of world literature that few of us even knew about. The Modern Library has done us a big favor."   —*Locus*

"What a find it is! Farooqi's translation is both elegant and earthy. . . . One is tempted to think that only a malevolent enchantress of great power could have kept *The Adventures of Amir Hamza* from a mainstream American audience for so long."
—*The Magazine of Fantasy and Science Fiction*

"The translation by Musharraf Ali Farooqi is a bravura performance. . . . Nothing that readers in India, or elsewhere, have read would have prepared them for its lightness, deftness and frothiness."
—*Hindustan Times*

"Stupendous . . . a major achievement . . . Farooqi has opened a window to a very different world."   —Calcutta *Telegraph*

THE ADVENTURES OF
AMIR HAMZA

GHALIB LAKHNAVI AND
ABDULLAH BILGRAMI

THE ADVENTURES OF
AMIR HAMZA

LORD OF THE AUSPICIOUS
PLANETARY CONJUNCTION

Translated, with an Introduction and Notes, by
Musharraf Ali Farooqi

THE MODERN LIBRARY
NEW YORK

2008 Modern Library Paperback Edition

Translation copyright © 2007 by Musharraf Ali Farooqi

Published in the United States by Modern Library,
an imprint of The Random House Publishing Group,
a division of Random House, Inc., New York.

MODERN LIBRARY and the TORCHBEARER Design are
registered trademarks of Random House, Inc.

Originally published in hardcover in the
United States by Modern Library, an imprint of The Random
House Publishing Group, a division of Random House, Inc., in 2007.

ISBN 978-0-8129-7743-1

Printed in the United States of America

www.modernlibrary.com

2 4 6 8 9 7 5 3 1

FOR AZHAR ABIDI
SORCERER OF THE ANTIPODES

CONTENTS

INTRODUCTION

Musharraf Ali Farooqi

I grew up in Hyderabad, Pakistan, whose climate during summertime closely resembles that of Hell. Temperatures can reach 50°C (approximately 120°F), and in the absence of air-conditioning, a three-hour nap is considered the best answer to nature's excesses.

My younger brother Arif and I came up with another, more entertaining alternative. We would improvise a spear by affixing a butter knife to the tip of a bamboo pole and go into the courtyard to hunt the lizards and chameleons that lived in the crevices of the brick walls and the wind catchers on the roof of our house. The authorities never learned of the carnage, because we always eliminated all signs of it. The corpses were fed to Mano—a fellow hunter and a fine specimen of a marmalade cat. That was how we passed our afternoons before we discovered books.

Everyone from my generation is familiar with the children's titles published by the house of Ferozsons. A few of these were translations of English-language classics, but the rest were written in Urdu. My older sisters had accumulated about a hundred of these titles, and in a city lacking in public libraries, this was a considerable treasure. After inheriting the collection from our sisters, Arif and I developed an unhealthy appetite for these stories. The schoolwork suffered, and I was often caught under the covers with bound paper and a pencil light. All this was probably enough to send my parents into a panic, and they decided to remove the temptation from the path. The storybooks were put in an iron chest, which was locked up and placed in the storage room. We tried but were unable to find the key during our periodic searches.

While sadly lacking in lock-picking skills at the time, we had not entirely wasted our time at school. Here was an opportunity to put our book learning to use. It was the principle of the lever that we applied—inserting a heavy shish-kebab skewer between the lid and the top of the trunk and giving it a little lift. The physics were flawless. The lid rose, then twisted, becoming almost dog-eared. Sliding our hands in and grabbing a book each was what we did next, before covering the lid with an old quilt and stealing away.

Our parents never suspected we had burglarized the iron chest. It was a little unimaginable for two quiet boys living a protected life to have committed such a heinous deed (may that be a lesson for parents not to put a limit to their imaginations). In that trunk, among other books, was the juvenile edition of the *Dastan-e Amir Hamza*, in a set of some eight or ten books. That was my first introduction to the *devs*, jinns, *peris*, cowfooted creatures, horse-headed beasts, and elephant-eared folks.

I remember that after spending an hour or two reading these stories my brother and I would undergo a transformation. One of us would become Amir Hamza, the other the king of India, Landhoor bin Saadan, or some other such mighty champion. We would head for the courtyard. Our arms and armor were ready and we would gird ourselves: swords improvised of hockey sticks, spears made of bamboo, body armor fashioned of sofa cushions. Mattresses would be spread on the courtyard floor to break the fall, and hostilities were declared. Once we tired of fighting with weapons, it would be time to wrestle. When that too was insufficient to dissipate the adrenaline rush, our focus would turn to the lizards. While our parents slept, Amir Hamza and Landhoor would indulge in the pleasures of the chase. Death to the infidel lizards and the faithless chameleons!

Meanwhile, at school I was having an existential crisis—or perhaps it was one of the spiritual kind. Often during the classes I would have an unworldly awakening. I would look around and find myself surrounded by uniformed creatures sitting in rows while an older person chalked something on a blackboard. I would try but could never figure out how I had ended up with them. I would have preferred to be a *dev*, running around swinging a tree trunk and clobbering humans with it. Or a jinn, throwing humans from the heavens into the mountains and seas. Thus, at a young age I had my first experience of alienation. I returned home worn, exhausted, and a little stupider, and sneaked away to the storage room where my real and true friends awaited me—the *devs*, jinns, and so forth. I felt one with them. In their company I never had any of my spiritual or existential dilemmas. I was back under the covers with bound paper and a pencil light. This time I took care not to be caught. And so the years passed.

Let me now fast-forward six years, to a time when I was having another crisis. I had ruined my eyes from reading with the pencil light and disqualified myself from my natural calling as a soldier. Then I had moved to Karachi and ended up in the electrical engineering program, where both the induction motor and the synchronous motor refused to reveal their secrets to me. I decided not to force the issue. But my parents were not prepared to hear of my dropping out. So I carried on, going in the morning to the university, where some considerate person had provided very comfortable sofas in the dining lounge. While the future builders of the country made their parents proud and strove mightily against the curriculum in rooms adjacent, a lonely truant grappled with his very own curriculum of assorted fiction scrounged from secondhand bookshops.

Most of the books I read at that time were in English, many of them classics. A story is a story, and I was too busy enjoying the books to pause and wonder where all the classics of the Urdu language were hiding. One did not see them in the bookstores.

After dropping out from engineering studies in the late 1980s, I spent a few years experimenting with learning languages, working as a journalist, and making films—and failing at all of them. During this time, I also made new friends who introduced me to good contemporary Urdu fiction. However, the fiction writers were unable to keep pace with my reading consumption and I soon ran out of Urdu books. In their absence I read in English, and later, when I tried to write fiction myself, I found it easier to structure sentences in English than in Urdu. Still, for a very long time, I needed to read something in Urdu before I could go to sleep.

Then I got married, and in 1994 I moved to Toronto. One day at the University of Toronto library I came across *Urdu Ki Nasri Dastanen.* It was a record of Urdu's classical literature compiled by Gyan Chand Jain. It contained information about a large number of classics written in the Urdu language in the nineteenth century and earlier. Most of this literature had originated in the oral narrative genres of *dastan* and *qissa.* They were packed with occult, magic, and sorcery. I realized that if I could find them, I would have more than a lifetime's supply of reading.

I also discovered the *Dastan-e Amir Hamza* a second time. I learned of one version of the *Dastan-e Amir Hamza* (1883–1917) that existed in forty-six volumes, each of them approximately a thousand pages long. It can no longer be found and exists only in one or two special collections in the form of microfilm. Another version of the *Dastan-e Amir Hamza* (1801) was compiled by Khalil Ali Khan Ashk. It was one of the many texts written at the Fort William College in Calcutta to teach Urdu to the officers of the British colonial administration. I obtained an undated reprint of this book but found Ashk's language rather insipid. It also lacked a large portion of Amir Hamza's adventures in Qaf. This Ashk fellow was probably some freedom fighter who had infiltrated the Fort William College to sabotage the education of the colonial officers. He must have feared that if the Brits began enjoying these stories too much they might become very difficult to get rid of. I could appreciate his motives, but I did not appreciate the fact that in the process he had also killed many of my friends. That was just not right. Finally, I discovered the most popular one-volume version of the *Dastan-e Amir Hamza*, first published by Ghalib Lakhnavi in 1855 and amended by Abdullah Bilgrami in 1871. Neither one of them were "authors" in the sense we understand today. They were compilers of this oral *dastan*, and in the process they rewrote and expanded the story.

When I started reading about the *Dastan-e Amir Hamza* in greater detail, I also discovered a family connection to its social history. My great-grand-uncle Ashraf Ali Thanvi (1864–1943) was a religious scholar and one of the spiritual leaders of the Indian Muslims. He found the story's ribald passages unsuitable for the sensibilities of proper women and in his book *Bahishti Zevar*, which is an introduction to social norms for women, he declared that they should avoid reading it. Now that I have read these passages, I have the same advice for proper women. Taking modern-day sensibilities into account, I would just add that men, too, must not sit down with this book without a bottle of smelling salts close at hand.

Through the writings of *dastan* scholar Shamsur Rahman Faruqi, I began to understand the significance of this legend, its complex theme of predestination and its thousand-year history in the South Asian subcontinent. At first, while reading the Lakhnavi-Bilgrami *Dastan-e Amir Hamza*, I had difficulty understanding the ornate passages. I had to look into classical dictionaries to understand what was being said. Three generations ago, those considered truly literate in our culture could read and write with equal facility in Arabic, Persian, and Urdu. My father's generation had lost Arabic and the ability to write in Persian. In my generation, reading classical Urdu had become an issue, too. With our literary heritage becoming inaccessible to us at this rate, it seemed reasonable to assume that—let alone being able to share it with other cultures—we would soon find ourselves alien to it.

This was a complex and weighty problem that lay far beyond my capacities to resolve. I worried about my friends—the *devs*, the cow-footed creatures, the horse-headed beasts, the elephant-eared folks. If the world ever forgot their existence I knew I would not be able to bear the tragedy.

I checked to see if the *Dastan-e Amir Hamza* had ever been translated into English or one of the European languages. I found out that in 1892, Sheik Sajjad Hosain published an abridgement of Book One titled *The Amir Hamza: An Oriental Novel*. By his own admission he tried to make a novel of it, but the results were disappointing, the experiment was left unfinished, and he was not heard from again. In 1895 Ph. S. Van Ronkel published his Dutch study of Amir Hamza's legend, titled *De Roman van Amir Hamza*. Then, in 1991, Frances Pritchett published *The Romance Tradition in Urdu: Adventures from the Dastan of Amir Hamzah*, which contained excerpts translated from a 1969 edition. That was it. The complete *Dastan-e Amir Hamza* had never been translated into English or any other Western language.

Someone simply had to be found who had enough time on his hands to translate a thousand-page book. Ideally, this person should not be bright enough to anticipate the distinct likelihood that the book might never be published. As the whole thing was to be done without any grant money, it also had to be someone whose spouse had a reliable job. Since everyone I knew seemed to have a purpose in life, and their spouses would not hear of any such nonsense, the search soon drew to a close. And the matter would have rested there but for a most eventful dream, which should be recounted here in its entirety due to its historic significance.

It was a wintry night. I was fast asleep when suddenly I heard galloping noises and woke up. A horse-headed creature appeared from the darkness. Behind him walked an elephant-eared lady carrying a candle. The horse-headed gent greeted me with a sly smile, congratulated me, and said that I had been chosen to do the translation. Then the elephant-eared lady came forward and said that everyone was counting on me. Before I could say anything or ask any questions, they plunged back into darkness. I heard sniggering, galloping sounds, and then all was quiet.

It is not every day that one receives such distinguished visitors in dreams and is declared their chosen one. Naturally, I could not forget the dream. And didn't the lady tell me that *everyone* was counting on me? I could not ignore that, for sure. I finally told my wife what the horse-headed gent and the elephant-eared lady expected of her, and threw myself wholeheartedly into the task.

I had thought that with such auspicious beginnings the translation itself would be a breeze. But I ran into major problems with the very first passage. It took me several hours and left me somewhat disillusioned and embittered. I persevered and tried not to think too much about the meaning of my dream visitor's sly smile. After Book One the language becomes simpler, the ornate passages shorter, and the poetry less frequent. I also had more practice. A few years earlier, I had translated the Urdu poetry and fables of Afzal Ahmed Syed. This exposure to translating one of our contemporary masters helped me. But I think the real breakthrough came when I learned to keep three fat dictionaries open in my lap at the same time.

Because I visited the text over and over again, the structure of the tale began to reveal itself. I was happy that I was beginning to see structure in fiction, but I could not say the same about my life. I was piling up rejection slips for my own writings. Naturally, I felt jealous of Ghalib Lakhnavi and Abdullah Bilgrami, who had found publishers in their time and were important enough to be translated. The evil thought often crossed my mind to stop the translation. That would teach Messrs. Lakhnavi and Bilgrami a nice lesson! But my friends began calling to inquire when the book would be ready. For the last few years I had constantly bragged to them about it, and they had remembered. Now I had to finish it just to save face. Later, when the Modern Library decided to publish it, it became a contractual obligation as well. In short, as always I was caught in a web of my own follies, and the only way out was to finish the thing.

Now that the translation is done, after seven years of intermittent work, I hope that *everyone* is satisfied. If they feel a need to express their gratitude I would very much prefer it if they did not appear in my dreams and communicated instead by e-mail.

I also have a message for all young boys and girls. They should take warning from my example and get themselves a good education. I now realize its virtues. If I had had one, the horse-headed fellow and the elephant-eared lady could not possibly have made such a capital fool out of me.

—Toronto, July 3, 2007

A Note on the Text

In 1855, the obscure press Matba-e Hakim Sahib in the Indian city of Calcutta published a book titled *Tarjuma-e Dastan-e Sahibqiran Giti-sitan Aal-e Paighambar-e Aakhiruz Zaman Amir Hamza bin Abdul-Muttalib bin Hashim bin Abdul Munaf* (A Translation of the Adventures of the Lord of the Auspicious Planetary Conjunction, the World Conqueror, Uncle of the Last Prophet of the Times, Amir Hamza Son of Abdul Muttalib Son of Hashim Son of Abdul Munaf).[1] Its writer, Navab Mirza Aman Ali Khan Bahadur Ghalib Lakhnavi, identified himself as the son-in-law of Prince Fatah Haider, the oldest son of Sultan Tipu of Mysore. According to one account, the writer was a new convert to Islam and a public official.[2]

This book by Navab Mirza Aman Ali Khan Bahadur Ghalib Lakhnavi (Ghalib Lakhnavi, for short) was one of the earlier versions of the *Dastan-e Amir Hamza* (Adventures of Amir Hamza) printed in India in the Urdu language. It already existed in multiple handwritten manuscripts and was a long-established legend in the South Asian oral narrative tradition of *dastan-goi* (*dastan* narration). It was a narrative of composite authorship, and different versions of the same event existed in different narrative traditions.

Ghalib Lakhnavi's use of the term "translation" is confusing. Unless it was a translation from a Persian-language version of the *Dastan-e Amir Hamza* originally composed in South Asia, it is difficult to explain the overwhelming number of references particular to the social life and culture of South Asia found in the book. Certain passages which are in regional Indian dialect could not possibly have originated in any foreign language. It is more probable that Ghalib Lakhnavi compiled the text from various versions and attributed it to an older source to give his story an ancient pedigree, a practice common among *dastan* writers.

Ghalib Lakhnavi's text became the basis of a very popular edition that remained in print until recently, although these later editions were drastically abridged. In November 1871, sixteen years after Ghalib Lakhnavi published the book, the Naval Kishore Press in Lucknow brought out its own version of the *Dastan-e Amir Hamza*.[3] The book was identified as an amended version of a tale previously published in Calcutta, Bombay, Delhi, and Lucknow.[4] However, the author of the text of the Naval Kishore Press version was not acknowledged, only the man who amended it: Abdullah Bilgrami, an instructor of the Arabic language in Kanpur. We now know that it was, in fact, Ghalib Lakhnavi's text, modified by Abdullah Bilgrami by adding ornate passages and poetry to it. This translation is made from Abdullah Bilgrami's 1871 edition of the *Dastan-e Amir Hamza*.

The oral narrative tradition of the *Dastan-e Amir Hamza* heavily influenced its written version. The text of the *Dastan-e Amir Hamza* was used both for reading and as a guide for the narrator of the *dastan*. In a few places, instructions appear to guide the person narrating the story. A *dastan* narrator knew more than one version of a particular episode of the *dastan* and used the one most suited for the audience being addressed. In addition, a *dastan* was never narrated in its entirety during a session. Only certain episodes from it were narrated. Therefore, considerations of continuity and structural integrity were not important. The histories of multiple versions of the same event and the loosely woven oral tradition sometimes intervene in the text. In some places parallel traditions and discrepancies have crept in (see notes 18, 32, 49, and 62 to Book Two, notes 11, 12, 16, 17, and 20 to Book Three, and notes 36, 37, and 46 to Book Four).

I have not tried to straighten out these inconsistencies, not only because to do so would compromise the story, but also because they allow for a comparison of different traditions and texts, which can be very helpful in the study of the *dastan* genre. These inconsistencies reveal that this text was compiled using at least three variant traditions (see note 49 to Book Two, note 12 to Book Three, and note 46 to Book Four).

Consistent with the classical *dastan* literature, the Urdu text of the *Dastan-e Amir Hamza* is unpunctuated and has no text breaks except where a new chapter is marked. While this offers a translator great flexibility in structuring a sentence, it is a challenge to identify and isolate individual phrases and sentences in a continuous text before translating them. In some instances, the print was not legible and an approximation was made in choosing the missing text. Such instances have been marked with a question mark following in brackets.

The title *amir* (meaning "commander" or "leader") has become an inseparable part of the hero's name and has been used as such throughout the text. The title *khusrau* (meaning "king") has likewise become part of Landhoor's name and is similarly used.

The characters and the numerous legendary kings, warriors, sorcerers, historical figures, deities, and mythical beings mentioned in the story are grouped together in the List of Characters, Historic Figures, Deities, and Mythical Beings.

NOTES

1. The Library of Congress has a microfiche of this title (Control Number: 85908676; Call Number: Microfiche 85/61479 [P] So. Asia).
2. Shamsur Rahman Faruqi, *Sahiri, Shahi, Sahibqirani: Dastan-e Amir Hamza ka Mutalaa,* Volume I, *Nazari Mubahis* (New Delhi: National Council for the Promotion of Urdu Language, 1999), 209.
3. The only known copy of this text is in the British Library (Reference No. 306.24.B.21).
4. *Dastan-e Amir Hamza Sahibqiran* (Lucknow, India: Naval Kishore Press, 1871), 752.

ACKNOWLEDGMENTS

My understanding of the many facets of the *dastan* literature has been shaped by the Urdu language's foremost writer and critic, Shamsur Rahman Faruqi. His unparalleled insight into the poetics of Urdu's classical literature in his monumental study *Sahiri, Shahi, Sahibqirani,* which analyzes the known Urdu and Persian versions of the *Dastan-e Amir Hamza* and their sources, has laid the foundations of a serious study of the *dastan* genre and was immensely useful during my work.

In the course of translating this text, I have been fortunate to have had the help and encouragement of many other friends as well. At a very early stage of this translation, Professor Muhammad Umar Memon published an excerpt from it in the *Annual of Urdu Studies.* Mr. Salimur Rahman read that excerpt and offered his valuable advice. Professor C. M. Naim's testimonial underlined the importance of this book's publication. Ms. Elham Eshraghi helped in translating the Persian verses and phrases. My wife, Michelle, put up with me during the time it took to finish the translation and let me clutter up the living room with dictionaries and printouts.

The publication of this work owes a great deal to Frances and Bill Hanna of Acacia House Publishing Services, who placed this work with the Modern Library. My editor at the Modern Library, Judy Sternlight, deserves special thanks for her thoughtful editing advice and all her help in seeing this project to completion. Thanks are also due to Rebecca Shapiro and to production editor Evan Camfield. Lastly, a big thank-you to Medi Blum for her truly marvelous copyediting work. For any remaining shortcomings in the translation, I alone am responsible.

BOOK ONE

The First Book of the Dastan *of the Sahibqiran,
Amir Hamza bin Abdul Muttalib, and of the
Events Preceding His Birth*

The florid news writers, the sweet-lipped historians, revivers of old tales and renewers of past legends, relate that there ruled at Ctesiphon[1] in Persia (image of Heaven!) Emperor Qubad Kamran, who cherished his subjects and was a succor to the impecunious in their distress. He was unsurpassed in dispensing justice, and so rigorous in this exercise that the best justice appeared an injustice compared to his decree. Prosperity and affluence thrived in his dominions while wrong and inequity slumbered in death, and, rara avis—like, mendicants and the destitute were extinct in his lands. The wealthy were at a loss to find an object for their charity. The weak and the powerful were equals, and the hawk and the sparrow roosted in the same nest. The young and the old sought one another's pleasure, neither ever deeming himself the sole benefactor. The portals of houses remained open day and night like the eyes of the vigil, for if someone stole even the color of henna from the palm,[2] he was ground in the mill of justice. The thief therefore did not even dream of thieving, and if perchance a wayfarer should come upon someone's property on the road, he took it upon himself to restore it to its owner. Compared with Qubad Kamran's fearlessness, might, and valor, Rustam was the same as a hag most decrepit and cowardly.

This imperious monarch had forty viziers,[3] who were the epitomes of learning, wisdom, and prudence; and seven hundred wise men before whom even the likes of Plato and Aristotle were abecedarians.[4] All these viziers were peerless in intellect and cognition, and so accomplished in physics, arithmetic, *ramal, jafar,*[5] and astrology that they did not consider the likes of Galen and Euclid and Pythagoras fit company for themselves, let alone their equals. The emperor had seven hundred privy counselors, each more adept than ancient masters in arts and letters and in the decorum of assembly. And at the emperor's command were four thousand champion warriors, to whom Sam and Nariman and Rustam and Zal would alike present the sword of humility in combat and accept from their hands the badge of slavery. Three hundred sovereigns who reigned over vast tracts paid tribute to Emperor Qubad Kamran, and bowed their heads in vassalage and obeisance before him. And one million mounted warriors, intrepid and fierce, and forty troops of slaves, clad in gold and finery, waited, deft and adroit, upon the emperor at his court—the envy of Heaven, the adornment of Paradise!

In the same city there also resided a savant by the name of Khvaja[6] Bakht Jamal, who traced his lineage to the prophet Danyal (God's favors and mercies be upon his soul!). He was unrivaled in learning and the sciences of *hikmat*,[7] *ramal*, astrology, and *jafar*, and was truly a successor beyond compare of the ancient philosophers. Malik[8] Alqash, the emperor's vizier who had often made use of the divinations of this sage, offered himself as a pupil to Khvaja Bakht Jamal, and became so attached and devoted to him that he would not hear of parting even for a moment from his master. Before long, Alqash, too, became adept at *ramal*. His fame spread far and wide, and he proved himself such a consummate practitioner of the art, that he was deservedly labeled Khvaja's distinguished disciple, second only to his master.

One day Alqash said to Khvaja Bakht Jamal, "The other night as idleness weighed on my heart, I decided to cast lots in your name. Reading the pattern, I discovered that your star is in the descendent, and some vicissitude of fortune will befall you. Your star shall remain in the same house for forty days. Thus it would not bode well for you to step out of the house during this period, or trust anyone. Even I must suffer under this burden of separation, and not see you!"

Following Alqash's advice, Bakht Jamal secluded himself from the world, declining to receive either visitors or friends. Of the foretold days of ill-boding, thirty-nine had passed without mishap. On the fortieth day, Khvaja felt wretched to be shut inside his house, and set out carrying his staff to see vizier Alqash, to bring his only faithful and affectionate friend the news of his health and welfare.

By chance, instead of the thoroughfare, he followed a deserted road to the riverside. As it was summer he took refuge from the burning sun under a tree's shade. While he sat there, his eyes suddenly beheld a building most imposing, save for its outer walls that had fallen to ruin. Some curiosity led him toward it, and as he drew near, he found most of the apartments inside in a state of decay, and the vestibules in ruins, but for one that had survived ravaging and still stood—in desolation and disarray like a lover's heart. In that vestibule there was an antechamber whose

entrance was bricked up. Removing the bricks he found to his right a
door with a padlock. Khvaja thought of forcing it open with a brick or
stone, but when he held the padlock in his hand, it came open of its own
accord and fell to the floor. Stepping inside Khvaja discovered a cellar.
There he found buried Shaddad's seven boundless treasures of gold and
jewels. Seized by fright, Khvaja was unable to take anything, and retraced
his steps out of the cellar, then hastened to Alqash's house to give him the
propitious news.

Alqash's face brightened at the sight of Khvaja. He made room for
him on his throne, and after expressing joy at seeing his friend, said,
"Today was the fortieth day. Why did you take such trouble and inconvenience yourself? Come tomorrow, I had intended to present myself at
your door and receive great joy from the grace of your genial company."
After making small talk Khvaja mentioned the seven treasures to Alqash,
and recounted the windfall, saying, "Though I was blessed in my stars to
have come upon such an untold fortune, it was found on royal land, and
lowly me, I cannot lay claim to it, nor is it indeed my station! I resolved
in my heart that since you are the emperor's vizier, and an excellent patron and friend to me, I should inform you of this bountiful treasure.
Then, if you saw fit to confer a little something upon your humble servant, then that bit only would I consider—like my mother's milk—
warranted and rightful!"

Alqash was beside himself with joy when he heard of the seven treasures, and ordered two horses to be saddled forthwith; then he mounted
one, and Khvaja the other, and they galloped off in the direction of the
wasteland. By and by, they arrived at their destination. Alqash became
greatly agitated and ecstatic the moment he set eyes on the seven hoards,
and so violent indeed were his raptures of delight on the occasion, that
he was almost carried away from this world.

While murmuring gratitude to his Creator for bestowing such a
windfall on him, the thought suddenly flashed across Alqash's mind that
Khvaja Bakht Jamal was privy to this secret, and all that had come about.
Alqash reasoned that if some day Khvaja Bakht Jamal chose to betray him
to the emperor in order to gain influence at the court, the vizier would
find himself in a sorry plight. That would indeed put his life in great
peril, and not only would he have to wash his hands of this God-given
bounty, but also the emperor might declare him an embezzler and depose him. It would be small wonder if at that point the contents of his
house were confiscated and the building razed; he himself would be

thrown into the dungeon, and his family exposed to humiliation and ruin, with all traces of his honorable name forever erased from the face of the earth. It would be by far the lesser evil, Alqash thought, to kill Khvaja right there, and then lay claim to the boundless treasure without the least anxiety that the secret would some day come to light, or that someone might one day reveal the secret.

Once resolved, he immediately bore down upon Khvaja and put the dagger to his throat. Confounded by this turn of events, Khvaja cried out, "What has got into your head, Alqash? Does a good deed deserve evil? Is that how a favor is returned? What injury have I done you that you resolve to punish me thus?" And much did the poor old man groan in the same vein, and seek compassion, but to no avail. The heart of that villain did not soften, and his sympathy remained unstirred.

When the frail man saw that there was no escape from the clutches of this blackguard, and that it was only a matter of a few breaths before the candle of his life would be snuffed out by those hands, he entreated in despair:

> *Advertise well how I was laid low by your hand,*
> *That no one shall consider being faithful again.*

"O Alqash! I see that you are bent upon my murder, and on dyeing your villainous hands with my innocent blood. But if you could find it in your heart to act upon my last words, I shall entrust them to you and die with at least this debt toward you." The ungrateful wretch shouted back, "Make haste! For the cup of your life is now ready to overflow, and the thirst of my inclement dagger is ordained to be quenched in your blood!" The poor man spoke:

> *Such was my lot that friend proves a foe*
> *And the guide waylays me on the trail.*[9]

"There is hardly any money in my house to last my family beyond tomorrow," Khvaja continued, "and even less food. I would to God that you might send them enough to survive. And inform my wife, who is expecting, that if a boy is born to her, she must name him Buzurjmehr, and if a girl is born, she may follow her own counsel." After saying this he closed his eyes and began reciting the *kalma*,[10] seeking divine absolution, as he was to die an innocent man. Whereupon that heartless villain cut off

Khvaja's head with his unrelenting dagger, destroyed his horse, too, and interred the two of them in the same vault where the treasures were buried.

After sealing the door, Alqash went to the river to cleanse the blood from his hands and the dagger, and also to wash his hands of the faith that he had forfeited in exchange for short-lived riches. Then he rode away to his house, glad in his heart and thrilled. The next day, he returned to the place with great pomp, and after surveying it, ordered the prefect to build a garden for him on the site, bound by walls of marble, and a turquoise chamber erected over the vestibule, where he would give audience, and to have this heavenly abode furnished with rarities and wondrous curiosities. As soon as the order was given, the prefect sent for masons, laborers, and sculptors from the city, and began the construction. In a matter of days, the garden, the marble walls, and the turquoise chamber were ready, all of which delighted Alqash greatly, and he named the place Bagh-e Bedad.

Then he called at Khvaja Bakht Jamal's house, and told the family that he had sent Khvaja off to China to conduct trade, and he should soon return after turning a profit. He then communicated to them Khvaja's wishes. He consoled and comforted the family, and bestowed on them a rich purse, mentioning that more would be available whenever there was need, and that they ought not entertain any fears of adversity. Then Alqash returned home, with the grim truth buried in his heart.

My life passed as passeth the wind on the plains;
Alike with bitterness and joy, coarseness and beauty
All the harm the tyrant inflicted on us
Passeth over us, and resides with him.[11]

OF BUZURJMEHR'S BIRTH, AND OF THE CONTENTS OF THE BOOK BECOMING CONSPICUOUS

The singing reed of the knowers of tales of yore, and the mellifluent quill of claimants to past knowledge thus luxuriously modulate their song, and in a thousand voices delightfully trill their notes to proclaim that by the grace of God Almighty (Maker of this and the Future State!) the auspicious day arrived when, at a propitious hour on a Friday, a boy of high fortune was born to Khvaja Bakht Jamal's wife.

A sun today lifts the darkness from my life
And stirs fortune with its resplendence.[12]

At first his mother shed many a tear, thinking of Khvaja and reminded of her lonesomeness. Then she doted on the comely newborn, and offered thanks to the Progenitor. Remembering Khvaja's wish, she named him Buzurjmehr, and the child began to blossom in her care. A clement God safeguarded him from all evil, and the Insuperable Artist endowed him with such perfect beauty that before him even paragons of beauty were ashamed to show their faces. His stately forehead bespoke nobility, and his princely face shone with the light of eminence.

When Buzurjmehr was five years of age, he was taken to an instructor who tutored neighborhood children, and had been a pupil of Khvaja Bakht Jamal. He was told he could repay Khvaja's debt and earn acclaim by imparting knowledge to his son. The man very gladly accepted the charge, and put all his heart into educating Buzurjmehr.

A propitious year's augur is in its spring.

It was Buzurjmehr's routine to spend the whole day at his teacher's side, learning reading and writing skills, and to return home when a few hours remained before the close of day, to partake of whatever his mother had provided for him with her labors. One day, it so happened that there was nothing to eat. Buzurjmehr said to his mother, "I am perishing with hunger. Please give me something that I might sell it and buy some food." His mother replied, "Son, your father left us nothing that I can spare to be sold for meat and drink. But on the shelf there lies an ancient book, belonging to my father, and written long ago. Many a time, when your father was in need of money, he resolved to sell it. But every time he reached for it, a black serpent would dart out hissing from the shelf, and your father would turn back in fright. See if you can fetch it from there and sell it. I have nothing else at present to offer you to sell to buy food."

Buzurjmehr went and fetched the book as his mother had bid, but he did not find the serpent. As he turned a few pages and read them, he at first began to wail loudly, and cried copious tears like a cloud in springtime; then, having read a little further, he burst into riotous laughter. From his raptures of joy his pallid face—which before was the envy of the taper's amber glow—now became as scarlet as a ruby's honor.

Those present were greatly astonished, and marveled at what might have caused such a reversal of humor in him. Suspecting a fit of lunacy, his mother beseeched some of the witnesses to send for a bloodletter to bleed him, and others to get an amulet to put around his neck, wailing all the while that he was her only son and if he were seized by madness she would have no support in her adversity.

Noticing his mother's agitation, Buzurjmehr comforted her, and said, "Do not grieve, Mother, and stop worrying in your heart. God willing, the days of affliction shall soon end, and for all our suffering we shall be more than compensated. I see our slumbering fortunes stirring, our well-wishers rejoicing, and our enemies coming to humiliation and grief."

> Pass the wine! O cupbearer, 'tis the morn of the fest:
> Delay not the rounds until the sun sets.[13]

> His bounty does not long demur;
> The petitioner must not despair.[14]

"Suffice it to say, Mother, that I have become neither deluded nor taken with delirium. The reason I cried and laughed was that from reading this book I have learned all that has gone before and all that shall come to pass. I cried to discover that the vizier Alqash had murdered my innocent father, and that his corpse still lies above the ground, awaiting last rites. And I laughed upon finding out that I will avenge my father's blood, and shall become our emperor's vizier. Vex yourself no further! We shall have enough for ourselves—and to feed ten others besides."

Having said this, Buzurjmehr took a handmaiden to the grocer's and asked him to weigh out daily as much in victuals, butter, and sugar as she might ask for, without bothering about payment. The grocer asked, "But when would I be paid? Why should I bestow this largesse upon you?" Buzurjmehr said, "Do you ask payment of me? Perhaps you have forgotten how you poisoned the farmer Chand along with his four sons to avoid payment for the several thousand *maunds*[15] of wheat you had bought from him. What would become of you if I were to reveal this before the royal court, and what would be your payback then?" Hearing this the grocer was seized with fright, threw his turban at Buzurjmehr's feet, and pleaded in a trembling voice, "My son, as Ram is my witness, this shop is at your disposal. Whenever your desire anything, send for it from here, but pray keep to yourself what you have just uttered."

From there Buzurjmehr took the servant girl to the butcher's shop, and asked him to apportion one Tabrizi *maund*[16] of meat to her daily. The butcher asked, "And when shall I be paid and the account settled?" Buzurjmehr answered, "Remember shepherd Qaus, from whom you received several thousand heads of sheep? When it was time for his settlement, you slaughtered and buried him in your shop's cellar, and appropriated thousands upon thousands of rupees from that innocent man. Would you desire that I send his heirs to the Court of Justice, and show you how his blood calls out? Have you taken leave of your senses that you demand payment of me for this viand?" Upon hearing that, the meat vendor began to tremble like a cow at the sight of a butcher, and threw himself violently at Buzurjmehr's feet declaring, "My provisions and my life may both be ransom of your life! As much as Your Honor's girl shall desire shall be weighed out to her, and never even in my dreams would I desire compensation. But please safeguard my life and honor, and keep your lips sealed!"

Buzurjmehr dealt with the jeweler similarly, unnerving him by telling him of his past heinous deeds, and settling at the jeweler's expense a daily stipend of five dinars for himself. Then he returned home and bided his time in happy anticipation. He was thronged by newfound acquaintances and friends, and he indulged himself in all sorts of pleasant amusements.

All reverses are reversed in the face of God's bounty.

OF THE EMPEROR'S VISIT TO ALQASH'S BAGH-E BEDAD, AND OF THE FESTIVITIES HELD IN THAT HEAVENLY ABODE

Gardeners of annals and singers of the nursery of articulation plant the trees of words row after row, and thus embellish the brightness of the page with the flowers and redolent blossoms of colorful contents, making it the envy of Mani's tablet, telling how when Bagh-e Bedad was ready, and the form of Shaddad's Heaven realized, the euphoric Alqash, in his giddiness, forgot all cares of this world and the next.

Enthralled and enchanted at the sight, and beside himself with joy, he submitted to the emperor, saying, "By virtue of Your Highness's blessings and prestige, your slave has built a garden full of multitudinous flowers and fruit trees. A host of rare plants has been collected at great expense, and choice landscapists, past masters of the art, have been employed to tend to them. Thousands upon thousands have been spent to gather hundreds of uniquely skilled masters in the art, who have adorned the grounds with flowers and shrubs with such industry that Mani and Bahzad would be ashamed of their skill. But none of it brings any joy to your follower, for whom it shall remain a figure of autumn, until Your Eminence, the Shadow and Regent of God, sets his blessed foot there.

Trodden under your foot, the verdure grows greener;
The tree whose shade you patronize deems itself redeemed.[17]

"I desire Your Excellency, Emperor of the world, the Immortal Soul of the Age, to crown it with your presence and come for recreation and with your condescension raise the prestige of your ancestral vassal to high heavens. Then shall the garden taste of spring, and every bud and flower sprout in majestic splendor. And should Your Highness deign to partake of a fruit or two, this slave's prayers will be granted, and his trees of hope will bear fruit." The emperor consented to his request, and gave sanction to the wish expressed by Alqash. Gratified, Alqash bowed low and after making his offering, departed to busy himself with preparations for the feast.

Before long, everything needed for the feast was provided. An array of delicacies were prepared. Trays laden with fruits of all kind were set on tables. Dancers and musicians were sent for. Pyrotechnicians planned a fireworks display. Special lighting was prepared: Thousands of lamps were hung from the walls; chandeliers and wall-lamps were dusted; and wax and camphor candles were lit. And presently there arrived, exalted as the heavens, bright as the sun, most just and clement, His Imperial Majesty, attended by his retinue of nobles and viziers, to increase the beauty of Bagh-e Bedad with his presence. Thus, at long last, Alqash's prayer was answered.

Alqash had constructed for the emperor an extravagant throne over-laid with diamonds and rubies in the shapes of flowers and leaves. And four emerald peacocks were installed in its four corners in whose cavities incense burned in jewel-encrusted cassolettes. Embedded on either side of each bird were pots of narcissi set with gold and precious stones, the leaves fashioned of emeralds, the flowers of diamonds, and pollen from sparks of topaz—a work of art to rival the Incomparable God's Creation itself.

At the approach of the royal procession, the lookouts and riders posted by Alqash to gather intelligence proclaimed the emperor's arrival:

As the Shadow of God approached the Garden,
The blossoms in ecstasy bloomed out of scope.[18]

Alqash, escorted by his sons and aides-de-camp, came out to wel-come his sovereign lord with that throne carried aloft beside him, along with forty elephants draped in sheets of brocade and fitted out with be-jeweled howdahs[19] and litters worked with gold inlay. From the necks of the behemoths hung golden and silver carcanets and talismanic signs. Their foreheads were covered in brocade, their tusks sheathed in scab-bards of painted silver, and their trunks in gold leaf. The elephant drivers were all furnished with diamond-inlaid goads. The mahouts sported Banarasi[20] turbans of crushed silk, and wore brocade robes with cummerbunds of brocaded silk around their waists. The ostlers[21] walked along-side them, wielding studded staffs and spears, and wearing drawers of patterned silk and embroidered doublets. They were dressed in Banarasi garters, with dressings of figured brocade wrapped around their heads.

They were flanked on three sides by a host of pikemen riding, pranc-ing, galloping, and displaying their prowess atop their horses. Surrounding them were two hundred steeds, Tazi, Iraqi, Arabian, European, Kathiawari, Kacchis, Chaugoshia,[22] Bhumra, Thalay, Turkish, Tartar, Najdi, Cape Vella, Mujannas,[23] Dahunay; and a hundred and twenty-five Galloway, Rangpur, Pegwa, Syrian, Rangoonese, Tibetan, Javanese, Bukharan, Banol, Terhi, and Kusgi horses. All were nimble-footed, fast as wind, and of a zephyric nature. Fairy-faced but demon-spirited, their gait outpaced thought, and their hooves barely touched the ground. Their manes were thinned and cropped, and washed with lavender. They were fitted out with golden saddles and covered with embroidered saddlecloths. They pranced about, bobbing their plumes, sporting chamfrons, belts, leather cruppers covered with velvet and small metal bosses, breast harnesses, tassels, golden charms, richly decorated fly whisks, and jewel-studded armor over the gold thread nets covering their stifles. They had gold rat-tles around their fetlocks, and woolen martingales[24] tied to their withers with surcingles[25] of silk.

Each bridle was attended by two equerries who led the horse by hal-ters woven of gold thread. Their hair plaited with red silken fringe, the grooms wore golden bracelets and were dressed in drawers of Gujarati *mashru*[26] and jerkins of broadcloth. Even as they kept watch on the ani-mals, they whisked right and left, and fore and aft, with massive fly whisks, each strand of which was strung with pearls, and the handles were worked in gold inlay.

Then followed several thousand bridled camels: Arabian, Baghdadi, Bactrian, Marwari, Jaipuri, and Bikaneeri, clad in embroidered broad-cloth and brocade sheets, and fitted out with studded panniers.[27] Their muzzles were caparisoned with golden and silver plumes, and they had cavessons of silk galloon[28] in their noses. Every camel-rider was dressed to make himself conspicuous, and each she-camel strutted about osten-tatiously. Never once looking at the ground, she held her muzzle up with a lofty air and every so often couched her head in the rider's lap with the utmost affection and pride.

Then followed slaves bearing several thousand golden and silver salvers heaped with rubies, garnets, diamonds, emeralds, topazes, sapphires, chrysolites, star rubies, corals, turquoises, and similar lustrous, costly, and inestimable jewels and jewelry.

The salvers were followed by many thousand platters laden with miscellaneous blades and weapons: Khorasani, Isfahani, Qazvini, Portuguese, Gujarati, Alamani, Maghrebi, Janubi, Egyptian, *Farrukh-Begi,* Tirah, Sirohi, *kaj-bhuj;* and *chhuri, qarauli, peshqabz, bichhawa, baank, katar, dashnah, qama,* and *bahbudi;*[29] as well as European percussion locks, flintlocks, matchlocks, pellet guns, and single- and double-barreled musketoons, and pepperboxes in holsters of woven silk. (Begone malicious glances, and the like!)

Then thousands of rolls of brocade were brought: damask silk, *chanaboot,*[30] *mashru,* and *gulbadan.*[31] Delicate and elegant kerchiefs, doublebreadth mantles, and turbancloths from Banaras and Gujarat made of *jamdani, kamdani, mahmoodi, chandeli, shabnam, chaqan, tar-shumar, tarandaam,* muslin, gauze, *neno, nen-sukh,* and *tanzeb,*[32] all of these lined up in salvers with great ornamentation. And for winter raiment there were pairs of shawls, kerchiefs, gloves, neckerchiefs, *jamawars,*[33] pectorals, long gowns, quilted cloaks, *kaleecha,*[34] cloaks, and long coats, all decorously presented in excellent taste over silver trays and salvers.

Alqash went to the entrance of the house at the head of this procession to make his offering. Then, holding a post of the royal litter, he escorted the emperor into the garden. When he entered that heavenly sphere, the emperor found the garden an indulging and alluring retreat—a resort most sublime and sumptuous.

The towering doors of the garden gate were most elegantly and laudably worked, with the sill and lintel made of sandalwood, and the portals of ebony riveted with silver and steel ingots, which made it impregnable. There was jewel-encrusted lettering on the crevices of the marble enclosure. Trees with branches and leaves of emerald, and flowers of pearls and rubies, were embedded in the walls, and in their branches were perched nightingales, parrots, mynahs, turtledoves, ringdoves, *laals,*[35] quails, *sina-baz,*[36] doves, green pigeons, and black cuckoos, all made of turquoise, emerald, sapphire, and rubies. The lower part of the walls was trellised with bamboo frameworks on which emerald vines laden with clusters of real fruit were trained. The fruit clusters were enclosed in purses made of variegated silk brocade and gold foil, which were hung from the vine by silken strings and lace. The landscaping was of such fine quality that the promenade looked as if it were made of crystal, affording no rest to the glance and leaving the spectator awestruck.

In the flowerpots was a luxuriant growth of tulips, violets, calendula, chrysanthemums, chamomile, marigolds, double poppies, *phirki*,[37] jasmines, double jasmines, Tuscan jasmines, gardenias, *juhi*, lilies, *ra'e-bel*, eglantine, *keora, ketki,* balsam, coxcomb, *farang*,[38] marvel of Peru, bachelor's buttons, tuberoses, sunflowers, narcissi, basil, Cupid's arrows, *gul-e Abbasi*, saffron, and *chiraghan*.[39] Some gardens were fenced by Indian myrtle and some hedged by *chapni*.[40] Some boasted in their four corners stretches of clipped and pruned *maulsari*[41] trees that rivaled a man's height. From other areas wafted the redolence of cypresses, pines, boxwoods, and weeping Nyctanthes (peace be upon the Holy Prophet!).[42] The flower boughs commingled, locked in embrace, kissing one another with their blossom lips. Heavy with flowers, the boughs of fruit trees swayed in the breeze.

Flamingos, demoiselle and Indian cranes, and Greek and Bartavelle partridges preened on the promenades. Thousands of wrens and nightingales warbled from the rosebushes. Ringdoves and turtledoves sporting their ash-colored coats retorted in song from cypresses, boxwoods, and firs. Four arbors of silver wire enameled in green stood in each garden, bound on four sides by elegantly erected silver-encased columns. Peacocks preened themselves on the walls.

Then the female nursery attendants arrived who were in the full bloom of adolescence, dressed in red, parti-colored sheets hemmed with gold lace, which they wore over embroidered skirts. Their foreheads were adorned with *maang-tikas*[43] and spangles, and they sported golden wristlets and armbands studded with garnets, and gold bead necklaces. Tinkling their toe rings, and toe bands, and carrying in their henna-dyed hands hoes fitted with gold and silver handles with small chimes, they began weeding the wild growth from the promenades and plant beds. Sifting straw and gleaning fallen blossoms, the maids delighted the hearts of the onlookers with their enterprise. More tenuous than boughs of the sandalwood tree were their soft and tender wrists, and their slender fingers were the envy of the coral-tree branches. The maidens' ruddy breasts (begone malicious glances!) and the delicious swellings of their bosoms—each more sublime than the other!—put to shame citrons and apples, and outshone many a citrus and pomegranate. Exchanging pleasantries and carolling on the sly, they irrigated the gardens in groups: now weeding dry grass from one patch, now sowing verdant panic grass else-where; now making water basins from flowerpots at the base of trees, now training bellflowers and vines on bamboo frameworks.

On either side of the rivulets that streamed through the garden were arrayed herons, cranes, ruddy geese, teals, and snipes in groups of two. The branches and boughs of the taller trees were wrapped in silk tissue sacks—white and golden and green. At every step octagonal terraces of marble, alabaster, and veined jet met the eye. Before every terrace were basins filled with rose water, essence of musk, and *keora* water. In the middle of the basins were *jets d'eau* and fountains, with their golden and silver spouts mounted with nightingales, ringdoves, and turtledoves carved out of gems. The spray jetting out from between their feathers and wings was a most ravishing sight, which soothed the eyes and gladdened the heart.

In the nave of the garden stood a chamber, unrivaled in architecture, made of turquoise and surrounded by canopies of variegated gold leaf fixed on gold-inlaid posts. Galloon-plaited orris lattices hung over them, and gold-leaf curtains suspended by garnet bobbins were drawn up with strings of gold brocade. A platform made of seven hundred thousand gold pieces was built in the courtyard of the chamber, on which sat a be-jeweled throne.

At this platform, the emperor ascended and graced the throne, and received offerings. Alqash was in seventh heaven and felt himself most extraordinarily distinguished. When the emperor regarded the splendor and glory of Bagh-e Bedad his own munificence seemed lacking, and he declared: "Indeed, this garden would hold its own in magnificence before that of Shaddad! The sight of it has delighted us! Its sparkling avenues, symmetrical promenades, succulent fruits, luscious fare, rare and curious flowers, sculpted trees, refreshing pools, and the agreeable and blissful air, are all very luxurious and elegant indeed. We used to hear of its air and landscaping, and now we have witnessed it! A most excellent garden it is, praise be to Allah!"

A garden most wondrous, envy of Paradise,
To dazzle the eyes of Rizwan himself,
To drive from his mind the thoughts of Heaven;
A splendor such as this he would have nowhere seen in Heaven.
The avenues and gardens are strewn
With roses and tulips and the dog rose;
Here blooms the jasmine, there the eglantine

And somewhere the beds of keora;
The narcissus locks its gaze with a blossom,
Some flower returns the nightingale's glance;
From one corner trill the wrens,
Cock pheasants chortle from another;
Obeisant the cypresses stand around the garden,
Truckle the fir its expanse;
In the cypress boughs the turtledoves
Warble after the carolling of Daud,
Fruit trees fill the eyes with abundance:
Quince, pear, apple, and pomegranates,
The golden kernels hung from the vine
Brew already in the vats of the drinkers' eyes;
Peacocks preen on the promenades
And are a-singing on the ledges.

Alqash the wretch relished every last word of his praise and, flattered beyond measure, responded in a transport of delight, "It is all in oblation to His Majesty, the Shadow of God. His abject slave could never have dreamed that he would be chosen to wait on His Eminence! The honor of your devoted slave was today redoubled. Unsurpassed pride was determined his lot. He was held twice and thrice esteemed among his fellows!" Thereafter the emperor sat down for the meal. The festivities and entertainments set to rolling following Alqash's orchestration. Fairy-faced dancers flitted to the tunes of silver-bosomed courtesans. Red wine gurgled into goblets held by ruddy-cheeked cupbearers. The rounds of drink set in motion the firmament of the heavens. The wine unfurled a new world before their eyes. Fireworks were set off, further bedazzling the onlookers' eyes.

For twenty-one days the emperor thus indulged in convivialities and merriment. On the twenty-second day he conferred on Alqash the Jamshedi robe of honor.[44] The royal litter arrived presently, and the emperor then repaired to his palace, fully content. He was soon occupied in matters of state.

Of Alqash Taking the Innocent Buzurjmehr Prisoner, and of His Deliverance from Alqash's Clutches, and of the Emperor's Assembling His Prudent Ministers to Ask Them of the Dream, and Vowing Punishment on Them

One day when I ventured into the garden to regard its bloom,
My eyes beheld on a bower a withered rose.
When I inquired what had caused that blight,
"My lips for a moment opened in a smile in this garden," it replied.

Such is the decree of Destiny's Gardener that every instant a new flower should bloom in Life's Green. The farsighted one regards in it His transcendent art, and disengages his mind from this world and all things worldly. No sooner does one laugh than he feels some grief prick his side. The bough that bows in humility procures forthwith desire's fruit. A branch that overreaches, the Gardener's hand promptly prunes.

In this abode of inconstancy one must mind one's deeds,
For a sea's existence could turn to a bubble in a breath.

Regard what new blossom flowered in that garden, and what fresh colored bud sprouted there. We return to Buzurjmehr and his story. Regard how times change and fortunes ebb and flow.

Thus narrate the legend writers and the raconteurs of yore that since Buzurjmehr was wise, sagacious, virtuous, and discerning, he had given himself to a solitary life, and the hours of his nights and days were spent venerating the Almighty. One day his mother said to him, "Son! Of a sudden I am taken with a longing for some greens. If you were to inconvenience yourself, your mother's craving would be fulfilled." Buzurjmehr gladly acquiesced to his mother's wishes, and bent his legs toward Bagh-e Bedad.

Arriving at the gate he found it locked. He called the garden keeper, who came directly. As he was about to unlock the gate, Buzurjmehr said to him, "Do not touch the lock. The female of the snake you killed the other day is secreted away in the catch of the lock to bite you and avenge her mate." When the keeper looked closely he did indeed find a female snake in the catch. He killed her, too, and opening the gate, threw himself at Buzurjmehr's feet declaring, "It was your forewarning that saved me! Otherwise nothing stood between me and my death, and certainly I would have breathed my last." Then he asked Buzurjmehr, "What is your pleasure, my dear boy? What was it that brought you here today?" Buzurjmehr answered, "I needed some greens. I will pay for them with pleasure, and then go my way." The keeper replied, "I will fetch the greens directly. But I cannot accept payment from my savior, and shall make a present of them to you."

When the gardener went to get the greens, he noticed a goat plundering the saffron fields with great abandon. He struck her with his mattock in irritation, and her chapter of life soon ended with her throes. Buzurjmehr called out, "O cruel man! Why did you kill for no reason, and take the blood of three innocent lives on your neck?" The gardener smiled and said, "Here I killed one goat, son, and you count her as three! Are you in your right mind?" Buzurjmehr told him that the goat had two kids of such and such color inside her womb, and when the gardener killed her, they died with her, too.

Unbeknownst to them, as they stood there talking, they had attracted Alqash's ears, who was sitting on his throne, listening. He called the garden keeper over, and inquired what they had been discussing and what had come about. The keeper narrated all that had passed. When Alqash ordered the goat's belly cut open, it did reveal two kids of the same color as Buzurjmehr had described. Greatly surprised, Alqash called Buzurjmehr over, and seating him by his side on the throne, asked him to introduce himself, his father, and where he had come from.

Buzurjmehr said, "I am Buzurjmehr, Khvaja Bakht Jamal's son, and the grandson of Hakim Jamasp. Afflicted by fortune, as some tyrant has murdered my father, I long for revenge. I have become a recluse, and bide my time in patience and equanimity in the worship of the True Avenger, and am always consumed by my bereavement!"

Alqash asked, "Did you find your father's killer, then?" Buzurjmehr said, "God is the True Avenger, and there is nothing beyond His scope. One of these days some mark will be discovered, and the blood of the innocent victim shall call out." Alqash asked, "Could you divine what was in my heart that night?" Buzurjmehr replied, "You had it in your heart to divulge to your wife the treasure that you had discovered and what was your windfall. But something decided you against telling her, and you resolved to maintain your quiet."

Alqash's wits took flight at these words, he became out of sorts, and all his composure was thrown awry. He began trembling like a willow, fearing that, if his dark deed became known, all the wealth and fortune he had hoarded would invite disaster upon him. This boy has the gift of clairvoyance, he thought, and anyone who would eat the vital organs of such a one would become all-seeing, too. He decided to kill Buzurjmehr and devour his heart and liver. That would nip in the bud any evil that might be afoot, he thought, and silence any words that could spell trouble for him before they were uttered.

Thus decided, Alqash called for his Nubian slave, Bakhtiar, and secretly told him that if he were to slaughter Buzurjmehr, and bring him kebabs of his heart and liver, he would grant him his heart's desire. The slave took Buzurjmehr to a dark cellar, as he was bid, and there he bore down upon Buzurjmehr and was about to slit open his throat with a knife, when Buzurjmehr involuntarily broke into laughter, and said to the slave, "The hope for which you sully yourself with my murder shall never be fulfilled by Alqash's false promise, and the honor and prestige that you have at present will also be lost. However, if you refrain from killing me, you shall find success with me, God willing!" The slave said, "If you were to reveal to me my motive, I would set you free this instant!"

Buzurjmehr replied, "You are in love with Alqash's daughter, but he will never give you her hand. I, however, shall arrange for you to marry her and, moreover, shall settle all your wedding expenses, too. Set me free now! Ten days from now, the emperor will have a dream that he shall forget. He will assemble all his viziers to quiz them and ask them of the dream and its interpretation. When all of them fail him, he will be taken by passion. Then your master will come asking for me. But beware, not until he has slapped you thrice should you divulge the truth about me. And remember not to breathe a word of it until then!" The slave said, "He had sent me to bring him kebabs of your vitals. If I took him some made from an animal, he would discover it at once—as he is a hakim[45]— and punish me." Buzurjmehr said, "At the gates of the city a woman is selling a kid raised on human milk. Take money from me and slaughter it and take Alqash its vitals. Use the remainder of the meat yourself!"

At length the slave relented, from fear of God, and also from the hope of having his ambition satisfied. He did not kill Buzurjmehr but did as he had told him. Alqash ate the kid's kebabs, and believing that he too had now become oracular and sapient, rejoiced exceedingly while sitting in his garden.

Delivered from death, Buzurjmehr returned home, reckoning, as the saying goes, that

Disaster had struck, but we were spared the tragedy,

and narrated all to his mother. That poor, star-crossed woman, thinking now of her husband, and now of her son's distress and tribulation, was overcome with tears. She offered many thanks to God for her son's safe return home and said, "My son, confine yourself to the safety of our house, and do not step out. Whatever God will provide by the close of the day we will graciously accept. The enemy lies in wait! God forfend that he should set in motion any evil, and God forbid that your enemies should come to any harm."[46] Buzurjmehr replied, "You must not torment yourself with thoughts of disaster. Regard what comes forth by the grace of God, and wait and see how God manifests His will!"

It so befell that on the tenth day, the emperor had a dream that he in no way remembered. In the morning, he said to his wise counselors and viziers: "Last night I had a dream that I do not now recall, and no matter how hard I try to recollect, it does not come to me. You must narrate it to me and tell me its interpretation to ingratiate yourselves with me!"

All of them replied that they would exert their wise minds and all their learning to their utmost, and oblige him with an interpretation if they only knew the dream. The emperor replied: "The wise men in Sikander's times would often narrate to him dreams that he could not recollect and tell him their interpretations, for which they were liberally rewarded. I have employed you for similar offices, and you have received all manners of favors and kindnesses from me. If you fail to narrate the dream and tell me what it signifies, I shall have every single one of you put to the sword, and order your wife and children to be pulverized in the oil press and your households plundered. For mercy's sake, I give you a reprieve of forty days. By that time, if you come up with an interpretation to my liking, very well and good, otherwise yours will be a most unenviable lot!"

The emperor was irked most by Alqash, as he was the most celebrated among the viziers. All the counselors and wise men were at a loss as to how to relate an unseen and unheard-of dream, and wondered how and by what device to ward off the scourge from their heads.

After forty days had passed, the emperor again assembled the company and asked them if they had succeeded in finding out the content of his dream and all that it entailed. Everyone remained silent, but Alqash spoke: "This slave has divined from geomancy that Your Majesty dreamt of a bird that swooped down from the heavens and dropped Your Eminence into a river of fire. Your Excellency started in your sleep in fright, and woke up without remembrance of the dream."

The emperor replied angrily, "O vile and brazen-faced liar, I give you the lie! A fine story you have concocted. On this basis you call yourself learned and prudent and sagacious and a celebrated geomancer! Never did I have such a dream that you relate to be mine. I shall allow you two days more of respite. If you have not related the dream by the end of that time, I swear by Namrud's pyre that you shall be the first to be buried alive. My wrath shall visit every one of you assembled here, and not a single one of you will be shown mercy!"

Greatly distressed at the emperor's words, Alqash returned home, and immediately sent for Bakhtiar and asked him, "Tell me verily where the boy is hidden! Did you spare his life or was he consigned to some cellar?" Bakhtiar answered, "I killed him just as I was ordered, and roasted his vitals and brought them to you, and today I am being asked to produce the boy!" Alqash replied, "As he was most wise and sapient, I am convinced that he escaped from your hands and you do not confess for fear that I would chastise you for disobedience. But I swear by the gods Lat and Manat that I shall not punish you but shall invest you instead with estate and high office. Bring him to me that my life, and the life and honor of countless other innocent people shall be spared."

When Bakhtiar reiterated his statement, his master in annoyance slapped him three times so hard that Bakhtiar's eardrum was ruptured and spurted blood, and Bakhtiar fell on the floor in pain. When he came to in a few moments, he replied, "Do not punish your slave. I shall go and bring Buzurjmehr as you command!" Alqash said, "I wonder at your foolishness! How many times did I ask you for him, and so kindly, but got nothing except denial? And now you confess after I have punished you." Bakhtiar said, "He had strictly forbidden me to disclose his whereabouts to you until you had struck me thrice." Thereupon Alqash embraced

Bakhtiar, and said, "Hurry and bring him at once! I shall make you a happy man, and shower you with gold and jewels."

Buzurjmehr came out directly when Bakhtiar knocked at the door, and after inquiring about what had transpired, accompanied him to Alqash's house. The vizier showed Buzurjmehr much respect and deference, and excused his past conduct. Then, to inform him of his present predicament, Alqash spoke thus: "The emperor had a dream that he forgot and we are made to bear the brunt of it. The emperor said that if we did not narrate his dream to him, he would kill every single one of us to punish us collectively. But no one but you has the power to describe what is hidden and to save us and our families from imminent ruin. If you would be kind enough to relate the dream to me, it would be as if you granted us all a reprieve from death."

Buzurjmehr replied, "I cannot disclose the dream here. But come morning, tell the emperor that you had only been testing the wise and learned counselors and viziers in his employ, to see if they had any claim to omniscience. And that, as their knowledge and worth had now become amply manifest to His Majesty, you would like to bring forward your pupil, that if His Highness were to send for him, he would presently relate the dream and all its particulars. Then, when the emperor shall send for me, I will relate the dream and its interpretation, which shall earn you great distinction in the emperor's eyes, save hundreds of innocent lives, and you will be advanced in your office in the bargain."

OF BUZURJMEHR'S RELATING THE EMPEROR'S DREAM AT THE APPOINTED HOUR, AND OF ALQASH'S LIFE BEING CLAIMED IN RETRIBUTION

Do not be neglectful of the retribution for your works;
For a grain of wheat begets wheat, and the barley its kind.

*   *   *

No two days pass alike in this world;
There is no garden that could avert autumn.[47]

The world is the abode of retribution. Oftentimes every deed is accounted for here, and occasionally something remains in abeyance, to be settled on Judgment Day. It behooves every man therefore to bear in mind the deserts for every deed, and not settle for dishonor in this life—and reproof in the Future State—for this vile world and its short-lived riches. What this adage verifies and where the discourse drifts is the story of unworthy Alqash, tyrant and malefactor, who at long last reaped the harvest of his sins, and paid for his benefactor's blood.

Those versed in past legends and privy to the episodes of history thus interpret the night's sable dream by the tongue of the stylus in the paper's bright morn, and tell that the next day Alqash presented himself before his sovereign, narrating verbatim Buzurjmehr's words. Orders were given that Buzurjmehr be produced and presented before the emperor.

A mace bearer called at Buzurjmehr's house and said, "Come at once! The Imperial Highness wishes to see you!" Buzurjmehr said, "What conveyance have you brought me from his Highness that I may present myself at the threshold of the Shadow of God?" The mace bearer replied, "I did not bring a conveyance, as I did not receive any orders to that effect. But I shall return and request a conveyance for you from the nobles."

Returning to the court the mace bearer said, "He could not come without a conveyance, as he is a man of great pride." Thereupon the mace bearer was ordered to take a steed, and bring him forthwith. When the mace bearer arrived with the horse, Buzurjmehr said, "In its essence the horse is made of wind, and I am fashioned of clay. Wind and clay are manifest opposites, and I shall not, therefore, ride the horse. But if you bring me a conveyance that is suited to me, I will presently go with you, that I may solicit the audience of the Regent of the Most Benevolent."

The mace bearer returned with Buzurjmehr's reply, whereupon the emperor ordered all kinds of conveyances to be sent to Buzurjmehr's house so that from among them he might choose one that suited him. According to the royal orders, the conveyances were immediately readied, and brought to Buzurjmehr's door. Buzurjmehr looked at them and said, "I cannot possibly ride the elephant, as it is reserved for the emperor. To ride it would be a breach of deference. And only the sick ride litters. I am neither sick, nor dead, that I should be carried on the shoulders of four men, and imagine myself dead while I am still alive. God be praised, I am robust of health, and neither have illness of any kind nor am at all lethargic. The camel is seraphic in nature, and I am but an insignificant mortal. I neither find the courage nor the talent in myself to warrant riding such a beast. The mule is misbegotten, and I am of noble birth. Therefore it does not behoove me to ride it, nor is it indeed my desire. As to the ox, corn-chandlers and launderers ride it, and I belong to neither trade but am of gentle birth, learned and discerning. And the ass is reserved for the guilty and the culprits, and I am innocent of any crime, and am a law-abiding, God-fearing subject of the Refuge of the World. Return them all, and convey my words to the sagacious ears of the one who is a just emperor."

The messengers again returned without Buzurjmehr and communicated word-for-word his reply to the emperor's summons. The emperor said, "Ask him what conveyance he desires. Whatever he wishes for shall be provided, and we shall prepare to send it." The royal pages took the emperor's message to Buzurjmehr, who said, "If His Highness wishes me to narrate his dream, he should send me Alqash saddled. Because as the saying goes, everyone tends toward his own, and I will ride him and present myself before His Majesty and describe his dream in its entirety. Again, as I profess to be wise, and Alqash is the Mount of Wisdom,[48] it is only meet and proper that I ride only him, and to do that would reflect most properly on my part, and not otherwise."

Those assembled at the court marveled at Buzurjmehr's audacity and at the utter disregard of royal orders implicit in his replies, as it was a matter of great pride to be chosen for royal commissions, and even if one were ordered through the agency of a vizier or noble, one felt greatly indebted. And here, they wondered, the emperor himself requested his presence, and that noble personage had so high a mind that he showed supreme indifference. They speculated that either there was something the matter with Buzurjmehr's head, or else they themselves were mistaken, and Buzurjmehr was indeed a man of great nobility and eminence.

When the messengers brought back Buzurjmehr's reply, the emperor broke into laughter, and ordered that Alqash be saddled and sent to bring back Buzurjmehr. No sooner was the order given than Alqash was bridled and saddled, and he trotted over to Buzurjmehr's house to carry out Buzurjmehr's wish. Buzurjmehr mounted Alqash and spurred him on, proclaiming every step of the way, "I have redeemed myself this day, because I caught the one who had murdered my father!"

Whoever saw them along the way—young and old alike—found the sight a curiosity and followed them in the train.

When Buzurjmehr was presented before the emperor in such state, the emperor showed him great regard and honor. After commending him highly on his deep knowledge and observance of form and etiquette, he said, "First you must explain what Alqash has done to you that caused him to be treated so scandalously at your hands, and made you wish to hold him up to shame?" Buzurjmehr replied, "In the first place he is an embezzler, who had for his master Your Highness—the Shadow of God, a Hatim of his times, and so generous and bountiful a lord—and yet he stole from Your Highness, and with such flagrant obduracy! He never once feared what would become of him if his theft came to light! The thought never crossed his mind that he would invoke the emperor's wrath and be buried alive! That all manner of calamities would befall him! That this theft would lead him into a terrible predicament!

"In the second place, he studied geomancy with my father. And my father in his great generosity imparted to him every word of the knowledge at his command. His own father in his life would not have shown him the generosity that my father did. He was the teacher of this depraved man, and was trustworthy, faithful, and unsuspecting. My father took pride in his progress, loved him as a pupil, and showed this vicious man more preference than one would his own child. He never concealed any useful knowledge from this miscreant nor kept any secrets.

When my father came upon the seven treasures of Shaddad,[49] he never took anything, and due to the camaraderie that he felt for this man, divulged to him the find. And he took not even a farthing, but handed the entire treasure over to him. And this man here, worrying lest the riches should be transferred to another and he be deprived of the treasure if the news reached Your Highness from this or that source, murdered my innocent father and consigned him to the cellar where the treasure is buried. And he felt neither fear of God nor any scruples that he was murdering his benefactor, and inculpating himself by shedding innocent blood. And thus, at the same place lies my father's cadaver still, half buried in gravel, without coffin or grave. This man did not once realize that the blood of the innocent cries out and brings about retribution for the guilty in unknown ways, and the culprit finds no respite upon discovery.

"I now beseech Your Majesty, my equitable sovereign, in the hope that I shall be dealt with fairly. If Your Highness does not settle with me and refuses me justice this day, on the arrival of Judgment Day, I shall petition before the Supreme Justice and seek redress from that Diviner and the Avenger of Deeds and the Arbiter of Arbiters. There Your Eminence would also be summoned, and you would have to answer for yourself. You would be called to account for your part in not rectifying the wrong done to the victim, and for not punishing the tyrant. Oh, how would you explain your conduct then, before the Omniscient Master?"

When he heard these words, the emperor cast a fiery glance at Alqash, and said, "Did you hear what he said? What injury did his father do to you that you perpetrated such a diabolic felony against him, and ruthlessly killed him in disregard of all obligations due him, making his son an orphan and inflicting widowhood on his spouse? If you did not fear me, did you also not fear God? Did it not occur to you that the murder of the man who dies innocent at your hands would one day come to light, and show you the dark day? Indeed, he deserved it for doing good to an ingrate like you and instructing you in geomancy! Death's arrow would not have found him had he not guided you in its secrets."

Never did I instruct one in archery
But he made me his arrow's mark.[50]

"And if he had not disclosed to you the seven treasures, would you have so gruesomely abused him?

> To give a boon to the tyrant
> Is the same as to do the good a bad turn.[51]

"But regard now, O villain (who deserves to be roasted alive!), what just punishment you shall receive for this unjust deed, and how expeditiously you will be dispatched to Hell! If I do not have you riddled with the arrows of Justice, I shall hold myself guilty of an equal wrong and have the blood of equity on my head."

Alqash replied, "Your Majesty, he calumniates me and plots my undoing for no reason!" Buzurjmehr spoke: "Put me to the proof! I have no use for idle talk! Who needs a mirror to see how a bracelet sits on the wrist! Whoever cares to come with me, I shall prove what I profess. Then see if this liar's claim of innocence holds up!" The emperor accompanied Buzurjmehr with his royal cortege to the place where Khvaja Bakht Jamal lay murdered. He had ordered that Alqash be brought on foot in chains, and led behind a horse like a prisoner.

All these developments caused much stir in the city, and the populace turned out to see what the villain had been brought to. Some solicited mercy before divine wrath. Some of the commoners who accompanied the procession, when told of Alqash's murder of his benefactor, reviled him. Some commented, "Foul begets foul!" Some said, "Every evil deed is accounted for!" Some took admonition from his example. Others marveled at his unwarranted crime. By and by, surrounded by officers of law and the public, Alqash was brought to the gates of Bagh-e Bedad.

Buzurjmehr guided the emperor to the cellar and showed him the site. The emperor saw the seven treasures consigned there and also saw lying in a corner Khvaja Bakht Jamal's withered corpse—a picture of innocence violated. The dead man's steed, too, lay murdered beside him, wasted to a shadow.

The emperor was delighted to see the treasure, and ordered that it be removed without delay to the royal treasury and consigned to the vaults with great care. His orders were carried out, and thus came true the proverbial saying that "In the world gold attracts gold, and treasure, more treasures!"

The emperor then ordered that Khvaja's corpse be removed with a great deal of decorum and protocol, his last rites performed with high ceremony according to the custom of his people, and a shrine built to his memory. Then he granted Buzurjmehr forty days' leave to pass in bereavement and in arranging prayers for Khvaja's *fateha*,[52] and conferred on him thousands of rupees from the imperial treasury. Buzurjmehr brought home elephant-loads of money and placed them before his worthy mother, and told her all that had transpired. Buzurjmehr then busied himself with the *chehlum*[53] arrangements.

All kinds of attendants and retainers appeared at his door when the news of his wealth spread; and friends, acquaintances, and relatives gathered around when the tidings of his increase in fortunes circulated. Cauldrons were put on the fire and, at Buzurjmehr's expense, food was distributed in the city every day. Thousands of salvers and trays of food were sent out all over the city with great ceremony. After the community and the local nobility had been attended to, it was the turn of the laity, and the needy and the destitute. In short, for the duration of forty days, all the rituals of *fateha* and *chehlum* were observed, and all the particulars and formalities in that regard were more than met.

Then, Buzurjmehr appeared before the emperor. He was bestowed with a robe of condolence, and was ordered to be in regular attendance at the court. Buzurjmehr began attending the court every day. One day he found occasion to say to the emperor: "If it is Your Majesty's pleasure, I shall now narrate your dream to you, that I am not deemed an impostor in your eyes." The emperor said, "Nothing would be more opportune! If you describe the dream properly, you shall be richly rewarded. My worries will be put to rest and my heart will find solace."

Buzurjmehr thus spoke: "Your Majesty dreamt that forty-one dishes of all varieties were laid out on a spread. Your Eminence took a morsel of halva from a dish and raised it to your mouth, when a black cur darted forward, snatched the piece from Your Majesty's hand, and devoured it. Your Highness started in fright and forgot the dream." The emperor declared, "I swear by Namrud's pyre, it is indeed the very dream I had. Verily this was my dream! Now interpret it, too, and gladden my heart!"

Buzurjmehr replied, "Allow your slave to be conducted to your palace, and order all your harem to be assembled. Then I shall tell you the interpretation of this dream, and shall present to you the true picture of things." The emperor took Buzurjmehr to the palace and ordered his harem assembled. After everyone had congregated as ordered, there arrived, walking with dignity and state in the cortege of her consorts and mates, a damsel of comely features and great pride: handsome, fairylike, and *houri*-faced,[54] wearing a most exquisite robe adorned with lustrous gems and jewels, like a cypress sapling in beauty's green.

Among her consorts there was also a black woman. Buzurjmehr caught her hand, and said to the emperor, "This is the black dog, Your Honor, who took the morsel away from Your Majesty's hands. And that morsel was this princess, who is guilty of the most grievous ingratitude to the emperor, who is the equal of the sun and the moon in gracefulness."

The emperor was transfixed with wonder upon hearing this and when he asked what it all meant, it came out that in reality it was a man who lived in great luxury with the princess, disguised as a woman, who imbibed, unrestrained, the wine of her charms at all hours of night and day. The emperor raged most wonderfully when he discovered this. The lord porter became the object of severe chastisement, and the gatekeeper of the palace was censured even more severely. The black man was thrown before the hounds at the emperor's orders, and that ill-starred princess's face was blackened, and she was paraded around the city mounted on an ass and then bricked-up alive in a tower on a thoroughfare. A robe of honor was conferred upon Buzurjmehr, and that same day Alqash was taken outside the city walls and, before a crowd of onlookers, buried up to his waist and riddled with arrows by expert archers. All the goods and chattels belonging to Alqash, with the inclusion of his wife and daughter, were awarded to Buzurjmehr, and all those riches and estate changed masters in no time.

After making his offering to the emperor, Buzurjmehr took the slave Bakhtiar to Alqash's palace and said to Alqash's wife, "I do not desire this estate and its riches. It is futile to put store in such transient wealth. May its possession afford you happiness. However, I did promise Bakhtiar that after avenging my father, I would arrange for him to be married to your daughter, and shall satisfy his heart's desire by fulfilling my promise. I would that you give him your daughter's hand in marriage for my sake, and fill his goblet of expectancy with desire's wine. I promise you that if a boy is born to your daughter from Bakhtiar, I shall educate him myself and, when he comes of age, shall prevail upon the emperor to have him instituted as a vizier in Alqash's stead."

Alqash's wife replied, "I have no objection to your wishes. We are your slaves. Whatever is your pleasure shall agree with us, too. My daughter is your handmaiden, and we will accept whosoever you wish to give her to in marriage." In short, Alqash's wife acted on Buzurjmehr's request gladly, and married her daughter to Bakhtiar the Nubian.

When these tidings reached the emperor, he was overwhelmed by Buzurjmehr's act of generosity. After many days, when all the emperor's viziers, privy counselors, learned men, commanders, and sovereigns were assembled in the royal court, he spoke to them thus: "I have found Buzurjmehr to be pious and devout, of noble blood, courageous, and unrivaled. He is Khvaja Bakht Jamal's son, grandson of Hakim Jamasp, and unsurpassed in wisdom and learning. I have rarely seen one so upright, constant, and generous. All the wealth and riches of treacherous Alqash that I had bestowed upon him, he returned untouched to Alqash's wife and daughter. He is well versed in etymology and syntax, logic, ethics, mathematics, rhetoric, astronomy, geometry, letters, arithmetic, philosophy, geomancy, astrology, and so forth. And he is no ordinary lay cleric either, but adept at statecraft, economics, etiquette, judgment, administration of finances and state, attention to forms, and is liberal, brave, and most civil. He is also virtuous and an eloquent speaker. One rarely comes across such a capable and dignified man. Even if one were to search for a man of such qualities, such a one as this would never appear. And he is oracular, moreover. Previously, all the viziers of our empire were ignoramuses and rank idiots. They were corrupt, base, and indolent, and deficient in the performance of their offices. Therefore, I desire to make Buzurjmehr my vizier, and confer upon him the robe of ministerial rank."

The courtiers unanimously sounded their praise and approval of the emperor's propitious opinion, and with one voice announced: "Indeed a man of such qualities has been neither seen nor heard of before. No opinion could surpass the capital opinion of Your Highness! Before His Majesty's precious thoughts, all other thoughts perish! In this matter your beneficent eye has alighted on the ideal candidate. We desire with all our heart that Buzurjmehr be promoted and advanced in rank!" The emperor conferred the robe of ministerial honor on Buzurjmehr without delay, and granted him a seat to the right of his throne. Thereupon, the court was adjourned.

Buzurjmehr returned home with great pomp and ceremony, lavishing gifts and offerings, and dispensing alms. Witnessing this, his mother offered thanks to the Omnipotent King. Before long Buzurjmehr occupied himself with ministerial affairs and immersed himself in the administration and reform of the finances and state.

Of Dil-Aaram's Expulsion from the Emperor's Favor and of Her Returning to His Good Graces

How man is reduced to a mere trick in the hands of the celestial juggler! What enchanting antics does this trickster world play on man! Here a beggar is made king! There a whole empire is wiped from earth's face! Those who once longed for dry bread now distribute alms and food! Those who never saw a farthing today command untold wealth! Such is the story of the poor man here told.

Reliable chroniclers report that, once exposed to the culpable princess's deceit, the emperor became wary of all women—with the exception of Dil-Aaram—who, apart from her natural beauty and grace, and chastity and virtue, was most accomplished in musical arts and a lute player par excellence. Aside from her, no other woman dared show herself before the emperor, and whenever one did, she would quickly fall into disgrace and disfavor.

One day the emperor rode out to the chase with a bevy of hawks, ospreys, merlins, ossifrage,[55] sparrow hawks, peregrines, tercelets,[56] falcons, stannels,[57] pigeon hawks, goshawks, and kestrels; packs of hounds, cheetahs, and lynx; and with a troop of gamekeepers in the train. Not too far from the seat of his empire there stood a sky-high mountain, huge and imposing: a sight both magnificent and enticing. The Gardener of Nature had strewn the mountainside with fields, and there the Gardener of Perfect Art had grown a multitude of diverse trees. On one side, grand and towering trees rose high, half-hidden in clouds; and vines carpeted the expanse on the other. At the foot of the mountain was a game reserve, most worthy and fair beyond description. Every single blade of grass that grew there was the envy of the rose and tulip. A tangle of rivulets and springs ran there—and every single spring that flowed there was like the

Fountain of Life.[58] The air, laden with the fragrance of flowers and trees, was more redolent than musk. And its pleasant smell of flowering blossoms was the envy of the jasmine-breathing gale of spring. The trees exuded divine grace, and were in full bloom from the agreeable air. From its spontaneous growth of flowers, the grove presented the ideal portrait of a garden. And there was such an abundance of game that it could not be described. The hunter was overwhelmed by their sheer numbers. The expanse teemed with geese, cranes, ruddy-geese, teals, Indian cranes, flamingos, *buzi*,[59] grouse, demoiselle cranes, pheasants, partridges, cranes, peacocks, storks, bustards, *Shirazi, kavak*,[60] waterfowl, and the like. On the other side of the field grazed numerous herds of deer, axis deer, hog deer, stags, *paseen, ghora-roz*,[61] antelopes, and ravine deer. The place abounded with birds and beasts of game, and, covered with lush growth, the ground stretched like an emerald carpet for miles. Water rushed in the rivulers, and in places springs and lovely ravines gushed. Several miles across in width, a grand river flowed on one side. Its water was transparent and clear and bright like the hearts of the pure. Its banks were bounded by green fields, and the lagoons swarmed with blue water lilies.

There the emperor dismounted to admire the landscape. By chance, his eyes espied an old man coming out of the forest, carrying a load of bundled sticks on his head. He was most feeble and decrepit and staggered at every step, being unable to walk properly. Pitying his plight, the emperor asked members of his party to inquire after the woodcutter's name, and the whereabouts of his domicile. It emerged that the miserable old man, so ravaged and ill-treated at the hands of fate, was also named Qubad. Upon hearing this the emperor marveled greatly, and wondered at finding his namesake in such dire straits. He asked Buzurjmehr, "How do you account for this variance in fortunes? Despite our having the same name, I am the Emperor of the Seven Climes,[62] and he is all but a beggar!" Buzurjmehr answered according to the established codes of his knowledge, "Your Highness and this man were born under the same star, but at the moment of your auspicious birth, the sun and the moon were together in the constellation Aries, while upon his birth they were in Pisces."

Dil-Aaram, who was present there, could not help but remark: "I do not believe in all that, and cannot for a moment subscribe to these notions! It seems that his woman is a slovenly frump, and this poor man is an ignorant simpleton. Otherwise, he would not have fared so ill. He would not have found himself so wretched, and his life in such distress!"

Already virulently set against women, the emperor was incensed by Dil-Aaram's words. He said, "Her words suggest that all our wealth and riches are indebted to her good management! That we rule an empire simply because she has arranged it so! Strip her naked, and let the woodcutter have her! Drive this insolent wench from before our presence this instant!" The imperial orders were carried out the moment they were given. Then and there before thousands of onlookers, Dil-Aaram was dishonored and disgraced. She declared, "I submit to whatever fate ordains!" and then said to the woodcutter, "Take me to your home! God has shown you favor by bestowing upon you a woman such as myself. Offer thanks to the Beneficent Succor that your adverse days are now over, and hard times lie behind you. Do not worry how you shall provide for me, or that in your advanced age you are further encumbered. I shall provide for myself and a thousand others, and earn you honor and acclaim." Upon hearing that, the old woodcutter was very well pleased and took Dil-Aaram to his house.

When they arrived near the house, the woodcutter's wife saw that her man had brought along a fresh blossom. She saw that a new flower had sprouted that day in the woods. Beside her man walked a nubile, *houri*-faced, silver-bosomed, moonlike nymph of a woman. And he took long strides, beside himself with joy. She came out flying like a fiend, and screamed, "Doddering fool! Have you become senile that you bring a rival on my head in my dotage?" Speaking thus she gave the old man such a powerful blow that he fell to the floor in pain, and began thrashing around like a ground-tumbler pigeon.

Dil-Aaram said to the woman:

For nothing do you seethe and rage:
Your husband he is, my father before God;
With solicitudes beset yourself no more
To all anxieties shut your heart.

"O *houri*-faced mistress of chosen virtue! I consider our relationship now as that of mother and daughter! Consider me one among your issue, and give me your scraps to eat. I shall not be a burden on your hearth but a support to you." At Dil-Aaram's words, the old woman relented, and was ashamed of herself and her behavior. She said, "My daughter! I make you the keeper of my life and domestic realm. You are now in charge of everything in this household. Whatever you shall apportion as my share I will graciously accept, and will serve you faithfully."

It was the old man's custom to sell his wood in the bazaar every day for bread. His twelve or thirteen children, who were all blind and handicapped, swarmed over him when he returned home and wolfed down the bread amongst themselves, without the food ever satiating their appetites, or satisfying their hunger. And thus helplessly they had continued in their hapless lot. Dil-Aaram saw this on the first day and kept quiet. But the second day she could no longer contain herself, and said to the woodcutter, "Dear father! Today sell the wood for wheat, and under no circumstances must you buy bread from the bazaar." He replied, "My daughter, I shall do as you say and bring you wheat instead."

That day the woodcutter sold the wood for grain and brought it home to Dil-Aaram. She took it to the neighbor's to grind it and made enough bread from it to suffice them all for three days. The woodcutter's family blessed her, and in the shadow of her benevolence began enjoying life's comforts. With the money saved from two days Dil-Aaram bought wool, strung it into ropes, and gave them to the old man to sell at a nominal price in the bazaar. In the days that followed, it became her custom that she would barter the wheat saved from several days for wool and string it and sell the ropes. In a few days she gradually saved enough money to buy the old man a mule for carting wood from the forest, and asked him not to exert himself so much in his old age. This way, he could fetch ever greater quantities of wood without exhausting himself, and the remainder of the wood would be used for fuel in the house.

To cut a long story short, in a matter of just two years, Dil-Aaram bought some five or six mules and several slaves, and put together enough money from renting them out to buy an estate and houses as well. By this time the circumstances of the woodcutter's household had undergone a complete reversal. Adversity had given way to prosperity. The children were all hale and hearty, and the woodcutter's complexion had improved beyond recognition and he beamed with complacence.

When it was summertime, Dil-Aaram said to the old man, "Ask your slaves not to bring wood into the city from now until the end of summer but to store it instead in some mountain cavern. During the rains and in the winter, they will sell it at a higher price and fetch a better profit." The patriarch did as Dil-Aaram had advised him. And when the rains ended and it was the outbreak of winter, there was a great demand for wood in public baths and other places.

The weather completely changed and the winter started in earnest. One day the emperor returned to the mountainside to hunt. The follow-

ing night it suddenly snowed so hard and became so bitingly cold that
tongues froze inside people's mouths. Their teeth chattered and their
hands and feet did not show from under their garments. There was no
refuge except in cotton or near fire. The emperor's cortege came very
near to dying from frost. They began scouring the forest and plains for
wood and, by chance, they happened upon Qubad's store in the mountain cavern. Their spirits revived upon finding the wood. Color returned
to their cheeks and light to their eyes. They made a great big fire and
began warming themselves, repossessed of their senses and breathing
easily.

In the morning the emperor finished hunting and returned with his
great entourage to the seat of the empire to give audience at court. And
Qubad the woodcutter returned to remove the wood from his cavern, as
was his custom. When he arrived there and found a great heap of coal instead of wood, he was so shocked that he collapsed on the ground clutching his sides, and began lamenting his fate and crying at his ruin.

Once the workings of fortune were brought into play, Qubad's lot
then changed for the better. Fortuitous tidings escorted him into his new
circumstances. As the saying goes, he touched clay and it turned into
gold dust. It turned out that where the wood was stored in the cavern
there was a gold mine. Heated by the fire, the ore melted and gathered in
one place. The old man began excavating the coal. Thinking that the
scorched floor was also coal, he dug it up when underneath he found
some slabs. Not knowing that he had found gold, Qubad loaded up two
mules with coal, threw a few slabs in with it, and brought it all home to
show Dil-Aaram what had happened. There he piled up all the coal before Dil-Aaram and with tears coursing down his face told her the whole
story.

Having reached the end of his story he said, "There were several
stone slabs besides what I found there. I brought home a few lest you not
believe my story, and suspect me of falsehood. Here, you may witness it
with your own eyes! Once you are done with them you could use them as
grating slabs for grinding spices, and perhaps I could even sell them in
the bazaar." When Dil-Aaram scratched a slab with the point of a knife to
see what it was, she discovered it to be gold, and then prostrating herself
before Allah and offering thanks, she declared: "It is His will to raise a
particle to a mountain." Then she said to the woodcutter, "Return immediately with the mules and cart back all the slabs that are there!" The patriarch did as she had bid him and brought home all the gold slabs.

Dil-Aaram then wrote out a note to the goldwright Faisal and, after loading a mule with as many slabs as it could carry, said to Qubad, "Take the mule to Basra and hand this note and these slabs to the goldwright Faisal there, telling him that I send my regards. Just as you are my father, he is my brother before God, and has shown me compassion always. Tell him that I have sent you as my representative and what I desire is written in that note. He will melt these slabs into gold pieces and give them back to you. But be extremely wary along the way of the thieves, thugs, and ruffians and their many lures!"

While Qubad headed for Basra, Dil-Aaram had a large, deep hole dug in the courtyard and buried the rest of the slabs there. Then she sent a slave with a message to the goldsmith Suhail, who sojourned in Ctesiphon, which read, "For several years I was in disfavor with the emperor. Made a plaything of the fickle heavens, I was holed up in a wasteland. But God willing, I shall very soon regain prestige and acclaim at the imperial assemblage. You must immediately come here with craftsmen, masons, laborers, and carpenters, without wasting or idling a single moment. I wish you to supervise the construction of a building in the image of the royal palace. If it is built under your care and is to my liking, I shall forever remember your loyalty and diligent exertion. At present you will defray the expenses that are incurred in the construction of that regal abode, and settle with the laborers; and God willing, I shall reimburse you very soon to the last farthing."

As Suhail put great store in Dil-Aaram's words, he hired skilled masons and accomplished carpenters as soon as he received her message and, presenting himself before Dil-Aaram, said, "I am your obedient servant. I shall perform whatever you command. Speak nothing of money matters now. Whenever God shall redeem you and promote you to high office, He will recompense me, too, and will not be forgetful of me!" Speaking thus, he set to work and laid the foundation of the building at an auspicious hour.

Thousands of masons and workmen and sculptors busied themselves with the construction, and that wasteland bustled with life. Before long God's will manifested itself in that wilderness, and a splendid building was made ready. The borders of all of its gates and walls were painted with portraits of Dil-Aaram and the emperor. Thousands of intoxicating, charming, and delightful images were made by painters of enchanting and alluring skill, and the palace was furnished with such regal trappings and paraphernalia that it became the image of the house of Mani. Choice footmen, guards, soldiers, chamberlains, valets, betel-box bearers, water carriers, mace bearers, and wardrobe attendants were employed. Champions in all disciplines and of all distinctions—jesters, cudgelers, dagger throwers, horse trainers, spearmen, and archers—were sent for from far and wide.

In the meanwhile, Qubad had arrived from Basra with the gold pieces. Dil-Aaram had him sent to the baths. Neither Qubad nor any of his forefathers had seen the inside of a bath in seven generations, and he panicked when the bath attendant began undressing him. Throwing himself at the attendant's feet, he cried out, "Forgive me if in my thoughtlessness I have done you an injury, and for God's sake do not throw me naked into the seething waters of the hothouse!" The bath attendant had a good laugh at the callow man and comforting him, said, "Nothing like what you imagine will happen. Have no fear in that regard! After the bath your body will feel light and clean, and no harm will come to you!" When Qubad was given the waistcloth, he began tying it on his head. In short, he was cleaned and bathed after much trouble and a thousand instructions. Then he was decked out in such a stately robe that, except for the gowns of mighty and imperious monarchs, no one had laid eyes on its equal. Dil-Aaram announced that from then on everyone must call him Qubad the Merchant, and anyone caught calling him a woodcutter would be severely punished and have his tongue extracted through the back of his neck. After a few days Dil-Aaram furnished Qubad with choice gifts and curiosities from all over the world, instructed him in the etiquette and decorum of presenting himself before the nobility and viziers, and sent him to see Buzurjmehr.

By and by Qubad arrived at the ministry. When Buzurjmehr was informed, he had him shown in to his court and greeted him with an embrace. Observing that he was an old man, the vizier treated him with honor and deference, showing him many kindnesses. After the exchange of greetings and words of gratification, Qubad, in accordance with Dil-Aaram's advice, asked permission to wait upon the emperor, and expressed his eagerness to kiss the emperor's feet. Buzurjmehr said, "Very well! I shall mention you to His Imperial Highness today and arrange for an audience commensurate with your station and dignity. Tomorrow is an auspicious day and the emperor shall also be at leisure. Present yourself in the early hours of the morning and you shall be ennobled by waiting upon His Majesty."

Qubad took his leave, returned home, and narrated to Dil-Aaram all that had passed with Buzurjmehr. The next day Dil-Aaram verified from Suhail the goldsmith how the emperor was dressed and appareled. Procuring for Qubad exactly the same dress that Suhail had described, she sent him for his audience with the emperor. Qubad first called on Buzurjmehr, who took him along to the royal court as he had promised. Lodging him in the chamber of audience, Buzurjmehr went forth to have counsel with the emperor, and introduced Qubad to him in most excellent terms. The emperor granted Buzurjmehr's request, allowing Qubad the Merchant to be presented before him.

Now, after a life of cutting and splitting wood, the poor bumpkin knew nothing of the value of royal audience. Therefore, Dil-Aaram had explained to Qubad before he left how he should put his right foot forward in the court of the Shadow of God, and make seven low bows. Qubad soon forgot all about it. But when he laid eyes on the emperor, he suddenly remembered Dil-Aaram's injunction. He collected his feet together and leapt; but slipping on the polished marble floor, landed flat on his ass.

The emperor smiled at this caper, and the courtiers, too, grinned when they noticed their sovereign smiling. Everyone present was greatly amused by Qubad's comical entry, but because he had been presented with Buzurjmehr's reference, they did not dare breathe a word. The emperor accepted Qubad's offering, and as a mark of singular favor, conferred upon him a piece of sugar candy from his own hand. Qubad took the candy and, after making salaam, put it in his mouth thus making his impudence and ill-breeding manifest to everyone assembled there. Buzurjmehr, too, felt greatly embarrassed by his actions.

When the court adjourned Qubad went home and narrated to Dil-Aaram how the emperor had given him the sugar candy and how he bolted it down. Feeling ashamed at his folly, she felt greatly embarrassed in her heart and said to him, "You showed extreme irreverence and impertinence when you ate before the emperor what he had conferred upon you. You should have made an offering upon receiving it, made low bows, and placed it on your head. Then you should have brought it home as a souvenir from the sovereign." Qubad asked, "What must I do so as not to let my ignorance show at court?"

Dil-Aaram replied, "The next time the emperor gives you something, make three low bows and put the gift on your head. And where making offerings is warranted, you must not be unmindful either." Qubad committed these injunctions to memory and the next day again presented himself at the court.

The emperor was having his meal, but as he had found Qubad's antics amusing, he had ordered that the man be announced upon arrival. When the presenter of petitions announced Qubad, the emperor ordered him to be shown in directly. Then, when Qubad presented himself, the emperor accorded him a most uncommon preference by giving him a bowl of curry. Qubad made a low bow upon receiving the bowl and, remembering Dil-Aaram's words, poured it over his head, besmearing not only his clothes, but drenching as well his beard, whiskers, and his whole body with the gravy. The emperor said in his heart, *He is absolutely untouched by manners! His every deed is a marvel of folly. And then he also calls himself a great merchant! Wonders never cease!*

That day Dil-Aaram had asked Qubad to invite the emperor to a banquet, using the good offices of Buzurjmehr. She had told Qubad that if the emperor accepted his invitation it would confer unique honor upon him and bring him prestige to no end. Acting on Dil-Aaram's advice, Qubad mentioned the banquet to the emperor, and recited the verse he had been taught by Dil-Aaram:

> *An emperor's honor would be in no way diminished*
> *If he were to show indulgence to a husbandman as his guest.*

Buzurjmehr, who indulged Qubad, petitioned in his favor, too. The emperor, already amused with Qubad's antics and simple ways, granted his request to appear at the banquet. Qubad returned home joyous and elated and communicated the news to Dil-Aaram, who immediately busied herself with arrangements for the banquet and began providing for the occasion.

OF THE EMPEROR'S ARRIVAL AT QUBAD'S HOUSE AND HIS RESTORING DIL-AARAM TO HONOR, AND OF HIS FEASTING AND DRINKING

When the diligent orderlies of faultless Nature unfurled the bright spread of morn across the heavens, and with great excellence decked them with the golden dish of the world-brightening sun, the emperor, accompanied by Buzurjmehr and his viziers, arrived at the woodcutter's palace. Qubad received him in the approved custom and made an offering.

Thou whose advent is the spring of my welfare!

Having graced the house with his venerable presence, when the emperor looked around he saw portraits of himself and Dil-Aaram staring down at him from every gallery, balcony, and wall. Remembering his courtesan, the emperor expressed great remorse at her loss. Upon discovering that wherever he looked, he found in every niche and corner an exact likeness of the royal palace, the emperor remarked to Buzurjmehr, "This house looks an exact replica of my palace. What a wonderful correspondence and resemblance has been achieved!"

Then the emperor moved to the bejeweled throne in the summerhouse, where the tabla began to play and the dancers to perform. Presently the meal was ordered. The table deckers laid out the spread and the head cook started bringing out all kinds of sweet and savory delights: halva, meats, naan, broiled meat, grated sweet apples, and a variety of fresh and dried fruits laid out in china and celadon bowls. Qubad, as per Dil-Aaram's orders, sent for a jewel-encrusted ewer and basin, and doing the honors of washing the emperor's hands, put choice delicacies before him with his own hand. After the emperor had finished the meal,

Dil-Aaram, appareled exquisitely and dressed in a regal robe, showed a beloved view of herself to the emperor from behind a lattice, and lured the emperor behind the curtain and toward herself. Having caught a glimpse of her, the emperor asked Qubad, "How are you related to the woman behind the lattice and what is her name? She appears to have excellent taste, and to my mind it seems all these preparations are owing to her organization and industry!"

Respectfully folding his arms before him, Qubad responded, "She is your slave's daughter! And all that you see is indeed the fruit of her diligence and industry. There are no personal confidences from the Refuge of the World. If Your Eminence were to grant the women the charity of visiting their quarters, Your Honor's slaves would be most exalted. Your Majesty's slave girl, my daughter, is herself most desirous of audience and eager to wait upon Your Eminence!"

When the emperor went into the women's quarters, from a distance he thought his eyes were deceiving him. And when she approached nearer and made an obeisance, the emperor exclaimed, "What do I see here, Dil-Aaram? Is that you?" Dil-Aaram flung herself at the emperor's feet and began to unburden her heart by way of shedding copious tears. The emperor raised her head and embraced her, and offered her many kind words of consolation.

Dil-Aaram revealed that it was the selfsame woodcutter, Qubad, to whom she had been given away, handed over in utter disgrace. And that by virtue of His Highness's prestige he had risen in the world to be called the Prince of Merchants and was so honored that the Emperor of the World had directed his august and distinction-bestowing feet hither to grace his house with his presence.

The emperor was most embarrassed to hear this and, taking Dil-Aaram by her hand, brought her to the summerhouse. Praising her industry highly, he seated her near the throne.

The emperor invested Qubad with a robe of honor and confirmed him as Prince of Merchants. Then, to show Dil-Aaram his former favor, he asked her to play on the lute. Acquiescing to his wish, Dil-Aaram began strumming on the lute and played it more wondrously than she had ever played before. Intoxicated by her music, even Venus in the heavens began to sway and flutter like a kite. The air became so suffused that all those present were overwhelmed, and transfixed with wonder became frozen like portraits. After Dil-Aaram had finished playing and regaling the emperor, it was the turn of the *bhands, bhagats, kathaks, kashmiris, qawwals, dharis, kalanots,*[63] and courtesans to perform. Some time having passed in these regalements, the emperor invested another robe of honor on Qubad. Then, taking Dil-Aaram alongside him, he repaired to the royal palace. The emperor's misogyny having thus changed into fondness for women, he was royally wedded to his uncle's daughter, Mohtram Bano, before long.

Regarding the Birth of Naushervan and Bakhtak, and Buzurjmehr's Predictions, and of Naushervan's Falling in Love with Mehr-Angez

A year after the emperor's marriage the empress showed signs of expecting a boy, and by God Almighty's grace, when the gestation was over she went into labor. The emperor sent for Buzurjmehr, and informing him that the empress's labor pains had started, asked him to prepare an account of his heir's fortunes and draw the horoscope.

To ascertain the precise moment of birth, Buzurjmehr put Indian, European, Roman, Dutch, and Gaelic clocks before him. Then, after setting an astrolabe[64] to determine the movement of the stars, he sat alert with the dice ready in his hand and the astrological table spread before him, to await the illustrious birth of the emperor's heir. By the grace of the Incomparable Progenitor, a sun of magnificence and prestige, a luminary of grandeur and dignity, the light of the empire's eyes, and the spring of the empire's garden—to wit, a worthy son arrived securely into the midwife's arms under the constellation Aries at an auspicious moment. Buzurjmehr immediately wrote down the time of birth and threw the dice on the astrological table. Then drawing the horoscope, when Buzurjmehr matched the forms, he found the sun and the moon in Aries, and discovered Venus, Jupiter, Mercury, Saturn, and Mars also in auspicious constellations.

Beside himself with joy, Buzurjmehr went to the emperor and recited the verses:

Felicitations on the son of happy omen!
May his friends prosper and his foes perish,
He is the Emperor of the Seven Climes
Illuminator of the Crown and Diadem!

Then Buzurjmehr announced: "This glorious child will grow up to reign over countless kingdoms and realms. He will be just and equitable, and the sovereign of a bountiful land, and shall rule for seventy years with great magnificence and grandeur. However, from the knavery of one of his counselors he will often find himself in dire straits." Having said this Buzurjmehr was about to propose a name, when two *ayyars*[65] presented themselves and pronounced to the emperor: "The chosen spring for royal consumption that had dried up long ago has begun to flow of itself today, and gushes with water." Deeming it a propitious augur, Buzurjmehr named the prince Naushervan.[66] Some chroniclers have written that at the moment of the child's birth the emperor was holding a cup of red wine, and Buzurjmehr said to him in Persian:

Qibla aalam jam ra nosh-o-ravan ba farmayıd
Pray imbibe from the goblet, O Guide of the World!

It is said that the emperor was so pleased at Buzurjmehr's words that he invested him with a robe of honor, and named the prince Naushervan.

The trumpeters were ordered to sound abroad the eminent birth, and the cannoneers to discharge their muskets. Kettledrums were sounded and the fuses of cannons were lit. Shouts of "Congratulations!" and "Salutations!" rose from the Earth and reached the ears of the dwellers of the heavens. The commonality and the elite, the plebeians and the nobles, the attendants and the viziers, all celebrated and exchanged felicitations and benedictions. All the apparatus for amusement and regalement were provided for, and everywhere there was singing and dancing. The old man of the heavens, elated at the birth of this illustrious infant, began playing at the tambourine of the sun and the moon, and every single planet was set to whirling, so enchantingly did Jupiter and Venus dance. The doors of the royal treasury were thrown open, and by the emperor's scattering of wealth, every single beggar was made rich. The subjects were all forgiven a whole year's tribute, and every last household in the empire was visited by prosperity.

On the eleventh day after the birth, even as the emperor was occupied with the festivities, informers brought word that another slave had appeared from his mother's womb into the service of the Prince of the Heavens,[67] for a boy had been born to Alqash's daughter. The emperor turned to Buzurjmehr and said, "It would do well to do away with Alqash's grandson forthwith. If allowed to live, this boy would bestir great evil. If he ever obtained power over you, he would turn against you, and of a certainty would avenge his grandfather's blood. To kill the snake but nurse its young is not the way of the wise! In my view it is seemly to remove this threat. However, I leave the matter to your esteemed opinion, and shall give it precedence over mine!"

Buzurjmehr replied, "No religion ever sanctioned punishing a man before he is guilty of an offense! And it is inadmissible to murder an innocent child!" The emperor said, "I believe that a villain should be destroyed before he causes injury! We must extinguish his existence, or we shall have the foundation of evil laid today. Mark my words, if he lives, it will bode ill for you, and sooner or later you will certainly come to grief at his hands!"

But Buzurjmehr protected the infant and persuaded the emperor against murdering him. Then he took his leave of the emperor and went to Alqash's house. And he named Bakhtiar's son Bakhtak.

When Naushervan reached the age of four years and four months, the emperor put him under Buzurjmehr's care to be educated. A week later, Buzurjmehr arranged for Bakhtak to make an offering to the emperor, and used his good offices to have him appointed the beneficiary of Alqash's estate. Then he began educating Bakhtak alongside Naushervan, and occupied himself in this with equal diligence.

As Naushervan was intelligent and bright, he very soon mastered all the sciences of council: including etymology and syntax, rhetoric, logic, philosophy, letters, mathematics, astrology, geomancy, geometry, astronomy, geography, and history; and he excelled as well in martial sciences, making a name for himself in those fields, too.

It so happened that merchants from China arrived in the city one day. After they had made their offerings to the emperor, they sought permission to call on the prince and make offerings to him, too. The emperor granted them permission to wait on the prince. After the merchants had presented Naushervan with gifts and curiosities and lavished many delicate and wondrous marvels on him, Naushervan desired that they tell him about the emperor of China.

Having discoursed at length about the Chinese emperor, the merchants said, "The emperor of China also has a daughter, Mehr-Angez of name, whose face is like the moon, whose forehead is bright as the sun, and whose bearing is as elegant as a flower's, who is jasmine-bosomed, whose waist is thin as hair, and who is *houri*-like and fairy-limbed. The renown of her beauty has traveled the world from one end to the other.

The whole world dotes on her sovereign grace. Thousands of princes draw water from her love's well, and hundreds of kings sigh after her Venus-like charms."

Love is not engendered by a beautiful aspect alone;
By comely speech, too, it is oftentimes implanted.

These words about Mehr-Angez's charms evoked a passionate longing in Naushervan's heart and the flame of love kindled in the prince's breast for this beloved. His heart pierced by the arrow of love, Naushervan was overcome by passion's potent spell. By degrees his verve and endurance gave way and his patience and composure took their leave. Eating and drinking became things of the past and Naushervan was struck silent. He gave up merriment and society altogether and soliloquized night and day in his heart thinking of her. And sometimes, imagining himself before her, he would passionately intone these verses:

There was a time that in spring time
I would long to hasten outdoors,
My ardor having brought me to the grove
The boisterous morning air would make offerings of flowers.
Together with friends and singing,
Now sweetly laughing, now cavorting,
In life's mead my heart was not a bud unblossomed;
Its splendorous sprouting made flowers transfixed with wonder.
Night and day the cup of delight remained filled
And in the heart every moment a new joy awakened;
I had neither mind for lovely damsels
Nor was I enamoured of some fair mistress's cheeks;
I was a stranger to the winds of grief
And my ears were unacquainted with melancholic strains.
Given to toasting life's pleasures all night
I ever saw my morns melt into eves without a shade of anguish;
Garden walks, the company of friends, and wine were my only employments
And amusement and liberty from sorrow were all the burden of my cares.
Surely there was nothing that clouded my countenance;
The only visions before my eyes being the garden and spring
Ever saluting the Mistress of Delights and in her embrace.
By the heavens I was apportioned a new fate in night and morn:

The winds of love have made me desolate,
Stripped bare of its foliage is the tree of my heart;
Like the autumn leaf, of a sudden it has gained pallor,
The bloom of spring has departed from Delight's flower,
The Bride of Bliss has withdrawn herself from my side,
And the heavens have served me with the company of sorrow instead.
Like a withered flower my head is bowed low
And like the narcissus I look about wide-eyed and astonished;
My vermilion tongue has become thin like a lily petal
And of itself my tunic is become rent; like a bud sprouting to flower,
All laughter is forgotten, no memory remains of the mead
I sit by, my head lowered, like a broken-winged bird,
Like a ringdove I wear gloom's collar around my neck,
And under its shadow, life is become a burden to carry.
A sea of blood issues constantly from my eyes
And only my heart knows what it must endure;
I can bear it no further, oh God, how must I act?
To whom must I tell my grief, and how to allay this pain?
I am fallen into a drowning sea of sorrow
Whose shores are nowhere in sight,
Its every single wave a chain of blight and grief.
And much else that shall befall from fate lies in waiting still;
Now there is no familiar, and none who could afford me succor;
Who but God is my friend and companion in this hour?
How to give it words, and to whom shall I convey this grief?
That night and day I am consumed by love's pyre,
When I breathe flames dart from my tongue.
How much longer can I contain this blaze within?
How much longer must I keep silent and let this fire sear my heart
And burn secretly within and keep my secret sealed?

However much Nausheryan tried to disguise his condition, he was betrayed by his wan appearance, his chapped lips, and the cold sighs flowing from the well of his ailing heart. As his condition began to deteriorate with each passing day, well-wishers declared to the emperor: "We do not know what malady has befallen the prince (from the good fortune of his foes!) that he has stopped eating and drinking altogether. He neither listens to anyone nor speaks his heart and sits by himself transfixed by wonder." Upon hearing this, the emperor became agitated and distraught, and sent Buzurjmehr to inform him of the prince's condition.

Buzurjmehr comforted the emperor and went to see Naushervan. After arranging a private audience with Naushervan, he said to him, "Are you keeping well? What is the reason for the state I find you in? What is it that has weighed you down? Why are you so distressed? You would be well advised to confide in me, so that I may busy myself in finding some cure for it and effecting a remedy!"

Naushervan replied, "Dearest Khvaja! In the first instance you are vizier to my excellent father, and in the second place, my teacher! You are older and wiser and I consider you my guide! Still, considerations of seemliness and propriety forbid me to speak. Revealing the secret would show my error, and decency prevents me from broaching this matter with you, or revealing to you my condition and confiding to you my heartache. And yet, as considerations of modesty must not preclude the statement of truth, I must summon the courage to state that I have become enamored of the daughter of the emperor of China, Princess Mehr-Angez, just from hearing of her charms and never having set eyes on her. Claimed by the arrow of her love, I am fully confident that I shall not survive if I do not wed her. If unrequited in my passion and kept away from this beloved, I will forfeit my life."

As he tried to stifle the soul-searing sigh
His heart caught fire and was set ablaze,
He fell into unceasing stupors from the heat;
In a strange struggle were his soul and his heart locked.

Buzurjmehr said, "My dear Prince! One must not become derelict and let go of one's reason so completely, as it does not behoove the high-minded! One must not take leave of one's senses entirely. What you are out of sorts about, and unnecessarily distressed over, is not something that lies beyond the realm of possibility. For God's sake cast this burden from your heart! Partake of food and drink! Amuse yourself with merry pursuits and pleasures! And in God's name, show some consideration for your tender years before you set yourself to renouncing the world! The beauties of the world would offer their hearts and souls in love to you! Emperors of the world would feel honor in offering to you their daughters' hands! Get a hold on your passion and preserve your self-possession.

Your prospects are not so dire that you should feel that your life is at stake. Set your mind at ease! I shall take charge of this affair myself and fill your cup of longing with the wine of desire!"

Comforted by Buzurjmehr's compassionate words, and with his hopes of union with Mehr-Angez now revived, Naushervan leapt out of his bed. After having a bath and sending for his friends and companions, he changed clothes and sat down to have his meal.

After speaking with Naushervan, Buzurjmehr went to see the emperor and conveyed to his ears the amorous affliction of the prince. The emperor said, "Khvaja, this matter will not be resolved without your agency. Only your wisdom can solve it amicably. The emperor of China is a proud and mighty king, and the monarch of numerous lands and illustrious tribes. Such delicate matters of alliances and unions need the diplomatic offices of august and illustrious men if they are to be brought to fruition. Only a wise and gifted man could unravel these intricate affairs."

Through their mutual counsel it was decided that Buzurjmehr would go with an embassy to the emperor of China, and undertake to arrange Naushervan's marriage to Mehr-Angez by his own agency. Arrangements were made to this effect, and Buzurjmehr proceeded to China at the head of fifty thousand foot soldiers and cavalrymen.

————

Now we return to Bakhtak, who, ever since he had come of age and heard about his grandfather, would daily say to his mother, "Whenever I lay eyes on Buzurjmehr, blood rushes into them; and thinking of my poor grandfather, my heart becomes overcast with grief. I shall remain restless until I have avenged his blood. Once Buzurjmehr is in my snare, he will find no escape. I only wait for the day when he falls into my power!" Bakhtak always spoke ill of Buzurjmehr, and tried to incite Naushervan against him with his slander and by using all he could think of to paint Buzurjmehr as the devil incarnate. But Naushervan always censured and reproved him. Reminding him of Buzurjmehr's kindnesses toward him ever since he was a child, he would tell Bakhtak, "Regard how nobly he treats you, and then see what diabolical aspersions you cast on him. O ungrateful wretch! He is in every way your benefactor. Repent before you find instruction to your detriment in this world and the next. Not only would you lose face before God, you would be made wretched and debased in this world, too!"

Of Buzurjmehr's Journey to China with Troops and Retinue, His Return with Princess Mehr-Angez, and the Nuptials of the Seeker and the Sought

The singers of the pleasure garden of ecstasy and the melodists of the assembly of discourse thus create a rollicking rumpus by playing the dulcimer[68] of delightful verbiage and the lute of enchanting story, and thus warm the nuptial assembly most exquisitely. Having taken leave of his emperor, Khvaja Buzurjmehr proceeded with his retinue in wondrous pomp, state, and grandeur, and traversed league after league, bridging stretch after hazardous stretch, until he entered the frontiers of China. Once he had set foot in the country, the informers of the emperor of China brought their leader news that the prudent vizier of the Emperor of the Seven Concentric Circles[69] had arrived with an embassy from his sovereign, Qubad Kamran, the Emperor of the World.

Upon hearing this news, the emperor of China sent forth his ministers to welcome Khvaja Buzurjmehr, and when the vizier's retinue approached the precincts of the seat of his kingdom, the emperor ordered his sons to go forth with the kings of Scythia and Tartary to welcome their guest and escort them. Upon entering the Hall of Private Audiences, Buzurjmehr made obeisance according to the imperial custom and conveyed the words of fond greetings and happy wishes from his sovereign in a most becoming manner. Then he presented the expensive jewels, horses, elephants, weapons, and artefacts gathered from every corner of the world, which he had brought from his sovereign as offerings for the emperor of China, and placed those souvenirs before him.

The emperor of China was greatly taken with Buzurjmehr's fine manners and refined ways. Most gratified with his gracious address, the emperor invested him with a robe of honor and bestowed immense riches and gold upon Buzurjmehr. It is written that during the first audience alone, he conferred the robe of honor upon Buzurjmehr eleven times and showed him great honor and wonderful preference. For every time that the emperor asked something of Buzurjmehr, he received a becoming answer. When the emperor asked Buzurjmehr the purpose of his visit, he explained the matter in so courteous and refined a manner, that the emperor agreed to Naushervan's marriage with his daughter with all his heart. Indeed he could think of no other reply but to offer his consent, exclaiming with great pride in the court, "It is my good fortune to have such an august son-in-law as Naushervan!"

He then ordered his subjects to commence the preparations for the princess's departure forthwith, and to make sure that her journey to Ctesiphon was not delayed for a moment longer than necessary. To cut a long story short, no sooner were the preparations ordered than Mehr-Angez's entourage was made ready. The emperor placed her in the protection of his worthy sons, Kebaba Chini and Qulaba Chini, at the head of forty thousand Turkish troops, and gave away in her dowry numerous heirlooms and family treasures of gold, jewels, dresses, and fine and rare objects, together with several hundred slave girls, and Turkish, Ethiopian, Scythian, and Tartary slaves.

After a journey of many months, Buzurjmehr arrived near Persia safe and happy, and ordered Mehr-Angez's chaste retinue to settle there for the night. In the morning the commanders organized their respective troops and with great discipline and ceremony the Chinese princes took the dowry and the bridal gifts under their care, and the entourage proceeded toward Ctesiphon. Upon hearing the portentous tidings, the citizenry gathered in droves to see the majestic arrival of the bridal procession. A jubilant and exulting emperor and prince greeted the cavalcade and distributed salver after salver of gold and jewels from Mehr-Angez's litter among the poor, making them wealthy and opulent. They embraced Buzurjmehr with grateful affection, and conferred upon him numerous robes of honor. Imperial arrangements were then set afoot for the nuptials, and at a propitious hour Naushervan was married to Mehr-Angez. All these festivities lasted for a year after the wedding ceremony.

> So magnificent and splendorous were the nuptials
> That commonality and elite alike were satisfied.
> The delivered woman[70] set foot out of doors
> As the bridegroom set out in the starry night:
> His resplendence made the dark night bright

As the bridegroom was the world-illuminating sun.
The beds of roses and tulips and jasmine were blossoming
In the flower beds all over the garden,
That night must needs have preference over the brightest day
For that night was indeed the Shab-e Baraat.[71]
From every corner rose the clamor: "Congratulations!" and "Salutations!"
For the sum total of God's creations had become one in their great joy
And from the wealth scattering over the bridegroom,
The poor of the world became affluent.

It is said that when the emperor gracefully broached with Buzurj-mehr his heart's desire to step down in Naushervan's favor, and sought his vizier's opinion on the decision, Buzurjmehr replied, "You may vacate the throne for him after forty days have passed, and duly celebrate the coronation and appoint an heir apparent. But until then, give the prince into my power to do with him as I see fit, and have no one interfere in this matter!" The emperor acquiesced to Buzurjmehr's wishes with all his heart, and gave him the powers he desired.

Buzurjmehr ordered Naushervan to be shackled and consigned to the jail forthwith, where he remained for forty days. On the forty-first day, pulling a running Naushervan behind his steed, Buzurjmehr brought him to the royal palace and lashed his back with his whip three times so severely that Naushervan cried out from its violence. The burning sun, the flying sand, and these hardships all compounded with this incessant toil and greatly agitated Naushervan. Then Buzurjmehr un-sheathed his sword, and presenting it to Naushervan, lowered his neck and humbly said, "I deserve to be beheaded for this outrage, for such is the punishment for this contumely!" Putting his arms around Buzurj-mehr's neck, Naushervan violently embraced him, and said, "Khwaja! There must be some logic behind what you did, or else you would not have put me through this trial and suffered yourself at my pain!"

According to Buzurjmehr's advice, the emperor stepped down from the throne in Naushervan's favor. He went into seclusion and, in the custom of those renouncing the world, became a recluse. But he enjoined Naushervan again and again before his coronation: "Do not take any step without first consulting Buzurjmehr, and do not heed Bakhtak at all or allow him to have any say in the state affairs, lest the empire slip into the hands of ruin and the sun of your prestige become clouded."

But when Qubad Kamran died two years later, Bakhtak gained influence in Naushervan's court and rose to command great authority. There was no audacity or evil but that wretch had forced Naushervan's hand to commit it, and at Bakhtak's inciting the emperor let loose all manner of grief and injury on his subjects. His trespasses increased to such an extent that he came to be called Naushervan the Tyrant, and word of his injustice and despotism spread far and wide.

One day a convict was brought before Naushervan on the charge of banditry. He was the chief of highway robbers and a most bloodthirsty and consummate rascal who had taken thousands of innocent lives, strung up hundreds, beheaded many, and poisoned and waylaid countless travelers. Naushervan ordered him to be put to the sword. When the executioner arrived to drag him to the execution ground, the convict submitted: "I understand that I shall be killed and awarded my due punishment. But I have a wondrous gift and knowledge that no one in the imperial assemblage has heard of, let alone possesses. If I were to be given forty days' reprieve from death, and besides that grace period the emperor also were to allow me the pleasures of food, wine, and women, I shall impart that knowledge—after forty days have passed—to the one in whom Your Excellency reposes his trust. Then my life would be entirely at your disposal!" Naushervan asked, "What is this knowledge? Is it at all useful?" The convict replied, "I know the language of all beasts, but I am particularly versed in the speech of birds."

Granting him the desired reprieve, Naushervan put the convict under Buzurjmehr's charge. Buzurjmehr provided him a mansion furnished with every last comfort and amenity that he desired, and had it well stocked with food and drink and robes. And there the convict lived in great luxury for forty days and imbibed the nectar of all earthly charms.

On the forty-first day, Buzurjmehr said to the convict, "Now that forty days have passed, instruct me in the language of animals, as you promised." The thief replied, "I am a complete stranger to all learning, and never crossed ways with any kind of knowledge. I am nothing but an idler and an imbecile. But, all praise to the bountiful God and His amazing ways, even His donkeys feast nobly! It was His will to save me from impending doom, and keep me in food and drink most wonderfully, and thus apportion these pleasures to my lot. I craved that luxury and by this ruse my longing was fulfilled. Now I am at your mercy, to be beheaded, lynched, or put to death in any which way you find seemly!"

Buzurjmehr laughed heartily upon hearing his speech, and after securing a pledge from him that he would never again rob or steal, set the man free.

One day Naushervan separated from his hunting party, with only Buzurjmehr and Bakhtak remaining by his side. They came upon two owls perched atop a tree hooting and screeching, and Naushervan asked Buzurjmehr, "What are they deliberating on? What is it that they confer and argue about?" Buzurjmehr replied, "They are discussing the plans for their children's wedding, and argue regarding the settlement. The boy's parent says that he will not give his consent unless the girl's parent agrees to give three wastelands in her daughter's dowry. He says that only then would he let his son marry her; otherwise he will arrange for his son's match elsewhere. The girl's parent replies that if Naushervan were to live and continue in his cruel and audacious ways, he would give Naushervan's whole empire, not just three wastelands, as a bridal gift and fill up the other's skirts of expectancy with more flowers of desire than it could hold!"

Naushervan said, "Now our despotism has become so widespread that the word of our injustice and tyranny has reached even the animals!" Naushervan took warning from this, and shed many a tear of compunction and remorse, feeling ashamed and miserable at his vile deeds. Upon his return he had a bell hung from the Court of Justice fitted out with a chain,[72] and had it proclaimed throughout the country that any petitioner might ring the bell without having himself announced or being routed through mace bearers and functionaries. Thus it became the custom that any petitioner who arrived was meted out justice upon ringing the bell. From that day forward Naushervan's justice became legendary, and to this day he is remembered by the young and old as Naushervan the Just.

But why go into these details! After many years the emperor was blessed with a daughter and two sons from Mehr-Angez, and stars of nobility decorated the sky of his prestige and grandeur. He named his daughter Mehr-Nigar, and his sons Hurmuz and Faramurz. They were raised in the imperial custom and their instruction and education was entrusted to Buzurjmehr's care. Two sons were born to Buzurjmehr. He named the one Daryadil and the other Siyavush, and applied himself to their breeding and supervision. God also sent a son to Bakhtak, who named him Bakhtiarak.

Storytellers relate that one night the emperor had a dream that a jackdaw came flying from the east and flew off with his crown; then a hawk appeared from the west and killed the jackdaw and restored the crown to his head. Naushervan woke up from the dream and in the morning narrated it to Buzurjmehr, then asked for its interpretation. Buzurjmehr said, "Toward the east there is a city called Khaibar. From those regions a prince by the name of Hashsham bin Alqamah Khaibari will rise against Your Highness and wage war against the emperor's armies, causing much turmoil and bloodshed. He will rout the imperial armies and claim Your Highness's crown and throne. Then a youth named Hamza will come from the city of Mecca in the west. He will kill that villain and restore the crown and throne to Your Majesty, and avenge your defeat."

Naushervan became jubilant upon hearing these words, and invested Buzurjmehr with a robe of honor. He then sent him to Mecca to announce that when the boy was born he should be proclaimed the emperor's protégé, and raised with great honor under imperial tutelage.

Carrying numerous gifts, jewels, and riches, Khvaja Buzurjmehr repaired to Mecca to seek out that worthy boy, and went searching for signs of his birth in every house.

OF BUZURJMEHR'S ARRIVAL IN MECCA AND
SEARCHING FOR SIGNS OF HAMZA'S BIRTH, AND OF
THE BIRTH OF HAMZA, MUQBIL, AND AMAR

The gazetteers of miscellanies, tale-bearers of varied annals, the enlightened in the ethereal realms of legend writing, and reckoners of the subtle issues of eloquence thus gallop the noble steed of the pen through the field of composition, and spur on the delightful tale. Arriving near Mecca (the hallowed!) after journeying long and traversing leagues, Khvaja Buzurjmehr sent a missive to Khvaja Abdul Muttalib, chieftain of the Banu Hashim tribe, which read: "This humble servant has come on a pilgrimage to Mecca, and is also desirous of waiting upon you. He hopes to enjoy your audience, and awaits permission to partake of your hospitality."

Khvaja Abdul Muttalib was most pleased to read Buzurjmehr's communiqué, and proceeded, together with all the nobles of Mecca, to welcome Buzurjmehr. He brought him and his cortege into the city, bestowing on them great honor and prestige, and vacated illuminated houses for their stay. Buzurjmehr first went with Khvaja Abdul Muttalib to pay homage to Kaaba.[73] Then he greeted the elite of Mecca with great propriety, and conferred riches and gold pieces on every last one of them.

Buzurjmehr said to them, "The emperor of Persia has sent word that he is very well content with you, and always counts you among his well-wishers. He hopes to remain forever in your prayers, and seeks and prays for your friendly favors and noble gestures." Then, sending for the town crier, he had it announced that the next boy born from that date would be raised in the service of the emperor of Persia; and that as soon as he was born, his parents should bring him to the vizier, that he may be named and bequeathed his legacy from the emperor.

As Buzurjmehr had arrived with a substantial entourage, he had camped outside the city, but he regularly called on Khvaja Abdul Muttalib in the city, and on occasion Khvaja Abdul Muttalib also returned his visits. Some fifteen or twenty days had passed since Buzurjmehr's arrival in Mecca, when on one of his visits, after they had exchanged the customary greetings, Khvaja Abdul Muttalib said to the vizier, "The Eternal God conferred upon me a firstborn; yesterday your slave was blessed with a male issue!"

Buzurjmehr immediately had the boy brought to him, and upon looking at his face, then throwing dice, and drawing the horoscope, he discovered that it was the selfsame boy destined to exact tribute from the emperors of the Seven Climes and conquer the whole world: he who would humble all the great and mighty on Earth and on Mount Qaf;[74] the star of the height of prestige before whom mighty warriors and rulers of the world would make obeisance; the one who would cause the True Faith to flourish and idol worship to be stamped out; and the one who would make tyranny give way to the rule of justice. Buzurjmehr kissed the child's forehead and named him Hamza, and congratulated Khvaja Abdul Muttalib most warmly, and felicitations and salutations were exchanged all around.

Then, Buzurjmehr included, those assembled there turned toward the sanctified Kaaba and offered prayers for Hamza's well-being and benediction, and said their thanks to the Almighty. Buzurjmehr then presented Khvaja Abdul Muttalib with several chests filled with gold pieces and the rarest of garments and robes.

Khvaja Abdul Muttalib was going to offer sherbet to the assembly according to the Arabian custom when Buzurjmehr said, "Wait a while! Let two others arrive, whose boys shall be your son's companions and peers, his devoted mates and supporters, and steadfast friends." Even as Buzurjmehr spoke, Abdul Muttalib's slave Basheer brought in an infant, and said to his master: "Your slave has also been blessed with a son!" Buzurjmehr named the boy Muqbil Vafadar, and conferred a purse of one thousand gold pieces on Basheer, prophesying, "This boy will be an accomplished archer and a peerless marksman and bowman!"

As Basheer was returning home after seeing Buzurjmehr, he crossed paths with the cameleer, Umayya Zamiri. Umayya asked Basheer where he was returning from and how he had come into the purse of gold pieces, and Basheer gave him all the details. Then Umayya went home all excited and happy, and narrated the whole episode to his wife. He said to her, "You keep telling me you are with child; now quickly bear me a son that we may take him to receive gold pieces, and find at last peace and comfort, and begin a life of luxury."

His wife said to him, "Are you mad? Knock some sense into yourself! I am hardly into my seventh month! Heaven forfend I bear the child now! May my enemies go into labor in the seventh month!" Umayya said, "Just begin straining and I am sure the boy will drop! We need him hatched between today and tomorrow. Plenty of good it will do me if he is born two months from now!"

His wife, who had worked herself into a rage, shouted, "The brains of this wretch have gone woolgathering! How wantonly he forces me into labor! O wretch! You do this not out of viciousness, but because you are a prize ass! You would do well to take all your snarling elsewhere!"

In a fit of rage, Umayya kicked her in the abdomen with such violence that she fell to the floor rolling in an ecstasy of pain. The boy burst out of the womb from the impact, and the woman's spasms ended soon afterward.

Umayya quickly wrapped up the infant in the sleeves of his coat, took him to Buzurjmehr, and declared, "Propitious fortune has smiled at your slave and blessed him with a son! I have brought him here to present before you and to give him into imperial tutelage." Khvaja Buzurjmehr laughed when he looked at the boy's face, and turning to Khvaja Abdul Muttalib, remarked, "This boy will be the prince of all tricksters, unsurpassed in cunning, guile, and deceit. Great and mighty kings and champions of the order of Rustam and Nariman will tremble at his mention and soil their pants from fright upon hearing his name. He will take hundreds, nay, thousands of castles all by himself, and will rout great armies all alone. He will be excessively greedy, most insidious, and a consummate perjurer. He will be cruel, tyrannical, and coldhearted, yet he shall prove a trustworthy friend and confidant to Hamza, remaining staunch and steadfast in his fellowship!"

After speaking, Buzurjmehr took him into his arms, and the boy fell to screaming and yelping lustily. To quiet him Buzurjmehr gave him his finger to suck. The boy slipped off the ring from Buzurjmehr's finger into his mouth and fell silent and did not cry anymore. When Buzurjmehr noticed the ring missing from his finger, he searched the pockets of his robe and, not finding it there, remained purposely quiet. When sherbet was brought for everyone, Buzurjmehr put a few drops in the infant's mouth, too, and as he opened his mouth the ring fell out of it. Buzurjmehr picked it up, and remarked jestingly to Khvaja Abdul Muttalib, "This is his first theft, and he has chosen me as his first victim!"

Then Buzurjmehr said, "I name him Amar bil Fatah!" Thereupon he conferred two chests of gold pieces on Umayya, and enjoined him to raise the boy with every care and show great diligence in his instruction and education. Umayya first secured the chests of gold coins, then said, "How can I raise him? How does Your Honor propose that I care for him, when his mother died in childbirth!" Buzurjmehr said to Khvaja Abdul Muttalib, "Hamza's mother died in childbirth too, as did the mothers of these two boys here. It would be best that all three of them stay under your roof. Presently, there shall arrive at your door Aadiya Bano, the mother of Aadi Madi-Karib, whom Prophet Ibrahim has converted to the True Faith in the realm of dreams and sent here to be Hamza's wet nurse. Go forth to greet her and let her nurse Hamza on her right breast, and Muqbil and Amar on her left."

Following Buzurjmehr's advice, Khvaja Abdul Muttalib welcomed Aadiya Bano in the finest traditions of hospitality, offered her sherbet, and had the honor performed of having her hands and feet washed for her. He gave the three boys into her care and appointed her their wet nurse.

When six days had passed after Hamza's birth and he had been bathed, Buzurjmehr said to Khvaja Abdul Muttalib, "Come morning, have Hamza's cradle removed to the roof of your house and do not despair if it goes missing! With his unbounded might, the Maker of the World has created a host of wonderful creatures, and has prescribed to each species a separate abode and a diverse way of life. The inhabited part of the Earth is bounded on all sides by a great sea whose vast expanse is interspersed with populous islands and ports. Beside it lies Mount Qaf, the domain of the dormant folk and the children of Jan, surrounded by numerous colonies of the jinn, *peris, devs, ghols, Shutar-pas, Gao-sars, Gosh-fils, Nim-tans, tasma-pas, Ghur-munhas,* and others. The emperor of those dominions is Shahpal bin Shahrukh, a most dignified and handsome monarch, beautiful as the sun and the moon. His vizier, Abdur Rahman, has no peer or equal in present times. He is just and wise, and moreover prudent, and an administrator of the first magnitude who prays night and day to the Almighty. He will send for Hamza's cradle for his emperor, and have it returned after seven days. Many advantages will be gained from this, and it will serve Hamza's cause and profit him to no end." Then Buzurjmehr took his leave and returned to his encampment, and Khvaja Abdul Muttalib began biding his time in anticipation of the augured moment.

Hamza's Cradle Is Carried Off to Mount Qaf, and That Sun of Excellence Shines on the Mount of Brilliance

The zephyr-paced sojourner, the stylus of fascinating accounts of the expert chroniclers, and the flying arrowhead—to wit, the pen that must detail the messages of intelligencers—also records a few words concerning events on Mount Qaf, and regales those enamored of fables and legends of the past with some choice phrases from this wondrous tale.

One day the sovereign lord and potentate of Mount Qaf, Shahpal bin Shahrukh, was giving audience on King Suleiman's throne at his seat of government with all imperial pomp and majesty and boundless splendor and dignity. In the court were assembled the monarchs who ruled the eighteen realms of Mount Qaf, who paid him allegiance and were his tributaries and feudatories. Numerous lords and nobles from the neighboring lands and regions were paying court and receiving royal audience, when the porter of the harem presented himself, made obeisance, and communicated the propitious tidings that a star of the constellation of blessedness and virtue, and Venus of the skies of rectitude and continence—to wit, a princess, like the Sun in beauty, and in nature the like of Jupiter, had risen forth to shine over the emperor's house by gracing the cradle from her mother's womb.

Emperor Shahpal turned to his vizier, Abdur Rahman—a most eminent jinn who had seen the court of Suleiman and served there, and was a past master of all sciences—and asked him to name the girl, cast her horoscope to see what it foretold, and determine what should be the star of her reputation and dignity. As per his sovereign's wishes, Abdur Rahman named the girl Aasman Peri. Throwing dice, casting the horoscope, relating the shapes together, and rejoicing greatly at what he had deciphered, he conveyed the news to Emperor Shahpal: "My felicitations to

Your Honor! This girl will rule the eighteen realms of Mount Qaf and hold sway over these dominions. But eighteen years from this day, the mighty jinns, who pay vassalage today, shall rise as a body in rebellion. They shall make an insurrection most contumaciously, violate the bounds of obedience and propriety, and show impudence toward Your Highness. With the exception of Gulistan, Irum, Zarrin, Simin, and Qaqum, all cities shall slip out of Your Majesty's control. In those days a human will come from the inhabited quarters of the Earth, and will rout those rebels and inflict upon them a most resounding defeat. And he shall conquer the occupied countries by his might and return them to Your Majesty's rule!"

Emperor Shahpal greatly rejoiced upon hearing these tidings, and thus ecstatic with delight, told Abdur Rahman, "See if that boy has been born yet, and if he has blessed his mother's lap! Of what land is he a native, and of what prestigious constellation is he the luminous star?" Vizier Abdur Rahman cast the dice and said, "In the land of Arabia there is a city called Mecca. He is the son of its chieftain and today is the sixth day since his birth. He has been named Hamza and this day his father has sent his cradle to the roof of his house." The emperor ordered four *perizads* to bring the cradle and forthwith present before him that bliss of rank and dignity to the eyes.

Then the emperor busied himself with the necessary festivities and ordered celebrations at the expense of the royal treasury. The emperor was still occupied in these celebrations when the *perizads* brought Hamza's cradle before him, and solicited rewards for carrying out the royal commission. All those present were amazed and spellbound when they gazed upon Hamza's beauty, and upon setting eyes on his features and graceful airs, the *peris* lost their senses. The emperor lifted Hamza from his cradle, kissed his forehead, and had his eyes lined with the collyrium of Suleiman.[75] Then he sent for the wet nurses and dry nurses and handmaidens, who came bustling upon hearing the summons, and had Hamza nursed by *devs, peris,* jinns, *ghols,* lions, and panthers for seven days.

Khvaja Abdur Rahman then said, "My knowledge of *ramal* tells me that Aasman Peri shall be betrothed to this boy, and the ties of man and wife shall be established between the son of Aadam and the daughter of Jan." The emperor rejoiced at the news, and sent for a cradle from his palace encrusted with various costly jewels, with legs and poles cast of emerald, and the side pieces of ruby. He placed Hamza in it and gently put him to sleep. He hung the cradle with several lustrous carbuncles,[76] woven into red and green silk, and lined it with all sorts of rare and expensive jewels. Then he ordered the *perizads* who had brought him: "Conduct him safely whence you brought him. Then return with the word of his well-being, of what passed on the journey, and the intelligence of that land!"

The *perizads* took Hamza's cradle back to Khvaja Abdul Muttalib's roof. Returned home a short while later, they happily and joyously narrated in great detail to the emperor all they had witnessed on their journey.

The swift-paced traveler of the quill hastens through its journey along
the stretches of the ream, and thus diligently passes the landmarks of this
new history with its digressions, revealing that a week later Buzurjmehr
sent word to Khvaja Abdul Muttalib to inquire if Hamza's cradle had returned from Mount Qaf, and whether or not he had been reunited with
his lost Yusuf.[77] Upon receiving Buzurjmehr's message, Khvaja Ab-dul
Muttalib sent a man to the roof to verify, who was startled upon setting
eyes on the cradle. Blinded from the refulgence of the cradle, everyone
who saw it was transfixed with wonder. Khvaja Abdul Muttalib was informed that Hamza had brought back a cradle the likes of which even the
eyes of Heaven had not seen—a cradle that had brightened up the whole
upper story with its luminance, and caused the whole roof to glimmer
like a trove of jewels and rubies.

Despair not, your lost Yusuf will be restored to you.

A joyous Khvaja Abdul Muttalib immediately sent for Buzurjmehr,
who arrived directly upon receiving the news to procure bliss for his eyes
by gazing upon Hamza.

Then Buzurjmehr said to Abdul Muttalib, "It has been ages since I
last touched the feet of my sovereign, the Shadow of God. God only
knows what has passed with my wife and children in my absence. Now I
am become melancholy and seek the audience of my liege. I am consumed with the desire to set eyes again on my homeland and the reins of
my resolve steer me violently thither. Therefore, I shall beg your leave
now, hoping always to remain in your prayers of benefaction! Pray do not

be neglectful in raising Hamza, Muqbil, and Amar, and apply yourself with due diligence and to the best of your ability in their instruction and education. Whenever you receive a missive from me, pray grace it with a prompt reply, providing detailed answers to all questions asked therein. Proclaim Hamza the protégé of the Emperor of the Seven Climes, and have this fact announced in all regions to all men."

Khwaja Abdul Muttalib acquiesced to these requests with all his heart and soul and wrote out a note of gratitude to Naushervan, and charged Buzurjmehr with its delivery to the emperor. He also requested Buzurjmehr to convey to the emperor his respects, fond greetings, salutations, and benedictions.

Buzurjmehr then returned to Ctesiphon with Khwaja Abdul Muttalib's letter. Arriving in his country after some time, he ennobled himself with the emperor's audience and paid court to him according to the royal custom. He presented Abdul Muttalib's epistle to the emperor and sang his encomiums, highly praising his manners, his exalted rank, and his many kindnesses. Immensely pleased to read the letter, the emperor invested Buzurjmehr with a robe of honor.

One day, many months later, Naushervan was seated on the Throne of Kaikaus,[78] and viziers and nobles of every rank, minor and eminent, men of excellence and men of dignity, were all basking in the glory of his blessed audience. The nobles were standing at their respective stations, and plenipotentiaries from around the world and merchants from the neighboring regions were in attendance at the court. Gazettes from diverse territories and cities were being continuously recited, when the report of the gazetteer from China came to be read out. It brought intelligence that Bahram Gurd, the son of the grand emperor, had been enthroned as the emperor of China and had become the master of crown and power. He had no peer or equal in power and might, and Rustam and Nariman were as feeble crones before him. He could bring the feral elephant to its knees trumpeting in agony with one blow to its skull. The desert lion he considered of even less consequence than a mangy cur. Every champion and warrior swore by his superior mettle. Besides the whole empire of China, several cities had also fallen to his sword, and he had claimed many great and fertile lands with his might. He was loath to submit his due part of the four years' tribute and averse to remitting land taxes to the emperor's auspicious coffers. As his force and might had made him arrogant, he brazenly averred that the Emperor of the Seven Climes would do well to forget about his unpaid debts, but pay him some tribute instead, or else he would devastate and plunder Ctesiphon, and raze every last hut and hovel in the empire to the ground.

Naushervan became greatly alarmed upon hearing this news, and said to Buzurjmehr, "What do you advise we do regarding this menace? We would like to hear your sage counsel and the strategy you suggest." Buzurjmehr replied, "As Bahram Gurd has yet to consolidate his power and resources, I would suggest that you detail some fierce and seasoned warrior from among your royal commanders to apprehend and bring this insurrectionist before Your Highness—or to present Your Majesty with his contumacious and boastful head. For if he were allowed to gain power, it would become exceedingly hard to exterminate him, and he would turn China into a hotbed of rebellion and strife." Naushervan said, "I authorize you to appoint whomever you find worthy of leading this campaign and crushing this recreant!"

Buzurjmehr chose Gustham bin Ashk Zarrin Kafsh Sasani for the task, a renowned commander who was eminent among warriors, and upon whom the emperor conferred a robe of honor. He was sent at the head of twelve thousand fierce and bloodthirsty troops, in the retinue of many valiant lords and ferocious and lionhearted veterans, for the correction and chastisement of Bahram Gurd, the emperor of China. Gustham was under strict orders to exact from Bahram Gurd, in addition to the four years' tribute due in arrears, an offering in the way of a fine. And in the event of the least show of resistance, Gustham was to inflict a humiliating defeat upon him, and bring him to Ctesiphon chained and fettered. Gustham was sternly enjoined not to depart or detract from those commands, and receiving his orders he made obeisance and left for China.

OF AMAR STEALING THE RUBY, AND THE THREE BOYS BEING SENT TO THE ACADEMY

Children on their reed horses gallop about the pages inscribing with ink drops the delightful episodes of Hamza and Amar's time at the academy. It was Aadiya Bano's custom to nurse Hamza on one breast alone and have Muqbil and Amar share the other one, and she had cultivated greater affection for Hamza than the other two boys. But with every passing day Hamza grew thinner and Amar fatter, even though Amar shared with another the breast he sucked on. Everyone wondered why he was fleshier than the other two, and so marvelously rotund and plump.

One night Aadiya Bano started in her sleep and woke up to find Amar sucking the milk from both her breasts with great abandon, having pushed both Hamza and Muqbil from the bed. In the morning she recounted the episode to everyone and said, "This boy will grow up to become an infamous and notorious thief, that such are his deeds at birth and so outrageous his antics!"

After some time when Amar began to crawl on his hands and knees, he made it a custom to go crawling into the vestibules at night after everyone had gone to bed. Slipping away with women's rings and bracelets, or any jewelry he could lay his hands on, he stowed them away in Aadiya Bano's betel box or under her pillow, and quietly went to sleep. In the morning, when people searched for the lost objects, they were recovered from Aadiya Bano's betel box or found under her pillow. They would come to reclaim their things and Aadiya would be most puzzled and embarrassed, but could offer neither any explanation nor voice a suspicion of who could have placed the things there.

One day, without anyone noticing, Amar stole a carbuncle from Hamza's cradle and put it into his mouth. Khvaja Abdul Muttalib was informed that there was one ruby less in the cradle, that it had gone missing from within the house. By chance Khvaja Abdul Muttalib caught a glance of Amar's face, and noticed that one of his cheeks was swollen. He grew even angrier with Aadiya Bano and the attendant maidservants, and calling Amar over, looked to see what had caused the swelling. When he pressed Amar's cheeks, the carbuncle fell out of his mouth. Khvaja Abdul Muttalib exclaimed, "Heaven's mercy! If such are his deeds in infancy, what will he grow up to be? There will be no outrage that he will not commit!"

Amar thus vexed and tormented everyone, and they could only grit their teeth at him and his pranks. When Hamza, Muqbil, and Amar were five years of age, Khvaja Abdul Muttalib sent them to study with a mulla who taught the boys of Banu Hashim and Banu Umayya, and they began going to the academy, as was the custom of the day.

Their Bismillah[79] was performed the first day, and all celebratory rituals were carried out as per tradition. On the second day the mulla began their lessons. Hamza and Muqbil read as the mulla instructed them, but when he said to Amar, "Say *aleph!*" Amar answered, "The Upright and Righteous!" The mulla said, "What kind of a fool are you? I ask you to say *aleph* and you say *the Upright and Righteous*! What is this stupidity?" Amar replied, "I only respond to what you ask. What I understand is what I submit before you. That is, you say *aleph* and I say *the Upright and Righteous*! I see absolutely no ambiguity or the least discrepancy in that! That is, aleph is upright[80] and its numeric value is one.[81] And the person of God, alone and without a partner, is also singular. If what I say is wrong and I speak preposterously, instruct and admonish me and explain how I am wrong, and convince me in some manner how you maintain that God is not One, and that He has an equal, and that there is another besides Him who claims singularity!"

In short, Amar went through the first tablet with much ado, and finally progressed to the second slate with great difficulty. When it was time to learn that aleph is blank, *be* has a dot under it, *te* two dots over it, and *se* three, Amar expressed ever greater wonderment and perplexity, and his mischievous nature found greater play. He would neglect his lessons and while away his time in horseplay. However much the mulla admonished him, Amar paid him no heed. He always made light of the mulla's instruction, and followed his own bidding. Sometimes Amar would say to Hamza, "You are free to waste your time with the mulla and continue with your lessons. But I shall have nothing further to do with it.

I have had enough of this teaching and instruction, and I renounce this learning. I came here to read the primer or do math! A lot I care if aleph happens to be blank; and what concern is it of mine if something has one, two, or three dots!" Such were the roguish, nonsensical remarks that Amar often made.

One evening the mulla called on Khvaja Abdul Muttalib, and after bitterly complaining about Amar, spake thus: "He neither studies nor lets Hamza or anybody else learn anything! If you wish me to continue teaching Hamza, you should give Amar into someone else's care. I refuse to teach this rascal and, if you don't remove him, you might as well recall the other boys too!" Khvaja Abdul Muttalib resolved to send Amar elsewhere, but Hamza would not hear of it; indeed, he began crying at the very mention of such a proposition, and said, "Where Amar goes, I will also go, or else I shall refuse to learn a single letter!" Khvaja Abdul Muttalib found himself helpless, and desisted from separating the boys.

It was the custom that the parents of these young scholars sent food for them to the academy in accordance with what their financial circumstances allowed. One day, as was the routine, the food had arrived from the homes, and was sitting out, arrayed in pots and pans. Except for Amar, who was wide awake, everyone had fallen asleep, including the mulla. Amar bolted down everything he could eat, and hid away the rest under the mulla's gear. When everyone woke up and looked for food, it was nowhere to be found. Famished with hunger the boys began to complain. The mulla said, "Who else could be behind this except Amar? Nobody besides him could even dare think of it!" Amar replied, "Fie! Fie! It reminds me of the proverb in which the master searches for the camel high and low when it is in plain sight in the city. O Master, first conduct a thorough investigation into the matter. The guilty party is the one from whose possession the food is recovered. It will prove it to be his doing, and he will deserve the severest chastisement then!" The mulla said, "Why don't you search for the thief yourself?"

Feigning supreme ignorance, Amar first frisked all the boys most thoroughly. Then he looked this way and that, and began searching under the mulla's mattresses and pillows, and turned all of the mulla's clothes and gear upside down. Then everyone saw the food hidden inside, whereupon Amar immediately raised a great hue and cry, and began shouting and clamoring, "Witness this, O people, how fares Faith when the Kaaba itself becomes the hotbed of Untruth! When a mulla has such vile designs and such a monstrous nature as this great scholar has, what can we expect of the unlettered? Get up, Hamza! Tell your father we shall not study with a thieving mulla, and would much rather remain illiterate. He will be better off sending us to an honest grocer, or ask him to arrange our lessons with a guileless teacher!"

Abashed and embarrassed, the mulla gave Amar a few tight slaps, and when that failed to silence him, dealt him the whip. But Hamza intervened and did not let the mulla have his way with Amar.

The next day, when the mulla and the boys went to sleep in the afternoon, Amar took the mulla's turban to the sweetmeat vendor. He pawned it for five rupees' worth of sweets and stored them in the academy, then curled up in a corner to sleep. When the mulla woke up and saw such a huge amount of sweets, he rejoiced in his heart, but also feared lest it should turn out to be one of Amar's pranks. He inquired of every single boy the occasion for those sweets, and who had brought them, but all of them expressed ignorance as none of them knew the truth.

When the mulla woke up Amar and asked him, Amar replied, "Father brought these sweets as an offering he had pledged. Some acquaintances were also with him, and he thought it improper to wake you up. He left instructions with me to have you say the *fateha*[82] on the sweets when you wake up, and to distribute them; and asked me to keep his share myself." The mulla asked, "In whose name should I say the benediction, and to whom must I apportion the benison?"[83] Amar replied, "In the name—and for the soul—of Baba Shimla!"[84] The mulla said, "What kind of a strange name is that, so odd and confounding?" Amar answered, "The reclusive have such appellations, with which their patron saints address them!" In the end the mulla said the benediction, and gleaning the choice morsels from the top of the bowl partook of them himself. Amar distributed the rest among the boys and also ate some himself.

Now, Amar had laced the inviting *peras*[85] the mulla ate with croton oil, and presently the teacher began experiencing cramps and tenesmus. His stomach began to churn and his bowels to grumble. Stricken with a severe case of diarrhea, he rushed to the toilet every few moments. Soon he was unable even to bear himself to the toilet, and his hands began to shiver and tremble. He groaned, "O Amar! What was in those sweets that has brought me to this?"

Amar replied, "You are so fluent in the primer of insinuation that it has become a refrain in your speech, and as I have myself become well versed in such vile parlance I, too, shall not refrain from this language.[86] All of us here had the sweets, and we did not suffer the least belch or burp. How are we to blame if you have come to this end from eating them? There is always the possibility, as the saying goes, that some consume the eggplant and some are by the eggplant consumed. Or it could be that before I woke up, you incited some boy to bring you some sweets on the sly. You might have eaten them without good faith, or else, with abandon. Baba Shimla is not someone to disrespect, and he does not visit you with a great turmoil of the bowels. But if this is not the cause it must be your greed! Why eat so unrestrainedly as to suffer bad digestion and become sick?"

Hamza discovered Amar's hand in this and sent for buttermilk for the mulla, and having it administered to him, said, "It must be the sugar's warmth that caused your body to become heated. Have this buttermilk and do not give yourself any anxiety!" In the end, the mulla was delivered from unforeseen calamity, and barely escaped with his life.

Some hours then remaining until the close of the day, the mulla sent the boys home. After everyone had left, the mulla also donned his robe and gown and prepared to leave, but he could not find his turban. Giving it up for lost, the mulla wrapped his cummerbund around his head and set out for home. When he approached the sweetmeat shop, the vendor came running out with the mulla's turban and said, "You did not have to insult me by pawning your turban if you wanted to buy sweets from my shop! What is a sum of five rupees that I would not trust you with it, and leave you alone for a week or ten days! Please feel under no obligation to pay. Settle the account whenever you are paid. Consider it your own shop, and always send for any kind of sweets that you feel a fancy for."

The mulla made up a reply, and was obliged to pay him five rupees from his own pocket to ransom his turban. He said in his heart, *Those were the same sweets that Amar made me say the* fateha *on! Very well! Let the night pass! Come morning, it will be Amar and myself, and his back and the whip in my hand!*

Now hear of the next morning when Amar arrived before anybody else had entered the academy. He spread out and tidied up the mulla's mattress, and arranged his cushion and pillows. Then he opened up the primer and began reading it with great engrossment. When the mulla arrived and saw Amar in the academy, he said in his heart, *My terror has plainly overwhelmed him. That is the reason why he arrived before everybody else today. Rather than chastise him, today I must seize the opportunity to show him some indulgence!*

After setting them the lesson for the day, the mulla said to the boys, "I am going to the baths and shall be back presently. Read and learn your lesson while I am away!" The mulla then set out for the baths, having already prepared his hair dye and sent it ahead of him with Amar. On the way Amar found time to mix a *tola*[87] of very fine ground ratsbane into the dye. In the baths, after he had applied the dye, the mulla rinsed it with warm water, and his beard and whiskers were washed away, too, along with the dye.

Then it was with tears of bitter remorse that the mulla washed his face, and was unable to show it around for his shame. The whole day he remained in hiding, and come night, presented himself before Khvaja Abdul Muttalib clad in a burqa.[88] Then unveiling his face before him, and remonstrating and lamenting much, the mulla said to him in a voice choked with tears, "This is what I have been brought to in my old age, at the hands of Amar. In this manner Amar has embarrassed and humiliated me on the last leg of my life! Now I cannot show my face for the shame, and while I am in this state, I must remain hidden from my friends and acquaintances!" The mulla also narrated the episode of the turban and sweetmeats, explaining how Amar had tainted them with the purgative.

Khvaja Abdul Muttalib sent him away after comforting and consoling him, and then he punished Amar and banished him from the house. He then said to Hamza, "I shall be angry with you if I ever hear you mention Amar's name again. Who has ever heard of keeping company with such a rogue and a ruffian? The only gain to be had in the company of such a one is disrepute and coming to a bad end oneself!" But Hamza could not think of parting with Amar and he went without food and drink for two days, going every now and then to the roof to cry his eyes out. When Khvaja Abdul Muttalib learned of this, he found he had no choice but to send for Amar, forgive his conduct, and reunite him with Hamza. Khvaja also wrote a note to the mulla, interceding on Amar's behalf. The mulla forgave Amar, and he was allowed into the academy as before.

One day food was sent to the mulla from a pupil's house. The mulla said to Amar, "Take it to my house, but see that you do not play any tricks on the way, as there is a chicken inside that will fly away if you open the pot, and no matter how hard you tried, you would never be able to catch it!" Amar replied, "What business do I have opening the pot? I am not bitten by a mad dog so that I'd do such a thing! I shall hand it to your wife and bring back a receipt." Speaking thus, Amar set out carrying the tray over his head.

Approaching the mulla's house, Amar found a safe spot and put down the tray. Upon opening the pot he found it full of sweet rice and began salivating with greed. Hungry to begin with, he now sat down with the bowl and ate to his heart's content. Then throwing the remainder before the dogs, he tore off the tray cover and the wrapping cloth, and went forth and knocked on the mulla's door, calling for his wife. When she came to the door, Amar handed her the tray, and said, "The mulla has forbidden you from opening it. He has asked you not to cook anything, and to ask your friends in the neighborhood not to cook anything either, as food will be sent to them from your house today!" That poor woman knew nothing of Amar's treacherous and deceitful ways. She did not cook anything, and kept her two close friends in the neighborhood also from cooking that day.

It so happened that when the mulla finished at the academy, he decided to stop by a friend's house to talk and inquire after his welfare. His friend held him up at his house until quite late, but much as he tried, he could not prevail upon the mulla to have dinner with him, as the latter, in anticipation of the sweet rice waiting for him at home, declined his offer. Obtaining his friend's leave much later, the mulla returned home and said to his wife, "I put you through a lot of trouble today by keeping you waiting for me. Bring whatever you have cooked today, and tell me if you have eaten anything yourself!" His wife replied, "How was I supposed to cook anything today, as you forbade me from cooking yourself. Then you returned home so late, and the two women in the neighborhood I had invited because of you were also kept waiting along with their sons and husbands! Indeed you have shown very little consideration for your guests! However, the food that you sent is here. First send some to our neighbors, and then we can have some ourselves too."

The mulla's heart sank upon hearing this, and he said to himself, *God have mercy! There is more to Amar's prank than meets the eye! I smell something foul in this, and it bodes great mischief!* And sure enough, upon opening the pot, the mulla found it empty. He said in his heart, *Indeed, there is no greater folly than to place trust in one proven false! What came over me that I once again trusted Amar, after he had duped and deceived me so many times before!* That night the mulla's whole family slept on empty stomachs, and when their neighbors heard what had happened, they did likewise.

After scraping together some breakfast in the morning, the mulla went to the academy and asked Amar, "Whatever became of the food that I had sent home with you yesterday?" Amar replied, "I know nothing about any food, but the chicken you sent flew off on the way, after tearing the tray cover and its cloth. I tried my level best, but could not find it anywhere!" The mulla then asked, "Why did you forbid my wife from cooking anything, and when did I ask you to invite the neighbors and put them all through the ordeal of going without food?" Amar replied, "In doing that I was indeed in the wrong!"

At this, the mulla bound Amar's hands and feet and punished him severely. But Hamza again interceded, and begged the mulla to forgive Amar, promising that Amar would never again do such a thing or trouble him in any way. But now Amar swore enmity against the poor mulla, and waited for a chance to even scores with him.

Abu Jahal and Abu Sufyan studied in the same academy. One afternoon, when the boys were asleep and deep in slumber, Amar slipped Abu Jahal's ring from his finger, and sneaking inside the mulla's house, hid it inside the mulla's daughter's betel box. Then he called on the mulla's daughter, and asked her to give him her earring in the mulla's name. Returning to the academy, he slipped the earring onto Abu Jahal's finger, and lay quietly in a corner without stirring.

When the boys woke up and returned to their studies after sprinkling their faces with water and refreshing themselves, the mulla gave a start upon noticing his daughter's earring on Abu Jahal's finger. But he did not challenge him outright, but asked him instead, "How did you come upon the earring on your finger?" Greatly startled himself upon noticing it on his finger, Abu Jahal became frightened and replied, "I cannot say who slipped the ring onto my finger!" Thereupon Amar interjected, saying, "Ask me, respected master, for I know all too well, and have become privy to this secret. Ask me, although propriety requires that I hold my tongue!" The mulla said, "I bid you speak!"

Upon that Amar said, "In the afternoon when yourself and the boys go to sleep, Abu Jahal visits your house, then retraces his steps and sneaks back inside. It was his ill luck that just when he was stealing out today, I woke up and quietly followed him. Upon arriving at your house he shook the door chain and your daughter came running out. They first exchanged kisses, arranged future trysts, and then indulged in loving prattle. When they parted, Abu Jahal gave her his ring and himself took her earring. I returned after witnessing the whole episode and pretended to be asleep."

When he heard these words, blood rushed to the mulla's eyes. He snatched the earring from Abu Jahal and, spreading him on the floor on his face and securing his limbs, gave him such an unmerciful thrashing that Abu Jahal forgot he had ever partaken of any comfort since the day he was born. Fuming, the mulla then went home, and told his daughter to bring out her betel box. When the mulla looked inside, he found Abu Jahal's ring put away very securely. Immediately upon discovering the ring, the mulla lay violent hands upon his daughter and, seizing her by her hair, slapped her rosy cheeks black and blue until the girl cried out in pain and fainted. Her mother came rushing to her rescue, shouting abuses at the mulla at the top of her voice: "What has come over you? What devil has taken possession of you that you are bent upon murdering her? What is her crime, in God's name?" She then landed a powerful blow to the mulla's back with her clenched fists, and the mulla let go of his daughter and turned upon his wife. Soon the mulla was pulling at her plaits and she was hanging from his beard.

The racket reached even the neighbors, who came running upon hearing the rumpus, and demanded of the mulla, "Who has instructed you in molesting a woman? Who is the teacher of this violent practice? Show us the book that commands that a man beat his wife! Give us the source from which you draw this authority!" In the end the neighbors intervened between the mulla and his wife, after heaping many rebukes on his head and severely remonstrating with him for assaulting his wife.

The next day being a Friday, the boys had a holiday and they were busy in recreation and play. Amar had an idea, and he went to the haberdasher's shop and said to him, "Your wife is on her death bed, and I have come to inform you at the pleading of your family!" Immediately upon hearing this, the haberdasher rushed home, crying and lamenting and pulling at his beard.

Amar accompanied him a short distance, then retraced his steps to the haberdasher's shop, and said to his apprentice, "Your master has sent for the large box of needles. He has a buyer willing to pay a good price for them. As your master cannot come himself, he sent me in his stead. But it is entirely your decision whether or not you wish to trust me with the goods!" The apprentice looked at Amar's face and, thinking that he looked truthful, not like one who would cheat or deceive him, handed Amar the box of needles. Amar headed straight for the academy and, finding the place to himself, riddled the mulla's bed and bedding with the needles, and went home.

As the mulla and his wife had quarreled that day and come to blows, the whole house was in turmoil, and nothing had been cooked. Estranged from his wife, the mulla headed for the academy and spread out his mattress, resolved to keep away from his wife and home and spend the night at the academy. The moment he set foot on the mattress, needles pricked the soles of his feet. Screaming with pain, the mulla sank onto the mattress. The needles now bore into his rear, piercing him painfully. As he lay down to allay his anguish, his back and stomach were all run through, and he began rolling about in fits of agony and his whole body swelled up like a crocodile's. As the children were away on holiday, there was no one in the academy who could remove the needles from the mulla's body and deliver him from his pain and distress. His whole body became like a sieve, and blood oozed out from every single pore.

When the pupils arrived on Saturday, they found the mulla groaning and rolling on the floor like a fish out of water and spread out all pale and withered. They began plucking the needles out, and they had a hard time of it with the mulla screaming loudly every time one was removed and becoming inconsolable with pain. Meanwhile, Amar arrived at the academy late on purpose, and set up crying loudly upon finding the mulla in such a state. Swearing most solemnly, he declared, "If I ever find out who has done this to my master, I will inflict a similar fate upon him and avenge him for what he has done to my dear teacher!" Then Amar called for a litter, and had the mulla carried on it to the surgeon's.

When the litter passed by the haberdasher's shop, the shopkeeper recognized Amar, and came rushing out, saying, "O vile boy! Indeed you are a wanton seditionist and a great fomenter of mischief! Duping me and sending me home by claiming my wife to be on her last breath, you cheated my apprentice in my name, and made away with the box of needles! But now I have caught you. I shall not rest until I have made mincemeat of you and taught you a good lesson for your trickery—and recovered my goods!" The mulla pricked up his ears when he heard mention of the needles, and asked the peddler, "When did he make away with your box of needles?"

Realizing that the secret would be out before long, Amar gave them both the slip, and returned to the academy posthaste. Addressing Hamza and Muqbil, he said, "So long, my friends! My time is up as this city has become too small for me!" Hamza became agitated when Amar spoke of parting, as he could not think of a life separated from his friend. He asked, "What is the matter? Tell me verily why you look so pale with worry!" Amar said, "I cannot at present make answer, as I am not in command of my faculties. But I will convey the entire story to your blessed ears and narrate to you in detail the account of my misfortunes, when I am a little more composed!"

Hamza said, "Come, take us where you will, as I shall be miserable without you! I pledge my lot with you this moment, even though I am all too familiar with you and your pranks!" Hamza, Muqbil, and other boys who had become attached to Hamza, followed trembling with fear in Amar's train, casting terrified glances at every step, with their hearts in their mouths. Amar brought them to a pass in the hills of Abu Qubais where they hid for a night and a day.

After they had gone hungry for a whole day, Hamza said to Amar, "Now we are consumed with hunger and dying of starvation. We must look around for something that we may eat or drink and satisfy our hunger." Amar replied, "This humble servant shall procure food and drink. While I am gone, pass the time by conversing with each other, and wait and see what wonderful delicacies I shall provide for you in this wasteland!"

Thus having spoken, Amar went into the town, and bought a length of clean intestine from the butcher. Then he headed for the dunghill in the backyard of an old woman's house, where her pullets were pecking. Amar tied a knot on one end of the intestine and threw it on the dunghill. When a pullet swallowed it, Amar blew into the intestine from the other end and it inflated and choked the bird. Then Amar quickly slaughtered it, and wrapped it in a kerchief.

In this manner Amar had caught some fifteen or sixteen pullets, when he began to think of stealing something else. He showered a hail of stones on the old woman's roof and then lay in wait. Frightened by that barrage of stones, the terrified crone rushed out shouting and screaming from the front entrance, and Amar sneaked into her house by the back door and began looking around. He stole some eggs lying there in a pot, then headed out.

Farther down the road was a kebab shop where Amar had the chickens roasted and a *khagina*[89] made of the eggs. He also bought five rupees' worth of *shir-maals*[90] and *nihari*.[91] After putting all the food on a tray, securing it with a cloth and placing it on his head, Amar asked the kebabist to send a man with him to Khwaja Abdul Muttalib's house, and told him that he would be paid for the food there, as it was meant for a banquet that Khwaja Abdul Muttalib had arranged for his friends. When the kebabist heard Khwaja Abdul Muttalib's name, he did not question Amar, and accompanied his man with Amar to collect the payment.

After they had gone a little way, Amar said to the man, "Go ahead and wait for me at Khwaja Abdul Muttalib's guesthouse. I shall be there soon after I buy some cheese, and will pay you for your trouble!" The man headed toward Khvaja Abdul Muttalib's house, and Amar for the hills of Abu Qubais.

When Amar returned to his companions, they marveled greatly at the package of food that he put before them. Tearing its cloth open in their hunger, they found it full of delicious food. Hamza in particular was delighted to see the *shir-maals*, the roast chicken, and the *khagina*, and knowing Amar's trickery all too well, asked him, "First of all, tell us with what ruse you came into all this food, and what fraud and trickery did you work this time?" Amar replied, "Eat first and talk later! First have the food and then ask me what you may!" Thereupon Hamza and all his companions fell upon the food.

In the meanwhile, the man sent by the kebabist arrived at Khvaja Abdul Muttalib's house and said, "My master has sent this humble servant with his respectful regards to request of you the payment for the five rupees' worth of *shir-maals* that you had sent for by Amar!" Now, the mulla had already arrived and detailed his woes, and a bewildered Khvaja Abdul Muttalib was listening to the kebabist's man when suddenly crying and wailing was heard, and the old woman presented herself. She petitioned Khvaja Abdul Muttalib: "Oh, poor me! With what treachery Amar deprived me of my chickens and eggs, and in so foul a manner tricked an invalid old widow like myself!"

Khvaja Abdul Muttalib now asked the kebabist's man, "Did you see where Amar went?" He replied, "I saw him heading toward the hills of Abu Qubais shuffling furtively."

Khvaja Abdul Muttalib paid him the five rupees, compensated the old widow, too, for her eggs and chickens, and said to the mulla, "I ask that you take the trouble to go to the hills of Abu Qubais with your pupils to apprehend Amar and bring him before me!"

His ill luck drove the mulla to lead his pupils to the hills of Abu Qubais to catch Amar. When they drew near the hilly pass, Amar roared with laughter upon espying them in the distance, and said to Hamza, "Here comes the mulla with his novices to catch us! They will have Hell to pay for this, and I will send them home in such a sorry state that their own mothers will not recognize them!" Overhearing this, the mulla stopped in his tracks, but urged Abu Jahal and Abu Sufyan and some others to go forward and capture Amar, shouting commands at them from a safe distance.

When Abu Jahal and the other boys closed in upon them, Amar cried out, "Do not call this calamity upon your heads! The mulla is indeed insane, but what rabid dog has bitten you that you wish to sell your lives at such a bargain? It would be best for you to return in one piece to your folks!" But Abu Jahal was never one to heed a warning. He mustered his courage and went forward. When he came close, Amar let fly a barrage of pebbles at him with such violence that his whole face was cut and bruised, and the sharp points of the pebbles lacerated Abu Jahal's whole body. Those pebbles were the devil's own pellets! They pierced Abu Jahal's forehead and cheeks and pockmarked his face like a sieve. Rubbing his eyes and screaming with pain, Abu Jahal turned tail. And when they saw Abu Jahal's state, the other boys dared not take a step forward either.

The mulla, imagining that Amar would give up in terror if he saw him coming, went boldly ahead. But as soon as he drew close, Amar hurled a stone at the man with such savage fury that it broke open his head and a stream of blood came gushing out from his wound, blinding him and rendering him unable to go forward a single step. Finding his business done there, the mulla also beat a retreat and headed back to town drenched in blood. He went straight to Khvaja Abdul Muttalib's house and showed him Abu Jahal's face and the state he himself was in. He recounted the whole episode, and said, "I have had enough of teaching and educating Amar, as he makes me wonderful recompense for all my pains!"

Upon hearing this, Khvaja Abdul Muttalib himself rode out to the hills of Abu Qubais, and headed to the spot where the mulla had told him the boys were hiding. Amar recognized Khvaja Abdul Muttalib from far away, and said to Hamza, "I see Khvaja Abdul Muttalib coming, and over him I have no power! There is no knowing what punishment he will mete out, if he finds me. I remain true to you, but now I must go my way and leave you to your own devices!" Arriving at the pass, Khvaja Abdul Muttalib did not find Amar. He sent Muqbil and the other boys to their homes escorted by his slave and consoled and comforted Hamza. Then seating the boy on his camel, Khvaja Abdul Muttalib returned home, his mission fulfilled.

Once they were home, he said to Hamza, "Now beware and take heed from this event! Never must you utter Amar's name again! Never, ever invite him to your house! Boys from good homes do not mingle with such vicious liars and cheats; they avoid such low company. He will lead you on the path of wrong and evil. He will earn you a bad name, and sully the honor of your forefathers!"

But when was Hamza ever comforted or consoled without his friend? He began to sob most uncontrollably and, no matter how hard Khvaja Abdul Muttalib tried to reason with him or explain things, Hamza made no answer and sealed his lips, and did not touch food or drink for seven days. When seven days passed in this state that neither a morsel of food nor a droplet of water had found its way into Hamza's mouth, Abdul Muttalib panicked. Worried that his son might forfeit his life over a trifle, he was forced to send people to look for Amar and bring him back.

But at the same time, Khvaja Abdul Muttalib also enjoined Hamza, "Never must you follow Amar's bidding, my son! And never again lend your ears to what that rascal says. If you feel the need for recreation, visit our gardens and amuse yourself there. But never, oh never must you venture into someone else's garden. And remember to adhere strictly to my words!"

OF AMAR LEADING HAMZA INTO THE NEIGHBOR'S GARDEN, AND OF AMAR STEALING DATES AND HAMZA PULLING DOWN THREE TREES

I persuaded him to venture into the garden by the lure
Of visiting the grove where nightingales sang their welcome.[92]

One day Amar persuaded Hamza to visit the garden and take a walk in the grove. At Amar's incitement, Hamza took him and Muqbil to his garden, and they were soon happily engrossed in the scenery. From there Amar sneaked into a neighbor's garden. He came back after having his fill of the fruits and delicacies, and said, "My lords! There is such a paradisiacal garden close by, before which the blooming splendor of this garden is reduced to an image of autumn!" Hamza asked him, "Where is this garden of which you speak, and how far away?" Amar replied, "Right close by your own!"

With Muqbil and Amar alongside him, Hamza headed there. By and by, when they reached the garden, they indeed found its flower beds blossoming with a dense growth of all sorts of lovely flowers. Rivulets ran along the garden and it was adorned with flowerpots and planting beds. There were also some date palms laden with fruit so luscious that the moment one set eyes on them, one began salivating with greed, and forgot the taste of all fruits of the world, desirous of tasting only this particular fruit. In the nave of the garden was a beautiful marble terrace so bright and smooth that it did not afford a rest to the eyes.

Hamza sat down there and occupied himself with admiring the scenery, while Amar went around, climbing over the trees and stealing fruit. Presently he returned with his hands and mouth full of dates. Hamza said to him, "Let me have some, too, that I may also taste and enjoy these delicious dates!" Amar replied, "Sit quietly! Why must I give you a single fruit, and not eat all of them myself, after all the trouble I have undergone in picking them, climbing trees and imperiling my neck? If you are so consumed with greed, here is the tree. Come and help yourself!"

As Hamza got up to climb the tree, Amar chided him, and said, "Such labors become thin people like your humble servant! Fat people are well advised not to climb trees! If I had a physique like yours, I would have pulled down this tree from its very roots!" Hamza felt the challenge in Amar's words, and he dealt a blow to the tree in his rage. It broke from the base, and came crashing down. Amar said, "What is so great about bringing down a sapling of a tree like this one? Even a weakling like me could have brought it down and proven my strength. It is no great show of strength to fell such a cankerous plant that would have fallen of its own accord!"

Upon hearing that, Hamza grew even more furious and pulled out a second tree from its roots. Amar said, "Now, this is what I call a proper tree! However, the real test of strength would be to fell that big, strong, firmly rooted tree over yonder. That would indeed be a manly feat, and would prove your mettle beyond a shadow of a doubt!" In his anger Hamza felled that tree as well. At this point, Amar said, "O Arab! What has come over you? Why are you set upon destroying someone else's property? Have you no fear of God? What is this arrogant pride in your strength that makes you forget all other considerations?"

Amar then ran to inform the garden's owner. He also called the gardener over, saying to him, "A while ago such a strong storm blew that it brought down three of your trees. First it snapped some branches and then in one swoop laid down three trees." The gardener said, "There was hardly enough wind here to stir a leaf, let alone bring down trees! Nor do I see a single flower or fruit fallen on the ground to believe what you say." Amar replied, "Do not take my word for it. Go and see for yourself! Then you will know whether I speak true or false. Once you are in the garden, you can judge for yourself the veracity or fabrication of my words."

When the gardener went over to investigate, he did find three trees, the pride of his garden, lying on the ground. He began to cry and lament loudly, as he earned his bread from selling the fruit from those trees, and the subsistence of his whole family depended on them. Hamza took pity on the gardener, and comforted and consoled him by promising to give him three camels in lieu of the three trees. He immediately sent a man to bring the camels. Beside himself with joy, the gardener blessed Hamza from his heart, and the withered sapling of his hope became green again with foliage.

But Amar said to the gardener, "Do not for a moment think that you can dupe boys and trick them into parting with camels! Or do you believe that I would allow you to benefit from this arrangement, and let you have a moment's peace until you have shared the spoils with me? O ye unbridled camel! You will have Hell to pay for this mischief!" The gardener was frightened out of his wits by Amar's dark and ominous threats, and gave one of the camels to Amar. Then he went his way with the other two, thanking Heaven for his deliverance from that devilish boy.

Of Hamza, Muqbil, and Amar Becoming Blessed and Acquiring Occult Gifts

The fingers of ancient scribes straddle the provident dark reed, galloping their mount in the sphere of rhetoric, and in this enchanting wise, speed the fleet gray steed of the pen in the domains of the page. One day Hamza was seated with his friends Muqbil and Amar in the vestibule of his mansion, along with their companions and acquaintances, when Hamza noticed a stream of people heading in one direction. Regarding this activity, Hamza said to Amar, "Find out where these people are going in droves, and make haste to return and tell me what it is that attracts them!" Amar brought news that there were horses on display in a merchants' caravan. The people had gone to see the animals and to freely indulge in the display. And if Hamza so desired they, too, could join them and view the steeds on show. When he heard of an exhibit of horses, Hamza was resolved to go and, in their eagerness, the three friends set out on foot. Upon arriving there they found horses of fine breeds—Turkic, European, Arab, Najdi, Hindi, Cape Vella, and so forth—tied to posts at short distances from one another.

Also in that caravan was a stallion, heavily restrained with chains instead of ropes, with a muzzle over its face and blinders on its eyes, and secured with iron shackles instead of front and heel ropes. Housed inside a pavilion, the charger stood fierce and proud like a lion.

Amar made contact with the horse's owner and asked, "What is this horse's crime that you have chained and fettered him thus?" The merchant replied, "This horse is a great biter, and has all five vices[93] defined in the sharia.[94] Nobody can go near him, let alone mount him. He is fed with the muzzle on, and eats and drinks with much ado!" Amar said,

"This is all stuff and nonsense! What senseless talk is this that nobody can mount this horse. A great lot of fuss you make over this animal! Tell me what you wish to wager for someone to ride this horse." The man answered, "I have tested and tried the mettle of everyone here to my contentment, and find no one around here man enough to ride him. If someone could mount this horse and manage him even a few paces I would present him with this horse worth thousands and never ask for a farthing!" When he heard that, Amar made him pledge the offer in the presence of some neighboring merchants, and made them witnesses to the wager. Then Amar returned to Hamza and repeated the terms of the wager to him, inciting him to ride the horse.

Hamza went forth to have the horse saddled and brought to the grounds with its fetters and blinders removed. The unchained beast began to display its vile temper the moment Hamza put his hands on its mane with the intention of mounting him. He reared and clawed the air with his forelegs. But Hamza closed in and with one leap seated himself upon the animal's back. The horse nipped Hamza's leg, bucked, lurched sideways, and kicked his hindlegs into the air. Then Hamza landed such a powerful blow to the horse's head that he was beset with agony and became bereft of his wits. His ears drooped like a goat's, and sweat poured from every pore on his hide. Hamza pulled him together and made him amble, then trot, then break into a gallop. As Hamza pressed him under his thighs and sat firmly, the horse got his second wind. As he was a headstrong stallion, no matter how much Hamza tried to rein him in, the beast could not be controlled, and he bolted and ran at a gallop for fifty leagues. Finally, Hamza weighted himself down in the saddle and broke the horse's back in retribution for his wickedness and malevolence. The horse collapsed to his death, and Hamza turned homeward. As he was not used to traveling on foot, and his legs were not familiar with such an arduous march, the soles of his feet got blistered and imperiled his safe return home. He tried to lift his feet but they failed him. Exhausted, Hamza sat down to rest under a tree.

Presently he espied an approaching rider, his face veiled, leading a parti-colored horse adorned with a jewel-encrusted saddle.

If one were to write down the praise of that steed,
His speed would be attributed to the zephyr, his color to red wine;
The charger of the heavens is not fleeter,
The zephyr itself that horse outpaces.

As he drew nearer, the veiled rider greeted Hamza and said to him, "O Hamza! This horse here is the mount of Prophet Ishaq (may the blessings of God be upon him!), and answers to the name of Siyah Qitas. He has properties of the zephyr, and at God's bidding I have brought him to be your mount. As it is ordained by the Omnipotent One, I make you my favored one, and pronounce this blessing that no warrior will ever overcome you, and the height of your prestige shall forever remain ascendant over your opponent's. The might of your arm will bring them all low, and they will pay you the court of allegiance. Remove that stone standing on the heap over yonder, and dig into the earth underneath. It will reveal a chest containing the arms and armor of the prophets. You shall find therein an endless array of choice weapons. Decorate yourself with them, and test their mettle when the occasion presents itself!"

Hamza directly removed the stone and doing so discovered such power and force in his limbs that he had never suspected himself of possessing even a fourth part of it. He removed the earth, and upon uncovering the reliquary, found within the vest of Ismail, the helmet of Hud, the chain mail of Daud, the arm guard of Yusuf, the ankle guards of Saleh, the cummerbund and dagger of Rustam, the swords Samsam and Qumqam of Barkhia, the shield of Garshasp, the mace of Sam bin Nariman, the scimitar of Sohrab, and the lance of Nuh. Hamza took them out, and dressed and decorated himself with these arms and armor, pronounced the name of the Almighty, and mounted Siyah Qitas.

Mounted on that great ambler, it was proclaimed,
He was like a jewel mounted on the ring of the saddle!

The veiled one was gone within the blink of an eye, and had vanished from Hamza's sight. It is recorded that the veiled ancient was none other than the angel Jibrail (may the blessings of God be upon him!) who assisted and succored Hamza that instant (God alone is the perceiver of the truth!). Then Hamza turned the reins of his mount toward Mecca, and took himself to his mansion.

Now we turn to Amar, who followed Hamza on foot for ten leagues and did not let up but kept him within sight. When the soles of his feet became as porous as a beehive from acacia thorns, he could carry on no longer, and collapsed unconscious under a tree. As per God's decree, the prophet Khizr reached his side, and offered him words of encouragement and solace. He lifted Amar from where he lay on the ground, and made him his favored one.

Then Khizr declared: "Rise, O Amar! I bless you by the command of Allah, and declare that no one shall outpace you in this world!" With this proclamation, Prophet Khizr vanished; God alone knows whence he disappeared. Amar got to his feet and, in order to test the veracity of what Khizr had pronounced and discover its truth, sprinted a short distance. He learned that he could indeed run swifter than the wind itself, and that it was impossible even for the speed of thought to best him. He prostrated himself to say thanks to the Almighty, and set out in search of Hamza in the direction he had seen him disappear.

He had gone but a few paces when he saw Hamza coming. Both friends expressing joy at their reunion, they recounted the hardships they had faced in their respective adventures. Amar marveled greatly at the horse and armor, and said to Hamza, "O Arab! What did you make of that merchant's horse? Tell me verily, whom did you waylay to come into this horse and armor?"

Hamza replied, "Indulging in purposeless talk is your vocation. As to murdering people, it is an office best suited to the likes of you! God has ordained that I be blessed by the angel Jibrail and inherit the arms and armor of prophets! This horse named Siyah Qitas was the mount of the prophet Ishaq, and the arms and armor you see are the belongings of the prophets that are a gift from God!" Amar said, "I would believe your word as true, and hold you in earnest, if your horse would outrace me and I lagged behind even a single step!"

Hamza thought Amar deliberately talked nonsense, or was speaking like a buffoon as was his wont. For how could a human ever run beside such a horse as this! What power did a mortal have to outpace such a steed? He then said to Amar, "Here! Come show me how you fare alongside my horse." Amar replied, "First wager something that I may derive some consolation from it." Hamza said, "Make any wager that you wish!"

Upon that Amar said, "If I get ahead of your horse, I shall win ten camels from you; and if the horse outpaces me, my father will graze your father's herd of camels for a whole year free of charge and all recompense!" Hamza accepted the wager and spurred on the horse, and Amar, too, set off. They both raced for ten leagues, disconcerting the wind with their swiftness, and remained shoulder to shoulder and head to head. Hamza was amazed at Amar's speed and marveled greatly. Amar then admitted, "Hear this, O Hamza, that I, too, have been blessed by Prophet Khizr and made his favored one!"

Now let us hear what passed with Khvaja Abdul Muttalib when the merchant's horse ran away with Hamza in the saddle, and after Amar had gone in his pursuit. The news was communicated to him in its entirety, and upon hearing it he became very agitated. Along with the notables of Mecca he had left the city to join in the search, and had gone only a few steps when he saw Hamza approaching in the distance astride Siyah Qitas with Amar alongside him, holding the saddle ropes. Hamza was sporting regal accoutrements and wearing a helmet and body armor. Signs of eminence and grandeur were manifest on his august and glorious forehead, and his face shone with happiness and bliss.

Beholding this sight, the grief on Khvaja Abdul Muttalib's face and his dejection at Hamza's feared loss gave way. He beamed with ruddiness of delight from the rush of blood to his face, and prostrated himself before God in gratitude. Hamza dismounted at Khvaja's sight and, making obeisance, kissed his feet. Khvaja Abdul Muttalib embraced Hamza with tears of joy coursing down his face. The entire search party returned homeward jubilant and happy, offering many thanks at Hamza's safe return. Khvaja Abdul Muttalib also made many sacrifices in Hamza's name and, with his scattering of alms, the cup of desire of beggars and mendicants was filled to the brim. Then Khvaja questioned Hamza about the horse and armor, and was delighted when Hamza provided him with all the particulars, and then he offered many more thanks to the True Benefactor.

———

Now listen to the story of Muqbil Vafadar, and hear of the fidelity of that faithful one. When Muqbil heard that Hamza and Amar had been blessed and proclaimed favored ones of the angel Jibrail and the prophet Khizr (may God bless their souls), and had become elected among mortals by the grace of God Almighty, he said in his heart, *Now I cannot possibly hope to prevail alongside these favored personages. They are now invested with high aims and lofty ambitions, and poor me, I could not pass muster in their company. It would be best to offer myself into Emperor Naushervan's service and become his courtier. God willing, I shall secure some honorable post and become esteemed and creditable. My slumbering fortunes may revive, and my lot shall change for the better. In Naushervan's court everyone is worthy of respect, and in the emperor's service, all are equals and coevals!*

Engrossed in these vain reveries and absurd fancies, Muqbil set out toward Ctesiphon. He had barely gone some five leagues when he sat down under a tree from exhaustion, and said to himself, *Death is far better a prospect than a life such as mine! It is better to give up my life than to continue in this wretched existence, with neither a farthing for traveling provisions, nor a mount for transport. What an utterly disgraceful state is mine!* Giving in to despair, Muqbil climbed up the tree and tied one end of his cummerbund to a branch. Then making a noose of the other end and putting it around his neck, he let himself go, and his limbs began to flail from suffocation.

The avis of his soul was on the verge of fluttering out of his body and flying heavenward, and he himself was on the brink of being dispatched from the abode of mortality, when there arrived the Lion of God, the Exalted One, *Sahib-e Hal Ata*,[95] the Feller of Khaibar's fort, the Second of the Five Holies.[96] He called out to him, whereupon Muqbil fell to the ground. That holy personage helped him to his feet and, presenting him with a bow and five arrows, proclaimed, "I bless you with the art of archery, and pronounce you peerless and unmatched in this skill. Many a master archer will feel honored to be accepted as your pupil, and the archest of arch archers will never best your aim!"

Muqbil replied, "If someone were to ask me by whom I had been blessed, how must I answer, and make reply?" The Exalted One said to Muqbil, "Say that you have been blessed by the Triumphant Lion of God, to whose selfsame house you swear vassalage, duty-bound!" Hearing these words Muqbil turned toward Mecca jubilant and happy, carrying his bow and arrows.

When Hamza and Amar did not find Muqbil, they became apprehensive, and Amar set out to search for him. As he left the city he saw Muqbil approaching. They ran into each other's arms and happily embraced each other, and Amar took him to Hamza. Muqbil presented his bow and arrows to Hamza and told him how he had come into them and how he had received blessings. Hamza expressed great delight upon hearing Muqbil's adventure, and together they bided their time in happiness and joy.

OF HAMZA EXACTING TRIBUTE FROM THE KING OF YEMEN, AND OF THE FORTUNATE KING'S CONVERSION TO THE FOLDS OF THE TRUE FAITH

The inkwell's closure is opened by the reed's key, manifesting to the connoisseurs' eyes a treasure store of florid locutions, and the trinket box of the ocean floor is pried open, revealing pearls of eloquence that thus decorate the ears of the listeners. Hamza was into his seventh year when one day he happened by the bazaar in the company of Muqbil and Amar. There they came upon some deputies of Suhail Yemeni, the commander under the king of Yemen, exacting treasury revenues from the shopkeepers by their king's orders. Those shopkeepers who had nothing to give them pleaded with them and made pledges, but those tyrants would not have mercy, and cuffed and buffeted them and used them ill. Hamza asked Amar to go and find out the cause of the commotion. Amar brought news that the deputies of Suhail Yemeni were exacting a toll, and when a shop owner made excuses, they molested him with saddle ropes.

Hamza took pity on the victims and asked Amar to tell the deputies to desist from their vicious and high-handed methods. Amar went as ordered, but nobody would listen to a boy. Then Hamza himself went forth, and ordered Amar to tell the shopkeepers not to pay anything, and to seize from the deputies all they had collected. At this command Muqbil and Amar at once confronted the deputies, to stop them from their brutality and coercion. Thinking of them as mere boys, the deputies tried to disperse them. At this, Hamza severely punished some of the deputies, breaking their arms and legs and cracking open their skulls. They soon turned tail and sought refuge in Suhail Yemeni's pavilion, and recounted to him how a seven-year-old boy[97] interfered with the collection of taxes and tried to stop them and, when they resisted, charged at them along with two other boys, battering them into this state and confiscating all they had collected.

Even as they were narrating, Hamza arrived astride Siyah Qitas outside Suhail Yemeni's pavilion, flanked by Muqbil on his right and Amar on his left side. Suhail Yemeni came out of his pavilion and addressed Hamza. "Hear, O youth, that I greatly admire your mount and armor. It seems fortune has smiled on me by sending me this windfall. Waste not a moment and forthwith make a present of them to me, that I may forgive your trespasses and pardon your transgression; or else you shall pay dearly for your offense, and be severely disciplined for this felony!"

Upon hearing this, Hamza laughed loudly and replied, "Convert first to the True Faith if you value your life, then dare speak before me! Submit to my allegiance, or else you will grievously lament your ways and bitterly repent your end!" Suhail Yemeni thundered, "What is come over this boy that he utters threats so far beyond his scope! Pull him down from the horse and snatch all his arms and armor!"

At these orders his soldiers surrounded Hamza on all sides, and resolved to lay violent hands upon him. Hamza killed some on the spot with a hail of arrows, beat a few more to pulp with his mace, and dispatched some to Hell with his sword. Some others were trampled under the horse's hooves and found in the Erebus of Hell[98] a permanent abode. Then arrows began to fly from Muqbil's bow and anyone who made a false move presently found himself pierced with one.

When Suhail Yemeni regarded thousands of his men lying murdered,[99] he grew livid with rage, and himself came charging at Hamza to avenge the dead. Catching a hold of his cummerbund, Hamza raised him over his head, and resolved to smash him against the ground and to lay low that recreant. Suhail Yemeni then begged for mercy. At this, Hamza put him gently on the ground, and Suhail Yemeni converted to the True Faith with one thousand of his champion warriors. Embracing him, Hamza seated him by his side, showed him great affection and kindness, and promoted him greatly in honor and esteem.

Then Muqbil, Amar, and Suhail Yemeni—and the thousand champion warriors who had converted with him—declared Hamza their amir,[100] in tribute to Hamza's ferocity and grandeur and in recognition of the superior strength of the one aware of the Divine. They made offerings and lowered their heads in obedience and allegiance before him. Hamza smiled and conferred robes of honor upon each and every one of them according to his station, and rewarded them in consideration of their individual rank and prowess.

Upon entering the city Hamza first paid homage to Kaaba and said his prayers of gratefulness to Allah. Then presenting himself before Khvaja Abdul Muttalib, Hamza kissed his feet and narrated how he had been made an amir, and how he had battered, routed, and massacred infidels, and converted Suhail Yemeni to the True Faith. Khvaja Abdul Muttalib said, "Although it is an occasion for me to rejoice and say a thousand thanks to God Almighty, who honored you thus, won you this glory with his unbounded grace, and made you the leader of august people, yet I fear that the nobles of Mecca would resent it and smolder with envy at this news. The king of Yemen commands forty thousand fierce mounted troops and hundreds of thousands of foot soldiers and auxiliaries besides, and he receives tribute and vassalage from many kings. Should he advance against Mecca, drawn here by this incident, the citizens of this city would be thrown into turmoil, and would hold you to blame!"

Hamza replied, "All I count on are your prayers and divine favor. God willing, I shall keep the king of Yemen from attacking Mecca. Indeed, yours truly will himself advance against him and visit his head with a calamity, should he refuse conversion to the True Faith!"

After a few days Amir Hamza took leave of Khvaja Abdul Muttalib and left the city with Muqbil, Amar, and Suhail Yemeni at the head of one thousand mounted warriors. The army charted its course toward Yemen with great pomp and glory, riding under the banners of the signs of victory and prestige. Friends and travel companions were in their retinue and, to bid them adieu, chiefs and nobles mounted and on foot flanked their sides. At the time of parting some said prayers on their heads, others tied amulets to their arms. Khvaja Abdul Muttalib embraced Hamza and vouchsafed him into God's care, and offered him advice for the journey. Thus all of the soldiers took their leave and departed for their destination.

The first leg of their journey over, Amir Hamza was riding at some distance from his entourage, conversing with Amar and enjoying the lush fields of evergreens and the pleasant breeze, when he beheld a youth of ten or eleven, dressed like a mendicant. He sat with his head on his knees, looking all distracted and distraught, presenting a woeful mien with grief and sorrow etched on his face.

Taking pity on the boy's condition, Hamza turned the horse toward him to discover why a youth of these parts had renounced the world and become a recluse, wasting the prime of his life in such wretchedness and misery. Hamza greeted him and expressed a desire to know what had caused him to suffer such a state. When the youth did not answer, Hamza persisted all the more, and the resistance of the youth finally weakened before Hamza's insistence. The boy saw that nothing short of hearing his story would satisfy this kind stranger, and of a certain he would force his heart's secret out of him.

> *Oh, why did I cross paths with that rider,*
> *That the reins of my restraint I let go.*[101]

Before Hamza's perseverance the youth could not hold and, heaving a cold sigh, he exclaimed (as my verse reads):

> *I am with such a unique malady afflicted*
> *That the Messiah prescribes me death as cure.*[102]

"Hear then, O kind friend, that I am afflicted with that pain to which the world offers no cure! A malady of which there is no remedy in this life!" And thus speaking, the youth recited these verses of Mian Bahr in the *vasokht* style:[103]

> *I would to God none is snared in the love for a mistress,*
> *He may sooner die rather than be so afflicted.*
> *May one never set one's mind on beauty's flame,*
> *May one never bid for a Yusuf*[104] *even should he sell at a bargain,*
> *May the eyes lose the power of admiring beauty*
> *And the moonfaced ones offend the sense of sight;*
> *The beasts of the forest would die if they were to regard love,*
> *A desert's expanse would be torn asunder disentangling from this thorn;*
> *A whiff of its breath turns a garden to chaff,*
> *A droplet of its essence brings a river to silt,*
> *The heavens burst where love rages,*
> *Mount Sinai would turn to dust should this scourge descend;*
> *Far too bitter with salt is this inviting roast,*
> *Like a bane is this sweet for the youth;*
> *Ever for the soul's harvest love has been the rain of fire:*
> *Shy away like quicksilver from this fire;*
> *One claimed by its hand the Messiah himself could not revive,*
> *A single spark of it would set ablaze a river,*
> *Love is the keen-edged dagger with which one may violate his life,*

And a virtual tempest to force his heart's vessel to capsize;
It is the chink in the soul's armor, a scalpel for life's artery,
A dungeon from which even death does not bring release.
May God never put one through this trial,
Should one utter love's name he must immediately repent;
Heaven forfend that a mortal should think of love;
The straw the wind blows around does not ride it to mountain summits,
With all their tribulations, Qais and Farhad came to naught;
Many a caravan has love ransacked, many a house has it burnt to ashes,
It vents into the world the ashes of charred hearts,
To angels[105] it dictates terms as readily as it does to men;
When the clouds of love gather over a heart
The lovelorn eye soon rains tears of blood,
With a lightning bolt of fire-raining sigh
It sinks all reputation, rank, and grace;
Where it rains, all verdure is obliterated,
And in the rose and hyacinth garden one looks in vain for their chaff;
The blooming sapling of youth is reduced to a dried thorn
And from the neck's stem the executioner's sword reaps harvest;
Love is that spring which cultivates its own colors,
And the fragile soul becomes a veritable flower bed from scars;
Hyacinth-like one remains all wrapped in gloom
And nightingale-like the heart's bird breaks into a dirge;
Never did he emerge who once took the plunge,
And the pearl of the soul was extracted from his body's oyster;
The heart was seen to burn in its fire like a moth
And, taperlike, the body to dissolve from its heat;
Many comely men it introduced to the wardrobe of dust
And they changed it only to be clothed in a winding-sheet;
Being charmed by someone's gait may one never exchange his peace for love
Or invite this calamity on his head after witnessing a charmer wear her hair
*   loose;*
The beauty of these enchantresses is inimical to a man's riches and honor;
May God avert even the dreams of these enchantresses,
May one never long for maidens graceful and courtly;
Shun these well-groomed ones, keep no cause with them,
Setting heart on someone is the start of one's undoing
And before long the Seven Climes know him as a madman;
Now one loses honor, now he earns rebuke:

To love and to earn disgrace are indeed fully commensurate;
One is well advised to keep a safe distance from Love,
Rather than become enamored he would do well to poison or drown himself.

Upon hearing this, Hamza said, "There is no malady save death but has a cure in this world!"

In view of Hamza's compassionate indulgence, the youth opened his heart to him and, with fiery tears of blood flowing down his pallid and sunken cheeks, told his story thus:

My humor distraught and my heart frosty,
I am like a tulip marked by affliction and pain.

"I am the heir to the throne of Maghreb, which is the country and domicile of my fathers, and Sultan Bakht is my name. I have been brought into this terrifying wilderness by my love for Huma-e Tajdar, the daughter of the king of Yemen. It is my passion that has shown me this day in this reduced state; honor and repute are of little regard to me and, parted from my friends and dear ones, I have abandoned my home.

They do not sojourn in one place, the ill-famed lovers,
Changing stations night and day, every morn and eve.

"As I could not meet the demands of my beloved, grief-stricken and helpless I have turned my back to the world, and taken to mendicancy!"

Hamza replied, "It is neither a difficult undertaking, nor an occasion to despair! What issue is there to which there is not a resolution? What adversity, that cannot be converted into prosperity? One must not take leave of one's senses and despair, becoming derelict after such trivial considerations!

There is no problem but has a solution,
No man but stands resolute against odds.

"Anchor your hopes in the bounty of your Lord. Exercise patience and restraint. Rise from this place as a favor to yours truly! Renounce this wasteland and accompany me back into civilization. God willing I myself shall bring your wishes to fruition, and fill up your skirts of desire with the pearls of requited longing!"

That day Amir Hamza camped at that place, and converted Sultan Bakht Maghrebi to the True Faith. The attendants and menials were ordered to wash and clean the prince and exchange his beggarly garb with a princely attire. Tents and livery and all the accessories required by a prince were provided for Sultan Bakht, and he was shown every token of honor, esteem, and prestige. The prince entered the aegis of Hamza's patronage, spending his nights and days in great comfort and luxury.

After they had gone a long way and traversed many fathoms, Amir Hamza beheld a youth wearing a cap and robe of lion skin seated in their path with a fierce lion tethered by his side. Hamza went forward and asked him, "Who might you be, O youth? What are your name and particulars, and why is that lion chained by your side?" The youth answered, "I am a robber and a highwayman, and my name is Tauq bin Heyran. I am most dexterous and skilled and unmatched in my trade, and this very plain is my domain and abode. Whenever someone happens by and when a wayfarer takes this path, I let my lion loose at him. After the lion has killed him, I seize his goods and chattels, and make a living from their sale, while my lion here devours him and feeds on the carcass!"

Amir Hamza said to him, "O youth! Repent from this carnage of the innocent, or you will find yourself a loser in this world and the next. You invoke abasement and discredit on your head in this world, and also in the Future State. One day you shall be held up to shame and made abject!" The highwayman replied, "O stranger! Your beauty and graceful airs move me to have pity on you. But if you waste your time in purposeless talk, you will forfeit your life! It would bode well for you to surrender your horse and your arms and accoutrements and vestments, and peaceably go your way, with my promise of safe conduct and pardon for your life!" Amir Hamza said, "What great swagger, and what an impetuous speech! Witness that you yourself summon trouble on your head! Let loose the lion and behold a little show of my divinely gifted might!"

Immediately the man let the lion loose at him. As the lion leapt at Amir Hamza, he skewered him with his spear and flung him back at the bandit. That man was amazed at Hamza's might, and unsheathed his sword and attacked him. With one blow from the shaft of his spear, Amir Hamza made him bite dust. Then dismounting and catching him by the scruff of his neck, he lifted him over his head and would have gladly crashed him against the ground and erased his name from the roll of the living, when Tauq bin Heyran asked for forbearance, and pleaded for mercy. At this, Amir Hamza gently put him down. He made Tauq bin

Heyran profess a complete break from his infidel ways, and the robber repented with all his heart. Amir Hamza converted him to the True Faith and appointed him the standard-bearer of his army and, with his indulgence and kindnesses, made him venerable and worthy of honor.

When they neared the end of their journey, and the fortress of Yemen lay just five leagues farther, Hamza gave the order to set up camp, and they bivouacked with ease and comfort in a verdant pasture. As per his orders, pavilions were unloaded from the camels, and unfurled and put up at short distances from one another.

Now we return to Munzir Shah, the king of Yemen. Those from Suhail Yemeni's army who had escaped with their lives during their skirmish with Amir Hamza returned to their homeland and narrated all the details of Amir Hamza's battle with Suhail Yemeni. They also told of the latter's conversion to the True Faith, and recounted the manly deeds of Amir Hamza, the lion of the forest of valor. Thereupon Munzir Shah left his son Noman with ten thousand troops to guard the fortress, and himself advanced toward Mecca at the head of thirty thousand mounted troops. But the paths of Munzir Shah and Amir Hamza did not cross, as they had taken separate routes to and from Mecca.

Amir Hamza sent an embassy to Noman with a missive stating that he represented a friend who sought the hand of Huma-e Tajdar, the daughter of the king of Yemen, in marriage. He conveyed to Noman his desire to find out Huma-e Tajdar's terms for marriage, so that he might fulfill them. When Noman communicated Amir Hamza's message to his sister, she said, "Very well! Let the ground be made ready. After routing Hamza at the game of horse-shinty,[106] I shall behead him and spike his head over the fort parapet! That shall teach him a lesson in soldiering, bravery, and might, and erase from his mind all presumptions of his manhood. And it will quell all his mutinous humors." Noman wrote back to Hamza, "We express our deference to your wish. Tomorrow we shall play at horse-shinty, and the mettle of each combatant will be thereby tested. If you should bear the ball away from the field, you shall also bear away the princess. Otherwise, your head shall be spiked at the fort parapet. There will be slaughter and carnage between the two camps, and the curse of it shall be on your head!"

Amir Hamza was delighted to hear of a match of horse-shinty. He busied himself in encouraging his mountain-crumbling warriors and behemoth-bodied champions, and ordered the kettledrums to be sounded. The whole night battle drums pounded, and kettledrums were played in the two camps. Amir Hamza remained awake the whole night, engrossed in fervid prayers and solicitations to the Almighty.

When the kingly sun ascended its heavenly throne and speared the terraqueous globe with its shaft of light, Noman marched to the battlefield at the head of his army, and took position in the field with his phalanx of rank-destroying and formidable skirmishers arrayed behind him. The august king, Lord of the Auspicious Planetary Conjunction of the Age, the distinguished Amir—to wit, Hamza the Illustrious, also armed himself with a helmet over his head, his body clad in armor, and a sword girded to his side, and mounted Siyah Qitas, carrying a lance in his hand and with his companions and friends and retainers in his retinue. Tauq bin Heyran took him under the shadow of his standard, and the Avis of the Height of Fortune took him under its wing. To his right marched Sultan Bakht Maghrebi, to his left Suhail Yemeni, both decorated with bejeweled and encrusted armor; their minds filled with the heady wine of youth. The illustrious champion sprinter Amar Ayyar, that heart-splitter and dagger thrower, went leaping and bounding before Amir's charger, making pleasantries and cajoling the army with his quips, chortling with great flourish and dazzle and display. That day Amir Hamza put Muqbil Vafadar at the vanguard of the army leading the thousand troopers who had converted alongside Suhail Yemeni. Amar configured the battle array with such skill that the enemy was confounded by the appearance of an overwhelming host, and Amir's army appeared several thousand in number.

When it was time to seek combat after the battle lines were drawn on both sides, Amir stood opposite Noman bin Munzir Shah, and bellowed like a ferocious lion and recited a poem in the *rajaz* meter[107] in anticipation of Huma-e Tajdar. Suddenly, a rider hidden by a green veil and covered from head to heel in a sea of jewels, like his steed, leapt onto the battlefield astride his horse, and sauntered into the arena with a stately and graceful air, sporting his armor, sword, dagger, Khatti spear,[108] bow, and quiver, and carrying in his hand the horse-shinty stick. Addressing Amir Hamza, he declared, "Show thyself, the one who seeks Huma-e Tajdar! Here is the ball and here the field. Show what you have got to offer of your skill!" The moment Amir heard the challenge, he spurred on the charger of the prophet Ishaq in a flash, and lunged atop the horse with a roar, now giving him head, now administering restraint. Advancing the ambling stallion into the arena, he declared, "O youth, take heed! Here is the field, the stick, and the ball!"

The opponent's attendants threw the ball into the field, and that darling veiled youth urged the horse with strong legs, and struck the ball with the stick and bore it away, manifesting his alacrity, speed, and prowess to all. Whereupon Amir Hamza took the stick from Amar's hands, and spurred his horse forward, pressing with his seat at that lightning-quick charger. He swung the pole and struck the ball with great precision, displaying his divinely gifted might. When that youth saw the game slipping from his hands and his skill and cunning brought to naught, he directly threw back the veil from his face and displayed a luminous aspect, making the whole field resplendent with a damsel's world-ornamenting charm. For it was no other than Huma-e Tajdar.

A sun was witnessed on Earth
When she threw back her veil;
Hamza's gaze became transfixed mirrorlike
With marvel upon meeting her eyes.

As Amir sat thunderstruck by her beauty and confounded by this display of the Creator's handiwork, Huma-e Tajdar saw her chance. She again nudged the horse and struck the ball. She was on the verge of carrying it away, and had all but borne away the ball, when Amir steeled his heart and proclaimed, "There is no power or might save in Allah!" Then, resorting to his perseverance and courage, he urged his horse forward and declared, "I see your fraud and deceit, and your chicanery and treacherous ways. This explains how you bear the ball away from the field, and how you win the wager to spike men's heads on the fort parapet. But methinks you never once encountered a man of skill, nor ever came upon a man of valor! I will show you the essence of courage and valor and how the ball is borne away from the field! Behold! Beware! Be warned! Here I take the ball and, with the attendant grace of God, win this game!" He bore away the ball and handed Huma-e Tajdar a resounding defeat. Much though Huma-e Tajdar tried to reach for the ball with her stick, and showed excellent skill and speed, she never stood a chance against Amir, and could never have surpassed that lion of the forest of valor.

After he had borne away the ball, Amir Hamza addressed her thus: "O Huma-e Tajdar! Speak if you have anything to say! Are you satisfied, or do you wish to put yourself to further test?" She replied, "Let us match ourselves once more! Let the field be a witness to our skills yet again!" In honor of her request Amir threw the ball once more into the field and, again flourishing the stick, he won the game with his superior speed and skill. Recognizing that she had lost the competition, and had ground all her honor and celebrity into the dust before thousands, Huma-e Tajdar sought retreat. She turned tail, and spurred her horse to reach her brother Noman and the safety of her camp. But Amir Hamza spurred his horse forward in pursuit and, catching her by her cummerbund, lifted her up from her saddle and threw her like a ball toward Amar, who fastened her arms with his lasso, and headed toward his camp after having secured that bird of the apex of beauty and grace.

Upon noticing this turn of events, Noman shouted to his soldiers, "My men, this youth has made scandalously short work of this affair! Make haste and cut him off. Come to the defense of your honor and virtue, lest the man bent upon vanquishing our renown and repute should carry away Huma-e Tajdar!"

Upon his call, ten thousand armed troops took rein and exerted themselves faithfully as one. They besieged Amir Hamza and attacked him from all sides. Amir's Hashimi blood[109] rushed to his face, and his heart settled on a holy battle. Wielding his sword he fell upon them and, every which way he lunged, he cleared the field of men and their bodies of their heads.

At his approach that malevolent host scattered away like moss on water's surface. The slain carpeted the battlefield, and villains who had before made bold claims now all meekly laid down their arms. Our gallant warrior duly showered them with many well-aimed arrows. The enemy commanders were cleaved in two upon their saddles when his sword landed on their heads. To whomever Hamza dealt a blow of his saber, to the Erebus of Hell he was forthwith dispatched—his head, neck, and full torso sundered. And the one who took his blow on the back found himself split in two. At this point, Noman bin Munzir Shah Yemeni came with his sword raised over Amir's head, and brought down his villainous arm to unleash his vigor. Amir took the blow on his shield, and then plucked Noman clear off his saddle by his cummerbund. Like an intrepid hawk clutching a timid sparrow, he thus gave him into Amar's custody. As the rest took to their heels in terror, the crocodile of the saber continued his attack, also dispatching to Hell those in flight.

Amir Hamza designated all the booty from pillage to his army, and returned glorious and victorious to his pavilion. Drums of victory and triumph were sounded, and tumultuous roars of rapture and joy rose to the heavens. At night when the revelries began, Amir sent for Noman, and said to him, "Speak your mind and let your tongue unburden your heart!" Noman relented, "It was not given to one among mankind to come before my numerous host of swashbucklers and dagger fighters and escape with his life! God alone knows whether you are seraph or man; in either case you are the most select of the Beneficent One. I have nothing further to say but that I convert hereby to the True Faith!"

Amir initiated Noman into the True Faith, embraced him, and had a seat spread out for him by his side. Then drinks were passed in rounds; Noman became one of the legion of the faithful; and Amar began to croon a festive song. Before Amir gave them leave of parting, he decorated Noman and Princess Huma-e Tajdar—who had also been ennobled in the True Faith—with robes of distinction. Then the assembly adjourned, and Amir himself retired to his bedchamber.

In the morning, Noman summoned his army and extended to them the invitation to convert to the True Faith. All of them lowered their heads as one in acquiescence, and were initiated in due succession. All the commanders of Noman's forces found the ennoblement of the True Faith and were presented before Amir Hamza. They were granted leave to wait upon him, and he conferred upon every one of them a robe of honor as well.

When the tidings reached Munzir Shah Yemeni that Amir Hamza had routed Huma-e Tajdar in the match of horse-shinty and accorded her honor commensurate with her status, and that Noman was captured in the battle and was converted to the True Faith with his army, a blaze of rage flared up in Munzir Shah's breast. Aborting his advance on Mecca, he returned posthaste and, upon his arrival in the fort, sounded the war drums. Thereupon Amir also ordered kettledrums to be sounded in his camp in response to the challenge, and his victorious army once again made battle preparations.

At the crack of dawn the two armies marched into the arena. Lion-hearted skirmishers, pearls of valor, and intrepid warriors girded themselves, ready to wager their lives to earn renown. Munzir Shah sauntered into the arena astride his horse, and bellowed out thus from the ranks of his heathenish horde: "Declare thyself who is Amir Hamza, the commander of the army. Where hides he? Let him show himself and his wits, and display the might and stature he claims as a man. Let him test his mettle with me.

His own arm he humbles,
He who wrestles it with steel.[110]

"It is certain that the one who thirsts after his own blood and calls out for swift death to visit him, never crossed paths with a man, nor ever before stood in the presence of a veteran warrior!"

In response, Amir Hamza rode up to him and said, "Why bark so boastfully, and brag thus? What is this mad desire you nurse? In just one stroke, God willing, you shall bite dust. In an instant the sword of True Faith shall put paid to you! I shall give you the first blow so that all your heart's desires may be realized and they do not die unrequited with you!"

As Munzir Shah aimed his spear, Amir urged his horse alongside Munzir Shah's, wrested the spear from his hands, and threw it over his shoulder after breaking its shaft. Munzir Shah attacked with his sword, but Amir Hamza parried that, too, and grasping him from behind, lifted him off his saddle and snatched his sword from him. He would have dashed Munzir to the ground, but the latter asked for mercy, and thus escaped certain doom. Amir released him lightly to the ground. Munzir Shah kissed Amir's feet, and converted to the True Faith with all his heart by reciting the Act of Faith. Amir brought him into his pavilion, showed him great regard and indulgence, and augmented his rank. He conferred robes of honor upon him and his boon companions, and on the commanders of his army.

For a whole month Munzir Shah hosted Amir Hamza, and with great zeal and devotion performed the offices of allegiance and fealty. From the first day Munzir Shah began preparations commensurate with his status for the wedding, and in accordance with Hamza's wishes arranged for Huma-e Tajdar to be wedded to Sultan Bakht Maghrebi. Then Bakht Maghrebi pleaded before Hamza, "Huma-e Tajdar is now affianced to me; through the auspicious fortunes of Your Majesty, this unimagined windfall was apportioned my lot. I will marry her and set up house, God willing, on the day when Your Honor shall celebrate his own nuptials. Until then, Huma-e Tajdar may stay in her father's house, and there bide her time!"

Thereupon Amir said their engagement sermon and had the ceremony grandly solemnized. When the festivities ended, Amir Hamza said to Munzir Shah, "Now I shall take my leave and head back home, where my father shall be anxiously awaiting my return, giving himself to worry and disquiet over thoughts of my welfare." Munzir Shah replied, "I shall be your riding companion, as I am consumed by a desire to make a pilgrimage to the Kaaba and wait upon Khvaja Abdul Muttalib myself." Thus speaking, he appointed his deputy to run the affairs of the state and, along with Noman and thirty thousand fierce grapplers in his train, rode toward Mecca with Amir.

OF THE RISE OF HASHSHAM BIN ALQAMAH KHAIBARI AND HIS MARCH ON CTESIPHON FROM KHAIBAR

Thus unfolds the account of authentic historiographers and this tale of great import and moment, that Hashsham had turned twelve and come of age when he set foot out of doors with lofty aspirations, and heard a great tumult in the marketplace. When he inquired what had caused all that agitation, and why the city of Khaibar rang with lamentations, people told him that collectors sent by Naushervan were exacting taxes, and punishing anyone who offered the least excuse for not promptly submitting the levy. Galled by anger, Hashsham had a few collectors arrested, and banished them from the city after cutting off their ears and noses. Then he proclaimed a ban declaring that no one should pay even a farthing in tribute, and should submit an equivalent amount into Hashsham's coffers instead. He set about enlisting an army, and focused his undivided attention on matters of governance. Before long he assembled an intrepid army, and marched on Ctesiphon.

When tidings dispatched by gazetteers were conveyed to the auspicious ears of the just emperor, relaying that Hashsham bin Alqamah Khaibari had sallied forth, with great pomp and magnificence, the emperor assembled the ministers of state and sought Buzurjmehr's counsel. Buzurjmehr said, "In my judgment it would be improper that your Excellent Highness skirmish with the offender yourself. In this vassal's opinion it would be indecorous in the extreme, for there is no glory to be gained in vanquishing such a one as he. And should the results be otherwise (we seek God's refuge from such a terrible thought!), this would be most inauspicious and your enemies shall have the occasion to say that the Emperor of the Seven Climes was humbled by an abject fellow. Then anyone and everyone would find courage in defiance, and every individual would become contumacious and refractory. It would be far more seemly if Your Highness should depart on a hunting expedition before his ingress, leaving some commander in charge of affairs in Ctesiphon. That way, when that wretch (deserving to be beheaded!) should arrive, he will be accorded such a chastisement that the wind will be taken out of the sails of all, high and low, and they never again will raise their heads from your obedience and vassalage."

The emperor found Buzurjmehr's advice to his liking, and highly commended his well-intentioned counsel. Then deputing the celebrated champion Antar Filgosh with a force of fifty thousand troops to guard Ctesiphon and rout Hashsham, the emperor took himself to the hunting fields, and busied himself with the routines of the chase. In a matter of a week or ten days Hashsham bin Alqamah Khaibari descended with forty thousand ruthless troops, besieged the fort, and threatened the populace with his tyranny.

Antar Filgosh proved worth his salt; his hot cannonade did not allow a soul to approach the protection moat, nor a single trooper from the enemy host to advance an inch. One day a thought crossed Antar Filgosh's mind: *I am fortified within, and Hashsham bin Alqamah Khaibari continues his siege of some days. When was Hashsham ever such a renowned warrior that I should hide my face from him? Why not give him combat outside the city walls, rout him speedily, and hand him a most inglorious defeat, to earn myself renown in the world and receive rank and estate from the emperor!*

Rustam is gone from the face of the earth, and also Bahram;
A man's legacy to posterity is only his renown.

Thus resolved, Antar departed from the city with five thousand troops. Upon catching sight of him, Hashsham laughed with contempt, and said, "Death flutters above his head seeking a perch, and doom spurs him forward, since he has come forth to skirmish and dares show me his face!" Then urging his rhinoceros alongside Antar's mount, Hashsham said, "What is it that you seek? Why do you desire the massacre of your troops, and wish to lay down your life!"

Antar answered, "O infidel, perfidious dog, and slave of slave stock! You dared raise the flag of rebellion and, for the sake of this world and its short-lived fame, dared bite the hand that fed you! Did you not realize that a humble slave of the Emperor of the Seven Concentric Circles could call you to account, and forthwith trample all your pomp and show and dignity into dust!" Hashsham replied, "O ignoramus! Take heed! In matters of conquest and statecraft when did anyone ever show any consideration to who is a master and who is his subject and vassal?

He who wields the sword shall have the sermon read in his name![111]

"With this sword I shall claim tribute from your emperor and lay claim to all his lands and treasures soon!"

As Hashsham made this utterance, Antar couched his spear, then thrust it at Hashsham's evil bosom. The point of the spear piercing Hashsham's breast, it exited from the back. But despite receiving this deadly wound, Hashsham yet cleaved Antar in two with his sword, and then attacked his army. Deprived of its commander, Antar's army retreated toward the gates of the city. Hashsham gave them chase with his troops and, following them into Ctesiphon, pillaged the whole city, took seventy thousand prisoners, deployed his men at all the entry points of the city, and secured the crown and the throne. After this, he returned to his pavilion in a royal procession. Spending the night in festive revelries, he then set out toward Khaibar with his grandees.

After traversing many leagues, they arrived at a forking path, whence one road led to the Kaaba, and the other toward Khaibar. Hashsham's companions counseled him, and his ministers advised thus, that in this battle for worldly renown, having earned victory and triumph this once, he must fight on for benediction, and earn a high laurel by marching further, razing the Kaaba to the ground, and effacing from the face of the Earth the temple of the Faithful (we seek God's refuge from such wickedness!).[112] Hashsham's luck now being exhausted, his misfortune thus ordained that these improvident words inveigled him to advance toward Mecca and head for the House of God.

This news circulated in Mecca, and the rumor reached all, high and low, that Hashsham bin Alqamah Khaibari, who had pillaged Ctesiphon, was now headed there, bent upon violating the Kaaba; and that he brought in his train a large host with great majesty and grandeur, and much magnificence and might to demolish the House of God. Whosoever heard the news set to shaking like a willow branch, and shivered in ecstasies of fear.

That very day Amir Hamza the Renowned arrived triumphant and victorious in Mecca with his intrepid army. After paying homage to the Kaaba, he presented himself to kiss his father's feet. Khvaja Abdul Muttalib raised Hamza's head from his feet, and embraced him with exceeding affection, and paid respect also to his companions according to their rank. He sent for vats of sherbet, and prostrated himself several times to say thanks to the Beneficent God. And then he broke into a cascade of tears.

Amir Hamza cried, "O Father! This is a day for rejoicing. What is the occasion for your grief and sorrow? I have returned safe and sound from the perils of war, and have won for myself a fair victory, the likes of which—were it not for God's grace—could not have been imagined to be my lot! But instead of reveling in it, my father gives way to grief, and let alone celebrating and ordering a feast, he indulges in woe and sorrow!"

Khvaja replied, "O my illustrious son! The reason I shed tears is that in just a few days we will face a great terror. Hashsham bin Alqamah Khaibari, having ravaged Ctesiphon, is now headed to destroy the Kaaba. With great bustle and array he brings an intrepid force and a bloodthirsty host. The nobles of the city are in great consternation about what to do, as he is a fierce and mighty warrior, the commander of a sanguinary army, and the fountainhead of tyranny. Therefore, I wish to send you off quietly to Abyssinia on some pretext."

Amir responded, "O Father, the source of all my devotions! It is hardly warranted to lament before the end is reached! Mightier and stronger yet is the True Progenitor! It would be little wonder if we should triumph over the enemy with your prayers and His grace. Have no fear that Hashsham will ever set foot in Mecca. I will intercept him outside the city, and dispatch him speedily to Hell." Having spoken thus Amir took short leave of his father. He went to the Kaaba where he offered prayers, with a view to soliciting victory, and sought help from the True Assistant (His name be glorified and exalted!). Then arraying his army, Amir Hamza set out to overtake Hashsham and put paid to that impious despot.

After traversing many stretches expeditiously, they received intelligence at one of the stations. The scouts brought news that Hashsham's army was encamped two stations away, and his forces were strung out for miles. Upon receiving this news Amir halted and arranged his army. And four hours into the night, Amir chose several thousand soldiers from his army, and advanced to ravage the enemy force.

Before long Amir's troops alighted like an unforeseen calamity at the enemy's camp. Hashsham's troops were thrown into turmoil. Bellowing the cry, "God is Mighty!" Amir then proclaimed, "Wake up, ye of slumbering fortunes, and take heed, O ill-starred men! The wrath of God has closed in upon you! The staunchest of infidels has lost heart and the most refractory has yielded his appetite for life, for the Angel of Death has come to extract your souls!" Before it was daybreak, ten thousand men of Hashsham's army lay slain.

Hashsham lay sleeping in his tent when cries of "Slay and Slaughter! Slay and Slaughter!" reached his ears, and a cry of "God is Mighty!" rang out. Hashsham immediately awoke from his sleep, and asked his men the cause of all the pandemonium and stir. His people told him that some Arab named Hamza had made a night assault and perpetrated wholesale slaughter, and had butchered His Lordship's troops. If the carnage continued a few hours longer, not one soul would remain to speak of, and come morning, neither man nor beast would be left alive in the army.

Hashsham rode his rhinoceros forthwith into the camp, witnessed his whole army in trepidation and disarray, and discovered some dead and others bleeding. Just then the kingly orb ascended the throne of the heavens; the night melted away and the day shone bright upon the field, to reveal Hashsham with thirty thousand troops and Amir with ten thousand mounted warriors and a great sufficiency of commanders and foot soldiers.

Riding his rhinoceros into the field, Hashsham regarded Hamza and declared, "O Arab lad! Whose horse and weapons are these that you borrowed to use them as your mainstay to dare challenge me? You showed little regard for your life, indeed, in troubling my army to no purpose. But my compassion is stirred by your youthfulness, and I withhold the order to put you to a swift death! Were you to make me the offering of this horse and armor and present me these goods with folded arms and supplicate my forgiveness for your crime, I should yet forgive your trespass, and exempt you from the levy of my revenge for your night assault on my army. Your contumely was grievous, and your manner most rebellious. If you go against these commands, however, you shall be meted out an untimely death at my hands, neither grave nor a winding-sheet[113] will you find, and your existence shall be prematurely effaced from this world!"

Upon hearing this babble Amir could not contain his rage any longer, and bellowed out in his wrath, "O abject dog (who deserves decapitation!), little do you know who I am, and to which noble house I belong— I am the son of Abdul Muttalib bin Hashim! Has the renown of my sword not reached your ears? Are you deaf to the loud advertisements of my courage? Come to your senses, you hellbound dog, and do not commit such reckless words to your tongue! Why do you wish to call this calamity upon your head? Why do you wish to throw away your life?"

Hashsham raged marvelously upon hearing this speech, and attacked, thrusting the spear he was wielding at Amir's unpolluted breast. With the point of his javelin Amir blocked Hashsham's spear, and then they sparred on with lances. After a hundred thrusts of their spears had been exchanged without injury to either party, Hashsham threw away his spear in vexation and unsheathed his sword to close in and strike Amir. But Amir wrested the sword from his hand and, throwing it to his companions, spoke to Hashsham thus: "You had your chance, now take my blow and watch for your weapons and mount. And impute not afterward that I did not warn you before I attacked, or that you were denied your chance!"

Hashsham covered his head with his shield, but when Amir landed his sword on that refractory's head with the cry of "None but God alone is powerful!" it cleft his shield in two, splitting his steel helm and smashing his cranium into splinters. Carving up his long neck and thrusting out of the back, the sword did not vanish into the confines of his breast; it descended through the felt saddle and cleaved the rhinoceros's back, and emerged shining with the putrescence from the animal's belly. Friends and foes alike bit their fingers in stupefaction, for never had one seen or heard of such a sword.

> *The keenness of that blade be told, it did not stop at the head;*
> *Let alone the head, even the cupola of the helmet had not stopped it,*
> *Neither did the arch of the tyrant's snout hinder its progress,*
> *Nor did the charging sword repose on the shield's escutcheoned flower bed,*
> *But flashing to-and-fro like thought*
> *There was not a single head it alighted on but cut it through;*
> *Call it sword, that veritable lightning crack of doom,*
> *The mortal hand, which is the hand of God.*

Thus dispatching Hashsham to Hell, Amir broke into his army flanks like a ferocious lion charging into a herd of goats, and before long heaped up piles of the slain. Many a blackguard then turned tail and fled, and several converted to the True Faith. Amir sanctioned full rights to pillage to his army—with the exception of Naushervan's crown and throne—

and set free the prisoners, conferred a robe of honor upon each according to his status, and equipped each of them with a mount and money for the journey, directing them to return to their homes. Thereafter, Amir wrote out an epistle to Naushervan, which read:

> God's grace accompanied me, and by virtue of Your Eminence's Majesty I dispatched the tyrant Hashsham to the Erebus of Hell, and seventy thousand of your subjects and vassals were freed from his captivity. I hereby send that rebel's head by the agency of Muqbil Vafadar to your illustrious presence, and await orders regarding the restoration of the crown and throne of Kaikaus, whether I must bear them into your presence myself, or entrust them to one designated by Your Royal Highness.

Then charging Muqbil Vafadar with the delivery of Hashsham's head and the letter, Amir Hamza sent him to Naushervan's court, and himself embarked toward Mecca, triumphant and victorious. It is related that after this one time, Amir never again made a night assault, nor ever sought to assault and ravage a foe in the darkness of the night.

OF MUQBIL VAFADAR'S AUDIENCE BEFORE
NAUSHERVAN, RULER OF THE EMPYREAN

The Philomel of the pen sings a new story and thus makes the expanse of the leaf a flower bed, narrating that after forty days of absence, when Naushervan returned to Ctesiphon from his hunting expedition, he found the city an image of desolation, and his crown and throne plundered. With moist eyes he said to Buzurjmehr, "This adverse fortune has befallen me by the vicissitudes of the heaven. Your interpretation of the dream has thus far come true; time alone will tell when the rest shall come true, and whether our anxiety will be addressed." Buzurjmehr replied, "It is ordained that some hour between today and tomorrow, God willing, your spirits shall revive and there will be reason to celebrate.

Meanwhile, the Sassanids who had survived carnage and enslavement said to Bakhtak, "All our troubles stem from the doings of Buzurjmehr. Had he not inveigled the emperor away from Ctesiphon on a hunting expedition, we would have been spared the terrors Hashsham unleashed upon us. Our kith and kin were waylaid for no purpose by untimely death; they were violated and enslaved and herded to their graves. Indeed, Buzurjmehr's religious prejudice against us became our undoing, and the cockles of his heart were warmed by the slaughter of our kinsfolk. Pray plead our case before the emperor and have justice done to our cause, and thus earn exceeding benison by wailing on our behalf!"

While this commotion was rising, Sabir Namdposh Ayyar presented himself before the emperor, all covered in dust from head to foot, bearing joyous tidings and auspicious news, and declared: "Hashsham bin

Alqamah Khaibari, who had despoiled and ravaged Ctesiphon, and enslaved seventy thousand men, was headed toward Khaibar. Moreover, the selfsame Hashsham, who in his excessive vanity and arrogance thought nothing of individuals, human beings, kings, or emperors, was checked in his retreat by the glory of Your Lordship, and killed by Hamza's hand, who had dispatched the head of that villain with his companion, Muqbil Vafadar of name. Hamza has routed and ravaged Hashsham's army and liberated your subjects and invested them with robes of freedom, after securing their release from slavery."

The emperor became ecstatic upon receiving this delightful intelligence and hastened to embrace Buzurjmehr, and ordered that all nobles should go forth to welcome Muqbil Vafadar and escort him into his presence with the utmost honor. These orders were carried out forthwith, and the leading nobles and powerful lords decked themselves out and went in a body to welcome Muqbil Vafadar outside the city walls, escorting him into the emperor's presence with great esteem and immense honor. Muqbil was presented before the emperor, and he kissed the throne. When he produced Hamza's epistle, the emperor showed most singular esteem to Amir Hamza by himself taking his letter from Muqbil's hands. First he read to himself, then handing it next to Buzurjmehr, he said, "Read it aloud and advertise well its contents in all the provinces of our dominion."

All the Sassanids and Kianids and Majdakids assembled there rejoiced upon hearing the letter's contents, and congratulated the emperor on his triumph. Thereupon the emperor conferred a most sumptuous robe of honor upon Muqbil Vafadar, had his mouth stuffed with gold and precious jewels, and ordered that during the length of his stay in Ctesiphon Muqbil would have the freedom of the court in order to bestow the honor of his daily attendance.

The scribe has recorded that on the day Muqbil presented himself to wait upon the emperor, people witnessed a ringdove perched on a cypress branch[114] in the court of Jamshed,[115] with a black snake curled ringlike around her neck. The informers conveyed these details to the righteous ears of the emperor, who said, "It appears she has come to seek redress. Is there such a clever archer in the assembly whose arrow will not falter, nor fail to pierce the serpent? For it would cause me inexpressible grief if the ringdove were harmed!" No one came forward for this undertaking, and none dared accept the challenge. Not a soul stirred at his place, nor did anyone move a muscle. Then Muqbil rose from his station, and kissed the foot of the emperor's throne, and then ventured forth having obtained his leave.

Positioning a mirror at the point of a javelin, he appointed a man to hold it steady before the snake's head and enjoined him not to let fear of the snake cause his hand to sway. The serpent lifted his hood when he saw the image appear in the mirror, and lunged at it, darting his tongue. Finding his chance, Muqbil joined the arrow's notch with the bowstring and drew the bow to his ear. He let loose death's bird of prey at the bird of the serpent's soul. The arrow lodged itself into the serpent's head, and not a feather of the ringdove was harmed. The serpent fell to the ground, Muqbil withdrew his arrow, and the bird flew away to its nest striking her wings. A spontaneous chorus of "Bravo!" and "Well done!" rose from the assembly. The emperor kissed Muqbil's hands and decorated him with a golden robe of honor.

Then he wrote out the reply to Amir's letter and, along with a robe of honor, entrusted it to Bakhtak to stamp it with the royal seal. Bahman Sakkan and Bahman Hazan were ordered to hasten before Amir Hamza's presence and to present these items with great decorum and esteem. It is reported that the emperor had written the following words in his reply to Hamza:

O Indomitable Champion and Wringer of Rebellious Necks of the World, you showed excellent regard to your status as my protégé and, fighting my foe whose head was filled with the wine of sedition, effaced his existence from the face of the world. Indeed, were Rustam and Nariman alive today, they would have been proud to decorate their ears and necks with the tokens of your slavery. And Sohrab and Rustam would never have contested a claim against your power and might. I herewith send Bahman Sakkan and Bahman Hazan to you with a robe of honor as a token of my regard. Send with them the crown and the royal assets that you recovered from that villain's possession, and also present yourself at my court without further delay, so that my longing eyes may be brightened by the light of your beauty, and my heart regaled.

But Bakhtak the wretch did not send that note. He changed the sumptuous robe with a shabby one, and wrote out a letter to this effect: "O Arab stripling! Before I was intent on inflicting a wholesale slaughter on the Arab race, and exterminating every single soul among the Banu Hashim, but you performed a deed that regaled my heart. Therefore, I forgive your trespass and send Bahman Sakkan and Bahman Hazan with this robe." Then having included a similar message for Khvaja Abdul Muttalib, Bakhtak sent the emissaries to Mecca.

OF AMIR HAMZA'S ENCOUNTER WITH AADI MADI-KARIB

On the way to Mecca was the fortress of Tang-e Rawahil where tarried the mighty swashbuckler Aadi Madi-Karib, who passed his nights and days in that choice domicile. Upon hearing of the rise and exploits of Hashsham bin Alqamah Khaibari, he vacated his residence and, with a force of eighteen thousand men, laid an ambush at the foot of the hills with the intent of devastating and ravaging Hashsham bin Alqamah Khaibari when he should pass by that place. While he lay in wait a scout brought Aadi the news that Hashsham bin Alqamah Khaibari was put to death by one Hamza, who was heading toward the fortress on his way to his homeland, Mecca, with his booty. Upon hearing this news Aadi declared, "Very well, we must take our share from the booty as well; and give fight should he dither in the least!" When Hamza's army reached the environs of the citadel of Tang-e Rawahil and entered that treacherous terrain, Aadi chose a commander of his fortress as the emissary, and sent him to Hamza's camp with this message:

I had marked Hashsham bin Alqamah Khaibari as my prey, and for many a day I lay waiting for him, having laid an ambush in his anticipation. But you snatched my prey for your own, and my desire thus remains unfulfilled. Therefore I enjoin you to amiably share your booty with me in equal proportions, as well as all the spoils that have befallen you of his treasure and estate. Then you may carry on safely toward your destination with your share. Otherwise, your share will go the way of the rest, and longing and bitter grief will be your sole inheritance.

Amir Hamza laughed heartily upon receiving this message and, conferring many honors upon the messenger, said to him, "Report this to

Aadi after conveying to him my blessings: Should peace be to his liking, he will find me ready to celebrate it with a goblet of wine; but should he desire to venture forth on the path of confrontation and war, he will not find me lagging, but ready in every wise. The ball and the field are already provided, and I will indulge him to his taste!"

Greatly taken with Hamza's courteous manner, the ambassador carried Aadi the reply to his message, and further admitted, "Never have I come across so gentle and courtly a commander, and never seen a noble of greater vigor and courage. That his ambitions are lofty is evident, and it would be small wonder if his name is proclaimed sovereign in the Seven Climes and before long the countries of the region fall into his power." But Aadi made preparations for battle upon the receipt of Hamza's message, and the next day rode into the field with eighteen thousand mounted warriors to clarions of war. Amir encountered him with his triumphant, billowing army, poised himself for battle, and sought combat.

Aadi entered the arena in such an impressive array that many a heart sank in Hamza's army. They regarded a giant twenty-one cubits high, with a girth and bulk to match, wonderfully corpulent and of surpassing power and strength. His steel helmet was wrapped in seven turbans of seven folds each, and his whiskers jutted out from their end cloths. His waist—which may only be called superhuman—measured a full twenty-one yards. He was clad in a steel cummerbund and body armor, and displayed cuirass, scimitar, dagger, and katar; and sported arm guards, foot guards, thigh guards, and the hatchet. With a shield and quiver slung on his back, he carried a bow five hand spans high, and wielded a cudgel and a spear. When Amar Ayyar laid eyes upon Aadi's form, he said to Hamza, "You put great store in your might, but today the truth will out, and even your teeth will pour sweat!" Amir laughed, and replied, "The One in whom I put store is far more powerful.

If the enemy is mighty, the Protector is mightier still!

"Fret not, for my Assistant and Succor is the All Powerful and Indomitable God. Wait and see how things take shape."

Amir Hamza then turned his heart to his Creator in prayer and, giving no thought to his foe's mighty stature, urged his steed forward until the horses stood touching ear to ear. Immediately thereafter Amir gave such a powerful blow of his shield to the forehead of the enemy's mount that it staggered back some steps confounded by the blow, and his head set to shaking. When Aadi saw this show of Hamza's strength, he reckoned that his adversary was one who was both worthy and drunk on the heady wine of adolescence. He called out: "O youth! I see that you, too, have a claim on might, and a title to courage and vigor! Give your name so that a champion of your stature does not die at my hands unsung— and the name of a courageous, elegant, and handsome lad can be vouchsafed to the memory of time!"

Amir answered, "Do you not know that the name of a brave man is engraved on the hilt of his sword, on the notch of his bow, and on his arrow's point? Be warned that I am Abul-Ala;[116] that I was driven here to gauge for myself the might of your arm, and to discover what you have to show for skill and strength. Show what power you have—and do not hold back what your arm can deliver!"

Aadi couched his massive mace in his hand, closed in on Hamza, and raising it over Hamza's head with great might, declared, "O Abul-Ala! One blow of this mace will be your undoing! From this strike you will find no refuge!" He struck Amir's head with his bludgeon and unleashed wonderful vigor and might.

Amir parried the blow, then said, "Now give another blow, too, so that all your heart's desires are fulfilled and all cravings in your breast are sated. If I survive it, I shall deal one blow in return, whose memory will accompany you all your living days, and whose taste you will never forget!"

Upon hearing these words Aadi waxed ever more wrathful, and returned the mace to its hold in the saddle. He unsheathed his sword and, locking the stirrups together, made to land a blow on Hamza's head to show the error of his infidel ways. But Amir laid hold of Aadi's hilt with one hand, and with the other grasped his cummerbund.

As Aadi tried to break loose of Hamza's clasp, Amar approached and said, "O warriors! While you are at each other's throats, your combat takes its toll on your mounts. Why are you bent upon breaking the spines of these dumb beasts? If you wish to match your might against each other, then dismount and skirmish, and display your vigor and valor to the world!"

Both Amir Hamza and Aadi found Amar's counsel to their liking. They broke off their combat, dismounted, and stood facing each other. Aadi then said, "O Hamza! We were both evenly matched in armed combat, and are equals in plying the lance, mace, and sword. Now let us try

Maghrebi wrestling,[117] and exert our skill and vigor in this discipline! Whoever is victorious shall command the obedience of the vanquished, and the feeble one shall pledge everlasting submission to the mighty!"

Amir replied, "I am ready either way; and am willing to test and be put to trial!" Amir then sat down cross-legged. Aadi exerted himself mightily, so that sweat coursed from every pore on his skin. Yet he could not move Hamza an inch; Amir remained rooted to his place.

Then Aadi spoke thus: "O Hamza! I exerted myself all I could, and crossed the threshold of my strength; now it is your turn to exert your-self, and show what power you have." Hardly had Aadi squatted on the ground than Amir in his first attempt lifted Aadi's massive ass above his shoulders. Wheeling him several times around his head, he said, "What do you say now, and what are your intentions?"

Aadi answered, "I shall be faithful to you, and swear allegiance with all my heart and soul to your God gifted might!" At this, Hamza set him lightly upon the ground. Aadi kissed Amir's feet and, reciting the Act of Faith, was ennobled in the True Faith. Aadi brought Amir with all his army to the citadel of Tang-e Rawahil and arranged for a great feast and presented his brothers also into Hamza's service. Amir embraced every one of them, and conferred upon each a warrior's robe.

When the feasting and the celebration were over, Amir spoke to Aadi thus: "Farewell now, I am headed to my homeland to show my face to my compatriots, and to kiss my dear father's feet!" Aadi replied, "When was I ever such a crapulous glutton that you would be unable to feed me, and would refuse to take me along? Why, I will manage to survive even if I am only apportioned a thousand *maunds* in grains, and shall restrict myself to one meal per day, instead of two!"

Amar said, "The Almighty God be thanked, Aadi has no appetite at all! A wonderfully sparse eater he is, too. Who would turn down such an abstemious guest, and break the heart of one who eats like a sparrow?" Amir laughed, and replied, "Rest assured that it was never a considera-tion. The one who feeds both you and me is the True Provider, even as he is responsible for feeding all his creatures. Should Aadi wish to ac-company us, he will be my honored guest!"

At length Aadi mustered his eighteen thousand troops, and accompa-nied Hamza, who charted his course triumphantly and jubilantly toward Mecca.

OF AMIR HAMZA'S ARRIVAL IN MECCA AND HIS RECEIPT OF NAUSHERVAN'S EPISTLE

Sweet-lipped narrators and historians of honeyed discourse report that upon arrival in Mecca, Amir first paid homage to the Kaaba and, thus ennobling himself, offered the promissory prayer in gratitude for his victory. Obtaining Aadi's oath to renounce brigandry, Hamza secured from him also a promise to lead a virtuous life and to observe all rituals of the True Faith. Thereafter, Hamza attended to paying court to his father, and to presenting himself before his patriarch.

When Khvaja Abdul Muttalib received the news of Hamza's arrival, and the denizens of the city cheered him on the news of Hamza's return, he took the nobles of the city with him and went forth to welcome Amir, sallying forth to escort Hamza into the city with his near and dear ones walking in his retinue. The meeting of the father and son took place along the way. Amir kissed his father's feet, who in his turn raised him and embraced him to his heart, and scattered gold and silver among the destitute. All the paupers and the mendicants claimed their share of the sacrifices. The nobles of the city offered benedictions upon Hamza's head, praying that the True Triumphant One, always, forever, and for all future, return him victorious from his exploits; and that he might always vanquish and ravage his blackguard foes.

Khvaja returned to his house with Hamza, and they reposed in the Hall of Audience. Other notables of the city also called on them, and Amir introduced Munzir Shah, Noman bin Munzir Shah, Suhail Yemeni, Sultan Bakht Maghrebi, Aadi Madi-Karib, and Tauq bin Heyran into Khvaja's service, lauding them and praising their individual virtues. Khvaja was greatly pleased and showed great regard and affection for each of them, and accorded due prestige, honor, and hospitality to each one of them.

One day in the course of the conversation Amir chanced to learn that Aadi was Aadiya Bano's son. Amir rejoiced upon discovering that Aadi was his foster brother, and on that very day Amir appointed him the commander in chief of his armies and commander of his vanguard, and conferred on him the titles of Master of the Hall of Assembly, Keeper of the Carpets-Chamber, and Maestro of the Assembly of Kettledrums. Along with these designations he also bestowed on Aadi a title and a robe of honor comprising eighteen pieces.

Following Amir's directions, Amar said to Aadi, "Let us know what quantity of rations and other victuals you require, so that the Master of the Kitchen may send you daily that quantity, or have it delivered to your camp cooked should you so wish." Aadi answered, "This now is my home. And I just need food enough to keep body and soul together so that I may guard the gates of Amir's court with strength commensurate with the responsibilities of my station!" Amar said, "Speak plainly to me what quantity you need, and do not beat about the bush, so that the Master of the Kitchen may allot the necessary provisions for your table. The considerations of duty and submission to your master do not warrant all this modesty and coyness!"

Then Aadi said, "Verily spoken, my brother! Inform the Master of the Kitchen, then, that I eat a *nihari* of twenty-one camels in the morning; and in the afternoon the kebabs of twenty-one deer and as many fat-tailed sheep, with twenty-one flagons of grape wine to wash it all down. For dinner I have a fricassee of twenty-one camels and as many deer, fat-tailed sheep, and buffalo; and for the two principal meals, I have by my side a pile of bread made from twenty-one *maunds* of flour. As to the sweetmeats, they are never enough to my liking, but somehow I manage to ward off the pangs of hunger!"

When Amir was informed of Aadi's demands, he said, "Direct the Master of the Kitchen to have twice this amount—neither more, nor less—sent daily to Aadi's camp!" Thus it was apportioned Aadi's allowance, and was routinely sent to his camp.

After several days Amir heard of the arrival of Naushervan's emissaries, and the news that they had brought him a letter and a robe of honor from Naushervan. Khvaja Abdul Muttalib and Amir Hamza along with the other dignitaries of the city went outside the city walls to greet the ambassadors. They brought them first to their own homes with commensurate honor and prestige, and then had equipped illuminated residences for the ambassadors. Then many salvers of sweetmeats were put before them and, come evening, an array of delicacies were cooked and delivered to them.

Amir Hamza was greatly vexed upon reading the letter they had brought and regarding the shabby robe, and gave himself to disquiet and distress. When Khvaja Abdul Muttalib discovered the cause of Hamza's grief, he spoke thus: "My son! Such are the humors of kings. At times your salutations will invite their opprobrium; yet at other times your imprecations will gratify them and earn you a robe of honor. This is no occasion to become unhappy and dispirited; and not the hour for giving yourself to sorrows!"

The next day when Nature's Table-Layer produced the blazing hot sun from the Heavenly Oven, and spread out the spangled cloth of its luminance on the earth's expanse, Khvaja Abdul Muttalib held a feast in honor of Naushervan's emissaries, and also invited all the nobles and dignitaries of the city. After the ambassadors had been plied with meat and drink, they handed to Khvaja the letter addressed to him. Upon reading the letter, Hamza bitterly resented his fidelity toward Naushervan and the many exertions he had undertaken on the emperor's behalf.

The appellations of the emissaries, as written in the letter, greatly intrigued those assembled, who marveled at the spelling of their names. They misspelled the dot in Bahman Hazan's name, rendering it Bahman Kharan, or Bahman the Ass; and misusing the Arabic letter *kaaf* as written in the Persian convention, spelled Bahman Sakkan's name Bahman Sagan, or Bahman the Cur. And thus it came about that the two emissaries became famous in the length and breadth of Mecca by these remarkable names, and were remembered in near and far lands by these marvelous epithets.

Upon learning of the content of Naushervan's letter, Amar waxed even more furious than Hamza. When food was laid out on the spread, he brought before the assembly two salvers covered with pack cloths, and made to abuse the emissaries, but Hamza kept him from this intention. Then Amar said, "I have prepared this feast for our two honoured guests!" He then laid the two salvers with great ceremony before the emissaries, and said, "Here is food worthy of your palates!" and undid the pack cloths, producing a salver piled up with grass. Amar put this before

Bahman Hazan; and the other one filled with the bones of the dead he put before Bahman Sakkan.

All those assembled were astonished by Amar's deeds, and said, "What is meant by this? What is the place and occasion for this prank?" Amar replied, "What other delicacies are fit for the ass and the cur? This is what these creatures crave, and as I was obliged to show them hospitality and provide them a feast, I did my utmost to indulge their pleasure!"

The two emissaries could only grind their teeth at Amar with rage, as to say a word against him would have been indecorous. When the meal was over and everyone was well sated, Amar ordered two trays of robes placed before the ambassadors. Then removing the cover from the first, he produced a golden packsaddle and laid it on the back of Bahman the Ass; and producing from the other tray a jewel-studded halter and wrap, he draped them over the shoulders of Bahman the Cur. Unable to restrain themselves any further, the two emissaries drew their daggers, and ran after Amar to savage him. But Tauq bin Heyran wrested the daggers from their hands, and with well-aimed fists knocked them flat on the floor. Confounded by this turn of events, the emissaries escaped with their lives as fast as their feet could carry them.

Amir now wrote a letter to Naushervan, which read:

> Your humble servant received wonderful recompense for whatever service he had rendered you and for all the fidelity that he manifested toward Your Highness. Indeed, the services of your faithful merited just such a letter and robe as he got, and the note of disapprobation he received instead of a worthy letter of exaltation!

Along with his epistle, Amir also returned the letter and the robe he had received from Naushervan by the agency of Mehtar[118] Aqiq, and gave him sundry other instructions as well.

Meanwhile, the two emissaries arrived in Naushervan's court and narrated their woes amid great lamentations, making a great to-do about their treatment, larding the facts with falsehood, slandering much, and perjuring themselves greatly. Upon hearing all this Naushervan became vexed, and addressing Buzurjmehr, said, "These Arabs are a most rebellious lot and show great ambitions and giddiness of mind. It is manifest from the emissaries' account that they have embarked upon the path to revolt!"

Buzurjmehr replied, "Your Honor! No one more courteous, civil, courageous, or valiant, generous or polite—nor a better judge of character—was ever born in this world than Hamza. There is no one like him in prudence and precocity, in learning and intellect. If the account of the emissaries is true, and not adulterated with calumny, then there must be a good enough reason for it. In either case, we will come to know the facts, and the true picture of things will emerge before long!"

Even as this conversation was in progress, Muqbil presented himself with Hamza's letter delivered by Aqiq, as well as the note and robe received from Naushervan.

Upon reading Hamza's letter, and discovering the false note and the robe, the likes of which he would not have deigned to confer even on his privy attendant, the emperor raged marvelously, and severely rebuked Bakhtak: "O vile wretch! What baseness is this? What prompted you to act in so mean and sordid a manner?" The emperor fined Bakhtak a thousand gold *tomans*[119] there and then, and for several days afterward did not allow him to attend the court.

The emperor then wrote out an apology with his own hand, which read:

> The letter and the robe you received were subverted by the evildoings of Bakhtak. Considerations of obedience and duty demand that you do not let this incident cloud your judgment, nor let any resentment find harbor in your heart. This letter and robe are being sent to you with Khvaja Buzurg Ummid, Khvaja Buzurjmehr's worthy son, so that Bakhtak is afforded no further opportunity for mischief and my presents remain unmolested by all evil and resistant to the long hand of devilment. You must conduct yourself into the royal presence alongside Khvaja Buzurg Ummid, and bring back our crown and throne to present to us with your own hands.

Then handing Khvaja Buzurjmehr this letter and a far costlier and more resplendent robe of honor than before, the emperor bid him send them with Khvaja Buzurg Ummid, under strict injunction that no one should meddle or make delays in the fulfillment of this royal trust.

After returning home, at an auspicious moment Khvaja Buzurjmehr constructed a dragon-shaped standard of such subtlety that when the wind entered its mouth and filled its cavity, it resounded thrice with the cry of "O Sahibqiran!" The sound was designed to reach friend and foe alike. And while a perfume that put to shame the fragrances of musk and ambergris would suffuse the minds of the soldiers marching under this standard, the enemy would be struck with terror when laying eyes upon it. Along with this standard, Buzurjmehr also sent Hamza the tent of the prophet Danyal.[120] He also vouchsafed to Buzurg Ummid's care four hundred and forty-four devices of manifold virtues packed inside a costume of trickery meant for Amar. He enjoined Buzurg Ummid to present these to Amar on his behalf, and provided him with instructions on how to outfit Amar in the garb with his own hands. After imparting all these instructions, Buzurjmehr accompanied an army of troops to escort Buzurg Ummid, and instructed him well on the perils and pitfalls of the journey, and of its various stages and stations.

At a distance of four leagues from Mecca, Buzurg Ummid halted and set up camp. It so happened that that day Amar chanced by those environs during the course of his daily exercises. From the runner's physiognomy, Buzurg Ummid ascertained him to be Amar and called him over. He embraced Amar, and said, "You and I are like brothers. Our fraternal love yearns to make us one. In the name of Allah, stop here and rest a while, as my honorable father has sent you a present in this costume of trickery that I have brought you. Take off your Arabian vestments that you may be decked out in this livery and instructed in how to array yourself in your new attire." When Amar took off his clothes, Buzurg Ummid handed them to his companions, and left Amar standing naked. Then Buzurg Ummid said, "Never strip again in vain expectations! Clothed in your nakedness, now resign yourself to the will of God, and remain thus denuded and carefree like a child!"

Hearing this speech Amar became greatly alarmed, and cried abundant tears pleading movingly, "Return my clothes to me, and don't leave me in this disarray, denuded before so many people. For this favor I shall forever remain in your debt, and will renounce the costume of trickery and all gifts and take myself straight home!" Thereupon Buzurg Ummid burst out laughing, and said, "O Father of the Racers of the World! You, Amar, will thus consternate many by stripping them naked, and will steal the mantles and robes of many a person. I left you standing naked for a while so that the memory of this humiliation may accompany you on those occasions." Amar replied, "I submit myself to your instruction!"

Then Buzurg Ummid sent for the parcel from the wardrobe, and first made Amar put on breeches lacking in a codpiece. The moment the pants were pulled up, Amar's privates protruded from them. Then Amar said, "The generosity of your noble father perhaps could not afford to provide a handbreadth of cloth for the codpiece!" Thereupon Buzurg Ummid produced a piece of cloth, which Amar saw to be a brocade pouch with flowers and leaves embroidered on it in seven colored silken threads, and a priceless ruby hanging from its sash for a button. Buzurg Ummid strapped it over Amar's privates and said, "This is called an *aafat-band*.[121] Even in your many generations nobody has seen or heard of such a garment!" Thereafter, instructing Amar in its advantages, Buzurg Ummid said, "First, your testicles will not be exerted as you run, leap, or gambol. Second, you will not need to undo your drawers before swimming." Amar said, "All praise to your father, who provided a robe for me, and one also for my apparatus!"

Buzurg Ummid then dressed Amar in two shifts—one made of silk, the other of linen—and said, "The softer of the two is meant to provide comfort to the body, and the other is to afford ventilation." Then he dressed Amar in a singlet of green brocade, and placed on Amar's head a golden headdress decorated with a bejeweled aigrette and fillet[122] and surmounted by an emerald parakeet whose cavities were stuffed with musk and ambergris to delight the mind. He furnished Amar with a parasol made from the skin of the musk deer to protect his forehead from the violence of the sun; a sling wrapped in seven-colored silk, richly decorated with a variety of brocade patterns; and a lasso with emeralds and garnets that outshone the brilliance of the sun strung in every noose to serve as its knots.

Amar was given five daggers with bejeweled hilts, and forty-four rattles to strap around his waist. Then he was taught twelve musical styles, twenty-eight manners of improvisation, six high-key notes, twenty-four songs, and instructed in six methods of sporting stockings and false whiskers. Buzurg Ummid girded a naphtha flask securely around Amar's waist, and gave him a ball of dried silk cotton steeped in a blend of medicinal wines of such a potency that were even a small plug of it dissolved in water, that liquid would turn to liquor, and for all purposes would substitute for roseate wine.

Also, Amar received a gallipot of lip balm; a scent box of marvelously intricate pattern full of a remarkable fragrance of delirious power; a finely worked box of theriaca;[123] a fly whisk made of peacock plumules; a flask filled with water; a glittering and deadly sword; a shield polished to a sheen as bright as the sun's orb; a quiver; a bow before whose perfection a rainbow would appear shabby; and peerless Khorasani and Isfahani daggers.

Buzurg Ummid also gave Amar a cloak of trickery of vast length and breadth that covered his entire body from head to foot, reticulated like a bird net so that one wrapped in its folds would not feel his breath strangulated and would neither agitate nor suffocate; a pair of shoes decorated with broadcloth tassels, softer than cotton, light, and weightless; and two *hava-mohra*[124] plaited in silken cords for tying around the thighs so that even a thousand mile sprint would not tire out his legs nor would his legs ever falter. Buzurg Ummid then decorated Amar with four hundred and forty-four similarly marvelous devices contrived by Buzurjmehr, and also provided Amar with choice, rare, priceless, and glittering arms.

Amar then took his leave of Khvaja Buzurg Ummid, and presented himself in this array before Amir. After providing him a detailed account of his encounter, Amar said, "Naushervan has sent you an apology in answer to your letter, along with a most sumptuous robe by the agency of Khvaja Buzurjmehr's son, Buzurg Ummid, who is camped four leagues from the city. Khvaja Buzurjmehr has also sent you the present of a dragon-shaped standard and the tent of the prophet Danyal; and the selfsame hand has conferred upon me this robe of honor and four hundred and forty-four pieces of trickery that I am sporting on my person. His son has decked me out in this outfit and initiated me in the use of each one of these various items!"

Amir rejoiced greatly upon receiving these glad tidings, and rode out to greet Khvaja Buzurg Ummid in stately pomp and array with his companions and army. Buzurg Ummid received Hamza with affection, and presented the apology and the costly robe that Naushervan had sent for him. So gladdened was Amir upon reading the royal epistle, that he immediately decorated himself with parts of the robe of honor. Then Buzurg Ummid presented the dragon-shaped standard and Danyal's tent, and declared to Amir with great respect: "My father sends you his many benedictions with these presents—rare gifts that are wonders of time, whose possession truly becomes someone as august as yourself!"

Amir was greatly taken with Buzurg Ummid's ways, and felt a great debt of gratitude toward Khvaja Buzurjmehr. He vouchsafed the standard to Tauq bin Heyran, and gave Danyal's tent into Aadi's keeping. With his triumphant army, he escorted Buzurg Ummid into the city, presenting him before Khvaja Abdul Muttalib and other nobles and hosting a welcoming feast that lasted for several days.

One day Buzurg Ummid said to Amir, "The emperor will be expecting you and mentioning your name in his court with every breath. It would now be appropriate that you present yourself in Ctesiphon and, with your graceful presence so steeped in exaltation, regale and gladden the populace there!"

Therefore Amir rendered homage to the Kaaba with Buzurg Ummid and, having taken his leave of Khvaja Abdul Muttalib, headed toward Ctesiphon with Munzir Shah, Noman bin Munzir Shah, Suhail Yemeni, Sultan Bakhat Maghrebi, Aadi Madi-Karib, and Tauq bin Heyran at the head of thirty thousand sanguinary foe-slayers. They made regular stops on their journey, then setting out again toward their destination, and admiring the scenery on land and water.

One day they came upon a forked path, and Amir asked Buzurg Ummid, "Since you passed here on your way to Mecca, you would know where these roads lead, and to whose borders." Buzurg Ummid replied, "Both these paths lead to Ctesiphon. The one does not offer any perils, but it takes a longer journey of six months' duration; the other shall bring you to your destination much sooner, but this road has lain forsaken for the past five years as it passes through a dense forest where a mighty lion has hidden himself in a reed thicket. The lion comes out of the thicket when he catches the scent of man, and deals death to even the hardiest and most intrepid man with just one blow. Therefore no one ventures on this path any longer; fearing for their lives, everyone avoids this road!" Then Amir said, "That villainous beast torments God's creatures, therefore it is incumbent upon me to put an end to his mischief!"

And with that, Amir embarked on the perilous road to Ctesiphon, taking only the dagger thrower Khvaja Amar Ayyar along, and sending Buzurg Ummid on the road of safety to Ctesiphon with his companions and army, enjoining them to travel expeditiously. Much though Munzir Shah and others pleaded to accompany him, Amir did not grant their requests.

On the afternoon of the second day, Amir Hamza and Khvaja Amar arrived at the reed thicket adjoining the forest and dismounted by a spring—akin to the Fountain of Life in its clarity, and in the true sweetness of its water—to restore themselves with the delightful air. They strolled amid the pleasing verdure and the leafy trees that lined the expanse and rang with the chatter of lovely and colorful songbirds. Amir spread his saddlecloth by the spring and sat down to rest. Amar took the horse for grazing and occupied himself with enjoying the forest air, when of a sudden a rustling of leaves was heard in the forest, and the snapping of twigs announced the arrival of a beast. A great lion emerged soon thereafter. Amar, who had never beheld even the clay effigy of a lion, was frightened beyond measure and let go of the horse, climbed up a tall tree, and called out, "O Hamza! A great big lion has emerged out of the thicket and is headed toward you! For the sake of God leave your place by the spring and run to me, or take refuge in the branches of some tree!"

Amir laughed heartily upon hearing Amar's words, and said, "O rascal! Why have you become aflutter all of a sudden? Is it some madness or craze that has befallen you? I took this path for the sole purpose of exterminating this beast, and toward this end I journeyed on this path, having separated myself from my army! And now you wish to turn me from my purpose, instill fear in my heart with your words, and make me look a coward in this place?"

Amir pursued the lion and, stepping toward that horrible creature, discovered him to be a magnificent beast of terribly ferocious aspect, some forty cubits in length from nose to tail, and a full head taller than an ox. Amir challenged the lion and called to him: "Whither are you fleeing, O jackal-face? Behold here your adversary!"

Upon these words the lion leapt on Hamza, but the Amir turned to one side and foiled his charge. Then Amir bellowed "God is Mighty" with such clamor that the whole forest rang out with the cry. Catching hold of the lion by his hind legs, Amir shook him with such violence that the column of the beast's spine was shattered from the impact. Roaring with anguish, the lion soon breathed his last. Then Amar climbed down from his tree and kissed Amir's hands.

The next morning, Amar skinned the beast, cleaned it thoroughly inside, and stuffed it with straw. Then he gathered some branches from the forest while he schemed his new caper. He made a pedestal with the branches and installed the stuffed lion on it, so that whoever might see it would take it for a live beast. Then Amar hired a laborer to carry the contraption on his back, and they thus accompanied Amir. Having judged that his army would take longer to reach Ctesiphon, Amir made frequent stops in the meads at scenic, pleasing, and breezy stations so that he could occupy himself in the interim with hunting. Thus it was that Amir Hamza and Buzurg Ummid arrived at Ctesiphon on the same day. And while Amir went to visit his army, Amar set up the lion at the side of a hillock near the castle's gates so that nobody could distinguish between his effigy and a real lion.

The gates of the city opened the next morning, and a group of scythemen issued forth to do their day's work on the hillock. By chance, the eyes of one of them alighted on the stuffed lion, and screaming in terror, he began trembling violently and then fell to the ground in a faint. As his companions darted their eyes here and there in search of the apparition that had so terrified their friend, they, too, discovered the lion and thereupon ran helter-skelter into the city in a state of great alarm and agitation, with cries of "Lion! Lion!" The scythemen began to circulate rumors in the city, saying, "A mighty and ferocious lion is resting on the hillock, and could come charging into the city at any moment! Our companion fainted with fright upon espying the beast, and it is not known whether he will make it home alive, or fall prey to the animal!"

A great stir was created in the city by this news, and everyone became aggravated and perturbed. Some bolted their doors, and some armed themselves and lay in ambush on their roofs. Nobody ventured out of their homes, or took repose outside the safety of their domiciles. Watches were set up at all entrances to the city. The city was rife with rumors that hundreds would fall prey when the lion headed into the city. When the emperor heard the news he sought shelter in the royal tower, escorted by his ministers, commanders, and champions. They witnessed that a ferocious lion indeed reposed in a corner of the hillock, and whoever laid eyes on him shuddered with fright.

It happened that at that time Muqbil Vafadar was headed to the royal court from his camp outside the city, when arriving near the hillock he saw the lion, and loaded his bow with a shaft from his quiver and approached the beast close. He saw no signs of life in the lion when he drew near, and quickly discovered the subterfuge. Immediately it occurred to Muqbil that no one but Amar could have pulled such a prank—it was a caper that had Amar's name written all over it. He reasoned that Amir Hamza must have taken the path through the dense forest upon hearing of the lion, and must have cleared the forest of the pest. And that once the lion was slain, Amar must have stuffed him and installed him here to play this trick and frighten the people.

Muqbil narrated these thoughts to the emperor, who believed his construction of the events. Rejoicing at the news, the Refuge of the World then conferred a robe of honor, precious jewels, and three chests of gold pieces upon Muqbil Vafadar, and said to him, "Go forth and find out where Amir Hamza is camped: Locate his whereabouts and find out where he has alighted and lodged himself. Journey there yourself, and send other messengers, too. Find out the news and send me intelligence at once." Muqbil took his leave of the emperor and headed for the forest path.

Coincidently, Amar was headed up that path toward the city, taking the news of Hamza's arrival to Naushervan, having already seen Amir off to his camp. From far away Amar saw a party emerge from the castle gates and head for the forest trail. He went toward them and, upon closing in, discovered that the head of the party was none other than his old bosom friend, Muqbil Vafadar. Upon recognizing Amar, Muqbil asked him where Amir sojourned and had pitched his camp. It displeased Amar that Muqbil neither greeted him nor asked of his welfare, nor had he even as much as proffered his hand—let alone dismounted or embraced him.

Addressing Muqbil he said, "O pitch-faced one! Did Amir send you here to wait upon the emperor, or to go gallivanting?" Muqbil replied, "I heard that Amir arrived in the land a short while ago. I was headed to present myself and seek his audience. This is no pleasure romp; I come straight from the court!" Amar said, "You would invite a great calamity on your head by so doing, I will tell you that much!" Then Muqbil replied, "O Amar! Have you become crazed that you address me as an equal?" Amar, who was looking for just such an excuse, said with vexation, "O slave of slave stock! How dare the likes of you address such language to me? The three chests of gold pieces that Naushervan has conferred upon you have so robbed you of your reason that you deem yourself a Khvaja!"

Thereupon, Amar instantly undid the sling from his headdress and produced from his trickster's girdle a carved and chiseled stone, polished in the riverbed and tempered by the light of the sun and the moon, and wheeled the loaded sling around his head, aimed, and let fly. Blood gushed immediately from Muqbil's forehead.

Muqbil hastened before Amir Hamza's presence in this wounded state, and raised a hue and cry. Amir seethed with rage imagining that the people of Ctesiphon had thus bathed his friend in blood, and that a terrible scourge had been inflicted upon him by some seditionist. But when Muqbil blamed Amar, Amir sent for the *ayyar* and said to them both, "What is this that I see? Why do you harbor such malice toward each other?" Amar replied, "This situation reminds me of the proverb that says, 'Satisfied is the one who pleads alone before the judge!' Hear me out, too, before you assign the blame." Amir then replied, "Speak what you have to say! Let us hear what you have to offer in your defense!"

Then Amar said, "O my Provider! In an alien land one expects even a stranger to greet him and make him welcome. And in this instance I had

134 · The Adventures of Amir Hamza

met my old companion after a long separation, but he did not greet me as the True Faith or even civil behavior warrants, nor did he show the least token of fidelity by dismounting and embracing me. That we are cut from the same cloth is obvious; and as I see it, we are both equally worthy associates and equals in your eyes. I stood there in anticipation of greeting him, and he pulled the reins of his horse in a greatly condescending manner, and inquired of me about you. In all friendliness I said to him, O pitch-faced one, did Amir send you to wait upon the emperor or go promenading; and I told him that these pleasure romps would be his undoing. And what was the first word he said in reply? How dare I claim an equal footing with him! Now, I ask that you do justice and redress the wrong he did me. In what way does he have preference over me—except that by the virtue of Your Honor's Majesty, God has shown him the day when he sports a golden robe conferred upon him by Naushervan, and he has the possession of three chests of gold pieces conferred by the bounty of the same hand? But there is no helping his crazy arrogance! The sage spoke verily when he said, May God never confer power on the ignoble or endow a bald man with nails, nor indeed bestow a high office in life on a vile man!"

Upon hearing Amar's address, Amir said to Muqbil, "Indeed the fault is yours that your pride made you keep reserved with Amar. It is a fault to display haughtiness and pomposity toward friends. Come now, and embrace each other!"

Muqbil readily stepped forward, but Amar refused, saying, "My lord! He is a man of riches and effects, all magnificence and grandeur, with a high station in life; and I am but a common trickster without any means! Where is the parity between us? How could I pass muster by his side?" When Muqbil saw that Amar was unwilling to bury the hatchet, he offered him one of the chests of gold pieces, and said, "Here, brother, take this! Now, forgive my wrong and wipe all spite from your heart!" Guided as he was by greed in all things, Amar readily accepted the chest of gold pieces and embraced Muqbil.

The next day Khvaja Buzurg Ummid presented himself before Naushervan, and narrated the whole account of his journey to Mecca and of Hamza's arrival at Ctesiphon. The emperor rejoiced exceedingly and, heeding Buzurjmehr's counsel, made ready to go forth with his nobles to welcome Amir. Bakhtak incited the Sassanids to persuade the emperor not to go, and they cried that indeed an unhappy hour had descended upon the honor, majesty, and glory of the empire when the Emperor of the Seven Climes should go forth to greet a vulgar Arab lad and confer such prestige and honor on a common vassal and a ward!

Then Khvaja Buzurjmehr said, "Besides the fact that Hamza enjoys the honor of being the emperor's protégé, you are indebted to him, too, for the great favor he showed you, securing the release of your kith and kin from the clutches of the foe and providing them with robes, conveyance, and money for their journey. It shows that all of you are utterly shameless, wretchedly ungrateful, and blind to all sense and intelligence!" At Buzurjmehr's words, all conspiratorial babble immediately died out, and everyone was struck silent at their respective stations.

Then the emperor had his throne mounted atop four elephants and, escorted by his nobles and ministers, he went forth with great royal splendor to greet Amir. The commanders and grandees of the state followed in his train. The procession had advanced two leagues when a dark cloud appeared on the horizon. The scissors of the billowing wind cut asunder the veil of dust, and the Beautifier of Light washed the face of the field. There then appeared on the horizon twenty standards, with a force of thirty thousand mounted warriors marching underneath. Hedged by a body of troops under the flags fluttering in the gusting wind, Amir Hamza was seen riding Siyah Qitas in the shadow of the dragon-shaped standard. To his right rode illustrious kings, and to his left renowned warriors. And in Amir's cortege marched the Father of Racers, the Lord of Mischief-mongers of the World, the King of Dagger-Throwing Tricksters, Khvaja Amar Ayyar, sporting his headdress of brocaded silk, brocade singlet, broadcloth tasseled shoes, and trickster's sling, and bedecked with many such contrivances. A glittering sword bright as lightning reposed in his scabbard; a shining dagger was lodged in his belt; on his back were slung the bow and the quiver, the tangles of the lasso, and the net—the scourge of the adversary. He was accompanied by his pupils and continuously sang in six high-key notes, twelve musical styles, and twenty-four melodies in twenty-eight manners of improvisation.[125]

The emperor saw veteran soldiers marching to the right and left, front and rear, mounted and on foot, drunk with valor (a sight to behold of God's power!). When the emperor trained his eyes on Hamza, he beheld a youth of fifteen or sixteen whose cheek was covered with down, and before whose beauty the sun in the heavens was a mere worthless speck. With manifest courage, valor, grandeur, majesty, and glory he rode Siyah Qitas. A youth of such glorious parts the eyes of the heavens had never beheld; nor could someone more affable, gentle, worthy, and majestic with the summation of worldly accomplishments and intrinsic virtues like his be found on the face of the Earth. While Naushervan's gaze was riveted on Hamza's person, the powerful and mighty champions in the emperor's cortege realized the falsity of their claim to dominance upon beholding this sun of majesty and glory, and were thrown into great despondency.

Amir dismounted upon beholding the emperor's throne, and came forward to present himself, kissing the legs of the emperor's throne. Amir Hamza bore on his head the Throne of Kai-Khusrau,[126] which the hellbound Hashsham had plundered from Ctesiphon, and submitted it into the emperor's presence, along with the crown and other regalia of the empire. Amir had borne the throne on his head because when Emperor Kai-Khusrau had vanquished Turan[127] and then occupied Iran, to render homage to the emperor, Rustam bin Zal had walked thirty steps bearing this throne on his head. In like manner Amir showed regard for Naushervan by carrying the throne on his head for forty steps—sporting it like the aigrette in his turban—to declare that he was ten times more powerful than Rustam, the Champion Warrior of the World, and the Reigning Lord of the Powers of Time.

Naushervan was mightily pleased by this deed of Amir Hamza, and signaled to his attendants and minions to transfer the burden from Amir's head to their own, as was proper. Then he himself dismounted and stepped toward Amir, looking upon him with great fondness and delight. Amir fervently stepped forward with signal humility and, hastening toward the emperor, kissed his feet in utmost submission. Then Naushervan raised Amir by his arms and clasped him to his breast with great effusion. He bid his sons Hurmuz and Faramurz also to embrace Amir, and introduced him to all the commanders, and gave him the name, particulars, and the rank of each according to his station.

Of Amir Hamza's Entry into Ctesiphon and His Occupying of Rustam's Throne[128]

Narrators who illuminate the assembly of discourse, and storytellers who relate ancient tales, recount that Buzurjmehr then presented Khvaja Amar Ayyar before the emperor, and conveyed choice words of praise to his ears regarding Amar's person, detailing all his many talents to Naushervan. As a sign of great affection and benefaction, the emperor stretched out his feet toward Amar that he might kiss them and placed his hands on his knees. Amar kissed the emperor's feet and pressed the emperor's hands, and with wonderful artistry slipped the signet ring from the emperor's finger, so dexterously that the emperor did not feel a thing. After the royal audience Amar met other nobles of the court, and when he was introduced to Bakhtak, that swine of the faith, he quietly slipped the signet ring into Bakhtak's pocket.

The emperor then mounted his steed and, taking Hamza the Lord of the Auspicious Planetary Conjunction by his side, headed for Ctesiphon. Amar also joined the emperor's cortege, gamboling and vaulting, and making raillery all the while. At these proceedings of Amar's, the commander of Naushervan's *ayyars*, Aatish, stewed like a roast with jealousy, and called out to Amar: "O lad! The ladder of privilege is climbed one step at a time. What you assume is not yours to claim. Of a certain, your privileges do not undermine my own. Walk at your station, and do not overreach the confines of your rank! The retinue of the Lord Potentate of the Universe is not open to your trespasses. How dare you go marching in the emperor's rout?"

Amar answered, "First, you are a shrine of old age in comparison with my youth and vigor; and second, earlier your status may have been unchallenged, but now that I, an *ayyar* of equal merit, have arrived, you cannot claim precedence over me. As the proverb goes, why make ablution with clay when water is close at hand? An old codger like you would do well to ask to have some small gratuity bestowed on you by His Majesty and to retire into oblivion!"

Aatish flared up like a blaze upon hearing Amar's words, and retorted with a vigorous tongue-lashing. Both Amir and Naushervan had heard the conversation between the two *ayyars,* and turned their attention to the men. The emperor asked Aatish, "What is all this argument for? Why do you dispute between yourselves?" Then Aatish said, "Your Highness! Your born slave has long been the chief of the royal *ayyars,* and has a claim to prestige and honor among the tricksters of this land as an homage to Your Majesty. But this greenhorn, a trickster-initiate, has usurped my station in the cortege of Your Majesty!"

Naushervan then turned to Amar, and said, "Speak what you have to say in this matter! Is it that pride in your *ayyari* has made you too giddy?" Amar answered, "Your Lordship! *Ayyari* is not accomplished in words alone, but has to do with art and deftness! In this trade speed is at a premium; and alertness and alacrity are its mainstay. If Aatish wishes to test his mettle against mine, we are in a field already. He must not dither further but show instead his fleetness!"

The emperor said: "O Amar! You speak verily, and your words are to our liking! The gates of the city are two *farsangs*[129] from here. Both of you take an arrow and remove yourself thither. Whoever shall return first after handing his arrow to the guard on gate, shall win precedence over the other!"

The two acquiesced, and at the emperor's orders they were each given an arrow. Both arrayed themselves and set off like lightning, running shoulder to shoulder, flying like sparks, like arrows shot from a well-strung bow. They had gone some distance from the royal procession when Amar purposely lagged behind, and Aatish managed to put half-a-league's distance between them.

Those who witnessed this said, "To no purpose Amar lost all his prestige and distinction by making such a perilous wager with Aatish, who finally outpaced Amar!" Aatish was about to reach the gates of the city and show the soles of his feet to Amar, when Amar leapt into the air realizing that people would be throwing ridicule at him. The Father of Racers and Tumblers of the World turned a somersault alongside Aatish, delivered him a kick in flight, and bit him hard and so strangled his neck that Aatish fell flat on his back, all his speed and quickness having fled him; the taste

of agony alone remained in his mouth. As a stone struck Aatish's head during his fall, it splintered his skull, and he lay all bathed in a rivulet of blood. Thus shocked and confounded he fell unconscious.

Amar then took Aatish's headdress of an *ayyar* and, handing his arrow to the guard, said to him, "Mark me well! I am Amar Ayyar! The renown of my *ayyari* has reached the lands and kingdoms of far and near! In me the deceiver finds no refuge for his device, and I give the liar the lie! Beware, lest you be prevailed upon through bribery to bear false witness and state that it was Aatish who first handed you the shaft, and that Amar arrived and delivered his later! Woe betide you, O lad, should you lie! Beware and be warned, and let not greed be your undoing! Speak verily before the emperor, and do not dissemble or speak false!"

The guard was much bewildered at these words, and marveled to the limits of marveling at their import and at the calamity that had thus visited him uninvited. Amar retraced his steps, and took himself to the emperor's presence. After kissing his stirrup, Amar produced Aatish's headdress to him, at which the emperor broke out laughing at Amar's roguery. Then all the flash and flourish of Aatish became things of the past, and he was so embarrassed that he never again showed his face in the court.

When the emperor's procession arrived at the city gates, he ordered that the army of the Lord of the Auspicious Planetary Conjunction might camp at Tal Shad-Kam. Thus Hamza's contingent camped at this scenic spot outside the city, and his pavilion was also set up there by the riverside. The troops and foot soldiers set camp a short distance from each other. The mounted warriors formed themselves into protective hedges, and the auxiliaries[130] ranged themselves in ranks.

Then Hamza entered the city gates with the emperor, and found the citadel and every nook and corner of the city adorned for his welcome. The whole populace had turned out to set eyes on the Lord of the Auspicious Planetary Conjunction, and young and old alike were rejoicing because Amir had secured their freedom and shown them great favor. Whoever set eyes on Amir prayed for his benediction and petitioned that the Benevolent God might forever guard and promote his fortune; bestow on him ever-increasing riches and prestige; and with His bounty augment his majesty and grandeur. Amid these prayers Amir entered the Court of Jamshed with the emperor. They arrived in the royal court accompanied by the companions, counselors, and noble champions of both groups.

The emperor ordered that the nobles belonging to the True Faith be seated to the right of his throne, and that the rest take their allotted stations. Before anybody else had a chance to do so Amar made himself comfortable, and sat on a couch twirling his whiskers. The emperor then addressed Hamza, saying, "Consider this your own house, and find a seat for yourself where you will!" Amir said in his heart, *One must nip evil in the bud! I should set a lasting precedent by finding myself a station that will not be contested!*

By the throne was a chair inlaid with jewels, which traditionally had been the seat of Rustam. Amir made obeisance to the emperor and stepped thither. The moment he lifted the insignial covering of the chair and made to sit on it, a shaft of grief pierced the hearts of the Sassanids. But they held their tongues, realizing that it would be futile to contest this privilege that day or reprove Amir or foment sedition; they restrained themselves and resolved to bring up the issue and plead it before the emperor the next day. The emperor sent for many trays of gold pieces, and had them distributed as the sacrifice of Amir, and Hamza offered the gifts he had brought for the emperor.

At a signal from the emperor, richly adorned, fairy-limbed, and sweet-lipped youths brought goblets of sherbet and offered cups of the rose and sugar concoction. Amir drank first, then passed the cup to his companions. Later the table attendant laid out the bejeweled tablecloth and lined it with a multitude of choice food. Once the repast was over, goblets of wine were passed around, and clamor of "Drink! Drink!" rose from every quarter. Then revelries that were the climax of the carousing were set in motion, and silver-thighed cupbearers carrying in one hand a carafe holding roseate wine, and in the other a goblet of worked crystal, walked in enacting a hundred coquetries. At the height of this delirious event, the emperor requested Amar to sing.

Producing the prophet Daud's *do-tara*,[131] Amar began to strum at it, and his music attracted the ears of all assembled, young and old alike. Before Amar's melodious song Shora's melodies would have lost all allure; the cherubim in the heavens strained their ears to hear every chord of his song. From every corner of the assembly rose such a cry of "Marvelous!" and "Well done!" that Taan Sen's memory was revived. Then Naushervan thought of conferring his signet ring on Amar as a token of royal praise for his gift of song. But finding his finger bereft of the ring, he asked in all surprise, "Who took Our ring? It went missing from Our finger lately. Has it fallen somewhere?"

Amar responded with folded arms, "Your Honor! Except for those present in this assembly, no stranger has set foot here who could be suspected of this infraction. Who could have made away with the signet ring of the Emperor of the Universe in the presence of all his attendants assembled here? If you allow me, I shall search everyone present and recover the ring by the blessings of Your Honor's glory!"

Then Amar began to call out, "Hearken ye, O friends! Whoever has come upon the ring must needs submit it before His Highness to claim just recompense, or else the noose of scourge will tighten around his neck!"

Everyone began looking all about them for the ring, and murmured among themselves such words as "God be praised we never even as much as set foot outside the court!" Then at the emperor's signal, Amar made a pretense of searching people and looking into their pockets. Then the emperor said to him, "I have no suspicions regarding the nobles of the True Faith, as their creed does not warrant such an act. I would have you examine my courtiers, and conduct a search of their body!" After Amar had finished searching the warriors and commanders, the emperor ordered Buzurjmehr to search all the philosophers and nobles, and to check their garments. Following the emperor's orders, Buzurjmehr searched well their robes, girdles, and mantles, and upon Bakhtak's turn, discovered the signet ring in his pocket. Buzurjmehr was greatly surprised and all the nobles bit their fingers in astonishment. And Bakhtak was sunk into the mire of shame.

Then Amar declared with folded arms before the emperor in a loud voice: "*Ayyars* have been known to play such capers, but until today we neither saw or heard of a vizier thieving. Yet now that Bakhtak's example is before us, we can assume that viziers, too, are embezzlers. If the merchandise were worth a million a two, one could perhaps understand his motive. But to demonstrate an appetite for a trifle such as this, was allotted to Bakhtak alone, and serves as the crown of his ministerial career! Although his house must certainly contain far more precious jewels than this one bestowed by His Majesty as his oblation, yet those did not suffice for his greed! Indeed he is a worthy grandson of Alqash, and molded in his cast. It is little wonder he has stolen Your Honor's ring, since that ungrateful sanguinary, Alqash, kept Shaddad's seven treasures a secret from your patriarch; but by this theft Bakhtak has overreached the deed of even his own villainous progenitor!"

Naushervan blazed into a rage against Bakhtak, and heaped rebuke on his head before the whole assembly, showering him with insults. Then Amar said, "The just punishment for a thief is to cut off his hands. Such punishment—nay, one even harsher—befits the man before you!" Bakhtak said in his heart, *Confound this trickster! He clamors to have my hands severed! What retribution he has served me!*

At Buzurjmehr's interceding, Bakhtak's hands were not severed, and the infliction of that punishment was removed from his head. But ever more abuse and defamation was bestowed on him, and it was ordered that he be laid hold of by the scruff of his neck and driven away from court, never to be allowed back in. The orders were executed as soon as they were given. That very moment Bakhtak was shamed before the court, and thrown out.

After some time had passed, Amir Hamza told the emperor that Bakhtak was innocent of the theft and that it was Amar's roguery: one of his capers and caprices. The emperor was astonished at this display of Amar's sleight of hand and, at Amir's intercession, Bakhtak was allowed into the court as before. The emperor conferred the ring on Amar, and was mightily pleased by his sharpness and deceit. The emperor said to Amir Hamza, "You have my leave to retire and rest in your camp. But take it upon yourself to be in daily attendance at the court with your associates." Having thus spoken, the emperor retired into his palace, and Amir returned to Tal Shad-Kam after taking his leave.

Of Gustham's Entry into Ctesiphon Along with Bahram Gurd, Emperor of China

The writing finger of the storyteller shows its might and exerts itself in the arena of the paper in this majestic manner, relating that while Amir reached Tal Shad-Kam, changed his court livery, undid his arms, and made to retire, there arrived a note addressed to Khvaja Amar from Bakhtak. It read:

> I hereby send an offering of five hundred *tomans,* and a promissory note for an equal amount. Before long that amount owing will be sent to you, and the note redeemed. Other offerings will be made in the future at all suitable occasions in the hope that you shall never again play such jokes on me that threaten to condemn me to grievous insults, and render me vulnerable to humiliation, shame, and disgrace. By virtue of Your Honor's Majesty, I have a claim to respect amid the Sassanids, and among them I am considered worthy of note.

Upon receiving this money and promissory note, Amar rejoiced greatly, and said in his heart, *God be praised that I see the face of riches for the first time, and a little fortune has come my way of itself. God showered me with this wealth without my having to exert myself for it. This is a good omen, forsooth!* Immediately Amar wrote out an apology to Bakhtak, and sent with it the receipt for the money and the note.

The next day Amir Hamza presented himself in the court with his companions, and as before seated himself at the same station. The Sassanid nobles prickled with jealousy at this gesture, and schemed to reduce Hamza in the emperor's esteem somehow—to hold Hamza up to be unworthy of his station, and thus give him just deserts for arrogantly claiming that exalted station.

One day Amir Hamza was seated at this spot when a towering youth presented himself before the emperor, clad all in armor and sporting a helmet, cuirass, foot guards, hatchet, and *ragay*[132] on his person, the skirts of his robe rolled up around his waist, his sleeves drawn to his elbows, with steel gloves upon his hands grasping the hilt of his sword. He made an obeisance to the emperor showing utmost devotion and honor to his sovereign, and after he sat down, he regarded Hamza with a sideways glance and submitted to the emperor: "Your Honor sent my father on a campaign to Zabul, and in his absence seated an Arab lad in his chair. Is this fair consideration of my father's estimation in the emperor's eyes, or even warranted by justice? Is this how the ancient servants of the crown are dispensed their due? Soon, when my father returns in all triumph, it will be seen how this contumacy bodes for this Arab's merriment!"

Amir could not abide listening to this idle swagger, and said to the emperor, "What is the name and rank of this youth? His words smell of rebelliousness and sedition! What is the meaning of all his banter?" Naushervan said, "He is Faulad bin Gustham. I sent his father to chastise the rebellious emperor of China, Bahram Gurd, and he will soon return successful from having captured Bahram Gurd. He will soon make his entry, and then he will be granted all due honor and his wishes will be met. The chair in which you are seated belongs to him—it was allotted to him. This boy is vexed that you have taken over his father's privilege, and your sitting there torments him no end. He asserts that the seat belongs to his father and demands to know why I let you occupy a station that belonged to him!"

Amir replied: "I am desirous, then, that his father test his mettle against mine. And may the vanquished then forever pledge obedience to the victor!"

Upon hearing this, Faulad entered a wild rage and said with knitted brow, "O Arab! Wrestle my father later, when you have first wrestled down the hand of his son and shown all you have to show!" Amir responded, "As you please!" Then Faulad sat alongside Hamza and they interlocked their hands and exerted their strength. Before long Amir wrestled the boy's arm down, and Faulad fell from his seat. Embarrassed beyond measure, he drew his dagger and came rushing at Hamza. When Amir then wrested the dagger from his hands, Hurmuz said to Faulad, "O Faulad! Do you wish to disrupt the royal court? You have been suitably humiliated and yet you remain relentless in your conceit. Take yourself quietly to a seat, and then do not stir or say a word, lest you be humiliated further and are disgraced and shamed before the court!" From that day Amir attended the court every day with his companions, and when it adjourned, retired to Tal Shad-Kam to rest.

Some ten or twelve days had passed when news reached the emperor that Gustham was nearing Ctesiphon, with Emperor of China Bahram Gurd and four thousand of his Uzbek warriors as captives, and had halted four leagues from the city. Gustham awaited royal orders to approach, and as soon as he received the summons, he would present himself and kiss the feet of His Highness. Now, Bakhtak's heart was full of rancor toward Hamza, and he was always seeking a pretext to abase Amir and reduce his prestige and honor. The emperor had gone in person to welcome Hamza, and this news had become famous in far and near lands—this fact rankled Bakhtak's heart and he resolved to use the precedent to Gustham's advantage. Bakhtak would persuade the emperor to go in person to welcome Gustham, so that it would become clear that if the emperor had thus welcomed Amir earlier, it was no privilege exclusive to Hamza; but instead whenever any of the royal retainers returned successful from a campaign, the emperor personally greeted him to raise him in honor and prestige with his august and glorious presence.

In short, Bakhtak was successful in his scheme, and managed to prevail upon the emperor to ride out and welcome Gustham, and Bakhtak, too, went riding alongside. On the way Buzurjmehr said to the emperor, "Amir Hamza must needs ride in the royal cortege, too, as the escort of such a noble, valorous, and renowned champion would augment the prestige of Your Highness's retinue no end!" The emperor immediately sent word to Hamza's camp that he was headed to receive Gustham, and that Amir Hamza with his army, friends, and associates should also join the emperor.

The emperor's procession had gone a league outside the city when they saw Gustham bin Ashk Zarrin Kafsh approach, clad in mail and armor, twirling his whiskers, and riding a rhinoceros under the shadow of a wolf-shaped standard. It was abundantly manifest from his appearance that he gave no thought to anybody else's valor, bravery, or might, for he himself had taken captive a warrior of such repute as Bahram Gurd, emperor of China. Regarding this sight, the Sassanid nobles rejoiced in their hearts, thinking that now that Gustham had arrived, he would soon rout Hamza; and they indulged their minds with many such fantasies.

Upon coming close, Gustham dismounted, kissed the leg of the royal throne, and with great eloquence narrated the account of his bravery in taking captive Bahram Gurd and of the skirmishes of the battle. The emperor then made a gratuitous prostration to his one hundred and seventy-five gods, and turned back toward the city. But Gustham lagged behind at a sign from Bakhtak, and did not accompany the emperor. On his return the emperor crossed paths with Hamza and said to him, "Go forth and meet Gustham, and please yourself for a while listening to his adventures!" Amir acquiesced, and said, "I hear and I obey! Your bidding shall be done without fail. The execution of royal orders is an honor, and a reason for me to feel my increased worth."

Now we turn to Bakhtak, who bitterly complained to Gustham about Amir, and said, "Besides committing other misdemeanors that Arab lad had such pride and haughtiness in his valor that he committed the grave disrespect of couching himself in your chair. Then he grossly humiliated and disgraced Faulad before the whole court, overpowering him in arm wrestling. But God be thanked that now you are finally here and did not keep away long! When embracing him, press him in your grasp so that all his bones are set out of joint and he learns to reckon with your strength, and does not commit any further acts of pride and contumacy in your presence." Gustham replied, "I shall see to it!"

In the meanwhile Amir's party arrived and entered Gustham's camp. Gustham dismounted upon beholding Amir and stepped forward to greet him. Amir, too, got down from his steed, and both came forward for the embrace. As he embraced Amir, Gustham pressed him with his arms for all he was worth, offering him sweet words of welcome expressing his pleasure and delight. Amir returned his compliments and pressed him back so powerfully that Gustham's rear trumpeted many a note from an abundant release of wind. Greatly confounded by this mishap, Gustham whispered in Amir's ear, "O Amir! I trust to your chivalry never to breathe word of this to anyone, and not to work my humiliation and ruin before the world. Let that forever remain a secret between us!" Amir said, "Have no fear in this regard."

Then Gustham returned to the fort with his army in train, and Amir occupied himself with admiring the scenery, making quips, and jesting with his friends and companions who had escorted him. Thus occupied Amir noticed a chest being brought forward, heavily secured with chains, with four thousand menacing troops marching in the rear. When he inquired of the guards about the contents of the chest, they replied, "Within is enclosed Bahram Gurd, the emperor of China, whose chivalry and valor are famous to the whole world!" Amir exclaimed, "Who has ever heard of champions and kings transporting a prisoner in this manner? Who has ever seen chivalrous men put to such indignity?"

He ordered the chest put on the ground, and when his attendants opened it they beheld within a beautiful youth wrapped in chains and lying in a faint. Amir had him taken out of the chest, released him from his prison, and had his face sprinkled with rose water and musk willow and his mouth fed a sherbet of apples and pomegranates from the baggage train.

When the youth regained consciousness, Amir asked him, "Who might you be, O brave one?" He replied, "I shall give a detailed account once I have reached your camp, and then I will narrate you my whole story. At present my strength fails me from speaking a single word, and my senses are all in disarray!" Amir forthwith provided a horse for him and released his imprisoned men, and brought them all with great honor to his camp. He laid Bahram Gurd in his own bed, sent for aromatic unguents to revive him, plied him with a delightful and nourishing pap of almond milk, and fed his men on excellent food.

When Bahram Gurd came to, and regained the command of his faculties, he said to Amir, "Your auspicious aspect betokens nobility and majesty. Although it is against the norm, beneath all civil behavior, and contrary to decorum, to ask your particulars, I do not regard anyone else here worthy of this inquiry and, as my patience grows weak and my curiosity stronger, I request that you tell your pedigree and lineage and satisfy me regarding the title and station of the one whose hand warded off certain death from my head, and granted me a new lease of life. For I had reached death's door, and certainly would have been carried away by its hand! Many a day I lay entombed in that coffin without food or drink, and had all but resigned myself to death when God put my destiny in your path and showed me this happy day! It seems that some borrowed life remains to me still; that I shall live a while longer."

When Amir had satisfied Bahram regarding his particulars, Bahram rejoiced exceedingly and exclaimed, "Oh, happy hour! That I incurred a debt of gratitude toward one peerless in the Seven Climes!" Then Amir asked him, "O Bahram, how did Gustham manage to overwhelm you? How did you fall captive to his hands?"

Bahram replied, "After I had overpowered him in the battle, ravaged and destroyed his army, and taken him prisoner, he vowed fidelity to me, and for four whole years he remained constant in his devotion and servitude. On a hunt one day, I rode far away from my army and, as I was dying of thirst, I asked him for some water. He found the opportunity to drug it, and offered it to me. When I fell unconscious, he sent for his companions and abettors in my army, who had until now kept up the pretense of loyalty to me. They put me in irons, shut me in that chest, and inflicted all manner of torture and suffering upon me!"

Upon hearing this, Amir Hamza offered Bahram Gurd many words of consolation and solace.

When the news reached Gustham that Amir had taken Bahram and all the other prisoners into his camp, had given freedom to the emperor of China and his troops, and had regaled Bahram by hosting and feasting him, he hurried before the emperor with rage blazing in his breast and detailed the whole episode to him. The emperor was also greatly vexed upon hearing Hamza's conduct in this matter, and forthwith sent for him, and said to Amir, "O Abul-Ala! You knew well that in the Seven Climes I have no greater enemy than Bahram Gurd, yet you showed no regard for this consideration. Why did you grant him his freedom?"

Amir said, "Your Majesty being the Emperor of the Seven Concentric Circles, if champions and brave men are to be taken captive by wile in your time, there will be no stopping people from uttering inauspicious words about you. History will bear witness and to all eternity it will be mentioned in the assembly of Kings that Naushervan was such a coward that champions were subdued with guile in his reign—and that his retainers and ministers and warriors were ever skillful with the weapons of chicanery and fraud! When was Bahram Gurd ever such a mighty champion that he could not have been subdued in fair combat or prevailed against and vanquished by a valiant warrior?"

Hearing this the emperor said, "Where is Bahram Gurd? Send for him forthwith and bring him into my presence so that I may verify the circumstances of his capture and hear his account with my own ears!"

Amir had left Bahram in Naushervan's antechamber and immediately sent for him. Addressing Bahram, the emperor asked, "Did Gustham take you prisoner in the traditions of valor, or were you captured and imprisoned by treachery?" Bahram replied, "Your Honor will judge the facts with your own eyes, and will weigh the veracity of my account when I say that I have been kept on starvation rations for four months and have been denied food and water until today. While chained inside that chest I longed to see the outside world and breathe its air. If Amir was any later in securing my release from those confines, that chest would have served me for a bier, and I would have passed into the Future State. All that is abundantly plain as I stand before you in a most feeble and decrepit state. But were I to encounter Gustham even in these reduced circumstances, I could still wrest the sword from his hand, or else I should gladly forfeit my head to the executioner's sword!"

Gustham was present in the court with the Sassanid army. The emperor turned to him and said, "Do you hear what he states?" Embarrassed, Gustham hung his head and made no reply for his shame. The emperor then said to Bahram, "Would you be ready to wrestle with Hamza?" Bahram answered, "Most willingly! Once I have proclaimed myself a champion, I cannot disregard a challenge."

Then Amir said to the emperor, "O Guide of the World! At the moment he is most weak, and lacks any real vigor and strength. But were he to be carefully indulged and plied with nourishment for forty days, he would recover all his lost vigor, and then it would afford some joy to see a display of his strength against mine."

The emperor highly commended Hamza's suggestion and conferred robes of honor and a multitude of royal favors on both Hamza and Bahram, and then said, "O Hamza, I trust Bahram to your care and appoint you to attend to his needs of nourishment and welfare. You may then wrestle together and we shall judge the power and skill of both of you!"

Amir returned safe and happy to his camp with Bahram, and fed him on choice food for forty days. On the forty-first day, with Bahram alongside, Amir presented himself before the emperor, and said, "I am ready now to be matched with Bahram, as he is now well nourished and restored to his previous strength. Now you may see us wrestle!" The emperor asked Bahram, "Speak your heart's desire before me, and say what you have to say!" Bahram replied, "I am ready! To go against the emperor's wishes is beyond me."

Then Naushervan said, "Very well! We will witness the spectacle, and judge your skill." He ordered that the arena be prepared, and the ground was made ready forthwith. Both Amir and Bahram clad themselves in loincloths and caps of lion skin and girded themselves. Striking their arms with their hands in challenging postures, they were soon locked in combat.

Clasping each other's necks, they butted so mightily that a mound of steel would have turned to powder from the impact, but neither one even shed a hair. For a full three hours they wrestled together, and resorted to all manner of stratagems without either having any success in lifting the other over the shoulder, to say nothing of stretching the adversary on his back.

Finally, Amir yelled out "God is Mighty!" and lifted Bahram over his head. Bahram cried, "O Amir! You are clearly endowed with a might that is divinely gifted. In the whole world there lives no one more powerful than you—indeed you have no peer or equal! I surrender and vow submission. Stretch me not on the floor before these thousands, and deliver me not into such ignominy before other champions!"

Amir set Bahram lightly on ground. Voices of praise clamored from all corners in a chorus of "Bravo!" and "Well done!" The emperor commended Amir, who made obeisance, and said to Bahram, "Now, O Bahram, enter into the folds of the emperor's service, and ennoble yourself with the prestige found in his servitude." Bahram replied, "I shall never commit myself to anyone's service save yours! I am bound to your vassalage, and would dare not set foot outside my allegiance to you." The emperor said to Hamza, "To be admitted into your service is the same as to be brought into Ours!" He then conferred robes of honor on both Amir Hamza and Bahram.

Afterward, Amir brought Bahram to his camp and indulged him with his patronage. Bahram was allotted his own kitchen; a livery furnished with forty chosen horses from Amir's stables, fitted out with gold and silver bridles and saddles; seven strings of Bactrian pack camels; forty asses bearing loads of gold and silver; and a fourth part of the tribute from Yemen, as well as from the goods and chattels of Hashsham. Then Amir wrote a detailed account of these events, and charged Amar to deliver it to Khvaja Abdul Muttalib.

———

Now to the Sassanids, who in Bakhtak's company went to visit Gustham, lamenting and clamoring for redress. Both young and old, openly and covertly they seized the skirts of his robe and raised a great hue and cry, complaining that they had been robbed of their due honor and abased because of Hamza, that they were used ill and deemed worthless, and that if no serious attempts were made to rid them of the man, they would renounce all comfort and pleasure in life. They related how the emperor conferred increasing honors upon Hamza, and how with every passing hour their esteem and worth diminished as a result.

Gustham said to them, "Nobody can best Hamza in strength, and none can overpower him in combat. But soon I will work a stratagem in the guise of amity and concord, and will put paid to Hamza and erase all vestiges of his name from this land!" This counsel being held at night, the next morning Gustham rode out to present himself before Amir, and ingratiated himself with great deeds of flattery, debasing himself thoroughly with his humility and making a doormat of himself. Amir showed him great solicitousness and regard, and that day they both rode side-by-side to the court, with many words of conciliation and friendship exchanged between them.

When the court adjourned, and Amir left the palace to return to his pavilion, Gustham was on hand to escort him to his camp. Thus he spread out his net of treachery and dissimulation further. Gustham presented himself before Amir twice a day, performing new feats of fawning and cringing, and outdoing himself in his avowals of fidelity and servitude. Slowly Amir developed a fondness for Gustham, and all traces of his former spite were cleansed from his heart.

One day Gustham said to Amir, "The whole of Ctesiphon is witness to your favors and kindnesses toward me. It warrants some token of graciousness and gratitude also on my part, and therefore I make bold to ask that you spend some days in festivities in my garden and thus increase my worth and prestige in the eyes of my contemporaries." As Amir was simple-hearted and of pure disposition, he would not turn down Gustham's overture, and accepted his invitation.

It was the emperor's routine to hold court for one week, and spend the next carousing with moonfaced beauties in private, indulging in revelries. When the emperor next retired to attend to his private commerce and occupy himself with song and music, Gustham announced to Amir, "We have leisure this week. It would be a great boon to your orderly and a signal honor for him if you would deem it proper to set foot in his garden and spend this week there in feasting and revelry!"

Amir took Bahram Gurd and Muqbil and a few other associates, and with great pomp and ceremony they proceeded forthwith and arrived in all happiness and joy at the garden gates.

Gustham had spread out a floor covering of satin, brocade, and gold tissue from the gates of the garden to the summerhouse; and the summerhouse itself was furnished with a sumptuous carpet. Amir was greatly pleased with Gustham's exertions, and praised his fine taste to his companions. Fresh and dried fruits were put before them, and then Gustham sent for the silver-limbed cupbearers, and they began to drink in rounds.

Gustham for his part employed himself like a servant, with the skirts of his robes all rolled up, but he kept an eye out for his tyrannical, cowardly, and pusillanimous mates and accomplices. Before Amir's arrival, he had secreted away four hundred trusted intrepid warriors, with instructions that when he clapped his hands thrice and beckoned to them thus, they must come in force, and with relentless swords fall upon Hamza and all his sympathizers and cohorts, and not have the least fear regarding censure from either the emperor or Buzurjmehr.

In short, when Gustham saw the night spread its dark shades, and Amir and his companions had become befuddled and robbed of their senses by drink, he stepped into the corridor of the summerhouse and struck his hands in succession three times, and thus loudly gave his signal. His accomplices emerged from their hideout and followed Gustham's lead to where Hamza and his companions lay in the summerhouse.

Gustham looked squarely into Hamza's eyes, and spoke thus: "Hearken, O Arab lad! You displayed great rebelliousness, and deemed the nobles of the empire insignificant and worthless! Now behold the death that stands above your head, ready to carry you away!" He closed in, and dealt Amir a blow from his sword. Although Bahram was himself addled by drink, he threw himself on Hamza to act as his shield. Gustham's blow was thwarted and it landed on Bahram's back, cutting him open from back to front. The wound was most grievous and caused his intestines to fall out from his abdomen.

Muqbil had been prudent and had imbibed very little wine, and when he saw these events unfold before him, he secured his bow and arrows without further delay. He unleashed a hail of shots, riddling so many bodies with shafts that he brought down one hundred-odd men, and heaps of the slain were piled up in the garden. Gustham, mistakenly believing that he had killed Hamza, said in his heart that it would be futile to remain and become a target of Muqbil's aim, thus forfeiting life to no purpose since he had already finished off his main enemy. Therefore, mustering together the men who had survived Muqbil's barrage, he escaped with his life.

Upon regaining his senses, Amir Hamza beheld the truly remarkable view that lay before him: the whole summerhouse and the promenades outside were washed in gore like a veritable rose garden, and the garden bloomed with a new manner of spring. Nearby he saw Bahram lying on the ground and groaning with his stomach slit open, and more than a hundred men scattered around stuck with shafts. Upon inquiring of Muqbil, Amir discovered that all of this was the doing of the redoubtable Gustham, who in the veil of camaraderie had made him the target of a murderous plot (may such be his enemies' fate!). His treacherous attack had become known to all, and he had fled the scene of the crime.

The news circulated in every corner of Ctesiphon that Gustham had invited Hamza to his garden, and then worked his treachery. The emperor became inconsolable with grief upon hearing of it, and sent the crown prince Hurmuz, along with Buzurjmehr and Bakhtak, to attend to Hamza and administer him aid and relief; With the promise of rich reward, he dispatched Alqamah Satoor-Dast at the head of three thousand troops to arrest Gustham. When Gustham heard of the summons for his arrest, he absconded from the city in great disarray.

When the crown prince Hurmuz, Buzurjmehr, and Bakhtak arrived in Gustham's garden, they prostrated themselves in gratitude upon finding Hamza intact, and expressed great remorse at Bahram's injury. Amir said to Buzurjmehr, "You are a learned physician. Make haste to attend to Bahram's wound, and cure my cherished friend. For mark well that should Bahram die (perish the thought!), I vow by Holy Mecca that I will put every last Sassanid to the sword!" When Buzurjmehr investigated Bahram's wicked wound, he was thrown into a great doubt, and pondering how to prescribe medication and affect a cure, he was brought to his wits' end by anxiety and dread.

In the meanwhile there arrived the Father of Racers, Lord of the Conjurers of the World, the Clipper of Infidels' Whiskers, and the Trickster of All Time—to wit, Khvaja Amar bin Umayya Zamiri, who narrated to Hamza the joyous news of Khvaja Abdul Muttalib's welfare. But when Amar beheld Bahram's state, he shed many a tear, and said to Amir, "O Lord of the Auspicious Planetary Conjunction, is this the treatment one metes out to his associates? Is this how one upholds the traditions of nobility and patronage—that the one whom they patronize finds himself in such dire straits, and so ill-used?" Amir replied, "O Amar! This is not the time or the occasion to make injunctions or to revile and reproach me with these thinly veiled words! We must occupy ourselves in finding some relief for Bahram and succoring our unlucky friend!"

Amar turned to Khvaja Buzurjmehr and said, "I, too, am racking my brain to contrive some cure! But what do you suggest, as you are by the grace of God the most learned of physicians?" Buzurjmehr replied, "The wound is grave and past all art and modes of surgery. It could not be stitched up without the intestines first being returned inside and restored to their place; but to return them to the stomach cavity will be the devil's own work! The viscera are a most delicate affair, and just touching the artery of the heart would kill him—then nothing whatsoever could save him! And it is well-nigh impossible to stitch up the wound without handling the viscera!" Amar said, "Indeed Khvaja! You are a great, astute physician and my veritable teacher! Yet truth be told the province of medicine is a most abstruse domain, and none may claim command over it."

And having thus spoken, Amar produced a razor from his pocket and, pressing Bahram between his legs, reached for his gut. Khvaja Buzurjmehr asked Amar, "What is your intention? What have you resolved on in your mind?" Amar replied, "With a nimble hand I will first crop the intestines that are protruding out, so that they may be used to sew up the wound. Then I will apply a salve and make him well." Confounded beyond belief, Buzurjmehr cried out, "What is this disastrous course that you have embarked on? Do you wish to do away with this miserable man?"

Bahram was mortified by Amar's speech, and lost all hope for his life. He heaved such a deep sigh of resignation that it caused his viscera to return to the cavity of his abdomen, secure again in their place. Then Amar said to Khvaja, "There you have it! The problem stands resolved. As I had believed, it did not prove at all difficult! Now apply the sutures and sew up the wound." Buzurjmehr commended Amar highly for his judgment, and all those present broke into fits of laughter and unanimously extolled and praised the clever stratagem employed by Amar.

Buzurjmehr sutured Bahram's wound, and ordered that he be plied with sherbet so that the corrupted blood could be purged and all other contaminated matter expelled. Then he said to Amir Hamza, "Have Bahram's limbs secured well so that his movement does not cause his sutures to come loose and break the mouth of the wound. This would imperil his survival, and there would be no hope left for his life. I will come twice every day to check how the wound is healing, and shall do all in my capacity to make him well." Khvaja Buzurjmehr, Crown Prince Hurmuz, and Bakhtak then took leave of Amir and retired. Since Amir held Bahram dear in his heart, he decided to stay by his side with his friends, and ordered his attendants also to set up camp there.

When Buzurjmehr detailed all these events to the emperor, he responded, "Khvaja! There is no dwelling more sumptuous in Ctesiphon than the Bagh-e Bedad, and there is no building in the city that could surpass it in beauty. I wish to invite Hamza to stay there for some days, and make him the recipient of my best hospitality, and confer on him some gift, that the ire in his heart should be palliated. For he might think ill of me, imagining that Gustham committed this pusillanimous, dastardly act at my behest. Indeed, his act inflicted much pain and suffering upon me. Never did my ears hear a word of Gustham's intentions and I vow by the fire temple of Namrud that I did not have the least intimation of it. You yourself are witness that immediately upon my receiving this inauspicious news, I dispatched men in all directions to apprehend Gustham, and also sent out dispatches and criers everywhere!" Next the emperor sent a sacrifice for Amir, and also set out to call on him in person.

When Buzurjmehr went to see Bahram again, he said to Amir, "The emperor sends news that he has dispatched six commanders to all points of the compass to arrest Gustham, and has also sent a sufficient number of secret summoners and heralds. The moment Gustham is seized and produced, he will be disemboweled and stuffed with straw! The emperor offers many thanks that you escaped unhurt from the hands of that villain, and also for the great refuge and privilege that God bestowed on you. The emperor confers to you these gifts, and makes a present of these rarities with great affection. He has enjoined me to inform him of Bahram's condition and to confer on him royal favors, and has given me detailed instructions regarding his treatment, and has also asked me to devise a way for his wound to heal quickly. He sends the message that it would afford him great delight if he could have your company for a weeklong sojourn at Bagh-e Bedad, and if you would stay there with his attendants and nobles. However, Bakhtak and Amar must be excluded from the company, as they are both the very essence of knavery, and their hearts are bitter toward each other!" Amir acquiesced and accepted the wishes of the emperor.

The next day the emperor sent for Hamza to come to Bagh-e Bedad, and allotted him a seat close to the imperial throne. Amir brought Muqbil Vafadar and Aadi along, and presented himself before the emperor. He beheld the garden that was some four *farsangs* in length, and was abloom with all the ardor of the spring. But nothing would be gained by describing its beauty here, as I have already sung its praises before. And in order not to prolong the narrative, I vouchsafe all further exposition to the agency of the storyteller.

Amir Hamza sat to the emperor's right, and Buzurjmehr and the other commanders took their stations to the emperor's left. Then musicians of alluring art and singers of enchanting voice appeared, regaling and rejoicing this reveling assembly. The wassails began and drinks were served. The first day the emperor held the festivities in the summer-house. When the golden lute of the sun was encased in twilight, and the silver tambourine of the moon appeared out of the gloaming to preside over the assembly, moonfaced cupbearers carrying inlaid goblets and flagons of roseate wine presented themselves, and many rounds of red wine were imbibed. The emperor conferred a goblet of crimson wine with his own hands on Hamza, who made obeisance and drank it.

Then, the goblet reigned supreme, and the sunfaced cupbearers began to fill and serve cup after cup of crimson wine, and the drinkers quaffed heartily and embarked for the land of intoxication, until the sun's blossom bloomed in the heavens' garden, and like the beloved's eye the flower of moon closed its petals of the moonlight. Then silver-faced cup-bearers brought in flagons of elixir to help slough off headiness, and yet again the sinful lovers of wine gave themselves to their mistress, and the enchanting singers intoned so amazingly that the floor and the walls beat time about them.

———

Now a few words about the yearning of the Lord of the Cunning Ones, Khvaja Amar Ayyar, and some delightful phrases in praise of the cunning and roguery of the Lord of Mischief-mongers. When Amar did not see Hamza for a whole night and day, he set out worriedly, and his search and curiosity brought him to the gates of Bagh-e Bedad. There he found Aadi installed in a sumptuous chair, guzzling wine, with attendants at regular intervals plying him with delicacies that he would fall on with great relish. He noticed that the vigil that had been set up around the garden was such that even the avis of fancy could not gain admittance to its environs, let alone a mere bird. Amar began to inquire among his friends and companions as to the cause for all these arrangements and why it was that Aadi was keeping watch outside, while Amir was occupied within. Someone told him that the emperor had ordered Amar and Bakhtak to be kept out of the garden and that this was the reason why Aadi was deployed there: to intercept and bar entrance to both Amar and Bakhtak.

Then Amar went forward and, after greeting Aadi, took a seat next to him. Aadi said, "O Khvaja! How did you happen to come here? What was it that brought you to this neighborhood?" Amar replied, "Having not set eyes upon your countenance for two whole days, all the light in my eyes was beginning to darken, so I threaded my way stumbling and staggering to behold again your graceful aspect, and my good luck led me here into your presence! Even though you had forsaken me, I never once faltered in my fealty toward you!"

Aadi put wine and roast and other delicacies before Amar, who emptied one cup, then said, "I bought a ruby today, and I believe I made an excellent bargain! But you take a look at it, and assure me that I was not duped." Greatly flattered, Aadi puffed up with happiness thinking that Amar considered him a connoisseur of jewels—for why else would he come to him to have the ruby examined, and bring it for the inspection. He said, "Khvaja, no jeweler in the world could claim your astute judgment. Who would dare cheat you? But allow me, in obedience to your wishes, to have a look at it." Amar put his hand in his pocket, took out a handful of earth, and shoved it into Aadi's eyes. Aadi began rubbing his eyes, crying, "Confound you, Amar, you have blinded me!"

All those around them worriedly turned to attend to Aadi, and began to clean the dirt from his clothes and face. In one leap Amar got inside the garden, and reached the courtyard. When Aadi washed his eyes and cleared them of dirt, and the irritation subsided and his senses returned, he asked those about him where they had seen Amar go. But when nobody could tell him where Amar had disappeared to, or even the direction he had taken, Aadi thought that Amar had run away for fear of him.

When Amar saw the delightful beauty of the garden he was beside himself with ecstasy, as never in his whole life had he laid eyes on, or heard the mention of, such beauty. Then he sauntered off toward the palace where the emperor and Amir were assembled, carousing with their companions. A poplar tree stood aside the stream that ran along the palace. Amar sat under the tree, and, strumming, began a prelude on his *do-tara*.

Now, Amar's song could resurrect the dead and rob the sleepers in their graves of slumber. When the voice reached Hamza, he said to Muqbil Vafadar, "I believe that I hear Amar singing, and my ears recognize the strumming of his *do-tara*! How did he gain entrance since I had enjoined Aadi not to let Amar set foot in the garden, and not to allow him admittance? Go and bring Aadi before me forthwith!" When the emperor noticed Hamza's discomfiture, he said, "Do not send for Aadi as I exonerate Amar! But instead send for Amar by the mace bearer, and invite him here to join us!"

When the mace bearer called on Amar, he answered, "In such august company where the emperor and Amir preside, there is no place for a common, worthless *ayyar* like myself! Indeed, such a lowly creature as I is not fit to be admitted into such an illustrious and glorious carousal. I was brought to these parts because I had heard of the beauty and air of Bagh-e Bedad, where I might sit in a nook and regard the smile of the blossoms and fill my ears with the lamentations of the nightingale! Yet should I set foot in your assembly and by chance my presence clouds the mirror of someone's heart, I stand to receive harm from his hand. Also, as the proverb goes, safety is in being single, and calamity in being amid others! It is by far a better indulgence to keep one's own company, and I much prefer to be a recluse, all solitary and detached."

> Neither in Paradise nor in Hell
> Is there my solitude's better or match.

The mace bearer returned alone and narrated Amar Ayyar's entire speech to the emperor. The emperor laughed involuntarily upon hearing it, and all those present rolled up, catching their sides in a riot of laughter. The emperor then stepped out of the palace holding Amir's hand, and they made their way promenading between the gardens to where Amar sat singing. When Amar saw the emperor and Amir arriving with all their cupfellows, and regarded them coming toward him, he made a leap and fell before the emperor, kissing his feet, and calling down many blessings on him. Then he said, "I never once imagined that Your Highness, too, would consider my person as a nuisance and would forbid my presence at this feasting and carousing assemblage! As to Hamza, his singular devotion and faithfulness to his friends is amply manifest in the fact that he indulges in feasting by himself, and in no time forsakes old friends in pursuit of the least pleasure!" The emperor laughed at this speech and, leading Amar by the hand, brought him to the Qasr-e Firoza-Nigar. When he was seated on the throne, the emperor ordered Amar to be the cupbearer.

Amar began passing out cup after cup of wine, and making pleasantries. The whole night Amar performed his office, and at the outbreak of dusk he improvised and played so harmoniously on the pipe of seven joints[133] and intoned with such pathos in the style of the caroling of Daud, that a flood of tears issued from the emperor's eyes, as well as those of Amir and all their cupfellows, and they drenched many a kerchief with their weeping. At the emperor's orders, Amar's pockets and the skirts of his robe were filled with pearls, and very many gifts and robes of honor were conferred upon him. Then the emperor rose from the Qasr-e Firoza-Nigar and retired with Amir to the Qasr-e Zarrin, where the walls were made of gold bricks and the crevices inlaid with jewel slabs.

———

Now a few words regarding Bakhtak, that listeners may be afforded some mirth.

When Bakhtak heard that Amar had found his way into Bagh-e Bedad, he was greatly chafed and vexed. He paced to and fro clutching his sides and muttered to himself, "It is a great disaster that Amar has wormed his way into the garden, while I am not allowed and am denied admittance to an assembly that compares to the assembly in Heaven. There is no knowing what thorns Amar may sow against me in people's hearts, finding the field to himself. God alone knows what flowers of mischief will bloom there by his agency!" Weighed down by all these thoughts Bakhtak left for the garden, carrying with him salvers laden with bales of velvet, brocade, and gold-worked satin, and arrived at the gates of Bagh-e Bedad, where he greeted Aadi with a great show and avowal of friendship.

At this, Aadi said to him, "Where are you headed and what has brought you here?" Bakhtak replied, "I have brought some gifts for you, and present myself to make you these offerings. It would be a show of great indulgence on your part, and I will be forever indebted, if you would accept these tokens of my gratitude and allow me into the garden!" At these words Aadi flew into a rage, and with great anger exclaimed, "O Bakhtak, it is condemnation you invite, and your bad luck has led you here! Did you think me a bribe taker, that you could gain admittance to the garden by thus luring me? If you do not wish to be publicly chastised, you would do well to take yourself from my presence, or else I shall strip you of all honor before Amir and order the soldiers to drive you out of here by the scruff of your neck!"

Thwarted and downcast, Bakhtak returned home and bided his day in weeping and gnashing his teeth. But come evening, he donned a felt mantle and, carrying his clothes under his arm in a bundle, stole away in the manner of thieves and arrived under the walls of Bagh-e Bedad after giving the slip to the guards. There, he threw the bundle over the wall into the garden, and made himself ready to enter by way of the sewer.

Now, Khvaja Amar was performing the services of cupbearer in the Qasr-e Zarrin by order of the emperor, filling up the crystal goblets with crimson wine, when all of a sudden he had a premonition, and the notion that some roguery was afoot took powerful hold of him. He said in his heart, *Gustham, too, had arranged a similar feast in Hamza's honor, and for all appearances showed him similar hospitality and warm indulgence. I must go investigate and sniff around, lest some mischief should stir as before and some devilry be enacted!*

On the pretext of going to the toilet, Amar stepped out of the Qasr-e Zarrin and sneaked outside on the promenade. Looking cautiously to his right and left, and admiring the beauty of the garden, he arrived near the gates of the garden, where at that very moment Aadi was telling someone, "Bakhtak came today to bribe me, taking me for one as unfaithful as his own grandfather, Alqash, hoping to tempt me and gain admittance to the garden!" Amar started upon hearing these words, thinking that if Bakhtak had approached Aadi with that intention, he would certainly attempt to get inside the garden by all means fair or foul. Then Amar began inspecting every thicket, hedge, and shrub, and applied himself to examining every promenade and grove, in order to find some sign of Bakhtak's entry.

Suddenly Amar spotted Bakhtak's wares, and his eyes caught sight of the bundle lying under the garden wall heavy with robe and regalia. Upon opening it, Amar discovered Bakhtak's robe inside and his happiness knew no bounds, nor could he contain himself for joy. He hid the bundle in a nook under some leaves, and then sought the place where Bakhtak would stage his entry—for no thief could have dared break into the garden through the gates and hope to live to enjoy the fruits of his trespass. Amar's eyes fell on the sewer and when he looked closely he saw a man's head emerge from the hole and withdraw after looking around here and there. Amar decided that it could be no one but Bakhtak, the same man who was blind in his disloyalty to the emperor!

Amar hurried to Khvaja Alaf Posh, who was the chief garden keeper, and said to him, "While you drowse here peacefully in a stupor of indolence, a thief is about to break into the garden by way of the sewer! When I heard him stirring I came to alert you, and I have brought you this intelligence anonymously in the confidence that you are a man of reason and good sense. Now it is up to you and your sense of duty, and to the emperor's retribution, to decide what to do. If some mischief were to happen, come morning you would lose your garden and be consigned to jail!"

Khvaja Alaf Posh became duly alarmed and bandied together some gardeners. Armed with mattocks they took up positions at the sewer by the garden wall. The moment Bakhtak crept out, the gardeners fell upon him and tied him up in no time. Although Bakhtak shouted, "I am Bakhtak!" they paid absolutely no heed to his declarations, and began beating him after suspending him from the branch of a tree. The chastisement they accorded Bakhtak was as thorough and relentless as their exertions.

When Bakhtak had been beaten to a pulp, and his ribs and back were all swollen from the thrashing he had received, Amar called out to ask Khvaja Alaf Posh, "What is all this noise that I hear, Khvaja Alaf Posh? What is the cause for all this rumpus?" Khvaja Alaf Posh replied, "Everything is in order now! We have caught a thief, and tied him to a tree."

When Bakhtak heard Amar's voice and his words reached his ears, he called out to him, addressing Amar in the language of *ayyars.* "O Khvaja Amar! In God's name, release me from the clutches of these ruffians, and deliver me from the power of these gardeners! I shall remain indebted to you all my life for this, and there shall be nothing that I would deny you!"

Amar then spoke to Khvaja Alaf Posh and interceded on Bakhtak's behalf, telling him that this man was indeed Bakhtak the emperor's vizier, who by the machinations of fate had been caught in that scrape. When he asked Alaf Posh to release Bakhtak and set him free forthwith, the mouths of the gardeners blossomed like so many buds, and they accosted Amar in a thousand ways, and said, "O Khvaja Amar, what is this that you propose? What a prodigious story you tell us! Why would Bakhtak call such a calamity on his head, that he would strip naked and attempt to worm his way into the garden through the sewer and settle for the ways of a thief, when he is a close associate of the emperor? This man here is indeed a thieving burglar, and the strumpet's son has shown great nerve by thus breaking into the garden! Now he must receive just reward for his courage, and enjoy the springtide that awaited him in the garden. And should the real Bakhtak himself be caught in this manner, we would neither set him free nor let go of him. Come morning, what may come to pass before the emperor shall come to pass!"

Then Bakhtak said to Amar, "If you would at least allow me to have my robe back, I may clothe my nakedness!" Amar replied, "I know nothing about your clothes, and if these men have taken them I have no power to prevail on them to return your vestment to you and have you clothed. I know not who took them, nor do I know who may have filched them!" And having thus spoken Amar returned into the emperor's presence to resume his duties, and remained occupied thus for the course of the night.

When day broke, Amar declared before the emperor,

It is springtide, and clothed all in fragrance is the garden,
How the flowers have bloomed, and how charmingly the nightingales sing.[134]

"There is a spicy gale and the air is sweetened by the zephyr. The dawn is breaking and it is a fit time to promenade in the garden where the sweet birds chirp and the buds turn to blossoms. The dust is settled by the morning dew, and the soil is wet from the shower of dewdrops!"

Thus was the emperor inveigled, and leading Hamza by the hand, he headed to the flower garden for a jaunt, with his attendants in the train. Amar led the emperor to the place where Bakhtak was tied up against the tree, naked as the day when he emerged from his mother's womb. Bakhtak raised a hue and cry when he saw the emperor and began to shout, "O my guide and mentor! I was brought to this state at the hands of the gardeners!" Then Khvaja Alaf Posh presented himself before the emperor and admitted, "Your Honor! Last night this thief tried to break into the garden by way of the sewer, and your slave caught him and tied him here. When we thrashed him he made claims to be Your Honor's vizier, Bakhtak, and alleged that he was delivered into this calamity by the hands of fate and fatuity!" When the emperor and Amir Hamza looked closely, they discovered that it was indeed Bakhtak who was tied to the tree.

Then Amar stepped forward and said, "A fabulous flower has blossomed today in the garden! Bakhtak is most astute and discerning, a man of distinction and dignity. Why in the world would he take it into his head to break into the garden and invite this calamity on his head? In all likelihood it is some demon who has come in Bakhtak's guise and now enthralls Your Honor with this prank. It is most probable that within moments he will dissolve into thin air, and become invisible to all those assembled here!" Beholding Bakhtak in this state, the emperor blossomed into laughter, and those in his retinue split their sides laughing. So taken were they by mirth, that they laughed out loud before the emperor in a most unbecoming manner.

After Amar had spoken and the emperor made to move onward with his stroll, Hamza determined in his heart that the episode bespoke Amar's hand—the telltale marks of his agency were visible everywhere.

He pleaded for Bakhtak's release and delivered him from that unforeseen scourge. Bakhtak's whole body was lacerated, his wounds bled in many places, and the crown of his head was swollen like a great gourd. The emperor was so chafed with him that he ordered Bakhtak to be thrown out of the garden in that same state and to be driven from his presence. But Hamza obtained a pardon for Bakhtak, and paid Amar three hundred *tomans* to return Bakhtak's robe, and then took Bakhtak aside, offering him many words of comfort and consolation.

The emperor then headed for Bagh-e Hasht Bahisht, which was situated in the center of Bagh-e Bedad, set like a precious stone in a ring. The emperor entered the garden with Amir, Buzurjmehr, Prince Hurmuz, Muqbil, Bakhtak, and other commanders. Indeed that garden was worthy of the name it bore, and was a veritable image of Heaven.

Amar had written Bakhtak's name first and foremost in the Book of Idiocy, and in the Catalog of Fools had registered it at the head of the roster. Amar started his capers before the emperor, and said to him, "O Guide of the World! The gardeners' mattocks have pounded Bakhtak's bones to powder, and not a hair is left on his pate, which shines from the swelling as brilliantly as marble. To allow him some little *momiyai*[135] would be to show him great privilege and indulgence. It was indeed grave folly on his part to trespass against Your Highness's wishes and step into the garden without Your Honor's permission, for which exploit he has been amply rewarded. But he will never again embark upon so perilous an undertaking, and never in the future will this errant dolt set foot outside Your Majesty's wishes!" Amar then turned to Bakhtak and said, "Seek repentance now with clasped hands, and say, 'Never in my life would I even think of such a folly, nor ever commit such an unwarranted act, nor even dream of an offense of its like!' " In short, Amar made a veritable clown of Bakhtak, and afforded those present a great source of mirth at Bakhtak's expense.

Then the emperor said, "Send for Aadi, and produce him before us without delay." When Aadi was presented before him, the emperor said to him, "O Aadi, when I appointed you the vigil at the gate, I conferred a duty on you, deeming you worthy of my trust. Why did you show such callous disregard and think so little of my orders that Bakhtak managed to break into the garden and you never found out? How is it that Bakhtak barged into our garden without your knowledge?" Aadi replied, "O Guide of the World, Bakhtak does not have the wherewithal to set foot in the garden or to even reach its precincts without your ordering it so! He had come and brought me offerings to let him into the garden, but I rebuked him severely and sent him home in humiliation!"

To this, the emperor said, "Look over there, and see whether it is Bakhtak or somebody else!" Upon finding Bakhtak present, Aadi flew into a great rage and, securing him by the scruff of his neck, said to the vizier, "Mark now how I shall serve you after you have already been ejected from the garden, and see how befittingly you shall be buffeted!" But Hamza kept Aadi from such an undertaking, and stopped him from making threats and casting imprecations, saying to him, "Do not accost Bakhtak now, as the emperor has pardoned his misdemeanor and forgiven his offense. Return to your station and your duty!" Upon that, Aadi returned to the gate to resume his duty.

Then drinks were passed around in the assembly. And when the sun's peacock retired to its nest in the mountain of the West, and the ruddy goose of the moon appeared on the scene to promenade by the shores of the Dark Sea, torchbearers lit camphor candles in the chandeliers; dancers, singers, and musicians presented themselves, and the revelries began anew. The whole night Amar satiated the company with roseate wine and entertained them with his quips.

In this manner, the emperor conducted Hamza into a new palace every day and regaled him there in numerous ways with feasting and revelry. When it was morning again, the emperor removed himself to Qasr-e Chahal Sutoon. Amir was taken with the beauty of that palace and was greatly enthralled by its architecture. As the emperor had not closed his eyes even for a moment for the past five days and nights, he was overtaken by sleep, and Amir stepped out of the palace to retrieve a change of livery, accompanied by his associates and attendants.

During their stroll, they came upon a stream in a corner of the garden, the purity of whose water was such that it would have shamed the mirror of the moon enough to hide its face in the clouds. The stream's water was channeled into the palace through porous goglets. Amir expressed his desire to bathe and change his clothes to Muqbil, who took Amir's old livery and sent for a fresh change, while Amir occupied himself with bathing.

It so happened that at that time Princess Mehr-Nigar, the daughter of Naushervan the Just, was looking out the window from the palace roof.

In the reflection of her luminance even a mote sparkled starlike
And every pore of her lattice window shone bright like a sparkling star.[136]

When she laid eyes on Hamza, the shaft of Amir's love pierced her heart, and she fell into a swoon.

The garden caught fire from the lightning of her beauty's force;
Now when the gardeners pick flowers they must needs use fire irons.[137]

Thus love-struck, she said in her heart, *Those arched eyebrows have shot my heart with love's arrow. It was without inducement that I became besotted and was branded by love's iron. It would be a fitting response to give him a taste of his own medicine, as I must not allow him to escape retribution.* She took the *ambar-cha*[138] from her neck and threw it at Amir. It fell on Amir's shoulders, and upon looking upward, he beheld the handiwork of the Perfect Artist.

I beheld a beloved, fairylike, in elegance and grace unique;
In her years an adolescent, in her parts, a calamitous firebrand.

Presently Amir was overwhelmed and he fell on his back in the water. Muqbil jumped in to rescue him and helped him out of the water in his arms.

Then Amir heaved such a soul-searing sigh that his garden of pleasure was set ablaze, the flames of love conflagrated his heart, and tears of longing began to issue forth from his eyes.

Love's fire is one that would set ablaze a sea,
And should a stone catch it, likewise it must burn.[139]

Amir then recited verses composed in the *vasokht* style:

Oh, memory of the days when my heart was not love afflicted,
And neither warm heavings nor cold sighs were my familiars,
Neither did my eyes shed blood tears nor was my aspect wan,
Nor indeed was my skin enveloped in a cloak of dust;
Never did I have any traffic with those of the arrogant bent,
And in bliss I bided my life—as my days, so my nights;
My heart was not aflutter like a fish out of water,
Nor was there anxiety, nor sleepless nights, nor crying;
All a-bustle and fertile was my fancy's garden,
Alien to any grief, any longing, the least anguish or pining,
No gloom clouded my heart from the spicy gale of the world's garden;

My soul's colorful blossom was not a wilted flower,
When I heard someone cry I would exclaim, Oh, why cry!
What is grief, and why do people wash their face with tears!
Why become besotted! Why dote on your beloveds!
Why lose faith and heart! Why abandon sense and reason!
Why do lovers subscribe to the tyranny of their beloveds,
What is lovesickness, and what indeed is love!
Become known to it myself, I now regard love as akin to doomsday:
A calamity, an oppression, an outrage, and a scourge;
Indeed it invites a thousand reproaches and condemnations,
It is the flame that chars all—faith, heart, resolve;
In its path the very man whom you set out to guide will waylay you
And whoever you befriend you shall make your enemy;
Of love's kindling power I was full unaware
How its mere spark turned to cinder my heart's abode,
A soul-searing plaint, and a flamelike sigh issues from my lips
For by the selfsame fire I was scorched indeed,
The fiery planet in the heavens seeks refuge from this spark, too,
Which has reduced many a home to cinders;
It made Qais inhabit the desert of frenzy,
And who indeed is Shirin if not the one guilty of Farhad's death,
Love had made Wamiq besotted with Azra,
This author of enchantments holds me, too, in its thrall;
There is no provision for joy in the travails of love
Now the heart longs for tranquility, but where is peace?
The archfoe of life is my adversary
And in my bosom tuliplike my heart is smitten,
Blood admixed, the plaint rises from my heart to my lips;
I invited love's scourge on myself with open eyes, well knowing the
    implications!
I would have done well to indulge in the rose and the spikenard[140]
Rather than make her aspect and her locks my indulgence;
I was entangled at last in the coils of those dark locks,
Longer and darker than the poor wayfarer's dark night,
More wretched is my heart than the darkest of dark nights
And my home has become dreary and prisonlike to me;
What need had I to interrupt the continuous pleasure of my grief-free heart?
In what wise was musk less pleasant than the beloved's locks?
Forsooth I should never have set eyes on that moonlike forehead,

But this calamity was foreordained in the path of love;
Better to attain martyrdom by the agency of the shining sword
Than fall prey to the sword of her eyebrows,
I should have suffered the dread of parting,
Better to be riddled with spears, and those eyelashes evaded,
I should have eluded those half-opened eyes;
I never sensed the bloodthirstiness of that beloved,
Ready for carnage her eyes were, like a hundred daggers,
I should have run from them like the wild gazelle,
I should have regarded instead the eyes of the narcissi
And indulged myself with the gazelle's coquettish eyes,
Even though her aspect was full and luminous as the moon
And my heart tore me asunder from reason like the katan[141]
Were I to be resurrected by the one who laid me low
Never again would my tongue dwell on the praise of her inspiring lips
Oh, woe, that I became enamored of those missi-tinged[142] teeth
When I should have chosen the stars that brighten dark nights,
I fell like one purblind headlong into the dimple in her chin,
To drown in some well would have been a far better fate;
Her lovely spherical neck enamored my heart,
Like the finish of a crystal decanter it is, behold!
Her bosom no doubt is the envy of dusk,
I should have regarded instead the effulgent mirror;
Oh, woe, that I became enamored of her dainty hands,
My heart is mine no longer, with remorse I wring my hands,
I should have sought my pleasure from holding coral buds;
Her hair-thin waist coiled about and snared me and affords no escape,
It was indeed love that made me stoop,
For what business had I with her soles and ankles;
May none be thus trampled, as I was used,
May none ever be possessed by this scourge,
May none ever suffer from my malady,
He may well suffer from all ailments but this;
The passing of the day brings on the dread of the descending night,
The very mention of love sets fever in me,
A distant prospect is my release from the snares of love,
A distant prospect is rising from the sea where I am thrown
Fallen from the heights, a distant prospect is regaining my balance,
A distant prospect is obtaining any solace from the garden's charm;

My lamentations put to flight even the nightingale's reason,
Whenever I see a bud blossom, I wash my face with tears,
This passion has left my soul so branded
That even the garden appears to me now a fireplace,
The redolence of the rose is a detriment to my reason,
From grief I have no leisure, like a bud enclosed in grief;
Sometimes dewlike under the rosebush I drop crying,
Sometimes crying I embrace the cypress in my passion,
I writhe shut inside my house night and day
Without companion or consoler, without friend or solace,
My days and nights are spent thus strangely
And my restive heart allows me no repose in any one place,
At times from the city I wander away into the desert
And torrentlike I head to the river at times;
Oh, how to bring cheer to this cheerless heart?
Oh, how must I populate this desolate quarter?
Who would hear me! Before whom should I plead!
From whom should I seek redress for the wrong love did me?
Myself shamed, why must I drag another into this mire
To what purpose does one remonstrate with his own beloved!
None but my stars should bear the blame,
Even to declare my foe as the enemy is a meaningless exercise!
Constancy is a lover's retort to the beloved's tyranny
And should the beloved hurl abuses one must visit blessings on her,
For as long as the world where the fair one's reign remains
One must show a constancy that should become a thing of legend![143]

At this, Muqbil counseled Amir, "Now is not the hour to become derelict or cultivate the familiarity further! You must change into your new livery and return to the assembly!"

Acting on Muqbil's advice, Amir changed and returned to Qasr-e Chahal Sutoon. But all his humors were in disarray, and his senses were in confusion. And likewise Princess Mehr-Nigar was in no better state.

In a faint she fell onto the bedstead,
Falling into a swoon like one possessed.

Her nannies, domestics, and female attendants surrounded her. One brought her water in the bowl engraved with the *Chahal-kunji*;[144] one recited the *Ayat al-Kursi*[145] over her; another recited the *Naad-e Ali;*[146] yet another massaged her hands and feet. The princess stopped partaking of all food and drink, and her eyes were robbed of sleep. When she recovered and realized that her secret might leak out and her passion compromise her, she said to her attendants, "Do not give yourself to disquiet, as it was a momentary giddiness that overtook me. Now it is passed and I am recovered. Stop all this rumpus and speaking, and allay your anxiety!"

Amir Hamza, meanwhile, bided his time by vacantly staring about and waiting for the day to come to a close, so that he might find some remedy for his disconsolate heart, and the pangs of his yearning might be softened by the prospect of the evening drawing nigh. He passed his day somehow, and restrained himself until the evening hour, but then his restive heart prevailed upon him to say to the emperor, "Today marks the sixth night since your devoted servant slept a wink. If I may be granted leave, I would take some rest and remove myself to a garden nook for a little repose!" The emperor replied, "By all means! I give you to the protection of God!"

Then Amir stepped out with Muqbil and arrived under Mehr-Nigar's lattice window, but he found no foothold there save a great tall tree that stood by the palace wall, its canopy spread over the palace roof and touching the coping. Amir left Muqbil standing under the tree and climbed up himself.

Of Amir Hamza's First Tryst with the Apogee of Elegance, Princess Mehr-Nigar

Love is ever fertile in ploy and stratagem,
Ready with a new trick for every occasion:
Sometimes it becomes a contagion of tears,
Sometimes it reads like a fable of blood and gore,
Sometimes it becomes the salt with which a wound is sealed,
Sometimes it takes the form of a moth headed for the flame,
Sometimes it is the seeker, sometimes the sought,
An engaging subject it is in any guise.

The melancholic pen fathoms the affliction of lovers and discerns the humors of those languishing in parting; and with the tip of its tongue the love-stricken reed records the history of yearning and desire, and narrates this tale of separation and meeting thus: Hamza saw from the palace roof that Mehr-Nigar sat with a cluster of her moonfaced and fairy-limbed companions, with a flagon of crimson wine placed before her and a full crystal goblet held in her hand.

The wine of her beauty she pours in a goblet and herself takes pleasure,
Her hand the wine server, her lips drinking companions, what pure company
she keeps.[147]

But pearls of tears rolled down ceaselessly from the tips of her eye-lashes onto the skirts of her dress. The fire of love blazed in the chafing dish of her bosom; cold sighs abundantly issued from her lips; and plentiful was her indulgence in lamentations.

That morning Amir had beheld her from afar. When he regarded her now in proximity, he witnessed that the resplendent sun confessed its inferiority before her beauty; and the luminous moon borrowed its radiance from a single ray emanated by her dazzling aspect. Had Harut and Marut[148] seen her dimple's well, they would have presently drowned in it. The sight of her full chin made the citron abashed; her stature showed the cypress to have an awkward bearing; her cheeks made the tulips cover themselves with grief; her eyes drove the gazelles of Tartary into the desert from shame. In comparison with her eyebrows the moon's crescent would have been pointed at with scorn; her locks taught the spikenard how to curl; her eyelashes were a barrage of arrows for the lover's heart; flower buds would have wilted away in a gale of envy without ever opening their mouths if they had beheld hers; leaves of jasmine would have been held in contempt compared to her lips; the moon would have worn the ring of her servitude just from beholding the becoming way her ear sported the earring; if the lustrous pearl had witnessed the whiteness of her evenly arrayed teeth, the cockles of its heart would have been chilled with envy; the sharpest eye would have failed miserably if it had made an attempt to discern her slender waist; her abdomen was surmounted by two cupolas of excellence; her navel was a veritable whirlpool for those who would dive into the sea of love; and such were her feet that the lover's hands would itch just to feel them.

> Should the sun lock its gaze with her eyes
> It would be dazzled by a greater brilliance,
> Should the full moon behold her face
> From shame it would be scarred abundantly,
> If Yusuf, the epitome of beauty, had beheld her
> The knife would have cut his hand, not the citron,[149]
> And should Zulekha have regarded her
> She would not have looked at Yusuf twice.

VERSES IN THE *VASOKHT* DETAILING MEHR-NIGAR'S *SARAPA*[150]

> The bright nose on her luminous aspect
> Is like a shaft of light on the moon's illuminated face,
> Ears that would outshine a mine of jewels, such are her ears,
> The mirror is like a cloud of dust before her cheeks,
> Lips that would drain the Yemeni agate of all blood, such are her lips,

Teeth so keen as would make the diamond's edge seem blunt
Her mouth an imaginary mote, neither to be made out nor to be discerned,
It doubtless betokens the handiwork of God;
When was a bud so firmly closed that
The Fountain of Life hid itself in shame over her mouth's dissimulation
Who could do justice to the beauty of her embouchement?
The lips declaim, but may as well remain shut;
Her dimple is a marvel of the Creator's industry,
How lovely is this whirlpool in beauty's sea,
The heart marvels at the dimple in her chin
Which sinks the lover sooner than the lover's heart sinks,
Never would a lover find release should he drown in it,
Never would Yusuf's heart have sought release from this well's depths;
A neck the likes of which the eyes indeed never beheld,
Radiating most alluringly like roseate twilight,
It is a worthy dais for the codex of her face,
It is sheer bliss for my hands to clasp it in embrace,
As long as the gaze of my thought beheld that neck
It was as if the sun's taper had transfixed me;
Her hands burning torchlike from the tinge of henna
Have seared further my poor heart,
My heart flounders, alas her hand is not in my hand;
I was brought to love not by my heart but by my doom,
It is torture to break contact with her wrists,
My disconsolation was not born today—long I have had no succor;
By the Progenitor's hand were her hands so marvelously cast
That Musa's miraculous White Hand[151] would become their sacrifice,
However brilliantly the sun's rays might shine
They, too, are bedazzled before the luminance of her fingers,
Even the sun's radiant flower would bite its fingers in marveling;
A hundred times the soul would offer itself as sacrifice to that flower garden,
What delightful pomegranates this cypress-statured one bears:
Are they two combed birds of prey,
Or two luminous, round lanterns together hung?
Are they two nosegays decorating a mantel,
Or two goblets full of light incarnate?
How bashfully she withdraws her form
When the mantle slips away from her bosom,
As she turns her face away to adjust her mantle,
Unable to withstand the sight the lover draws his last breath;
At all hours the bodice straps remain fastened,
With what unique restraint are my heart and soul restrained!

So fair a stomach that the mirror will be mortified with shame;
This cake of the moon, delivered on earth by God's own decree,
It would make the sun hide its face in shame with its effulgence;
No star could compare with the luminosity of her navel,
To seize her waist is for me to secure eternal bliss;
I would that luck should favor me with capture of that rara avis;
The tongue is struck silent when it must advance praise
And in secret is described the thing that is secret,
But the lover's heart is forever restive
And disguises the secret thing in this similitude of veils;
Here one must cultivate the concerns of modesty
And suffice with painting two waxing crescents together joined:
Such were her thighs that every time one desired to couch one's head on them
They would make the heart dolorous, and in grief indulge;
Even if a thousand velvet pillows should be provided
My head would not find solace until couched in her lap;
God's hands alone could have fashioned such milky-white calves:
The heavenly columns do not stand taller in beauty,
The luminous face of the moon pales in comparison,
What wherewithal hath a mortal's glance that it should dare to behold them;
Rich in beauty and comeliness are both her shins:
On what wonderful columns is poised the house of beauty!
Before her feet the emissions of the sun feel abashed
And the face of the moon from the luminous face of her heel;
Every star fades before the sparkle of her nails,
The roseate twilight blushes before her henna-tinged soles,
The partridge dove learns from her his gait,[152]
The fairies apply to their eyes as collyrium the dust from her shoes,
If her form is the likeness of doom, her demure ways are a calamity:
Her gait is enough to stop even the chhalawa[153] *in his tracks,*
So slender is her waist that her walk sends it into a hundred twists and turns,
And she shows favor in ways that would leave the heart bereft,
Her coquetry will accomplish wonders;
May God preserve her! All self-conceit is far from her mind,
She has not yet begun admiring herself in the mirror,
She has not yet estimated her beauty's grace,
She has not yet fathomed her innate worth,
She is as yet innocent of these conceits, oh, lucky me!
No arrogance hath her beauty, her comely aspect shows no conceit,
Nor is her glance initiated in amorous exchanges,
The locks covering her face are an annoyance to her,
And an annoyance to her, too, is the untwining of her ringlets,

She is loath to comb her hair for long
Or to have her dress rubbed with perfume,
Or indeed to make herself a coquette in any way,
So she would not know if someone were to throw away his life for her;
Such inamoratas are indeed rare in the world
Who find their common garb a lavish raiment:
The necklet interferes with my breathing, says she,
Who would lift the garland's weight, I am too dainty;
She covets neither bracelets nor indeed missi,
Not necklaces but one charm alone adorns her neck,
She shies from looking in the mirror,
Becomes bashful, blushes, and hides her face,
She becomes all distressed when clothed in lavish vestments
And all restless when her bodice straps are fastened;
She could never endure a lover's plaints
When the mere sprinkle of gold dust on her hair brings on a headache,
The kohl lining is a great weight for her eyes,
Her shoulders give way under the mantle's weight;
How could her neck ever lift the amulet's chain?
A lighter burden would injure it, she is so fragile;
How could her hands be exposed to the violence of henna's application
When they are liable to be injured just from the weight of its tinge!

Amir's senses fled when he beheld Mehr-Nigar's ravishing beauty, and in his heart the flames of love raged ever more furiously. Princess Mehr-Nigar, too, was counseled by her companions and confidantes, who did all they could to bring solace to her heart. They would say, "Who is to know what further ruin these lamentations would invoke; and who is to know how ill you would then fare (may such be your enemies' fate)? Become not derelict. Show some restraint, and control your passion! The one after whom you long so violently has also regarded you, and separation from you indeed will never give him peace and will keep him disconsolate! He will contrive some way to see you, and find a ruse to obtain a tryst with you."

At long last all those many counselors prevailed, and Princess Mehr-Nigar ceased her crying. Then Fitna Bano, the daughter of Princess Mehr-Nigar's nanny, handed her a goblet of wine to drink.

Drink, for the days of sorrow will soon pass;
As they had passed away before, so they would pass away now.[154]

The princess said, "I shall drink in a little while, after all of you have sipped first and made toasts to the ones who have captured your hearts!" Before anyone else, Fitna Bano raised a cup filled to the brim, and drank it in one go, toasting the name of Amar Ayyar.

Hamza was confounded upon hearing Amar's name, and wondered how Amar had found his way there. While he was occupied in these speculations and anxious musings, yet another beauty, Tarar Khooban, raised her goblet and drank the roseate wine, announcing the name of Muqbil Vafadar. And in like manner, one after another, the companions and mates of the princess made toasts in their turn. Hamza said in his heart, *Good heavens! Until now I lived in ignorance of these secrets, and as God is my witness, I never had the least foreboding of this state of affairs!*

Then the princess raised the goblet of crimson wine and brought it to her lips, exclaiming, "I drink this to the memory of the slayer of Hashsham bin Alqamah Khaibari, who secured the release of all of you present here!" At these words Hamza was thrown into transports of joy. Many a lover's secrets were then exchanged as the company was occupied for some hours in bouts of drinking, and during that time the princess quaffed every cup of the rose wine calling out a toast to the Lord of the Auspicious Planetary Conjunction.

After six hours had passed, the assembly adjourned and the princess retired to her bed, but though she tossed and turned, her eyes found no sleep in memory of the Sahibqiran,[155] and she cried on without cease until she was exhausted. Hamza saw that at last the princess had fallen asleep, and all her attendants had retreated, too, and were taken with slumber. He came down the palace roof from the stairwell, and stole quietly toward the princess's bedstead. He beheld that her eyes were closed in sleep, but the eyes of her longing had remained open.

The eyes are open in dreams of coquetry,
The mischief sleeps, but mischief's portals are open.

For a long while Hamza stood there admiring her luminous face and musing, *I have made my way here after so much effort, and at great hazard to my person. I must satisfy the yearning of my heart by some ruse!* As the Sahibqiran rested his hands on the pillows to lean over and kiss her sweet lips and also plant a token of his love on her rosy cheeks, his hands accidentally slipped down to the princess's bosom. The princess started and, having no suspicion of Amir's presence, screamed lustily with cries of "Thief!

Thief!" Her attendants rose immediately and rushed to her aid from all corners of the palace. Then Amir said, "O sweetheart! The slayer of Hashsham bin Alqamah Khaibari stands before you—in love with, and all but slain by, the coquetry of the fairy, Princess Mehr-Nigar!"

Upon recognizing Hamza, the princess was embarrassed by her screaming and offered him many excuses and apologies. Without delay she hid Amir under the bed. Then she said to her attendants, "I screamed as I started in a nightmare. You may return to your stations and go back to sleep now!" Already intoxicated with sleep, her attendants returned to their posts. After they were gone, Amir came out from under the bed and sat beside Princess Mehr-Nigar. In the morning the princess had seen him from a distance. Now upon regarding him in proximity, she fell into a greater swoon and took leave of her senses. But after a while she revived when Amir joined his mouth to hers and she inhaled his scent. The roseate twilight having appeared, Amir said to her after filling his narcissus eyes with dewlike tears of longing, "Farewell, O sweet one. The slayer of Hashsham bin Alqamah Khaibari can stay no longer!

It dawned on me as the night melted away
That the moon branded me and stole away![156]

"I fear lest the secret come out, as I had taken my leave of the emperor on the pretext of getting some sleep. Should I live, I will return tonight, after warding off and averting all hazard!

Instead of the sable spikenard I beheld the dark night of parting,
And separation was determined my lot even as I became enamored;
A heart whose longing would fain be satisfied with meeting,
That heart the heavens doomed to be separated![157]

"But erase not the memory of this victim of the dagger of your charms, and do not lose remembrance of one afflicted by separation!"

The princess sighed deeply and with tears in her eyes spoke thus: "How I shall while away this dismal day and bring solace to my heart remains to be seen!

The night of parting somehow found an end,
The task ahead now is to while away the gloomy, interminable day.

"Farewell now, and godspeed! I vouchsafe you to God's care!" the princess said.

Enough now and away with thee,
So that what is preordained shall not be hindered!
As sure as my soul shall pine for you
By and by it shall be calmed!

Thereafter Amir took his leave, climbed down from the palace roof the same way he had climbed up, and returned to the royal assemblage in Muqbil's company.

At that time the emperor exited his bedchamber to give audience and make his appearance in the assembly, and each and every station bearer, minister, and noble was enriched by the wealth of the monarch's audience. When the morning breeze freshened up the flower of the sun, and the sunflower blossomed, the emperor arrived in Char-Chaman holding Amir's hand, with his companions and mates in his train. But Amir was all restless like quicksilver in fire, and he no longer had any control on his heart.

A singular malady is your lover's frenzy, whom
Neither the company of men nor the desert affords peace.[158]

Every so often Amir would venture outside the assembly to behold again the sight of Princess Mehr-Nigar's palace.

Not friends but love now occupies him,
All decorum is cast to the winds by passion's frenzy;
I wished to emulate Ayub in my patience,
But lo! This restive heart no patience hath![159]

When Buzurjmehr noticed Hamza's restiveness, he surmised that Hamza must have become enamored of someone's charm. He signaled to Amar, who said, "I had come to this conclusion long before you did, and have suspicions that our dear Amir has fallen head over heels in love with someone, and the caprices of his heart are responsible for his state!"

Amir Hamza's restlessness had not escaped Bakhtak's notice either, and he concluded, too, that Hamza was in love. His restlessness bore telltale signs, and his trips in and out of the assembly were nothing if not the work of a strong passion. Bakhtak submitted to the emperor, "Your Honor! People disturb the assembly with their constant coming and going, and with their movements to and fro, they disrupt the harmony of the gathering. Pray declare that whoever shall now step out of the assembly without cause will be made to pay a fine of a hundred *tomans* for the disruption!"

The emperor found the counsel to his liking, and said to Amir, "If anyone now wanders out, he will invite a fine of a hundred *tomans* for doing so!" Amir acquiesced, yet his impatience made him rise twice from the assembly, and he was obliged to pay two hundred *tomans* in fines.

> *The buyers throng in your alley*
> *And hot and brisk is the trade,*
> *After beholding you I cannot move a step forward*
> *As I stand transfixed like a wall marveling at your looks.*[160]

Buzurjmehr now said to Amar, "We must arrange it so that somehow Bakhtak is made to leave the assembly, or is ejected on some pretense so we are rid of him for the present!" Amar replied, "Nothing could be simpler! In no time he shall vanish and be dismissed at one word!" Having said this, Amar approached the emperor and conveyed the following to the royal ears: "The festive assembly is now at a new height of elation. Should Your Highness so decree by your order, this slave would present a few cups of wine to Your Majesty!" The emperor answered, "Nothing would be better! Indeed I would like this very much!" Amar took the charge and with great zeal put the cup and the flagon into circulation. After passing three or four cups to the emperor in quick succession, Amar filled a cup for Prince Hurmuz and another for Hamza, and after serving them, presented one to Buzurjmehr. And going around in this manner he then put a wine cup to the lips of the Lord Swine of Faith, Bakhtak.

Then suspicion arose in Bakhtak's heart that something foul and villainous was behind this—some new flower of Amar's roguery was about to blossom—and Amar's request to be made the cupbearer hid some nefarious intent. He said to Amar: "The past day I gave up drinking, and therefore I shall abstain!" At this, Amar announced loudly for everyone to hear: "It is a prodigious thing that all the cupfellows of the emperor, and even His Highness himself, would deign to drink out of my hand, but

Bakhtak deems it unworthy of his station and is loath to do so! Indeed little does he know that if Satan himself had drunk a cup from my hand, he would have made a thousand prostrations before Aadam and never once raised his head in vainglory!"

The emperor included, all those present laughed heartily at Amar's quip, and the courtiers said to Bakhtak, "Indeed it is a signal honor to have Amar for one's cupbearer. Surely you cannot be blind to this consideration! It is most remarkable that you spurn this honor in your insistence not to drink!" Helpless, Bakhtak was left with no choice but to take the cup from Amar's hand. Overwhelmed by those who persuaded him to do so, he reluctantly drank it like one imbibing hemlock.

Now, Amar had admixed Bakhtak's drink with a drug, procured with great trouble, that was a most potent purgative. Hardly a moment had passed when Bakhtak's stomach began to churn and he felt a great turmoil in his bowels. Bakhtak submitted to the emperor, "Your born slave seeks leave to attend to the call of nature, and will return presently!" But hardly had he returned after relieving himself than he again felt a grinding in his bowels, and he was again obliged to rise. Amar said to him, "Whither go you now, as you ventured out only a moment ago!" Bakhtak said, "I am going to the toilet!" Amar replied, "Is something the matter with you? You just returned from the toilet!" Bakhtak then paid a hundred *tomans* in fine and attended to his need. No sooner had he returned when he again felt the urge to go. But the fear of incurring the fine kept him rooted to his station, until the urge became unbearable and, unable to control it any longer, Bakhtak relieved himself in his chair. The scat filled up his pants and flooded out from its cuffs.

Amar, who had been waiting for that moment, put down the goblet in his hands, and declared to the emperor, "Your Highness is now pleasantly intoxicated. Your pleasure would double if Your Highness were to take a stroll in the garden, and further his elation. The others, too, would be afforded as a sacrifice of His Majesty an opportunity to promenade and fill up the skirts of their longing with bliss!" The emperor replied, "O Amar! At this moment I would like it very much indeed!" The emperor took Hamza's hand and directed his steps to the garden, and those present also rose and followed in the emperor's train.

As Bakhtak, too, was obliged to rise, people soon noticed that his whole chair was smeared with excrement, which also flowed from the bottoms of his pants and defiled the Kirmani carpet upon the floor. Amar bore the news to the emperor, who was already tipsy from drink. Naushervan sent for Aadi, and said to him, "This uncouth, ill-mannered man is not fit for our company! Throw him out of the garden and drive him from our presence this instant!" Aadi, who was already furious with Bakhtak, immediately took him away upon receiving his orders, dragging him along by his beard.

Then Buzurjmehr said in his heart, *Bakhtak was gotten rid of by this stratagem, but Hamza's restiveness grows by the moment—God alone knows what has caused it. If the emperor should discover it, some new misgiving might find way into the emperor's heart!* Therefore, he declared with folded arms before the emperor, "Hamza is greatly indebted to the honor Your Majesty has accorded him. He shall forever be in thrall to Your Highness, and for all his life shall sing adulations and acclamations to the Emperor of the Universe for the esteem accorded him! The Guide of the World may now ascend the throne of the empire, as God's creatures await him for the dispensation of justice, and the royal subjects are waiting to receive his audience!" The emperor greatly appreciated Buzurjmehr's counsel and, after investing Amir Hamza with a sumptuous robe of honor, gave him leave to retire, while he himself repaired to the court.

Of Princess Mehr-Nigar's Anxiety After Parting with Amir Hamza and of Her Going Forth to Seek Him in His Camp

Scribes of love chronicles and cherishers of tales of love, passion, and desire write that the Lord of the Auspicious Planetary Conjunction returned to Tal Shad-Kam to count the moments and hours left until night, and in this manner bided the day of separation with prospects of the night meeting. When the sun's simurgh[161] returned to its nest in the West, and the moon's partridge dove[162] sauntered out to display its gait across the expanse of the heavens, Amir sent for his nocturnal livery. He put on a robe of black satin, girded himself with a cummerbund of black brocade, and tied a black mantle in a turban around his head. Securing a dagger to his waist and a sword to his sword belt, he donned woolen socks, put on felt shoes, and slung a rope ladder in a loop over his shoulder. Then covering his luminous aspect in a veil of black silk, he stepped out from his pavilion with Muqbil, and in this array headed for the palace of Princess Mehr-Nigar.

Amar lay in hiding along the way, and as they passed by he leapt out and shouted, "Beware, O thieves! Whither go you, and why do you hide your faces from me? Do you not know that I stand here on night watch, and make the rounds of vigil? How would you enjoy the prospect of my summoning the guards on duty and putting you under incarceration until morning?" Amir responded, "Verily spoken, O rogue and ruffian! Why must you needs thrust your nose in this affair?"

Amar answered, "It is now become amply manifest to me that I am not among your confidants, and so you kept this affair a secret from me and deem me unworthy of your trust and one who bears ill will toward you!"

Amir replied to him, "There is no one worthier of my confidence than yourself! I did not confide this matter in you for the reason that you would counsel me against this undertaking, and I have no control over my passion and no power over my heart. Come follow me, as I am headed for the alley of my sweetheart to bring solace to my heart with a tryst with my beloved!" Amar said, "O my lord and potentate! Who might she be, and what is she like—is she of the human kind, or is she a *houri* or a fairy creature—that she has thus melted a man of tenacious perseverance like yourself, and left you all shaken and aflutter?" Amir replied, "It is better to behold than be told. Come and witness with your own eyes, and pay homage to God's most charming creature!" After thus conversing with Amar, Hamza bent his legs toward Bagh-e Bedad and proceeded thither with great precipitation by the vigor of his passion.

———

Now hear how miserably Princess Mehr-Nigar fared, and how she passed her day in separation from Amir. Grief and lamentation filled up that morning, and she clung to her bedstead the whole day. Neither getting up nor getting out of her bed, she recited these verses all the while:

> *I pray, O my beloved, as I lay myself to repose*
> *That the sound of your approaching feet awakens me;*
> *My eyes are unclosed in the arms of sleep*
> *Like the languor-eyed narcissus.*[163]

She did not do her toilette, she neither ate a morsel nor drank a drop, nor raised her head from the pillows; she did not change clothes, nor brush nor plait her hair. The whole day she washed her face with tears, and cried from the pain of separation. For food she gnawed on morsels of her heart; for water she shed rivers of tears, and restrained them only when she felt someone's presence near. Her only combing and plaiting was to ruffle her hair with her dainty paw. She hid her face in the coverlet, and when she noticed someone approach, she stared wild-eyed, heaved cold sighs, and recited these verses:

> *My tears issue at the thought of those alluring narcissus eyes,*
> *The likes of a goblet are my wet eyes, a wine ewer my heart,*
> *Indulgence in that intoxicating gaze has made my heart a drinking house*
> *And my plight a goblet from which I partake and become inebriated with my*
>   *passion;*
> *Branded is my heart from the memory of those lips,*

From that ruby's fire is my desire lit,
My heart is become a chandelier lit by the tapers of my lover's luminous
    cheeks;
Like the moth my soul has fluttered out of my body,
It is springtime and every bough carries the goblet of intoxicating flowers,
And the zephyr is rollicking everywhere on the promenades.
Pain drives me away, but longing sends me back;
You are a candle, O tyrant, and my heart is like a moth,
Night and day those locks of night's hue engross me
And the sun's rays, too, have become the teeth of an ebony comb,
A veritable garden of desire's wounds is my breast
So that it shall forever be in need of a curative balm,
My Yusuf's purchase is a most perilous commerce:
Where the heart is merely the pledge money, life itself the price.
The restless billows of the morning breeze are perhaps a sign
That the destroyer of my garden of peace has set out on another pleasure romp;
Pay him no heed, O imprudent ones, occupy yourselves with your lives,
Nasikh is nothing if not a madman.[164]

And having recited these verses, she then sang out this *ghazal*, even as
she broke into a cascade of tears:

When I became enamored of that fairy creature
All my friends and foes arrayed themselves against me;
I am the moth of the kindled taper of her cheeks
Whose glance would strike even the houri breathless,
The cup of my eye has become the goblet
To behold and drink of her love's wine,
The bait of the dark mole on her face
Snared the bird of my heart in her locks,
The shoulders of my flower have become all blue from their weight
The very shadow of her tendrils is a ponderous weight for her;
After many a year, by the grace of my beloved's love,
The desolate mansion of my house is again brought to life;
How do you propose to escape with your life, O Ghalib,
Now that your archfoe is become your beloved![165]

When her female attendants noticed Mehr-Nigar in this state, they
said to Fitna Bano, "It appears that the princess has lost her heart to love,

as she neither eats nor sleeps, and neither in day nor in night finds any peace! Go take these tidings to your mother the nanny, and divulge to her the secret and convey her these tidings, so that she may busy herself in effecting a remedy, and the violence of the princess's passion might subside in some way. Or else love—that destroyer of house and home—will spread roots, and its victim loses all sense of shame and decorum, and soils all name and honor. It disrupts the sane functioning of the mind, blanches the bright-red rose to a saffron-yellow hue, brings on raving madness, exposes one to the urchins' stone pelting; blights the one exposed to its breath, inverts the reason, makes one suffer cold sighs and hot lamentations with every breath, bids one to impetuously shatter the fragile glass of his name and honor, leaves one in complete stupefaction, causes one's head to be broken by stones, plugs one's ears with the cotton of heedlessness, and commands one not to lend his ear to any counsel!

> *How light and nimble is love's hand in the world's garden:*
> *No one it despoils notices his disarray.*[166]

"And how well this issue has been addressed and how marvelously composed and constructed it is in the *vasokht* style."

> *Come to my succor, O streaming tears, for I*
> *Burn from the heat of love's blaze;*
> *I cannot withstand the searing of its burning*
> *And cry out, "Oh, it is a veritable inferno!"*
> *It never cools—the fire in my hapless heart,*
> *Love burns it with the fire stolen from someone's ruddy cheeks;*
> *When love's effulgence abated my heart's darkness*
> *Like an unclouded mirror the world appeared clear to my eyes,*
> *Beauty began to work its wonders and I*
> *Was snared by it at the outset of my youth;*
> *My heart would never be snared, it had seemed;*
> *Once snared it would never be released, it seems;*
> *To all creation love's faith is prescribed*
> *For there is no honor greater than love itself;*
> *Be sure that just as Khizr is designated a trustworthy guide*
> *The heart has been made a bezel for the signet of love [?],*[167]
> *If love's wealth in the world would become abundant*
> *Every humble ant would become the mighty Suleiman,*[168]

Were beauty and love not manifest in the world
All mysteries of the world would have remained concealed,
The heart would have discovered no peace in the world
And the least pleasure the young and old would never have tasted;
The guidance of love every soul must needs esteem,
From love's creation all creatures learned of God;
Had love never made itself manifest
The moon would not have shown his blighted heart,
If beauty had not initiated your heart in love
Your eyes would never have put on the veil of tears,
No hearts would have become enamored of Venus-like[169] *charms*
And in Babylon's well angels would not have been jailed;
If love's message Majnun's heart had not received
Never in his dreams would he have uttered Laila's name,
If passion had not found in Farhad's heart a seat
Separation from Shirin would never have ruined him;
Everyone in the world has found a unique master in love,
If a beloved was discovered the longing of the hapless heart was answered,
If love's warmth had not found a way into their hearts
Why did the moth plunge into the candle's flame with an eye to burn himself,
Why did the nightingale's heart become fixed on the rose,
And why did Zulekha yearn for the Moon of Canaan[170]
If love had not become incarnate in the moon?
Why did the sight of it rend the katan?
Unique from all charms is love's passion,
It was God's model for investing charm in all creation:
By this property the yellow amber attracts straws
And by it stone hearts of beloveds melt waxlike by the hundreds;
It is a scourge from which no heart finds refuge,
It is a calamity from which no soul shall find reprieve;
Oh, what is this distress in which my unhappy life is caught?
My heart finds never an instant's peace;
There are no two worse enemies of life than love and beauty,
It shall not escape their clutches, I have but one life—
In my grieving heart they wreak havoc,
Doom is spelled in a congress between straw and fire;
If beauty is the light the creation was endowed with, love is the fire
And there is no doubt that both have the power to burn;
With their fervor they bestir the world

And they have scorched hearts without count or number;
Both are incendiaries, and confounders both,
The likes of a flash of lightning they are to one's poise,
In their making a great blaze was consumed,
In every heart they conflagrate a blaze,
In every place they accomplish a new mischief,
All fires are humbled before their incendiary power,
They engender a rare manner of heat
And even without kindling consume both heart and soul;
Love and beauty are found everywhere locked in combat
And everywhere both exchange lovers' glances;
Both are fomenters of mischief, and ruinous of faith both,
They are the two who kindle a concealed blaze;
They deform strangely the forms in life,
Unleashing all manners of prodigies;
Love is the cultivator, if beauty is the garden;
Like so many flowers a thousand beauties smile,
Their arrays in various guises are a sight to marvel at;
If one is the agreeable tulip, another is the wild rose,
In a hundred colors they flower, like the double flower;
Begone malicious glances! How rich is their spring!
What everyone calls by the names "springtime" and "autumn"
Are indeed "separation" and "meeting," there is no question;
Just as alongside roses grow prickly thorns
Around roselike creatures strangers throng;
Cold sighs are as constant in their pledge to the lover's heart
As the zephyr is true in its pledge to the garden flowers;
May the Gardener's hand keep this garden ever in bloom,
May the hands of autumn never waste this beauty's grove,
May the least hurt never cloud a rosebud's heart
For they are the garden's envy, more fragile than flowers cast,
May a dainty beloved never wilt away like a flower,
May the winds of grief never blow over lovers' hearts;
O Benevolent One! Such are the works of Your Nature
That beauty and love are everywhere found in diverse equations:
Here an eye sheds blood tears, there a heart is rent asunder,
In a hundred different guises has love made its home in hearts;
Every tongue narrates a new tale of love
And reproach's arrows everywhere have made hearts their mark;

Only the wise and sagacious would comprehend
That for love alone the lover's breast was endowed with a heart,
And that the eyes were fashioned to behold beauty
And ears were made to receive the beloved's voice,
The lover's hands were made for the beloved's locks a comb
And lover's feet the conveyance to the beloved's door;
Never did I suspect the horrors that love would unleash
And in the flower of my youth claim my life,
That this seditionist would foment many an intrigue
And blisterlike would burst my heart,
That it would find a thousand places to ensnare my heart
And with marvels of deceit fill the lover's sight;
Love is one who has a seat in every bosom,
And its touch is more powerful than the philosopher's stone;
Who could escape with his life from its arrows of tyranny?
Every single soul was erased that it had marked
When it went raging, the many it claimed
Were speedily dispatched to the embrace of living doom.[171]

Hearing this, Fitna Bano said, "Indeed I must not bear this message to my dear mother, but you may do so and speak to her of this state of affairs. It would carry more weight if you carried this message to her and heard what she recommended and counseled!" In the end, some female attendants went in a body to narrate the whole situation to the nanny, who rushed before the princess in a state of great anxiety and beheld that indeed the princess was entirely out of sorts, caring neither for food nor drink, nor attending to her toilette or adorning herself. The princess's face held a wild expression, and she lay in bed with her head covered. The nanny lifted the coverlet from her face, and said, "O my lady, what is the matter? How do you feel? (May your ills befall your enemy!) Why do you lie here so dismal and forlorn? Hide nothing from me, but confide in me your heart's grief without fear or inhibition! I have been your confidante since childhood. May my life become your sacrifice: I shall lay down my life for you, and scatter it away to bring you cheer."

The princess said to her nurse, "Though considerations of modesty forbid me, yet there is no recourse left to me but to confide in you, as the fire in my heart sears also yours! Hear then, O Nanny, that the love dart of the slayer of Hashsham bin Alqamah Khaibari has shot my heart. There is scarce hope this wound will heal except by the medicine of a tryst!" The nanny replied, "Consider this proposition well, O Princess! For a host of renowned and mighty Kianid and Sassanid princes have sought your hand in marriage; but you turned down all of them. And he is a follower of the True Faith, someone who shares neither your faith nor your language. In my view it is improper for you to attach and tie yourself to him!"

The princess replied, "O dear Nanny! When did love ever have scruples about coreligionists or those who are not coreligionists! Bear it well in mind that I shall not have long to live if I am not united with the Sahibqiran, for my heart violently longs for him and has become most restive!" She then took off her *ambarcha* worth three thousand rupees, and conferred it upon the nanny, promising that hag many additional rewards from the Sahibqiran, as well as many rich gifts that she herself would bestow.

The greed of the nanny was no less voracious than Khvaja Amar's own. Her mouth watered when she set eyes on the *ambarcha,* and she agreed to do the princess's bidding, reasoning in her mind that since no amount of persuasion would turn the princess from her purpose, why should she turn down the advantages she stood to gain. She said to the princess, "If such is your desire and you are set upon it in your heart, then rise. Bathe and change, and put on jewels and decorate yourself with the seven adornments.[172] Once the night has spread its dark shades, I will dress you in nocturnal livery and take you to visit the Sahibqiran, and thus satiate your heart's yearning. But do not lose patience, lest the secret should out, as there is no gain but only loss to be earned from its disclosure!"

Her anxiety a little allayed, the princess became pacified, and at once went to bathe and put on lavish vestments. When the court timekeeper gonged with his mallet and rang the third hour of the night, the nanny dressed the princess in night attire. Donning a manly garb herself, she and the princess climbed down a rope tied from the tower on the palace roof, and headed for Tal Shad-Kam.

Amir Hamza's encampment was still some distance farther from them when they saw three persons clad in black coming toward them from their destination. Upon espying them the princess and the nanny took cover behind a tree and set about making themselves inconspicuous.

Amir Hamza, as it was none other than he and his companions, saw these two dark-clad figures seek cover. He remarked in a loud voice, "Behold, O Muqbil, these ladies clad in black who have ventured out of their house without the escort of men, and haven stolen away after giving the slip!" Recognizing Hamza's voice, the princess recited aloud these verses:

> *In whose longing my soul strains to flutter out,*
> *How nonchalantly he passes by me, and how close,*
> *Oblivious to the fact that my poor soul is beset with dereliction and*
>   *craze for him*
> *He comes to inquire my well-being of me.*

When Muqbil neared the tree, he saw it was the selfsame dainty, silver-bosomed, rosy-cheeked, and moonfaced Princess Mehr-Nigar, and he shouted joyously. Upon the discovery of this most delightful windfall, he called out to Amir, "Bring yourself here, sire, and behold and recognize these personages; discover whither they are headed, and after whom!"

> *There is no one but longs to hear news of you;*
> *I walk about barefoot like a thread without end.*

When Hamza saw the princess he was beside himself with joy, and grinned from ear to ear. It was like Khizr approaching the wayfarer himself before he had set foot without.[173] Such were Hamza's transports of joy that he cared not a whit for the empire of the Seven Climes. Holding Princess Mehr-Nigar's hand, he returned to his pavilion, and thus both Venus and Jupiter progressed in conjunction.

Soon Amar presented himself before them and, after making salutations, declared with great deference, "O Princess! Indeed it was a signal honor you bestowed on us by being attracted to this place by your love for my dear friend. Thus you kept us from our nocturnal wanderings, and as his sacrifice we, too, are blessed by your audience, and our heart's desire is fulfilled!"

> *What is there to wonder that lovers wonderworkers are?*
> *What is there to wonder that they discover whom they seek?*

When Amar finished, the princess asked Muqbil, "Who is this man and what are his name and particulars?" Muqbil replied, "He is none other than Khvaja Amar, who is renowned to the ends of the world for his roguery!" The princess was much fascinated by Amar's general cast and mien, and every so often looked at him from the corner of her eye, reciting these verses:

> *From your brilliance the sun in the East is ashamed to rise,*
> *There is none in the summerhouse but is astounded.*

Upon entering his court, Hamza had seated Mehr-Nigar by his side and poured crimson wine for her into crystal goblets. The princess, too, picked up a ewer and cup, and plied Hamza with wine while Amar sat and sang. Hamza conferred several thousand *tomans* on the nanny and bestowed on her a tray laden with jewels, promising her many other rewards besides.

> *The whole of night in revelries bided,*
> *In wholesome bliss the night of tryst bided.*[174]

Before the dawn appeared, Hamza, accompanied by Muqbil and Amar, escorted Princess Mehr-Nigar to her palace, and parted from her with the firm promise to meet again.

> *The prospect of parting makes togetherness pleasuresome,*
> *Drinking is delightful only from the ensuing intoxication.*[175]

Some eunuchs lay awake when the princess and the nanny entered the palace and, sighting these two dark-clad figures, they raised the roof with cries of "Thief! Thief!" But when dawn broke, no sign even of the thief of henna could be descried.

In the morning the head of the eunuchs sounded his drum, and submitted to Empress Mehr-Angez: "Only God is privy to what passes in people's hearts! And all tribes of men have their share of people who practice evil in the guise of piety, as well as those who are pious despite their wicked semblance! It would be seemly to appoint some commander at the princess's palace on night watch who will do the rounds of vigil with adroitness and skill!" The empress found his counsel to her liking, and informed the emperor who delegated the warrior Antar Teghzan with a contingent of four hundred troops and foot soldiers to watch over the princess's palace, with orders to set up watch posts, appoint guards, and make rounds.

Now to Hamza who waited for Princess Mehr-Nigar until the middle of the night. But when the princess did not arrive and he learned of the deputation of Antar Teghzan's guard to the princess's palace, he became most inconsolable from the pangs of his heart, and sent for his nocturnal costume.

> *Like the jonquil flower my eyes do not close,*
> *In whose quest do these portals remain open?*

When Amar noticed Amir in this state, he broke into tears and threw himself at Hamza's feet, imploring him thus with folded arms: "O Hamza! I would to God that you not set foot from your pavilion this night, and restrain your heart! It is rumored that Antar Teghzan has been deputized by the emperor to watch over the princess's palace, and he has orders to safeguard the place and look sharp about him. May God forbid even the likelihood that Antar should see you, and inflict some harm upon you by the propitious luck of your enemies! Then all the honor and renown you have earned would be ruined in no time, and your enemies would rejoice. They will heap reproaches on your head, cast slurs at you, and all your happiness will be destroyed!"

Hamza, who was in tears until now, involuntarily burst out laughing, and said, "O Amar! What has got hold of your senses that you frighten me with the prospect of death? Have you forgotten that I am the slayer of Hashsham bin Alqamah Khaibari, and that by the grace of the Almighty God I do not give the least thought to the day of my dying? When did I ever turn back from encountering these cowards! But indeed, if you should put a premium on your life, you are at liberty not to accompany me. You are free not to set foot outdoors!" Having said this, Hamza took Muqbil and headed for the palace of Princess Mehr-Nigar. And as Amar could not help but accompany him for better or for worse, he followed in his train.

Approaching Bagh-e Bedad, they saw Antar's night patrol armed with torches and *chor mahtabs*,[176] and a great sufficiency of auxiliaries doing their rounds, calling out, "Remain awake! Remain alert!" Amir Hamza and his companions hid themselves in a dense coppice that was close by, and after the night patrol had passed, Hamza left Muqbil to stand guard as before under the palace wall, while he climbed up it with Amar. Having gained the palace wall, Hamza found Princess Mehr-Nigar sitting dressed in her finery awaiting him, with all the paraphernalia of the assembly—salvers bearing goblets and wine ewers—laid before her. She was surrounded by a profusion of wax tapers, and flanked on one side by Tarar Khooban, the lover of Muqbil Vafadar, and on the other side by Fitna Bano, the nanny's daughter and Amar's faithful beloved. Aside from these two, the princess's other female attendants who were privy to her secret sat before her with instruments of music and song, awaiting the princess's pleasure like faithful friends. The princess's eyes were riveted on the roof, and cheerfully but with yearning eyes she kept watch for Hamza's arrival.

The arrow of the beloved's separation pierced through the heart,
And the chink of the wound became the waiting eye.

The nanny said, "May all your misfortunes spend themselves on me, O Princess. Today it is well-nigh impossible for the Sahibqiran to find his way here, as Antar is on night vigil with four hundred troops and foot soldiers, and everywhere there is a clamor of 'Remain awake!' and 'Remain alert!' " The princess replied, "O Nanny! If the Sahibqiran is at all constant in his love, then even if the emperor's whole army had been put on vigil duty—let alone this night patrol—he would yet make sure to visit before long! Indeed, I have a premonition that he shall be here soon!"

At these words Hamza rejoiced in his heart and came down from the palace roof. Then the princess said to the nanny, "Witness now how I had told you that the Sahibqiran would be here any moment! He had to come since he could not have found any peace without visiting us!"

From the enticement of my heart, straight
To the house of sorrow the lover was led.[177]
* * *
It was a wonder of God that he sets foot in my house;
I behold him and behold the prestige of my poor abode.[178]

The princess rose and led the Sahibqiran by the hand to her throne, and the two exchanged many words of mutual longing and desire. Fiery wine was poured out, and goblets of the crimson drink were passed around. The princess filled cups of roseate wine with her own hand and plied Amir with them, who drank with his arm around the princess's neck. Presently their lips joined, their bosoms pressed together in the frenzy of passion, and Amar began to sing and prelude.

Greatly taken with Amar's pleasantries, the princess said to him, "Do you feel a desire for any of these beauties? Do you yearn for someone among those assembled here?" Amar said to her, "I dare not broach this subject as she is one of your boon companions and enjoys precedence over all your other attendants. There is no likelihood of her welcoming my advances. Nay, she will answer the very mention of my name with abuse and vilification!" The princess gave her pledge that Amar was at liberty to seek the company of the one he preferred, and granted him leave to sit next to her with all intimacy. Then Amar nimbly leapt over to snuggle next to Tarar Khooban, and began making sheep's eyes at her. She began to abuse Amar at once, and with knitted brows rose in great indignation from his side.

The princess asked Amar, "What says she? Does she dare to revile and imprecate you?" Amar responded, "What has she to say? She indulges in dalliance and plays the coquette, but rejoices in her heart of hearts!"

"Oh, good gracious me!" the princess let out, and rolled down laughing. Then she said, "O Amar, tell me truly what attracted you to her, and caused you to give expression to your love and ardor!" Amar answered, "She is laden with jewels, and first and foremost that was what attracted me to her."

At this reply the princess and the assembly again burst out laughing. As Tarar Khooban began to feel the teasing, the princess said to her, "Indeed you are a veritable jade and a grump! How dryasdust are you, and what a spoilsport! Amar is of the same rank as Amir Hamza, and he is the Lord of Tricksters and Rogues. To be his beloved would afford you a status no less prestigious than my own! I swear by your head that you shall find no better man to attach yourself to!"

After these pleasantries had passed, Amir taught the princess the vow of fidelity to the One God and instructed her in the Act of Faith. The princess converted to the True Faith and said to Amir Hamza, "I shall remain faithful to you, and never step out of your authority for as long as I shall live!" Amir replied, "And until I have taken you as my wife with betrothal, I shall never have eyes for another woman!"

While these vows were being mutually exchanged, the morning star rose in the heavens. Amir Hamza took leave of the princess, and climbed down from the palace roof along with Amar and Muqbil and headed for his encampment.

The morn cometh, the night passeth and the beloved moon leaves my abode;
The face of morn extinguishes me, my beloved employs the ruse.

On their way they were challenged by Antar's night patrol, and the guards gave them chase with cries of "Thief! Thief!" Amir drew his sword and dispatched a dozen or so of his pursuers to Hell, and then returned safe and sound to his camp.

When it was daylight, Antar Teghzan found only his own men among those slain and discovered no stranger among them, and saw that everything else besides appeared normal. He narrated the details to the emperor and gave him a complete account of what had passed in the night. As per custom, when the Sahibqiran presented himself at the court that day, the emperor said to him, "O Abul-Ala, hear this portentous event: When rumors of thieves reached my ears, I deputized Antar to safeguard the palace. Last night some ten or so guards of his contingent were killed, and no trace was found of the thieves! I would like that you take the trouble to guard the palace yourself, so that the thief is captured or put to death, since your men are renowned for their vigilance!"

Amir replied, "I am faithful as ever, and I hear and obey! I shall act on your command with great diligence!" When people heard of this arrangement, they said, "Indeed the emperor has found a wonderful solution in appointing the Sahibqiran to guard the palace. If the thief is one of the Sassanids, he will never dare set foot outside again hearing of Hamza's name. And should he be one of the Arabs or the Turks, he will likewise think twice, and never find the courage!"

But Bakhtak said in his heart upon hearing these tidings, *This scheme of things reminds me of the proverb that says, All fear is dispelled from one's heart when his kin becomes the commander of police! The emperor has given the lamb into the guardianship of the wolf. Alas and alack, and a thousand plagues on such sagacity!*

After receiving the royal orders, and once the court had adjourned, Amir returned rejoicing to his pavilion, and ordered his confidants, attendants, and soldiers to be brought into his presence. Hamza delegated Muqbil with a strong force of two hundred for the night vigil and, at the third hour of the night he took Amar along as before to pay a visit to the princess, and they spent the whole night drinking and listening to Amar's songs. At the approach of dawn Amir took leave of the princess, after biding the whole night in great merriment, and returned to Tal Shad-Kam without the least foreboding of threat or the slightest shade of danger.

When the court assembled that day, Amir presented himself and submitted to the emperor: "Your humble servant stood vigil the whole night, but never did I see even the ghost of a thief!" The emperor said, "It was from fear of you that nobody set foot there, realizing that he could only do so at the cost of forfeiting his life!" The emperor then conferred a robe of honor on Hamza, and gave him occasion to rejoice further by lavishing him with praise.

Bakhtak then begged of the emperor, "Pray deputize Qaran Deoband today to night patrol as he is a Sassanid commander of noble birth, and this shall test his skill and diligence!" The emperor agreed to Bakhtak's counsel and appointed Qaran Deoband to night patrol.

Then Bakhtak said to Qaran, "O intrepid warrior, you are among the progeny of Tahmuras Deoband! Do your vigil with extreme diligence, and make an arrest immediately should you see a soul. And should he recourse to arms, you must answer in the same coin. Beware! Show not the least fear even if you discover it to be a veritable giant!" Qaran answered, "Calm your anxiety in this regard. I shall perform my duty in complete adherence to your orders, and also acquit myself honorably before the emperor!"

When the court adjourned, Amir returned to Tal Shad-Kam accompanied by his friends and companions. Qaran Deoband picked three hundred warriors from among his troops and deployed his night patrol at the onset of evening. The princess was most perturbed upon hearing the news of Qaran's deputation, and said to her nanny, "Today Qaran Deoband is appointed on night vigil. It is nonetheless certain that Amir will not be deterred in his resolve to pay me a visit. I wish somebody would take my message to him that he must not plan on visiting today, or even give it a thought!" The nanny replied, "Amir is not such an arrant fool: He will master his passion, as he puts a premium on his name and honor. It is certain that he will mark the peril and keep away!"

Now hear of Hamza who sent for his nocturnal livery when the night was a little advanced in hours. Amar beat his head at this, and said, "O Hamza! What devil has possessed you that your patience runs short for the length of a night?"

Amir said: "O Amar! Indeed love and patience have no affinity with each other. The fire of love conflagrates in my breast such that no one may turn me from my purpose. Who has the wherewithal to deter me from this undertaking?" Amar said in response, "But Qaran Deoband is not one to show any qualms in confronting you and he will not look the other way!" Amir replied, "If I should let the fear of Qaran prevail upon me I might as well give up all thoughts of love and desire now!" Thus, he donned his nocturnal livery and headed out of his pavilion toward the princess's palace, with Muqbil and Amar alongside him.

From far away they made out small coveys of guards patrolling the place carrying *chor mahtabs*, and upon arriving near Bagh-e Bedad, Amir saw Qaran installed in a chair, commanding his troops to be on the alert and look sharp. Muqbil said to Amir, "If you should so order I would take my bow from my shoulders, and with an arrow rivet Qaran forever to his chair so that he may never rise again!"

Amir said, "Let him alone, as I have no intention of killing anyone. I little care what preparations he makes. But if he tries to deter me I will deal with him severely, and in a most befitting manner, too!" Hamza then stole toward the palace walls evading the eyes of the vigils. Leaving Muqbil to stand guard, he climbed up with Amar and gained the roof.

When he beheld the princess, Amir was beside himself with joy and hurried to embrace her. They passed the night in great merriment and, at the approach of dawn, Amir sought to leave, making preparations for his departure while bidding the princess adieu. Amar climbed down the rope first, and when it was Hamza's turn, Qaran rushed upon him and dealt him a blow of the sword.

Amir escaped the blow, which fell on the rope instead, cutting it in two. Although Muqbil tried to break Hamza's fall, he never stood a chance under Hamza's weight, and the Sahibqiran's head struck against the wall, wounding him enough to bleed. Muqbil then unleashed a barrage of arrows and Amar a hail of stones from his slingshot, and they injured several of Qaran's companions. When Qaran realized that the thief was Hamza, he did not pursue him. Instead, he took the rope, which was marked with Hamza's name, and presented it to the emperor.

The emperor flew into a rage when he saw this evidence. He sent for Buzurjmehr and said to him, "Regard this deed of Hamza, O Khvaja! Tell me if it is commensurate with the profession of nobility, or fair recompense for my hospitality!" Buzurjmehr replied, "This evidence is fabricated! Someone has counterfeited Hamza's rope! Hamza is not one to commit so indelicate an act, and raise his eyes at the royal harem with nefarious intent!"

Qaran responded to this, saying, "Hamza's head struck against the wall and he was wounded and bloodied. You may send for him and witness it for yourself!" The emperor dispatched a mace bearer with the summons to bring back Amir.

Now hear how after Hamza had reached his pavilion, and was back among his confidants, he thought in his heart, *Qaran will surely give an account of my injury before the emperor and then I will be held up to shame and my name will be made to bear the greatest ignominy!*

He supplicated without cease to the Shielder of Blemishes and Hearer of Petitions, and with tears flowing from his eyes, prayed thus to the Almighty God: "Conceal my secret from the eyes of my enemies, and safeguard my honor and name from the malice of my foes! It was You who bestowed on me my name and renown, and all my power and might is a divine gift from You, O God! You are the Beholder of what is hidden! My intentions were not corrupt! I did not indulge in the proscribed! I brought a woman of the infidels to the folds of the True Faith! Remove all marks of injury from my head, and let not this secret become known to a soul!"

Hamza was thus occupied with prayers when sleep at last overcame him and he was suddenly lost in dream. He beheld that he was in the presence of the prophet Ibrahim who stroked his head gently with his hand, and said to him, "Rise, O Hamza! The injury of your head is healed, and not the least sign of a wound now remains!" When Amir opened his eyes and felt his head with his hands, he discovered that indeed no sign of injury was left on his head.

Presently he was informed of the emperor's summons, and asked to report posthaste before the emperor. Therefore Amir brought himself to the emperor's presence accompanied by his companions. By a clever stratagem the emperor made him uncover his head, and upon looking closely he could not find even a sign of a swelling, let alone a wound. Then the emperor held Buzurjmehr's words as true, and severely rebuked Qaran for casting malicious aspersions on Hamza, and for attempting to malign someone's good name. He conferred a rich robe of honor on Hamza, and had Qaran driven away from the court.

While all of this had been going on, Bahram Gurd had taken the ritual bath to celebrate his recovery to health, and had begun to wait upon the emperor.

———

One day Buzurjmehr said to the emperor before the whole court, "Ever since the Khusrau[179] of the dominion of India, King Landhoor bin Saadan Shah, has ascended the throne, the royal treasury has not received the required tribute from his dominion. And things have come to this pass because the Khusrau of the Clime of India is most powerful, and a marvel of girth and bulk. The war club that he wields alone weighs one thousand and seven hundred Tabrizi *maunds*. He is the best of the elite swashbucklers, and commands great pomp and array. An elephant serves him for his mount, and on the Arch of Khusrau he has mounted an image of himself astride his elephant and wielding his war club. From the terror it instills, not a single horse of the Kianids will approach it, nor any horse that spies it—whether of Arab, Tazi, Turkish, or Iraqi breed—will advance a step." The emperor's response was: "What is to be done about this menace?"

Now, as Buzurjmehr was a most sagacious man of great address, well versed in the ways of the world, and the choice among all ancients, he had quickly determined by the signs on Amir's aspect that he had become enamored of someone in the royal palace—and moreover, that his beloved could be none other than Princess Mehr-Nigar. And when the thief could not be apprehended, Buzurjmehr became further convinced in his view that these night exploits were indeed Hamza's doings. He said in his heart, *Amir's head is filled with the wine of adolescence, and he is blind to all considerations of what is seemly and what is aberrant! If this leads to an untoward incident, and some strumpet's son should report it, nothing will be gained but disrepute. And as I am Hamza's aid and abettor, I shall also be vilified, and my name will be sullied.* He therefore resolved on a course of action, and thought of bringing up the matter of Landhoor's revolt. He well knew that nobody would consent to undertake this perilous adventure, except for Hamza.

Thinking that Hamza would be cured of his calamitous love if he were sent on a campaign for a while, Buzurjmehr said to the emperor, "The best way to go about this would be to broach the subject when all the nobles are assembled. Have it declared that arrogance in his might has led the Khusrau of India astray from obedience to you, and that he thinks there is no one more powerful on the face of the Earth than himself, and assumes that the world has nobody to offer as his equal. Let us then see who pledges to undertake the campaign against Landhoor and subjugate that rebel."

Of King Saadan Shah's Brother Shahpal Sending an Epistle in Condemnation of Landhoor, and of Hamza's Resolve to Depart for India to Chastise Him

The steed of all riders of the arena of narrative, that charger of horse breakers of the field of ancient legends, thus springs with ardor and gallops through the expanse of the page, revealing that talk of King Landhoor's refractory ways had not yet been brought up in court when cries of "Redress!" and "Succor!" were heard, and a plaintiff's lamentations and pleadings for mercy were conveyed to the righteous ears of Naushervan the Just.

Following the emperor's orders, Bakhtak emerged from the court and received a memorandum from the plenipotentiary of the king of Ceylon. Presenting it before Naushervan, he broke open the seal, unfolded the epistle, and read it out before the whole court in a loud voice. In this letter, after making adulations to Lat and Manat and singing the praises of the faith and religion of Faridun and Qubad and of the fire temple of Namrud, the king of Ceylon, Shahpal, had written:

May it be known to the discerning regard of the Emperor of the Seven Climes, and become fully manifest to the one who commands an all-encompassing gaze, that in the past my brother, Saadan Shah, used to be the master of crown and writ.

One day he was separated from his party while chasing a quarry, and he wandered for three days. He arrived near a fountain half dead with thirst, and beheld a woman of extraordinary stature about to lift three filled water skins on her shoulders and carry them away. Saadan Shah said to her, "I have gone thirsty for three days: Give me some water and extinguish the searing thirstiness in my heart." Immediately that woman threw out the water in the water skins and set about refilling them. Greatly vexed by her deed, Saadan Shah resolved in his heart that once he had quenched his thirst he would spill the blood of her life as she had spilled the water of the water skins.

Later, that woman filled up a bowl with water and put it before Saadan Shah. But hardly had he taken a few draughts when she stayed his hand and began to ask him who he was, what his name was, and from which land and city he hailed. Saadan Shah said to her, "O woman of evil fate! Allow me to quench my thirst, and then ask me what you may!" But the woman did not desist, and paid no heed to his request. King Saadan Shah had a few sips more, and once his thirst was quenched, he drew his sword with the intention to murder the woman. She said, "O stranger, what is my crime that you are bent upon my murder?" Saadan Shah replied, "First, I had told you that I had gone thirsty for three days and was dying for a drop of water! But you drained away the three water skins that were full, emptying them before my eyes. Then you began refilling them, purposely indulging in procrastination, and I was kept waiting in my thirst! And when at last you did give me some water and I began drinking, you did not let me have my fill, but interrupted my drinking every few sips by asking me who I was, where I had come from, and why I was so thirsty!"

Upon hearing this the woman laughed out, and then said, "Verily a good deed receives little regard! First give me your name and particulars, then I will answer your questions, and satisfy and convince you well as to the peculiarity of my behavior!" Saadan Shah said, "I am the king of these dominions, and my name is Saadan Shah. I set out with a hunting party and wandered off course." She answered, "Fie on you that even though you are the potentate of twelve thousand isles, you are bereft of all sense and reason, and a great distance from the realm of intelligence and wisdom!" To this Saadan Shah said, "Can you prove what you say, or do you speak idly, trying to make a fool out of me?"

She replied, "Hear then, that when you told me that you had gone thirsty for three days and had come in search of water from afar, I threw away the contents of the water skins, and even when I refilled them and gave you some water to drink, kept you from drinking too quickly for the reason that you were thirsty of many days, and in your greed you would have drunk with excess. I reasoned that if you drank the water swiftly, and it affected the lungs, you would die to no purpose and if someone witnessed me I would be apprehended in retribution. Then it would have been impossible to win my release, and my name and honor would have been tarnished!"

When Saadan Shah heard the rationale for her conduct, he marveled to the limits of marveling at her sagacity, and became hopelessly enamored of her propriety and sense. He said to her, "Where do you live? Do you have any dependents or do you live by yourself?" She replied, "I have no protector but God. I earn my bread from the sweat of my brow, and for all practical purposes I have no guardian to speak of."

Saadan Shah brought her with him to the city and betrothed her, and after some days the woman was with child. And then Saadan Shah died and I ascended the throne.

After the period appointed for gestation the woman bore a son who measured five yards in height. After some time the woman also died, and I named the boy Landhoor and busied myself with his caring. I appointed milch she-camels to be his wet nurses, and also appointed numerous dry nurses and attendants to nurture and suckle him. God had also blessed me with a boy the day Landhoor was born, and I named that boy Jaipur and busied myself in the care and guardianship of both boys.

When the boys were five years old, one day in the way of disciplining him, a dry nurse slapped Landhoor, which caused his cheek to swell. Landhoor picked up that dry nurse and smashed her to the ground, and she soon grew cold and met her end. The guards escaped in terror of Landhoor, rushed into my presence, and gave me a detailed account of the incident, narrating all the particulars. I ordered that Landhoor be driven from the house that very instant and thrown before a rutting elephant. As ordered, the elephant was brought, and Landhoor thrown before him. When the elephant made to pick up Landhoor with his trunk, Landhoor caught hold of it and gave it such a violent pull that it tore from the root. Roaring with agony, the elephant ran amok and, breaking into the elephant house, it brought down a column, which killed all the elephants, besides causing great upheaval in the city.

I ordered that Landhoor be put in chains and led straight to jail, but no one found the courage to come forward, except for one vizier, who said, "I take it upon myself to apprehend Landhoor and bring him into the presence of Your Majesty!" He took a big dish of halva for Landhoor, and placed it before him. After Landhoor had eaten the halva, the vizier made him follow him into my presence.

Upon beholding me, Landhoor asked the vizier, "Who is this man, and what is his name?" The vizier said, "This here is your venerable uncle, who is the king and master of these lands!" Landhoor said, "And who was the king before him, and whose writ was held supreme in the past?" The vizier answered, "It was your father!" Then Landhoor said of me, "Then who is this man when I am the heir to the crown and throne? Why must he rule and I become dispossessed?" The vizier said, "Indeed you are our lord and master, and the land belongs to you. You are the Refuge of the World!" Landhoor said, "Depose him then! I shall ascend the throne, and issue writs from today onward, and govern the kingdom." The vizier said to me, "It would be expedient to oblige, and step down from the throne and let Landhoor ascend it!" Then I stepped down from the throne, and Landhoor was enthroned.

After a while Landhoor asked for food, and the vizier laid out drugged food before him. Landhoor said, "Call also Shahpal and Jaipur to eat with me and accompany me in this meal, in case someone should have poisoned it with the intent of taking my life!" Judging the situation plainly, I sent for Jaipur and we ate with Landhoor. After a while all three of us were taken unconscious and lay there senseless.

After a moment, the vizier administered to us some smelling essence and brought me and my son Jaipur to our senses, restoring us to consciousness as before. I ordered that Landhoor be put in irons from head to foot, and given into the charge of Aurang and Gaurang, the princes of Lakhnauti. The vizier executed my orders forthwith, and sent for the two princes and informed them of the royal decree. They took Landhoor away and, after throwing him into the well of Lakhnauti, sealed its mouth.

For twenty-five years Landhoor remained imprisoned in that dark well, and passed his existence out of sight. As Landhoor's mother was the progeny of Prophet Shis, one day the sister of Aurang and Gaurang had a dream in which she saw a throne come down from the heavens with Prophet Shis seated on it. And after informing her of all the particulars about Landhoor and his status, the prophet said to her, "I have made you and Landhoor a pair, and from him you will be borne of a child who will grow up to be the sun of glory!" She started from her dream, and went to the prison well carrying a salver of food.

The guards asked her, "Who are you, what have you brought, and whence do you come at this hour?" She said, "I have brought food for Landhoor and come to convey to him the annunciations of a saint."

The guards made no reply, whereupon she climbed down the well and fed Landhoor, and filed away at his fetters with a rasp. After narrating her dream to Landhoor, she went away, and returned to her abode. Landhoor put the chain irons to his side, and released from that encumbrance after such a long while, fell asleep like a log. The guards wondered why they did not hear his wailing and lamentations, and what might have stopped them, as Landhoor never was wont to let up his cries. When one of them went to investigate the matter, he found Landhoor sleeping peacefully with his feet outstretched, deep in the depths of repose, with the irons that chained him lying broken by his side.

Immediately a stir arose among the guards, and Aurang and Gaurang were forthwith informed. They rushed to the well in the company of many champions, and saw that indeed Landhoor lay sleeping all unfettered. As they made to take him unaware and secure him again with the chains, Landhoor woke up and pinned the two princes to the ground, and narrated all that had passed, saying, "Your sister came and fed me. She pledged me her troth, cut the links of my chains with a rasp, and restored me to freedom. For that reason I spared your lives; otherwise, the two of you would have been relieved of your lives' burden!" Then Landhoor narrated to them their sister's dream with all veracity. The two princes rejoiced in their hearts upon hearing these auspicious tidings, and led Landhoor out of the dark pit. They enthroned him, with all the attendant rituals and regalia of coronation and ascension, upon the empire's throne.

Landhoor ordered a war club to be made for him weighing one thousand and seven hundred Tabrizi *maunds,* and he mounted a giant elephant wielding that club. He began to make inquiries as to the way to the land of Ceylon. Aurang and Gaurang submitted to him with folded arms: "O Refuge of the World! Wait a while! You may march on Ceylon once you have enlisted an army!" Landhoor found this counsel to his liking and, aborting his plans for the march, set about enlisting an army, and directed his attention to provisioning the force. When an intrepid army was raised, he advanced toward Ceylon with great might and magnificence, pomp and array, and in a few days arrived at the seashore. From there he sailed and soon arrived at the fort of Ceylon.

My lookouts brought me this intelligence, and the isles rang out with advertisement of this news. I sent Jaipur at the head of a force of two hundred thousand to battle Landhoor, and myself accompanied several hundred veteran and intrepid champions with him. Then battle lines were drawn on both sides, and the two armies skirmished.

Jaipur observed that with each blow of Landhoor's war club, scores of his champions were macerated, their bodies reduced to pulp and their bones crushed to powder. Jaipur retreated and fortified himself, and unleashed a hail of fire and cannonade on Landhoor's army. Landhoor advanced to the gate of the fort and gave a mighty blow with his war club, which shattered the gate to pieces. The keepers of the fort were beaten and thrown down, and the moment the gate fell, Landhoor entered the fort and indulged in wholesale carnage, causing rivers of blood to flow within the fort walls.

I saw no recourse left to me but to present myself before Landhoor and ask for mercy. Landhoor said, "On what terms do you seek reprieve? With what intention do you bring this plea before me?" I said, "I rule this kingdom in trust for Naushervan the Just, the Emperor of the Seven Climes. He appoints the one who ascends the throne. Wait a while until a reply to my epistle has arrived from his court!" Landhoor said, "Remove yourself to some isle until your pleas and entreaties are answered, and a reply to your missive is received! What do I care about Nausher-van or yourself? Am I some cowardly weakling that I should abide by his wishes or yours, or fear a soul?"

Helpless, I escaped from the city with my life, and Landhoor was enthroned. As I was duty bound to inform you, I have made my report. Now I leave it to the judgment of Your Highness, for faithful men like us are become exiles from our land, and our children have been ruth-lessly persecuted. If Landhoor is not speedily routed as he deserves, he will not stop short of committing the gravest outrages against Your Highness!

After listening to this message the emperor sought Buzurjmehr's counsel in private, and also sought the advice of his viziers and nobles to find a way to ward off this unforeseen calamity, bearing in mind that if nobody was able to vanquish Landhoor, it would reflect most disgrace-fully on the empire.

Buzurjmehr said, "First, order Gustham to advance on Ceylon. Then announce before the whole court that you will pledge the troth of Princess Mehr-Nigar to the one who brings Landhoor back a prisoner to Your Majesty; and that you shall also augment him in riches and domin-ions. In my view there is no Sassanid warrior who will undertake to bring Landhoor's head. But Hamza is ever enamored of renown and honor, and it is certain that he will make this pledge. And this plan is also not with-out ingenuity in that, should Hamza be killed in the undertaking, you will be saved from humiliation; and should he prevail against Landhoor, all of the lands of India will fall to your lot!"

Upon hearing Buzurjmehr's thoughtful opinion and counsel, the em-peror rejoiced in his heart. And that very moment he sent a precept by the agency of a camel rider to Gustham, who was in hiding in Zabul after wounding Bahram for fear of the emperor's wrath. Through this messen-ger, he ordered Gustham to proceed to Ceylon with his forty thousand troops and bring back Landhoor's head, in order that his past misde-meanors might be pardoned. He was told that he would be rewarded for this service to the emperor and restored to royal patronage.

The next day, when the philosophers, nobles, and royal cupfellows assembled in the court, the emperor said to them, "O renowned warriors and champions of time! The Khusrau of India has raised the flag of rebel-lion and foments sedition against me. Whoever among you will bring me his head, I shall adopt him as son, and he shall be proclaimed my kin. The head of the Khusrau of India would be considered the jointure of Mehr-Nigar."

All the Sassanid and Majdakid nobles and champions did not breathe the least word, and no one came forward to accept this undertaking, thinking in their hearts that it was well-nigh impossible to escape with one's life from the Indian Ocean, and even should one survive it, nobody would find the courage to fight such a powerful enemy; that there was no wisdom in jeopardizing one's life for a faint hope; and that the whole proposition was counter to all precepts of good sense.

But Sahibqiran rose from his seat and visited blessings on the emperor's head, saying,

May you live as long as Venus remains in the heavens,
And may we enjoy your patronage and you a long life.

Then he submitted to the emperor thus: "Should you order this faithful servant, he will produce the Khusrau of India before you in person! It is only a matter of my arriving there for Landhoor to be led in chains to your presence. Should I be killed in the undertaking, I shall become a sacrifice of Your Majesty!"

The emperor rose from his throne and embraced Amir, and said, "O Abul-Ala! I have even greater hope in you, and I give you my full confidence."

A king's scepter and the emperor's crown
Will never devolve on one of low station.
Begone malicious glances!
A propitious year's augur is in its spring.

"How could you have laid claim to the august station you hold if you did not have such courage and valiancy! For this reason you have a title to manliness and exaltation!" Having said this, the emperor conferred a royal robe of honor on Amir, and ordered thirty ships carrying a thousand men each to be furnished for the campaign.

Amir Hamza took his leave and returned to his camp. There, he began making preparations for the advance, and busied himself in consoling his heart and affording it solace. He ordered his troops to march that very day and to wait for him in Basra. Then he sent for Amar, and said to him, "O Amar, if I could have had a glimpse of the princess before I left, I would have left with a pacified heart!"

Amar said, "Write a note to Buzurjmehr, for such an arrangement could only be made by the intercession of the nobles. And since Buzurjmehr is well-disposed toward you and truly sincere to you—and also your aid and abettor—he would be the one to consult in this matter!"

Hamza therefore wrote a note to Buzurjmehr with his own hand, and Amar took it to Buzurjmehr's place and handed it to him.

Upon reading the note, Buzurjmehr took Amar along before the emperor, and said to him, "From Ctesiphon to the dominion of India, Hamza will be proclaimed your son-in-law; and the news of his campaign against Landhoor will travel to the ends of the Earth. But what is to be said about such a relationship when not even a drop of sherbet was imbibed to celebrate it, and Hamza had to lay down his life in order to execute your commands?"

Then Naushervan laughed, and said, "Indeed there is no harm in what you suggest. Send for Hamza, and order the keeper of beverages to dissolve the finest sherbet to celebrate the nuptials." Upon the emperor's orders Buzurjmehr sent for Hamza directly, and had several *maunds* of sugar and rose sherbet dissolved for the ceremony. Amir presented himself at once, and arrived all prepared to embark on the campaign. As a show of great affection, the emperor seated Amir by his side, and sent for the sherbet.

Then Khvaja Buzurjmehr said, "It would be more seemly to imbibe the nuptial drinks and serve the *gilauris*[180] in the palace, as it would be improper to hold the ceremony in the men's quarters, in the absence of Her Highness the Empress!" Naushervan gave his consent and said to Buzurjmehr, "You may accompany Hamza into the palace, and have him served the sherbet. Hamza will drink the sherbet out of the hands of Mehr-Nigar's mother. Instruct them to perform all the rituals of engagement, and to feast Hamza after the drinks and inform him that we will keep Mehr-Nigar for him in trust. Now our name and honor have become his name and honor, and he must hasten to vanquish the emperor's enemy, or bring back that calumniator in chains, and marry Mehr-Nigar and provide solace to our heart!" Buzurjmehr went into the palace without Amir, and conveyed all that the emperor had just said to Empress Mehr-Angez.

When Bakhtak received these tidings he said in his heart, *If Hamza goes inside the palace, it is certain that he will view Princess Mehr-Nigar. I should go there, too, so that his heart's desire remains unfulfilled and he is denied even a glimpse of the princess!* Directly Bakhtak mounted a mule and rode to the palace gates.

When he saw Bakhtak coming, Hamza said to Amar, "One must somehow ward off this bird of ill omen at this time, and dispel this unforeseen calamity! I will give you two hundred *tomans* and other rewards besides if this is so arranged!" Amar replied to Hamza in the language of *ayyars,* "You may go forth and enjoy yourself at the palace without the least worry. I shall deal with him presently, and not let this villain set foot there!"

The moment Hamza left, Amar stopped Bakhtak by catching hold of his mule's reins, and said to him, "O Khvaja Bakhtak, I am headed for India, and God alone knows whether I shall return safe and sound or whether my grave shall be made there! Here is your promissory note of five hundred *tomans:* Please make good on the payment so that it may be used as money for the journey, and you may also be relieved from the burden of your debt!" Bakhtak responded, "A wondrously ill-timed rooster you are! This is neither the place nor the occasion to make such demands. At the moment I am accompanying Hamza on an assignment, and proceeding in the cortege of your master. And you make yourself an obstacle, and ask me to clear this debt, demanding the money! Go lodge your complaint in the royal court of appeals. I shall make the payment duly if the debt is proven against me! But should you try to bar my way, I will bring suit against you for defamation of character, and ensure that you pay the damages through your nose!"

Amar cried, "Sire! Prithee give these instructions to one weaker than thou! I would move the royal court if I did not find it in my power to extract my debt myself. You are warned not to take a step forward without first clearing my debt. Once it is clear, however, you may gladly take yourself wherever you like!"

Riled upon hearing these words, Bakhtak said to his slaves, "Move Amar aside! Push him away from before my mule!" Now Amar could no longer restrain himself, and in one leap he mounted the mule behind Bakhtak. Drawing his dagger and pressing it into Bakhtak's side, he said, "You rascal! Why do you wish to call calamity on yourself? I will bring you to your final rewards before your time if you so wish, and pile up your entrails right here!" Bakhtak was terrified and began to shake like an aspen leaf. He made fervent pleas to Amar, who then let him go, but first clouted his head with the dagger's hilt as a parting gift so that blood issued out.

Bakhtak rushed before the emperor drenched in blood and, throwing his headdress at the emperor's feet, said, "Things have come to such a pass that your servant has been publicly dishonored by a common trickster, and is bathed in blood!" Displeased at this spectacle, Naushervan sent for Amar, and asked him, "What harm did you receive at Bakhtak's hand that you perpetrated this felony against him?"

Amar replied, "Your Honor, My Lord is known as the Just One. Pray first dispense the justice that is due before you pardon or punish the guilty one. I, your slave, have a duly signed and sealed promissory note for five hundred *tomans* against Bakhtak, but he dithers and hesitates in making good the payment! Just now, I, your slave, told him that I was headed for India, and there was no knowing when I shall return—supposing I survive at all—and I asked him to kindly redeem this promissory note. But he became angry at my words, and ordered his slaves to use violence to throw me out and drive me away from before him. Thereupon his slaves rushed at me shouting abuses, with the intention of laying violent hands on my person. Your Honor will kindly take into account that I, your slave, am not some butcher's boy or greengrocer to be meted out such public abuse or made to hear the rebuke of footmen! I then became vexed with Bakhtak and clouted him with my dagger's hilt, so that his crown swelled up a little. I plead before you to do justice: Blame the blameworthy; and decide who was the instigator of this feud!" Then Amar produced the promissory note from his pocket, and laid it before the emperor, seeking justice.

The emperor said to Bakhtak, "You are entirely to blame in this whole affair, and indeed your high-handedness is now proved beyond a shadow of the doubt. Yet you have the cheek to present yourself before me as the aggrieved party! Make haste to pay the money due on the promissory note to Amar, or else you will be held guilty and thrown into the mire of ignomily upon failing to make good the payment!" Bakhtak was obliged to bring every last bit of money from the treasurer that very moment. Then, while he returned home moaning and groaning, Amar headed for the emperor's quarters in the harem.

While Amar was thus entangled, Hamza and Muqbil had entered the palace and arrived in the royal gallery. Empress Mehr-Angez seated Hamza on a throne in the gallery, and called for all the paraphernalia of festive revelry to be set up. The empress herself sat in the annex with Princess Mehr-Nigar. The festive assembly began in a most regal manner and sherbet was soon served, with the company drinking it in rounds.

When Amar reached the gallery's threshold and made to enter, the porter barred his way with his staff, and said to him, "Who might you be that you dare to enter the palace in this impetuous manner, and set foot on the royal threshold without permission?" Covering his eyes with his hands, Amar fell to the floor crying and rolling, and screaming all the while, "Confound you, Porter, that you have poked out my eyes and blinded me, depriving me of my sight!" At this, the porter was dumbfounded and began pleading with Amar profusely.

When Empress Mehr-Angez heard the noise, she said to her attendants, "See what the row is all about, and who is crying at the gates!" Upon discerning Amar's voice, Hamza himself ran out in great trepidation with Buzurjmehr at his heels. They found Amar on the floor, rolling around and covering his eyes, exhibiting signs of great suffering. Hamza said, "O Amar, open your eyes and tell me if, God forbid, some harm has come to your eyes. Khvaja Buzurjmehr will treat you and prescribe some cure!" But Amar would not open his eyes, and said nothing but "Gone are my eyes, alas, gone!"

Finally Hamza forced Amar's hands from his face, and saw that his eyes twinkled like stars and showed no sign of having come to any harm. Hamza then said, "O Amar! Why did you make Khvaja and myself come rushing to no purpose with this prank and roguery of yours—and also distressed the empress?"

Amar replied, "I swear by your life that the porter had raised his staff to hit me, and had I been hit, it is a foregone conclusion that my eyes once wounded would have lost their sight!" Hamza and Khvaja Buzurjmehr laughed out loud at this, and brought Amar into the palace. When Empress Mehr-Angez was informed of the episode she, too, had a good laugh.

Hamza sat on the throne and was served sherbet according to the royal custom, and shouts of "Congratulations!" and "Salutations!" rose to the skies. The companions and confidantes of Princess Mehr-Nigar began frolicking and making merry, and the singers, dancers, and musicians were all rewarded according to their merit. Then Empress Mehr-Angez said, "O Sahibqiran, we shall hold Princess Mehr-Nigar in trust for you. She is now your adornment and honor. When you return triumphant and victorious from India, she will be married to you and the skirts of your hope will be filled with the flowers of desire!"

Amar exchanged glances with Buzurjmehr at this speech, and addressed the empress thus, "A thousand accolades on this signal act of beneficence and indulgence on your part! It is an act of the utmost propriety, and the most wondrous rite of hosting, that while we head for India and wager our lives at the orders of the emperor, you deny us even a glimpse of the princess. If God returns us alive and triumphant with our mission accomplished, there is no knowing to whom Hamza will be married off and with whom he may be saddled! We know not whether the emperor's daughter is dark or fair, lean or plump! If we were allowed a glance of her now, we will not be sold into some deception later. Indeed, we swear by the salt we have eaten at the emperor's table that we shall not set foot out of doors before we have been granted a view of Princess Mehr-Nigar!"

Empress Mehr-Angez laughed at Amar's speech, and said, "Who has ever heard of men inspecting the bride-to-be? It is the women who view the girl when they come to arrange the ceremonies of engagement and betrothal!" Amar humbly replied, "Your Majesty speaks the very truth! But we have neither mothers nor aunts who would perform these offices for us, or who may see the princess! In this house you are our patron and elder. We leave it to your discretion to arrange for the necessary examination and thus indulge our pleas!" The empress said, "Now that the princess is become your honor and adornment, you are free to view her whenever you may desire!" Then she said to Khvaja Buzurjmehr, "O Khvaja, pray bring Amir inside the *purdah*,[181] and let him view the princess!"

Buzurjmehr stepped forward with Hamza, who made obeisance upon beholding Empress Mehr-Angez, and made an offering himself, too. Princess Mehr-Nigar sat by the empress's side with her head lowered, and would not raise it for considerations of bashfulness and decency. The empress visited blessings on Hamza's head, as she was greatly pleased when she saw Amir in proximity and accepted him as her son-in-law with all her heart. Upon beholding the princess, Hamza was beside himself with joy and rejoiced exceedingly.

Buzurjmehr said to Princess Mehr-Nigar, "Hamza is about to embark on a journey of great length. Prithee confer some memento on him that keeps him engrossed with your memory, so that he may always carry it with him!" Mehr-Nigar took an emerald ring from her finger and gave it to Hamza, who put it on. Then exchanging for it the ring from his finger, he said to Princess Mehr-Nigar, "Take this as a memento from me, so that it may always remain with you, in order that you shall never become forgetful of me but instead think of me often!"

Then Amar submitted before Empress Mehr-Angez with folded arms, saying, "Should I be granted license, I would wish to speak the desire of my heart, too!" She answered, "Speak what you have to say!" Amar said, "God willing, when Hamza is married to Princess Mehr-Nigar, the nanny's daughter, too, *nolens volens,* shall be married to me! Therefore, have some memento conferred on me, too, and request that respected nanny to serve me the sherbet of nuptials with her hands!" Empress Mehr-Angez said, "How delightful, O Nanny! Do you hear what Amar asks for, and listen to his intentions?" The nanny said, "May the princess flourish, God willing, as it was on her account that these happy words were addressed to me! Indeed my daughter cannot leave the princess's servitude. She will obey whatever the princess shall order!"

Princess Mehr-Nigar then made a gesture to the nanny that revealed her consent. Then Empress Mehr-Angez said to Fitna Bano, "You, too, must give Amar some memento of yourself!" She gave Amar a scent box worth several hundred *tomans.* Empress Mehr-Angez said, "Now, O Fitna Bano, receive from Amar a memento for yourself!" Amar put a date and two walnuts into Fitna Bano's palm, and said, "Here! Keep them with you, and safeguard them well!" At this new caper of Amar's all those present collapsed in a fit of laughter.

When Hamza took his leave from these revelries and went to present himself before the emperor, Khvaja Buzurjmehr said to Amar, "My son, proceed to the camp of the faithful, and give the tidings to the renowned nobles that Amir Hamza is on his way there and shall arrive presently. That way no one shall feel any anxiety at his absence, and they shall not give in to worry on his account! I shall escort Hamza myself, so that he is seen off by the emperor and granted a robe of honor commensurate with the emperor's inclinations!"

While Amar headed off to perform the task, Buzurjmehr seated Hamza and Muqbil in his house, and then went before the emperor and reported that Empress Mehr-Angez, too, had accepted Amir Hamza as her son-in-law with open arms, and had invested him with the robe of the son-in-law. Then Buzurjmehr took Amir to a workshop, and after imparting some instructions to him regarding the mission, served sherbet to him. Upon drinking this, Hamza fell unconscious immediately, and lost all sense of himself. Buzurjmehr cut open Hamza's side, and after planting the Shah Mohra[182] inside him, sutured up the wound and rubbed it with the salve of Daud.[183] Witnessing this, Muqbil asked, "What was that physic, O venerated Buzurjmehr?" He replied, "A man scheming to work Hamza's death (may such be his enemies' fate!) will poison him in India, and for that poison this is the sole antidote and there is no other remedy for it in the whole world! But beware and be warned that you must not divulge this secret to Amar, until you are beaten with his hand first!" Buzurjmehr then dribbled a few drops of some liquid into Hamza's mouth, whereupon he immediately came to senses. And as the wound had completely healed by then, he never felt the least sensation or discovered a thing.

In the meanwhile Amar also returned from his errand, and Buzurjmehr bade them all adieu. Hamza arrived in his camp and soon rode out to the sea in the manner becoming a commander. A multitude of ministers and nobles of the royal court who were well-disposed toward Hamza escorted him to the outer fortifications of the city to see him off, and bade him Godspeed. Hamza vouchsafed them to God's care, and marched on from there forthwith. Within a few days he reached Basra and, arriving at the port with his triumphant, large army, Hamza beheld thirty ships anchored there at the emperor's orders awaiting him and ready to set sail. Hamza boarded them with his thirty thousand men, and made ready to sail for the campaign against India.

At this point, Amar got off the ship, calling up to Hamza, "As yours truly is most frightened of jinns, magic, and water, I will not sail for India, but will head for Mecca instead, where I will pray for your victory before the True Triumphant One, and supplicate before the Grantor of Petitions!" Hamza saw that it would be futile to try to persuade Amar to accompany him, as he would make all manner of excuses. He said, "O Amar, I would not force you into an undertaking that is not in accordance with your pleasure, but do wait a while so that I may write you a note for my father!"

Thinking that after writing the letter Hamza would see him off, Amar went aboard to Hamza, who wrote out a letter, handed it to Amar, and then said: "Come, Brother, let's embrace once, for God alone knows when we shall meet again and the anguish of our parting will be dispelled!" Tears rushed to Amar's eyes at these words and rolled down his cheeks. Then Hamza caught Amar in his embrace and said, "Dearest friend! How could I bear separation from you in this campaign when you have never left my side in the most trying of times!"

Farewell, for I set sail over seas!

Next thing, Hamza called out to the captain, "Weigh the anchor!" No sooner were the orders given than the ships weighed anchor. It was only after they had left the shore behind that Hamza released Amar, who began running on the deck in confusion, muttering with dismay, "I was always true in my camaraderie toward this Arab, but he has become my mortal foe!"

After some time had passed they sighted an isle some thirty yards in both length and breadth, and upon spotting it Amar said in his heart, *I will jump on it and from there find some way to return home!* But what Amar had mistaken for an island, was in fact a great fish that had swum to the surface of water to bask in the sun. When Amar jumped on it, the fish felt the thump of his feet and dived; and a panic-stricken Amar began to flounder in the open sea.

Beholding this, the Sahibqiran said to the sailors, "Beware! Make sure that Amar does not drown or go down a second time! The one who pulls him up and restores him to me shall win a reward!" The sailors threw ropes and tackle into the ocean, fished Amar out of the sea, and seated him next to Hamza. The maxim that the value of security is truly realized by one in adversity, is truthful indeed. After Amar was pulled out from the sea, he quietly took himself to a corner of the ship like a beaten dog, and then did not stir at all.

Many days later they arrived on the shores of an island, and the ships dropped anchor. Amar was the first one to leap onto shore and go running freely in all directions. By chance, he espied a man with a strap around his waist sitting under a tree. Upon beholding Amar the man began to smile from ear to ear, as if his heart's desire had been answered, and he called to Amar, "Come hither, my nephew! It is a wonder of wonders that the two of us have been brought together! I can only attribute your arrival on this island to Divine Providence. I had become convinced that I would die and all my riches would go waste, but God sent their rightful owner and showed great mercy to one in my condition!" At hearing the mention of riches, Amar kept quiet; otherwise, he would have objected to the old man's calling him his nephew, and his claiming himself to be Amar's uncle. He also resisted questioning why the man did not show reserve toward a complete stranger.

When Amar inquired about his particulars, the old man said, "You would not recognize me, since you were a mere toddler when I left for

Ceylon. When I had accumulated a great fortune there, I resolved in my heart to leave that place and return to my homeland. On my return passage, a contrary wind took hold of the ship. A storm began to blow and the sea began to rage, and the ship capsized at this place. When I noticed the ship was going down, I laid hold of my chest of jewels and jumped overboard, and swam to the land. But in that undertaking my foot was injured and it rendered me an invalid. A surgeon who is a past master of his trade lives on this island. People took pity on me and carried me to him, and also left me some food and drink. The surgeon rented me a house near his own abode and gave me oil made from earthworms to rub on my leg from his own store. My condition is now improved to the extent that when I felt my heart becoming overcast, I brought myself here. For the longest time now I have been trying to muster the strength to return to my house, but I hesitate for the pain. I do not have the strength to stand on my feet, let alone walk! If you were to carry me to my house on your back, I would be doubly indebted to you, in that I would not only reach my house but would get there without any strain and shall also vouchsafe to you what by rights is yours! That is to say, I would hand over that chest of jewels to you. Then the due would be restored to its rightful owner, and I would return home aboard the ship with you!"

Amar's mouth watered upon hearing this talk of the chest of jewels, and he said in his heart, *Fortune must be smiling on me, since I appear to complete strangers as one of their kin! I must be favored by luck that this windfall is about to become mine!* Without further thought, Amar loaded up that *tasma-pa* on his back.

The moment the *tasma-pa* climbed on Amar's back, he strapped his legs tightly around Amar's waist, then goaded him forward with his knees, exclaiming, "Come, my ambler! Now trot along, and show me how you gallop!" Amar was thoroughly tied up and howsoever he tried to free himself and obtain release from the grasp of that monster, he was unable to do so, as his arms were also secured. The old man began to slap Amar's cheeks and clout his head. Cuffing his face and kicking him in the ribs, the old man said, "Run! Why don't you run? Do you wish to obtain all the riches without taking a single step, and establish yourself as an heir without the least labor?" Amar was taken with a great panic and alarm, and all his roguery and trickery left him.

In all helplessness, Amar ran toward the ship, thinking that Hamza would grant him release from this monster and give him freedom from the *tasma-pa*'s power. But upon arriving near the ship Amar beheld a marvel of marvels. Hamza and all his companions were caught in the same calamity, and all those who had a claim to horsemanship were themselves being ridden hard and fast. Upon regarding Amar in his state, Hamza said to him in the trickster's language, "We had thought that you would not be caught in this evil, and would bring us release, too, but I see that you are also taken prisoner!" Helpless, Amar drew away from Hamza but kept considering some way to secure his release.

Every so often the *tasma-pa* would command Amar to jog, then order him to leap and gambol. When he saw others of his race likewise furnished with mounts, he said to them, "Race your mounts, and show how your chargers stride and gallop! I will race my mount, too. Let us see whose horse wins the race, and whose steed lags behind and loses. After having our fun we will kill them and roast them on skewers!" Upon hearing these words, Hamza's companions lost all their senses, and they began heaving cold, despondent sighs. Their riders again spurred them on and started forward. Aadi fared worst of all: Due to his corpulence he stumbled at every step. Reciting "Whatever calamity visits the son of Aadam passeth," Amar charged forward at a pace so fleet that nobody even caught up with the dust he raised in his wake, and he soon put a distance of two leagues between him and his companions. Then that rascally *tasma-pa* rejoiced exceedingly, and said, "My charger is the fastest among them, a great runner and as fleet as the zephyr itself!"

At one place in that wilderness, Amar saw a profuse growth of grapevines that stretched for miles on end, from which clusters of fruit were hanging, and juice flowed from them in a veritable river. Adjacent to this was a growth of gourds, with hundreds of goblet-shaped fruits hanging down, their tendrils spread over a great expanse. Beside himself with joy, Amar approached the gourd vine, and said to the *tasma-pa*, "Pick me a big gourd and fill it up with the juice that drips from the grape clusters. Give me sips from it along the way, so that after drinking it I can stride even more nimbly, and display to you my speed and spirits: how I lounge and strut and jump and dance!"

That dolt did as Amar had bade him and, plucking off a gourd, filled it up with grape juice. Then he dripped some into Amar's mouth and gave him also some grapes to eat. Amar began to leap forward and gambol, and then he broke into an air and carried his rider sprinting at ever greater speed. That rascal was mightily pleased, and said, "Oh, my charger! For as long as I shall live, I will never release you from between my legs, as you make me laugh and lighten my heart with your pranks and by running so swiftly!" Amar said to him, "Mind that you drink none of this liquid, but leave it all for me!"

The *tasma-pa* now thought in his heart, *It seems that this juice is some sovereign elixir! That is why he forbids me to drink it and the very mention of it makes his mouth water!* Thus thinking he took two sips from the gourd and, immensely enjoying the taste, he put the gourd to his lips and guzzled down its entire contents. Now when the forest breeze billowed against the *tasma-pa*'s face from Amar's running, all his rascality and horsemanship left him. From the giddiness in his head he fell down unconscious from Amar's back. Then Amar took out his dagger and slit open the *tasma-pa*'s belly.

From there Amar returned to Hamza and said, "You imperiled the lives of the followers of the True Faith for the sake of an infidel's daughter, and put me to great distress and made me labor under great hardship. What shall become of you on the Day of Judgment, and what deserts will befall your adventure, remain to be seen!" Hamza said, "Indeed I am guilty of the charge, as well as inexperienced. But you now have the chance to earn great recompense by delivering us believers from this scourge!" Amar replied, "What is in it for me if I kill this multitude of *tasma-pas* and have the blood of these invalids on my neck?" Hamza said, "Their blood will be on my neck, and I shall give you two hundred gold pieces for every one of them that you kill, and shall be greatly indebted to you moreover!"

Amar accepted the offer, killed every single *tasma-pa* by picking them clean off their mounts with well-aimed slingshots, and made piles of the dead. After everyone had been released from the clutches of those beings, they breathed freely once more. Hamza said, "This is an isle of India, and there is no knowing what further troubles await us here or what new misadventures may befall our army." He then ordered the ships to weigh anchor without further delay and set sail.

Two months later, they discovered another island, and the captains said to Hamza, "If you should order it, we would fill up the ship with drinking water from the island and collect some provisions and provender there, too!" Hamza said, "Very well! The soldiers' clothes have also become soiled. We could quickly rinse our clothes while you fill the ship with water, and then sail onward!" The captains dropped anchor and everyone waded ashore to the isle. Finding a cold breeze blowing, Amar went on a romp, and happened by a pool of a most pleasant appearance.

Amar found its water to be pearl-bright, and was immediately seized by a longing to bathe and wash his clothes. He undressed, leaving his clothes by the side of the pool, and dived in.

When he emerged, he found that his clothes had disappeared from the side of the pool. Thinking that perhaps Hamza had had the clothes removed in jest, and had asked someone to hide them, he began calling out, "Hamza! Hamza!" and set up a most vigorous yelling. When Hamza heard Amar's voice, he ran to him in great anxiety, and said, "O Amar, what has now befallen you, my brother? Are you again caught in some calamity?" Amar replied, "I have no appetite for such capers that leave me standing here naked in the pool! Return my clothes to me: Send your servants to fetch them immediately!" When Hamza swore that he knew nothing of his clothes, and made God his witness that he had no knowledge as to where Amar's vesture had disappeared, Amar panicked, and thought, *If my clothes were not removed by Hamza's direction, and his attendants have not taken them away, who could have played this caper and pulled this trick on me?*

It so happened that his glance traveled up the surrounding trees, and he saw monkeys perched atop them, pulling and tearing at his clothes. One had his headdress, another his drawers, and while one fondled his robe, another was busy winding his cummerbund over his head. After sending for and changing into another dress, Amar tossed his new headdress in the air. Mimicry being a principle with the ape, the monkey who had Amar's headdress threw his also into the air. But he could not catch it, and it fell to the ground where Amar picked it up. In similar fashion Amar retrieved all his clothes from the monkeys. Then after smearing the trees with naphtha, he set them ablaze. All the monkeys were burned to death, and their very existence was effaced from that island.

Hamza ordered his ships to weigh anchor straightaway, and they sailed on. After many days a speck of cloud appeared on the horizon, and in no time it covered the entire firmament, and suddenly a tempest began to rage and a storm to brew. The bright day became darker than the dark of *Shab-e Yalda*[184] and everything drowned in such pitch darkness that one could not even make out the hair on one's arms. The wind raged so fiercely that the water of the sea mixed violently with the water of the sky, and every wave lashed with greater force than the Deluge.[185] When they saw the waves beating mercilessly against the prow of the ship, the riders of the ship's steed were overtaken by distress. Giving up all hope for their lives' bubble, they shed copious tears of remorse at the prospect that they had reached the shores of death instead of the shores of their destination.

Addressing his men, Hamza said, "One must not throw oneself into such a medley of dissipation and distress, but must always anchor one's hopes in the mercy of the True Succor."

Not everything has an auspicious end,
Of auspicious fortune is the one who foresees the end.

Now, Amar presented the picture of one who had drowned in the very sea of doom, and he wept, saying, "O Skipper of the Vessel of Oneness![186] This fleet of believers will anchor in safety only through the Agency of Your Grace!" Then he would call out, "O venerable Ilyas! If you were to anchor this storm-tossed vessel to safe shores, and deliver it from this calamity, I would throw the offering of a sugar packet in your name in the river, even though my existence is but a minim,[187] and my wealth but a farthing! Yet you will earn recompense and moreover, as I was blessed by your brother Khizr, he, too, would be most gratified by your deed!"

Then Amar said to Hamza, "O Hamza, these storms are the deserts of your deeds! Should we die here, our remains will fall into desecration, without a grave or a winding-sheet, a wake or even a bier! I hold you entirely to blame for this state of affairs! Fearing just this fate, I did not come on board at first, and declined to call this trouble on my head. Even though it was plainly conspicuous to your heart and as brightly manifest as day that I run from water like the torrent, keep away from the sea by staying always on shore, and that I have never in all my many years wetted my feet even in a cistern nor indeed poured water on my head when taking a bath—still you forced me into this voyage, and sank the vessel of my heart in the middle of the ocean, and lost me to both worlds!" The audience who until now had been floundering in lamentation and outcry in the abysmal depths of their anguish and distress, bloomed like flowers into laughter from the refreshing breeze of Amar's speech.

After three days the tempest gradually blew away and no signs of it remained, just as tears die in the longing eyes of those drowned in a sea of wonderment. The darkness put on a dress woven of the sun's rays, and light appeared in the heavens. The lashing of the waves subsided and the boars[188] of the sea were slaughtered. The raging swells suddenly disappeared like the waves of the mirage, and the sea was sapped of all its vigor and might. Rejoicing, the royal servants embraced, and said to each other, "We had washed our hands of all hopes of survival and were as good as dead, but the Progenitor gave us a new lease on life!" Someone said, "Nothing stood between us and the certainty of drowning, but the True Skipper delivered us into safety!"

Amar said to them, "Dear friends, it was nothing but my prayers that saved those who were destined to drown and delivered you from the clutches of calamity. It was due only to the pledges I made, and the offerings that I resolved to make! Give me a little something that I may arrange for offerings and oblations for the saints!" Everyone gave a few dinars to Amar, and some pledged him larger sums. Then Amar called out, "O Uncle Ilyas! I shall purchase some sugar and make you a sugar offering upon reaching the shores of Ceylon, as there is no place in this turbulent sea where I can buy any sugar!" All those present laughed at Amar's words, and enjoyed them a great deal.

The pall of this calamity was not yet cast from their hearts when it was discovered that the ships of Emperor of China Bahram Gurd could not be accounted for. All four of his ships had disappeared without sign or trace, and even though the ships had been searched for by spyglass, no sign of them could be found. Upon hearing these tidings Hamza immediately drowned in the abyss of sorrow, and cried out, "A great leviathan of the sea of courage and valor has drowned! The one who was the pride and honor of the whole army—only his ships have not made it to safety!" His companions said, "Sire, God forbid the possibility that his ships were destroyed! They have perhaps found a port and the Sailor of Fate has taken them to shores of safety. He is the Collector of the Dispersed. By virtue of His great beneficence He will bring us together again!"

Amar said to him, "O Hamza, pledge some offering! Witness that I was saved when I pledged an offering, and your salvation was also achieved through me." Hamza replied, "Pray be mindful of the occasion, as it is not one for gaiety! You are free to make a pledge on my behalf. When I set eyes on Bahram's face again I shall furnish you with all you ask for." Amar responded, "Very well! But were you to sacrifice a louse upon reaching the shores of safety, then I would be helpless. That is to say that I would be powerless were you to order me to arrange for a parsimonious offering, and then I would be obliged to spend out of my own purse!" Hamza now laughed at his friend, and said, "I promise that that will not be the case. Everything will be arranged in accordance with your wishes!"

OF ANOTHER STORM, AND HAMZA'S SHIPS BEING
DRIVEN INTO THE WHIRLPOOL OF SIKANDER, AND OF
THE DELIVERANCE OF THESE POOR SOULS FROM THE
TEMPEST; AND OF THEIR ARRIVING IN THE LANDS OF
CEYLON AND EXACTING TRIBUTE FROM THE KHUSRAU OF
INDIA, LANDHOOR BIN SAADAN SHAH

The divers of the ocean of historiography and the excavators of the sea of ancient tales bring up the pearls of legends, and thus display them by stringing them into prose, that after the storm had blown away, the fleet found favorable winds for a few days and the travelers remained safe from any catastrophes, and the captains gave full sails and sped on their vessels. Then one day the lookout of the ship shouted, "Hear ye, O friends! A great storm is about to engulf us, and compared with its intensity the tempest we experienced earlier was like a minim to a veritable sea! It remains to be seen how God will deliver us from this adversity! And a greater calamity still is the Whirlpool of Sikander that lies a short distance from here. Should the ships be led into it (perish the thought!), they will go whirling down and will founder in no time. Then every man will find himself at the mercy of the open sea!"

Upon hearing this news Amar was terribly frightened and was thrown into a great panic. Troubled by thoughts of an imminent drowning, he set to crying profusely. Now he would call out, "O Uncle Ilyas! I already promised you an offering upon reaching Ceylon!" and then he would exclaim, "O venerable Khizr, please intercede on my behalf with your brother Ilyas, that he may help me out of the whirlpool of calamity and this fierce tempest, and pray for me to God! I shall duly make my pledged offering upon reaching the shore!" When Hamza heard Amar's moaning and groaning, he said, "Why are you importuning Khizr and Ilyas now, and setting up these lamentations anew?" The helmsmen answered for Amar, "Sire! A mighty storm is brewing most violently, and God alone can save us from its vengeance!"

They were still engaged in these discussions when the storm came upon them, and the sea began to rage, and before long the ships were driven into the Whirlpool of Sikander. Then all of them lost their senses and were thrown into ecstasies of terror. As Hamza peered into the storm, he beheld a stone obelisk of great length and breadth that rose from the center of the whirlpool. Affixed to it was a tablet of white stone. When he looked closely, Hamza saw words in Arabic letters chased on it in black stone, which read:

> There will come a time when the fleet of the Sahibqiran shall arrive at this place and be caught in the Whirlpool of Sikander. Then the Sahibqiran must climb up the obelisk and sound the Timbal of Sikander that is kept here, or else order his deputy to climb up, and do what is needful. Then the ships will find escape from this whirlpool, and the Sahibqiran shall be delivered from this difficulty.

Hamza said to Amar, "Adieu, my brother! I shall head for the obelisk and sound the timbal, in the name of God Almighty! There will be no harm done if the sacrifice of my one life saves the lives of thousands. I am resolved to save the lives of God's creatures!" Amar said, "The same command applies also to your deputy; he is similarly commanded to sound the timbal. And thus, as I am your deputy, I shall climb this obelisk and sound the Timbal of Sikander!" But in his heart Amar thought, *Once I have climbed to the safety of the column, I will be saved from the raging sea, and when some ship happens by, I will board it, and go anywhere it will take me! As I have neither wife nor issue, I would happily bide my life in celibacy!*

Then he turned to Hamza's commanders and said, "O noble chiefs! I am now become your sacrificial lamb! Prithee show the generosity of your pockets, in order that I may reap the reward of my perilous labor should I survive!" Everyone present there wrote out promissory notes— a hundred where one was due, and a hundred thousand where a hundred were asked for—and handed them to Amar, who took them. Reciting,

> *In this endless sea and in this calamitous storm*
> *In God who causes things to flow*
> *And in God who is the anchor*
> *We repose our trust*

he held his breath and leapt. But he landed short of the obelisk, and fell into the sea with a splash.

As he began to sink, he saw a mighty leviathan awaiting with open jaws to make him his fodder. Upon beholding this new scourge Amar's senses were all disarrayed. But thinking that he would thus forfeit his life for certain, even should he escape drowning, Amar rallied his senses, and using the jaws of the beast as leverage he jumped up and landed on the summit of the obelisk, crowning all his previous tricks. Upon witnessing Amar's feat everyone shouted "Bravo!" and "Well done!" and highly commended Amar on his courage and alacrity.

Amar saw that a timbal was indeed placed there and the name of Sikander Zulqarnain was inscribed on its head. Proclaiming, "In the name of Allah!" Amar hit it with a mallet, whereupon a most deafening rumble was created, and for sixty-four leagues the sea was thrown into a turmoil, as a most unearthly sound was produced. All the marine life appeared on the surface, and all the seabirds within a circumference of ten miles suddenly cried and drummed. The wind from the constant fluttering of their wings filled the sails of the ships, and they sailed on. Amar stayed on the obelisk as he had planned, but soon his heart became overcast with loneliness.

In a few days the ships dropped anchor in the isles of Ceylon, and the Sahibqiran landed on the island with his armies. Amar, however, was in great distress from solitude. Finding the violence of the sun unbearable, he supplicated before the True Lord and wept for his deliverance when suddenly he heard someone say, "Blessings of Allah be upon you!" Upon hearing this, Amar became ever more disconsolate, and startled by the voice looked to his left and right with great surprise, and then said to himself, *Beside myself there is no soul here who would greet me, and ask after my welfare. It could only be Izrail who has come to extract my soul, resolved upon taking my life! A hundred disgraces on a death such as this, and in so unbecoming a place, where neither a winding-sheet nor grave will I receive!*

Amar was in these thoughts when the holy Khizr appeared to him, and Amar saw a green-clad personage of illuminated aspect standing before him with a veil over his august face. Amar made a profusely humble salutation, and said, "What is your good name, O venerated sir, and how did you happen by this place?" The holy Khizr said, "I am Khizr and have brought you deliverance. God willing, I shall soon grant you release from here!" Amar kissed Khizr's feet, and made a prostration of gratitude.

But the scurrilous trickster who was famished with hunger had no trouble telling Khizr impertinently, "O venerated sir! I now put my store of hope in your hospitality as I am consumed with hunger!" The holy Khizr offered him a bread-cake, and said, "Eat this! Then I will also give you water to drink, and give you release from this confinement and trial." Amar grew wrathful in his heart upon beholding the bread-cake, and said, "How can I eat my fill with this bread-cake?"

Amar started muttering and grumbling impatiently to be fed, and said to Khizr, "Sire! Indeed you are Allah's prophet, and I have no claim to your venerated station, but I, too, am a favorite of God. And yet you make jests with me in a time of distress, when I am dying of hunger! When one's belly is full, he readily thinks of gibes and quips but when one's belly is deprived of food, he is not fit even to converse!" Khizr said: "Who jests? You complained to me of hunger, so I offered you this bread-cake and also promised you water!" Amar said to this, "It reminds me of the analogy about a caraway seed in the camel's jaw! Never mind filling me up, the bread-cake would not satisfy even a length of my intestine! You just offered me a memento of a morsel!" Khizr answered, "My good fellow, start eating in good faith and then you shall judge for yourself whether you are able to finish it, or if you spoke prematurely from your impetuosity!"

Then Amar began eating the bread-cake, and even after he had eaten his fill, the bread-cake remained whole as before. Next Khizr produced a water flask the size of a hand's length and a quarter, and gave it to Amar to drink from, asking, "How is it that you did not finish the bread-cake, since you were so hungry to begin with?" Amar saw that the flask also remained full as before, although his thirst was fully quenched. He thought up a ruse to keep them both, and expressing his gratitude to Khizr, said to him, "O venerated sir! Once you are gone, I see no reason why you should return! But thirst and hunger follow a man everywhere. When I am again consumed by the pangs of hunger, there will be nobody I can petition for relief! I would be most indebted and forever relieved of all cares of sustenance, if you would confer this bread-cake and water flask upon me!"

The holy Khizr granted Amar's request, and conferred the objects on him, and said, "This bread-cake and water flask will show you their wonder in many great difficulties, and will succor you in numerous ordeals! Give this Timbal of Sikander to Hamza along with all its regalia, but mind that you keep none of it yourself!" Amar said to the prophet, "How will I carry this great load, and travel under its burden?" The holy Khizr gave him a sheet of cloth, and said, "Wrap it all in this, and you shall feel no weight whatsoever." Amar said to himself, *This sheet is also a good thing to have. It will come in handy, and keep me warm in the winter besides!*

Wrapping all the goods and the Timbal of Sikander in the sheet, Amar carried the bundle on his head, and climbing onto the instep of Khizr's feet he closed his eyes and began to recite the Most Great Name—as Khizr had instructed him—and he was carried away from one place to another in just an instant. Soon Khizr said, "Open up your eyes, Amar! Behold the wonder of your Lord, who brought you such a great distance in the blink of an eye! See where you have arrived, out of your distress!" When Amar opened his eyes he found himself standing on land. He performed a prostration of gratitude to the True God, and headed in search of Hamza.

Now hear of Hamza, how when he landed in the port of Ceylon and reached the safety of its shore with his troops, he made offerings of great bounty and munificence to Khizr and Ilyas, and said to his men, "We shall sojourn here for two months, and occupy ourselves in grieving and mourning Amar's death, and make offerings to Allah in Amar's name. Indeed I held Amar as dear as my own life, and preferred his fellowship to that of all other men. Nor was he ever backward in returning the camaraderie, and in the end laid down his life for me!" Then all the commanders and their troops dressed themselves in black, and with great solemnity occupied themselves with grieving and lamentations.

We return to Amar's account. After he had traveled for some days, Amar saw a mosque of most holy, noble, and august aspect in the forest, and when he approached, he saw five men inside saying their prayers. Amar joined them, saying his prayers with the group. After they were finished with their prayers and visiting blessings and thanksgivings, four of the men mounted their steeds and rode away, while the fifth set out on foot. Amar hailed him and inquired after his particulars and welfare with great compassion. The man said to him, "Dear friend! The five of us are martyrs. We have laid down our lives in the path of Allah, and in recompense He has granted us absolution from the Day of Reckoning. Our salvation is now assured by the Grace of His Beneficence. The other four men were martyred with their mounts, while I died fighting on foot. Hence they have mounts and I do not. But if you would do me a kindness, I, too, will acquire a mount, and you shall receive my blessings."

Amar replied, "I would consider any service that I could render you an honor, as obedience and ministration to men of your station would be

the very means of my salvation." The man told Amar that a short distance from there was a town in which he had his house in such and such
a neighborhood. There was a quince tree in the courtyard of the martyr's
house under whose roots he had buried two thousand gold pieces in an
earthen pot. He asked Amar to dig it out, give a third to his heirs, keep a
third for himself, and with the rest buy a horse and its trappings and give
it away in the name of Allah as an offering by the martyr in order that he
might cease traveling on foot.

Amar took his leave and went to the house of the martyr. He carried
out his command and then went forth on his way. After traveling for several leagues he sat down in the shade of a tree to rest a while. Some time
had elapsed when he saw an ancient standing to his right. Amar kissed his
feet, and said, "Who are you, O venerated sire?" He replied, "My name is
Ilyas, and I have brought you these gifts, and have come to confer what
was kept in trust for you. Take this net and mantle! All that you carry in
this net will become light, and when you wrap yourself in this mantle,
you shall become invisible to all, but see everyone yourself!" Having
spoken, Ilyas disappeared before Amar's eyes and dissolved without a
trace.

In a few days Amar approached the Sahibqiran's camp. Having finally
made it to his companions he was beside himself with joy. Then he noticed that everyone there was clad in black, and appeared grief-stricken
and woebegone. Amar said to himself, *I hope that by God's clemency I receive
news of Hamza's well-being and am united with him in all happiness!* Pretending to be a stranger, he asked a passerby, "Whose army is this, and why are
all of them dressed in mourning?" The man answered, "This is the army
of the Sahibqiran, who set up camp here some time ago. Amir had a
brother, Amar Ayyar by name, whom he held very dear. He died in
climbing an obelisk in the Indian Ocean, and the Sahibqiran dressed
himself in black to lament his death. His entire entourage are also clad in
black since they, too, are in mourning. Today being Amar's *chehlum*, food
and victuals over which *fateha*[189] has been said are being distributed
among the beggars and the indigent."

Upon hearing this Amar said in his heart, *Now I have obtained proof of
Hamza's love for me!* He spent the day among the beggars who received the
food offered for Amar's salvation, and that night he put on the mantle
given him by Ilyas and entered Madi-Karib's pavilion. He found him
lying fast asleep. Amar clambered over his chest, whereupon Madi-Karib
woke up, and said, "Who are you, whence have you descended, and what

is your issue with me?" Amar replied, "I am the Angel of Death! Today when Amar's soul was bidden to enter Paradise, he refused, and told the keeper of Heaven that Madi-Karib was his bosom friend, that he would not enter Heaven without him, and that he would not set foot there except in Madi-Karib's company!"

> To promenade alone in the garden I am not the one,
> Even were it Heaven I would refuse it!

"Much though it was explained to him that Aadi's death was a long time away, and his entering Heaven lay in the distant future, Amar would hear nothing of it, and in the end I was ordered to extract Madi-Karib's soul. Thus I am come on the mission to take possession of your soul and claim your life!"

Madi-Karib replied, "I am most certainly not Amar's friend, and have no real love for him! Indeed I was his mortal foe and prayed for his death! There was never any love lost between us, nor did we ever get along!" Amar now said, "If you were to offer me a little something, I would spare your life, and take your words to God Almighty!" Madi-Karib said, "A chest of gold pieces is kept over yonder. Pray take it and refrain from taking my life!"

After securing the chest Amar left, and next entered Sultan Bakht Maghrebi's pavilion. He repeated similar words there, and Sultan Bakht Maghrebi, too, offered Amar a chest of gold pieces, thinking in his mind that he had escaped with his life from the clutches of the Angel of Death.

The long and short of it is that Amar visited all the commanders that night, and received gold pieces from all of them after leading them into deception. All the chiefs came down with the ague on account of Amar's phantom, and none found any sleep the whole night from terror.

Come morning, when Aadi first narrated what had passed with him the previous night, Amir Hamza laughed heartily listening to his account, reckoning that Aadi had probably had a nightmare. But then Sultan Bakht Maghrebi arrived and narrated his story, and other nobles as well related identical details. Then Amir said, "Make haste to move the camp and bivouac the army elsewhere! It is now become abundantly manifest that this place is under the influence of the devil: How else could all the men have an identical dream? Our troops should be moved elsewhere, lest they be taken by madness and fall into the power of the devils!"

The next day Amar played the trick on Hamza, pulling the same prank. Hamza said aloud, "It is a marvel that I hear the voice, but do not see the man who speaks! I wonder what is behind it all!" When he groped with his hands, Hamza felt a body. Thinking it was a jinn, Hamza caught hold of it by one hand, and made to clout it with the other hand and make it bite dust, when suddenly Amar called out, "Beware, O Arab! Don't hit me or I will be grievously wounded and hurt!" Amar then threw off the mantle. Hamza had recognized his voice and now embraced him with great delight. Amar narrated all that had passed with him and recounted all his adventures, and handed the Timbal of Sikander and other effects to Hamza. He showed him the bread-cake, the water flask, the net, and the mantle, and said, "Khizr and Ilyas bestowed these on me, and none has a claim on them except me!" Then Amar put them away for his own use.

The next morning Hamza moved his camp to the foot of Mount Ceylon, and having trekked all that distance of his journey, at last arrived at his destination. The news spread to the four corners of the world that Amir Hamza, the son-in-law of Naushervan the Just, had arrived to skirmish with the Khusrau of India, King Landhoor bin Saadan, that Hamza's men made up in valor what they lacked in numbers, that every single one of them held Rustam and Nariman and Afrasiyab of no account, and that Amir Hamza himself was a mighty warrior, and a man who had a great claim on power and might.

Amir had arrived at Mount Ceylon at the time of the festival commemorating the day Prophet Aadam's expiation was accepted by God and the Merciful Lord released him from his anguish and grief. People were converging there from surrounding regions to celebrate the festival. On the mountain was a stone that bore an imprint of Aadam's foot, and the Hindus and the True Believers made their pilgrimage to that site. They would undertake journeys of two to four months' duration and set camp at the foot of the mountain, and make pilgrimage on the appointed day.

Amar said to Hamza, "If you would allow me, I shall go and visit the mountain and bring you news from there!" Hamza gave permission, and Amar made his way to the place. Arriving at a steep slope Amar found no pathway that he could take up to visit the holy site. By chance, he spied a hut and went toward it, and he found an ancient praying inside. When the old man visited blessings on Amar, and addressed him by his name, Amar frowned and reached for his dagger, thinking this was a *tasma-pa*.

The ancient smiled, and said, "O Amar! I am not of the race of the *tasma-pas* but of the line of Nuh, and my name is Saalim! I recognized you by virtue of receiving annunciation about you last night in a dream, otherwise I would know nothing of you or your name!" He handed Amar an iron club, and said, "Go to that nook, and dig in the ground to this club's length, and there you will find what is apportioned your share, and what is ordained by fate to be conferred upon you from the blessings of the True Lord. Mind not to give in to greed, but be content with whatever you find!"

Amar dug up the ground to the measure, and found a bright grain of ruby. He put this in his bag and kept digging, but despite the continuous labor he found nothing else. He felt embarrassed, and returned to Saalim to show the ruby to him. The old man said, "Now go to the mountain and make pilgrimage to the imprint of Aadam's foot!" Amar replied, "I see no pathway to climb up the mountain, and my head swoons from the prospect of the upward climb! If I must make pilgrimage, how am I to find the way?" Saalim said, "Follow that narrow trail over yonder, and do not let fear find a foothold in your heart!"

Amar took the trail the old man advised to the mountain, and came very near to dying from the arduous uphill climb. Then he came upon a most sumptuous enclosure surrounding a garden furnished with rivulets of pearl-bright water and a coppice of giant trees. When Amar drew close, he saw there a white stone with the imprint of Aadam's foot. Amar kissed it, pressed his eyes to it, and smeared his eyelids with the dust from that place. Amar's mouth watered when he saw tall heaps of jewels piled up around the stone. Then his heart was possessed by a powerful greed and he reasoned thus in his heart: *I have already made pilgrimage to Aadam's footprint. Now I must pack up these jewels and return hastily to my camp! There is nobody here to witness the deed and apprehend me!*

Amar spread the mantle on the ground and gathered up all the jewels inside it, but when he neared the door of the enclosure carrying his burden, the door disappeared from before his eyes, as if it had never existed. He retraced his steps and put the jewels back, and now when he looked toward the door, he found it there as before, whole and entire. Deciding to mark the door before carrying away the loot, he put his headdress by the threshold. Then standing by the heap of jewels and looking at the door, he observed that he could see both the door and the headdress. He again lifted the bundle of jewels and headed out, but again as he approached the door, the consequences of his deed became manifest and he found that the door had again disappeared as well as his headdress. Amar said in his heart, *Now it is becoming plain to me that grandfather Aadam was not one to leave anything to chance! His riches shall forever remain before his eyes and nobody may swallow or plunder them!*

When Amar returned the jewels to their place, he was again able to see his headdress and the door. Noting that it was time to say prayers, Amar made his ablution with water from the spring and offered his prayers. He broke into tears thinking of his mercenary act and, deeming that this holy site was a place where prayers would be granted, he supplicated to God with all sincerity. In the midst of his weeping and importuning he was overtaken by sleep of a sudden, and beheld a group of ancients standing around him, regarding him with affection.

One among them who was tall of stature gave Amar a lion skin, and said, "Put this on! It is called the *dev-jama*.[190] Once you have dressed yourself in it, you shall become immune to any and all calamities and troubles, and will be safeguarded from the harm of all demons and malignant jinns. The *zambil*[191] that you see with it can accommodate the entire contents of the world in it, will produce all that you may wish for, and will safeguard what you vouchsafe to its care. Such is the miraculous power of this *zambil* that when you place your hand on it and recite, 'Grandfather Aadam! May I acquire such and such an aspect!' you shall presently convert to that form. Moreover, you will be able to speak and comprehend all the languages of the world. Learn ye now that I am Aadam!" At this, Amar made obeisance, and knelt down and kissed Aadam's feet.

The second ancient gave Amar a goblet, and said, "Commit to memory the Most Great Name written on this, as it will be of great value to you, and you stand to gain much advantage from it! Learn ye now that I am Ishaq, the prophet of God!"

The third ancient introduced himself as Prophet Daud. Giving Amar a *do-tara*,[192] he said to him, "When you shall play this *do-tara* and sing, you will surpass even the greatest musician, and even if your audience is alien to the science of music, their hearts will be overwhelmed by your singing, and they will adore you and love you with a great passion!"

The fourth ancient gave his name as Prophet Saleh and, stroking Amar's back with his hand, said to him, "Nobody will ever outpace you, and the finest charger will be unable to match your speed! You shall run faster than the wind, and never tire!"[193]

As Prophet Saleh was saying these words, a throne descended from the heavens on which an ancient was seated. Amar's eyes were bedazzled upon beholding the face of this ancient, and he was awed and overcome by his majesty. The other four prophets greeted him with great reverence and honor. Amar asked them, "Who is this personage?" And they replied, "He is the Last Prophet of Time, Muhammad the Messenger of Allah (peace be upon him)!"

Amar made obeisance, and with folded arms spoke thus: "Sire! All the prophets assembled here have conferred on me a gift each. I plead you to grant my wish that the Angel of Death not extract my soul, that I may not die until I myself ask for my death three times!" Then Prophet Muhammad (peace be upon him!) said, "Should it be Allah's pleasure, your wish shall be granted!"

Then Amar woke up, and saw lying around him all the gifts that he had received from the prophets. Amar gathered all those gifts and displayed them before Saalim, and narrated the whole incident to him as it had happened. Saalim said, "Send Hamza here, too, Amar, so that he may also receive what is apportioned to him by destiny!" Then Amar left, and on his way back, he put his hand on the *zambil* to try it out, and called out, "O Grandfather Aadam! Make me tall and change the color of my skin to a hue darker than pitch. May I not shrink in stature unless I ask for it myself, and may my height and bulk and whole being become distinct from those of all other denizens of Earth!"

Immediately Amar noticed that he had risen in height, and when he held a mirror to his face, he was himself terrified by his features. Fearing that perhaps his changed color, feature, and stature had become permanent, Amar again put his hand on the *zambil* and asked to be returned to his original form and likeness—whereupon he immediately reverted to his natural self. He then breathed easily and was beside himself with joy thinking that now he could acquire any shape and form at will, and find new opportunities for amusement with every disguise.

Then changing again to his former disguise, he entered the camp of the faithfuls and started playing on his *do-tara*. Whoever heard its sound left their work unattended, and followed in his train. People brought news to Hamza that an Indian of such and such an aspect had arrived in the camp and played the *do-tara* so melodiously that he left his audience completely in raptures. The Sahibqiran ordered that the Indian be presented before him, and found him to be of a form exceedingly strange that nobody had seen before, not even in the world of dreams. Riveted by his singing and music, Hamza and all his nobles became so engrossed that they lost command of their senses and were thrown into reverie as if somebody had cast a spell over them.

After Amar finished his song and stopped playing, Hamza asked him, "Where have you come from, stranger, and what is your name?" Amar answered, "I go by the name Mahmud Siyah-Tan! I am a denizen of this very land, and am known to the Khusrau of India, who rewards me according to his liberality, albeit always short of my expectations, thus obliging me to put out my hand and solicit before other princes!" The Sahibqiran ordered his men, saying, "Take this Indian to our treasury, and allow him to take all the money and gold pieces and jewels that he can carry!" Thereupon Sultan Bakht Maghrebi took Amar to Hamza's treasury, and asked him to collect his reward.

One after another, Amar started bringing each and every chest out of the treasury, whereupon Sultan Bakht Maghrebi said, "All this is worth hundreds of cart-loads. Why display such greed, and scatter the chests in the treasury! As Amir has ordered, take only what you can carry, and only the goods and riches that your cloth can hold!" Amar replied, "My lord, do you see any cart or curricle with me, or some hired hand around to be my porter? Rest assured that I am only doing what I was bid!"

Thinking that the Indian was perhaps a lunatic, Sultan Bakht Maghrebi kept quiet. The other employees of the treasury also watched in silence, and no one else asked further questions of Amar while he spread his net and piled up all those chests on it, and then secured them with his rope. When he slung the entire load over his shoulder and made to head out to the mountains, those assembled were unable to call reason to their aid, and they became bereft of their senses from marveling.

Sultan Bakht Maghrebi stopped Amar from leaving, saying, "Wait a while until I have informed my commander and conveyed the news to his ears." Amar put down his load and sat there to wait. Sultan Bakht then narrated the whole episode to Hamza, and said, "O Sahibqiran, he seems to be some jinn or a *ghol* of the desert, or else he is some wizard. He is a veritable calamity on two feet and a scourge descended from the heavens. He tied up all the chests in the treasury in a net and, carrying them all upon his shoulders, walked with a light foot, without his legs faltering in the least, or his shoulders giving way! I held him up on the pretext of informing you, and with the ruse of obtaining your leave before he departs."

Upon hearing this, Hamza discerned that this could only be Amar, returned with some new artifice, and that it was certainly another one of his capers. He then went himself, and said to Amar, "What a surprise, my friend, that we are the lucky victims of your prank, and you picked us to be the target of this trickery!" Amar could not hold back his laughter then, and Hamza embraced him. Amar related his whole adventure, and said, "Saalim has sent for you, and he has put away gifts for you as well!"

Hamza rested that night, and in the morning headed for the vale with Amar and other nobles in his entourage, promenading by the springs, lakes, and glades. During his romp, he came upon an arena whose floor was leveled with a mix of white sandalwood powder and roses. The arena was most marvelously smooth and admirably planed, without the least unevenness. Stone quoits, dumbbells, a *lezam*,[194] a pike, a mace, and other such exercise apparatus were kept in a corner of the arena, and a body of men stood guard over them. When Amir asked them to whom the arena belonged, they replied, "It is the arena of the Khusrau of India, who is the king of these dominions!" Hamza turned to Amar and said, "Let me also exercise my skill, and show a display of my strength to these people!" Amar replied, "In the name of Allah, so be it! May this arena prove auspicious for you!"

Then Hamza stepped into the arena, and lifted up all the quoits, dumbbells, the pike, and the *lezam* easily, but he could not lift the mace. Hamza became most distraught and depressed in his heart, and cried out, "O Almighty God! You are the One who upholds a man's name and honor! When I am unable to lift up Landhoor's mace, it is certain that combat with him will be most perilous!"

Then Hamza left the arena despairing, and visited Saalim, who embraced him and handed him the same mace he had given Amar, and told him to dig at such and such a spot measuring the length of that club, and when he had found what was apportioned for him by fate, to bring it over to him. Hamza did as Saalim had bid him, and upon digging at the ground, found a grain of ruby, which he brought to Saalim, who said, "This is for you! Put it in your pocket, and make your pilgrimage to the mountain, and may God be your assistance and your guardian! Without divine help you shall not prevail upon the Khusrau of India or defeat him at all!"

Hamza went to the mountain and made his pilgrimage to Aadam's footprint and offered prayers at that site. He occupied himself in petitioning for, importuning, and soliciting divine assistance. In the course of his penultimate prostration, all of a sudden he was overtaken by stupor and fell into a deep sleep.

In his sleep he witnessed a throne descending on the face of the Earth from the heavens and lighting up the place with its brilliance. On that throne a group of ancients of illuminated aspects were seated, whose faces were surrounded with halos of light. One among them, who was of a tall stature, greeted Hamza by his name and, after visiting God's blessings upon him, said, "O Hamza, take this armlet and wear it. Your arm will never be lowered by your adversary then, nor will anyone ever prevail against your arm's might. And even should your adversary be a thousand yards tall, by virtue of this blessed armlet your sword will yet surmount his head, and no harm will ever come to you. But do not ever be the first to sound the war drums, never take precedence in seeking combat, and not until your adversary has first dealt you three blows should you deal him one yourself! Never kill one of noble soul, offer reprieve to the one who asks for it, do not pursue a retreating enemy, and never break the heart of one down in spirits! Never turn a mendicant empty-handed from your door. Never give yourself airs of vanity, and never be a braggart, nor let yourself be the agency through which the least injury is inflicted on the weak and humble. You are the one who shall weed out the reed of infidelity from the face of the world, and establish the standard of Faith!"

> *Better to be as dust and the burden of wind*
> *Than to be the king and the burden of men.*

"And take heed when you bellow your war cry, as its sound will travel sixteen *farsangs*, and instill great fear in the hearts of those who hear it!"

After imparting these injunctions Prophet Aadam embraced Hamza, and other prophets showed him their favor also, whereupon Amir's eyes opened in ecstasies of joy. He rose from there and recited invocations for his auspicious dream and, after making ablution, offered prayers. And having recited the *fateha,* he returned to Saalim and narrated to him the details of his propitious annunciation. Saalim congratulated Amir and, vouchsafing his last wishes to Amir's ears, said, "This traveler to the land of Death awaited you only, as guiding and initiating you on your destiny was entrusted to me[?]. Adieu, as I must now depart for the final leg of my journey! But I would request that you yourself attend to my last rites and burial!"

Having said this, Saalim stretched his legs out on his mat, withdrew himself from the cares of the world, recited the Act of Faith, and was entered into Heaven.

Betimes my rectitude is the angels' envy,
Betimes at my transgressions demons sneer;
It would be a commendable marvel of skill
To retain unviolated my faith to the grave.

Amir shed many tears of remorse over the fickle nature of human existence, and attended to Saalim's burial. Then he headed to Landhoor's arena. He lifted up the mace weighing one thousand and seven hundred Tabrizi *maunds* with ease upon reciting, "In the name of Allah!" as if it were a twig, and removed it to another corner of the arena. Then he returned joyously to his camp, and offered several thousand dinars in the name of Allah to the mendicants.

The guards carried news of this incident to Landhoor's ears, who presently arrived at the arena. He marveled greatly upon finding the mace placed in another corner, and reasoned that someone who was his equal in might had arrived on the island. He gave orders to the guards that if the man who had displayed his might by removing the mace to another corner of the enclosure returned, Landhoor should be informed at once, and the man conducted into his presence.

Now hear of Amar, who, having separated from Hamza on the pretext of going on a jaunt, entered Landhoor's camp in the guise of a Khorasani, with the *do-tara* in his hand, and approached the threshold of Landhoor's court. The mace bearer asked him, "Who are you, what is your trade, whence have you come and from what land?" Amar answered, "I have come to these lands with the son-in-law of the Emperor of the Seven Climes, and the fame of the liberality of the Khusrau of India has brought me to his august threshold. Give him the news of my arrival, and take me before him!" The ushers informed the head porter who informed the king. He ordered that the Khorasani be brought into his presence and, according to his orders, Amar was led before Landhoor.

Amar's appearance greatly intrigued Landhoor, who had never seen a man of such aspect, nor ever set eyes on such a mien and physique. He asked Amar, "What is your name, of which country are you a native, and where are you domiciled?" After visiting blessings on Landhoor's head, Amar made answer: "I am known as Baba Zud Burd, and I call Khorasan my home!" Landhoor said, "A matchless name you have, and strange is your discourse! From your account it appears that you assault men and plunder their property!" Amar replied, "The only strikes this vassal makes are with a plectrum on the cords of my instrument; and I plunder only the hearts of my listeners and connoisseurs, and make them mellow!" Landhoor was greatly delighted by this quip, and ordered Amar to sing.

Amar sat ahead of all the singers and minstrels in the court, and began tuning his *do-tara*. All the musicians assembled took offense at this and began to whine, and asked, "What is his great talent that he claims station above all of us, like some great maestro, and shows such vanity!" Landhoor answered, "In the first place, he is one of the True Believers, and has arrived in the entourage of an illustrious prince. Furthermore, he has the appearance of an ascetic, and I must not break his heart as he would then go traveling from land to land, narrating everywhere how he was received at my court. Mark it well that if I do not indulge him, I will be reproached and reviled by his tongue. But if I show him honor, he will praise me and mention my name kindly! Do consider this! Moreover, as I wish him to be seated near me when he sings, it is no reflection on your merit, and you have no cause to become at all chagrined!"

After the musicians were calmed, Landhoor signaled to Amar, who began to sing. The whole assembly including the musicians was thrown into raptures, and they said, "This man has a fife for a gullet! It would be a wonder if his throat has any bone at all!" While the assembly was engrossed in his song, Amar's greedy eyes were glued to the four emerald peacocks affixed to the four corners of Landhoor's throne, and he surveyed them with an eye to finding a chance of stealing them.

Greatly pleased by Amar's singing, Landhoor said, "Ask me for anything, O Baba Zud Burd! Speak what you most desire!" Amar replied, "May God increase your life! Your Honor be thanked, Naushervan's son-in-law has bestowed much on your vassal, and freed me from all material concerns!" After a while, Landhoor again said to him, "You must ask for something, as I wish to reward you for bringing such delight to my heart with your singing!" Amar answered, "By the glory of Your Honor, I have no material needs! Your slave does not crave gold and riches, but desires instead to be your cupbearer, should the permission be granted, and to offer you a cup or two of roseate wine!"

Landhoor signaled to the head cupbearer who handed Amar the goblet and ewer. Amar poured crimson wine in bejeweled goblets and began the rounds. After the cup had been passed for some two or three rounds, and Amar saw that Landhoor's eyes showed the effects of intoxication and signs of losing control of his senses, he stretched out his hand and plucked out one of the emerald peacocks, and hid it under his arm. Landhoor saw him from the corner of his eye, and said, "What is this you are doing, O Zud Burd! Why did you put the peacock in your bag?" Amar winked at him, and said, "Be quiet lest someone hear this and the thing become known!"

Then Landhoor laughed out loud at Amar's clowning at asking the one from whom he stole to keep quiet lest someone hear him and catch him in his act. He said to Amar, "Hear this, O Baba Zud Burd! Little do I care should someone hear me, since the goods belong to me and it is not I who steals them! But since even your theft is so deliciously audacious, I willingly grant you the other three peacocks as well. Tell me if you are now satisfied."

Amar made obeisance and, after putting away the peacocks, thought of lining his pockets further. Without the Khusrau catching him this time, he mixed four *mithcals*[195] of an inebriant in the wine ewer, and poured out two cups each for Landhoor and all his courtiers. Hardly a moment had passed before the eyes of all those present became glazed.

Completely oblivious of their own actions, and imagining themselves swimmers in their inebriation, they began to call out, "The sea is becoming turbulent! Dive now and swim for the shores as hard as you can!" Landhoor was the first to jump from his throne, and fell flat on his face. His courtiers likewise jumped from their stations alongside him, and with resounding thuds fell unconscious on the floor one after another. Without loss of time Amar began his pillaging and looting, and stuffed all the effects and regalia of the court into his *zambil*, down to the last carpet in the room. Then he made his way out, and reaching his camp before long, sat dragonlike upon all the treasure he had gathered.

It so happened that just then Amir Hamza ordered a search to be made to determine Amar's whereabouts, to discover whether he was inside the camp or out, as he had not been seen around for some time; and also to find out what he was occupied with, and to have him conducted into Hamza's presence in whatever condition he was found. When the members of the search party reached Amar's pavilion, they found Amar busy sorting the choice bits from the great heap of goods piled there. They said to Amar, "Come along with us as the Sahibqiran has sent for you, and ordered us to produce you before him, however and wherever we find you!" Amar replied, "Very well, my friends! But do let me take care of all these effects. Then I will readily come along and leave here in your company." They said, "Do not bother about the goods! You must come with us now with all these goods to see Amir; otherwise the Sahibqiran will be made unhappy, as he gave us orders to this effect."

When Amar was led before Hamza with all these goods and effects, Amir laughed, thinking that Amar must have robbed someone again. He asked his friend, "How did you come into these possessions?" When Amar replied that everything was a gift from the Khusrau of India, the Sahibqiran did not believe him, and had all the effects put away into safe-keeping for the night.

The following morning, Hamza said to Aadi, "Convey my regards to the Khusrau of India and take to him all these things, in addition to the other gifts that I shall also give into your care. Also, give the Khusrau this message from me: 'It appears Amar visited your court last night in disguise and he maintains that the Khusrau of India made him a gift of all these effects, and conferred them on him of his own volition; but as I do not believe his account and version of events, and moreover, as he is a most notorious trickster, I am returning all these goods, and sending them back to you. And should you deign to accept my small token as a gift—the acceptance of which would be meet and proper for you—it would afford me great joy. And I beseech you to inform me if Amar is guilty of any offense, so that I may chastise him accordingly!'" Aadi Madi-Karib loaded all the goods on curricles and took himself to Landhoor's court, arriving at the threshold of that court with great pomp and glory.

In Landhoor's court, meanwhile, the Khusrau of India and the nobles of his court regained their senses when the sun of the new day rose to take its seat on the throne of the heavens. Upon beholding the whole court looted bare, they looked for Baba Zud Burd, and made inquiries as to his whereabouts. But people answered that they did not know where he went, or how he disappeared. As Landhoor was busy conducting these inquiries, he noticed a note tied to his neck. After opening it and reading its message, he discovered that it was in fact Amar who had visited him the previous night in the guise of Baba Zud Burd. The Khusrau then went to the baths, and prepared to hold court.

While he was thus occupied, the housekeepers spread out carpets in the court, and decorated the halls anew. As these preparations were taking place, couriers and mace bearers arrived to announce that Aadi Madi-Karib, the emissary of Naushervan's son-in-law, had arrived to seek audience, and had brought an abundance of gifts for King Landhoor, the Refuge of the World. Landhoor sent his prominent commanders to greet Aadi, and they went in a body and escorted Aadi into the court. After performing the rituals of royal audience, Aadi conveyed the Sahibqiran's message to Landhoor, and placed before him all the things Amar had looted from the court, as well as all the gifts that Hamza had sent. Landhoor was greatly pleased and much taken with Aadi's manners. He seated him above all his nobles, and accepted from him the gifts sent by the Sahibqiran. As to the things stolen by Amar from his court, however, he declared that he had conferred their possession to Amar and given them over willingly.

Landhoor said to Aadi, "After offering him my humble greetings, convey this message to Amir Hamza: Even if the tiniest shadow of spite passed over my heart against Amar, it has now been forgotten, and not the least modicum of displeasure remains in my mind in that regard. I request that he, too, be sparing in this matter, and not let it cloud his heart. Indeed I am most desirous of seeing Amar's face, and I would be beholden to Hamza if he would send Amar to visit me without a disguise!" After speaking, Landhoor conferred a robe of honor on Aadi and gave him leave to depart. At the time of parting he expressed great ardor and love for Amir Hamza.

When he returned, Aadi narrated all that he had seen and heard, and upon hearing this Hamza was greatly pleased, and said to Amar, "O Baba Zud Burd! The Khusrau of India desires to see you in your real person, and has returned your booty as a gift." Amar was in seventh heaven when he heard these words, and headed for Landhoor's court after stashing away all the goods.

Along his way Amar saw a group of merchants who were also headed for the Khusrau's court. They were carrying very many excellent and choice objects, and one of the merchants had a crown worth the hundreds of thousands in his possession, which was studded with such a marvel of jewels that nobody had seen or heard the likes of them. Amar donned the garb of a merchant, and followed along in their entourage. When the party reached the threshold of Landhoor's court, and presented themselves at that august station, the messenger took the news of their arrival, and they were ordered to enter and display their goods.

Landhoor was most delighted when the crown was presented before him, and sent for the keeper of his state treasury, and said to him, "Reward these merchants over and above the cost of the crown, and send them away delighted and pleased! I shall wear this crown on my head this instant, and adorn myself with it forthwith!" When Amar overheard this, he said, "We must first be paid the price of the crown, then the Khusrau may freely put it on his head, or send it to his wardrobe keeper!"

At these words, Landhoor instantly returned the crown to the broker to hand it back to the owner, and said to the keeper, "Bring it to me once its price has been paid to the merchants. I would never dream of acquiring anyone's property by force, and will not stand for such talk!" The broker took the crown to the merchants, and asked them to name its price. Amar took the crown from his hand, and said, "I shall judge its worth once I have appraised it in the sunlight—as one must speak judiciously regarding business matters in the court of kings!" The broker replied, "Verily said! Your opinion is aright in this matter!"

Amar stepped out of the Hall of Audience and, peering intently in the sky, spoke thus to those present, "What a dark cloud is rising in the skies! I imagine it is the harbinger of a severe dust storm, as a great mist is upon us!" Thus speaking Amar stepped to one side, and then made away, giving them all the slip. The merchants and royal retainers meanwhile looked over the entire sky, and said, "There is not even the hint of a cloud in the sky, dear friend! Why do you make so false a claim?" When they turned to look, they saw Amar running away with the crown, having already put a great distance between them.

The news was immediately conveyed to the Khusrau and proclaimed throughout the camp. The Khusrau mounted his elephant and went in pursuit, and intercepted Amar, who tried to hide himself in a thicket. But finding no escape from there, he was distressfully looking around when he beheld a hut, with a man inside grinding a hand mill. Amar immediately barged into his house, and said, "Do you have any idea how precariously your life hangs in the balance? The Khusrau has had a dream, and philosophers have interpreted that the king will be delivered from the evil boded in his dream, if he beats a drum with a head made of a miller's scalp. A party is on their way here to catch you, and they bring the executioner along!"

When he heard that, the poor man almost died of fright, reckoning that he would lose his life for nothing. Terrified, he asked Amar, "How can I escape from the power of these tyrants and live to claim the remainder of my natural life?" Amar replied, "Give me your waistcloth so that I may wear it and sit here grinding the hand mill in your stead, and I shall think of some ruse to deliver you from certain death! You must dive into this pool here and must not stir at all. If someone comes looking for you I will answer for you, and divert them from your house by some trick!" Seeing a new lease of life being offered to him, the miller immediately handed his waistcloth and dress to Amar, and dived into the pool stark naked and settled there without moving.

Amar tied on the waistcloth, and sat grinding the mill. Soon Landhoor arrived and dismounted from his elephant. He entered the miller's house, and told Amar that a man of such and such a description had entered his house just a moment ago, and to tell him truthfully where he was hiding. Amar replied, "That man jumped into the pool and has been hiding there!" Landhoor then undressed and jumped into the pool after him, and Amar picked up his dress and headed out of the house, asking people along the way directions to the office of the royal treasurer.

When he found the treasurer, he showed him Landhoor's dress, and said to him, "The Khusrau of India has sent me with this token to collect two hundred *tomans* from you and return to him posthaste to bring him the money without delay!" The treasurer handed him the two hundred *tomans* without asking any questions, and Amar headed for his camp after thus lining his pockets.

Now, when Landhoor tried to get the miller out of the pool, pushing and heaving him out of the water, the miller banged his head against the stones of the pool. After inflicting this injury on himself, he said to Landhoor, "Now my scalp is damaged and shall be of no use! You must look for another miller now, and fit out the drum with *his* scalp, and present it to the Khusrau so that he may drum it and ward off the evil boded by his dream, and that you may receive the reward and the robe of honor due you!" Landhoor was most utterly confounded upon hearing the miller, and wondered what insanity might have come over him to utter such crazy words. He reasoned that the man was certainly possessed by some madness or craze.

When the miller got out of the pool Landhoor saw that he was not the person he had been looking for; indeed there was a world of difference between him and Amar. Landhoor stepped from the pool and asked the people gathered outside if they had seen anyone come out of the house and pass their way. They replied, "We did not see anyone pass here except for the man whom Your Excellency sent with his robe as a token of identity to collect two hundred *tomans* from the treasurer—and whom Your Honor yourself had sent with the royal dress to receive the sum. He passed by here again after collecting the money from the treasurer. But we know not where he lives!" At this, Landhoor understood that it was

Amar, and he marveled at his ingenuity, cunning, and stratagem. After changing into a new robe, he mounted his elephant, and headed in a straight line toward Hamza's camp by himself.

His *ayyars* informed Amir that the Khusrau of India, King Landhoor bin Saadan, was approaching His Honor's pavilion alone on an elephant, without any nobles, courtiers, or soldiers in his train. The Sahibqiran said to them, "Wait here without stirring, and let him come!"

When Landhoor dismounted and stepped toward Hamza's pavilion, Hamza received and welcomed him at the threshold, escorted him inside, and seated him on his own bejeweled seat, showing him great honor and prestige according to his station. Hamza ordered that preparations be made for festivities, and the assembly of revelry was made ready at once. Landhoor became greatly enamored of Hamza's manners and fell in love with his gentle ways. Thanking him profusely for his kindnesses, he said, "Where is Amar? Please send for him! But do ask him to appear in his own person as I am most desirous of seeing him, and wish to behold his true face! Every time that he has visited me, he has done so in disguise and left after committing some roguery!"

Upon these orders, Amar immediately presented himself in his true self, and took a seat after making obeisance to Landhoor. Fair-bodied cupbearers, clad in gold finery, arrived carrying goblets and ewers, and began passing drinks in rounds by pouring the sun of the yellow wine into moon-shaped goblets. With his own hand, Hamza offered the first cup to Landhoor, and then drank one himself. When the assembly became steeped in inebriation and their eyes intoxicated with delight, Landhoor requested Amar to sing and asked him to send for musical instruments. Amar sent for the *do-tara* and after tuning it, sang a song of such subtlety and elegance that the whole assembly sat enraptured, and Landhoor involuntarily called out "Bravo!" and "What excellence!" He took off his pearl necklace and conferred it on Amar, and bestowed on him as well the stolen crown.

The Sahibqiran and Landhoor next conferred together privately, and many a word of affection and goodwill was exchanged between the two. When King Sol entered his pavilion in the West, and it was time for parting, Landhoor said to Hamza, "Did my plea find favor with you, and did my request reach the threshold of your munificent dispensation?" Amir answered, "You practice the ways of fidelity and oblige me with your excellent manners, but the position that I am in, I am helpless to find a way out of my obligation to the Emperor of the Seven Concentric Circles, who sent me here to wage war upon you!" Landhoor replied: "Abandon this intention for all pleasure is in making peace, not in making war! You must turn your mind from thoughts of waging war. Indeed, Naushervan did not send you here to fight with me. It is clear to me that he planned it as a collusive war to your detriment! It is manifest that he bears enmity toward you! When he could not overpower you with the means at his disposal, he sent you this way. And his plan in sending you here was most nefarious, too. I wish that you would renounce your plans for war, and take me along with you. I shall kill Naushervan and seat you on his throne. You will reign in peace, and bide your nights and days in revelries with your beloved in your arms!"

Amir answered, "I gave my pledge to Naushervan to efface your existence from this world. How could I go back on my word and break my pledge?" Then Landhoor drew his sword and, presenting it to Hamza, lowered his neck before him, and said, "If this is your pleasure, go ahead and behead this unworthy one, and take my head and present it to Naushervan without subjecting yourself to the least labor or toil on my account!" The Sahibqiran embraced Landhoor and greatly extolled his manliness and courage, and delighted Landhoor with his praise.

Then Amir said to him, "Such an act is suited either to a coward or an executioner! Sound the war drums and let us descend tomorrow into the arena, and let the course of events be determined by the results in the battlefield!" Landhoor answered, "Adieu, then! If this is what you desire, you must sound the clarion of war today from your camp, and alert your army!"

Amir replied, "You may sound the drums in your camp and take precedence! Then I shall also give orders to that effect and answer your call!" The Khusrau was obliged to return to his camp and sound the war drums. Upon hearing them, the Sahibqiran ordered that the Timbal of Sikander be sounded. It was duly struck and shook the whole expanse of the arena with its impact.

> *And from the music assembly issued forth the song*
> *That dreadful is the world and despicable and foul.*

For those brave souls who had awaited the alluring show of swords in battle, that night was like the night of Eid.[196] Their slumbering fortunes began to awaken at the approach of this auspicious day. They declared that the time had come when they were to obtain a tryst with their beloved sharp blades, and on that day the fairy-limbed scimitars and daggers would be arrayed in glory. They bathed and changed and rubbed the perfume of good fortune[197] on themselves, lined their eyes with collyrium, and consulted among themselves, chewing betel leaves the while. They made vows of valor for the morrow in the battlefield: some making them with considerations of propriety, some without reserve, discussing who among them should return victorious from the arena and who pale-faced. Embracing their comrades, they said, "Tonight the oblation is due for the festival of sacrifices! Let us embrace now, as tomorrow the Butcher of Doom will gird himself and descend into the arena bent on wholesale slaughter, and it remains to be seen whether or not we shall find leave again to see one another! Let us now clasp ourselves in one another's happy embrace as God alone knows who will be slaughtered and who slain!"

Some had a sharp edge put to their blades so that their adversary's neck would be severed without fail. Others had their blades cleft so that neither muscle nor sinew should remain on the bones of the enemy. One said, "Come tomorrow, see the flash and sparkle of my sword!" Another declared, "I wish to see the face of my Isfahani sword dripping with gore!" Some polished their steel gauntlets bright to lure victory to them and make their hand ascendant. Someone commented, "God is the sole Preserver of Honor, and victory in battle is never certain! One must only repose his hopes in His Person!" Another exclaimed, "Watch out for the Indian sword, and take stock of the valor of the Indians and their stratagems!"

Some burnished their steel helmets into prestigious emblems of the height of lordship and victory. Some brightened their cuirasses to reflect therein the propitious image of the bride of victory. Some tempered their daggers so that with just one blow the foe would be so unsettled, that never again would he show the least temper, and would retire to the Future State in the cold shadow of steel. Some inspected their spears and lances, and some sharpened the spearheads and pike points, so that they would not get lodged in the enemy's malicious breast, but instead thrust clear past it and come out shining on the other side of the rib cage. Some whetted their knives and stilettos to a mean edge, and resolved in their hearts to make the foe taste unimaginable sorrow. Some cleaved the points of their poniards, so that the enemy's life would be put out. Some emptied their quivers to trim the feathers on their arrows, and straightened their bows over fire, so that they might shoot straight in battle and not twist.

And upon hearing the thunder of the war drums, the lowborn pansies set about emptying their bowels with abandon. With pale complexions, dry lips, and a look of great terror etched on their aspects, they broke into a calamitous bout of weeping and crying, and pledged offerings thus with their litanies: "O Madar Sahib! If peace be declared without the hostilities of war, I shall make a pilgrimage to your shrine to make an offering of a banner."[198] One malignant coward spoke thus: "I shall make a pilgrimage to Pir Jalilan,[199] and make an offering of Pir Bhuchri's halva."[200] Someone else said, "I shall celebrate the festival of Pir-ul-Wali!" Thus each one of their lot made these pledges, and said to his syce,[201] "My friend! Make haste and get the horse ready before daybreak, so that we may retire under the canopy of stars while it is still dark and pleasant, and then head for our homes. The combat could last for hours on end! Amir has Princess Mehr-Nigar ever before his eyes, but why must we lay down our lives in this idle cause?"

The syce would reply, "Dear master, how could you commit such words to your speech, in view of the fact that you are a soldier? Do you have no consideration for how the whole world would judge such a one as yourself, who received soldier's wages for years and on the day of trial turned tail? How would you show your face to your comrades? It is most unmanly to flee in the face of an enemy! This is a time to show valor, not a time to retire! If you take the latter course, your cowardice will become the subject of your comrades' taunts and slurs, and they will make your life a living Hell by heaping rebuke on your head in every assembly in which you set foot! Besides that, your name will carry the most denigrating shame, and the word of your cowardice will be borne everywhere by gossip! Then you shall find no employer, and never will a noble deem you worthy of his employ! If you were so pigeon-hearted, why did you enlist in the soldiery in the first place, to come to see this day? Moreover, what gave you the idea that your death is certain in combat, or that the good fortune of your enemies shall ordain that you are speared or claimed by an arrow? Consider that when the gram is split for horse fodder, the grain destined not to be split remains whole despite all the heavy grinding! Do not lose your heart, for God's sake! Go forward and ply your sword, and manlike fight your foe, and should you prevail, claim the reward and robe of honor from your master. Today you may be a common trooper, but tomorrow might see you the commander of ten! And the future holds ever more prestige should you win further laurels!"

Greatly vexed by these words, the coward turned upon his syce, and replied to him thus: "I have the frail parakeet of my soul at stake, whereas you stand to lose nothing, and no harm shall come to you in battle! Indeed in your heart of hearts you desire (may the devil's ears become deaf!) that I am brought to a bad end, while you sit comfortably here in shelter. And in the event of my falling on the battlefield (perish the thought!) you shall attire yourself in my dress, adorn yourself with my armor, and, registering my horse in your name and enlisting yourself among the troops, lay claim to my wages and go roistering!

"I hope that God makes Hell's fodder of nurse Rae-bel and nanny Chambeli, who led my mother and elder sister into temptation to sell their gold. For then those two witches gathered enough money from their numerous paramours to buy a horse, and let themselves be sodomized by the paymaster to have the horse branded, only to land me into this royal mess! Time and again I reminded them that I fall unconscious at the very sight of blood, and that even if a sparrow whirs past my head my whole soul is thrown into ecstasies of terror, and I tremble and shiver with fright, imagining that someone has shot at me! Never was there any association between myself and horse and armor, war and carnage! Since childhood my mother raised me in the lap of luxury, and never allowed me to enter into the company of soldiers. I never had to do with anything besides play the *sitar*[202] and chess and cards, and indulge in the pleasures of song and dance! Then all of a sudden I find myself enlisted among warriors, and turned out of my house! Hardly have a few years passed since I was married! How will my poor wife fare should things come to a bad pass? Who will take care of her, still in the flower of her youth? It would have been far better a fate to become a day laborer and earn my bread embroidering *augi*[203] or manufacturing hookah snakes. Although it would have only furnished me with meager wages to take home, yet I would have sat in the evenings by my mother and sisters, regaled myself in their company, and at night had a full, peaceful sleep by my wife's side, with my legs stretched wide.

"As to taunts and slurs they will only come my way if I am found in this sanguinary horde! My life is not so burdensome to me that having once quit the army, I would ever again enroll in soldiery's ill-starred trade or even think of enlisting in the ranks of this tribe in my wildest dreams! As to your allegory of the grams for the horse, I see myself among those who shall be split. I wish to survive with my life somehow.

Don't you know that we are like the face of the fleeing hare that the hound never sees and the rear of the chasing hound that the hare never looks upon? In like manner no one sees us.

"Give me your loincloth and waistcloth, if you are faithful and sincere to me in truth, and I will take your hoe and grass net and from tomorrow will fetch the grass in your place, feed the horse in the evening, and make bread for you, while you may dress yourself up in my vesture, decorate yourself with my arms, ride my horse into the battle, and fight alongside the warriors' ranks and lay claim to whatever rewards and robes of honor are dispensed to them!"

In short, brave men and cowards occupied themselves in their respective preparations for the coming battle the whole night. While the courageous and valiant warriors busied themselves in supplications to the Almighty God to safeguard their honor in the field of combat, many a coward slipped away, taking advantage of the dark night, and others suffered bouts of diarrhea from fear.

When the standard of sunlight flashed in the skies and the imminent ascent of King Sol to his throne was declared, the Sahibqiran said his prayers, and prepared for battle alongside his seraphic-faced, impeccably virtuous, upright, and pure-hearted troops. On the other side King Landhoor bin Saadan organized his armies in battle array with evil intention, and final preparations were made by the warriors on both sides. The hatchet men cleared the arena of bushes and shrubbery, and the hoemen made the surface smooth and level. Water carriers fitted out their water skins with sprinklers and settled the dust in the arena, making its expanse the envy of the Vale of Kashmir in beauty and freshness. The right wing of the army and the left wing, the center of the army and the advance guard, the rearguard and the ambuscade, in short, fourteen battle divisions were drawn, complete with the advance guard in the front and the rearguard in the back, and with great glory the two armies filed out onto the two sides of the battlefield.

But none from either side had yet come forward to seek combat when the horizon was darkened by a great cloud of dust that arose in the sky with dark and malignant shadows. When scissors of wind cut the skirts of this dark cloud and blew away the dust from the face of the land, forty new standards came into view. On account of this new development both of the assembled armies raised their guards. It was soon revealed that this approaching host numbered forty thousand troops marching under these standards with mien and might.

When this unannounced army came to a halt, the Sahibqiran saw Gustham bin Ashk Zarrin Kafsh standing in the front row under his swine-headed standard, busily arranging his troops. Hamza brought this scene to Amar's attention, who thought of a stratagem. Separating from his army, he headed toward Gustham's camp. Having arrived there he made a profusely humble salutation to Gustham, and the two indulged in small talk.

Gustham said, "How are you, Khvaja Amar? It has been ages since I last saw you!" Amar replied, "What is there to be said about the existence of such a one as I, who counts himself neither among the dead nor the living! It was an evil day when I entered the service of that Arab, and invited all these troubles upon myself without receiving recompense!" Gustham asked, "What is the matter? What is wrong with your state of affairs?"

Amar replied, "Since you ask me, everything is falling apart! Thinking that he is already Naushervan's son-in-law, Hamza is riding such a high horse these days that he cares not a whit for anybody else! In his false opinion he imagines that there is no champion in the whole world who is his equal, and that he is born peerless in wisdom and might. Gone are the days when he would beg me to sit on the throne by his side. Things have come to such a pass now that he begrudges me even a seat in his court! There is absolutely no rank or honor left for me even though I was most diligent in his service and served him most faithfully without ever giving a thought for my own life. I would like to see someone who would serve him with the same zeal! Now I have resolved to relinquish his service, and go elsewhere. The unbounded benevolence of the Almighty God is proverbial and, as the saying goes, the world is opened wide and I am not lame of foot! If I cannot find myself an equally illustrious service, I will willingly settle for one half as august, in order to save myself my present degradation."

When he heard this, Gustham replied, "Do not speak so despondently! Wherever you go, you are sure to find all that you wish for, and all manner of prestige and offices of authority will be bestowed you. If you would condescend to enter my service, I would hold you dear as my own life, and ensure that you are accorded all due care and comfort!"

Then Amar said, "Indeed this was the reason for my leaving behind that camp and those shameful days, and for approaching you! But you must first ensure that Hamza does not engage in combat with Landhoor. You would do well to be the first to spur your charger into the arena and seek combat with Landhoor, in order that Hamza will seem a fool and his army put to shame. Landhoor has absolutely no might or power. I inspected his mace and found it to be nothing more than a lump of wood covered in iron shell for appearances! As to Landhoor himself, he is the worst coward in the whole world, and I have never seen anyone more craven or pusillanimous. Thus, if Hamza were to kill him, he would become Naushervan's son-in-law. And then any excesses that he might commit will be too little, and he will perpetrate all manner of atrocities!"

Gustham said, "It was a happy moment when you came to me and augmented our honor with your visit! I shall put to sword both Landhoor and Hamza and dispatch them to Hell! Since there are no secrets between us now, I must confess the truth of the matter that after wounding Bahram I took refuge in Zabul, and was spending my days in great luxury and comfort when Naushervan sent me a note to the effect that in order to regain his favor I must immediately proceed to Ceylon and cut off Landhoor's head and also put Hamza to death, and then present myself at his court so that he might marry me to Princess Mehr-Nigar and take me into his kinship."

At length Amar goaded Gustham to step into the arena, and then walked in disguise by Gustham's side toward the field. Gustham rode his rhinoceros forward, and called out, "Let Landhoor bin Saadan emerge from hiding and present himself here! The day of reckoning is come! Let him now witness the dexterity of my sword, and prepare to taste my arms' sharp edge!" Landhoor spurred his she-elephant Maimoona forward, and said to Gustham, "What rot do you speak, O wretch? Give your blow, and deal what you have to present!" Then Gustham drew his sword from his scabbard and aimed a blow to Landhoor's head, but Landhoor blocked it with his mace, rendering the sword blunt. Then Landhoor dealt him a strike with his mace. As Gustham was destined to live yet some more days and receive his allotted dishonor and disgrace in this world, the mace did not come down squarely on him, but the shaft brushed his side, breaking his ribs and mixing all his courage and valor into dust. He fell face forward from his rhinoceros, was taken unconscious, and lost the power of his senses. His comrades rushed in and carried him away by stealth, and soon sounded the drums of retreat.

Then Landhoor turned toward Hamza with a smile, and said, "Come tomorrow, we two shall settle our account, and witness how your sword shall fare and what it has to offer!" Amir replied, "There is nothing stopping us from settling the account now! We are both in the arena that tests the skill. What could be dispensed with today must not be put off until tomorrow! Come, let us combat in the name of Allah." Landhoor replied, "It would be well to sound the drums of retreat, and put off the combat until tomorrow."

After the drums of retreat were sounded, the two armies withdrew from the battlefield. Amir returned with his army to his camp, and Landhoor retired with his troops to his own. Gustham escaped, taking advantage of the cover of darkness, and took refuge on the slope of a mountain where he resolved on this cowardly plan in his heart: Should Hamza kill Landhoor, he would certainly pass by this slope, and then Gustham would ambush him from his hiding place, and rout his army by taking him unaware.

But little did Gustham know that:

If the enemy is mighty, the Protector is mightier still!

OF LANDHOOR DOING BATTLE WITH THE SAHIBQIRAN, AND HIS SURRENDERING TO THE WORLD CONQUEROR

The might of the reed is tested by the narrative's power, and the vigor of the swashbucklers of colorful accounts is now manifested in the arena of the page. Hear now this history of the war of the clime of India, and an account of the combat between two lions of the forest of courage and valor. Gustham had made an absconding retreat after having his ribs broken at Landhoor's hands and, having fled the battlefield, took refuge on the slope of a mountain. But in the Sahibqiran's camp, brave men reiterated their resolve of the first night, and solicited the aid of the Grantor of Petitions to safeguard their name and honor. Each brave one called out to his fellow, "Tomorrow is the day of the trial! Like goldsmiths the recording angels will adjudge the gold of our courage for its purity and veracity, and the battlefield is a veritable touchstone for the essence of courage, where the trial tests the quality of one's valor. Let us then see who is purified by the fire of the sword and declared of perfect standard, and who shows weakness in his character. Let us see whose coin gains currency in the clime of bravery. And let us discover the alchemist able to transform his mercurial heart in the blaze of the swords to distinguish himself in the battlefield, and the one whose brimstone essence survives the heat of the battle. Tomorrow everyone's mettle will come to light and our true natures will be revealed!"

A similar clamor rose also from Landhoor's camp. Those who had rivalries with one another would comment, "We shall see how dexterous is the dagger thrower with his dagger, and what claim the champions have to might and strength! Let us see who plunges headlong into the sea of valor, and who casts challenges with drawn sword to the warriors steeped in might! Let us see who hunts the crocodile-natured foe and who sinks the boat of the enemy's soul into the squall of doom!" In short, this was the import of the conferences held that day in both camps, and they rang with these cries the whole night as well.

When the seraph of the morning routed the night's foe in the arena of ascendancy and raised the standard of light in the clime of the heavens, the Sahibqiran decorated himself with helmet, coat of mail, cuirass, armlet, doublet, foot guard, *ragay*, and hatchet. Also sporting his shining sword in his sword belt, and his sparkling dagger at his waist, he mounted his steed Siyah Qitas. The aides-de-camp and the mace bearers shouted, "In the name of Allah!" and visited prayers of victory and triumph on Amir's head. Amir presented the proof incarnate of the Progenitor's unbounded glory with his bow case secured by his saddle straps, his bow slung from one shoulder and his heavy mace supported on the other, and a spear in his hand that was like in its length to the sighs of lovers and the tresses of their beloveds.

Tauq bin Heyran took him under the shadow of his dragon-shaped standard, and Amir went forth at the head of a thirty-thousand-strong host of soldiers, flanked by Muqbil Vafadar on one side, and Sultan Bakht on another. The renowned dagger thrower, the clipper of wizards' necks, the bearder of infidels, Khvaja Amar Ayyar went forward leaping and gamboling, sounding the six high-key notes, twelve musical modes, and twenty-four airs, in the twenty-eight manners of improvisation[204] surrounded by twelve hundred *ayyars*. Amar was adorned with his brocade singlet, his broadcloth tasselled shoes, the loops of his lasso, the net that was the entrapper of the enemies' lives, and he also wore his grease cloth gauntlets, the clever stratagems of trickery, with the lightning-bright scimitar and keen-edged dagger stuck at his waist.

The Khusrau of India, King Landhoor bin Saadan, came forth from the other side, armed to the teeth and mounted on his she-elephant Maimoona, in a cortege a hundred-thousand-strong of Khamachi, Sandli, Bengali, Karnataki, Maratha, Dakhani, Gujarati, Rangar, Bhil, Siyar, Khorra, Kaein, Bhojpuri, Bundela, Rajput, Mandraji, Assamese, Bunaki, and Bhutanese soldiers, all of whom were clad in steel. The Bais from Baiswara, Chhatris from Awadh, Thakur, Dichhit, Panwar, Brahmin, Shukla, Tiwari, Pand, Dube, Chaube, Bhar, and miscellaneous other tribes from the country, carried shining and glittering *katars, sirohis,* swords, cudgels, *bannas* [?], firelocks, carbines, pistols, lances, and javelins.

Wave after wave, horseman after horseman, troop after troop, steed after steed, rank after rank, body after body, and file after file, the two armies descended into the arena, took rein, and arranged their forces for battle. The Angel of Death set up his pavilion between the two armies, and Mars, the Executioner of the Heavens, brightened the forehead of every warrior.

The Sahibqiran spurred his steed and stood face to face with Landhoor. Bellowing like a lion and firmly mounted atop his steed, Amir delivered these words with his graceful tongue: "O King Landhoor! I have issue with you, and you with me! Nothing shall be gained from the carnage of God's creatures, and therefore we must needs abstain from it! Deal me a blow with your greatest claim and with the pride of your might, and thus fulfill your heart's desire!" Landhoor replied, "O Sahibqiran! If I were the first to deal the blow, you would perish with all the desires of your heart unrequited, and never would any of your hopes come to fruition! I ask that you deal the first blow yourself, and show your ability!" The Sahibqiran replied: "My teacher enjoined me from such a course! I would not give you a blow myself until you have given me three blows first, and only then will I return your blow!"

As Landhoor was much taken with Amir, he did not touch his mace but attacked Sahibqiran with his lance instead. The Sahibqiran blocked the point of Landhoor's lance with the point of his own lance, and they sparred this way for a while. After a hundred thrusts of the spear had been made and foiled on each side without the combatants receiving any injury, and the horses were all drenched in sweat, the Sahibqiran locked Landhoor's spear with his own, and gave a blow with its shaft which sent the lance flying out of Landhoor's hands into the air. Landhoor's face turned deathly pale from mortification, as if the point of Amir's spear had pierced through his breast.

But Landhoor quickly regained self-possession and, by way of commendation said to Hamza, "O Sahibqiran! The cloak of spearsmanship sewn by the Seamstress of Death befits you alone! Indeed on you alone the Omnipotent God has bestowed the gift of this art! If I were to deem myself a champion in the arena of valor, never ever would I touch a lance again."

Thus having spoken, he weighed his mace in his hands, and said, "O Sahibqiran, the opportunity for making peace is not yet lost, as it is always preferable to the prospect of war. The grief of losing you to no purpose would leave its mark on me for all my living days! I request that you spare me the grief of having to kill you!" Amir replied, "This is a time for seeking combat and dying, not a time for making exhortations and establishing bonds of love! I told you before that I am bound by my word of honor, and must needs remain faithful to Naushervan. Come, I would like to see what your mace has to deliver. This is still the beginning of combat!"

Then Landhoor was obliged to proceed. He sat back on his haunches and, weighing his mace in both his hands, brought it down with great force on the Sahibqiran's head. Amir now reflecting on the unbounded might of the True Protector, received Landhoor's blow on the shield of Garshasp, which was not affected by the impact in the least. Even though sweat broke from every pore on Hamza's body, still his arm did not flinch from the grace of Prophet Aadam's armlet. Then Landhoor said in his heart, *Whenever a blow of this mace had landed on someone, every single one of his limbs was crushed and his bones were reduced to powder, but Sahibqiran seems unruffled and even his brow was not clouded!*

Then Landhoor dealt a second blow with greater might, and even though the Sahibqiran remained steadfast as Sikander's rampart,[205] he was suddenly reminded of the taste of the milk on the day he was born. Irritated, Landhoor now brought down his mace with such force that had it landed on the *Koh-e Besutoon*,[206] it would have caused water to flow from it. The Sahibqiran blocked this blow on his shield again, but from the impact of the blow the legs of his steed Siyah Qitas were driven into the ground to the shanks, and Amir himself was enveloped in a cloud of dust, and the screen of dirt that rose billowing from the ground veiled him.

The hue of Landhoor's face underwent a sea change upon beholding this scene, and involuntarily these words escaped his mouth: "At last I killed him, and a great and illustrious warrior was laid low! But what a disgrace that a youth such as the Sahibqiran was killed! Much as I tried to keep him from embarking on his disastrous course, he would not desist from it for the word he had given to Naushervan!" Landhoor then dismounted his elephant and approached, anxiously stroking his limbs, and called out, "O august and illustrious lord! Answer me if you are alive so that I may rejoice; and if you are dead, we shall meet again on the Day of Reckoning! Indeed I would forever bear the gravest remorse in my heart for the loss of your life!"

Having regained possession of his senses, the Sahibqiran struck Siyah Qitas with the whip of Prophet Daud, whereupon Siyah Qitas extricated his legs and jumped up from the pit and emerged clear of its depression. Amir said, "O Khusrau! I do not see the one whom you killed and laid low! Who is the one you prevailed upon and the one you triumphed over?

Give another blow and satiate every last desire of your heart! Our combat has just begun. It is given to God alone to bestow honor. Why such anxiety? It seems you neither encountered a man nor indulged in fierce combat before!"

Landhoor was most astonished and, mounting a horse, he drew the steel blue Bardwani[207] sword from his belt—quicksilver in nature, the slayer of foes, and as free from stain as a perfumer's counter—and dealt a blow to Amir's head with it. Amir raised his bejeweled shield adorned with studs of woven seven-colored silk, and blocked that devastating blow. Then he spoke thus: "O King Landhoor! I blocked all your five strikes, and indeed the best of all blows were arrayed in them! It is my turn, and now I shall return your blows. Beware now, and say not that you were not alerted and were taken unaware and were not afforded ample opportunity to take stock and be forewarned!"

Amir now locked his stirrup with Landhoor's and, drawing his sword Samsam, dealt a blow to Landhoor's head with wonderful deftness, address, and technique. The Khusrau attempted to block the blow with his shield and lock Amir's arm, but Amir's sword cut through Landhoor's shield as if it were made of fresh cheese. Landing on his horse's neck, the sword severed his head from the neck and felled it. The Khusrau of India was obliged to empty his saddle and, flying into a fierce rage, he drew his sword and came charging furiously at Hamza. Thinking in his heart that if Siyah Qitas was wounded or felled by Landhoor, the loss would deprive him of one half of his capacity and never again would he come by such a noble steed, Amir, too, emptied his saddle with great alacrity. Wresting Landhoor's hand and wrenching the sword from it, Amir threw it toward his camp. Then Landhoor locked his arms around Amir's neck in a tight clasp, and the two of them began to wrestle, turning the gall of the onlookers to water.

Now, when the wrestler of the day retired for repose to its Westerly pavilion, and the night's master began to take up his daily exercise rituals with his celestial novices, torches were lit in both camps. They burned continuously through the following nights, for Amir and Landhoor remained locked in combat for three nights and three days fist to fist, breast to breast, and cheek to cheek, and neither could overthrow his adversary. Then on the fourth day Amir bellowed "God is Mighty!" and heaved Landhoor up, lifting him to the height of his breast, and maintained his stupendous weight above the ground but failed to hoist Landhoor over his head.

Hamza resolved to release Landhoor and plunge the dagger chivalrously into his own breast and put out the lamp of his precious life. But Landhoor stayed his hand and submitted to him thus with folded arms: "O Sahibqiran! It was not given to anyone besides yourself to lift me or even to heave me up from the ground! I declare my allegiance and fealty to you from the bottom of my heart, and claim my fellowship to you!"

Amir embraced Landhoor and made a prostration of gratitude before the Almighty God, and said, "O Khusrau! I pronounce you my right arm! I shall treat you like a brother, and hold you more dear than my life. But I desire that you accompany me before Naushervan, and help me fulfill my promise to him." Landhoor replied, "I shall be obedient to your wishes and go anywhere that you command me to! In the name of Allah, proceed, and I shall follow. Dispatch the advance camp thither! In this matter as well as in others, I am bound to your orders now that I have submitted my allegiance to you!" Landhoor then sent for the commanders of his army, entered them also into Amir's service, and described to him the rank and station of each man among them.

Landhoor accompanied Amir to his pavilion, and the Sahibqiran scattered a great quantity of gold and jewels as Landhoor's oblation, and ordered an assembly of merriment arranged. Then he set about filling his eyes' goblets with tears of blood in remembrance of Princess Mehr-Nigar. Noticing this, Landhoor surmised that thoughts of the princess occupied him, and he wiped at Amir's blood-red tears with a kerchief, saying, "The days of parting are coming to an end, and the day of meeting is approaching! Why cry now?" Then the Sahibqiran regained the control of his heart, and asked Amar to sing.

With great ceremony Amar sat on his haunches and, wearing the plectrum on his fingertip, began to tune and strum the *do-tara*. He then played a canzonet and accompanied it with the *do-tara* to affect a veritable *raga*.[208] Then he broke into a song in the manner of Prophet Daud with such an air that all those present—whether or not they were lovelorn—were transported into a trance. Both Hamza and Landhoor were enchanted by Amar's singing and conferred riches and heaps of gold and jewels on him.

Landhoor presented the keys of his treasury to Amir, and conferred many choice objects from the lands of India on him as gifts. Landhoor then ennobled himself by converting to the True Faith, renouncing idol worship. He gave orders to the keeper of the pantry, the steward, and the chamberlain, and arranged for a table cover of perfumed goat leather[209] to be spread in the hall and decked out with all manners of delicacies.

Amir sat down for the meal with Landhoor by his side, and after they had finished the meal, Landhoor said to him, "I long to be blessed by a visit from you. And for a long time I have nursed this desire that you set foot (the rival of Heaven!) in my house and make my humble abode the envy of Paradise, and by eating bread and salt with me afford the palate of my soul an occasion to experience the taste of your charity."

If you were to set foot in my house a while,
As a doorstep the stone of Kaaba would honor find.

Amir answered, "This proposition is most agreeable to me! Indeed it would be a shame not to taste the cuisine of India." Landhoor soon sought his leave. Amir conferred a royal robe of honor on him, and thus obtaining leave to part, Landhoor retired to his palace and ordered preparations for a royal feast. Then he escorted the Sahibqiran with all his renowned nobles and august champions to the feast, and the assembly began to warm up and the tabla to play.

———

Now we leave Amir and Landhoor occupied in these revelries, and turn to Gustham. We recall that after being disgraced by Landhoor crushing his ribs, the weak Gustham retreated from the battlefield and for several days did not once look back until he found refuge on the slope of a mountain. There he occupied himself night and day with the sole thought of finding some way to kill Amir, when *ayyars* brought him intelligence that Hamza had prevailed over Landhoor, the armies of True Faith had returned triumphant, and that for several days festivities had been celebrated in which Landhoor had supped with Hamza. Indeed in these festivities there was no pleasure that went untested, and the days recalled the day of Eid and the nights recalled the night of Shab-e Baraat.[210] The *ayyars* also informed Gustham that aside from Muqbil Vafadar there was no commander present in Hamza's camp and no one left to defend the army, as all the champions and nobles were occupied along with Amir in the festivities. Finding the field to himself, Gustham thought of raiding Hamza's encampment and routing his army.

Gustham had brought with him two attendants of Princess Mehr-Nigar, whom Amir knew by sight. He filled up two flagons with the choicest grape wine, and mixed it with four *mithcals* of such a potent poison that were a drop of it to fall into the Indian Ocean it would suffice to kill all marine life. After counterfeiting Mehr-Nigar's signet, and sealing the flagons with it, Gustham dressed her attendants in travelers' attire, and then forged an amorous missive from the princess. Handing the letter to the attendants, he explained in detail that they must first present themselves before Muqbil Vafadar and announce that Princess Mehr-Nigar had sent them in utmost confidence and at great risk of exposing herself. This would put Muqbil under obligation to take them to Amir and conduct them into the Sahibqiran's presence, whereupon the attendants were to convey to Amir a great deal of love talk from Mehr-Nigar, and present him the wine and the letter. Gustham made it known to them that if they succeeded, he would induct them into his harem and take them as his wives.

Then those two vixens garbed themselves in manly clothes and set out. When they approached Amir's encampment and the sentries on patrol hailed them and the vigils challenged them, they replied, "We are the messengers of Princess Mehr-Nigar! We have come from Persia and are headed to see your Amir!" The men then escorted them to Muqbil Vafadar. After hearing them out, he took himself to the festive assembly where Amir was seated, and whispered into his ear that two attendants sent by Princess Mehr-Nigar had arrived with two bottles of wine and a letter from their mistress, and sought leave to be presented before His Honor. Already a little under the influence of wine, Hamza became ever so intoxicated with joy upon hearing this news that he rose from his seat excitedly and said to the Khusrau, "I must needs attend to a matter of utmost importance, and shall soon return after taking care of this affair. In the meanwhile pray continue with the festivities!" Then he commanded Amar to regale Landhoor and keep him company in his stead.

Amir ordered privacy and sent for the attendants the moment he arrived in his pavilion. Upon hearing their account, Amir kissed the princess's seal on the letter and pressed it to his eyes, and in his transports of joy he would put it down on his lap and pick it up again every so often. In short, he felt so exulted in his heart upon reading the contents of the letter, that, beside himself with joy, he threw all caution to the wind. Breaking open the seal of the flagon, and holding it up against the light, he made a toast to Princess Mehr-Nigar's name, and drained its contents.

No sooner had the wine traveled down his throat than Amir fell into a daze. He began to foam at the mouth, his limbs began to convulse, and with tearful eyes he recited the following verses, and was taken unconscious:

Even a drop that I imbibed without your company
From the gorge it rose and issued out as blood tears from my eyes.

Thinking that Amir was at death's door, and that his life was only a matter of a few more breaths—and that their mission had been accomplished—those two strumpets pulled out a peg of the pavilion by some artifice to escape unseen, and happily made their way out of there to take these tidings to Gustham.

It so happened that at that moment, Landhoor mentioned to Amar that the absence of the guest of honor had deprived the assembly of all joy, and that such a state of affairs should not be allowed to continue. He promised Amar a gift of four hundred *tomans* and pledged to fill up his *zambil* if he would bring back Hamza that instant. Once Amar heard of the reward, he did not need further persuasion and immediately set out on his errand.

He found Muqbil guarding the entrance to Hamza's pavilion, and asked him what Amir was occupied with. Muqbil said, "Two female attendants sent by Mehr-Nigar arrived, and Amir is conferring with them." When he heard the mention of the female attendants, Amar's heart skipped a beat from some unknown foreboding, and he was suddenly seized by the gravest misgiving.

Exclaiming, "May God have mercy on us!" he entered Amir's pavilion where he found all the tapers extinguished. Without loss of time Amar lit up one of his trickster's flares and witnessed that Hamza's whole body was covered with blisters, his coloration had turned dark, spume flowed from his mouth, and he was writhing in convulsions while unconscious on the floor. One flagon of wine stood upright while the other lay shattered on the floor. Where its contents had splashed, the earth had cracked. When Amar looked around, he found nobody there, but discovering that one peg of the pavilion had been pulled out from the ground, he immediately followed where the footprints nearby it led him.

Those slogging and plodding bawds were no match for Amar's superior speed and reach, and any comparison between the two of them would be idle. They were still on their way when Amar caught up and descended upon them. They were just discussing how the moment they had set out was most auspicious in that they finished off Amir in no time and were already returning in triumph. One of them was saying, "Come friend, let us go and receive the reward that Gustham had promised us!" when Amar called out from behind them, "O villainous witches! Behold here your Angel of Death! And I send you to the House of Death as you deserve!" Thus speaking, Amar drew his dagger from his waist, and relieved their shoulders of the burden of their heads.

Then Amar retraced his steps and returned to his camp. He took Muqbil along to show him Hamza's state, and said, "It all came about thanks to your negligence and lax guard! Now tell me what is to be done about it! How must this issue be addressed and a remedy wrought?"

When Muqbil began to beat his head in remorse, Amar said, "Quiet! Lest word of it leak out and the armies of India revert upon us, and they overrun our camp and we are surrounded! Guard Amir and do not set foot outside the pavilion until I have returned. In the meantime do not allow anyone to enter into Amir's pavilion, nor must you at all budge from your post!"

Then Amar went before Landhoor, and privately addressed him thus: "Amir Hamza is unable to return at present, nor is he able to send for you, as two commanders have arrived from Naushervan's court. They have brought word that should Hamza wish to remain true to his promise to the emperor, he must immediately take Landhoor prisoner, and not release him at any cost! Amir has requested that if you oblige him by pretending to be taken prisoner for the sake of appearances, not the least harm will come to you, and it will serve his purpose and promote his cause!"

The Khusrau replied, "Let aside such a thing as imprisonment, I would have thought nothing of it even if Amir had asked for my head! Never in the least would I dither from obedience to him, but find it right in accordance with my pleasure!" Amar said then, "I fear lest your camp take offense and rebel." The Khusrau replied, "There is no one who would even contemplate such a thing! No one would have the cheek or the wherewithal!" Then Landhoor gave out orders to the commanders of his camp and, with his hands bound by a kerchief in the token of willful surrender, he entered the camp of the Faithful.

Amar removed Landhoor to a secluded place and had him attended to with great honor, and offered him a goblet of drugged wine. The moment Landhoor was taken unconscious, Amar put him in chains and confined him in a chest perforated with holes for air, so that he would not suffocate. Then Amar attended to his army and set out from there to find some cure for Hamza.

He spotted two horsemen, and much though Amar tried to escape notice, the encounter could not be avoided. Amar boldly went forth and confronted them. The two riders dismounted, and inquired after Amar's well-being. When Amar asked them to introduce themselves, they replied, "We are the sons of Shahpal Hindi. Our names are Sabir and Sabur, and we have undertaken a long journey in search of you. Our father professes to the True Faith, but at heart he has remained an infidel and that is his true creed and faith! Last night, when he heard the news of Amir's poisoning, he went over to the side of Gustham, and became an aider and abettor of that perpetrator of iniquity. Thus we have come to remove Amir to our fort, and to treat him with all due diligence!"

Amar was mightily glad upon hearing these words, and exclaimed, "A blind man needs nothing but seeing eyes! You may remove Amir to your fort. Make God a witness to your pledge of his safety, to dispel the doubts of treachery and fraud from my heart!" They readily swore by God, and said to Amar, "If we had any evil intent, we would never have come hither!"

Amar brought Sabir and Sabur into his camp, and put them up in a separate pavilion. When the timekeeper announced the middle hour of the night, Amar had Hamza carried in a litter to the fort of Sabir and Sabur. After making all arrangements to his satisfaction, he said to the brothers, "Now, tell me what must be done to cure Amir?" They answered, "Ten days' journey from here is the isle of Narvan, where Hakim Aqlimun lives. He can restore Amir to health, as he is veritably possessed of the breath of the Messiah! We shall write out a note for him. If you were to bring the hakim here, Amir would be cured before long and would receive all the right medicaments and appropriate physics!"

At first Amar thought he might lose Hamza by the time the hakim arrived, but then he realized that nothing at all could be done to cure Amir, and he would not get well without the hakim being present. Thus he resolved to go and fetch the hakim.

Sabir and Sabur sent Darab the trickster to accompany Amar and guide him on the way. Stepping out of the fort, Amar addressed the wind thus: "O Mother Wind! I need to get ahead so that Darab does not overtake me!" Darab had not quite traversed half a day's journey when he stretched out on the ground, and said to Amar, "If we could have employed a conveyance, we might have proceeded on and gone a few leagues farther! My feet are unable to move, but you seem to be riding the wind's charger, traveling at such staggering pace!" Amar answered, "Rest a while, then! Go sit under a tree and catch your breath!"

A little distance farther on was a garden where they both sat down under a tree's shade. Amar offered Darab drugged food, and said to him, "Eat a little so that you may find the energy to proceed!" Then Amar began to ask directions of Darab, who said, "Go straight forward as the crow flies, without looking or stepping to the right or left! To your right you will find a winding trail close to the island, which you must follow to the bank. You will find other pathways, too, on that road, but you must not let yourself stray from your course. The river is some four leagues in width. Once you have been ferried across to the other side, and have gone a few steps, you will see houses on the island. From there onward you should be able to find your way yourself."

When Amar saw Darab's eyes becoming glazed, and noticed that he was growing all torpid and limp, Amar said to him, "Come, friend! Let us hurry. Gird yourself, as we have far to go!" As soon as Darab rose, he dropped again like a lump of dough, and Amar tied him to a tree trunk and went forth with great dispatch.

It was not yet evening when Amar arrived at the riverbank. He waited for the ferry, but when it did not materialize, Amar walked on the water by the miracle of Ilyas, and in no time he had crossed the river and arrived on the other side. The sun was setting when, dressed as a Hindu, he entered the bazaar, and said to a man, "Which is the way to Hakim Aqlimun's house, and how may I recognize it and proceed to that august abode?" The man answered, "Hakim Aqlimun is the lord of this town! The gates that you see over yonder are the entrance to his dwelling."

Arriving at the house, Amar went to the porter, and said to him, "I have brought a message for the hakim from Sabir and Sabur. Prithee take the trouble of informing the hakim of my arrival!" The porter informed the hakim that a messenger had arrived with a letter from Sabir and Sabur, and sought leave to be admitted into his august presence. The hakim said, "Let him come and make sure no one impedes him on his way." The porter informed Amar, and sent him before the hakim. Approaching the hakim, Amar made the ritual salutations and handed over the letter. The hakim took the letter from Amar's hand, but bristled upon reading it, and said to Amar, "How royally Sabir and Sabur have written that if I come posthaste and make Hamza well, they will fill up my pockets with jewels that would afford me great joy. Praise the Lord! They take me for an avaricious man to address me thus. I would have certainly gone if they had not mentioned it, but now I would never go, and am determined never again to set foot in that place!"

Amar said, "O reverend sage! They were clearly in the wrong and made a mistake by thus addressing an ascetic puritan like yourself in that manner. But pray overlook their error, and send for a conveyance!" The hakim flew into a rage, and said, "How dare you step out of the norms of propriety? What business have you poking your nose in, suggesting how I must reason! It has ever been my motto never to take my word back once I have said no! You shall gain nothing by your insistence!"

Amar said, "Pray save me a long-winded speech! The gist of the matter is that one of God's creatures will lose his life if you do not attend to him. Thus, by coming along you would do a good deed and earn great recompense from God!" The hakim replied, "I would still not go even if I were to receive the Most Great Recompense!" Amar replied: "I know nothing of the most great and the inferior-most! But show me the vade mecum that enjoins a hakim not to budge from his place after hearing of a man lying sick! And how is it a great merit in a hakim not to attend to a man whose life stands to benefit thousands?" Hakim Aqlimun answered, "Are you a judge or an expounder of law, or just someone whose death is nigh? Or is it that you are a messenger parrot? Stop eating my brains, and go your way with the reply I have given you!"

Amar said, "Sire, I fail to see what great hurdle blocks your accompanying me. It would be far more desirable that you come. We must needs find some way that you do!" Hakim Aqlimun replied, "What melancholy is it that drives a base creature like yourself to reason with the Pride of Creation in this manner, and to make exhortations beyond your scope?" Amar answered, "Sire, if I were a madman of any sort, no doubt I would have been followed to your door by shouting and abusing urchins. As it is, during my long journey here no one even snapped a finger at me. But you adjudge me as crazed. Indeed you do me a grave injustice!"

Then Hakim Aqlimun called out to his slaves, "Secure this man's hands and feet as he suffers from contumaciousness of speech. And then bastinado him, for it is a sovereign remedy and a veritable cure for madmen like him!" Amar saw the matter getting out of hand and the hakim's disposition taking a turn for the worse. He realized, too, that while Aqlimun would not come with him, he would be punished to no purpose, and thus he set to weeping and wailing, and submitted to the hakim thus with folded arms: "Sire, I spoke idly! The speech that I made before you was put into my mouth by Sabir and Sabur. Indeed, why must you take this trouble on your head, and to what purpose? Sabir and Sabur are strange birds indeed, who made me traverse dark leagues and sent me on such a long and tedious journey. However, now I cannot leave as the dark of the night has fallen, and also since I am a foreigner in this place and I would not be able to find my way out of here! If you would be so kind to give me permission, I will lodge myself in the servants' quarters for the night, and go my way come morning!" Then Aqlimun ordered his slaves to conduct Amar into the kitchen, feed him something, let him sleep the night over, and send him on his way in the morning.

Amar had diagnosed Hakim Aqlimun's symptoms as the telltale signs of stupidity, for despite being a hakim he was unable to distinguish between right and wrong, the sure mark of all dolts. And thus he had decided to effect a remedy and administer Aqlimun a physic that would bring him to his senses. With this intent Amar began to butter up the cook in the kitchen, and the cook melted like so much ghee and sugar from the stirring of Amar's glib tongue. Then Amar produced several sweetmeats from his trickster's pouch, and said to the cook, "Have a taste of these, too, as you are an experienced pantryman, and have prepared many a sweetmeats in your life and trained with the past masters of the trade!" Amar tricked him into eating the sweetmeats, and the cook stuffed himself in his gluttony, and spoke thus: "Verily the sweetness of these sweetmeats is such as to seal one's mouth from the very pleasure! Never in my whole life has my palate known such heavenly taste!" Amar replied, "Sire, say nothing of your mouth being sealed, as it is only a matter of time before your fate shall follow the same course, and you will find yourself transported into an altogether heavenly realm!"

Amar took the raving cook to one side, and said to him, "Have a taste now of something savory!" The cook answered, "With the sweetmeats being so delicious, I can only imagine how delightful the savory treats will be!" Amar produced a loaf of bread from his bag of tricks, and that ever greedy man gobbled it down as well. When Amar saw that the cook's body had begun to waver and swing from side to side, he abused him with great sarcasm. That made the cook fly into a rage, and he laid hold of a billet of wood and rose to clobber Amar with it when his legs gave way underneath him and he fell down at Amar's feet.

Amar dug a deep hole underneath the kitchen's kiln and interred the cook there. After covering him up with a great pile of billets, he kindled a fire and put a cauldron of water to boil on top of it. Then he dressed himself in the cook's garb and began to prepare the hakim's breakfast with great skill.

Amar used black poppy seed from his own stores in preparing the naan, the bread loaf, and the *gao-dida*,[211] and then sprinkled sweet fennel over them. Then he produced some ghee from his *zambil,* and seasoned the fricassee, *qorma,*²¹² fritters, *pulao,*²¹³ and boiled rice. Amar put salt into the gruel from his own provisions, too, and also laid out on a plate the confection of almonds that lay prepared in his *zambil,* and he put a syrup of trickery on the kebabs for the relish. In short, Amar prepared all manner of delicacies for Aqlimun's breakfast, and early the next morning he decked them out on the table spread, and sat down himself with a fly whisk to fan the hakim.

The hakim was lost for words, praising every last dish that he tasted. Amar said, "Sire! What you eat is nothing other than the recipes you prescribed yourself, which have been judiciously prepared and cooked! You must always eat such dishes as they will renew your mental energy, and make your prognosis ever more acute! Then no malignant disease will escape your diagnosis, and just from touching a patient you will obtain his pulse!" The hakim was most satisfied by his sumptuous meal and began to burp out loud once he had finished eating. Addressing Amar, he said, "You have a most sublime talent! I shall dictate other recipes to you as well, and share many a trick of preparing the food with you!"

Amar now took a few steps back, and said, "Indeed, O hakim! When it comes to recipes, you are another one! Look at all your knowledge and learning, and how it has been totally lost on you, and what a first class dolt you have turned out to be!" Hakim Aqlimun flew into a great passion, and as he rose, saying, "What is this buffoonery, you fool! How dare you presume thus, and commit such words of impropriety with your speech!" Amar gave him a shove and the hakim fell flat on his face on the floor. Amar tied him up in his mantle, and took the leftovers and fed them to the servants. When those unsuspecting fools, too, lost the power of their senses, Amar put the hakim into the *zambil* along with his whole library and pharmacopoeia, and all the goods and chattels of his house. He then wrote out a bill of passage, which stated that it was incumbent upon the ferryman at the wharf to take the carrier of the bill across the river with great care and dispatch, without asking any questions or charging him a farthing. And that if the ferryman dithered in the least from obeying these instructions, he would find himself floundering in the sea of the hakim's ire. Then sealing the document with the hakim's signet, Amar cheerfully made his way out of the house.

In a few moments he arrived at the wharf carrying the bundle on his back, and handed the note to the ferryman. The ferryman set diligently to work, and ferried Amar across the river in a trice. And in a few hours Amar reached the spot where he had tied Darab to the tree. Amar untied Darab and gave him a physic that restored him to his senses. When Darab came to, he said, "If only we had not slept here so long, we could have advanced well past the halfway mark of our journey to the island. Confound this slumber that kept us from reaching our destination! Let us now hie on our way, to get there without further delay!" Then Amar narrated his adventure from the beginning to the end of how he had come to bring back Hakim Aqlimun, giving the details of all that had passed with him. Darab was so utterly confounded upon hearing the account that he threw himself down at Amar's feet exclaiming, "You are the master!" and became Amar's professed pupil.

Amar said to him, "Follow me at your sweet pace, as I must now speed away to bring these tidings to Sabir and Sabur!" Then Amar kicked the air and disappeared from Darab's sight. Before long he approached the fort, and there a wonder of wonders awaited him. Gustham stood before the fort with his own host, and with the armies of the Khusrau of India arrayed opposite his. Hot cannonade was coming from the battlements, and the cannoneers were lighting the fuses of the batteries. Amar speedily threw his rope ladder on the crenelations, and shot upward like a rocket, but as he climbed an archer on the ground took aim and shot at him. The arrow pierced the bundle but its progress was stopped by the golden mortar and pestle inside. Amar jumped inside the fort and laid the bundle before Sabir and Sabur, and told them of the strategy he had employed in bringing Hakim Aqlimun. Both brothers praised Amar's cleverness and wisdom to the high heavens, and greatly marveled at his cunning.

Amar then gathered all of Hakim Aqlimun's goods and possessions around the hakim, and administered him a drug to dispel his faint. Once again dressed up as the messenger, he said to the hakim, "O sire! Sabir and Sabur have sent for you as they are in great distress, and they have asked me to fetch you!" The hakim sourly called out, "Is there someone here who will secure this madman and deliver him into my power, so that I may bleed him for his pestering me thus, and cure him of all his pestilence?" Amar replied, "Sire, I am not a madman to be cured by your applying the blade to his veins! How would you treat one who has method to his madness?" The hakim replied, "Madmen do not have horns growing from their heads that you may be exempted from their ranks! And I see no such sovereign virtue in you to make an exception in your case! I told you a hundred thousand times that I will not go, and yet you do not cease from your refrain!"

As nobody answered the hakim's call, he looked around and was utterly perplexed and confounded to find that while all the goods and paraphernalia of his trade were there, it was not his house, nor was it the city and the people of his land, as he could well see. During this time Sabir and Sabur presented themselves, and greeted the hakim, and busied themselves in making him welcome. Hakim Aqlimun asked them, "How do I happen to be here with all my things?" Amar replied, "Sire! It is no malady that you may diagnose without being told about it, or one which you may cure by forcibly bleeding someone! It was yours truly who brought you here, after traversing such a long journey!" When Aqlimun found out that it was Amar and not some common messenger who had called on him, he rose to embrace him, and said, "O Khvaja! Had I known that it was you, I would have come without arguing in the least or uttering a single word of refusal!" Amar replied, "I am still indebted to you for the kindness you showed me. Pray now make haste and find some way to exude the poison from the Sahibqiran's body, so that this traveler in fatal exile may find cure from his affliction!"

When he examined Amir, Hakim Aqlimun wrung his hands in great anguish, and said remorsefully, "Alas! Except Naushervan no one has a cure for this illness on the face of the Earth, and its antidote can only be found in the coffers of his dynasty!" Amar said, "O sage, what is this sovereign elixir that is like the rara avis in its properties?" The hakim replied, "The name of this antidote is Shah Mohra, and it has been in the possession of the Kianids for many generations. Amir will not recuperate without it, as the toxin has invaded the veins, and every single organ in his body has been affected by the deadly poison!" Amar then said, "O sage, it reminds me of the proverb that the poisoned man died by the time the antidote had arrived from Iraq![214] How will Hamza survive by the time the Shah Mohra is sent for, and brought back from Ctesiphon? In his present precarious state how do you see him breathing until then?" The hakim replied, "Indeed, I see no other way to cure Hamza. His condition is most grave!"

Amar went weeping and wailing and throwing dirt on his head to the gates of the fort, where Muqbil Vafadar was standing guard. He asked Amar, "Say, O Khvaja, what was it that the hakim prescribed as a remedy for Amir?" Amar said, "I cannot even begin to tell you! I put myself to all that hazard in bringing the hakim here, only to hear that bird of bad omen tell me that there is no cure for Hamza's affliction except for the Shah Mohra, which can be found neither in the perfumeries of the world nor anywhere else but the coffers of Naushervan!"

Muqbil remained silent upon hearing this, but when Amar had taken a few steps, he called out from behind him, "O Khvaja! If you go to Ctesiphon, give my salutations and regards to the old woman of Ctesiphon[215] who dwells by Naushervan's palace!" Amar turned upon him in great vexation, and struck him on the head with his staff so hard that Muqbil was bathed in blood and fell to the ground in a swoon. Then Muqbil addressed Amar gently thus: "O Khvaja, do not be angry with me. The Shah Mohra is right here!" Then Amar became even more wroth with Muqbil, and began to rebuke him, and said, "Then why did you not say so right away instead of sending me off on a wild goose chase?" Muqbil replied, "O Khvaja! When Hamza's side is opened, the Shah Mohra will be revealed! It will be there where Buzurjmehr secreted it before my eyes, sewed up the wound, and informed me of its properties!" Amar then embraced Muqbil joyfully and went to see Hamza.

When Hakim Aqlimun saw him, he said, "O Khvaja! I thought that you would have left for Ctesiphon to fetch the Shah Mohra, and would be on your way back now after securing it, but I see you are still here!" Amar said, "How would it please you if I told you that I have already returned from Ctesiphon, and have possession of the Shah Mohra and brought it with me?" Aqlimun replied, "Knowing you, I would not be surprised if you have indeed accomplished what you claim. Come, hand me the Shah Mohra now if you have it on your person!" Amar replied, "It is buried in Amir's side, and had been in his possession all along!" When Aqlimun examined Amir's body, he discovered that while the rest of it had turned crystal blue, the poison had not affected the part where the Shah Mohra was embedded, and there the skin had retained its natural color. Aqlimun said, "Amir would not have survived this long for his body is all darkened, and would have died long ago if the Shah Mohra was not buried in his side. And for certain his last breath would have left him long ago!"

Then Aqlimun ordered that a large cauldron be filled with several hundred *maunds* of milk. After opening Amir's side with his blade, he removed the Shah Mohra, wrapped it in silk, and inserted it into Amir's stomach by way of his mouth. And after leaving it inside for a while, the hakim extracted it and dipped it into the cauldron of milk. The milk began to change color and turned rusty. In this manner, the hakim lowered the Shah Mohra some five or six times into Amir's stomach, kept it there for a few moments, and then dipped it into the milk. Then the milk stopped changing color, and showed no further variation in its hue, and the coloration of Amir's skin began to turn natural, and he sneezed. Aqlimun covered him with *katan* sheets, and busied himself in restoring him to his senses.

Hakim Aqlimun said to those around him, "Beware! You must take care never to utter even the word *poison* before Amir! Nor even by mistake must you allude to his condition!" A few hours had passed when Amir began to sweat profusely from every pore in his body, and the whole bed was drenched. The next day when Amir had regained a little sense, he asked for food, and Hakim Aqlimun ordered partridge soup to be prepared and administered to him.

When he regained control of his senses, Amir sat himself up with the help of pillows, and asked, "Where is King Landhoor, and what became of all the festivities?" Amar immediately restored Landhoor to consciousness, and took him to Amir, on the way recounting all the events that had transpired to Landhoor, and saying, "My fear of your reverting was the reason I was guilty of this contumely! Pray do not mention any of it to Amir, as what came to pass was ordained by fate!" Then Landhoor and all the illustrious nobles presented themselves before Amir, and scattered over him gold and jewels for the mendicants and the indigent, and showered the poor with alms and oblations for the health of Amir.

Upon noticing Hakim Aqlimun there, Amir asked, "Who is this person, and from where has he arrived? Is he the plenipotentiary of some land, or is he a merchant who has brought merchandise for trade?" Unable to hold his tongue, Aadi spoke thus: "The two female attendants, who claimed to have brought the flagons of grape wine from Mehr-Nigar, were in reality the angels of death sent by Gustham with poisoned wine to put an end to Your Honor's life (may such be your enemies' fate!). The flagon that Your Honor imbibed was admixed with the deadliest poison. It invaded your entire body (by the good fortune of Your Honor's foes!). Then Sabir and Sabur, who are the sons of Shahpal Hindi, brought you to their fort, and attended to you in your sickness, and treated us, too, in the finest traditions of hospitality. Amar was sent to the isle of Narvan to fetch Hakim Aqlimun here, so that Your Honor could be treated, and the All Powerful God brought you out from your grave state. Gustham has now laid siege to the fort, and is putting up an unremitting fight!"

Upon hearing this, Landhoor flew into a fiery rage, and said, "I shall dispatch this blundering dog to Hell! His angel of death is now here, in my person, and with just one huff of breath I shall wipe him from the face of the Earth!" But Amir kept him from following through on this, and asked Landhoor to be patient while he found a way to deal with the menace.

In the meantime the news reached them that Shahpal Hindi, who was aiding and abetting Gustham, had attempted to storm the battlements, but his elder son, Sabir, had dispatched him to Hell with a fiery missile, and because of the incident Gustham had resolved to charge the fortress, and it was only a matter of time before he forded the moat and put the escalades to the fortress walls. Hamza said to Amar, "Go and convey to Gustham on my behalf the message that I have shown restraint until now for the sake of Naushervan, and did not retaliate. But that he has been blind to my consideration and is unable to desist from his malevolent ways and remains hell-bent on raising Cain! Tell him to make his dark face scarce soon, or else he will receive the deserts of his deeds and be taken to task before long!"

When Amar conveyed Hamza's message to that man of evil-omened aspect, Gustham replied thus: "O cameleer's son, play these tricks on someone else! It has been a long time since Hamza died, and no mark remains even of his grave. Have you resurrected the dead to bring me this message from him?" Amar said to him in a fit of anger, "O strumpet's son (deserving of beheading!), watch your mouth before you speak these ill-boding words against the Sahibqiran's honor! Indeed your death grows nigh when you utter such balderdash! Amir has not ordered so—and therefore my hands are tied—otherwise, I would smash your teeth with the sling stone and stuff them down your throat, and make you pay dearly for all your big talk and tall claims!" Gustham replied, "O Amar, if Hamza is alive, as you claim, then go and ask him what secret of mine he is privy to! I will believe the veracity of your claim if you bring me the right answer; otherwise I will know that you made up this story due to your fidelity toward Hamza!"

Amar returned to Hamza and narrated word for word what Gustham had told him, and then said, "O Sahibqiran, I would never have believed that you were on such intimate terms with a cad like Gustham, and cannot fathom how you could ignore all the intrigues of that strumpet's son whose very essence is fermented with mischief and who tried to kill you with everything in his power! First it was Bahram who barely survived his villainous plot, and then he poisoned you! May God recompense Buzurj-mehr, who hid the Shah Mohra in your side, or else there would have been no hope of your escaping with your life."

Then Hamza narrated the incident of Gustham breaking wind in his embrace, and said to Amar, "This is the secret that he alluded to. Go and tell him this and bring me his reply, and find how he reacts to it." Amar returned to Gustham, and said to him, "Hear this, you dolt! Amir replies that just from the force of his embrace you broke wind three times! If you were to receive a blow from his arm you would fill up the whole arena with your scat!"

When Gustham heard Amar reveal the secret, he knew that Hamza was alive and well, and that some new calamity now lay in store for him. For which reason he decided that the wisest course of action would be to turn tail. He headed for Sindh without further loss of time and, unable to give up his seditionist ways, he obtained the severed heads of two men in Sindh, and sent them by messenger to Naushervan, and wrote this in the accompanying note:

Landhoor has defeated Hamza in battle, and by the grace of Your Highness I managed to kill Landhoor, and many an adventure befell me in the undertaking. I am herewith sending you the heads of both Hamza and Landhoor!

Gustham also wrote a detailed note to Bakhtak, which read:

In my letter to the emperor, I have written the exact opposite of what I write here, so that the emperor may marry off Princess Mehr-Nigar with someone else, and that heart-ravishing beauty does not fall to Hamza's lot! However, the truth of the matter is that Hamza had prevailed over Landhoor, who has vowed allegiance and fidelity to Hamza from the bottom of his heart. Since Landhoor lowered his neck in earnest obedience before Hamza and submitted himself to his authority, I could do little else but have Hamza poisoned, as I had no other recourse. But Hamza is verily a great drinker, and has the most unflagging constitution, so that even poison had no effect on him, and not the least harm seems to have come to him from it. Helpless, to escape with my life, I then retreated and arrived in Sindh! Therefore, I reiterate that you must prevail upon the emperor to have Princess Mehr-Nigar married off to someone else, and obtain the support of others, too, in this matter. When Hamza hears of it, his heart will burst from grief. Our purpose is to put an end to his life, and there are more ways than one of gaining that end!

When the two severed heads and the note were presented to Naushervan, his eyes filled up with tears, and he said to Buzurjmehr, "Alas for the youth of Hamza! I know it for a fact that if the vaults of the heavens were to turn for a thousand years, one who is Hamza's match would never be born!" Buzurjmehr said, "I cannot say anything, as Hamza's horoscope testifies to his well-being—although it does clearly manifest and attest to great physical suffering. However, the knowledge of the future is only with Allah!"

OF AMIR'S SETTING OUT FOR CTESIPHON ACCOMPANIED BY LANDHOOR WITH GREAT POMP AND ARRAY AFTER HIS TRIUMPH AND VICTORY

The reins of the steed of the pen are turned and it is spurred into a gallop to traverse the stations of the narrative, thus revealing that when Hamza's strength was a little recovered, his heart again began to pine in the memory of his charming beloved, and he said to Landhoor, "Now I wish for us to proceed to Ctesiphon!" The Khusrau replied, "As Your Honor pleases! Indeed you have spent many a day away in your adventures! Proceed in the name of Allah, if you now wish to seek audience with the emperor. But don't you wish to have coins minted in your name, and appoint a vice-regent to be in charge of affairs in India during your absence?" Amir replied, "O King Landhoor, may the possession of your kingdom be a source of continuous joy to you! I shall only have your friendship, as my heart is conquered by your hospitality, enterprise, and ability!" The Khusrau appointed his uncle's son, Jaipur, as his deputy, and then Landhoor himself with his army in his train accompanied the Sahibqiran as his riding companion.

Aadi had set out a day earlier with the advance camp and, finding a pasture by the banks of a river, he pitched Prophet Danyal's tent in that spot. Amir, who had started out with the Khusrau and the army, then entered the encampment with great pomp and splendor. The following day they again set out, and in this manner the army daily pitched camp and moved it forward the next day. Although the violence of the poison had reduced Amir to little more than skin and bones, yet his desire to set eyes again on Princess Mehr-Nigar made him persevere station after station of all-day journeying, and the ardor of his love and passion propelled him forward.

Now hear of the machinations of Bakhtak, who applied himself to devising a strategy after reading Gustham's note. It occurred to him that Aulad bin Marzaban, the relative of Zhopin who traced his lineage to Kaikaus, might be inveigled to ask for Princess Mehr-Nigar's hand, and therefore must be sent for without delay. In his letter to Aulad, Bakhtak wrote,

> The daughter of the Emperor of the Seven Climes, Princess Mehr-Nigar, has passed from adolescence into nubile age. An Arab named Hamza had sought her hand, but the emperor turned down his suit on account of his not speaking the same tongue, and he was sent to India on the campaign against Landhoor. It has now become known that he was killed at Landhoor's hands, and joined the caravan of the travelers to the Future State. Therefore, it is my well-intentioned counsel that you proceed here posthaste, finding all means to arrive in Ctesiphon soon. I will arrange to have you married to Princess Mehr-Nigar and have you declared Naushervan's son-in-law!

Upon reading this letter, Aulad bin Marzaban was near to bursting with joy, and he left Zabul with thirty thousand troops, arriving in Ctesiphon within a few days. Upon receiving the news of his arrival, Bakhtak began making preparations for his welcome and, in a moment of private audience with the emperor, spoke thus: "Aulad bin Marzaban Kaikausi has arrived from Zabul to enter the service of Your Majesty. As he is the scion of an illustrious family, it would be in the order of things for you to welcome him!" The emperor ordered the nobles to welcome Aulad, arrange for his camp to be set up at Tal Shad-Kam, and attend to hosting and feasting him. Keeping with the emperor's orders, Aulad was received with great fanfare, and all due arrangements were made to provide him with the amenities he needed. The following day Bakhtak arranged for Aulad to have an audience with the emperor, and enter the royal service and receive a robe of honor.

After some days had passed, Bakhtak again found an opportunity to speak privately with the emperor, and said to him, "Now that Hamza is dead and departed from this world with all his many hopes unrequited, we must needs attend to the marriage of Princess Mehr-Nigar, as she has reached the nubile period and the age of majority (Begone malicious glances!) and is sensible and ready for marriage. As to Your Highness's considerations of Gustham, he is well advanced in years, and is knocking at the threshold of dotage. Clearly it is a recipe for disaster to make a match between a decrepit dotard and a nubile, youthful girl. It would be more suitable to marry her to someone young and honorable, who has a claim to personal ability and title to noble birth. Your Highness must acquit himself of this duty at Your Honor's first leisure—this also being the need of the moment—as the times are changing for the worse!"

Naushervan said to him, "Then, why do you not propose someone yourself, and make it easier for me to attend to this obligation!" Bakhtak replied, "In my humble opinion, there is no better match than Aulad bin Marzaban, who not only traces his lineage to Kaikaus, but is also someone gifted with fair looks and charming manners. But only the discretion of Your Highness and Her Highness the Empress can best decide the matter!"

Most satisfied with Bakhtak's counsel, the emperor informed Empress Mehr-Angez of the proposition. As no one in the female quarters of the royal palace yet knew the news of Hamza's death, it brought Empress Mehr-Angez great distress to hear it, and she strictly forbade anyone from conveying the news to the ears of Princess Mehr-Nigar, or breathing a word of it in her presence. But the news soon circulated and reached Mehr-Nigar, who was struck with such violent pains of grief that everyone who saw her state was taken with surprise, and her woe and sorrow and fury were the cause of great anxiety for all of them. Empress Mehr-Angez herself went and offered her many words of consolation, and tried to allay her grief, but the princess paid no heed.

Finding herself helpless in this matter, the empress informed Naushervan of their daughter's state, who said to Buzurjmehr, "Go to the princess and bring her around to the prospect of marrying Aulad bin Marzaban!" Then Buzurjmehr took Mehr-Nigar aside, and said to her, "O Princess! Amir is safe in all ways, and is secure and unharmed by the grace of God! All these rumors circulating regarding him (may such be his enemies' fate!) are baseless, to say the least. These tidings have been spread to ensure that Amir does not gain a foothold in the empire. However, Amir did undergo great physical suffering after being poisoned by Gustham. You shall see this on the fortieth day from today—you will meet him of a certain. In the meanwhile, reasons of expediency dictate that you accept Aulad bin Marzaban's suit, as it will please the emperor. But make him pledge that until forty days have passed Aulad must not present himself before you or be admitted in hours of seclusion." At Buzurjmehr's counsel, the princess agreed to the proposition, and Buzurjmehr congratulated the emperor and conveyed him Mehr-Nigar's message.

The following day Naushervan conferred the robe of son-in-law on Aulad bin Marzaban before the whole assembly, and told him that the nuptials would be celebrated forty days hence. Bakhtak said to Aulad, "This delay does not bode well for your plans, as news has reached here that Hamza is alive and well and headed for Ctesiphon! If he were to arrive here during this period, it would unravel the whole scheme. I suggest that tomorrow you should declare to the emperor, before obtaining leave of parting from him, that you wish to celebrate the nuptials in Zabul, and that by the time the princess's procession reaches Zabul, the forty days will have elapsed, and your kith and kin will be afforded an opportunity to participate in the celebrations and rejoice on the joyous occasion. Then I will second your request, and obtain the emperor's consent."

Aulad's countenance brightened to a ruddy hue from relishing this prospect, and he was greatly overjoyed to hear this counsel. The next day he made his plea before Naushervan, and Bakhtak also petitioned on his behalf, and instigated the emperor on his own as well. The emperor consented and ordered the dowry and all such preparations to be made ready, and said to Bakhtak, "I am relinquishing to you the office of making all arrangements for sending off Princess Mehr-Nigar to Zabul. I wish to acquit myself of this obligation now."

Bakhtak spent prodigiously in arranging for the necessary dowry and money for the journey. The emperor sent Mehr-Nigar off with great pomp and ceremony, and himself accompanied the procession for a day, and all the nobles of the court also joined the emperor in the wedding train.

Aulad made progress toward Zabul happily and joyously, but at Mehr-Nigar's instructions, his pavilion was always pitched three leagues away from her own, and her tent was guarded by twelve thousand Nubian and Turkish slaves, making it well-nigh impossible for even a bird to fly into the princess's camp. When thirty-nine days had passed, the princess knew that the day of her meeting with Amir had come.

Aulad had ordered his camp to be set up at a picturesque hillside, where the breeze was so refreshing that it caused the buds of one's heart to blossom, and where the verdure filled the landscape with its sheer abundance. Aulad said, "Tomorrow we shall remain camped here, as it is also the day when my promise to the princess will be fulfilled. We shall celebrate the nuptials at this very spot, and indulge ourselves in pleasures and jollity!"

Mehr-Nigar had resolved in her heart that the moment Aulad entered her pavilion, she would kill herself and put an end to her life.

OF AULAD BIN MARZABAN BEING TAKEN CAPTIVE, AND A GRIEF-STRICKEN AND REMORSE-BITTEN AULAD BEING SENT AS PRISONER TO NAUSHERVAN AT AMIR HAMZA'S ORDERS

His bounty does not long demur,
The petitioner must not despair.[216]

Regard this marvel of the work of the Gatherer of the Separated that a new flower blossomed in the wild. The nightingale of the pen thus chirps that the Almighty God ordained that the Sahibqiran would arrive in that neighborhood the same day, and he, too, set up his camp on the acclivity of that hillside. He said, "My heart derives strength from the refreshing breeze of this place, and I wish to sojourn here a while. I would like to camp here for a week, and rest a while before moving on!" All those present submitted their agreement and declared that Amir's command was their pleasure.

Hakim Aqlimun said to Amar, "Go to the pasture with your hunting gear, and bring me a deer! The smell of the roast will serve to invigorate Amir's heart, and the two of us will do it justice thereafter." Immediately upon hearing Aqlimun's words, Amar took his lasso and sling, and set forth, leaping and bounding to the pasture. There he espied a flock of deer, and ran toward it. The flock pricked up their ears and took flight, and they all ran in one direction. Amar went gamboling alongside a stag, and when they were adjacent to the mountain, Amar lassoed the stag's horns with such alacrity and precision that all the creature's speed and flight left him, and he was trapped in the net of death. Amar then tied his legs and buried him under a rock away from the main passage, and he climbed up the hill to enjoy the scenery.

Amar beheld a pavilion by the rivulet that bordered on the royal encampment. Two men, who for all appearances seemed to be waiting on someone, were standing by the rivulet, holding in their hands a ewer and basin made of gold and silver. Amar hung one of his arms loose and, swinging it from side to side, he approached them, limping with one foot, and addressed them in a most sweet and affable manner thus: "My friends, whose camp is this, and who are you, and what are your particulars?"

They replied, "This is the encampment of Princess Mehr-Nigar, the daughter of the Emperor of the Seven Climes. We are her slaves, and it is our charge to attend to her faithfully. At first the princess was pledged to an Arab named Hamza, but he died in India at the hands of Landhoor, and the days in this world of that unfortunate man came to an end without his hopes being realized!

"Much though the princess wept and wailed for him, and the emperor was also grief-stricken, one cannot defy the decrees of fate. Bakhtak the bawd prevailed on the emperor to pledge the princess to Aulad bin Marzaban Kaikausi, who is taking her to Zabul to marry her. The princess had learned from Buzurjmehr that she would meet the Sahibqiran along the way after forty days, and would be able to satiate herself with the sight of the one torn from her. Therefore, she extracted a pledge from Aulad that he would not come near her pavilion until forty days had elapsed.

"Today the fortieth day will come to a close, and if the Sahibqiran should arrive by this evening, the princess will live; otherwise, tomorrow, the moment Aulad steps up to the threshold of her pavilion, she will swallow the dose of deadly poison in her possession! Alas and alack the fair young princess who has not yet tasted any of life's pleasures will die innocent and to no purpose!"

Amar replied, "Sirs, have faith in the Provident God! It is not beyond His power to send the Sahibqiran here this very day, and grant the princess's desire despite all odds! I only have this to ask of you: My arm and leg are paralyzed, and a hakim had told me that if I were to wash my arm and leg with a ewer and basin made of gold and silver, my limbs would become well again. A recourse to this remedy is not in the power of a poor man like myself, but it appears I have some days of happy life remaining to my lot to have come upon such kindly folk as yourselves, who have the possession of such utensils. If you were to lend them to me for a moment, I shall wash my arm and leg before your eyes with the water of this rivulet. It is unlikely that I will again find such an opportunity, and no one else would trust me with such precious wares!"

These men took pity on Amar, and after conferring together decided that no harm would be done if a poor man were to benefit from the use of those wares. They also knew that he could not run away from the camp and would certainly return them. Having come to this conclusion they handed the ewer and the basin to Amar, who made a profusely humble bow to them and then went to the rivulet and filled the vessels with water. He washed his arm and leg, but did not return the utensils when he was done. The men said, "Come, brother! Return to us the basin and ewer, as your need has been fulfilled!"

Then Amar leapt away from them, and said, "I am no fool to return them and restore these wares to you, or hand back my medicament once I have its possession! I may have regained the use of my limbs, but if the ailment were to relapse, where would I find you again, and who would lend me this ewer and basin?" And with these words Amar fled toward Aulad bin Marzaban's camp. Realizing that it would be futile to try to catch him, the two men did not give chase; and indeed they could not have caught Amar, who fled before them like the wind.

Before long Amar reached Aulad's encampment, where he made his way disguised as a geomancer and, spreading out his mantle, sat there with the board and dice. When Mehr-Nigar's attendants found a throng clustered around Amar, they decided they, too, should solicit his help in tracing the thief, and ask him to draw lots using the art of geomancy for that purpose. With that intent they drew near to see him at work, and observed that the geomancer would most miraculously relate the secret of a man's heart when someone asked him for it. They, too, went and sat before him and asked him to tell them what might have occurred to them. The geomancer said, "It appears that you have lost some utensils, that they were two in number and were made of gold and silver!" Now the two attendants became convinced that the geomancer was entirely genuine, and they consulted together a while, after which one of them stayed behind and the other went to the threshold of the princess's pavilion, and sent message that he sought leave to announce something of great importance to the princess.

The princess had been waiting for nightfall so that she could take poison and set her soul free from the prison of her existence. Upon hearing this message she rose at once, imagining that the slave had perhaps brought the awaited auspicious tidings of the arrival of the caravan that carried her long lost Yusuf. She approached the curtain, and said, "Speak what you have to say! I hope that you are the harbinger of propitious tidings!" The attendant first narrated the details of how he had lost the ewer and basin, and then recounted the story of the geomancer.

The princess was gifted with intelligence, and reasoned that nobody but Amar could display the cheek to steal her goods so close to her encampment, and then make his way out, dodging thousands of guards. It would be little wonder, she thought, if the geomancer, too, was Amar in disguise. Immediately she sent out a train of messengers and mace bearers to have the geomancer conducted into her presence. After arranging for privacy, she had him seated by the curtain and said, "O geomancer, pray narrate to me the secrets that I hide in my bosom and give an account of my grief-stricken heart!" Amar replied, "Your ladyship should know that I am not initiated in the art of recounting the secrets in people's hearts without examining their aspects, as I never learned the art of divining secrets from behind a curtain!"

The princess thought a while and decided that since she had already resolved to kill herself that day, no great harm would come from exposing her face before that ancient, and besides, nobody other than he would become privy to her secret. She had the curtain lifted from between them, and showed her face to Amar who held out the dice to Princess Mehr-Nigar, and said, "Take these dice and throw them over the charts. Then I will interpret them and narrate the secrets of your heart and draw the horoscope and make the predictions!" When the princess took the dice in her hand, she found their shape strangely different from the dice ordinarily used by geomancers, for she herself had studied geomancy with Buzurjmehr. But she maintained her silence to see what the geomancer had to say and what he would predict.

After she had thrown the dice, Amar narrated the whole story of her love from its beginning up to that moment, and told her that she would receive tidings of Hamza's arrival that very day. Then deducing that this was indeed Amar, and that the geomancer was in reality that infamous juggler and trickster in person, Mehr-Nigar reached out and pulled at his false beard, which came off in her hands to reveal Amar's face. Unable to contain herself any longer, the princess fell crying at Amar's neck, and with tears coursing down her cheeks in a flood, she asked him, "Tell me verily where Amir is now. Where is the caravan that brings to me that Yusuf?" Amar replied, "This very morning Amir set up camp on the slope of this hill. By the grace of God he is alive and out of danger, but he is foundering in the depths of the sea of grief and sorrow because of his separation from you."

Then the princess was near to bursting with joy and wished to inquire after Hamza's welfare and give Amar an account of her own days, but just at that moment a train of messengers arrived at the threshold of the princess's pavilion to announce that Aulad had requisitioned the geomancer to ascertain the proper hour and moment for the nuptials, as all the arrangements had been made for the wedding, and only the arrival of the geomancer was awaited. Amar said to Mehr-Nigar, "My ladyship may now breathe easily, and not fall prey to any worries. Observe what terrible calamities I shall now visit on Aulad's head in lieu of the bliss he anticipates, and how I take this man to task!" With these words, Amar took his leave, and the princess conferred on him a purse of gold and a robe of honor for his departure.

Then Amar went before Aulad and beheld a Gueber[217] stripling seated on a bejeweled throne, covered from head to foot with gold and jewels, with all the paraphernalia for the nuptials strewn about him. Aulad asked Amar, "Why did the princess send for you?" Amar replied, "She inquired of me regarding one who is deceased, and lamented his loss a great deal. I told her that the man was dead and departed, but that she had great happiness in store in a marriage with Aulad bin Marzaban. At first she would hear nothing of it but she softened after I advised and counseled her, and thus made her reconciled to her lot."

Upon hearing these words Aulad began to grin from ear to ear, and ordered a host of celebrations at the news. He conferred a costly robe of honor on Amar, and asked him, "When should I celebrate the nuptials and consummate my troth with that moonfaced beauty?" Amar replied, "Arrange it at your earliest pleasure!" Aulad was even more delighted by this reply and further conferred a purse of red gold on Amar.

Upon receiving that purse Amar visited blessings on Aulad, and said to him, "This humble servant of yours has four sons. One of them indulges himself with plying the mace and is peerless in that art, another excels in the art of cudgeling, my third son is a great drummer, and the fourth is a legendary master of the hautbois. It would afford you the greatest pleasure, and delight you no end if you were to see a display of their talents!" Aulad replied, "Come morning, send your sons into my presence. Indeed it would be a pleasure to watch a display of your sons' talents since they must surely be as well versed in their respective trades as you are in yours."

Amar took his leave and, having reached the hillside, got rid of his disguise and brought the deer to Hakim Aqlimun, who slaughtered it and had Hamza smell the roast to invigorate his spirits. From there Amar headed straight for Landhoor's pavilion. On the way he met Muqbil, whom he asked to come posthaste to Landhoor's pavilion and bring Aadi with him. The Khusrau asked Amar, "What brings you here, O Khvaja, looking so perturbed?" Amar replied, "I have come to plead to you today for a favor! You know well how the Sahibqiran pines for Princess Mehr-Nigar, and indeed it was on account of her that he undertook all these troubles. It would be a great disgrace should a Gueber youth steal Princess Mehr-Nigar from right under your nose and the Sahibqiran poison himself as a result of separation from her." Amar gave a complete account of the events to Landhoor, and informed him that Aulad's encampment lay on the acclivity of the hill and all the arrangements for the nuptials had been made, and everything would be over by that evening. Upon hearing this Landhoor flew into a terrible rage. He rose from his seat carrying his mace, and said, "I shall go forth and crush Aulad's bones and joints to powder, and visit the most terrible fate upon his head! Now I cannot rest without washing my hands in his blood!" Amar replied, "Dispel all such thoughts from your mind, lest Amir take exception to them! We must plan to take him alive." The Khusrau said, "Then I shall abide by your counsel. I am willing to help out in any way I can and shall do so in accordance with your plans." In the meanwhile Muqbil arrived there with Aadi in tow. Amar also counseled with them and took them into his confidence regarding his plans, and in their turn they, too, reiterated what Landhoor had avowed.

When the master of the sky stood at the framework of the vaults of the heavens wielding the cudgel of the sun's beam, Amar hung a big drum from Aadi's neck, furnished Muqbil with a hautbois, and asking Landhoor to take along his mace, and with Amar himself dressed as a fair youth sporting a cudgel, the four arrived at the threshold of Aulad's pavilion.

When Aulad was informed that the geomancer's sons had arrived, he sent for them and ordered them to display their talents in his court. Amar produced eleven brass cudgels from his bag of trickery, and plied them so dexterously that the whole assembly sat entranced and praised his talent to the skies, commenting that they had never seen a cudgeler of such excellence in their whole lives, and Aulad, too, showered him with gifts. Muqbil on the hautbois and Aadi with the drum also delighted the company, and they as well received robes of satin and many other gifts and rewards besides. When Landhoor began to swing his mace around, it caused such powerful blasts of air that the onlookers started to be blown to the ground from their seats and thrones, and they shouted from all corners "Stop!" and "Enough!"

Then Amar gestured to Landhoor that the time had come for him to put his mace to the test in the name of Allah, and show a real display of his power to those assembled there. Landhoor swung his mace and brought it down on the supports of the pavilion whereupon Aulad was buried inside with all his courtiers. Then they turned to attack his army, and a battle ensued. Landhoor raised the mace over his head and bellowed, "Anyone who does not know, learn that I am Landhoor bin Saadan, the Khusrau of India!"

Upon hearing Landhoor's war cry his twelve thousand warriors, who had lain waiting in their positions, fell upon Aulad's army with drawn swords. Ten thousand men from Aulad's host died in the battle, another ten thousand were taken prisoner, while five thousand escaped with their lives.

Now we turn to Aadi, to whom it suddenly occurred in the midst of the battle that food must have been cooked in great abundance in Aulad's camp that day and the finest delicacies would have been prepared to celebrate the nuptials. And this thought convinced Aadi that he ought to break into the pantry and gorge on and gobble up all that he could lay his hands on, and so he headed for the kitchen with that intent. On his way Aadi noticed a man crawling out from under Aulad's pavilion. Aadi squashed him with his drum, which caused the drum's skin to rupture and the man to be transported inside it. Aadi quickly secured the drum's mouth tightly, and barged into the kitchen. And it was indeed the case that food had been prepared there in great plenty, and Aadi helped himself to whatever took his fancy without the least anxiety of having to share it with anyone. He was an image of the proverb that when everything is thrown to a man's disposal, if he does not help himself it is his own loss.

Amar searched for Aulad high and low, but could find no trace of him. Looking for Aulad among the slain, Amar happened by the kitchen and saw Aadi sitting before a great pile of delicacies, bolting them down like there would be no tomorrow. Casting an angry glance at him, Amar addressed him thus: "O drum-bellied one! In Hamza's camp you give yourself the airs of a great champion, but when the time comes for skirmishing, you shirk your duty and hide in this nook to nurse your gluttonous gut! Verily it is a most likely time to attend to one's appetite! You have absolutely no regard for your name and honor!" Aadi replied, "I have taken a man prisoner, and that justifies my freedom to have my meal!" Amar said, "I would like to be blessed by the sight of him and see the one you have caught!" Aadi replied: "He is trapped inside the drum. Go and take a look at him, and leave me to have my food in peace!" Stealing a glimpse of the captive, Amar said to Aadi, "This one man alone is worth a hundred thousand prisoners! Indeed, O Aadi, you accomplished a great deed, and acquitted yourself most honorably by catching this Gueber stripling and netting this prize fish!"

Thus speaking Amar had Aadi carry the drum to Landhoor, and put it before him with great fanfare and triumph. Then Amar said to him, "O Khusrau! I have brought you a veritable bird of paradise, and solicit your munificent indulgence!" Landhoor replied, "Show me whom you have caught." The moment Aadi opened the drum's mouth, Aulad emerged from it with a drawn dagger, and came charging at Landhoor, who wrested the dagger from Aulad's hand and slammed him against the floor. Amar tied him up like a skein of yarn with his lasso, and took these glad tidings to the princess. The princess made a prostration of gratitude, and lavished a great many rewards on Amar. From there he went to Hamza and narrated from the beginning to the end all that had come to pass. Hamza embraced Amar, and then said to Landhoor, "Indeed our prestige and honor are now one! Who would come to the defense of my honor if not you yourself! Without one's friends and well-wishers there is no one to bring succor in such times of need!"

It was decided that Sultan Bakht Maghrebi would escort Princess Mehr-Nigar back to Ctesiphon, and Aulad would be sent back in chains to the emperor, to let Naushervan exercise his own discretion in dealing with him. Hamza then wrote a missive to the Emperor of the Seven Climes, which read:

Your humble servant had taken himself to Ceylon as per Your Excellency's orders. It is beyond the scope of human expression to give a full account of all the hardships and calamities that befell us on the way. I prevailed over King Landhoor and Almighty God preserved my name and honor. I am bringing Landhoor along and shall soon present him before Your Highness, the Shadow of God.

In the meantime, my enemies had circulated the rumors of my death, and propagated this falsehood far and wide. Your Honor believed it to be true and pledged Princess Mehr-Nigar to Aulad bin Marzaban at the instigation of shallow and perfidious counselors. Your Majesty did not pause even for a moment to show the least sympathy for my cause, nor attempted to research the veracity of these rumors. On my way back from battle Aulad and I crossed paths, and I am now sending him as a prisoner to Your Honor. What passed has been recompensed now, and Your Highness may deal with him as you see fit, and censure also those who were instrumental in misleading you in this matter, should you so wish!

I am also sending back Princess Mehr-Nigar, who shall be kept there in trust for me. God willing, I shall soon present myself and celebrate my nuptials with her and put paid to the mischief of all seditionists and calumniators!

Postscriptum, I should inform you that I survived Gustham's attempt to poison me, albeit it caused me untold suffering!

Amir vouchsafed this missive to the care of Sultan Bakht Maghrebi, and conferred robes of honor on everyone in the cortege of Princess Mehr-Nigar.

Mehr-Nigar then sent for Amar, and said to him, "I made all preparations and arranged for festivities, but Amir did not once send for me to come into his presence, and has ordered that I be forthwith dispatched to Ctesiphon! What great crime is mine that I am no longer worthy of showing my face before him?" Amar went to Hamza and told him that Mehr-Nigar had sent this message from the depths of grief and sorrow. Amir said, "You see that the poison has disfigured me, and my body has been stripped of all its glory! It is not my desire to present myself before the princess in this reduced state, or to send for her here. God willing, I shall be restored to my natural looks and health by the time I arrive in Ctesiphon. Then the True God, the Gatherer of the Separated, will arrange for us to meet in happiness! Go and gently advise the princess that she must not take offense at this arrangement nor give herself to any anguish. I shall reach Ctesiphon at her heels since I am headed there myself. Once you have safely deposited the princess, you must return and meet us on the way, and join us without delay!"

Hakim Aqlimun said to Amar, "Khvaja, since you are headed for Ctesiphon, pray bring some *noshidaru*[218] with you. But do not ask for it in Hamza's name because then you will be denied it!"

Then Amar took his leave of Hamza and went before Mehr-Nigar and delicately advised her and offered her consolation. He then had her carried in a litter toward Ctesiphon. In a few days the princess's litter arrived in Ctesiphon, and Naushervan came out to receive her and escorted her into the palace. He conferred a robe of honor on Sultan Bakht Maghrebi, and expressed great delight upon receiving news of Hamza's well-being.

Now hear of Amar, who dressed himself as a peasant and went to a butcher's shop and threw before him two coins that had been completely worn smooth, and said, "Take this money and give me some *noshidaru* for it!" As the butcher had never even heard its name, he asked, "What animal is *noshidaru*? How do you describe its appearance and its size? I have never set eyes on this beast in my life!"

Then Amar went to a grocer, and likewise flung the coins before him, and asked for *noshidaru*. The grocer replied, "Sire, if you would like to buy flour, pulses, rice, salt, wood, ghee, oil, *mandwa, kodon*,[219] millet, gram, peas, barley, or lentils, I have all of them in ready supply, and you are welcome to consider this shop as your own and buy them freely. But I do not have any *noshidaru* to give you. I never heard of this commodity to even confirm that it exists! Ask some spice merchant, as he might have it!"

When Amar went to the spice merchant, the man said, "There is no spice in my trade that is called *noshidaru*. I have never even heard the mention of this condiment. If you would go to the greengrocer, perchance he might have it!" When Amar went to the greengrocer to ask for *noshidaru*, he was told, "Sire, ask me for the freshest in carrots, radishes, greens, melons, and all kinds of vegetables, but I know of no legume that is called *noshidaru*! Go and look for it in some other shop!" Thus going from shop to shop Amar finally arrived at the perfumer's shop, and asked him for *noshidaru*. The perfumer said, "I have never even set eyes on *noshidaru*, let alone carry it in my shop! But go and move the chain of justice[220] at Naushervan's court, as it is to be found in the emperor's pharmacopoeia, and if your luck favors you, you will obtain it there!"

Amar in his peasant's disguise went and moved the chain of justice, whereupon the emperor sent for him, and asked him what it was that he sought. Amar took two farthings from his pocket and, putting them on Naushervan's throne, said, "Your Honor, I require two farthings' worth of *noshidaru*, as my son was bitten by a snake, and the village doctor said that he would make him well if I were to bring him three *mithcals* of *noshidaru* from Ctesiphon. I have been to the butcher, the grocer, the spice merchant, and the greengrocer, but none of them know of it. A man I met on the way told me today that I would find it at the emperor's court, so I present myself before Your Highness, and throw myself at the feet of my

Lord. Take this money and give me a three *mithcals'* measure of *noshidaru*, but if it is even a grain short of three *mithcals,* it will not serve the purpose! I will have the full three *mithcals'* measure, or I will not pay!"²²¹

Upon hearing Amar's speech the emperor and all the nobles in the court broke into laughter, and were most amused by his mien and air. They said to him, "Take your money back! You shall receive from His Lordship what you seek!" Amar replied, "I may be poor, but I would not accept a thing without making payment for it. I shall not receive anything gratis even from the emperor, or burden myself with receiving any favors!" The emperor said to Buzurjmehr, "Take him to the royal treasury, and give him three *mithcals* of *noshidaru*, and make sure that you do not measure it even a grain short!"

Buzurjmehr took Amar to the treasury and lifted the lid of a chest to take out a jewel-encrusted box, from which he gave three *mithcals* of *noshidaru* to Amar. Then Buzurjmehr took out another three *mithcals,* and quietly slipped them into his pocket, for since discovering Hamza's poisoning at Gustham's hands, he knew that Amar would arrive there any day to ask for *noshidaru.* On the way back to the court, Amar said to Buzurjmehr, "It is a thing to marvel at, sire, that you steal even though you are the emperor's attendant! And your being such a respectable and honorable man does not keep you from coveting even this thing worth but a farthing! Hand me the *noshidaru* that you have stolen and secreted away in your pocket. Did it not occur to you that you will be shamed and dishonored for your theft?" Buzurjmehr was obliged to give the *noshidaru* to Amar for fear of inviting scandal, and from the realization that everything would be ruined if the yokel betrayed him.

Now we turn to Bakhtak who also knew of Hamza's poisoning. The knowledge gave him no peace but constantly worried him that Buzurjmehr would certainly reserve some *noshidaru* from the pharmacopoeia for Hamza. Unable to overpower his base nature, Bakhtak said to the emperor, "Regard Buzurjmehr's status, and then consider his theft of *noshidaru*! Behold his prestige and honor, and see how he has crowned it with his embezzlement! If he needed the *noshidaru,* why would he not ask Your Majesty for it? If Your Honor had conferred it on that peasant, it is certain Buzurjmehr would not have been denied it."

Incited by Bakhtak, the emperor gave orders that Buzurjmehr be subjected to a full search. But nothing at all was found on Buzurjmehr, and Bakhtak was taken to task and penalized, and the emperor offered an apology to Buzurjmehr. When Buzurjmehr learned that it was Amar himself who had expropriated *noshidaru* from him in the guise of a peasant, he rejoiced exceedingly that Amar had saved him the humiliation of being branded a thief.

Once Amar was outside Ctesiphon, he took off his disguise and headed for Hamza's camp. Hamza had fallen into paroxysms of tears one day, distressed by suffering this weakness that had reduced him to the last extremity. He cursed himself, thinking that death would be far more preferable than a life such as his, since he became increasingly decrepit with each passing day. Then Prophet Ibrahim appeared to him in the realm of dreams and offered him consolation and many words of solace.

In the morning Hamza offered prayers in gratitude, and had propped himself up in his bed, when Amar arrived. Not recognizing Hamza, he addressed him as one would a stranger, and asked, "Who are you, and where have you come from? Do you happen to know where Hamza's pavilion is?" Hamza replied, "I am Aulad bin Marzaban's brother, and I came here to secure my brother's release from prison. When I did not find my brother, I set Hamza's soul free from the chains of existence!"

Upon hearing this Amar rushed toward Hamza brandishing a dagger, but Hamza wrested the dagger from him, and embracing Amar, said to him, "I am Hamza! Save yourself all purposeless fretting and fuming!"

Amar handed the *noshidaru* to Hakim Aqlimun, but did not say a word to him about how he had obtained it. Aqlimun began administering Hamza several *mashas*[222] of that confection, in order that he might regain his strength and fully recover the power of his faculties.

———

Now hear of what passed with Bahram Gurd, the emperor of China. After his four ships had been separated from Hamza's fleet by the storm, he was tossed around in the turbulent sea for six months. After the storm abated, he anchored near Sindh and thought of stocking his ships with provisions, and went ashore with that intent.

He had gone a little distance when he saw a bow and a purse of a thousand gold pieces lying on a pedestal under a great tree. Bahram asked some passersby, "Why are this bow and this purse of gold kept in this place, and what is the purpose in keeping them here?" The people answered, "This bow belongs to Koh Bakht Hindi, who is the brother of our ruler Sarkash Hindi, and one who has a title to great strength. He put the bow and the purse here as a challenge, so that the one who could draw the bowstring might claim the purse of gold!"

Thinking in his heart that these riches were a windfall and he must not lose this opportunity of claiming them, Bahram walked up to the pedestal and drew the bowstring, pulling its notch up to his ear. Then he picked up the purse of gold pieces and placed the bow back on the pedestal, and made to leave after handing the purse over to his attendant.

The guards took the news to Koh Bakht Hindi that a merchant had arrived who drew the bowstring and then took the purse of gold pieces. By chance, an *ayyar* had also witnessed the incident and, like an arrow shot from a well-strung bow, he hied before Sarkash Hindi and narrated the whole incident to him. Sarkash Hindi ordered him to produce the merchant and the bow before him at once. Immediately upon receiving these orders, people rushed to fetch Bahram, proclaiming, "The ruler of the city has sent for the merchant, and expressed the desire to see him!"

Bahram went as demanded by traditions of chivalry, and Sarkash Hindi received him with great kindness and showed him much honor. When the men sent by Sarkash Hindi had returned with the bow, and the nobles had also assembled, Sarkash Hindi asked Bahram, "Were you the one who handled this bow?" Bahram replied, "Indeed it was I, God's weakest creature, and I thank God a thousand times for endowing me with the strength to do it!" Sarkash Hindi said, "I wish you to draw it once more in my presence and display your might and strength before us, as the audience are desirous of a repetition of this feat before their eyes!"

Bahram grasped the handle of the bow, and pulled at the bowstring with such force that the bow snapped into two. Then as a token of his respect Sarkash Hindi gestured to Bahram to be seated, and Bahram stepped up to the gold-inlaid steel chair next to Sarkash Hindi's throne, and sat down after removing its coverlet.

Hardly had Bahram seated himself when Koh Bakht Hindi walked into the court like a fierce lion. When he saw his bow lying broken, and Bahram seated at his station, he flew into a great passion. Brandishing his dagger, he charged at Bahram, bellowing, "Not only did you break my bow, but you dared also to sit in my seat! Now you shall taste the deserts of your presumptions!"

Bahram twisted Koh Bakht Hindi's arm and, wresting the dagger from his hand, he threw him to the floor by catching him from behind. Then Bahram said to him, "Is this all the strength you had to show or is there some left in you still?" Sarkash Hindi apologized to Bahram, obtained pardon for Koh Bakht's contumacious behavior, and then addressing Bahram, spoke thus: "In the name of your creed and your people, I ask you to tell me verily who you are, what is your appellation, of which land you are denizen, and where is your homeland!" Bahram gave a complete account of his particulars, and told Sarkash Hindi all that had led him to this land.

Upon hearing Amir Hamza's name, Sarkash Hindi heaved a cold sigh, and said, "I forever nursed a desire to some day kiss Amir's feet, but may the devil take Gustham, who killed such a peerless youth and champion without match, and mixed the prime of such a noble and illustrious youth into dust!" At these words Bahram let out a cry, and was taken unconscious.

When he was restored to his senses with the help of aromatic unguents, he said, "Pray tell me in detail who is your source for this news, and how these tidings reached you!" Sarkash replied, "Gustham himself was here, and although he tried to obtain an audience with me, I would not grant it. He sent the heads of Hamza and Landhoor to Naushervan's court from here by the agency of one of his companions. His destination upon leaving this place I could not determine, but I did not believe a word he said as he was an idle talker and an unmatched liar, much given to making tall claims and assuming false airs. For this reason I have dispatched my *ayyars* to Ceylon to research this news and bring me all the details concerning this matter!"

Bahram said, "Now that you have mentioned Gustham's name, I no longer doubt the truth of his claim. Surely, that wretch (deserving of beheading!) must have killed Hamza by deceit. That witless fool had been plotting it for a long time, and must have found an opportune moment to spring his treachery. I cannot stay here a moment longer, but must needs head immediately for Ctesiphon! If I do not rout Naushervan's army with these selfsame four thousand troops and do not quench my dagger's thirst with the blood of Naushervan's life, I shall never again show my face among brave and valiant men, and will eat poison or extinguish my life with this very dagger!"

When Sarkash Hindi saw that nothing could turn Bahram from his purpose, he ordered that Bahram's ships be provisioned with enough rations for six months, and saw him off. Bahram boarded his ship lamenting and grieving, and ordered the fleet to weigh anchor. They reached the port of Basra in six months and from there Bahram headed for Ctesiphon at the head of his four thousand Uzbek warriors, giving orders to pillage and plunder and raze to the ground every village, town, city, and tract of land, and burn down every last hut and hovel on the way to Ctesiphon.

The news reached Naushervan that Bahram had raised the standard of rebellion upon hearing the rumors of Hamza's death, and was marching on Ctesiphon with impious intent, laying siege to all the villages and towns and cities that he passed on the way. Naushervan sent Faulad bin Gustham with ten thousand mounted troops to go and comfort Bahram with the news that Hamza was alive. Faulad was asked to tell Bahram that seditionists and enemies had propagated these rumors and spread falsehoods and black lies, and to tell Bahram that it was incumbent on him to present himself humbly at the court in Ctesiphon, and no longer give himself over to any worries on Hamza's account.

Faulad bin Gustham encountered Bahram on the way, but try as he would to convince him of Hamza's well-being, Bahram did not believe him. Flying into a murderous rage, Bahram spoke to Faulad thus: "O progeny of sedition! Since when has your word become worthy of believing that I must give it any credence? Why in the world must I trust anything you say after your own father has been responsible for this treachery? Come and show what you have to offer if you have a title to courage, so that you may take with you the memory of a good fight!"

Then Faulad bin Gustham was obliged to draw battle arrangements, and launched combat by thrusting his spear at Bahram's breast. Catching hold of Faulad's spear, Bahram tore it from his hand and, turning it upon Faulad, picked him clear off his saddle by driving his steed forward and skewering Faulad on his own lance. Bahram threw the spear from his hand when he saw that Faulad was killed. With his troops surrounding Faulad's army on all sides, Bahram cut down Faulad's men with his four thousand Uzbeks. Of the Sassanids' ten-thousand-strong force a mere five-hundred-odd men survived the slaughter. They fled and went before Naushervan to give a complete account of the encounter.

This news greatly agitated Naushervan. On the fourth day, while the emperor was still occupied with thoughts of somehow dispelling this calamity, Bahram's Uzbek troops arrived within sight of the fort. Many tried in vain to persuade him that Hamza was alive by the grace of God and that it would cause Amir the greatest displeasure if Bahram were to inculpate himself with any offense against the emperor. None of this convinced Bahram, however, who thought that Naushervan was using this ruse to gain time to save his life.

Before long the emperor's besieged army was obliged to shower Bahram's force with Greek fire,[223] and fiery missiles were exchanged by the two camps. Bahram used a clever stratagem to advance to the parapets of the fort, whereupon Naushervan underwent ecstasies of fear, knowing that it was only a matter of time before Bahram would enter the city after felling the gate, and would inflict carnage to no purpose and put the whole populace to the sword.

Bahram was about to bring his mace down on the gates of the fort when the arrow of Naushervan's supplications for divine succor reached the mark of God's approval. A dust cloud rose on the horizon, revealing a body of approaching troops. The besieged innocent people cried out, "There! The Sahibqiran has arrived!" When he turned to look, Bahram beheld that the dragon-shaped standard had manifested itself from the cloud of dust, like the sun appearing from behind a lining of clouds. Bahram spurred on his steed and rode at a gallop to kiss the stirrup of Amir Hamza, who jumped down from his mount and embraced Bahram. He introduced Bahram to Landhoor, and said, "Just as you are my one arm, he is the other! He is an illustrious person, a valiant warrior, and a faithful friend!"

They had not yet mounted their steeds when a camel rider dispatched by Naushervan arrived and reverently kissed the ground in front of Amir. The rider conveyed the message that the Emperor of the Seven Climes sent his fond prayers and good wishes and expressed the desire that Amir should camp at that station that day, and the following morning, His Majesty would come himself to welcome him and to escort him in his cortege into the city. As per the royal orders, the Sahibqiran ordered that his camp be set up right there, and sent his salutations and humble regards to the emperor as demanded by royal etiquette.

When the King of the Four Climes[224] ascended the throne of the heavens and filled the whole world with the grace of his luminance, the Sahibqiran mounted his steed and rode out to kiss the royal threshold in the cortege of the Khusrau of India, Landhoor bin Saadan, the Emperor of China, Bahram Gurd, and other illustrious nobles. From the opposite direction Naushervan came forth to welcome the Sahibqiran, riding upon a throne and flanked by his Sassanid and Kianid grandees. When Amir sighted Naushervan's throne draw near, he dismounted and kissed its leg. Naushervan ordered his throne to be put down, and embraced Hamza, and then the two headed toward the city, regaling each other with clever repartee and conversation. Naushervan ordered that Amir's entourage be billeted at Tal Shad-Kam as before, and Amir's pavilion was assembled there as usual.

Upon entering the court of Kai Khusrau, the emperor ascended the imperial throne to give audience, and Amir was seated on the throne of Rustam. Naushervan scattered gold and jewels to the destitute and the indigent in oblation for Amir and, at the time of Amir's leave-taking, conferred a robe of honor on him. Amir retired to Tal Shad-Kam contented and joyous, decorated with the robe of honor, and at once arranged for an assembly of revelry and jollity.

And while Amir was thus occupied, the malicious Bakhtak declared to Naushervan, "Before, everyone was in awe of Hamza and there was no one but was terrified of him. Now that he has Landhoor and Bahram by his side, no one dares look him in the eye or stand against their combined might! I fear that they may overthrow Your Majesty and usurp Your Highness's crown!" Bakhtak's words smote terror in the emperor's heart, and becoming panic-stricken, he asked, "What must be done about it?" Bakhtak answered, "You must dispose of them one by one, each in his own turn, and gradually rid yourself of their menace! Tomorrow when Hamza presents himself into Your Honor's presence, Your Majesty must tell him that he had been ordered to bring Landhoor's head, not to bring Landhoor alive, contradicting Your Majesty's commands!" Naushervan said to Bakhtak, "I give you the authority to speak to Hamza as you deem proper." Then Bakhtak returned home rejoicing in his heart, and after passing the night in anxious anticipation of the coming day, arrived in the court at the crack of dawn.

In the morning when Amir arrived in Naushervan's court, Bakhtak addressed him in a loud voice even before greetings had been exchanged: "His Majesty states that he ordered you to bring him Landhoor's head, not descend on His Majesty with Landhoor and conduct this menace into the city!" Amir took offense at these words, and replied, "Rather than beheading people unwarrantedly, gaining their fidelity should be the desired end. Landhoor has come here with his army to offer servitude. There are no thoughts of rebellion in his heart, as he has brought his entire force along with him." Bakhtak replied. "His servitude has no meaning! It would not bode well to allow him to live! Today he may lay down his head at the emperor's feet, but who would answer for him should he revert tomorrow?"

Amir replied, "For as long as I live, he will not have the gall to raise his head from His Majesty's servitude or rebel or go against the emperor's orders. But should the emperor so desire, I will presently go and bring his head, as His Majesty's pleasure is my command!"

Bakhtak said, "The emperor is loath even to behold Landhoor's face and will settle only for his head. But how could you claim with any certitude that he will submit his neck at your command, and will not instead rebel and display his headstrong ways?" Amir replied, "Speak not of rebellion. At a word from me Landhoor shall willingly submit his head to the inclement sword and would not show the least hesitation! Indeed, my own order would be enough for him to sever his head with his own hands!"

Bakhtak said, "Then why this delay? What is it that you await? Send for Landhoor and tell him what you must!"

The Sahibqiran ordered Amar to bring Landhoor to him. Amar went before Landhoor, and said, "Come along! The emperor has ordered you to be put to death, and Amir has sent for you to fulfill the emperor's wishes!"

Then Landhoor rose, reciting the lines:

Intoxicated on the wine of love, I am oblivious of myself;
Little do I care for my head if it should roll in this path.

He said to Amar, "My sole consideration is a life that is spent seeking the Sahibqiran's pleasure! What do I care whether my head stands on my neck or rolls? Indeed now it has become a veritable burden upon my shoulders.

My shoulders can no longer bear my head's burden, nor must I
Have qualms about my severed head filling the skirts of my beloved's desire.

"Come, tie my hands with a kerchief and lead me to the emperor's court!" Landhoor declared.

Hearing Landhoor's words, Amar embraced him, and spoke warmly thus: "O Khusrau! No power on Earth could cast an evil glance at you or even presume to harm a single hair on your body. Come along with me. Hamza's head shall fall before any injury will come to you! And after him all the nobles, the champions, and I myself will lay down our lives before your person is exposed to the least detriment! Decorate yourself with all your arms and armor, and follow me on your she-elephant Maimoona." Then the Khusrau placed all his arms on his person and, carrying his mace resting on his shoulder, rode his she-elephant to the Hall of Audience.

Amar went into the court, and said to Hamza, "Landhoor who is to be executed has arrived, for the sole purpose of his life is to submit to Amir's pleasure!" In the Hall of Audience Landhoor began playing with his mace by tossing it into the air. It occasioned a great uproar, and people cried, "If the mace should slip from his hands, some ten or twenty lives will be lost immediately, the bones of hundreds will be crushed and they will lose the use of their limbs!" Upon hearing the hue and cry the emperor asked, "What is this noise? What has caused this din to erupt all of a sudden?" When the people explained the reason, the emperor was struck silent.

Then Hamza said, "Go and show Landhoor in!" Amar went outside and brought Landhoor with him to the Hall of Assembly. Landhoor submitted to Hamza with folded arms, saying, "What is your pleasure, my lord? What caused Your Honor to remember this slave today?" Amir replied, "The emperor wishes to have your head, as he has become distrustful of you." Landhoor replied, "I am a slave to your orders! I will obey whatever you shall command, and submit to it fully!"

Amir said: "Very well then! You must take leave of His Majesty, and wait outside in the yard of the Hall of Audience with bowed head. The one who shall receive the orders to behead you will be sent there."

Landhoor made obeisance, went into the yard, and sat there resting against his mace. Amir then ordered Aadi to go and bring him Landhoor's head. When Aadi expressed his duty to Landhoor, the emperor of India lowered his neck and recited:

My darling severed my head from my body
And put an end to a long story and much headache.

Then he said, "I am most grateful to God that my submission to Amir does not show the least variance even as I am being beheaded at his command!" Struck by the degree of Landhoor's devotion, Aadi sat down next to him, saying, "Before anyone could cast an impious glance at Landhoor, he would first have to behead me."

Upon hearing of this turn of events Amir Hamza bid Bahram to behead Landhoor with his own hands. But Bahram, too, became enamored of Landhoor's noble sentiments, and sat down by Landhoor's other side himself, pronouncing, "My head will also fall with Landhoor's head! If Amir wishes to behead us with his own hands, he has the freedom to do so!" When the Sahibqiran heard Bahram's words, he sent Sultan Bakht Maghrebi, who also sat down next to Landhoor, and said, "A fine thing is this purposeless slaughter that Amir has taken into his head. But if he is set upon this course, my head will also roll with my friends' heads!"

The emperor was notified of these men's comments by spies who narrated the speeches of these nobles before him. Bakhtak said to this, "Why is the royal executioner not ordered to go forth and bring His Majesty the heads of all of the men that His Highness desires, and put an end to this scandalous state of affairs instantly?" Hamza replied, "You are at liberty to send whomever you choose!"

Bakhtak immediately signaled to an executioner. Amar quietly shadowed the executioner when he noticed him walk up to Landhoor wielding a Bardwani blade, dressed in a lion skin robe, with a bloodied butcher's towel stuck at his waist. The executioner arrived at Landhoor's head, and called out, "Who is the one whose life's sun is become pale? Who is the one whose sun of life is about to set?"

All of a sudden a great clamor arose when a carriage passed by, and the cries of crowd dispersers and the shouting of the royal proclaimers began to fill the air at intervals, gradually reaching the threshold of the royal palace. It was revealed that Empress Mehr-Angez and Princess Mehr-Nigar were passing by in a litter on their way to the palace. The empress looked out from the curtains of the carriage, and asked Mehr-Nigar, "Who is this man, and what is all this bustle about?" When Mehr-Nigar told her that it was Landhoor, the empress ordered the carriage to slow down, and sent eunuchs out to find out the reason for the tumult and report to her why a throng was gathered at the royal threshold.

When the eunuchs had made queries and brought the details to Empress Mehr-Angez, she said, "A fine bloodlust this is that prompts the emperor to shed the blood of innocent men! Go and conduct Landhoor to our palace!" When the eunuchs went to fetch Landhoor, the executioner obstructed them from carrying out their commands. Learning of this, the empress said, "Cut off the executioner's nose and ears and have him thrown outside the city walls after dragging him out of the Hall of Audience and disemboweling him!" At this, the executioner became deathly pale, and did not offer the least resistance to Landhoor's removal.

Landhoor was released from that scourge, and taken to the empress's palace, where the empress conferred a robe of honor on him and gave him leave to depart. Then Landhoor retired happily and joyously to Tal Shad-Kam, alongside Bahram, Aadi, and Sultan Bakht Maghrebi. When spies took this intelligence to the emperor and gave an account of how the empress had sent for Landhoor and then let him off after conferring a robe of honor on him, the emperor said, "The empress would not have acted in this manner without good cause! She must have seen some wisdom in so doing. I shall come to learn the reason before long and then this mystery will unfold." He then adjourned the court and retired to his palace.

Of Rumors of Princess Mehr-Nigar's Death Being Spread by Bakhtak's Mother, Saqar Ghar Bano, of Hamza Becoming Distressed upon Hearing Them, and of Amar Killing Saqar Ghar Bano and Burying the Bawd in the Leaves

The ebb and flow of time is proverbial, and the juggling of the heavens is ever evident and fully manifest. At times grief will strike amid transports of joy; sometimes in the depths of sorrow the face of hope will gleam. Similar is the course of the story here told.

The connoisseurs of the tale recount that when the emperor entered the royal harem, he asked Empress Mehr-Angez, "What was the reason that you granted pardon to Landhoor and saved him from execution?" The empress answered, "In the first place, Landhoor was not guilty and did not put up the least resistance despite all the power and might at his command, for his hands were tied by his love for Hamza. In the second place, Landhoor is also the sovereign of a clime, and monarchs do not mete out such treatment to their equals, and do not show such callous disregard for the changed circumstances of other kings. My third reason was that if the news of this incident had been carried abroad, your reputation would have been forever lost, people would have heaped rebuke on your head, and never again reposed faith in your word or believed in your promises. Again, if Landhoor had died in this manner, in retribution for his blood, Hamza himself would have laid your whole empire to ruin. Did you not consider that if Landhoor had not submitted his neck himself at Hamza's bidding, no one among your royal retainers could have dared cut off his head? These were the reasons why I conferred a robe of honor on Landhoor, and sent him away in safety!"

Then the emperor praised to the skies the empress's reasoning, and greatly lauded her judgment, and rejoiced exceedingly. But then he became listless, and said, "Alas, no ruse has yet been found to dispel Hamza's menace!" Bakhtak's mother, Saqar Ghar Bano, who was present

there, submitted before the emperor with folded arms saying, "If Your
Majesty would so order, I could rid you of Hamza's life in a most suitable
way and in no time nip his menace in the bud." Nausherkvan asked, "How
do you propose to go about it?"

She answered, "Tomorrow Your Majesty should tell Hamza before
the whole court that he will be wedded to Mehr-Nigar after a week and
should therefore start the preparations for the wedding, and that Your
Highness will order royal orderlies to assist with the preparations. This
slave will hide Princess Mehr-Nigar in a cellar on the pretext of her
maiyoon[225] ceremony. After two days news of Princess Mehr-Nigar's
being ill will be spread, and then on the sixth day her demise (may such
be her enemies' fate!) will be proclaimed."

> From the artifice of women, are men's hearts cleft,
> Mighty indeed are the stratagems of the female mind.

Saqar Ghar Bano continued, "When Hamza hears this sorrowful
news, he will kill himself and thus die at his own hands!"

The emperor was greatly taken with Saqar Ghar Bano's plan, and the
next day before the assembled court he ordered Hamza to make preparations for the wedding, whereupon Amir retired to his camp rejoicing
and occupied himself with the necessary preparations.

Then Saqar Ghar Bano went and congratulated the princess in the
palace, and using the *maiyoon* ceremony as an excuse, removed her to a
cellar, where she spoke to her thus: "My lady! Now, you must not set foot
outside this cellar for an entire week, because such are the formalities of
this ritual!" Mehr-Nigar's companions gathered around her, and they all
began to frolic and make merry, celebrating in anticipation of her nuptials and instructing Mehr-Nigar in all that she needed to learn. Mehr-
Nigar proceeded happily to the cellar and remained enclosed within it.

After two days that harridan, Saqar Ghar Bano, spread the news that
Mehr-Nigar had taken ill (may such be her enemies' fate!), and four days
later, the palace rang out with lamentations that Mehr-Nigar had moved
out of the confines of the Garden of Night and Day to promenade in the
Copse of Paradise, and sauntered out now on her journey to the Grove of
the Future State.

Amir was struck with the most violent anguish from hearing merely
of the Princess's sickness. Now that he heard the news of her death, he
made to plunge his dagger into his bosom. But Landhoor and Bahram

took away his dagger and threw themselves at Amir's feet, comforting him with many a word of solace and saying, "While there is no helping the ordinances of fate, who has ever heard of the living departing to join the dead?" Amir replied, "In the creed of love, life is forfeit for the lover when the beloved has died! No matter what you say, I shall put an end to my existence yet, as I no longer have any business with life!"

When Amar saw that Hamza would not listen to their advice, he said, "Hear me first! Let me go and confirm the news of the princess's death, lest some perfidious mind have thought up this plan to be rid of you. Perhaps some bawd circulated this rumor so that you would kill yourself, even though Mehr-Nigar lives. Then, she would be alive and well while you put an end to your life! Have a little patience until I return after finding out the truth of the matter." Hamza found Amar's proposition to his liking and when they heard of it the others also greatly admired its wisdom. Amar set out with great dispatch and had his arrival announced upon reaching the threshold of the empress's palace.

On his arrival Saqar Ghar Bano said to Empress Mehr-Angez, "It would be well to invite Amar into the palace. When he witnesses the lamentations and wailings here, he will go and narrate them to Hamza, who will kill himself immediately upon learning this state of affairs!" The empress sent for Amar to enter the palace, and when Amar arrived, he saw every last person there dressed in black, and found both young and old in mourning. But a while later he caught sight of Saqar Ghar Bano walking up to the empress and then retiring whence she had come after whispering something into her ear. Amar said in his heart, *There is some mystery behind this. It is all the working of this bawd and it is certain that she is the author of this farce!*

Night had fallen and the whole palace was covered in darkness in keeping with the rites of mourning. Looking around and making sure that nobody saw him, Amar disguised himself as an old woman. Then Amar followed Saqar Ghar Bano at a slow pace. The harlot halted at hearing a sound when she entered the back garden of the palace, and called out, "Who is there?" Amar replied, "It's only me, and only a matter of time before the Angel of Death carries you off instead of the princess!" The moment Saqar Ghar Bano took a forward step, Amar caught her neck in the loop of his lasso and pulled it, knocking her flat on her back. Then Amar throttled her, and the avis of Saqar Ghar Bano's soul flew away to roost in the Erebus of Hell.

Amar buried her body under a pile of dry leaves, and after disguising himself in her person, he went up the promenade. He stood there perplexed, unable to decide which direction to take and whom to ask where the princess was concealed, when a young courtesan came up to him from a corner of the garden holding a taper, and addressed Amar thus: "O Saqar Ghar Bano, the princess has sent for you, and it has been some time since she inquired after you!" Amar said nothing in reply, but followed the courtesan to the cellar.

There Amar beheld Princess Mehr-Nigar sitting all made up on the bridal throne, making repartee with her attendants in perfect bliss and happiness. A wine ewer and goblet lay close at hand, and every so often Fitna Bano would fill up the cup and pass it on to the princess who would drink to the well-being of the Sahibqiran.

Seeing Amar, Mehr-Nigar said, "Saqar Ghar Bano, what is the reason for your acting so kindly toward me of late, as you never showed such fond devotion to me before?" Amar replied, "I was afraid to occasion any ill boding in your heart for fear that since I am Bakhtak's mother I might cause you some harm—or lest you imagine that like Bakhtak I also bear malice toward those who do not bear me any. For these reasons I kept myself out of Your Honor's way, but you remained always in my prayers, even though I was not before you in person, and my head was not laid down at your feet. You can judge for yourself that I wish you well, and witness that I am so busy making preparations for your wedding that I find no rest from it, but am constantly attending to this thing and that!" Mehr-Nigar replied, "Indeed all that you have stated is true! Now tell me: How long must I wait before the bridegroom will arrive, and what are the preparations on the other side?"

Then Amar took her aside, and said, "A wedding procession, indeed! The whole palace is ringing with lamentations on news that you have died (may such be your enemies' fate!). Our camp is also in great upheaval, and upon hearing the news Amir was very near killing himself when something occurred to me, and I asked him to have a little patience while I went and researched the rumors and brought him the truth. I fear that his enemies have worked this treachery to kill him, and those perfidious minds thought of this insidious plan from their malicious natures. I killed that bawd Saqar Ghar Bano upon arriving here, and hid her body in the leaves and gained access to you in her disguise! Now I shall return posthaste to Hamza, and bring him the happy tidings of your well-being so that he may find a new lease on life, regain command of his senses, and breathe easily once more!"

Mehr-Nigar was overjoyed upon hearing this news, and sent Amar away after conferring five purses of gold pieces on him. So that Hamza would believe the veracity of the news Amar also made Mehr-Nigar write a note in her own hand. He brought the note to Hamza whose spirits revived upon reading it, and he, too, conferred a reward of ten thousand gold pieces on him.

Amar then said, "Now, if you would grant me leave, I will let the cat out of the bag with such marvelous subterfuge that the bastards who have colluded in this plot will themselves be most fittingly humiliated, and for this indelicate act the emperor will be branded with everlasting shame and will never again think of going back on his word to a noble man!" Hamza replied, "Nothing could be more to the purpose. I shall do as you bid me, and shall not act but in full accordance with your advice."

Amar said, "Then proceed to the Kai Khusrau's court with Landhoor, Bahram, Aadi, and the other nobles, dressed in black, and prevail on the emperor that he must bring out the funeral procession of princess Mehr-Nigar without delay, to stop malicious tongues from speculating why the daughter of the Emperor of the Seven Climes lies unburied so long after her demise!"

Hamza found Amar's proposal greatly to his liking, and went to the Kai Khusrau's court escorted by Landhoor, Bahram, and the others, all clad in black, with grief and mourning amply visible on their aspects, and they all took their allotted stations. They saw that the emperor along with all his Sassanid and Kianid grandees was also wearing black, and they heard heartrending lamentations and passionate wailings that arose from all corners of the palace, where weeping and crying seemed to be the order of the day.

After a while, Amir said to the emperor, "The decree of fate is now passed, and no appeal can overturn it. But keeping the princess's corpse in the palace so long will invite scandal, and it will reflect poorly on the crown to delay the funeral any further. Pray order that the funeral procession is brought out now and the body is carried outside the palace!" The emperor sent the message to Empress Mehr-Angez, who sent back the reply that the princess's corpse would be kept in the palace for the duration of the day, and the funeral procession would be brought out that night.

In short, that whole day was spent in wailing and lamentation, and the whole palace remained in a state of great upheaval. When darkness fell, hundreds of Brahmins began ringing wooden gongs and rattles and chanting the names of their one hundred and seventy-five gods and goddesses. When people searched for Saqar Ghar Bano in the palace, they discovered her body buried under leaves, and her corpse was placed in a casket at Empress Mehr-Angez's orders and taken in a funeral procession from the palace.

The path was lit with hundreds of thousands of torches, and thousands of mourners followed the bier. Amar observed the Brahmins ringing their gongs and rattles, chanting the praise of their one hundred and seventy-five gods,[226] letting off fireworks at every step, and embracing their fellow worshippers. Amar dressed himself as a Brahmin and, carrying a rattle in his hand and singing the praises of Lat and Manat, he, too, began embracing the fire worshippers.

Slowly Amar made his way toward Bakhtak, and after dropping a squib[227] inside Bakhtak's collar, he caught him in his embrace. Realizing that only Amar could have done such a deed, Bakhtak involuntarily cried out, "Oh! Oh! I burn! Oh, Amar! For the sake of Hamza, let me go as my stomach and my breast are burning, and my whole body is turning to a blister!" Amar replied, "Since it is your own mother who has died it would reflect most nobly on your filial love if you were to burn in her memory like the cypress chandelier!"[227]

At this, Amar let go of the ill-starred Bakhtak and moved back. The firecracker flew out of Bakhtak's collar after it had scorched his whole stomach and breast and thoroughly scalded his skin. To bring himself relief, Bakhtak plunged headlong into a nearby water hole, and lost power of his senses. The mourners who had followed the procession weeping and crying were unable to suppress their mirth at the sight, and broke into uncontrollable laughter. Some Brahmins rushed to put the fire out and stop it from burning Bakhtak further. But he was inconsolable with pain and, leaving his mother's bier with the Brahmins, he returned crying and wailing to his house.

When the crowd returned after burying Saqar Ghar Bano in the grave she had dug for herself with her own deeds, they found the emperor weeping and grieving in the Hall of Private Audience, and they, too, broke into a flood of tears at the sight. When Amar regarded closely, he saw that the emperor held an onion root in his kerchief, and when he applied it to his eyes the burning sensation caused the eyes to bring forth tears. Amar stole close to the emperor, and in a whisper spoke to him thus: "Never has the world known or heard of a more treacherous emperor who so grossly violates his promises to men willing to lay down their lives for him!"

The emperor laughed this off, saying, "The one who wrought the deceitful plan has received his just deserts!" But even though the emperor dismissed Amar's comment, he was mortified with shame in his heart, and felt unable to countenance his humiliation. Hamza now asked, "How is it that Bakhtak was meted out his punishment?" Amar answered, "Your Honor, this funeral procession carried the bier of Bakhtak's mother, and after reaping the harvest of his deed he is now left to mourn the loss of his kindly mother and reflect on his privation in the quiet of his home!"

Naushervan then offered many excuses to Hamza, and said, "I was myself completely in the dark regarding this deception! Pray do not allow this incident to cloud your heart toward me! The one who hatched this perfidious plan was sent to her rewards." Hamza replied, "I am fully obedient to your commands, and regardless of everything am still faithful to you with all my heart and soul. Pray tell me now when my wedding shall be celebrated, and when I will be afforded an opportunity to set up house." The emperor replied, "It shall come to pass after forty days, and then your heart's desire will bear fruit!"

Upon hearing this, Hamza took his leave and retired to Tal Shad-Kam, but Amar stayed behind. And once the emperor had adjourned the court for the day, Amar solicited Buzurjmehr's help and petitioned on Hamza's behalf that the forty-day delay in the wedding was not agreeable to him, as it was not warranted to defer the auspicious occasion.

The emperor replied, "The dowry is not yet prepared, and we wait for it to be furnished!" Amar said to this, "Your Majesty is the emperor! It is only a matter of Your Majesty ordering it so, and everything is provided for." After some consultation, Buzurjmehr obtained the emperor's consent to hold the wedding ceremony after twenty days, which delighted Amar, and he submitted to the emperor, saying, "O my lord and master! Prithee write a note to this effect to the Sahibqiran so that he is reassured and may begin his preparations for the ceremony." The emperor wrote out a note as a letter of consent, and Amar brought it to Hamza. Reading the note and realizing its import, Hamza was beside himself with joy, and embraced Amar at this show of fidelity and conferred on him a reward of ten thousand gold pieces. He ordered celebrations to begin, and cries of "Congratulations!" and "Salutations!" rose from all corners of the camp.

The emperor embraced Mehr-Nigar upon returning to the palace, and informed her of his consent to Hamza that after twenty days the princess would be wedded to him. Next, the emperor gave an account of all the rogueries Amar had committed during Saqar Ghar Bano's last rites, and listening to Amar's exploits both Empress Mehr-Angez and Princess Mehr-Nigar rolled in laughter.

Now hear of Bakhtak, who smoldered in the fire of envy and whose soul was burnt to a cinder in the blaze of grief when he learned that the emperor had written a letter to Hamza, giving consent to his marriage to Princess Mehr-Nigar after twenty days; that the emperor had committed the thing in writing and would not go back on his word; that five days of that twenty-day period had already elapsed, and only fifteen remained before the wedding would be celebrated, for which preparations were being made on both sides; and that the whole city was ringing with the news of that event.

Even though Bakhtak's burns and his scalded skin were not yet healed, he yet mustered enough strength to present himself before the emperor in order to vent his inconsolable grief. And after they had found privacy, he spoke ardently thus: "I have come to learn that Your Majesty has given Hamza a letter of consent to the effect that his marriage with Princess Mehr-Nigar will be celebrated after twenty days, and the wedding preparations are already under way, and the populace is celebrating the news. Alas and alack, Your Honor disregarded all considerations of constancy! It will not bode well at all to marry Princess Mehr-Nigar with Hamza! The whole world has learned that the Emperor of the Seven Climes was loath to marry his daughter to Hamza, and those who heard it agreed that indeed the emperor could not have given his daughter in marriage to someone who did not speak the same language and who worshipped an invisible God. They saw that the emperor could not possibly have married his daughter into an alien people, an alien religion, and an alien land! But I see Your Highness set upon proceeding with plans for this marriage! What will the whole world say on such a match? How will all those high and low adjudge Your Honor's prestige?"

Naushervan answered, "I could not help but give my consent, even though I was in great anguish myself, as all my strategies have come to naught and none of my plans have come to fruition." Bakhtak replied, "Your Honor need not worry any longer, as I have thought of a most disingenuous and artful scheme!" Naushervan asked, "What plan is it that you have devised now?"

Bakhtak replied, "Tomorrow, when the nobles and the royal attendants assemble in the court, Hamza will also present himself escorted by his companions and associates, as is his wont. I will send some men whose ears and noses have been mutilated, and they will rattle the chain of justice. Then Your Majesty will send for them as per custom, and demand to know their grievance. They will identify themselves as Your Majesty's faithful old servants, and relate that every year they collect the revenue from the Seven Climes and send it to the royal treasury. But this year not only were they kept from collecting a single farthing in revenue, they were also rebuked, and told that the Emperor of the Seven Climes was no longer worthy of receiving land revenues because as a fire worshipper he had shown utter disregard for the name and honor of his forefathers by marrying off his daughter to Hamza—an adherent of the True Faith. And that the monarchs throughout the Seven Climes have declared that should the emperor's son-in-law dare, he can come and collect the revenue himself! These plaintiffs will claim that they were meted out this treatment when they asserted their rights to collect land revenues. When Hamza hears this speech, he will fly into a passion and seek Your Majesty's leave to depart on a campaign against them!" This counsel immensely pleased the emperor and then the villainous Bakhtak took his leave and departed.

In the court the next day, when the emperor ascended the throne to give audience, and the sages and philosophers of the persuasion of Namrud's creed gathered along with his intrepid warriors, and Amir also presented himself and took his seat on the throne of Rustam, someone was heard to rattle the chain of justice. When the noise reached Naushervan's ears, he sent for the petitioners, and called the plaintiffs before him. He soon beheld some men with severed ears and noses enter the court presenting a picture of great distress and with all their senses in complete disarray.

Upon regarding this spectacle, those assembled in the court called out, "Who could have reduced them to this state by severing their extremities at the root?" Then the petitioners gave a complete account of the events, as instructed by Bakhtak, in a most effective manner, whereupon every single hair on Amir Hamza's skin bristled with rage, his Hashimi blood was stirred, and unable to control his fury he avowed, "I swear by the God of Kaaba, that I shall not marry the princess until I have exacted revenge on those recalcitrants!" He ordered Aadi to move the vanguard and the impedimenta of the army toward the lands of the

Seven Climes, and declared that it was proscribed for the army to sup or drink in the city any longer.

Naushervan said, "Oh, Abul-Ala, if such is your desire, then attend first to the matter of your nuptials, and then you may embark on the campaign to punish the rebels." Amir replied, "I, your humble servant, have avowed not even to think about marriage until I have exacted revenue from those rebels! Your Honor should not insist in this matter, but send me off with your prayers and with a glad heart." The emperor said, "If this is the course you are resolved on, leave behind Landhoor or Bahram to attend to the princess's safety in your absence." Amir rejoiced exceedingly on hearing this proposition, and appointed Bahram to remain in attendance at Naushervan's court.

The emperor conferred a robe of honor on Amir, gave him seven epistles addressed to the seven monarchs of the Seven Climes, and gave him injunctions that in making terms with the monarchs, he should use force only as a last resort. The emperor then appointed Qaran Deoband at the head of twelve thousand Sassanid troops to accompany Amir, giving him express orders to obey Amir in all matters and not dither in the least in subordinating to Amir's commands. Amir said to the emperor, "Pray accompany me with some other Sassanid noble, and let Qaran remain in Your Honor's presence, as he is the scion of a illustrious Sassanid house and counts himself among Your Majesty's kin! Moreover, we have crossed paths at times, and it would not bode well for him should he pick a feud with me along the way. For even if I were to forgive him, he would die at the hands of my companions." Then Qaran wrote out a letter of obedience to the effect that if he were guilty of any wrong, he would forfeit his life to Amir without recourse to any appeal. Then Amir said, "I shall forgive you two offenses, but your third offense will not go unpunished!" Amir then took his leave, and retired to Tal Shad-Kam.

Then the emperor wrote out and handed Qaran another set of seven missives addressed to the monarchs of the Seven Climes stating that reasons of expediency made him send Hamza toward their dominions. They must ensure that he is not allowed even to trespass the boundaries of their lands, let alone collect any land revenues. And they must see to it that Hamza is beheaded and his head sent to the court. The emperor also gave seven *mithcals* of the deadliest poison to Qaran, with instructions that he administer it to Hamza at the first opportunity. Then the emperor conferred a robe of honor on Qaran and sent him off.

Qaran presented himself at Hamza's camp, who ordered the march drums to be sounded, and headed toward his destination with his triumph-incarnate host.

Then Amar said to Hamza, "Your love for Mehr-Nigar is only a pretense, and your true love lies in the skirmishes of the battlefield! However, you are your own master and may go wherever you will, passing the days of your life conquering lands, tasting foreign waters, fighting wars, shining in the amphitheaters of battle, and regarding the spectacle of the armies fighting and the champions facing combat together! Yours truly has whiled away a great many days of his life accompanying you in your adventures and overcoming all manners of perils. Now I am headed for Mecca, and shall pray for you there. If you would like to send a letter for your honorable father, I would most gladly carry it for you."

Then Hamza wrote out a letter to his father, and gave it to Amar, who departed for Mecca.

• • •

All praise is merited for God alone, through Whose agency Book One came to an end and reached its culmination with facility. Should it be the will of Allah (Whose aid we solicit and in Whom we trust!), the second book shall detail the bravery and the munificence of Amir Hamza (a thing to try the limits of the pen's expression!), the departure of the Sahibqiran (the world conqueror, Uncle to the Most Holy Prophet of God, the Last Prophet of the Times—upon whom be peace!) toward the Seven Climes with his companions, and the adventures that befell them.

Completed this day, Thursday, dated the 29th day of the holy month of Moharram, Anno Hegirae 1288, corresponding to the 20th day of April, Anno Domini 1870.[229]

BOOK TWO

The Second Book of the Dastan *of the Sahibqiran,*
Amir Hamza bin Abdul Muttalib,
and of His Departure for Mount Qaf

The imperious pen departs to conquer the dominions of rhetoric, girding itself to trek the blank stretches of paper, and delivers the account of Amir's journey, painting a host of new episodes and choice encounters before the mind's eye.

Amir had put seven days' journey under his belt after embarking on his campaign to the Seven Climes, when Qaran Deoband pulled up his steed at a forked path. Upon Amir asking his reason for stopping, Qaran replied, "From here two roads lead to the Seven Climes. The first one is lengthy and full of peril, and if we were to march on it without rest it would take us at least a month before we arrived at our destination. The other road is shorter and would get us there within a week or ten days' time, but while there is no hazard to be met on the way, we shall not find any water for three days, and the dread of dying from thirst would be our constant companion." Amir said, "Store enough water in the water bags to last three days, so we do not have to take the longer route and inconvenience the army with an arduous trek!"

The army loaded enough water on the camels to last three days, and set out upon the shorter route. Not a single drop remained in the water skins, goatskins, or water bags after three days had passed, and on the fourth day the whole army suffered from severe thirst, and Amir himself felt as if his tongue was covered with thorns. Although they searched their surroundings, they found no river, spring, lake, pool, or tarn.

Amir asked Qaran, "Where is the water source you said we would find on the fourth day? This whole situation presents an ominous picture."

Qaran replied, "Heaven forfend that any misgiving should enter your heart! I had passed this way twelve years ago and it seems that the springs, rivers, and rivulets have silted up in the interim, and neither pond, spring, nor pool has survived. However, I have in my flask enough water to quench your thirst. You only have to say the word and it will be yours!"

Amir replied, "Very well, then! I am beside myself with thirst!"

Qaran poisoned the water and offered it to Amir, who took the goblet in his hand and said to himself, *It would be most unbecoming if I were to quench my thirst while a friend like Landhoor remained thirsty.* He handed the goblet to Landhoor and said, "I am a denizen of Arabia and have much greater resilience against thirst compared to you who hail from a clime where water is plentiful and abundantly found. You are ill-equipped to bear the pains of thirst indeed. Drink this and afford some solace to your mouth and lips!"

Khusrau thought, *It would be contrary to all the norms of camaraderie if I were to quench my thirst while Amir remained thirsty, and it would reflect most ignobly on me to guzzle down this water, depriving Amir of his drink!* Thus Landhoor did not drink it and offered it instead to Aadi who had been struck silent, with his mouth dried of all moisture and his tongue parched from the violence of his thirst.

Aadi reasoned that drinking the draught of water would be like throwing oil on a fire, and would only make the thirst worse. He offered the goblet to Muqbil, and said, "This water is enough to quench your thirst. Drink it and moisten your dry tongue!" Muqbil deemed it against all considerations of fidelity that Amir should remain dry-lipped while others satiated themselves and drank up that water. Thus the goblet passed from hand to hand without anyone drinking it.

In the end, all of them handed the goblet back to Amir and said to him, "We cannot see you suffer from thirst! It would be unseemly for us to drink without your drinking first." Nobody consented to Amir's demand that one of them should drink it.

OF THE MYSTERIOUS VOICE ENJOINING AMIR FROM DRINKING, AND OF AMAR KEEPING HAMZA FROM IMBIBING THE POISONED WATER BY PROPHET KHIZR'S INJUNCTIONS

Divers of the sea of traditions extract treasures of discourse from the oyster of imagination, and bear forth the luminous offering of the pearls of narrative thus, telling that Amar was on his way to Mecca when he beheld an old man in the distance. He considered that the journey would pass amiably if they were to strike up a conversation together and, moreover, he would find some pleasant company to occupy himself on the way. When Amar tried to catch up with the old man, he was unable to bridge the distance between them. Even when Amar leapt, gamboled, and sped faster, he remained as far behind the man as before. After the sweat from his brow flowed down to reach his heels from the effort, Amar began importuning and beseeching the man in God's name, "O venerated sir! I ask you in the name of your faith and creed to wait for me. Do not take a step forward or move another pace!"

The moment that old man stopped Amar saw that he was the holy Khizr, and upon finding him there Amar asked him the reason for his haste. Khizr replied, "O Amar! At this moment Hamza is thirsty and Qaran has offered him a goblet of water mixed with a deadly poison. The cup is still in Hamza's hands. Rush and take it from him and throw it on the ground. Hasten forth, crying, 'Drink it not! Drink it not!' The True Protector shall cause your words to be carried to Hamza's hearing, and shall save his life from that tyrant's hands!" Amar hurried from there in a state of great despair, crying out every step of his way: "Beware! Drink it not! Here I come! Drink it not! Here I come!"

Hamza had raised the goblet to his lips when his ears heard a voice calling out, "Drink it not! Drink it not!" He lowered the goblet and looked around to see who stopped him from drinking. When he could not see the one who forbade him, he made to imbibe the drink and heard the same words: Someone warned him again in the same manner. Greatly perplexed, Amir looked around to see who it was who enjoined him from drinking but did not see the one who issued the call or the one who warned him. He raised the goblet again a third time and the same voice again reached his ears, calling, "Drink it not! Drink it not!"

Amir now put away the goblet and stared wonder-struck, thinking the phenomenon a veritable marvel of God, and contemplating who might be keeping him from drinking every time he attempted to. In short, Amir was stupefied and unable to decide whether he should drink the water or throw it away. He was still caught in this bewilderment when a dust cloud rose on the horizon, and Amar appeared from it rushing forth like a storm, shouting, "Drink it not! Drink it not!" The moment Amar reached Amir Hamza's side, he took the goblet from his hand and smashed it to the ground. Wherever the water splashed, the earth bubbled and broke open. At beholding this sight, the faces of the onlookers were drained of all blood in horror. A drop had also splashed on Amir's face and it penetrated his skin and bones to reach through his body and cause a boil on his back. Amar quickly rubbed the Shah Mohra and applied it on the sore, which counteracted the poison's effect and healed the wound completely.

Qaran ran with all haste toward his army when he saw that his secret had been exposed. He had already instructed them to stand at the ready. Immediately, that twelve thousand-strong host fell upon Hamza's camp. Qaran aimed his lance at Landhoor's chaste chest. Wrenching the lance from his hand, Landhoor struck a blow with its shaft and sent Qaran rolling in the dust. Without loss of time, the rest of Qaran's troops removed that coward from the scene, carrying him off to the forest.

Amar took Hamza's army to a spring whose location the holy Khizr had disclosed to him, where he quenched his thirst and drank to his heart's content along with the rest of the soldiers. Amir and the Landhoor embraced Amar there with gratitude. Then Amir said, "Your voice saved my life today. Nothing else remained between me and my death, and I would have certainly departed from the world. Now we must look for a way to exit from this arid valley, and somehow find a route that will lead us safely to our destination."

Amar left the army behind and went into a nearby village, where its people ran from his sight and took all manner of perilous risks trying to flee from him. Amar chased and caught hold of one of them and, after comforting him, asked, "What is the reason for this mad flight?" The man replied, "A host of troops descended on our town a few days ago, took us captive, and appropriated our riches. They put us to great hardship and torment, and also carried away several of our people as slaves. The memory of that terror made all of us flee to save our lives at your sight!"

Amar offered him many words of consolation and comfort, and said, "It is not our wont to behave in such a manner nor is it our practice to show injustice and cruelty to anyone. Our leader is a most kind and compassionate man. You stand to profit from his friendship, and he may yet bring cheer to your people. Go with confidence to your people to ask them to return, and admonish them for this display of unwarranted fear."

The man went and comforted and reassured the others and led them before Amar, who took them to Amir Hamza and had their needs liberally provided for. Then Amir asked the man, "Tell us, how far does this forest extend and how much farther along do we have to go before we discover a source of potable water? Tell us also, what is the name of the first land of the Seven Climes, and who rules over it?"

That man answered, "This forest goes on for twelve *kos*. After you have emerged from the forest you will come upon a sweet-water ravine. The first city lies a day's journey from there. It is known as Antabia and the name of its governor is Haam. Beside Antabia is the city of Antaqia, which is joined on its border by another city, Antakia. Haam's younger brother, Mehd Zarrin Kamar, rules over Antaqia, and their youngest brother, Saam, is the ruler of Antakia. All three brothers are most courageous and valiant and each has ten thousand troops under his command. Should you wish it, I would willingly lead you along your way there and see you to safety!"

Amir richly rewarded him, and they charted their way out of that place with the man as their guide. After they had exited the forest and reached the banks of the ravine they discovered that its water had turned green. Amir asked the guide, "Has this water recently turned green or did it always have this coloration?" He replied, "Once the clarity of this water was such that the luster of a pearl would have faded before it and the fountainhead of the sun's brilliance would have appeared dark in comparison. It seems that someone has contaminated it with poison grass which has caused this change in its properties and color, and now this water has become a deadly poison itself and is no longer potable!"

Amar said to Hamza, "It is the work of that same despicable wretch who has no modicum of shame left in him!" Their army then dug out several wells, and quenched their thirst and filled up their leather bags with this water as a precautionary measure. The next day they arrived at their destination, and pitched their tents near the fort of Antabia.

———

Now hear of Qaran, that viper who poisoned all the ravines and wells in Amir's path with poison grass. He presented himself before Haam, gave him Naushervan's letter, and said, "Hamza, who worships an invisible God, is headed this way and brings his companions and faithful along. If he asks you for tribute, you should refuse it and instead kill both Hamza and Landhoor or take them captive in any manner you see fit. No tribute will be levied on you for three years as a reward for producing their heads, and the emperor shall richly reward you for this service besides." Qaran later communicated the same message to Saam and Mehd Zarrin Kamar, and then marched away with his troops.

When Haam saw that his own ten thousand troops would be unable to overcome Hamza's numerous host, and he stood no chance to defeat and triumph over Hamza's army, he sent a communiqué to his brothers asking them to join him urgently for deliberations, and hurry to his aid with their forces. He informed them that Amir Hamza had brought a large army, and if he took his fort by storm, the forts of his brothers would not stand for long, and then there would be none left in the area to challenge Hamza's power.

Upon receiving their brother's letter, Saam and Mehd Zarrin Kamar both arrived at Haam's fort with their armies to hold counsel together. Saam proposed that they make a night raid on Hamza's camp as he had a vast army with him. Mehd Zarrin Kamar said, "Night raids are the choice of pusillanimous cowards! We should instead draw battle arrays and give fight with the thirty thousand troops at our command!"

Their elder brother Haam said, "To my ears both these suggestions sound impracticable. I propose that we call on Hamza with mementos and gifts. Should he show us due regard, we must swear allegiance to him and pay the tribute gladly. The option to fight would remain available to us, and we could decide upon the desired course once we return to our fort. This is by far the most preferable line of action.

"It would be little wonder if Hamza showed us favor and received us nobly in accordance with the traditions of hospitality. Kings and illustrious men comprise his entourage, and Hamza himself is inebriated with the heady wine of courage. The renown of his valor, benevolence, and fortitude has reached lands and cities far and wide. Brave men always venerate others who are brave, and show honor and esteem to those who are valiant. Hamza's bravery is also manifest in the fact that the Emperor of the Seven Climes found himself helpless before it, and wrote to us to overpower and kill him and behead him at his behest. The emperor suggested that we do so by treachery and deceit, which is plainly the way of cowards and a course not in the least commensurate with our dignity!"

Saam and Mehd Zarrin Kamar found Haam's counsel to their liking and put off any plans of resistance. They resolved instead to make peace with Hamza. The following day they presented themselves in Amir Hamza's court carrying mementos and gifts, and ennobled themselves with his audience.

OF HAAM, SAAM, AND MEHD ZARRIN KAMAR
CONVERTING TO THE TRUE FAITH AND SWEARING
ALLEGIANCE TO AMIR, AND OF THEIR PAYING THE
TRIBUTE AND BECOMING HIS FOLLOWERS

The charging pen gallops forth in the domains of composition, and thus recounts with great ardor Amir's journeys through the stations and stages. Amir Hamza received the three brothers in the finest traditions of hospitality. He arranged festivities in their honor for three continuous days and attended to their comfort and pleasure in all ways. When he saw that they had been won over by his excellent manners, he counseled them with great love and affection, thus: "It is a wonder that wise and courageous men such as yourselves should choose to worship fire instead of the True God, and scatter your devotions on an idol devoid of omnipotence—an idol carved by human hands that does not even have the power of mobility!"

Because the three brothers were endowed with intelligence, they recited the Act of Faith and converted to the True Faith with sincere hearts. They renounced their infidel ways and publicly exalted themselves by professing the True Faith. Amir conferred a robe of honor on each of them and said, "Now the three of you are my brothers, and if your treasury is empty by any chance, I shall make good on the payment of your tribute to the emperor from my own, and there will be no mention between us of any tribute or levy of even a farthing!" They answered him, "By virtue of your grace our treasuries are full, and because your pleasure is paramount to us, we shall also, should you so command, remit the advance tribute for the next few years!" Amir Hamza said, "It is not necessary to make advance payment of the tribute. Only the rightful amount should be remitted, and the keepers of the tributary office and the treasury will issue the receipts."

Then Haam and his brothers showed Amir the letters that Qaran had brought them. At first, Amir became dispirited upon reading them, but then, thinking that perhaps the letters had been forged by Qaran, he did not allow them to cloud the mirror of his heart, and drew no conclusions.

He said to the brothers, "Tell me what the name of the land we shall come upon next is, who its ruler is, and how long a journey will take us there. Tell us, too, about the pleasant and captivating stations on the way." Haam replied, "Fifteen days' journey will bring you to Alania, whose ruler goes by the name of Anis Shah. He is a most noble-minded and august man!"

Amir then said to the brothers, "Adieu now! You may return to your affairs of state while I head for Alania. I shall soon return from there after conquering it by the grace of God!" They replied, "We have sworn ourselves into your slavery now! Even if you were to release us from this bond, we would not step outside the bounds of your service. Pray accept our levy and direct the keeper of treasury to issue the receipt. Then grant us leave to be your riding companions so that we may ennoble ourselves in your august service!"

Amir Hamza tried everything in his power to dissuade them from embarking on their chosen course, but they would not back down. After remitting payment to Amir's treasury and appointing their deputies to look after the affairs of state in their absence, all three brothers joined Amir's entourage.

When the fort of Alania was two *kos* away, the group happened upon a most pleasant and scenic stretch of land. Amir dismounted there and the army pitched its tents. When Anis Shah learned of their arrival, he drew battle arrays with the intention to skirmish with them. Then he reasoned that he would be wiped out of existence by an encounter with Amir's powerful force. He dismounted his steed and went and kissed Amir's stirrup, and recited the Act of Faith and converted to the True Faith in fear for his life.

Amir welcomed him into his camp and lavished all manner of kindnesses and preferences upon him. The knave remained in Amir's presence for several days, fawning on Amir and flattering him. Finding the opportunity one day, he said to Amir, "Your slave has constructed a most pleasant and agreeable bathhouse. I desire that you visit it some day and divest yourself of both the fatigue of your journey and your bodily pollutions." Amir Hamza tried to evade the subject but could not prevail against Anis Shah's insistence and, finally acquiescing to his wishes, paid him a visit.

That bath attendant's child (deserving to be burnt!) had constructed a bathhouse of such marvelous design that whoever set eyes on it was immediately taken with the desire to bathe there, whether or not the person was in need of doing so. The roof was raised on iron pillars and suspended by a contraption[?] with four chains minded by four slaves. If they let go of the chains the roof collapsed on the bathers below—that bath becoming their last—and they were buried underneath without even a winding-sheet. That day Anis Shah appointed four sturdy Nubian slaves to mind the chains and instructed them that the moment he struck the drum and they heard its sound, they should let go of the chains and flee. Amir Hamza had brought Landhoor, Muqbil, and others along with him and they occupied themselves with bathing. Amir invited Amar and Aadi to join, but they would not consent to set foot in the bathhouse.

It suddenly occurred to Amar to investigate the bathhouse from the inside to explore all its novelties. He entered by the back door disguised as an old man. The Nubians took pity on him and called out, "Run for your dear life, old man! We will let go of the chains at the sound of the drum and then, as the saying goes, the weevils will be ground in the mill with the wheat, and we will have your innocent blood on our necks!"

Upon hearing these words Amar immediately retraced his steps and, arriving at the gate of the bathhouse, communicated the whole story to Amir Hamza in the secret language of *ayyars*. Amir Hamza stepped outside, locked the door of his enclosure, and got dressed. Anis Shah said, "There is an adjacent private chamber where I have laid out fruit both fresh and dried for Your Honor!" Amir replied, "Pray arrange for everyone to be served. I shall be there presently with my companions. Then we will do justice to those delicacies and enjoy your hospitality."

The moment Anis Shah set foot into that private chamber, Amar struck the drum with the mallet with all his might, whereupon the Nubian slaves let go of the chains. The roof of the bathhouse collapsed on Anis Shah. He was released from the worries of the sensory world, and hastened on his way to Hell even as his body became cold. And thus Anis Shah landed in the pit he had dug with his own hands.

Hamza greatly extolled Amar's wisdom. He converted Anis Shah's underage son along with his whole army to the True Faith and gave him to the tutelage of Mehd Zarrin Kamar so that he might educate him and raise him in the finest traditions, leaving nothing to chance.

The commanders of Anis Shah's army then disclosed that Qaran had brought a note from Naushervan ordering the deaths of Hamza and King

Landhoor. After delivering the letter that perjurer had left for Aleppo, to
the kingdom of Hadees Shah. Upon hearing this, Amir's heart filled with
rage and he dispatched the advance camp toward Aleppo the same day.

———

Now hear of that unsurpassable Qaran. Upon arriving in Aleppo the pre-
varicator made much sweet prattle with Hadees Shah. Qaran gave him
the emperor's note and told him that Naushervan had also conveyed the
verbal message that he would be forever indebted to the one who would
finish off both Hamza and Landhoor, and would never be able to recompense him fully for that service. Thus Qaran filled up Hadees Shah's ears
with all manner of gossip—some true, some fabricated—and after poisoning his mind sufficiently toward Hamza, prepared to depart for
Greece.

Hadees Shah said to him, "Stay a while! Do not leave for Greece yet.
Wait and see how I kill Hamza before your eyes and relieve that rebel's
neck of the burden of his head!" Qaran replied, "It is mere wishful thinking that you will conquer Hamza in the battlefield and hand him a resounding defeat. Hamza is not one to be laid low by your hand, nor will
his army be routed by your troops!"

Hadees Shah replied, "If you advise against open combat, I will have
a pit filled with pointed arms and sharp-edged weapons dug in the arena.
I will play horse-shinty with Hamza and lead him to it, and put paid to
his existence before long."

Qaran replied, "Indeed this is a much preferable strategy, and one
certain to yield results!"

———

When Amir's army arrived near Aleppo, Hadees Shah came to them with
gifts and mementos and made an offering of three years' land revenue to
Amir. He willingly recited the Act of Faith, and to all appearances acted
out the rituals of obedience and allegiance. Amir Hamza arranged a feast
in his honor, accorded him great distinction and preference, and conferred a costly robe of honor upon him. For a few days Hadees Shah
made great blandishments and fawned upon Amir.

One day Hadees Shah said, "This slave had come to learn that you
hold your own in the arts and crafts of the war. I nurse a desire in my
heart to match my talent with yours. My good luck ordained that you set
foot in these parts, causing my slumbering fortunes to awaken. This slave

is now desirous to be initiated in the finer points of the game of horse-shinty and to excel in this sport as a sacrifice of Your Honor!" Amir Hamza replied, "I am at your command."

The next morning Hadees Shah addressed his troops and gave them these stern orders: "Disguise the pit by skillfully covering its mouth with grass so that nobody will harbor the least suspicion that a pit or a moat has been dug there. The moment Hamza falls into it, fall upon the armies of the True Faith and put them to the sword and vanquish them. I grant you pillage and shall confer the spoils of war on you, whole and entire!"

When the horse-shintier of the heavens bore away the ball of the moon and the world-illuminating sun descended on Earth sporting its lance of rays, Hadees Shah and Amir Hamza stepped from either side into the arena, and the nobles and peers settled down to watch the contest. Hadees Shah kissed Amir's stirrup and said, "Here is the ball and here the field!" Amir replied, "My preceptor instructed me against taking the lead in any matter. You should strike the ball first and then I shall handle the stick next and show you what I have to display!" Hadees Shah made a bow and spurred his steed.

When he had advanced by a distance of a bow shot, Amir grabbed his stick and urged his horse onward. Hadees Shah was left behind, and Amir went forward toward the pit without entertaining the least suspicion of that knave's treachery. Amir's horse, Siyah Qitas, vacillated at approaching the pit whereupon Amir gave him a cut with Prophet Daud's lash. While the horse did its best to clear the chasm it could not fully escape it, and its hind legs landed on the inner walls of the pit. Amir exited the saddle and, holding the reins and clucking his tongue, brought the horse out. Once Siyah Qitas had cleared the moat, Amir leapt back into the saddle. Suddenly Amir found himself face-to-face with Qaran, who was standing close by keeping an eye on things. At the sight of Amir, Qaran fled toward the nearby mountain range and Amir gave him pursuit.

Thinking that the waters of death had closed over Amir Hamza in the pit, Hadees Shah fell upon the armies of the True Faith with his twenty thousand troops, and many a follower of the True Faith met martyrdom at the hand of the infidels. In the end, however, Hadees Shah died at Landhoor's hand, and his army took flight.

When Landhoor could not find Amir he became worried and said to Amar, "We should search for Amir and look for our lost Yusuf!" Thereupon Amar set out following the tracks made by Siyah Qitas.

Qaran reached a field of melons and, taking a melon from the field's farmer and lacing it with poison, addressed him thus: "Make an offering of this melon to the rider who comes behind me, and accept what he gives you in return! If he eats it, I will give you a hundred gold pieces as a reward and will make it well worth your while if my desired end is achieved!" The wily Qaran then headed for the mountain pass and waited there to reap the harvest of his seditious deeds.

When Amir reached the field in pursuit of him, the farmer made him the offering of the melon. Amir accepted it and asked him, "A rider passed this way before me. Which direction did he take?" The man replied, "He went toward the mountain pass over there, but the path offers no refuge to the one who travels there as a ferocious lion stalks those parts and no human being has the gall to confront the lion and escape with his life!"

As he was extremely parched, Amir made to eat the melon and quench his thirst. The farmer stopped him and submitted himself before him with folded arms, saying, "O youth! Although I stand to gain a hundred gold pieces from it, yet I cannot bear to see the least harm or disadvantage befall you, as I have never set eyes on a more beautiful or handsome youth! That first rider laced this melon with something, and I am certain that it was some kind of poison. He told me to feed it to the one who comes following him, and he would give me a hundred gold pieces as a reward if you died through this device!" Amir threw the melon from his hands, and conferred jewels worth a thousand gold pieces on the farmer. Then he spurred his horse toward the mountain pass.

He had hardly entered the pass when a lion leapt at him with a mighty roar. Amir dealt him a blow of his sword and the beast fell in two parts to the ground. When Amir entered the mountain pass he saw Qaran hiding behind a rock, lying motionless without so much as breathing. Amir was of a mind to strike him with his dagger and cut off the rogue's neck when Qaran said, "O Hamza! If you spare my life I will confer three things on you!" Amir Hamza answered, "Give me whatever you have to offer and thus take out another short lease on your life!" Qaran produced a dagger from his belt and presented it to Amir. He said, "This dagger belonged to Tahmuras Deoband and I came into its possession after great effort and hardship!" Then he took off his armband, which sported twelve carbuncles, each weighing three *mithcals*. After handing Hamza these objects, Qaran said, "The third object is kept in a cavern in this mountain. Come, let me lead you to it and make a present of it to you as well, since it is your destiny to claim it!"

Amar arrived there in the meanwhile. After securing Qaran's hands, Hamza delivered him to Amar and said, "See what treasure it is that he was going to divulge, or if it was one of his fibs. If he has spoken the truth, you may take the treasure, and if he proves false deal with him as he deserves!" Amar bound a rope around Qaran and led him out of the pass with his hands tied behind his back. As Qaran tried to force the knots to free his hands and escape from Amar's clutches, Amar said to him, "Why do you exert yourself needlessly? Lead me to the treasure and I shall plead on your behalf to Hamza and intercede in your favor. You will surely be freed!" Qaran replied, "I mentioned the treasure only to purchase more time. However, if you were to set me free I would confer two hundred thousand *tomans* on you when I reach Ctesiphon!"

Amar answered, "O tyrant! I would never allow you to escape with your life! You wasted no time in demonstrating your animosity and hostility toward Amir and myself at every opportunity! Now that you are in my power, do you expect me to let you go free? Do you judge me to be such a blundering fool?" Amar drew out his dagger and killed Qaran then and there. Afterward, Amar went before Amir Hamza and after giving a detailed account, said, "O Amir, there was no treasure to speak of! That liar tried to cheat his death by inveigling us with the mention of treasure, and by buying himself more time with that ruse. When he was unable to deceive me, he tried to break loose and escape, whereupon I inflicted on him a death deserved by a cur like him!" Amir rejoiced greatly and said, "O Amar! You did well indeed by eradicating that fountainhead of sedition and strife!"

Of Amir Marching on Greece, and of His Betrothing His Heart-Ravishingly Beloved Naheed Maryam

The beautifiers of discourse adorn their rhetoric with the ornament of narrative, and evoke in multitudinous new ways the beauty of the story. With Amir's heart filled with pleasure from his triumph, he returned to the fort of Aleppo and indulged in festivities and celebrations for seven days. He sent Muqbil Vafadar to Naushervan's court with the tribute from the five lands, along with a missive describing events with Qaran and other incidents. Then he marched toward Greece and, having arrived at the frontiers of that land in a few days, pitched his tents.

Faridun Shah, the potentate of Greece, had already come to learn of Hamza's exploits through his chroniclers' reports, and upon hearing of Amir's arrival he gathered together a worthy offering and came forth with his brothers to meet him. At the meeting, which took place midway between Amir's camp and Faridun Shah's dominion, Faridun Shah made his offering to Amir. He entered Amir's service and exalted himself by kissing Amir's feet with pious zeal. He also recited the Act of Faith with a sincere heart, and ennobled himself by converting to the True Faith along with his brothers. Amir was much delighted by his worthy demeanor and disposition. He conferred sumptuous robes of honor on Faridun Shah and his brothers, and proclaimed a period of festivities, so that the whole camp indulged in celebrations and conviviality for several days.

One day Faridun Shah found a suitable occasion and said to Amir Hamza, "O Amir! I am faced with three challenges, each of which I find most daunting! Indeed they are such mammoth tasks that they are beyond the scope of ordinary mortals and well-nigh impossible! If you were to help resolve them, it would be a supreme token of indulgence from you toward this slave!" Amir said, "What are these challenges? I would like you to give me an account of them." He replied, "The first is posed by a dragon who has haunted these parts for some years and on whose account whole lands have been depopulated, causing the loss of hundreds of thousand of rupees! The second challenge is Shankavah, a pitch-faced Nubian, who has built a castle on a mountaintop several *farsangs* from the fortifications of my city and who raids the surrounding area every hundredth day, putting thousands of people to the sword. Once these two challenges have been resolved, I shall tell you the details of the third, and will beseech you to bring that to a happy resolution as well!"

Amir answered, "I shall not rest now until I have killed the dragon! Accompany me in the morning, and lead me to the dragon's lair. Then you may stand aside and witness what unfolds." Landhoor said, "It would not become Your Honor's eminence to challenge the pitch-faced Shankavah! Pray order me to go finish him off in a trice and produce his rebellious head to you!" Amir answered, "If it is the will of God, I shall go to slay the dragon tomorrow while you march out to rout the black-faced tyrant and dispatch him to the Erebus of Hell!"

When the pitch-skinned dark night was laid low by the Turk of the bright morn, and the Emperor Sun routed the armies of the stars, the Sahibqiran sallied forth to kill the dragon, taking along Faridun Shah and some of his devoted followers and faithful comrades. Landhoor marched against Shankavah with Faridun Shah's brother, Asif.

Three *farsangs* from the dragon's lair, Faridun Shah dismounted his horse and said to Amir Hamza, "Pray witness that there is no sign of vegetation left except for some charred stumps and branches. The whole expanse of the mountain and the forest has been scorched! When that abominable creature awakens from his slumber and exhales, the tongue of flame reaches as far as this spot from his hiss. At present he is blissfully asleep, otherwise, even a bird of the air or a beast of land—let alone a human being—could not have approached this far or dared to come this close!"

Amir also dismounted and, taking Amar and Faridun Shah with him, went toward the dragon's lair. When they approached, they beheld a dark hillock and upon closer inspection discovered it to be the dragon himself. Amir said, "It is contrary to the traditions of chivalry to kill an enemy in his sleep, let alone a despicable worm!" He broke the dragon's sleep with a loud cry, and the dragon raised his head, which was the size of a Palmyra palm. Seeing Amir there, the beast rushed hissing and charging at him. Amir took out his bow and let fly a two-pronged arrow at the dragon's eyes, which soon became the arrowhead's nest. As the dragon pounded his head against the ground in agony, Amir stepped close and dealt him a blow of his dragon-slaying sword so that one hillock became two, and all signs of life departed the monster. Faridun Shah rushed forward and kissed Amir's hands and arms profusely, and by performing the ritualistic act of circling seven times around Amir, offered his own life as a sacrifice for Amir's.[1]

Amir then returned to the saddle and headed back. The moment he entered the fortifications of the city, he saw Landhoor arrive there bearing Shankavah's head and treasure. After he had made an offering of it to Amir, Faridun Shah scattered all of the riches and jewels as the sacrifice for Amir Hamza and Landhoor's lives and arranged for an assembly of revelry, where they all remained occupied with festivities and celebrations for a long time.

Toward the end of the night, when the revelries were at their height, Faridun Shah said to Amir, "Two of my troubles have ended as the result of Your Honor setting his auspicious foot here. Those great scourges have been warded off now. My third petition is that Your Honor take your slave's daughter as his handmaiden and make her an attendant in your harem, so that I may gain eminence among my peers, and it may strike fear and terror in the heart of my enemies!" The Sahibqiran replied, "This is a most difficult proposition, and I shall be unable to agree to it. The idea is not feasible because I promised Princess Mehr-Nigar that until I have married her I will never have eyes for another woman, even if her beauty be equal to the sun!"

Faridun Shah was thwarted in his plan. After he found privacy, he said to his brother, Asif, "I very much wish that I had never approached Amir with the proposal to wed my daughter, and had saved myself the humiliation and disgrace of his rejection. Now the whole world will come to learn that Amir refused Faridun Shah's daughter's hand because he deemed the king unworthy of such an alliance. They will think that to be the real reason he did not betroth my daughter. Death would be a far better prospect than a life such as mine!"

Having said this, Faridun Shah made to disembowel himself with his dagger and seek an exit through the door of violent death, but his brother stopped his hand and said, "The solution of such issues must be sought in stratagem. Send for Amar and I will see to it that Naheed Maryam is married to Amir Hamza. I will ensure that your end is achieved, and humiliation and disgrace are meted out to your enemies!"

Faridun Shah sent for Amar and seated him by his side. He showed Amar much favor and honor, and after making him an offering of five thousand gold pieces, said, "O Khvaja! You are as much a guardian of my honor as God Himself! In God's name pray find some way to resolve my problem, and have the Sahibqiran marry my daughter. After their betrothal I promise to make you a further offering of ten thousand gold pieces! Otherwise, I will be unable to show my face among my peers, and the only recourse left to me will be to eat poison or put an end to my life by disemboweling myself!"

Amar offered him many words of consolation and said, "This should not prove such a daunting task! I shall see to it that the betrothal takes place before the day is past. Have no worries in this regard, and begin the preparations for the wedding privately." Amar took the gold pieces and returned to his camp and when privacy was arranged, he broached the subject of Naheed Maryam's beauty and fair looks with Amir and planted the seed of desire in Hamza's heart.

Amir said, "O Khvaja, I would readily marry Faridun Shah's daughter, but how would I show my face to Princess Mehr-Nigar afterward? I gave her my word that until I had taken her as my lawful wife I would consider even a *peri* a monstrous beast!" Amar replied, "Sahibqiran, what has come over you? When did men ever hold true to their word in such matters? They are known to go back on their word after making far greater promises to women! How can the Lord of the Auspicious Planetary Conjunction, the master of crown and writ, and a receiver of tributes, repress his desire and devote it singularly to Mehr-Nigar's person alone? Do you not recall the lover's faith in the dictum, 'When a woman closes her door another opens hers'? What of the spectator's belief, 'When one spectacle ends another begins'? Pledge your troth to Naheed Maryam freely and take your pleasure of her. Leave it to me to deal with Princess Mehr-Nigar. If she reproaches you later, tell her that you did it at my bidding. Then it will be my responsibility to bring her around!"

At Amar's counseling and advice, Amir at last assented to betroth Naheed Maryam on the condition that he would not consummate their marriage until he had first married Princess Mehr-Nigar. Faridun Shah gladly consented to that condition and was greatly beholden to Amar. To cut a long story short, that very day Naheed Maryam's limbs were rubbed with oil,[2] and wedding preparations began.

In addition to the promised ten thousand gold pieces, Faridun Shah conferred a most sumptuous robe of honor on Amar along with priceless gems and said to him, "O Khvaja! You have won my heart into your service. You will receive the tokens of my indebtedness from time to time." The ever-greedy Amar offered words of comfort to Faridun Shah and from there went to Hamza. He sang such praises of Naheed Maryam's beauty to him that Amir's desire was fully aroused.

On the eve of the day that henna was applied to Naheed Maryam's hands,[3] Amir pledged his troth to her, and for the length of a fortnight remained in his harem occupied with the exercise of nuptial pleasures, while the festivities continued without. On the sixteenth day he conferred on Naheed Maryam one of the twelve carbuncles Qaran had presented to him. Afterward, Amir came out of the harem affording great joy to his devotees who all this while had not had an opportunity to ennoble themselves by kissing his feet. Amir sent Landhoor and Amar with the tribute from the five lands and the goods and chattels of Shankavah to Naushervan, and ordered his advance camp to move toward Egypt.

OF AMIR'S MARCHING TO CONQUER EGYPT AND OF THE RULER OF EGYPT TAKING HIM PRISONER BY DECEIT

The historians of kingdoms and metropolises, and the account bearers of provinces and cities report that, after traversing many *farsangs* and miles, King Landhoor bin Saadan approached Ctesiphon, and Naushervan sent many a Sassanid noble to welcome him. During the audience Naushervan showed him many preferences and a multitude of favors, and inquired at length about the Sahibqiran's welfare.

In accordance with royal etiquette, after some time had passed, Landhoor made an offering to the emperor of the gold received in tribute and presented him with the letter and gifts sent by the Sahibqiran. He narrated all the adventures that had befallen them on the way, including the villainies perpetrated by Qaran and Hadees Shah, and said, "Amir has declared that if the Emperor of the Seven Climes were to bid him to jump into fire, he would gladly rush in like one does into a flower garden, without offering the least ruse or excuse. Indeed the ideals of nobility ordain that the greatest honor is laying down one's life in the service of one's master. It is beneath all considerations of nobility for a man to allow his heart to become clouded if his benefactor becomes less indulgent—provided the situation does not compromise one's honor and dignity!"

The king had the gold tribute removed to the royal treasury and conferred two luxurious robes of honor upon Amar and Landhoor. He ordered them to remain in daily attendance at the court and wait upon him as before. Then, while Landhoor took himself to his camp at Tal Shad-Kam, Amar headed for the gates of the royal palace. Upon Amar's announcing himself Queen Mehr-Angez immediately sent for him, and inquired after the Sahibqiran's welfare. Amar presented Amir Hamza's letter to her and after narrating exactly all that he had witnessed, next called upon Princess Mehr-Nigar. He gave her Amir's letter of fond remembrance and told her all the adventures that had befallen them during the journey.

Amar then said to her, "O Princess! The Sahibqiran thinks of aught else but you. Every breath that he takes revives your memory in his mind!" The princess replied, "Khvaja! The night of parting and the day of separation weigh so heavily upon my soul that from the burden that it was before, my life has become a veritable curse!

My day passeth occupied in your thoughts,
And every night in my sleep I dream of your face.

"O God! Thou art the Gatherer of the Separated! Rejoin me with Hamza or else ordain death for me so that I may be saved this anguish!" She then spoke these lines:

Separation from Hamza has brought me to the brink of death,
My soul oft escapes my lips from its abode in my heart;
Death would be like a new lease on life for one in my state,
From the jail of grief it shall bring me release.

Amar replied, "Princess, you have shown exemplary patience thus far. Hold on a while longer, and do not lose your poise and equanimity. None but the Almighty God shielded Amir from calamities, and freed him from the power of a despot. By the decree of the same Omnipotent God the day will come when you shall be blissfully reunited with Hamza. Only the tribute from Egypt remains to be collected. I am fully confident that the Sahibqiran will have successfully exacted it by now. Indeed it would be small wonder if he was not already on his way here, exultant and triumphant, returning in complete safety to you!"

In short, Amar reassured Mehr-Nigar with words of comfort, and took his leave and arrived at Tal Shad-Kam. There Amar called on Bahram Gurd and Muqbil Vafadar, and they held a lengthy and pleasant meeting. They arranged a festive assembly in honor of Amar and Landhoor, and indulged themselves in conviviality. After they had finished feasting, Amar addressed Landhoor, Bahram, and Muqbil, saying, "Remain in daily attendance at Naushervan's court, but do not for a moment drop your guard or let the slumber of negligence overtake you. Because of Bakhtak's presence, there is no knowing how the emperor will act toward you from one day to the next as he has shown himself to be irresolute and fickle. Take it upon yourselves to keep in contact with Khvaja Buzurj-mehr, and depend on his advice and counsel as he is genuinely well-disposed toward Amir Hamza and has his best interests at heart. Now I am headed for Mecca to bring Khvaja Abdul Muttalib the news of Amir's well-being!" Amar then donned his brocade vest and broadcloth sandals and, decking himself in the *ayyar*'s livery, headed toward Mecca.

―――

Now to satisfy those seeking the news of more adventures, a short account of Amir Hamza. The Sahibqiran arrived near Egypt's frontiers and set up Prophet Danyal's pavilion and pitched his tents by the banks of the Nile. That day was spent in the pleasures of the cup, and when it was evening and the shades of night began to fall, the carpet attendants dressed the pavilion with crystal chandeliers, candlesticks, and candelabra. Wax and camphor candles were lit and began to flicker like the flames in ardent hearts. The Sahibqiran ordered that the drapes of the pavilion be raised to open up the view of the river. The sight became doubly delightful when the lights in the pavilion were reflected in the river and the scene of revelry extended into the water. The wind that wafted over the Nile brought solace to the hearts of those being consumed by the flames of separation. The Sahibqiran ordered meat and wine to be served, and fairy-limbed dancers enlivened the assembly with their singing and dancing. The whole night was spent in imbibing roseate wine and listening to the lyrics accompanying the *sarod* and the *arghanun*.[4]

The king of Egypt, Abdul Aziz, had learned that Hamza had been sent there by Naushervan to levy tribute on him. The news of Hamza's arrival had also reached him and he discovered that Hamza had come at the head of an invincible army and an array of intrepid warriors and commanders. The king had a wise counselor in the person of his vizier, Karvan. He sent for him in private and sought his opinion about the course of action they must follow regarding Hamza's advance.

Since Karvan was a prudent and sagacious man, he said to the king, "The whole world is ringing with news of Hamza's valor, and reports of his victories and triumphs have reached far and wide. The accounts of the chroniclers also attest that he is a great tactician and an invincible warrior. It would be imprudent to jeopardize your reputation by challenging such a man. It would be wiser in my humble opinion to take the lead and call on him and make him a royal offering. It is well-known that just as he is without match in courage and valor, he is peerless, too, in fortitude and generosity of spirit. He would show an equal degree of preference and partiality should your excellent manners and sincerity be revealed to him!"

Abdul Aziz was incensed by his vizier's counsel and said irritably, "Your advice in this matter is most injudicious. The preferable course of action is the one I have resolved upon in my mind!" Karvan thought to himself that even though this king lacked the wherewithal, he considered himself no less in stature than the great pharaoh just because he ruled over Egypt. Even if Musa himself were to counsel him, let alone a mere vizier, it would have no effect on him.[5] Karvan decided to hold his tongue and let the king hang himself with his own rope if he so desired. Having come to this decision the vizier kept quiet.

Early the next morning, Abdul Aziz called on Amir with the three years' tribute and many gifts. During his audience, he made an offering of all that he had brought, and expressed much warmth and affection toward Amir. He said to Hamza, "Why did Your Honor choose to camp in a field when the comforts of the city are available to you? You took all the trouble of setting up camp here to no purpose! Pray come into the city and ennoble my humble abode by setting foot there."

The kings often condescend to indulge the beggarly.

Amir conferred a robe of honor upon him and said, "Indeed one always has the freedom to visit a friend's house. I have no objections to accompanying you to your place!" Amir stood up after reciting the holy name of God, and leaving his army stationed at that place, headed for the city in the company of some of his illustrious nobles.

When Amir set foot in the city, every last person came out to feast their eyes on his face. Nobles and pelebians alike, upon seeing Amir Hamza's visage, called out,

I pray to God that destiny shows you favor,
That you become propitious of fortune, and achieve great power and youth
*   everlasting.*

Amir gave audience on a bejeweled throne in the royal court and the eminent nobles of his entourage occupied seats and thrones according to their established ranks. The king of Egypt ordered moonfaced cupbearers to bring goblets and ewers and directed the Venus-like dancers and exquisite musicians to dance and sing. The chorus of "Drink unto oblivion!" rose from all corners of the court, and the medley of songs and music was carried to the ears of the heavens.

All this while, Abdul Aziz employed himself in officiating and looking after the party's arrangements with the skirts of his robe tied up like a menial. When Amir insisted that he should rest and let others take care of the arrangements, he replied with folded arms, "It is a signal honor for me to wait upon the son-in-law of the Emperor of the Seven Climes. One is not afforded an opportunity to wait upon such illustrious personages every day!" Amir was greatly pleased by his talk, and the glib tongue of that wily man led Hamza into such deception that he threw all caution to the wind.

When evening drew to a close, that deceitful devil went into the wine cellar and drugged the wine with his own vile hands. Then he instructed the cupbearers to serve wine only from those ewers. The cupbearers carried out his orders and poured wine into the goblets from the flagons filled with drugged wine. After drinking the very first cup of that wine, the Sahibqiran said to the king, "It tastes different and its color and effect are unlike the one served earlier!"

That malevolent king replied humbly with folded arms, "Indeed it is a different wine, and a finer one it would be impossible to find. Your Honor's visit is a fit occasion to bring out this wine, which is much headier and stronger than the first. I had kept it cellared for the longest time."

Amir, who had never tasted drugged wine in his life, believed the king's word. After the wine had made a few rounds, one after another, Amir's companions began to swoon, falling down from their stations. As Amir stood up from his seat upon regarding this alarming state of affairs, his legs gave way under him, and he, too, fell unconscious to the floor.

The king of Egypt said to his vizier, "Behold this now and see how well my plan worked to bring low such a mighty one as he! Send for the executioner this moment to behead Hamza and his companions, and without wasting a moment have their heads dispatched with a camel rider to Naushervan's court!"

Karvan humbly replied, "Indeed Your Honor overpowered the adversary with great facility and without loss of time, but I see good reason why you must not act hastily in executing and beheading Hamza. First, Hamza has powerful friends who would wipe the kingdom of Egypt from the face of the earth if they heard of his murder. There is Khusrau of India Landhoor bin Saadan, who commands a hundred thousand troops and auxiliaries, each of whom is more intrepid and formidable than the other. They would wager their sweet lives at a moment's notice at one word from him. There is Bahram Gurd, the emperor of China, who has at his command several thousand mounted warriors and foot soldiers from the lands of China and Tartary, each one of whom is a swordsman without match. Then there is Muqbil Vafadar, who commands several thousand flawless archers. And last, but not least, is Amar Ayyar, who is such a terrible scourge that he could rout tens of millions all by himself! Therefore I deem it advisable that you put Hamza and his companions in chains and incarcerate them, and send this news to the Emperor of the Seven Concentric Circles. If he writes back to sanction Hamza's execution, then you may proceed to fulfill your heart's desire!"

The king of Egypt said, "Indeed in this matter I deem your advice most judicious and propitious, O Karvan! I am of the same mind, too, but I fear that if Amar arrives here before the courier can return from his two thousand *farsangs* journey to Ctesiphon, all my labor will come to naught. Then there will be no punishment that Hamza would consider too harsh for me, and his mischief would then know no boundaries!"

Karvan replied, "I could arrange for the emperor's reply to be received here within two days, provided it is not delayed at his end and no misadventure befalls the messenger. Pray hand me the letter and I shall dispatch it in the morning by tying it to a courier pigeon's neck, as I have a pair of Ctesiphon pigeons at my house. By evening it will have reached Ctesiphon, and if the emperor immediately grants a reply, it should arrive here the next day!"

The king greatly praised Karvan's counsel and highly commended him, and that very moment he sent for blacksmiths and had Amir and his companions put in irons. They were imprisoned in the well where Yusuf's brothers had once incarcerated Yusuf.[6] Then the king summoned Sarhang Misri, the chief of his *ayyars*, and said, "Keep strict watch on these prisoners with your men and do not exchange a single word of intimacy or allegiance with a soul, lest it attract Amar here to seek their release, which would bring us humiliation and disgrace to no purpose. Have it proclaimed in the city that anyone who utters Hamza's name is to be killed on the spot!" His edict was so severe that the denizens of the city refrained from even uttering the name of the followers of the True Faith. The next day, the king of Egypt wrote out a missive to Naushervan, and fastened it to the pigeon's neck. Then the bird was sent toward Ctesiphon, and it flew there astride the wind's charger.

OF THE PIGEON BRINGING THE MISSIVE INTO
CTESIPHON; OF THE CONSPIRACY TO KILL LANDHOOR,
BAHRAM, AND OTHERS; AND OF AMAR MAKING AN
UNEXPECTED APPEARANCE

The dove of the narrative is entrapped in the cage of these lines by lovers of sweet discourse and admirers of high-flying fancy. They expound on all manner of singular and propitious subjects thus.

When released from Egypt, the pigeon rose into the air fluttering its wings and reached Ctesiphon and perched atop Naushervan's pigeon tower before evening had cast it shadows. When the pigeon keeper saw a new pigeon sitting on the tower, he released the birds in the pigeon tower and, keeping his net on the ready, threw feed to the pigeons and presented them water in an earthenware bowl. Because the carrier pigeon had gone without food or water the whole day, he descended into the net along with the other pigeons. The keeper pulled at his net and when he took out the new pigeon, he found a letter tied to his neck. Leaving the pigeon to forage in the net, he took the letter to Bakhtak and said, "A short while ago I caught a pigeon and discovered this letter inside a small pouch attached to his neck. I have brought the letter for Your Honor to inspect, and left the pigeon to feed himself!"

Beside himself with joy upon reading it, Bakhtak's morose face cracked into a grimace, and that very moment he hurried before the emperor. He congratulated him warmly and presented the letter to him. Upon reading it, Naushervan, too, came very near to bursting with joy. Bakhtak declared, "Your Honor must send a reply forthwith sanctioning Hamza's death, and not let Your Honor's resolve in this matter be swayed by anyone's counsel or advice! This humble slave of yours has in his possession a pigeon from Egypt. He shall be dispatched early in the morning with the reply fastened to his neck to take the letter to its destination and deliver it to the addressee!" Naushervan replied, "I must needs, however, take Buzurjmehr's advice in this difficult matter, since I am honor-bound to follow my father's last wishes."

The cowardly Bakhtak (deserving of decapitation) replied, "Very well! But Buzurjmehr is a follower of the True Faith himself, and his opinion will incline in the favor of his coreligionists. It is not every day that a powerful foe like Hamza falls into one's power. Such an opportunity will not present itself again!" The emperor replied, "Buzurjmehr's belief will also be put to the test in this matter and his creed will be revealed!" The emperor summoned Buzurjmehr and gave him the letter to read.

The avis of Buzurjmehr's reason flew away[7] upon reading the devastating news in the letter. However, he summoned his senses to his aid and said, "Congratulations! Your greatest anxiety was addressed without your becoming involved yourself. However, it will not bode well to sanction Hamza's death this instant. I counsel this for the reason that if the news is leaked to Landhoor, Bahram, and Muqbil—let alone any other human beings—neither bird nor beast will be found alive in Ctesiphon before the pigeon has even reached its destination. I shudder to think the terrible fate that will visit Egypt itself! You should first address these matters. Then you may give the orders for Hamza's death!"

Bakhtak replied, "It can be arranged with facility, and they can be killed without any great ado. Tomorrow, when these men present themselves in the court, Your Honor must arrange for wine and meat to be served and then take them unconscious with drugged wine. Thereafter, the sanction for Hamza's death may be dispatched to the king of Egypt by pigeon post, and the services of your humble servant's own bird may be employed for the task. When Hamza's head arrives in the court, Your Honor may have Landhoor and the others beheaded at your pleasure, and put an end to all this sedition and strife that has blown into our kingdom from foreign lands!" Naushervan was delighted by Bakhtak's counsel and greatly praised his wisdom.

Because Bakhtak considered Buzurjmehr a follower of the True Faith, he counseled the king not to let Buzurjmehr go home that night and stayed over at the court himself, too. When it was morning, Landhoor, Bahram, and Muqbil arrived in the court according to their custom and each took their seat according to their station. The king received them with great kindness and following the plan, gave orders for an assembly of revelry to be arranged. Portuguese and Frankish wines were poured out and drugged wine began to circulate. Buzurjmehr tried to

warn the men by making signs with his eyes in vain. They did not understand his message and remained oblivious to his signals.

After Muqbil had had two cups, he sensed some mischief. He rose
from the assembly on the pretext of a headache, and headed straight for
Buzurjmehr's house where he fell unconscious on the floor. Landhoor
and Bahram had had four and five cups each and, once fully drugged,
they tumbled from their seats and thrones and collapsed to the ground.
At the emperor's orders they were manacled and put in leg irons, and
thrown into the jail with yokes tied around their necks and spiked steel
balls placed under their arms. Then Naushervan wrote these words to
the sovereign of Egypt:

> Indeed, you showed great loyalty toward me by taking Hamza captive.
> You should behead him and dispatch me his head upon receiving this
> letter, and carry out this order with the greatest expedience!

After writing this note Naushervan said to Bakhtak, "Seal it with the
royal seal and send it early tomorrow morning. Take heed that you not
breathe a word of it to anyone!" After giving these orders the emperor
adjourned the court and retired to the royal bedchamber.

Buzurjmehr took his leave and returned home, where he found Muqbil lying unconscious on the floor like a dead man. He administered him
a physic that dispelled the effects of the drugged wine and brought Muqbil back to his senses. Then Buzurjmehr gave him a detailed account of
all that had come to pass, narrating the whole story from the beginning.
Upon hearing it, Muqbil tore at the collar of his robe in grief. He began
wailing and lamenting and was fully disposed to put an end to his life.
Buzurjmehr said to him, "This is not the occasion to indulge in wailing
and lamentation but to think of some clever scheme! It would be a great
folly not to seek recourse to some stratagem at this crucial juncture. I
have a camel that can traverse eighty *farsangs* in a day. Ride him full tilt
and when you catch sight of the pigeon, kill him at the first opportunity,
for our salvation lies in his destruction. This should be our chosen strategy as it will turn the tide of the events in our favor."

Muqbil set out astride the camel that very moment. After he was
gone, Buzurjmehr learned through *ramal* that all obstacles would be removed and their dilemma resolved only with the help and participation
of Amar. His anxiety grew greatly upon discovering this, and he wondered how and where he could track down Amar that moment. His eldest

son, Buzurg Ummid, arrived at his father's house while he was engrossed in these meditations and, noticing the shadow of distress on his father's face, said, "My dear father, I hope that nothing is the matter with you! What is it that has caused this anxiety to reflect on your face?" Buzurjmehr replied, "I wish you to tell me the reason for my anxiety yourself by drawing lots, and describing the matter that weighs so heavy on my mind!" Khvaja Buzurg Ummid drew lots and answered, "It seems that you are distressed on account of someone you await. He will present himself by this evening and call upon you without fail!"

Buzurjmehr then himself read the pattern of the lots, and was over-joyed upon interpreting it. He called out to his slave, "Go and see who stands at the door, and bring me the particulars regarding his appearance, stature, and countenance!" The slave returned and answered, "A tall man with a white beard is at the door. He sends his regards and asks to see you!" Upon hearing this Khvaja Buzurjmehr ran out barefoot and brought Amar into the house, and after narrating the whole story to him, broke into tears and said, "O Amar! Everything depends on you killing that pigeon on the way! Then all this will come to a happy conclusion; otherwise our goose is as good as cooked, and things will take a turn for the worse!"

At these words tears also came to Amar's eyes, and he said, "How do you think that I can travel a thousand *farsangs* in one day, since I do not have a bird's feathers and wings to go fluttering and flying into air?" Buzurjmehr replied, "O Amar, I have learned from studying your horo-scope that during your life there will be three occasions when you will run so swiftly that the feat will surpass those of great men who have gone before, and remain unequaled by those who will come after! The first time you shall travel a thousand *farsangs* in pursuit of this pigeon; the sec-ond time will be when Amir's enemies have hung him from the pole of *uqabain*[8] and you will gather the nobles of the True Faith from the sur-rounding expanse of eleven thousand *farsangs* in a matter of twelve days. On the third occasion, you will travel seven thousand *farsangs* in seven days for the sake of Hamza's son in Bayaben-e Sikanderi. Never in all these expeditions will you tire in the least!"

Amar replied, "O Khvaja! Verily these are happy tidings! Indeed a pretty picture you paint of my fate where my lot is to spend my life run-ning errands and playing the courier." Khvaja Buzurjmehr replied, "Re-joice, O Amar! For in recompense for these labors you will receive such inestimable treasures that none have ever dreamed of, nor the mightiest kings heard of! Now make haste and be off, for this is not a time to make delays or show laziness and indolence. I have also dispatched Muqbil by camel whom you will surely meet on the way."

Taking his leave of Buzurjmehr, Amar went to Tal Shad-Kam and said to the nobles of India and China, "It is not advisable for you to camp here, as Naushervan might pick a quarrel with you in finding you without a leader. You should move camp to the forest, and wait and pray for God's favor and see what fate unfolds and the Will of God ordains!"

OF AMAR SETTING OUT FOR EGYPT IN PURSUIT OF THE PIGEON AND KILLING HIM CLOSE TO ITS CITY GATES, AND OF HIS SECURING HAMZA'S RELEASE AFTER MUCH TOIL AND AFFLICTION

The dove of the stylus trills its notes inside the vestibule of the page and the pen's homing pigeon makes circles around the pigeon tower of the ream. When the hour of dawn struck, Amar decked himself in an *ayyar*'s attire and stationed himself under the royal pigeon house. The moment Bakhtak took the bird out of the pigeon house and released him in the direction of Egypt with the note tied to its neck, Amar locked his gaze with Bakhtak and said, "Mark it well that if, God forbid, even a single hair of Hamza or his companions is harmed, I will pluck clean the avis of Naushervan's soul[9] and annihilate those party to this treacherous counsel along with their kin. What an unenviable lot yours will be you cannot even imagine! At this moment I am going after the pigeon, but soon you will taste the terrible scourge I shall visit on your head!" At these words the avis of Bakhtak's soul very nearly fluttered out of his body's cage. People had to help him down from the roof, and he lay in a faint for a long time afterward. However, as all errant cads have a hardy constitution, he survived the shock.

Amar, the Father of Racers and Tumblers, sped on under the pigeon's shadow reciting "Help, O Immortal One! Help, O Imperishable One!" He surmounted any hillocks or declivities that presented themselves with a leap, thinking nothing of any obstructions however big or small. At every step of the way his eyes remained transfixed on the bird like a hawk chasing a pigeon.

Now to those eager to hear a brief account of Muqbil Vafadar. He went at full gallop for seventy *kos* after setting out from Ctesiphon, and dismounted at a rivulet where the water was more sparkling and lustrous than a pearl. He took out some bread from his belt and ate a little. Letting his camel graze in the forest, he lay down a while to rest himself. It so happened that this forest abounded in poisonous grass, and upon eating it the dromedary fell dead. Muqbil set out from there on foot feeling completely at a loss, and trekked onward for several *kos* until his feet became swollen, and every step that he put forward was met by one backward. Feeling completely powerless, he sat down under a tree and fell unconscious from a paroxysm of tears.

Amar, who had been following the pigeon, found the camel lying dead on the way and reasoned he must be the one Muqbil had ridden there. A little farther ahead he found Muqbil also lying unconscious under a tree with his feet swollen and his body sapped of all strength. Amar immediately dripped some water into his mouth. Muqbil opened his eyes and began crying upon finding Amar there. Amar said, "This is no time to waste in crying tears. Make haste and climb on my shoulders, and let us find some way to hunt down that pigeon!" Muqbil fitted the notch of an arrow in his bowstring and climbed atop Amar, who set out at a comet's pace.

It is recounted by Amar Ayyar[10] that at times he found himself ahead of the pigeon by the length of a bow shot and sometimes the pigeon bridged the distance. The westbound bird[11] had not yet retired to its nest when the pigeon approached the ramparts of the castle of Egypt. As the pigeon was about to fly over the castle walls into the city, Muqbil released the falcon of his arrow from his bow's nest and the talons of the death's hawk caught the pigeon at once. Try as it might to escape the arrow's clutches, the pigeon came spiraling down and fell dead into the moat, where Amar fished him out. He opened the bird's letter and after reading it, put it safely into his *zambil* to show to Hamza.

Amar slaughtered and roasted the pigeon and gave it to Muqbil to eat, and then accompanied Muqbil into the camp of the followers of the True Faith, which stood along the banks of the Nile. Sultan Bakht Maghrebi broke into lamentations upon beholding Amar, whereupon Amar wiped the man's tears with the kerchief of consoling words, and said to him, "Abandon all your anxiety and grief and disquiet and sorrow. God willing, I shall soon secure Hamza's release, and once I have delivered you from this anxiety, you shall see how I will chastise this deceitful king!"

As Amar was exhausted by the day's journey he slept like a log the whole night and when the first light of the morn appeared and the world-illuminating sun manifested itself in the heavens, he went into the city disguised as an Arab. He made the rounds of the city until it was time for the *asr* prayers,[12] but never heard anyone so much as mention Hamza's name.

Around the time of the *maghreb* prayers,[13] he saw a water carrier who looked astute, wise, and discerning, who was making the rounds of the bazaar with a water skin slung over his shoulder, clinking his water bowl and quenching people's thirst. When Amar asked him for some water, the water carrier poured some into the bowl and handed it to him. Amar drank some and then threw away the rest, then secured the bowl inside his bag and took long strides to get away from him. The water carrier came running after him, crying, "Where are you off to with my water bowl! Never have I seen such a bandit and highwayman!"

Once Amar had cleared the square he came to a stop. The water carrier caught up with him, and after snatching the water bowl from his hands, made to depart. Amar led him by his arm to a corner and said, "O water carrier! Though I have been doing the rounds of the city since morning, I have not come across anyone who looks as kindly as yourself! I beseech you in the name of holy Khizr to tell me where the king of Egypt has imprisoned Hamza and what calamity has befallen that scion of the House of Hashim!"[14] That infidel (marked for hell fodder!) caught hold of Amar's arm and began screeching, "Hasten to my aid, friends, for I have caught Amar!" Upon these words people rushed toward them from all corners of the bazaar.

Amar wondered how the man had recognized him. Wasting no time in these speculations, however, he bit the water carrier's hands, and won release from his grip. He climbed atop the upper story of a nearby house in one leap, and sped away leaping and gamboling from roof to roof. When Sarhang Misri heard this news, he began searching for Amar and spread out with his deputies all over the city. When he could not find a trace of Amar he ordered them to arrest any stranger they came upon, in the likelihood that it would be the notorious *ayyar* in disguise.

To cut a long story short, Amar found his way into another bazaar in due time. He made an exploratory circuit of it and saw a blind beggar resting against a pillow by the roadside. Amar produced a false coin from his *zambil* and gave it to the beggar, who then showered Amar with blessings. When Amar drew near him and inquired about Hamza's whereabouts, the beggar caught the skirts of Amar's robe and began to scream loudly for Sarhang Misri. Amar wondered endlessly how a man born from his mother's womb blind could have recognized him. As people began gathering in throngs from all sides to apprehend him, Amar again escaped after cutting off the skirts of his robe, and disappeared in the flash of an eye like the wind.

Night fell in the meanwhile and the vigils had begun to do their rounds. Amar hid himself in a temple in a priest's garb for the fear of being spotted by the chief vigil. He passed the night in great anxiety and neither ate nor drank. In the morning, he went out disguised as a merchant and ambled around exploring the sections of the city. On his way he passed the magistrate's chair where he saw Sarhang Misri sitting decked out in his *ayyar*'s attire, observing his deputies perform their exercise regime. Amar stopped to watch them when Sarhang Misri saw him and their eyes met. He walked up to Amar and asked, "Who are you and what is your name? Where have you come from and what has brought you to this city?"

Amar replied, "I am a merchant and have arrived from China. The fame of your city has brought me here, and I have set up camp at the gates of the city. My name is Khvaja Taifus bin Mayus bin Sarbus bin Taq bin Tamtaraq Bazargan, and I am one who has disgraced a few good men in his time." Sarhang Misri replied, "Until today I had not heard such a strange name!" He called two of his *ayyars* and said to them, "Go with Khvaja here and see what goods are there in his caravan and what kind of merchandise is stocked in his shop!"

Amar said, "The saying that the grass always looks greener on the other side is indeed most truthful and accurate, for I used to hear in my town that Egypt is a safe and secure place, and everyone could travel there without anxiety. But I see that it is a city reigned over by turmoil, where the ruler's deputies expose tradesmen to the hardship of searches, and heap insults upon travelers and merchants!"

Sarhang Misri replied, "This is a most secure and peaceful place where you will find all manner of amenities and comfort, and never encounter any threat or peril. I am sending you to your camp accompanied by my men so that they may post a night vigil in the evening to guard you and attend to your comfort and needs!"

Amar replied, "In that case I appreciate your offer and will have no further worries for the future!" He then set out from there taking the two *ayyars* with him.

OF AMAR SWINDLING AND DUPING
SARHANG MISRI'S AYYARS

Truthful spies and wise and cunning scribes recount that Amar took along the two *ayyars* and marched about the city's neighborhoods. He paraded them all over town until afternoon, keeping them constantly occupied in conversation. At last, the *ayyars* said to him, "Pray tell us at which gate of the city you have set up camp, and why you seem so fretful and uneasy!" Amar replied, "I am camped at the Yemen Gate, but the truth is that I have lost my bearings and God alone knows where I am headed in my perambulations!" They answered, "If you had mentioned that to us earlier, we would have conducted you there at once. You would not have been discomfited, and we would have gone on our way sooner. Come with us now and we will lead you to the Yemen Gate and take you to your place!"

Amar replied, "Afternoon has come and I have not had food or drink as yet. I am famished with hunger and my soul is about to flutter out from my body's cage!"

The *ayyars* said, "The market by the royal palace is close by and there you would find shops selling all kinds of delicacies. Have some food first and then we will show you to your abode and take our leave!" Amar inquired, "How much would it cost for the three of us to have a meal?" They replied, "One *shahi*[15] will be sufficient!"

Amar said: "What would one *shahi* purchase? I would like to order food worth at least five *shahis* to feed us better and to our satisfaction!" Upon hearing this the *ayyars* thought that the merchant had a most liberal disposition and must be some eminent man.

At a confectioner's shop, Amar made the *ayyars* order five *shahis'* worth of the finest food, and sat down to eat with them in the upper chamber of the shop. He got up once he had had his fill, saying, "My hunger has been satisfied, but you may continue. Stuff yourselves to your hearts' content and eat all that your guts can hold!" He washed his hands and began inspecting the jewels in their headdresses and said, "I have several chests full of bigger and costlier stones. I shall show them to you and you will be welcome to fill up the skirts of your robes with them and carry them away!" Those dimwits rejoiced immensely in their hearts thinking this was indeed a generous man whom their master had sent them to accompany, and convinced they must have beheld some most auspicious augur in the morning to have come into such marvelous good luck. Amar began pacing about holding their headdresses and aigrettes, and as soon as an opportunity presented itself, he stole down from the upper chamber and made away.

After the *ayyars* had eaten, they came down from the gallery and asked the confectioner, "Where is Khvaja Taifus who bought the food? Pray take us to his abode as we have been wandering with him since morning!" The confectioner replied, "Talk some sense and do not rave on nonsensically! I know nothing of him, but I know the two of you very well. It was to you that I sold the food. How am I supposed to know where he went?" The *ayyars* replied, "He had in his hands our headdresses and aigrettes! Tell us where he has gone, and if you have any knowledge of him at all."

The confectioner replied, "I will not let you move a single step without first recovering my five *shahis* from you, and if you continue to talk balderdash, I will give you a severe lashing with my ladle. Then your cheeks will puff up like butter loaves and become red as *shir-maals*, and all the gibberish and bombast will be drained out of you!"

The *ayyars* replied, "This is a most presumptious speech for a confectioner, and one that merits a good chastisement!" The man answered back, "You have already had an entree of kebabs, how about some dessert of skewer lashings now, that would make you retch out all that you have eaten? You swallowed my food like your mother's milk, and when it is time to pay up your greasy tongues churn in glib talk and your asses are all ablaze! You had better pay me, or be cudgeled and beaten so mercilessly that in the end a dried mango paring will offer a prospect more handsome than your face. This is not the house from which those scullion mothers of yours can steal bread to feed you!"

So liberally did the confectioner sprinkle the *ayyars* with ignominious words that their hearts began to blaze with rage and spew flames like an oven. The two parties fell on each other, and became like the layers of a *paratha*.[16] Most furious with the confectioner, the *ayyars* doled out a wealth of obscenities at him, and the confectioner on his part served them the thrashing of their lives with the help of his kitchen workers. He beat them to an inch of their lives, dealing them such chops with the cleaver that he very nearly made mincemeat of them.

Their hearts all parched and roasted, the *ayyars* hardly had any breath left in them and murmured to passersby, "If someone would take news of our plight to Sarhang Misri, it would grant us a new lease on life!" A kindhearted person took the news to Sarhang Misri that two of his *ayyars* and a confectioner were at each other's throats, and if he did not hasten to their aid they would be beaten to a fine pulp and their brains would flow out of their noses from the violence of the assault. Upon arriving at the scene Sarhang Misri discovered the facts of the matter, and after paying the five *shahis* to the confectioner from his own purse, he expelled the two *ayyars* unceremoniously from his service and severed all connections with them.

———

Now hear an account of Amar. He roamed around until evening and then went to a grain parcher's kiln to sleep there. In the morning he disguised himself as a beggar and began reciting verses and asking for alms outdoors. By chance, Sarhang Misri happened by that place along with two of his *ayyars*. The moment their eyes met, Sarhang was convinced that this was none other than Amar, and nobody else but that *ayyar*. He sidled up to Amar, and after giving him a gold piece from his pocket caught hold of his hand. It was Amar's wont to always wear an *ayyar*'s greased gauntlet. When Sarhang Misri called out to his *ayyars*, Amar laughed loudly and withdrew his hand from the gauntlet. Leaving it in Sarhang Misri's hand, he snatched his headdress and jumped onto the roof of a nearby shop. Then he escaped, leaping and bounding from roof to roof as before.

Bareheaded and crying bitter tears of remorse, Sarhang Misri went to the magistrate's station. The realization dawned upon him that he had not only lost his honor but also risked the discontentment of his sovereign and the scorn of men. He said to his *ayyars*, "If one among you would apprehend Amar for me, he will be rewarded handsomely. I would intercede in the royal court for his promotion in office and have him given the role and robe of my deputy!" At this, the *ayyars* spread out prowling all over the city like the Ursa Major and Ursa Minor prowl the expanse of skies and started searching for Amar in each nook and corner.

Never easy prey, Amar hid in a ravine the whole day and trotted out from his hiding place in the evening disguised as a dervish. Two hours of the night had passed when he presented himself at a kebab seller's shop. The kebab seller asked him, "Where do you come from, venerated sir, and what is the name given you by your patron saint?" Amar replied, "What business do you have with the name and domicile of a dervish? I have been wandering around this city for a long time and now I am your guest!" When the kebab seller realized that he had the privilege of hosting a holy man, he stepped down from his shop and led Amar upstairs, seating him with great cordiality and affection and then serving him meat and wine.

After a while he said to Amar, "If it is not offensive to you, there is no harm in giving out your name and domicile, for it is purposeless to hide one's particulars in a foreign city from a well-wisher who happens to be a resident!" Amar replied, "I am the son of a beggar and have arrived from Ctesiphon." The kebab seller said, "Did you ever come across Amar Ayyar, and do you know if he is living or dead?" Amar answered, "I stayed at his house for several days before coming here and was his guest for a long period of time!" The kebab seller said, "Indeed he is a most ungrateful wretch. If I ever laid hands on him I would visit on him the punishment he deserves!"

Amar asked, "What harm has he done you that you are so bitterly set against him?" He answered, "What possible harm could he have done me? I am angry with him because he earned all his prestige, honor, and fame on account of Amir Hamza and yet he is oblivious to the welfare of Hamza, who has been held prisoner by the king of Egypt for so many days!" Amar replied, "Even if he did arrive here, what could he possibly do, as every traveler who arrives here is taken prisoner on suspicion of being Amar in disguise!" The kebab seller answered, "If he came to me, I would lead him straight to Hamza!"

Upon hearing this, Amar said, "O kebab seller! Amar presents himself before you! Now take me to Hamza!" The man replied, "My dear friend! Just two cups of wine have made you giddy, and you have started raving and ranting! What resemblance do you have with Amar? Don't you realize how far Ctesiphon is from this city? Even though I have not seen Amar, still his appearance is well-known to me, for I have heard it described often!" The kebab seller then pointed toward his shop and continued, "In the bygone days of my youth, I was also an *ayyar*. You can still see my *ayyar*'s attire hanging over there. I gave up that profession once I became advanced in years. Then I set up this kebab shop, and now earn my living in this profession."

Amar took off his disguise and said, "Judge for yourself whether or not I am Amar, or if it is somebody else in my guise!" Upon regarding this, the man embraced Amar and said, "The king of Egypt has imprisoned Hamza in the well where Yusuf was incarcerated by his brothers. Come, let me lead you there so that you can see the torments poor Hamza is suffering!"

The kebab seller also donned the trappings of trickery and set out alongside Amar, the two of them evading the watchful eyes of thief catchers and any encounters with vigils. They had gone a short distance when they saw a man sitting outside a shop. The old *ayyar* challenged the man and asked, "Who are you, O stranger, and what is the reason you wait here?" When the addressee disregarded his question, the old *ayyar* rushed at him with a drawn sword. The man wrenched the sword from his hands and slammed him to the ground.

Amar then drew his dagger and charged the man, but on drawing close he noticed that it was none other than Muqbil Vafadar. He embraced him and asked, "How did you find your way here and happen to be in this place?" Muqbil answered, "For several days now I have been fruitlessly searching the city for any signs of Amir!" When the old *ayyar* saw Amar embracing the stranger, he began remonstrating and said, "You embrace the one who threw me to the ground! A marvel this is, and a most seemly manner of showing camaraderie with me!" Amar said to him, "He is not some stranger but my affectionate friend and benefactor, Muqbil Vafadar, who is a supporter and devotee of Hamza!" At this, the old man embraced Muqbil and expressed his heartfelt pleasure at meeting him.

The three of them then headed for the fort and in good time arrived under its ramparts. Amar threw his rope at one of the towers, but it fell back on his face without finding a hold. After trying a second time and failing, he asked the old *ayyar* to try his luck. He also tried, but the rope did not catch on. Then Amar said to Muqbil, "Throw the rope at the tower and see how you fare!" Muqbil's attempt was successful and the rope caught hold, whereupon the three of them gained the wall with its help, and climbed up the ramparts by force of fate.

On the roof they saw a person wearing a veil standing in wait. As Amar approached, the masked one reached for him. Thinking that the person was making an attempt to capture him, Amar was greatly alarmed. He realized that everyone in the fort would come running there if the veiled person raised the alarm. Then even if he himself slipped away by some subterfuge, his companions would certainly be arrested and all their efforts would come to naught. Therefore Amar decided to subdue the masked one. But the veiled person, seeing that it was Amar, came forward and placated him and kissed his hand and said, "My name is Zehra and I am the daughter of the king of Egypt! Prophet Ibrahim converted me to the True Faith in the realm of dreams and betrothed me to Muqbil. He gave me your whereabouts, and told me that Muqbil and Amar would come from such and such a tower and I should employ myself in ministering help and hospitality to them. I have been standing here since evening in anticipation of your arrival!"

She took off an *ambarcha* worth five thousand rupees and gave it to Amar as an offering, and promised him a further reward of five thousand gold pieces. Amar kissed her forehead and, securing the *ambarcha* in his possession, congratulated Muqbil and said, "Consider this a good omen. God willing, we shall soon find what we seek!" Then Zehra came down from the ramparts of the fort with these three companions, and they headed for the well of Yusuf where Amir was incarcerated.

OF AMIR HAMZA'S RELEASE FROM THE WELL OF YUSUF, AND OF HIS REGAINING HIS FREEDOM WITH ZEHRA MISRI'S ASSISTANCE

The pen draws out new fictions from the pit of nothingness, and the fingers exert themselves to unfold this wondrous tale on the paper's bright expanse. When the four of them arrived near the well of Yusuf, Sarhang Misri appeared there, and as they turned toward him, he visited blessings upon them in a loud voice and said, "O Khvaja Amar! I was deep in my slumber when Prophet Ibrahim appeared to me in a dream and showed me visions of Heaven and Hell. He converted me to the True Faith and bade me to hasten to join the four of you to secure Hamza's release and ennoble myself by accomplishing this deed. Immediately upon waking up, I put on my *ayyar*'s attire and hurried here as fast as my legs could carry me, without a single moment's hesitation or delay. Now hide yourselves for the moment, and once I have made the arrangements I will accompany you to the well of Yusuf and conduct you inside!" Delighted, Amar embraced Sarhang Misri, and along with Muqbil, Zehra Misri, and the old man, he hid in a corner.

Sarhang Misri rendered unconscious the guards at the well of Yusuf and then beheaded them. Next he conducted Amar and his companions to the mouth of the well. Amar dropped a rope down its shaft after uncovering its mouth and, giving one end to Sarhang Misri to hold for support, he lowered himself into the well reciting the name of God.

The captives of that terrible well were themselves occupied in prayers. While they were counting the days of their lives they heard a noise and reasoned that the king of Egypt had sent his executioner to execute them, and that their link to life was about to be severed. Then Amar approached them and asked, "O believers in the True Faith, who among you is Aadi, as I have business with him!" Imagining that he was soon to be killed, Aadi was frightened out of his wits. He pointed toward Munzir Shah Yemeni and said, "That's him!" All the other prisoners laughed at his words. Amar said to Munzir Shah Yemeni, "O Aadi! The king of Egypt has ordered your release!"

Aadi bitterly repented his words then and, unable to restrain himself, cried out, "Sire! Aadi is, in fact, my name. I was merely jesting with you!" Amar said to him, "Indeed you were described to me as one with a tremendous gut, who has defiled the well from his excessive defecating, and made the lives of other prisoners a living misery with the stench. You should be taken out of the well, executed, and flung away as a corpse!" Upon hearing these words, Aadi's blood curdled in his veins from terror, and he felt ever more embarrassed and ashamed.

It became obvious to Amir Hamza from the conversation that the visitor could be none other than Amar, for such jesting and quipping was in his blood. Amir sat on his haunches and bellowed, "God is Great!" whereupon all the links of his chains and the collar on his neck snapped open as if made of gossamer. To give Amar a good scare, Amir charged at him swinging the chains. Realizing that if these chains even so much as touched him he would not draw another breath, Amar cried out, "O Arab! Is this how one conducts oneself with friends? Mark that I am your old faithful, your sworn slave, and the one beholden to the salt of your table!" Amir Hamza embraced Amar and removed the chains of his companions. Then he climbed out of the well with them.

Amar related to Amir all that had come to pass since Hamza's imprisonment, and lowered his head in gratitude before the True God. As he looked toward the skies, he saw the morning star shining in the heavens like a symbol of Amir's prestige and a sign of the approaching hour of dawn. Amir headed straight to the king of Egypt's palace with all his companions in his train. They searched for the king, but did not find any trace of him. Amir's companions entered the back garden and began feasting on the guavas, apricots, and mulberries they found there.

Aadi presently felt an overpowering urge to empty his bowels, since he in his bovine greed had eaten several *maunds* of fruit. He took himself to the royal toilet chamber and began attending to nature's call. The ill-starred king of Egypt had hid in the toilet for some reason, and he was soon sunk up to his head in Aadi's ordure. Realizing that he would have no refuge there, he caught hold of Aadi's testicles and hung from them for dear life. Feeling the terrible pain in his balls, Aadi jumped up and ran out of the chamber without washing himself, dragging the king of Egypt along with him. He ran raising a great hue and cry, shouting, "Terrible is the effect of this city's air and water that it causes a man to excrete men!" Munzir Shah Yemeni and others came rushing to him and, upon seeing the king of Egypt dragging from Aadi's testicles, rolled on the floor in fits of laughter. They had the king bathed and then conducted before Amir in his sorrowful state.

Amir Hamza said to him, "O King, you were meted out your just deserts! Now do not resist recognizing the One and Only God who has no partner. Speak what is on your mind, and tell me what keeps you from reciting the Act of Faith. I have no desire for your kingdom, and you may possess it with joy, but convert to the True Faith you must, or else it will not bode well for you, and you will come to a bad end!" Then the king of Egypt, who was a Yezid[17] incarnate, made vile imprecations, whereupon Amir's attendant, Agha Bulbul, who stood beside him, dealt him a blow of his sword which sent the king's head flying, and his torso began to writhe like that of a slaughtered chicken.

Amir put Zehra Misri on the throne of Egypt and bestowed the charge of public offices on Sarhang Misri and conferred a sumptuous robe of honor upon him. Then Amir asked Muqbil to marry Zehra Misri to bring her anguishing wait to an end. Muqbil replied with folded arms, "Until Your Honor marries Mehr-Nigar, this slave shall also remain unwed!"

The palace scouts brought intelligence that mass carnage was now under way in the city and the populace sought refuge, and a great crowd of them had gathered outside the royal threshold. Amir allowed them inside and gave them reprieve. Then along with his companions he indulged himself in festivities. The royal musicians began playing notes of rejoicing and merriment, and the sound of salutations and greetings was carried even to the ears of the heavens.

Once the celebrations were over, Amar gave Amir an account of his imprisonment and of Landhoor and Bahram Gurd, and showed him Naushervan's letter that he had recovered from the pigeon's neck. Upon reading the letter Amir let out a cry of anguish and wept, and then addressed his eminent nobles, saying, "Consider, my friends, that I underwent all kinds of ordeals and trials on Naushervan's account, and assented to all that he commanded me to do, but he always played me false and ever occupied himself in causing me dreadful afflictions. Now, God willing, I shall march on Ctesiphon and reduce it to ruins, and give every single Sassanid's wife and daughter to the equerries and cameleers to do with them as they please, as sure as my name is Hamza. I promise to keep my word and make all of you witness to my pledge so that I do not break my vow and earn humiliation and disgrace in the eyes of God and my companions!"

Everyone present replied with one voice, "Your Honor speaks the very truth in maintaining that you fulfilled every last bidding of that ungrateful wretch! You must not countenance his evil further, or suffer any more calamities at his fickle whims, for he always finds some pretext or other to foment mischief!"

From there Amir rode back to his camp and gave orders to prepare to march, and arrangements were made for the campaign forthwith. Zehra Misri came before Amir and said, "Your Honor's handmaiden has always nursed a desire to feast her eyes on Princess Mehr-Nigar. Being chosen to wait upon her would augment my honor to no end! I deem waiting upon the princess a far better proposition than the throne of Egypt."

My every breath intones my wish to line my eyes with the collyrium
Of the dust that lies under my beloved's feet.

"I wish you to command me to ride alongside you as your riding companion and to wait upon the princess until she is married to Your Honor!" Amir finally acquiesced to her wishes and, leaving vizier Karvan behind as their deputy in the city, marched on Ctesiphon with Zehra Misri by his side.

———

Now hear of Naushervan, who was seated on his throne one day when he suddenly proclaimed, "Go fetch Landhoor and Bahram from the prison and hang them on the scaffold before my eyes, and thus relieve the custodians of the jail from their duty!" Buzurjmehr said, "It would not be expeditious to kill them. Heaven forfend, you should be under fear to act speedily in killing these men, for it is unlikely that their supporters are nigh. From the divination of *ramal* it appears that Hamza is still alive and Your Honor's star is in the house of bad omen. It would be judicious for Your Honor to go with the nobles of your court and harem on an excursion by arranging a hunting party. Choose some mountainside or desert to adorn with your presence until this evil presage is dispelled from over Your Honor's fortunes. When the news of Hamza's death reaches here, Your Honor may hang Landhoor and Bahram and rid the world of their existence!"

Naushervan then asked Bakhtak, "What is your counsel in this matter?" He replied, "The Khvaja counsels well. When I was releasing the pigeon, Amar suddenly appeared from nowhere and threatened me! It would be most suitable for Your Honor to leave Ctesiphon according to Khvaja's commendable advice. In fact, Your Honor should set out for Egypt, and order the organizers of the journey to make preparations for that destination. In the event Hamza is not killed, Your Honor can have him executed in his presence, and upon returning to Ctesiphon have Landhoor and Bahram also sent to the gallows!"

Naushervan agreed to Bakhtak's counsel and, leaving his commanders Harut Guraz-Dandan and Marut Guraz-Dandan behind with forty thousand troops to guard the city and the prisoners, he himself headed for Egypt at the head of a vast force.

Now hear an account of Hamza. In his high dudgeon he traveled two and three days' distances without resting and arrived at Ctesiphon within a matter of days to set camp at Tal Shad-Kam as before. There many of his troops who had bivouacked in the woods in his absence also joined him and hundreds of thousands felt their slumbering fortunes awaken. Two *ayyars* presented themselves to Amir and reported that Naushervan had left behind Harut and Marut Guraz-Dandan to guard the city and the prisoners with forty thousand troops, and Bakhtak had also escaped. Amir replied, "I have my business with the custodian[?]. God willing, you shall soon see the city fall into my hands!" Amir then said to Amar Ayyar, "Go and tell Harut and Marut to send Landhoor and Bahram over. They will have not the least blame in the matter for I myself shall answer to the emperor!"

As Harut and Marut wished to invite an untimely death, they answered, "What authority does Hamza have that we should release the prisoners at his bidding? If he has any wherewithal he may come and take them himself!" Amar returned to Hamza and recounted their exact speech. Amir Hamza's face turned crimson with rage. Trembling with fury, he said, "Sound the war drums this very moment! I shall no longer lay claim to my honor and will renounce all title to courage and valor if I do not speedily secure their release!" Immediately upon his orders, the Timbal of Sikander was rung and Ctesiphon was thrown into turmoil at its sound.

Amir passed the night in ecstasies of grief and rage, and early the next morning he charged the fort, besieging and attacking it from all sides. When Harut and Marut tasted Hamza's wrath and witnessed the might of his force, they became worried lest he break down the fortifications, lay the city to ruin, and bring the royal army and citizenry to grief. They immediately led Landhoor and Bahram from their prison to the ramparts of the fort and proclaimed, "O Hamza, your companions shall pay with their lives if a single troop advances from your army. Their heads will be cast into the moat and their remains scattered before crows and kites. Then whatever comes to pass we will all suffer the consequences!"

Apprehensive that Landhoor and Bahram would die pointlessly if those wittols carried out their threat, Amir commanded his army to advance not one step nor launch any attacks without his express orders. Then he said to Amar, "O Khvaja, to this day I have not taken back one step that I put forward. If today I were to retreat for the sake of Landhoor and Bahram, it would earn me the most denigrating shame. Think of some ruse to save their lives and punish those bastards at the same time. If you accomplish this, I will confer a hundred thousand gold dinars on you, and indeed, I will reward you over and above this promise." Amar replied, "It is hardly a challenge beyond my scope. Those bastards and eunuchs are certain to fail in their strategy!"

Amar jumped across the moat, and addressed Harut and Marut, calling up to them, "Amir Hamza asks you not to kill Landhoor and Bahram. In return we shall retreat and not extend a single hand of molestation toward your city!" Then addressing Landhoor in Hindi and Bahram in the Chinese language, Amar said, "Amir states that the two of you are unfit to be called men, and are indeed nothing but craven cowards, the way you stand idle without moving a muscle! Recall how Amir broke his chains in the well of Yusuf as if they were made of gossamer thread, but you with all your might are unable to snap open the two chains upon you that are as thin as wire!"

Landhoor and Bahram both felt the sting of these words and, bellowing "God is Great!" exerted themselves so that the links of their fetters snapped open like so many crude linkages. Upon this sight Harut and Marut Guraz-Dandan charged at them with drawn swords, but Bahram and Landhoor wrested the swords from their hands and dispatched them to Hell in a shower of powerful blows. They also killed those doing duty on the ramparts before Amar gained the wall and joined them. Some twelve or thirteen thousand Indian troops stormed the ramparts and rivers of blood flowed in the battle that ensued. Amar flung the fort gates wide open immediately and the army of the True Faith entered the city and handed a humiliating defeat to the royal army. Amir gave orders for wholesale carnage, sanctioned plundering, and ordered all men and women taken prisoner.

Then Amir Hamza entered the royal bedchamber accompanied by Amar and began searching for Princess Mehr-Nigar. When Amir could find no trace of her, he asked Queen Mehr-Angez, who answered, "I have nothing to gain by telling you a falsehood! The emperor has taken her along with him." Amir answered, "It defies reason that the emperor would invite her to join the chase and scour the forests while leaving you behind." Queen Mehr-Angez replied, "The royal palace is open to you, and you have the freedom to search all its chambers." Amir then said to Amar, "This shall be your responsibility, and for this service I will pay you twelve thousand gold dinars. Your lucky star is today at the height of its glory. Now we must find Princess Mehr-Nigar, who is like to Venus in beauty!"

Amar searched for the princess in the palace's back gardens and in the gardens of Qasr-e Chahal Sutoon and Bagh-e Hasht Bahisht, but Mehr-Nigar seemed to have disappeared like the rara avis, and he could catch no trace of her. He was almost out of ideas for her search when his eyes suddenly beheld a marble well in the foyer of one garden and thought, *If I am not mistaken, with God's grace, I will find Mehr-Nigar imprisoned in this well!* When Amar approached the well, he found it covered with a slab weighing several hundred Tabrizi *maunds*. It so completely covered the mouth of the well that there was not a crevice even for air to pass through. To move that slab was beyond Amar's strength so he called Amir Hamza over and said, "Come over here and inspect this!" When Amir neared, Amar said, "O Amir, I have not the least doubt that Mehr-Nigar is imprisoned in this well and that treasure trove of beauty is secreted away therein. However, I find myself unable to move this slab for the Almighty God has gifted you alone with such strength!"

Amir slid the slab over to one side and lowered himself into the well. At first he could make out nothing for the darkness, but slowly a tiled vestibule became visible to his eyes. As he lowered himself further, he saw Princess Mehr-Nigar sitting there with her head cradled on her knees filling the skirts of her robe with tears. Raising her head at the sound of approaching steps, she caught sight of Amir and ran to him, falling upon his neck and proclaiming in a cascade of tears:

Not knowing this fate I fell in love,
For I fell in love and not in some error,
Thinking that our lives would be spent in blissful union
Never once knowing the pain of the day of separation.

"O Hamza! Do not tear me away from you again for I will be unable to withstand the pain of separation and my heart will not be able to bear the burden of disunion!"

My bosom is the sky in which the sun of separation dawns,
The break of the morn of doom a mere rent from which my grief outpours.

Amir wiped her rose-tinted tears with his sleeve and said, "O soul of Hamza! The night of separation is over and the day of union has arrived. Delivered into the days of rejoicing, the pain of parting is waning away.

Today I have been afforded union with my beloved,
After many a day the eve of separation has departed.

"Come, take this rope and help yourself out of this well. Behold the light outside this dark hole!"

Amir first helped Mehr-Nigar out of the well, then had all her attendants conducted out of there, and then he climbed out himself. He forthwith sent for a gold-inlaid litter for Mehr-Nigar's conveyance, and headed for his camp at Tal Shad-Kam. All the illustrious nobles conferred offerings upon him in celebration of his victory, and the chorus of "Congratulations!" and "Salutations!" rose from all corners.

Mehr-Nigar said to Amir, "O Abul-Ala! You sought me, and now the Gatherer of the Separated has united me with you. He was the one who kept me alive and saved you from a thousand calamities and other evils. For my sake now release the men of Ctesiphon, and restore the prisoners to freedom as your sacrifice." Amir replied, "Your wish is my command!" He ordered all the prisoners to be set free instantly and all pillaged goods to be returned. His orders were carried out that same moment, and the war booty was returned to the owners.

Now hear of Aadi, who was posted by the kettle drums when Amir gave his earlier orders for assault. While at his post, he espied a damsel, barely twelve years of age, who was like the sun in beauty, wandering in great confusion with some ten or twelve attendants. She stumbled at every step from daintiness as she was clearly unused to such exertions. Aadi was greatly charmed by her ways and rushed from his post to catch her. He soon found out that she was Bakhtak's daughter. Not having entered adolescence yet, she was an unopened bud and a unripe grape. This delighted Aadi even more, and he thought, *It is meet and proper that the Sahibqiran should have Naushervan's daughter and I should have Bakhtak's!* Reckoning that it was fate that had sent her his way, he took her into his pavilion. That night, when he tried to ravish her, she was unable to bear the pain and cried loudly. Aadi desisted from his pursuits fearing that Amir would visit the most terrible chastisement upon his head should the alarm reach his ears. The dread of this kept him from molesting her.

But after so many days of hard austerity he was unable to keep his hands off such succulent fruit. Throwing all modesty to the wind, he ordered the Timbal of Sikander to be sounded. Then he returned to his pavilion to renew congress with the girl, ignoring all considerations of her age, size, and stature. Lust prodded him on, and the devil was his counselor. She was too frail to receive Aadi's phallus without injury, and their sizes were incompatible to say the least. The moment he squeezed her rear, her mouth opened like a sparrow's and the avis of her soul flew from the confines of its corporeal prison.

When they heard the Timbal of Sikander, Landhoor, Bahram, Muqbil, and other commanders armed themselves and gathered in the Hall of Audience. When the camp heard the call the whole army girded itself in preparation and the troops began to array themselves in platoons and detachments. At that very moment Amir was sitting on his throne with Mehr-Nigar and Amar was singing and playing the *do-tara* and acting as their cupbearer. Amir started upon hearing the sound of the Timbal of Sikander and, much astonished by the event, said to Amar, "Quickly go and find out why the Timbal was sounded and for what reason it was struck!" Amir rose from the throne himself as well and, hastily decorating himself with his weapons, began pacing to and fro while awaiting Amar's return.

When Amar arrived at the Hall of Audience, he found all the illustrious nobles and kings armed to the teeth and in their saddles, and the entire army arrayed outside the hall ready for battle. Amar asked Landhoor and Bahram, "Why do you stand here armed, and who ordered you out?" They replied, "We know nothing of the matter. We armed ourselves and came forth as is customary upon hearing the Timbal of Sikander, to await

Amir's orders and sacrifice our lives at his command! You should know the rest of the details yourself as you were with the Sahibqiran and must have known about this and had a say in the matter."

Amar marveled greatly, wondering what had caused the alarm and what fresh mischief and new devilry was afoot. He kept his quiet for the moment and went to the assembly of trumpeters and said to Kebaba Chini and Qulaba Chini, "Amir demands to know at whose command the Timbal was sounded. Who brought you the orders?" They replied that it was Aadi who had ordered them to sound the Timbal.

Perplexed, Amar went to Aadi's pavilion where he saw a truly marvelous calamity unfold before his eyes. He regarded the singular turn of events that had taken place and the most peculiar scene that now showed itself to him. Having killed a dainty damsel in her pubescence by forcing her maidenhead, Aadi sat with her corpse before him, contemplating his deed with his head in his hands. Amar asked Aadi about the circumstances of her death, whereupon Aadi shamefacedly narrated the whole account of how he had brought Bakhtak's daughter there and ravished her by force, and how she had died in the act.

Amar returned to Amir Hamza and narrated to him the entire account. Amir was enraged and said, "Have Aadi arrested so that I can bury him alive in the same grave where that girl is interred!" Mehr-Nigar interceded with Amir to pardon Aadi, and Amar added to her petition by saying, "Just imagine that in the same way Your Honor took a fortress by storm, he, too, forced open a citadel of virtue!" Amir then left the court and entered the Hall of Audience, and after narrating the whole account and tendering an apology to each of the commanders assembled there individually, he asked them to let down their guard and retire. Amir went back to his station to lie down, and his entire army also returned to their posts to stretch and relax.

When it was morning, Amir ordered a weeklong period of festivities to celebrate his victory. Before long all the festivities were prepared and enjoyed. After that merrymaking was over, Amir Hamza was about to give marching orders to his army when Aadi presented him a letter from Jaipal Hindi, whom Landhoor had left behind to look after the affairs of his land in his absence. His brow clouded after he perused its contents and he handed it to Landhoor, who also became apprehensive after reading it. Jaipal Hindi had written:

Firoz Shah the Turk has attacked us with an army of three hundred and fifty thousand troops and foot soldiers. We have already had a few encounters, but because Firoz Shah came with a vast army, he has returned victorious from the battlefield after each skirmish. Your humble servant was forced to shelter himself in Sabir Shah's fortress, and if the Sahibqiran or the Khusrau of India should fail to come to our aid, the Turks will soon have the run of the place, and we shall all become Your Honor's sacrifice by the good fortune of your foes.

Amir said to Landhoor, "I want you to advance on India and chastise that headstrong rebel. May the grace of God ordain that you return victorious." Landhoor replied, "It has always been my fervent desire to spend the days of my life under the shadow of Your Grace's feet, and one day to become a sacrifice of your life. But Your Honor wishes to part me from himself, and thus inflicts on me the anguish of separation!" Amir answered, "God forbid I should ever wish separation between us, but if I do not send you on this campaign, the entire land of India will needlessly slip out of our hands. God willing, when you write to inform me of your triumphal victory, I will immediately send for you. Moreover, I shall not marry Mehr-Nigar until you return."

Amir dispatched Mehr-Nigar and Zehra Misri toward Mecca escorted by Amar and Muqbil with forty thousand troops, and furnished them with a large purse for supplies and travel expenses and said to them all, "I shall have the pleasure of your company as soon as I have seen off Landhoor on his campaign." Then Amir ordered Aadi to move the advance camp toward Basra for the purpose.

In a few days Amar and Muqbil arrived in Mecca with Mehr-Nigar and Zehra Misri, and the Sahibqiran reached Basra accompanied by Landhoor and Bahram and his army. Amir sent for the skipper to commission the ships. Then reading the prayer for safe journey once Landhoor and his army had boarded the ships, Amir ordered the ships to weigh anchor.

The next morning Amir said to Bahram, "O Bahram! Though I suffer greatly at the prospect of separation from you, the heavens that take pleasure in sequestering friends are bent upon putting distance between us still. You well know that I consider the Khusrau of India and yourself as the mainstays of my power, and indeed it is by dint of your help and assistance that I have been able to entertain my lofty ambitions. I had no choice but to send Landhoor on the campaign to India, and now I count on you to proceed there and assist him in his undertaking, for I can think of no one else to nominate for this mission. Besides the fact that Firoz

Shah is a mighty warrior, he also commands a great army, and is counted among the most illustrious warriors in that part of the world. I would counsel that you advance toward China, sack Firoz Shah's country, and lay it to ruin, razing his cities to the ground. From one end Landhoor shall visit scourges on him, and from the other you shall despoil his land and spring a surprise on his rear. Once you have accomplished your mission, I will send for you along with Landhoor. Until the two of you have joined me, I promise not to marry Mehr-Nigar."

Bahram replied, "I would to God that you live until the end of times! Nothing can deter me from carrying out Your Honor's commands. Although leaving my station at Your Honor's feet is indeed a cause for grief for me, it is a greater privilege to lay down my life in your service, and an unparalleled favor it is to become a sacrifice of Your Honor's life." In short, that same day Bahram also boarded a ship with his army; and after seeing him off on his campaign, Amir himself headed for Mecca with his victory-clinching army. It is related in another account that a mighty foe had invaded China, and that was why Amir had dispatched Bahram to chastise him.[18]

Amir had traversed seven stretches of the journey to Mecca when the chiefs of Tang-e Rawahil told him that a mighty and splendid river lay two *kos* farther to their right whose bank was bounded by the pasture of Alang Zamarrud, a place whose ambience no words could describe and whose beauty—which put to shame even the gardens of Farkhar[19]—had to be seen to be believed. Amir said to Aadi, "Set up my pavilion in Alang Zamarrud and bivouac the army there!" Aadi went immediately and pitched Prophet Danyal's pavilion on the riverbank, where Amir and his army dismounted.

After resting in his pavilion overnight, Amir stepped out in the morning to find that indeed this was a scenic place the likes of which his eyes had never beheld. On one side a lush growth of grass bound the horizon and this emerald green expanse filled the vision. On the other side blossomed a vast stretch of marigolds that presented a view both serene and blissful. On one side of the river stood a mighty mountain whose slopes bore countless fields of blooming flowers and all manner of trees laden with flowers and fruit. Flocks of deer, antelope, hog deer, blue antelope, and ravine deer frolicked there and thousands of varieties of caroling birds perched on the branches of the fruit trees. Flock upon flock of demoiselle cranes, teals, buntings, ruddy geese, and black-barreled geese sat by the banks of the rivulets, springs, lakes, and ravines that limned the pasture, and the foliage of its trees bustled with countless partridges, painted quails, Greek partridges, and cock pheasants.

Greatly delighted by the sight, Amir spent the whole day hunting birds and beasts. In the evening when he entered his camp, he sent game worthy of his own table to the royal kitchen and distributed the rest among the nobles, kings, champions, and commanders of his army. He spent the night in revelry and pleasure seeking as was his wont, and come morning, stepped out of his bedchamber, and performed his toilet and changed, and ascended his throne. He had not yet ordered his army to move camp when two *ayyars* presented themselves to him. After paying their respects and making salutations, they announced that the warrior Zhopin Kaus was headed there to challenge him, accompanied by many illustrious warriors at the head of a seventy-thousand-strong intrepid army.

Accounting for why Zhopin Kaus had come forth for battle, they explained that while Naushervan was on his way to Egypt to murder Amar, he received intelligence that Ctesiphon had been sacked and ruined by Hamza, who had put the populace to the sword and absconded with Mehr-Nigar from the royal palace. The news distressed and grieved Naushervan to no end, and he hastily retraced his steps to the seat of his empire. Beating his head in remorse when he saw the devastation in his city and found Mehr-Nigar missing, he cursed Bakhtak and attributed his reverses and the ruin of his city to his advice. The emperor declared that his prestige and honor had been tarnished by the city being sacked and the princess taken away. He pronounced himself unable to countenance his equals tainted with such a blemish on his prestige, and commented that if he had heeded Buzurjmehr's counsel, he would not have lived to see that dark day.

Presently Bakhtak also returned to the court from his home and, flinging his turban on the floor before the emperor, wailed that after Amar had killed his mother, now his daughter had died at Aadi's hands. He cried that the potentates of the Seven Climes would judge Naushervan a fine emperor if they learned how he had allowed an Arab lad to forget his place, and moreover how he had left his entire land exposed to sack and ruin while he watched on in silence, unable to do a single thing to put a stop to it. Naushervan replied to Bakhtak with tears in his eyes that he was at a loss to find a remedy for the plague that was Hamza. He had done all that Bakhtak had asked him to do, the emperor avowed, and yet it had proven beyond his power to behead Hamza and feed his com-

364 • *The Adventures of Amir Hamza*

panions to the crows and kites. Bakhtak answered that none but Gustham might be pitted against Hamza and sent to do battle against him at the head of an intrepid army. Then Naushervan immediately sent a communiqué summoning Gustham to his presence, and thereby allayed the fears of the Sassanids.

The next day intelligence reached the emperor that Zhopin Kaus had issued forth with forty thousand troops and was encamped two *kos* from the city in order to present himself and wait upon the emperor. Naushervan sent Bakhtak and his courtiers forthwith to welcome him. On their way back Bakhtak narrated the emperor's feud with Amir Hamza to Zhopin Kaus in its entirety, whereupon that coward asked Bakhtak to calm the emperor's apprehensions regarding Hamza, and wagered his name that he should slay Hamza before long. When Zhopin presented himself before Naushervan, the emperor dwelt in great detail on his misfortune and afflictions. Zhopin offered him many words of consolation and encouragement, and asked to be granted leave to depart on a campaign against Hamza. Zhopin declared that he found every passing moment weighing like an hour on his mind, as he was loath to idle away a single instant in inaction. He vowed to punish Hamza and bring back Mehr-Nigar—or never again deem himself worthy of his name. He also declared that day before Naushervan that if he failed he would hide his face from his equals, let alone present himself before the emperor, and a handful of water would suffice him to drown himself from mortification.

Delighted to hear such words, Naushervan conferred on Zhopin the robe of son-in-law, and told him to set out without further loss of time with his intrepid army and his bloodthirsty champions. The emperor asked him to kill Hamza and bring back Mehr-Nigar so that he might give him her hand in wedlock, and moreover appoint him as his heir. Naushervan then accompanied him with two nobles of his court, one of whom was Ayashan Malik, with a force of thirty thousand warriors. Thus it had come about that the army was headed toward Hamza's camp.

Upon hearing this account Amir smiled and said to his men, "Today we shall remain encamped at this spot and our army shall continue to bivouac here! Zhopin shall be dealt with when he arrives. Our troops have become despondent from lack of action and this shall afford them a good opportunity to exercise their limbs and distinguish themselves in the theater of war and carnage!" Having said this, Amir turned his attention to revelries and awaited Zhopin's arrival.

Around the time of *asr* prayers, the horizon was darkened by a foul dust cloud rising to the heavens, and an army was seen approaching. When the scissors of wind tore apart this collar of dust, Hamza's men beheld seventy standards and many detachments of one-thousand-strong troops marching under them. By and by Zhopin's army settled down before them and set about making preparations for battle. When the darkness of night had fallen, two *ayyars*, Namian and Tomian, presented themselves before Amir and proclaimed that the drums of war were being beaten in Zhopin's camp. Amir ordered that the drums of war should answer from his camp, too, and that all the preparations for war should be completed. The moment these orders were given, Kebaba Chini and Qulaba Chini struck the Timbal of Sikander with a mallet weighing eighteen Tabrizi *maunds*, and its thunderous clap made many a man in Zhopin's army lose their hearing, and filled their hearts with terror. In short, the two camps spent the night in preparations and everyone's mind was occupied by matters relating to the pending battle.

Before long, King Sol routed the Potentate of the First Heaven[20] along with his army of stars, and ascended the throne of the fourth heaven. Zhopin entered one end of the battlefield with his seventy-thousand-strong army, and the Sahibqiran arrayed his five hundred thousand valiant troops at the other. The men of Arabia prepared themselves for battle and the soldiers and champions in the enemy's army fell to marveling at the strength of the followers of the True Faith. Once the groundsmen had cleared the field of all shrubbery, bushes, and roots and leveled it, the water carriers hastily wetted the ground with their water skins fitted with sprinklers. Criers and heralds started calling out, "Whoever has a claim to courage and valor should step forward and win acclaim, for today the mettle of the brave and intrepid shall be tested, and the ball and the field are provided."

At hearing this clamor each man's hair stood on end and they regarded one another's faces anxiously. The Angel of Death pitched his pavilion in the battlefield, and Mars, the Executioner of the Heavens, brightened the brow of each soldier. The warriors felt their steel armor soft as wax against their necks and knew that fierce combat awaited them. Every trooper saw the face of death reflected in his cuirass, and some hurled taunts at one another, while others berated their rivals with the talk of their supreme strength, saying:

Every warrior who came to skirmish with me
Kept a tryst with Hell and found a hard grave!

The braggarts said, "The ability of the dagger throwers shall be tested today! Look whose headgear is trampled under the horses' hooves! Observe whose step advances forth and whose step beats a retreat, and who loses his betel satchel[21] to his rival!"

While the armies exchanged these slurs, Zhopin Kaus spurred his horse from out of the center of his army. He brought him to a halt in the middle of the field and called out, "O worshippers of the True God! May the one who yearns for death come forward to face me, and taste the blade of my sword and the point of my life-drawing spear!" Unable to countenance this vain and boastful talk, Amir spurred on Siyah Qitas and descended like lightning on Zhopin's head, ramming his steed so powerfully against Zhopin's own that the latter was thrown back a full twenty paces. Not a little unnerved by this show of Amir's strength, Zhopin said, "It seems to me that you are the one who goes by the appellation of Hamza and commands the army of the followers of the True Faith!" Amir replied, "Indeed, I am Hamza, an abject servant of God the Creator, and a slave to those who worship Him!"

Zhopin said, "O Hamza! What idle fancy drives you, and why do you wish to imperil your life? Surrender Princess Mehr-Nigar to me so that I may take her as my wife, and follow me yourself with your hands tied in voluntary submission, so that I may intercede for you and have your calumny pardoned by the Emperor of the Seven Concentric Circles!"

The Sahibqiran answered, "O wretch! Save your tongue such ravings! Fulfill your heart's desire and deal me a blow if you have any claim to valor. Afterward, you should prepare to receive mine!"

Upon hearing this Zhopin thrust his spear at Amir's immaculate chest. Amir pulled the weapon lightly by its point, at which it came loose from Zhopin's hands as if it were a loose twig in the sweeper's broom. Enraged, Zhopin next attacked with his mace, but Amir received its blows on the shield of Garshasp, foiling every single one of his strikes. Mortified and humiliated beyond measure, Zhopin brought down his mace ceaselessly and repeatedly, yet Amir foiled every blow, which landed on the ground causing a cloud of dust to rise over their heads. As that dust cloud screened Amir, Zhopin fell to boasting and swaggering and said, "There! I have killed him and made him dust, and trampled him under my feet! Where are his well-wishers? I wager them riches and high office if they can find me even a single shard of his bones!"

When Amir heard his bragging, he spurred on Siyah Qitas like a blinding bolt of lightning and advanced on his adversary, saying, "O dastard! Who do you claim to have killed, and boast to have made into dust? The Angel of Death stands before you in my person seeking your soul. God willing, you shall see how I dispatch you forthwith to the Erebus of Hell! Come, I shall give you another blow, so that your desire is fully requited!" Zhopin weighed his mace in his hands and attacked again. Amir again foiled the blow and wrested the mace from his hands. He plucked Zhopin off his saddle like a hawk picks up a wagtail, or a kestrel a pigeon, and slammed him against the ground.

After dismounting his steed, Amir pinned Zhopin down by sitting on his chest, and with his dagger pressed against his throat, addressed him thus: "Speak what you have to say now! Now that you have tasted the fruit of your boasting, do you have any gallantry left?" While nursing malice in his heart Zhopin pleaded for mercy, and made a pretense of conversion to the True Faith. Amir got off his chest and stepped away, and Zhopin got up and then fell at the feet of Amir, who embraced him. Drums of victory were sounded in the camp of the followers of the True Faith, and while Amir's standard-bearers unfurled the flags of victory, Zhopin's army retreated in great disgrace and humiliation to its resting place, bemoaning their fate after their crushing defeat that day.

Amir returned triumphant and victorious to his camp along with Zhopin, occasioning a chorus of congratulations and salutations to rise from all sides, and then preparations for festivities were started anew. Zhopin's toilet was attended to, and when the cloth was spread and food served, Amir broke bread with him. After the repast, cups of roseate wine began to make rounds and they all indulged themselves to their satisfaction. Zhopin said to Amir, "I ask your leave now to return to my camp and convert my army to the True Faith. Come tomorrow morning, I shall present the commanders of my army before you, to enter them into your service!" Amir was immensely delighted by his words and said, "A most propitious idea that is, too! I give you leave to embark in the name of God, for in such matters one must brook no delay! Go forth with my blessings and convert all of them to the True Faith!" Then Zhopin departed and went back to his men, and busied himself in spawning deceit and subterfuge.

Of Zhopin Conducting a Night Raid on Amir Hamza's Camp, and of Amir Disappearing Wounded from the Battlefield

Rancor does not find way into the heart of the one who is pure;
Dust and mirror are friends never: one obscures, the other reveals.

Those who are pure of heart do not nurse grudges once they have made peace, and never brood on what lies in the past nor think of settling old scores. Hear what Zhopin the wretch planned and plotted in his camp while Amir put his trust in that wretch and awaited his return. Upon entering his own camp Zhopin comforted and consoled his army, and said, "I converted to the True Faith upon finding my life in peril, and managed to slip away from their camp after hoodwinking that young fool, Hamza. Now, gird yourselves for ambushing his camp tonight and routing and scattering his army speedily. Defeat shall be meted out to them then, and we shall be victorious!" His army stood at the ready, and when night fell Zhopin headed for Amir's camp with his seventy thousand men to conduct the night raid.

On the way he ran into Amir Hamza's commander, Shis Yemeni, who was on vigil duty with four thousand troops. Hearing the sound of horses' hooves, he called out, "Who is it who dares to come forward? Do not advance a single pace or step an inch without first identifying yourselves!" Upon taking a closer look, Shis Yemeni beheld Zhopin advancing with hostile intent at the head of seventy thousand troops and foot soldiers. He challenged Zhopin, and the two parties drew swords and were locked into fierce combat which lasted four hours. But since it is ordained that the more numerous shall prevail, Shis Yemeni met his martyrdom at Zhopin's hands. The enemy then fell upon Hamza's camp.

Amir's army was deep in peaceful slumber, untroubled by the least fear or apprehension, when Zhopin's seventy thousand troops took them by surprise. There was no time to take stock of the situation, gird oneself, or secure weapons. The men snatched the first thing they laid their hands on, and faced the enemy. The cling-clang of swords, the rattle of weapons, and cries of "Bravo!" filled the air until they at last interrupted Amir's serene repose. He got up and inquired about the source of that clamor. His spies informed him of Zhopin's night raid on their camp. Fearful lest some harm should come to his mount, Amir headed for Siyah Qitas's stable from his pavilion without dressing, and bridled the horse and rode out bareback.

Naushervan's commander, Ayashan Malik, attacked Amir with a bloodied sword, but Amir foiled his blow and, wresting the sword from Ayashan Malik's hand, dispatched him to Hell with his own weapon. Ayashan Malik's younger brother then called out, "O Hamza! You committed a terrible act in murdering my older brother, but you shall not have long to live to reflect upon your deed! Little do you know what a terrible scourge I am!" Amir answered, "Grieve not, you shall soon keep company with your brother, for I am resolved to pack you off to the Erebus of Hell, too!" When Ayashan Malik's brother attacked, Amir parried his blow and returned it with such a blow to his back that it sliced him in two like a cucumber.

In the meanwhile, Zhopin stole up behind Amir and, calling all his power to his aid, landed a lethal blow on Amir's head, and the blade of his sword pierced Hamza's skull and wounded him gravely. Nevertheless, Amir turned back and answered with a blow to Zhopin's head that—although the sword missed its mark when Zhopin leapt aside—left a four-digit-deep impression in the skull of that brainless ape. Amir's second blow cut through his ribs on one side, and his next blow wounded him similarly on the other side. Disconcerted by these blows, Zhopin swung forward in his saddle, and his derriere presented itself to Amir, who drove the point of his sword nearly a handspan's measure into Zhopin's ass, causing it to burst forth in a veritable fountain of blood. As Zhopin fell unconscious from his horse, ten thousand men from his army rushed to his aid and carried him off to Ctesiphon without loss of time.

Of Zhopin's seventy thousand men, sixty thousand made their permanent abode in Hell. Several thousand men in the camp of the followers of the True Faith entered the gates of Paradise after attaining martyrdom in the night raid. Amir lost consciousness from the continuous bleeding of his head wound. Noticing that his master had been injured, Siyah Qitas carried him into the forest and away from the battle-field.

Aadi and other commanders from Amir's army looked for him among the dead and searched high and low the surrounding area of the battlefield for some trace of him, but they found none. Then the clamor of the mourners rose from the camp of the followers of the True Faith, and all the commanders and their men ripped open their collars in grief and clad themselves in sable. Amir's companions, disciples, well-wishers, and nobles threw dust on their heads and lost themselves in the depths of sorrow. On the third day following the incident, Aadi arrived in Mecca with his entire army and gave news of the tragedy to Khvaja Abdul Muttalib and Amar. Upon hearing the news, all the nobles of Mecca clad themselves in black, too, and occupied themselves with weeping, wailing, and lamenting their loss. The heartrending wails and cries of the mourners rose from Earth and unsettled even the angels of the first heaven. Stunned by grief, Khvaja Abdul Muttalib clutched his heart and neither listened further nor uttered a word. Amar and Muqbil tore the collars off their garments. Mehr-Nigar slapped her rose-colored cheeks purple as the iris, and pulled out her locks until she was far from all cares of combing and plaiting them, and her face looked like that of a woman recently widowed.

While that unearthly ruckus was going on, Amar had a thought. He offered comfort and reassurance to everyone and said, "Believe me when I tell you that by God's grace the Sahibqiran is alive and well and safe. If the least harm had come to him (may such become his enemies' fate!), Siyah Qitas would not have failed to return to camp. Yet the horse has not returned, which means that the Sahibqiran has only suffered a minor reverse. Pin your hopes on the bounty of the merciful God while I go and find news of Sahibqiran. God willing, I shall soon return to bring you tidings of his well-being!"

Amar deployed the army in and around the fort, and said to Muqbil, "Beware and look sharp and guard this place with great care until my return. Do not let anyone approach, either friend or foe, and never let down your guard!" Then, clad in the livery of *ayyars*, Amar embarked on his search for Amir Hamza, and headed toward that field in Alang Zamarrud which had been the scene of the battle.

OF THE ARRIVAL OF ABDUR RAHMAN JINN, MINISTER OF THE EMPEROR OF QAF, FOR THE PURPOSE OF CARRYING AWAY AMIR HAMZA TO HIS DOMINION

The chroniclers of news and the copyists of traditions relate that at the appointed time the infamous *devs* of Qaf rebelled against Shahpal bin Shahrukh, the emperor of the realm of Qaf, and wrested control of Shehr Simin, Zarrin, Shehr Baqm, Shehr Qaqum, the Bayaban-e Mina, Qasr-e Bilour, Qasr-e Abyez, Qasr-e Murassa', Qasr-e Gohar, Qasr-e Zamarrud, Qasr-e Yaqut, Qasr-e Mina and Qasr-e Chahal Sutoon and Bagh-e Sada Bahar, Bagh-e Farhat, Bagh-e Hasht Bahisht, and Bagh-e Janan, taking control of the talismanic wonders created by Suleiman, and also over-running the cities of the *shutar-sars, gao-sars, gao-pas, galeem-gosh,* and the *nim-tans.* The emperor was reduced to taking refuge in Gulistan-e Irum, where he and his family hid in a fort.

One day the emperor of Qaf recalled something. He sent for his minister Abdur Rahman and said, "Find out what became of that boy Hamza, from the race of man, whose cradle was sent for from the land of Arabia, and about whom it was foretold that after the rebellion of the *devs* of Qaf and our taking refuge in Gulistan-e Irum, he would arrive and root out the rebels, and return the land to our control after freeing it from their domination. Find out where he is now, and what is his present domain and domicile!"

Abdur Rahman cast lots and said, "He has lately seen action in a fierce battle and received a wound from a poisoned blade! If Your Honor so desires, he can be presented before you!" Shahpal said, "I would like nothing better!" He forthwith sent for the salve of Suleiman[22] and gave it to Abdur Rahman along with plentiful fruit from the lands of Qaf, saying, "Go forth without further delay and apply this tincture to Hamza's head so that his wound is healed, and feed him these fruits so that he regains his lost strength. Then bring him along once he has recuperated!"

Abdur Rahman left the realm of Qaf mounted on a throne, accompanied by an entourage of several hundred jinns, and departed in a flash to fulfill his mission. Arriving in the pasture that stretched from the slope of the hill of Abu Qubais, he looked around and discovered Amir Hamza lying on the grass, unconscious from the grievous wound to his head. Abdur Rahman carried Hamza away on the throne and moved him to a cave in the hills of Abu Qubais.

There he cleansed his wound gently and carefully, and bandaged it after applying the salve of Suleiman. He placed salvers of fruit from Qaf around Amir, so that the aroma might revive his mental powers and invigorate his soul. After the third bandage was changed, Amir opened his eyes and regained consciousness. Abdur Rahman offered his blessings to the Sahibqiran, whereupon Amir returned them and said, "Who are you, whence have you come, and what is your appellation and your station? Tell me if it was you who brought me here and laid me on this throne!"

Abdur Rahman answered, "I am Abdur Rahman, the minister to Shahpal bin Shahrukh, the potentate of the realm of Qaf, and I am bound to that monarch's vassalage. When you were an infant I had your cradle carried to Qaf from your house at the orders of the emperor, who kept you there for seven days and had you nursed by *devs, ghols,* and jinns so that when you grew up you could meet their glance. Your eyes were lined with the collyrium of Suleiman, and you were returned to your home with the gift of many precious jewels in a most luxurious cradle!

"Lately, when the emperor sought news of you, I cast lots and learned that you were lying here wounded by a poisoned sword—separated from your companions and far from your camp. The emperor sent me here with the salve of Suleiman and these fruit offerings to attend to you in your affliction and make my services available to you. When I arrived here I found you in the condition that divination had indicated, and you were put on the throne and brought here. By the grace of God your wound is now healed and I can breathe easily once more. As regards the restoration of your strength, pray partake of these fruits, and you shall presently find all your past vigor returned and experience all your languor and weariness departing with every moment."

Amir said, "How and by what signs did you recognize me?" Abdur Rahman replied, "By the exercise of deduction, from remembering your dark mole, and by your curled locks, which are the telltale mark of Prophet Ibrahim's progeny!"

Abdur Rahman's manners greatly pleased Amir Hamza, and he praised them in becoming words suited to the personage of the addressee. Then Abdur Rahman introduced the several hundred jinns who had accompanied him and entered them into Amir's service. Next he told Amir, "I have a favor to ask of you, and I put my hope in your manly courage! Once you are fully recovered, I shall submit my plea before you, and await your pleasure to grant it!" Amir replied, "Your word is my command! I grant you your request without your asking for it, and there's an end to the matter!"

————

Now hear of Amar. When he set out in search of Hamza, he scoured Alang Zamarrud and the hills of Abu Qubais, but found no trace of him. In his wanderings he happened upon a pasture where he saw Siyah Qitas grazing and casting about rueful glances every few moments. Siyah Qitas at first did not recognize Amar as he ran to catch him. Siyah Qitas came charging at Amar with his tail raised like a feral lion. But he showed no further belligerence and came to a stop after Amar clucked his tongue and he recognized the voice. Siyah Qitas then stood obediently by Amar's side.

Amar kissed the horse's forehead and said, "Lead me to your master!" Siyah Qitas neighed and pointed with his muzzle toward the cave. But the gesture was lost on Amar and, unable to comprehend it, he made a futile search of the surrounding area. Amar decided that he would resume his search after taking Siyah Qitas home, so that the sight of Amir's mount could afford some comfort to the mourners. With that in mind, Amar led Siyah Qitas back to his camp and presented him before the illustrious champions, kings, nobles, and Khvaja Abdul Muttalib and Mehr-Nigar, and then said, "Siyah Qitas has been found, and I have led him here so that the sight of him may afford you relief. Now I am headed back to find Amir!"

Amar set out again, and this time his path led him to the slope of Abu Qubais where his ears picked up the buzzing of human speech. He thought he heard people talking, and upon entering the hill's cave he beheld Amir seated on a throne, partaking of a variety of fruits the likes of which Amar had never before seen. He rushed forward and fell at Amir's feet. His friend raised him and embraced him affectionately, and asked news of Mehr-Nigar's well-being.

Amar narrated all that had happened up to that point, and then stood with folded arms before Amir. Because Amar's eyes were not lined with the collyrium of Suleiman, he could not see any of the jinns present there. The jinns were greatly amused by Amar's mien and appearance, and began jesting and playing among themselves. One of them pulled Amar's feet out from under him, and Amar fell flat on his face. When Amir laughed at the caper, Amar said to him, "Do not laugh at me O Sahibqiran, since I am exhausted after wandering in the forest and hills in search of you. I fell down because there was no strength left in my legs!" Then Amir asked him to draw near, and as Amar stepped forward one of the jinns sat down on his haunches in front of him. Amir Hamza again broke into laughter as Amar stumbled over the jinn and fell. Another jinn removed Amar's headgear with such a light hand that he never felt a thing. Hamza asked, "Why are you bareheaded, Amar? What did you do with your headgear?" Amar felt his head with his hand and, finding his headgear gone, raised a great hue and cry, and gave vent to his anger.

Seeing Amar become so nettled, Hamza said to him, "You should know that Shahpal bin Shahrukh, the potentate of the realm of Qaf, has sent his vizier Abdur Rahman Jinn here with an assignment that he has not told me as of yet. He will deliver the message and inform me of the task once I have fully convalesced. He was the one who tended to my injury and made it well, and made my wound to heal rapidly. He also brought me these fruits so that I may quickly regain my lost strength. Those who jested with you were jinns who accompanied him here."

Amir took back Amar's headgear from the jinn who had removed it, and restored it to Amar. He praised Amar highly before Abdur Rahman, and had Amar's eyes lined with the collyrium of Suleiman as well. Amar was then able to see everyone present there, and the Sahibqiran introduced him to Abdur Rahman. Afterward, Hamza said to Amar, "You may go back to Mecca and take news of my well-being, but do not breathe a word to anyone about my whereabouts!" After Amar had departed for Mecca, the Sahibqiran said to Abdur Rahman, "Now you may relate the matter regarding which your lord and master sent you here!"

Abdur Rahman replied, "I have already told you that when you were seven days old I determined from *ramal,* and informed my sovereign, that a time would come when the *devs* of Qaf would rebel against his authority and wrest control of his empire from his hands—they would ignore all considerations of obedience and behave most fractiously toward him. I also told him that the scion of a noble house, who had already been born to Mecca's chieftain, would arrive in Qaf and rout the mighty and indomitable *devs*, and dispatch a great many of them to Hell with his unrelenting sword. I saw that he would take thousands of *devs* prisoner, would restore the emperor's dominions to his control by the dint of his arm, and would wipe out all evil and iniquity from his land.

"Thus it came about that the emperor sent me to bring him your cradle and he kept you in Qaf for seven days nursing you on the milk of *devs*, *ghols*, jinns, lions, and other ferocious beasts so that these creatures would be unable to outstare you in an encounter. Your fierceness always overwhelms them, and they quail before you by Almighty God's grace. On the eighth day you were taken back to Mecca in a bejeweled cradle from Qaf, and your father, who had been grieved by your disappearance, was delighted and overjoyed to have you back.

"Lately, it came to pass that Ifrit the *dev* gained such power that he took control of the entire realm of Qaf. The emperor is now fortified in Gulistan-e Irum, yet he is under an ultimatum from Ifrit to vacate that abode as well. The good fortune of the emperor's enemies has brought about his disarray and distress, and he longs for death to relieve him of his unenviable situation. He asked for news of the one I had mentioned in the past in such glowing terms, whose cradle he had sent for, and who I had predicted would slay all his enemies and restore control of his land to him. The emperor mentioned that the infant would now have become a youth, having attained intelligence, learning, wisdom, and perspicacity, and must have become the pride of his age and the envy of his contemporaries. He asked me for your whereabouts and for information on where you were to be found.

"Following the emperor's orders, I cast lots and discovered through *ramal* that you were lying wounded in this pasture. When the emperor heard this, he asked me to come forthwith and heal your wound with salve of Suleiman and restore you to strength by making you partake of these fruits, so that every passing day brings you health and you are fully restored to your former vigor. The emperor asked me to convey to you his blessings with the message that the infidel Ifrit, who was a mere pawn of a foot soldier in the times of his ancestors, has deviated from the path of righteousness. Cultivating influence among the ranks of soldiers and giant-riders, Ifrit has followed a twisted path like the chessboard's bishop, and caused him no end of trouble, finally driving him to hide himself at Gulistan-e Irum. Emperor Shahpal sends you the message that he is unable to move either fore or aft, or left or right, and has been exhausted of all options. If a master strategist like yourself does not come to his suc-cor, the tables will completely turn upon him. Then his options will be exhausted as the successive victories of his opponent, who is bent upon effecting a change of regime, will have blocked all his moves. You know that my emperor is among the followers of Suleiman, as you yourself are from the line of Ibrahim. The progeny of one prophet must needs assist another's in their time of need to their utmost extent and capacity."

Amir replied, "O Abdur Rahman! The prospect of that *dev* dying at my hand and the emperor's land being freed and restored to him by the dint of my arm affords me immense delight. I will accompany you most willingly!" Abdur Rahman answered, "I have already divined the certainty through *ramal*—and I am convinced of it in my heart as well—that you are the slayer of Ifrit, and that that renegade *dev* will be dispatched to Hell by your hand alone, and the land of Qaf will return to the emperor's authority!"

———

Now hear an account of Amar. After leaving the Sahibqiran, he pre-sented himself before Khvaja Abdul Muttalib, the nobles of Mecca, the commanders of Hamza's army, and Princess Mehr-Nigar. Giving them the news of Amir's well-being, he said, "If these happy tidings of which I am the bearer do not stir your hearts to confer rich rewards on the mes-senger, I wonder if I can ever entertain hopes of receiving anything from you, or obtaining what my covetous heart desires!" Then everyone lav-ished rewards on Amar according to their capacity, and busied them-selves in celebrating the happy news.

The next morning Amar again presented himself before Hamza and conveyed the whole account of his visit and the ensuing celebrations to Amir's chaste ears. Amir said to him, "Dear friend, I am obliged to under-take a journey that will last a number of days. Now let us see what the will of God ordains!" When Amar asked about the particulars, Hamza re-peated all that Abdur Rahman had told him. Then Amar said, "Whatever is the matter with you, O Hamza? What leads you on this fruitless en-deavor to that far-off place, after you went to all that trouble to rescue Mehr-Nigar? Declining to partake of all the pleasure you merited from that exercise is an act that defies all logic!"

Amir answered, "I am obliged to Abdur Rahman because he healed my wound and tended to me as I lay injured, and took great pains to see to my comfort. You well know that the mightiest *dev* or *ghol* or sorcerer holds no terror for me because the True Savior is my protector, and I have no reason to entertain the least dread toward any creature!"

At that point, Abdur Rahman said, "O Sahibqiran! The journey to Qaf will take you three days. Allowing another three days for the return journey, one for rest, one for killing Ifrit, and another to celebrate your victory, the entire trip will last nine days." Amir said, "That is agreeable to me. Indeed I would still agree to your request even if the journey took twice that time, and a full eighteen days! To bury my head in the sand during your time of need, and deny you any assistance that I can offer, would be counter to the dictates of courage and valor!"

Amar said to Hamza, "Do as you wish! I shall guard Mehr-Nigar for another eighteen days. But my responsibility will end on the nineteenth day, and I shall go my way, leaving you the master of your own affairs!" Hamza answered, "You have my consent! Bring me my inkstand, so that I may write out my instructions to Mehr-Nigar and the commanders of the army, enjoining all of them to obey your orders and seek your pleasure and consent in all matters. But I would to God that you not give way to your quirks of temperament or ride your authority roughshod over the commanders of the army!"

Amar left the cave with tears in his eyes, and headed for Mecca. When he arrived there, and Khvaja Abdul Muttalib learned Hamza's intent of journeying to Qaf, he became greatly alarmed and said to Amar, "Do something to convince Hamza not to execute what he has taken into his head, and bring him to see me!" Amar admitted, "My words were entirely wasted on him, but if you were to write him a letter arguing against this adventure, it might prove more conducive to your wishes!" Khvaja Abdul Muttalib sent for Amir's writing desk and wrote out a letter to Hamza and handed it to Amar.

From there Amar went to his camp, where a pandemonium like the Day of Judgment broke out: The assembly erupted in protestations when the commanders heard the news of Amir's impending journey. When Amar revealed the Sahibqiran's intentions to Mehr-Nigar, she fell to the floor crying, and tossed and turned and writhed in agony, and then washed her face with her copious tears. Amar said to her, "Princess! All this crying and wailing will serve no purpose! Get ahold of yourself and your humors. Write a letter to Amir as Khvaja Abdul Muttalib has done and see what he writes in reply so that his true intentions may become known!"

As Amar counseled, Mehr-Nigar wrote a letter lamenting how Hamza was forcing a separation on them. At the end of the letter she asked him to allow her to accompany him, in the event that she was unable to prevail upon him to reconsider his decision. She warned Hamza that if he left her behind, he would discover upon returning that she had put an end to her life and sacrificed herself for his safety.

Amar put her letter together with Khvaja Abdul Muttalib's and carried them secretly to Hamza. Placing the inkstand before him, he produced the letters and also gave Amir a personal account of all that had transpired. Amir first answered his father's letter and then addressed one to the commanders of his army, writing to the effect that he was obliged to undertake a campaign under circumstances that allowed no neglect or disregard on his part, and that in his absence those who held dear his leadership and companionship should consider Khvaja Amar their leader, and under no circumstances violate his orders. In reply to Mehr-Nigar's letter, Amir wrote:

I am going away for a mere eighteen days. I shall not be away longer, and will be reunited with you at the end of that period. The emperor of Qaf sent his vizier to look after me and he made me well with his ministrations. It will be a blot on my virtue, generosity, and bravery to show disregard for his plight and hold back my help from him in his hour of need. I ask that you accept another eighteen days of separation for my sake, and resign yourself patiently and contentedly to the will of God. It is not the custom of soldiers to take their women on campaigns with them. I shall adhere to this rule and not have cares for your pavilion weighing on my mind in my campaigns and battles. I would have had no qualms, however, in taking you along if I were embarking on an excursion or hunting expedition. Until my return you must act on Amar's advice, and always consider him a well-wisher and as someone devoted to you with his life. He will never be culpable of breaking my trust, and you must never entertain any thought of his acting deceitfully or with connivance in your affairs.

Amir gave these letters to Amar to deliver to the addressees, and asked him to return with his arms and armor, forbidding him to breathe a word of these proceedings to a soul or even allow a slip of the tongue in the matter. Amar returned to Mecca and gathered Amir's arms and armor for him, but he did not deliver any of the letters. Satisfied, Amir Hamza decorated himself with his weapons and made preparations for his departure to Qaf.

OF GUSTHAM DYING AT AMIR'S HANDS AND OF HIS BEING SLAIN ALONG WITH HIS ARMY

Regard how fate displays its machinations and how death calls out to the one whose end is nigh. Now the battle with Gustham and the encounter between jinn and men shall be related.

After Amir left for his homeland, along with his intrepid army and Princess Mehr-Nigar, Naushervan's summons to Gustham were dispatched. Receiving them, that wretch set out and presented himself in Ctesiphon expeditiously. Naushervan narrated to Gustham Amir's sack of Ctesiphon and his abduction of Princess Mehr-Nigar, and then said, "It has been several days since Zhopin Kaus arrived here with forty thousand troops. I sent another thirty thousand troops with him under the command of Ayashan Malik, charging him to punish Hamza and bring Mehr-Nigar back. You should also join them, and with help from Zhopin and Ayashan Malik, kill Hamza and return with Mehr-Nigar."

Gustham then left for Mecca with thirty thousand troops and led his army forward with great speed. But Zhopin Kaus had taken the route from the pasture of Alang Zamarrud, and Gustham made his way from the forest. As he approached Mecca, Gustham learned that Hamza had received a fatal wound at Zhopin's hand and that nobody had heard any news of him since. It was not known whether he was alive or dead; and even if he were alive, nobody had seen the evidence. However, a small contingent of followers of the True Faith had arrived in Mecca and were said to be in a sad plight. Gustham was mightily pleased upon receiving this intelligence. He pitched his camp three *kos* from Mecca and ordered the drums of war to be sounded.

Hamza, who had not yet departed for Qaf, heard the sound of these war drums. But since there was no army within sight, he said to Amar,

"Dear friend, go find out who has sounded these drums, and whose army has announced its arrival!" After receiving these instructions, Amar went out, and he beheld an army of several thousand troops. Amar learned upon making inquiries that Naushervan had sent Gustham with thirty thousand troops to kill Amir and take back Mehr-Nigar.

First Amar went to the walls of the city and delegated soldiers to man the towers and the ramparts, and stationed archers, thunder throwers, lightning throwers, and naphtha throwers at every few paces. Amar was still thinking about presenting himself before Amir and informing him of the news, when Gustham attacked the fort with his thirty thousand men, ordering them to charge the walls. Amar answered their assault with a thunderous hail of Greek fire whose burns caused a great many enemy deaths. Terror seized the rest and they did not dare move a step, and became rooted to their spots. Gustham sounded the drum of retreat for the day and said to his men, "Rest for today and, come tomorrow, we shall settle scores with them! They will be defeated before long! In Hamza's absence it will not take long for the city to fall to us. This small army of a handful of followers of the True Faith cannot make a determined stand before our army or fight steadfastly. Tomorrow morning we shall attack and take the city, and return home with the princess after putting an end to their evil."

Then Amar found his chance and went before Amir to tell him the details of all that had come to pass. Amir said, "Go and sound the drums of war, and lead your army out into the battlefield. I shall come and settle this menace, and God willing, hand him a resounding defeat. Send Siyah Qitas to me before the first light of the day appears, and convey to our army my words of consolation and solace!" Abdur Rahman said, "If you wish to embark for the battlefield without delay, you need not send for Siyah Qitas. Instead of your mount, ride the throne to the battlefield!" Amir said, "Very well, then! I shall do as you suggest and ride the throne!" After rescinding the order to send for Siyah Qitas, Amir said to Amar, "Farewell, dear friend! Come tomorrow morning, deploy your men in the field in battle array, and await my arrival. I shall deal with that wretch and, God willing, teach him an unforgettable lesson for presuming to come this way!"

Amar returned to the city and conveyed the fortuitous news to all and sundry, saying to everyone he met, "Come tomorrow morning, you shall see the Sahibqiran and have an audience with your lord and commander. When I gave him the news about Gustham and narrated the details of all that had transpired, the Sahibqiran ordered me to return and sound the drums of war and array the army in the battlefield to await his arrival in the morning. He told me that he would arrive there to chastise Gustham and bury all his sedition in the dust!" Amar ordered Kebaba Chini and Qulaba Chini to sound the Timbal of Sikander, and made himself busy as well in preparations for battle. Once they heard the auspicious news, the whole camp passed that night in celebrations, as if it were the night of Eid or the Shab-e Baraat. The shadows of gloom and misery departed from their minds and the prospect of the coming day threw them into transports of joy and exultation. The drums of war sounded in the two camps the whole night, and the affairs and concerns of war occupied the fancies of the men in both camps.

In the morning Amar rode a handsome mule into the battlefield, and arrayed his troops, who positioned themselves in a state of great high spirits and preparedness opposite the enemy. Gustham also brought his army into the field, and upon looking closely, he discovered to his great surprise that it was not the Sahibqiran but Amar who had led the army into battle. He rode his rhinoceros into the field ecstatically and joyously, and was about to bark out his vain war slogans and order his army to charge into battle, when Amar espied the Sahibqiran's throne in the sky. Amar called out to the commanders of his army, "There! See the Sahibqiran coming to ennoble you with his magnificent presence!"

When the throne approached, everyone saw Amir Hamza seated on it fully dressed for battle, and observed that his face did not appear the least bit transformed by any sign of illness. He looked hale and hearty and in the best of spirits. Beholding this, his followers hastened to dismount their steeds, and in their joyful eagerness to rush forward to kiss Amir's feet, some of them even fell over, as their feet were still caught in their stirrups.

While Gustham laughed out loud and made jests with the commanders of his army at this sight, Amar called out to him, "Laugh not so hard, O sniveling one, for you shall soon be crying harder when you are dispatched to Hell! Mark that the Angel of Death has come to claim you!" The Sahibqiran's throne descended from the sky in the meanwhile, and Gustham and his companions marveled greatly when they beheld this sight. They wondered how and from where Hamza descended like some heavenly calamity, and how he had suddenly come alive after no news had been heard of him for so long.

The Sahibqiran alighted from the throne and challenged Gustham forthwith, saying, "O worthless knave! Come now and face me, for which reason you made your long journey!" As Gustham was drunk on the wine of pride and vanity, he made a thrust with his spear at Amir's immaculate chest. Amir wrested the spear from his hand and brained the rhinoceros with a mighty blow of its shaft. The beast fell dead to the ground. Relieved of his mount, Gustham unsheathed his sword and came charging at Amir on foot. Gustham's sword broke as Amir parried his blow, and he was left holding the hilt. He ducked his head the first few times Amir dealt him blows, but then his luck ran out. An excellent thrust of the sword from Amir's hand cut Gustham in two like a raw cucumber and sent him to Hell. Witnessing this scene, Gustham's army charged the followers of the True Faith.

Then Abdur Rahman said to the jinns, "Do not stand idly thus! Fall upon Amir's enemy!" Each of the four hundred jinns who had accompanied Abdur Rahman caught two men in his arms, flew heavenward, and then smashed the soldiers against their companions on the ground. In this manner they killed twenty thousand men from Gustham's army and sent them to keep their master company in Hell. Three thousand had already become Hell fodder on the first day of the battle, when Amar had let lose his fireworks after Gustham's attack on the city walls. The remaining seven thousand realized that they must not sell their lives cheaply, and headed for Ctesiphon carrying Gustham's cleft corpse. With Amir's triumph secured in his battle with Gustham, Abdur Rahman carried him off toward Mount Qaf, leaving his army bivouacked in that place.

OF AMIR'S JOURNEY TO MOUNT QAF AND THE
BEGINNING OF HIS EIGHTEEN-YEAR STAY

The *dastan*[23] writer's pen traverses the vast expanse of the page as a jour ney to a far-off land is afoot. The circumstances of Gustham's death and the routing and retreat of his army have all been related. After Hamza departed for Qaf, Amar gathered the booty the enemy had left behind in gold, provisions, tents, and pavilions, and having appropriated the gold and the provisions himself, distributed the rest among his soldiers. Then Amar handed out the letters Amir had written earlier to Khvaja Abdul Muttalib, Mehr-Nigar, and the commanders of the army, and announced to everyone the news of Amir's departure for Qaf.

Khvaja Abdul Muttalib prostrated himself in gratitude before the Almighty God upon word of Amir's victory. Resigned to his fate, he laid the burden of patience on his heart and busied himself in prayers for Amir's safe return. The commanders of the army said to Amar, "O Khvaja, we always deemed you worthy of the same honor as the Sahibqi- ran himself, and carried out your orders in the same spirit. We shall not dither or vacillate in obeying you, or falter in the least in executing your commands! Even if you were to order us to walk into blazing fires or jump into the deep sea you shall find us at your beck and call!"

Amar embraced all of the commanders and expressed his heartfelt gratitude to them. He then told them, "All of you are companions of the Sahibqiran. Do not speak of obedience to my person, for I shall be happy only if we share the obligation brothers have toward one another. I de- clare that I would lay down my life for you, and pledge so with all my heart and soul! My concern for Mehr-Nigar's safety now prompts me to seek your counsel for I am afraid that when a mighty emperor like Naushervan hears of Amir's departure to the realm of Qaf, he will not leave any stone unturned to have Mehr-Nigar back. She is the light of his eyes and he has been endeavoring to have her spirited away all this time!"

The commanders replied, "Khvaja! If one of his commanders, nay, even if Naushervan himself, should descend on us with his army, God willing, he will take back nothing but humiliation and defeat as long as a single one of us keeps drawing breath!"

Amar replied, "Indeed I have even greater faith in your courage! This is what nobility and the principles of gallantry demand! This is the very soul of courage and high-mindedness! If Amir did not have such faith in you, why would he entrust his honor to your custody, and not seek some other succor and refuge?" Amar conducted the army inside the fort, ordered them to lift up the drawbridge, and after fitting out the whole city, flooded the moats around the fortifications. Then he laid out a bejeweled chair for himself to give audience with great pomp under a pavilion of embroidered Kashani velvet.[24]

After giving audience, Amar went before Mehr-Nigar, and spoke to her of Amir's victory over Gustham. Mehr-Nigar said to him, "O Khvaja, I consider you the same as my father, and therefore obey you in all matters. Amir wrote to admonish me not to act vainly or take any step without first securing your counsel and advice. God forbid I ever take into my head to act in defiance of your wishes. I would to God that I should perish the moment in which any of my acts contravene your commands!"

Upon hearing that, Amar praised Mehr-Nigar for her probity and noble nature and said to her, "O Princess! You can be sure that if I ever request anything of you it will be in your own best interest. Your well-being shall ever be foremost in my mind, and my actions will always reflect my dutiful devotion to you. Amir asked you to obey me in his absence because he knows that women are unsophisticated and are not privy to the devious ways of men. For this reason, participation in wars and battles is proscribed to them for their honor and virtue are threatened in such situations. Except as it regards your father—who nurses a grievance and is bent upon settling the score and harboring a grudge—I shall remain your faithful servant at all times!" Mehr-Nigar answered, "Khvaja, you shall have my obedience always, regardless of whether Amir is present or away!"

Amar was greatly pleased by Mehr-Nigar's replies. He bought enough provisions to last for six months and then said to himself, *Now even if the armies of the entire world should congregate here in an effort to drive us out of the fort, they are sure to leave empty-handed. We have taken refuge in the House of the Almighty and the favor of the Most High God is with us!* He deployed his commanders and champions to guard the ramparts, and cladding himself in a regal robe waited in his pavilion for the Sahibqiran's promised return.

Now an account of the Sahibqiran's journey and the continuation of this singular tale. The jinns carrying the Sahibqiran's throne soared so high that all the mountains and fortresses on land were lost to view. Around the time of *zuhr* prayers,[25] they descended and set the throne in a pasture. Amir asked Abdur Rahman, "What is the name of this place where we have landed?" He replied, "We are still within the dominion of man. A human reigns over this land and it is the place where the arena of Rustam bin Zal is situated."

After saying his *zuhr* prayers, Amir headed toward Rustam's arena for an excursion accompanied by a few close aides of Abdur Rahman. There they beheld a dome, and upon entering it, found a huge locked iron chest hanging from the roof, which no ordinary mortal could have brought down. Amir retrieved it and put it gently on the ground. When he opened it he discovered lying within a cummerbund, a dagger, a bow, and a stone tablet that read: "These artifacts belong to Rustam, and nobody may lay hands on them. But the Sahibqiran will acquire them and will be made our beneficiary heir[?]." Overjoyed, the Sahibqiran brought the artifacts and stone tablet to Abdur Rahman, who said, "This is an auspicious augur that has been bestowed on you from the future state."

They rested in this place that day and in the morning Amir again mounted the throne and resumed the journey. At night they descended to a spot where an iron wall of indeterminate antiquity rose to the high heavens and stretched for miles on end. No doors were marked in the wall, and there were no signs there of bird or beast or human. Upon Amir's orders the jinns searched, and discovered a door hidden in the wall. Amir opened it and gained entrance to the other side, where he beheld a saintly man saying his prayers inside a dome in a pasture.

When he caught sight of Amir, the man visited blessings on him and said, "O Sahibqiran! I have waited for you for two hundred years!" Amir returned his blessings and asked, "How did you learn my name, and know that I am the Sahibqiran?" The man answered, "I heard from my elders that in this domain of Qaf no human would set foot except for a man called Hamza! All praise to the Almighty God that the happy day has come when I set eyes on your face. Now the time has arrived for me to return to my Lord, and I request that you give me my funeral bath and bury me with your own hands and return my body to its element in the Earth!" The man then recited the Act of Faith and died, and set out for the land of the Future State. Amir was grieved to behold that scene, and carried out the saintly man's last wishes. After the funeral rites were over, Amir had his meal and again mounted the throne.

Abdur Rahman's entourage flew continuously for a night and a day and around the time of the *zuhr* prayers they again descended into a desert. Amir said to him, "Only a quarter of the day has elapsed as yet. Why alight here now?" Abdur Rahman answered, "I asked the jinns to descend now and brought down your throne for good reason. A little distance from here is the abode of Rahdar the *dev*, who plies the trades of banditry and murder. Anyone who escapes his notice escapes with his life. Others become his prey and meet their deaths. I descended here so that we could renew our journey in the middle of the night. Then we will have no fear of attracting his eye, and will be relieved of all dread and anxiety regarding him."

Amir replied, "I wish you to lead me to his den so that I may take stock of him—and kill him should the opportunity offer itself, to free God's creatures from his depredations." Abdur Rahman remarked, "O Sahibqiran! He is a veritable monster. It would be best to wait here for night to fall, as confronting him is against all reason!"

Amir demanded, "I would like you to tell me if Rahdar Dev is an even greater menace than the dastardly Ifrit!"

Abdur Rahman responded, "Rahdar is of absolutely no significance before the monster Ifrit! Indeed, he stands nowhere in relation to Ifrit, and any comparison between the two would be idle!"

Amir replied: "It begs reason then that while you are conducting me to Qaf to slay the mighty Ifrit, you forbid me an encounter with a smaller menace like Rahdar!"

Abdur Rahman was at last convinced by this argument and said, "There is yet another monster who infests these grounds and inspires such fear that nobody ventures here, for he strikes terrible terror in the hearts of men." Amir asked, "What is this monster? Give me its particulars!" Abdur Rahman replied, "This monster is a most feral and ferocious two-headed lion!"

Amir was mightily pleased upon hearing mention of a lion, and at once headed for the desert. When the scent of Amir reached the lion he left his desert lair to search for its source. Amir beheld a mighty beast, some sixty cubits in length from head to tail, whose ferociousness could not have been matched even by a thousand lions. Amir challenged it, and the lion charged him with a mighty roar. The moment it came within reach Amir leapt to one side and brought down his sword on the lion's back, cutting it in two. The faces of the jinns were drained of blood when they witnessed this show of Amir's strength, and they were mightily amazed and terrified. Abdur Rahman kissed the hilt of Amir's sword, and from there they carried Amir's throne to Rahdar Dev's den.

The whole night Amir did not sleep a wink from anxiety that the jinns' concern for his safety and fear that he was not a match for Rahdar would force them to divert him from the encounter. Dawn was breaking as they arrived at the *dev*'s abode, but the jinns became panic-stricken from fear and, putting the throne down, they rushed away in a frenzy to hide themselves in any nook or corner that offered them refuge. Amir dismounted his throne and set out in search of Rahdar Dev.

Now hear of Rahdar Dev. He inhabited that abode with three hundred *devs*, and kept watch on the proceedings of the emperor of Qaf, staying abreast of all his deeds. One day, a *dev* brought him news that the emperor of Qaf had dispatched his minister, Abdur Rahman, to the dominion of men to bring back a human. It was said that the man was a valiant champion, unsurpassed in courage and peerless in might and valor, who would slay the *devs* of Qaf and reinstate Emperor Shahpal on the throne. Ever since he had caught wind of this news, Rahdar Dev had lain in wait for that human to pass his way so that he could sink his fangs into Hamza's tasty and luscious flesh and make a meal of him.

It so happened that Rahdar was sitting on the summit of the mountain, gazing on the splendid scenery, when he espied the Sahibqiran. Seeing him from afar, Rahdar reasoned that the anticipated human must have arrived, and the man he saw was probably one of his companions. Rejoicing in his good luck to have found such a delicious tidbit, Rahdar ordered one of his *devs* to bring the human being alive into his presence. As the *dev* approached Amir and extended his arm to take him to Rahdar, Amir caught hold of his hand and wrenched it so mightily that the *dev*'s knees buckled and he came very near to dying from the violence of the tug. Amir then clouted him so powerfully over the head that his brains were smashed into his neck and he departed forthwith from the Qaf of the present to the Qaf of the Future State. Watching all of this, Rahdar decided that this must be the selfsame champion whom Abdur Rahman had gone to fetch. Feeling certain of this fact, he descended upon Amir's entourage with a force of three hundred *devs*. Amir bellowed "God is Great!" so powerfully that the entire expanse of the desert reverberated with the sound and the jinns very nearly died from fright.

Rahdar arranged his three hundred *devs* opposite Amir and made preparations for combat. Amir beheld a veritable monster some three hundred yards in height, sporting two horns that measured fifty yards each and resembled a cedar's dried branches. His mouth, which was like the opening of a well, spewed flames more copiously than the pit of Hell. His bloodshot eyes were the size of an executioner's tray, his eyelashes like a porcupine's quills, and his nose resembled a casket affixed between his eyes and lips. He was girded in a loincloth made of lion skins, and his tail was wrapped around his waist. Wearing golden, ornate chains and rattles on his arms, feet, and neck, he accosted Amir and said, "O dark-headed, white-toothed one, why did you kill one of my *devs*, disregarding all consideration and deference due me? Now you will never be delivered from my clutches, or escape with your life!"

Rahdar swung a box-tree branch tied with several millstones and brought it down on Amir with full force, but he foiled the blow. Then stepping to the *dev*'s side, Amir dealt him such a fierce blow with Rustam's dagger that it exited clean from Rahdar's other side. With the link to his senses permanently severed, the *dev* gave up the ghost from just that one blow. Amir put his dagger in its scabbard and, unsheathing the sword, he fell upon the three hundred *devs* that stood by. Whoever received a blow from his hand that day did not draw another breath.

Abdur Rahman said to the jinns in his entourage, "You should feel no fear or anxiety now that Rahdar is dead! Go forth and help the Sahibqiran!" At this command, all the jinns fell upon the *devs* and fought mightily. A great many *devs* were dispatched to Hell and entered the dominion of the Future State. Amir did not pursue the few who managed to escape with their lives but allowed them to flee. Then Amir went to Rahdar's abode with Abdur Rahman, where there were heaps upon heaps of countless priceless jewels and valuables. The sight reminded Hamza of Amar Ayyar, and he said, "Amar's station is empty today, but my heart is full of his memory." Then he said to Abdur Rahman, "All these goods here are the property of Emperor Shahpal bin Shahrukh, and I am not going to touch these ephemeral riches or be tempted by them. Present them to your emperor so that the recovery of his goods may give him some occasion for rejoicing."

All the jinns present there warmly lauded Amir's gestures of courage and munificence, and commented to each other that they little knew that such noble men were born among the sons of Aadam who could dispense such great riches without a moment's hesitation. From there Amir set out again mounted on his throne. The jinns clustered around him like loving moths around a burning taper. Four jinns brought up the rear carrying Rahdar's head.

When they reached the castle of Ghaneem, Salasal Perizad, who was one of the companions of Emperor Shahpal, came out with an entourage of forty thousand *perizads* to welcome Amir. After he conducted Amir Hamza into the castle, he feasted him in a right royal manner. The next day Amir set out again with Salasal Perizad toward Gulistan-e Irum.

The scribe writes that upon hearing of Amir's arrival, Shahpal rejoiced exceedingly and ordered that the news be reported abroad to all and sundry, and that a sumptuous royal procession should be organized so that he might welcome Hamza in person. The commands were carried out as soon as they were uttered, and with great pomp and array the emperor of Qaf set out to receive Amir.

Now we continue the account of Amir Hamza. His throne was flanked by Abdur Rahman on the right and by Salasal Perizad on the left. They were making their way, discoursing together, when scores of *perizads* of such luminous aspect that they overwhelmed one's vision materialized before them. They came flying toward them mounted on hundreds of thrones, chanting and playing musical instruments. They were followed by several thousand more—of such beauty as to bereft a human being of all senses—carrying bouquets of flowers, incense, and aromatic unguents, which fragranced the whole desert. They all clustered around Shahpal's throne, affording great delight to the eyes of their beholders. Spotting them in the distance, Abdur Rahman and Salasal Perizad said to the Sahibqiran, "What a marvel! The emperor himself has come out to receive you!" When Shahpal's throne approached, Amir ordered that his own throne be set down on the ground, whereupon Shahpal said to the *perizads,* "Set down our throne, too, next to Amir's so that we may derive wholesome bliss from our meeting!"

When Emperor Shahpal's throne alighted, Amir dismounted and kissed its foot. Shahpal embraced Amir, kissed his forehead, and said, "I took the liberty to inconvenience you by sending for you. It is well-known that only upright men can succor a righteous party in distress. It is through them that supplicants find the fulfillment of their wishes." The Sahibqiran said, "I would consider it an honor to sacrifice my life in your service. Indeed, as your sincere well-wisher, I would not hesitate in this undertaking in the least, and would deem it a bestowal of great glory upon myself!" Amir presented the emperor with Rahdar's head, along with all the jewels and valuables collected as war prizes. Shahpal was delighted by Amir's acts, and all those present became transfixed with wonder at the might of Amir's arm. They regarded him with great marvel, lauded him warmly, and praised his strength highly.

The emperor granted a robe of distinction to Abdur Rahman on the occasion, and thus raised him in esteem among his coequals. Then seating Amir by his side, the emperor repaired to Gulistan-e Irum, where he conducted Amir into the Hall of Suleiman, offering him a bejeweled throne for his station and scattering precious jewels as a sacrifice to Amir. All the illustrious *perizads* stood with folded wings before Amir. Taking delight in Amir's beauty and comely aspect, they said to one another, "Who would have thought that the Creator endowed feeble humans with such beauty and might, and made them so courageous and suave?" As for the emperor, he had eyes only for Amir and gazed on him like one spellbound. The emperor ordered that wines of Qaf be served in order to break the timidity of Amir, who sat quiet with his gaze lowered.

This scribe now returns to the realm of Earth to discourse on what passed there until the wine is brought out for Hamza.

The historians of chronicles of yore relate that Naushervan was already floundering in a sea of sorrow after hearing of the reverses suffered by Zhopin and Ayashan Malik, when Gustham's corpse was brought before him, and the companions of this slain commander narrated how Hamza's throne had descended from the skies like an unforeseen calamity after Gustham had arranged his army for battle. They recounted how Hamza killed Gustham and their troops were lifted to the high heavens by some unseen force that then hurled them at their compatriots on the ground, so that both were killed from the impact, and how, in that manner, twenty thousand troops died without anyone finding out who or what had killed them.

After these tidings, Naushervan looked askance at Buzurjmehr, who from his foreknowledge narrated the entire account of the realm of Qaf and said to the emperor, "Shahpal bin Shahrukh sent for Hamza to assist him, and he came to Hamza's aid in this adventure. Hamza has promised to return after eighteen days, but he will remain held up in Qaf for eighteen years. He will return after slaying the *devs* of Qaf, none of whom will be able to lay him low. Gustham declared war the day Hamza was to depart toward Qaf. While Hamza killed Gustham, Gustham's troops were killed by the jinns."

Naushervan rejoiced upon hearing Buzurjmehr's account, thinking that eighteen years were an eternity, and that Hamza would certainly die at the hands of some *dev* or another as it was well-nigh impossible to find release from the clutches of that malicious race. It occurred to Naushervan that now was a most opportune time to settle the score with the followers of the True Faith and wipe them out of existence when they least expected an attack. Thus resolved, he ordered Wailum and Qailum, who were the mightiest warriors among the Sassanids, to advance on Mecca with thirty thousand troops. He told them that with Hamza gone to Qaf, they would find the field to themselves and should have no fear of any kind. They should lay Mecca to ruin, and bring back Princess Mehr-Nigar and restore her to his sight. Having received their orders, the two commanders took their leave and headed for Mecca.

———

Now hear an account of Amar Ayyar, the exterminator of all infidels. After eighteen days had come and gone, and another few days had passed beyond the period stipulated by Hamza, Amar broke into loud cries and began to wash his face with tears. When he went to see Mehr-Nigar, he found her also in a state of great agitation. She said to him, "O Amar, Amir Hamza has not returned, and separation from him weighs heavily on my heart. God alone knows what passed with him, as he—a mere human, all by himself—has gone to the land where *devs* and *peris* dwell! God alone now is his custodian. I can think of nothing else but taking poison to die, and removing from life's page the mark of my existence. Then you may bury me wherever you deem proper, and inter me where you will."

Khvaja Amar responded, "O Queen of Heavens! What is this I hear? When did you ever hear of anyone taking poison due to separation from his beloved? Do you not recall the words, *Do not sever your hopes from God's Beneficence?* Why do you not put your hopes in God's aid and assistance? I am now headed to Ctesiphon to seek Buzurjmehr's opinion on this matter. Pray take charge of yourself and do not let any anxiety find its way into your heart!"

After counseling Mehr-Nigar, Amar went to see Muqbil and said to him, "I am off to Ctesiphon to get some news of Amir from Buzurjmehr. I would like you to employ yourself in guarding Mehr-Nigar with forty thousand faultless archers. Also depute strong warriors to guard the ramparts of the fort." Having imparted these instructions, Amar put on his *ayyar*'s attire and set out for Ctesiphon by way of the forest. He accomplished the journey in a few days and arrived at Buzurjmehr's door in the guise of a farmer. Buzurjmehr was just returning from court, and finding Amar there, asked him who he was.

Amar replied, "I work as a farmhand on your estate. I have suffered many injustices, and have come to you as a supplicant. If I do not find redress at your door, I will go and rattle the chain of justice at the emperor's court, and narrate my sufferings before him."

Upon hearing his story, Buzurjmehr determined that this was Amar in disguise. Finding privacy for them, he then embraced Amar and asked after his welfare. Amar replied, "I do not know how to begin to tell you the problems that burden my mind, and what anxiety and distress I have suffered. Hamza left with the promise to return after eighteen days, but several days have now passed beyond that time and I have no news of what became of him or if he was overtaken by some calamity. Mehr-Nigar is also greatly distressed by this situation, and all but resolved to take poison and put an end to her life!"

Khvaja Buzurjmehr said, "It is true that Hamza promised to return after eighteen days. You will see him at the Castle of Tanj-e Maghreb, but not until eighteen years have passed. He shall slay all the rebellious *devs* of Qaf and come to no harm himself. In the meanwhile, you will have to undertake and surmount many challenges. You will be assailed from all sides by kings and warriors from all over the world, and they will do all in their power to harm you. But rest assured that none of them shall prevail against you, and you will triumph over them in the end. Have no fear of anybody now. Repair to Mecca posthaste, and employ yourself in fortifying your defenses, because Naushervan has dispatched Wailum and Qailum at the head of thirty thousand troops to kill you and bring back Mehr-Nigar."

Amar replied, "I will not mind it in the least even if I should lose my life in Hamza's service. Fidelity to him is a thing impressed deep on the tablet of my heart. I shall remain faithful to him until my last breath. As to Wailum and Qailum, even if the mighty emperors Jamshed and Kai Khusrau were to rise from their graves, I would send them back whence they came if they should as much as utter Mehr-Nigar's name, let alone abduct her. Pray write out a letter of instruction to Mehr-Nigar, so that she may find some solace from your words and act upon my counsel."

Buzurjmehr sent for his inkstand and wrote a letter to Mehr-Nigar, wherein he stipulated the long waiting period before Hamza would return, and offered her many words of consolation. He gave the letter to Amar who set out toward Mecca by way of the forest. Passing all of the stations of the journey without taking rest night or day, Amar reached his fort and gave Buzurjmehr's letter to Mehr-Nigar. Reading it, she shed tears without cease and cried out, "Alas, such was my destiny that I should burn in the fire of separation from Hamza for eighteen years, and waste away like a taper by the flame of disunion from him. I know not how to survive the wait until the day I set eyes on Hamza's face again!"

Amar consoled her and said, "O Queen of Heavens, may you live long! God willing, these eighteen years will pass like eighteen days, and Hamza will return to you in perfect safety. Now pray to God and make supplication to the Almighty to safeguard Hamza, and afford your heart some solace. The Almighty God is the Unifier of the Separated. He will ease your separation until the day you meet Hamza and your eyes finally rejoice in beholding his face."

After comforting Mehr-Nigar with these words, Amar went into the camp and mustered the army, and then addressed all of them thus. "My friends, I have learned through Buzurjmehr that Hamza will remain in Qaf for eighteen years. Therefore, anyone among you who desires to leave may leave now, and those who wish to stay may stay in the spirit of fraternity. Upon his return, finding that you have been staunch in his friendship, Hamza will increase you in honor and esteem you more highly than before."

Regardless of rank, the whole camp replied with one voice, "O Khvaja! We have vowed to be true and faithful to Hamza with all our hearts! We shall not break our vow as long as we live! Now that you are with us in place of Hamza, we will never leave you, or ever dream of setting foot outside the bounds of obedience due you!" Rejoicing at their words, Amar embraced every one of them and said, "I put the same value on your person that I set upon my own life. Indeed I am the one who has incurred your debt of gratitude, and all of you are like my brothers!" He delegated the necessary force to the ramparts of the fort, and instructed them to remain alert at all times. Then he donned a regal robe and retired to a pavilion made of gold tissue, furnished with a sumptuous carpet. He deputized Muqbil Vafadar with his faultless archers to man the defenses, and sat waiting for Wailum and Qailum.

Hardly a few watches had passed when a dark dust cloud rose on the horizon, enveloping the whole expanse. As it drew closer, and the wafts of air dispersed it a little, Amar's army saw a host carrying thirty standards. At its head rode two mighty and valiant champions clad in armor, whom Amar reasoned to be Wailum and Qailum.

In their greed to receive robes of honor and rich rewards from Naushervan, those fools made the blunder of ordering their forces to surround the fort and to take away Mehr-Nigar by force after slaying the followers of the True Faith. They incited their army with the prospect of a quick return to Ctesiphon with their mission fulfilled, and promised the men promotions to high stations by the emperor.

Under these orders, their troops spurred on their horses and approached the fortifications. When they came within range, Amar let loose a hail of Greek fire that burnt alive all those who had advanced close and stopped the rear ranks in their tracks. When Wailum and Qailum saw that the day was nearing its end and their army had suffered a reverse, they sounded the clarion for the cessation of hostilities, and set up camp beyond the fort's firing range, ordering their army to carry out vigils.

Since the Sahibqiran left, it was Amar's custom to accompany Mehr-Nigar when she took her meals, and to revive her spirits and offer words of consolation. That evening as well, he arrived when Mehr-Nigar was sitting down to dinner, and ministered to her for several hours. Then he sent for Sarhang Misri and said to him, "Go and fetch Munzir Shah Yemeni's daughter, Huma-e Tajdar, and employ yourself in this errand. She and Zehra Misri should keep Mehr-Nigar company until the Sahibqiran's return and keep the princess occupied with their sweet prattle." After giving these instructions, Amar retired to bed and slept soundly. In the morning after he had performed his toilet, he gave orders to everyone to carry out their assigned duties and himself sat in his pavilion as before. All those attending on him were honored and ennobled in his service.

Wailum and Qailum sallied forth with their army and when their troops were opposite the fort, they ordered them to storm the ramparts. As on the first day, Amar again fired salvos of Greek fire from the fort and showered the advancing soldiers with rocks and stones. A great tumult broke loose among the enemy ranks as a result, and they retreated in great disarray. Wailum and Qailum revived the spirits of their troops and confronted those retreating with accusations of cowardly behavior. They shouted, "No man ever takes back the step he puts forward! The valiant and the courageous never turn their backs in the face of danger." These words induced his army to take the reins again and muster courage, but they could not withstand the continuous salvos of Greek fire, and were unable to advance. Wailum and Qailum covered their heads with their shields and spurred their mounts forward until they reached the edge of the trenches around the fort. Mortified with shame at seeing their commanders standing alone at the moat, their army charged in to fight beside them.

The sight of the enemy reaching the trenches greatly distressed Amar. He immediately took out a missile filled with naphtha and, setting it afire, he then swung it a few times and let it fly at Wailum's breast. The naphtha soaked Wailum when the missile burst on impact, and set him ablaze. When he tried to put the fire out with his hands, his fingers lit up like so many fuses. The liquid splashed on his beard, too, and it began burning like a wad of cotton. As he felt his face with his hands, he singed his eyebrows and whiskers. When Qailum saw Wailum burning and unable to put out the flames by himself, he was alarmed. He approached him and tried to help, but he fared the same as Wailum, and writhed in agony from the pain of burning. Both brothers began rolling on the ground like tumbler pigeons. Catching sight of their commanders burning away and unable to put out the fire, their army covered them with mud and dirt. The fire was at last put out, and then the two of them found release from their scourge after great suffering and painful moaning. The fight called off for the day, their army retreated to its camp and employed itself in ministering to those who had been wounded in battle.

Amar went back to his jewel-encrusted seat under his pavilion. When about an hour remained until the close of day, Amar thought of employing his guile in another adventure and playing another trick on the enemy. He got up and put on the attire of *ayyars*, and disguised himself as Naushervan's *ayyar*, Aatish. Then he brazenly entered the pavilion of the enemy commanders and, calling on Wailum and Qailum, spoke to them with great warmth. Just the sight of Aatish brought Wailum and Qailum to sobbing, and they set about stringing a necklace of tears. They said to him, "Brother Aatish! See how ill we have fared at Amar's hands and what a calamity he has visited upon our heads!"

The fake Aatish replied, "Mark my words well: Only an *ayyar* can be an *ayyar*'s match. A soldier who sets out to fill an *ayyar*'s shoes will surely come to grief. And you know that Amar is a consummate *ayyar* who has no equal in the whole world. There is none more accomplished than he is. With this in mind, the emperor sent me to safeguard you from him. You were in too much of a hurry and did not wait for my arrival, and spoiled things for yourselves in your haste. No purpose is served in crying over spilled milk, however. Now that I have arrived here, you shall see how Amar fares at my hands, and what a terrible retribution I will visit on him for the offenses he has committed against you."

At that moment the agony of their pain again overwhelmed Wailum and Qailum, and they resumed crying and wailing. Again the false Aatish spoke: "You should both imbibe a few goblets of the finest wine to recuperate your energy and allay the pain." Wailum and Qailum said, "If this is what you prescribe then pass us a few round of drinks to allay our pain and suffering for there could be no better cupbearer than yourself!" Amar, who was waiting for just such an opportunity, immediately picked up the goblets and the wine ewer, and handed out two rounds of pure wine to the brothers and the rest of the assembly, but then drugged the wine when serving the third round. After having only a few cups, everyone assembled became bereft of his faculties and fell unconscious to the floor. Amar went to the entrance of the pavilion and served the same wine to all the servants and menials as well, and thus got them out of the way, too. Once he had secured the pavilion from without and within, he stripped everyone naked and put all the furnishings of that pavilion, carpet and all, into his *zambil*. Then shaving one side of each man's face of its mustache and beard, and tying small bells to the mustache on the other side, he marked each bare cheek with lime, catechu, and kohl,[26] and blackened the other cheek entirely. After that Amar tied a note around Wailum's neck that read:

> It was I, Amar in person, who visited you today. I spared your lives this once and saved you the fate of the dead. You had better wind up your circus tomorrow and depart for Ctesiphon, or else I will slaughter all of you and exile you from the realm of the living.

Then hanging them upside down and naked from the posts of the pavilion, he headed out. After reaching his fort he changed, had his meal, and slept the sleep of the pure, having done his bit for the day.

In the morning, when the commanders of Wailum and Qailum's army arrived to pay court to their leaders, they found every one of them in a most singular state. They untied them one by one, and no one spoke a word for shame. After having their faces washed and dressing in new clothes, the attendants read the note tied to Wailum's neck and discovered that it was Amar Ayyar who had visited them in disguise as Aatish. Wailum and Qailum veiled their faces out of mortification, and immediately broke camp and headed for Ctesiphon, returning to Naushervan's court in their sorry state.

Of Nausheran Sending His Elder Son, Hurmuz, to Chastise Amar Ayyar

The narrator writes that after Wailum and Qailum departed toward Ctesiphon with their tails between their legs, Amar packed the fort with enough provisions to last his army for six months, and bided his time in peace.

Now, to return to the account of Wailum and Qailum: When they arrived battered and beaten in Ctesiphon and complained to Nausheran of Amar's ravages, he involuntarily laughed out loud at the sight they presented and said, "Indeed, Amar is a consummate rascal. Every time, he comes up with some new trick. I wonder how our army will ever triumph over him, and defeat and put an end to his mischief." Nausheran sent for Hurmuz and said to him, "I would like you to go and bring back Mehr-Nigar after killing Amar. Proceed with great pomp and array, as many a battle is won from the propitious presence and good fortune of kings and princes. Our faithful commanders have put themselves to great pains for the glory of our name." In addition to forty thousand armor-clad warriors, he dispatched Hurmuz with several mighty, swashbuckling champions, and provided them for all eventualities. Nausheran also sent Bakhtak's son Bakhtiarak to accompany them, and obtained a promise from him to exert his utmost for the success of the mission.

But while they head toward Mecca, let me narrate what passed with Amar, the master of all speedsters of the world. One day Amar realized that he had not enjoyed a good sprint for some time. Deciding not to put it off any longer, he exchanged his regal clothes for the attire of an *ayyar,* and headed in the direction of Ctesiphon. He had gone some twenty-odd *farsangs* in that direction when he beheld a great dust cloud on the horizon. Thinking that he should investigate the cause and learn what new calamity lay hidden therein, Amar disguised himself as a water carrier, and went toward it with a water skin slung over his shoulder.

When Amar drew near the cloud he beheld Crown Prince Hurmuz marching forward with such a grand and intrepid army and so vast a force that the Earth shook from their advance. The soldiers, however, were unable to open their mouths from the violence of their thirst and their tongues seared in their mouths from the fire of this need. Upon catching sight of a water carrier, they rejoiced as if they had encountered the holy Khizr in person. Their eyes lit up and their hearts were filled with cheer at the prospect of quenching their thirst. One commander said that the water carrier should first be taken to the prince as he was the thirstiest, and near to dying from the hardship. Amar witnessed the prince's tongue hanging out of his mouth and his eyes all clouded. In his state, stranger and kin were as one to Hurmuz; he was lying flat on his back, rubbing his heels in anguish and delirium, with his face distorted from loss of water. A few of his men stood around him, holding a sheet over him for shade, wondering if he would survive.

Amar dripped a few drops of water into his mouth whereupon Hurmuz regained his senses a little and opened his eyes. Seeing a water carrier, he gestured with his hands for more water as he was yet unable to speak. Amar again dripped a small amount into his mouth. After some time had passed Amar cupped his hand and gave Hurmuz more water to drink, which gave him a new lease on life. When Hurmuz regained his senses and felt somewhat satiated, he got up. After drinking a goblet of water, he cried out, "O water carrier! You have indeed performed the office of the holy Khizr, and for this deed you shall receive blessings. Indeed the water you gave me to drink was the veritable elixir of life. Pray put aside a little water for me, and serve the rest to my army, and resurrect them, too."

Amar had with him the gift given him by Prophet Khizr, which worked the miracle that even if ten million people were to drink from it, the source never dried and it remained as full as before. Amar satiated the thirst of the whole army including its beasts, feeding them all from the same source. Seeing that it was not exhausted, Amar offered thanks to God. Hurmuz gave him several hundred gold coins in reward and said, "O water carrier! I am headed at the emperor's orders toward Mecca. If I am successful in killing Amar, I will make you the ruler of that city. Now show me a way to Mecca that has some water sources so that my army can advance without suffering."

Amar led Hurmuz and his army deep into the heart of a forest where for miles around there was not a drop of water to be found, and the torrid wasteland seared the hearts within their breasts. After they had traveled a little deeper into the forest, Amar said to Hurmuz, "O Hurmuz, it is only an idle fancy to think that you can fight Amar! How do you suppose you can overcome him? For he is a most dreadful villain, and God knows what calamity or dreadful deception he might set up against you!" Hurmuz replied, "O water carrier, Amar is a mere *ayyar*! If I did not rout him in our very first encounter, I would deem myself most unworthy."

The false water carrier laughed loudly at this, and leaping away from Hurmuz, exclaimed, "O Hurmuz! You are a mere slip of a boy! But even if your father, the Emperor of the Seven Climes, were to advance against Amar with his entire army, he would be unable to harm him in the least. Little did you know that I am Amar in person! Even though I am by myself in the midst of your whole army, there is nothing you can do to harm me!"

Amar then dove away and made off after taking away Hurmuz's crown and leaving him standing there bareheaded. The troops gave him chase, yet none could catch even the cloud of dust he raised in his wake, and all of them returned confounded and baffled back to their army. Then some battered and ravaged troops from Wailum and Qailum's army whom they had met on the way led Hurmuz's army out of that pass after many a false start, and put them on the right path to Mecca.

On the fourth day, around evening, they arrived within sight of Mecca, and pitched their tents. The preparations for the battle were made, and the army arrayed in battle formations. Come night, when the commanders of the army presented themselves before Hurmuz, the followers of the True Faith were referred to during the course of the discussion, whereupon every person gave his opinion on the subject. Then the warrior Zura Zarah-Posh yielded to Hurmuz with folded arms, saying, "My lord, neither Amar nor the armies of the faithful stand anywhere in comparison to the prestige and glory of Your Honor. All of the followers of the True Faith will be wiped out in the flash of an eye and you will see that they will be exterminated as if they had never existed. If it should please Your Honor, I shall go forth and, with this very battle-ax I hold in my hand, break open the gates of the fort, put to the sword all followers of the True Faith along with Amar, and retrieve Mehr-Nigar to show you a sample of my courage and valor!"

Hurmuz replied, "I know well that your deeds will match your words, and in battle you are a veritable lion, but I want a plan that will put an end to their menace without imperiling us in the least. I wish for triumph in this campaign—which appears a most daunting prospect to all purposes—with the fewest complications, and I wish to earn great glory and renown in the world for my signal deed. It would bring me no end of ridicule and shame to have battled with a lowly *ayyar*. It would be entirely beneath my station to employ all this majesty and glory against a vulgar fellow."

Bakhtiarak praised Hurmuz's judgment and lauded him to the high heavens, and observed that princes and kings must show such sagacity for they are noble and highborn, and there are none others whose honor must be more closely watched over. Then he said, "If you were to command me, I would be willing to counsel Amar and persuade him to surrender before Your Honor. I will explain to him the many facets of his current situation and what would be profitable for him and what not profitable!" Hurmuz replied, "Nothing would be more to the purpose. You are yourself prudent and discerning. I leave the whole thing to your judgment."

In short, they passed the whole night in these machinations, and come morning, Bakhtiarak mounted his mule and trotted up to the trenches around the fort. He saw Amar turned out in a regal robe and seated under a canopy with great pomp on a golden throne, flanked on his right and left by the rulers and kings of Tang-e Rawahil, Yemen, and Haft Shehr, all of whom stood before him with folded arms awaiting his orders. Muqbil stood behind Amar with his bow slung over his shoulders and his quiver around his waist, along with his twelve thousand faultless archers.

Bakhtiarak made a low bow and greeted Amar, calling out, "O Khvaja! Since I consider you as my cousin and have the greatest regard for your person, I have come to counsel you as a well-wisher, and have brought you a message that is to your benefit in whatever way you may choose to look at it. What I have to tell you is this: Hamza has left for Qaf, and to imagine that he will escape the clutches of the *devs* is against all reason. There is no possibility at all that he will return in safety; indeed he is as good as dead. You are also aware that all the princes and kings of the Seven Climes are enamored of the very name of Mehr-Nigar, and they have cultivated such an ardor and ravishing passion for her that they would think little of dying a thousand times in pursuit of her hand. There is not one among them who can be kept from advancing against you or who accepts matters where they presently stand. It is contrary to all dictates of prudence, and against all sense and reason, to imperil one's life with hardships in vain. You would do well to hand Princess Mehr-Nigar over to Prince Hurmuz, and receive from him in exchange the authority to rule Mecca."

Amar replied, "O coward! Do not make sport of my beard. Know that if Naushervan, the Emperor of the Seven Climes, should himself advance here with all his army, he would not be able to lay hands on Mehr-Nigar. Do you mean to frighten me with your deceitful words and glib talk? Eighteen years will pass before you know it, so save your loquacious tongue its gymnastics for someone else's ears. The *devs* of Qaf will soon find out to their peril where they stand with Hamza. They will be unable to harm him in the least, let alone triumph over him. Now leave before I put you to the sword in retribution for your words!"

Upon hearing this, Bakhtiarak said despite his better judgment, "O cameleer's son! You'll see now how your unbridled manner lands you in untold calamities and afflictions, and how it shall ensnare you in untold hardships. I shall have lived to no purpose if I do not soon put a halter through your nose!"

At this, Amar swung his sling and let fly a stone at Bakhtiarak with such fury that it inflicted a two-digit-deep wound on his brow. Bakhtiarak spurred his mule on before he should receive another dose of the same and bite the dust. He arrived before Hurmuz covered in blood from head to foot and showed the sorry state he was in. After he was bandaged and had recovered command of his faculties, Bakhtiarak narrated the words exchanged between Amar and himself, whereupon Hurmuz flew into a towering rage and rebuked Amar in harsh and severe terms.

THE PEN'S CHARGER, COERCED BY THE REINS OF DISCOURSE, RENDERS AN ACCOUNT OF THE LORD OF THE AUSPICIOUS PLANETARY CONJUNCTION, THE CONQUEROR OF THE WORLD, THE MOST MUNIFICENT AND BOUNTEOUS, AMIR HAMZA THE MAGNIFICENT

The nurturers of narrative relate that when the *perizads* brought out the grape wine, Shahpal served Amir a goblet with his own hands, and the flower bud of Amir's fancy opened up in delight from the amiable effect of that pleasant and temperate wine. After he had quaffed the contents of the goblet, the Sahibqiran kissed the foot of Shahpal's throne and offered him many thanks for his kindnesses and favors. He drank cup after cup from the hands of moonfaced cupbearers until his heart was filled with bliss and the effects of inebriation swam into his eyes. He felt himself being rocked in the lap of rapture and ecstasy, and his senses surrendered themselves entirely to the power of intoxication.

As his gaze traveled around, he beheld four hundred velvet and vari-colored satin canopies of such beauty that they robbed the eyes of wonder with their magnificence. These marvels, whose creation had exhausted every talent of the heirs of Mani and Bahzad's art, left the mind stupefied. Such workmanship had been employed in fashioning these fine specimens of art that the agencies of intellect and wisdom could hardly penetrate it. On the fabric of some of these canopies illustrations of revelry were so finely worked that one's eyes were duped into believing that they were gazing on a living assembly of song and dance. On others, scenes from battlefields were so effectively displayed that those who looked at them could even see the flash of swords, and found the same thrill beholding these canopies as one did witnessing actual fields of battle and carnage. Lovers of the chase longed to set out on hunting expeditions upon seeing scenes on the canopies that depicted pastures and hunting fields. One canopy installed in the center bore an image of Suleiman and his courtiers, outlined with embedded jewels. Anyone who saw this vision believed to all purposes that this was King Suleiman himself who was giving audience in his court, with all his courtiers occupied in their respective offices. All of the canopies were supported on bejeweled poles, their fabric strung with buttons of rubies, emeralds, garnets, and diamonds. Golden vessels were embedded in the poles, and jewels made with great skill, finesse, and craftsmanship cascaded down their sides in clusters.

In the nave of the court chandeliers made of precious stones were hanging. The columns supporting the roof held lamps made of multicolored precious stones. Surrounding the court was an array of garnet lanterns hung by gold chains, interspersed at every third lantern by one made of diamonds. These, too, presented a sight most magnificent and sumptuous. The whole edifice of the court was supported by four thousand silk tent ropes, and ropes woven of silk, gold, and silver threads secured with golden tent pegs. Inside the court, a floor made of gold and silver was so intricately detailed with jewel-inlaid crevices that the soles of one's feet never felt any variation in the smoothness of the floor. Those who beheld the sight of this place lost their senses from marveling. Four thousand four hundred and forty-four thrones and chairs made of gold, silver, ivory, ebony, and sandalwood, and bejeweled steel benches inlaid with gold were set out as the allotted stations for the chiefs of the realm of Qaf.

In the midst of all these marvels stood a grand and finely worked throne that was once the seat of King Suleiman and was now occupied by Emperor Shahpal. It was a spectacle of enchantment, and painstaking labor was taken to fashion it. Its four corners held emerald peacocks that were a wonder to behold. One of them grasped in its beak a wriggling and writhing snake, which whipped its tail and raised its hood like a live snake. From the beak of another, a pearl necklace was suspended, which the bird swallowed and disgorged in turns. On their backs these peacocks carried garnet vases filled with bouquets of jewels cut in the shapes of flowers. Such art went into their fashioning that each one of them gave off the particular fragrance of that flower, and delighted beyond measure those who inhaled its perfume. When the emperor stepped onto his throne, the peacocks called out and preened and entertained onlookers with their dancing.

The rails of the balustrade around the throne were topped with narcissus-shaped pots made of emeralds and garnets, flanked by a most delicately worked cassolette. On four diamond poles a canopy was stretched to shield the emperor from dew, edged with pearls strung in the pattern of a ewer, and with a *shabchiragh*[27] ruby hanging from its roof. At the four corners of the throne sat basins that provided support to square, pentagonal, and spherical ornaments made of marble, jasper, and crystal and inlaid with jewels. The basins were filled with rose water, *keora* water, and essences of musk and saffron, which gushed out from *jets d'eau* and sprinklers. The creator of these marvels had taken care to see that the basin filled with rose water bore a spout carved in the shape of the rose stem. Some of those stems were laden with roses in full blossom and the rest had flowers in different stages of bloom, all of these inundating the whole place with their fragrance. The basin filled with *keora* water had its spout carved in the shape of a musk deer, and the basin containing the essence of saffron had a spout shaped like a saffron plant in flower. Anyone who caught sight of these basins or caught their scent broke into riots of laughter and was rendered unconscious from the transports of mirth.

Six hundred priceless canopies raised on twelve thousand columns, and four thousand tent ropes dotted the expanse of the court. The Hall of Audience alone was spread over two and a half *farsangs*. It was a most sumptuous abode where King Suleiman's conveyance once stood at the ready with great majesty. The court also contained an enclosure three *farsangs* wide for the encampment of the court nobles. There the gongs sounded and reverberated like the mighty crack of thunder. An indoor garden, which would have put even the pastures of Eden out of countenance, led to a richly adorned private chamber adjacent to the court and furnished on the same scale as the court itself, which was constructed for the purpose of pleasure seeking. In front of it stretched a promenade entirely laid with bricks of golden and rainbow-colored hues. The garden abounded in trees made of precious stones, where nightingales, doves, turtledoves, ringdoves, parrots, mynahs, *laals, sina-baz,* and *char-kovay*[28] cut out of jewels were perched and opened the portals of rapture and ecstasy to their audience's hearts with their singing. The smooth flowing water of the brooks circling the garden was the pride of the spring breeze. Along the water's edge, ducks, waterfowl, teals, *chaha*,[29] storks, ruddy geese, sandpipers, and peewits sat leisurely, preening their wings with their beaks and delighting the onlookers. Partridges, quails, *chanaks*,[30] Greek partridges, cock pheasants, painted quails, and peacocks made of jewels promenaded in the garden. Upon beholding these wonders the Sahibqiran was thrown into ecstasies of delight.

Let it be known that Emperor Shahpal's daughter, Aasman Peri, who was one of the comeliest fairies and unsurpassed in charm and beauty, was screened off sitting on a throne behind Shahpal's station, and although her bejeweled station was doubly masked in the front, she was able to catch sight of the Sahibqiran from behind the screen. Upon beholding his peerless, youthful beauty she became enamored of him, smitten by love to the very core of heart and soul. Becoming disconsolate, she began to pine away that very instant.

After one night and one day had passed in feasting, Abdur Rahman said to Shahpal, "The Sahibqiran is pressed for time, and I brought him here on the promise that I would bear the blame and be at his mercy if he spent more than nine days in Qaf. I told him that he would be occupied on this errand for a full nine days—the time required to bring matters to a happy close—with three days spent on the journey to Qaf, a day of feasting upon arrival, a day spent in the campaign to kill Ifrit, another day for celebrations, and three days for the return journey."

Shahpal then said to Hamza, "O Sahibqiran! I cannot even begin to tell you how I have suffered at the hands of these *devs,* and what grief I bear as a result of their vileness. I will live under a debt of obligation to you all my life and will offer my whole empire in your service if you would do me the kindness of eliminating them!"

The Sahibqiran replied: "It is no great favor that you ask. God is my assistant and my abettor. By the grace of Your Excellency, and God willing, I shall behead every single one of these rebels and restore your lands to your control, or else I will deem myself unworthy of my title, and then no success could be expected of me in the least of tasks. Pray let the drums of war be beaten, and see how God's will manifests itself."

Shahpal rejoiced at Amir Hamza's words and said to Abdur Rahman, "Bring out the four swords of King Suleiman so that from among them he may choose the one to his liking!" Abdur Rahman produced the swords without delay. Shahpal put them before the Sahibqiran and said, "These are Samsam, Qumqam, Aqrab-e Suleimani, and Zul-Hajam,[31] all of them peerless and without compare. You may pick the one that you prefer!" Amir chose the Aqrab-e Suleimani and girded himself with it, whereupon all the *perizads* broke into joyous cheers. They congratulated the emperor and made vows to take all his troubles upon their heads.

When Amir regarded this, he asked Abdur Rahman what it signified. Abdur Rahman replied, "O Sahibqiran, these four swords once decorated the belt of King Suleiman who is reputed to have said that after his days were done, the heads of the contumacious *devs* would be severed by the

Aqrab-e Suleimani, and that by that selfsame sword they would reap the harvest of their refractory ways. Everyone here rejoiced because you picked up the Aqrab-e Suleimani and must have chosen it by divine prescience since you were unfamiliar with its legend!" Amir was very glad to hear these tidings.

Then Abdur Rahman said, "One last test remains in this matter, and you may hear of it now and believe its truth!" When Amir inquired about the details, Abdur Rahman replied, "There is a poplar tree that the *perizads* consider to match the height and dimensions of Ifrit. It is also a legend known all over Qaf and a belief firmly held by all its denizens that the one who brings down the poplar with one blow of the Aqrab-e Suleimani will be the one to dispatch Ifrit to Hell."

Amir then went to this tree and, reciting the name of Allah, dealt one blow to its trunk, which sliced through the wood as if it were made of soap; however, the tree did not fall. Thinking that it had withstood his blow, Amir was cut to the quick, and tears rose to his eyes. Abdur Rahman congratulated Amir, joyfully embraced him, and said, "The trunk was cut through entirely by your hand. Pray test it by giving it a little push!" When Amir put one hand to the trunk and pushed it, the tree came crashing down.

Shahpal kissed Amir's hand and arm and, embracing him with great joy, said, "O Hamza! Indeed you have been blessed by King Suleiman and for that reason you command such power and might. There is none other than you who has the wherewithal to kill Ifrit and undertake this perilous adventure with such courage and valor!"

Amir replied, "God willing, by the grace of the emperor of Qaf, I will wipe out the entire lot of these rebels from your dominions. I will not stop at Ifrit alone. The refractory *devs* will lie slaughtered in heaps in the battlefield. Pray order your army to sally forth from Gulistan-e Irum and pitch their tents in the battlefield. Have the drums of war sounded and give your enemy a taste of your army-routing glory!"

The moment the emperor mustered his troops his entire force armed itself to the teeth and marched out from Gulistan-e Irum. The emperor had the Court of Suleiman moved to the battlefield, too, and joined his army with his companions.

Ifrit received the tidings that Emperor Shahpal had sent for a man from the realm of Earth to assist him, and heard that this man had reached Qaf with great pomp, array, and acclaim, and that by dint of his help Shahpal had come to the battlefield and arrayed his troops to give fight. Ifrit roared with laughter upon hearing this news and then said, "How could there ever be a match between a human being and a *dev*? It is well, I suppose, that it brought Shahpal out of his hole!" He ordered his side to answer the drums of war, and commanded his armies to prepare for battle and carnage.

Emperor Shahpal ordered his army to beat the battle drums and see to it that claims of his valor were emblazoned abroad. The rumble of twelve hundred pairs of golden and silver drums rose like reverberations of thunder. In Ifrit's camp the *devs* struck stones together, and by way of drumming thumped their asses. In short, the whole night the two camps engaged in clamoring and shouting. The next morning, Ifrit stepped into the battlefield with hundreds of thousands of *devs*. Some *devs* sported lion skins around their necks, some dragon skins, and others elephant skins. Their horns were sheathed in steel. Steel chains and talismans were tied around their necks, arms, waists, and thighs, and they wore necklaces of skulls around their necks. Armed with flint spears, millstones, box trees, and saws made of crocodile backs, they descended to the battlefield, but were struck with marvel upon seeing Shahpal. Mounted on one throne himself, and with the Sahibqiran seated on another, Shahpal had fanned out his troops in a daunting formation designed to strike terror in the heart of the *devs* and instill fear in the enemy.

When the *devs* beheld the Sahibqiran they indulged themselves in all manner of foolish capers and horseplay. Some rushed into the center of the arena, prancing about and thumping their asses. Others jumped up and down and tittered riotously; some did leg squats while holding their beards in their hands; yet others flew toward the sky and came tumbling back down doing somersaults in the air. One gnashed his teeth at the Sahibqiran to frighten him, another swung his tail around in his hand, and another rode his companion's back. Amir could not help but laugh watching their antics. He found them fatuous and, watching their unbridled horseplay, formed a low opinion of their shameless lot.

The first to seek combat was Ifrit's father, Ahriman, who stood five hundred yards high. He stepped out of the ranks to confront Shahpal's army, holding a box tree in his hands. He let out a war cry and bellowed, "Where is the Quake of Qaf, the Latter-day Suleiman who puts great store in his valor and gallantry? Let him come forward and face me so that I can make him taste death's relish, and reward him for his intrepid entry into Qaf and his presumption in battling the *devs*!"

Amir, with Shahpal's permission, descended into the battlefield without allowing the least fear or terror to find foothold in his heart. He bellowed "God is Great!" so lustily that the whole desert reverberated with the sound. Ahriman said, "O Quake of Qaf! You make a big squeak for one your size, just to frighten us! Come deal me the great blow that you have!" The Sahibqiran replied, "It is not my way to take precedence in dealing blows. I would not contravene my tradition. Deal me a blow first, and then I shall return it and show you my mettle!"

Ahriman replied: "How would all the *devs* judge me if I were to attack a diminutive being like you whose very creation is tainted with infirmity. Indeed, they would deem me an unworthy warrior and marvel greatly at my actions. Neither would you survive my blow to live to return it!"

Hamza said to this, "You got your fill when nature was distributing stature and height, and I got mine when it distributed power and might! Little do you know that I am your Angel of Death. I have come all the way from the realm of Earth to extract your soul, and brought you the goblet of death to drink!" At this, Ahriman brought down the box tree on his opponent. Amir foiled the blow and, unsheathing the Aqrab-e Suleimani, said, "O vile creature! Now you cannot say that you were killed without due warning. Be on your guard, for I am about to deal you a blow and smear my shining sword with your foul blood."

Even as he finished speaking those words, Amir struck a blow that cut that carrion-eater in two, and his carcass fell to the ground. Shahpal prostrated himself before God in gratitude and ordered the *perizads* to play festive music. Ifrit Dev heaved a searing sigh and said, "O human! You committed a terrible deed in killing a great warrior like my father and beheading him. But you shall not escape your deserts. Witness what terrible calamity shall visit you!" He sent a *dev* of even more imposing stature than Ahriman to combat with the Sahibqiran. Amir Hamza dispatched him to Hell as well, and entered another *dev*'s name in the catalog of the dead. In short, within no time Amir destroyed nine mighty *devs* who were the pride of Ifrit's army, leaving their master confounded and baffled.

Then Ifrit shivered and groaned and immediately had drums sounded to announce the cessation of hostilities for the day. He had his father's corpse carried away, and returned to his camp crying and wailing in ecstasies of grief and fear. Emperor Shahpal retired to Gulistan-e Irum scattering gold and jewels on Amir's head as the sacrifice of his life, and was most pleased by Amir's valor and courage.

THE *DASTAN* CHANGES COURSE TO GIVE AN ACCOUNT
OF KHVAJA AMAR AYYAR

Now hear a short account of the father of racers of the world, the King of *Ayyars*, Khvaja Amar bin Umayya Zamiri. When Bakhtiarak returned to his camp wounded by Amar's hand, Zura Zarah-Posh declared to Hurmuz, "If Your Honor so orders, we will beat the drums of war so that Amar Ayyar may receive a reward for his treachery and never again raise his head in rebellion." Hurmuz answered, "On no account do I wish to inculpate myself with the blood of God's creatures. The thought of unleashing war and carnage is not pleasuring to me. Order the guards to keep vigils night and day so that Amar's fort receives no outside aid, its rations are cut off, and those within begin to suffer from thirst and hunger. Chop down the forest to make ladders for use at the appointed time when we charge the fort!"

Everyone admired the prince's counsel, and they busied themselves in getting the ladders constructed. In four months' time, when the ladders were ready, Hurmuz said, "Deploy the ladders at the fort and gather them alongside. The drums of war should be beaten now, as tomorrow we will charge the fort and clash swords!"

The news was brought to Amar that ladders had been erected opposite the fort and were ready. The soldiers in Hurmuz's camp had been ordered to charge the fort, and drums of war were beating. Hearing that all the preparations for war had been made by the foe, Amar said to Aadi, "I am off to take a stroll and shall return shortly. In the meanwhile, you may strike the Timbal of Sikander."

Amar changed out of his regal garb into an *ayyar*'s attire, and, carrying all the paraphernalia of his trade and dressed like a foot soldier, headed to the site of the ladders. There he saw four hundred soldiers armed to the teeth doing vigil duty bearing torches. Amar went up to them and said, "Hurmuz has sent me to check on the guards of the ladders to see who is vigilant and who is unmindful, and whether or not everyone is employed in their respective duties. Draw up a record of witnesses to identify those negligent in their duties. Bring me the list so that the idlers may be chastised in the morning and reap the deserts of their indolence, while those standing alert are sent some provisions from the royal table and rewarded handsomely." Upon hearing his words, the diligent and the indolent all began fawning on him. They threw themselves at Amar's feet and cried, "Pray report that no one was lethargic, but that all performed their responsibilities with great vigilance and were assiduously engaged in discharging their respective assignments."

Amar then returned to his fort and, taking some *ayyars* in disguise, carried several salvers holding *maunds* of sweetmeats laced with soporific drugs back to the site of the ladders. Amar now said to the guards, "Hurmuz has sent these sweets for you, but I will distribute them in the morning since I do not see your commander here." One of the guards stepped forward and said, "I am the commander of these guards and am familiar with each of these men. My name is Mehtar Shatir. I am an *ayyar* and my turquoise signet ring here has been given to me by Prince Hurmuz as a sign of recognition. Tell me, brother, what is your name and office?"

Amar replied, "I am Mehtar Aqiq, and many men serve under my stewardship. The keeper of the carpets rugs is my father-in-law." Amar then took the ring from Shatir and gave him the salvers of sweets. Mehtar Shatir distributed these among his men and also ate his own share. All the foot soldiers licked their chops and took great pleasure from the confection. Then, at once, all of them fell unconscious into dreams of oblivion.

Amar had already ordered his *ayyars* to keep an eye on how things transpired. The moment they heard tell of Amar's success, they descended on the enemy and cut off their heads with their daggers, filling the ground with their corpses. Then Amar sprinkled the ladders with naphtha and set them aflame. Once the fire flared up, he returned to his fort and fell into a deep and peaceful slumber, having rid himself of that cause of anxiety. All the ladders were fully consumed by fire in the night. When the sun's oven again became warm, Hurmuz ascended a throne mounted on four elephants and with his army in tow headed to the fort so that they might charge its walls that day. They planned to gain the ramparts with the help of the ladders, murder the followers of the True Faith, and visit revenge on them. Hurmuz had gone some distance from his camp when his *ayyars* brought news that all that was left of the ladders was a giant heap of ashes, and not a single guard was left, for they all had been beheaded.

Upon hearing this, a ball of fiery rage traveled from the soles of Hurmuz's feet to his head, and he was beside himself with anger and dismay. He said to Bakhtiarak, "Amar's dastardly deed put paid to four months' labor!" He replied, "Your Honor knows well that he is a mischievous soul and a master strategist. You have already ridden forth to mount the assault; now order the attack and fulfill your heart's desire. You might court victory yet, and it may turn out that you were fated to receive it today."

When he finally arrived at the fort, Hurmuz assigned companies of ten thousand troops on each side of the fortress to press the siege, and gave them all necessary instructions. Amar recognized the impending peril as well as the fact that his fortified army feared the great numbers of the enemy host. He unleashed his full force of Greek fire, missiles, flaming arrows, barbs, and ballistae on Hurmuz's army from all sides, throwing the attacking force into terror. They were unable to defend themselves against Amar's fiery onslaught, and thousands of Guebers were burned to death. All Hell broke loose in Hurmuz's camp as this calamity befell them, and the survivors beat a retreat from the fort, their forces broken.

Then Hurmuz said to Zura Zarah-Posh, "The other day you claimed that you would break down the gate of the fortress, that your Zarah-Posh warriors would slay the followers of the True Faith, and that you'd carry away Mehr-Nigar. Go forth! Display your valor and bring down the gates this instant and take Mehr-Nigar!" Zura Zarah-Posh replied, "I shall carry out Your Honor's command at once!" Zura and his four thousand-strong Zarah-Posh troops took to their horses and galloped forth and arrived outside the fort. Zura's horse crossed the moat in one leap, and Zura arrived safe on the other side covering his head with a shield. His men, however, were unable to cross over and could not move a step forward. Amar kept them at the moat with a hail of Greek fire, but Zura Zarah-Posh showed great courage and stayed on the near side of the moat, refusing to budge an inch.

Bakhtiarak said to Hurmuz, "Zura is indeed a most valiant man. It has been established beyond the shadow of a doubt that he is courageous. He was as good as his word, but he cannot do any more all by himself. His army made a mistake by retreating under Amar's shower of Greek fire. Your Honor should order your army to go to Zura's aid and not to fear death at all at this juncture." Then Hurmuz said to his army, "Zura is standing by himself at the doors of the castle in honor of the pledge he gave us. If you were to assist him now, the fort would fall to us forthwith." All the Sassanid warriors now spurred on their horses and rode to the edge of the moat, yet none of them could cross to the other side.

Amar appeared on the ramparts of the fort and, addressing Zura, said, "O brave man! Indeed you have as good as conquered the castle and defeated all of us! I beseech you now to follow the custom of the valiant men who give quarter to their defeated foes and earn eminence by offering them the refuge of their mercy. I would be greatly indebted to you if you could prevail upon Hurmuz to forgive my trespass. I will then order my men to leave the fortress and hand over Mehr-Nigar."

Zura brought his horse a little closer to the fort and removed the shield from his head to give an answer. The moment he lifted the shield from his head, Amar let fly from his sling a well-chiseled stone aimed at the bridge formed by Zura's brows. From the impact, Zura's brain was blown out of his head by way of his nose. He fell into the waters of the moat, which soon cooled his death throes. The Sassanids who were standing at the edge of the moat jumped into the water to retrieve his corpse and then hauled it away.

The murder of his eminent commander turned Hurmuz's face deathly pale. He wrung his hands in grief, and he burned in fires of remorse. Greatly flustered, he asked Bakhtiarak what to do next and how to avenge Zura's death and punish Amar. Bakhtiarak answered, "At this moment the troops are reeling under this setback and the whole army is panic-stricken. Beat the drums to cease hostilities for the day and let us retreat to our encampment. Tomorrow will be a new day, and then we shall see what other stratagem shall avail us." Hurmuz ordered the drums beaten, and his army returned to its camp. Dispirited and dejected, Hurmuz returned to his pavilion and sent a missive to Naushervan with a complete account of the situation.

When Naushervan received that missive and became aware of the latest news, he also suffered untold anguish. Addressing Buzurjmehr, he said, "Consider Amar's dastardly deeds and how he keeps murdering my eminent commanders without the least regard for my grandeur and majesty." Buzurjmehr replied, "Indeed he is such a rascal that these considerations are as nothing to him. You should advise the prince to stop all warfare and devise some other strategy to catch Amar alive."

Buzurjmehr had hardly stopped speaking when the Sassanids began airing their grievances about Amar. They said, "Your Honor should note the status of this cameleer's son and how he vitiates and even kills commanders of the rank of Wailum, Qailum, and Zura. We shall not rest in peace until we have avenged their deaths on that incorrigible *ayyar* and properly punished him for his monstrous villainy." Naushervan consoled them and asked them to take heart. He sent Akhzar Filgosh, an eminent Sassanid commander, at the head of a force of seventy thousand intrepid troops to Hurmuz's aid. He also sent a missive to Hurmuz that read: "You must not lose heart or panic, or give thought to the prospect of retreating, for I have dispatched Akhzar Filgosh with detailed orders to help your mission."

Later, Naushervan dismissed the court and retired to the royal bedchamber. When Queen Mehr-Angez saw him looking dejected and dispirited, she asked him why he was so forlorn. Naushervan replied, "It is on account of your daughter that I remain mired in grief and suffer a thousand barbs and arrows of woe and sorrow. Since I sent Hurmuz on this campaign, that cameleer's son has already handed him three defeats. As to the loss of my peerless and unmatched commanders whom he murdered and beheaded ruthlessly, only my heart and I can account for the grief." Upon hearing this, Mehr-Angez said, "May Your Honor, the Shelter of the World, never come to grief. In my opinion Amar will not be killed by these efforts. I wish that you would send Khvaja Nihal, who raised Mehr-Nigar in his care as a child, along with gifts and offerings to Mehr-Nigar. Secretly you may send with him a missive addressed to Mehr-Nigar that should speak to her thus:

Fie on you that your own blood does not call to you anymore, even though your parents burn in the searing fire of separation from you and dissolve away like candles in this disunion. But the thought never visits your heart to quench the fire in our hearts by showing us your face and presenting yourself before us. Show us the mercy of accompanying Khvaja Nihal back to us, for our lives now depend upon it.

The queen continued, "With this missive also send some gold and riches for Amar, and inveigle him with money so that he invites Khvaja Nihal into the fort and allows him indoors. Within a few days of gaining admittance into the fort, Khvaja Nihal will conspire to poison Amar.

Then throwing open the fort gates, and admitting our forces inside, he will slay the followers of the True Faith. He will return with Mehr-Nigar and relieve us of this terrible suffering on her account." The king greatly commended Mehr-Angez's advice, and after instructing Khvaja Nihal in all aspects of his delicate mission, dispatched him to Mecca bearing gifts and offerings, gold and riches.

Of Khvaja Nihal's Departure for Mecca to Bring Back Mehr-Nigar, and of His Dying at Amar's Hands

Narrators of honeyed discourse have passed down that after dispatching Khvaja Nihal, the king wrote out a missive and entrusted Paik Ayyar with its delivery to Hurmuz. It read:

> My dear son! It has been two days now since I dispatched Akhzar Filgosh with seventy thousand troops to come to your aid, and he has departed with great preparations. I also sent Khvaja Nihal today with separate instructions, as enclosed, as well as gifts and offerings. I have briefed him well in all aspects of the case. I want you to help him somehow find a way inside the fort, so that he may carry out my orders and afford you release from the bane that is Amar's existence. However, if for some reason Khvaja Nihal is unable to gain entry to the fort, you should rely on Akhzar Filgosh's might to capture the fort and achieve your end.

Now hear of Khvaja Nihal, who left Ctesiphon with only a day's journey separating him from Akhzar Filgosh. Traveling with great speed, Nihal soon caught up with him, and informed him of the nature of his mission and its strategy. The two of them passed all the stops and stations of the journey together, and in approximately three months' time from the day that they left Ctesiphon, they joined Hurmuz's camp. They presented to him the letters sent by Naushervan, and informed him of all the particulars of their respective missions. Hurmuz had already learned of the contents of these missives from the king's note he received earlier by the agency of the *ayyar*. He presented both Khvaja Nihal and Akhzar Filgosh with robes of honor after reading the letters they had brought, and indulged both men by showing them great preference and favor. Because both were exhausted from their journey, they soon took leave of Hurmuz and retired to their pavilions to rest. An *ayyar* brought news of this to Amar, and gave him all the particulars of the large force that had come to the aid of Hurmuz and of the arrival of Akhzar Filgosh and Khvaja Nihal.

Amar decided to learn more about the new enemy commander sent there from Naushervan's court. After disguising himself as a washerman, he infiltrated Hurmuz's camp and stopped to eavesdrop wherever he saw a few people conversing. In one place where he found several people standing and talking, Amar heard one man say, "This time Naushervan has sent Akhzar Filgosh to assist Hurmuz with seventy thousand intrepid troops. The fort would surely fall to us now, and Amar will be killed and our army will return victorious." Another replied, "Naushervan has also sent Khvaja Nihal!" To that a third man said, "He is not sent here to fight but to find some way to infiltrate the fort, kill Amar by deceit, and take away Mehr-Nigar so he may earn renown, rich rewards, and robes of honor. To me this appears an unlikely prospect, however, for Amar is not one to be fooled by any tricks or duped by guile. It is more likely that Akhzar Filgosh will secure Naushervan's end, although I have serious reservations about his chances of success, too. As to the rest, all will be dictated by fate!"

Amar removed himself from there and, changing his disguise from that of a washerman to a stable groom's, he decided on yet another deceit. With a feed bag full of grain in his hands, he started calling out loudly, "Direct me to Khvaja Nihal's pavilion, my friends. I went to get the fodder in the evening, and have lost my way since night has fallen. My poor horse will be scraping at the ground from hunger. If someone would do me the kindness of taking me there, I will recompense him for the good deed." One man answered his call, saying to Amar, "Come with me, my brother, so that I may take you to Khvaja Nihal's pavilion and his camp." After they had gone a few steps the man pointed out Khvaja Nihal's camp and said, "There before you stands Khvaja Nihal's pavilion whose search has made you so distraught!" Amar then removed his disguise and, entering Khvaja Nihal's camp, told the mace bearers to announce him to Khvaja Nihal and tell him that Amar Ayyar had arrived with auspicious tidings.

Hearing of Amar's arrival at his door, Khvaja Nihal became very perturbed and uneasy, and at the same time he was surprised and puzzled. He wondered why Amar would call on him and what important business had brought him there. He went out and greeted Amar and seated him on the throne next to his own. Khvaja Nihal then spoke with great ardor and fervor: "You showed this insignificant mortal tremendous favor by calling on him yourself. If you had not come today, I would have presented myself at your fort on the morrow to seek the bliss gained from the beauty of your wonderful countenance. Friendship naturally results in convivial gatherings, and indeed if we reflect on it in greater depth, such friendships are the *summum bonum* of the borrowed existence that is our lot."

Amar's eyes shone with tears at these words, and he said, "O Khvaja! I know not where to begin the tale of the woes and afflictions that make me weary of my life!" Khvaja Nihal replied, "Tell me in detail what has brought you to this pass that you utter such terrible words. I hope to God that all is well with your affairs!"

Amar answered: "There is not a single affair of mine that is not a cause of anxiety. Do lend me your ear and offer any solution that you think might address my anxiety. The facts are that Hamza gave Mehr-Nigar into my custody and departed to Qaf with a promise to return in eighteen days. However, a long time has passed and there is no knowing whether he is alive or if he has died at the hand of some *dev*. Now I can no longer keep Mehr-Nigar: She despairs constantly and is wont to give in to terrible despondency on account of her loneliness. I tremble at the prospect of handing her over to Hurmuz as I have been guilty of many incivilities toward him and have caused him much grief. I wonder whether the emperor will pardon my transgressions or if he will inflict revenge on me and punish me for my trespasses.

"I set my hopes in Naushervan's forgiving and merciful nature, and would not be surprised if he pardoned me and did not seek revenge. However, I have enemies in both Bakhtak and Bakhtiarak, who are full of evil, and unable as they are to act against their malicious natures, they will certainly incite the emperor and prevail upon him to have me put to death. I had already resolved in my mind that today I should present myself before Hurmuz and seek his forgiveness, and then let what may come to pass come to pass. Imagine my happiness then, when I arrived into camp and heard of your arrival. Now I shall hand responsibility for Mehr-Nigar into your able hands and relinquish my trust with an easy mind. As for myself, I shall remove myself to wherever on the good lord's earth I might find some shelter."

Amar's speech rang like heavenly music in Khvaja Nihal's ears; he was beside himself with joy. He embraced Amar and said, "O Khvaja

Amar, nobody has the power to influence the emperor's judgment in this affair now that you and I have fostered this trust between the two of us, nor will anyone be able to sow seeds of rancor in the emperor's breast against you! I take it upon myself not only to have your trespass forgiven, but also to have the kingdom of Mecca bestowed upon you! This is my irrevocable word to you and you can rest assured that I shall not betray it!" Amar replied, "Indeed I place even greater hope in you!" He produced dates from the skirts of his robe and, offering them to Khvaja Nihal, said, "This is a present from the holy land of Mecca. Pray partake of them and savor their luscious taste." It was an evil hour for Khvaja Nihal when he put those dates in his mouth without suspicion or further thought.

Amar then took his leave of him, saying that he was going home to bring back Mehr-Nigar. Stepping outside, he distributed the dates among the attendants and duped those fools also with the story that they were a present from Mecca. Khvaja Nihal thought to himself that fate was smiling on him, for his mission was accomplished without his moving a finger. But hardly a few moments had passed before Khvaja Nihal and all his servants fell unconscious and became bereft of their senses. Amar now returned to the pavilion and, producing the keys from his *zambil*, unlocked the chests and helped himself to the gold and valuables stored there. After he had packed them into his *zambil*, he came upon a most finely crafted chest. Inside, he found the emperor's letter addressed to Mehr-Nigar wrapped in many folds of cloth, and Amar put this also in his *zambil*. He replaced the locks on the chests as they were before, and after finishing with that affair, dug a hole and buried Khvaja Nihal alive.[32] Then Amar put his disguise back on and, finally finished with his business for the day, went to sleep in Khvaja Nihal's bed.

———

Now hear of Hurmuz. Around this time he said to Bakhtiarak, "I wish to give a feast in honor of Akhzar Filgosh and Khvaja Nihal, and invite them here for the banquet." Bakhtiarak replied, "Nothing would be more appropriate! It would be entirely to the purpose, and indeed the demands of etiquette also make it incumbent on you!" Hurmuz therefore prepared for the feast. He ordered the workers to make preparations for the occasion, and sent the invitation to Akhzar Filgosh and Khvaja Nihal.

When the time came to pass all the commanders presented themselves along with Akhzar Filgosh and were seated at their stations. A short while later the false Khvaja Nihal, that is, Amar Ayyar in disguise, also presented himself, made obeisance, and stood with great propriety with folded hands before Hurmuz. Hurmuz was greatly taken by his gesture of submission. He conferred a robe of distinction upon him and showed him great favor, and said, "O Khvaja Nihal! You have acquitted yourself with great distinction in the decorum of assembly and etiquette, and I admire your discernment of the court protocol greatly. Come join us in this assembly in a fraternal spirit and cast off all worries of this pitiable world for a while!" The false Khvaja Nihal replied, "It is not the place of this slave to sit before you, as it would be presumptuous for someone of my lowly station!" Hurmuz said, "Be a good fellow now, and do not indulge in this idle talk!" He led Amar by the hand and made him sit next to him, and showed him even greater favor.

All the musicians and singers who had accompanied the army, and other musicians besides them who had gathered there from the vicinity of Mecca, sounded the opening notes. They started playing their instruments and singing, and regaled the assembly with the sweet strains of their lyrics and melodious airs. The chorus of "Drink unto oblivion!" rose from all corners, and everyone derived the utmost pleasure from the revelries. The entire day was passed in such conviviality, and come evening, the torchbearers lit wax and camphor tapers on two-, three- and five-pronged candleholders. Hurmuz poured out a goblet of fine wine with his own hands and offered it to Akhzar Filgosh. He made a salutation and quaffed it, then himself offered a goblet of wine to Hurmuz, for it was the etiquette that whoever was offered a drink should return the favor. In short, the participants of the assembly began offering one another drinks and imbibing wine with pleasure.

After some hours of the night had passed in this way, the false Khvaja Nihal rose from his station and announced, "This slave is desirous of being the cupbearer, for this ambrosial assembly is now at its apex." Delighted to hear this, Hurmuz said, "What could be better than that? Appoint yourself the cupbearer and pass the drinks with your own hand!" The false Khvaja Nihal took the goblet and ewer into his possession, and first offered Hurmuz a drink, astonishing him with his dexterity. Then Amar circulated throughout the assembly. For the first two rounds he poured out the wine that had already been put out, but in the third round he laced the wine with a sedative and began handing out goblets and making everyone drink with abandon. Already drunk, everyone now became comatose with just two rounds, and were rendered totally unconscious. When the false Khvaja Nihal saw the whole assembly stretched unconscious on the floor, he went out with the goblet and ewer, and served drugged wine to all the servants and menials, too.

He returned to the royal pavilion, and cleaned the place of everything—all the carpentry and drapery and apparel and effects, sparing not even the humble mat used in the servants' dwelling. Then forming a great bundle of the unconscious Hurmuz, Amar stuffed him into his *zambil*. He shaved off Akhzar Filgosh's whiskers on one side and made seven colored spots on that cheek, then painted the other cheek black and tied a small bell from its mustache. He draped an ibex pelt over Akhzar, making him into the very likeness of a mountain goat. Amar turned to Bakhtiarak next and, after shaving his face clean of whiskers, he blackened it and disguised him as a woman—with his forehead colored with a mixture of cinnabar and oil, and his legs tied up around his neck with laces. Amar then placed him in Akhzar Filgosh's lap and put them in a bed together. Amar played a new prank on everyone, stripping all the commanders and everyone else in the assembly of their clothes, shaving their faces clean and blackening them, and tying them upside down from the columns in their unconscious state. Still disguised as Khvaja Nihal, he left the pavilion and headed to the fort, his mind finally at peace after all the mischief he had performed.

Now hear of Akhzar Filgosh. When he came to his senses, he found a woman sleeping naked in his lap with her legs around her neck, oblivious to all considerations of modesty. Akhzar said to himself, *Perhaps Prince Hurmuz sent her to me, so that she might help me recover from the toils of the journey. A thousand curses on foolish me! Why did I become so derelict by sleep that I slumbered the whole night in ignorance of this succulent morsel? In the morning she will carry the story everywhere that I am impotent and unendowed because I showed no desire for a woman. While it is still dark, I must take my pleasure of her at least once, and take delight in ravishing her.*

The moment Akhzar penetrated Bakhtiarak, the latter opened his eyes with a bloodcurdling scream, and his racket woke up everyone, who soon discovered their individual shameful states. Those in the court who had been tied up were unable to rise, but when the attendants, mace bearers, floor keepers, and torchbearers rushed in, they were shocked to see a grotesquely attired man and an even more peculiar woman engaged in a vulgar act in the royal court, oblivious to any sense of propriety or shame. They castigated them well, shouting, "Fools! This is the court of the prince. To commit such acts here is to show utter defiance of etiquette. Certainly you scoundrels should be taken to task for this deed!"

When the servants descended on them, Bakhtiarak found his chance and escaped with his life, but they continued to pummel Akhzar. A messy brawl developed. Many men gave up the ghost when Akhzar's punches landed on them. At last when it was light outside, they were able to discern that it was none other than Akhzar whom they had fought, and they beheld all the commanders of the army hanging upside down, tied up from the columns. As the servants untied them, none of them spoke a word for the shame. Their garments were brought from their quarters, their faces washed, and those idiots then returned to the state of respectability.

In the meanwhile, Bakhtiarak had also returned after putting on clothes and washing his face. He said to Akhzar, "My good fellow! There is none on the face of the Earth except Amar who has the power to deliver us into such ignominy and bring us to this sorry pass." When Akhzar replied with the words, "Now Amar will hear from me. You shall see what a terrible fate I visit on his head and what condign punishment I accord him for his deeds!" and swore upon his beard, the bell tied to his mustache jingled. Discovering then that one side of his face had been shaved of its mustache and beard, Akhzar grew even more furious.

Bakhtiarak said to him, "We at least know the fate that visited us, but who knows what passed with Hurmuz and Khvaja Nihal. The person we saw acting as the cupbearer last evening was surely Amar in disguise. He must have killed the man to masquerade under his identity. When I searched for him just now, I discovered that Khvaja Nihal is missing from his pavilion, as are all of his belongings. Amar has also taken away Hurmuz, and this is a great ignominy for us!"

Akhzar was now exceedingly infuriated. After ordering the drums of war to be sounded, he said, "If I do not raze that fort to the ground, feed the flesh of that cameleer's son to the crows and kites, and make this desert flow with the streams of blood of the followers of the True Faith, I will no longer call myself Akhzar and will never have another moment's rest!" The next day he led thirty thousand troops from Hurmuz's army along with the seventy thousand men who were under his direct command to besiege the fort, after exacting the oath of valor and self-sacrifice from all the troops.

At that time Amar pulled Hurmuz from his *zambil*. Seeing that he was still unconscious, Amar dripped a few drops of strong vinegar into his mouth. Hurmuz opened his eyes and beheld Amar perched on a bejeweled throne, giving audience to the commanders and potentates of

Yemen, Tang-e Rawahil, and Haft Shehr, who flanked him on his left and right. He saw Muqbil Vafadar who stood by Amar's side with his twelve thousand faultless archers while stalwart champions deployed to man the defenses looked on, and musketeers, grenadiers, naphtha throwers, and sling bearers were alert on the ramparts of the fort. Finding himself caught in the clutches of the adversary, and despairing for his life, Hurmuz broke into uncontrollable sobs. Terror and dread sunk their talons into his heart, and he was thrown into the depths of despondency.

Seeing Hurmuz in tears, Amar offered him consolation and words of solace and said, "Have no fear, O Prince! I shall never do you any injury, and will inflict no harm upon you. However, I will put three propositions before you. If you were to agree to even one of them, you would do both of us a great favor, and then you would be able to rest assured of your safety." Hurmuz asked, "What are these three propositions? Let me hear them so that I could offer a reply." Amar replied, "My first proposal to you is that you convert to the True Faith and become the commander of the faithful, and do yourself the favor of giving up the ways of the infidels!" Hurmuz answered, "I find myself unable to give up my ancestral creed and turn my face away from the faith of my forefathers."

Then Amar said, "Although it would have been to your advantage to convert to the True Faith—you would have fared well in this life and the Future State, and slept in peace in your grave—there is nothing to be done, since fated as you are to remain unblessed, the idea does not find favor with you. My second proposition is that you prevail upon Naushervan not to wage war with me until the Sahibqiran has returned from Qaf, and not to trespass the boundaries of my dominion.

"Once the Sahibqiran has returned, the emperor may deal with him as he sees fit. Hamza has entrusted Mehr-Nigar to my custody and until he relieves me of that trust, I will make every endeavor to guard her. I cannot show, or even think, any infidelity to Hamza and the trust he has reposed in me. If Naushervan continues to persecute me, however, I cannot promise that I will restrain myself from initiating steps that would inflict indignity on his person and engender further acrimony in his heart toward me. Understand well that nothing stops me from visiting mischief on you, and there is nothing of which I am afraid."

Hurmuz replied to this, "It seems more likely that Naushervan would consent to this second proposition of yours!"

Amar answered, "O Hurmuz! I know well that Naushervan would not consent to it, and even if he did, there are Bakhtak and Bakhtiarak who would never abandon their malignant natures and would continue to influence his judgment. In any case, I excuse you from committing to this proposal as well. My third proposition is that you must forswear ever fielding an army against me in the future. Powerless as I am to influence your judgment in the matter, if you ever do decide to cross my path, you must not then complain of the means I employ to counter you." Hurmuz replied, "I give you my word that I shall never challenge you again in the future and will not even think of confronting you!"

While they were having this discussion, Akhzar Filgosh arrived with his armies before Amar's fort. When Amar saw that Akhzar Filgosh had come forward with a vast host in battle array, he took Hurmuz to the rampart of the fort and declared, "O Akhzar! You had better believe my words when I say that if any of your troops advance a single step, I will sever Hurmuz's head from his body and toss it into the moat. Then let what may come to pass come to pass!"

Bakhtiarak said to Akhzar, "There would be little wonder if this cameleer's son proves as good as his word and Hurmuz dies at his hand. We ought to sound the drums of retreat and leave, or else we endanger the life of our prince." Akhzar heeded this advice and, beating a retreat with his forces, returned to his pavilion.

Then Amar had Hurmuz dressed in a princely robe, supplied him with a steed, and holding his saddle straps, led him to Hurmuz's camp. From there Amar went to Mehr-Nigar, informed her of his doings, and acquainted her well with the facts of his triumph and the enemy's debacle. Overjoyed to hear this, Mehr-Nigar replied, "O dear Amar! Night and day I pray for your victory! However, when I compare their vast army to our own, and their superior power to wage war to our lesser resources, I become most apprehensive!"

Now we turn to Hurmuz. He returned to his camp and told Bakhtiarak and Akhzar Filgosh, "I have made a pact with Amar and given him my word that from this day onward I shall abandon all my intentions to fight him or step in the arena of war against him. I shall also counsel the emperor to desist from waging warfare, and will do all in my power to turn him from his enmity toward Amar. Thus, O Bakhtiarak, I ask you to refrain from your perfidy and deceit, and give up your chicanery. Renounce your malice and villainy and your guileful, malevolent ways."

Bakhtiarak replied, "I hear and I obey, as I fervently desire your pleasure with all my heart and soul! This slave shall do as he is commanded!" Akhzar, on the other hand, took exception to Hurmuz's words and said,

"We were sent here to destroy the fort, slay the followers of the True Faith, and capture Mehr-Nigar. These were the very orders given by the emperor. Without carrying out his orders and accomplishing these goals, I shall not turn back."

Hurmuz was furious to hear Akhzar speak thus. He said, "I have had occasion to notice that those whose corpulence is caused by their phlegmatic humors are unable to perform any deed of valor and gallantry. They taste reverses in every endeavor they make!"

Akhzar now seethed with rage and replied, "My prince! I think that perhaps you are a stranger to the war cries of valiant men in battle that burst the eardrums, and have never witnessed the sparks flying from the swords of gallant men that blind the eyes of the foe. This is why you have resolved as you did. It is beneath the station of royalty to sell such absurd reasoning to their troops!" Riled at these words, that very moment Hurmuz had the drums of retreat sounded, and set out for Ctesiphon with his army. Akhzar, on the other hand, ordered the drums of war to be sounded, and could not be restrained from his mischief.

Amar became alert to the sound of war drums and said to himself, *It is a wonder that Hurmuz broke his word so soon. Only a short while ago he made profuse vows to me never to wage war against me for as long as he lived and to have nothing to do with this feud. The moment he returned to his camp, he had the drums of war sounded and forgot all of his promises. I must go and find out what is afoot and what is its cause.* As Amar went toward Hurmuz's camp, he found out that Hurmuz had returned to Ctesiphon with his troops but Akhzar had stayed on after exchanging words with him. Amar also learned that it was Akhzar who had sounded the drums of war, and that he had extracted an oath from his army that the next day they would either conquer the fort or die in the effort.

After Amar had gathered this intelligence, he whiled away his day in petty chores, but come evening, he disguised himself as a foot soldier and infiltrated Akhzar's camp. There he saw all the commanders busy with preparations for the impending battle. Taking care that nobody should notice him, Amar sneaked up on Akhzar's pavilion at whose entrance several torches were burning. The vigils were all fast asleep and deep in the oblivion of slumber. Amar pulled up the pavilion's tent rope from one corner and slipped inside, where he heard Akhzar loudly trilling the trumpet of snores. Amar extinguished the lights with his *ayyar*'s mantle and plunged the place into darkness but for one taper that he kept lit to work his trickery[?]. Filling his seven-jointed reed pipe with two *mithcals* of drugged ambergris, he put it to Akhzar's nostrils and blew into it. The powder traveled to Akhzar's brain, and he sneezed once and fell unconscious; from the effect of the soporific, he entered a coma. Amar then made all of his attendants unconscious, too.

Every article that Amar could lay hands on in the pavilion he tied into a bundle and stored in his *zambil*. He made a bundle of Akhzar Filgosh, too, and slung him over his shoulder. After removing one of the supporting poles from the pavilion, Amar planted that pole on a crossway in the center of Akhzar's camp. He cut off one of Akhzar's ears, blackened his whole body, and made seven spots on it in seven colors. Then he performed more mischief and humiliated Akhzar further by hanging him upside down from the pole. He inserted a flagstaff into his ass, and affixed to it a multicolored piece of paper bearing a message, in place of a flag. After all this was done, Amar headed back to his fort without further thought about Akhzar's vengeance and assault.

At the gates of his fort, Amar saw that a small group was gathered, and this made him apprehensive. He wondered what it portended. As he leapt across the moat, someone called out, "Who goes there?" Amar replied, "It's me, Amar! But do tell me who has arrived outside the gates of the fort." Mehtar Aqiq answered him, "Sarhang Misri has arrived with three hundred *ayyars* bearing seventy thousand *tomans* in red gold coins, seven trains of Baroi and Baghdadi camels, as well as trains of carting mules, all as an offering for you." Amar was overjoyed and his worries were dispelled. He sent for Sarhang Misri and embraced him, and they entered the fort with all the baggage and impedimenta. Sarhang Misri's arrival and the aid he had brought in goods and men greatly rejuvenated Amar's spirits.

The next morning, Amar conferred on Sarhang Misri a braided shift of brocade, a gold-covered crown embedded with two costly royal pearls, a jewel-studded dagger, a scimitar, and a shield, and said, "Present all that you have brought to Zehra Misri, and offer it all to her!" Sarhang Misri carried out Amar's orders, immediately acting on Amar's wishes. Zehra Misri then took all these goods and presented them to Mehr-Nigar, displaying every individual item for her. Mehr-Nigar sent for Amar and conferred the whole lot on him, and presented Zehra Misri the dress and jewels she was wearing.

When Amar told Mehr-Nigar about the trick he had played on Akhzar Filgosh, she laughed and said, "O Khvaja! God has appointed you the king of the followers of the True Faith. It is an eminent station, and the prayers of the forty saints[33] shall always be with you. You will always be triumphant and victorious in your adventures and none will be able to defeat you." Delighted to hear her words, Amar blessed Mehr-Nigar, passed his hands over her head, and cracked the joints of his fingers over his temples in the token of taking all her misfortunes upon himself. Then he said to her, "I have decided to spend thirty thousand *tomans* to fill the granaries in the fort, and thus allay everyone's anxiety as to the availability of food. I will send Sarhang Misri with a purse of forty thousand *tomans* to buy twelve thousand Abyssinian and Ethiopian slaves, who will be of service to us and perform many useful deeds. I shall train them in musketry, the sling, and javelin throwing, and then you will see what a terrible scourge they will prove for the armies of the foe." Mehr-Nigar replied, "Dear friend, what you propose is most suitable, and there is none who could match your wisdom!"

Now hear a few words of the adventures of Akhzar Filgosh. The tent pole stood in its place, and Akhzar spent the whole night tied there with the flagstaff stuck in his ass, while the drums of war kept beating. When it was morning and his army presented itself at his threshold, they beheld a man hanging upside down from a tent pole. His limbs were motionless and a flag was flying from his derriere. Upon stepping close they found him in a most pitiable state with his one ear severed, and his body covered with soot from head to toe. He was marked with spots of yellow, white, blue, red, and various other colors, and he had been subjected to other miscellaneous clownish tricks. The soldiers tried to identify him, but nobody was able to recognize the man despite their best efforts. All failed to see through Amar's wonderful handiwork. When they examined the paper attached to the flagstaff, they found it inscribed with the following message:

> O Gueber, because you exchanged words with Hurmuz and stayed back to kill me and raze the fort and carry away Mehr-Nigar, I have offered you a little chastisement. You will find your ear severed, a flagpole stuck in your ass, and your countenance appalling and awful. If you take heed from this and remove the plug of ignorance from your ears that has made you deaf to sense, you may yet spare your life from my hand. Otherwise you will learn that I, Khvaja Amar Ayyar—known to the world as the King of *Ayyars*, the bearder of infidels, the lopper of the heads of fractious men, the chastiser of those deaf to sense, the ripper of the bellies of knaves, and one whose trickery is the dread of all men—am notorious for good reason. I spared you this time with this little warning,

and visited only small rebuke on your head. If you cross my path again, you shall find yourself with far worse a fate and shall learn what awful humiliation and disgrace shall become your lot.

Upon reading this note, the men reasoned that this was Akhzar Filgosh. They quickly untied him and carried him into his pavilion. They cleaned those black marks off him, rid him of that repugnant guise, and changed his dress.

Akhzar began crying and said through his tears, "How will I now show my face in Ctesiphon? I have been so humiliated and disgraced that I shall never set foot there!" He suddenly plunged a dagger into his own ribs, and it came out the other side. He drove a second dagger into his neck, and engulfed in pain and misery, departed for Hell.

When has an army ever fought without a commander, or stood their ground alone in a battlefield? All seventy thousand men of his army headed for Ctesiphon carrying his corpse, and all signs of their camp soon vanished with them.

Amar was informed of these developments in due course. He discovered how Akhzar had died by his own hand, tearing the neck band that had kept his soul captive. He also found out that Akhzar's army had returned to Ctesiphon with his corpse. Jubilant, Amar went to the Kaaba and offered prayers of gratitude. He had the gates of the fort opened and carried the happy tidings himself to Mehr-Nigar. She, too, offered prayers of thanks, and congratulated Amar on the victory.

Amar organized a feast in honor of the grandees of Mecca and asked them to do him the kindness of supplying him with thirty thousand *tomans'* worth of grain. They replied, "O Khvaja! May the Exalted and Glorified Lord always return you triumphant from all danger! The grain can be provided easily, but we are concerned that when the corpse of Akhzar is presented before Naushervan, he will fall into a towering rage. There is no knowing how great a force he will send, or if he would descend on us himself with his whole army. Then we will certainly be killed since confronting and resisting his might is beyond our power. It would be better to find another strong fort and fill it up with grain, and think of some way to save the city afterward. All of us, young and old alike, will pray for your success. We shall go into the Kaaba and solicit God for your victory and triumph, and shall also secretly watch out for your interests."

Amar informed Khvaja Abul Muttalib of the message he had received from the nobles of Mecca. Khvaja Abdul Muttalib replied, "Indeed what they say is true and they have reason to feel the danger and dread that they have shared with you." Amar realized then that Khvaja Abdul Muttalib also desired that they move away from Mecca so that their citizens might breathe more easily, delivered from the threat of Naushervan's revenge.

Amar narrated all these developments to the commanders of his army and sought their advice as to where they should find refuge. Aadi replied, "For the moment we should retire in the fortress of Tang-e Rawahil, and make that our abode. Then we may make other plans and take over some impregnable fort." That very moment, Amar ordered his army to move out of the fort. After some hours of the night had passed, he had Mehr-Nigar borne upon a litter and delegated the commanders of Yemen, Tang-e Rawahil, and Haft-Shehr to escort her. Toward the end of the night the caravan proceeded on its way.

When it was morning, Amar made them all bivouac in a desert. He rested there for a while, and then provided fodder and grass for the beasts and food for his men. After some hours of the morning had passed, Amar ordered Muqbil and all the commanders of the army to safeguard Mehr-Nigar. Then after putting on the disguise of a saintly man with a prophetic visage, he headed for the fort of Tang-e Rawahil.

By noon he was close to the fort, but due to the excessive heat, the ground burned like a gram parcher's kiln, and gusts of hot wind blew with such intensity that Amar's bones felt to him like melting wax. As it was a vast desert, there were no trees under which he could find refuge and take some comfort. Bewildered and disconcerted, Amar trekked all over looking for a place where he might find some rest and where his heart might glean a few moments' peace from the violence of the heat. Finally, he found a few shady trees. He gathered his senses and happily headed toward the place where he saw a wizened old shepherd sitting on a mantle spread under the trees.

When the shepherd beheld Amar he saluted him and asked, "Sire, whence have you come, and how did you happen to pass here?" Amar replied, "I have come from my mother's womb. I am a human being and human born!" The shepherd replied, "Everyone has used the same doorway to this world, and you have no distinction over others in that particular. Do tell me whence you have come and where you are headed, and why you undergo the rigors of a dervish's life."

Amar replied, "O brother! I come from Greece and am headed

toward Ctesiphon. Only when I have reached my destination will I find peace. At this moment, I am famished with hunger and my life seems like a burden to me!"

The shepherd milked a few goats and, putting the milk before Amar, said, "My lord and master, at present I have only this. There are no victuals that I can offer you at this time!" Amar replied, "My friend, to the pious man the thought of the Creator alone is fulfilling. Whether in wellness or adversity, his heart and soul are occupied by thoughts of Him. I was just testing you to see whether or not you would show mercy to a man of God. May God show you His munificence and favor, and recompense you for the kindness you have shown me."

After a while, Amar again asked the old man in all innocence, "What is the name of this fort? Are mendicants and paupers welcomed and shown favor at the court?" The shepherd answered, "There was a time when the ways of the believers in God were supreme in this place. But ever since an *ayyar* named Amar has rebelled, the Emperor of the Seven Concentric Circles has dispatched many of his commanders to different fronts. The commander who has arrived at this fort, Humran Zarrin Kamar, is a most prudent man."

Amar froze upon hearing these words and said to himself, *God's hand stopped me from taking Mehr-Nigar into the fort. Great mischief would have been done if I had. I would have cursed myself to my dying day for landing myself in a dragon's lair and burying myself alive with my own hands.* Thinking thus, Amar took out a pipe and placed it before the shepherd. When the shepherd saw it, he said, "Sire, I also used to have a pipe, but some days past it went missing; I haven't seen a wonderful pipe like this one even in my dreams. Indeed, no words could be found to praise it enough." Amar said, "All right, my brother! If you have taken such a liking to the pipe, here, take it and be happy! As long as this memento of this mendicant shall remain with you, melancholy shall never find a foothold in your heart."

The shepherd took the pipe from Amar's hands and said, "Your giving me this pipe is like granting me a whole kingdom. There is no way I could thank you enough for this gift. If I were to sacrifice my life for you it would only be appropriate!" Amar replied, "I am a mere fakir.[34] From excessive devotion my heart has become like a mirror, and what lies in people's hearts is manifest to me. This is no idle boast! Pipe a song for me, and play it to show me how you perform and trill the notes!" Without the least misgiving, the shepherd put the pipe to his mouth. As he breathed in to play a note, the powder inside the pipe flew into his mouth. He began coughing, sneezed once, and fell comatose and unconscious all of a sudden.

Amar dug a hole in the same spot and buried the old man there. Once finished with that labor, he disguised himself as the old shepherd and went to the gates of the fort, where he began rolling on the ground and protesting. He worked himself into such a frenzy that everyone there wondered what had happened to him. They gathered around him and beheld the shepherd, who was the servant of that selfsame grandee, Humran Zarrin Kamar. A footman brought Humran the news of his shepherd's sorry state. The shepherd happened to be in Humran's favor. He ordered that this man be conducted into his presence without delay so that he might witness his condition himself, redress his grievances, and afford him comfort and solace.

It was nearly evening when the shepherd was brought before Humran, who shed many a tear upon beholding the old man's state. When the false shepherd beheld Humran, he began rolling on the ground again and became more disconsolate than ever. Humran grew very troubled and said to him, "Tell me what has passed with you! What calamity befell you?"

Amar replied, "I don't know where to begin to tell my tale of woe to Your Honor. As is customary, your slave was watching over the grazing herd and enjoying the forest breeze when in the late afternoon a cavalcade arrived from the direction of Kaaba. They were escorting a palanquin[35] and some litters carried on camels that were surrounded by several hundred men. Some *ayyars* dressed in brocade vests and broadcloth socks were also among them. One of them, who appeared to be their commander, asked me whose herd I guarded. I gave him Your Honor's name and acquainted him with your magnificence and glory. He herded away the flock saying that his men had starved for the last few days in Mecca, and had undergone great discomfort on their journey. Now, he said, they would eat those goats and quench the fire of their hunger. When I protested, he called out to his *ayyars* who beat me so severely that I lay unconscious for a long time. Even now every fiber in my body aches, and I am in great pain and misery."

Humran asked him, "Where did that cavalcade proceed to afterward?" The false shepherd replied, "It went toward Yemen!" Humran felt overjoyed at this and said, "Now I know that the *ayyar* was Amar, and the citizens of Mecca have driven him away from their city for fear of

Naushervan. He has departed from Mecca, and is now headed toward Yemen with Mehr-Nigar!"

Humran headed out of the fort without delay with all the troops in his command to snatch Mehr-Nigar and take possession of her and thus earn himself favor and renown at Naushervan's court. Amar also left and headed toward his camp. Disguising Sultan Bakht Maghrebi as Humran, he entered Humran's fort with his army and the women's litters. Amar ruthlessly slew the remaining men in the fort, deputized his men to guard the walls and ramparts of the fortress and, raising the drawbridge, made himself at home, earning great glory for himself as an *ayyar* by this successful subterfuge.

Now hear of Humran. He carried on with his wild-goose chase for forty or forty-five miles but found no signs of the cavalcade that the false shepherd had reported seeing. In the end, he returned dejected to his fortress around dawn the next day. As he approached the moat around the fortress, he suddenly came under a shower of fiery projectiles, stones, and arrows. His troops fell in this attack in great numbers, and he suffered a huge loss. Humran was confounded and wondered what had come over his men that they had turned against him and attacked, and were bent upon rioting and mischief. He was forced to escape from the range of the projectiles.

When he scanned the fortress with his spyglass he did not recognize a single person; the faces he saw manning the fortifications were complete strangers. After much thought it occured to Humran that the shepherd who had shed tears and made lamentations in his presence must have been Amar in disguise, and he had thus driven him out of the fortress by artifice in order to occupy it. Humran's commanders advised him that there was nothing to be done except to besiege the fortress and wait. They advised him not to take any offensive measures but to bide his time in silence until the rations in the fortress ran out; Amar would then be distressed, unable to get provisions from outside. They counseled Humran to take steps so that no provisions could get inside the fort, so the fortress would fall by itself, since no one would be able to hold it without food. Humran replied, "Who is going to wait for that day to come to pass? It would be far better for me to go before Naushervan to inform him of this situation and brief him regarding these details. Then he shall do as he deems suitable and issue orders as per his wishes." Thus resolved in his mind, Humran headed toward Ctesiphon.

Now for a short account of Prince Hurmuz: He had also set out for

Ctesiphon after giving his solemn promise to Amar. He arrived at the seat of the empire after a few days' journey. At the moment of his arrival, the emperor was giving audience and was occupied with matters of state. Hurmuz presented himself and kissed his father's feet. The emperor embraced him and showed him much favor and asked him what news he had brought. Hurmuz gave him a detailed account and afterward said, "In my opinion, it would be best if Your Honor leaves Amar alone until Hamza returns. Such a course of action would prove expedient and would become our lofty status!"

The emperor was furious with his son's words and said, "I would have followed your advice if I, too, were impotent like yourself!" Buzurjmehr said, "Do not call it impotence, for Hurmuz is wise and has acted in the finest traditions of chivalry. There were two reasons why the prince returned from the campaign. In the first place, it does not become the prestige of a prince to battle a lowly *ayyar*; it would tarnish his glorious renown among illustrious men. Then there was also the matter of a long separation from Your Honor. He wished to return from the desire to kiss Your Honor's feet, and also as he suffered anxiety about your well-being."

The emperor turned toward Bakhtak and asked, "Bakhtiarak accompanied Hurmuz on the campaign. Was he also trumped by Amar and equally unable to find some means of capturing that cameleer's son?" Hurmuz replied, "Amar doused Bakhtiarak's face with urine and shaved it clean of mustache and beard. After that he stripped him naked and placed him in Akhzar Filgosh's lap, who, in his drunkenness, committed sodomy with him and plunged Bakhtiarak deeper into ignominy." The emperor burst into laughter upon hearing this and marveled at Amar's trickery. Buzurjmehr said, "Your Honor, a champion of Akhzar Filgosh's caliber is rare even among the Sassanids. He will certainly chastise Amar well now that he has decided to stay behind!" The Sassanids were very pleased to hear Buzurjmehr sing praises of Akhzar Filgosh. They voiced their agreement with Buzurjmehr's counsel and fawned on him a great deal that day.

The emperor dismissed the court and, taking along Hurmuz, retired to the royal palace. He feasted for three days and thus became oblivious to any distress or pain. On the fourth day he held court and ordered all nobles to be assembled. Hardly an hour had passed when the chain of justice was pulled by a plaintiff calling for redress. Naushervan demanded, "Go and see who has moved the chain and produce him before replied, "Of course! This is how I make a living!"[36] Amar asked him next, "Do you live in that castle?" He replied, "Indeed that is my abode, I tell you in all truth!" Amar asked him, "What is the name of this castle and who is its ruler? Is he a follower of the True Faith or is he an infidel, a just man or a tyrant?" The grass cutter replied, "The fort is called Kurgistan and it is ruled by two brothers, Darab and Sohrab. But the entry and exit points of the fort are rigorously guarded."

Amar was still talking to the grass cutter when a youth, some twenty-odd years of age, arrived on the scene mounted on a fleet horse. An entourage of five thousand troops and *ayyars* were with him, and his footmen walked before him holding the bridle of his horse, dispersing any who might come in the way. Amar asked who he was, and the grass cutter replied, "He is the one called Sohrab!" Amar was overjoyed to hear this and said to the grass cutter, "Wait here a moment while I go and behold this beautiful youth in proximity, and acquaint myself with his charm." Amar then retired behind a clump of trees and removed his disguise and put on his *ayyar*'s attire. Approaching Sohrab, he made a great display of deference, and after performing all the rituals of veneration and reverence, started crying copious tears and put on a show of great disquiet for Sohrab.

Sohrab beheld an *ayyar* attired in a bejeweled costume crying before him and wondered what calamity had made the man so completely out of sorts. He pulled on the reins of his horse and asked, "Dear man, who are you and why do you cry and inflict such woeful lamentations on the world?" Amar spoke to him with folded arms: "Your Honor will have heard the name of Amar Ayyar. It is that selfsame Amar who stands before you. I have brought you a message regarding Mehr-Nigar, the daughter of Naushervan, which I shall only share in complete privacy. Then I shall acquaint you with all the details."

At the mention of Mehr-Nigar's name, Sohrab's whiskers began trembling with joy, and he very nearly burst from happy anticipation. He ordered Amar to draw nearer, and sent the men in his entourage a bow shot's distance from them. Then he said to Amar, "Make haste and give me the message, for my heart is unable to bear the suspense any longer. I am dying to hear the tidings you have brought me!"

Amar wiped his tears with a kerchief and replied, "You must have heard of a most queer fellow, Hamza the Arab. He carried away Mehr-Nigar forcibly from Naushervan's house and kept her in his possession. The garden of his hopes had not yet seen the bloom from the breeze of

us!" The order was carried out promptly and the plaintiffs were produced before the emperor, carrying a bier with grief writ large on their countenances. Upon questioning they replied, "We carry the corpse of Akhzar Filgosh in this bier, whose demise is being mourned by the whole army, which has clad itself in black in grief." The emperor asked, "What happened to him and how did he die?" When the men narrated the whole catalog of Amar's rascality in great detail, the emperor came into a towering rage and declared, "That cameleer's son has completely forgotten his place, and set himself up as a great deviser of stratagems! Very well, then! Dispatch our advance camp and order the army to assemble. We shall ourselves march to punish that rebel and avenge ourselves fully."

The advance camp was sent off, and within four days an army of one hundred thousand men was gathered. The emperor had not yet given orders for the march when it was announced that Zhopin Kaus had arrived from Zabul with his army with a desire to kiss his sovereign's feet. The emperor ordered some commanders to go out to welcome him so that he might enjoy the sight of Zhopin's face. At that moment Humran Zarrin Kamar also presented himself and gave an account of how the fortress had been lost to Amar's forces, and informed the emperor of all the particulars of the incident.

Then Buzurjmehr said, "It appears that the citizens of Mecca have expelled Amar and driven him out of their city. Now it will not take much for Amar to be overpowered. Anyone who is dispatched against him will return victorious. Your Honor may now cancel your resolve to fight, and not incommode yourself with such an expedition." The emperor replied, "Very well! Our advance camp should return, the expedition be deferred, and the troops return to their places. And instead, you yourself should march along with the princes to exterminate Amar's menace by some stratagem." Buzurjmehr replied, "I have no objections. I hear and obey. I am ready for the campaign!"

The emperor sent Buzurjmehr with Zhopin, Bakhtiarak, and five renowned commanders at the head of forty thousand troops to punish Amar. He also commanded his sons, Hurmuz and Faramurz, to join the campaign and bring back Mehr-Nigar. The army was well provisioned with all that it might need and each of the commanders was decorated with robes of honor according to his station.

When the force arrived at the fortress of Tang-e Rawahil, Zhopin saw a pavilion of Scythian yellow satin worked with gold thread, richly and profusely appointed with all amenities and erected at the tallest tower of the fort. Under that sat a bejeweled throne on which the Prince of *Ayyars*, Khwaja Amar bin Umayya Zamiri, was giving audience clad in a regal robe. All his deputies were assembled before him in a row and Muqbil Vafadar stood guard at his back, along with his twelve thousand faultless archers. To Amar's left and right the commanders and kings of Yemen, Tang-e Rawahil, and Haft Shehr sat on their thrones. Every tower and rampart was manned by musketeers, lancers, sling bearers, Greek-fire launchers, and firework throwers on the ready. Large standards and flags fluttered, affixed to the towers of the fort.

The princes asked Buzurjmehr for some plan for taking over the fortress. Buzurjmehr replied, "The men guarding the fort are on alert and are armed with all manner of weapons. They seem ready to lay down their lives in its defense. We will be throwing away the lives of our men if we storm the fort now. We will lose many men on our side, weakening our army's strength, and will be unable to inflict any losses on them."

The princes then asked Bakhtiarak, "What do you counsel would be a more appropriate course of action?" Bakhtiarak replied, "Although Khwaja Buzurjmehr's counsel is good, and he has an acute sense of the intricacies of the situation, yet there appears no great benefit in setting up a siege. It does not appear it would yield us much good. In my opinion our army is fresh and well suited to undertake any challenge. I say we should storm the fort. If the fort falls to us, all the better; if not we will look for some other tactic. Moreover, those within will panic at our attack and it would instill fear and terror in their hearts." The princes then turned to Zhopin and said to him, "Sally forth into the land of valor and storm the fort!" Zhopin took over command of the army and spurred on his horse in the direction of the fort to show the mettle of his valor.

At first Amar sat quietly watching them all. The moment Zhopin's army came within range of his weapons, he called out to his valiant men, "Now, my men! Make sure that they are unable to step an inch forward and are stopped in their tracks!" The defenses of the fort were immediately unleashed and the infidels destined for Hell were claimed by their graves, while the rest retreated with their hearts bursting with terror.

It was an evil hour for Zhopin when he spurred his horse forward, covering his head with a shield. Amar put a stone in his sling and let fly at him with full force. As it struck Zhopin on the chest, he was knocked down from his horse. He was still reeling from the pain and trying to recover himself and regain the saddle when Amar let fly another stone that completely unnerved him. All his senses took flight and he began rolling

on the ground like a tumbler pigeon from the pain. His companions were shocked to see him in that state and lifted him off the ground, for Zhopin had not completely run out of his store of good luck yet.

The princes asked Bakhtiarak, "What should we do now? Amar's jiggery-pokery has confounded us and seems beyond our means to counter." Bakhtiarak replied, "Sires! If you had it in your head to take a fort by these simple sallies, pray understand that it is well-nigh impossible, and drive such ideas from your mind." The princes cried, "O son of a whore! It was at your suggestion that we ordered the attack and were handed these losses! Now you have the temerity to preach to us that the fort cannot be taken by these means?"

That cad answered, "It did not turn out all that badly for us! Those inside the fort learned that we have come to do battle and have brought all our men and arms for that purpose. Sound the drums for cessation of hostilities now and begin the siege. You should do nothing for the next few days but bide your time in peace. When all the provisions in the fort run out, and those inside are assailed by pangs of hunger, then you may show them a piece of bread and catch them one by one."

The princes ordered the cessation of hostilities as Bakhtiarak had counseled, and all of them retired to their pavilions.

Now hear of Amar. When he saw that the armies of Hurmuz and Faramurz had stopped fighting and had set a blockade around the fort, he said to his commanders, "We shall easily fall into the hands of our foe if we remain besieged within. It is necessary for us to take over another, stronger fort so that our foe is unable to overwhelm us with the large army it has brought. Carefully keep watch on the situation, and guard the fort with great alertness until my return. Within the next few days I will find some fort where all of us may find shelter." Amar put on the *ayyar*'s attire then and went looking for a suitable place, searching every mountaintop, desert, and forest, and enduring all manner of hardships in his pursuit.

The following day, after a westward journey of seven *kos* from the fort of Tang-e Rawahil, Amar spotted an imposing castle and headed toward it. He circled around it and found it highly impregnable and secure. As he was cudgeling his brains to find some way to secure the fort for his army, pondering some means to achieve his end, he espied a poor grass cutter carrying a bale of grass on his head and selling his merchandise. Amar immediately dressed himself as a stable groom, and approached the man and said, "Would you sell me your grass?" The grass cutter

fulfillment, however, when an adventure befell him, and he went away to Qaf with the promise to return in eighteen days, leaving me the custodian of Princess Mehr-Nigar. He put me under strict orders to protect her until his return without letting my guard down for a moment, or allowing anyone to intimidate me. I carried out his trust as best I could, and took good care of Mehr-Nigar.

"Now that Hamza's eighteen days have turned into as many years, I no longer know whether he is alive or dead, or if some *dev* has made a snack of him. After the Arabs conspired to snatch Mehr-Nigar from me and send me to Naushervan as prisoner, I escaped from Mecca and took her with me. They are unable to lay their hands on her, and my promise to Hamza has not been violated. Yet five thousand Arabs are in pursuit of me right now to murder me and send me off to the Future State and to take possession of Mehr-Nigar.

"In view of this, Mehr-Nigar recently said to me, 'O Khvaja! I address you with the title of brother and consider you my guardian who has never failed me. Do me the kindness now of finding me a suitable man so that I may find happiness with him, and am never, ever brought to see the face of disgrace.' I set out to find such a man, and when I saw you I recalled Hamza's face since you bear a striking resemblance to him.

"That was the reason for my tears. I wish to declare to Your Honor that if you were to show me the same patronage as Hamza, I would hand Princess Mehr-Nigar over to you. I would feel that I have done well by both her and myself. However, I am apprehensive that after securing Mehr-Nigar, you may decide that you would find distinction at Naushervan's court by sending me there as a prisoner."

With the repeated mention of Mehr-Nigar's name, Sohrab's desire was so violently stirred that he was unable to maintain his self-restraint. He jumped down from his mount, embraced Amar, and said, "O Khvaja, you shall find with me a far better station than the one you enjoyed with Hamza, and shall have no reason for complaints. Even if the whole world should stir into a boiling frenzy, let alone Naushervan, nothing would make me surrender you into anyone else's hands. This fort was erected by Sikander Zulqarnain, and if all the monarchs of the world exert themselves as one against it, they will find it beyond their power to conquer it. Indeed, they would be entirely frustrated in their plans as the makers of this fort made it completely impregnable. Accompany me now so that I may take you on a visit and show you the various sections of the fort!" Sohrab took Amar along and they headed toward the fort.

When they arrived there, Amar thought, *Thank Heaven I was able to beguile him and find my way here. God willing, I shall conquer this fort, too, through the majesty of Hamza's glory, and Sohrab shall live to rue his stupidity.* Amar was greatly pleased to inspect the defenses of the fort: The structure was indeed an unparalleled rarity, for none had reached the apex of glory that Sikander Zulqarnain had held in his time in the world. After seating Amar in his hall of assembly and providing him all comforts and pleasures, Sohrab went to relay Amar's account to his elder brother, Darab, and thus acquaint him with the whole history of Amar's arrival. Sohrab said, "The gods Lat and Manat must be looking upon me with favor, for they have sent me a beloved of the likes of Mehr-Nigar, and an *ayyar* of the caliber of Amar!"

In contrast to his brother, Darab was a wise man of lofty intelligence and sound perception. He listened to his account and said, "It appears that your luck has turned for the worse and your prestige has gone into decline if you have taken these idle fancies into your mind. It remains to be seen what disaster Amar has prepared for you and how you will fall into his power without any recourse to help!" However, Amar's words had left such a profound impression on Sohrab's mind that nothing that Darab said could erase it, or cause him to reconsider what was good for him. He replied, "Amar's speech was not idle talk. His words had the ring of sincerity and truth. I suggest that you speak to him and judge for yourself, then make up your own mind regarding the truth or untruth of what he states." Darab said, "There is certainly no harm in sending for Amar and hearing him out." Sohrab then sent for Amar and brought him before Darab.

Upon arriving into Darab's presence, Amar made a most reverential obeisance, and after making salutations and visiting blessings on him, gave him a convincing presentation as well. As a result, Darab also embraced Amar and offered him words of comfort and encouragement. When Amar saw that he had duped Darab, too, he made another bow and said, "Now I shall take my leave to go fetch Mehr-Nigar and ennoble her with an audience with you. Pray order the sentinel to open the fort gates for me whether I return by day or night, and to offer no impediments to my entry, nor wait for Your Honor to grant my admittance!" Darab sent for the sentinel and told him to make sure he opened the gates for Amar the moment he arrived, so that Amar might have unimpeded entry to the fort. He instructed him to offer no resistance to Amar's entry and to grant similar access to any who accompanied him. Darab also told everyone that from that day onward Amar should be considered the master of the castle and anyone who disobeyed him would be suitably chastised. Having no interest in the matter, the servants assented to these orders without offering any objections, and circulated the injunctions among their ranks.

When Amar took his leave and headed out of the fort, Sohrab said to Darab, "I shall accompany Amar to take stock of the situation lest the Arabs fall upon his party on the way and snatch away Mehr-Nigar. Then our interests would be compromised, our aims thwarted, and the windfall snatched from our hands, causing us much heartache and distress." Darab said to him, "In my opinion your accompanying him would be entirely inadvisable. I remember Amar's words very well. He will bring Mehr-Nigar here in the manner he finds most suitable, and there is no one who can outfox him!"

Sohrab could not be persuaded, however. He took five thousand fully armed archers with him and went along with Amar, who advised Sohrab and his army to stop and rest at a distance of five *kos* from the fort of Tang-e Rawahil. Amar thought of a new artifice and said to Sohrab, "Pray camp here while I go and inform the princess and bring her along when the opportunity presents itself." Sohrab was so completely in Amar's power that he bivouacked with his army at that place, while Amar went to Tang-e Rawahil. He gave a detailed account of his adventures to his commanders and said, "By the grace of God the fort of Kurgistan is as good as ours, as I have fooled the master of the castle with a most singular trick!"

Amar acquainted his commanders with the strengths of the fort in praiseworthy terms whereupon they all rejoiced greatly, extolled Amar's cunning and wisdom to high heavens, and lauded him on his exploits. In the morning, Amar racked his brains to come up with some ruse that would rid him of Sohrab and allow him to go about his business without fear of finding him in his way. Unable to find a person suited for the task, Amar decided to go into the enemy camp himself to try his luck with Hurmuz by pulling the wool over his eyes.

Dressed as someone on a spying mission, he passed by the guard post of Hurmuz's army, raising suspicions with his conspicuous appearance. The foot soldiers arrested him and asked him time and again who he was and where he had come from, but Amar only cried incoherently like one dumb and made no answer. The head guard went to Buzurjmehr and said, "We have arrested a man who appears to be a spy, but despite our rigorous interrogation, he only makes unintelligible sounds like a dumb man and does not reveal his identity, origins, or employer. We have been greatly frustrated by his gibberish in our questioning."

Buzurjmehr ordered them to produce the captive before him. Once Amar was led before Buzurjmehr, he tried to interrogate him in the Arabic, Persian, Turkish, Kashmiri, Pushto, Maghrebi, Ethiopian, Zanzibarian, English, Portuguese, French, Russian, Latin, Greek, Hindi, Karnataki, Bhojpuri, Deccani, Chinese, Tartar, Rangari, and Sindhi languages, each time asking, "Who are you? And which land have you come from that you seem so alien to all known features of the human race? I will reward you and set you free presently, and you will have reason to feel happy again if you tell me your story in detail."

When Amar continued in silence, the champion warriors sitting by Buzurjmehr commented, "Sire! This is not the kind of pot from which you can extract butter just by dipping you fingers into it! Who ever heard of wax being melted without the application of heat? Put him in the stock and whip him. When he is thoroughly broken he will readily yield the information you seek and reveal whence he has come."

Buzurjmehr replied, "Such affairs are best settled using gentle persuasion. The application of force does not yield results in these matters and only serves to ruin them!" Buzurjmehr then took off the robe of honor given to him by Naushervan and, putting five purses full of gold pieces on top of that, placed them before Amar to tempt him. Then Buzurjmehr pleaded with him, "O friend! Tell me verily who you are. I swear by Naushervan's head that if you share the truth with me, I will present you this robe of honor and these gold pieces, and immediately set you free." Upon beholding the robe of honor and the gold pieces, Amar began to salivate with greed.

Speaking in the Maghrebi language,[37] he revealed himself, giving all the particulars of his mission to Buzurjmehr and telling him how he intended to capture the fort of Kurgistan with this ruse, for which reason he had deceived Sohrab and brought him there. Amar also told Buzurjmehr that he had come in disguise to give him the news that Sohrab planned to conduct a night raid on Hurmuz's camp that evening. Amar asked Buzurjmehr to strengthen his hand by seeing to it that Sohrab was either killed or captured; so that with the nuisance of Sohrab's existence dispelled from his head, he would again find peace of mind. Buzurjmehr added another thousand gold pieces to the reward he had already presented to Amar, and sent him away.

Afterward, Buzurjmehr went to Hurmuz and said, "One of the enemy's spies was caught by our men and brought to me as a prisoner. When I interrogated him and promised him a reward, I learned that Amar has brought here the master of the fort of Kurgistan, Sohrab, who is greatly in his influence and plans to conduct a raid on our camp tonight!" Hurmuz and Faramurz asked what Buzurjmehr's judgment of the situation was, and what his counsel would be under the circumstances. Buzurjmehr replied, "Assemble the commanders of the army. Ask them to take their meals early this evening and after four hours of the night have elapsed set up an ambush on the slope of the hill. When the night raiders fall upon the camp and begin its plunder, our army should emerge from its hiding place and slay them. Then our prospects will meet with success. We should try to catch Amar and Sohrab alive as that will result in the fort falling to us." Hurmuz and Faramurz immediately sent for the commanders of their army to brief them on the new developments and ordered them to make preparations as Buzurjmehr had advised.

We return now to give an account of Amar: He went to his fort and told the commanders of his army to have their mounts ready early in the evening. He instructed them to be armed and in the saddle so that the moment he returned they could leave with him for the fort of Kurgistan. After making these arrangements, Amar presented himself before Sohrab with a long face. Sohrab asked him, "What is wrong, Khvaja? Why do you look so sad and woebegone?"

Amar answered, "I don't know where to begin or find the words to explain what has happened except to say that I am heartbroken at the new turn of the events. I had taken leave of Your Honor and presented myself before Mehr-Nigar, and there I painted such a efficacious account of Your Honor's glory, magnificence, and courage that she became ardently enamored of your youthful beauty and most eager for a meeting. When I made preparations to send for a litter to bring her here and fulfill my promise to you, an *ayyar* suddenly came to me with the intelligence that an army had arrived near our fort and camped out of its range. He could not find out whose army it was, where it had come from or why, and whom they intended to fight. I went myself and discovered that Naushervan had sent Buzurjmehr here to counsel Mehr-Nigar and bring her back after securing her release from her confinement. Ever since that discovery, I have felt very anxious because Buzurjmehr is a sage who commands great power of persuasion, and there is wonderful strategy in all his actions. It would be little wonder if Mehr-Nigar is won over by his words and enticed by his honeyed tones. If I had had a mere thousand men at my command, I would have made a night raid on Buzurjmehr's camp to rout his force and drive him away from this place."

Sohrab replied, "What you propose is well within the realm of possibility, O Amar, as I will explain. Do not give yourself to such anxiety on this account. After all, there would be no point to my commanding five thousand troops and accompanying you here if I could not aid you with my arms. Show me the place where the army is camped and then leave everything else to me. I shall see to it that they are routed." Amar expressed great joy at this and incited him even further by saying, "Indeed such are the ways of true lovers, as Your Honor has professed! Verily you are a most gallant man, and this is a most auspicious omen for Mehr-Nigar that she will find a loving husband in yourself. Her slumbering fortunes have been awakened by propitious fate."

Sohrab puffed up even more upon hearing Amar's praise, and the flower of his heart blossomed with a thousand hopes. Accompanied by Amar, he sallied forth with his army with great pomp and ceremony, twirling his mustaches. When they reached an area close to the enemy fort, Amar asked Sohrab to halt and went himself into Hurmuz's camp. There he saw the pavilions of all the commanders lying empty and no one present to challenge him. Amar returned to Sohrab and after pointing out the location of Hurmuz's camp from afar to him, made himself scarce.

Sohrab advanced and found the pavilions empty and the goods lying around without anyone there to guard them. Not a soul was to be seen, nor were there any signs of the army. He thought that perhaps some spy had alerted them to the raid and they had escaped, fearing the assault, and hidden themselves, or that perhaps they had some other good reason not to fight him. Sohrab's troops bundled up everything they could lay their hands on from Hurmuz's camp and loaded themselves with the loot. But they had not yet departed when Hurmuz's forty thousand troops fell upon them from all sides and shouts of "Slaughter them!" and "Slay them!" rose from every corner. All avenues of retreat were sealed on Sohrab's army, and very many of his men were killed, and the rest were captured along with Sohrab. Finding themselves in this unenviable situation, they quietly surrendered. Hurmuz sent for blacksmiths to put them in chains and then imprisoned them.

Now hear of Amar. After herding Sohrab's army toward the camp of

Hurmuz, he returned to his own fort and said to his commanders, "Put Mehr-Nigar and the other womenfolk into their litters, take the army along, and head out westward. I shall follow you there and direct you to our destination." His army left with the women's litters and Amar busied himself with installing a mannequin made in his likeness on his throne. Afterward, he installed several hundred mannequins on the battlements and towers, and put miscellaneous strange contraptions in their hands[?]. He also tied up two dogs close to each other, so that they would bark at each other and fill the night with their racket. Then he roped an ass to the gate of the fort and placed caparison[?] on him to give a frightful aspect. Finally, putting a few cockerels at the casements, he raised the drawbridge, leapt over the moat, flew like the wind in the direction of his army, and caught up with them after traversing a distance of several *kos*. He kept his army on the march all through the night.

With some hours of the night remaining, they arrived at the gates of the fort of Kurgistan. Amar said to the commanders of his forces, "I will go and get the gates opened. Enter the fort with the womenfolk, and without further thought take hold of your inclement swords and start the wholesale slaughter. Do not pay heed to any hue or cry you may hear. Any who convert to the True Faith must be pardoned, but the rest should be laid low by your swords." Then Amar went and called out to the sentinel at the fort's gate, "Hurry up and open the door! This is Amar! I have brought Sohrab's beloved, Mehr-Nigar, as I promised." Already under orders to open the doors for him, the sentinels threw them open without any qualms.

Amar entered the fort with his army and Mehr-Nigar as he had planned. He conducted her and her companions to a safe place and delegated Muqbil Vafadar to guard them, with instructions to keep the princess in his protection and custody. Then taking along his army, Amar busied himself in wreaking carnage on the fort dwellers who suddenly found God's wrath upon them. Those who converted to the True Faith survived with their lives; the rest were dispatched to Hell to augment the ranks of the condemned. Upon beholding this state of affairs Darab realized that Amar had attacked the castle and it was as good as lost. He wondered what had become of Sohrab and what misadventure had overtaken him. When Amar assaulted Darab, he cried out, "O Khvaja, I convert to the True Faith! Stay your hand and initiate me into the Act of Faith!"

Amar embraced Darab and showed him mercy and said, "I have no designs on your fort or your goods and riches, nor will I reside here for the rest of my life. We only seek temporary shelter from our enemies here so that Hamza's honor will remain unviolated by the hands of his detractors, and he does not heap opprobrium on my head for not exerting myself in his cause to the best of my ability. You will continue to be the master of your fort as before once all this is over. I shall have no further business with either you or your castle afterward, as I nurse no enmity or rancor toward you." Darab recited the Act of Faith sincerely that very moment, and entered the ranks of the followers of the True Faith by virtue of his auspicious fortune. Amar settled down in the castle and the dwellers of the fort resigned themselves to their fate.

Now hear of Sohrab. He languished as a prisoner in Hurmuz's camp, cursing his fate and the trick Amar had played on him. Bakhtiarak and Zhopin said to the two princes and Buzurjmehr, "One can surmise that Amar must have left for the fort of Kurgistan and will have entered it and put it under his control." At the first light of the morning they sent out *ayyars* to find out whether the fortress of Tang-e Rawahil had been emptied. After conducting their reconnaissance, the *ayyars* returned and reported, "We saw soldiers manning the battlements as before, and heard the racket made by dogs and an ass and the crowing of cockerels. The fortress is not empty and there are no signs that it could be. We find it populated as before." Bakhtiarak commented that he found this impossible to believe and said to Hurmuz and Faramurz, "Order the drums of war to be sounded. You may then determine the veracity or falsehood of what I state!" Hurmuz and Faramurz commanded Buzurjmehr to safeguard the prisoners, and after ordering the drums to be beaten, they marched toward the fortress of Tang-e Rawahil themselves.

Upon their arrival, Zhopin said to Bakhtiarak, "Regard that what you said was false: The fortress is not empty and everything is as before. At every few paces soldiers are manning the battlements, Amar is standing alert with his slingshot, and all the standards are flying from their stations." Bahtiarak again inspected the fortress facade and said, "O Zhopin, that is not Amar! The rogue has played a new trick by making a dummy in his likeness and arming it with a sling. All the men you see on the fort are also mannequins. See how the sling does revolutions with the wind and the stones move?" As Zhopin stepped forward, the movement of the air discharged the sling. The stone hit Zhopin's head at the same place where Amar had earlier inscribed his signature, and the old wound reopened. Now Zhopin became absolutely certain that the figure was not a dummy but Amar in person. His retreat from there was helter-skelter, as he was all drenched in blood and inconsolable with pain.

Bakhtiarak called after him, "O Zhopin! Where are you running off to? Why earn ignominy with this show of cowardice? A thousand pities on the House of Kaikaus, which had to countenance a pusillanimous cad like yourself among its progeny, for you were born to sully the glory of their ancestral valor, and are not ashamed to show your cowardice even before your own men!" Zhopin replied, "A marvel it is that even when Amar clearly stones me, you maintain that it is not him! Tell me yourself who else is playing such havoc here with my life!" Bakhtiarak replied, "You poltroon! It was the wind that discharged the sling and fired the stone that hit your head and caused the injury. Rest assured that it was only chance that made it happen! If it was indeed Amar, he would have launched a hail of stones and none of us would have been able to escape. He would have unleashed such fireworks from the battlements that everyone would have died an untimely death, roasted like grain inside the parcher's kiln and dispatched to the land of the dead. Go break down the gate of the fort, and do not ignore my advice!"

At Bakhtiarak's bidding, Zhopin crossed the moat and broke open the gates of the fort with his mace. When he entered with the princes, Bakhtiarak, and other commanders of his army, he marveled greatly to see an ass tied up there. Then he saw the roosters crowing in the casements and two dogs roped together and [?] several hundred paper dummies installed on the battlements. With these marvels taunting them in the fort, Zhopin felt he had been made a fool. He angrily struck Amar's dummy with his mace, which unleashed the final spectacle: When the mannequin burst, a baby jackal Amar had put inside its belly scampered out, frightening Zhopin into believing it was some new calamity. He said to Bakhtiarak, "What is this new scourge? Marvels keep unfolding in this fort one after another!" Bakhtiarak replied, "Catch him, someone, don't let him escape! He is none other than Amar's spouse!" Everyone present bent over in laughter at Bakhtiarak's joke and kept bursting into guffaws when they recalled it later.

Upon return to his camp, Hurmuz said to Bakhtiarak, "Now that we have been dealt an unexpected hand, we must think of some new strategy and a new course of action." Bakhtiarak replied, "It would be unwise to leave Amar to his devices. Whether or not we score a victory we must continue to pursue our mission, especially at this juncture when Amar has found himself a new haven. It is likely that he has not settled down yet in the new fort since he has only secured it recently. His faculties will still be in a state of disorder and his affairs in disarray." Hurmuz agreed with this opinion and sent for Buzurjmehr and said to him, "O Khvaja! Take Sohrab along and go before the emperor to narrate in detail all that you have witnessed, and also present my missive to him and find out what it pleases His Highness to command!"

While Buzurjmehr headed for Ctesiphon with Sohrab, the princes, Zhopin, and Bakhtiarak went with an eighty-thousand-strong force toward the fortress of Kurgistan and upon arrival besieged it, cutting off its supplies.

Now again for Amar: Having found a few moments of respite, he had thought of providing himself with provisions and stored up six months' worth of rations in the fort, filling the stores with all kinds of victuals. Then he decorated the exterior of the castle so that it resembled a preening peacock, and took his seat under a canopy on a bejeweled throne at the gate with such splendor as would rob the Emperor of the Seven Climes of all grandeur, and strip him of all magnificence and glory.

In the meantime, Hurmuz and Faramurz had arrived there with their army. Acting on Bakhtiarak's advice they stormed the fort, and ordered the army to launch an assault without delay. When Amar saw that the enemy was within range, he signaled to his army and called out to them, "There they are, my men! Get them now and don't let them escape! Let them all find their graves where they stand!" Presently a barrage of arrows, Greek fire, stones, and fireworks was unleashed on Hurmuz's army. The hellish heat from the discharge of fire made the victims long for even a single drop of water. Sapped of their life force by the hail of fire, several thousand troops rode off to the inn of Malik, the keeper of Hell. Their strength thus squandered, the remainder of the army retreated.

Bakhtiarak then said to Hurmuz and Faramurz, "This will not do! If we carry on in this manner, we will lose our whole army without ever seeing the slightest chance of a victory!" This sent the princes into a rage and they shouted at him: "What is this drivel that you commit to your tongue now, O coward! The fort was attacked and the army sent to storm it at your own suggestion. It seems that you have changed your song now. Indeed you are entirely without shame and deserve befitting punishment!" Bakhtiarak answered, "What great harm was done by my advice except a few thousand soldiers finding release from the misery of their existence and bartering their lives for the pleasures of Heaven? It has been made amply manifest to those within the fortress that Your Highnesses have come determined to fight at the head of a most grand and noble army. Now declare the cessation of hostilities and find a nice level plain on which to camp and rest the horses and men. When the fort runs out of their provisions and no aid reaches them from without, it will fall by itself!" The princes ordered the drums of retreat beaten, and the army bivouacked there and continued its siege.

Now hear of Buzurjmehr. He arrived in Ctesiphon at a time when the emperor was giving audience in his Hall of Assembly and was occupied with affairs of state. Buzurjmehr headed straight there to present himself before his sovereign, and made a royal obeisance. After presenting Sohrab, he narrated all that had come to pass, greatly distressing the emperor with the news of the losses sustained by his army. Buzurjmehr also gave the emperor the missive sent by the princes Hurmuz and Faramurz. Naushervan said to Sohrab, "If you wish me to spare your life, explain truthfully all that passed with you without any fear that I will throw you into the dungeon!" Sohrab related the whole story of Amar duping him into conducting the night raid and how he then fell prisoner. Having told that much he proclaimed, "If the emperor would pardon my transgression and dispel from his heart the rancor that my actions must have caused him, I will offer my life in his service and visit blessings on him for the rest of my borrowed existence."

The emperor pardoned Sohrab's crime and then ordered Hurmuz's missive to be read out to him, and applied himself to understanding its contents. It read:

In the four years that your slaves have been waging war against Amar at your orders, we have never seen the face of triumph even once, and none of our strategies have brought us any closer to victory. We have become convinced that it is not our destiny to defeat Amar. Instead we daily live in terror of him murdering us in our sleep, extracting our dear souls from our bodies, kidnapping us from our beds to remove us to his camp, snaring us into some calamitous proceeding, or visiting some untold trouble on our heads. In any event, it would be most appropriate for Your Honor to consider coming to our avail since offering assistance and succor to your obedient servants will reflect nobly on Your Honor's prestige. There is no question in our minds that the very sight of Your Honor's intrepid armies would unnerve Amar, and his aiders and abettors would turn their backs on him. Then it would be little wonder indeed if they came with their heads bowed to surrender themselves.

450 • *The Adventures of Amir Hamza*

Lives are being lost and our men forfeit their existence to no purpose in the manner in which we have continued so far. But Your Honor's word is final, and we shall carry out the commands that you dictate to us!

Naushervan first asked Bakhtak what he would suggest in the matter. He answered, "The princes have not indicated that I should interfere in their business or offer any advice against their wishes!" The emperor then turned to Buzurjmehr and asked, "What do you say? Would it be fitting or inappropriate in your opinion to pay heed to the wishes of the princes?" Buzurjmehr replied, "My advice is the same that I submitted earlier: that it would be entirely inappropriate for Your Honor personally to lead a campaign against Amar. It is unbecoming to the glory of a sovereign of the Sassanid dynasty, and great mischief lies in the undertaking. When illustrious kings heard that the Emperor of the Seven Climes had judged a common *ayyar* a fit adversary for himself, they would lose the reverential fear in which they hold Your Honor now, and everyone would become emboldened to raise their heads in rebellion. Then you would hear of sedition breaking out in every corner of the empire and the whole edifice of your power would crumble. Besides, Your Honor well knows that Amar is a terrible scourge and marvelously versed in the art of deceit. God forbid he should carry away Your Honor like he did Hurmuz and act disrespectfully toward you—it would be a most unwarranted calamity for all of us. If Your Honor escaped alive it would still be a blemish on your dignity, and should he kill you (perish the thought!) it would put out the luminous light of the Seven Climes!"

Upon hearing Buzurjmehr's last words, Naushervan began to shake like an aspen leaf and called out, "Throw this wretch Bakhtak out of our court and drive him away from our sight, for the vile man always leads us into deception and disgraces himself as well[?]!" Bakhtak was thrown from the court by the scruff of his neck. Following Buzurjmehr's advice, the emperor then ordered Qaran Fil-Gardan, a most renowned warrior whose strength was held equal to that of ten thousand troops, to march at the head of an army of a hundred thousand troops and foot soldiers to capture Amar alive along with his companions.

Of Qaran Fil-Gardan's Departure to Chastise Amar, and of His Being Killed at the Hands of the Naqabdar[38]

The narrator has related that when Qaran Fil-Gardan arrived in Hurmuz's camp after passing all the stations of his journey, he was greatly gratified in his meeting with the prince. In the evening, all the commanders of the army gathered in a convivial assembly and goblets of wine were passed around. Qaran Fil-Gardan became the cupbearer and passed goblet after goblet of wine to the prince. At the height of his intoxication, Qaran Fil-Gardan asked Hurmuz, "How is it that Your Honor was stationed here with the army for such a long period of time—becoming a veritable fixture of the Earth like some mountain—and yet you were unable to kill or capture a common *ayyar*? Why was Your Honor unable to exercise any power over him or thwart him in any way? Anyone who heard of this marvel would wonder at it and find it hard to understand how such a thing came to pass!"

Hurmuz replied, "You have come here with a hundred thousand-strong force and count many intrepid warriors among your ranks. If there is anything more manifest than the bright sun it is the valor of your arms, since there is none who may count himself your equal in courage! This talk will suit you better, however, and the praise of your intrepidity will be more justified once you have killed or captured Amar. You have but freshly arrived here. It would be best to take a few days' rest and acquaint yourself with the state of affairs here. Then together we will take care of the situation, and we will sing your accolades loudly once you have captured or killed Amar!"

Qaran Fil-Gardan replied angrily, "We are warriors and have no need of respite! A soldier is not hindered by such considerations. Have some patience and let the night pass. Come morning, you may ride your charger to the battlefield and see from afar how we inflict great losses on Amar and his companions and have the fort emptied!" Qaran Fil-Gardan then ordered the drums of war to be beaten in his camp and made all arrangements for battle. Immediately, the chorus of fifes, trumpets, clarions, and war drums rose to the sky so that the whole Earth shook from this thunderous fanfare.

Meanwhile, the *ayyars* submitted themselves before Amar with folded arms, saying, "O most noble and excellent Prince of all Kings, may you live long! Qaran Fil-Gardan has arrived here this evening at Naushervan's command to assist Hurmuz with a hundred thousand troops and foot soldiers, and now he has sounded the drums of war!" Amar answered, "Strike the Timbal of Sikander in our camp, too, so that Qaran Fil-Gardan may learn the grandeur of our arms, and our awe is implanted in his heart."

In short, the drums of war were beaten in both camps all night long while the vigils made their rounds. On account of having already tasted the bitter fruit of skirmishing with Amar and having lost all appetite for it, Hurmuz, Faramurz, and Zhopin mustered their armies at a safe distance from the fort on the morning of the battle to let Qaran Fil-Gardan reap the fruit of his valor on his own, without harm coming to them and their men. Undeterred, Qaran Fil-Gardan split his army into four parts. Having surrounded the fort from all sides, his troops took rein and galloped toward the fort with great flash and flourish, assaulting it from all sides.

When Amar saw the foe approaching all sides of the fort with great grandeur and bravery, he called out to the commanders of his army, "The fortress will be assailed fiercely today. The foe has descended on us for a great show. Now is the time to prove your alertness and prowess! The field shall be won today by the one who stands his ground. Make sure that anyone who steps an inch within our range does not retreat alive but dies in his tracks." The moment he gave the orders, Muqbil Vafadar and his twelve thousand archers affixed arrows in their bowstrings, drew up to their ears, and let fly the bird of the arrow's shaft. Each arrow felled four or five enemy combatants, piercing through their chests. From just one barrage of arrows several thousand men lay rolling on the ground in raptures of death like slaughtered chickens, the avis of their souls butchered. Those who the darts did not pierce in the breast screamed in fear and, buckling like a faulty bow, retreated and gave up all thought of attack.

On another front, the sling shooters loaded chiseled and sculpted stones that could fell mammoths into their slings, and let fly after swinging them thrice, bursting open the foreheads of the infidels, and speedily dispatching throng after throng of them to Hell. Accursed in this world and in their faith, several thousand Guebers fell on their faces bereft of life. The rest turned tail in great terror and turmoil without knowing where they ran, often falling flat on their faces in retreat.

On the third front the musketeers discharged salvos of fire at which thousands died at once. Death's thunderbolts struck them, and fate's knife slashed their necks. The survivors retreated whence they had come, screaming loudly in terror. On the fourth front the masters of Greek fire unleashed the might of their fiery missiles and naphtha projectiles, and unleashed such a blistering sea of fire on the foe that everyone on whom these missiles landed perished in the mouth of death's flame along with three or four of his companions. In just an instant all of them became travelers to the land of doom. And those who showed great fervor in retreat were singed by searing grief for their companions, if not by the fire itself.

Although Qaran Fil-Gardan's army was routed and his forces badly battered, in his fury he himself thought nothing of the danger to his life. With his shield covering his face, he approached the gates of Amar's fort like a rutting elephant, with the intention of breaking it down with his mace. Seeing this turn of events, Amar was disconcerted and dread gripped his heart. Quickly resolving on a course of action, he said to the commanders of his army, "There is no remedy left now and no solution offers itself except to throng the gates of the fort and wait for the moment when that coward strikes with his mace and breaks down the door. Then we must draw our weapons and either kill him or die fighting, without giving a thought to our lives. We must put our faith in God, for indeed this is a time to entreat for divine help. All of us must solicit God's help with all our hearts. If He sends us assistance from the Future State, and heeds the prayers of our distressed lot, we shall be rid of this infidel, and our wishes will be answered. Otherwise no recourse is left to us but to kill or die fighting, as there is no other solution to our predicament that comes to mind!"

Even as the armies of the True Faith raised their hands in prayer, a dark dust cloud rose on the horizon that soon enveloped the vast expanse of the field. The scissors of the wind had yet to cut the dust's collar when Amar's spirits revived and he called out to the followers of the True Faith, "Congratulations, my friends! The Grantor of Petitions has answered your prayers. Behold that relief has come from Providence, and now all of you shall find release from the hands of this infidel!" Then Amar addressed Qaran Fil-Gardan, who stood below, calling, "Prepare to die, you dead-drunk elephant! Behold that your mahout has come to drive you all the way to the gates of Hell!" When Qaran Fil-Gardan turned to look, he was confounded with wonder when he saw forty standards appear through the veil of dust.

Naqabdar Naranji-Posh, a veiled warrior clad in orange vestments, raced his horse forward like lightning and approached the moat with an awe-striking mien. He said to Qaran Fil-Gardan, "O Gueber! Who is fortified within this castle, and why do you stand at the gates of the fort and advance on it like a specter?" Qaran Fil-Gardan answered, "The nation of the followers of the True Faith who have been declared felons by the Emperor of the Seven Climes are enclosed within these gates. They have become delinquent and have no reverence or dread left for their sovereign. I am about to break down the gate of the fort and slay them. Tell me now who you are and what business has brought you here."

The Naqabdar replied, "It is to aid and succor the followers of the True Faith that my army and I have arrived here. Before you even think of breaking the door of this fortress, you will have to reckon with me! Only when I am dead can you have your revenge on them!"

Qaran Fil-Gardan answered. "I cannot use a weapon against you as you seem a mere boy to me. You will be blown away like a leaf from its impact!"

The Naqabdar replied with great vexation, "O dastard, stop these idle ravings and bring yourself over to this side of the moat so that I may extract your soul and make a fitting answer to your deranged nonsense!" Qaran Fil-Gardan took great umbrage at these words. In his rage he leapt with his horse across the moat and faced the Naqabdar, who said, "Let us see what you have to show! Instantly you shall reap the reward for your villainy[?]!" Qaran Fil-Gardan attacked the Naqabdar with his heavy mace, but the veiled one foiled his blow and, drawing his sword—whose metal was tempered by lightning—dealt a blow to Qaran Fil-Gardan's head that put out the light in that coward's eyes. Qaran Fil-Gardan tried to take cover under his steel shield, but undeterred like a thunderbolt, the Naqabdar's blade cut the shield like a piece of cheese; and slicing his helmet and cleaving his head, it flashed down through his neck. Without resting in his breast, the sword carved through Qaran Fil-Gardan's spine and came out shining after severing his horse's martingale. In this marvelous fashion Qaran Fil-Gardan's limbs were bisected by this blade that flashed like lightning. He and his charger fell lifeless to the ground in four pieces. Thus Qaran Fil-Gardan's name was struck from the register of the living in but an instant.

When his army saw him meet this grisly end, they attacked the Naqabdar from all sides. The army of the Naqabdar also drew swords and unsheathed glittering scimitars. Amar recognized that although they were forty thousand-strong and every one of them was an intrepid warrior, there was too great a disparity in the sizes of the armies for valor alone to surmount the odds, and for the foe's numerous horde of one hundred and seventy-five thousand to be routed. Amar had the gates of the fort thrown open and sallied out at the head of his force to battle alongside the Naqabdar and annihilate Qaran Fil-Gardan's army. In the fierce battle that ensued seventy thousand men lost their lives on Hurmuz's side whereas not one man was even slightly wounded in Amar's camp. Their whole force thrown into disarray, the army of the infidels turned tail and fled.

Amar said to the Naqabdar, "Give me your name, your station, and your particulars so that when Hamza returns from Qaf to restore our spirits and bring us joy, we can tell him that it was your opportune arrival today that saved us and gave us a new lease on life. Nothing else stood between us and the fort falling to the enemy and the wholesale slaughter that would have resulted!" The Naqabdar answered, "The Sahibqiran shall learn of my identity upon his return. I do not feel the need to disclose it at this juncture, nor have I any desire to flaunt my deeds. Carry on with the duty of guarding the fort in peace, and free your heart of all fears. I shall come to your avail in your hour of need to succor you!" The Naqabdar then returned whence he had come. Amar gathered all the booty of the routed army, including their goods and chattels, the pavilions and supply trains, and retired to the fortress, with all his fears and apprehensions quelled by God's favor.

Now hear of Hurmuz and Faramurz, who after their defeat by the Naqabdar did not even turn to look back or take a moment's rest for a full twelve *kos*. At Bakhtiarak's counsel, they sent the details of the whole affair to the emperor, describing how the fickle heavens had visited that scourge on their heads and how their whole army had suffered a setback.

In reply, Naushervan dispatched riches, pavilions, supply trains, and a renowned warrior to the aid of his sons. Naushervan wrote them a missive detailing all the supplies that were being sent to them and mentioned that a large army would also be sent to augment their ranks as soon as possible. He enjoined them not to give up in the pursuit of Amar, or turn their backs from the encounter. Hurmuz and Faramurz derived consolation from the missive, and after gathering their broken, dispersed, and disheartened army, put together a force of forty thousand and returned to besiege the fortress as before.

Now hear of the army of the followers of the True Faith. When the provisions in the fort ran out, the men said to Aadi Madi-Karib, "Now the provisions are finished and our end is near. Whatever remains will not last us more than four days, and then all of us will be exposed to the pains of hunger. We must inform Khvaja Amar of the situation and make arrangements to forestall this eventuality." Aadi answered, "All of you must come with me to make this presentation. If I were to go by myself to Amar, he would doubt my words, thinking that I was being untruthful. He would presume that I had made up the story to serve my own needs. Until he is convinced otherwise, my words would only serve to compromise our cause."

Therefore, everyone went in a group before Amar. After informing him about the depleted state of the rations, they told him of the anxiety felt by those within the fort and declared, "Either you must find some way to acquire provisions so that we do not die miserably from hunger and end our lives to no purpose, or else order that the gates of the fort be thrown open so that we may kill the enemy or die fighting!" Amar answered, "Friends! We still have enough provisions to last us four days. Go about your business as before and keep your trust in God's bounty. I have sowed a crop at great expense and soon it will be ready for reaping. There will be grain aplenty for everyone!" Reassured by Amar's words, everyone was relieved and returned to his business.

Amar was deep in the sea of thought in the meanwhile. He surfaced happily soon enough, as a trick had presented itself to him, and the idea gave him immense satisfaction. Putting his army on the alert, he left the fort and went to a pass in the desert. There he put his hand on the *zambil* and utilized the power of its marvelous attributes to turn him into a forty-yard-tall giant with a beard two handspans in length on his face. Thus wonderfully disguised, Amar put on his wooden shoes, and holding a sack of lion skins under his arm, he stood looking in turn at his fort and Hurmuz's camp with wonderment, and started a bizarre conversation with himself.

Zhopin's nephew, Katara Kabuli Ayyar, happened to pass by there, and was transfixed with awe upon beholding Amar's face and height. The hue of Katara's face was transformed from the sheer terror that seized him at this sight, as he had never laid eyes on such a strange being before. He approached Amar trembling and shaking with fear, and made a profusely respectful salutation to him, showing him many tokens of honor and respect. Then he said to him with folded arms, "Whence have you come, sire, and what has brought you to these parts? Why do you look in wonderment at the fort and the army camped opposite, staring at them in an unhappy manner?"

Amar replied, "What is your name, and who are you to ask me all this? What interest do you have in all this information?" He answered, "I am known as Katara Kabuli. I am the commander of Hurmuz's *ayyars* and the nephew of Naushervan's son-in-law, and I bide my time blithely in the shadow of Naushervan's bounty."

Amar replied, "My name is Sa'ad Zulmati, and I have arrived here on an important errand. I am the younger brother of Sikander Zulmati, the emperor of Zulmat. A man called Hamza went to the realm of Qaf to help Emperor Shahpal of Qaf. He showed great courage and daring, but a human being is after all no match for a *dev*. In their encounter Ifrit Dev crushed Hamza to a pulp with just one blow. Emperor Shahpal sent Hamza's bones to my brother in a leather sack with the message that because our realm was situated closer to the realm of men we should bear the sack to Naushervan; then the emperor may bury Hamza's bones in the graveyard of men, and release Shahpal from his obligation to the deceased.

"My brother waited a long time for some human being to pass by our realm, so that he might entrust him with taking the sack to Naushervan, thus releasing him from his duty. When no man came by, my brother ordered me to deliver the sack myself and earn blessings through this duty to the dead. I was wondering if this was the fort of Ctesiphon and if the army I see camped here was Hamza's. I have been occupied with these thoughts for a long time and passed many a day pondering them."

Upon hearing the news Katara was beside himself with cheer and his lamp of joy flickered brightly. He replied, "Sire, the army that you see camped there belongs to Naushervan's sons and son-in-law. Come, that I may take you there and introduce them to you." Amar answered, "A blind man needs aught but two eyes. Nothing would be better!"

Katara led Amar before Zhopin and narrated the whole story to him. Showing great respect and deference to him, Zhopin seated Amar on a jewel-encrusted throne, asked about his welfare, and bestowed on him the very best of his hospitality and bounty. Amar repeated to Zhopin what he had told Katara, whereupon Zhopin fawned on him and said, "Where is the sack that you spoke of? Deliver it to me and I will write you a receipt. I will make sure the sack is dispatched to the emperor with an elaborate missive acquainting him with the whole course of events." Amar took the lion-skin sack from his bag and handed it to Zhopin in trust. Amar said, "You have taken a great burden off my chest. I am greatly indebted to you and am delighted by our meeting. Now I take my leave of you and bid you adieu!" For appearances alone Zhopin said to Amar, "Show us the favor of staying a few days more so that you may fully recover from the hardship of your journey. You must also regale the princes with your presence, as you have a right to every token of honor in this camp!" Amar did not accept their request and departed after making an excuse. Then he changed his shape again and returned to human form.

When the commanders of his army asked Amar about their provisions upon his return, he answered, "My dear friends, I have been busy sowing the crop all this time and in the next couple of days it will be harvesttime. Then you may have your fill of food and stuff your guts to your hearts' desire!"

Now hear of Zhopin. He showed the sack to Hurmuz and Faramurz and detailed to them the entire story of Sa'ad Zulmati's arrival, his mien and bearing, and the circumstances of his journey and mission. Hurmuz and Faramurz grew so elated upon hearing the news of Hamza's death that they very nearly burst with joy. Bakhtiarak, however, laughed after hearing the account and said, "To me this seems like another one of Amar's pranks; the hoax has his signature mark. May the gods Lat and Manat prevent me from speaking an untruth and prove me veritable in my conjecture that because his fortress has run out of provisions, Amar finds himself in a pickle and has thought of this trick to replenish supplies. With this deceit he is trying to pull the wool over our eyes. If Hamza were indeed dead, the *perizads* would have brought the news to Amar and acquainted him with Hamza's fate. As to the height of the man you saw, Amar has the miraculous power to assume any size he wishes and become even a thousand yards tall, let alone a mere forty yards."

Zhopin said to this, "How are we to believe your evil notion without any proof, and assume this a hoax when the sack is sealed with the signets of the four hundred kings of Qaf!" Bakhtiarak answered, "You are well within your right to make that judgment. As for me I cannot believe this news any more than I believe any fib. That man's account is laced with falsehoods!"

Zhopin said, "Silence would become you in this matter, and it would be best for you to keep your counsel to yourself! I shall send for the news from the fortress, and make up my mind on the intelligence I receive!"

Zhopin enjoined his *ayyars* to find out what was going on inside the fortress, ordering them to exert themselves to the best of their ability to find out how Amar and the commanders of the army were doing—whether a convivial mood prevailed among them, or if everyone was lost in lamentations over Hamza's death.

Now hear of Amar. That very day he had ordered his musicians to quit playing, and the fortress was shrouded in a dismal and dreary air. For three days, Zhopin's *ayyars* made their rounds outside but saw nothing in the fortress of its past joyous and convivial spirit, neither did they notice any tokens of cheer within. On the fourth day they presented themselves before Zhopin and said, "The fortress wears an utterly doleful and gloomy air. We did not hear the musicians trill their notes even once in three days, nor did we see a single happy face. Previously the music played five times daily, and people went about gaily with carefree countenances!" Upon hearing this, Bakhtiarak said, "If all this is true then there must be good reason. Something has indeed happened then, and Hamza must have died in Qaf!" That prospect gave untold joy to Hurmuz, Faramurz, Bakhtiarak, and Zhopin, and all anxiety was erased from the tablets of their hearts.

In the meanwhile, Amar was busy in his camp with his machinations. He ordered his camp to set up lamentations in the middle of the night and to call out the name of Amir Hamza amid loud moaning and wailing. Soon cries of "Alas, O Sahibqiran!" rent the silence of the night. The princes, Zhopin, and Bakhtiarak were already on the lookout for any such signs; the plaints of those inside the fort rang like heavenly music to their ears, and brought them no end of happiness. They ordered their own musicians to play festive airs and everyone young and old received the news that Amir Hamza had died.

The next day Amar left the fort with his collar torn, his face smeared with dust, his head bare, and his feet unshod. He kept striking his head and breast in the manner of an utterly devastated man while headed toward the threshold of Zhopin's pavilion. When he reached that place, he said to the mace bearers, "Brothers! Take the news of my arrival to the prince of Zabul and tell him that Amar has presented himself!" The mace bearers went before Zhopin and said, "Amar is standing at the threshold of your pavilion bareheaded and barefoot, with his collar rent, and his face covered with dust. He is crying and looking most distressed, agitated, anxiety-ridden, and devastated. He declares that his arrival should be announced to Your Honor and that he should be shown the kindness due a victim of tragedy and cataclysm." Zhopin said, "Grant him entry and send him into our presence!" The moment Amar was admitted, he immediately prostrated himself before Zhopin, who asked him, "What is the matter with you, Amar? Tell me what has passed and what calamity has befallen you!"

After moaning and groaning a great deal, Amar replied, "How can I tell you that I have been rendered without refuge and all my days of peace and comfort are now forever gone! It was five days ago that the *perizads* brought me news that Hamza had died in Qaf at the hands of the *dev* Ifrit who beheaded him. Right away, the mouth of doom began to close around me. For four days I guarded the secret and kept everyone in the dark, but on the fifth day it leaked out, and now everyone young and old alike have heard the news. The whole fort is in turmoil from the impact of the report: Everyone is afflicted by the tragedy and there is no eye that is dry. I present myself before you because I could not muster the courage to show my face before the princes. I know well in my heart that because of my camaraderie with Hamza I have been incriminated in every possible outrage against them; I single-handedly bear the blame of every abuse and affront meted out to them. Now I have decided to deliver Mehr-Nigar into Your Honor's hands, and I intend to smash my head against some rock and die. I will never again find a benefactor and patron like Hamza. Nobody else would accord me a station commensurate with my rank where I could wait attendance on him and sing his praises and adulation night and day!"

Zhopin embraced Amar and showed him much favor. Then he said, "Why do you torment yourself, O Amar, and give yourself to such melancholy speculations? I shall keep you as close as the amulet around my neck and will never be unmindful of the patronage you deserve!" Amar answered, "I am willing to wager upon your honor that I will receive even greater kindnesses from yourself—a scion of the royal family and the pride of the peerless offspring of the world's nobility. However, I dread the malevolence of Bakhtak and Bakhtiarak, and have apprehensions about their influence lest they incite and turn you against me, prevailing upon you with their wily natures to do me injury!"

Zhopin answered: "Those small fry will not dare cast a harmful glance at you, or affront you in any way. Nor can they create any rift between us or nurse enmity in me against you. If they should show any affront to you, I shall crush their mischief forthwith and annihilate them along with their aiders and abettors. You may go and bring Mehr-Nigar to me now without any fear!"

Amar answered, "I am willing to bring Mehr-Nigar this very instant, but I fear that the commanders of my army will not consent to her departure. They will challenge me with all the trespasses they have committed against the princes at my bidding, and the grief they have caused them. They will state that I propose to escape punishment by surrendering Mehr-Nigar while they are left to take the blame and bear the brunt of the princes' wrath!"

Zhopin replied, "Under my patronage all of them shall receive greater honor and distinction than they did under Hamza. I shall grant all of them ranks commensurate with their skill. Persuade them to come to me, and reassure them by spelling out my offer to them!" Amar said, "But they will not believe my word, and will never agree with me. I could only persuade them if Your Honor were to write out a missive addressed to them. Nothing that I may say would make them change their mind!" Zhopin declared, "I would gladly write out ten missives to them if it would serve your purpose!"

That very moment Zhopin sent for his inkstand and wrote out a letter to all the commanders of Amar's army. In that missive he allayed any and all fears they might entertain, and then he handed the sealed letter to Amar, who carried it to his fort and showed it to the commanders of his army. He then said to them, "The crop is now ready and all that is needed is someone to reap it! Come with me first to have a feast and taste these delicacies. Afterward we shall see what needs to be done and shall act as opportunity warrants." With the exception of Muqbil Vafadar, who stayed behind to guard the fort and protect the garrison with forty thousand troops, all the commanders of the army accompanied Amar to Zhopin's camp.

Zhopin meanwhile narrated the details of his meeting with Amar to Hurmuz and Faramurz, to which Bakhtiarak said, "May the gods Lat and Manat keep us in the shadow of their protection, and save us from falling into the hands of calamity. Not just one or two but every single one of

Amar's commanders are headed here to take up residence! Any calamity that might occur now will be too little!" Then Bakhtiarak said to Zhopin directly, "O Zhopin! Amar is full of guile and is a most sly customer. Do not succumb to his deceitfulness or be fooled by his tricks, and don't act recklessly. Believe me when I say that his fort has run out of provisions and therefore Amar has thought of this ruse and has laid this trap for you and all of us here!"

Zhopin was greatly peeved at these words and said, "O Bakhtiarak, do not interfere in this matter, as it is an agreement made between Amar and myself. I would never listen to a word from a fool like yourself. Amar already warned me that you would try to start a quarrel and would rush forward to ruin our understanding!" Bakhtiarak replied, "Indeed he would forewarn you of that for both Amar and I know what passes in each other's hearts. Very well, then! You shall not hear another word from me and I will not open my mouth to comment on this affair. One can only guide someone who is amenable to advice. Now you and Amar may settle this between yourselves. I shall make myself scarce when things begin to unravel!"

Zhopin went to his pavilion and made arrangements for a feast and had all manner of dishes prepared for the occasion. Then he sent his *ayyars* to go and find out if Amar had set out yet and whether or not he was bringing Mehr-Nigar along with him. As the *ayyars* stepped out of their camp they saw Amar coming toward them with an entourage of four hundred bloodthirsty warriors—a sight to instill terror in the hearts of the beholders. The *ayyars* retraced their steps and told Zhopin that Amar was approaching in the company of four hundred warriors to be ennobled by waiting on him. Zhopin went to the two princes and said to them, "It appears that Amar is as good as his word! My *ayyars* have told me that he is coming here with four hundred warriors, all of whom wish to ennoble themselves by waiting upon your Highness!" Bakhtiarak became paralyzed with fear at this news and wondered what might happen next with Amar arriving there like a calamity and bringing his whole entourage of warriors.

In the meanwhile, Amar entered Zhopin's pavilion with the commanders of his army, where Zhopin greeted and welcomed them, and moreover embraced each man and inquired about his welfare individually. He showed them great favor and took them with him to wait upon the princes. He seated them on gold-inlaid thrones and showed them every token of kindness. Zhopin set up Amar's throne beside his own and showed him even greater honor than anybody else. After making some friendly small talk, Zhopin summoned cupbearers whose bodies shone like silver and gave them instructions that the ewer and the goblet should be set in motion and the finest wines poured out. Aadi Madi-Karib said, "It is customary for a round of dining to precede the round of discourse. It would therefore be preferable to have food first and imbibe wine later so that it may also taste better and affect us to advantage!"

At these orders, the attendant unfurled the dining cloth and laid out fine, choice dishes. As the head cook started laying out the dishes, Aadi asked him to put each one before him. The cook finally lost his temper and replied in anger, "Sire, do I have leave to serve anybody else or shall I pile up all the food only before you?" Aadi replied, "Let me first eat to my heart's content. Then you may serve whosoever you please. Let others have a taste afterward, and you should also partake some yourself!" The head cook put all the dishes before Aadi, and soon the whole feast was piled up before him. Aadi began eating and did not stop until the food disappeared from the dining cloth and was firmly tucked away in his gut. Zhopin, who had witnessed the whole scene, asked Aadi, "Shall I send for something else or have you had your fill?"

Aadi had received this miracle from the benediction of the fakirs that no matter how much he ate, it never sated him, and did not send him away from the table fulfilled! He replied, "Whatever you have to offer will suffice." Zhopin sent for more food and laid it out before Aadi, who bolted that down, too, without even as much as asking for a glass of water. Zhopin asked him, "Do you feel sated now or shall I order more food so that you do not rise hungry from this feast?" Aadi replied, "No harm would be done if some curry and bread were ordered. Pray send for it and set it before yours truly without delay." Immediately a bowl of curry was put before Aadi along with bread made with several *maunds* of flour. Aadi swallowed that down as well and desired that even more be sent for and that everyone should see the spectacle of him polishing that off as well, when Bakhtiarak said to Zhopin, "O Zhopin, it is impossible to ever satisfy the hunger of that man or feed him to his capacity! It is all part of Amar's plan that our whole army's rations are fed to him so that in the end you are unable to serve a single meal to your men, and their hunger lead them to break ranks with you."

Hurmuz made a sign to the attendent and said to Aadi, "Cauldrons of food are cooking, O warrior, and all the cooks are employed in preparing food. Until it is ready we shall order whatever you desire from the market so that your belly is not troubled by hunger." Aadi answered, "Sire, I am not such a glutton that I would put you to the trouble of sending for food from the bazaar on my account!" He then washed his hands and retired for a siesta.

The table was then laid a second time and all the commanders of the army were served, and still more food was sent for. After all of them had eaten, goblets of roseate wine were passed to the guests and the gathering took on a festive air. Singers and dancers joined the assembly and the musicians tuned their instruments and sounded the opening notes. The shouts of "Drink unto oblivion!" rose from the assembly and everyone there was lost to raptures and transports of joy. They chatted amiably among themselves, with the cups of wine washing all the rancor from their hearts. Zhopin now said to Amar, "What is the delay in bringing Mehr-Nigar? It seems inappropriate to delay her arrival any further!"

Amar replied, "My commanders are of the opinion that to hand over the princess in such a uncivilized manner would be entirely unbecoming of us and beneath our dignity. You must first make preparations for your marriage and start the wedding rituals and ceremonies of the nuptials in your camp. A feast should be arranged for the army in the fortress as well so that everyone may enjoy the pleasurable assembly!" Zhopin said, "Nothing would be better! What you say is fair and reasonable indeed!" Amar then told him, "Since we are of the same mind, I shall require gold to defray the expenses. Without spending money such assemblies never come to fruition!" Zhopin said, "Have no worries on that account. Whatever you require is available and at hand. You may go ahead and arrange the festivities to your liking!" For three days and three nights Amar and his commanders remained there as Zhopin's guests and showed him every token of their debt and obligation toward him. In the meantime, Amar took provisions and gold from Zhopin to his fort and gave everyone the glad tidings of the riches procured.

After Amar had stockpiled six months' worth of provisions in the fort, he returned to Zhopin and said to him, "Make preparations now to bring out the wedding procession from your camp, and get ready to enjoy the fruit of your nuptials while I make arrangements at my end." Zhopin bid farewell to Amar and the commanders of his army, and sent them off with gifts of gold and other items. Amar fortified his fort on a much larger scale than before and informed everyone there of his secret plan.

For seven days Zhopin had *ubtan*[39] rubbed on his body and dined on delicacies to improve his skin's tint and texture. He occupied himself with assemblies of song and dance, and remained engrossed in happy thoughts of ravishing Mehr-Nigar while his army feasted and made merry. After seven days had passed, during which Amar had not turned up once, Zhopin panicked and gave in to anxiety. Bakhtiarak asked Zhopin, "Say, sire, when are you going to lead the wedding procession to enjoy congress with your bride? A full seven days have now passed." Nettled by this remark, Zhopin cursed Bakhtiarak and sent his *ayyars* to ask Amar what was causing the delay in the wedding as all the needed items had been procured, the preparations made, and everything in his fort adorned to best advantage.

The *ayyars* observed that Amar's fortress seemed four times as guarded and impregnable as before. Every commander in Amar's camp was on watch and Amar himself was seated under a canopy near the gate of the fort on a jewel-encrusted throne, carrying out his duties and supervising miscellaneous affairs. The *ayyars* made a humble salutation to Amar from afar and gave him Zhopin's message, narrating all that their master had asked them to convey to him. In reply to Zhopin, Amar sent a message that for the next six months he would be loath to entertain any communication with him or the two princes, and that he looked now upon their army and camp with scorn. Furthermore, said Amar, if Jamshed himself were to rise from his grave and wage war against him he would bury him again; and, even if Afrasiyab descended into the battle arena against him in person, he would lay him low with just one blow.

The *ayyars* retraced their steps back to Zhopin. They told him what Amar had said and informed Zhopin of his intentions. The avis of Zhopin's senses now took flight, and he turned deathly pale. Much disconcerted that events had taken this turn, he chewed his lips in impotent fury and seethed with rage realizing what a capital fool Amar had made of him by deceiving him so completely. Amar had impaired Zhopin's standing in such a way that he would be held up to ridicule not only in his own camp but in the entire length and breadth of Ctesiphon. He could do little else but keep silent as it was not easy to exact revenge on Amar or chastise him.

Now hear of Amar. Well protected in his castle, he scanned the environs with a spyglass and settled his glance on the forest. He was engrossed by the sight of its dense jungle, which was home to all kinds of beasts. He asked Darab, "Do you believe that the forest is teeming with wild beasts?" Darab answered, "True indeed: The forest is infested with lions, some six or seven thousand of them. No other forest has a greater number of these beasts, and you will find an even larger number of other animals there. The human eye has never beheld a forest to match this one. Its very name strikes terror in men's hearts as one could spend hundreds of days traveling its length without coming to an end. Indeed there is no question about its immense expanse."

Amar now thought of a trick and immediately sent for his *ayyars*. He ordered them to cut down the trees on three sides of the forest leaving standing only the side abutting Hurmuz's camp, and to close all avenues of escape from the forest. Amar instructed them to smear the felled trees with naphtha and set them afire to start a great blaze, and to inform him afterward when it was all done. In obedience to Amar's orders, the *ayyars* set out together for the forest. A few hours into the night, tongues of fire from the trees joined to make a great ball of flame that reached up to the revolving heavens. Troubled by the searing heat, lions, cheetahs, wolves, leopards, wild bulls, rhinoceroses, monkeys, langurs, hyenas, apes, and other beasts of the forest thronged together. Finding their path blocked by fire on all sides except one, they settled upon that as their exit. Whole herds and packs of these beasts raced toward Hurmuz's camp and devoured anyone who stood in their way. Hundreds of men became their fodder and the whole camp was fully exposed to this unforeseen calamity and was overrun.

Hurmuz's army panicked and their senses took leave of them. They put on undergarments in the place of mail, and armor where they should wear undergarments. Such was their terror that when saddling their mounts they could not distinguish the crupper of the horse from the bit. A great ruckus broke out in the camp and rumors abounded that Amar had made a night raid. Swords were drawn forthwith and put into violent service. By the time it was dawn, thousands of men had been laid low by that crocodile of the soul-extracting sword,[40] and many thousands more became the meal of the beasts and departed to the Future State. When it was daylight, Hurmuz, Faramurz, Zhopin, and Bakhtiarak, who had all survived the onslaught, went to inspect the field along with their commanders to determine how many of their men had died in the battle and how many of the enemy lost their lives and were felled by the sword of death.

Upon inspection, however, they discovered only their own men in the piles of the slain with the occasional dead beast among them. It seemed as if a curse had fallen over their men that had made them think they were fighting against men while they were really skirmishing with beasts.

Zhopin, the two princes, and their commanders were confounded by this discovery; they marveled greatly at the sight of all the dead and deemed it a calamity sent by the heavens.

Bakhtiarak said, "What lies before you and confounds you so utterly is just a taste of what Amar is capable of. May Lat and Manat keep me from uttering an untruth, but I believe he must have set fire to the forest on three sides and left open only the one side opposite our camp. When the fire spread, the beasts of the forest stampeded in the direction of our camp, finding their exits blocked on all other sides. They descended on the camp and tore up anyone who stood in their way." Bakhtiarak sent his *ayyars* to spy on Amar's camp and they soon returned, verifying the truth of his conjecture.

Amar, meanwhile, was looking through his spyglass at the state of confusion and turmoil in Hurmuz's camp, and he decided to play another trick on them. He said to Aadi, "I have good mind to conduct a night raid on the camp of that Gueber and visit a new calamity on those cowards." Aadi answered, "We shall carry out whatever you order us. Obedience to you only brings us greater honor." Amar told him then that when they attacked he wanted him to pronounce the war cries and pretend to be Landhoor. Amar next acquainted the commanders of his army with his plan and made them privy to his secret. They all armed themselves to the teeth and readied themselves.

After the first half of the night had passed, Amar marched out from the castle with his force and conducted a night raid on his foes of slumbering fortune. Aadi Madi-Karib drew his sword and exclaimed, "Beware all you who do not know that I am the Rustam of my times and my name is Landhoor bin Saadan! Where are Hurmuz, Faramurz, and Zhopin to savor a taste of my blade and rub their foreheads on my feet?" The flash of Aadi's sword led those who were of a cowardly cast to hide themselves forthwith in bales of hay set before their horses and tightly shut their eyes. Others concealed themselves in pavilions and tents. Some took Aadi's cry to be a crack of thunder and stuffed cotton in their ears. In short, everyone acted upon their first impulse to save their own lives. Hurmuz, Faramurz, Zhopin, and Bakhtiarak also rose from their slumber of oblivion and quickly experienced flights of confusion and bewilderment. Baffled, they asked one another how Landhoor had possibly descended on them and found his way there. Bakhtiarak replied, "This is another one of Amar's tricks: to conduct a night raid under the war cry of Landhoor, and cause fear in our camp with the deception."

In short, the army of the followers of the True Faith slew thousands of infidels in that raid and dispatched them to Hell, leaving the battlefield littered with heaps of corpses. Some hours still remained before morning when the *ayyars* told Amar, "Naushervan has sent Zhopin's brothers Jahandar Kabuli and Jahangir Kabuli to aid Hurmuz and Faramurz with a force more numerous than armies of ants and swarms of locusts, and their mighty armies are nigh. If you look you can see the great dust cloud rising on the horizon at their advance, which leaves no room for any question or doubt!" When Amar looked he saw a dark dust storm on the horizon that darkened the vision of the beholder. Filled with terror, he wrung his hands in anxiety and said to himself, *No hope remains now for our army, as it is impossible to stop the onslaught of the approaching foe. How will I ever show my face to Hamza, and excuse myself for failing his trust?*

Now, Amar was blessed with miraculous powers and whenever he was unable to conjure up some strategem and felt some anxiety on this account, he recited the benediction to the holy Prophet forty times, blew it on the back of his palm, and beseeched Almighty God to help him devise some subterfuge. Three hundred and sixty cunning tricks that he had never thought of before would immediately divulge themselves to him and would gratify his mind with their ingeniousness. Amar sought recourse to this same method now, and immediately thought of all manner of tricks, and his mind became even sharper and more fertile than before. Immediately, Amar blew into the Sufaid Mohra to summon the champions of his army and then declared to them, "O Rustams of time, remain steadfast in the fields of carnage and hold aloft your titles of courage! We must not let a single soul from the army of the infidels escape alive but dispatch them all to Hell. The emperor of China, Bahram Gurd, has arrived to your avail with a force more numerous than an army of ants or a swarm of locusts. Understand well that his army—the very embodiment of triumph—has been sent to you as divine help! The great dust storm that you see before you rises at its advance!"

Soon rumor spread to the enemy camp about the approach of the emperor of China, Bahram Gurd, and when they saw the great dust cloud on the horizon, they completely lost their nerve. Dread weighed down their hearts when they realized that the intrepid and numerous army pitted against them could never be surmounted. Without further thought, they escaped to save their lives and not one man among them showed the courage to encounter the foe or even show him his face.

Bakhtiarak proclaimed to his force, "Friends, do not give in to fear, for morning is nigh! Remain steadfast as we have no evidence that the approaching army belongs to Bahram Gurd. No friend has brought you the news. Pay heed to me when I say that perhaps this is an army sent by divine help to assist you!" In all turmoil, however, none had the ear for that old singer's strains; everyone sought to save his own neck and escape with his life. The remainder of the army stampeded away like camels without halters, never once stopping to think or take a break to rest. On the pretext of coaxing them back, Hurmuz, Faramurz, Zhopin, and Bakhtiarak followed after them, really to save their own lives. Indeed, they could think of little else to do at that time. Amar plundered the retreating army so thoroughly that not even a twig was left behind. Upon returning triumphant and victorious with his army to his fortress, he informed his commanders of the strategy he had employed. He ordered the defenses of the fort to be strengthened without delay and allowed his army some leisure to rest and relax.

Of the Arrival of Zhopin's Brothers Jahandar Kabuli and Jahangir Kabuli at Naushervan's Orders to Assist Hurmuz and Faramurz

The nimble scribes of fancy inform us that the army of the infidels lost its nerve and was in full retreat. They had gone some two or three *farsangs* without breaking for rest when informers brought them intelligence that the army that had been declared to be Bahram's and proclaimed by Amar as the provision sent to aid him was in fact a great army sent by Emperor Naushervan under the command of Jahandar Kabuli and Jahangir Kabuli to aid the princes. Indeed, it was such a powerful and mighty army that no force in the world could withstand its onslaught. They learned that now their anxiety ought to end as gods had shown them their favor.

Jahangir and Jahandar had arrived in the meanwhile, and after they presented themselves to Zhopin, they waited upon the princes and offered them their consolation. They told them it was a pity that they had been unable to stand their ground until help arrived to battle the foe. Bakhtiarak replied, "I advised against retreat and offered objections, but no one listened to what I said, instead judging my advice to be the ravings of an idiot. We let ourselves be beaten, and allowed ourselves to be plundered and disgraced without reason." Jahangir and Jahandar then said, "What is past cannot be undone, but we shall presently make amends by taking the fort and routing those within it." Thus speaking, they headed for Amar's fort. The moment they came within range, Amar showered them with Greek fire and launched a barrage of projectiles and flaming rockets at them. Their army could not advance further, but both Jahangir and Jahandar crossed the moat under the cover of their shields. However, the moment they raised their maces to break down the gates of the fort and force entry, Naqabdar Naranji-Posh arrived there with his forty thousand troops.

Amar ordered his musicians to play festive tunes and said, "Now the one who punishes Guebers and avenges us on the infidels has arrived!" The Naqabdar spurred his horse forward and, standing at the edge of the moat, roared, "Beware, O infidel dogs! If you dare even to touch that gate with your maces I shall visit on you such terrible punishment that you will not recognize your own faces! You must reckon with me before you break down the fort's gate!" The brothers crossed back over the moat and assaulted the Naqabdar from both sides. The Naqabdar wrested the swords from their hands and threw them away; then catching hold of their cummerbunds, he raised them over his head with Rustam-like might. The two of them still retained some share of the life allotted to them: When their cummerbunds broke, they fell down and escaped from the Naqabdar's clutches. Their army deemed it expedient to take rein and carry their commanders from the battlefield, and judged it fortunate that their masters had survived with their lives.

In the meanwhile, the Naqabdar attacked the forces of Jahandar and Jahangir with his army, and started piling up the corpses of infidels in the battlefield. If the slaughter had continued a little longer, not a single soul would have survived in the enemy army. Realizing this, Bakhtiarak judged it prudent to retire from the battlefield and immediately announced the cessation of hostilities. Victorious and triumphant, the Naqabdar returned whence he had come, seeing no further need for his presence there. With tearful eyes and wounded hearts the army of the infidels retired to its camp in a state of great disarray and ruin. In the fort, everyone congratulated Amar on his triumph and presented offerings to him for his victory.

The following day, the keeper of the storehouse told Aadi that the fort had been emptied of provisions. When Aadi informed Amar, he replied that they should move to another place if they could find a strong fortress. Darab told them, "There is a fort called Nestan two days' journey from here, which is the envy even of rose gardens for its beauty. All the armies of the Seven Climes may storm it and yet remain unsuccessful in wresting control of it from the one who holds it. The name of its ruler is Quful Nestani and the fort is populated by those of his race." Amar now said to his commanders, "I am going away to think up a scheme by which to take over the fortress of Nestan. When you receive news that I have secured the fort and placed it under my control and writ, send some palanquins conspicuously carrying langurs, monkeys, wolves, and lions, in plain view of Zhopin's camp. At the same time, you should also send Mehr-Nigar and the other women from the exit at the back of the fortress. But you must carry out the business in such a manner that nobody gets wind of your plan. Later, make haste and reach the fortress of Nestan along with everybody else left behind."

Without telling anyone what he intended to do, Amar headed for the fortress of Nestan taking two *ayyars* with him. Some two hours remained until the close of day when he reached the fortress of Nestan and saw that it was indeed a most strong and robust fort the likes of which did not exist in those parts. While circling the fortifications, he discovered that the main gate and the wickets were all secure, the moat was flooded, and there was no possible way of gaining entry; he wondered how to break in and secure control of the fortress. After passing two watches of the night brooding over this problem, he caught sight of a pack of five or six dogs coming toward him from the fort. As they crossed over the moat and drew near, Amar fed them bread and meat, and gave the famished dogs a new lease on life. They ate until their bellies could hold no more and then returned to their domicile, and Amar followed them in order to glean some information about the citizens of the fort. The dogs crossed the moat and entered a tunnel that went into the fort, with Amar following them, happy to find only the watchmen lying awake. He successfully evaded them, and reached the palace of Quful Nestani without anyone noticing.

There was a big tree adjacent to the walls of the palace, which Amar climbed to reach the roof of the fortress. From there Amar descended into the summerhouse in the fort's garden, where he found Quful Nestani fast asleep in his bed. His companions were also deep in slumber and the attendants were spread out on the floor, snoring away by the light of the wax candles that illuminated the place. Amar extinguished the candles with his *ayyar*'s mantle and lit a small fuse to help carry out his plan. He put together his seven-jointed reed pipe and filled it up with four *mithcals* of ambergris, then blew it into Quful Nestani's nostrils. When the powder reached his brain, he sneezed once and lost consciousness, losing his senses and falling comatose from its effect. Amar put his body in his *zambil*; then he disguised himself as Quful Nestani and slept in his place, having accomplished what he had planned to do.

In the morning, Amar washed his hands and face and gave audience as Quful Nestani with all pomp and glory. When the nobles of his court presented themselves, he said to them, "Naushervan's daughter, Mehr-Nigar, has fallen in love with me and longs with all her heart and soul for a tryst with me. She sent me a love letter yesterday and as a result I have sent for her and told her to come without any ceremony. Take heed that when her conveyance arrives no sentinel should hinder its way. The keeper of the main gate should open it to admit her along with her companions without waiting for my permission, so that she may seek the bliss and pleasure of my company without delay." Several of his nobles acquiesced, but others questioned his decision. They told him that the devious and cunning Amar Ayyar was in Mehr-Nigar's entourage and that this accorded with the usual way he went about occupying fortresses and hoodwinking people. Amar ordered the naysayers thrown into prison, and then he reiterated his orders to the main gatekeeper to open them for Mehr-Nigar, and allow her admission without delay or hindrance.

Here it must be mentioned that Amar had stationed his two *ayyars* outside the main gate who were fully aware of his scheme. When they got wind of these orders they reasoned that Amar was now the ruler of the fort and had it under his control. They went to the gatekeeper and asked him to tell his master that two *ayyars* sent by Mehr-Nigar had arrived with a message from her. Amar sent for them and, consulting with them in private, he said, "Return to Sarhang Misri and tell him and the other commanders to carry out the plan without fear or delay according to my instructions, and to arrive here quickly to observe my trickery at work. By the grace of God I have become the ruler of this fort, the whole populace is under my writ, and all our anxieties are now over." The *ayyars* returned to the fort of Kurgistan with a few hours remaining before the break of day. They conveyed Amar's message to Sarhang Misri and the other commanders, informing them of the whole situation, which dispelled any remaining apprehensions that they had. All of them now prepared for the journey. After one and a half watches of the night had elapsed, they sent some *ayyars* with palanquins carrying beasts from the gate opposite Zhopin's pavilion. They then sent conveyances for Mehr-Nigar and her companions and, accompanied by the armies of the True Faith, set out from the back door themselves.

One of Zhopin's *ayyars* espied the palanquins and ran to inform Zhopin that Mehr-Nigar was headed out of the fort. Zhopin exited his pavilion gladly and ran to lift the covers of the most ornate palanquin in the forefront of the procession. Finding a ferocious bear tied inside it, he let out a scream and his blood curdled with fear. Zhopin ran from there after ordering his men to search all the litters to make sure Mehr-Nigar was not inside any of them. Whoever raised the curtain of a litter found a beast riding it, and they, too, ran away in fear, leaving the litters behind. In the meantime, another *ayyar* informed Zhopin that the gates of the Kurgistan fort were open. They told him that it seemed empty, as no signs of life were to be witnessed there. Upon hearing this, Zhopin immediately sent for his mount and set out at a gallop, soon catching up with Mehr-Nigar's procession.

As for Mehr-Nigar, tired of riding in the litter, midway through the journey she threw a veil over her face and mounted a horse. Having drawn up alongside, Zhopin now jumped down from his own horse and caught hold of the saddle straps of Mehr-Nigar's mount. He began singing her praises, making loud protestations of love, and avowing his great passion and ardor for her. Mehr-Nigar tried her best to spurn his advances, but that shameless dog did not desist, reasoning that it was to his advantage to carry on in this manner. Driven to despair, Mehr-Nigar finally unsheathed a dagger and struck him a blow that cracked his forehead. That poltroon ran away in shock of the injury and then stood by watching the princess from a distance. Mehr-Nigar then put an arrow in her bow and drew the string, letting fly at the cad. Trying to dodge the arrow and avoid a second injury, Zhopin turned away, whereupon the arrow breached his armor and underpants, piercing his derriere a handspan deep. Crying in pain, Zhopin ran far away from there.

Meanwhile, the armies of the True Faith also arrived on the scene and escorted Mehr-Nigar into the fortress of Nestan, and Amar was finally relieved of all his anxieties about the foe. Everyone in the fortress who converted to the True Faith was spared and those who spurned the invitation were put to the sword. Presently, the law of the followers of the True Faith became supreme in Nestan, and their enemies were plunged into the depths of despair. Amar brought Quful Nestani out from his *zambil* and asked him, "What do you say now about the One God who is alone and without partners? Do you wish to convert to the True Faith or continue with your infidel ways as before?" The man saw that he had already lost his fort and was on the verge of losing his life as well; there were no avenues of escape for him. He recited the Act of Faith, sincerely converted to the True Faith, and ennobled himself at Amar's insistence and by God's grace.

Amar embraced Quful Nestani and said, "My friend! May you have the pleasure of your fort as I have no interest in either it or your property. Indeed I wish you no harm at all. I am your guest here only for a few days, after which I will go wherever fate shall ordain. The two of us have a bond of friendship between us now, and I shall return to inquire after your welfare after I have disposed of my affairs!"

Amar adorned and trimmed out the fort to resemble a preening peacock and as before positioned himself with great contentment under a pavilion of Chinese silk on a bejeweled throne at its gate, having been successful in his schemes and earning celebrity through his deeds.

Now hear of Zhopin. Unable to bear the pain from the arrow in his rear, he fell from his horse in the middle of his journey. In an act of manifest unfaithfulness toward him, his horse dashed off into the forest, leaving him sprawled behind. In the meanwhile, Hurmuz and Faramurz heard that the fort had been emptied and Zhopin had gone in pursuit of Amar's men. They, too, followed after that army with Jahangir and Jahandar, hoping to overtake them and exact revenge on the followers of the True Faith. Finding Zhopin lying injured and unconscious along the way they grieved at his pain and misery, and cursed Amar's high-handedness. They picked Zhopin up and carried him away in a litter for treatment, so that he might be cured and find relief from that wicked wound. They learned from their *ayyars* that Amar had taken refuge in the fort of Nestan along with his whole army. Helpless to do anything about it, they pitched their camp out of range of that fort so they would not be exposed to any hazard.

When Amar saw the army of the infidels camped there, he devised another trick to inflict on them. He dressed himself as a surgeon and, carrying a surgeon's gear tucked under his arm, appeared in the vicinity of Zhopin's pavilion. The *ayyars* alerted Zhopin and brought him intelligence that a surgeon who seemed a past master in his trade was close at hand. Zhopin said to them, "Send for him and show him in without delay!" Thereupon the *ayyars* brought Amar to see him. Zhopin showed him his wound, and after narrating his whole tale of woes, said, "O surgeon, use your art to make me well as soon as possible and I shall reward you richly and make you the happiest of men!" Amar said to him, "Your forehead injury will not take long to heal, but the wound to your rear is most malicious. It will require great art to treat it. If you can bear a little distress and hold up under the pain, I have the art to make you well before five watches of the day have elapsed."

Zhopin replied, "I will accept the pain of the cure, for I have been driven to distress by this wound!" Amar said, "If you are thus decided, then order your men not to approach here until five watches of the day have elapsed regardless of any screams or painful cries they may hear, and to pay no heed to your clamoring." Zhopin ordered his attendants and his companions accordingly, and all of them moved away from his pavilion. Once the curtains of the pavilion were drawn and all the men sent away, Amar turned Zhopin over onto his stomach and secured his limbs at four posts. Then with a blade he cut the wound even deeper, and mixing ratsbane with limestone made it into rolls, which he poked into his wound, plastering this now with an ointment of the same, and leaving Zhopin in a state far worse than before. Zhopin began raising Cain and screaming from the burning sensation that plagued him. His attendants outside reckoned that the surgeon was busy with him and they must not meddle, as they had been forewarned in advance and enjoined from interfering. Thus none paid any heed to Zhopin's cries for help and, unable to bear the violence of the pain any longer, Zhopin finally fell unconscious.

Amar stuffed all the gold and effects to be found in Zhopin's pavilion into his *zambil*. Richer for all that gold and wealth, he pulled a tent peg out from the pavilion and escaped. When Zhopin's attendants entered his pavilion after five watches, they found him in a miserable state, inconsolable with agony and torment. They lamented his condition, untied his hands and feet, and were confounded into silence with embarrassment at the situation. Without speaking a word, they washed his wounds and bandaged them with camphor and other tried and tested salves. When Bakhtiarak heard of Zhopin's fate two days after Zhopin had regained consciousness and felt a little relief from his misery, he declared, "That was no surgeon but Amar himself disguised as a surgeon who visited this scourge on Zhopin."

News also reached them that Naushervan had sent one of his courtiers, Hakim Majdak, bearing treasures and gifts, to ennoble himself by waiting upon the princes. Hurmuz and Faramurz rejoiced greatly upon hearing this and sent Jahangir and Jahandar Kabuli along with many brave warriors to welcome him. When this news reached Amar, he disguised himself as one of Zhopin's *ayyars* and set out to lead Hakim Majdak into deception by means of some artifice. After he had traveled a distance of some five *kos,* Amar saw Hakim Majdak's conveyance approaching and also saw Jahangir Kabuli and Jahandar Kabuli arrive there and dismount. After embracing and exchanging pleasantries, they all headed for a pavilion making small talk. Amar noticed that apart from their mounts, no other baggage trains were in sight and Hakim Majdak's conveyance had traveled alone. He reasoned that perhaps the baggage was following him, accompanied by his servants. Amar slipped outdoors without anyone detecting him.

A few hours of the night had elapsed when he observed many camel- and cartloads of treasure arrive accompanied by five hundred troops. Amar's eyes lit up with happiness as they approached. He then asked one of the troops, "Who is your commander and what is his name and rank? Tell me what manner of man he is." The soldier replied, "He is the one wearing felt headgear, and he is responsible for the safety and security of the treasure!" Amar approached and greeted him and said, "I have been awaiting your arrival here for some time, and was apprehensive about the delay. The princes have dispatched me with orders to make sure the treasure and goods are conveyed by a secure route. If Amar Ayyar got wind of it, he would steal them and dispatch you into the care of the Angel of Death. I have received orders to camp here should you arrive when the shades of night have fallen, and to set out when it is light."

The leader of the troops replied, "It would be well, then, to stop to rest here and order everyone among us to bivouac here as well, since they are also tired. We shall set out again in the morning. We see no danger here and have no fear of thieves and brigands." Once their commander bivouacked there, Amar said to the troops, "I shall now take this news to the princes and inform them of your arrival!" They replied, "Go and inform the princes of these particulars!"

Amar had deployed some of his *ayyars* in the forest in advance. Returning to them immediately, he dressed himself as a state messenger and disguised his *ayyars* as palanquin carriers. Then, with his *ayyars* carrying platters of sweetmeats laced with soporifics, Amar returned to the guards of the treasure and said to them, "The princes have sent you these platters to help you recover from the long journey." The commander of the guards distributed the sweets among his men and ate his share without the least fear or doubt. To cut a long story short, there was not one man among them who did not taste of those treats. Once all of them had lost their heads, fallen unconscious, and become bereft of their senses, Amar secured the gifts and treasure they had brought, stuffing everything into his *zambil.* He then filled up the chests with gravel, stones, and animal bones, and locked them up as before. Afterward, Amar returned to his fort to repose, having procured the whole horde of riches without the least harm to his person.

In the morning the guards regained consciousness and renewed their journey. Around midday, they reached their destination at the camp of the princes. Hurmuz and Faramurz sent for the chests and with the keys from Hakim Majdak opened them. They anticipated the many wonders locked within, and found stones, gravel, and animal bones instead of gold pieces and precious stones. Bakhtiarak said, "Indeed a slier *ayyar* than Amar cannot be found on the face of the Earth. There is none so sharp and insidious in the whole race of Aadam. At his hands Zhopin came to grief, and he inflicted endless woes on our army." The princes asked the guards of the treasure, "Did you meet any stranger last evening or come by someone who had the appearance of an *ayyar*?" They answered, "We saw no such person but we did meet the *ayyar* Zhopin had sent to guide us. At his suggestion we bivouacked in the night to recover from the fatigue of the journey. Later, a cook with several palanquin bearers brought the sweetmeat platters you had sent for us and performed their duties with great attentiveness and diligence." Bakhtiarak said to them, "The *ayyar* you met was Amar, and the same accursed crook also brought you the sweetmeat platters disguised as a cook." The princes and the commanders grieved a great deal at the loss of those riches, but they were unable to do anything about it and incapable of exacting revenge. They could see no other answer but to write a petition to Naushervan describing the entire episode.

OF IFRIT DEV SEEKING REFUGE IN TILISM-E SHEHRISTAN-E ZARRIN AT THE COUNSEL OF HIS MOTHER, MALOONA JADU

Before I resume the narration of the events mentioned above, let me give a few sentences to relate an account of the Quake of Qaf, the Latter-day Suleiman, the World Conqueror, the Lord of the Auspicious Planetary Conjunction, Abul-Ala, Amir Hamza. Earlier, we told how the Sahibqiran killed the murderous Ahriman, the father of Ifrit, and inflicted a most ignominious death on him, which had sent Ifrit into mourning. The *dev* had retired to commit himself to wailing and lamentation, and rivers of tears issued from his eyes. Emperor Shahpal ordered a week of festivities in honor of the Sahibqiran. That festive assembly was decorated with such wonders that whoever laid eyes upon it was sent into transports of delight, and wished to barter away a hundred existences for such luxury.

On the eighth day of festivities the Sahibqiran said to Shahpal, "Your Majesty, Ifrit's intentions remain uncertain and his designs obscure. It is not known whether he will bide his time in solitude or stir into skirmishing. In any event, if he does not sound the war drums and keeps off the battlefield, Your Honor should take precedence and imprint your awe and dread on his heart. I came here on the promise of an eighteen-day sojourn. That period is long past, and God knows what became of my relatives and dear ones. I cannot imagine their grief at having received no news of me and my not returning to them as promised. Anxiety about my welfare will be tormenting them and they must be weeping and wailing night and day. Besides, Emperor Naushervan nurses malice toward them, and there is nobody there now who can stand in opposition to him."

Shahpal ordered the war drums to be beaten, and all preparations were made for battle. Immediately upon receiving their orders, the drummers produced twelve hundred pairs of golden cymbals and an equal number of silver ones and began beating them. The sound of those instruments began to shake the mountains and the Earth. This was the Music Band of Suleiman whose power no other instrument could match, and whose report reached even far-off places that lay a distance of three days' journey from there.

Ifrit himself was not too far away from there. Upon hearing the war drums and their thunderous, cacophonous noise, he became agitated and his senses were thrown into disarray. He said to his accomplices, "I am still in mourning for my father. While my heart has yet to find solace and comfort from this terrible loss, Hamza has already sounded war drums and is arming for battle. Indeed he tortures me like no other, and I am sure he is my slayer." Then Ifrit broke into sobs and washed his face with tears of anguish.

He dispatched a swift *dev* to fetch his mother, Maloona Jadu. That woman, accursed as her name,[41] was a matchless sorceress who considered Kamru's[42] magic mere child's play. Immediately upon receiving these tidings, she arrived flying like a whirlwind, and descended like a scourge from the heavens. Ifrit fell upon her neck crying loudly. He shed many a bitter tear, stringing a veritable garland of pearls that he wept in lamentation. Giving her a detailed account of the Sahibqiran, he informed her of all the occult details about him. Upon hearing this, she replied, "Indeed, this human who has arrived to assist Shahpal is your sworn enemy. Nay, he is the enemy of the whole tribe of the rebel *devs*. It would be best for you to retire to the *tilism*[43] I have created in Shehristan-e Zarrin. We will settle our account with Shahpal and chastise him for these excesses once that human being has returned to the realm of men!"

Ifrit liked his mother's counsel and admired her strategy. Along with his accursed mother, he departed forthwith for the *tilism* of Shehristan-e Zarrin, and took no one into his confidence regarding his plans. His entire army was routed and all his might and grandeur were undone. Many of his warriors went their own way; many others consulted together and decided that Emperor Shahpal was their old master and a man of great munificence, nobility, generosity, and kindness. They decided to present themselves before him and repent, seeking permission to wait upon him again and showing remorse for absconding from his service.

When pitch-faced night was laid low at the hands of morn's Turkoman and chose retreat over standing his ground, and the world-illuminating sun with its sword of light did away with the darkness of the world, Shahpal and the Sahibqiran rode their thrones and headed for the battleground accompanied by their army. On the way, the jinns brought this intelligence to the emperor: "Upon hearing the drums of war and out of the fear of the Lord of the Auspicious Planetary Conjunction and the Emperor of Qaf, Ifrit the Damned has turned tail. He could not find the least courage or resolve for the encounter. Ever since his father's death, the greatest misfortunes have befallen him and his army has been scattered to the skies like the Daughters of the Deceased.[44] Some parties of *devs* with shame clearly marked on their faces have also arrived here to renew their pledge of obedience, hoping for clemency for their past crimes. They stand in humility in His Majesty's court with their heads bowed low from shame and remorse."

Upon hearing these happy tidings the emperor bestowed gold and jewels to Amir Hamza as the sacrifice for his life and the favorable news that Ifrit's army had come to pledge obedience to him gave him great joy. All the lords of Qaf made offerings to Shahpal and scattered gold and jewels as the Sahibqiran's sacrifice. The celebrations continued for many days on a grand scale and everyone in the empire participated in the festivities. After the revelries had ended, Amir Hamza said to Emperor Shahpal, "Kindly give me leave to depart, and send me back, as many obligations have been lying in abeyance and await my return. Moreover, my heart is most distressed at having received no news of my near and dear ones."

Emperor Shahpal replied, "O Sahibqiran, it was our agreement that you would leave Qaf after slaying Ifrit. Once this task has been fulfilled, you will be given leave to return. As you know, Ifrit is still at large. If you left without killing him and dispatching him to Hell with your sword, he would again raise his rebellious head and take vengeance on me, and this would again compel me to send for you and disturb your peace. It would be far better for you to return to the realm of men after putting an end to his menace and delivering all of us from this devil's clutches. God willing, I shall send you back sooner than soon, and rejoicing with triumph shall see you off to your land!"

Amir lowered his head and, after a moment's silence, said to Shahpal, "I am willing to oblige you in this instance as well, as it is not my place to act against your wishes. However, I would like to find out where Ifrit Dev has retreated and is now hiding so that I may go there myself, kill him, and bring you his head." Shahpal replied, "His present abode will not be revealed until we have reached Qasr-e Bilour." Amir said, "Then we must not delay in starting for Qasr-e Bilour. Your humble servant is prepared to depart this very moment!"

Shahpal sent his advance camp at once to Qasr-e Bilour and the next day departed for the city in Amir Hamza's company. When they arrived, the nobles of Qasr-e Bilour presented themselves to make offerings. After performing all the offices of submission, they reported, "Ifrit along with his mother, Maloona Jadu, is hiding in Tilism-e Shehristan-e Zarrin, which was constructed by that harridan. He has gone into seclusion in that *tilism*—a most immaculate enchantment built in a frightful, desolate land."

At this, Amir said to Shahpal, "Give your faithful servant leave to depart! Trusting in God, grant me permission to dispatch that wretched *dev* to Hell along with his mother so that they may populate the region of fire together. As he is hiding at the *tilism* by himself, I shall also confront him alone, and shall triumph over him with the grace of God." Shahpal looked toward Abdur Rahman upon hearing Amir's speech. Abdur Rahman replied, "Pray have no anxiety in your heart and give him leave to depart. I have discovered by the calculations of *jafar* and astrology that Amir will triumph over Ifrit and defeat him immediately upon his arrival."

Shahpal seated Amir on a throne and ordered four swift *perizads* to carry him to Shehristan-e Zarrin with great comfort. The *perizads* immediately flew off with the throne, and after three nights and three days alighted atop a green mountain known by the name of Zehr Mohra, which was home to a race of singular beings. Amir asked the *perizads*, "Do you know how far Shehristan-e Zarrin lies from here, and which is the way there?" They replied that it lay at a distance of six *kos* from there. Amir then said, "Why did you bring my throne and descend here instead of flying straight to our destination? What fear oppresses your hearts?" The *perizads* replied, "O Sahibqiran! We have come across an impediment! Magical *tilisms* created by Maloona Jadu are strewn all along the path from this slope to the boundaries of Shehristan-e Zarrin. One also comes across all kinds of wonders along the way. If we were to take a single step farther, we would be combusted by magical devices. Behold that radiance in the distance: It is the same Shehristan-e Zarrin where that reprobate *dev* has made his abode!"

In the end, the Sahibqiran camped for the night on the mountain. After saying his prayers in the morning, he petitioned God to grant him victory. He said to the *perizads,* "Pray stay here without anxiety or fear and remain alert to my call. I am now headed toward Shehristan-e Zarrin. I forewarn you that I shall make three war cries: the first one when I encounter Ifrit; the second during combat; and a third cry upon my victory. If you do not hear the third war cry, you should understand that I have been beheaded and have died at the hands of Ifrit. You may then take the news of my death to Emperor Shahpal and inform him of the event."

Amir Hamza girded himself and, rolling up his sleeves and drawing out the Aqrab-e Suleimani, he descended the mountain. However, when he suddenly could not take a step forward for the darkness and was unable to advance even a handspan, he was forced again to climb the mountain. From there he saw light all around as before, and wondered why it had disappeared when he descended. Amir went down once again and plunged into the same pitch darkness that had utterly blinded and confounded him. He climbed back up again to look around. When the *perizads* saw him climb up and down the mountain five or six times in that manner, they figured that he was perhaps exercising his body. They said to him, "O Sahibqiran! Is this how the humans exercise their bodies on Earth, and is this the regime they follow to prepare their physique and strengthen their limbs?" Amir Hamza answered, "I am not exercising my body. When I climb down the mountain I am enveloped in such pitch darkness that even the darkness of the *Shab-e Yalda* would seem a bright morn in comparison, and no words can be found to describe it. When I climb up, however, I see light as before. I greatly marvel at the phenomenon and wonder what might be its root cause."

The *perizads* replied, "These wonders are due to the *tilisms* created by Ifrit's mother, Maloona Jadu, which are spread from here to the castle where she lives. It was that which confounded you and made you wonder." Amir said, "Come what may, I shall now head into this darkness with God as my guide!" He climbed down the mountain and had gone some distance when he heard a voice from the heavens, and someone invisible called out to him, "O Sahibqiran! Pray do not advance! Beware! Do not to take another step! Have patience until I come!" Amir stopped and saw Salasal Perizad appear there. He made salutations to Amir and handed him an emerald tablet inscribed with the names of God and said, "Abdur Rahman has sent this tablet for you and instructed you not to take a single step without first consulting it. You must not act against its advice or else you will fall into great error and suffer terribly!" After handing him the tablet, Salasal Perizad disappeared whence he had come. As Amir looked at the tablet, he saw written there:

In the Name of Allah

O Destroyer of *Tilisms,* the Exalted and Illustrious God showed you unique favor that you have come into possession of this tablet and secured the key to victory and triumph. Read the word written on the margin and blow at the sky. Then the darkness will part, all gloom will disappear, and the path will become illuminated.

The Sahibqiran recited that word and blew at the sky. His yearning was fulfilled and the darkness was completely cast away. Amir made a prostration of gratitude before God and stepped onward, carrying that tablet.

When he arrived close to the castle, he saw a dragon whose lower jaw touched the foundation of the gate and whose upper jaw sat atop the portals, as if he held the door to the castle in his mouth. As Amir was looking upon that sight in wonder, the dragon called out to him, "O Destroyer of *Tilisms,* walk into my mouth and entertain not the least fear or anxiety in your heart!" When the Sahibqiran consulted the tablet, it read:

Recite this word and breathe on yourself and jump into the dragon's mouth without fear of it. It is nothing more than an illusion and deception to frighten you. It is neither a real dragon nor is it a ghost.

The moment the Sahibqiran jumped into the dragon's mouth, a loud and mournful cry rose to the heavens and a thunderous clamor was heard, as if doomsday itself had burst upon him.

When Amir opened his eyes after a moment, he saw no signs of the dragon or the castle but instead a garden in full bloom that was the very envy of the garden of Paradise, blossoming with flowers of every season. Trees laden with flowers and fruits not in season lined it in a beautiful array. Birds made of jewels were chirping in the trees, creating a most angelic music with their caroling. Amir Hamza sat down beside a lake and indulged himself with the scenery, when he suddenly heard a most doleful voice calling out from the summerhouse in the garden, "Alas, there is no man of God to release me from my dreadful prison and receive from the Almighty the reward for this deed!" Amir looked around but saw nobody there. He followed the voice to its source in the summerhouse and beheld a nubile maiden of great charm and beauty sitting prisoner on a throne. She wore iron chains instead of jewlery on her hands and feet, and from her oppressive imprisonment she was beside herself with grief and distress.

Amir felt great pity for her and was struck with remorse at the sight of her virtuous face. He asked her with compassion, "O maiden, tell me who you are and who has imprisoned you here. Who is the tyrannical hunter who has snared a charming doe like you in this terrible prison?" She answered, "I wish for you to take precedence in introductions and give me your particulars. Tell me who you are, whence you have come, and how you found your way in these *tilisms*." Amir replied, "I am the Quake of Qaf, the Latter-day Suleiman, Lord of the Auspicious Planetary Conjunction, World Conqueror, Slayer of Sly Ifrit, and a believer in God Almighty. I count myself among the kin of the Holy Prophet (praise be unto him!) and am a follower of the True Faith!"

She said, "And I am Susan Peri, the daughter of Saleem Kohi. I don't know where to begin the tale of my woes: Ifrit became enamored of me and asked my father for my hand in marriage. Upon my father's refusal, Ifrit descended on us with his army. After my father was unable to prevail over him in battle, he came and narrated the account of his defeat to me. I said to him, 'Marry me to Ifrit and have not the least trepidation or anxiety regarding my welfare. I shall drug him with deceit and throw him in prison. You may then send him to Emperor Shahpal, who will be pleased with you and most gratified to hear of his enemy's arrest. I am certain that he will bestow even greater honors upon you and promote you to high office.'

"My father then married me to Ifrit. One day the *dev* drank himself unconscious. The wine completely befuddled his senses, and he became inebriated, intoxicated, and entirely senseless. I immediately tied up his hands and feet to send him as a prisoner to Emperor Shahpal and gratify my sovereign with this service to his throne. But before I could carry out my plans, someone took the news of these proceedings to Ifrit's mother, Maloona Jadu, who arrived instantly. She released him and left me imprisoned here. Since that time I have lived here as a captive. A life such as mine is a fate worse than death. I would prefer to die than to continue this existence. If you were to liberate me from my prison now and release me from this affliction, I would conduct you very easily to where Ifrit is hiding, and would remember you in my prayers for all my living days."

The Sahibqiran released her and gave her a new lease on life. She led the Sahibqiran into another garden and showed him Ifrit's dwelling, and instructed him in all the signs from which Amir Hamza could ascertain the *dev*'s presence. The Sahibqiran saw that twelve hundred armed *devs* were standing guard there, alert in their vigil.

After reciting magical incantations Susan Peri suddenly rose before Amir's eyes into the air, and forgetting the great favor Amir had bestowed on her, revealed her true ingrate self. Once she had risen high, she called out loudly to the *devs*, "O *devs*! Don't continue to warm your rears! The Slayer of Ifrit and the Destroyer of *Tilisms* is standing within your sight. Put him to death in any manner you see fit."

The Sahibqiran sorely regretted having set that creature free. He felt vexed at her treachery and was troubled and annoyed by her perfidy. The *devs* surrounded Amir on all sides, brandishing their weapons to kill him. Amir drew the Aqrab-e Suleimani from its scabbard and any *dev* to whom he dealt a blow he cut in two and dispatched to Hell. The *devs'* blood fell on the ground and quickly created new *devs*. Amir's hands and arms became worn from the fatigue of fighting them, and he felt sapped of all energy from doing battle. Amir then remembered the tablet, and transfixed his eyes on its words. Therein he saw written:

O Destroyer of *Tilisms*, do not be duped by the chicanery of Susan Peri or release her from captivity. She is a consummate charlatan and will beguile and betray you in a most abominable manner. If by chance you commit this error and she is released from captivity and rises to the sky and the *devs* attack you, read the Most Great Name on the point of your arrow and shoot at her so that the scourge of her existence vanishes and is not seen again!

Amir carried out the tablet's instructions and directly a great hue and cry arose: "There he is! The Slayer of Ifrit has arrived at the *tilism*. Don't let him get away! Kill him without mercy!" After this clamor subsided, Amir looked around, and saw neither Susan Peri nor any *devs* nor any signs of the recent pandemonium.

From behind the garden wall he heard *perizads'* voices and thought he could discern the speech of the people of Qaf. When he went to the other side to investigate, Amir saw another garden, as sumptuous and lavish as before, and a fourteen-year-old comely beauty whose splendor was the envy of the moon, sitting in chains in the summerhouse. An ancient whose mien betrayed his royal lineage sat beside her with his head hanging down from grief. Some four hundred jinns and *perizads*—innocent of any crime—were also gathered there as prisoners. When she beheld Hamza, the girl called out, "O Sahibqiran! Release us from this confinement and earn great recompense for the deed!" Once bitten, twice shy, Amir Hamza reasoned that this was a case like the one he had encountered earlier. He felt apprehensive that this woman would also do him an ill turn and deceive him like the other *peri*. Drawing his sword, he advanced to kill her.

The old man accompanying her interceded with a thousand solicitations and said, "O dear friend! Why do you wish to exhaust your wrath on ill-fated people? Have some fear of God and show mercy on our sorry plight. Listen to our account first and then decide how you must act toward us. You may then, as you wish, slay us or set us free. I am Junaid Shah Sabz-Posh, the elder brother of Emperor Shahpal, and this girl is my daughter, Rehan Peri. The land of Qaf is our home. When Ifrit defeated Shahpal, he asked me to give him my daughter's hand in marriage. He asked me to swear allegiance to him and fear his wrath. I did not give in to his threats, but he defeated me in battle, and imprisoned me with my daughter and our four hundred companions. He has given us this garden for our dwelling. Now you know my story and have the power to kill us or set us free and grant us a new lease on life. Do as you wish!"

When Amir consulted the tablet it corroborated the old man's account. Amir was overcome with feelings of pity for them, and that very instant he freed them and sent them to their home. He said to them, "Pray give my salutations to Emperor Shahpal and convey him the message that after facing many hardships and suffering great asperity, I have advanced thus far in my journey by the grace of the Almighty. God willing, I shall soon slay Ifrit and return triumphant to receive the honor of waiting upon you again. I beg you to pray for my victory and beseech you not to let any anxiety or apprehension find room in your hearts."

It is written that Junaid Shah Sabz-Posh took his leave of Amir and rediscovered the joy of life in his freedom. Amir went ahead in his mission and came upon a most magnificent building that was sumptuously and ornately furnished. He marveled, however, to see its courtyard inundated with water. In the nave of the courtyard he saw a chest lying with its lid open. When he put his foot in to judge the depth of the water, Amir Hamza discovered that it was not water but an illusion created by a crystalline surface: Such was its amazing brilliance that it appeared more clear and transparent than water itself. He wished to look into the chest and inspect its contents, certain that it would contain some magical wonder or talismanic marvel.

The moment he peered down to look into the chest, he found himself in the clutches of a *dev* who was hiding inside, who caught his neck with both hands and began squeezing the breath out of him with great vigor. With one hand Amir held on to the edge of the chest to keep his balance, and used the other hand to consult the tablet, on which was written:

> O Trampler of *Tilisms,* protect yourself from this calamity and do not enter the chest. If you do, you will never find release from this *tilism* until your dying day, and will meet your end here. There is a hair like a thick rope on the chest of the *dev*—which is not a rope but a terrible calamity—to which a tablet is attached. Pluck this along with the hair so that you find release from the hands of the *dev* and your prayers are answered. Afterward, recite the Most Great Name on this tablet, then strike it on the *dev*'s head and witness what transpires by the marvels of God, and how the grace of the Almighty releases you from all your present woes.

Amir pulled out the tablet attached to the *dev*'s hair, and thanked God for his success. Then he recited the Most Great Name on the first tablet and struck it on the *dev*'s head. The *dev* was dispatched to Hell directly with a blazing flame rising from his head, and the wooden chest began to burn and crackle in the blaze that sprang up. Terrible cries that reverberated as far away as the mountains rose to the heavens, echoing, "Kill him! Butcher him! Do not let the Slayer of Zaraq Jadu escape! Finish him soon, in any way possible!"

When that pandemonium subsided, Amir saw neither the crystalline surface he had witnessed earlier, nor the *dev,* nor any building at all. There remained only a desolate wasteland with a pool of blood with a pulley hanging above at its center. The blood was conducted by means of the pulley into a big pond, but Amir could not make out its mechanism, or the nature of the *tilism* and its magic. He only marveled and then proceeded forward. He had gone some distance when he encountered another curiosity. He came upon a garden where a boy stood guard at the entrance. Amir asked him repeatedly to tell him his name and to disclose his particulars, but the boy uttered not one word. He stood quiet without offering Amir any answer. However, the moment Amir stepped into the garden, the boy called out, "Beware, O *dev,* the Destroyer of *Tilisms* has turned all your marvelous devices to naught and gained entrance into the garden!" Amir turned and dealt him a powerful blow of his sword, which cut the boy's head off like a corncob, and it landed fifty paces away.

When Amir advanced he witnessed another prodigious sight: The boy's head flew back through the air and became fixed again to his torso at the neck. He came back to life immediately as if resurrected by the waters of the Fountain of Life. Surprised, Amir consulted the tablet and found the following written there:

> O Destroyer of *Tilisms,* beware not to attack Darban Jadu as he will not die until the end of time, and no weapon will prove successful against him. However, if you were to recite the Most Great Name on the point of your arrow and then successfully lodge it in his breast, he will die from it and his existence will not be renewed in this life. Congratulations to you for closing in upon Ifrit and arriving at his lair.

When Amir recited the Most Great Name and shot the arrow at the boy's breast, a dark dust storm bore down upon him. It was as if the entire world were plunged into darkness. Thunderbolts began falling and sparks of lightning started dancing all around. A clamor greater than thunder was heard and robbed the birds and beasts of their senses. Amir huddled down with the tablet, covering his eyes lest any harm should come to them and deprive him of sight.

After the clamor had subsided and the gale had blown away, Amir Hamza looked around and beheld beds of tulips stretching for miles on end. Everywhere he turned his gaze he saw flowers and fragrant plants in full bloom. He saw flower beds whose ornate construction and delicate adornment were beyond human expression, and represented a labor to humble the most eloquent tongue. Some *perizads* were there singing harmonious notes and deriving pleasure from one another's company. Amir approached the place, and when the *perizads* spotted him, one of them came rushing toward him with a goblet of wine, cooing, "O Sahibqiran, you are all exhausted and spent from your adventures. Come, drink this and wash away all your woes and revive your spirits. You may spend a few hours listening to our music and songs, which will bring joy to your heart. All your hardships will be forgotten and you will find contentment!"

Amir consulted the tablet and, following its instructions, took the goblet from her hand and reciting the Most Great Name poured it over her head. Directly, a flame rose from her body, and she thoroughly combusted in just a few moments, all her flesh and bones melting away like wax. Even greater clamor was heard then, and voices called out, "The Destroyer of *Tilisms* has killed Asrar Jadu as well! He has left her a corpse and struck terror in the hearts of her companions."

After a moment, Amir's eyes fell upon a mountain of unfathomable height and a riverbank, with the hill of Koh-e Besutoon[45] between them. From its cave emanated the enchanting peal of kettledrums. Amir stepped into the cave and beheld Ifrit sleeping like a log, and saw that it was his snores that sounded like kettledrums, echoing far and wide. It was a sight to make one cataleptic with fear. The Sahibqiran thought, *It would be a heartless act and the worse kind of pusillanimity to kill someone in his sleep.* He drew Rustam's dagger and struck Ifrit Dev with such great force that the blade sunk up to its hilt into his foot. Ifrit thumped his foot irritably and grumbled, "What troublesome mosquitoes! God knows where this pestering horde has come from that attacks so relentlessly and does not let one sleep a wink." The Sahibqiran thought, *God be praised! If he considers that blow a mere mosquito bite, how shall I ever wake him up?* Amir caught Ifrit's neck and arms in a lock and securing his grip, bellowed "God is Great!" so mightily that mountains and deserts—indeed the whole firmament— were thrown into turmoil.

Terrified, Ifrit arose, his head all in a swoon from the shock of the blow. In his half-wakeful state he wondered whether the Earth had been cleft asunder or if the sky had fallen. As he rubbed his eyes and looked around, he saw the face of the Quake of Qaf. A great fear seized Ifrit then, he was all atremble and said, "O son of Aadam! I know and recognize only too well that you are my Angel of Death, and I will lose my life at your hands. For that reason I had hidden myself here, thinking that perhaps in this cave I would find refuge from your hand. You followed me here as well and now find me in your power. I am determined that whether I live or die, I shall not turn away from the encounter, and you will meet your death at my hands." Ifrit Dev came at Amir Hamza swinging a box tree tied with millstones to exhibit his demonic might and attacked Amir Hamza. Amir stopped the blow with the Aqrab-e Suleimani and cut the tree in two. Without wasting another moment Amir dealt Ifrit a blow of the sword that struck his back. It cut Ifrit in two, but the halves remained attached by a cord of flesh and kept his soul enchained.

Ifrit cried out, "O son of Aadam! Now that you have killed me, sever this last cord, too, with another blow so that my soul shall be released from this receptacle and be freed of its pain and misery." The Sahibqiran dealt him another blow and did as requested. The moment the cord was severed, the two halves of Ifrit's body flew toward Heaven and fell down before the Sahibqiran as two Ifrits, each fully alive as before. In short, within a few hours thousands of Ifrits were produced and *devs* tall as mountains surrounded the Sahibqiran. He was utterly confounded and marveled at this turn of events and said to himself, *What is this devilry that whoever I kill comes back as two, and plies his force and strength against me?*

At that moment Amir received divine help in the form of someone calling out from his right, "May the blessings of God be upon you!" When Amir turned to look he found holy Khizr, that ambassador of happy omens. After returning his salutations, Amir kissed his feet and pleaded with him. "Sire, my arms are numb from plying the sword. The situation I find myself in is a marvel to stupefy reason. I am in a terrible fix, for whoever I kill becomes two and then both skirmish with me. Not a single one of them has been dispatched to Hell from the wounds received at my hand."

The holy Khizr replied, "O Sahibqiran! It is a menace of your own making. You went about the whole affair recklessly, otherwise things would not have come to this pass and you would not have lost your countenance in this manner! You know well that this is a *tilism*, the greatest of all conjurings. You act here as it pleases you, without consulting the tablet or showing any regard for the *tilisms* and this manufactory of witchcraft. Do as I tell you now, and recite the blessed word I instruct to you in the manner I suggest. Then bless an arrow with that word and aim for the head of the *dev* whose face glows like a ruby and on whose forehead you see a mole like a carnelian. Then this calamity would be dispelled and you will find deliverance from the magic of these *devs*." The Sahibqiran acted upon Prophet Khizr's directions and used the blessed word and the arrow as he had been instructed.

Then Amir Hamza saw not one single *dev* and found Ifrit lying dead before him, carved in two. The whole field was empty without any sign of *dev* or monster. Amir saw that Ifrit's head was missing. When he could not find the head and saw no sign of it anywhere, holy Khizr asked him, "O Sahibqiran, did you or did you not comprehend the reason for the *devs* multiplying?" Amir replied, "The cause is either known to God Almighty or to yourself, as you are the guide of those lost in error." Prophet Khizr replied, "Ifrit's mother, Maloona Jadu, is sitting in this cave holding Ifrit's head. It was that harridan who set in motion this sorcery. She would dip a coriander leaf in his blood and throw it up to the sky after reciting incantations over it. From that magic one Ifrit would become two and both would do battle with you. You saw this illusion through her power of sorcery. Now go into the cave and kill her as well and sever her filthy head from her torso, so that the *tilism* can be finally conquered." The Sahibqiran went with holy Khizr into the cave, the two of them stepping into it together.

When Maloona saw Khizr along with the Sahibqiran, she flew into a rage and with great anger declared, "O ancient, now I know that this is all your mischief, and it is your cherished desire to see death and destruction befall our race. It was you who had my son killed at the hands of this human, and acted on the malice you bear toward us in your heart. Come what may, I shall not let you escape without harm, and will seek my revenge!" As she began reciting some incantation, Prophet Khizr recited an incantation himself and blew it on her head. She was dispatched to Hell in the flash of an eye, and there joined the rest of her tribe. All signs of the *tilism* then dissolved away, and the hearts of the two men of God became filled with joy.

Holy Khizr congratulated the Sahibqiran on the conquest of the *tilism* and praised his courage and said, "Take off the golden helmet and the *shab chiragh* jewel from the head of Ifrit Dev. You shall acquire a similar *shab chiragh* jewel from the Sufaid Dev as well, and many benefits will come to you from these rare objects. You may put them in your crown and then your headgear shall be unrivaled under the heavens!" Then Khizr made a gift to the Sahibqiran of a huge goblet that could hold three and a half Tabrizi *maunds* of sherbet, and said to him, "This vessel will serve in your assembly and reveal its marvelous properties to you!"

Amir said, "I feel famished, O sire! Perform another miracle and provide me with something to eat!" Holy Khizr produced a small loaf from his leather bag and offered it to Amir. He had his fill of it and found relief from the pangs of hunger, but the loaf remained the same size as before and did not diminish in size at all. The holy Khizr also gave Amir a flask of water to satisfy his thirst and said, "Keep these two articles with you so that you do not go hungry or thirsty throughout your sojourn in Qaf and do not have to rely on anyone for provisions. When these two objects disappear from your possession, and you are unable to find them, then you should understand that you will be returning to the realm of Earth soon, and your house will become illuminated with your presence." After conveying this message to Amir, the holy Khizr disappeared.

After many days of hunger Amir had eaten his fill and became a little torpid. He stretched himself out to rest on the same rock where Ifrit lay in the sleep of death. Having become oblivious in his sweet slumber, Amir forgot to make the third war cry, and the *perizads* who were waiting on the mountain of Zehr Mohra for his signal, having not heard it returned to Shahpal to give him the news of Amir's death, telling him the whole story of Amir's adventure from beginning to the end.

When Shahpal heard the news of Amir's death from the *perizads,* he involuntarily broke into tears, and the pain of his grief threatened to endanger his life. He turned to Abdur Rahman and said, "Alas, the blood of one of Ibrahim's descendants will now be on my neck, for it was I who sent him on the errand to search and kill Ifrit Dev!" That very moment Abdur Rahman made calculations by *jafar* and astrology and said, "The Sahibqiran has already slain Maloona Jadu and Ifrit Dev. He has severed their necks and relieved the land of their filthy burden! However, a little iniquitous influence of the stars yet prevails, which is the reason why he forgot to make his third signal. That evil influence shall be dispelled soon, too, and his heart's desire fulfilled. Let us go, so that we may bring him back and everyone here can receive great bliss from the sight of him, and any misgivings regarding his welfare may be dispelled."

Shahpal ordered his musicians to start playing festive tunes and made elaborate preparations for the journey. Then, along with the nobles of Qaf, he rode out to Shehristan-e Zarrin and the *perizads'* hopes were revived[?].

When Aasman Peri heard the auspicious tidings of Amir's victory, she could not contain her joy and hastened there herself like a gale of wind to indulge herself with the sight of the Sahibqiran[?]. She reached the place before the others, and descended where Amir lay. She found him asleep in a cave with his face exposed to the sun, whose rays had painted his complexion with a tinge of bronze. With her one wing Aasman Peri shaded Amir's face from the sun, providing him relief from its scorching rays and withering heat, and with her other wing she began fanning him. From the tender emotions engendered in her heart, she made a pledge to take all his troubles and misfortunes upon herself.

Feeling relief from her ministrations, Amir Hamza opened his eyes and looked around, and he saw Aasman Peri shading him with one wing and fanning him with the other, earning great blessings in her labor of love. Amir rose and embraced her and kissed her many times. He planted a kiss on her cheek that was as beautiful as the moon, and became greatly enamored of her upon witnessing such ardor and love on her part. Greatly charmed and won over upon seeing her affectionate nature and loving manner, he said to her, "O soul of the world and life of the Sahibqiran! It is a marvel that I see you here, and I wonder about the reason for your presence." Aasman Peri replied, "I arrived upon hearing the news of your victory. I have brought the happy tidings that the emperor himself is on his way here. He is beside himself with joy from the news of your victory and the death of his enemies."

Amir was most gratified to hear this. He seated that beauty beside him and showed her much affection. While he was still making love vows and swearing devotion to her, the conveyance of Emperor Shahpal arrived there like the gale of spring. Noticing the emperor's throne, Amir rose to his feet. The emperor stepped down from the throne to kiss Amir's victorious hand and arm, and embraced him. He seated Amir on the throne by his side, and flew him back to Gulistan-e Irum. As all his wishes had been fulfilled, a most sumptuous royal assembly was arranged to celebrate the festivities on a grand scale. The *perizads,* kings, and nobles of Qaf scattered gold and jewels over Amir's head as a sacrifice for his life, and offered gold coins and rupees to the poor and needy. After offering Amir their congratulations on the victory, everyone also wished him happiness in life.

Then the *perizads* began to dance and unburden their hearts long heavy with sorrow with the strains of song and music. The emperor said to Abdur Rahman, "I recall you telling me that Hamza has the ability to couple with Aasman Peri, since he is superior to the whole race of human beings in all matters. I cannot think of any time more auspicious than the present for the occasion, for all the kings and nobles of Qaf are present, and by the grace of God young and old alike are pleased with Hamza's courage. There should be no delay in joining Aasman Peri in the bonds of matrimony to Amir Hamza, and no reason for postponing such a good cause."

Abdur Rahman got up and threw a perfumed orange at Amir's breast.[46] He congratulated Amir and showed him much favor. The Sahibqiran asked, "What does the orange signify, and why have you congratulated me?" Abdur Rahman answered, "The emperor has accepted you as his son-in-law, and shown you preference over the entire race of the *perizads*!"

Amir replied, "I cannot accept this honor under any circumstances. It is not my way to undertake matrimonial commitments during the course of my journeys. If I married Aasman Peri, my return to the realm of Earth would be deferred. I would become occupied with her here in pursuit of pleasure seeking. The other qualm I have is that I promised Mehr-Nigar, the daughter of Emperor Naushervan, that until I married her, I would never even look at any woman with the eye of desire. I cannot go back on my word and break my promise and pledge to her, as I cannot violate my pact without disgrace to my name. It is binding on every man to remain true to his covenant!"

Abdur Rahman then said, "O Sahibqiran! You made that promise on the realm of Earth and this is the realm of Qaf. Your actions here will not contravene your compacts there! It is my responsibility and part of my promise to you to return you to the realm of men!" At this, Amir asked, "How long will it be before you see me off and return me to Earth?" Abdur Rahman said, "O Sahibqiran, this is a promise made in the land of Qaf. Pray do not press me in this matter. Please agree to what we ask without insisting otherwise! One year from now I shall take you back to Earth and then you can return in all safety and welfare to set eyes on your homeland!"

Amir saw no recourse except acquiescence and found no path open to him beside submission. Discord with them would make it impossible for him to leave Qaf, as he could not go back to his world without their permission. Emperor Shahpal busied himself with preparations for the wedding, ordering all the nobles and kings of Qaf to be present and making all manner of festive arrangements. The kings of the realms of Tareeki, Zulmat, and other dominions arrived in Gulistan-e Irum bearing gifts from their lands, and joined that festive assembly[?].

The news of Amir Hamza's defeat of Ifrit and Maloona Jadu had spread all over Qaf. When it reached the ears of the *dev* Samandun Hazar-Dast, he became angry and rueful, and a blaze of fury burned his heart to ashes. He said to himself, *The emperor of Qaf sent for a human being called the Quake of Qaf and the Latter-day Suleiman from the realm of Earth, and had mighty* devs *such as Ifrit and his parents murdered. He showed no consideration for our people. The Tilism-e Zarrin was destroyed and our thousand-year-old works demolished. Then the emperor himself conducted him to Gulistan-e Irum and betrothed his daughter to him, admitting an alien species into his palace. On the emperor's part this was an appalling act, and now it is incumbent on me to avenge Ifrit's blood and chastise the guilty party severely for his impropriety!* He dispatched his commander in chief, Sufaid Dev, a brave and intrepid warrior, along with four hundred *devs,* to speedily produce that human being before him, exhorting them to permit no delay in carrying out his commands.

Emperor Shahpal was giving audience on the Peacock Throne[47] in the Court of Suleiman, where Amir Hamza's marriage to Aasman Peri was being celebrated. All major and minor nobles and grandees of Qaf derived the bliss of his audience. The Sahibqiran was seated with a lordly mien in all his glory and magnificence on the throne, which was inlaid with thousands of jewels of a great variety and which Prophet Suleiman had had constructed for his minister Asif bin Barkhia. The kings and nobles of Qaf were seated alongside Hamza on seats and couches according to their stations. Everyone was enjoying the sumptuous gathering and indulging themselves with that joyous assembly when Sufaid Dev burst in upon the assembly without any fear or trepidation, along with his four hundred *devs,* who carried lances, *zangala,*[48] box trees, millstones, and crocodiles[?].

Sufaid Dev shouted, "O Emperor, Samandun Hazar-Dast sends you the message that Your Lordship visited a great injustice on the race of the *devs* by taking upon your neck the terrible penalty of inviting a human being from the realm of men to murder a commander of Ifrit's stature as well as his parents. The emperor's heart felt no stirring of passion at the consequences and he made a mistake by venturing on this path. It would bode well for him to send that human being to Samandun Hazar-Dast now, surrendering that cruel and bloodthirsty creature to my master without further ado, so that he may distribute his flesh and bones among the *devs* to avenge Ifrit's death and exact retribution on that sanguinary man for the murder of Ifrit and his parents."

Greatly enraged by the speech of that vile creature and most thoroughly displeased with his foul talk, the Sahibqiran said, "O wretch deserving of beheading, what is this inane speech? Rein in your loose tongue and suppress your profane words, or else I shall chastise you and give you your just deserts for these scandalous words! Go and tell your master that if he has a desire to meet Ifrit, he should come here himself and I will dispatch him to the same abode where I earlier dispatched his friend, packing him off to Hell as well!"

Displeased at hearing Amir's words, Sufaid Dev said, "O dark-haired, white-toothed creature, I see that you are the slayer of Ifrit! Come with me as my commander has sent for you, and this whole contingent of *devs* has accompanied me for the purpose of carrying you away!" Sufaid Dev then extended his hand toward Amir to demonstrate his strength. The

Sahibqiran turned his mind to thoughts of God and, catching the *dev*'s arm, gave it such a violent tug that he fell to his knees. Then, drawing his dagger, Amir stabbed him in the breast with a powerful thrust from which the *dev* gave up the ghost with just one cry.[49] Amir was able to overcome that villainous *dev* with God's assistance. The *devs* who had accompanied Sufaid Dev marveled at the ease with which the Sahibqiran had killed their commander. Unable to muster the courage to challenge Amir Hamza, every one of them fled from there with their tails between their legs.

All the kings and nobles of Qaf applauded the Sahibqiran's power and extolled his courage and valor to the high heavens. The emperor offered salvers of gold and jewels as the sacrifice for the Sahibqiran's life and distributed thousands of rupees among the mendicants as an offering of gratitude. He had the corpse of Sufaid Dev left exposed in the desert, and that recalcitrant villain was meted out humiliation even after his death.

As it was yet a day of festivities, rows of lights mounted on bamboo frameworks lined the streets of Qaf on both sides. In the middle of these pathways pyrotechnicians had mounted fireworks, and they had planted lights to create a garden of luminence that afforded the eyes another delight. The decorations there were extraordinary, and anyone who looked at them imagined that he saw a real garden, and was pleased at the sight.

The Sahibqiran was dressed in a royal robe of honor and was led from the Court of Suleiman to the royal harem. All articles and accessories necessary for the festivities were amply provided. The Sahibqiran proceeded in the circle of the kings, nobles, *perizads,* and mace bearers of Qaf like the moon surrounded by clusters of stars. Heralds and mace bearers walked before them, announcing their proclamations, and the Music Band of Suleiman marched alongside them, mounted on a throne. Every lutenist and minstrel played joyous songs. The *perizads* flew in the air ahead of the thrones singing and dancing, and affording all onlookers a taste of Qaf's musical fanfare. As the rockets set off by the pyrotechnicians fell from the sky and burst on the ground, it appeared that the Earth was receiving a shower of stars from the heavens.

As I do not wish to unduly lengthen this book, and am averse to the scribe's tendency to embellish, I have vouchsafed the details of the wedding procession to the narrator of the *dastan,* and do not expand them here due to my preference for brevity. In short, the bridegroom's procession reached the bride's house with great pomp and fanfare, and by the workings of Almighty God the human entered into new enchantments. With one watch remaining for the night, Abdur Rahman tied the nuptial knot between Amir Hamza and Aasman Peri. The proposal and assent were concluded between the parties, and the desire of the two yearning hearts came to fruition. The emperor included several lands of Qaf in Aasman Peri's dowry and showed many other favors to Amir Hamza. Then the Sahibqiran entered the bedchamber. After the necessary rituals and ceremonies were finished, he took Aasman Peri in his embrace and took his pleasure of her on the bed, fulfilling his desire. By the grace of God, that same night, his seed was planted in Aasman Peri's womb, and by the work of God the union between the man made of clay and a *peri* whose essence was fire bore fruit. In the morning, Amir arrived in the court after bathing and changing and a festive party was held in which the newlyweds cast off all inhibitions. In short, night after night the revelries continued for Amir Hamza, and everything that he desired was provided to him.

However, Amir still counted the days and nights of his sojourn in Qaf, waiting for the year to be over so that he could return to the realm of men and enjoy once again the company of his near and dear ones. He looked forward to narrating to them all that had passed with him and showing them the many wondrous gifts that he had acquired in Peristan, the land of *peris*, jinns, and *devs*.

———

Leaving the Sahibqiran thus busy in enumerating the years, months, days, and hours, I shall now give a few words regarding the King of the Land of Might and Power, the Rustam of His Times, the Pillar of the Empire of the Sahibqiran, the Khusrau of India, King Landhoor bin Saadan, so that what passed with him may also be presented in brief. Let it be made clear that when King Landhoor took leave of Amir Hamza and boarded the ship, he was tearful at the prospect of separation from his friend. But the ship had weighed anchor and soon it advanced on its journey. The next day Landhoor's vessel crossed paths with Bahram's ship and the two of them exchanged news. Upon learning that Amir Hamza had sent Bahram Gurd to his assistance, Landhoor was very gratified and felt a great debt of gratitude toward Amir.

On the fifth day a storm brewed in the sea and brought hazard to both ships. For three whole days the raging sea tossed their ships about. It returned to calm on the fourth day, and the ships and those inside them found a measure of peace. However, before long they learned that the ship carrying Bahram had gone missing and no signs of it were visible anywhere. Upon learning this, Landhoor was plunged into the deepest sorrow. He said to himself, *If Amir Hamza should ask me about Bahram, how would I break the news to him and account for Bahram's loss? Amir Hamza sent Bahram to assist me. Indeed his loss is a great calamity, and I feel most miserable at this accident of fate!*

Now hear of Bahram. His ship was driven away by the tempest and after traveling some distance it broke apart from the violence of the sea. Bahram caught hold of a wooden board and drifted upon it toward shore. With the aid of that plank he arrived on land, whereupon he offered prayers of gratitude to God for saving him from drowning. He then set out on foot to explore, going without food or water for a few days. One day, after he had traveled some two or three *farsangs,* he saw a caravan of merchants encamped at some distance from him. Because Bahram felt wretched, dispirited, and miserable, he feared that if someone in the caravan happened to recognize his identity, he would lose his honor in the eyes of men and earn their contempt. He sat down far away from them under a tree, and cast his glance around hopelessly, lamenting his ruin and reversal of fortune with many cold sighs.

Fate ordained that the leader of the caravan came along and passed by the very spot where Bahram was sitting. He said to Bahram, "O youth, who are you and whence have you come? What is your mission, and to what land are you traveling?" Bahram replied, "I am a merchant. My ship capsized in the tempest and I caught hold of a plank. I had another few days remaining to my life so that piece of wood drifted ashore. I await the decree of fate now to see what new hand it will deal me. I wonder what adventure will befall me next!" The leader of the caravan said to him, "Dear friend, I do not lack for riches. Indeed you can say that this slave of God is quite wealthy and prosperous. What I do not have, however, is a son and heir. For that reason nothing can buy me happiness. I hereby declare you my son and give you the status of my heir. Come along with me and you shall never again see a hard day, for the good God has given me a bounty to which even the treasure hordes and fortunes of kings cannot compare!"

Bahram went along with the man, who had him bathed and clothed in a sumptuous manner, and manifested all the signs of his wealth and magnificence to him. He then gave Bahram control of the entire trade. Bahram asked the merchant, "Where will you travel from here, and in which city will you next stop?" The man answered, "I will travel next to the land of Mando, which is the seat of governance of Malik Shuaib and is close to the land of Ceylon. That is where I will camp next to recover from the fatigue of the journey!" Bahram felt glad to hear this and he thought that if fortune continued to smile upon him, God willing, he would soon have occasion to meet Landhoor again.

After several days the caravan arrived in the land of Mando, and lodged at the caravansary. The next day the merchant visited the baths with Bahram and arranged for him to be attended to lavishly. Then they changed and went into the bazaar and saw a sight to behold: a bow and a purse of gold coins lying on a small table on an octagonal platform. Bahram asked the guards about the bow and the purse of gold. He demanded to know the reason and significance of why they were kept there. They answered, "This bow belongs to the commander in chief of our king's forces, Zaigham, who is a courageous man and unsurpassed in virtue. Because he finds himself unable to draw the bow and pull the arrow across the bowstring, he has had it placed here with a purse of red gold coins, and has declared that anyone who is able to draw the bow can claim the purse of gold coins. Being the owner of this purse he is free to do with it as he pleases and bestow it on anyone he chooses!"

Bahram said to a guard, "I would like to draw the bow if you permit, and display my strength!" The guard said, "A mere cotton merchant? What do you know about drawing bows and such?" Bahram retorted, "My friend, strength is a gift from God, and whether one is a cotton merchant, a mighty warrior, or a lowly man, nobody has a monopoly over God's bounty. Thus you spoke idly!"

While Bahram was thus engaged in his argument with the guards, Naik Rai, Malik Shuaib's vizier, happened to pass by with his entourage. Bahram was struck with the great pomp and glory with which he arrived. His scouts brought Naik Rai the news of what had passed between Bahram and the guards, informing him of all particulars. Then Naik Rai himself went into the crowd and, addressing Bahram, said, "O youth, do you wish to draw this bow?" Bahram answered, "Try me and test my strength, for one does not need the confirmation of a mirror to see what is obvious!" Naik Rai said, "Very well then, we would also like to see this. Go ahead and draw it!" Reciting "In the Name of Allah!" Bahram picked up the bow and, securing the bow's grip in his hand, pulled the bowstring to his ear and flexed it seven times. Upon this marvelous show of strength, everyone there cried out "Bravo" and "Well done" and praised him greatly. Everyone, that is, except for Zaigham's servants, who took offense at Bahram's success with the bow, and all of them felt great humiliation. They began barking inanities at him and shouting nonsense in the manner of lunatics. Irritated, Bahram clouted some of them on their heads, causing their brains to flow from their noses. Naik Rai warned the rest and had them sent away. Then he took Bahram to his house.

Zaigham soon learned that a merchant had bent his bow and taken the purse of gold coins along with the lives of several of his servants, but despite that Naik Rai felt no regard for Zaigham. Instead, he took the merchant to his house, showing much favor to the transgressor. In a towering rage, Zaigham armed himself and headed for Naik Rai's house, searching for Bahram with bloodthirsty eyes. When he found Bahram, he uttered these words with great harshness: "O vendor of cheap stuff, you found the strength and gained the impudence to draw my bow and brain my men and kill them with your hand!" Declaring this, he drew his dagger and rushed at Bahram to kill him and avenge the blood of his men. But Bahram caught his arm and wrested the dagger from his hand, and then hit him on the head with such force that his brain flowed out of his nose and the avis of his soul found a perch in Hell along with his men. When this news reached Malik Shuaib, he immediately sent for his vizier Naik Rai along with Bahram and gave orders that they should present themselves before him. When Bahram presented himself, the king said to him acidly, "O contumacious man, how dare you kill my commander in chief and my chief warrior, Zaigham?" Bahram answered, "O King, you must not keep such pusillanimous men as the commanders of your forces who depart from the world and give up their lives with just one blow of the fist!"

Bahram's retort went straight to the king's heart and pleased him immensely. Then and there he offered the robe and office of commander in chief to Bahram, and appointed him to that august post, giving him Zaigham's throne to sit on. Bahram then drew that bow a few times before the king and then ordered it to be placed on the same platform as before with a purse of gold, with the instructions that he should be notified if anyone was able to draw the bow. The king was persuaded of Bahram's humanity by that gesture, and he was convinced of Bahram's rectitude. That very day he married his daughter to Bahram and made lavish arrangements for the nuptials as were demanded by the occasion. He also said to him, "I make you the lord of one half of my kingdom, and make you its absolute ruler. For two quarters of the day you may sit on the throne and administer the law and redress the needs of your subjects. For the other two quarters I shall rule, and administer all affairs."

Now hear a few words regarding Landhoor, the Khusrau of India, and hear an account of that king of lofty eminence who arrived in Ceylon and dropped his ships' anchors. Along with his army he came ashore and suggested a scenic place for camp, and they bivouacked there. After resting there for a few days he mustered his army and gave orders to every individual as he saw fit. Then he headed for the fort of Sabir and Sabur and everyone among the nobility and laity came to know that Landhoor had returned.

Of the Arrival of King Landhoor bin Saadan, the Khusrau of India, at the Gates of the Fort of Sabir and Sabur

The narrator relates that Jaipur had been left behind by Landhoor on the throne of India when he went to Ctesiphon with the Sahibqiran, and had been named his vice-regent in charge of all administration and defenses. He had been forced to seek refuge in a fortress after suffering reverses at the hands of Malik Siraj, Firoz Turk, Ajrook Khwarzami, and Muhlil Sagsar. All those imprisoned in the fort had become distressed and weary of their lives on account of the siege. In the end, the army said to Jaipur, "How long will you resist the enemy keeping us fortified here, and put up with the miserable fate imposed on us by those fiends? If you were to order us, we would march out to encounter the enemy and either kill them or die fighting so that our suffering might end in some manner." Jaipur said to them, "I shall do as you ask. Truth be told, it is not the way of the brave to lie hiding in dark corners!" That very instant he sent a messenger to the enemy camp to say that if they were to remove their armies from the gates of his fort, his army would then arrange itself for a final encounter.

The joy of Malik Siraj and his accomplices knew no bounds upon receiving this message. They assented to the request and pulled their armies away from the fort. They had the drums of war sounded in their camp, ordering the army and the whole camp to prepare for battle. Drums of war were also sounded inside the fort the whole night, where all preparations were made for war. In the morning, the two armies emerged from their respective encampments, and the two forces arrayed against each other.

Before anyone else, Muhlil Sagsar urged his rhinoceros forward into the arena to do battle and slaughter the foe. From the other camp Jaipur spurred on his mount and steeled his heart to answer the challenge. No one had yet dealt a blow or raised his arms against the adversary when a great dark cloud rose on the horizon that covered the whole expanse of the field by its dust. When the wind blew away the dust and parted its veil, seventy gleaming standards emerged over a force of seventy thousand, insignias before whose brilliance and refulgence the likes of the sun and moon would have faded. Marching ahead of those standards was Landhoor on his she-elephant Maimoona, carrying in his hands the pulverizer of foes, the younger brother to the Angel of Death—to wit, his massive mace engraved with the inscription "Everyone and all will die!"—the sight of which weapon instilled such terror in its beholders that they very nearly lost consciousness.

When Landhoor entered the arena, he approached Muhlil Sagsar and bellowed "God is Great!" and said to him, "O man on the brink of doom, I am your Angel of Death! Come deal me the blow you have and drink at once the cup of death from my hand." At this, Muhlil brought his mace down on Landhoor's head. The Khusrau took the blow on his mace and then retorted with such a powerful blow of his own that his adversary never again raised his head, for Muhlil Sagsar's bones were powdered and ground to dust. Upon witnessing this scene, Muhlil's camp changed its mood, their hopes crushed and their vigor drained. When Landhoor cried out, "Is there anyone who will skirmish with me, and come forth against me and show his courage?" not a single soldier replied or took up the challenge. Landhoor then goaded his she-elephant Maimoona to charge the enemy's forces, and the entire army of the foe forgot its skittishness. The army of India also took up the reins, spurred on their horses, and charged. Many an infidel lost his life in the attack and paid with his poor existence for his superiors' poor designs. Those who survived the slaughter thought it best to escape with their lives. The armies of India secured great quantities of the booty the foe had left behind in its retreat, and everyone reckoned himself as rich as a Qaroon. Each one of them became wealthy men of means. The Khusrau of India entered the fort greatly contented, with the tablet of his heart cleansed of all his troubles and sorrows. He ordered royal revelries to be held and a festive, carousing assembly was arranged.

Meanwhile, Malik Siraj and Ajrook Khwarzami sent for two brothers who were renowned warriors to aid them, each of whom alone could take on a thousand troops by himself. They arrived amidst great pomp and fanfare and making mighty claims of valor. One of them was Haras Fil-Dandan, who was extremely proud of his strength and puissance; the other was Maghlub Fil-Zor, who was the source of great terror for many intrepid men. The enemy assembled again with three hundred thousand men and besieged the fort of the Indians, and their column-smashing warriors again gathered in clusters. They struck the drums of war at once and produced a noise more awful than the clamor of doomsday. Landhoor also ordered the drums of war to be beaten and instructed his forces to prepare for skirmishing and battle.

In the morning the opposing armies advanced from opposite directions. Before anybody else, Haras Fil-Dandan stepped into the arena and sought combat. Landhoor approached him on his she-elephant Maimoona and bravely issued this challenge: "O warrior, give me a blow and show me what art you possess in combat!" Haras Fil-Dandan unsheathed his sword from its saddle scabbard, a weapon that had a striking impact of four hundred *maunds*. He brought this down on Landhoor's head, dealing a blow to that lion with great force. But Landhoor withstood it with his prodigious strength and thwarted the blow through agile maneuvering. Then Landhoor drew his sword glittering like a diamond from his scabbard and called out, "Be warned now, O coward! Be alert! Do not say later that I attacked you unawares, not giving you warning before launching my attack!" With this declaration, Landhoor brought down his glittering sword on his adversary's head. It was a blow more potent than a hundred powerful blows. Although Haras Fil-Dandan tried to shield his head to thwart it, neither the sword nor the blow could be foiled or warded off. Cutting through his shield as if it were a ball of cheese, Landhoor's sword did not stop there but slashed straight through his breast, killing him in no time at all. Haras Fil-Dandan thus died a dog's death, dispatched to the land of the dead by Landhoor's sword.

When Maghlub Fil-Zor saw his brother lying dead, blood rushed to his eyes and, maddened by fraternal grief and roiling in pain, he raced on his rhinoceros to confront Landhoor and said to him, "You committed a terrible deed by killing my brother. Now I shall not spare your life, and you will witness how I shall crush your bones!" Landhoor replied, "Grieve not your parting with your brother, for I shall soon send you to him, and without doubt you shall be reunited in the pit of Hell. Now give me the greatest blow that you have!" Maghlub Fil-Zor packed his utmost might in the blow he dealt Landhoor, but the Khusrau foiled it and, in turn, gave him a blow on his back with the bloodied sword, which came out shining from the other side. Maghlub was cut down like a fresh cucumber and fell to the ground, split in two.

Upon seeing Maghlub lose his life as well, Malik Siraj and Ajrook Khwarzami took rein and attacked with their three-hundred-thousand-strong army, unleashing a most ferocious assault. The armies of India also spurred their mounts forward and encountered the foe. The battle carried on for a full six hours. However, after witnessing a great portion of their army fall prey to the crocodile of death[50]—and seeing the armies of India prevailing—the infidels decided that it would be unwise to fight any longer. With heavy hearts they sounded the drums to announce the cessation of hostilities for the day and returned to their encampment crying and bleeding, utterly humiliated by their defeat. King Landhoor entered his court regaled by the sound of festive music, with every soldier in his army drunk on the heady wine of victory.

When Malik Siraj entered his harem looking the very picture of grief and sorrow, his wife and daughter inquired the reason for his woe and distress and were much dismayed by his dolor. He told them, "It appears that Landhoor's hand will snuff out my life. There is no commander who finds himself up to the challenge of fighting him. I do not have words to describe how he routed us in the very first battle or to explain the valor he showed. Although we were four kings striving against him as one, we could not turn the tide of his onslaught, and were soundly defeated. Our entire army was thrown into disarray and the whole camp cowered before him. In the second skirmish he killed two such renowned warriors that the army completely lost heart, and all our hopes for victory perished. To no avail I fought a pitched battle with three hundred thousand troops, and tried to raise the spirits of my forces: I had nothing to show for all my efforts. More than a hundred thousand of my men were slaughtered, and yet our desired end was not achieved and reverses piled upon us from all fronts. Now I see no recourse left to me but to commit suicide, and take poison!"

His daughter was much grieved at his words and said, "If you allow me, I can bring Landhoor prisoner to you, and show you my talent!" Siraj asked her, "How would you be able to undertake this mission and carry out this momentous task?" She replied, "To see to this is my responsibility. I only seek your permission. Then you may see how I bring it to fruition!" He said, "A blind man needs aught but seeing eyes! I would like nothing better. You have my permission to make the preparations!" That artful vixen had a most sumptuous pavilion erected next to a pasture, and then adorning her person with such cosmetics, jewelry, and lavish costumes that she became the envy of *peris* in beauty, she entered that pavilion in the company of four hundred maidens as beautiful and comely as the moon, and arranged such enticing entertainments that anyone who beheld them was struck with wonder. She organized an assembly of song and music, endowing the celebrations and carousals with a most delightful air.

When King Landhoor saw that the enemy had retired in the face of defeat to nurse its broken heart in the recesses of grief, he decided that until the foe sounded the drums of war and descended into the arena, he need not waste his time but instead should seek some diversion in the beauty of the forest and occupy himself with hunting. He equipped himself with the necessary accessories and headed out to the meadow.

There Landhoor beheld a most magnificent pavilion and saw it thronged by *peri*-like, moonfaced beauties. He asked bystanders whose pavilion it was and the name of its occupant, and whether it was a man or someone of the fair sex. He found out that it was the camp of the daughter of Malik Siraj who was visiting there to amuse herself in miscellaneous diversions. Desirous of catching a glimpse of her, Landhoor settled himself on a rock near the pavilion of that stone-hearted beauty and remained rooted to the spot. When that vixen caught sight of Landhoor from behind her curtains, she sent him a goblet of wine in the hands of one of her beautiful maids.

Landhoor asked the maid, "Does she know me or at all recognize me?" The maid answered, "Ever since she laid eyes you in the battlefield, she has been enamored of your looks and your beauty, and your love would make her sacrifice a thousand lives given her!" Upon hearing this, Landhoor became even more smitten with love and madly enamored of her.

In the meanwhile, another one of her maids arrived with the auspicious news that her mistress had sent for him, and he should hurry to her presence lest she take the trouble to come to him herself. Landhoor felt he was in seventh heaven, and he happily stepped into her pavilion, where he saw a fourteen-year-old beauty, the envy of the sun in resplendence and the *houris* in beauty, sitting and sipping wine on a throne adorned and decked with jewels. She sat surrounded by several hundred beauties, who sat around her as the stars encircle the moon. These maidens were themselves paragons of beauty, as comely as eglantine and the China rose. Dancers like *peris* and singers gifted with the melodious tones of Prophet Daud were busy dancing and caroling ecstatically, and the whole scene resembled the Court of Indar.[51]

Landhoor was beside himself with joy to see this assembly. He was thrown into ecstasies of rapture and cast eyes full of wonder all around him. The daughter of Malik Siraj seated Landhoor beside her on the throne and further spread her net of deceit. She offered him many goblets of roseate wine with her own her hand, and with every goblet exposed him to her coquetry and flirtatious manner. Landhoor was so badly smitten that he was utterly disarmed by her charm and became completely oblivious of himself. All distinctions of friend and foe became blurred in his mind and, throwing his arms around her neck, he said to her, "O life of Landhoor! Come with me to my court, where a life of great luxury and comfort awaits you." That bawd answered, "It is broad daylight now! If you were to take me with you once night had fallen, I would spend the night with you!" Landhoor agreed to the rendezvous and she pledged her commitment. Forced to take his leave, Landhoor returned to his court much against his will, where he ordered the attendants to decorate his pavilion lavishly, and himself lay engrossed in loving thoughts of her awaiting nightfall. His anxiety grew as the day passed, and in the evening he donned his nocturnal livery and went to call on that vixen. As he had become all nervous and distraught in anticipation of their tryst, she offered him some goblets of drugged wine, which soon made Landhoor comatose, its potion rendering him unconscious.

At first she had a mind to send him to her father all tied up so that her father might take his revenge, but the Transformer of Hearts changed her decision and she did not carry out her plan. Instead, she put Landhoor in a chest and had it thrown into the Dead Sea, which was nearby. Then she went and told her father that she had had his enemy killed and thrown into the sea to avenge his humiliation. That coward was mightily pleased with the young vamp and lavishly praised her and commended her actions. Malik Siraj had the drums of war sounded that very moment and made all preparations for battle on a grand scale. The two armies were arrayed against each other again in the morning. When the army of India did not see King Landhoor and could not find that mighty warrior among their ranks, each man, young and old, lost his heart and became bereft of courage. Malik Siraj fought a pitched battle and martyred many a follower of the True Faith, and urged his army to avenge their defeat on the adversary. Jaipur realized that his army was completely demoralized by Landhoor's absence and it was well-nigh impossible to pull victory from the jaws of defeat. Also noticing that the foe was bent upon earning greater renown and prevailing in the battlefield, he sounded the drums of retreat. He sought refuge in the fort as before and made efforts to find out what had become of Landhoor.

Now hear of what passed with Landhoor. The chest was carried away by water, bobbing up and down at the mercy of the waves. By a stroke of luck, it crossed paths with a merchant's ship coming from Sindh. The sailors hoisted the chest up and sold it unopened to a merchant, who was foolish enough to purchase it on the spot without determining its origin or contents. Later, he opened the lid and found a strapping young man lying there unconscious and still. The merchant felt great pity and compassion toward him and he took Landhoor out from the chest and laid him in a bed. He administered an antidote to him to restore him to consciousness, and thus woke him up. When Landhoor opened his eyes he saw neither the pavilion nor his beloved, and discovered himself lying in a bed aboard a vessel, wrapped up in many clothes. Greatly surprised he asked the merchant, "Who are you and what is this place? How did I come here, and who brought me on this ship?" The man replied, "I am a merchant by trade. I am returning from Sindh bearing merchandise. You were found in a chest floating in the sea. When the sailors retrieved it and I opened it, I found you lying inside. I put you to bed and gave you a drug to bring you back to consciousness. This was all the service I did you. Thank God that you have regained consciousness. We are most pleased to feast our eyes on your visage. Pray give some particulars about yourself, who you are and how you ended up in this manner, and what caused this calamity to befall you."

As Landhoor gave his name and particulars, and informed the merchant of his story, the merchant, who was himself a follower of the True Faith and believer in the True God, dropped down at Landhoor's feet and said, "God willing, I shall conduct you to Ceylon in safety and take all possible care of you!" Landhoor asked him, "Where are you headed now? How long will it be before you shall return?" The merchant replied, "I am heading toward the land of Mando, and will stop there for a few days!"

After several days, the ship arrived in Mando and anchored, and the merchant set up residence in the city with Landhoor. One day, Landhoor went out into the Mando bazaar and happened to pass by the place where Bahram had placed the bow and the purse of gold coins. Landhoor saw a contingent of soldiers standing guard there. He asked them whose bow it was and why it was lying there. They answered, "This bow belongs to Bahram. Whoever is able to draw it may lay claim to the purse of gold and earn great renown!" At the mention of Bahram's name, Landhoor's heart filled with joy, his mind was finally at peace, and he felt mightily glad. But he said to the guards, "The one you call Bahram is my runaway slave who had been missing for a long time. Thank God that I hear his name today and am finally able to trace him." He picked up the bow and flexed it a few times to display his great might. Then he took the purse of gold coins and dispensed them all in charity on the spot, distributing them among the needy and the destitute.

The guards took these tidings to Bahram and gave him a detailed account of all that had happened. Upon hearing that the man had called him his slave, Bahram was enraged, and he ordered several men to hurry without delay and bring the man to him. Those men had traveled only a short distance when they saw Landhoor himself coming toward them. They immediately returned to Bahram and said, "The glory of Your Highness draws the man in question to the court. He is himself headed here." As Bahram left the court and took a few steps, he beheld this scene. He ran and bowed down his head at Landhoor's feet, showing him many tokens of honor and devotion. Landhoor raised him and kissed his forehead, and they embraced. Raptures of joy and ecstasies of affection caused them both to be taken unconscious.

Upon hearing news of this, Malik Shuaib himself came out of his court and beheld their state. He had their faces sprinkled with the perfumes of musk willow and rose water, and after they were restored to their senses and had regained their consciousness, Malik Shuaib asked them about their history. Until that day Bahram had kept his particulars a secret from Malik Shuaib, but he now disclosed his secret and revealed his own and Landhoor's full identities. Upon hearing the name of Landhoor, Malik Shuaib kissed the Khusrau's feet. He took the two men to his court and seated Landhoor on the throne and offered him many tokens of honor and devotion. He himself sat on a chair and gave orders for a regal feast to be arranged and a musical assembly to be prepared without delay. For a whole week Landhoor remained engrossed in festivities, where everything needed to complete a revelry was provided. Later he gathered together an army and all the necessary equipment and, taking Bahram along with him, headed for Ceylon with great pomp and glory.

AN ACCOUNT OF THE EVENTS THAT PASSED WITH THE SAHIBQIRAN, THE CONQUEROR OF THE WORLD, THE QUAKE OF QAF, THE LATTER-DAY SULEIMAN, AMIR HAMZA THE MAGNIFICENT

The narrators of past legends thus continue their tale: When the year neared completion and the days of gestation were over, a girl whose visage was as resplendent as the sun was born from the womb of Aasman Peri, and everyone was greatly taken with her charm and beauty.

The emperor was most pleased at the news of her birth. However, the Sahibqiran was extremely unhappy and apprehensive. Upon learning that the Sahibqiran was displeased by the birth of a daughter and was aggrieved, the emperor conferred the Robe of Suleiman on him and said, "O Amir, it was the will of God that it should be so, and nobody is to blame for this event! It is not an occasion for you to be sad, nor is such emotion warranted by the dictates of reason!"

Abdur Rahman said, "O Sahibqiran, this girl shall prove very fortunate and will overpower all the rebellious *devs* of Qaf. She will earn the title of the Sahibqiran of Qaf, and earn great distinction throughout the length and breadth of the realm of Qaf." Amir's sadness was dispelled upon hearing these words and joy was restored to his heart. The emperor celebrated the birth of his granddaughter for several months and distributed riches, gold, and other items among the destitute, the needy, and the invalids.

One day when the girl was six months old the Sahibqiran said to the emperor, "I have carried out all that you asked me to do. Now pray return me to the realm of Earth and honor your promise to me!" The emperor answered, "O Sahibqiran! Indeed I am most indebted to you. In view of your personal qualities I have no objection in granting you leave to depart, for I have the utmost regard for your happiness, but the fort of Simin, which is to the north of Qaf, has been taken over by two malicious and vicious *devs,* Kharchal and Kharpal, who lead a force of ten thousand *devs.* As that is my ancestral castle, I hope that you will grant me my request and slay them and liberate the fort from their hold before you leave. If not, you have the right to your decision in this matter, and we will be most happy to acquiesce to your pleasure, since we are already greatly in your debt."

Amir replied, "I am bound to obey your wishes. After all, I am truly and veritably your faithful friend. Let us begin in the name of Allah. Pray send for a conveyance and have the preparations made for my departure so that I may set out for the castle of Simin and put an end to the menace of these foul creatures as well!"

The emperor sent for a throne for Amir Hamza and made all the necessary arrangements for his journey. Then Amir seated himself on the throne and took command over ten thousand terrible *devs,* all of whom pledged allegiance to him. The Sahibqiran then set out from there on his new adventure. At a distance of some five *kos* from the castle of Simin, Amir saw a vast field and ordered the *devs* to descend there. He said to them, "It would be best for us to bivouac here as this arena is well suited as a battlefield."

The news of Hamza's arrival reached Kharpal and Kharchal and they also readied themselves for skirmishing and carnage. They arrayed themselves opposite Amir Hamza's camp with a force of twenty thousand *devs.* Amir assembled his fighters and observed two *devs* of most singular appearance and unsightly countenance standing some distance from the enemy ranks. One of them had ears like an ass, and the other had the face and features of that beast. Anyone who set eyes on them marveled with wonder. Amir learned that they were the commanders of the enemy forces, Kharchal and Kharpal in person.

Kharchal was the first to challenge Amir. He entered the arena wielding a box tree and called out, "Where is the slayer of Ifrit and the murderer of Ahriman? Come forward and demonstrate your valor, so that I may kill you with just one blow and avenge the death of the *devs* of Qaf!" Amir stepped out to meet him and said, "Deal me your blow! Come near me and show me how courageous you are!" Kharchal laughed uproariously and replied, "Look at your size! *You* ask me to deal you a blow? Surely I would not ruin my reputation by attacking a puny creature like yourself!"

Amir replied, "It was with this small stature that I prevailed over those of mighty stature, like Ahriman and Ifrit, and sent them into the sleep of death. If you do not first deal me a blow, your heart's desire will remain buried in it, and with that terrible yearning you would depart toward your abode in Hell, for I am your Angel of Death. Your death is as truly written on my sword as it is in your destiny!"

Kharchal was infuriated by this, and dealt a blow to the Sahibqiran with the trunk of the box tree. Amir foiled this blow and countered with a thrust of the Aqrab-e Suleimani that hit with such finesse that the *dev* and the box tree fell in four pieces to the ground, and Kharchal stretched himself on the bed of death.

When Kharpal saw his brother lying dead, he rushed at Amir and struck him with his *zangala.* Amir foiled his attack and, securing a hold on him by his cummerbund, forced the *dev* to the ground. Amir Hamza then drew his dagger with the intention to send Kharpal to the same land where he had earlier dispatched his brother when Kharpal cried out, "If you spare my life, I will pledge obedience to you for the rest of my life and will never act contrary to your wishes!" The Sahibqiran then stood up from the *dev*'s chest once he had secured Kharpal's word, and asked him, "O Kharpal, would you carry me back to Earth and take that duty upon yourself?" The *dev* answered, "I would do so with the greatest pleasure, but pray rest a while in the castle of Simin and take relief from your arduous journey here. Then I will carry you wherever you command me to, and will transport you where you wish!"

Amir dispatched four *devs* to Shahpal to convey news of the victory to him, and himself sojourned in the fortress of Simin, where he lodged himself with great comfort and made himself entirely at home.

Simin had a beautiful garden that blew with gales of bracing wind. Amir dived in its lake, bathing and cleansing his body well, and also washed in its water the bloodied blade of his sword, cleaning it of all taint of death. Thereafter Amir went into the summerhouse and sat on its throne, where he partook of and relished the strange fruits of that orchard. As he felt himself slipping into a deep calm, he stretched himself out on the throne to take a nap and was soon lost to sleep.

When Kharpal saw that deep slumber had wrapped the Sahibqiran in its arms, he decided that it would prove an easy task to kill him. He picked up the Aqrab-e Suleimani from Amir's side and unsheathed it and dealt Amir a blow. It is proverbial that no one can kill the man who is in the protection of God: The sword struck instead one of the room's arches and, by chance, Amir also turned over at the same moment. Thinking that the Sahibqiran had awakened, Kharpal sheathed the sword and fled in terror. The circumstances appeared ominous to the Sahibqiran when he awoke. Not a single soul was around, nor could he find the Aqrab-e Suleimani anywhere. He became most anxious. He assembled the *devs* and said, "Where is Kharpal, that ass of the Dajjal?"[52] They answered, "He is in the Bayaban-e Mina, but no other *dev* can gain admittance there to find the way to him." However much Amir pleaded with the *devs* to carry him to the Bayaban-e Mina and guide him once there, none of them would consent or even give him the directions. Amir therefore gave them leave to depart and set out on foot by himself, pinning his hopes on God Almighty in his lonesome journey.

On the seventh day he arrived in the Bayaban-e Mina, where he beheld a mountain of a height that was impossible to surmount by human endeavor. The rocks of that mountain were of a lustrous topaz color that put to shame the luminance of the sun. The flora that grew on it seemed enameled on the slopes, as if the Incomparable Maker by His Insuperable Art had given the mountain a glaze of verdant coloration. At the foot of the mountain lay another pleasant vista, where for miles on end spread fields of saffron. In the middle of the fields there was a crystalline platform of great luminosity on which Kharpal lay in deep slumber like his fortune, and the Aqrab-e Suleimani lay beside him like an omen of death. First the Sahibqiran secured the Aqrab-e Suleimani, taking it into his possession without delay. Then Amir bellowed so mightily that the whole mountain shook. Kharpal awoke to this and began to tremble like an aspen leaf. He attempted to escape the Sahibqiran, but Amir stepped forward and dealt a blow of the Aqrab-e Suleimani to his waist. Kharpal fell to the ground in two like a withered poplar. His life fled and his soul departed from him. After killing him, the Sahibqiran rested on the same platform using his sword as support and sat there in calm and tranquility having dispatched that villain to Hell.

In the meanwhile, the *devs* returned to Shahpal and narrated to him all the events that they had witnessed. After they had given him a detailed account of all that had passed, Shahpal became troubled and said to Khvaja Abdur Rahman, "We must hastily get news of the Sahibqiran and hurry to his aid, as the *devs* who accompanied him have returned with adverse news!" Khvaja mounted a throne and set out in search of Amir Hamza. After several days' journey, he finally arrived in the Bayaban-e Mina. There he beheld the corpse of Kharpal lying in two pieces with not a single fiber connecting the two, so precise was the blow dealt him by the Sahibqiran. Abdur Rahman saluted Amir, kissed his hand and arm, and conveyed to him the emperor's message. Then Abdur Rahman returned to Gulistan-e Irum with Amir Hamza seated beside him on the throne and presented him to the emperor with great deference and decorum. The emperor embraced the Sahibqiran, showed him many tokens of kindness, and said, "Let six months pass and then I shall certainly send you back to the realm of Earth, and see you off with great ceremony." Amir returned to his chamber and sat there counting the days, exercising great equanimity in the face of the emperor's wishes while trying to restrain his yearning to return to his world.

OF THE NOTORIOUS KHVAJA AMAR, THE PRINCE OF AYYARS, AND OF THE PRINCES HURMUZ AND FARAMURZ

Artful storytellers and crafty narrators thus record the account of these men: When the fort of Nestan also ran out of provisions, Amar became anxious to use some artifice to procure rations for his camp. He asked Quful Nestani, "Is there another fort close by where I can seek refuge from the hands of these infidels and make some arrangement to save the lives of those in my camp?" Quful Nestani replied, "At a distance of twelve *farsangs* from here is a fort called Rahtas Gadh whose citizens lead their lives without fear of any foe. It is a well-fortified and impregnable castle and in my opinion there are not too many castles on the face of Earth that could match its defenses. It would be an idle fancy and mere wishful thinking to imagine that the fort could be taken by force. Two men rule over it: One of them is called Tahmuras Shah, and the other is known as Sabit Shah. Both men are renowned for their magnificence and grandeur."

Amar said to Muqbil Vafadar, "Be watchful of our fort's defenses while I think of some scheme to capture the fort of Rahtas Gadh, and work out some plan to secure its control." Amar changed from his royal robe to the *ayyar*'s attire and, sporting his weapons, set out from his fort speeding like the wind's charge. In a few hours, he arrived at Rahtas Gadh. However, despite making several rounds of the fortifications, he saw no means to gain entrance and no path that led inside. Foiled in his initial plan, he sat down dejected on a mound of earth in front of a tree, trying to think of some other way to gain admittance and worm his way inside. After an hour he saw a grass cutter emerge from the fort riding a mule, with his sickle and net tied around his waist.

Amar disguised himself as a saintly man and followed the grass cutter without addressing him or divulging to him what he had in mind. When that man dismounted after some miles and began cutting grass, Amar called out *"Ishq-Allah!"*[53] from behind him, and then was silent. The man returned his salutation and then said, "Reverend sir, whence have you come, and what errand has made you take the hardships of journey upon yourself?" Amar answered, "You have no business to ask that of us! We find pleasure in our hardships. We go where the one God instructs us to, and convey His message to the one He has chosen! Indeed you have become His favored one, since I was ordered to visit you. Now that I am in your presence, consider all your wishes answered!" Amar produced two dates from his sack and offered the fresh and succulent fruit to the grass cutter and said, "Eat these after reciting God's name, and relish their taste!" That simpleton took the dates from Amar's hand and ate them. Hardly any time had passed before the dates worked their effect and the grass cutter became comatose. Amar blew the drug into his nose as well so that he would not regain consciousness for the next three or four days and would lie there without stirring. Then Amar hid the man in the grass and, after disposing of him in this manner, disguised himself as the grass cutter. He tied his net and sickle around his waist and, after mounting the mule, headed for the fort.

Upon reaching its gates, Amar began shaking terribly and panting like someone worn out by fatigue. Recognizing the grass cutter, the gatekeeper opened the portal for him and let him pass without questioning. Amar let the mule have free rein, knowing that it would be familiar with the route and would lead him to the right house. Surely enough, in the quarter where the grass cutters lived, the mule stopped outside a hut. Amar let himself slip down from the mule and, with an exhausted expression on his face, began trembling violently. The grass cutter's wife came out of the hut and said, "Manwa's father, I hope nothing's the matter. What is wrong with you?" Amar answered, "I have come down with the ague!" She carried him into the hut and put him on a mat. She began massaging his arm and legs while worrying at his sorry condition. Amar had a good sleep that day and in the evening asked the woman to make some rice gruel for him. After polishing it off, he set about his business.

After one half of the night had passed, he donned his night livery and slipped out of the hut. He evaded the eyes of the night watchmen and arrived at the foot of the walls of Tahmuras Shah's palace. With the help of his rope he soon gained entrance into the palace. Finally, after all his efforts at dissimulation, he came near to accomplishing his mission when he saw Tahmuras Shah lying asleep on a bed of lapis lazuli. He was all wrapped up in a pair of shawls and a few tapers were burning nearby.

It is a veritable truth that there is not much that separates a man lying dead and a man lying asleep. Amar extinguished all the tapers but one, which he needed to perform his trickery. When Amar lifted the fold of a shawl to uncover Tahmuras Shah's face, the man caught Amar's hand. Amar usually wore a greased glove for such occasions and had taken that precaution for just such eventualities. He pulled out his hand, securing his release, and jumped back ten paces. Tahmuras Shah said to him, "Khvaja Amar, pray have no fear! You may approach me without entertaining the least fear or apprehension. Just now Prophet Ibrahim appeared to me in the realm of dreams to convert me to the True Faith and gave me tidings of all the efforts you have made and news of your arrival. There is no other way that I could have known you were Khvaja Amar otherwise. Think for yourself how anyone could have recognized you in disguise and learned your name without being told it."

Finally Amar drew near again, and Tahmuras Shah embraced him and said, "I shall do as you command so that I may receive blessings from attending to you!" Amar narrated the whole story of his woes to him from beginning to end and told him the facts in great detail. Tahmuras Shah responded, "Please take my word sincerely when I say that you should consider this castle as your own. Bring Mehr-Nigar and your army here, and camp in this place!" The two passed the rest of the night in these discussions. In the morning Tahmuras Shah said to his attendants, "I have converted to the True Faith. The Hand of God guided me in this, and I was ennobled by accepting the True Faith; indeed I received a signal honor. I have given the freedom of the fort to Khvaja Amar and made him the master of this castle in all matters. Take care that when Amar's entourage arrives nobody stops it, and the gates are opened for him without delay, and he is admitted without questioning!"

Amar returned happily to his fort and gave this news to all his companions. Providing conveyances for the princess and others, and with his army in train, Amar headed out by way of a tunnel in the direction of the fort of Rahtas Gadh.

Meanwhile, news of Tahmuras Shah's conversion to the True Faith spread by word of mouth. Upon learning of this from his vizier Shamim, Sabit Shah, Rahtas Gadh's co-ruler, murdered Tahmuras Shah, putting him to the sword for converting to the True Faith. Then Sabit Shah went together with Shamim to the gates of the fort to await Amar's arrival and murder him, too.

Oblivious to these machinations, Amar approached the walls of the fort along with the conveyances carrying the women and took a few steps forward to ask that the gates be opened. As he approached the moat, he was targeted by soldiers in the battlements, and lances and swords were pointed at him. Amar said to the gatekeepers, "My name is Amar and Tahmuras Shah has given me permission to enter the fort and offered me his friendship."

Sabit Shah called out to him, "O cameleer's son! Do you come here with a mind to ply your deceit and snare me, too, in your web of perfidy? Tahmuras Shah fell to your tricks and paid for it with his life and was beheaded. Be warned that you will also receive your just deserts if you take a single step forward, and you too will be dispatched to Hell if you do not pay heed."

Amar was troubled by this trick played on him by the contemptible heavens. He had lost the fort he had and now failed to seek possession of the other one. He said to himself that if Hurmuz and Faramurz were to follow him, all his months of hardships would come to naught and the enemy would make merry. However, he had no choice but to erect Mehr-Nigar's pavilion out in the open and persuade his companions to safeguard her.

The following day the vizier Shamim said to Sabit Shah, "Pray write a letter to Hurmuz and Faramurz informing them of these circumstances, and send them this intelligence. If they were to arrive now with their forces, our combined effort would certainly vanquish our foe. Amar would be killed and his army defeated. As soon as they regain possession of Mehr-Nigar, the princes would be unburdened of their constant anxiety." Sabit Shah greatly admired Shamim's counsel and immediately wrote out a letter and entrusted it to an *ayyar*, Mehtar Sayyad. He ordered him to take the message immediately to Hurmuz and return with his answer.

Mehtar Sayyad was the chief of Tahmuras Shah's *ayyars* and excelled in the accomplishments of trickery above all others. Tahmuras Shah had raised him from a child and trained him in his care as if he were his own son. For this reason Mehtar Sayyad had swallowed tears of blood and kept his rage in check ever since Tahmuras Shah had been murdered. He had not shared his grief with anyone for fear of Sabit Shah. He carried the letter straight to Amar and showed it to him. Upon reading the letter Amar embraced Sayyad and showed him much favor. Amar said, "God willing, I shall kill Sabit Shah. I will make you the ruler of that fort in his place, and bestow his governing powers on you." Then Amar quickly forged a reply from Hurmuz and Faramurz in which he wrote:

> O Sabit Shah! Indeed you did us a great service by sending us such auspicious intelligence. As a result your stature will rise and your honor shall be redoubled in Naushervan's court. Since Amar is a most devious *ayyar* and most deft in artifice, we are sending Katara Kabuli Ayyar to your court so that he may make arrangements to secure the fort until our arrival there, and render you every assistance.

Then forging the letter with the princes' seal, Amar decorated it like a royal communiqué; disguising himself as Katara Kabuli Ayyar, he then went along with Sayyad into the garrison.

Amar handed Sabit Shah the reply letter and also responded to other questions he asked. Sabit Shah turned to Sayyad and said, "Who is this man, why has he come along with you, and why did you bring him here?" Sayyad answered, "He is the commander of the *ayyars* of the princes' court and the head of all *ayyars*. Moreover, he is the nephew of the prince of Kabul. He is called Katara Kabuli, and he commands a high office and great honor!" Sabit Shah embraced Amar and seated him by his side with great honor, and gave a most sumptuous feast for him, treating him like royalty and according him a lavish reception.

When it was night, Amar said to Sabit Shah, "The princes have given me strict injunctions and stern orders to guard the garrison myself. Thus I will now go and station myself at the gate and do sentry duty there for the duration of the night. Tomorrow the princes themselves will arrive with their army!" Amar took Sayyad along and took his position at the gates of the fort. After two watches of the night had passed, all the other guards fell prey to the merciless crocodile of Amar's sword. He flung open the gates and admitted his men, all of whom had girded themselves for slaughter. The denizens of the fort awoke to the cling-clang of swords and saber cuts disfiguring their persons. Those who converted to the True Faith were saved, and those who hesitated were dispatched to Hell.

Amar secured the fortifications and battlements with his men and consolidated control of the garrison. He had Sabit Shah and vizier Shamim hanged and made Mehtar Sayyad the king of the castle, investing him with all the powers of a sovereign lord. Then Amar sent for provisions from all corners of the region, and after stocking them in the fort, sat down with great magnificence to rest with a peaceful mind.

Hurmuz and Faramurz received intelligence from their *ayyars* that the gates of the Nestan fort lay open, with not a single guard to be seen there and not a soul stirring within.

Nobody seemed to know where everyone had gone. It was as if they all had disappeared from the face of the Earth, or Amar had tunneled his way to Rahtas Gadh.

The princes first made a foray into the fort of Nestan and themselves encountered nobody there. Thereafter they returned to their camp and dispatched a communiqué to the emperor and enclosed the following message within:

> It has been eight years since we began wasting our lives in pursuit of Amar, and the exercise has now become a torture for us. Either Your Honor should deign to take direct charge of this mission or else send us someone who can undertake the responsibility and annihilate Amar along with his companions. We have been so completely humbled and frustrated by the antics of this notorious *ayyar* that there are no words left to describe our plight.

They sent the letter to the emperor's court by the agency of Kargas Sasani, ordering him to acquaint the emperor in detail with the situation on the ground, while they themselves headed to Rahtas Gadh with their army to encounter Amar and give him battle. There they found the fort fully decked out like a prancing peacock. It was so well guarded that not even a bird could have found its way inside or entered by any means. Feeling powerless, they laid siege outside the castle and set up camp there to keep an eye on Amar and study the defenses of the fort. In the camp of the infidels everyone took turns sleeping during the day for fear of Amar and kept awake at night to forestall any night raids by him.

One evening Hurmuz, Faramurz, and Bakhtiarak were drinking with their army commanders when the real Katara Kabuli Ayyar, who was making his rounds, happened by their assembly. Bakhtiarak said to Katara, "Why, Katara, Amar is an *ayyar* just like yourself, but while the whole world rings with the acclaim of his deeds and marvels at the cunning subterfuges he invents and the spectacular devices he employs to safeguard himself, you are not even good enough to bring him to us as a prisoner, or employ even a single trick that would land him in your clutches." Katara felt most ashamed and embarrassed by these chastening words and said, "If I do not bring Amar to you as a prisoner today, I shall renounce my name." Katara then headed for the fort. He circled around it but saw no way to enter and no way to sneak inside. There was one tower, however, from which he heard no human voice, and saw no guards there either. He reasoned that perhaps the guards, the watchmen, and the vigils in that tower had all fallen asleep. He threw his rope over the tower and gained the wall and saw that everyone there was indeed in as deep a slumber as their fortunes, drunk on the potent wine of slumber and made oblivious by it. Katara severed the heads of every single one of them and found his way into the royal tower.

At that time Amar had gone into Mehr-Nigar's quarters to offer her words of consolation and dine with her. Katara sneaked beneath Amar's bed and clung to one of its legs. After some time Amar returned from Mehr-Nigar's quarters and lay down on his bed. Since the shades of night had fallen a long time ago, his eyes soon closed and he sank into deep slumber. When Katara heard Amar snoring, he came out from under the bed and, assembling his *ayyar*'s seven-jointed pipe, filled it with ambergris and put it to Amar's nostrils, finally finding his chance to make Amar unconscious. Amar sneezed and fell comatose and immediately lost all sense of his person. Rendered totally helpless, he fell into his enemy's clutches. Katara tied four knots around Amar's neck and, tying his hands and feet together, completely secured his limbs. He wrapped Amar in his *ayyar*'s mantle and, carrying the bundle on his shoulder, headed for the same tower where he had entered the fort and found his way inside. He climbed down from the tower and swam across the moat. He was in seventh heaven to have taken Amar captive by trickery. He placed the bundle before Hurmuz and Faramurz and said, "Here is Amar! Tell me whether or not I deserve your commendation now!"

Hurmuz, Faramurz, Zhopin, and Bakhtiarak did not know how to express their happiness at Katara's success, and were beside themselves with joy. They tossed their headgear into the air and kept shouting "Bravo!" and "Well done!" and they embraced Katara and praised him highly. They conferred a robe of honor upon him and increased him greatly in rank. The blacksmith was sent for and Amar was put in irons so that his every limb was secured with iron clasps. All of them forgot to sleep in their joy, and when toward morning Amar began to return to his senses and found himself bound in chains, he said, "I seek God's refuge from wily Satan! What a terrible nightmare and a horrible state of affairs!"

Hurmuz said to him, "O cameleer's son! This is not a dream, but true wakefulness! This prison is a just reward for your deeds! You raised your rebellious head too high and thousands have come to grief at your hands: Now you shall see what retributive justice is meted out to you, and never will you escape from our power now." Amar replied, "You well know that I am favored by God, and was trained in the occult arts by Ali. I am not used to languishing in captivity and no one has the power to keep me in chains for long. Indeed you are ruining your life's prospects and destroying your chances of a happy and peaceful existence. The moment I find release, I shall chastise every single one of you here, or else I will consider myself to have cheapened the art of trickery, and will renounce my name!" Hurmuz replied, "Do you still nurse hopes of finding release from your captivity and going on living? Who could possibly free you now that you are in our power?" Amar answered, "God Almighty shows me much favor and He is the one who has the titles of Benevolent and Merciful. I am not afraid of captivity such as this nor do I have the least fear of you. You are free to do all that is in your power: Spend all your efforts and show me no mercy, for all I care!"

Hurmuz fell into a rage after Amar's speech and gave him over to the executioner, ordering him to take Amar away and behead him with his inclement sword and relieve his body of the burden of his head.

Of Naqabdar Naranji-Posh's *Ayyar* Securing
Amar's Release from His Captivity

The narrator states that the executioner took Amar along, seated him on a sand platform, and approached him after drawing his sword. When Amar saw that no hope remained of his being saved and that his soul would depart his body for the Future State in the flash of an eye, he recited in his heart the names of God and Prophet Muhammad (praise be unto him!) and said under his breath, "Help me, O Holy Khizr, and come to my aid in my helplessness. If I survive, I promise to say the *fateha* and make an offering of a full five cowries' worth[54] of porridge by the riverside in your name."

When Bakhtiarak saw Amar's lips moving, he said to Hurmuz, "Pray signal the executioner to finish his work and waste not a moment further in killing him so that the sword may set the sun on Amar's life. Otherwise, he will find release before long, and if he survives there is no end to the mischief he would do. Regard him mumbling his incantations. Indeed there is great power in his bidding, and if he is successful he will come to no harm!"

Hurmuz thereupon gave a second command to the executioner. The executioner said to Amar, "You may now eat or drink whatever that you wish as you will lose your life in just a few moments and the Angel of Death is on its way to extract your soul!" Amar replied, "I have had my share of anger and grief and tasted all the pleasures of life. Now I have nothing more to desire. Hasten to do your work and bother me no more with your idle talk!"

Upon receiving a third order, the executioner stepped up to Amar's neck and raised his arm to behead Amar, who sat with a lowered head.

Amar suddenly looked up at the executioner and said, "O friend! Pray kill me with a sharp sword so that my head is severed from my body in just one stroke and my soul is spared the contortions of death. But I wonder how you will be able to do this with a dull and broken sword like yours!" As the executioner paused to look at his sword, Amar found his chance and swung his hands to the ground to land a powerful kick on the executioner's chest. It proved such a fatal kick that the sword dropped from his hands, and the executioner began rolling around in pain on the ground like a tumbler pigeon. He died from the impact of the kick and never rose again. A cry of "Bravo!" rose from all corners. Hurmuz thought that the executioner had killed Amar and his name had finally been erased from the chapter of the living, but Bakhtiarak said to him, "Your Honor, it was Amar who killed the executioner. Indeed, it was the executioner who forfeited his existence."

Hurmuz said, "Indeed he is a vicious *ayyar*, and most sly and intrepid. Even in the mouth of death he took another man along. Regard how he squared accounts with the executioner!" Then Hurmuz sent for another executioner who approached with a drawn sword and raised his arm to deal Amar the stroke of death. Amar's eyes welled up with tears, he lost all hope for living, and his face turned deathly pale from despondency. At that moment, a young *ayyar* clad in the livery of *ayyars* presented himself before Hurmuz, made a humble prostration, and said, "I am in the employ of the king of Turkistan, the great Khan Sultan bin Zal Shamama Jadu. I am the commander of his *ayyars*. Naushervan has sent me here to inform you that the king of Turkistan along with his Turkish army is coming to your aid, and will soon present himself before you." Hurmuz and Faramurz rejoiced greatly and their minds were relieved by the prospect of the arrival of reinforcements. After making his statement, the young *ayyar* looked toward Amar and asked, "Who is the man sitting under the shadow of the sword with his head lowered, despondent and lacking all hope for his life?"

Hurmuz replied: "It is the notorious Amar Ayyar about whom you must have certainly heard a great deal. We were reduced to despair and humiliation at his hands. He constantly tormented us and made us most uneasy and anxious by his machinations. Last night Katara Ayyar, the commander of our *ayyars*, overpowered him and brought him to us, and it is thanks to Katara's subterfuge and cunning that Amar fell into our hands after a long time. Even in his present state he took the life of one executioner, such a powerful kick did he land on his breast. Now we have ordered another executioner to deal him a stroke of the sword and dispatch him to the Future State."

The young *ayyar* replied, "What a simple matter it is indeed to kill him! He is neither armed in any way nor does he have any hope left for life. At the orders of the great Khan I have killed many a rebellious champion the sight of whom alone was enough to strike terror in the hearts of men, and who could single-handedly destroy a thousand-strong force. If you should bid me, I would make his head roll with just one stroke of my sword and show you a sample of my mighty arm and glittering sword!" Hurmuz said, "Very well, then!" He recalled the executioner and sent the young *ayyar* to do his bidding.

The young *ayyar* approached Amar and said to him, "Lower your head and stretch out your neck before me!" Amar answered, "I am already sitting with a lowered head. Approach and deal the blow!" The young *ayyar* replied, "I am not such an errant fool that I will be deceived like the other executioner by approaching you in such a way that if you support yourself on your hands and land a kick on me like you did the other man I would be totally vulnerable and defenseless against it." Amar thought, *This young* ayyar *seems sharp and artful. He is guilefully ingenious. Certainly he will be my death!* Amar's eyes welled up with tears then, and he lost all hope for his life.

Then the young *ayyar* spoke to him in the Greek language and said, "O Khvaja Amar, do not cry! And do not grieve in your heart. I am the *ayyar* of Naqabdar Naranji-Posh and I have come to rescue you. It was with a thousand artifices and machinations that I brought myself here. Now, stretch out your feet so that I may cut your chains and release you from their harsh binds. Then I will mount you on my shoulders and get you out of here. You shall see with what cunning and bravery I will help you escape from this place."

Amar felt as if he had won a second lease on life. He offered many thanks to the young *ayyar* for the favor and stretched out his feet. The *ayyar* dealt a blow that rent asunder the chains on Amar's feet with one stroke. Then carrying Amar on his shoulders, he ran off before anyone could see where he went. A great uproar rose in the Hall of Audience and people rushed in from all sides with drawn swords. With many foot soldiers and troops giving him chase, the *ayyar* lad unsheathed his sword, and anyone to whom he dealt a blow did not raise his head again. Amar, who was seated on his shoulders, started knocking off people's headgear and kicking at anyone who came within his reach. Finally, the *ayyar* lad brought Amar out of the camp of the infidels and freed him from the clutches of his bloodthirsty enemy, and no one was even able to catch the dust he raised in his wake.

When he reached the forest he put Amar down and said, "I will say adieu now! You should head for your fortress and I shall head home. I now take my leave and make my bow!" Amar replied, "Wait a while! I shall come with you and accompany you!" The *ayyar* answered, "I am not such a fool to stand here a moment longer. How would I be able to free myself from you if you found a chance to bind my hands and feet and then demanded to know the Naqabdar's name and particulars?" With those words the *ayyar* left Amar and headed for the forest.

Amar entered his fortress and regained his peace of mind. He saw young and old alike, supplicating tearfully, "O God! Pray return Amar alive to us, and restore him safe and sound!" As their eyes beheld Amar the followers of the True Faith made prostrations of gratitude to God and made good on all the pledges they had made while praying for his safety. Mehr-Nigar had been severely affected by grieving for the loss of Amar. When she set eyes on him again she felt as if a corpse had been resurrected with the breath of life. She broke into ecstasies of joy as if she had suddenly found herself the Empress of the Seven Climes. She sent for Amar and fell on his neck, crying tears of joy. She sent for platters of jewels that very moment and distributed them among the poor and the destitute as a sacrifice for Amar's life. For one whole week festive revelries were held there and everyone was lifted up in transports of pleasure and joy.

Meanwhile, Hurmuz asked Bakhtiarak, "Who was it who deceived us so plainly and made away with Amar?" Bakhtiarak replied, "Verily Amar spoke the truth when he claimed that the chosen of God can neither be killed nor imprisoned. Each time heavenly succor comes to their aid, the Creator of this universe sends them relief, and none may torment them." Upon hearing this speech Hurmuz kept his silence.

Now hear of those inside the fort. When the rations were again about to run out, some men went with Aadi to inform Amar that they had provisions for another couple of days and acquainted him with the state of their stores. Amar said, "Now we must capture another fort, and move elsewhere." Mehtar Sayyad said, "At a distance of five days' journey from here is another fort called Salasal Hisar, which is not only known for the strength of its walls and fortifications, but is also a pleasant place for establishing quarters. The king of that place is Salasal Shah and he is a man of great magnificence and grandeur. If you wish you may take over that fort and use it for our habitation." Amar answered, "Very well, then! Watch over the affairs of this place with alertness while I think of some means and find some way of conquering it." He changed his royal dress for an *ayyar*'s attire and stepped out of the fort. Speeding along with lightning dash and flourish, he arrived near Salasal Hisar after just one day and one night, overcoming the entire length of the journey by dint of his courage and bravery. He discovered that indeed it was an impregnable fort and fully furnished with all amenities. He turned his attention next to finding some way for capturing it and gaining entrance.

After some time had passed Amar beheld a youth some fourteen or fifteen years of age and dressed in royal attire, coming out of the fort. He rode with a majestic mien, carrying a falcon on his wrist. One-hundred-odd troops and as many foot soldiers, musketeers, falconers, hawk masters, mace bearers, soldiers, attendants, messengers, heralds, and high-ranking courtiers rode with him in his entourage, all of whom were matchless in their devotion to their master and adroit in their duties.

Amar got to his feet and followed this entourage, keeping his eyes and ears open and trailing behind foxily, reasoning that the youth must be the prince of the dominion, for which reason all that fanfare accompanied him. When he judged that the prince had ridden out some two *kos* from the fort, Amar dressed himself as an Azad fakir[55] by drawing the perpendicular mark of their tribe on his forehead and putting on the crown of thorns worn by beggars on his head. He appeared before the prince sporting a *seli*[56] and wearing a necklace of crystal and carnelian on his neck. He tied a knot in his waistcloth, carried a forked cane on his shoulder, and held a kerchief, the Rashidiya staff, and a cleaver in his hands. Amar now called out in the manner of the Azads, "*Ishq-Allah Faqir-Allah!* Early this morning I laid eyes on the favored one of God! It seems that my fortunes have turned auspicious, that this fakir has attracted your attention. Would you have a little something for someone who has devoted his life to God, my lord?"

The prince was pleased to find the fakir before him and drew the reins of his mount and asked him, "Whence have you come, my lord, and where are you headed?" Amar answered, "Like the wind from the camel's bowels, I am neither of the Earth nor of the heavens but from a world all its own! This fakir's domicile is beyond existence, having neither address nor abode. Verily, the fakirs have no fixed station in this world. You tell me if the fakirs have a fixed abode. They are here today and tomorrow they are in another land. There is no homeland that they call their own. It would be well-nigh impossible to furnish you with an answer even if were to try. If there were a place I could call my own, I would disclose it to you."

The prince said, "My lord, all that you say is indeed correct, and your discourse is nothing but truth itself. Yet, upon arrival in this world, one needs a place to call his own, even if it is barely the length of two arms and is one's own for just one night." Amar answered, "The fakirs' presence is like the presence of mirages. When do houses ever hold them? For worldly appearances, however, my lords and masters are scattered all over Baghdad, the city that is the image of Heaven on this world."

The prince asked, "What is your good name, my lord?" Amar replied, "Ask me my ignoble name instead: My master gave me the name of Shidai Qalandar,[57] but in truth I am Saudai Qalandar."[58] The prince was pleased by this discourse of the false dervish and said, "My lord, I am desirous that you set foot in my house and stay there a while. You may rest yourself and explore the captivating sights of my land and take pleasure from them." The false fakir replied, "There is no harm in this indeed. The house of fakirs is among people and they sojourn where they deem a place hospitable. But you asked me my name and never gave me yours." The prince answered, "My name is Bahman bin Salasal Shah. I am held in reverence for the dignity bestowed on me by my father's name." Amar said to him, "Do not hold yourself back from proceeding on the hunt. This fakir will await your return on the mound in front of the fortress. I will give myself in your power to do with me as you please."

Bahman immediately returned to the fortress, however, taking Amar along with him. He put him up in his palace, housed him in a luxurious residence, and offered him all manner of courtesies and favors. After consorting with the fakir for a couple of hours, Bahman said, "I shall take your leave for a few moments now. Have no anxieties while I am away. If you need anything to eat or drink, feel free to send for my attendants without ceremony and ask them for anything you wish." The fakir replied, "Very well, take yourself where you may, but do tell me what it is that calls you at this hour. Is it a fit subject for a fakir's ears or not? I would like to hear about it if you see no harm in telling me so that I may also learn the details!"

Bahman replied, "I am in the habit of drinking a few goblets of wine at this hour. You well know that disrupting a habit is the same as killing it. Since drinking before you might be offensive to your holy nature, I am removing myself to fulfill my craving, but will soon return." Amar said, "Dear sir, send for it here and drink in my presence. I, too, shall have a cup or two and take pleasure from the roseate wine. No matter what the state of a person, he must not disregard his Creator and become forgetful of His omnipresence. And to the fakirs wine is like milk: We indulge in it sometimes to give pleasure to our senses."

Bahman sent for the wine and drank a few cups in the company of the fakir, who also became intoxicated. Deep in his cups, the fakir took Prophet Daud's *do-tara* from his *zambil*. He began playing it and singing, regaling the company with the music. It is said that Amar's singing could put life into the dead: His audience sat rapt, deriving the utmost bliss from this performance and heaping praise on him. It so happened that Mansoor Ayyar, who was in Salasal Shah's employ, happened to pass by there in the company of two other *ayyars*. After paying his respects to the prince, he asked him, "Who is this fakir in your court? Whence has he arrived?" When Bahman had answered him in detail, Mansoor asked again, "What is his name and what is the reason of his appearance in your court?" Bahman replied, "He goes by the name of Shidai Qalandar and has no fixed address or abode." Upon hearing this Mansoor pounced on Amar and arrested him. Having caught him in his clutches, he asked his *ayyars* to tie him up well and secure his limbs so that he could not escape. Mansoor's men immediately carried out the orders of their commander, and Amar was incarcerated in no time.

Amar said to Bahman, "My dear man, you treat the fakirs who make the mistake of accepting your hospitality in a most fitting manner. Indeed you are a great host and your sense of justice will earn you great renown." Bahman became unhappy with Mansoor and said to him, "What harm did this fakir do you that you took the liberty of tying him up and inflicting this retribution on him?" Mansoor answered, "My lord, this is the selfsame fakir who has led hundreds, nay, thousands to the pit of penury and has killed countless men by his deceit and chicanery. If you have ever heard the name of Amar Ayyar, then know that he stands before you in the person of this fakir. It is he who has made Emperor Naushervan's life a constant misery and inflicted all manner of harm on him."

In the end, Mansoor took Amar to Salasal Shah's court and pronounced, "My lord, Amar Ayyar is now in your power!" Salasal Shah replied, "Produce him before me without delay!" When Amar was brought into his presence, Salasal Shah said to him, "O Amar, it is said in the praise of your singing ability that it delights and captivates all who hear it. Sing to me and show your prowess, for I have long desired to be your audience. Now that I have you before me, I am doubly keen!" Amar replied, "Much as I wish, I won't be able to perform before you since I cannot play my *do-tara* with my hands tied." Upon that Salasal Shah ordered that Amar's hands be untied. Accompanying himself on the *do-tara*, Amar then sang with such skill that it sent everyone into ecstasies of pleasure. Salasal Shah was greatly pleased and said to Mansoor, "Do not tie his hands again since we do not wish to torment him. Keep him as your prisoner and produce him again tomorrow when I send for him. But make sure not to distress him." Thereupon, Mansoor took Amar away and locked him up in a chamber.

Once locked up, Amar called out, "I am languishing in prison here, O God. I wonder if the armies of the True Faith have suffered any calamities or privations in my absence!" Amar was plagued by these thoughts when, a few hours into the night, Mansoor opened the door of his prison chamber. He led Amar out, fell at his feet, and exclaimed, "Pray forgive me for I was unaware of your stature and did not know your status. Some time ago Prophet Ibrahim converted me to the True Faith in the realm of dreams, and told me that when you arrived here I would be exalted by your esteemed company. He instructed me that I was duty-bound to help you in your mission and follow your commands. Ever since that day I have kept a lookout for your arrival. The reason I took all those excesses and liberties with you was in an effort to research well and make sure that it was you yourself, and not someone else, to whom I was unburdening my heart and declaring my secret. Now I proclaim myself your servant and am at your disposal to do whatever you command me to do, so that I may earn blessings."

Amar embraced Mansoor and said to him, "We must find a way to secure control of this fortress so that the armies of the True Faith can make it their refuge for some days. It will alleviate their hardships and they will find some pleasure in their lives again." Mansoor replied, "In the name of God, let us rise without further ado and capture Salasal Shah and take control of the fortress!" Amar put on his livery of *ayyars* and they both broke into Salasal Shah's bedchamber. After rendering him unconscious, Amar gave him into Mansoor's custody with strict injunctions to keep a close eye on him lest he try to break away from prison, as a precious bird like him might take flight. Then Amar put on the guise of Salasal Shah and slept in his bed as the king.

Come morning, he sent for Bahman and said to him, "My son! Prophet Ibrahim has converted me to the True Faith in the realm of dreams and I would that you too should enter the fold of this faith by renouncing the ways of infidels and joining the nation of believers." That wretch, deserving of beheading, did not accept the proposition, whereupon Amar hanged him. Then he sent for Salasal Shah in his private chamber and told him that he would fare well if he converted to the True Faith. Salasal Shah marveled upon seeing someone of his own appearance sitting on the throne, and when he heard that he was being asked to renounce his faith, the fear that he was about to lose his kingdom changed the complexion of his face. He said to Amar, "I would like you to explain to me fully who you are, the reason why I see you on my throne, and the person who allowed you to infringe thus on my rights?" Amar replied, "I have nothing to say to you except that you would save both your skin and time by accepting belief in the one and only True God who shares His divinity with no one." When he heard Salasal Shah utter a blasphemy, Amar hanged him, too, without delay. Then he left Mansoor as his vice-regent on the throne and asked the nobility and commonality to make offerings to him and proclaimed, "Anyone who does not obey the orders of King Mansoor will die at my hands and will meet the end that his disobedience merits." All those present gave themselves into Mansoor's service and none disobeyed him.

After Amar had laid his enemies low and made his preparations, he said to Mansoor, "You are now the ruler and lord of this fortress. I will come back with the armies of the True Faith and lead them into the fortress. Then and only then will I be able to take rest. During the time that I am gone, buy and store provisions in the fortress." As soon as Amar had departed, Mansoor did as he was told and carried out his orders.

Upon reaching his companions, Amar informed all his commanders of the conquest of the fortress and gave them a full report of his accomplishments. They secured conveyances and moved under the cover of the night, bringing the princess and her whole camp to Salasal's fortress in order to take refuge there. Completing a journey of five days in just two days and two nights, they reached their destination and found peace within the walls of the fortress. As before, Amar set about making it secure and then took charge of the fortress with great fanfare.

On the third day the *ayyars* in the other camp brought news to Hurmuz and Faramurz that Amar had already left camp and was now ensconced in Salasal's fort with the princess and his whole army. Hurmuz was most upset upon receiving this intelligence and sent for a scribe who wrote a message to the emperor, detailing their circumstances, the story of Amar escaping to Salasal Shah's fort, and the many factors responsible for the *ayyar's* success. He dispatched the letter with a fleet messenger, enjoining him to take it expeditiously to the emperor's court.

OF THE RETURN JOURNEY OF THE LORD OF THE AUSPICIOUS PLANETARY CONJUNCTION FROM THE LANDS OF QAF TO THE CONFINES OF EARTH

It has been narrated thus far that after slaying Kharpal and Kharchal, Amir spent another six months in Qaf at the pleading of Emperor Shahpal, obliged to do so because he was powerless to do otherwise. One night he was lying with Aasman Peri on a bejeweled bed in the Pavilion of Suleiman, when Mehr-Nigar appeared in his dreams looking gaunt and withered. Her appearance was as scrawny as a crescent, and all her beauty had been ravaged from grief at their separation. She was wasted like a skeleton and a stream of tears flowed from her eyes. As she cried bitter tears, she accosted him thus: "O Abul-Ala, indeed I must be culpable of some terrible sin, and must have wronged you terribly that you find it fit to burn me in the fire of separation while you yourself take pleasure in the company of *peris.* I suffer a hundred thousand bitter woes that the heavens do not take me and the Earth refuses me, or else my soul would have flown to Heaven and I would have buried myself, releasing me from this horrible existence."

Amir cried out in his sleep and opened his eyes and realized that it was a dream and he was still in Qaf. Sobbing uncontrollably as grief and sorrow overpowered him, he became inconsolable with anguish. Upon hearing Amir's cries, Aasman Peri woke up and asked, "Is all well with you? What terrible grief has gripped your heart that you suffer such pangs and make such heartrending complaints?" Amir replied, "Such as it is, I cannot even begin to tell you my terrible and wretched state. I feel so weary and downtrodden that I wish to end my life with my own hands." Aasman Peri said, "Pray tell me about your sad state of affairs, and share this with me." Amir answered, "O Aasman Peri, I implore you to send me back to the realm of men and use any means possible to grant me this wish. Just now I saw Mehr-Nigar in my dream, who appeared in a most wretched state brought on by the pain and agony of separation from me."

Aasman Peri asked, "O Abul-Ala, how is Mehr-Nigar related to you? I wish to know every detail about her!" Amir replied, "She is my beloved and the daughter of Naushervan, the Emperor of the Seven Climes. There is none who surpasses her in beauty and comeliness, and she is in love with this wretch who has lost his heart to her." Upon hearing this, Aasman Peri said, "So why didn't you plainly admit to me that you were carrying on a love affair elsewhere, and there is someone from the race of humans whom you love as well? Now I understand why you cry for your beloved in this manner, and are willing to throw your life away at the prospect of separation from her. Listen, O Amir, and speak the truth to me: Is she more beautiful than I? Does she really surpass me in allure, charm, beauty, and coquetry that you long for her in my presence, and are willing to scatter your love at her feet?" Amir could not hold back his words, and said, "You cannot be compared with Mehr-Nigar; you cannot even hold a candle to the charm of her maids."

Turning crimson with rage upon hearing these words, Aasman Peri said, "O Hamza, woe to you that you put me below her maids and prefer them over me! I swear that for as long as I live you will never get out of my clutches or find your way back to the world of humans!" As Amir Hamza was already eaten by frustration, he replied, "I will find my way there all the same! And if you become an obstacle, then I shall have to travel upon your dead body." Aasman Peri said, "O Sahibqiran! Do not let the facts that you are the Lord of the Auspicious Planetary Conjunction, the progeny of Prophet Ibrahim, and superior to the race of jinns cause you to entertain any illusions about me. If you are the Sahibqiran and descended from the line of prophets, I also am highborn and come from the line of a mighty prophet, Suleiman. Nor indeed am I any weaker than you. When you think of killing me, know well that I can also kill you."

Amir was most vexed by her words, which sent him into a mad rage. He drew his sword and leapt at Aasman Peri, who also drew her dagger and charged at him. The *perizads* swarmed over them to break up the fight and separated the warring parties. Someone took this news to Emperor Shahpal and informed him of all that had passed. It caused him great distress to hear about it. He rushed to the scene and rebuked his daughter, saying, "O impudent girl! How dare you talk back to your husband and fight with him? Have you no shame before God and His

Prophet? Did you not even think of my displeasure or fear earning notoriety? Go away and remove yourself from my presence." After admonishing his daughter, Shahpal took Amir to his court and said to him, "Pray have some more patience as it is now night. Come morning, I will send you off and say farewell to you."

In the morning, the emperor sent for a throne for Amir, and after equipping him with all necessities, ordered four swift *devs* to take him immediately to the world of humans. When Aasman Peri received the news that the emperor had bidden farewell to Amir Hamza and ordered him to be sent to his world, she took their daughter, Quraisha, into her arms and went to see Amir Hamza so that he might relent upon seeing his daughter's face and cancel his plans. Upon seeing Amir Hamza sitting on the throne ready to depart, Aasman Peri began crying and said, "O Sahibqiran! I can understand if you do not love me, but do you not feel any pity for this girl? Doesn't your heart soften with love upon seeing her face? For God's sake forgive my offense. I shall never fight with you again or commit any such transgression."

Amir replied, "I am not angry with you and I do love the girl, but I must needs return to the land of the humans. As I depart for there, I would like to tell you that I made a promise to my followers that I would return from Qaf in eighteen days. That was the reason why I refused to bring anyone here with me. Many years have passed since then, and they will all be wondering what became of me and whether I am alive or dead. I shall return to you when you invite me, and will come here without hesitation. Indeed, why should you invite me when you can come to see me in the realm of the humans whenever you wish, and also bring Quraisha with you? You can get yourself there in the flash of an eye. I trust you now to the safety of God Almighty!" Amir then ordered the *devs* to carry his throne aloft and set out toward his homeland.

Aasman Peri returned to her quarters and gave herself over to fits of sorrow and grief at Amir's parting. Salasal Perizad, who happened to be visiting Aasman Peri, became sorrowful upon finding her in that state. He asked, "What calamity has sunk you to such depths of unhappiness?" With tears streaming from her eyes, Aasman Peri replied, "Today the emperor sent Hamza back to the world of men, and gave him leave to depart freely. It is my wish that you go to the *devs* and caution them not to carry Hamza to the world of men but to abandon him instead in the Bayaban-e Heyrat. I will show you much favor if you carry out my wishes, and if you refuse I shall not touch food or water again. Should

Hamza ask you the reason for your visit, tell him that you have come to bid farewell to him and that you have come to see him out of the great fondness you feel for him."

Salasal Perizad carried out Aasman Peri's orders and instructed the *devs* as he was told. The *devs* consulted together and concluded that if they went against Aasman Peri's wishes and transgressed her commands, it would be impossible for them to inhabit the lands of Qaf in peace, and their whole race would be maligned and vilified for disobedience. They decided at last to leave Hamza where Aasman Peri had ordered. Having settled on this course of action, they descended with the throne into the Bayaban-e Heyrat and lay down there to rest their backs. When Amir asked why they had alighted there, they replied, "We are hungry and thirsty. We would like to go hunting to satisfy our pangs of hunger, for we will not feel the heaviness of your throne once we have eaten." Amir said, "Very well! Have something to eat and drink, and I will use the time to say my prayers and fulfill my obligations to God." Amir made his ablutions in a nearby river and said his prayers atop a rock.

After he was done he sat down on the throne to wait for the *devs'* return so that they could carry him on his way. But he saw neither hide nor hair of any *dev* after keeping wide awake the whole night. At dawn he said his morning prayers and again continued to wait for the *devs*. When it was broad daylight and there was still no sign of the *devs'* return, Amir reasoned that it must be fear of Aasman Peri that caused them to deceive and abandon him. He decided to submit to fate and go forth on his own on foot. As the saying goes, "Whatever calamity visits the son of Aadam passeth," Amir started from that desolate desert relying solely on the succor of God Almighty.

Around noon he reached another bleak desert where neither grass nor any shrubbery, let alone trees, grew. It was a place to turn even a *dev*'s gall to water. Water itself was nowhere to be found and there was no sign of any life, plant, animal, or human. Wherever he looked, mounds of sand shone like mercury and flames danced on the sand from the blazing sun. A pen's tongue itself would blister and the leafs of a book turn ashen in describing the searing wind that blew over that wasteland in gusts. So ardently did that expanse burn in the scorching sun that it shamed the empyrean[59] and made the desert call out for mercy.

The armor Amir wore on his body became so hot that merely touching it burned his hands, and the tongue uttering its name broke out in blisters. Amir threw his weapons on the ground and relieved himself from their oppressive burden. From the pain of thirst he came very near to dying and the avis of his soul fluttered violently trying to break the confines of his body and fly heavenward to make its nest in the branches of the tree of Tooba.[60] He dug a pit in the sand and pressed his breast against the cool, moist sand underground, affording some comfort to his body and solace to his soul. When that sand became hot, too, he dug even deeper and lay there. Amir had dug under a dune, and it collapsed over him. Amir was buried underneath, making it impossible for him to extricate himself as he was unable to move his limbs.

Meanwhile, one day Emperor Shahpal asked Abdur Rahman, "Tell me how Hamza has fared in his journey. I imagine that when he entered the realm of the humans he would have felt very happy to be reunited with his loved ones." Abdur Rahman set the divining board before him. He drew lots to determine an answer to the emperor's question, and after reckoning every figure, he filled out the sixteen chambers of the geomancer's board. From drawing the horoscope, he determined that Hamza lay buried under the sand. Discovering this state of affairs caused Abdur Rahman great grief. He sighed, then said, "A hundred thousand bitter woes that Hamza's youth and his life were thus squandered for nothing!" Then he turned to the emperor and said, "Once it becomes known that you committed such an unconscionable crime against a person like Hamza, and reduced him to the sorry state he finds himself in, nobody will ever trust your word again. And if things continue in this vein, no one will pledge obedience to you either, since it was he who killed your bloodthirsty foes and delivered you from them, veritably enthroning you anew as emperor."

The emperor sent for the *devs* who had been ordered to carry Amir's throne and angrily asked them, "Where did you take Hamza?" The *devs* replied, "We left him in the Bayaban-e Heyrat as Aasman Peri commanded, for if we had carried him to the world of humans, the princess would have ordered us to be killed or exiled from Qaf. If we had dared to cross her we would have lost both house and home and imperiled our near and dear ones."

This propelled the emperor into a fit of passion and he turned crimson with rage. Sorely grieved, he looked toward Aasman Peri and said, "Indeed you are a most worthless creature! How do you explain yourself?" She replied, "I have no desire to send Hamza to the world of humans. Parting from him even for a moment sends me to the depths of misery. But I will go in search of him now and shall bring him back myself." The emperor replied, "Don't waste your time in this endeavor. Not knowing where to find him you will torment yourself in vain." The emperor prepared to depart and set out on the quest taking his *devs* along. Upon reaching the Bayaban-e Heyrat he ordered the *devs,* jinns, and *peris* to search for Hamza high and low, and to comb the area thoroughly to locate him. He promised to elevate the rank of the one who found him and to present him with wings made of jewels. All of them went in search of Hamza, and at last came upon his arms and armor, which lay scattered on the desert floor. When they carried those weapons to the emperor, he grew greatly distraught and distressed. He again enjoined their group to search for Hamza and leave no stone unturned in the pursuit. They searched everywhere, but returned empty-handed without finding any trace of Hamza. Then Aasman Peri lamented her actions and began weeping, with streams of tears issuing from her eyes.

One *perizad* happened upon the dune where Amir lay buried under mounds of sand. As if it were conspiring to aid Amir's release, by God's will the wind had removed some sand from the dune. The *perizad* saw the glow of the *shabchiragh* jewel in Amir's headgear and signs of his presence underneath the sand. He removed the sand and discovered Amir lying unconscious in a sorry state with his eyes shut and his body drained of all vigor. He called out, "The Quake of Qaf lies here! That worthy creature is buried under the sands of this dune!" The moment these words reached Shahpal's ears, he ran barefoot in his anxiety to the spot. After extricating Amir, he had him carried to his throne and put all kinds of aromatics and smelling salts near him to help him regain consciousness.

After some hours, Amir woke up and found himself lying on the throne in a strange place with Shahpal sitting near him, the picture of sorrow and despair. He gathered his strength and rose and addressed the emperor thus: "What wrong have I done you that you acted in this manner toward me?" Shahpal replied, "O Sahibqiran! I swear by the name of King Suleiman and by your life that these actions were not carried out at my behest. I could never even dream of causing you any injury! You have done me such favors that I can never return, and all of us feel most indebted to you and pledge our service to you. None of these circumstances had anything to do with me. It was all done at the command of my thoughtless daughter, Aasman Peri. It was she who made you suffer thus."

Upon these words Aasman Peri rushed in and threw herself at Amir's feet, and then offered herself as Amir's sacrifice by circling several times around him. Then she said, "O Sahibqiran! Indeed I am the guilty one, and have been clearly in the wrong. Pray forgive me this once, and clear your heart of any ill feelings toward me. Come with me to Shehristan-e Zarrin to rest and enjoy yourself, for you have been through this terrible hardship and have suffered greatly. I promise to send you to the world of men after six months, and will fulfill this promise to you most certainly." Amir answered, "I trust neither your words nor your actions, for I judge you to be perfidious." Aasman Peri swore upon the name of King Suleiman and finally prevailed on Amir to return with her to Shehristan-e Zarrin. Shahpal's armies also camped there for the next six months until Amir recovered and discovered the same vigor in his body as before.

However, the appointed time came and passed, and Amir did not receive leave to return to the world of humans. He again saw Mehr-Nigar in his dreams one night and discovered her in the same anguish and torment as before. She cried continuously and accosted Amir Hamza with these words:

It is a strange tradition among men
That they tend not to remember the one out of sight!

"You promised to return to me after eighteen days. Eighteen years have now passed and I can no longer bear separation from you, for my sorrowful heart will burst and kill me certainly. In the name of God, pray return soon and do not delay this journey further, or else you will not meet me again in this life, and you will sorely regret it if this comes to pass."

The Sahibqiran started in his dream and when he opened his eyes he saw neither Mehr-Nigar nor her palace. He saw that he was still languishing in Qaf, in a state of bleak despair and hopelessness. He began to weep and cold sighs issued from his lips.

Aasman Peri opened her eyes and saw Amir inconsolable with despair crying bitter tears of helplessness. She got up and wiped the tears from his face and said, "Is everything all right? What has caused you such grief at this hour? What has made you so listless and sunk you into the depths of sorrow?" Amir replied, "It is nothing! All is well! It is in the temperament of humankind to become doleful sometimes." Although Aasman Peri tried all kinds of pretexts and subterfuge to discover the cause of his sadness and tears, and wished to learn why he looked so dejected and downhearted, Amir kept absolutely silent, drenching kerchief after kerchief with his tears and weeping without cease.

When the emperor came out of his bedchamber, Amir made salutations to him, and after performing all the acts of obeisance, said to him, "Your promise to me is due to be honored! Grant me leave now to depart, and allow me to say farewell to you!" The emperor immediately consented and provided a throne for Amir, ordering four *devs* to transport him to the world of humans with comfort and bring back a receipt from him of his arrival at his destination, duly witnessed and sealed. Upon receiving their orders, the *devs* departed carrying the throne on their shoulders. Aasman Peri abandoned herself again to the same state of lamentation and grief and presented the same signs of suffering as before.

She told Salasal Perizad to do all he must to take a message to the *devs* carrying Amir's throne that if they valued their lives at all, they would carry out her orders and abandon Amir on the enchanted Jazira-e Sargardan, where he might wander around for a few days by himself and have some time to reflect on his fate. She threatened to have the *devs'* wives and children ground in the mill if they did not carry out her commands and to punish every single one of them with an ignominious death.

Salasal spread his wings and flew away. Upon seeing Amir, he made his salutations and greeted him with much humility and reverence. Amir replied, "O Salasal Perizad! I find your arrival here at this moment a bad omen. Do not come near me or show me your face!" He replied, "I came only to say farewell, O Sahibqiran! God knows when you will set foot in Qaf again, or if my destiny will ever favor me again by affording me an opportunity to wait upon you!" Amir replied, "Now we have bid farewell to each other. I say adieu to you now, and ask you to leave. Pray do not let me keep you from attending to your affairs!" Before he returned, Salasal managed to communicate Aasman Peri's message to the *devs* and persuaded them to carry out her wishes.

The *devs* flew the whole day and, come evening, they alighted in the arid plains of Jazira-e Sargardan to carry out Aasman Peri's orders. Amir asked them, "Why did you descend here with the throne in such a wasteland that makes one's heart fill with dread?" They answered, "Now the shades of night have fallen. It is not wise to travel in the night and fly in darkness. Moreover, we must needs eat and rest. We will occupy ourselves with these concerns and depart in the morning." The Sahibqiran replied, "Do not conduct yourself in the manner of your predecessors and act with the perfidy those *devs* showed me!" They answered, "We would not dare to do so, for there is no betrayal in our bones." Upon hearing this, Amir kept his silence. The *devs* set Amir's throne down in that place and themselves departed toward Gulistan-e Irum to hunt.

As before, Amir sat awake on the throne the whole night. When it was morning and the *devs* did not return, Amir reckoned that they, too, had deceived him and returned whence they came. He said to himself, *O Hamza, the emperor of Qaf will never let you go back to the world of humans, and will always dupe you in this manner! You should set out on your own. It is not beyond the scope of possibility and God's unlimited bounty that you will be guided back to the world of humans and your homeland.* Having made up his mind, Amir embarked on the journey. Whenever he became tired, he sat down to rest under some tree for a few hours and then continued on his way, wringing his hands at his hardships and the dissembling of the emperor of Qaf. When it was evening, Amir realized that after traveling the whole day he was still in the same expanse of the very same wilderness where he had been abandoned by the *devs*. Amir was astounded, and it bewildered him that after journeying the entire day and facing the hardships of the passage he arrived at the same point at the end of day where he had set out at its beginning. Amir had no choice but to spend the night there. He wondered at the mysterious ways in which God unfolds the functions of the world and pondered what might have occasioned such a marvel. In the morning he again set out. Even though he took a different direction this time, in the evening he again ended up where the *devs* had left him on the first day. In short, he underwent the same trial for three days. On the fourth day he took a fourth direction and traveled well into the afternoon and even inconvenienced himself with the labor of walking barefoot. When the desert began to burn with heat, the violence of the sun exhausted him and he felt greatly aggravated by his debility. He saw a few green trees in one spot and headed there to lie down to rest his back a while in their shade. Amir saw an octagonal marble platform there from which a cold breeze issued, and anyone who stopped there even for a few seconds would be enlivened and invigorated by it. Amir sat on the platform and rested his back against its columns.

Hardly an hour had passed when a great din was heard from the direction of the forest, from which a most singular creature now appeared. It was a *dev* with the head of a peacock who was as tall as a tower and wielding the trunk of a box tree. His appearance alone was sufficient to turn one's gall to water. Upon arriving before Amir, he said, "O son of man! Woe to the ill will and the hand that sent you here! Now you will not escape with your life, and no power can release you from your impending death!" He swung the tree and brought it down on Amir, delivering a mighty blow. The Sahibqiran answered with a strike from the Aqrab-e Suleimani, which cut the tree trunk in two and also struck the dev but produced not even a scratch on his body. The dev escaped in the blink of an eye, but before long he reappeared in a new array, carrying a dragon in his hands, and calling out, "O human child, beware and prepare for this blow which you shall receive from my hands!" He swung the dragon to bludgeon Amir with it, who cut the dragon in two with one blow of his sword and also dealt the dev a blow as before. That dastard remained unmarked and the blade had the same effect on his skin as a washerwoman's club has on an alligator's hide—he was not harmed by it in the least. Once again the dev ran away from Amir Hamza. When he appeared and attacked a third time, Amir dealt him a mighty blow of his sword, but this time again the blade failed to cut him and the dev felt not a thing. Amir pleaded to Almighty God and his eyes welled up with tears.

Suddenly Prophet Khizr materialized there, having come to assist him. After reciting the Most Great Name, Khizr himself killed the dev, and after ridding Amir of his foe disappeared whence he had come. Amir was greatly pleased by the slaying of that dev, as he was now relieved of a cause of great distress. He sat down on the platform and occupied himself with admiring the expanse and the surrounding sea. All the worries plaguing him were cast away when a cold breeze suddenly picked up and lulled him to sleep; and before long all his grief and sorrow were sent into slumberous exile.

As he lay sleeping, Amir had a dream in which he saw Mehr-Nigar crying, her eyes streaming with endless tears from the pain of separation. Amir let out a cry of grief in his sleep and awoke to the familiar sight of the desolate plains surrounded by tumultuous waters. He thought to himself, *It remains to be seen how God will convey me to my world, and how I will ever be afforded the sight of Mehr-Nigar's face again!* Then it occurred to Amir Hamza that he should trust his fate and follow the path of the river that flowed there to find his way out of that wasteland.

Thus determined, Amir cut down tree branches to make himself a raft, and then he put it in the water. The raft had traversed half the length of the river when suddenly a great current came over the water and sent the raft back to the shore where Amir had embarked. He set off into the river a second time, and again its turbulence drove the raft ashore as before. It is said that Amir put the raft in the water seventy-two times and each time when the raft reached the middle of the river, either a great turbulence or a great storm returned it to the shore where it had begun its journey. Amir spent a whole week trying his luck but was foiled every single time.

Finally Amir was once again on shore and said his prayers in preparation for taking to the water, supplicating with passionate fervor to the Captain of the Ship of the World, praising the Resolver of Crises with great ardor, and beseeching His Almighty Eminence to help him overcome this obstacle and assist him in his distress by conveying his vessel safely through the river. At once Amir was overtaken by sleep, and in a dream he saw a saint dressed in a green robe who said to him, "My son! I am Prophet Nuh, and I am aware of the workings of this river. My lance is implanted in its waters and therefore the river does not allow you to pass over it but stops whatever floats above. Once you have reached the middle of the river, recite the words that I will give you and that lance will come into your possession, and from the power of these words you will prevail over the turbulence." Amir was delighted to hear these tidings in the realm of dreams and kissed Prophet Nuh's feet. When he rose from his sleep and regained wakefulness, he discovered his senses were overwhelmed by the scents of ambergris and musk and his anxiety was addressed from receiving an audience from Prophet Nuh.

Amir again climbed onto the raft after seeking God's assistance for the journey across the river and kept reciting the words disclosed to him by the prophet Nuh, his lips continuously uttering the same words. When he reached the middle of the river, a sudden commotion was produced in the water as if a great turbulence brewed within it, and then a small chest rose from the bottom of the river and floated toward him. The waves brought the chest to the raft, and Amir picked it up and placed it in his raft without the least apprehension. When he opened the chest he found a coiled spear of snake stick[61] tied with a string. He took the spear out of the chest and cut the string whereupon it became straight as flax leaf and assumed the shape of a long spear. Amir was very pleased by this and rowed the raft forward with the lance. Whenever Amir grew hungry he took out the bread-cake that the holy Khizr had given him and sated his hunger pangs. When it was time for prayers, he would tie his raft to the shore and say his prayers, asking the Lord Chancellor of Heaven to make him successful in his quest. He then continued on his way, without resting his back or closing his eyes in sleep. In this manner he passed twenty days and twenty nights.

On the twenty-first day he arrived along a pleasant expanse of field most refreshing to the senses. Amir disembarked and walked inland a little ways. Before he had gone two or three *kos,* he came upon seven great wolves who were the mightiest examples of their species. The largest among them was white and its fur grew well over its feet. It is said that these were the Seven Wolves of Suleiman and they lived off whatever they found in that land. According to tradition, Prophet Suleiman raised them and left them in that expanse with the command that they make it their home. When the wolves saw Amir, they surrounded him on all sides, cordoning him off. The Sahibqiran retreated with his back to a tree, and then unsheathed the Aqrab-e Suleimani and defended himself with the sword whenever a wolf attacked. After he had killed all seven of them and rid himself of their menace, he grew lighthearted again and skinned each of them with his dagger. He said to himself, *I have to journey through Qaf, where their hides will be useful and their possession will prove beneficial to me!* He draped the pelts around his shoulders like ascetics wear their antelope skins and traveled on.

He walked that whole day and slept inside a cavern in a hill that evening. In the morning he again started out, after saying his prayers. It was now summer, and around noon Amir tried to find some escape from the burning sun and went looking for a shade. As luck would have it, he spotted the outer walls of a garden, and this prospect offered him some relief. Amir Hamza headed toward it, but upon reaching the walls he found that the door of the garden was locked. He tried to find some way to enter the garden and get inside its walls, and at last he broke the lock with his dagger and stepped inside without the least fear or apprehension. He found that the garden was most tastefully planted with all kinds of odiferous fruit trees, and a stream flowed through this place where spring reigned supreme. Residences made of gold and silver had been constructed there, and every house was appointed in a most wonderful fashion. It was truly a sight to behold.

Amir entered one of the houses and saw a throne of emerald luxuriously decorated with bolsters and cushions. Amir stepped up and reclined on the throne as if that garden, which was the envy of the Gardens of Irum, had been constructed for him alone and was endowed to him as a gift. Amir reasoned that all these dwellings must be the property of

Prophet Suleiman and had been constructed by the race of jinns, who overran the place after his demise and ruled it as they pleased.

Amir was comfortably and peacefully seated on the throne when a two-headed *dev* named Ra'ad arrived there thundering and roaring. The commotion and tumult he created was the same as if an ensemble of a thousand musicians had suddenly started playing simultaneously. The din penetrated Amir's ears and struck terror in his heart. He dismounted the throne to investigate the cause of that uproar and to see if the Day of Judgment had been declared by the heavens.

Instead, he beheld a two-headed *dev* making noises like thunder and threatening the world thus: "If I lay my hands on the one who opened the door to my garden without my permission, I will squash him and swallow him, and eat him skin and all!" Amir challenged him, calling out, "O rebellious giant, don't give in to such idle talk, for you will not last before me for even a moment. Don't you know that I am the Quake of Qaf, the Latter-day Suleiman, the Slayer of Ahriman and Ifrit the Wretch, and a fearless killer of all *devs* big and small?" Ra'ad the two-headed *dev* answered, "O human born! You destroyed the flower garden that was Qaf and entered my grounds! I have heard that you killed thousands and sent them to their death, but I tell you this: Even if you have a hundred thousand legs, they will not help you get away from this place or escape with you life from my hands!"

Ra'ad swung the steel mace that he carried and brought it down on Amir's head with all his might, but Amir snatched the weapon from his hands with great cunning and dexterity before it could injure him. Now Ra'ad saw that his adversary merited all his notoriety and more, and was as valiant and mighty as his reputation announced. As soon as he realized this, he turned tail and ran, unable to stand his ground, and Amir pursued him and gave him chase. Upon seeing that Amir was fleet-footed and close upon his heels, Ra'ad threw himself into a well that lay in the way, as he could think of nothing else to do in his panic. The Sahibqiran sat on the edge of the well, hoping that sooner or later the two-headed *dev* would be forced to come out. After Amir had spent three full watches in this vigil and Ra'ad had still not come out, Amir grew anxious and tired, and sleep soon overtook him. Then Amar Ayyar appeared to him in a dream and said to him, "O Hamza! You could wait there until the end of time and continue your watch in vain. You will not see him come out of that well until he is sure that you have moved away. Therefore, I will share with you an artifice and teach you a stratagem: Divert the water of the pond that lies close by so that the water begins to fill up the well. Then that wicked *dev* will come out hastily in panic." Amir woke up when the dream ended. He dug a drain from the pond to the well and the water began to fill it up, causing Ra'ad to emerge from the well. The *dev* tried to escape, but Amir leapt forward and dealt him a blow of his sword which sliced Ra'ad like a cucumber, and he fell to the ground in two halves. The flames of Hell immediately engulfed his corpse.

A female *dev* who was a monument to old age arrived there before long. She cried, lamenting the loss of Ra'ad Dev, and said to Amir, "O human child! You have murdered my child who was only three hundred years of age! Indeed you killed without reason my baby who had not even lost his milk teeth! You never feared that someone in his family may survive him? I am here to avenge his death now. Sharara Jadu is my name, and you will find no escape from the flames of my wrath. There is no way now that you can escape from my hands with your life." Sharara Jadu began to call out an incantation whereupon Amir recited the Holy Names for counteracting enchantments, which made Sharara Jadu forget all her magic. Amir stepped forward and struck her with his sword and dispatched that harridan to Hell. Then Amir bathed and said prayers of gratitude to God who had helped him overcome such vicious foes. He decided that since he had to undertake a long journey, he should sleep in that place that day and rest his body. He therefore spent the night there and started out again in the morning.

On the thirteenth day of his travels, his feet became blistered and he was forced to stop. Because his feet were swollen and full of sores he sat down and said to himself, *My destination is still far away. I am tired and blisters have broken out on my feet. It remains to be seen how God will conduct me to my world and permit me to behold my homeland with my eyes.* Not too much time passed when a dust cloud rose on the horizon. When it settled Amir saw a black stallion heading toward him. He had a lovely gait that was pleasant to behold and was fully dressed and saddled. Upon approaching Amir, he came to a standstill. Amir said to himself, *This conveyance has been sent to me by God through some mysterious source. He has taken pity on my sorry state!* Amir got to his feet and mounted the horse, deeply grateful to God for his assistance.

He had hardly seated himself in the saddle than the horse reared like Burraq, shot forward, and then flew away like a *peri*. Amir tried to rein him in, but he did not stop and flew on for three days and three nights without ever breaking for rest. On the fourth day Amir espied the wall of a garden in the distance and his heart found some relief at the sight. His steed entered the garden, where a herd of horses of the same color were grazing. Amir's horse joined them foraging on the grass, which was of a quality superior even to sweet basil and hyacinth. Amir was amazed by the spectacle. When he looked closely he saw a fourteen-year-old girl, whose beauty was the envy of the sun, riding one of the horses. She was armed with a bejeweled staff and herded and guided the horses with great coquetry and coyness. She laughed and cried in turns, manifesting a new humor every instant.

Upon sighting Amir, she said, "O friend, were you exhausted when you saw this horse and found him yours to mount?" Amir replied, "O life of the world, indeed I was so tired that I had no strength left even to keep standing, let alone walk a single step. Upon finding the horse I mounted him, reasoning it was a sign and gift from God. Then this horse took flight and brought me all the way here into this garden. Pray tell me now who you are, and what is this place and its name." She answered, "This is the Tilism-e Shatranj-e Slaimani, and the heavenly intellect that construed it is the reason for the look of wonder I see in your eyes. To this day nobody who has entered it has left it alive. Anyone who has come here has fallen prey to death's lion."

The girl had disclosed this much when her horse carried her away to the other side of the garden and she was unable to say more, having disappeared from Amir's view. When Amir Hamza looked to his right he noticed that Prophet Khizr had appeared to bring him aid. When Amir greeted him, the holy Khizr returned his salutations and said to him, "O Sahibqiran, there's an emerald tablet embedded with great skill in the neck of your mount. Remove it and keep it in your possession. I urge you to act wisely and never act without first consulting the tablet, for it is an enchantment from which one would not find release in a lifetime." Having imparted this advice, the holy Khizr disappeared.

Amir took the tablet from the horse's neck and upon inspecting it found the following written on it:

O Traveler and Voyager to *Tilisms*! God has shown you favor, for you have come into possession of this tablet of enchantment. It is a rare find. When you see the woman who laughs and cries in turn, recite the Most Great Name, draw your bow, and shoot an arrow at her face. Then you will see and experience what unfolds.

Amir shot an arrow at the girl when her mouth opened in laughter. It shot through her face like lightning and came out of the back of her neck. A ball of fire shot from the hole and began burning the horses' manes and tails. All the horses there were burned in the conflagration and were so utterly combusted that no sign remained of their presence. Only the horse on which Amir was mounted survived the blaze and no harm came to the animal.

Amir saw that along with the horses, the garden also disappeared and there rose a tumult of wailing voices that struck the heart with dread and terror. Amir found himself in a vast and desolate desert whose expanse was endless, and whose horrors no other place could match. Amir's horse had traveled just a few paces when Amir saw the boundaries of another garden, even more beautiful and scenic than the first. When Amir entered this garden he was most pleased by what he saw. It was as if he had entered a replica of the garden of Paradise, for verily it was one in spirit with the Garden of Eden. In the middle of the garden stood a great tree, with signs of enchantment written all over it. Each of its branches was as wide as a tree trunk, and the tree itself was of inestimable size and width. All manner of different colored animals were perched on its branches singing in their own manners and talking in their many voices. In the middle of those animals sat a woodpecker wearing a pearl necklace. It was the loveliest bird of its species and had a most captivating voice. When it beheld Amir, it rose five hundred yards in the air along with all the other birds. Surrounded by those birds it wailed in a human voice with such pathos that it would have melted the heart of a stone, for it was a plaintive wail and a heartrending cry such as would rob a heart of all peace. Amir cried upon hearing the lamentations of these birds and his soft and tender heart was affected by them. However—once bitten, twice shy—Amir said to himself, *What if these animals are also made by sorcery and their only use and purpose is to bait me into a trap?*

When Amir consulted the tablet, he found the following written there:

> Be warned and beware! Do not stand under this tree or you will be snared by its enchantments and will never find release from it. These animals are a part of the *tilism*. Recite over your arrow the word inscribed herein and kill the enchanted woodpecker with it, and release its spirit from its body's prison!

Amir drew his bow and rose to his feet. The enchanted woodpecker had just perched to rest before again taking flight and joining other birds. Amir called out, "In the name of Allah!" and shot his arrow, which pierced the woodpecker's breast. The bird began to flutter and a flame darted out of its breast that engulfed in fire the entire garden with all its birds. When all of them had been burned to death, the heaviness was lifted from Amir's heart.

Now becoming aware of more noise and commotion, Amir discovered he was in a different garden where yet another spectacle awaited him. Namely, a frenzied *ghol* of outlandish appearance stood before him holding a golden spade. Upon beholding Amir he said, "O human-born, of black head, white teeth, and frail body, how did you manage to find your way in? Who showed you the way here?" Then the *ghol* rushed forward and attacked Amir with the spade. Amir jumped to one side and then dealt him a blow of his sword, killing the *ghol* who fell to the ground in two pieces. Every piece that fell to the ground became another *ghol*, however, and then Amir was faced with two *ghols*, each mightier and more prodigious than the first. Both of them attacked Amir and surrounded him. In a matter of hours the garden became full of *ghols* that kept multiplying in the same manner. Amir dreaded this growing army of *ghols*, which firmly stood its ground. It was a blessing, however, that none of the *ghols* could inflict an injury on Amir and not a single one of their strikes and blows harmed him.

The *ghols* were nonetheless a sight to behold. They appeared every moment in a new guise to frighten Amir, with their heads embedded in their chests or their arms extended from their torsos like horns. Finally, Amir remembered the tablet he carried and read upon it the following message:

> The *ghols* will not die by sword and your blade will inflict no harm on them. On the forehead of the white *ghol* is a red mole that shines like a carnelian. This *tilism* will be conquered when an arrow hits the mole; and only then will you be rid of their menace.

Amir looked around and discovered that indeed there was a white *ghol* among them with a red mole on his forehead, who presented a strange sight. Amir recited the name of Allah and shot an arrow at the mole. Suddenly, a great clamor arose from all sides, as if the Day of Judgment had broken upon the world. It thundered and hail began to shower from the sky. In a short while, however, all that evil subsided and all the furniture of that *tilism* disappeared from view.

When Amir looked about he saw another dwelling, most magnificent and imposing, and found a most refreshing and invigorating garden that instantly captivated his heart. He saw that in the center of the garden was a well full of water that burbled with small waves. At the foot of the well a luxurious throne was set, where a *dev* sat propped up on pillows. A woman lay prostrated in front of him with her hands and feet tied, and a jinn sat atop her wielding a dagger, keeping her pinned down with great force. Upon seeing Amir, the woman cried out and supplicated very humbly, "O Destroyer of the *Tilisms,* pray release me from his power and secure my freedom from the hands of this tyrant!" The moment she let out this cry, the jinn cut off her head and threw it into the *dev*'s lap, who threw it into the well. In this manner the woman was dispatched to her fate by the *devs.* But then the head bounced out of the well and again connected itself to the woman's body, and she pleaded with Hamza as before. Again the jinn severed her head and threw it into the *dev*'s lap, who in his turn threw it into the well from which it bounced out and again became attached to the woman's body. Amir wondered at this marvel and said to himself, *Verily, this is a sight to behold and an occurrence most unique that unfolds itself thus!* When he looked at the tablet, it read:

> When the jinn throws the woman's severed head into the *dev*'s lap, recite the Most Great Name and shoot an arrow into his gullet, and destroy all the wizardry in this place.

Amir fired the arrow at the *dev*'s throat and carried out the tablet's instructions. A great commotion broke out the moment the *dev* died and a tremor like the tremors of the Day of Judgment shook the ground.

When it subsided, Amir beheld that he was surrounded by a desert and a boundless wasteland. He went forward and before long arrived at a marvelously constructed fortress made of jet stone. He approached one of its gates and found it ajar, with neither watchman nor gatekeeper standing on duty. As he could hear noises coming from within its walls, he reasoned that the fortress was populated, and when Amir entered the fortress he found it indeed fully inhabited. Shops were open with shopkeepers in attendance on both sides of the marketplace, but all of them were stock-still and there was no movement at all in their limbs. Amir addressed them and tried to engage them in conversation, but none of them so much as moved his lips or offered a single word in reply to him. From the marketplace, Amir turned toward the Hall of Announcements and found it also crowded, but as before the throngs stood motionless. A little farther along, Amir found luxurious residences, and saw heralds, attendants, mace bearers, guards, and servants at their stations—all in a similar state of stillness. No one Amir asked about the owner of the castle made reply, nor did anyone say a word to him.

A few steps ahead was the court, which contained a jewel-studded chamber in which Amir found a king seated in full regalia, enthroned on his seat encrusted with jewels, surrounded by his courtiers and circled by warriors at their respective stations. Amir approached the king and greeted him and made salutation, but when he did not receive an answer, he became irate and testily asked, "Is it your custom to disregard a person's salutations and disdain even a reply by way of common courtesy?" He received no answer to that either, and not a single lip broke its seal. Amir turned in anger to go back, but discovered that neither the door through which he had entered nor any signs of its presence could be seen anymore. Disappointed, when he returned to relate his woes to the king in the hope that he might get an answer this time, Amir saw a piece of paper in the king's hands with something written on it. He took the paper while the king sat silent and remained quiet. Amir read the note, which said:

O visitor to the *tilisms,* this court is a replica of the Court of Suleiman. In all respects it reflects that august assembly. All those who were in Suleiman's court have been reproduced here in effigies, and their respective stations and ranks are replicated in the manner you find them seated. All the figures that you see in the fortress were people who used to live here in the time of Suleiman, and had the positions depicted in their figures. It is useless to seek replies from effigies and figures who do not have the power of speech.

Amir was pondering over the contents of this paper when he saw another throne next to Suleiman's. He found a fourteen-year-old beautiful coquette sitting there covered in jewels, whose beauty was such that even *peris* could not hold a candle to her charms. Four hundred *perizads* stood behind her throne with arms folded in obedience, wearing exquisite gold chains strung with jewels. Amir approached her throne and greeted her, whereupon she returned his salutation and said, "O friend, how did you find your way through these enchantments and gain admission where no human is allowed?" Amir answered, "I know not how to tell my story, which is both long and arduous, or how to narrate a never-ending tale. It would be simpler if you were to tell me first who you are, what your name is, and how you came to settle in this remarkable place?"

She answered, "O fellow creature of God, I belonged to the harem of Suleiman and my name is Salim Shairan. It was none other than the potentate of the land of jinns and *peris* who bestowed this rank and prestige on me. When Suleiman bid adieu to this transitory world and Shahpal took over command of the jinns, he made me the sovereign of the realm of Zulmat. After I swore allegiance to Shahpal, Ifrit bin Ahriman rose his mutinous head and stirred a rebellious uprising. He took control of the lands of Qaf to manifest his ingratitude and defiance, and Shahpal lost power over many lands. Slowly and gradually Ifrit extended his influence to Zulmat and told me to accept his advances gladly and give myself in concubinage to him, or else he would make me suffer great ignominies and torture me relentlessly. I realized that since Shahpal himself was unable to challenge him, I had not the wherewithal to ward off Ifrit with all his armies and influence. I considered, therefore, that I would be putting my honor in jeopardy and besmirching the renown of my elders by continuing to live in Zulmat. Thus I decided to escape and willingly became a prisoner of this *tilism*.

"My heart counseled me that Ifrit would not be able to enter this place, and thus he would have no power over me here. I bide my time paying homage to the image of Prophet Suleiman and have taken residence in this nook to devote myself to God and pray fervently night and day. The four hundred *perizads* that you see here are my attendants, whom I brought with me when I decided to leave Zulmat. Now tell me who you are, where you have come from, and how you happened upon this place."

The Sahibqiran replied, "I am the Quake of Qaf, the Latter-day Suleiman, and a progeny of Prophet Ibrahim. My name is Hamza, and I come from the realm of human beings. Shahpal had sent for me to assist him and I came to Qaf in consideration of his request. Upon my arrival here I first killed Ahriman, then Ifrit and his mother, Maloona Jadu, and reinstated the emperor of Qaf as the rightful emperor of these lands. With God's help, and with my courage and valor, I annihilated his enemies and restored his writ in his land. I destroyed many *tilisms,* killed the rebellious *devs* to turn them to ashes, and disgraced and dishonored their aiders and abettors. You should rejoice and cast away all your fears and return to your land because all your enemies have been eliminated and obliterated, and you can again be the sovereign of your land."

Queen Salim Shairan said, "I came here willingly, but it is not mine to leave at will because no one who arrives here is allowed to go in freedom from this place." Hamza answered, "I make you my pledge that I will destroy this *tilism* as well and release you from here, provided you promise that you will do me a favor in return!" Salim Shairan asked, "What is that? Before I give my word you must tell me your proposition. I will not deny you it if it is something within my power."

Amir said, "I want you to promise me that after you are released from here, you will take me to the realm of the humans so that I can return to my world." Salim Shairan replied, "I make you this promise with all my heart and soul. I pledge to take you to your world and do you this favor!" Then Amir took out the tablet to read its instructions, but he could not discern a single letter on the tablet and found nothing written there to read. Amir was gripped by apprehension and feared that perhaps he would remain a prisoner of that *tilism* for the rest of his life, and that cruel fate had dealt him a most curious hand.

He put away the tablet and made his ablutions, and then said prayers outside. Amir untied his headgear and prostrated himself before God and prayed to be granted his wishes. He was soon overcome by sleep and in that state he saw Prophet Suleiman press Amir's head to his breast and speak thus:

> My son! Do not grieve! One of your sons, Badi-ul-Mulk,[62] will conquer
> this *tilism,* for the destruction and unraveling of this *tilism* is written in
> his name. To escape this *tilism,* walk toward the door reciting the words
> that I instruct you, and a path will appear to lead you out of here. As you
> step outdoors, keep reciting these words, whereupon a stag will appear
> and then flee from you. You must give him chase while continuing to re-
> cite these words. When that stag disappears and you cannot see it any-
> more, know then that you have come out of the boundaries of the *tilism,*
> and God in His munificence has granted your wishes.

Upon coming out of this reverie, Amir raised his head and offered another prayer of gratitude for divine help.

Then he related the dream to Queen Salim Shairan and said to her, "When I walk out of here, you should also hurry out behind me and do as I tell you." Reciting the words taught him by Prophet Suleiman, Amir began stepping toward the door and found it opened to him. Upon exiting Amir saw a stag appear sporting a saddle of gold brocade, and wearing golden anklets and jewel-encrusted metallic covers on his antlers. The antlers carried two rubies at their tips. Before Amir's eyes the stag went leaping and bounding toward the field jingling his bells. Amir sped after the stag reciting the prophet's words and realized that this was the same stag which Suleiman had mentioned in his dream. Queen Salim Shairan also followed Amir with her entourage of *perizads* and did not make delay. Immediately a great hue and cry rose from the palace as if the Day of Judgment had arrived, and loud cries were heard: "Seize them! Detain them! The prisoners are running away from the jail! The captives are nowhere to be seen!" None of Amir's party paid any heed to those cries, and running and scampering and falling over themselves, all of them exited that prison, and offered gratitude to God for their lucky escape.

As they continued their forward march they arrived near two hillocks. The stag disappeared between them, and nobody saw any sign of him again. Amir realized that he had come out of the boundaries of the *tilism,* and that he had been released from his terrible ordeal by God's grace. They crossed the first hill and camped at the foot of the next one, resting from their arduous ordeal. Queen Salim Shairan also camped there, and she was released from all her anxieties and fears in the company of Amir. She ordered her four hundred *perizads* to arrange an assembly of revelry. She entertained Amir and acted toward him reverentially and in consideration of her obligations to him. For a full seven days Amir occupied himself with assemblies of music and dance. He was entertained by the *perizads* and their coquetry and their charming and alluring ways.

On the eighth day, Queen Salim Shairan sought counsel from her companions and said to them, "Hamza is wedded to Aasman Peri, and it is for fear of her that nobody transports him back to the world of men, as her terror keeps everyone from helping him. I have promised Hamza that I will take him back to the world of men and I will fulfill my word. Advise me in this matter and tell me what means will secure an auspicious result."

They replied, "Understand this well that if Aasman Peri comes to know that you took her husband back to the world of men and acted against her known wishes, she will swear enmity to your life and honor, and you will suffer most grievously. Against her brazenness even the honor of her own parents is not safe, so you can imagine how others fare at her hands. Beware, since you know her well, that if you fulfill your promise to Hamza, she will dishonor and defile you and revoke your sovereignty over the realm of Zulmat. You would do well to leave this man where he lies sleeping, depart with your four hundred attendants, and never think of defying Aasman Peri." Salim Shairan found their advice to her liking and saw that it was in her own best interests. Leaving Amir asleep there, she flew away toward Zulmat with her *perizads* and disregarded her promise to Amir.

When Amir woke up the next morning he saw no signs of Salim Shairan or her entourage and realized that she, too, had succumbed to fear of Aasman Peri, and it had kept her from taking him to his world. Amir said to himself that he should put his faith in God whose will alone could accomplish his return to his world, and that he should never lose hope in his Creator's munificence and benevolence. Having made up his mind, Amir continued forward around the hill, and once he had put his trust in God, his troubles weighed less heavily on his mind. It is said that Amir walked for nine nights and nine days, and when he felt hungry he took a bite from the bread-cake given him by Prophet Khizr. In his journey on land, in water, and over the hills, he disposed of the leftovers of the bread-cake, but always found it whole whenever he felt hungry, and he would feast on it and found its sustenance necessary to undertake the tasks before him. On the tenth day he stopped under a clump of box trees to spend the night and, finding it a pleasant spot, made a bed of the wolf skins and went to sleep on the ground. In the morning he headed into the open field after saying his prayers, setting out again with the hope of reaching his destination. He had not gone far when he espied at the foot of a hill a flame that rose every so often whose source and origin he could not ascertain. When Amir approached, he saw it was a most scenic hill whose many charming sights made one marvel with wonder. Water spouted from springs and cascaded down its sides in thin sheets, and greenery covered the desert floor in a carpet of silken, emerald green. The entire expanse was verdant, and a magnificent palace constructed of bricks of gold ingots stood atop the hill, whose breaches were blocked with jewels of such brightness that the power of sight was rejuvenated from beholding it. All kinds of fowl and beasts abounded there.

At the foot of the hill on the huge mouth of a cave a *dev* sat roasting a buffalo, camels, and elephants over a pyre and gobbling them down with abandon. The flame that rose from the spit and traveled to the heavens

was the fire of that pyre. It is told that the *dev* Arnais who was the master
of that land had declared himself God and thus brought damnation on
himself. He had designated the palace as his heaven and the pyre and the
cave as his hell. He had also appointed four hundred *devs* who kept guard
on it as the keepers of that hell. Amir thought of approaching them to ask
what were these marvels beyond comprehension and understanding,
when one of the *devs* suddenly caught sight of Amir and said, "My skewers
were all bare, but the God of Qaf has sent me a prey and indeed it is
a tasty morsel that he has dispatched for me!" The *dev* rose and gestured
to Amir to approach and, speaking softly, offered him these happy tidings,
"O human child, come trotting here softly, and let no one hear your
footsteps lest another *dev* nab and gobble you up first and get all the pleasure,
depriving me of the gratification of eating you myself."

Amir began to laugh at his words, upon which the *dev* took offense
and wielding the skewer rushed forward to strike Amir and catch and eat
him. Amir drew the Aqrab-e Suleimani from his scabbard and dealt him
a blow before he could do any mischief. The *dev* fell to the ground in two
pieces along with his skewer. Witnessing that their companion had been
slaughtered, all the *devs* wielded their weapons and attacked Amir. He
stood in the middle of them with the shield of Garshasp in his left hand
and the Aqrab-e Suleimani in his right, putting his trust in God, and
fighting dexterously and displaying his Rustam-like might and belligerence.
Whoever received a blow by his hand fell to the ground in two.
Many were killed and the few who survived fled, clearing the field of
their contamination and emptying the grounds of their beastly presence.

When Amir saw that none of the *devs* remained, he climbed the hill
to Arnais's heavenly garden and saw that it was decorated in a most
splendid fashion with all manner of peerless jewels. Amir saw that it was
indeed a picture of the Garden of Eden and a jewel in the crown of
earthly beauty. Amir saw an emerald throne, also matchless in beauty,
where he seated himself and thought of taking a few hours of sleep to
rest himself and revive his spirits. Then he abandoned the thought realizing
that the *devs* who had fled would inform their leader, who would
certainly return with them to kill him, and it would be unwise and ill-advised
to drop one's guard in such a place.

As it happened, the *devs* who had fled went as a group to the castle
of Aqiq Nigar to inform their god, Arnais Dev, of the whole situation.
They related Amir's cruelty and merciless nature to him and told him
how Amir had killed his numerous guards, and that if they had not es-

caped with their lives they, too, would have been slain and would never have received reprieve. Arnais demanded to know where Amir had gone and asked them his whereabouts. The *devs* answered that the human being had trespassed into his heaven and at that moment he had the entire place at his disposal to take pleasure from it without any fear or apprehension. Upon hearing this Arnais was enraged. He asked, "Who is this man and where has he come from? How did he manage to get inside a place where it is well-nigh impossible for a human being to set foot? How dare he treat my slaves ill and humiliate them in this manner? Let me test how mighty he is and how courageous and brave in slaying *devs*."

Arnais flew from the castle of Aqiq Nigar along with several thousand *devs* and immediately laid siege to the palace occupied by Amir. He ordered the *devs*, "Storm the palace and apprehend that black-headed, white-toothed one, and have no fear of him!" They answered, "It is not in our power to step inside and challenge and apprehend him for you. You are our god; you should kill him by some ruse. Then we will witness how mighty you are, and see you slaying him with your sword!" Arnais waxed even more furious upon hearing their reply, and their jeering words rankled in his heart. Wielding a box tree, he barged inside, and said to Amir, "O child of man, why did you attack my angels? Didn't my fear and terror deter you in your actions?" With these words Arnais brought the box tree down on Amir to show him his power and might. Amir jumped to one side to foil his attack and, catching hold of the *dev* by his cummerbund, lifted him over his shoulders and slammed him to the ground. Arnais rolled away and attempted to escape, but Amir leapt up and came down on his chest, and drawing his dagger from his cummerbund pressed it against the *dev*'s neck, bringing low that mighty dev.

Then tears came to Arnais's eyes and fearful of losing his life, he pleaded, "O courageous man and the Quake of Qaf, give me quarter and spare my life!" Amir answered, "I will do so on two conditions: First, you must confess to me about your person and your origins, and second, you must convert to the True Faith and pledge allegiance to me!" Arnais Dev sincerely converted to the True Faith and was greatly indebted to Amir for sparing his life.

Then he related this story to Amir: "O Amir! I was employed among the mace bearers in the time of Suleiman, and was one of his confidants! When Suleiman passed away and went to his domicile in Heaven, anarchy took root and everyone laid their hands on whatever they could secure. I occupied this place and declared myself the god of *devs* and brought everyone under my rule. Now you have arrived to show me the righteous path and the wealth of the True Faith. I am grateful to God that I was saved the sin of professing partnership in His divinity, and glad that I have converted to the True Faith. I am at your command now, and shall obey your every word. I shall do what you order and through it receive grace in this world and the next."

Arnais next stepped out of his palace and said to all his *devs,* "I have converted to the True Faith and those among you who wish to convert to my new faith may stay; and the rest may go their own way for I spurn them as infidels as I am now a man of faith." Some of them converted, but most of them refused and turned away to follow their own path. Arnais returned to Amir, and said to him, "I have kept with me those *devs* who have converted to the True Faith, and those who did not I sent away and drove out of my service!" Amir answered, "You acquitted yourself well in this matter, but it would be a greater service to me if you conduct me back to my world, for I have sojourned in Qaf much longer than I had wanted."

Arnais replied, "It is no great hardship to take you back to your world, but nobody undertakes the task for fear of Aasman Peri, as everyone is scared of her tyranny. Indeed she is a despot, but I agree to bear the brunt of her cruelty, take you to your world, and defy her will for your pleasure, provided you help your faithful servant fulfill his desire and obtain what he covets." Amir asked, "What is it that you so ardently desire? Say it now and open your heart to me!" Arnais replied, "The castle where I live is called Aqiq Nigar. It is made of yellow carnelian and there is nothing on the face of the Earth that can compare with its beauty. Close by is the castle of Zamarrud Hisar, whose sovereign, Lahoot Shah, is a mighty and majestic king. He has a daughter called Laneesa, whom I love, but she has always remained beyond my reach. Without her I find no pleasure in this world. If you could help me get her, and make efforts on my behalf in this affair, I will undertake to take you to your world and put myself in opposition to Aasman Peri's wishes."

Amir answered, "I have no objection to you taking me there! I will do my best to join you with your beloved and take up this task to please you!" Arnais said, "Come then, climb on my neck and get ready to embark!" Amir adjusted his mail and armor and clambered upon Arnais, who sprang into action and headed toward Zamarrud Hisar, the city and land of his beloved Laneesa.

. . .

The second book of the tale of Amir Hamza, Lord of the Auspicious Planetary Conjunction and Conqueror of the World, is ended. The rest of the story will be told in Book Three, if it be the pleasure of Allah, whose aid and succor we seek.

BOOK THREE

The Third Book of the Dastan of the Sahibqiran, Abul-Ala Amir Hamza, the Conqueror of the World, the Quake of Qaf, the Latter-day Suleiman, and Uncle of the Last Prophet of the Times

Be it known that Arnais Dev carried Amir Hamza toward Zamarrud Hisar and descended around sunset to a resting place most bracing and wondrously refreshing. After saying his *maghreb* prayers, Amir asked Arnais about his plans and the course of action he wished to follow. He replied, "Zamarrud Hisar is not too far from here, but you see that the night is pitch dark. It would be best for you to spend the night here to revive your spirits. We will depart come morning." Amir answered, "The holy Khizr has given me instructions never to trust the word of the *devs* of Qaf or follow their counsel. Therefore, I will sleep only after I have tied you to a tree, so that my mind may rest easy on your account." Arnais Dev answered, "O Amir, far be it from me to betray you, but if you do not have faith in my word, do not hesitate to tie me to a tree and do what puts your mind at ease." Before he went to sleep, Amir tied Arnais to a giant tree. Then he spread the wolves' skins and settled down for a good night's rest, stretching himself out to sleep.

Arnais said to himself, *In Qaf I claimed the station of a god, but the one at whose persuasion I abandoned my claim considers me so unreliable that he tied me to this tree and then dozed off to sleep. He cares not a whit about my suffering and shows me not the least bit of mercy. It would be folly to remain in the company of such a man whose selfish needs are his only concern.* Thus resolved, Arnais flew away along with the tree, turning his back on Amir's company and leaving him alone in that desert.

When Amir woke up the next morning, he saw no trace of the *dev* or the tree, and the situation he had often been in before again met his view. He reasoned that perhaps Arnais had left him due to the displeasure he felt at being tied to the tree and might have stayed on if he had not been thus fastened. In the end, Amir reconciled himself to the event, thinking that perhaps it was all for the best. He said his prayers and then headed onward. When the sun climbed the skies, a blistering hot wind picked up, strong enough to melt one's bones. Amir saw a clump of trees at some distance, and in that scorching heat, he longed for their shade. As he went toward them, he discovered a breezy garden whose draftiness provided comfort and solace to the heart.

He sat down after spreading the wolves' skins on the ground, but hardly a moment had passed before a *dev* arrived wielding a millstone and said to him, "O child of man, before you decided on making this place your resting post, were you not at all troubled with fear of me?" Amir answered, "The *devs* of Qaf do not frighten me and I am not the least bit scared of your race." Upon hearing that, the *dev* brought the millstone down on Amir's head. Amir foiled this attack with the Aqrab-e Suleimani, answering with a sword thrust that cut the *dev* in two and dispatched him into the sleep of the afterlife. When the heat of the sun had subsided, Amir went forth. A couple of hours remained until the close of day when he heard sounds of weeping and wailing from the direction of the forest, and cries of someone begging for quarter and mercy reached his ears.

Surprised by this marvel, Amir stopped in his tracks and beheld Arnais Dev being prodded forward by some four hundred jinns who kept severely lashing and tormenting him. Upon spotting Amir, Arnais cried out, "O Sahibqiran, come quickly to my aid and help me, in the name of God!" Amir took pity on him and released him from the clutches of the jinns, securing his freedom from that tyrannical horde. Then he asked Arnais, "What passed with you that you ended up in this plight?"

Arnais answered, "I was seen by Lahoot Shah, who was out on a hunting expedition, and he captured me and put me in the power of these jinns. He ordered them to take me into the forest and kill me and make sure that an end was put to my existence. I must have a few more days remaining to my life, for I saw you and was released from the clutches of those villains; otherwise nothing stood between me and my death today, and I would have certainly found a home in the Future State." Amir asked, "Why did you flee from my service?" Arnais responded, "I was duly rewarded for my deeds and invited all this trouble in recompense for my conduct. I shall never again betray you or leave you in that manner!"

Amir again clambered onto his back and the two went forth toward Zamarrud Hisar. In the evening, they rested at another station and relieved themselves of the fatigue of the journey. As before, Amir again fastened Arnais to a tree before going to sleep, and again Arnais escaped, revealing his betrayal and treachery. In the morning when Amir did not find him, he finally realized that treachery was in the nature of the *devs,* and told himself that it was foolhardy to believe their word and cultivate their fidelity. Amir then said his prayers and journeyed on alone. After seven days spent passing all the stages of his journey, he espied a fortress that showed signs of being inhabited on the eighth day. When he drew close he saw some four hundred mighty and stalwart jinns guarding the ramparts. Two jinns with unbraided hair[1] were busy praying, while a force of four hundred *devs* surrounded the fortress wielding box trees, flint stones, millstones, *zangala*[?], and crocodile hides[?], as if they were assembled there for battle. Amir also observed a *dev* about to break down the fortress gate by releasing his weapon's might against the portals.

Amir challenged him, calling out, "Do not dare touch that fortress gate or you will pay for it dearly! Defy me and I will chastise you so severely that you will not even recognize your own face. You must fight me first before you touch the fortress gates!" The *dev* answered him, "O human child, you are my next meal! What makes you think I harbor any fear or dread of you? How could you ever fight and prevail against me?"

The Sahibqiran countered, "O wretch! You speak idly. Come before me and show me your might, and then see what you can make of me. Soon we will find out whether I become your next meal or if you fall prey to the crocodile of my sword. You will throw away your own life in no time! Do you not know me? I am the Quake of Qaf, the Latter-day Suleiman, the Slayer of Ifrit, the Killer of Ahriman, and the Intrepid Destroyer of *Tilisms!*" The *dev* replied, "Then *you* are the one who destroyed the garden that was the realm of Qaf and implanted there the seeds of strife and disharmony. It appears that you were sent to me so that I could exact revenge on you for the blood of all the *devs* of Qaf you have killed, and it was your impending death that dispatched you hither."

At this, the *dev* landed a blow of his *zangala* on Amir, which he foiled. Having frustrated his blow with great alacrity and swiftness, Amir cut the *dev* down with a single blow of the Aqrab-e Suleimani. At once, all the *devs* around the fortress attacked Amir. They charged him as a body and surrounded him on all sides. Amir killed a great many *devs* with his sword and the remainder escaped with their tails between their legs. In the end, a sea of blood was all that remained of the *devs'* existence, and the field was finally emptied of them.

Lahoot Shah now came out of the fort and conducted Amir back inside with great honor, seating him beside himself with much reverence. When Amir asked him his name, he answered, "I am called Lahoot Shah and these jinns are in my service!" Amir said to him, "I have a favor to ask of you. To grant it would be worthy of your magnificence and glory." La-hoot Shah replied, "Pray express your wishes so that I may carry them out!" Amir said, "You have a daughter, Laneesa of name. I ask that you marry her off to Arnais, and fulfill his most ardent longing with the jewel he desires. I have made him a promise and given him my word to champion his suit."

Amir's words rankled Lahoot Shah's heart and he was most upset. Keeping up appearances, however, he said to Amir, "Arnais is after all a king of the realm of Qaf. If you wished, I would give her in marriage even to a slave, as I could never refuse your wishes!" He led Amir by the hand to a chamber and insisted that he sit on a throne there that was suspended in the air above a well. It turned out to be a trap: The moment Amir sat down, he sank into the well, along with the throne, and fell into the hole. Then that ungrateful wretch Lahoot Shah placed a stone on top of the well and ordered two hundred jinns to stand guard around the prison chamber.

When news of this reached his daughter, Laneesa, she went to her fa-ther trembling with rage and exclaimed, "Indeed you have no fear of God to have paid the man who did you a good turn with the coin of wickedness! You have returned the favor to the Sahibqiran—through whose exertions your life and honor were saved, and who removed immi-nent harm from your head—by scheming to kill him." Lahoot Shah replied, "He wished me to marry you off to Arnais at his command. That was why I have incarcerated and punished him thus!" Laneesa did not re-spond to her father but remained silent while she continued to think of some way to secure Amir's release.

When it was night, she put on night livery and, after arming herself, went to the well and exerted herself in releasing Amir. She removed the stone from the mouth of the well, descended fearlessly into it, and proceeded gallantly, resolved on her mission. Amir saw before him a fourteen-year-old damsel clad in night livery whose beauty was the envy of the moon. He asked who she was, to which she answered, "My name is Laneesa, and I have come to release you from this prison. Have no fear because I have brought you the auspicious gift of freedom!" Amir prostrated himself before God in gratitude, praised Laneesa for her commendable actions, and then climbed out of the well with the help of the rope. When the guards tried to thwart Amir's escape, La-neesa unsheathed her sword and fell upon them, and many a jinn was killed in the skirmish. The rest ran off to inform Lahoot Shah, and un-nerved by the incident they repaired to him in great disarray. Lahoot Shah was stunned upon hearing of Laneesa's actions and his face be-came flushed with rage.

As Amir bid farewell to Laneesa, she said to him, "I have sold myself in slavery to you. Now I cannot think of an existence except in your ser-vice. I will remain beside you wherever you go, and won't be separated from you ever!" However much Amir asked her to desist from such thinking, she remained adamant and showed her preference for Amir's service over everything else. She thus came to accompany Amir, and they walked on foot for many days until they were exhausted and unable to take even a single step. Amir found himself in a quandary and felt greatly hindered and encumbered by Laneesa's companionship. What before had been a day's journey now took him four or five days. Yet he stead-fastly kept her by his side.

After several days' journey they saw a mountain far in the distance that was as bright as a flash of lightning, and they discovered that it was made of crystal. Fields of saffron spread for hundreds of miles around it, and in the middle of those fields there flowed a lake whose sparkling water outshone the luminance of the waters of Lake Kausar,[2] whose clar-ity humbled the Fountain of Life and whose refreshing gusts of breeze placated one's soul. As Amir sat by the lakeside to regard the scenery, a wild bull materialized and came straight toward him without showing the least hesitation. When Amir tried to catch the bull, he ran off toward the forest. Amir chased the bull and caught him, frustrating his attempt to escape. He then said to Laneesa, "It seems that God took pity on your miserable state and sent this animal to be your mount." When they started up again, Amir put Laneesa on the bull's back and relieved her from the trials of walking barefoot. To subdue the bull, he put a cavesson[3] on him, and handed the rope to Laneesa. After they had traveled some distance, the bull suddenly bolted toward the forest. Laneesa tried des-perately to stop him by violently tugging on the reins, but he would not slow. Flying like the wind he disappeared with her without a trace. Lamenting the loss of Laneesa, Amir headed in the direction where he had seen the wild bull disappear, but he could not track them farther.

Toward the end of afternoon Amir arrived near a hill where he saw a captivating and enchanting garden in which there was a jewel-studded golden dome encircled by pavilions of gold brocade decorated with lamps raised on ornamental poles. When Amir arrived at the door of the dome, he found it locked from within, and could not find any other entrance. He heard two people talking within. One of them made pleas and exclaimed, "Accept my love and do not break my heart by spurning me!" The other person replied, "I would sooner eat manure than have you for my life partner! I'll never have it!" Amir called out, "Who is inside? Open the door, for I wish to come in!" When nobody answered, Amir kicked in the door, breaking it to pieces and unhinging it. He entered and his eyes met a marvelous sight: Laneesa was sitting on a throne and Arnais stood before her, making entreaties with folded arms, and heaving cold sighs from his ardor.

When Arnais Dev saw Amir, he threw himself at his feet, and said, "Pray witness how I beseech Laneesa endlessly and put my head at the feet of this pitiless creature, but she does not accept my suit and does not requite my heart's desire. If you were to do me one more favor and have me betrothed to her with your bidding and persuasion, I shall remain loyal to you to the end of my days, and conduct you anywhere you desire." The Sahibqiran said to him, "You have deceived me twice and shown disloyalty to me by running off and leaving me alone in the desert!" Arnais countered, "You tethered me and went to sleep, and I ran away as it made me suffer. But pardon my misdemeanor now for God's sake and empty your breast of all malice toward me. Never again shall I repeat what I did and I shall remain faithful to you for the rest of my life."

Taking pity on the *dev*'s weeping and wailing, the Sahibqiran said to Laneesa, "O Laneesa, Arnais promises to conduct me to my world, and he also languishes in his love for you. I wish that you would accept his suit for my sake, for the pride that you display is akin to conceit, and your refusal is tantamount to cruelty." Laneesa replied with folded arms, "He is, after all, a *dev*! If you had wished to marry me off even to an ass, I would have accepted it with all my heart and never dared to go against your command! But I, too, will now set a condition that he must transport you to your world and not again deceive you like a cad!"

Arnais Dev accepted her condition, whereupon Amir wedded them together, joining Laneesa's hand with the hand of Arnais in matrimony. After making his salutations to Amir, Arnais said, "Pray give me leave to take her with me to my castle Aqiq Nigar, to conduct the wedding rituals and satisfy the desires of my heart now that my wishes have been granted, so that no craving remains unfulfilled either in my heart or hers, and nobody can mock or ridicule me. Aasman Peri will certainly come to hear that I transported you to your world against her wishes, and she will undoubtedly put me to death. Thus I wish to satisfy all my desires during the life that I have left, and take pleasure from all that I can of this life's joy. I will present myself in your service three days from today and will do as you command!"

Amir said to him, "I shall wait for you for three days. It would be to your advantage to hold true to the word you have given me, otherwise you will get your just deserts and long rue the day you decided to ply me with deceit." Arnais placed Laneesa atop his neck and together they set out for the castle of Aqiq Nigar.

Midway in the journey they came upon a scenic grassland whose beauty captivated Arnais Dev's heart. He set Laneesa down under a pear tree by the side of a pond and said to her, "Laneesa, my soul! Take rest here a while until I return from urgent business. I must now arrange a conveyance so that I may conduct you to the castle of Aqiq Nigar with fanfare and honor, for it would be a disgrace for you to be conducted thither in this unbecoming fashion." At once, he left for Aqiq Nigar.

When Laneesa grew oppressed by the heat of that place, she cast off her clothes and stepped into the pond to bathe and refresh herself, and to find refuge from the heat and reinvigorate her spirits in its cold water. Hardly a moment had passed when a horse resembling a wild bull appeared from the fields and came to stand at the side of the pond. Because its aspect was most strange and frightful, Laneesa was scared by its sight and rushed out of the pond to retrieve her clothes. The horse gave her chase and the terrified Laneesa fell flat on her back. The horse then took his pleasure of her and satisfied his carnal desire. As God had willed, Laneesa became impregnated in that act: The Gardener of Fate implanted the seed of an embryo in her womb in that manner and thus showed the marvel of His insuperable power to all His creation.

Now, that horse was none other than Arnais, and after he had relieved himself and satisfied his letch, he rolled around on the ground and returned to his original form. Be it known that Laneesa would bear a colt, and a wonder of the Progenitor's work would thus become manifest. He would be named Ashqar Devzad and was to become Amir's favored mount and would remain in his service for many a long year, and whoever saw him would marvel at his wondrous qualities.

Laneesa said to her husband, "O Arnais, why did you do this? What pleasure did you derive from this exercise?" Arnais replied, "God alone knows what tomorrow holds. For that reason I satisfied myself today. The heavens are in a constant whirl and events overtake us all too often, therefore I allowed myself the pleasure of ravishing you!" He lifted La-neesa onto his shoulders as before, and carried her to Aqiq Nigar. After conducting her into that marvelous castle, he held celebrations amid all the furnishings of pleasure and revelry as befitted the occasion. He devoted his time to these festivities during the day and at night took La-neesa to bed and coupled with her.

———

Let me now say a few words about Aasman Peri before we continue with the account of Arnais. One morning, dressed in a red costume and with a frown playing on her forehead, she sat on her throne to give audience with great splendor and grandeur. She sent out summonses to all the no-bles of the state, ordering them to present themselves. Anyone who then beheld her in this condition became deathly pale with fear and dreaded inviting her ire on their heads and being caught in her tyrannous clutches. Aasman Peri now turned toward Abdur Rahman and said, "Khvaja! I had Amir cast into the Bayaban-e Sargardan and ordered the *devs* who were commissioned to take him to his world to leave him there. Pray see what passes with the Sahibqiran these days and whether he is alive or dead. Tell me as well what occupies him and keeps him busy at present."

Abdur Rahman replied with folded arms, "O Queen of the Skies! My calculations by geomancy indicate that Amir still tarries in the Bayaban-e Sargardan, languishing in that wilderness from great hard-ships. However, Arnais Dev promised Amir that if he would favor him by interceding with his beloved Laneesa to accept his suit, he would carry out Amir's wishes and take him to the world of men. Thus Amir united him with Laneesa and did what Arnais asked for. It is the second day today that Arnais has been busy in nuptial festivities in the castle of Aqiq Nigar, where he is reveling with utmost abandon and deriving sweet gratification from his life. The day after tomorrow he will conduct Amir to the world of men and fulfill his word and make good on his promise."

Aasman Peri raged like a flame and ignited like a blaze from the fury of her anger at this news. She said, "How dare Arnais have the gall to sep-arate me from my husband, and cast off all fear of my wrath? Watch how I shall punish him now and avenge myself on that dim-witted, accursed creature!"

Taken with irrepressible furor, she immediately flew toward the cas-tle of Aqiq Nigar in the retinue of thousands of jinns, *devs,* and *perizads,* burning like a taper from the fire of her wrath. As she approached the castle, her scouts brought word that Arnais lay sleeping in the arms of Laneesa, and thus might be easily arrested and pinioned and handed over to the *devs*. Aasman Peri's ardor did not cool even a little until she had both Arnais and Laneesa arrested and taken to Gulistan-e Irum as prisoners. She had them severely thrashed and then imprisoned them in Zandan-e Suleimani,[4] from which one found release only in death. Aasman Peri had it proclaimed abroad that whoever took it into his head to convey the Sahibqiran to the world of men without her orders and defied her in the matter would have a similar or even worse fate visited on his head.

———

Now hear of Amir. After three days passed and Arnais did not return, Hamza said to himself, *In truth the race of* devs *is unsurpassed in perfidy and is most ungrateful and treacherous. To believe their word is utter folly. O Hamza, nobody will ever conduct you to the world of men, and even if from self-interest a* dev *promises it, he will betray you in the end. You should put your hope in God Almighty who is all-powerful and may have mercy on your condition and have you led back home.* Remembering Mehr-Nigar again, Amir cried bitter tears.

Suddenly he heard someone say, "Peace be with you!" Amir looked up and saw Prophet Khizr before him. He rose, paid his respects, and said, "O Prophet of God, am I fated to languish in Qaf and remain forever lost and bewildered in this wilderness? Nobody who makes me a promise ever fulfills it—or fails to reveal his rascality and maliciousness. The *dev* Arnais bound himself by oaths but never held true to his word!"

Holy Khizr replied: "O Abul-Ala! Everything has its hour. Do not let your heart become weighed down by aggravation, and close it to all fear and apprehension. By the grace of God, whose aid we solicit, you will return to your world and obtain that long-awaited pleasure of reunion with your near and dear ones. But some hardships remain to you still. As someone stated so appropriately, 'Though a lot has passed, some more yet remains to transpire!' Arnais Dev is not at fault, and there was no disparity in his word and deeds. He wished this time to be true to the word he gave you and made a firm resolve to take you to your world. However, Aasman Peri discovered the plan after consulting Abdur Rahman. She arrested Arnais and carried him off to Gulistan-e Irum, where she has punished him severely and imprisoned him with Laneesa in the Zandan-e Suleimani. Much he has been made to suffer on account of promising to help you!" After speaking these words, Khizr disappeared. Amir was so shaken up by Khizr's whole account that he did not notice when the holy one left his side.

Amir went forth, and after completing a journey of seventeen days arrived under a hill that held a crystal dome at its peak. Hamza surmounted the hill after great struggle and regarded its shining cupola whose brightness blinded the sun itself. Amir decided to observe it from closer quarters and learn what went on within the dome. He climbed the hill and came to the dome's boundary wall but found the door locked and saw nobody around. Amir broke open the lock and stepped into a garden, proceeding fearlessly and intrepidly. The garden rivaled the Garden of Heaven, and Amir reflected that since the day he had arrived in Qaf he had never seen a garden or an abode that was its equal or even came close in comparison. When he studied the cupola again he discovered there the likeness of the *shabchiragh* jewel, for he found it surmounted with an inestimably precious ruby. Using the miracle granted him by Prophet Aadam, Amir reached up and took the jewel from the cupola. Upon comparing it with the one in his headpiece, he found not the least disparity between the two. Amir's heart was most pleased by this memento of Qaf, and he thought that the kings and emperors of the world of men would never have beheld such jewels even in their dreams.

When Amir went inside the dome, his eyes caught upon a jewel-studded throne, and then wherever he looked, he found the place appointed with rarities and marvels of astonishing quality. He thought of resting there for a few moments to give his tired body some relief from the travails of his journey, but then thought the better of it, realizing that it was entirely likely that the custodian of the place was some *dev* who would become enraged to find him there and therefore harm him. Amir decided that it would not do well to tarry, and he must leave the place at once. He stepped out of the dome and sat down on a promenade after spreading out the wolves' skins, using his staff as a prop. Hardly a moment had passed when a mighty blast of wind issued from the forest and very nearly uprooted all the great trees in the garden and flattened them to the ground with its violent velocity. Amir saw Sufaid Dev, who was some five hundred yards in height, enter the garden shouting and making the heavens and Earth alike ring with his clamor.

Sufaid Dev called out, "Where is the thief who has taken the *shabchiragh* jewel from the cupola of the dome that was the relic of Prophet Suleiman, and thus extinguished the light of life in Gumbad-e Suleimani?"

Amir confronted him and challenged Sufaid Dev by bellowing his war cry of "God is Great!" Then Amir said, "You towering fool of hideous form and amorphous shape, your search has now ended! I wonder if you know me, and recognize the Slayer of *Devs* and Destroyer of *Tilisms*! If not, then approach and learn that I am the Quake of Qaf, the Latter-day Suleiman, the Killer of Ifrit, and the Destroyer of Ahriman. Indeed I am the one who has had the pleasure of removing *devs'* bodies from their necks!"

Sufaid Dev replied, "Today I learn that it was you who destroyed the garden that was the land of Qaf, and all the mayhem caused in this land is your doing! O human child, you will now taste my avenging wrath for the murder of those *devs,* and a terrible punishment will visit on your head. Even if you possessed a thousand lives, you would not be able to escape today with even a single one of them. Now there is no chance that you will not forfeit your life."

Amir responded, "To what purpose do you make all this prattle? If you really long to meet the *devs* I have killed and are so desirous of joining their companionship, I shall dispatch you to their abode forthwith and pack you off to their presence in no time! Come deal me your most potent blow; confront me and show the quality of your valor!"

The *dev* swung a box tree hung with millstones and aimed it with utmost force at Amir's head, imagining that he had dealt him a fatal blow. But the Sahibqiran cut the tree in two with the Aqrab-e Suleimani and, catching hold of the *dev*'s cummerbund, lifted him over his head and slammed him to the ground. Amir bore down on his chest and pressed the dagger of Rustam against his neck, overpowering him with his might and courage. Sufaid Dev's eyes filled up with tears, and he said, "O Quake of Qaf! Do not kill me, for I will prove of much help to you and will perform all that you order me with all my heart and soul!"

Amir said to him, "No harm will come to you if you convert to the True Faith. I will ward off death from your head if you do this; otherwise this very dagger will take your life."

The *dev* replied, "I have some enemies who dwell on the slope of this hill. If you were to kill them, I would convert to the True Faith and submit myself wholeheartedly into your service." The Sahibqiran said, "Give me a detailed account of these enemies, tell me where to find them, and give me all the particulars."

Sufaid Dev answered, "At the bottom of this hill is the place where Prophet Suleiman used to sit and admire the scenery. At the end of day he would retire there to comfort his eyes with the scenic fields of saffron, delighting freely in the sight of that beautiful meadow. There dwell in those saffron fields seven *Nasnaases* of Suleiman who are considered by all *devs* to be of unsurpassing might. It is, therefore, not just myself but all *devs* who fear and pledge submission to them. If you were to kill them, it would be an extraordinary favor to me. Your humble servant will forever owe a debt of gratitude to you." Amir said to him, "I wish you to take me to their dwelling!"

Sufaid Dev accompanied Amir to the bottom of the hill and showed him the home of the *Nasnaases*. Amir beheld an expanse bound by saffron fields and noticed that a rare bloom reigned there. In the midst of those fields was a lake of immeasurable length, some two hundred yards across, whose water was unsurpassable in its sparkling clarity. It was a luminescent, agreeable, and overflowing body of water that intensified the delight of the beholder. In the middle of the lake rose a most praiseworthy crystalline platform fifty yards across and a full fifty yards high, fitted with palisades of topaz. These were themselves surmounted with jewels of great art and refined workmanship. In the nave of that platform sat a diamond-inlaid throne that was a marvel of delicacy. The hill and the saffron fields were reflected in the surface of the platform, and when the verdure swayed with the motion of the wind, its movement was reflected in the platform. Amir jumped into the lake and climbed up to the platform, looking around in all directions. He asked Sufaid Dev, "Tell me, where are your enemies and where are they hidden?" He answered, "They are in these very saffron fields. If you were to call out, 'O seven *Nasnaases*, what are you eating?' they will answer and show themselves, appearing before you without delay."

Amir then called out, "O *Nasnaases*! What are you eating, and where are you hiding? Come out, for I am most desirous of seeing you—come out and and show yourselves to me!" The *Nasnaases* answered, "We are eating saffron! Wait a while and we will present ourselves to you!" Then all seven *Nasnaases* came out en masse and stood in a row at Amir's side. He regarded their singular form and bodies: They resembled humans, but they had sharp front teeth, keen as the point of a spear. If by chance a fly landed on them the teeth would impale her, and their sharp points offered clemency to none. Amir drew the Aqrab-e Suleimani and jumped into their midst. He killed all seven of them with his gleaming sword, quenching his blade in their blood. Then Amir said to Sufaid Dev, "Now all your enemies have been killed and your wishes fulfilled. All your worries and cares are now erased!" Sufaid Dev was so pleased that he placed one hand on his head and another on his ass, and began dancing with joy. Then he said, "O child of man, although you killed all my enemies, I remain sworn to your enmity! It is a rule with our race that we do evil to those who do good unto us without fear of God's retribution."

Sufaid Dev then lifted a heavy slab of stone and threw it at Amir's head. Amir dodged it, and then drawing his sword, attacked Sufaid Dev, who turned tail and ran speedily, neither stopping to take a breath nor hesitating even for a second. Amir called after him boldly, but the *dev* would not answer Amir's challenge. Instead he said, "I am not such a fool to squander my life away by answering your challenge, and foster my own death with my hands. I will come after you whenever I find you unawares." At this, he flew away. The Sahibqiran reasoned that it would not bode well for him to stay there longer and he must leave that place to save his life. Since Sufaid Dev was now his enemy, there was no knowing when he might strike him unaware and inflict harm on him. Thus Amir immediately departed from that place.

The narrator has said that for seven nights and seven days, fear of Sufaid Dev drove Amir onward without even a moment's rest, and he strove to get out of the reach of Sufaid Dev so that he would not receive injury from that scoundrel's hands. On the eighth day Amir came upon a place that showed signs of life and discovered another marvel waiting. The denizens of that city each possessed only half a body. When two of them stood together, they formed one person. It was on this account that those people were called *nim-tans,* and they were born and passed their lives in that shape. Their king was Futuh Nim-Tan, who was renowned for his excellent manners and his liberality. When he heard of Amir Hamza's arrival, he came to welcome him and conducted Amir with honor into his city. He insisted that Amir share his throne with him, served Amir with deference, and attended to all his needs with great care. He kissed Amir's feet and said, "I was told by Prophet Suleiman that a child of man would arrive in Qaf to lay low the *devs,* injuring thousands of them and beheading thousands more. I was told that he would be called the Latter-day Suleiman and would carry the signet of Suleiman.[5] Ever since that day I have been most desirous of seeing you and receiving grace from our meeting. I am grateful to God who has granted me the honor of kissing your feet and brought you here in safety at an auspicious moment."

After King Futuh Nim-Tan had feted Amir and showed him excellent hospitality, Amir asked him, "Is it possible for you to conduct me to my world and grant me the great favor of transporting me to my homeland?" The king answered, "We *nim-tans* cannot set foot beyond the boundaries of our city, and cannot move to another abode outside our own." Then Amir took his leave and traveled onward.

The *dastan*'s narrator tells that after overcoming many hardships, the Sahibqiran passed through a desolated stretch for ten days straight. On the eleventh day, he reached the shores of a turbulent sea that looked impossible to cross without a vessel, but he saw no sign of any ship or boat there. Amir looked at the sea with wonder and marveled that Qaf had such a mighty and dangerous sea that neither man nor beasts of air could cross. He told himself that it seemed unlikely that he would ever return to his world; more than ever it seemed to him that he was fated to languish in Qaf. Amir sat down upon a rock and, recalling Mehr-Nigar and his companions, began crying and wasting away his life in grief. In the course of his wailings, Amir was overtaken by sleep and fell into a deep slumber. The hardships of the last many days made him lose all consciousness.

Sufaid Dev, who had lain in wait for just such an chance, saw his opportunity when Amir grew lost to sleep. He flew away with the rock on which Amir lay sleeping. After the *dev* rose some two hundred *kos* into the sky, the blasts of wind finally awoke Amir. He saw Sufaid Dev flying away with him, carrying him on his back like one carries a pitcher of water. Amir called out to him, "O Sufaid Dev! The kindness I have done, you return with wickedness. Was ever good returned with evil? Have you no fear of God?" Sufaid Dev replied, "I already told you that it is the custom of *devs* to reward good with evil. We have forever acted in this wise. Now, tell me what is your pleasure—shall I throw you into the sea to drown or smash you against the mountains below?" Amir reasoned that since the *devs* have twisted minds, Sufaid Dev would do the very opposite of whatever he told him. Therefore, Amir said to him, "If that is what you desire, throw me into the mountains to avenge yourself!" Sufaid Dev said, "O human child! I will throw you into the sea instead, so that you will drown in it and never again perpetrate any tyranny or injustice against our race!"

Having said this, the *dev* indeed acted against Amir's bidding and threw him and the stone into the sea and flew away from there. At God's orders, the holy Khizr and Prophet Ilyas caught Amir in their arms in midair and carried him to safety to the shore. Amir greeted and thanked both prophets and said to them after much weeping and wailing, "Sires!

Aasman Peri persecutes me severely, and on account of her I have seen great misery. She prohibits my returning to my world and does not allow me to seek a remedy for my distress."

The holy Khizr said, "O Amir! This is not an occasion to be distressed. Everything depends on how much longer you are fated to eat and drink[6] in Qaf! When the time has come for you to partake food elsewhere, you will depart from here to your world and discover the pleasure of your homeland! A few more days of hardship remain and, God willing, they, too, will pass. Put your faith in God and have some patience, for that propitious time is just around the corner!"

———

Now hear an account of Emperor Shahpal and Aasman Peri: One day Emperor Shahpal was giving audience in his court when Aasman Peri arrived dressed all in red, with her face displaying all the passion of rage. After seating herself on her throne she sent for Khvaja Abdur Rahman, ordering him to appear before her. Eighteen *lakh* chiefs, *devs,* and *perizads* were present in the court at that moment, and all who beheld Aasman Peri in that condition trembled with fear. They tried to hide their faces from Aasman Peri, who had appeared in the color of Mars[7] and looked full of fury. They wondered who was destined to lose his life that day, and how many of them would suffer her anger.

At that moment, Abdur Rahman arrived and made obeisance to Emperor Shahpal and Princess Aasman Peri. Addressing him, Aasman Peri said, "Khvaja, pray tell us of Amir's whereabouts at this moment, and whether he is alive or dead, happy or miserable!" Upon studying the horoscope, Khvaja Abdur Rahman beat his head and shed many tears, and at last said to Shahpal, "What evil did Hamza do you that you take your revenge in this manner and make him suffer thus?" Shahpal was greatly alarmed and replied, "I hope all is well, Khvaja! How does Amir fare? Tell me verily what adversity confronts him and give me the whole account of him without delay!" Khvaja Abdur Rahman answered, "Where evil thrives, no good ever takes root. You are oblivious to his fate and not in the least concerned about his welfare. Sufaid Dev has thrown Amir into the Caspian Sea, and that villain has committed this crime against him. It remains to be seen whether Hamza will live or die, for someone thrown into such turbulent waters has a very small chance of survival."

When Emperor Shahpal heard this inauspicious news, he dashed his crown on the ground and was most saddened. Aasman Peri, too, began pulling out her hair by fistfuls. Uttering many plaintive cries, she occupied herself with lamentation and prayers. That very moment the emperor departed for the Caspian Sea with every member of his court in train. The *devs* of Qaf bore his throne heavenward, and in the flash of an eye they arrived over the waters of the Caspian.

The Sahibqiran had just finished saying his prayers with the prophets Khizr and Ilyas when Emperor Shahpal arrived with Aasman Peri. When Amir turned his face to the right, he beheld Shahpal, and Amir's brow became clouded. When he turned his face to his left, his gaze met Aasman Peri's. Amir turned his face away from her as well, and showed not the least favor to either of them. Both Emperor Shahpal and Aasman Peri threw themselves at Prophet Khizr's feet and said, "O holy Khizr! We give you our word and swear and pledge that six months from this day we will send Amir Hamza back to the world of humans, and will never break our word. If we go against our pledge we will deem ourselves in violation of God Almighty and also of your holiness, and shall be deserving of the most severe punishment. Pray have mercy on us and intercede on our behalf with the Sahibqiran just this once."

Holy Khizr then advised Amir, addressing him munificently, "Although you have stayed here for nine long years, dwell here another six months for my sake, and force yourself to bear all that happens as the dictates of God's predetermined fate. Both Aasman Peri and Shahpal swear and give their word. Try them once again and put your store in their pledges. It is said that one must give the lie to the liar, and the one who swears and makes a pledge is deserving of trust." Amir lowered his head and said, "O holy Khizr! You are a prophet of God, one of His favored creatures, and the chosen one in the Court of Heaven! What choice do I have but to show obedience and deference to your wishes? I accept what you suggest with all my heart and soul. Very well, I will stay here for another six months and promise not to doubt them as per your commands!"

Emperor Shahpal and Aasman Peri fell at Amir's feet and offered him many excuses for their trespasses. They sought Amir's forgiveness and forced him with their entreaties to pardon them. Prevailed upon by these circumstances, Amir took leave of Khizr and Ilyas, and sitting on the throne alongside Shahpal and Aasman Peri, returned to Gulistan-e Irum.

OF THE KHUSRAU OF INDIA, LANDHOOR BIN
SAADAN, ARRIVING AT THE FORTRESS OF CEYLON AND
ROUTING MUHLIL SAGSAR AND MALIK AJROOK; AND OF
THE DEPARTURE OF BAHRAM GURD, THE EMPEROR OF
CHINA, TOWARD THE CLIME OF CHINA, AND HIS GIVING
AUDIENCE AT THE SEAT OF HIS KINGDOM

The narrator now tells that many days had passed since Muhlil Sagsar and Malik Ajrook Khwarzami laid siege to the fortress of Ceylon, and they had had many skirmishes with those within the fortress walls. One day they sounded the battle drums, charged the fortress, and assailed the followers of the True Faith yet again. Those in the fortress raised their hands in prayer and entreated the Court of Heaven with their tearful solicitations.

Suddenly a dust cloud rose from the direction of the forest and when the scissors of wind cut through the skirts of dust, lion-head standards and lion-faced flags appeared on the horizon. The besieged men saw warriors come forward marching under those banners whose faces had never before been seen in that clime. When those in the fortress gazed upon the horde with spyglasses, they saw the Mighty Lord, a Pillar of the Empire of the Latter-day Suleiman, the Sahibqiran's next-in-command, the grandson of Prophet Shis, the Khusrau of India—to wit, Landhoor bin Saadan, clad in armor, carrying a colossal mace on his shoulder, and riding his she-elephant Maimoona with great pomp and glory.

It so happened that while Bahram Gurd, the emperor of China, departed for the lands of China on horseback, Landhoor had directed himself toward Ceylon with a vast and intrepid army. Those inside the fortress sounded notes of jubilation and trumpeted with thunderous clamor. As Malik Ajrook and Muhlil Sagsar looked around with surprise upon hearing these jubilant notes and wondered what had caused the garrisoned army to play triumphal music in their helpless state and in utter disregard of their foe's numerous and mighty army, Landhoor bin Saadan fell upon the Sagsar army with his warriors. When Jaipur saw

Landhoor leading the charge, he flung open the gates of the fortress and led his army out to join the battle. Then the prospects of the battle changed and it became an intense conflict.

Malik Ajrook led his elephant next to Maimoona and dealt a blow of his mace to Landhoor. While Landhoor successfully foiled the blow, it landed on the head of Maimoona, and the she-elephant's brains immediately gushed out her trunk, her life extinguished with great pain. The Khusrau jumped off his mount, and as Malik Ajrook landed a second blow on him, he foiled it and caught hold of the trunk of his enemy's elephant. He pulled it mightily, sending Malik Ajrook's elephant tumbling on its face, with a river of blood issuing from his trunk. Malik Ajrook now confronted Landhoor, resolved on battle. The Khusrau caught him by his cummerbund and, after whirling him above his head, slammed him to the ground so hard that it recalled to Malik Ajrook the moment of his birth.

Seeing the might and power of the Khusrau, all of Malik Ajrook's sense and wit took leave. He tried to rise to his feet and escape, but Landhoor caught him. Pressing one leg of his adversary under foot and securing the other in his hand, he then tore him apart like an old rag. After ripping that mighty man in two, Landhoor turned his attention toward the Sagsar army. But just at that moment a cloud suddenly appeared in the sky, a puff of darkness materialized in the heavens, and it thundered so loudly that it seemed the heavens would come crashing down to Earth. Everyone was blinded by the lightning and traumatized by terror, and wondered what strange calamity and new disaster had descended upon them.

Then a claw came down from the heavens and carried Landhoor away, just as a squall carries away a twig. Upon witnessing this the Sagsars fell like ferocious lions upon the armies of India, unleashing the full strength of their army in the charge. The armies of India again sequestered themselves in the fortress, apprehensive about their small numbers. The Sagsars encircled them and laid siege on the fortress as before.

Before I give their full account, let me say a few words about King Landhoor.

The claw that carried Landhoor from the battlefield was Rashida Peri, daughter of Rashid Jinn, the distinguished and celebrated king of the lands of Abyez Min Muzafat, one of the realms of Qaf. When Rashida Peri witnessed Landhoor's demonstration of power and might, she resolved in her heart to carry him away to slay Sufaid Dev. That blackguard *dev* had become enamored of Rashida Peri, and demanded of Rashid Jinn his daughter's hand in marriage, expressing a desire to attach himself to that beautiful and comely *peri*. When Rashid Jinn did not accept his suit but answered it instead with harsh words and a resounding rejection that was a veritable slap on the face for Sufaid Dev, the *dev* captured Rashid Jinn and imprisoned him in a cave that was adjacent to his abode. He then pursued Rashida Peri so that he could capture her, too, and ravish her.

Upon getting wind of the *dev*'s plans, Rashida Peri had escaped to Gulistan-e Irum so that she might find succor and a protector in Aasman Peri and be rid of Sufaid Dev, and protect herself and her honor from that wretch's advances. But upon arriving in Gulistan-e Irum, she discovered that Aasman Peri was visiting another land, so then Rashida Peri traveled to the world of humans to divert her mind and amuse herself for a few days with its sights and sounds. As she was returning from the realm of humans, she witnessed the display of Landhoor's power and ferociousness in Ceylon, and carried him away, enamored of his appearance and comely aspect. She placed Landhoor in her garden, and then bedecked with the seven adornments, she presented herself before him with such an exquisite appearance that her beauty and splendor would plant temptation even in an angel's bosom.

When Landhoor beheld Rashida Peri he fell head over heels in love, and upon regarding her *houri*-faced aspect, his own face grew wan from the pain of his longing. He asked her, "Who has brought me to this garden, how was I conducted here, and what land is it where I find myself?" Rashida Peri answered, "This slave girl that you see before you was guilty of bringing you here and of involuntarily committing this act. This is the land of Peristan. A *dev* who has imprisoned my father and inflicted much suffering upon him wished to take me for his wife and enjoy the pleasures of life through possession of me. However, the very idea was abhorrent to me and I found the prospect of this union most repugnant. Our emperor sent for a human being from the realm of men to slaughter thousands of *devs* and reclaim the land that was lost to him. He avenged himself on his enemies with that human's assistance, and gave him the hand of his daughter in marriage, betrothing him to his daughter, who is unsurpassed in beauty and comeliness. Therefore, I have brought you here likewise to avail myself of your aid and succor. If you kill this *dev*, I will give myself to you in slavery for the rest of my borrowed existence.

I will offer myself to your service, and you will never hear me utter a word against your wishes."

Landhoor asked only, "Where is that wretched *dev*?" Then Rashida Peri conducted him to the domicile of Sufaid Dev and gave him all the particulars of his station and abode. The *devs* who stood guard at Sufaid Dev's dwelling ran to their chief Saqra-e Barahman with news that a human had appeared, and that there was no knowing how he had found his way there. When Saqra-e Barahman saw Landhoor, he thought of capturing and making him a present to Sufaid Dev, and thus receiving some reward in return. As he approached and extended his hand to grab Landhoor, the Khusrau caught it and tore it from Saqra-e Barahman's shoulder with one mighty tug. Saqra-e Barahman was knocked out by the pain, and all his pomp and might were made dust. When the *devs* saw their chief in that sorry plight, they wielded their weapons and fell upon Landhoor. However, Landhoor did not allow them to land even a single blow on him and slaughtered many with his sword. The rest of them became deeply unnerved and escaped with their lives.

Landhoor then brought Rashid Jinn with him to Qasr-e Abyez, conducting him to the safety of his palace. The latter expressed his utmost gratitude to the Khusrau and arranged a royal feast for him, ordering revelries and assemblies of song and pleasure. In the midst of the revelries, the Khusrau turned to Khvaja Abdur Raheem, who was one of Rashid Jinn's ministers, and said, "Pray inform your king that I have fallen in love with Rashida Peri, and I desire that the king give me his daughter's hand in marriage. I will be willing to make any pledges that he may wish." Khvaja Abdur Raheem conveyed his message to the king whereupon Rashid Jinn replied, "Give him this message and convey these words to him in the most amiable terms: I would be honored to give him my daughter's hand in marriage. My only conditions are that he first kill my mortal enemy Sufaid Dev, and then clears the Qasr-e Marmar of the scourge of the *devs*. Then he may freely take Rashida Peri as his wife and find the pleasures of life in her company." Landhoor accepted these conditions. It being night, he then went to sleep, after making ready to leave the next morning to kill Sufaid Dev.

Now hear of Sufaid Dev. The *dev* named Palang-Sar took himself with great dispatch to Sufaid Dev and informed him that a human had descended upon them who had killed the *devs* guarding Rashid Jinn, secured his release, whisked him away to safety, and now sought Sufaid

Dev. Upon hearing this, the accursed Sufaid Dev flew into a passion and shouted, "I drowned the Quake of Qaf in the Caspian Sea and put an end to his existence! Whence has this second human come?" When Sufaid Dev went to look, he saw a gigantic youth cavorting with Rashida Peri. She sat in his lap, and he was kissing and fondling her and having a merry time of it. Upon seeing this marvel, Sufaid Dev rushed at Landhoor wielding a box tree and brought it down upon him. Landhoor foiled his attack and, snatching the box tree from his hands, smote the *dev* so powerfully on his head that Sufaid Dev was laid out flat on the ground. The Khusrau pinioned him and completely overpowered him, curing him of all his mutinous and rebellious humors.

Then he flushed out all the *devs* who stood by, cleaning the palace of every last one of them and securing its control. He produced Sufaid Dev before Rashid Jinn, who embraced the Khusrau and showed him every mark of fondness and affection. Rashid Jinn scattered much gold and many jewels over Landhoor's head as the sacrifice of his life. Then he incarcerated Sufaid Dev in a cave situated between two mountains. He appointed several thousand *devs* to guard him, with stern and strict orders regarding the vigil to be kept over him.

Rashid Jinn now again ordered festivities in Landhoor's honor and, pledging Rashida Peri's troth to him, gave her hand to Landhoor with immense pleasure and ordered Khvaja Abdur Raheem to prepare the dowry for his daughter. It took Khvaja several days to make preparations, but at last masters of crafts were commissioned to make all that was needed and the dowry was provided. Rashid Jinn married off his daughter to Landhoor with great fanfare in a manner befitting the ruler of a kingdom.

Since a lengthy account already weighs on the reader, I have not elaborated but left out the account of the marriage ceremony for the *dastan* narrator to embellish, in the interest of not unnecessarily prolonging this history.

In short, after the marriage Landhoor skirmished with the *devs* occupying Qasr-e Marmar, drove them out, and took over control of that palace as well. He bided his time in the pleasant company of Rashida Peri, satisfying all the demands of his love and affection.

It so happened that one hot day, Landhoor was enjoying a deep sleep on a marble platform under the shade of some trees, when Palang-Sar Dev, who had been on the lookout for any opportunity, released Sufaid

Dev from his prison, and informed him of the place where Landhoor lay sleeping and told him to take him unawares.

Thus, Sufaid Dev carried Landhoor away to his abode, and after putting him in chains and securing an iron ball around his neck, threw him into a cave, putting him into incarceration. Then he left to capture Rashida Peri so that he might also imprison her and avenge himself on her.

From fear of her enemy Rashida Peri cast herself into the Tilism-e Anjabal, which was a creation of the Seh-Chashmi Dev, and hid herself there from his wrath. Upon learning this news, Sufaid Dev resolved to enter that *tilism* and secure control over it. His companions, however, prevailed on him to banish such thoughts and told him that anyone who entered that *tilism* never left alive but brought on an end to his life. Sufaid Dev's heart became full of dread upon hearing the details of that *tilism*. He laid siege around it instead, and settled down to bide his time.

————

Now let me narrate a few words about the Sagsars and bring you intelligence of them. When the claw came down from the heavens and carried off Landhoor and Jaipur again shut himself inside the fortress, the Sagsars made life sheer misery for those garrisoned there. Finding himself in a difficult situation, Jaipur was forced to ask Muhlil Sagsar to grant him thirty days' reprieve so that he might make a decision about surrendering the castle. Jaipur wrote a missive to the emperor of China, Bahram Gurd, which read:

> We find ourselves in a terrible mess, and life has now become a burden for us all. Do not delay it if you can come to our avail, and use whatever sources you must to come to our relief; otherwise we will surely see our end.

Upon receiving this missive, the emperor of China headed for Ceylon with his army. When Bahram arrived in Bengal, two brothers, Zaad Khan and Samandar Khan, who were expert pyrotechnicians, presented themselves into his service and submitted with great resolve that if he were to take them along, they would roast the whole Sagsar army in no time. They promised to incinerate the Sagsars so completely that their every last trace would be forever lost, and even the ground on which they tread would vanish, to say nothing of the enemy itself. Bahram was most pleased by their speech. He conferred robes of distinction on both of them, and took them along, promising them many a reward besides.

Now hear of the Sagsars. When thirty days had passed, the duration of the reprieve requested by Jaipur, they again attacked the fortress and exposed Jaipur's army to new trials and tribulations. The followers of the True Faith helplessly raised their hands in prayer and beseeched God to save them from their calamity and release them from the clutches of those demons.

The Sagsar forces were about to breach the fortress when the armies of the emperor of China arrived on the scene, and brought assistance to the besieged at the command of God. The Sagsar army was unable to hold up against the explosions of Zaad Khan and Samandar Khan, unable to protect itself against their pyrotechnics. Many of them were burned to death and dispatched to Hell, and the few who survived fled pell-mell all over the land like unrestrained camels. The fear of explosives left such an indelible mark on the hearts of the Sagsars, and they were so traumatized by their showers, that even if they saw a blazing comet in the darkness of night, they started in terror, burst with laments like noisy firecrackers, and lost their minds from fear.

Bahram meanwhile entered the fortress of Ceylon amidst great jubilation, and the spirits of the people there were greatly bolstered by his arrival. However, Bahram was concerned about Landhoor's fate and was anxious and eager to hear some news of him. He sent his *ayyars* out in all directions to bring him back some intelligence of Landhoor and satisfy the longing and curiosity in his heart.

Now hear of Rashida Peri. At the time she cast herself into the Tilism-e Anjabal, she was with Landhoor's child. After nine months a son was born to her, and the oyster of her womb produced a lustrous pearl. Rashida named him Arshivan Perizad. She inscribed his name and the complete account of his birth on a piece of paper, and after attaching it to the point of an arrow, shot it out of the *tilism* in an attempt to convey her news to her father.

It so happened that a *perizad* found this arrow and carried it to Rashid Jinn, who instructed the *perizad* to carry it to Ceylon and deliver it to an elder of Arshivan Perizad, and ensure that the message was received by him. Upon arriving in Ceylon, the *perizad* put the letter in the lap of Bahram Gurd, and thus carried out Rashid Jinn's orders. Bahram Gurd made every attempt to learn the contents of the letter, but because it was written in Jinni, the language of the jinns, no one could read it, nor could

anyone be found who knew it. Bahram could do aught else but safely put
away the letter, in the hope that one day he would find someone who
knew the language and it would prove of use.

———

Now hear of Arshivan Perizad. When he turned eight, he saw his
mother's sorrow and dejection, and said to her, "Why do you remain so
grief-stricken and unhappy? And why do you not confide to me the cause
of your melancholy and distress?" Rashida Peri told him her whole story
then and everything regarding his birth. She said to him, "My son, I cast
myself in this *tilism* to save my honor. That was why I escaped from my
land. Now there is no hope that I will leave this *tilism* alive, and this anguish gnaws at me from within. Your father has also been imprisoned by
Sufaid Dev. If he were free I would nurse the hope that one day he might
find some way of releasing us from this prison and freeing us from this
trial!" Arshivan said, "Someone must have the tablet of this *tilism* in his
custody. I must find him and take possession of it!" Upon that Rashida
Peri wrote a letter to her father asking him to search for the tablet, and
dispatched that letter out of the *tilism* with an arrow as before.

One of the jinns who had been posted by Rashid Jinn outside the *tilism*
carried this letter to him, and Rashid Jinn mounted a search for the tablet
and did all that was in his power to do in this matter. When he was unable
to locate it, he wrote to Rashida Peri and gave the letter to a *perizad* to
throw into the *tilism* at the same place whence his daughter's letter had
come. The *perizad* immediately took wing and carried out his orders.
Upon reading her father's reply, Rashida Peri said to Arshivan, "Your
grandfather has written that no stone was left unturned in searching for
the tablet, but still it was not found. He thinks it probable that the tablet
is inside the *tilism* itself and may be discovered if searched for within!"

Arshivan now cried copious tears at the helplessness of his mother
and himself, and his feelings of powerlessness kept the tears cascading
down his face. During his lamentations he was suddenly overtaken by
sleep. He saw an old holy man in his dream, who said to him, "My son!
Why do you indulge so much in sorrow and cast such a burden of anguish on your heart? Open the gate of the dome that is opposite your
abode and there you will find a *dev* from whose neck hangs a tablet made
of carnelian inscribed with bold letters. You must act according to the
dictates of that tablet and have no fear even if you find yourself in a dis-

astrous situation. The *dev* will depart after handing you the tablet. Your wish will be fulfilled and you will conquer the *tilism* through the assistance of God."

When Arshivan awoke he narrated the dream to his mother, disclosing the secret to her. When he opened the door of their dome, he indeed found a *dev* there with a carnelian tablet tied to his neck, and he was met with the same circumstances described by the holy ancient in his dream. Peering closely at the tablet Arshivan read:

O Destroyer of *Tilisms*! Recite the following words and blow on the *dev*. He will hand the tablet over to you, and you will find that it will help you in your mission. After giving you the tablet the *dev* will turn back, and you must then strike him on his head, dispatching him to Hell and relieving you of the blackguard existence. Then two rutting elephants will materialize before you, fighting each other and trying to terrify you. You must throw the tablet between them. They will both battle hard to lay claim to the tablet and will mightily defend themselves. During their skirmish, sparks will fly from the clashing of their tusks, and the fire arising from this will combust them and turn them to ashes. Then they shall no longer have any power over you.

Arshivan carried out all the instructions on the tablet, and then he went forth to discover the secret of the *tilism* and the truth behind its enchantment. He came across a great empty desert whose terrible sight would turn any man's gall to water and drain his life blood. In the middle of the desert was a cedar tree covered in delicately patterned foliage. He saw a giant crane,[8] which was the size of a mastodon, sitting atop the tree. It was a beast of a shape and form rarely seen on Earth. Its mandible was like a beam, and its pouch was the depth of Amar Ayyar's *zambil*. Arshivan consulted the tablet and then recited the Most Great Name over the point of the arrow, aimed it at the bird's pouch, and let fly. No sooner had the arrow hit the bird than it fell to the ground and there arose a dark storm, which made the bright day darker than the *Shab-e Yalda*. The darkness was so profound that nobody could make out his one hand from the other, and everyone was engulfed in frenzy. A hue and cry arose of: "Catch him! Do not let him escape! Don't let him get away! The Destroyer of *Tilisms* is escaping after killing the *dev* of the cedar tree! Let us see who puts him to the sword!"

Arshivan began reciting the words on the tablet loudly, and when the commotion ended, he saw a black hill before him. Arshivan headed toward it and saw a marble staircase there that led to a huge pond. Standing there were twelve- and thirteen-year-old damsels who were the envy of the sun and the moon in beauty, carrying goblets of roseate wine in their hands. Many finely crafted and delicate ewers lay scattered about them. The moment they beheld Arshivan Perizad, they said with one voice, "O Destroyer of *Tilisms!* Indeed you have made us wait too long for you! We have stood here for an eternity, suffering the pangs of expectancy!"

Arshivan thought it a marvel and a wonder that thousands of beautiful women whose beauty and splendor surpassed that of the *houris* of Heaven were longing for him, bearing goblets of wine. He found himself in a quandary as he could not possibly drink up all the wine they offered him. Wondering whom he should favor with his acceptance and whom he should refuse, Arshivan looked at the tablet, which read:

> Be warned and beware, O visitor to this *tilism*. Do not even contemplate touching any of these women or even approaching one of them. Their leader is the woman who stands on the embankment clothed in a red dress. Her name is Sehba Jadu. She possesses complete power over the rest of them, and this rosy-cheeked beauty is indeed the commander of these sorceresses. Take the goblet from her hand and, reciting the Most Great Name on it, throw the goblet's contents in her face. Then you will witness the marvels of God and the sorceress will show you an unparalleled spectacle. Beware, however, not to let even a single drop of wine splash on you and take great care that not even a droplet comes in contact with your body or your clothes, or else you, too, will share the same fate as they and a similar adversity will befall you.

Arshivan took the goblet from the hand of Sehba Jadu, and after reciting the Most Great Name over it, threw it in her face. Then he jumped away fifty paces and kept running. The moment the wine touched the face of the sorceress, it caught fire. Sehba Jadu began moving about like a blazing flame and revolving like a top. The fire raged so potently that all the women standing around the pond began to burn like a candelabra and they wrung their hands with grief at their destruction. Within an hour they had completely burned away and not a single one of them remained.

Arshivan offered his thanks to God and when he looked to the tablet again, it read:

O Destroyer of *Tilisms*! Some *perizads* will appear before you singing and frolicking and will try to entice you with their spectacle. Then an old man will greet you and make salutations, and will speak to you in honeyed tones. You must not answer him but instead hold the tablet to him like a mirror. Remember to use this stratagem, and all of them will scatter away at the sight of the tablet. Then the *tilism* will be conquered and you will be successful in your mission.

Arshivan acted as he had been commanded and destroyed the *tilism*.

Rashida Peri was beside herself with joy at her son's victory. She embraced Arshivan and exited the *tilism*, and everyone there was delighted and released of their sorrow by the end of her internment. The *perizads* who had been posted there by Rashid Jinn marveled at the sight of her. They wondered how she had been able to secure her release from such a dreadful *tilism* and what subterfuge she had employed to break free from it. Rashid Jinn was immediately informed of Rashida Peri's well-being, and he forthwith arrived on his throne and embraced Arshivan fondly. Then seating both Rashida Peri and Arshivan on his throne, he returned to Qasr-e Abyez scattering gold and jewels as their sacrifice. All of them gave thanks to God Almighty on that happy occasion.

Arshivan then asked his grandfather, "Where has Sufaid Dev imprisoned my father? Pray do me the kindness of directing me to that place." Rashid Jinn took Arshivan with him to the domicile of Sufaid Dev, showing him where that dev dwelt and giving him all the particulars about that place.

———

Now hear of the Rustam of His Age, King Landhoor bin Saadan. One day he was bemoaning his helplessness and washing his face with tears at his sorry fate when he heard someone say the words, "Peace be with you!" Instantly, Landhoor was imbued with new life. He answered the greeting and saw that his interlocutor was Prophet Khizr. Landhoor tearfully supplicated him and said, "O holy Khizr! How much longer must I remain caught in this prison and suffer these privations and hardships?" The prophet answered, "I have come to set you free today, sent to you with this auspicious news of freedom from God!" The prophet removed the fetters from Landhoor's arms and legs, and then disappeared, having delivered Landhoor from the pain of incarceration.

When Landhoor left the cave, he beheld Rashid Jinn and Rashida

Peri sitting on a throne outside, looking in his direction. Rashida Peri held a boy in her lap. After kissing Rashid Jinn's feet and embracing Rashida Peri, Landhoor asked, "Who is this boy? Give me all the details and tell me the truth about the whole matter!"

Rashida Peri told Landhoor all about his son and then made Arshivan kiss Landhoor's feet. Landhoor embraced Arshivan and they returned to Qasr-e Abyez in the company of Rashid Jinn.

Of Khvaja Amar Ayyar's Moving to the Castle of Devdad from the Fortress of Qiamlam [?] Along with Mehr-Nigar and the Followers of the True Faith

The narrators of sweet discourse tell that after a year had passed, the commanders informed Amar that the fortress had run out of provisions, everyone was fearful of starvation, and anxiety was making the populace apprehensive and fretful. Khvaja Amar asked Mehtar Sayyad if there was another fortress nearby where they could take refuge for a few days and set their hearts at ease from all worries of sustenance.

Sayyad said, "Two days' journey from here is the fortress of Devdad, which was constructed by Jamshed and is equipped with all manner of luxuries. It is more impregnable than any other castle in the world and is a marvel of toughness and invincibility that puts to shame even the mountains of Alburz. Four mountains lie opposite it, which are themselves wonders of the Insuperable Maker's work. Jamshed secured the castle by riveting it with massive steel chains to the mountains. The rivets are driven deep into the rock and the castle is sheathed in steel plates that make its facade extremely strong and stable. At a distance of four cubits from the castle lie two concentric iron border walls with the intervening space filled with sand. The fortress encompasses such a huge tract of land that crops are cultivated within its own walls. Thus, the castle is self-sufficient in production of food and free of dependence on supplies from outside. Those who live there do not want for anything. There is only one entrance to the castle and it is such a narrow gap that only one person can make his way through at a time; more than one man cannot pass it simultaneously."

Amar was pleased to hear these qualities of the castle. He sent for his commanders and said to them, "Take care of this place while I go to plan a takeover of the other fortress and discover some way of providing for us." He then changed from his court regalia to his *ayyar*'s livery, rushed out of the fort bravely, and arrived at the fortress of Devdad in no time. He was amazed by the castle, as he had never before seen a fort like it or even heard of one that could compare to it.

Amar walked around the castle a few times to see if he could find an entrance, but he was disappointed, unable to find a way of gaining admission into it. He sat down on a rock and submerged himself in the river of thoughtfulness to think up some way of getting in when he caught sight of a water carrier standing on a iron platform in a turret of the castle, drawing up water from the lake and filling it into water skins. Amar said to himself that he would find no better means for getting inside the castle, and surely no other trick would get him within the fortress walls. He stole closer and, evading the notice of the water carrier, jumped into the lake and climbed into the bucket. The water carrier was surprised to find the bucket so heavy and when he looked down he saw a man of strange shape and form riding in it. In his foolishness he thought that luck had favored him and he had caught a merman in his bucket. Imagining it an invaluable treasure sent to him by auspicious fortune, he began pulling up the pail slowly lest the precious creature should escape and slip out of his grasp.

As the bucket neared the pulley, the water carrier extended his hands with the intention of catching the creature and taking it out. Amar leapt at him and, catching him by his neck, hurled him down into the lake, playing a trick on the water carrier. Because the lake was deep and the cup of life of the water carrier was already full, he sank and rose up flailing his arms a few times before drowning. Disguising himself as the water carrier, Amar then took over his duty and began drawing water. After he had filled the water skins, he tried to reason out where the water carrier took his water and what he used it for.

Before long other water carriers arrived there with their water skins. They waved to Amar and said, "Fattu, why do you lie here idling and not performing your duty carrying water?" Amar said to them, "I have been taken with fever and my heart is stifled by heat. I would be most grateful if you could do me the kindness of informing my family of my condition." One water carrier went and informed Fattu's family that he was lying near the ramparts of the fortress, shivering and panting from the heat and violence of a fever. His wife and children came running to him and carried him back to his house. Everyone who saw his condition was greatly distressed, and Amar meanwhile slept on peacefully and rested himself at leisure.

Some hours of night had passed when Fattu's wife woke him up and said, "Eat something, for you should get some nourishment." Amar answered, "I do not feel hungry!" She said, "I have made porridge with rice and lentils. Eat a little so that you do not become weak." Amar relented, "If it is your wish, then give it to me!" After eating it Amar washed his hands and mouth. He had begun smoking the hookah when someone suddenly called out to him from outdoors, shouting, "O Fattu! Are you awake or asleep? Come out quickly, as I have something to communicate to you!" Amar said in his heart, *God have mercy! Who is this man who calls me? Let us see what new marvel of fate awaits me! Who could have come to call on me in the middle of the night, and what important business is it that has brought him here?*

The false Fattu asked his wife to find out who it was. She called outside, "What is your name, and what business do you have with Fattu at this hour of the night? He has been taken ill and cannot come out. He is unable to take even a single step because of his malady!" The man answered, "I am Haam Devdadi, the commander and head of the king's *ayyars.* I have something of great importance to discuss with him." When Amar heard that it was an *ayyar* who had come to see him, suspicion and anxiety engulfed him. He asked the woman if the man had ever called there before or if she had seen him in the past. When she denied ever hearing from or seeing him, Amar became even more troubled and said to himself, *Running into an* ayyar *immediately upon arrival is not a good omen. May God protect me.*

Amar came out of the house coughing and clearing his throat, saying, "My God is now my protector against evil." When Haam saw Amar, he said, "Peace be with you, O King of the *Ayyars* of the World!" Amar replied, "This is the house of Fattu the water carrier! Maybe the king of the *ayyars* of the world lives farther down!" Haam Devdadi said, "O Khvaja! Why do you hide yourself from me? I, too, am a follower of the True Faith and have always nursed the desire to meet you. For two months I have awaited your arrival, and now I swear myself to your servitude." Haam Devdadi kissed Amar's feet, and then Amar embraced him and offered him many words of amity and encouragement.

Haam Devdadi said, "Come, let us carry out what you came here to do. We will worry about the consequences and deal with the situation as it unfolds. I am your companion now however dark the night." Evading the notice of the guards, the two of them climbed up a rope into the palace of King Antar Devdadi and found their way in with their cunning. Amar saw that the king was by himself, sleeping under a Cathay satin pavilion with the coverlet pulled up to his face. There was neither guard nor attendant and the king slept the sleep of those lost to the world. Amar removed the corner of the coverlet from the king's face. He was about to blow a drug into the king's nose to render him unconscious when the king caught his hand. Amar pulled away and shook off the hold, and the king was left holding the gauntlet Amar had been wearing. While Amar was pondering his escape, the king called out to him, "O Khvaja! Do not run away from me. Listen to what I have to say and think on it a while. This very moment Prophet Ibrahim converted me to the True Faith in the realm of dreams and gave me news of your arrival with orders to offer myself in your service. I do not possess the power of divination to have been able to recognize you otherwise, or to have known you without being acquainted with your particulars." Upon hearing this Amar stopped in his tracks. The king got up from his bed and embraced Amar and said to him with great love and sincerity, "In the morning bring your people to this fortress and conduct them here without delay. Consider this fortress your own. Even if Jamshed himself, let alone Hurmuz and Faramurz, charged the fortress he wouldn't be able to wrest it from me or inflict the least bit of harm on you."

Amar returned immediately to the fortress where his camp was currently lodged and gave news to the commanders of his camp that the fortress of Devdad had been secured. He rested for one day and, come night, put Mehr-Nigar into a palanquin covered with gold brocade and sent her to the fortress of Devdad along with his army. He installed paper puppets all over the empty fort and then headed himself toward Devdad. Within two days the whole camp had moved to the fortress of Devdad, and Amar was relieved of all his anxieties. In the fortress the king had already converted everyone to the True Faith and instructed his guards that they should let Amar pass without hesitation. The guards opened the gates the moment they heard Amar's call and he moved his entire camp within. After establishing matters to his liking at the new fortress, Amar settled down to bide his time and instructed all his companions to take some rest as well.

———

Now we turn to the camp of the infidels. On the third day after Amar's move *ayyars* brought news to Hurmuz and Faramurz that the fort of the followers of the True Faith seemed empty of people. They reported that nobody could be seen there, and yet it did not make sense that the whole fort could be empty all of a sudden. Bakhtiarak said, "There is no other fortress in this vicinity except the fortress of Devdad. It would be little wonder if Amar had taken it over by some cunning or subterfuge." The princes immediately rode to the fortress and saw that indeed it was empty of all people and, instead, decorated with men cut out of paper standing guard on the castle. An ass and a dog were tied to its gates, and except for a few birds stirring inside, there was no sign of guards, soldiers, or Mehr-Nigar's presence. The princes sent a note to the Emperor of the Seven Concentric Circles that Amar had left his castle for the fortress of Devdad, and that their campaign to attack him would not succeed without the emperor arriving in person or sending some master strategist in his stead, for without such assistance they would have a hard time of it. They sent the missive to Naushervan's court with the *ayyar* named Kargas Sasani and themselves marched forth with their camp. Three days after giving marching orders to their whole army, they arrived at the castle of Devdad and laid a siege.

Naushervan became grieved upon reading the princes' missive, and the news made him angry and enraged. Turning to Bakhtak he said, "I do not know how to overpower and punish this cameleer's son, yet I must avenge his transgressions against my people!" Bakhtak replied, "It would be proper for you to go and join your armies. His misdemeanors have now crossed all bounds and his punishment is long overdue. Without your presence this campaign will never come to fruition. If you advance there after making the requisite preparations, the tide will turn in your favor and bring you victory."

Naushervan then asked Buzurjmehr, "What is your advice in this matter? Would it be proper or improper for me to march there?" Buzurjmehr answered, "Your slave's advice will be the same as before. If you head there and Amar makes Your Excellency a target of his crimes, it will be a most terrible calamity, mortifying and humiliating for us all. However, Your Honor's opinion is superior to the advice of all of his slaves, and whatever you command we shall carry out without fail!" When Naushervan recalled Amar's past deeds, he trembled with fear and turned upon Bakhtak and said, "You reprobate fool! You are the one most disloyal to my interests and are nothing but a marvel of chicanery and mischief. You have always led me down the path of deceit and gained me false repute!"

At that moment the emperor received news that Zhopin's brother Bechin Kamran was on his way with two hundred thousand mounted warriors to present himself to his service and would arrive there before long. Naushervan was most pleased with this auspicious news and sent several nobles to receive him, ordering them to usher Bechin into his court with great respect and honor and to inform him of the emperor's desire of receiving him in his service. When Bechin Kamran arrived and kissed the throne and ennobled himself in the emperor's audience, Naushervan bestowed on him his highest favors by conferring on him the Jamshedi robe of honor and ordering festivities and revelries befitting the majesty and honor of his court. For three days and three nights the celebrations were held, and when the revelries were over Bechin Kamran asked, "O my lord and master, I do not see my brothers Zhopin, Jahandar, and Jahangir. I would be grateful if you could inform me of their whereabouts and tell me what has passed with them."

Naushervan heaved a cold sigh and said, "I cannot even begin to tell you how saddened and distraught I am by their absence. Your brothers are accompanying Hurmuz and Faramurz in their campaign to capture Amar Ayyar, a minion of Hamza. Nine years have passed and yet he avoids capture. He hatches mischief after mischief and moves from one fortress to the next, neither sitting still in one place himself nor letting anyone else have any peace."

Bechin Kamran replied, "If you so order this slave, I will charge the fortress where he is holed up and, without taking a moment's rest, lay waste to his fortress and produce him and Princess Mehr-Nigar before you! I will make him forget all his mischief and trickery and force him to eat the bread of humility!"

The emperor was most pleased to hear these words and said, "You are such a valiant warrior indeed as to fulfill this mission and a consummate soldier on the battlefield." He conferred on him an honorable robe of departure and gave him orders to march immediately on the fortress of Devdad. Bechin Kamran advanced toward the fortress at the head of two hundred thousand troops and within a few days arrived at his destination. He set up camp adjacent to the fortress. When Hurmuz and Faramurz heard news of his arrival they sent his brothers Jahangir Kabuli and Jahandar Kabuli to greet him so that he might be delighted by the reunion, and his fatigue of the journey might be dispelled in their company. When Bechin arrived in his camp, the princes received him with every mark of favor and provided him every amenity that he requested.

Bechin approached Zhopin and said to him before everyone, "Tell me, Zhopin, how is it that an ordinary pawn has proved such a mighty foe for you? Is this an accomplishment worthy of someone who desires to be the emperor's son-in-law and take his daughter in marriage?" Zhopin answered, "Indeed you speak the truth, but you say these words without knowing the one you call an ordinary pawn. Now that you have joined us, you will soon learn about him yourself, and I am certain that you will come to harm at his hands. That pawn is such a scourge that hundreds of thousands of troops are too few to put him down. He is a consummate *ayyar* against whose mischief none can prevail." Bechin declared, "What idle talk to say that a mere pawn renders hundreds of thousand of troops useless and no answer can be found to his machinations! Beat the drums of war in my name right now and get the army ready for battle!"

Hurmuz ordered the drums of war beaten in his camp and readied his forces for battle and slaughter. The moment the drums were sounded, the news was brought to Amar that the camp of the infidels had sounded the drums of war and was ready for battle in the morning. Then Amar ordered the Timbal of Sikander to be sounded. The drums of war were beaten in both camps the whole night while the armies carried out the duties of the vigil. In the morning, Hurmuz and Faramurz were carried on a throne to the battlefield, and all their commanders brought along their forces and joined the princes in the field. Bechin Kamran arranged his two hundred thousand troops on one side of the field, and the battle cries of the armies created a din like doomsday. The armies of Hurmuz and Faramurz, which were by now versed in Amar's battle tactics, did not advance but saved themselves from the possibility of Amar showering them with Greek fire. Bechin Kamran's army, who were newly inducted in that campaign, went forth to charge the fortress and drew close to it. As they came within range, they found themselves suddenly engulfed in a hail of fire and they all fled pell-mell, not being able to stand their ground or stay the course.

Upon seeing his army in such disarray, Bechin said to Zhopin, "It seems we will not be able to achieve our end with this force, as all the men are mortified of the fire and are as good for the purpose of warfare as dead bodies. Let us charge, you and I, and break down the fortress gates and barge into their hole and wring their necks." Zhopin answered, "Come! I am with you. Never would I refuse such a challenge!" The two brothers rode out and approached the fortress gates. From the smoke of the fireworks, the whole battlefield was enveloped in a darkness that rivaled the

Shab-e Yalda, and it was so completely dark that nobody could even make out his one hand from the other. When the garrisoned army stopped the fire, the wind carried the smoke to the skies and the air became clear and visibility was restored. People inside the fortress saw Zhopin and Bechin standing on the edge of the moat, resolved on breaking down the gates. Amar was devising a scheme for killing them when Naqabdar Naranji-Posh suddenly appeared with his forty thousand troops.

He rode up to Zhopin and Bechin and said, "O castrated curs, who are you to have taken it into your heads to wage war against the followers of the True Faith? Why do you wish to bring calamity upon yourselves?" They answered, "Who are you to interfere in the fight between us and the garrisoned army and take the side of the armies of the True Faith?" The Naqabdar replied, "I am your Angel of Death. I shall send you both to the Future State and herd you into the gates of Hell without delay!" The two brothers now drew their swords from their sheaths and attacked the Naqabdar, who snatched their swords and, holding them by their cummerbunds, lifted them above his head and rendered them completely helpless. He asked them, "Tell me, shall I throw you into the sea or onto land?"

Witnessing this turn of events, Hurmuz and Faramurz fell upon the Naqabdar with their army. The Naqabdar's men drew their swords and joined the battle and showed their mettle as men and warriors. Amar also came out of the fortress then, and joined in the slaughter of the foe. In the fight that ensued, the cummerbunds of the two brothers broke and they fell from the Naqabdar's grasp. Their wits left them and, looking neither left nor right, they fled the battlefield on horseback in all haste.

To cut a long story short, some eighty thousand men from the army of the infidels lost their lives in the pitched battle that was fought that day. Many important commanders of Naushervan's army were among the dead. Everyone in the armies of the True Faith remained unharmed and suffered not even a bloody nose—even their arms and armor escaped the slightest damage. Untold riches and treasures were claimed by the followers of the True Faith, and they acquired many goods and valuables in the war booty. Amar rushed to kiss the stirrup of the Naqabdar and said, "O valiant youth! What you accomplished today even Rustam could have only dreamed of doing. No one has ever witnessed or heard of such gallantry and valor. In the name of God, give me your name and remove the veil from your splendid aspect so that our longing gaze may find solace in beholding it."

The Naqabdar replied, "O Amar! I have yet to accomplish any such deed that would warrant disclosing my name with honor or showing you my face with pride! When Amir Hamza returns in safety and well-being to the world, you will then hear my name and see my face! Return to the fortress now and bide your time in safety. Let no fear or anxiety cast its shadow on your mind. Consider me always as one who has cast his lot with your own and will prevent the hand of evil from reaching you." He sent Amar back to the fortress, offering him many words of consolation and comfort, and then returned whence he had come—and nobody saw where he disappeared.

Hurmuz and Faramurz sent a missive to the emperor informing him of the particulars of the battle and their defeat. They submitted to him a detailed account of the events and beseeched him, "We request you to dispatch us pavilions, provisions, and gold, for without proper shelter we will be exposed to the sun during the day and the dew showers at night and will fall sick. Not even a single foot soldier will then remain with the army. If gold is not received in time we will die of starvation. Pray consider that we will have nothing to eat if the provisions run out."

The *dastan*'s narrator says that when that missive from Hurmuz and Faramurz reached Naushervan and he became aware of their plight, he said to Bakhtak, "You always claim that if I advance on the enemy, you will prove such a force that you will burn to ashes a thousand *ayyars* like Amar with your deceit and will drive him and his companions from the face of the Earth. Tell me what Bakhtiarak—that bastard son of yours—has accomplished in the nine long years he has accompanied Hurmuz and Faramurz that you think you can outdo. Why, you will also surely come to grief at the hands of Amar. By following your advice I have brought about my ruin with my own hands. I have myself invited all this humiliation and dishonor on my person and have given my enemies reason to take comfort from my misery. You are hereby warned not to present yourself at my court after today. Never again show me your star-crossed face at the risk of exposing yourself to my wrath and inviting the severest punishment on your head!"

Bakhtak returned weeping and wailing to his house, where he wrote a letter to his son and sent it with utmost dispatch. In that letter, he wrote:

O ill-begotten bastard! For a full nine years you have accompanied the princes and you have yet to accomplish a minor matter like putting Amar to death and carrying out what you were sent to do. You have besmirched the honor of your elders and deprived me the pleasure and prestige of both our world and the Future State. Your actions have resulted in my being driven from the emperor's court, and much suffering and humiliation have become my lot in this matter. It would bode well for you to carry out this mission at all costs; or else, risk my renouncing you as my son and forbidding you from ever showing me your face again. It surprises me no end that—rascal as I am—my own flesh and blood should not have turned out a consummate rascal and rogue. I have lost all hope for great deeds from you now, and fear you are not the fruit of my loins but of some common merchant or grocer.

Bakhtiarak became very troubled when he read this letter and wondered what he might do to save face and regain his father's approval. He spent the whole day occupied in anxious machinations and nervous scheming until finally he hit upon an idea and decided to carry out this cunning plan. Wearing his night livery he made a few rounds of the fortress but found the guards vigilant and alert at all posts, and felt much consternation at not being able to carry out his designs as he wished.

It so happened that one of King Antar Devdadi's sons, Khvaja Arbab, was drinking wine in one of the towers of the fortress. All the guards of that tower had gone to bed and were deep in the slumber of the lost. Upon hearing Bakhtiarak's footsteps, Khvaja Arbab called out, "Who goes there? What is your business, and what errand brings you here?" Bakhtiarak answered, "It is I, Bakhtiarak, come to submit something to your ears in earnest, and bringing you a weighty proposition to consider." In his stupor, Khvaja Arbab let Bakhtiarak climb up a rope into the tower without the least suspicion. Bakhtiarak gave a forged letter to Khvaja Arbab and said, "This missive has been sent to you by Naushervan!" Seeing Naushervan's seal on the letter, Khvaja Arbab believed it to be genuine, sent to him by the great and mighty emperor himself. He opened the envelope to peruse the letter, which read:

O Khvaja Arbab! Your father has proved false to the bounds of vassalage and has grievously deceived me by becoming an ally of my foe. I am therefore placing my hope in your fidelity. If you give the possession of this fortress to my men for a few days and arrest Amar and send him to me a prisoner, I swear by the fire temple of Namrud that I shall bestow this fortress on you and shower you with many other favors besides. I shall grant your every wish, induct you among my confidants, promote you to a high rank among them, and show you the utmost favor.

Khvaja Arbab was beside himself with joy upon reading the contents of the letter and prayed for the emperor and sang his praises and adulations. He said to Bakhtiarak, "You should attest this letter with your seal so that whoever sees it will believe it!" Bakhtiarak answered, "Nothing would be easier. If you wish I can even have the letter authenticated by the princes themselves." In short, Bakhtiarak was able to entice Khvaja Arbab to go with him that very moment to see Hurmuz and Faramurz. When he arrived in the presence of the princes, Bakhtiarak said to them, "Pray show me the kindness and favor of putting your seals on this letter that the emperor has sent to Khvaja Arbab." Hurmuz and Faramurz figured that Bakhtiarak had some ploy in mind and that this was all part of a ruse. They answered him with happy countenances, "We will gladly authenticate this letter with our seals and give you a letter of our own to that effect. Besides that, whatever you demand we shall undertake to get approved by the emperor as well and any favor that you ask we will have granted by the emperor." Then Hurmuz and Faramurz attested the letter with their seals, and plied Khvaja Arbab with much deceitful prattle.

Khvaja Arbab said, "Underneath your pavilion is the mouth of a tunnel whose other end is in my quarters. I request you to dig through the ground until you have reached the tunnel, while I go to my place and have the other end of the tunnel dug up from my end. Over the course of this night and tomorrow morning, the heat inside the tunnel will thus be dissipated and it will become well ventilated. I invite you to come to my humble abode early tomorrow evening by way of this tunnel and to augment the honor of your servant with your august and distinction-bestowing presence. Enjoy my feast for you and see my abode, and after a few hours have passed in the night, kill the followers of the True Faith and take Amar into custody. You may do with him as you wish once he is in your power and you may also bring Mehr-Nigar back with you and enjoy the company of your sister. I only request that you bring with you the most valiant commanders of your army who are sworn to valor and courage." Hurmuz and Faramurz sent Khvaja Arbab off after bestowing a robe of honor on him, and gave directions to their men that accorded with his plan. Khvaja Arbab returned to his fortress the same way that he had come, and brought diggers to his house and set busy. The men exerted themselves fully, and around morning, they had opened up the cavity of the tunnel. Khvaja Arbab then occupied himself with arranging for the feast and securing the necessities for the revelries.

Dil-Aavez, who was one of Khvaja Arbab's daughters, asked him,

"Pray tell me what is the occasion for all this ceremony and celebration, and the event for which this assembly is being arranged!" Khvaja Arbab decided to take his daughter into his confidence and gave her the entire account of the previous night. He reasoned that she was a member of his family, so he divulged the secret. Dil-Aavez felt great dismay that her villainous father was so blinded by avarice that he was ready and willing to take upon his head the blood of thousands of innocent followers of the True Faith and inflict a grievous wrong on them. She immediately wrote a note giving a detailed account of these proceedings, and entrusted her wet nurse to hand it to Amar, enjoining her to take it speedily to him and telling her that Amar would reward her richly and bestow much gold and many provisions on her. The wet nurse immediately brought the note to Amar and conveyed Dil-Aavez's message as well after giving him the letter. Amar offered many rewards to the wet nurse and also showered praise on Dil-Aavez, commending her on her generous gesture toward him and his camp.

Amar seated himself on his throne and ordered his commanders to assemble. First he addressed Aadi and said, "A food offering is being made somewhere today. I will take you along with me and feed you as you deserve. But you must first promise me that you will not show aversion to hard work, for if you do I will make sure that you sneeze out every single grain of food you eat and receive a severe punishment besides."

Aadi answered, "We will obey you in all respects. It is not our way to be disloyal to you. Consider that ever since Amir has left, I have been given only twenty *maunds* of flour and rice for my two daily meals. I eat all of it for one meal and go hungry the other part of the day. With that food my belly is not even half filled. But until Amir's return this loyal servant endures his lot and survives on a diet barely enough to keep him alive. I never utter a word of complaint for fear of displeasing you. If you were to let me have my fill of food, I would not turn away from hard work. You will see how I will exert myself and sweat in your cause. As the saying goes, 'First feed the beast of burden and then burden his back.' "

When a few hours remained until the close of day, Amar took his commanders and headed to the house of Khvaja Arbab. When Khvaja Arbab heard that Amar's entourage was on its way, he became pale with anxiety and paralyzed by fear. His senses began to take leave of him and the resolution of his aiders and abettors wavered. In the meanwhile, Amar's conveyance arrived and, along with his entourage, he descended at the entrance. Khvaja Arbab came out of his house to greet Amar, received him with great honor and prestige, and made him an offering. After receiving the offering, Amar said, "I have heard that you are making a food offering in the name of Prophet Ibrahim today and have arranged a feast for the followers of the True Faith. For that reason I have called on your house and brought my companions along so that we may partake."

Khvaja Arbab was greatly surprised and dismayed by these words, but there was nothing he could do. He could not hide the preparations of the feast, for they were visible everywhere and there was no possibility for him to deny them. He answered, "Indeed Your Honor is a veritable saint, and things hidden and manifest are as one to you. It is true that I have been busy since morning in the preparation of the feast, and that was the reason I could not appear before you any earlier to bring you an invitation. All my time has been taken up by these arrangements, and I was unable to present myself in your service. I had planned to inform Your Honor once the food was cooked and to augment my honor by kissing your feet afterward. It is well that you directed your feet hither and came without the formalities of an invitation, saving me the visit."

At this, he led Amar to the same chamber that he had equipped with luxuries and seating arrangements for the princes. He showed great honor to Amar, attending to him devotedly, and provided seating stations to his commanders according to their rank. Amar then asked that the food be served. He had Aadi stuffed to the gills with the finest foods first, and then asked that the rest be served to his commanders. In short, all of them had their fill of the food and delicacies prepared for the occasion.

When it neared evening, and the world was covered in darkness by the setting of the sun, Amar ordered Khvaja Arbab to be pinioned and taken into custody without delay. No sooner were the orders given than Khvaja Arbab was trussed up into a bundle. He said, "What is my crime that you have tied me up in this manner? Verily this is just recompense for my waiting on you as host and treating you to a feast." Amar answered, "Indeed you have committed no crime on your part, but I also have an obligation to remain true to the bounds of vassalage. What I have done is not without good reason." Amar had Khvaja Arbab locked up in a room and ordered that nobody should be allowed to visit him.

Then Amar said to Aadi, "The time to exert yourself has now come. Do it with diligence and do not let any vacillation jeopardize our mission." Aadi answered, "I offer myself with my heart and soul. Give me your orders and I will carry them out and show you how well I can reward your trust in me." Amar found the entrance to the tunnel and, deploying Aadi at its mouth, said to him, "Strangle anyone who emerges here with your hands and drag him out so that he does not make a sound or utter a word. All our commanders will stand by your side and won't move from their positions. You can hand over your prisoners to them, and they, too, will make sure that my orders are carried out and the men are silently transported to the prison. Beware not to let anyone slip from your hands, or else I will have you disemboweled with the same intensity with which I just fed you, and will pinion and slaughter you like a goat."

Aadi sat on his haunches at the mouth of the tunnel to carry out Amar's orders and pull out anyone who emerged from there just like a *nanbai*[9] pulls bread from an oven pit.

———

Now hear of Hurmuz and Faramurz. When a few hours remained before the close of day, they entered the tunnel with ten thousand troops and four hundred renowned warriors without the least fear or apprehension, as if they were headed to a house as invited guests. The thought of any ploy or trick staged by Amar never crossed their minds. When they neared the tunnel's end, Aadi alerted Amar and said, "I can hear footsteps and people approaching!" Amar told him, "Beware! Do not let a single one of them escape alive." In the meantime, a man poked his head out of the tunnel and Aadi, who was stationed there like the Angel of Death, caught his neck, pulled him out, and handed him to another commander who conducted him to the prison. Another man's head appeared from the tunnel and he fared the same, and the tunnel soon became the bane of his existence. In short, Aadi caught all four hundred of the renowned warriors in no time and handed them to his commanders, who took the prisoners to the guards of the jail, who put them in chains and incarcerated them under a strict and watchful vigil. All of them tasted the unhappy surprise that came from stepping into the tunnel that day.

Now, Zhopin followed behind his commanders and wondered why none of the four hundred men who had gone before him had brought back a report from the other side. Indeed he found it quite odd and suspicious. Before emerging from the tunnel, he peeped out just a little to see what was happening there. Aadi caught hold of his head, but since Zhopin had not extended his neck, and even his head was only partially thrust out, Aadi could not fully secure his grip on Zhopin. Wondering what terrible scourge and retribution he had been invited to instead of a feast,

Zhopin thought that perhaps Khvaja Arbab had orchestrated a way of killing the guests who came to him expecting dinner. Zhopin dug his feet into the walls of the tunnel and began calling out for his brothers, crying, "Come, brothers! Rush to my aid, for someone has caught my head and is pulling me out! God knows what scourge or demon it is that hauls me up!"

Bechin grabbed Zhopin's legs and pulled him so hard that Zhopin's head slipped from Aadi's hands, and they foiled Amar's strategy of catching him. Zhopin escaped with his life from Aadi's grip, but could not save his ears, both of which were left behind in Aadi's hands. Those following behind him became aware of the trouble when the alarm was raised, and they quickly retraced their steps. Aadi made a present of Zhopin's ears to Amar, who realized that everyone had been alerted to the trap. Figuring that now no one would be caught coming out of the tunnel because such a huc and cry had started, he began shooting fiery missiles into the tunnel and sending iron rockets to explode on their heads. The ten thousand troops who had entered with the princes found fiery graves in that tunnel, and not a single one of them escaped alive. Hurmuz and Faramurz got away with only a few men from their entourage.

In the morning Amar hanged all four hundred of the imprisoned commanders of the infidels along with Khvaja Arbab. He spared not a single one of them but executed all of them mercilessly. Then he poured molten lead into the tunnel and sealed the passage off to all traffic. Hurmuz and Faramurz reported the whole account of this misadventure in another missive to Naushervan and dispatched it to him with Sabir Namadposh, relating the particulars of the story and what passed with them.

———

Now for some news of the Sahibqiran. Aasman Peri had sworn before the prophets Khizr and Ilyas and given them her word that after six months she would send the Sahibqiran back to his world and never again break her promise. When six months had passed, Amir said to Aasman Peri, "Now the time has come to fulfill your promise. Send me back to my world, in the name of God, and carry out your pledge." Aasman Peri said, "I will send you back after one year has passed. Pray have patience for just one more year and repress your longing for my sake." Upon hearing these words Amir was enraged and said irately, "O Aasman Peri, do you have *any* fear of God in your heart? It is best for one to have fear of God and avoid a course of action that invites divine wrath. Six months ago you swore before two prophets that after this period you would send me to my world and dispatch me to the realm of humans without fail. Now again you make pledges and promises and vows to me about your reliability and veracity!" Aasman Peri answered, "The retribution for breaking my word will be mine alone, so have no worries on that account!"

Amir took his complaints to Emperor Shahpal, entering his presence looking distraught and woebegone. He said to Shahpal, "O emperor of the lands of Qaf! What ill have I done you that you are bent on wrecking my life and torturing me in this manner? I came here on the promise of remaining just eighteen days. A long time has passed since that brief period, and in all that time I have received no news of my family. God knows what has passed with them and what horrors they have suffered, for I have a virulent enemy there in the Emperor of the Seven Climes, whose fondest wish is to see me dead. Moreover, both you and Aasman Peri made a solemn vow before two prophets of God that after six months you would certainly and unfailingly send me back to the world of men and would make not the slightest delay in doing so. By the grace of God that period is now over. And now Aasman Peri tells me that since I have passed so many days languishing here, I should spend another whole year and continue to bear the pain of separation from my family. I have a good mind to ask you why you are desirous of taking my life with your own hands!"

Shahpal comforted Amir, showed him much favor, and offered him words of consolation. Seating Amir on a throne that very instant, he ordered four *devs* to carry Amir to his world and to carry out his orders with complete submission. When Aasman Peri received this news, she arrived there holding Quraisha in her arms and said to Amir, "O Abul-Ala, have you no love for your daughter either? If I have wronged you, what is her crime, and what grief have you received at her innocent hands?" Amir answered, "When you come to visit me in the world of humans, bring her with you. It is a simple matter for you to travel between Qaf and my world, and offers you no hardships. If you were to invite me here for a visit, I would come to see you without hesitation or the least misgiving. But now I must depart, and you would do well to let me go and not stop me." Thus speaking, Amir ordered the *devs* to carry his throne aloft and departed from there.

Aasman Peri returned to her quarters tearful and heartbroken from Amir's departure. She sent for Rizwan Perizad and said to him, "Go to the Sahibqiran on the pretext of bidding him adieu in order to convey my urgent orders to the throne bearers. Tell them that they are to travel no farther than the Dasht-e Ajaib, where they should leave Amir and then return here. In the event that they disobey this command, they will have to answer to me, and I will severely chastise them for their refractory behavior." Rizwan Perizad flew away and speedily approached Hamza's throne. Amir saw his arrival as an ominous sign, realizing that his coming could not be a good thing. Sensing that Rizwan had arrived on some covert mission at the bidding of the treacherous Aasman Peri, he said to the *devs* who were bearing his throne, "Return to Shahpal and do as I command you!" When the *devs* resisted, Amir grasped the hilt of his sword and said, "If you do not return, I will kill every single one of you by smashing your skulls!" The *devs* were thus forced to return Amir's throne to Shahpal's court in keeping with his wishes.

When the emperor saw Amir, he said, "O Amir, tell me that all is well with you! What has caused you to return to me and come back to my court?" Amir answered, "I have come to ask whether you sincerely wish to send me to my world, or if you instead wish me to languish again in some desert and wander in desolation." The emperor swore upon the sincerity of his intent and said, "I am gladly sending you back to your world, and it is my earnest wish that you return to your homeland and finally enjoy the company of your family!" Amir declared, "If that is the case then make these *devs* who are my bearers swear upon the name of Prophet Suleiman that they will take me to my world, and enjoin them to carry out your wishes under oath."

When the emperor asked the *devs* to swear upon the name of Prophet Suleiman, they balked and replied that they would not swear because it was not Aasman Peri's wish to send Amir to his world. They told Shahpal that they would not carry out orders in opposition to hers and would not cross her because they had not yet lost all regard for their safety and they knew what was beneficial for them. Then the emperor turned toward Aasman Peri and said, "What willfulness is this? Why is it that you always find an occasion to foment mischief?" Aasman Peri answered, "You have no say in this matter because he is my husband. I won't let him go because I wish him to remain before my eyes and because my heart can't bear separation from him."

Hearing this, Amir dismounted the throne and heaved such a terrible sigh of anguish that the whole castle shook from its impact. Then he said, "O Aasman Peri, you made the prophets witness your promise to me and then you betrayed your word. In doing so, you did something most unconscionable. God willing, His wrath will overtake you and the shadow of prestige will be stripped from you. As for me, I shall now take myself to the wilderness!" With these words, Amir headed for the wilderness crying with the frenzy of a man deranged and distraught.

Shahpal now said to his daughter, "O Aasman Peri, you committed a grievous wrong to the Quake of Qaf and have broadcast abroad that I am a vile and dishonorable person." Aasman Peri answered, "Your gaining ill repute from my deeds is a happier prospect for me than the idea of my family's destruction!" She had it immediately announced abroad that the Quake of Qaf had left Gulistan-e Irum and anyone found offering him shelter or any assistance in returning to his world would be put to death along with his entire family at her orders, and would receive terrible recompense for disobeying her command.

Now hear of the Sahibqiran. After leaving Gulistan-e Irum he walked continuously in the wilderness for seven days and nights. On the eighth day, he fell unconscious in a garden from lack of nourishment. When he regained consciousness the next day, he partook of the bread given him by holy Khizr. After some time, as he lay regarding the expanse, he saw approaching a towering *dev* of monstrous girth whose sight alone would turn one's gall to water. As he came closer, he recognized Amir and saluted him. Amir Hamza asked, "O *dev*, how far is the world of men from here? I wish to know its distance from this place." He answered, "O Quake of Qaf and Latter-day Suleiman! If a man should attempt to travel on foot to the realm of humans it would take him five hundred years; a common *dev* would need six months; messenger *devs* would require forty days because they are faster than their peers; and for someone of my stature and power it would take a period of seven days."

Amir said, "If you were to conduct me to my homeland it would be a great act of kindness to me, and I would forever be in your debt." The *dev* answered, "Indeed I would take you there if I did not ever hope to return to Qaf, or if I wished to defy my mistress Aasman Peri. She has proclaimed that anyone who conducts you to your world will have his head crushed and his family put to death with him." When Amir asked this *dev* to draw close and give a complete account of himself, the *dev* said, "I am not such a fool to come near you and fall into your clutches. Then you will climb on my back and force me to take you to your world; I will find myself helpless and be forced to submit to your will." With those words, he made a salutation and flew off.

Amir was deeply distressed and said to himself, *O Hamza! No dev or perizad will ever conduct you to your homeland, and your wishes will not be met through them. It would be better to set out on foot, believing in your own destiny, and in the benevolent God who will transport you thither and unite you with your family if it be His wish.* Led by such thoughts, Amir headed toward the open horizon. He went on his way crying and laughing by turns, traversing forest after forest, desert after desert, and plain after plain, suffering privations and a thousand hardships.

Amir Hamza had traveled in this wise for fifteen days when he came upon a castle where jinns with unbraided hair were busy praying, soliciting the court of heavens. It appeared that a towering *dev* with ears like an elephant was forcefully and relentlessly besieging them. Amir felt pity for those inside the castle, and his heart softened at the thought of the hardships faced by those garrisoned within.

Issuing a challenge to the *dev,* he said, "O infidel! Here I am, your Angel of Death, come to relieve you of your siege and visit a tempestuous calamity on your head!" When the *dev* saw Amir's face he recognized the Quake of Qaf, the Latter-day Suleiman, the Destroyer of *Tilisms,* and the Slayer of *Devs.* He attacked Amir with a box tree, but one blow from the Aqrab-e Suleimani cut him down, and Amir did not allow him even a second breath.

Then Amir plunged into the *devs'* ranks and gave them a taste of his swordsmanship. Half of the *devs'* army was slaughtered and the rest turned tail and ran. The king of the castle came out of the fortress and embraced Amir. He led him by the hand into the city, where he seated him on the throne with great honor and said, "I am the same jinn, Junaid Shah Sabz-Posh, the elder brother of Emperor Shahpal, whom you freed from the Tilism-e Shatranj-e Suleimani and saved from a horrible fate." He took Amir into the castle of Sabz Nigar and made all his courtiers wait upon the Amir. He lavished praises on Amir before everyone in attendance and organized a royal feast, and then asked Amir how he fared and what had brought him there.

Amir narrated his entire tale and then said, "O Sabz-Posh, I fear even you because you are Shahpal's older brother, and are, after all, a part of the same family. Thus I cannot expect any fidelity from you." The king answered, "What are these terrible words that you speak? What terrible things you utter! I am your loyal slave and will obey you with all my heart and soul. If my life can be of some service to you, I am willing to sacrifice it at a word from you." Amir replied, "May God preserve you! Indeed one can count on one's friends in every need! Rather than sacrifice your life for me, do me the kindness of having me transported to my world. For as long as I live, I will remain indebted to you and remember you in my prayers of gratitude."

Upon hearing this, the king contemplated for a while. Then he sent for Khvaja Rauf Jinni and said to him, "Tell Amir that if he marries my daughter, Rehan Peri, who is enamored of him, and does so happily and without the least vacillation, I will have him conducted to his homeland on the ninth day from today and will take upon me the fulfillment of this promise." After an initial refusal, Amir accepted the proposal and made Sabz-Posh give him his solemn word. Sabz-Posh married Amir to Rehan Peri with great fanfare and accepted Amir as his son-in-law, considering it a signal honor for himself.

However, on the first night Amir slept with a sword between Rehan Peri and himself. She thought that it was perhaps a human custom to sleep with a sword between man and wife, and lie in the nuptial bed in that manner. Each of them turned their backs to the other and went to sleep, neither disturbing nor taking pleasure from each other. That night Amir encountered Mehr-Nigar in his dreams yet again, and saw her suffering on account of their separation. He woke with a start and took to the desert like a frenzied man.

In the morning, Rehan Peri's mother, Durdana Peri, saw her daughter sleeping by herself. She woke her up and asked, "Where is the Sahibqiran? Tell me what happened with him, and what passed between you." She replied, "I do not know. In the night he slept with a sword between us. Then I do not know where he went because I, too, went to sleep, and I have no news of where he might be now. I do not know the whereabouts of him to share with you."

Durdana Peri was upset upon hearing this account and reported it to Sabz-Posh. He, too, was greatly saddened upon hearing it, and was grieved to learn how ill the Sahibqiran had treated his daughter. He said, "Why did Amir agree to marry my daughter if such was not his desire? Now I have been humiliated throughout all the lands of Qaf. Everyone will say that there must be some fault with my daughter that caused Amir to leave her after marrying her, for nobody would turn away from a day-old bride without good reason." He immediately sent for the *peris* and *devs* and ordered them to find Amir Hamza and to bring him into his court wherever he might be, without the least delay.

———

Now hear of Aasman Peri. One day she bedecked herself in a crimson dress and went to the court of her father. She turned toward Abdur Rahman and said, "Pray check where Amir is now and discover his whereabouts with your divinations and give me a true account of him." After interpreting the geomancy pattern, Abdur Rahman did not give the whole account. He said only, "On account of you Amir tarries all distressed and distraught, and he suffers many a hardship in the wilderness because of your ill treatment." As Aasman Peri was sitting next to Abdur Rahman and was well versed in geomancy herself, she glanced at the calculations of the horoscope and said, "How wonderful it is to see that Sabz-Posh, despite being my uncle, still married his daughter to my husband, and showed neither regard for my prestige and honor nor any fear of my burning wrath. I have learned today that he is not an uncle to me but a rival. If he were in truth my uncle, he would not have committed the wrong of making Rehan Peri a rival wife to me, his niece. Indeed, he felt no compassion for me. I shall no longer call myself by the name of Aasman Peri if I do not burn his land down to cinder and punish him most severely." She then mounted a throne and, taking along an intrepid army of *devs,* headed for the castle of Sabz Nigar.

OF AASMAN PERI MARCHING WITH AN INTREPID ARMY ON SABZ NIGAR AND LAYING THE CITY TO RUIN, AND OF HER TAKING SABZ-POSH AND REHAN PERI AS PRISONERS AND INCARCERATING THEM IN THE ZANDAN-E SULEIMANI

The narrator says that when Aasman Peri arrived at the castle of Sabz Nigar, her uncle Sabz-Posh came out with gifts to receive her and brought her into his city with utmost honor and prestige and attended to her with great love and care. When they had reached his court, Aasman Peri ordered her attendants to restrain Junaid Sabz-Posh and Rehan Peri at once without the least hesitation. Her compliant servants produced both of them before Aasman Peri in chains. Then Aasman Peri laid to ruin the city of Sabz Nigar and promptly returned to Gulistan-e Irum. For many days she punished Sabz-Posh and Rehan Peri with a thousand strokes of the lash each day. Then she had them thrown into the Zandan-e Suleimani and incarcerated there.

The news of Aasman Peri's ravages reached Shahpal, and he heard of the manner in which Sabz-Posh had been dishonored and defiled at her hands. He tore his collar in grief and rushed bareheaded and barefoot to the prison, crying in mortification at the horror of his daughter's deeds. By that time Aasman Peri had retired to her abode, and was ensconced in her quarters. Shahpal brought Sabz-Posh with him to his palace and showed him every possible kindness and favor. He threw himself at his brother's feet crying copious tears, and made every apology to attempt to wash away Sabz-Posh's rancor and cleanse his heart of the acrimony with which the circumstances had tainted it. Shahpal admitted that he was so distraught by the insults and injuries his elder brother had suffered at the hands of his refractory daughter that he felt as if they were visited upon himself. Although Shahpal said all this and more, he did not console Sabz-Posh in the least. His resentment and spite remained unabated.

Sabz-Posh rose from his brother's side like a man possessed and struck a powerful blow with both hands on the portal of the castle of Gulistan-e Irum. He opened his lips to entreat the Court of Heaven with utmost humility and submission, and said, "O Almighty Lord! Visit your wrath and retribution on Aasman Peri for the harsh treatment I suffered at her hands and the injuries inflicted on me without cause. Cast her lot among the damned!" He went away in tears to return to his land and cursed Aasman Peri without cease.

Now hear some news of that fickle creature, Aasman Peri. There lived in the seventh realm of Qaf a *dev*, Ra'ad Shatir, who was a powerful *dev* from the time of Prophet Suleiman and whom everyone considered peerless in courage and valor. The Seven Enchanted Seas of Suleiman[10] are renowned throughout the world and it is known that no *dev* or jinn can cross them, for their waters are so turbulent and tumultuous that no one can bear even to hear their noise and uproar. When Prophet Suleiman departed from this world for the Future State, Ra'ad Shatir, who was a nephew of Ifrit Dev, constructed two castles in the seas, which he named Siyah Boom and Sufaid Boom, furnishing the castles with luxurious trappings and devising an enchantment to guard them.

The news reached Ra'ad Shatir that Shahpal had sent for a man from the world of humans who was called the Quake of Qaf and the Latterday Suleiman, and that this man had killed and dispatched Ifrit, Ahriman, and Maloona to the hereafter, and that many *devs* of Qaf lost their lives at his hands. He furthermore received tidings that the land of the *peris* that they called the garden of Qaf had been destroyed and sown with strife. All of this intelligence enraged Ra'ad Shatir and he immediately flew from the castle of Siyah Boom carrying Suleiman's net, which he had acquired by some devious means after the prophet's death. Ra'ad Shatir imprisoned everyone in Gulistan-e Irum and ordered the guards of the jail to put them to torture. Only Abdur Rahman escaped imprisonment, for he had left earlier for his home on some errand. All other nobles and counselors who attended on Shahpal fell into Ra'ad Shatir's power and were caught in the calamity. When Abdur Rahman learned of this, he became distraught and grieved. He cast lots and discovered that Amir Hamza was to the north of the city, and he departed immediately upon a throne in search of him.

Now hear of the Sahibqiran. When he stepped out of the city of Sabz Nigar, he walked for several days in the desert, and after crossing it, rested at the foot of a hill that was situated not too far from the abode of Abdur Rahman. Hardly a moment had passed when he saw Abdur Rahman approaching on a throne. The moment their eyes met Abdur Rahman dismounted and kissed Amir's feet, and Hamza then asked him to rise and embraced him. Amir received him very kindly and asked why he was not in attendance at Shahpal's court. Then Abdur Rahman gave him a complete and detailed account of his chance escape and the capture of Shahpal, Aasman Peri, Quraisha, and the chiefs of the races of *devs* and jinns. Abdur Rahman told him of their imprisonment in the castle of Sufaid Boom and all the hardships that they were undergoing. Amir Hamza replied, "It was on account of their swearing false oaths and tormenting me that they were overtaken by God's wrath!" Abdur Rahman submitted to him with folded arms and said, "All that Your Honor states is true. It is indeed the just deserts of their breaking their word and swearing false oaths. However, Aasman Peri's honor is attached to your own, and you should consider whose name will be sullied by her continued imprisonment. In your view only Aasman Peri should be held guilty. Quraisha is completely innocent. As a sacrifice of her soul, you must release all the others from the prison with her, and make an effort to devise some way of securing their freedom."

At first Amir refused, but when Abdur Rahman interceded with him with humble entreaties, he said, "Where is the castle of Sufaid Boom, and how can I get there to conquer it?" Abdur Rahman answered, "The castle of Sufaid Boom is situated past the Seven Enchanted Seas. It is well-nigh impossible to ford those waters, and the only one who can take you there is Shah Simurgh; the difficulties that lie in your way are so extreme that none but him can help you get there." Amir asked, "Where does Shah Simurgh live? In which desert does he dwell?" Abdur Rahman answered, "I shall be able to take you to the land of Shah Simurgh and convey you to his dwelling!"

Abdur Rahman was finally able to persuade Amir to undertake the mission despite great reluctance on his part, and he then took him to his home and ordered a celebratory feast in Amir's honor. He decorated his house for the event and attended to Amir for several days. Amir recognized the castle and said, "I have been in this castle once before, and was much delighted then to behold its beauty. In those days this castle belonged to Lahoot Shah, the father of Laneesa." Abdur Rahman answered, "You speak the truth. He was my subordinate and was a wise man!"

After the feasting was over, Abdur Rahman seated Amir on a throne and ordered four jinns to take it to the abode of Shah Simurgh with the utmost diligence. The four jinns carried Amir's throne aloft and rose as high as the stars. Amir looked down but could see only an expanse of water stretched beneath him. The jinns carried his throne for seven days and seven nights and bore it away at great speed. On the eighth day, a few hours had passed before sunrise when they placed Amir's throne on the seashore and took a rest from their long journey.

Amir then beheld this sea whose waves rose to the vaults of heavens. The sight of it even took the wind out of the wings of the beasts of air. Huge tall trees grew by the shore whose branches almost reached up toward the lofty tree of Tooba in Paradise, and their boughs extended to the eighth heaven. The shade of each tree extended five *farsangs*, and was cast far and wide. On top of those trees was a wooden castle of great expanse and vastness, adorned with all kinds of trappings. Amir asked the jinns, "Who has constructed this castle that is the rival of Gulistan-e Irum?" They answered, "O Sahibqiran! This is not a castle but the abode of Shah Simurgh, and the nest of that singular bird." Amir was greatly surprised to learn this.

After a while the messenger jinns returned to their city and Amir sat down under a tree to regard the expanse of the desert and the many marvels it offered. Before long he heard a clamor arising from a tree. When Amir went close and looked up, he observed that Simurgh's young were making the noise. Even though they had yet to grow feathers and were only balls of meat, each one of them was bigger in size than an elephant, and mighty like a small mountain. Amir saw that they cried continuously, and when he looked around to see what had terrorized and frightened them, he beheld a dragon climbing their tree, a monster whose fiery breath was burning all vegetation to ashes. Amir killed the dragon by shooting arrows at him and saved the young ones from the beast. Then he cut the dragon into pieces and fed his meat to the chicks with the point of his pike. Having had their fill and being now relieved of the pangs of hunger, the young ones retired into their nest to sleep. After a few hours a pair of Simurghs returned carrying food for their young. It was usual for the young ones to come out of the nest upon hearing their parents arrive and beg for food. However, as they were asleep, they did not leave the nest. The Simurghs saw Amir Hamza sleeping under the tree and they said to each other, "It seems that this man who lies sleeping under the tree is the one who has long caused us much grief by eating up our children. Today as well he ate our young, and this is why they did not come out of the nest and we did not hear their cries. We must kill him without delay."

Upon hearing these words, the Simurghs' young became uneasy and emerged from their nest. They told their parents about the dragon and how Amir had slain him, narrating their story in their language. Shah Simurgh was at once very grateful to Amir Hamza. Witnessing that Amir was exposed to the sun, he shaded him with one wing and with the other began fanning him, providing him comfort and bliss. Feeling this pleasant sensation Amir opened his eyes. Witnessing the Simurgh standing over him, he reached for his bow and quiver and had already drawn an arrow when the Simurgh said, "O Quake of Qaf! First you put me in your debt and gratitude, and now you are bent on killing me. Those were my young on whom you took pity and whom you saved from the dragon!" Amir asked, "How did you learn my name and find out my particulars?" The Simurgh replied, "I heard from Prophet Suleiman that a man would arrive here some time in the future and save the Simurgh's young from the dragon. His name would be the Justice of Qaf and his mission would be to slay the *devs*. Whoever would confront him would come to harm at his hands, whereupon the people would give him the title of the Quake of Qaf and the reputation of his valor would make men tremble wherever his name was mentioned!" Amir was most pleased by these words and asked, "What is the name of this frontier, and who holds dominion over this land?" The Simurgh answered, "It is called the Baisha-e Qaza va Qadar and it lies outside the dominions of Qaf. All that lies within it is beyond the writ of the king of Peristan."

The Sahibqiran said, "I have come to you in need and in a most distressed state, as I am faced with a grave problem." The Simurgh replied, "I am obedient and loyal to you. Your word is my command and I will carry out your orders as a special honor to myself!" Amir said to him, "Ra'ad Shatir Dev has imprisoned Emperor Shahpal and Aasman Peri along with the nobles of their court in the castle of Sufaid Boom and is torturing them there. I ask that you carry me to where they are imprisoned and show me the place." The Simurgh answered, "Even though I shall earn the enmity of the *devs* of Qaf by doing so and they will nurse a grudge against me, yet I will take you there and do you this service. But make sure to bring seven rations of food and seven portions of water to carry on my back. When I feel hungry and thirsty you should give me a morsel to eat and a sip to drink!"

Amir caught seven blue antelopes on the plain and skinned them and made water skins of their hides and filled them with sweet water. Then he climbed on the Simurgh's back carrying the water skins and blue antelopes, and prepared to depart for the castle of Sufaid Boom. The Simurgh said to him, "O Sahibqiran, do not carry on your person any weapons of steel lest the mountain of magnet that lies in the middle of the magnetic sea draw and claim them." Amir asked, "What do you propose I do with my arms, and where should I leave them?" The Simurgh replied, "You may leave them here except for any small weapons that you can fit in your shoe." Amir took the dagger of the champion warrior Sohrab and tucked it away in his shoe with great care. The rest he handed to the Simurgh, who hid them in his feathers.

The Simurgh then reached for the heights of the heavens and when Amir looked down he saw that the earth was the size of a small jewel. For as far as he could see there was only water to behold. Amir asked the Simurgh, "What is the name of this sea?" The Simurgh answered, "It is the first of the Seven Magical Seas. Six more remain to be crossed." The Simurgh kept flying like an arrow and moving forward with great diligence. When he reached the middle of the sea, the Simurgh felt hungry. He said to Amir, "O Amir, quickly put a morsel in my mouth, for my strength is declining and the pangs of hunger have started." Amir put one water skin and a blue antelope in his mouth and he bolted them down. He took one day and one night to span the first sea and started flying over the second sea the next day. Observing that the sea seemed enveloped in darkness, Amir asked the Simurgh, "What is this darkness that oppresses the heart and is such that one cannot make out anything in it?" The Simurgh answered, "This is the sea of clay." When he reached the middle of the sea, the Simurgh asked Amir for food again, and Amir duly put it in his mouth. Thus he flew over the second sea as well. On the third and the fourth days he ate his rations as before and passed over the sea of mercury and the sea of blood, without a moment's rest.

When the Simurgh was passing over the magnetic sea, the waters began pulling the Simurgh toward them on account of the dagger of Sohrab that Amir had stuck in his shoe. The Simurgh observed that despite his efforts to fly high, he was pulled down and was unable to gain any height. He then recalled the dagger Amir had hidden in his shoe and reasoned that the weapon was interfering with his flight. He said, "O Amir, pray take the dagger from your shoe and throw it away quickly and without delay, otherwise any moment I will be pulled down by the magnetic mountain, as it draws me powerfully to it." Amir threw away the dagger but lamented its loss greatly. The Simurgh finally crossed this expanse, too, and then he reached the sky above the seventh sea, which was the sea of fire. Despite soaring close to the heavens, the Simurgh was unable to bear the heat of the flames from the sea, which reached up to the realm of fire in the heavens. The Simurgh felt his senses take leave of him from the violence of the heat although he tried to remain calm and composed. When the Simurgh reached the middle of the blazing sea, he said to Amir, "O Quake of Qaf! Do not make delay in giving me my rations. The time has come for me to exert myself and fly speedily and do all in my power and wager my life in your service."

Amir put a blue antelope in the Simurgh's mouth, but he withdrew his hand quickly because of the heat of the blaze and the antelope fell to the sea of fire unbeknownst to him and was burned bones and all. After a short while the Simurgh again demanded food. Amir said, "The seventh ration was what I just fed you. Now I have nothing left to give you and I cannot see another way to feed you!" The Simurgh said, "I did not receive the ration and was not fed!" The Simurgh's strength soon began to decline and Amir saw that it was only a matter of a few breaths before they would both fall into the sea of fire and drown. He immediately put the bread-cake given him by Prophet Khizr into the Simurgh's mouth and freed him of all hunger. From the sustenance of that piece of bread the Simurgh was able to cross the sea of fire without anxiety or mishap. He landed on the other side of the Seven Seas and congratulated Amir, who was equally pleased by the safe completion of their journey.

However, the loss of his weapons weighed heavily on Amir's heart. Suddenly someone called out, "Peace be with you!" Amir saw it was holy Khizr who had come to console him and restore to him all the weapons that he had left behind at the Simurgh's place along with the dagger that he had had to throw in the magnetic sea. Amir was beside himself with joy upon receiving his arms. He kissed the feet of holy Khizr and expressed his gratitude for the favor he had done him. Then holy Khizr went away, and Amir decorated himself with his weapons and gazed upon the expanse before him. Amir saw before them two hills: One was as white as the dawn and the other as dark as the night of lamentations, and both were otherwise quite similar. Amir said to the Simurgh, "Are these white and black hills or something else? They are unique in their construction." He answered, "These are the castles of Sufaid Boom and Siyah Boom." Amir said, "I now bid you adieu, and you will always have my gratitude for helping me reach this place!"

The Simurgh pulled out three feathers from his wing, gave them to Amir, and said, "If, God forbid, you ever fall into difficulty, you should burn one of these feathers and I will come to your help that very instant and will do all you ask me to do. The second feather you should put in the aigrette of your horse and adorn him with it. The third feather pray give to Khvaja Amar Ayyar as a gift from me and fulfill my request in this regard!"

Then the Simurgh flew away to his nest and Amir headed toward the castles. He had gone some distance when a lion appeared and attacked him. Amir dealt him a blow of his sword and cut him in two. Then he skinned him and draped the hide on his shoulders with the thought of making a robe of it when he returned to the world of men. He recalled that Rustam bin Zal also used to drape himself with a lion skin, which augmented his awe and majesty and brought him much glory. When Amir arrived at the castle of Siyah Boom, he saw that its gates were open and there was neither vigil nor keeper except four hundred *devs* seated at the gates to make sure that no stranger should enter or trespass there.

The commander of those *devs* caught sight of Amir, let out a cry, and said, "Aaargh! My friends, woe unto us that the Quake of Qaf and the Latter-day Suleiman has reached this place! The wrath of God is now upon our doorstep!" He ran at Amir and smote him with a box tree so mightily that from its shock the Earth cried out, "Have mercy on me!" Amir managed to foil his attack and dealt him a mighty blow with his sword. The *dev* received such a vicious cut from its blade that he fell to the ground in two pieces. When the *devs* saw their commander suffering a dog's death and witnessed this unforeseen calamity claiming him, they ran off like a herd of heedless camels. They thought it best to clear the field and escape with their lives and they did not just play at running. Ra'ad Shatir was away hunting, so the escapees headed for the hunting grounds to bring him intelligence, and rushed to alert him of the disaster that had visited them.

Amir was standing at the gates of the castle and wondering whether he would find Shahpal and Aasman Peri in the castle of Siyah Boom or Sufaid Boom when he heard a voice exclaim, "O Amir! Shahpal and Aasman Peri are imprisoned in the castle of Sufaid Boom. It is there that those beautiful gazelles are incarcerated by the relentless hunter."

Amir headed for Sufaid Boom, and when he reached its gates he saw that the castle had a hundred towers and each tower was manned by *devs* in different forms. Some had heads of lions, some horses, others peacocks, crows, or wolves, and all were reciting enchantments and fiercely guarding the castle. The gates of the castle were manned by a dragon that spewed fire so profusely that there was no estimating its quantity. His mouth was wide enough that it extended to the portals of the castle and was like a trap laid around the entrance. The whole scene made Amir fearful and he wondered how he would be able to gain entrance to the castle and find his way inside. Then he heard the same voice again, saying, "O Hamza! The destruction of this *tilism* is not given to you. Your grandson instead is destined to break it, and he will be titled the Latterday Rustam. He will be the one to destroy it and take on the mission valiantly."

Amir said to himself, *I am a boy myself yet! God knows when a son will be born to me and when my grandson will come into this world. Those who are imprisoned here will certainly not remain incarcerated until then and spend the rest of their lives in jail!* The voice again called out, "Beyond undertaking to secure the prisoners' release, do not take it into your head to destroy this *tilism*. You are free to release them and take them away. Recite the Most Great Name and then blow on the dragon, and he will turn away and you will prevail over him."

When the Sahibqiran recited the Most Great Name over the dragon, he turned away and left. Amir went inside and found a garden inside the castle where Emperor Shahpal was sitting with his companions, crying bitter tears and direly lamenting his wretched fate. At the sight of the Sahibqiran he lowered his head in shame. Hamza untied and unfettered all of them and released them, returning the light to their eyes and the smiles to their faces. Then he asked Emperor Shahpal, "Where is Aasman Peri?" Shahpal said, "She is imprisoned in the vault that you see before you!" Amir broke open the door of the castle's dome and found Aasman Peri hanging there upside down, close to her death, and Quraisha sitting and crying, as fully afflicted as her mother. The Sahibqiran removed Aasman Peri's fetters and brought her out of the vault with Quraisha and reunited them with Shahpal.

Aasman Peri was most remorseful and greatly mortified at her deeds. She threw herself at Hamza's feet and said, "O Hamza, forgive me my trespasses and empty your heart of any rancor that you feel toward me. I will send you to your world for certain six months from now, and will surely not deceive you this time."

Amir made no reply and did not show her any favor. He gathered all the prisoners he had freed and they headed out of the castle. As they exited they saw Ra'ad Shatir Dev coming toward them with several thousand *devs* whose footsteps made the whole world shake with terror. Ra'ad

Shatir came up to Amir and said, "O human! You destroyed the garden of Qaf and now you found your way here as well to release my prisoners and take them away. Now you cannot escape from my hands and must die this instant!" He lifted a heavy stone and threw it at Amir's head, but Amir eluded his attack and dealt him a sword blow that felled him with just one stroke: He came crashing down like a canker-ridden plane tree. The *devs* who accompanied him carried off his corpse to Samandun Hazar-Dast Dev.

Amir meanwhile brought Shahpal and his entourage back to Gulistan-e Irum and all of them relaxed upon reaching their homeland.

Six months later, however, Amir again had a disturbing dream. He started in his sleep and broke out crying, stringing together a chain of tears. The sound woke up Aasman Peri, who asked, "What is the matter, Amir? Why do you cry? And why have you become grief-stricken?" Amir replied, "O Aasman Peri! Pray show some faith and constancy and send me back to my world, for I am wasting away living in separation from my loved ones!" Aasman Peri answered, "O Sahibqiran! I will send you to your world after one year and will not break my promise this time!" Amir became livid upon hearing her words and took his complaint to Shahpal, telling him about her betrayal and inconstancy. Shahpal comforted Amir and provided a throne for him, and then ordered the *devs* to convey Amir to his world and promptly carry out his orders.

After the Sahibqiran departed, Aasman Peri sent a *perizad* with instructions for the *devs* carrying Amir's throne to leave him in Shikargah-e Suleiman and under no circumstances take him to the world of humans.

When the *perizad* intercepted Amir in his journey, Amir knew that the *perizad* had again come to forbid the *devs* to bear his throne and carry out their orders. Realizing that Aasman Peri had again sent the same message, Amir returned to Shahpal and once again complained to him. It so happened that Aasman Peri was also present in the court. Emperor Shahpal showed extreme displeasure toward her and said, "O Aasman Peri! Why do you not refrain from your mischief and show remorse for your deeds?" She answered, "Pray do not interfere in matters of my family and do not oppress me with your commands. You are sadly mistaken if you think that I will destroy my home with my own hands!" After this speech, Amir headed once more for the wilderness cursing Aasman Peri, with tears of blood issuing from his eyes. Some transcribers write that Amir Hamza divorced Aasman Peri that day, while some others contradict this account and consider it a false tradition.[11]

The narrator has it that Emperor Shahpal was so troubled by Aasman Peri's disobedient speech that he gave up his crown and throne. He retired to a mountain and Aasman Peri inherited his kingdom. She had it broadcast throughout Qaf that whoever dared to take Hamza to his world would answer to her and be punished severely and justly for the rebellious deed. Then Aasman Peri said to Khvaja Abdur Rahman, "Find out who the woman is whom Hamza loves, what she is like in her appearance, and where she lives, for I have heard that her beauty is unmatched in all creation!" Khvaja Abdur Rahman made calculations by geomancy and declared, "Indeed Hamza is justified in his passion for this woman. Her beauty is such that even her attendants surpass you by far in comeliness! Every one of her attendants is made in the image of the moon and their aspects evoke the beauty of Venus. The woman herself is secured within the walls of the castle of Devdad and resides there." Aasman Peri had a map made of the castle of Devdad, and then sent for the *perizads* and said to them, "Go to the world of humans and fetch Mehr-Nigar from this castle and bring her to me without delay!" Immediately at her orders, the *perizads* departed to fetch Mehr-Nigar for Aasman Peri.

———

Before I continue in this tale, let me first give an account of Landhoor bin Saadan.

Be it known that when Landhoor was released from prison and returned to the city, he occupied himself with festivities and indulged himself in revelries and feasting. One day a *perizad* brought him the news of the approach of Sufaid Dev and informed him that the *dev* would be upon them any instant. Landhoor directly rose from the festivities and went out to encounter Sufaid Dev. He killed him at once and did not let that blackguard draw another breath.[12]

Landhoor's war cry resounded throughout the whole expanse of Qaf and was also carried to the ears of Amir Hamza, who was at that moment skirmishing with Ra'ad Shatir. Amir's war cry was likewise carried to the ears of Landhoor. Hearing a familiar war cry, they both marveled and wondered at the incident. Hamza said to himself, "It can't be Landhoor. Surely, there is no likelihood of his being in Qaf!" And Landhoor convinced himself of the same.

After Landhoor had killed Sufaid Dev and relieved that wretch's accursed body of the burden of its unclean head, he said to the king, "I have slain your enemy. Pray send me to my home now and fulfill your promise." The king immediately ordered a throne for Landhoor and Arshivan Perizad, and ordered the *devs* to carry them to the world of humans.

Now hear of Bahram Gurd, the emperor of China. After prevailing over the Sagsars, he passed his days in anxiety over the disappearance of Landhoor. Night and day he wearied himself wondering who had taken away Landhoor and inflicted this burden of separation on his heart. One day he was again lamenting the loss to Jaipur and the commanders of the camp, and said to them, "Alas, my friends! To this day we have not learned what passed with the Khusrau, nor do we know where he went and who carried him away. I don't know where to search for him or how to find him!" At that very moment Landhoor's throne descended from the skies into Bahram's castle.

Bahram rushed to embrace him and everyone went forth to greet him and kiss his feet. Festive music played in the castle and the blaring of the trumpets sounded like thunder. The Khusrau of India gave audience from the throne and an assembly of revelry was held. Cries of "Congratulations!" filled the air. In the midst of the celebrations, Bahram said to Landhoor, "I was fighting the Sagsars when someone threw a letter before me, which I picked up. A palm was imprinted on the letter, and it was written in strange characters that I tried very hard to interpret, but no one was able to read them, and to this day none has been able to decipher it!" Landhoor said, "Show me the letter and I will see if I can read it!" Bahram sent for the letter and handed it to Landhoor, who took it into his hands and also marveled that he was unable to read it. Then Arshivan spoke up: "The palm imprinted on the letter is mine, and the letter is in my mother's hand. She wrote it and threw it out from the *tilism* in the hope that it might somehow reach you." Bahram then embraced Arshivan and kissed his forehead and showed him many tokens of affection. Everyone who beheld Arshivan was taken by his beauty and unanimously proclaimed that the spirits of the citizens of Ceylon would be rejuvenated by his auspicious arrival.

OF ZEHRA MISRI'S DISAPPEARANCE FROM THE ROOF OF THE CASTLE AND OF HER BEING PRESENTED BEFORE AASMAN PERI

Now hear a few words of the story of one afflicted by separation, who had become a human incarnation of the longing gaze, who sought to forget the night of parting with endless lamentation and wailing, who said farewell to the day of separation with a hundred cold sighs, who was dying of a grieving heart, whose wounded bosom was the chafing dish of sorrows, who had been stabbed by the dagger of grief, who sought death having become fully despairing of life: to wit, Princess Mehr-Nigar. Hear now of the one whose soul was ready to take flight from her earthly abode and whose heart was marked with the scars of grief. Night and day she occupied herself with mourning her separation from Amir and maintained herself in a most abject state due to the pain of her exile from her beloved's side. She fed on nothing but morsels of her own heart and drank only from the goblet of her life's blood. She would lie disheveled and unkempt in her bed and bore alone the burden of her boundless grief and countless sorrows.

When Zehra Misri or Tarar Khooban or any of her other companions asked her to freshen up, she washed her face with the tears of blood. If someone asked her to adorn herself, she strung her eyelashes with the pearls of tears, while reciting these lines composed by this narrator:[13]

> To live in the night of longing is to me as death;
> Come to me, Death, and be my Messiah from this life.

Her companions worried that Mehr-Nigar would slowly slide into a state of frenzy and that the extremes of her passion would overwhelm her senses. Each of them endeavored to console her grieving heart in some fashion and distract her by some amusement. They continued to advise her and bound her by oaths to believe that her sorrows would soon end, having nearly run their course. They assured her that Amir would return in a few days and that her grief would be allayed by the grace of the munificent God. They asked her to change her clothes, partake of food, and occupy her heart with some entertainment. They told her that if she killed herself by continuing in her current state, she would not be there to receive any pleasure from the sight of Amir when he returned, nor would he receive any pleasure from gazing on her face. One day they said to her, "Let us go to the roof and walk there and take some fresh air. In God's name, do not torment us in this manner!" They persuaded her with their entreaties to accompany them to the roof of the castle, where they showed her the greenery of the pastures and diverted her humors with gossip.

They had not been standing there long when a little cloud appeared in the sky along with a dark mist. Slowly that small cloud glided over the castle and covered its whole expanse. Blinding bolts of lightning began striking then, and deafening claps of thunder sounded. Suddenly and unexpectedly, a claw materialized in the sky from nowhere. This claw came down from the cloud and grabbed Zehra Misri, who was standing next to Mehr-Nigar, carrying her off in the flash of an eye. The terrified attendants and companions of the princess collapsed unconscious, while some fell on their faces in their rush to reach the staircase. Such a commotion was engendered that no one thought of the other's well-being. All of them were shaken and stunned and lost all awareness of themselves. When they came to their senses they saw that Zehra Misri had disappeared. They raised a great hue and cry, and the very image of doomsday was replicated in the shouting and chaos that ensued. Everyone, young or old, was distressed by this tragic disappearance.

———

Now hear a little of what passed with Zehra Misri. When she saw that she was sitting on a throne that was bearing her away in the sky and nothing but darkness could be seen all around her, she asked the *devs* carrying the throne, "Who are you and where are you taking me, destroying my household in this manner?" They answered, "Aasman Peri, who is Hamza's wife, ordered us to bring her Mehr-Nigar, the daughter of Naushervan, and not to make the slightest delay in carrying out her wishes. Therefore we are taking you to Aasman Peri."

Zehra Misri reasoned that Hamza must have made a marriage in Qaf and that his new wife had sent for Mehr-Nigar so that she might kill her and quench the rancor of her heart with her blood. She understood then that since the *devs* did not recognize Mehr-Nigar and were not aware of her identity, they mistook her for Mehr-Nigar. She felt grateful that such a calamity had been warded off from the princess and that she would be killed in her stead, chosen as the sacrifice of Princess Mehr-Nigar.

When Zehra Misri reached Gulistan-e Irum, her eyes were lined with the collyrium of Suleiman so that she might see all those present and neither *dev*, jinn, or *peri* might remain hidden from her eyes. Next Zehra Misri was presented before Aasman Peri, who was crestfallen to behold Zehra's beauty. Marveling at her comeliness, she said, "Hamza is not to blame for suffering such pangs of separation from this woman. The manner in which he wastes away in love for her is completely warranted." Then she looked up, and addressing Zehra Misri, said, "Are you Mehr-Nigar, the daughter of Naushervan, who is known throughout creation for her beauty and who is beloved by young and old alike?" Zehra Misri made obeisance and said, "My name is Zehra Misri and I am the daughter of Abdul Aziz, the king of Egypt, and the wife of Muqbil Vafadar. Even in my dreams I cannot seek an equal footing with Mehr-Nigar, who is attended by four hundred princesses from many lands of the world, all of whom far surpass me in all respects. They are all ennobled by waiting on the princess and being her confidantes."

Aasman Peri was very pleased by the manners and decorum of Zehra Misri and asked her, "Speak the truth, Zehra Misri, am I more beautiful or is Mehr-Nigar? Whose beauty, in your eyes, surpasses the other's?" Zehra Misri yielded with folded arms, saying, "I regret any disrespect to you, but there is greater beauty to be found in the soles of the feet of the attendants who wait on Mehr-Nigar than in your face! There is no comparison between the sun and a mote that shines in its beam!"

Aasman Peri was enraged by her reply and said to her slaves, "Take her away this instant for she is most wicked and willful and has no etiquette worthy of an attendant. Send her to the executioners and have them behead her!" At once, the executioners carried Zehra Misri to the execution grounds.

It so happened that Quraisha was headed at this time for the court sporting a dagger. Even though she was only seven years of age, her beauty made the full moon shrivel with envy and the *houris* of heaven hide their faces with shame. Seeing a crowd gathered, she went where Zehra Misri was sitting and asked the executioner, "Who is she and what

is her crime that you should behead her and mark her neck with the blade?"
He answered, "I do not know who she is or what her crime is. The sovereign of *peris* has ordered her beheading!" Quraisha then asked Zehra Misri about her particulars, and she gave her a detailed account. Upon hearing the story, Quraisha began trembling with rage. She took Zehra Misri along with her to the court and said to Aasman Peri, "What was her crime that you sent for her from the realm of men and ordered her killed? It appears that if Mehr-Nigar had been brought here she would have suffered the same fate. You would have cared neither for the feelings of the Sahibqiran nor for the wrath of God. Mehr-Nigar is also someone in whose person the honor of the Sahibqiran resides, and she is a hundred thousand times worthier of respect and reverence than you because she is the Sahibqiran's first wife. In all other respects as well she has preference over you. My hands are tied because you are my mother; otherwise, with a single stroke of my dagger I would cut you in two without fear of consequences."

Aasman Peri trembled to witness Quraisha's fury. She remained silent and neither said a word nor uttered a sound. Quraisha sent for a throne for Zehra Misri and ordered the bearers to carry it back to where they had caught her. They bore the throne aloft and departed.

Now, Samandun Hazar-Dast Dev's dwelling was along the path they took. It so happened that he was at his home drinking wine with some companions when he saw the throne flying away with a woman. He ordered the *devs* to bring it down and present it before him so that he might find out who she was and where she was being carried. The *devs* brought him the throne as ordered. Then Samandun Hazar-Dast asked Zehra Misri, "Who are you, where are you headed, and what is your rank that the *devs* bear you aloft on a throne?" Zehra Misri submitted her detailed account to him, whereupon he had the *devs* killed and said to Zehra Misri, "I am setting you the duty of rocking my son's cradle and making sure that he sleeps comfortably." Dealt this new hand by fortune, Zehra Misri was forced to accept the duty of tending the baby *dev*'s cradle.

———

Now hear of Khvaja Amar. When he heard the hue and cry in the women's quarters, he went there and learned that a claw had come down from the skies and taken away Zehra Misri. Amar trembled with rage and said to Mehr-Nigar, "I counseled you a hundred thousand times not to do anything without first seeking my advice, but all of that was to no avail. If that claw had carried you off, how would have I shown my face to Hamza or have ever found you? My twelve years of labor would have come to naught and I would have earned the disgrace and ignominy of everyone!" Having said this, he lashed Mehr-Nigar three times so hard that she was unable to bear the violence and fell to the floor writhing like a tumbler pigeon from the ecstasies of pain. Amar's treatment of her rankled in her heart. She felt loathing for him and said in her heart, *It was all because I fell in love with Hamza that I was lashed today at the hands of a lowly cameleer's son and had to bear this humiliation. The slaves of my palace fare better and are more respected than myself.*

She did not say anything at the time, but after night had fallen she scaled down the walls of the castle with a rope and headed toward the camp of her brothers. Then she had a change of heart and decided that she must not appear before her brothers or present herself at their court. She saw a horse that belonged to Hurmuz standing fully saddled and equipped at a post. The syce had been overtaken by slumber like his fortune. Donning a man's disguise and throwing a veil on her face, she rode the horse into the forest and removed herself from Amar's guard and vigil.

Now hear of Amar. When he left the women's quarters after lashing Mehr-Nigar, he felt too ashamed at his actions to return there. He decided that he would apologize to Mehr-Nigar in the morning and make every effort to win her over. At the end of the night, Amir Hamza appeared to Amar in his dreams and addressed him thus: "O Amar, was it a seemly manner in which you treated Mehr-Nigar and gave her such pain? Because of your treatment, she has now taken to the forest and fallen into a thousand hardships!" Amar awoke from that distressful dream, and when he rushed into the women's quarters plagued by a thousand misgivings, he discovered that Mehr-Nigar was not in her bed. A search was made for her, but she was not found, and Amar became very anxious for her safety. When he climbed to the top of the castle he saw the rope hanging there and discovered the method by which she had departed, yet he could not discern the direction in which she had headed. Amar climbed down by the same rope and followed Mehr-Nigar's footprints. Tracing them, he approached Hurmuz's pavilion and looked around to see where she may have gone from there. He regarded a syce snoring near a post with the trappings of a horse about him but without the horse. Amar woke him up and asked, "Where is your horse?" The syce looked around in all directions but did not find it. Then Amar reasoned that Mehr-Nigar had been there and had ridden away incensed at his treatment of her. Amar followed the hoofprints of the horse in the hope of discovering her path and finding some clue to her whereabouts.

Now hear of Mehr-Nigar. Before daylight she had traveled a distance of fifty *kos* when suddenly a sovereign of that land, King Ilyas[?], arrived there on horseback, hunting with a falcon. Mehr-Nigar hid herself behind the trunk of a tree to keep away from his sight, but the king saw from a distance that a veiled rider had hidden from him. He approached her and said, "Tell me who you are, what your name is, where you have come from, and what has brought you into this jungle." Mehr-Nigar answered, "I am a traveler and have been sent here by the revolutions of the heavens and a fated misfortune!" The king asked, "Would you like to enter my service?" She replied, "I have no need to enter anyone's service!" From her voice, the king suspected that the veiled rider was a woman. He extended his hand and pulled off her veil and beheld a woman whose beauty would have blinded the sun itself and whose aspect was so luminous that even the eye of the sun would have been unable to keep its gaze trained on her face. He immediately brought her down from her horse, put her into a litter, and comforted her with many sweet words. King Ilyas carried her to his abode and put her in excellently furnished quarters. He provided her with every item of luxury and comfort and gave her much in which to find delight and pleasure. When he tried to enter her quarters and ravish her, Mehr-Nigar said to him, "Beware not to take another step forward or you will receive a grievous injury!" Frightened by her threat, the king returned to his quarters gnashing his teeth with anger and thinking, *It will be a great loss if a fairy like her should slip away from my hands without my taking pleasure from her.*

It so happened that the same Khvaja Nihal[14] who was Naushervan's friend and from whose services the emperor had greatly benefited, and who had seen Mehr-Nigar grow up as a child, arrived in King Ilyas's service bearing him gifts and mementos as offerings. Finding King Ilyas looking downcast, he asked the reason for his low spirits. The king told him the secret of his sorrow and disclosed that he had caught a fairy-faced creature in the forest for whom he felt a great desire but who spurned him and rejected his advances.

Khvaja Nihal said, "If I could see her, I would say a charm over her that would make her surrender before you and would make her submit to your wishes at just one word from you." The king immediately led Khvaja Nihal to her quarters and, pointing out Mehr-Nigar's rooms from a distance, told him where he would find her. When Khvaja Nihal looked through a crack in her door, he recognized Mehr-Nigar and called her loudly by name. Mehr-Nigar recognized him as well and opened the door, telling him to step inside. After learning the whole story from Mehr-Nigar, Khvaja Nihal counseled her and told her that she must not give herself to distress as he would release her from the clutches of the king and secure her freedom. After allaying Mehr-Nigar's worries, he returned to the king and declared to him, "Pray order the guards to allow me to come and go freely to see her at any hour of night or day, and see to it that nobody should restrict my movements in any manner. By your auspicious fortune, I will be able to persuade her on the third day from today, and then she will receive you willingly and with open arms!" The king was very pleased with Khvaja Nihal and conferred a robe of honor on him and showed him many other favors besides.

After taking his leave, Khvaja Nihal went to inspect the horses that were for sale in the market. Finally, he settled on two of them to purchase and he brought them to the door of the house where Mehr-Nigar was kept. That same night he provided one to Mehr-Nigar and, riding the other himself, rode out of the city with her without stopping anywhere until morning.

The next day the king sent for Khvaja Nihal, but he was not found at his dwelling. Then the guards arrived to report that the woman the king had kept in the house was no longer there and the house was empty. Everyone marveled at the manner in which she had disappeared without anyone knowing. The king reasoned that Khvaja Nihal had eloped with her, and he went in pursuit of him at the head of an intrepid army.

It was getting close to afternoon when Mehr-Nigar saw a dust cloud rising behind them and said, "O Khvaja! Spur on your horse, for the king's army is approaching and that malevolent blackguard is on our heels!" While Khvaja Nihal stood still watching the approaching dust cloud, Mehr-Nigar entered the forest to hide from the eyes of that rascal and escape from his clutches. In the meantime, the king reached Khvaja Nihal, who now stood frozen with fear. The king killed him and thus avenged himself, and then he began searching for Mehr-Nigar. But like the rara avis, she had disappeared without a trace. After he had been thwarted and disappointed in his search, King Ilyas returned grieving to his palace.

By the next day Mehr-Nigar had already put several days' journey between herself and that place. She was feeling famished when she suddenly came across a field of melons. Her spirits revived and she asked the man who tended the field for one melon. He brought several melons and put them before her. Mehr-Nigar ate every single one of them ravenously and felt rejuvenated. That dotard, a harlot's son of a pimp, who was well into his nineties, said to Mehr-Nigar, "O life of the world! If you agree to live with me, I will maintain you in the finest possible way and make sure that whatever you wish for is provided." Mehr-Nigar marveled at that jester's words and thought that perhaps he suffered from melancholy.

After she had eaten her fill of the melons and was fully sated, she asked him, "Do you have any family or do you live all by yourself?" He answered, "I have ten sons, eleven daughters, and one wife, every single one of whom is of a kindly temperament." Mehr-Nigar then said, "How would I live with you when you already have a wife? What would I do here that would make me satisfied with my existence?" He answered, "I will divorce my wife and separate from her for your sake." Mehr-Nigar replied, "Very well, then, go and divorce her while I wait for you here!"

That simple man rushed home, and Mehr-Nigar left him money for the melons and rode away. When the melon grower returned to the fields after divorcing his wife, he did not find Mehr-Nigar there and began crying out loudly, "Oh, my *peri*! Ah, my *peri*! Where have you gone, leaving me all distraught?" Presently, his wife brought along the landlord to knock some sense into his senile head, and upon reaching there they saw him moaning and groaning and lamenting his loss. His wife and the landlord figured that he had been possessed by some demon or malicious spirit. All the bystanders told his wife and sons to take him to be cured for madness and have the evil spirits driven out of him through some treatment.

Mehr-Nigar continued riding until evening when she reached a forest that abounded in lions, cheetahs, hyenas, wolves, wild bulls, rhinoceroses, bears, langurs, and monkeys. Whenever these wild creatures came upon an animal they tore him apart and ate him. Mehr-Nigar dismounted her horse and climbed a tree to hide herself in its branches. In the morning a lion appeared, killed her horse, and went away. Mehr-Nigar lamented the loss of her horse. She tied all his trappings to a tree trunk and started out from there on foot.

That evening she reached the outskirts of a small village where there were some farms and a big pond where a huge tree stood. Mehr-Nigar climbed up that tree and spent the night in its branches. In the morning the head of the village sent his handmaiden to fetch him water from the

632 • *The Adventures of Amir Hamza*

pond for his bath. Looking into the water of the pond she saw the reflection of Mehr-Nigar's face and imagined that it was her own reflection. The sense of her own beauty made her so vain that she returned from the pond with an empty pitcher. When her master asked her if she had brought the water, she replied, "A marvel it is that you imagine that someone as lovely and beautiful as myself would fetch you water and serve you as a handmaiden!" He gave her a good thrashing with his shoe and said, "Go, you whore, and quickly fetch me water so that I may bathe and refresh myself by washing and ridding myself of the grime." She again took the vessel to the pond, but as Mehr-Nigar was still there and her face was still reflected in the water, the girl gazed on it for nearly an hour. It again filled her with conceit, and as before she returned to the house without filling the pitcher and again spoke with the same proud air as she had done before. Her master again admonished her and sent her back to the pond to fill up the pitcher. The third time, too, she returned without water after gazing upon Mehr-Nigar's image, and pride took such a powerful hold of her mind that she let go of all sense of respect and honor toward others.

Mehr-Nigar had noticed the handmaiden coming more than once to the pond. When she arrived there a third time, Mehr-Nigar figured that something was afoot that made her return to the pond three times. Fearing that some mischief would transpire now, Mehr-Nigar climbed down from the tree and rushed away.

After the girl returned to her master and made the familiar speech to him, he felt obliged to hold up a mirror to her face and said to her, "Regard your despicable face, O wretch, and tell me if this is the beauty that makes you so arrogant and causes you to imagine yourself a comely lass?" When the girl looked into the mirror her repulsive face stared back at her. She grew thoughtful for a few moments and then said, "Come with me to the pond and see the reflection of my face in the water, and then you will know whether I lie or tell the truth!" Her master took a few men along and they all went to the pond. When the girl looked at her face in the water she found it as hideous as she had been in the mirror, but shameless as she was she kept repeating the refrain that her beauty and comeliness did not warrant her fetching water or doing any menial work. Everyone was convinced that she had been possessed, and they occupied themselves with finding some way to cure her condition.

Mehr-Nigar continued onward and on the second day arrived at a mendicant's abode. He was the chief of a group of four hundred beggars and the lord and master of a large tribe. Upon encountering Mehr-Nigar he asked her story. Mehr-Nigar replied, "I am a weaver's daughter. My father has taken a wife in his old age and this stepmother has driven me away from the house. Now I wander around in a state of ruin and distress, and the insufferable temper and hatred of my stepmother drives me all over the face of the Earth." That man had a tender heart and when he heard Mehr-Nigar's account he said to her, "I take you as my child and declare you my daughter. I am taken by your gentle nature. Just do me the favor of distributing the food and the collection among the mendicants and make this your daily duty." He gave her full charge of his place and made her responsible for his duties. Mehr-Nigar offered thanks to God who had found her shelter. She expressed her gratitude to the mendicant night and day for showing her his kindness and favor.

Now hear of Amar Ayyar, King of All Tricksters. In his search for Mehr-Nigar, he arrived in the land of the king who had carried Mehr-Nigar away from the forest. He gathered some clues as to where she might have gone and headed in that direction. When he arrived at the fields of the melon farmer and heard his cries of "Oh, my *peri*!" and "Ah, my *peri*!" he reasoned that Mehr-Nigar had been there and her fate had placed her path through that man's life.

From there Amar came to the spot in the forest where Mehr-Nigar's horse had been killed by the lion and she had continued forward after tying its trappings to the tree trunk. Amar untied the trappings from the tree and put them in his *zambil*. He then came upon the settlement where the crazy handmaiden lived and from there found his way to the abode of the head of the mendicants. When he arrived at his destination after many ramblings and wanderings, he recognized Mehr-Nigar from afar, doling out food to the mendicants. Amar disguised himself as an old man and approached her. When Mehr-Nigar started serving him, Khvaja Amar became tearful and said to her, "O princess, I am not a mendicant but your slave, Amar. I am remorseful for what I did and I profess myself your humble slave. I have searched for you in every corner of the world, and the hardships I have encountered have made my existence a fate worse than death!" When Mehr-Nigar recognized Amar she rushed into his embrace and began crying. Hearing her crying the chief rushed there, calling out, "What has happened, my child, that you cry so inconsolably and waste away your existence with such a flood of tears?" Mehr-Nigar told him, "Everything is fine. This man here is my father whom I have told you about!" The beggar began counseling Amar and said, "My dear friend! Who has ever heard of a father treating his youthful daughter in such a manner?" Amar answered, "I am helpless because I have not one penny and cannot marry her off and arrange for all the dowry that will be needed!" The beggar gave Amar five hundred rupees and said, "Go find a match for her soon and fulfill your duty!" Amar took the money and left with Mehr-Nigar.

On the way back to his fortress, he put the money in his *zambil* and drugged Mehr-Nigar to render her unconscious. Then he made her into a bundle and carried her on his back to the fort so that he could bring her home safely and then take some rest.

As it happened, Hurmuz and Faramurz had received intelligence from their *ayyars* that Mehr-Nigar had come into their camp one night dressed as a man and had ridden away for some unknown destination on one of their horses tied at the post. They also learned that Amar had gone in search of her. The princes conferred together and decided that there was no way for Amar and the princess to return to their fort without entering the mountain pass. They ordered the *ayyars* of their camp to lay an ambush so that when they saw Amar returning with Mehr-Nigar, they could snatch her from him. They gave them strict orders not to allow Amar to take her to his castle under any circumstances, to kill him if the chance offered itself or better yet to take him alive so that they could ensure that they would be safe from his machinations in the future. At their orders, four hundred *ayyars* hid themselves on the slope of the mountain, and a few *ayyars* were also put on sentinel duty. The princes told the *ayyars*, "Inform us immediately when Amar arrives and the ambush is made so that we can bring some choice warriors with us to your aid and your men are not overwhelmed by the enemy but have reinforcements at hand." The princes also ordered those men whom they had chosen to take along to remain armed and ready with their horses.

The moment Amar entered the pass carrying Mehr-Nigar on his back in a bundle, he was surrounded on all sides by four hundred *ayyars*, who encircled him leaving Amar no escape route. Posed with many difficulties by the challenge from their group, Amar drew his sword and shield, the lustrous bird of his sword leaving the nest of its scabbard. When Hurmuz and Faramurz received word that Amar had been surrounded and the details of the ambush were conveyed to them, they charged with the commanders picked for the mission. Amar grew anxious seeing the reinforcements the foe had brought. Worried that his adversaries were very many and were only increasing in number, whereas he was all by himself and had a burden to carry moreover that handicapped him, Amar began praying to God for assistance.

All of a sudden Naqabdar Naranji-Posh arrived there with his forty thousand troops to assist Amar by the order of God Almighty. He killed Zhopin's brothers, Jahangir and Jahandar Kabuli, and routed the entire army of Hurmuz and Faramurz, also driving away their companions. Many an infidel was killed and only those who chose to turn tail and escape survived to tell the tale and avoided being written off as dead. After being handed this humiliating defeat, Hurmuz and Faramurz returned to their camp in a state of dejection, lamenting the loss of Jahangir and Jahandar Kabuli and marked by their terrible misfortune. Meanwhile, Naqabdar Naranji-Posh returned to his abode after seeing Amar to his castle. Amar conducted Mehr-Nigar to the women's quarters and his worried mind finally felt at east to see her safe. Later, Amar apologized to Mehr-Nigar all over again and had his offense pardoned by her. Everyone was greatly pleased by Amar's wonderful efforts in recovering Mehr-Nigar.

––––

Before we return to their account, a few words from the story of the Sahibqiran, the Conqueror of the World.

Amir Hamza frantically forged a path through the plains for forty days and forty nights after leaving Gulistan-e Irum, dismayed by the fickleness of the jinns. On the forty-first day, when he came to his senses, he saw before him a castle that was under siege by *devs* who were standing at its gates. Amir bellowed his powerful war cry, which shook the whole castle to its foundations. The eardrums of many *devs* burst from the noise and those who stood before Amir scattered. The commander of the army of the *devs* recognized Amir and approached him and said, "O Sahibqiran! You have caused havoc in Qaf and destroyed this land that was a veritable garden of flowers! I recognize you and know you well, and now that I have found you in my power, you will not live to see the end of day!" With these words, he brought a box tree down on Amir's head. Amir, however, foiled his blow and dealt him a sword blow that cleft his body in two from head to navel. He fell to the ground, and his army decamped upon witnessing the might and power of Amir's hand.

A race of *gao-pas* inhabited that castle and their king's name was Tulu

Gao-Pa. He came out of the castle, embraced Amir, and took him inside the fort with great respect and deference. He organized a feast in Amir's honor and waited upon him with great awe and reverence. After the feast was over, Amir said to him, "Would you be able to take me to my world and deliver me from the troubles and hardships of my wanderings?" He answered, "Indeed I can take you to your world, but the orders promulgated by Aasman Peri clearly stipulate that anyone found guilty of this offense will come to harm at her hands. However, I am willing to take the risk if you agree to take my daughter in marriage." Amir answered, "Verily, I am not inclined to marry anyone as I am not attracted to the people of this land!" Tulu Gao-Pa answered, "If you refuse my daughter's hand in marriage, then pray instead kill for me the monster Rukh who is my enemy and deliver me of the anxiety of his existence. If you were to accept either of these two conditions I would have you conveyed to the world and defy Aasman Peri and earn her condemnation." Amir replied, "I agree to the second condition. Take me to the beast who is your enemy." King Tulu Gao-Pa sent his men to accompany Amir Hamza to show him this creature from afar and give him the directions to his abode. When they arrived at a white hill Amir asked them, "What regal and majestic personage is it who lives here?" His companions answered, "This is not a hill but the egg of the selfsame Rukh who is the enemy of King Tulu Gao-Pa. It is this same creature that has made existence a veritable affliction for our king and causes him to live in constant terror. It seems that he has gone away to feed."

Amir went to sit close to that egg so that when the bird returned he might devise some way of overpowering it. When the bird returned to sit on the egg and spread his wings to settle down on his perch, Amir said in his heart, *This is a mighty and powerful bird and it would be well-nigh impossible to overpower it. It is also certain that this creature travels to the world of humans and circulates in all climes. I should catch his legs and scream loudly to frighten it into flying away, and he will head for the world of humans. He will thus become the means of transporting me to my world.* Deciding on this course of action, Amir caught hold of Rukh's leg and made a cry that frightened the bird into flying away with him. However, when the bird reached the Caspian Sea, he pecked at Amir's hand with his beak so hard that Amir's hold weakened and he lost his grip on the bird's leg, and the thread snapped from which all his hopes dangled.

The prophets Khizr and Ilyas caught Amir in their arms before he could fall into the sea. They carried Amir, who had lost consciousness

from the fall, out of harm's way and laid him down safely on the shore to
let him rest.

———

Now hear of Aasman Peri. One day she inquired of Abdur Rahman,
"Pray find out where Amir is, and whether he has returned to his world
or is still within our dominions."

Abdur Rahman drew the horoscope and wrote down the results, and
then read them out: "Amir had reached the fort of the *gao-pas* where Tulu
Gao-Pa had been surrounded by *devs*. Amir killed the *devs* and saved
Tulu Gao-Pa's life; by Amir's assistance that king warded off a great
calamity from his head. He arranged a feast for Amir and provided him
with every comfort. Amir asked the king to send him back to his world
and he agreed but mentioned your broadcast and said that he would go
against your command only if Amir accepted to marry his daughter and
make her his wife. When Amir avowed that he would never accept the
proposition and would not marry the king's daughter and cast himself
into greater trouble, Tulu Gao-Pa told Amir that if he was unwilling to
marry his daughter he should kill Rukh, a giant bird who was his enemy,
and pull that thorn of fear from his heart. Tulu Gao-Pa promised to convey Amir to his world and carry out the mission to return the favor. Amir
asked him to take him to the bird and show him his abode, and thus he
took Amir to that animal. Amir considered it likely that the bird might be
a visitor to the world of humans. He caught hold of the bird's leg and
made a loud cry, and the bird flew from there with Amir hanging from its
leg. Over the Caspian Sea the bird pecked at Amir's hand and thus freed
himself of Amir's hold, and the Sahibqiran fell down."

Upon hearing Abdur Rahman's account, Aasman Peri cried bitterly.
She sent Quraisha at the head of an intrepid army toward the fort of the
gao-pas with orders that no living creature should be left alive in their city
but all inhabitants be put to the sword. Aasman Peri herself flew toward
the Caspian Sea, but finding holy Khizr and Ilyas there she turned away
mortified with shame and hid herself from their sight.

When Amir came to, he complained to Khizr and Ilyas about Aasman
Peri. They said, "O Amir! Though a lot has transpired of the decree of fate,
more yet remains! Do not worry and torment yourself. Aasman Peri had
just arrived on the scene, but seeing us here she did not dare show her face
and returned shamefaced whence she had come without presenting herself." Amir said to them, "O holy personages! Pray send me back to the

castle of the *gao-pas*! Show me this kindness so that I may get my recompense from that wretch and overpower him!" Prophet Khizr conveyed Amir to the fort of the *gao-pas*, carrying out his wishes. Amir saw that the whole city was deserted: A deathly quiet prevailed there and not even a bird was to be seen. Amir Hamza asked Khizr, "O holy one, where have the inhabitants of this place disappeared, for not even a single person is to be seen here? Verily, the very sight of this city makes me shudder with fear." Khvaja Khizr replied, "Whatever passed with you here was discovered by Aasman Peri through Abdur Rahman, and she sent Quraisha here with an army to lay ruin to this fort and kill every single inhabitant." Khizr then disappeared and Amir stayed all by himself in that city for three days.

On the fourth day he headed out of the city and into the plains. After another four days of traveling he saw a fort with some signs of life. As he approached, it looked as if it were the fort of Ctesiphon: It had towers and ramparts identical to those of that kingdom and also had the building of Tal Shad-Kam. When he went inside he saw the same buildings that he had seen in Ctesiphon but did not see any people and found every building empty of human presence. Amir wondered what had become of the citizens of Ctesiphon if this was indeed the same city. When he went toward the quarters where Mehr-Nigar dwelt, he found the arch on which he had inscribed love sonnets for Mehr-Nigar with his own hand but again saw nobody in the building. After visiting Chehal Sutoon, Amir headed toward Bagh-e Bedad and from there arrived in Hasht-Bahisht. He encountered a towering *dev* of mighty build standing there, who sniggered upon catching sight of Amir Hamza and said, "O human! It is my greatest wish to populate this city, and night and day I am eaten by this sole desire. I have had it constructed on the model of the city of Ctesiphon in the world of humans and undergone many hardships in its construction. I have already brought two humans to populate it and will bring more of them in the future. Because you have come here by yourself and God has sent you into this city I will appoint you the king of this city and invest you with the writ of the land."

Amir asked him, "What is this clime where I am now?" He answered, "It is the land of Qaf." Amir asked him, "Do you at all recognize me or know my name?" The *dev* answered, "How could I recognize you when I have never before set eyes on you?" Amir said, "My title is the Quake of Qaf, and my courage and valor are common knowledge." The *dev* asked, "Were you the one who killed Ifrit and Ahriman and severed their heads with your lustrous sword?" Amir answered, "I have killed scores of *devs*, not just Ifrit and Ahriman!" The *dev* said, "Then you will destroy this fortress, too, and create the same strife here that you fomented in the rest of Qaf. I will avenge the blood of the *devs* of Qaf on you and crush your head to inflict ignominy on you!" At this, the *dev* flung a millstone at Amir's head. Amir deflected his attack and with one mighty blow of his sword, dispatched that unfortunate soul to Hell, and prevailed over him with great swiftness and alacrity.

After killing the *dev* Amir went into the city's courtyard, where he saw two beautiful and comely boys sitting with great poise, grace, and elegance. When Amir asked their particulars, they replied, "Our father was a merchant. When he died, a *dev* who lived here kidnapped us and the tyrant kept us incarcerated here. Now tell us, who are you?" Amir answered, "I am called the Sword of God, the Hand of God, the Proxy of the Beneficent, the Quake of Qaf, and the Latter-day Suleiman. Everyone considers me peerless in courage and valor. I have come from the world of men and have killed many a *dev*—including the one who kidnapped you—and sent him to Hell. Have no worries now, for I shall take you to the world of humans, and I make you this promise."

Upon hearing this, the boys were greatly pleased and threw themselves at Amir's feet to express their gratitude. When Amir asked their names, one of them said, "I am called Khvaja Aashob!" The other answered, "And I am Khvaja Bahlol!" Amir said, "When we return to our world, God willing, I will appoint one of you as my minister and promote him to a high rank, and the other I will make my paymaster." They replied, "We will be appointed the minister and paymaster *if* we return to the world. For now, that is nothing but a pipe dream that we do not hope to see come to fruition in our lives, as we are likely to die here in misery!" Amir consoled them and offered many kind words to lift their spirits and told them that they would soon return to their world, God willing, and be released of their hardships before long.

Amir Hamza left the castle along with the boys and sat down under a leafy tree to eat the bread-cake given him by Khizr. Some time had passed when a *dev* carrying a box tree on his shoulder came up to Amir and said, "O child of man, dark-headed, white-toothed, and weak of body! Where do you think you are taking these boys after killing my gatekeeper? Do you not have the least fear of me? Do you not know that I am called Maymar Dev, and am the most sanguinary of all the *devs* of Qaf?" Amir asked him, "Were you the one who made this fortress in the likeness of Ctesiphon and decorated it on its plan?" He answered, "Indeed it was I who made it, and all the buildings of Suleiman in the realms of Qaf were also constructed by my hand. All the wonders that you see here are all my creation alone. Now you tell me what your name is and what business brought you here." Amir replied, "I am the husband of Aasman Peri, who is the daughter of the emperor of *perizads*. My name is the Quake of Qaf and the Latter-day Suleiman, a name familiar to young and old alike in your land for reasons of my gallantry and pluck!" The *dev* said, "Then say that you are the one who destroyed the garden of Qaf! Today your death has sent you here! It seems that I am the one appointed to extract your soul from your body!" Having said this, the *dev* brought the box tree down on Amir's head, but as before, Amir foiled this attack and dealt him an unwavering sword thrust that sliced him in two like a cucumber, with not a fiber remaining attached between the two parts.

The boys were delighted to see this display of Amir's might and valor, and said jocularly, "Bravo, O Terror of God! You are indeed a strong and mighty person! God be praised, what bravery and what pluck! We will definitely keep your company, accompany you everywhere, and do what you ask us to do. It seems that you prevail over such mighty *devs* because of the power of your names, for no human being possesses the capacity and power to kill a *dev* with such ease and behead him with such facility. We, too, will change our names to match yours."

In this manner they proceeded onward making pleasantries. The boys were much taken with Amir and became attached to him. The lion skin that Amir had obtained by killing the beast at Siyah Boom he cut in two halves and gave one piece each to Khvaja Aashob and Khvaja Bahlol. He gave them the names of Jahandar Qalandar and Jahangir Qalandar, and treated both of them equally in all matters.

When it was noon Amir spread the wolves' skins under a shady tree and sat down to rest. As a cold breeze was blowing and he was tired from his journey, he was overtaken by sleep and was soon lost to slumber. The boys went for a bath in the river that flowed by the tree and began splashing around. Suddenly a *dev* appeared from the forest, and upon seeing him, Bahlol said to Aashob, "Do you remember the formula for killing the *dev*, brother? Let us now go forward, you and I, and kill him and put an end to the life of this filthy beast." They consulted together and then shouted at the *dev* in challenge, "Here, O carrion eater! Where do you think you are headed? You will see how we send you to Hell with dispatch! Do you not know that we are the Arm of God and the Sword of God and know all too well how to deal with your race?" After challenging the *dev* they went forth to skirmish with him. But as the *dev* kept advancing toward them without paying any heed to their words and did not turn tail, they took fright. They hastily woke Amir Hamza up and told him all that had happened.

Amir saw that a mighty *dev* was advancing on them huffing and puffing. When he came near, Amir let out his war cry, "God is Great!" and lifting him up in the air, slammed him to the ground. Then climbing atop him, Amir cut off his head with his dagger and dispatched him to Hell. He then told the two boys, "Beware and be warned never again to try such capers, or else you will surely die and never find release from the power of this wretched race!" After that, Amir headed onward in the company of the boys.

On the fifth day they saw a big ship being put to sea. Amir approached and asked the sailors, "Who owns this ship, where is it headed, and what is its port of call?" The sailors answered, "This ship belongs to Khvaja Saeed Bazargan. It is headed for the world of humans and will call there!" Amir said to them, "The three of us are also headed for the world of humans. We will gladly pay the fare to take accommodation on the ship and will be grateful to you for allowing us to travel with you!" The sailors replied, "We do not have authority in this matter. You should speak to the master of the ship and obtain his permission." Amir then met Khvaja Saeed Bazargan and said to him, "We are going to the world of humans, which is also your destination. We will gladly pay any fare that you ask and make no excuses." Khvaja Saeed received Amir very cordially and said, "To pay for the voyage you must marry my daughter." Amir touched his earlobes[15] to express his vow never to entertain such propositions and said, "I refuse to enter into any commitments of marriage as I am averse to all matrimonial proposals!" The merchant was angered by Amir's refusal. Amir got up and left the merchant as he was unhappy with his words, but the two boys said to Khvaja Saeed Bazargan, "If you were to find us wives, too, we would undertake to convince Amir and ensure that he marries your daughter as you propose!" The merchant said, "I promise it!"

The boys then said to the Amir, "O Arm of God, why don't you accept marriage with the merchant's daughter? You will return to the world and find a wife in the bargain. What wonderful fun it will be, just imagine!" Amir answered, "I will never accept marriage and won't be led down that path again!" The boys said, "Dear Arm of God, you will have to get married, and none of your refusals will hold up. We see that it will only increase your suffering." Amir said, "Do you think that by forcing me into it I will marry and allow matrimonial concerns to plague me?" The boys answered, "Indeed we will force you into accepting it!" Amir laughed at the boys' talk, and then said, "Very well, then! If you insist, then I will get married and won't give you any reason to be unhappy."

The boys rushed to Khvaja Saeed Bazargan and said, "There! We have persuaded Amir to get married and have made him give us his pledge. Now you may marry your daughter to him and arrange for the wedding ceremony." The merchant married Amir to his daughter and Khvaja Bahlol and Khvaja Aashob to two other girls. All the ceremonies concluded without incident. Amir Hamza and the two boys slept with their wives that night.

In the morning when Amir woke up he found that a new marvel had unfolded. Namely, he found Aasman Peri sleeping by his side and discovered that the merchant was none other than Khvaja Abdur Rahman. Because Amir had divorced[16] Aasman Peri in anger, Khvaja Abdur Rahman had found a way of uniting them again, and following the letter of religious law, made it permissible for Amir to sleep with Aasman Peri again.

Aasman Peri fell to Amir's feet and began begging and vowing her submissiveness to him. Abdur Rahman also touched Amir's feet and importuned him. "Please forgive all her misdemeanors you have suffered to date and do not look to past grievances. If she crosses you again in the future you will have the right not to forgive her, and may punish her as you see fit." Aasman Peri said, "O Amir, indeed this time I will send you to your world and I swear not to go against my vow!" Amir was then forced to return with Aasman Peri to Gulistan-e Irum along with the two boys, and there Aasman Peri held celebrations for six months.

One day Amir again said to Aasman Peri, "O Aasman Peri! Pray give me your leave now, as my heart has become oppressed from my sojourn in Qaf and I have suffered gravely from separation from my family and friends." Aasman Peri said, "Tomorrow morning I will send you off, God willing, but do tell me if you will ever come here again and offer me an opportunity to see your face." Amir answered, "O Queen of Qaf! Just as my heart longs for Mehr-Nigar in her absence here, it will crave you when I am back in my world and will long to behold your face." Aasman Peri was most pleased by Amir's words. In the morning when she ascended her throne, she sent for the four *devs* who always carried Amir's throne. First she gave them a reward and then had many gifts of Qaf loaded on another throne, and said to Amir, "Please ascend the throne in the name of God and prepare to depart."

Before Amir could ascend the throne, a great hue and cry suddenly broke out in a din like that of Judgment Day. When they looked they saw four hundred *devs* and jinns who used to attend Shahpal coming toward them in great anxiety. They were throwing ashes on their head and had torn their tunics in grief. Aasman Peri panicked at the sight of this and the world darkened before her eyes. She asked them, "What is the matter?" They submitted themselves to her, saying, "The emperor has departed from this world for the Eternal Kingdom and his caravan's course is now set for Heaven!" From the shock of this terrible news Aasman Peri fell from her throne and gave herself to weeping and wailing, beside herself with grief. The whole of Gulistan-e Irum rang with lamentations and a din like the din of the Day of Judgment rang out from their mourning. Young and old alike clad themselves in mourning and many fell unconscious from excess of crying.

Aasman Peri yielded to Amir with folded arms, "Although you have stayed here already for seventeen years, please stay another forty days for my sake and bear the separation from your near and dear ones while I take my father's body for burial in Shehristan-e Zarrin. I shall inter him in our ancient burial grounds and commemorate the forty-day mourning ritual and grieve for his demise. Upon my return from there I will send you off and give you leave to go." Amir answered, "Very well! You may go and I will stay here and do what you ask me to do." Aasman Peri said, "Do not become sad in my absence and leave and inflict on me the wound of your separation. I am leaving Salasal Perizad here with you. If you ever feel restive ask her for the keys and visit the Forty Wonders of Suleiman to entertain yourself so that your heart does not feel oppressed and you remain in good cheer."

She then departed for Shehristan-e Zarrin with Shahpal's body, and when she got there the celebrated kings of all dominions of Qaf— Tareeki, Zabarjad, Yaqut, Bayaban-e Mina, and Zamarrud—presented themselves, and the nobility and the laity, the young and the old, came to receive audience from her. Together they buried Shahpal and performed the last rites. For forty days everyone clad himself in black and remained in mourning, and all other work was suspended.

Now hear of the Sahibqiran. He passed two days with great difficulty indoors, but on the third day he prepared to head outdoors as he could no longer suffer to remain within. Salasal Perizad said to him, "Until the

Queen of the Skies returns after acquitting herself of her duties to the deceased, you may go and visit the Forty Wonders of Suleiman and entertain yourself with those marvels." He handed Amir a key and led him to the door of a building. Amir opened the lock and the moment he set foot inside, the door of that chamber closed behind him. After a moment the darkness subsided and he beheld a vast field. As he went onward and looked about, he saw a sumptuously decorated bejeweled throne. On that throne lay an apple that was half red and half green. Amir picked it up and smelled it and immediately fell unconscious and lost use of his senses. In his dream he saw a magnificent castle that was beautifully constructed. He went inside and entered a captivating garden where moonfaced damsels were promenading about and could be seen all over the garden in their splendid beauty. A comely maiden who was the envy of the stars was giving audience upon a luxurious throne, whose luminance outshone the sun in the heavens to the same degree that the midday sun outshines a lamp. Upon beholding her, Amir immediately became enamored of her and pledged his life and soul to her on the spot.

That moonfaced beauty arranged a festive assembly in Amir's honor and waited on him hand and foot. Some four hundred beauties tuned their musical instruments and began playing music and singing, demonstrating their talents. In the midst of these revels, the arrival of the woman's father was announced, and she became agitated and asked Amir, "Where should I hide and conceal myself?" The Sahibqiran answered, "There is no need for you to go into hiding. Remain seated where you are and let your father come if he wishes to visit you. All your anxiety on that account is unnecessary and to no purpose."

Her father arrived in the meanwhile and saw Amir sitting beside his daughter. He saluted Amir and kissed his feet. Amir embraced him and said, "Dear friend, how did you recognize me, since you could not have known me, having never set eyes on me before?" He answered, "We had heard from our forefathers that the Quake of Qaf would arrive here at some time in the future to regard the Wonders of Suleiman and lay low many *devs* with his lustrous sword. No common man would have had the capacity to enter this place and overcome the *devs*." Amir was greatly pleased to hear this. That man married Amir to his daughter and made him his son-in-law. The Sahibqiran passed seven years there and two sons were born to him in that period.

One day Amir was sitting with his beloved by the side of the pond when she said to him, "O Quake of Qaf! My anklet has fallen into the pond. I would be grateful if you could fetch it for me." As Amir dived into the pond, he suddenly started and discovered he was standing in the same chamber where he had entered this place, and found Salasal Perizad standing before him. Surprised at this turn of events, Amir looked around and said to him, "I would like to go into that chamber again, because my heart longs to see my boys. I lived there for seven years and one day when I dived into the pool I emerged here." Salasal Perizad said, "Your honor! These are the Wonders of Suleiman. All this talk of your sons and wife is a dream. You were away for less than an hour. Come with me now and partake of your dinner and take some rest as it is getting close to evening. All that you saw was an illusion and a dream. One encounters such marvels in a *tilism*. Drive all those memories from your heart now. Tomorrow you may go and visit the second chamber, where new marvels await you, and you will derive ever greater pleasure from visiting it." Then Salasal Perizad locked the chamber and escorted Amir back to the palace. Amir had his dinner and rested, and his heart again felt content and at peace.

The next day, after performing the morning rituals, Amir opened the second chamber and went inside. After walking some distance he saw a woman's portrait propped upon a throne. As Amir picked up the portrait to look at it, he swooned and fell on the throne, having lost consciousness. In that state he saw a garden in which many beautiful women were gathered and the one whose beauty had made him lose consciousness was dancing amidst a group of women who were playing music and singing. Amir also saw a number of *ghols* standing in a corner of the garden. When they saw Amir they rushed at him with wielded maces. Amir drew the Aqrab-e Suleimani and attacked them, unnerving and confusing their host. The shock also made Amir open his eyes and he saw there was neither garden nor *ghols* before him, but Salasal Perizad stood in the same chamber.

Amir marveled at this and returned to the palace, followed by Salasal Perizad, who took care to lock the second chamber. After having his dinner and resting, Amir again retired to his room to sleep. On the third day he visited the third chamber and went inside. After walking there for some distance, he lost his way and came upon a desert, a great wasteland where the sun was blazing. He wandered there for seven days and seven nights and on the eighth day he saw a *dev* of strange shape and form. He caught Amir by his cummerbund and flew toward the sky with him, and when he reached the Milky Way, he flung Amir back to Earth. Amir's eyes opened then and he saw neither the desert nor the *dev* but instead Salasal Perizad waiting for him in the same chamber where he had started. Amir asked him for an explanation of that chamber and he answered, "These chambers are full of wonders that the mind cannot unravel and that leave people amazed and astonished. However, they do not pose any danger to your safety." In short, Amir visited thirty-nine chambers for thirty-nine days and delighted himself immensely with their many remarkable wonders. On the fortieth day he asked Salasal Perizad to open the fortieth chamber for him so he could visit it as well and experience what wonders it held for him. He answered, "I cannot open the door of this chamber, for I do not have the authority to do so. It is the Zandan-e Suleimani." When Amir insisted, he told him that he did not have the key. Then Amir snatched the key ring from him, found the key to the fortieth door, and went inside. Salasal Perizad rushed off to tell Aasman Peri that Amir had opened the fortieth chamber despite his objections and had gone in.

The narrator tells that when Amir entered the fortieth chamber he saw thousands of *devs,* jinns, and *perizads* languishing in captivity. All of them made obeisance to Amir and said, "O Quake of Qaf, have mercy on our circumstances and release us from this captivity!" Amir asked them, "How did you recognize that I was the Quake of Qaf?" They replied, "Nobody imprisoned here escapes as long as he lives. But there are many here in this prison who were incarcerated by Prophet Suleiman himself, and he once stated that the Quake of Qaf would come someday to release those incarcerated here, and that he would be a human who had come to visit Qaf. Thus we recognized you as the Quake of Qaf. We beseech you in the name of God to secure our release! God will recompense you for relieving us of our misery."

Amir took pity on them and cut their chains and fetters and freed them from the prison. All of them kissed Amir's feet and went home after taking his leave. Suddenly Amir heard the sound of a horse's hooves and when he went to investigate, he saw a red colt with roseatte patches on his whole body, running about and galloping in a most captivating, sublime, and excellent manner. There were some four hundred rosettes on his skin and each one was comparable to a thousand roses in full bloom. Amir was delighted to see the colt, and when he caught sight of Amir he began prancing about and racing from one end of the chamber to the other in skittish excitement. Then the colt rushed toward Amir and stepped on his foot. Although he was clad in armor, Amir felt severe pain from the horse's weight and rushed after the colt in anger. The colt entered a building and Amir followed in pursuit without a second thought. Because inside the building was utter darkness, Amir took out the *shabchiragh* jewel to illuminate his path.

He had hardly taken a few steps when he heard a voice call out, "I cannot bear my misery any longer, O my master! Come quickly to our rescue and release us from this hardship." When Amir stepped closer, he saw Arnais Dev and Laneesa sitting there, weeping and wailing in a most terrible state. Amir said to them, "Hold on a while longer. I will come and rescue you after I have killed the colt that ran away after kicking me." Arnais and Laneesa said, "O Sahibqiran! He is our son! He committed that misdemeanor because he did not know who you were. Please pardon him and count us among your loyal subjects." Amir was surprised by this and asked Arnais, "You are a *dev* yourself and your wife a *peri*. How did you beget a horse for a child? Tell me how it came to pass and give me all the details." They narrated the whole story and said, "We have named our son Ashqar!" Arnais then called Ashqar, made him bow to Amir and kiss his feet, and secured pardon for him for offending Amir. Amir treated all of them with great kindness and released them from their prison and said to them, "Wait for me here while I go and discover the other wonders of this place to see what else it has to offer."

A little farther along Amir found a building in which two *perizads* were hanging upside down and hitting their heads in misery. Amir took pity on them, too, and freed them. When Amir went onward he saw his wives, Rehan Peri and Qamar Chehra, sitting clad in chains and looking dejected and forlorn. Tears came to Hamza's eyes to see them in that state and he was aggrieved and saddened by their lot. Upon seeing Amir they, too, began crying inconsolably. Amir brought them out of the chamber along with Arnais and Laneesa. That night he slept with Rehan Peri and Qamar Chehra in Aasman Peri's bed and ravished them both to his heart's delight. As God had willed, the same night both Qamar Chehra and Rehan Peri were impregnated with Amir's seed.

The narrator says that Rehan Peri's son was to be called Dur-Dur Posh and Qamar Chehra's son was to be known as Qamza-Zad. The stories of these princes will be written in the Book of Bala-Bakhtar and will be narrated in their turn.[17]

In the morning Amir sent the two *perizads* away and they returned to their homes. Then Amir asked Arnais, "Can you now take me to my world?" Arnais answered, "I am at your service!" Amir sat with the two

boys on the throne and both Arnais and Laneesa bore it heavenward and
rose as high as the lights of the heavens. When a few hours remained
until the end of day, they descended by the banks of a river. Amir saw a
shining and luminous building there and beheld with wonder its marvelous construction and the refreshing air about it. When he stepped inside he gazed raptly at the walls and fixtures of the place, for he had never
before seen such marvels elsewhere and such luxurious construction
was unknown to him. He discovered that this was the Shish-Mahal[18] of
Prophet Suleiman, a palace that was proverbial for its amazing construction. In the evening, the palace lit up by itself, becoming so resplendent
that a hundred thousand lamps would have proved insufficient for the
task. When a few hours remained until the end of night Amir and the
boys fell asleep, and Arnais closeted himself with Laneesa. Ashqar, however, went outdoors for a romp in the forest, preferring this to sleep.

———

Now a few words about Aasman Peri. After she had performed all the rituals and completed the forty days of mourning, she gave leave to the
kings and princes of Qaf to depart, conferring on each a robe of honor
and a gift according to his station. Then she headed for Gulistan-e Irum.
In the middle of her journey Salasal Perizad presented himself before her
and stated that the Quake of Qaf had released the prisoners of Zandan-e
Suleimani and let them out of the prison. Aasman Peri responded to this
news, "The prophecy made by Prophet Suleiman has been fulfilled and
what he foretold has come to pass! It was well that Amir did this!" Salasal
Perizad then said, "Amir showed the same kindness to Arnais and Laneesa and released them as well." Aasman Peri replied, "It is well that he
did that, too." Salasal Perizad next said, "Amir freed Rehan Peri and
Qamar Chehra as well." Then Aasman Peri said, "He did wrong in setting free my rivals! Tell me, what happened afterward?" Salasal Perizad
admitted, "That was all I witnessed before I left. I do not know what else
transpired afterward." While they were having this conversation, another
peri presented herself and added, "The Sahibqiran slept with Rehan Peri
and Qamar Chehra in your bed and passed the whole night in pleasure-
seeking with them. In the morning he sent them away and then departed
for his world with Arnais and Laneesa carrying his throne."

Aasman Peri came into a towering rage upon hearing this and said, "I
had resolved myself to send the Sahibqiran back to his world. Why
should the Sahibqiran have slept with my rivals in my marriage bed if not

to pour scorn on me and make me jealous? You will see how I repay the Sahibqiran for this deed and what terrors and calamities I unleash on his head!" With these words, she mounted a throne and took her intrepid army in search of Amir Hamza. Upon approaching the Shish-Mahal, she discovered that Amir was inside. As fate would have it, she found Arnais and Laneesa sleeping together in the very first chamber that she entered. Aasman Peri drew her sword and decapitated both of them with just one stroke and thus cooled the fires of her rage by killing the two of them.

Then she took the same bloodied sword to Amir's bedside and raised it over his head, resolved to murder him as well. But Quraisha, who had accompanied her, snatched the sword from her and said, "My hands are bound because you are my mother; otherwise I would draw my dagger this instant and disembowel you, putting an end to your life. How do you dare even think of harming my father while I still live and before my eyes, let alone kill him?" Then Aasman Peri withdrew from her plans, and after leaving a note at Amir's bedside, flew off to Gulistan-e Irum not staying there another instant.

When it was morning, Ashqar returned from the forest and set to screaming and howling and wasting away in lamentations upon finding his parents murdered. His cries woke Amir, who soon encountered Arnais and Laneesa lying murdered and beheaded on the floor. Amir grieved for them immensely and said to Ashqar, "There is no warding off what has been fated. Nobody can change the plans of God. If I can discover the identity of the murderer, I shall kill him this instant and avenge your parents' death. Cry no more and consider me now in the place of your mother and father. I will treat you like my son and never give you occasion to be sad."

Then Amir saw a note at his bedside, in which was written:

I had resolved this time to send you back to your world and fulfill my promise to you, but it seems that you were not fated—either now or ever—to partake of food and water anywhere except Qaf. I do not approve of the two deeds you committed: You slept in my bed with my rivals, and then you tried to depart for your world without my knowledge. I wanted to murder you for your first offense like I murdered Arnais and Laneesa, but Quraisha intervened and I was unable to carry out my plan. She was ready to fight me in your defense and snatched my sword and said harsh words to me. In retribution for your second deed, however, I murdered Arnais and Laneesa. Now I will see how you return to your world, find release from Qaf, or find anyone to take you there. I would like to see who even dares to utter a word about conducting you to your world.

Amir was terribly shaken by the words in the note. He buried Arnais and Laneesa and performed their last rites and sojourned in that place for seven days. On the eighth day, Amir said with tearful eyes, "How will I return now to my world and find release from Aasman Peri's clutches? It seems to me that I will ever wander helplessly in Qaf until I die." Upon hearing this, Ashqar said, "Do not grieve any longer, for I will take you to your world and will not fear Aasman Peri in the least. Climb on my back and be prepared to depart!" Amir asked, "What will become of the boys, and where will I leave them?" Ashqar answered, "Put them on my back as well."

Amir made two panniers and put Khvaja Aashob and Khvaja Bahlol in them on either side of his saddle. Then Amir took his seat and Ashqar took off carrying them all on his back. It is said that Ashqar took Amir toward his destination with lightning speed, bridging a thousands *farsangs* a day. Ashqar flew over the sea and when he landed and felt earth beneath his feet again, he sped faster than the wind's own charger, who could only exclaim "Bravo!" as it was left behind in Ashqar's cloud of dust.

A few hours still remained to the end of day when Amir reached the slope of the Koh-e Noor mountain and dismounted there with the boys. He soon saw the prophets Khizr and Ilyas coming toward them. Amir rushed to them and kissed their feet and cried out, "O holy personages! I am endlessly tormented by Aasman Peri and I have tired of my life in Qaf!" They answered, "Have no worries, O Amir! It is certain that this time you will return to your world and be united with your near and dear ones. Come with us, for our mother, Bibi Asifa Ba-Safa, has taken pity on your condition and sent for you so that she might give you her leave to depart to your world." Amir and the boys climbed the mountain and saw a dome at the top. Flashes of light moved between the dome and the sky and lit up every inch of the mountain. When they went inside the dome, they beheld an old woman of luminous aspect sitting on a mat, prayer beads in hand, absorbed in worship of God. Her venerated presence struck awe in Amir's heart, and he greeted her with extreme reverence. Bibi Asifa pressed Amir's head to her bosom and said, "My child, I have been most desirous of seeing you. It was well that you came this way and my eyes have the chance to behold your auspicious beauty. You shall soon return to your world." With this, she gave Amir a piece of rope that was no longer than a yard and quarter in length and said to him, "Give this lasso to Amar as a gift from me and tell him that I have made it with my own hands. Tell him to keep it in safe custody, for it will serve him on many occasions and reveal to him its many marvels. If he so wishes he will be able to catch a *dev* with it and use it for many other needs besides. When he recites a benediction for Prophet Muhammad (praise be unto Him!) and blows on it, it will increase a thousand yards in length."

After that she said to Amir, "Tonight you will be our guest here." Amir answered, "It is a source of honor and distinction for me to be admitted into your presence." In the morning, when Amir had finished with his prayers, the holy Khizr said to him, "You will have to shoe your horse, otherwise he will not be able to cross the desert of Qaf or journey across the length of that harsh expanse." Khizr then clipped Ashqar's wings and made shoes of them, which he nailed to Ashqar's hooves. Amir said, "O holy one! How long will these shoes made of wings last, and will they be at all durable?" Khizr answered, "They will last for the length of your life and won't come off. When the last wing falls from Ashqar's hooves, you should understand that your cup of life has become completely full, and your time has come to depart from this world to the Future State." Then he gave Amir a saddle and said, "Put this on Ashqar's back. It was made for Sikander himself, who ordered it at great expense by spending the tribute from the Seven Climes." Amir then saddled Ashqar, expressed his gratitude to Khizr, and prepared to depart.

———

Now let me say a few words about Aasman Peri to keep you abreast of her news. Several days after she returned to Gulistan-e Irum from the Shish-Mahal, she donned a crimson dress, sat on the throne, and said to Abdur Rahman, "Give me some news of Hamza. Tell me how he is keeping himself, where he is, and whether he is sad or happy." Khvaja Abdur Rahman made his geomancy calculations and said, "Amir Hamza has continued on his way. He reached Koh-e Noor, where Bibi Asifa Ba-Safa is about to send him off to his world." Upon hearing this, Aasman Peri became crimson with rage and the news made life a veritable burden for her. She said, "How dare Bibi Asifa Ba-Safa, who is my subject, send my husband off to the world of humans without my permission and against my wishes? Send for my throne this instant!"

The flying throne was produced at her command, and Aasman Peri immediately mounted it and arrived swiftly as the wind to lay siege to the Koh-e Noor, where she ordered the *devs* to set up a cordon around it. Then with drawn sword, Aasman Peri went before Bibi Asifa Ba-Safa and said, "O Bibi, have you lost all regard for me that you decided to send my husband off to his world? Are you not aware that my anger knows no bounds and my terror has been impressed on every heart? I am the one who makes my elders taste disgrace at the slightest offense. Do you think that I would hold you in greater regard than them?" Upon hearing her harsh words, Bibi Asifa Ba-Safa said, "Watch your mouth, you wretch! Do not take it into your head that you are someone of great consequence or that you have any power over me! Has all fear of God left your heart that you speak to me in this manner? I wish that your body would catch fire!"

The moment Bibi Asifa Ba-Safa said these words, a flame sprang up from Aasman Peri's body and it soon appeared as if her whole body had become a pyre. As she burned she cried, "Mercy! Mercy!" Abdur Rahman rushed to Quraisha and said to her, "Any moment now Aasman Peri will fully combust and you will be left without even the memory of her face to recall in dreams. Go and plead with Amir and prostrate yourself at his feet so that he may intercede with Bibi Asifa Ba-Safa for Aasman Peri and take pity on you and ask her to forgive your mother." Quraisha rushed and threw herself at Amir's feet, saying, "For God's sake do me this kindness, Father, and have my mother's offense pardoned!" Amir solicited Bibi Asifa's forgiveness for Aasman Peri and bound her by oaths to pardon her. At Amir's request Bibi Asifa sprinkled Aasman Peri with her ablution waters, which immediately put out the fire, and thus Aasman Peri was saved from being consumed by flames. She swooned and fell unconscious to the floor, and the *perizads* carried her away to Gulistan-e Irum on her throne.

Amir stayed there that night as Bibi Asifa's guest. In the morning, she said to Prophet Khizr, "Take Amir to the Darya-e Khunkhar this instant to carry out my wishes." Amir took his leave of Bibi Asifa, placed the boys in the panniers on either side of Ashqar, and departed with the holy Khizr. They had gone some fourteen or fifteen *kos* when they came upon a sea whose other end could not be seen even with the eye of imagination and whose magnificence and ferocity turned one's gall to water. The holy Khizr said to Amir Hamza, "This is the Darya-e Khunkhar, the same swarming and tumultuous sea of which you have heard. All of you must close your eyes now and refrain from looking at its turbulent waters." Amir Hamza and the boys closed their eyes. The holy Khizr took seven steps forward and said, "Now you may open your eyes!" Amir opened his eyes and saw that the Darya-e Khunkhar was behind them and the holy Khizr, their kindly guide, had disappeared.

The narrator of the *dastan* tells that Amir went onward from there for forty days, and on the forty-first day he arrived at the banks of the

Caspian Sea. He saw a great endless sea whose other end could not be seen, and none dared go near its shores for fear of its raging waters. Amir headed along its shores and on the tenth day saw a fort and stopped to rest near its walls. As Amir was looking up at the fort, someone there recognized him and informed the king, Samrat Shah Gao-Sar. He was very pleased to hear of the arrival of the Quake of Qaf and came out of the fort to welcome Amir Hamza. He rubbed his eyes from Amir's feet as a token of extreme humility and his people welcomed Amir with great respect. They took Amir inside the fort and organized a feast in his honor, conducting festivities for many days. While this took place, Amir asked Samrat Gao-Sar, "Can you help me ford the sea?" He answered, "I will help you ford the sea and will carry out your orders provided you marry my daughter, Arvana." Amir declined, but the boys said to Samrat Shah, "Make arrangements for the wedding and leave it to us to persuade Amir and get his consent." Then Samrat Shah made preparations according to his custom and gave leave to his attendants to put together his daughter's dowry. The boys finally prevailed on Amir to marry Samrat Shah's daughter, which made the king extremely pleased.

The night of their nuptials, when they went to bed, Arvana tried to hold Amir Hamza in her arms and kiss him and take her pleasure of him. Amir Hamza slapped her face so hard that her front teeth fell out. She went crying to her father in a state of great despair and unhappiness and gave him a detailed account of Amir's doings. He sent for the two boys and asked them, "Why did the Quake of Qaf behave in this manner toward my daughter and torment her in this wise?" The boys answered, "It is the custom of our land that on the wedding night a man knocks out his wife's teeth so that she may always remember it and learn a lesson from it for life. Also, humans do not bed their wives until they have forded a full half of the sea's length."

Because Samrat was from the race of the *devs* himself, he believed that they spoke the truth. He immediately sent for a ship and made his daughter board it. Then he provisioned it for the journey and said to the boys, "Inform the Amir that he, too, may board the ship." The two boys returned to Amir Hamza with smiling faces and told him all that had happened and said, "Come now and board the ship!" Amir could not help but laugh at the boys' antics and accompanied them aboard. When half the sea had been forded, Arvana wished to take Amir to bed again and expressed her desire for him. Amir Hamza tied her arms and legs and threw her overboard, drowning her and sending that poor creature to the depths of the sea of God's mercy. Afterward, he said to the skipper, "Speed the ship and take us to the other shore, or else I will kill every single one of you! None of you will escape without a cracked skull!" Terrorized by Amir's threats, the skipper obeyed him. The crew hoisted the sails and carried Amir fully across the ocean before long.

Amir disembarked at the shore with the boys. He spread the wolf skins and sat down to eat from the bread-cake given him by the holy Khizr, also offering it to Khvaja Aashob and Khvaja Bahlol. Once their hunger was sated, they headed onward. When Amir again felt hungry the next day, he said, "I am now tired of eating the bread-cake and putting up with these hardships. I feel an overpowering craving for something savory and tasty." As he was saying this, a deer appeared before them. Amir hunted it and he and the boys soon ate venison and camped on a rock and passed the night there. In the morning they got up and traveled on.

OF THE KING OF *AYYARS* AND THE PEERLESS DAGGER THROWER KHVAJA AMAR AYYAR

Honey-tongued narrators have said that when eighteen months had passed that Amar had been living in the castle of Devdad, he asked the master of the castle, King Antar Devdadi, if he knew of any other fort in the vicinity where they could pass a few days in peace. The king answered, "Twenty *kos* from here is the fort of Talva-Bahar, which is situated on a mountaintop. It is bounded on the three sides by a mighty sea and on the fourth side by land. There is only one path that leads to the fort and it is so narrow a passageway that only one person can pass it at a time and nobody can take over control of it. If one person rolls down a rock, a thousand men would be crushed below and forfeit their lives. Even if the Emperor of the Seven Concentric Circles were to attempt to charge the fortress, nothing but utter humiliation would be the result of his toils. All his plans would come to naught and he would suffer a grievous defeat." Amar said, "Taking over that fort is not so difficult a proposition as leaving this castle in peace without the enemy following us." Antar Devdadi said, "There is a tunnel in this castle. You may use that to get out of the castle." Amar replied, "Very well," and that very instant he had Amir's camp mounted on conveyances and took all the goods and provisions for the journey. Taking his army along and comforting everyone, he headed for the fortress of Talva-Bahar by way of the tunnel. The next day, with a few hours remaining to the close of day, he arrived close to the other fortress.

As Amar proceeded he wondered how he might take over the fortress that he had set out to conquer. He said to himself, *We will not be able to storm it, and it is idle to think that it could be taken by force. I made a terrible mistake in setting out with everyone young and old without first securing the fortress where we are headed. If Hurmuz and Faramurz were to come upon us with their armies, it would make life treacherous for us. The doors of Hell will be flung wide open and every one of us would die. Therefore, I must think of some subterfuge and take the castle by some trick.* As Amar racked his brain, a thought suddenly occurred to him.

He hid four hundred armed warriors inside wooden chests and, disguising himself as a merchant and two other *ayyars* as girls, he loaded the wooden chests on camels and arrived at the doors of the fortress. The people inside the fortress called to him from the ramparts, "Who are you, and from where have you come? What is your business, and what merchandise have you brought?" Amar answered, "I am a merchant. Naushervan sent me to Zulmat to buy some goods and I am returning with the purchases I made there. Among the goods I have brought with me are all kinds of strange and marvelous objects that no one has ever seen before. No other merchant possesses such rare merchandise."

When the news reached the master of the fortress, King Jamshed Shah, he sent his vizier Haman to go and find out where the merchant had come from and what goods he had brought.

Haman arrived at Amar's pavilion and said to his attendants, "Make haste and inform your master that the king's vizier has come to call, and that the king has sent for him." Upon receiving this message, Amar said to his attendants, "Tell him that your master is resting—that he does not have the leisure and finds it inconvenient to receive him." The poor vizier stood waiting for nearly an hour. Finally he said, "Very well! I shall leave now and will return at a more opportune time, and will let you know then what the king desires." When Amar heard that the vizier was going back, he sent his attendants to inform the vizier that their master had woken up. After a short while, Amar sent for him and received him with great honor.

Haman saw an old man of venerable aspect sitting on a throne with wax and camphor candles burning in front of him and men of talent sitting around him in a circle. Haman greeted him, and as Amar had discovered the particulars of Haman's ancestry in advance, he answered his greeting and asked, "Who are you, and what is your name?" The vizier answered, "I am Haman, Jamshed Shah's vizier and his adviser in all matters." Amar asked him, "Are you the son of Rahman?" He replied, "Indeed I am his son!" Amar inquired, "Where is he now?" Haman said, "Both he and my mother are now deceased, and it has been some time that they departed from this world." Amar cried out, "Ah! My brother!"

and threw his headgear on the ground. Then feigning to be immensely grieved by the news, Amar cried in a plaintive voice, "A thousand woes that I cannot see my brother's face again!" Then drawing his dagger, Amar said, "Now there is no pleasure left for me, and I, too, shall put an end to my life." Haman stayed Amar's hand and consoled him and said, "What is your name?" Amar answered, "I am Khvaja Shahpal bin Karbal bin Taveel Zulmati. You, my child, were born at the same time that Naushervan sent me to Zulmat to buy the merchandise. Now that I return I hear of my brother's death."

Haman said, "There is no one who will escape death: What was written came to pass. Bear this grief with fortitude and exercise control over your emotions. Come with me and rest inside the fortress." Amar went to the fortress with Haman and told his attendants to bring all his goods and possessions inside as well. On the way, Haman asked Amar, "What are the things that you brought from Zulmat?" Amar answered, "I have brought many artifacts, but in particular I have two slave girls of such beauty that the glow of their faces is the envy of the luminescence of the sun and the moon. The sight of those comely beings would make all the lovers of the world accept the badge of slavery from their hands." Haman said, "Our king has a great weakness for women. If you were to present them to him, he will be very pleased with you and reward you liberally."

After Amar set camp inside the fortress, he dressed up two *ayyars* as women, put them into a palanquin, and sent them to Haman along with some gifts. Haman happily took them along to present them to his king. Jamshed Shah became ecstatic upon seeing the girls and immediately sent for wine and asked the girls to act as his cupbearers. They plied him with a few cups of drugged wine and Jamshed Shah soon fell unconscious and dropped into a stupor from the effects of the soporific. Then Amar opened the chest lids and the stalwart warriors came out of their hiding places. Amar captured Haman alive and began to slaughter the populace in the fortress. He instructed his men to give shelter and reprieve only to those who converted to the True Faith, whereupon the entire populace converted to the True Faith. Amar revived Jamshed Shah and converted him to the True Faith as well and consoled him that no harm would come to him. When Haman saw that the king himself had converted, he, too, embraced the True Faith and obtained lasting blessings in the Future State.

In the morning, Amar stationed his army in the fortress according to his requirements, had a canopy installed for himself at the gate, and sat down at the fortified gate with a majestic mien and great haughtiness and pride.

After Amar had left the fortress of Devdad, Hurmuz and Faramurz received intelligence that Amar had moved to the fortress of Talva-Bahar, converted its keeper to the True Faith, and taken complete charge of the castle. They sent this news to Emperor Naushervan and moved with their camp to the vicinity of Talva-Bahar, camping well out of the fortress's range.

———

Now hear of Naushervan. As he was giving audience in his court one day, the missive arrived from Hurmuz and Faramurz. Upon learning its contents, the emperor held his head in his hands and said, "No stratagem has been found yet that can bring about the arrest or death of this cameleer's son so that all of us might rest easy that the mischief fomented by his existence has come to end." Bakhtak said, "You never follow my advice and do not consider what is opportune for you and what is not. You always follow the advice of Buzurjmehr, and that is why you do not achieve your desired end. Buzurjmehr will ruin you because of his religious prejudice and diminish the grandeur and luster of your empire. A long time ago Hamza died in Qaf, but because Buzurjmehr said he was alive he is still considered alive. I challenge Buzurjmehr to draw lots in competition with me before Your Excellency. We will find out who speaks the truth and who is the consummate geomancer." The emperor said, "We find this a good proposition!" Both Buzurjmehr and Bakhtak drew lots and wrote their readings.

At the moment when these lots were drawn, the Rukh had just dropped Amir from a height of two hundred *kos* into the Caspian Sea. Bakhtak wrote in his reading that an animal had dropped Amir from a height of two hundred *kos* and thus drowned him in the sea. Buzurjmehr wrote that Amir would arrive from Qaf any day and would be reunited with everyone in safety by the grace of God. Bakhtak's determination was read out first and the emperor looked at Buzurjmehr, who replied, "Indeed an animal threw Amir into the Caspian Sea, but holy Khizr and Prophet Ilyas caught him in their arms." The emperor now looked at Bakhtak, who replied, "Hamza is not alive to appear again in these environs or to cast his eyes ever on this world! Can Your Honor possibly believe that someone would survive after falling from a height of two hundred *kos*? No wise person would make such a claim." After a pause, Bakhtak added, "Qaf is, after all, a distant land. If you order a pregnant cow to be presented before you and forthwith brought here, I will draw lots to tell the color of the calf and Buzurjmehr may do the same. Then the belly of the cow may be cut open to determine the veracity of our respective statements. The truth of our talents will then become manifest to Your Highness. I would set a condition, however, that if Buzurjmehr is proven right, I should be given into his power to do with me as he pleases. It should be left to his choice to kill me or keep me as his slave. However, if I am proven right, Buzurjmehr should be given into my power and I be allowed to do as I wish—and treat him with honor or disgrace as I see fit."

The emperor asked Buzurjmehr, "What do you say to his proposition?" Buzurjmehr replied, "I find it a reasonable suggestion. I am ready to be tested, as I am not in any way deficient in my art." A gravid cow was produced that instant and Bakhtak drew the lots and said, "The calf is black and has a white forehead. I am hopeful that this statement will be proven true." Buzurjmehr said in his turn, "Indeed the calf is black in color and its forehead is black, too, I am certain. Its feet, however, are white." The cow's belly was cut open and the calf extracted and put to a close inspection. As chance would have it, the caul covered his forehead and it appeared white in color. Everyone thought it was the coloration of the calf's forehead and reasoned that Bakhtak had won the bet and Buzurjmehr had lost both the bet and his life to Bakhtak.

Bakhtak took Buzurjmehr to his house and attempted to murder him there, but his wife stopped him and said, "Do not ever think of killing Buzurjmehr, for you will rue the day and God's wrath will overtake you!" Bakhtak agreed to desist from Buzurjmehr's murder by fear of unknown consequences, but since his own conscience was blind, out of his evil nature he had Buzurjmehr's eyes lined with indigo and rendered him blind.

It so happened that Naushervan's nephews by his sister, Sa'ad Zarrin-Tarkash and Asad Zarrin-Tarkash, had presented themselves in his service. Upon seeing the calf they asked why it had been brought there and what had occasioned its presence. The emperor narrated the whole incident and told them what had come about. Then Sa'ad Zarrin-Tarkash removed the membrane from the calf's forehead with the point of his dagger. Everyone saw that the calf's forehead was black and did not hold even a single spot of white, and then they realized that Buzurjmehr's statement was true. The emperor immediately sent for Bakhtak, showed him the calf, and said, "You have lost the bet and Buzurjmehr has won it. Bring Buzurjmehr immediately before me!" Bakhtak replied, "I have blinded him in accordance to the conditions I set!" The emperor wrung his hands with grief and said, "You wretch, blind of all conscience! How dare you act in such an evil manner against a noble man like him?" Then he had Bakhtak tied to a column in the court and thrashed so severely that his bones broke into small pieces and he was rendered incapable either to sit or to stand on his feet.

The emperor went and released Buzurjmehr from Bakhtak's house and apologized to him profusely, saying, "Khvaja, you indeed won the bet, but fate had ordained that this tragedy should happen and therefore it deceived us. Now we will punish Bakhtak as you desire and give him his just deserts." Buzurjmehr answered, "It is not necessary to punish him. I have neither intention nor desire to take revenge on him. I was subjected to what was written by fate, and there is no denying the writ of God. I cannot interfere in the eternal decree of the Divine Essence[19] and the execution and declaration of that decree at the appointed time. When the Sahibqiran returns from Qaf he will bring two leaves of a tree whose sap will heal my eyes and sight will then be completely restored to them. Pray give me leave so that I may take myself to Basra until Hamza's arrival and stay there for some time. Remember that I have guarded your honor for seventeen years and I saved you from all harm with my advice. However, I cannot speak for the future. I am certain that from the advice of these treacherous fools you will bring great discredit and dishonor on yourself and the whole world will come to hear of your disgrace at the hands of Amar Ayyar. The day Hamza returns, first the heads of the kings of the East will be sent to your court, then a horse will make a night raid on your camp. The next morning Hamza will hand you a resounding defeat and humiliate you before the whole world." Thus speaking, Buzurjmehr went away to his house and departed for Basra.

Now, Bakhtak had fallen unconscious after being thrashed. In recompense for his deeds the emperor had had him thrown into the Hall of Audience for everyone to see his sorry state. When he regained consciousness and recovered the exercise of his senses, he got up and went home. He was treated for his wounds with a hot compress of turmeric for the next ten or so days. When he recovered, he again presented himself at the court. When he entered, Naushervan said, "Who allowed this shameless creature to enter the court and gave him permission to present himself?" Those present there interceded on Bakhtak's behalf and he was allowed to stay as before.

That reckless fool kept his quiet for a few days. Then he again urged the emperor to advance against Amar and incited him to battle. Slowly and gradually, Naushervan became convinced that Bakhtak spoke the truth. He was persuaded that his commanders would not be able to ward off his adversaries and the campaign would not be won without him leading his armies in person. Thus resolved, Naushervan marched on Talva-Bahar with hundreds of thousands of troops and foot soldiers. When he came to that place, Hurmuz, Faramurz, and Bakhtiarak greeted him and conducted him into their camp. Everyone's spirits were bolstered by his arrival.

When it was evening, Naushervan addressed all of them. He stated with scorn and derision that in all the time that they had been deployed there, they had not captured a common pawn or killed even an ordinary foot soldier. He claimed that they would now see how he would capture and kill the followers of the True Faith and put to the sword their stalwart warriors and champions. All of the men replied with one voice, "There is indeed no comparison between Your Highness's capabilities and our own. We are nothing before your power and might!" The emperor rested there for the duration of the night and ordered his armies to prepare for battle the following day. In the morning, Naushervan rose and, after performing his toilet, mounted his horse and prepared for skirmishing and slaughter. He went forth and began observing the castle with an eye to finding the place where its defenses were the weakest.

Amar was seated on a jewel-encrusted chair under a canopy of Chinese satin. Commanders, princes, and intrepid warriors stood behind him with folded arms, their livery and weapons richly decorated with jewels. At every few paces warriors guarded their posts and heralds and mace bearers stood alert at their stations. Amar picked up his bow and flexed it several times, aiming for Naushervan. Then he said, "O fire worshipper! You have come here walking on your own two feet, but you will be carried off on the shoulders of other men! You will see what an example I make of you and what terrors I unleash on your head. Come forward so that I may give you again a taste of the moment of your birth and teach you a lesson for your defiance." Naushervan trembled with fright at Amar's words and said to Bakhtak, "Did you hear what Amar said?" That shameless cur answered, "He may say what he likes from afar because he is the master of his tongue, but he speaks idly and is unable to do anything. Order the army to charge the castle!" Naushervan said to his army, "Advance, my brave men, and take the castle with your courage and valor!" The troops spurred on their mounts at his command. When they entered within the range of the castle, the garrisoned army unleashed the force of their weaponry on them. In no time, thousands of Naushervan's warriors died. His forces retreated, and no one was able to withstand the fire from the castle. Left alone, Naushervan also returned to his camp behind his men.

Then Bakhtak said, "Who has ever heard of forts being conquered in this manner? Thousands of men were killed at your orders, and still you earned the ignominy of defeat in the battle and did not taste even a sip from the cup of victory." Naushervan said, "You wretch! It was you yourself who suggested that I order the army to charge the fort. You advised me to take the fort in that fashion!" Bakhtak said, "You speak the truth, Your Excellency! I forgot about that. It was all for the best that a few thousand men died. At least our adversary now knows that Your Honor means business and has brought a vast army!" Naushervan said, "Truly, you are a bastard who speaks with a forked tongue and is never constant in his speech!"

Now hear of Amar. After this skirmish, he said to his commanders, "Remain alert in the defense of the fortress and be alert to what transpires in the battle. Let me go and twist Naushervan's ears a bit and show him a little example of my handiwork!" Amar exchanged his regal dress with his livery of *ayyars* and dressed himself up as a juggler. He disguised his gifted students in the craft of *ayyari*, Abu Saeed Langari and Aba Saeed Kharqa-Posh, as beautiful women and went out with them with a small drum hanging from his neck. When they neared Naushervan's pavilion, Amar began beating the drum and the two *ayyars* disguised as women started dancing. Before long, a large crowd gathered around them and everyone thronged the place where the *ayyars* were dancing.

It so happened that Zhopin and Bechin were riding past and, noticing a crowd, approached to investigate why everyone was congregated there and what spectacle occupied them. The *ayyars* made sheep's eyes at them and accentuated their breasts, displaying great coquetry. Both Zhopin and Bechin fell head over heels in love with them. Zhopin selected the *ayyar* dressed in red and Bechin chose for himself the one dressed in green. They consulted together and then went before Naushervan and praised the dancers' beauty and their talent in singing and dancing so highly that Naushervan immediately sent for them, ordering that they be presented before him.

Amar beat the drum so captivatingly and the *ayyars* disguised as girls sang with such passion that young and old alike were thrown into raptures. Naushervan asked those *ayyars* to be his cupbearers. Everyone in his court drank cups of wine from their hands, and after a while their heads began to swoon and their eyes saw many wonders before they lost their senses. Finally, it came to pass that all of them said with one voice, "Friends, let us dive into the river and celebrate the rising waters!" Their tongues became silent all of a sudden and not a word came from their lips—become absolutely quiet, they were all taken unconscious. Amar went out and also drugged the servants and attendants. Then he started looting the pavilion, and stuffed everything into his *zambil* down to the very last carpet on the floor. He lathered up Naushervan's beard and whiskers with his urine and shaved them all off. Amar then stripped Naushervan naked, dyed his hands and feet with indigo, and after blackening his face, made spots all over it with lime. He shaved Bakhtak and Bakhtiarak's beards and whiskers as well, and made seven plaits in their hair. Then he lined Bakhtiarak's hair with minium, fastened his legs around Bakhtak's waist, and after oiling the latter's penis pushed it a little way inside Bakhtiarak's ass. Amar then played the same trick on Zhopin and Bechin, leaving them similarly positioned. He also stripped the princes naked and marked them with spots of seven colors and disgraced every man according to his station. Turning his attention next toward the commanders, Amar dealt with them likewise. In short, nobody there escaped disgrace from his mischievous hands. Then Amar left a note tied from Naushervan's neck that read:

O fire worshipper! Make sure to send me the monthly tribute of your beard and whiskers and do as I order you. Otherwise not a single hair will be left on your body and you will find yourself humiliated forever in this way. Be warned that I did not murder you but let you off after performing this little service, only out of consideration for the fact that you are the father-in-law of the Sahibqiran.

Thereafter Amar and the two *ayyars* retired to their fortress.

In the morning the unconscious men regained awareness and those who had been drugged came out of its effects. Because Bakhtak's eyes were still shut in stupor, when he felt his member hardening, he began pushing it deeper and taking his pleasure, thinking he was inside a woman. Bakhtiarak thought his rear was being torn apart and he began shouting and wailing, "For shame! For shame! You act thus toward me even though you are my father!" Upon hearing his cries, people gathered and saw this marvel of marvels: a father sodomizing his own son and carrying on like a beast. People began laughing when they beheld the condition of others, without realizing that they themselves presented a sight that would embarrass even the devil.

When Naushervan woke up and saw his face in the mirror, he was deeply chagrined and wondered what had transpired in his court. Then he opened the note tied to his neck and discovered that it was Amar who had dealt him such devastating humiliation and who had brought this calamity on his courtiers. Naushervan bathed and changed, and upon ascending the throne, sent for Bakhtak. He had Bakhtak constrained and thrashed until he lost consciousness and his head took on the shape of a shoe from the beating it had received with that weapon. Naushervan did not pay any heed when the princes and the commanders interceded for Bakhtak but said to them, "This villain, who deserves beheading, is the one responsible for my disgrace and humiliation at Amar's hands. This feckless person is the one who invited all the shame and scandal on me with his advice. A hundred million bitter woes that I did not take Buzurjmehr's advice and recognize where my interests lay! Had I done so, I would have saved myself today from being made a spectacle." Finally, Naushervan had Bakhtak thrown into the Hall of Audience and incarcerated.

Naushervan then sent a letter with Sabir Namadposh to a king of that region who was called Haman in which he explained that Amar was a mischief maker and that Haman should not let his guard down. Naushervan ordered Haman to present himself in his service after handing over the command of the castle to some trusted friend and briefing him in all the intricacies of the matter. Naushervan dispatched the letter with a messenger, and sent a second letter containing the same message with Samawa Ayyar to Sher Shah, the king of Qirwan. Sabir Namadposh was the first to return with a reply from Haman Shah, who had written, "Even if angels were to charge the castle they would find it impossible to secure it. I will present myself and my army in the emperor's service before long. Your Excellency must not let the least worry or doubt oppress you."

Samawa Ayyar received a similar reply from Sher Shah Qirwani who also expressed his regard and reverence for Naushervan with a favorable answer. When Samawa was about to leave him, Sher Shah had said to him, "If you promise never to utter these words to anyone nor breathe a hint to a soul, I will make you a proposition. You must promise me also that you will find some way of carrying out my wishes and do as I tell you!"

When Samawa accepted, Sher Shah said, "Some time ago I saw a portrait of Mehr-Nigar, and since that day I have been enamored of her. I have no other wish but to have her before my eyes. If you could find some way of bringing her to me and producing her before me by some clever stratagem, I would give half my kingdom to you and appoint you its sovereign lord." Samawa said, "I would not trust the word of mouth and I do not know evasion. If you give me this promise in writing and make God a witness to this agreement between us, I will not hesitate to shed my life's blood in your service. I will busy myself in implementing this plan and will not care whether I live or die in pursuit of this end." Sher Shah Qirwani immediately wrote out the proposal he had made to Samawa and authenticated the promise as suggested.

From there Samawa headed straight for the fortress and made a few rounds to find some way of getting inside. After he was unable to find any point of entry on land, he rowed around in a boat to find some way into it from the sea, and found guards on vigil at the towers and watchmen doing their rounds. As he was scouting the place, he espied one tower that seemed deserted. When Samawa threw a stone at the tower and no-body came out or made reply, he reasoned that either the guards in the tower were asleep, or else there was nobody on duty there. He gained the wall of the tower with his rope and climbed down into the fort by a stair-well. He lay in a corner for the night and in the morning began searching for the sleeping quarters. Unable to find such a place, he went into the bathhouse and sat down in a corner to bathe himself and think of some way of achieving his end.

After a short while, Mehr-Nigar's cook, Khalifa Bulbul, arrived there. He pretended to have converted to the True Faith but in truth the cook was still sworn to fire worship. Drunk on the wine of infidelity, he regu-larly worshipped in that bathhouse. That day, too, he bathed and began worshipping. Samawa approached him and offered him greetings, at which Khalifa Bulbul's senses took flight and he feared that if Samawa took the news to Amar Ayyar, his head would not remain upon his neck for long and his brains would be extracted from his skull. He began mak-ing sweet talk and fawning on Samawa. The *ayyar* asked him, "What is your name and your designation?" He answered, "I am Mehr-Nigar's cook, but do keep your silence, my dear brother, and do not reveal to anyone the story of my worshipping fire." Samawa said, "Have no wor-ries, for I am not in the service of your master. I am in Naushervan's em-ploy and the chief of all his *ayyars*. I have come to take away Mehr-Nigar

666 • *The Adventures of Amir Hamza*

and have brought many marvelous gifts with me. If you help me in this mission, I would be greatly indebted to you." Khalifa Bulbul answered, "I have never stopped praying to Lat and Manat. I prostrate myself at their feet to pray that Mehr-Nigar might be somehow sent back to Naushervan. Lat and Manat have favored my prayers by sending you on this mission here. Come with me to the kitchen and see what prospects lie before you." Samawa gladly went toward the kitchen and there he drugged all kinds of foods at leisure.

When Mehr-Nigar took her meal, others also ate and everyone therefore tasted the drugged food. It so happened that Amar did not have his food that day nor did he go into the women's quarters. Within an hour, everyone fell unconscious and fainted from the drug's effects. Samawa tied Mehr-Nigar up in a bundle, and with Khalifa Bulbul, headed back whence he had come. When he headed in the direction of the fields away from Naushervan's pavilion, Khalifa Bulbul said to him, "Why are you headed there? How will entering the jungle help your mission?" Samawa said, "Sher Shah Qirwani asked me to bring him Mehr-Nigar. I am taking her there to hand her over to him." Khalifa Bulbul said, "I will not allow this at any cost! You told me that you were returning her to Naushervan and were taking her to him. I am incensed that you carried her away to give her to a stranger!"

The two of them started arguing and fighting. During the scuffle that ensued, Samawa pierced Khalifa Bulbul's heart with his dagger and thus released his soul into the Future State. After that, Samawa headed for Qirwan.

———

Now hear of Amar. He was asleep when Amir Hamza appeared to him in a dream. With an unhappy countenance, he said these words to him: "Why, Amar, is this how you carry out your trust? Tell me, where is Mehr-Nigar and what has happened to her? Do you not know that she has fallen into trouble?"

Amar started from his sleep and rushed to the women's quarters, where he found Mehr-Nigar's bed lying empty. After looking all over that place for her, Amar went to search the towers and the ramparts, and soon he found a rope hanging from one of the towers. Amar grew anxious to see this and, decorating himself immediately with his weapons of *ayyars*, he climbed down that same rope and followed the footprints that led from it on the ground. On the way Amar found Khalifa Bulbul's murdered body, and figured that perhaps the enemy had conspired with him to kidnap Mehr-Nigar. Amir made a detour from the trail and sat down on a deer skin under the shade of a tree disguised as a fakir. He placed a water pitcher close to him and, lighting up a fire, put a hookah before him to convince those who came down that path that he was a fakir.

Before long, Samawa came that way carrying his bundle and decided to rest a little realizing that he was at the post of a fakir. Tired from his burden, he sat down to relax a while and said to Amar, "I am thirsty. Please give me some water to drink and God will recompense you for it." Amar replied, "The water pitcher lies before you. Pour yourself some refreshing cold water and relieve the dryness of your tongue with it." Samawa poured himself some water, but his heart sank when he noticed that the water had been drugged: An *ayyar* himself, he knew all the signs of a drug's presence in water. He changed his tone and said, "O cameleer's son! You think you can trick me? I am not one to fall into your trap. Do you think that an *ayyar* would allow himself to be killed by your tricks? I am well versed in these artifices myself." With that, Samawa bolted away. Amar pursued him with his dagger drawn and overtook him in just one bound. Samawa then put down Mehr-Nigar's bundle and also drew his dagger to fight. He confronted Amar and they began struggling together. Amar took out his rope and, unfolding its loops, shouted, "Friends, do not stand by and watch! Murder and kill this deceptive and deceitful worm!" Samawa believed that Amar's pupils had arrived on the scene. The moment he turned to look for them, Amar put a noose around this neck and pulled, and Samawa fell on his face on the ground. Amar put Mehr-Nigar's bundle on his back and carried a shackled Samawa away as prisoner. In no time, he returned to the castle where he had first imprisoned Samawa. Amar carried Mehr-Nigar to her quarters and worked to restore her to consciousness. When Mehr-Nigar came to, she asked, "Why have I been bound with ropes and why am I being treated in this manner without reason?" Amar untied her and told her the whole story of her capture. Then he went out and had Samawa hanged and riddled with arrows.

When the news of Samawa's deeds and his end reached Naushervan, he was extremely pleased with Amar. Naushervan said "Bravo" and "Well done" and highly commended his actions. When Sher Shah Qirwani heard the story, he said to his whole court, "Indeed Amar is an exceptional *ayyar*, and all others are as dust beneath his feet. This is how he has battled the Emperor of the Seven Climes all these years and remained victorious while his adversaries receive only ruin and disgrace for their labors. I wish to call on him and bestow my friendship and favor upon him!" At this, Piran Maghrebi, who was Sher Shah Qirwani's commander in chief, said to him, "Leave it to me to triumph over Amar! I take up the challenge, and you will see with what excellence I will prevail over him. Pray write to the Emperor of Seven Concentric Circles with the notice that I will lead the charge and it is time to have the war drums sounded so that the ears of the adversary resound with the beating of the kettle-drums. I shall not waste a single moment in securing the castle, and shall lay low the enemy in no time." Sher Shah Qirwani immediately sent a note to this effect to Naushervan with his *ayyar* Qatran Maghrebi.

OF AMIR HAMZA'S ARRIVAL AT THE DOMICILE OF
SAMANDUN HAZAR-DAST DEV, AND OF HIS FREEING
ZEHRA MISRI FROM HIS CLUTCHES

The transcriber writes that after he had eaten the roasted venison, the Sahibqiran started from the shores of the Caspian Sea. On the tenth day he approached a castle and said to Khvaja Aashob, "Go forth and find out whether the castle is inhabited or not and whether its master is a follower of the True Faith or an infidel." Khvaja Aashob went into the castle armed with a dagger, and found the place inhabited. He saw a bustling marketplace with double rows of shops and everyone happily occupied with their business. He asked one shopkeeper, "Whose castle is this and who is its master? Whose writ is established in these dominions, and what else can you tell me about this place?" The shopkeeper did not answer. Khvaja Aashob again asked, "My friend, are you deaf or dumb? Why don't you tell me the name of the person who rules this fort?" The shopkeeper again did not answer. The third time Khvaja Aashob cursed the shopkeeper and asked the same question, but still he received no reply. Then Khvaja Aashob grew furious and dealt him a blow of the dagger, cutting the shopkeeper in two.

The moment Khvaja Aashob killed this man, the other shopkeepers charged him from all sides, swarming from all corners to surround him. Khvaja Aashob called out to Amir, "O Grandeur of God! Come to my rescue speedily and rush to my aid!" Upon hearing his cry of help, Amir Hamza rushed to his assistance and began fighting the crowd and driving it to the doors of the castle. However, Khvaja Bahlol, Khvaja Aashob, and Ashqar were all separated from him. Amir's fighting propelled him into the palace, but those with whom he fought would not set foot there for fear of offending the royal honor. They protested from outside and shouted empty threats at Amir. He sat down on the royal throne in the

Hall of Audience and suddenly heard someone call out, "Alas! Alas! God knows what has passed with Amir and what difficulties have met him!" Amir followed the direction of the voice and found Ashqar, Khvaja Bahlol, and Khvaja Aashob imprisoned by the *devs*. Amir Hamza found another person imprisoned there, too, who was clad in a regal dress and was in a miserable state from the hardships of his incarceration. When Amir asked him who he was, he replied, "I am the sovereign of this dominion, and there was a time when I possessed majesty and grandeur. A *dev* named Khalkhal imprisoned me here and usurped control of the castle." Amir freed him from his incarceration, seated him on his throne, and showed him much favor and honor. When the jinns witnessed Amir's liberality and kindness, they ended their rebellion and presented themselves to Amir's service and kissed his feet.

When Khalkhal Dev returned from a hunting trip and heard that a human being had released the king from prison and acted kindly toward him, he stewed in rage and immediately launched upon Amir with a saw made from a crocodile's back. Amir foiled his attack and dealt him a blow of the Aqrab-e Suleimani that cut him in two. He fell like a moth-eaten poplar. Those who had accompanied the *dev* turned tail and escaped upon witnessing this show of Amir's might. The king ordered seven days of celebrations in Amir's honor, and on the eighth day Amir took his leave and departed.

On the twenty-first day after traveling from there Amir saw another marvel: a building with ramparts shaped like dragons. As its gates were locked, Amir broke them open with his mace and went inside, where he saw a huge deserted field that contained a delicately constructed marble enclosure. He stepped inside this and found a refreshing garden that afforded great pleasure to the beholder and was of a beauty that he had not encountered throughout his long time in Qaf. Amir sat down under a tree upon the wolf skins holding his staff while the boys played and roamed in the garden. While they promenaded free of all cares, they came upon a summerhouse whose luminance made them forget the world itself. Khvaja Aashob and Khvaja Bahlol walked inside without a thought and saw a baby *dev* that was some three hundred yards in height sleeping happily and peacefully in a golden cradle while a woman whose aspect was as beautiful as the sun rocked the cradle with a golden cord. When she spotted the boys, she said, "You shouldn't have stepped here, boys. Get away quickly for he has cried himself to sleep from hunger. He has only just fallen into slumber and if he wakes up, he will eat you alive and will be most pleased to find such juicy morsels as yourselves." The boys said to her, "We are in the company of the Terror of God! We have not the least fear of him or even his elder. Indeed, why should we fear him? That wretch does not frighten us at all!"

The woman, who was none other than Zehra Misri, wondered if the man they had called the Terror of God was the Sahibqiran. She said to the boys, "Take a message to the man who accompanies you that Zehra Misri is imprisoned here, and inform him of this without delay!" Khvaja Aashob and Khvaja Bahlol rushed back to Amir and said to him, "There is a beautiful summerhouse in the garden that is without equal in this world. When we went inside we found a baby *dev* no less than three hundred yards in height asleep in a golden cradle. We also found a woman whose aspect was the envy of the sun and who was a veritable Venus of beauty, rocking the cradle with a string. She told us lovingly and in a most melancholy voice that we should get away without delay for if the baby *dev* woke up he would eat us and would have no mercy on our souls. We told her that the Terror of God was traveling with us, and that we are not afraid to confront either the baby *dev* or its father. Then that woman told us to inform the man who accompanies us that Zehra Misri is imprisoned there."

Amir rushed in panic toward the summerhouse the moment he heard Zehra Misri's name, thinking that if she had ended up in Qaf, God alone knew what had happened to Mehr-Nigar and what calamities had passed with her. When he went inside the summerhouse, he saw that the woman was indeed Zehra Misri. Amir broke into tears at the sight of her and wept copiously. He then asked her what had happened to her, whereupon she told him her whole story and then said, "Now I am a prisoner of this filthy *dev* and I am unable to find words to explain the hardships I have to bear. If the Sahibqiran were to come here, I would soon find release because he has conquered the entire land of Qaf. Otherwise, one day the father of this *dev* will make a meal of me when he is unable to find something else to eat, or I will give up my life from the hardships I face."

Amir said to her, "Do you recognize the Sahibqiran and know him?" She answered, "Of course I would recognize him, for I have been in his service for years. He is the one who has been my guardian and who has conferred honor upon me." Then Amir removed his headgear and showed her his Ibrahimi ringlets. The moment she saw them, Zehra Misri rushed forward and fell at Amir's feet, crying and offering her life in sacrifice to Amir.

The baby *dev* awoke from his sleep from the noise of her crying and saw humans standing all about him. He rushed toward Amir from the pain of his hunger so that he might eat him and fill up his belly. Amir caught him and tore him apart like an old cloth and then smashed his skull against the ground.

Then Amir sat on the promenade and said to Zehra Misri, "Did you not recognize me at first?" She answered, "I had last seen you in your youth. Now, by the grace of God, you have become a mature man. More-over, you are wearing a beggarly costume. How could I, your slave girl, have recognized you and identified you as the Sahibqiran?"

As Amir was conversing with Zehra Misri, Samandun Hazar-Dast Dev arrived there as fast as a whirlwind and descended on Amir like a calamity. He was already furious to see the enclosure's broken door. When he found his son lying dead, his rage knew no bounds and the world darkened before his eyes. He addressed Amir thus: "O human being! Dark-haired, white-toothed, and decrepit thing! Which whirlwind has blown you this way, and what accident had brought you here?" Amir replied, "I was not brought here by some whirlwind but by my own voli-tion to dispatch you to Hell and bring you the tidings of death. As to my decrepitude, know that with these very limbs I have killed Ifrit, Ahriman, and others of their ilk, and before long you, too, will join their company. I have not the least doubt that with just one blow from my hand you will become Hell fodder."

Then Samandun Hazar-Dast picked up a thousand stones in his thousand hands and flung them all at Amir at once. Amir jumped behind the *dev*'s back with a single leap and, crying "God is great!" brought down the Aqrab-e Suleimani on his shoulders. It severed his five hundred shoulders and they fell down to the ground, but Samandun escaped with his life. After a moment, however, he returned whole of body and at-tacked the Amir as before, unleashing his might against him. As before, Amir cut off his five hundred arms from the shoulders. The *dev* again ran away with his arms and soon returned whole of body and renewed his at-tack as before. Amir's endurance was severely tested and he was exasper-ated that the *dev* remained impervious to his blows.

Then Amir began to pray, and his prayers were not yet finished when the holy Khizr appeared and greeted him. Amir returned his greeting and said, "O Holy Khizr! I have greatly suffered because of this *dev*. No sooner do I cut off his arms than he returns whole of body and attacks me with all his might." Khizr answered, "O Sahibqiran, there exists a spring whose waters God has invested with the property to alleviate pain, cure injuries, and heal wounds. Let me take you to that spring and then I will make it disappear so that the *dev* can be killed once and for all and he does not return to attack you again after being wounded." Amir accompanied Prophet Khizr to that spring and beheld that it was the very Spring of Life and its waters were so refulgent that in comparison to them even the luster of pearls appeared dark. Holy Khizr stomped his foot on the ground and thus caused the spring to disappear, and then he told Amir all it secrets. Then Khizr broke two leaves from a tree that stood by the spring and whose every leaf was brighter and more luminous than the shining portals of Heaven. He gave the leaves to Amir and said, "Carry these leaves with you and put their sap into Buzurjmehr's eyes so that his sight is restored and his eyes regain their light, for Bakhtak has blinded him by lining them with indigo."

Amir Hamza put those leaves inside his headpiece and said, "Please do me the kindness of returning me again to that garden." The holy Khizr took him there and then disappeared after informing Hamza of all the stages of the adventure that faced him. The next time Samandun Hazar-Dast returned wounded to the spring and could not find it, he let out a terrible cry of *Aaargh!* and started smashing his head against the ground and thus he gave up his life and fell dead.[20]

Amir meanwhile discovered some chambers in that garden, and upon opening them, found them full of all kinds of wondrous jewels that pleased him no end. The boys said, "We must take some of these jewels from here. We really must, for we will never again see such priceless stones." Amir smiled and said, "If you took them to the world and showed them off, my brother Amar would snatch them from you and you would never again see a single one of them."

Amir Hamza spent two days in that garden. On the third day he put the boys into the panniers and Zehra Misri on the saddle and then led the horse by his reins like a groom and headed onward. On the eleventh day he reached the deep sea and wondered how he could cross its waters since he had neither a boat nor a vessel. This presented an insurmountable obstacle and seemed an impossible task. Amir was occupied with these concerns when the holy Khizr appeared and miraculously took them all across the sea. The next day Amir reached the place where he had killed Rahdar Dev and dispatched that noxious beast to the Erebus of Hell. He found the door of the enclosure open and realized then that it must be Friday, as the gates opened only on that day. Amir recited a benediction for Prophet Nuh's descendant Saalim at his grave and the soul of the deceased was gratified by Amir's reciting Quranic verses on his grave.

Amir started off from there and said, "By the grace of God Almighty! The frontiers of Qaf have ended today and I have been delivered from my troubles, for God has shown me the face of comfort and peace again."

Amir and his companions proceeded on their way and passed by the mountain range, plucking and sharing the fruit from the trees around it. As he stood under a mountain, looking for some place to spend the night, Amir heard a voice call out to him, "Peace be with you!" Amir heard these words without seeing who uttered them, and looking around he could not find anyone and saw no trace of the one who addressed him. Suddenly, his eyes caught sight of a tree that stood before him. He saw that the fruits of that tree were shaped liked human heads and that it was from that tree that the greeting had come, for God's will had arranged it thus. Amir marveled to the limits of marveling at the work of God and returned the greeting, answering in the manner of the followers of the True Faith. Then the voice called out, "O Sahibqiran, my name is Waq and once upon a time Sikander himself rested in my shade for the night. Just as I hosted him once, I will host you this day and it will be a pleasure for me to arrange a feast for you. Pray stay here for the length of the night and enjoy the sights and the sounds of this place."

After this conversation, a fruit fell into Amir's lap, which Amir carved and shared with Zehra Misri and the boys. He found the fruit tastier than any other fruit he had eaten in the past and it fully sated him. Amir then lay down under the tree. The whole night the tree and Amir conversed together and the tree regaled Amir with his sweet speech. Waq said to him, "O Sahibqiran, where you now lie Sikander once lay and took comfort from the same refreshing ambience. He asked me when he would die and depart from this world. I told him that when the ground turned ferrous and the skies turned golden, he would leave the world and his end would come about in an unexpected manner.

After a journey of two or three days, he reached the Bayaban-e Haft Gardish-e Suleimani, which lies some distance from here and where there is no sign of any tree. When the violence of the blistering sun overwhelmed him and the suffocating heat of the place became unbearable, Sikander's companions lay down their armor for him to lie on and shaded him with their shields to alleviate his suffering. At that moment Sikander's soul was extracted from his body. Amir asked the tree, "O tree, tell me when I will die." The tree answered, "When Ashqar's hooves lose all their shoes, you should recognize that it is time for you to leave the world. Know then that your cup of life has become full up and that twilight is nigh. But a long time lies between now and that day!" In that manner Waq the tree and Amir Hamza conversed together the whole night.

When it was morning, Amir took his leave of the tree and started out again. In the afternoon the desert began to heat up and a searing wind picked up that began to melt even the fat beneath their skin. Their hearts beat restlessly and quivered like mercury, and the piercing rays of the blazing sun made them wretched. If the Sahibqiran had not possessed Khizr's gift of the water flask, the souls of his companions would have flown from their bodies and none of them would have found a way to carry on his existence. Every now and then Hamza drank some water from the flask and gave some to his companions. They camped and took rest that evening in the sands of that desert, and then started again the next morning. In short, they suffered seven more days of the desert journey and never experienced any comforting shade.

On the eighth day they arrived at a city whose ruler was a woman named Shirin, a kindly and hospitable woman. She greeted the Sahibqiran and conducted him into the city and held a royal feast in his honor. When the Sahibqiran noticed that there were no men to be seen in the city, he asked her, "What is the matter? Why are there no men here, even in name?" Shirin answered, "A male child is never born to the women of this city." Amir said, "How do the women become impregnated?" She answered, "When a girl reaches puberty, she goes to embrace a tree outside the city, which bears neither flower nor fruit. During the embrace she lets out a scream and is taken unconscious. She regains her consciousness after some time and at that moment the seed begins to grow in her womb and in due time she bears a girl child."

Upon hearing this Amir marveled at God's enterprise. He found every woman there a paragon of beauty such as he had never before seen. The boys said to Amir, "The women of this city are extremely pretty. We should take some of them along with us." Shirin said, "The women of this city cannot leave its precincts, for God has appointed a guardian over them. Even if she does leave the guardian brings her back, and no matter where she goes the guardian always retrieves and brings her back here." The boys replied, "This is all idle talk. Send them with us and no one will be able to snatch them from us." Shirin argued and tried to convince them, but the boys did not listen to her and did not give in despite her best efforts to dissuade them.

So, with Shirin's permission they took fifty women with them. In the evening, Amir stopped to rest and spend the night. When he woke up in the morning he found that half of the women had disappeared. The boys then regretted not heeding Shirin's advice and having therefore unnecessarily put themselves in her debt. That night the boys fastened a rope around the waists of the remaining women, and tied the other end to themselves, thinking that they would be unable to disappear and would not be able to leave them as the others had earlier. Then they lay down to rest and were soon lost to sleep, certain that the women could not run away.

It so happened that the Simurgh's wife was the guardian God had appointed on those women. She plucked them all up and rose several yards above the ground. Now, the boys, too, were dangling from the rope with them, and they began shouting and screaming in fear. When Amir arose from his sleep, he saw someone taking away the women. It seemed almost impossible to grab hold of them and the boys seemed in great difficulty as they were hanging by the same rope. Thinking that this was the work of some *dev*, Amir shot an arrow, which pierced the shoulder of the Simurgh's wife. She swooped down with the women and said, "O Sahibqiran! What crime did I commit against you and what injury did I inflict on you that you shot me with an arrow? Is this how you return the kindness that my husband did you? I have been appointed by God to ensure that these women do not leave their city and am obliged to carry out my trust."

The Sahibqiran felt most embarrassed upon finding that it was the Simurgh's wife he had shot. He offered her an apology and said, "I mistook you for someone else and shot you in error. For the sake of God, forgive my offense and do not mention this incident to your husband, for I am greatly indebted to him and his kindness I will never be able to repay." Then Amir prayed fervently and devotedly to God to make her shoulder well. Amir's prayer was received with favor in the Court of Heaven and his entreaties were heard. The wound of the Simurgh's wife healed and no pain lingered. Then she took her leave of Amir and departed with the women.

After Naushervan had laid siege around the fortress of Talva-Bahar, arrayed his ferocious warriors as requested in Sher Shah Qirwani's message, and sounded the battle drums in the name of Piran Maghrebi, a dust cloud rose on the horizon all of a sudden. When the skirts of dust were cut asunder by the wind, two hundred standards appeared in the sky. Amar realized that this was an army of two hundred thousand troops. When the force approached the fortress, Amar found out that Sher Shah Qirwani had arrived with his commander, Piran Maghrebi, and all the troops under his command. Naushervan sent Bechin and Zhopin to receive Piran Maghrebi, who presented himself before Naushervan, kissed the leg of the emperor's throne, and gave a detailed account of himself. The emperor showed him many favors that buoyed his spirits. Then the emperor gave Piran Maghrebi leave to charge the castle and gave him injunctions to make his very best effort to capture it.

As Piran Maghrebi headed for the fortress with his two hundred thousand troops, Amar began praying, fearing because of the smaller size of his army. At that moment a dust cloud rose from the direction of the jungle and Naqabdar Naranji-Posh soon arrived with his forty thousand riders. The sight of the Naqabdar's valiant army revived Amar's spirits and gladdened his heart.

Upon sighting the Naqabdar, Bakhtiarak said to Naushervan, "This is the same Naqabdar who always comes to assist of the followers of the True Faith. It is with his aid that the armies of the True Faith remain victorious." That very moment Naqabdar Naranji-Posh approached Piran Maghrebi and gave him a powerful shove with his shield. Piran retreated several steps, as if all his power and strength had been sapped. He was enraged and dealt the Naqabdar a blow of his sword, but the Naqabdar secured his hold on his mount and snatched the sword from Piran's hands. Then he plucked Piran off his saddle and threw him into the air. As Piran fell, the Naqabdar cut him in two like a cucumber. Piran's army fell on the Naqabdar, and Naushervan's armies also came to their assistance, ready to battle and slaughter. The Naqabdar kept his advantage, however, and cut down the foe and then disappeared into the forest with his forty thousand troops.

Amar had the drums of victory sounded from the ramparts of his fortress and offered thanks to the Creator. The emperor retired with eyes brimming with tears and his heart burning with affliction. He conferred a robe of condolence on Sher Shah Qirwani and comforted and consoled him.

That same day, the king of the fortress of Tanj-e Maghreb, Misqal Shah, presented himself to Naushervan's service and offered him many reassurances that the next day he would win the fortress for the emperor and avenge Piran's death. He invited Naushervan to be his guest in his camp so that they might spend their time in harmony and comfort. He set up his camp next to Naushervan's and busied himself preparing a feast and made sure that every comfort was provided to the emperor and nothing was left to chance.

———

Now hear of Amar. When he heard that Misqal Shah had arranged a feast for Naushervan, he sent for the commanders of his army and their men and said to them, "If you were to apply yourself a little, you could treat yourself to all manner of delicacies. We will relish the most savory dishes imaginable, for Misqal Shah has given a feast in Naushervan's honor and made great efforts and sacrifices to arrange the revels. Perform this much labor for me: Make a night raid on the enemy camp making the war cries of Amir Hamza, Landhoor, and Bahram." All of them accepted his proposition. Then Amar said to his *ayyars,* "Make five hundred *devs* of paper, each of them four and five hundred yards high. They should be constructed so that they have wheels under them. When I sound the Sufaid Mohra and you hear its voice, roll them out without delay." The *ayyars* busied themselves the whole day in preparing *devs* made of paper.

When it was evening, Naushervan headed for Misqal Shah's camp. The whole expanse was bathed in moonlight, torches were burning, and fireworks were being set off. The emperor sat to watch a dance performance. After some hours had passed, Amar instructed Muqbil in all the details, gave him Siyah Qitas for his mount, and ordered him to bellow out Amir's war cry. He told Aadi to attack the foe by proclaiming Landhoor' name, and instructed Sultan Bakht Maghrebi to utter the war cry of Bahram. Amar then brought his force out of the castle and fell upon the camps of Misqal Shah and Naushervan.

Muqbil shouted, "I am the Sultan, Lord of the Auspicious Planetary Conjunction, Amir Hamza the Illustrious!" Aadi cried out, "I am the Rustam of the times, King Landhoor bin Saadan!" And Sultan Bakht Maghrebi exclaimed, "I am Bahram Gurd, the emperor of China!" The three armies began to fight together, and the lustrous sword of battle darted here one instant and flashed there the next. When Amar saw that a pitched battle was being waged, he feared that he might lose due to the small number of his men and receive defeat at the enemy's hands. He immediately sounded the Sufaid Mohra. Then he called out loudly enough for the enemy camp to hear, "Rush here, O fierce *devs* of Qaf, and make a meal of the infidels!" Upon those words and the blast of the Sufaid Mohra, the *ayyars* rolled out the paper *devs* and held them up with balls of fire darting out of their mouths. The sight of this convinced the entire army of the infidels that Hamza had brought an army of *devs* from Qaf and their own defeat was now certain. They turned tail from fear and retreated.

Bakhtak repeatedly called to them, "My friends, this is all a deception wrought by Amar—it is all his trickery and cozenage!" but they did not listen and kept running. And they did not just play at running; they stopped only after they had put a distance of twelve *kos* between them. When the kings saw their armies in full retreat, they reasoned that staying there was tantamount to surrendering and allowing the birds of prey to catch them in their talons like doves. They therefore retreated with their respective armies and ran away from there holding one another's hands.

Amar looted the goods and property of Misqal Shah and Naushervan's retreating armies to the extent that he was able. He stuffed it all in his *zambil* and took possession as if he were indeed the rightful owner. Then Amar ordered a feast for his army and all of them ate their fill and were greatly satisfied. Amar said to Muqbil, "Go into the fort and bring the women's conveyances and all the luggage back by camel. Leave nothing there so that we may depart for the fortress of Tanj-e Maghreb." No sooner were the orders given than Muqbil had brought all the conveyances and the luggage out of the castle and not even a single twig was left behind. Amar led his entire camp toward their new destination. Upon arriving at the castle, he showed a vizier there a letter forged in Misqal Shah's name and thus gained entry and finally secured what he desired. Immediately, he began putting the infidels to the sword and those villains partook of the elixir of death. Most of them converted to the True Faith and for that Amar offered them reprieve and the sword no longer threatened their lives. Then Amar set up the castle as he saw fit, and sat down at the gates on a gold-encrusted chair under a canopy of golden satin surrounded by his regalia.

———

Now hear of Naushervan. When it was morning, he dispatched his *ayyars* to gather intelligence about the *devs* of Qaf so that they could gather the news and witness what passed there. Before leaving, Amar had left the paper *devs* standing at the foot of the mountain. Upon witnessing them from a distance, the *ayyars* hastened back to the emperor with the news that the army of the *devs* of Qaf was standing under the mountain in battle array, each holding as steadfast as a rock. Bakhtak commented, "Verily those who utter such baseless words eat ordure! If they were real *devs,* there would be nothing stopping them from attacking us and none of us could ward them off! This is all Amar's doing and is only a trick that he is playing on us, and with this deceit he has inflicted defeat on us. Regard how that *ayyar* has made fools of us!"

In the meanwhile, Misqal Shah's *ayyars* arrived there and brought detailed intelligence that the *devs* were made of paper and that Amar had safely entered the fortress of Tanj-e Maghreb with all his companions. Naushervan lamented this news and derided all his men for their spinelessness. As they returned to their encampment, they witnessed that Amar had handed them yet another defeat by looting the entire royal treasury and provisions and carrying away all the soldiers' effects and property. Misqal Shah's camp was plundered to the extent that the very last broom twig had been taken away. The servants and the keepers of the pavilions tearfully complained that there was no place to lie down as the beds were also gone. They lamented the fate that had been apportioned them and worried that they might not find enough to eat to keep body and soul together—let alone set up a feast. The emperor departed with his army, and arriving at the fortress of Tanj-e Maghreb, surrounded it on all sides and made plans to battle Amar once again.

Now, Amar had gathered all his commanders and said to them, "My friends, the eighteenth year is coming to a close and Amir Hamza has yet to return from Qaf. Now everyone will get half the rations that would be enough to keep body and soul together. Whoever agrees to these conditions can stay and the others may freely leave. Those who are true friends will bear this hardship with the rest of us." Everyone consented to Amar's proposal except for Aadi, who said, "I shall not be able to carry on like this. Ever since Amir Hamza has left not a single day has passed when I have slept on a full belly. Now if these meager rations are halved, there is no hope that I will survive, and I shall certainly end my existence before my time." Amar told him, "You are free to decide whether you wish to stay here or leave." Upon that Aadi headed out of the castle.

Amar called after him, "O Aadi Madi-Karib! You are leaving now, but remember that you will be buried alive as sure as my name is Amar or else I shall never show you my face again!" Aadi retorted, "And as sure as my name is Aadi, you will fall into the embrace of a *dev*, or I, too, shall hide my face from you always!" With this, Aadi went straight to Naushervan and said, "If Your Excellency would take me into your service, I will attend on you and wait upon you with all my heart and soul!" Naushervan asked, "What happened that caused a rift between you and Amar?" Aadi gave him a detailed account, whereupon the emperor sent for the keeper of the kitchen and gave him orders to take Aadi with him and feed him until he was fully satisfied and had eaten to his heart's content. Then Naushervan said to Aadi Madi-Karib, "I have appointed you to do guard duty. You must not let anyone inside without my orders. Keep everyone from entering the garrison." Aadi immediately went and sat on guard duty outside the pavilion, and put his bed and bedding there at the sentry post.

That night a beautiful woman arrived to do some service for the emperor. Her pretty face and coquettish ways so inflamed Aadi's desire that letchery awoke violently within him and he immediately grabbed her and ravished her. But the delicate body of that damsel was no match for Aadi's size: Unable to bear the pain and survive the violence of his prodigious member, she died that instant. Aadi thought that in the morning he would be taken to task for his act and killed in retribution. He mounted the emperor's steed that stood tied to its post and headed for the forest. He rode all night long and was fairly famished by daybreak. Since the forest offered nothing to satisfy his hunger, he broke some tree branches to start a great fire, slaughtered and roasted the horse, and ate of its flesh to his heart's content. From there Aadi went on foot to a gathering place of fakirs. The head of the fakirs was distributing the daily rations among the assembly. Aadi sat down with the mendicants and the man gave him a portion as well. Aadi ate it and then said to the leader, "O master, this fakir cannot survive on such a meager ration." The leader gave him another ration and Aadi ate that as well and then said, "The fire of the Hell blazing in my belly is not at all quenched, O master!" The head of the fakirs gave him several portions more, which Aadi bolted down in no time and then said again, "I find it surprising that you do not give me enough just once to completely extinguish this Hell!"

There were some five hundred fakirs in that group and all of them said to one another, "Come, friends, let us all give him our shares and see how much he can eat and how all of it finds place in his belly." Aadi Madi-Karib ate every last portion and tucked it all away without the least trouble. The fakirs asked him, "Is your belly full now?" He answered, "This blazing Hell will not be put out by these tidbits, but now at least I feel I am ready to have a sip of water to wash it down." Then all the fakirs said to their leader, "It appears that he is not a human being but some *dev* or *ghol*. Pray send him away quickly after giving him his beggar's kerchief and staff, and let us ward off this *dev* from our heads." The head of the mendicants gave Aadi a kerchief and a staff and said to him, "The land of God is without limit or end. Go forth to beg and provide for yourself!"

That night Aadi slept at the gathering place of the fakirs and the next morning headed for a nearby city. Finding it a bustling and prosperous city, he started begging. A kindly baker took pity on him, and gave him two naans with some kebabs. Aadi ate them and asked for more. The baker said, "You still ask for more? It does not behoove someone of your size and girth to become a mendicant. Why don't you earn your bread by the sweat of your brow? Why do you disgrace yourself by begging?" Aadi replied, "I do not run away from honest work, provided someone undertakes to feed me and fill up my belly." The baker said, "Very well! Begin chopping wood for me and I will feed you to your heart's content." Aadi chopped up all the baker's logs in no time and cut up the wood into pieces. The baker offered him five leavened breads and some gravy. Aadi made a snack of this and said, "My belly is not filled. You told me that you would fill up my belly and fully satisfy my hunger." The baker gave Aadi another four or five breads and Aadi ate those as well, then said, "Why do you tease me in this manner? You are making pleasantries at my expense without really filling up my belly. Why don't you give me all of it at once? Why do you make me grovel in this manner and then dole out small trickles? It neither satisfies my hunger nor fills up my belly and feels a hardship to me besides. Come, stand aside from the place where you keep your bread. I will only eat as much as will satisfy my hunger. It is not as if I will give all your food to someone else. I am not such a glutton either that I would gobble up all your food!"

When the baker refused, Aadi caught him by his neck and threw him out of the shop. Then he sat down to eat. After he had eaten all the bread and gravy and was still feeling hungry, he went into another shop that was nearby and, similarly pushing out its owner, ate up all the bread and the gravy that was there as well. Then Aadi headed for a third shop. A great hue and cry rose in the marketplace and a big crowd gathered to watch this spectacle. The nobility and the laity assembled, and the magistrate arrived hastily to investigate the cause of the commotion. Witnessing Aadi's might and power, he did not dare challenge him. Without taking the risk of confronting Aadi, he returned and narrated the whole episode to his king, Me'aad Shah Maghrebi, and gave him a detailed account of the incident. Me'aad Shah Maghrebi rode out without delay to witness the scene with his courtiers and marveled at Aadi's shape and form and was taken by wonder for he had never set eyes on a creature like Aadi.

The aggrieved people of that city rushed before the king with their complaints and told him that Aadi had looted many shops, killed several men, and let loose a reign of terror. The king ordered, "Let no one accost him!" Then he sent for Aadi and asked him to explain himself. Aadi truthfully gave a full account of himself and narrated to the king all that had passed with him. The king said, "Have you ever heard of a great champion who inflicted hardships and sufferings on poor people?" Aadi said, "In my defense I can only say that I did all this to keep myself alive." The king said, "If you agree to fight the followers of the True Faith, I will induct you into my service, offer you a distinguished position, and marry you to my daughter. I will grant you all these favors; however, it is our custom that if the husband dies the wife is buried alive with him. Similarly, if the wife dies before the husband, he is buried alive with her and is not allowed to live." Aadi agreed to these conditions and the king married him to his daughter the same day.

That night when Aadi tried to take his pleasure of the princess, she was unable to bear Aadi's weight and the force of his penis penetrating her. After just one thrust, she was killed. She was put in a winding-sheet in the morning and taken for burial. The people caught Aadi as well and took him along to bury him in the same grave. When they lowered the woman's body into her grave they asked Aadi to climb down with it, but he refused to comply. The people around the grave tried to force him into it, but none of them were able to prevail against his might or could make him budge from his place. Aadi kept standing at graveside by sheer force of strength.

It so happened that the Sahibqiran had entered that city the same day. He was sitting on the wolf skins under a tree where he had discovered a nice shade. Noticing a crowd he said to Khvaja Aashob and Khvaja Bahlol, "Go and find out the reason why that crowd has gathered and the people have assembled there. See what it is that attracts them there." The boys went and saw that people were unsuccessfully trying to force a man into a grave but none was powerful enough to prevail over him. They returned to Amir Hamza and narrated what they had seen. Hamza, too, went to witness the scene, and by looking closely, discovered that it was Aadi whom the people were trying to push into the grave. Hamza wondered what crime Aadi had committed for which he was thus being penalized and why these people were bent on putting an end to his life.

Hamza asked him, "O champion, who are you? Tell me what are your circumstances, and what is your relationship to these people?" Aadi answered, "My name is Aadi Madi-Karib and I used to be in the service of Hamza the Arab who departed for Qaf, leaving me and his other companions and appointing Amar Ayyar as his deputy. Until now Amar gave me barely enough food to keep body and soul together and I survived on it and waited for Hamza's return. Lately, Amar told us that a full eighteen years are coming to pass since Hamza left and he cannot struggle further and find us more rations. He told us that he would cut down our share to half, for he will be unable to feed us otherwise and find more food. I had already seen myself brought to my grave on a diet that was quite frugal and that had extinguished all feeling of joy from my heart. Now that that, too, was being cut in half, I despaired of my life. I saw no hope of surviving this cruel blow and realized that I would be starved to death. I found it more agreeable to beg for food and thus I arrived in these parts. Fate dealt me yet another cruel hand when the king married me to his daughter. It was God's will that she should die and depart from this world. Now they desire to bury me along with her and pull the tree of my life out by its roots."

Hamza said, "If you were to see Hamza now, would you recognize him?" Aadi answered, "Indeed why not? It is true that he has been gone eighteen years and his appearance will have changed, but I will yet recognize him by his green mole, his Hashimi vein,[21] and his Ibrahimi ringlet." Hamza shifted his headgear slightly on the pretext of scratching his head and revealed the mark to Aadi. The moment Aadi caught sight of it, he broke his chains and fell at Amir Hamza's feet. Amir embraced him and said, "Nobody can dare touch you now or play false with you." Amir stood by Aadi's side and roared, "Those who know understand and those who do not know learn that I am the Lord of the Auspicious Planetary Conjunction, Amir Hamza, the slayer of the sanguinary *devs* of Qaf, the Destroyer of *Tilisms,* and the betrothed of Mehr-Nigar." Hearing this war cry, Me'aad Shah came out of his pavilion and stepped before Amir and said, "O Hamza, I had heard that you died at the hands of the *devs* of Qaf, but now that you have returned, you will not escape alive from your encounter with me and will receive your just deserts." Then he exhorted his men, "Kill this Arab without further ado!" Drawing a sword himself, he dealt Amir a blow, but Amir grabbed the hilt of his sword and wrenched it from his hands. Lifting him over his head, Amir slammed him down so mightily on the ground that his head was hammered into his torso and became level with his shoulders. After killing Me'aad Shah, Amir turned upon his army. He began to slaughter them all and did not allow them a chance to escape.

Aadi picked up the same sword Amir Hamza had snatched from Me'aad Shah's hands and joined in the slaughter of the infidels. When a great many infidels had been dispatched to Hell, Me'aad Shah's vizier, Aqil Khan, who was as wise as his name,[22] presented himself to Amir Hamza and asked for mercy and willingly converted to the True Faith. Then he conducted Amir into his palace, where he provided Zehra Misri with her own quarters and proved himself an excellent host. Aqil Khan feted Amir at his house for seven days and Amir received every comfort from his hands. Before leaving, Amir enthroned him in place of Me'aad Shah. Aqil Khan expressed a great desire to accompany Amir Hamza, but Amir would not allow him to do so and said to him, "You must stay behind and carry out my orders here before joining me." As before, Amir put Zehra Misri and the boys on Ashqar and set out with Aadi on foot. Aqil Khan converted the whole city to the True Faith and took oaths from them to remain steadfast in their new faith. Then he sent a missive to Naushervan containing an account of Amir Hamza's arrival and accompanied it with the severed head of Me'aad Shah Maghrebi.

The narrator has said that on the third day of his journey Amir arrived in a desolate place. Around midday he took refuge from the burning sun under the shade of a tree, sitting there on the wolf skins by the riverside. Aadi said to him, "I am melting from the heat and suffering terribly. If you would allow it, I will go and dive into the river to soothe and relieve my body." Amir replied, "Nothing would be better. Go ahead and have a good bath in the river." Aadi put his clothes by the riverside and began swimming and washing himself in the river. Suddenly he saw a chest floating toward him in the water. Aadi took the trunk to the shore and opened it, whereupon a *dev* came out of the chest. He caught Aadi in his hold and completely overwhelmed him. Aadi called out to Hamza for help, and the Sahibqiran overpowered the *dev* and put him back into the chest and made a present of the chest to Aadi, who said to himself, *What Amar said came to pass: I was almost buried alive and saw no hope of my release. But God will prove my words true, too, when I take this chest and give it to Amar. When the dev catches him in his embrace to throttle the life out of him, he will remember what I said.* Aadi carefully put away the chest.

When the heat subsided, they set out again. After they had traveled for a few days, Amir Hamza learned from Aadi that Amar was camped at the fortress of Tanj-e Maghreb along with Princess Mehr-Nigar and the armies of the True Faith, and that he and all his associates were stationed there. Amir said to Aadi, "Follow me at a slow pace accompanying Zehra Misri and Khvaja Aashob and Khvaja Bahlol, while I go ahead and get the bearings of the castle and learn what there is to learn about the place." Amir mounted Ashqar Devzad and arrived in the vicinity of the castle within a short time.

There was a hillock close to the castle, which he climbed to have a better view of the fortress. He regarded that even though it was small, the battlements and the ramparts of the fortress were well manned. Not even a bird could fly over the fortress without being trapped, and even the Simurgh risked capture in such an undertaking. There was a mountain on one side of the fortress and a river flowed on the other side, while a plain stretched on the third side of the fortress where the double flower blossomed for miles on end in numbers beyond estimation. There were also very many fruit trees whose very sight revived the spirits, not to mention their fruit. On the fourth side was the passage leading out of the fortress. There Naushervan was camped with his mighty armies well out of the firing range of the fortress and the pavilions of every champion of his court could be seen standing there. Amir Hamza also saw Amar sitting outside the fortified gates of the fortress under a canopy of Chinese yellow satin. He sat with such majesty and grandeur on the bejeweled throne that the Emperor of the Seven Climes would seem a low dog before him, and the magnificence he exuded was such that made everyone awestruck and silent with reverence. To Amar's right the kings and princes stood with folded arms, and to his left Muqbil Vafadar was at the ready with his twelve thousand archers.

Amir Hamza laughed at this vision of Amar's glory and sat down under the wall of the fortress spreading his wolves' skins and settling down like a fakir with his back against the castle walls. He addressed Ashqar in the language of the jinns, saying, "Go to the fields that are behind the fortress to graze as you please, but do not let anyone catch you and do not walk into a trap." Ashqar then headed for the plains and did as Amir had instructed him.

———

Now hear of the King of *Ayyars*. That day he had gone to meet Mehr-Nigar and, finding her in a miserable state from the grief of separation with Amir, both he and the princess shed many tears of sorrow. Amar suffered greatly to see her in this state and said to her, "O Princess, pray turn your thoughts toward the Maker, pin your hopes in His beneficence, and comfort your heart and wait and see what He unfolds. He is the Gatherer of the Separated. He alone converts our hopes into happy tidings and events. Undoubtedly He will reunite you with Amir Hamza and the Creator of Causes will bring you together with the one you long to meet."

Mehr-Nigar answered, "Khvaja, there is an end to my store of patience. How long will I carry this burden and console myself with hope? Today it has been full eighteen years since Amir departed." Amar said, "The evening of the day is yet far away. It is not at all beyond the power of the Almighty Lord to send Amir in safety and peace to you before the day is out. Take yourself to the roof of the fortress and enjoy the bloom of the double flowers that grow in profusion, and soothe your eyes with the view of the green velvet carpet of the grassland. Go there and for my sake enjoy yourself and take some fresh air."

Amar's suggestion pleased Mehr-Nigar and she did as he bid her. She went to the roof of the fortress and began admiring the bloom of the flowers and the grassy plain. It so happened that a flock of black-barred geese came flying overhead. Mehr-Nigar shot an arrow at them saying to herself, *If this hits a bird in the middle it would be an omen that I am destined to meet Hamza today, and I will see him and receive bliss from his sight and hold him in my arms after all this time.* Her arrow pierced the wing of a goose flying in the middle and the bird fell right before Amir Hamza. He slaughtered the bird and put it aside. Reading Mehr-Nigar's name on the arrowhead, he began kissing it with amorous fervor.

Amar witnessed this and became enraged at the man's actions. He walked up to him and said, "O wicked fakir! You do not know the majesty of the name written on the arrowhead that you so shamelessly kiss. Come, give me the arrow! I have forgiven you on this occasion since you are a mendicant, but if you show impertinence again in this manner, you will receive your due punishment. You will be dispatched from this temporary abode of life to the permanent abode of the Future State." Amir Hamza replied, "Do not waste my time with this idle talk, for I have dealt with many of your ilk and kind. Go and frighten someone who will believe you. I have had my share of impostors and frauds. I consider the Emperor of the Seven Concentric Circles as worthless as a common insect. A common *ayyar* like yourself will never frighten me."

Amar grew furious at these words and, untying the sling from his head and loading it with a carved and polished stone, let fly at Amir Hamza. Keeping his eyes on the stone, Hamza caught it between his hands as it reached his chest and called out to Amar in challenge, "Take this, O *ayyar*. Receive this example of my skill!" and flung the same stone at Amar. Seeing the stone come flying at him with great force, Amar leapt to the side and shot a second stone at Amir from the sling. Amir again foiled the attack and threw the same stone back at Amar, who threw himself down so that the stone shot past over his head. Amar then reasoned that the fakir was a consummate conjuror and an accomplished occult master and that he could not prevail over him with violence. To obtain the arrow from him, Amar thought of tempting him with money. Amar approached Hamza and said, "I will give you five hundred rupees if you hand over the arrow to me!" Hamza did not consent to the proposal. Then Amar said, "Take a thousand rupees and give me the arrow!" Amir answered, "In Qaf I scattered such amounts to common folk on account of Hamza. I do not think you can impress me with your wealth with offers of such paltry sums!"

Amar sat down when he heard those words and asked, "How long ago was it that you saw Hamza?" Amir Hamza answered, "Just six months ago, he and I happened to be in the same place." Amar inquired, "Was there anything that Amir told you?" Hamza answered, "As I was leaving he asked me to send his greetings to his father and give him the news of his welfare." Amar asked, "Did he say anything else?" Hamza answered,

"Yes, he also told me that should I meet his companions I should convey to them his fond wishes!" Amar asked, "Did he send any other messages for anyone else?" Hamza answered, "There is a message that he enjoined me to convey to Mehr-Nigar, his rosy-cheeked beloved and faithful lover!" Amar said, "Pray do not make delay and tell me what it was." Amir said, "I shall not tell you and go against his wishes. I shall only whisper it in Mehr-Nigar's ears, for that was Amir Hamza's wish and such is the import of the message brought by this fakir." Amar answered, "How can you make such an unreasonable demand and make this proposition? How can Mehr-Nigar appear before you? She remains behind the veil and is a person of great dignity and majesty!" Hamza answered, "Very well, then! If she does not wish to hear it, I have no desire to convey it to her either." Amar said, "O *qalandar*![23] Take five hundred *tomans* and vouchsafe Amir's message to me." Hamza answered, "If I have told you once I have told you a thousand times: If Mehr-Nigar wishes to hear the message, she may send for me and let me whisper it in her ear. If she does not wish to hear it, she will have only herself to blame and she should put an end to her pretense of being in love with Hamza."

Amar was thus forced to go before Mehr-Nigar. When he entered the palace he saw signs of celebration. Everyone was beside themselves with joy and seemed jubilant and happy. Amar inquired, "What is the cause for this jubilation? Has it been occasioned by some happy tidings someone has brought?" Princess Mehr-Nigar answered, "I shot an arrow at a goose to determine my lot of destiny and learn my fortune. That arrow pierced the wing of the goose, but the bird pierced with the arrow has fallen near the fortress walls. Pray fetch it from there and do me this kindness. I have often tried and tested this method of determining my fate and found it reliable and true. By all means Amir will arrive this evening, and for certain I will be reunited with him today."

Amar witnessed that there was great to-do in the women's quarters. One attendant girl would gaze at the clouds and say, "Hamza's throne is hidden inside this cloud for certain." Another would look toward the plain and comment, "If Amir returns by land, he will choose this way and no other!" Amar said to himself that it was for the best that Mehr-Nigar's attention was finally diverted. Mehr-Nigar again said to Amar, "Khvaja, the bird I shot with my arrow has fallen under the castle wall. Kindly fetch it yourself or send someone to bring it!" Amar answered, "A fakir arrived today and sat down under the wall. God alone knows the purpose for his visit. The bird pierced with the arrow fell before him and he slaughtered it and kept it with him as if it were his trophy. He is holding the arrow in his hand. He states that he has come from Qaf with a message from Amir for you, which he will whisper only in your ears in exact fulfillment of Amir Hamza's wishes. When I tried to tempt him with offers of money and pressed and cajoled him into giving me the message, he answered that he had spent greater sums in Qaf on account of Hamza and had himself distributed thousands of rupees among the invalids and the poor. He told me that he was fully content and needed nothing more. He will give me neither the arrow nor the message from Hamza."

As the couplet goes:

> *When the day of union approaches,*
> *Restiveness waxes greater.*

Upon hearing Amar's words, Mehr-Nigar's anxiety grew tenfold. She said to Amar, "Khvaja! For God's sake send that fakir into my presence without delay!" Amar returned to Hamza and said, "O fakir, I am now offering you a thousand *tomans* for giving me Hamza's message and obeying my wishes!" Hamza replied, "Your proclivity for idle talk is a source of constant wonder for me. Take me before Mehr-Nigar if you and the princess are interested in hearing Hamza's message. I have told you a thousand times that I will never tell it except to Mehr-Nigar, and I will not forfeit my principles." Unable to do anything, Amar said, "Come along with me!" Hamza handed the goose to Amar and followed behind carrying the arrow and the wolf skins. Amar took Hamza into the palace and seated him in front of a curtain and said, "O fakir! Mehr-Nigar is sitting behind this curtain. Now you may convey to her Hamza's message." Amir said, "Hamza made me swear on his head that I should whisper his message in Mehr-Nigar's ear alone. I will not go against my oath. If she wishes to hear the message, she must come before me and receive her husband's message, otherwise I will depart this instant." At this, Amir Hamza rose.

Unable to think of anything else, Amar went behind the curtain and brought out Fitna Bano, the daughter of Mehr-Nigar's nanny, draped in a mantle. He presented her to Amir Hamza and said, "O dervish, the rosy-cheeked beloved and Hamza's faithful lover is standing before you. Speak what you must and do not remain silent even a moment longer." Amir Hamza replied, "Let her show me her face so that I can ascertain whether it is Princess Mehr-Nigar or someone else with the grace and airs of a princess." When Amar removed the veil from Fitna Bano's face and let Hamza have a glimpse of her visage, Amir Hamza said, "This is not Mehr-Nigar but Fitna Bano. Hamza gave me a description of her as well and informed me about her." Having no further ruse or pretext to remain concealed, Mehr-Nigar appeared before Amir Hamza herself and was forced to expose her face to him. Amir saw her miserable state, her wan face, her dry lips, her tearful eyes, and the grimy clothes in which she was dressed. Tears welled up in Amir's eyes also to witness her condition, but he successfully hid them from the others so that his identity was not revealed and nobody recognized him as Hamza upon seeing him tearful.

Amar said, "O dervish, this is Mehr-Nigar! Now say what you wish to say." Hamza answered, "I would still make the same condition I made before. I shall whisper Hamza's message into Mehr-Nigar's ear." Amar was enraged and sent for Muqbil and a few other commanders and said to them, "Stand ready outside the chamber with drawn swords. The moment the fakir emerges, kill him and cut him into pieces." Then Mehr-Nigar bent her head close and brought her ear near Amir's lips. Amir Hamza said in a whisper, "O life of Hamza, it is not some fakir but I myself." At these words, he removed his headgear and Mehr-Nigar saw the dark mole, the Hashimi vein, and the Ibrahimi ringlet. The moment she saw them, Mehr-Nigar let out a cry, Amir also exclaimed a sigh, and both were taken unconscious, for the ardor of their passion had made them lose possession of their senses.

When Amar looked closely at Amir's forehead he finally recognized that the fakir was Hamza in person. He rushed forward and fell at his feet and offered his life in sacrifice to Hamza. Everyone heard the news of Amir Hamza's return. Rose water and the essence of orange blossoms were sprayed on the faces of Mehr-Nigar and Amir Hamza and the attendants fanned them.

The unconscious couple slowly regained consciousness before their eyes. Hamza embraced Amar and Muqbil and showed great favor to everyone. He broke into tears, and everyone cried copious tears of joy along with him. Jubilation spread within and without the castle. That very moment Princess Mehr-Nigar ordered a great feast. She bathed and put on her bridal dress and decorated herself with the seven adornments. Amir went outside and embraced every commander and conferred robes of honor on each of them. There was no hand that did not scatter gold and jewels over Hamza's head as the sacrifice of his life and every man

692 • *The Adventures of Amir Hamza*

pledged an offering to ward off the evil eye. Amar thought it necessary to offer two cowries as sacrifice and that was the extent of his offering, for he possessed a great sense of humor. Amar ordered the kettledrums to be sounded and the trumpets began blasting and thundering.

The narrator tells that when the noise of congratulations and felicitations and the music reached Naushervan's ears, he asked his *ayyars* the reason for it. They replied that Hamza's return has been announced at the fortress and by God's grace his safe arrival had been proclaimed. Bakhtak said, "Your Honor, it might very well be another one of Amar's tricks!" The emperor said to Buzurjmehr, "What is your opinion?" He answered, "According to my calculations it is very probable that Hamza has arrived and that is why I have returned from Basra to meet him and hear the news of Qaf from his mouth!"

———

Now hear of Ashqar Devzad. When he headed into the forest he beheld Naushervan's horses grazing there as well. This made him furious and he killed some of them with his hooves, and the others who tried to confront him were badly injured. The few who remained galloped toward their camp with Ashqar in pursuit. It was evening and the unnerved horses flooded into their camp, causing the tent ropes to snap and the ropes to drop from people's hands. People rushed to catch Ashqar, but he tore them apart with his jaws and disemboweled them with his hooves. He severed their heads with his powerful kicks and with his teeth he relieved their necks of the burden of their heads. Men fell on their faces to the ground and Ashqar killed thousands in the camp of the infidels. Naushervan's army thought that Hamza's forces had made a night raid on their camp. They armed themselves and, confusing their own army for the army of Hamza, killed and slaughtered one another until morning, battling and skirmishing with one another the whole night. When they looked around in the morning, they saw not a single enemy among the dead, and found not a single casualty except their own. When Naushervan beheld Ashqar, he was captivated by the sight of the majestic steed. He ordered that every effort be made to catch the horse. But Ashqar severely injured anyone who attempted to capture him.

Meanwhile, Amir Hamza said to Amar, "The whole night a commotion has been heard from Naushervan's camp that has continued until now. Find out what it is all about and the reason for the racket." At that moment an *ayyar* presented himself and gave a detailed account of what had passed in Naushervan's camp. Hamza said to Amar, "He is my horse. Go and say to him, 'O son of Arnais and Laneesa, the Sahibqiran has sent for you,' and tell him that you have come as my faithful servant to bring him to me. He will accompany you directly and you may lead him here without any fear or anxiety!" Following Amir's orders, Amar gave the message to Ashqar and summoned him in Amir's name, and the horse followed him quietly. Amir came down from the fortress and embraced Ashqar and praised Amar before him and said to the horse, "O Ashqar, Amar will take care of you and look after your every comfort." Then Amir told Amar to give Ashqar a place of honor in the stable and take care of his feeding and comfort himself.

The next day Aadi Madi-Karib arrived there with Zehra Misri, Khwaja Aashob, and Khwaja Bahlol. Amir sent Zehra Misri to Mehr-Nigar inside the fortress and provided quarters for her as well. Amir kept Khwaja Aashob and Khwaja Bahlol in his own company.

Aadi Madi-Karib took Amar quietly aside and, giving him the wooden chest, said to him, "This contains many jewels. I kept it for you in trust just as I found it. Kindly accept it and take these jewels as yours." Amar was delighted to receive the gift of the wooden chest from Aadi. He carried it into another room, and after latching the door to lock it from inside, opened the chest. The moment he opened it, the *dev* emerged and immediately caught him, securing his grip on Amar. Finding himself caught by this unexpected calamity, Amar blew on the Sufaid Mohra and raised the alarm. At that moment Amir was lying with Mehr-Nigar, kissing her ruby lips and ravishing her with great pleasure. Suddenly he heard the blast of the Sufaid Mohra and rushed out in dread and panic, taking Mehr-Nigar along and wondering what might have overtaken Amar that he had blown on the Sufaid Mohra. Amir thought that some calamity might have occurred for Amar to have made that signal.

At that moment, Muqbil Vafadar was ravishing Zehra Misri. Upon hearing Amir's footsteps outside, he also stepped out in anxiety. When Amir listened closely, he identified the chamber from which the blast of the Sufaid Mohra was sounding and noises were being heard. He headed there but found the entrance secured from inside. Amir Hamza kicked it in and entered. He saw the same *dev* that he had caught and given to Aadi standing in a corner, ready to attack Amar, who was blowing on the Sufaid Mohra in another corner of the room and signaling for assistance.

Amir caught the *dev* by his cummerbund and carried him like that before Princess Mehr-Nigar. He tore him apart like an old rag in full view of her and disemboweled him and extracted his heart. Everyone present there praised Amir's might and lauded him for his courage. Mehr-Nigar scattered many jewels and gold as the sacrifice of Amir's life. Amar was taken unconscious by the shock of the *dev*'s attack. When he came to, after his face was sprinkled with rose water, he said to Aadi, "O big-bellied creature, you made me suffer terribly by playing this trick on me! Now you will see how I get even with you and what terrors I make you suffer on account of it!" Aadi laughed and said, "Khvaja, I was almost buried alive at your prediction. I had to make sure that my words were not proven idle either." Finally, Amir Hamza made them embrace each other and renew their friendship. Then he said to Amar, "Have no worries, for Aasman Peri will bring you many gifts from Qaf that will please you greatly!" The news made Amar very happy. He blessed Amir Hamza and in all love and sincerity offered to sacrifice himself to ward off any calamities from Hamza's head.

• • •

The third book is ended. God willing, the remainder of the
narrative will be given in Book Four.

BOOK FOUR

The Beginning of the Fourth Book of the Dastan *of the Sahibqiran, the Conqueror of the World, the Quake of Qaf, the Latter-day Suleiman, Amir Hamza the Magnificent, Son of Khvaja Abdul Muttalib*

The warriors of the field of fables and the soldiers of the domain of legends thus gallop on the steeds of pens across the arena of the page to reveal that when Naushervan and Bakhtak and other nobles of his court learned of Hamza's arrival from Qaf and everyone became apprised of that intelligence, Bakhtak said to the emperor, "Hamza has returned from Qaf after eighteen years and did not pay his respects to Your Honor. He wishes to take the daughter of the Emperor of the Seven Concentric Circles by might and finds it convenient to achieve his end by force of arms. It would be most judicious to sound the drums of war and confront him in battle, as he has returned worn and exhausted, and Your Honor has a force of intrepid warriors at your command who are brave and clamor for battle. To rout Hamza and hand him a resounding defeat would be the work of a moment." Duped by Bakhtak's words, Naushervan's mind became set on this idea. He ordered the war drums beaten, and the clarion sounded. Upon hearing this, the Sahibqiran, too, ordered the call answered from his camp. The sound from the cymbal of Afrasiyab, the clarion of Turk, and the fife of Jamshed[1] was like the blast of the Last Trumpet. Kebaba Chini and Qulaba Chini picked up the eighteen-Tabrizi-*maund* mallet and rang the Timbal of Sikander with such might that it was heard up to sixty-four *kos* away. From the violence of the thunderous noise, the eardrums of many men burst in Naushervan's camp, scores of them were deafened, and even the brave men felt their blood curdle in their veins. Both camps prepared the whole night for battle and remained on the alert.

The courageous soldiers sought the day of battle with the same fervor that one seeks his beloved. They bathed and changed and put on the perfume of good fortune, lined their eyes with kohl, and reddened their lips by chewing on betel leaves. They prayed to God for victory with every breath and invoked the curse of cowardice on their foe. They polished each sword and every cuirass, replaced the broken arrows in their quivers, and deftly straightened bows that had become twisted by putting them into a furious flame. They whetted their daggers, took stock of their arms, and sharpened the edges of their spears. They attached double belts and martingales to their horses' cloth saddles.[2] Friends, companions, comrades, brothers, fathers, sons, commanders, officers, and troop leaders embraced one another, prayed for victory, and sought with great humility and meekness the assistance of the Almighty Victor.[3] Those who were on familiar terms with one another made taunting remarks such as "We shall now see the true ability of the soldiers and the resolve of the brave men! We shall see whose skull is trodden under the horses' hooves and whose sword shows its mettle!" Others said, "God has finally allowed us to see the day when we, adorned with valor, shall embrace the bride of victory. For years we have sought this day and prayed without cease to the Almighty to bring us near it."

The pansies who had never left their mother's room and board and who normally occupied themselves with drumming and strumming instruments, suffered terrible bouts of diarrhea from the sound of the drums of war. Indeed, their senses took leave of them. They were conspicuous by their wan faces, dried lips, tearful eyes, and their constant fearful sighs. These men exhorted their grooms to keep their mounts ready so that they might escape to their homes in the cover of night. They exclaimed such things as, "We shall not consent to sacrifice our lives with our own hands! The preparations for battle are now in full swing. A pitched battle will be fought tomorrow with hundreds of thousands losing their lives and falling to swords and spears." Their grooms would say, "Why do you exhibit such terror? Surely only those who are destined to die will meet their deaths. When the barley is ground, not every grain is pulverized in the mill, and so, too, is the fate of soldiers in battle. If you were always of such a cowardly heart, why did you ever seek employment as a soldier? You would have done better for yourself accompanying some dance girl on the tabla or *sarangi*[4] and singing songs in the safety of your shelter."

The cowards would respond, "You foolish ass, stick your advice where the sun does not shine! What if we are the barley grains destined for grinding? Do you think we enrolled in the ranks of soldiers and fell into this trap by choice? May God open Hell's window upon the graves of those whores, nurse Rae-bel and nanny Chambeli, who brought us up. May they never sleep in peace in their tombs. They were the ones who saved up enough to buy us a horse and enrolled us as soldiers. They were the ones who opened their legs to the paymaster so that we would be confirmed as soldiers and the horse would be branded for the army. May God strike us dead if we had a part in any of this, or if we ever attempted to dig our own graves with our own hands.

"When our nanny had herself bled and cupped once, we were taken unconscious from the sight of the blood alone. The whole family took us for dead and began lamentations. They only quieted down and found solace when we regained our senses. Do you think we have any great fondness for plying the sword and receiving wounds? Even if a splinter ever pierced us as children, we kept the neighbors awake with our crying and tormented the whole neighborhood with our roars. It could be extracted only after we had been drugged with hemp leaves.

"Ever since we enrolled as soldiers, we have always brought up the rear guard of the fighters and then been the vanguard of those in flight. We have yet to see the face of battle and its terrors. You certainly do not know this history for you have been here only a few days. We heard today that the Emperor of the Seven Concentric Circles will test the mettle of everyone in battle and put us to his bloody survey. Thus we have resolved to depart and make a strategic retreat long before such a possibility can come to pass. What do we stand to lose except the wages of the past fifteen days or our current positions? We will be only too willing to surrender those things to escape with our lives. This battlefield will not see our faces even if we have to make a living by selling matchsticks for the rest of our lives."

———

Now, Naushervan was in such a temper that dawn had not yet broken when he had the torches lit and rode to the battlefield under a moonlit sky in the company of the Sassanid, Kiyanid, and Kai Khusravi princes and kings. A vast horde marched behind him. When Amir Hamza received word of this, he sent for his chest of arms and armor and decorated himself with the weapons he had been given by the prophets. Thus fully armed, he mounted Ashqar Devzad and prepared to battle Naushervan's army. All the kings and princes in Amir Hamza's camp rode out with him with their respective armies, marching valiantly forth with great majesty and speed. Several thousand torchbearers carrying four- and five-tier gold and silver candelabra marched at the head of the armies letting off fireworks every few steps, their hearts delighting in thoughts of the impending fight. Two thousand *ayyars* also accompanied them, leading Amir's horse and wearing short braided garments of brocade and shoes of broadcloth. They carried their *ayyars'* slings and nets that were the bane of the foe, and had loops of ropes and daggers in their casings hanging from their waists.

Thus the whole army rode with great pomp and ceremony, inviting awestruck glances and enthralled looks. The Prince of *Ayyars,* the dagger thrower, the mighty trickster, the Bearder of the Infidels, the Scourge of Headstrong Princes, Khvaja Amar Ayyar bin Umayya Zamiri, who was dressed in his *ayyar's* livery and decorative headgear adorned with the Simurgh feather, and was chanting martial songs, advanced holding Amir's saddle ropes with an entourage of four hundred tricksters surrounding him. Thus the Lord of the Auspicious Planetary Conjunction advanced in an august and majestic manner. The hearts of brave men filled with a roaring sea of valor to behold the field lit up with the moon shining in the sky, fireworks being launched toward the enemies, shining standards and fluttering flags in the wind, the rattling of shields, the neighing of horses, and singers reciting martial songs and calling the ranks into battle array. Amir Hamza advanced with his entourage of commanders, princes, and kings as if he were the moon traveling among the stars at night, or as if the Sahibqiran was the groom and his men his wedding procession. This sight pleased everyone who laid eyes on it.

The Emperor of the Fourth Heaven[5] ascended his throne of dawn to look upon Amir Hamza's resplendence and began piercing the breast of the foe with the lance of its rays, drowning that horde of enemies in a sea of shame. Both camps arrayed their armies in left and right wings, a rear guard, a vanguard, and the core. After they were arranged in fourteen ranks and files, and had decorated the battlefield with their armed formations, the groundskeepers cleared the field of shrubbery and bushes, leveled the high and low points of the battlefield, and made the surface of the ground as smooth as the expanse of the heavens and as resplendent as a white sheet. The water carriers put sprinklers on their water skins and wetted down the field in the midst of which the pavilion of the Angel of Death[6] was established. The Extractor of Souls[7] made preparations to set about his work, and the sign of Mars shone forth from the foreheads of everyone assembled there. The crier proclaimed, "Where are the champions of the likes of Sam and Nariman? Sohrab the soldier and Rustam the warrior? We dare them to enter the field to test their mettle. If they are such brave men, let them come and stand before this intrepid army." A great clamor broke out in the two camps. The battlefield appeared to the soldiers' eyes to be the field of the day of Resurrection, and their armor felt like wax around their necks when they witnessed the field of slaughter ready for them.

From Naushervan's side, a Sassanid youth named Koh-Paikar rode forward, kissed the leg of the emperor's throne, and sought his permission for battle. Naushervan offered him a glass of wine with his own hands and lauded his valor. Koh-Paikar's cup of life having become completely full, he took the wine from Naushervan's hands and drank it to the dregs. He entered the battlefield with boastful words, as if he were the venerable Rustam, and proclaimed, "O followers of the True Faith, anyone among you who desires to meet his death should come forth to confront me. Let the one who has a claim to bravery show me what he's made of." The Sahibqiran recited a prayer and, racing Ashqar Devzad forward, brought him alongside Koh-Paikar's horse and whacked the head of the enemy's steed with his shield with such force that it retreated several steps. The face of that idle talker grew blanched with disgrace and he melted away with shame. He said to the Sahibqiran, "O Hamza, indeed you are a stalwart and comely youth. Truth be said, you are peerless in swiftness and alacrity, and your might and courage are the talk of the heavens. Do not rebel against the emperor; have your trespasses forgiven by him and join the august fellowship of the riding companions of the Emperor of Seven Concentric Circles, the lofty prince and monarch of the world."

The Sahibqiran said, "Did you come here to fight or to proselytize me? If you wish combat then follow the way of warriors; otherwise, go back to your camp with all your wily commandments." Then the Sassanid youth took a lance from his *ayyar* and, taking up the reins of his horse, turned to attack. The Sahibqiran took his spear from the hands of the Prince of Tricksters and spurred on Ashqar Devzad. The Sassanid approached and attacked Amir with his lance, demonstrating his artful excellence, but the Sahibqiran foiled his blow with his spear. After they had exchanged two blows each, Amir noticed that the Sassanid was unprotected on his right side. Amir turned his horse to attack from that flank. His adversary, who was also adept in such strategies, saw Amir's left side exposed so he wheeled his horse around and targeted it with his lance. Amir scurried out of the saddle and sat on his horse's rump, and the point of the enemy's lance missed his breast by a handspan. In the flash of an eye, Amir was back in the saddle and holding his spear under his arm. He turned his horse around once more and charged, breaking his adversary's lance in two: Its point fell to the ground and only the shaft remained in the hands of the Sassanid. Amir's swiftness was praised even by his enemies, who joined their voices with Amir's friends.

When Amar saw that the jewel-encrusted piece of Koh-Paikar's lance had fallen on the ground, he rushed forward to pick it up from the battlefield and put it inside his *zambil* after kissing it. Then he said to the Sassanid, "Give me the other half, too, as it is of no use to you now! I am sure I can find some use for it and turn it to my advantage!" Koh-Paikar's greed prompted him to demand his jewels back and retorted, "O cameleer's son! You must be mad to think that after you have stolen the point of my lance and put it in your *zambil*, you can have the other half as well." Amar Ayyar said, "Do you not know that I am in charge of this battlefield and the master of all that I find fallen on the ground? It would be better for you to surrender it willingly, or else I will take it by force and humiliate you in the bargain." Koh-Paikar answered angrily, "I would like to see how you do that!" He pointed the broken shaft of the lance toward Amar and tried to jab him with it and pin him down. Amar untied the sling from his headgear and hurled a stone that put Koh-Paikar out of commission. The other half of his lance fell to the ground, and Amar grabbed it without loss of time and said, "Now you have seen how it is done and how a fool is duped!" Then Amar returned to his army.

Koh-Paikar was mortified and said to Hamza, "Verily fighting with spears is like wielding a toothpick, and jousting with maces is just a mace bearer's duty by another name. You are renowned in the art of the spear in all cities and lands of the world and have proven yourself now its peerless master. I shall not test my skills against you with a spear or mace only to be humiliated by you. I would like to fight with swords, for swordplay is the soldier's true sport and a trooper's only worthy test." Amir answered, "Nothing would be more appropriate. Your words express my heart's desire. I am dying to learn what excellence you can show with your sword and how accomplished you are in this art." The Sassanid drew his sword, which was spotless like a perfumer's counter, and attacked Amir, who foiled the blow with his shield. Then Amir drew his sword Samsam, uttered his war cry, and said: "O Gueber, beware and take heed and do not blame me for taking you unawares! You will now see what are worthy of being called a sword and a blow in my eyes. My sword is what one would call a lustrous sword and a slayer of infidels." With these words, Amir dealt a blow to the enemy's head and unleashed his might with full force. The Sassanid tried to cover his head with his shield. A veritable incarnation of the light, Amir's sword flashed like lightning. It cut through the soldier's shield, helmet, and skull, and embedded itself in his horse's saddle, leaving nothing that it passed through whole, combusting everything in its way like a blaze.

The moment Koh-Paikar fell dead to the ground, Naushervan let out a terrible sigh and called out to his army, "Do not let this Arab escape alive! Kill him immediately, and use any means you can to achieve this end!" The moment the orders were given, the army fell upon Amir Hamza, and the armies of the True Faith also charged forward bellowing "God is great!" and wielding their shields, swords, maces, daggers, spears, bows, and arrows. The deafening clang of swords filled the field where forty thousand of Naushervan's men were cut down in the course of one hour. Naushervan's army beat a retreat, unable to withstand the blinding glimmer of the swords of the soldiers of the True Faith. Breaking with custom, Amir gave chase to the retreating army and kept cutting through swaths of them with his sword, following them up to a distance of four *kos*. From there Amir's forces returned, playing triumphant tunes of victory. The spoils of war were so immense that day that Naushervan's army was left utterly and completely impoverished. In Amir's camp on the other hand, even the most indigent man acquired the wealth of a prince. The immeasurable amounts of gold and loot plundered from Naushervan's camp that day made all of them men of affluence [?].

After God had sent him triumph and victory, Amir returned to the pavilion of Jamshed,[8] where he gave audience from the throne of Rustam. All the commanders of his camp positioned themselves on either side of him in rows, and all the heroes and brave men took their respective stations. Preparations for a feast were made, and before long the spring of song bubbled forth, music enveloped them, and the place rang with the sound of festivities.

The narrator has said that after the festivities were over, Amir Hamza asked Amar what had passed with him in his absence. Amar related everything to him in detail, from start to finish. Amir Hamza sent for Khvaja Aashob and Khvaja Bahlol, and asked them what their plans were and what they wished to do now. They answered, "We would like to become merchants and occupy ourselves with trading and making profit." Amir gave them gold pieces and bid them adieu and wrote them a note to the effect that they should never feel hindered in the course of their business.

Next, Amir asked Amar, "Did Landhoor or Bahram ever come to visit you in my absence and bring you any gifts?" Amar answered, "Many a time I wrote to them describing the vulnerability of my situation, but I never received a reply nor did they send anyone to assist me. However, when the enemy attacked, a Naqabdar clad in an orange veil would come to my aid with his forty thousand troops and kill thousands of the foe. Whenever I asked the identity of my benefactor he always said that he had done nothing remarkable to warrant making himself known or revealing his identity. When I insisted, he only said that when God returned Amir Hamza to his camp safe and sound, I would learn about him." Upon hearing this account, Amir became furious with rage and said, "From today onward, if I hear anyone even mention Landhoor or Bahram's name in my camp, I will have the speaker's tongue extracted from his neck and will visit a terrible punishment on him."

―――

The news of Amir's return from Qaf had been proclaimed abroad. Many powerful kings and princes presented themselves to him to pay their respects and offer him felicitations. Those who were unable to come in person sent gold and jewels as a sacrifice for Amir Hamza, along with congratulatory missives and fine gifts brought by their trusted representatives. When the news of Amir Hamza's return reached Ceylon, Landhoor and Bahram were similarly overjoyed. Landhoor said to Bahram, "We have been in this land some twenty or twenty-two years. It is a pity that evil still infests it. In all this time, we have not won even a single laurel. There was no end to the terrors the infidels visited on Amar and the hardships to which they put him. Yet none of us were able to bring him any aid. I am sure that the story of our indolence must grieve Amir no end, and he must be upset with us. Come what may, we must present ourselves now before the Sahibqiran to kiss his feet and seek his forgiveness for the injury we have done him. If we fail to do so, we will earn everyone's condemnation, and people will brand us as ingrates." Bahram replied, "Very well. You may proceed ahead. I will present myself in due time to earn the honor of kissing Amir's feet." After that Bahram headed for China and Landhoor put in place a valiant force against his enemy, the Sagsars, and arrived at Amir's court within a few days.

After allowing Landhoor to see him, Amir criticized him harshly and censured him publicly. Landhoor recounted his adventures and offered many apologies to Amir, and he apprised Amir of Bahram's circumstances as well. Then Amir pardoned him and seated him by his side and restored him to the rank of his companion. Amir then asked Amar, "Do you have any news of where Naushervan has escaped to?" Amar folded his arms humbly and replied, "He had gone to Maghreb, whose king deputized one of his commanders with an army of five hundred thousand warriors to assist him with his arms. It is a magnificent and imposing army, one part of which is camped on the same side of the river as ourselves, and the other is with Naushervan on the other side." Amir then ordered, "Set up our pavilion in the pasture by the riverside at the foot of the hill, and provide for festivities to be arranged. Proclaim it to our soldiers that they should make ready to overwhelm Naushervan's army!" The royal pavilion was set up where Amir had indicated and all preparations were made for revels. The Sahibqiran and his worthy companions and venerable champions entered the court and all of them indulged in that assembly of revelry with conviviality and warm spirits. Rosy-cheeked cupbearers and singers as beautiful as Venus appeared carrying gold-encrusted ewers and jewel inlaid goblets, and bearing an assortment of musical instruments. The Sahibqiran was occupied with these matters when his *ayyars* brought intelligence that Muqbil Vafadar was on his way there, having taken captive both Prince Hurmuz and the ill-fated Bakhtak.

Be it known that the day the pitched battle was fought, Prince Hurmuz and the wily Bakhtak had sneaked away with five thousand troops in the middle of the war to seize Mehr-Nigar from the fortress. There Muqbil lay in wait for them with his forty thousand archers. He slaughtered the enemy force and took Hurmuz and Bakhtak prisoner. He now led them before Amir Hamza, who expressed great pleasure at the valuable work done by Muqbil.

The Sahibqiran said to Hurmuz, "If you will convert to the True Faith, you can have this throne and empire and rule it happily." Bakhtak, whose heart was fast sinking, told himself that Hurmuz was destined to receive whatever fate had in store for the prince, but his own survival surely did not seem at all likely. He made a signal to Hurmuz and the two of them pretended, fearing for their lives, to convert to the True Faith and enter its fellowship. The Sahibqiran surrendered Kai Khusrau's throne to Hurmuz, made him the king of his armies, and handed him the charge of his entire camp. He made an offering to Hurmuz himself and ordered all the kings, princes, and commanders of his camp to make offerings to Hurmuz as well, and appointed Bakhtak his vizier and counselor in all matters big and small. Amir was overjoyed by this turn of events. His heart blossomed with happiness and delight, and he ordered festive music to start playing.

Three days later, when approximately four of the daily watches had passed, Amir was happily admiring the view of the green expanse that stretched around him, with nothing to impede his pleasure, when three beautiful peacocks descended from the sky into the pasture, alighting in that invigorating field that was the envy of the beautiful Farkhar. Amir dispatched Muqbil Vafadar and Amar Ayyar to investigate the occurrence, whereupon the three peacocks disappeared into thin air, leaving the onlookers perplexed. The narrator tells that those peacocks were in fact Aasman Peri's agents, who had traveled there from some two *kos* away, where she had camped on a mountainside with her sanguinary army, as she had taken a liking to that pleasant and scenic spot. Aasman Peri had dispatched Abdur Rahman Jinn, Salasal Perizad, and Akvana Peri disguised as peacocks to bring her news of Amir Hamza.

After some time passed, they again presented themselves before Amir Hamza, this time in their true shape, and after making obeisance and performing all the rituals of submission and deference, they gave him news of Aasman Peri's arrival. Amir was delighted to see them and seated them at his side and showed them much favor. He also conveyed the auspicious news of Aasman Peri's arrival to Prince Hurmuz and the commanders of his camp, and then he said to Amar, "Congratulations are in order because Aasman Peri has arrived with great fanfare bearing gifts from Qaf for you." Amar was most pleased to hear these happy tidings. The whole night was spent in festive assembly and in the morning Amir Hamza got ready and mounted his steed to go welcome Aasman Peri. Dressed in their finery, all the kings, princes, chiefs, commanders, and companions of Amir Hamza—with the exception of Prince Hurmuz—went in an entourage, advancing with great majesty and fanfare in the company of their peerless lord.

Abdur Rahman Jinn, Salasal Perizad, and Akvana Peri had already returned to alert Aasman Peri about the imminent arrival of the grand procession of the Sahibqiran. Her heart overflowed with joy to hear the news and she spread carpets of velvet, ermine, brocade, and satin brocade in their path and adorned her whole camp like the Garden of Eden. When Amir arrived at the Pavilion of Suleiman, he left everyone to wait outside and entered it alone. Aasman Peri came with Quraisha and her companions and attendants to the entrance of the pavilion to greet Amir, and with a small laugh, addressed Amir thus: "You left us behind so we came by ourselves to visit you. We have also brought wedding gifts for Mehr-Nigar." Amir said, "Give me the details now of all you have brought with

you, and present everything to me." Aasman Peri answered, "I have
brought the Pavilion of Suleiman, the Music Band of Suleiman, the
Char-Bazar of Bilqis,[9] all kinds of jewels, ermine, miniver, velvet, and
gold-worked satin cloth, and other gifts from Qaf." Amir was delighted
with it all. He kissed Quraisha's forehead and embraced her, and he also
embraced Aasman Peri and kissed her many times. Aasman Peri said to
him, "You should seat yourself on my throne." Amir declined the invitation and took the throne of Asif bin Barkhia instead. All the *devs, peris,* and
jinns who had accompanied Aasman Peri presented themselves and
made obeisance to Amir, who looked upon them with favor and inquired
after the welfare of each one of them individually. Then Amir said to
Aasman Peri, "In Qaf, I often used to mention the name of Amar Ayyar
to you. He has come with me, desirous to see you and make you an offering. You should send for him." Aasman Peri said, "Send for Amar Ayyar
and present him before us."

As Amar entered that place, his senses took flight when he regarded
the beauty and splendor of that unique and exquisite royal pavilion. But
when Amar looked around, he saw no one but Hamza, and said, "Where
is the queen of the heavens whose praises you used to sing? I would like
to see the face of that beauty who kept your heart occupied in Qaf for a
full eighteen years and snared you in her love." Amir answered, "Queen
Aasman Peri is giving audience on the throne, O Amar. It is a thing to
marvel at that you have not offered her your salutations!" Amar said, "I
cannot see anyone to whom I may offer my greetings. I myself marvel at
these strange circumstances. My salutations are not so worthless as to be
given freely to an empty throne and chairs, and I am not going to break
from my custom today." Aasman Peri ordered her attendants to put the
collyrium of Suleiman into Amar's right eye and let him see the wonders
that it would reveal. Be it known that when this collyrium is put in one's
right eye *devs* become visible, and when it is applied to one's left eye one
can see *peris* and *perizads.* When the collyrium was put into Amar's right
eye, he instantly could see the faces of the *devs* who thronged about him.
Amar was seized by terror at seeing them, and he renounced his sins and
repeatedly sought God's protection. He said to Amir, "Which one of
them is the queen and your dear wife? Pray tell me so that I may regard
her face." Amir Hamza laughed at Amar's words and Aasman Peri also
shook with laughter. Then she ordered that Amar's left eye should also be
lined with collyrium so that he could at last see her.

When his left eye was lined, Amar saw the *peris* and the *perizads* as-

sembled there, and he also saw a woman whose beauty was as luminescent as the sun seated with great majesty and glory on the throne. Beside
her was a girl whose face bore a striking resemblance to Amir and whose
beauty struck its beholders with wonderment. Amar said to himself that
the girl must be Amir's daughter. He approached the throne, made a
salutation to Aasman Peri, and said to the Sahibqiran, "Is this the Queen
Aasman Peri for whom you wasted eighteen years in Qaf? May God protect us from the devil, I myself would not have spent even a single day
there for someone so plain looking and put up with all those hardships.
In fact I would not even let her carry the water bowl to my toilet chamber."

These words mortified Aasman Peri with shame, and tears welled up
in her eyes. Amir said to her in the Jinni language, "Do not become sad at
his words. He is a clown, and everything he said was in jest. Indeed it was
nothing compared to what he is capable of saying. You will soon see the
tricks he performs and all the rogueries he commits. When I mentioned
his name to you in Qaf, did I not tell you that he is such a rogue and a
trickster that his antics send people into ecstasies of confusion, and they
cannot believe their mind and senses? Do as I ask you: Make him an offering of something, and then you will see how he undergoes a complete
change." Aasman Peri did as Amir had told her and offered Amar a decorated robe of honor along with some jewels and gold pieces. Amar put
the robe of honor on and made a bow and began snapping his fingers and
singing these words repeatedly in a clownish manner:

> *How wonderful is the picture of your beauty: Hurrah! Bravo!*
> *Your beauty is the exegesis of the Chapter of Light.*[10]

Then looking at Hamza, Amar said, "O Sahibqiran, I suspected from
the start that you had found a moonfaced beauty in Qaf and that was
why you were unwilling to leave there and return to the world of humans. Indeed, anyone who comes upon such a beautiful mistress is
within his rights to be oblivious to all worldly and otherworldly cares.
Before I beheld this woman, I thought that Mehr-Nigar was the only
paragon of beauty in the world and the very soul of charm. But after
regarding this luminous sun of beauty, I realize that our princess cannot rightfully be judged even a ray of light compared to this one's resplendence. Before such a comely and charming face—whose luster
and delicacy would shame the sun and would embarrass the glowing

moon to show its face—Mehr-Nigar's charm cannot at all compete. It is hardly surprising, for one is born of man and the other born of peris."

Aasman Peri was charmed and delighted by Amar's words. She laughed and said, "What a turncoat!" Then she showered Amar with jewels and gifts from Qaf that satisfied even Amar's insatiable greed. Thereafter, Aasman Peri sent for the commanders and chiefs of Amir's camp and offered each one a robe of honor commensurate with his rank, and lavished gifts and gold pieces on each of them according to his station. Her gifts were treasures that had never before been seen either with the eye or the imagination. She said to Amir, "Order your attendants to make preparations for your wedding to Mehr-Nigar and to arrange all the necessities for the ceremonies. Although I have brought the wedding paraphernalia from Qaf and have come ready to organize the affair, I am not familiar with the rituals and ceremonies of your land, and you should make the preparations according to local customs. I will be on hand to facilitate and enliven the ceremonies." Amir Hamza spent three days with Aasman Peri and returned to his camp on the fourth day, unable to tear himself away from her sooner.

Then Amir went before Mehr-Nigar and broke his pleasant news to her, addressing her sweetly, "Aasman Peri has brought you all the accoutrements of marriage from Qaf, among which are many rare and delicate gifts, and she exhorts me to make no further delay in getting married but to do it as soon as possible." Mehr-Nigar lowered her head from modesty and did not answer. Amir Hamza then went before Prince Hurmuz and gave the same account to him with all necessary details. Next, he ordered the gongs to be struck to announce the impending ceremony, and all preparations to be made with no detail overlooked. Amir then wrote a missive to Naushervan that read:

In effect, you already gave me the hand of Mehr-Nigar, but due to the vagaries of time and the tide of events, I was kept from solemnizing the marriage. Many an unseemly event intruded in this and kept me away. There is no use crying over the past, however. I am writing to let you know that yours truly is solemnizing his marriage with Mehr-Nigar and is hopeful that you will give your permission for it to proceed. Show me this favor so that I may happily celebrate my nuptials with your daughter with great fanfare and ceremony. It would be unimaginable for us not to receive the gift of your presence in this heavenly assembly and joyous gathering. It would not be too much to expect of your munificence that you would consent to attend this ceremony and thus honor your humble servant.

Amar Ayyar took Hamza's note to Naushervan, who read it and asked Amar, "I have heard that Aasman Peri has arrived there with much fanfare bearing wedding articles and mementoes from Qaf for Mehr-Nigar. Is the news true or false?" Amar answered, "The news is absolutely true and has not the least bit of falsehood in it." In the meanwhile a note also arrived for Naushervan from Hurmuz and Bakhtak that read: "Your Honor should not hold back permission to Hamza so that you are not accused of going back on your word and Hamza is not disheartened. Even without your permission he will marry Mehr-Nigar and that would show Your Honor a dishonor." Naushervan sent for his companions and commanders, and he shared Hurmuz's note with them, reading it aloud in the meeting. All of them unanimously voiced their approval of the prince's opinion, so Naushervan sent for his inkwell and wrote out an answer to Amir's letter. He gave his consent for the marriage to proceed, but declined the invitation to attend himself.

Many of the emperor's courtiers had objected that the manner in which Amir was going about the business of solemnizing his marriage to Mehr-Nigar was more unseemly than a beggar's. They stated that it was not the wont of great lords to celebrate their nuptials in a careless and casual manner, for marriages are momentous events in a person's life. Buzurjmehr said to Naushervan, "If you were to attend the ceremony, Hamza would receive you with honor and respect. You could take part in the festivities for a few days and return without unnecessarily prolonging your visit. If Your Honor does not wish to announce his visit, Your Honor may give Amar a reward and show him some favor. He will respectfully conduct you to a place where you can witness the ceremonies without being seen yourself, and he, too, would show you every honor." The emperor replied, "I have no objections to this proposition." Then he told Amar, "I will come there disguised as a beggar," and Amar deferred to his wishes. The emperor conferred a robe of honor on Amar and gave him leave to go. Buzurjmehr accompanied Amar back in order to see Amir Hamza.

The narrator of the dastan tells that Amir Hamza was delighted to receive a positive answer to his missive and showed it to everyone present. He embraced Buzurjmehr, and then with his own hands he squeezed the juice of the leaves that the holy Khizr had given him. When he applied this to Buzurjmehr's eyes, they instantly regained their sight and his blindness was cast away. Buzurjmehr congratulated Amir on the auspicious occasion of his wedding and the musicians struck up playing nuptial tunes. The *devs* and *perizads* set up the Pavilion of Suleiman on a high rock and lavishly decorated it with all the paraphernalia of the court. The Char-Bazar of Bilqis was set up adjacent to it and four hundred *devs* were appointed to sweep the place and spread the carpets. The Music Band of Suleiman also began playing festive wedding music. Heaps of multicolored jewels and tasteful decorations of lustrous pearls were scattered all around. Aasman Peri took Mehr-Nigar into the Private Chamber of Suleiman inside the tent where the nuptials and all other ceremonies of the marriage would be celebrated. On the day of his wedding procession, Amir dressed in a royal robe and mounted Ashqar Devzad. Kings and princes from all over the world formed a procession with Amir Hamza's steed in the middle, and they went forth scattering gold and jewels over his head as the sacrifice of his life. Twelve thousand beautiful and comely jinn children carrying crystal lamps and wax and camphor candles in goblets of red glass led the procession. The attendants carried out their respective duties with diligence and alertness. Forty thousand jinns from Qaf marched with them, sniggering, making pleasantries with one another, and letting off fireworks. Twenty thousand *perizads* arranged in two rows rode atop flying thrones singing and dancing and playing music. The Music Band of Suleiman was borne aloft by flying camels. In short, the human eye beheld wonders it had never seen until that day. The Prince of *Ayyars,* the Hunter of the Foe, Amar bin Umayya Zamiri, advanced in the vanguard, marshaling Amir Hamza's procession with his entourage of four thousand four hundred and forty-four *ayyars* in richly wrought costumes, who helped organize and arrange everything with great joy and delight. Ashqar Devzad stepped magnificently at a regal pace, preening like a dancing peacock. His captivating gait made the partridge dove feel envious and enamored and long to sacrifice a thousand lives to its beauty.

> *The balanced stride of the happy steed*
> *Whisking left and right his tail;*
> *Hordes of them and herds*
> *All around, some near some far;*
> *By the manner in which the procession advanced*
> *One would imagine it was the conveyance of Zephyrus.*

In this way Amir's procession arrived with great fanfare at the Pavilion of Suleiman, where he alighted. The *peris* danced as Amir Hamza ascended the throne and sat beside Prince Hurmuz. Aasman Peri went with Quraisha and her attendants into the Char-Bazar of Bilqis and adorned Mehr-Nigar with inestimable and precious jewels the likes of which none but the wives of the emperors of Qaf had ever seen, and beautified her with the seven adornments. She embellished the princess to such stunning effect that the heavens longed to kiss Aasman Peri's hand. She declared Mehr-Nigar her protégée, and scattered salvers full of gold and jewels as a sacrifice for her until the offerings lay in heaps. Mehr-Nigar's beauty robbed Aasman Peri of her senses and faculties; she had fallen in love with her charm instantly. Before long Aasman Peri had thrown herself completely into the wedding ceremonies.

———

Now hear of Naushervan. He marked his forehead like a mendicant, put a snake [?] around his neck, wore an amulet, rosary, necklace, and kerchief, and put a quilted cap on his head. Then, with a stick in his hand, he headed to see the marriage ceremonies in the company of his seven nobles. Amar recognized Naushervan and offered to conduct him into the assembly so he could participate in all of the events, but the emperor would not accept. Then Amar offered to take him to a place where he could observe everything. Naushervan liked that proposition better and gladly agreed. Amar brought him to the Pavilion of Suleiman and gave him a jewel-embedded chair, seating him there with great respect. Then Amar ordered the rosy-cheeked and silver-limbed cupbearers to pass around the goblets of colorful wines, and they offered these to Naushervan with great coquetry. After spending some time there Naushervan rose and, offering his blessing to Amir, said, "I am only a beggar. I came to see the sights and sounds and shall now retire. I wish to be excused and granted your leave to depart." Amir told Amar in the language of the *ayyars* to conduct Naushervan to the Char-Bazar of Bilqis and attend to him diligently so that he might continue to participate in the ceremonies and enjoy his time without any interference, and to provide for his entertainment and pleasure. Amar did as he was told. He accompanied Naushervan to the tent, provided for his every comfort, and made sure that he was well looked after.

With a few hours left to the night, Khvaja Buzurjmehr read out the wedding sermon following holy tradition. As it was getting close to dawn, the female quarters buzzed with word of the arrival of the bridegroom.

At the first of the seven doors to the women's quarters Amir was accosted by Aasman Peri who closed the door on him and told him that it would only be opened once he had paid the marriage money promised to Mehr-Nigar and honored the pledge he made when the wedding sermon was read. Amir settled his pledge by offering Muqbil Vafadar along with forty thousand slaves in golden livery to Mehr-Nigar. At this, Aasman Peri opened the door. Then she closed the second door and asked him for another offering for Mehr-Nigar in return for the privilege to behold her. Amir did as Aasman Peri asked him and offered his sword, the Aqrab-e Suleimani, and his steed Siyah Qitas. In this manner Aasman Peri exacted a toll for Mehr-Nigar at all seven doors of the women's quarters and Amir paid without argument before he was allowed to set foot in Mehr-Nigar's private chamber.

Amir Hamza blossomed forth in smiles upon seeing Mehr-Nigar dressed in wedding costume, sitting among a cluster of moonfaced damsels who were lovely as *peris,* and offered many a thanks to God for the gift of Mehr-Nigar, whose beauty could trick anyone into believing she was a *houri.* After the rituals of *banat* and the *aarsi-mushaf* [11] were completed, Amir carried Mehr-Nigar to the bedstead. Like the frenzied Majnun he pledged his soul to his Laila and embraced her and sucked the jujube fruit of her lips. After some time had passed, a physical struggle broke out between the bride and the bridegroom, but Amir retrieved the desired pearl from love's sea after offering his bride many words of comfort and consolation, and then he fulfilled his desire with great facility and leisure. By the Grace of God a precious pearl [12] was conceived within the oyster of the sea of love.

In the morning, Amir took a bath and dressed and, smiling and joyous, arrived at the Pavilion of Suleiman. All his courtiers presented themselves to him and received great bliss from his audience. Festivities were held for the rest of the day. In the evening Amir shared his bed with Aasman Peri, and the next day it was Rehan Peri's turn to spend the night with Amir and for him to take his pleasure of her. The next night he slept with Saman Seema Peri and ravished her as well. In this way, Amir took his pleasure of a different woman each night for forty nights and tasted the finest pleasure that life can offer. And during each of those forty days, the kings of Qaf and the princes of the world engaged in festivities with Amir. Aside from pleasure seeking and reveling, all other matters were postponed.

One day, after the conclusion of the festivities, Amir mounted his steed to go to visit the Char-Bazar of Bilqis preceded by heralds and mace bearers. The moment he set foot outside, a *dev* who was the brother of Ra'ad Shatir whom Amir had slain in Qaf descended before him. Finding Amir by himself for a moment, he aimed a blow of his mace at Amir's head. Amir jumped from his saddle and foiled the blow, and then catching the *dev* by his waist, whirled him overhead three times and slammed him to the ground so hard that the *dev* recalled the days of his infancy and all his senses and faculties were dislodged from their stations. He tried to get up and escape, but Amir pressed his one leg underfoot and, holding the other leg in his hands, ripped the *dev*'s body in two with utmost ease like a piece of old cloth, and tore him up in two as if he were made of paper. The onlookers were shocked to immobility by this sight and marveled greatly. All the brave and valiant lords hung their heads in embarrassment at this unsurpassable feat, and Naushervan fainted at this display of Amir's might.

Later, having finished his romp, Amir Hamza returned to his court, where everyone expressed delight at his victory over the *dev*. Amar Ayyar restored Naushervan to his senses by sprinkling rose water and the perfume of orange blossoms over him, and brought him back to his senses. Amar then conducted him before Amir for his leave-taking, and the emperor announced his departure in terms suited to the purpose. Seeing Naushervan clad in the garb of beggars, Amir Hamza gently demanded, "O Emperor of the Princes of Seven Climes, renounce your idol worship and proclaim that there is only one True God. Then I will give myself in service to your most humble servants and will always remain faithful to you." Naushervan did not consent but forthrightly answered, "A change of religion is unacceptable to me! Moreover, it would be unbecoming to the traditions of my dynasty!" In the end, Amir was obliged to present Naushervan with gold and jewels and gifts from Qaf as offerings, and he bestowed Suleiman's robes of honor on the emperor's companions. Naushervan returned to his camp and ordered everyone to assemble and prepare to return to Ctesiphon the next day.

Aasman Peri, meanwhile, made Amir an offering of the gifts she had brought for him especially and then took her leave of him. Amir embraced her and said to her, "I am as happy and grateful to see you as I was once unhappy and discontented with you. You have put me into your debt. Whenever you send for me I will immediately prepare to come to you, provided I am not entangled in some battle here, and will make no delay. Consider this your second home always. Whenever you wish, you may show your august face here and join my company." Then Amir embraced Quraisha and kissed her forehead and sent them both off with many gifts. Rehan Peri and Saman Seema Peri also took their leave of Amir and departed. The Sahibqiran bestowed all the lands of Maghreb on the King of Tanj-e Maghreb and made him the sovereign of those lands, but the new king appointed a deputy to rule in his stead and joined Amir as his riding companion.

The next day Hamza ordered his advance camp to move toward Mecca and designated Amar bin Hamza, his son by Naheed Maryam, the daughter of the king of Greece, as the commander of his camp in his stead. Amir then closeted himself with Mehr-Nigar to enjoy the sensual pleasures of life. Amir Hamza surrendered all offices of command and put his son Amar bin Hamza in charge of them completely.

One day, Amar bin Hamza was busy drinking in the assembly with others when suddenly Aadi knitted his brow and said to Landhoor, "You giant, how did you find the courage to occupy my chair and take it into your head to commit this trespass?" Landhoor answered, "You are already out of your depth after guzzling just a few cups. You make a false claim, O monster-bellied one! It is a marvel that you prattle and babble in this manner with me and use harsh words and show no fear of my majesty and power. If I sit in this chair it is with permission from the commander!" Aadi called out loudly, "I am sure that the commander has not asked you to warm my seat for me. It is you who make a false and idle claim!" Landhoor said, "O Aadi, it is not you talking but the wine, and now you have proved your mettle by your mental collapse." Aadi then rose from his place and punched Landhoor. The Khusrau laughed and said, "O Aadi, you should not let this incident drive you mad. Take stock of your senses and control yourself."

When Amar bin Hamza noticed the situation, he confronted Aadi and said, "Stop this drunken madness and wake up from your egotistical reveries!" In his drunken state Aadi answered him, "You have no business poking your nose in our affair. This is between Landhoor and me: You have no right to speak in an issue that concerns only the two of us." Amar bin Hamza rose from his station and punched Aadi so hard that he fell to the ground. Then Aadi started complaining loudly, saying, "If Amir's son feels he has license to humiliate us in this manner and visit unwarranted cruelty on us, we will not remain long in this court." All the commanders and champion warriors had taken exception to Amar bin Hamza's actions, and a great din arose from the assembly that brought Amir Hamza out of his bedchamber. When he was informed of the situation he admonished his son and said, "I am warning you never again to act in this manner against anyone here. Landhoor and Aadi would have sorted out the matter between themselves. You had no business interfering in their personal feud." His son flew into a rage and said, "If Aadi ever speaks to me with such impertinence again, I will cut off his ears and drive him away from the camp." Now Amir Hamza became angry and replied, "Hold your tongue! I do not care to listen to such words. If you use such language again, I will pick you up and smash you on the ground and make your brains flow out of your ears. That will make you forget all your arrogance."

Amar bin Hamza was in the prime of his youth and his father's words rankled his heart. He shouted, "Who dares to touch me? There is no one who has the guts or the courage!" Furious, Amir Hamza led him by his hand into the arena. Father and son mounted their steeds and prepared for combat. Those present gathered around to see the fight between them and witness their skill. Amir asked his son to begin the combat, and Amar bin Hamza lashed his horse, but the animal refused to charge. Then Amir Hamza said, "O unwise man, learn comportment from this dumb animal." Amar bin Hamza left his saddle and Amir also dismounted and prepared for hand-to-hand combat. His son caught hold of Amir Hamza's cummerbund and exerted all his might trying to dislodge him, but was unable to do so. Then he let go his hold in frustration and stepped away, but now Amir caught him in a hold and lifted him over his head. Then he gently put his son down and kissed his forehead. Amir's son prostrated himself at his feet and sought forgiveness for his arrogance. Amir embraced him and said, "O light of my life, one rules with the support of one's champions. We enjoy all manner of privileges because of them. Regardless of circumstances, one must always treat them with great indulgence, show them the utmost respect, and take every care that they feel gratified and honored." His son felt shame from his deed and mortification for his actions and returned to the assembly, where singing and dancing soon resumed.

The news gatherers report that after nine months a son was born to Amir by Mehr-Nigar and his son Amar bin Hamza also became the father of a son. Amir Hamza named his grandson Sa'ad, but did not name his own son. He said to Amar Ayyar, "Take this news to Naushervan and request him to give a name to the child." Within a few days Amar reached

Ctesiphon, and after making salutations, said to Naushervan, "Congratulations on the birth of your grandson. Amir Hamza has stated that he would be indebted to Your Honor if you would name him yourself." Naushervan was greatly pleased by this auspicious news and bestowed a robe of honor on Amar Ayyar and ordered forty days of celebrations in his kingdom, arranging himself for the revels. Naushervan named his grandson Qubad. When Queen Mehr-Angez received these joyous tidings she sent for Amar and inquired about the welfare of Mehr-Nigar and Amir Hamza, and about her grandson's looks and features. She offered Amar a robe of honor, gave him precious jewels, gold, and other gifts, and then granted him leave to depart. Before long Amar returned and related to Amir Hamza all that Naushervan and Mehr-Angez had said and gave him a detailed account of his visit.

When both Qubad and Sa'ad reached the age of four, Amir Hamza gave them to the tutelage of Amar Ayyar. By the time the boys had turned five years old, all who beheld them prayed that the evil eye be warded off them and said, "We have never seen or heard of such comely and well-mannered boys. Even the eye of Heaven could not have ever regarded such paragons. The signs of valor are already evident in their aspects and courage speaks in their faces and features." Amir would recite benedictions [?] to bless the two of them every day and vowed to offer his own life as their sacrifice.

———

The narrator tells that when Zhopin Kaus of Zabul heard the news of Qubad's birth, he wrote a note to Naushervan that read:

> If Hamza has allowed you to keep your throne until now and has not intervened in your affairs, it was because he had no son from Mehr-Nigar. Now a son has been born to him by your daughter. It is highly improbable that he will allow you to continue reigning in peace without attempting to take over control of the empire from you. It is certain that he will overthrow and kill you and seat his son on the throne. In my opinion it would be most wise for you to seek Bahman Jasap's assistance immediately. It was my duty to alert you to the situation and now I have performed it. The next step is your prerogative, for I am but a slave and you are the master.

After reading Zhopin's note, Naushervan said, "I have complete confidence that Hamza would never do me any wrong, as I have often been in his debt." Buzurjmehr answered, "Verily said and most just!" However, Bakhtak and other Sassanid nobles prevailed on the emperor to set out from Ctesiphon to meet Bahman Jasap, and thus planted the seed of fear and misgiving in his heart with their deceitful and devious words. When Bahman Jasap received news that the emperor's procession was approaching his lands, he came out of the city to welcome him and brought Naushervan into the city with great fanfare after the exchange of salutations. Bahman seated Naushervan on the throne and said to him, "Have no fear now. If Hamza should dare to attack us, he will be killed. I shall undertake this task myself." Then Bahman sent a letter to Hamza that read:

Emperor Naushervan has sought refuge in my lands because of your tyranny, and has complained of your brutality and high-handedness. Therefore, I feel it is my duty to apprehend you and hand you over to Naushervan, producing you to him as a prisoner. If you have a claim to manhood, come here and test your mettle against mine and show your courage by facing me.

Amir Hamza laughed heartily upon reading this letter and said, "Alas! God is my witness that I never wished to overthrow Naushervan or to treat him in this vile manner and enthrone Qubad. But now that he has gone over to Bahman to seek refuge and has complained about me, it has become imperative for me to depose him and seat Qubad on his throne and drive him away from his lands." All his counselors and advisers piped up in a chorus, "Indeed, O Sahibqiran! There is no better manner of dealing with this situation. You must first hand over your own throne to Prince Qubad, and make him your heir and order everyone to make offerings to him. Then you may take the next steps and do as you intend." After determining an auspicious moment, Amir Hamza enthroned Prince Qubad as his heir and everyone came and made offerings to him, showering innumerable quantities of gold and jewels upon him in sacrifice. The destitute and the debilitated were also lavished with charity.

Amir headed toward Bahman's lands after forty days of celebrations. When Amir Hamza approached Kohistan and pitched his tents, Bahman sent his son Homan with a body of soldiers to take position on the mountainside so that Hamza would be unable to ascend it and reach high ground and would be foiled in his attempt to control the mountain. When Aadi tried to gain the mountain, Homan, who had already established himself there, started throwing stones at Aadi and his troops, making it impossible for Aadi to advance. In the meanwhile, Amar bin Hamza and Landhoor had arrived there with their armies and saw stones being thrown from the mountaintop and Aadi holding his ground with great courage and determination. Amar bin Hamza, King Landhoor, and Istaftanosh began scaling the mountain in order to dislodge the foe. Homan let loose a barrage of stones at them, but the three managed to climb up, using their shields to ward off the projectiles. Then they pulled out their swords and fell on the infidels, striking at the nation of mischief makers like bolts of lightning. Thousands of Guebers were dispatched to Hell, and with heads hanging in shame, they entered the chambers of God's wrath.

Homan escaped with his life, and in great disarray he went to Bahman and narrated the whole account of the skirmish to him. Bahman grew angry with Homan and said, "It was proved today that you are not my son; otherwise you would never have abandoned the field or run away from facing the sword. Moreover, you give me this account of your pusillanimity and cowardice so merrily." While Bahman was talking, a great dust cloud rose on the horizon and thousands of standards appeared from under its veil. It was announced that the Sahibqiran was approaching with great majesty and grandeur. Bahman said to Bakhtak, "I am very desirous of seeing the Sahibqiran, as his legend precedes him. I would like to see his face now to witness his appearance and features." Bakhtak answered, "If you mount your steed and stand along the way, I shall be able to show you Amir Hamza and you can have a close look at him." Bahman mounted his horse and accompanied Bakhtak.

The first person to appear from under the dragon-shaped standard was Aadi Madi-Karib. Bahman asked Bakhtak, "Is this youth the Sahibqiran whose name is renowned all over the world?" Bakhtak answered, "This champion belongs to the advance guard of Amir Hamza's camp and he is the foremost warrior of his intrepid army." As the champions of Amir Hamza's army came marching forward, Bakhtak gave their names and stations to Bahman with a short account of their talents. Behind the champions marched Amar Ayyar. Bahman asked Bakhtak, "Who is this oddly shaped creature?" Bakhtak answered, "That is the notorious Amar Ayyar, whose trickeries are renowned throughout the world. He is the terror of the kings of the Seven Climes and strikes fear in their hearts with his cunning and resourcefulness." The throne of Prince Qubad approached them now, and it seemed as if the resplendent sun had descended to the Earth. Bakhtak said to Bahman, "This is the majestic and magnificent Prince Qubad, Amir Hamza's worthy son and the grandson of Naushervan, and one beloved by young and old."

Then Amir Hamza himself came by riding Ashqar Devzad with great hauteur and ceremony. Bakhtak said, "This is Hamza of whom you have heard. Regard him well now!" Bahman was astonished to witness Amir Hamza's stateliness and magnificence, and said, "With *this* short stature he killed the *devs* of Qaf and prevailed over mighty champions of the world? How could even he—with all his valor—have routed the rebellious hordes of Qaf?" Bakhtak answered, "Once you get into the arena with him you will realize the truth behind his small stature and seemingly weak constitution. Beware, O Bahman, that there is no refuge from his sword, for once he unsheathes it, he single-handedly puts to flight a thousand-strong force. There is such power in his arms and he is so courageous and gallant, that even the mighty Rustam himself—let alone mere men—would have asked for reprieve from his might." Bahman replied, "It would be improper to challenge him today as he has just arrived tired, worn, and exhausted from his journey. But, come tomorrow, I will settle the score with him and inflict on him a humiliation he will never forget."

The next morning Amir wrote a letter to Bahman. After detailing his exploits in Qaf and describing his many victories over renowned champions of the world, he stated: "I have arrived here at your calling. You would do well to send Naushervan, Bakhtak, and Zhopin as prisoners to me and then present yourself to me with your treasury and ennoble yourself by converting to the True Faith. Otherwise, the day of your refusal will become for you an evil day, and a most shameful defeat would become your lot."

Amir Hamza did not send the letter with Amar Ayyar for fear that he might show disregard for Bahman's honor and harass, humiliate, and terrorize him. Hamza sent it instead with his son Amar bin Hamza, and also sent along a wise man to accompany him. Amar bin Hamza set out on his steed, and along the way he came across the keeper of Amir Hamza's horses, who was calling out for his master's help. When Amar bin Hamza asked him the reason for his distress, he answered, "I graze Your Honor's herd of horses. I had brought them to this pasture when Bahman's men appeared and took them away." Amar bin Hamza asked him, "How far do you think they would have gone?" He replied, "You can see them riding away in the distance. The dust cloud that you see is raised by their hooves. Look hard and tell me if you can see them." Amir's son gave Bah- man's men chase, and upon approaching them, challenged them fero- ciously. Their gall turned to water at his cry, and they trembled with fear.

Seeing Amar bin Hamza approach all by himself, Homan stopped in his tracks. When Amir's son drew near, Homan asked him, "Who are you?" Amar bin Hamza answered, "I am the son of Amir Hamza and your Angel of Death." At these words Homan rushed toward him with a drawn sword. Amar bin Hamza brought his horse up alongside him and lifted him clear out of the saddle.

He swung Homan over his head, threw him on his back to the ground and, pressing his dagger to Homan's throat, said, "Proclaim that God is one and there is no other God but Him, and declare the truth of the Faith of Ibrahim, or else I will slaughter you this instant and pollute my shin- ing dagger with your filthy blood." Homan asked for reprieve and said, "O Amar! Spare my life and keep yourself from murdering me! When my father converts to the True Faith I shall have no objection to converting as well. Then I, too, shall claim it as my faith without the least scruple and shall never set foot outside the bounds of obedience to you." When Amar bin Hamza got up off his chest, Homan kissed his feet and asked, "Whence did you come and where are you now headed?" Amar bin Hamza answered, "I am carrying the Sahibqiran's message to present it before your father in his court." Homan said, "I would request that you do not share today's unfortunate incident with anyone in the court." Amar bin Hamza granted his request. Homan then departed for his court, and after returning the horses to his groom, Amar bin Hamza himself headed for Bahman's court.

Bahman was present in the court along with Naushervan, Zhopin, Bakhtak, and Buzurjmehr, and they were conversing together and enjoy- ing one another's company. After offering salutations to Buzurjmehr, Amar bin Hamza threw Hamza's letter before Bahman, but said nothing to him. After reading the letter, Bahman tore it up, thus portraying his re- sentment. Amar bin Hamza said, "Alas, my father forbade me from taking any excesses, or else I would have torn you up in the same way that you tore up that letter, and extracted your imprudent brains from your heed- less skull." At a signal from Bahman, Homan rushed at Amar bin Hamza with his sword drawn and dealt him a blow with great prowess and cun- ning. Amar bin Hamza twisted his arm and wrested the sword from Homan's hand with great alacrity, and lifted him over his shoulders and slammed him to the floor. Homan's younger brother then charged Amar bin Hamza with a drawn sword, but met the same fate, his own daring having proved too costly for him. Seeing this example of Amar bin Hamza's courage and strength, Bahman greatly praised him and said without reserve, "I am not surprised at his bravery and might, for a lion's cub is born of a lion, and a valiant man's progeny will always prove brave." With these words, he put a robe of honor on Amar bin Hamza with his own hands, and kissed the young man's hands before giving him leave to depart.

Upon his return to camp, Amar bin Hamza recounted the whole story of his trip to Amir Hamza and narrated the details of all that had transpired. Amir embraced his son—the light of his life—and showered him with gold and jewels.

The following day Bahman took to the battlefield with his army. Amir Hamza also arrayed his force there. Amar bin Hamza kissed the leg of his father's throne to seek his permission for combat, turned his steed to face the battlefield, and issued a challenge to his adversaries, at which point Bahman signaled to Homan. He rode into the arena carrying a mace and raised it above his head to strike a blow against Amar bin Hamza, who foiled it. Amar bin Hamza lifted Homan clear off his saddle, whirled him seven times above his head, and slammed him to the ground. Then he tied Homan up and presented him to Amir Hamza, who gave him into Amar Ayyar's custody. Bahman sent his second son into combat and he fared the same as his brother. Bahman's side sounded the signal to announce the end of hostitilies for the day and the king returned sorrowfully to his camp.

Amir Hamza, on the other hand, returned to his camp accompanied by trumpets of victory. All of his men presented themselves to make offerings to congratulate him on his victory. In the evening, Amir Hamza sent for Bahman's sons and said to them, "Convert to the True Faith and refrain from fire worship." They answered, "O Amir! We will convert to the True Faith the day our father does so. Pray show us this kindness and do not force us to convert this day." Amir Hamza set them free that instant and conferred robes of honor upon them. The brothers returned to their father, and after kissing his feet, told him what had happened, upon which Bahman praised Amir Hamza's conduct. The next day, he again sounded the drums of war and entered the arena, and Amir Hamza arrayed his army opposite his as before. Amar bin Hamza went forth for combat wielding his lance in his hands. That day Bahman himself came out to fight. Amar bin Hamza said, "It is not our tradition to deal the first blow, and I cannot violate this tradition. I will show you what I possess by way of courage and unleash my warring might after you have dealt me the first blow." Bahman brought his mace down on him with all the might he possessed, but Amar bin Hamza foiled the blow and said, "I give you two more blows, and then it will be my turn." Bahman dealt two more strikes with all his might and Amar bin Hamza foiled them both with great adroitness and effort. Then he wheeled around Prophet Ishaq's steed Siyah Qitas, and said, "Beware now, O Bahman! Summon all your senses to the ready. Now it is my turn to deal you the blow that will lay you flat!"

At this, Amar bin Hamza dealt Bahman such a mighty blow that sweat broke from every pore of Bahman's body. In that manner the two of them continued battling from morning to sunset until their maces shattered and their senses were disordered. As neither one was able to declare victory or subdue his adversary, both of them finally returned to their camps. Amir Hamza embraced his son and made many offerings in sacrifice for him. He distributed alms and charity among the poor and the destitute and then asked his son, "What manner of combatant is Bahman, and how do you reckon him in power and might?" He answered, "If there ever existed a man worthy of being called a champion warrior besides yourself, it is Bahman. Indeed he is a consummate swordsman."

In the morning the trumpet of war was sounded in both camps and Bahman again descended into the arena seeking combat. The battlefield soon rang again with the preparations of the two armies. Landhoor took his leave of Amir and confronted Bahman, who said to him, "O warrior, give me your name and rank." Landhoor answered, "I am Landhoor bin Saadan, the Khusrau of India. My purpose in life is to lay low mighty warriors and brave men." Bahman said to this, "Your great renown has reached me, and when you fight me today it will become manifest whether or not your reputation is deserved." Having said this, Bahman dealt Landhoor a mighty blow with his mace and witnesses on both sides saw a spark rise from the weapon's impact. Both armies heard the landing of the blow and every man held his breath in anticipation. But Landhoor escaped unscathed from the blow and returned such a mighty blow himself that a spark of fire arose from it up to the fires of Hell in the heavens. Bahman marveled at this and said, "Indeed your reputation has done you justice. You are a man worthy of your name, and none among the champion warriors can compare with your mettle." The two champions fought until evening using all kinds of devices, but neither was able to best the other or inflict the least harm on his adversary. When the drums announced the day's end and both champions returned to their respective camps, Amir Hamza asked Landhoor, "Tell me what Bahman is worth as a warrior, and give me an account of his prowess." Landhoor answered, "What your son stated was indeed true."

In the morning the armies again prepared for battle. Bahman came out into the arena and once again sought combat. Aadi Madi-Karib rode out this time to meet him. Bahman asked, "Who are you, O warrior?" Aadi answered, "I lead the advance guard of Amir Hamza's army. I am devoted to his service and my name is Aadi Madi-Karib." Bahman answered, "O big gut! Your mission should be stuffing your belly, not answering warriors' challenges in battle. I invite you to my camp's kitchen today to share food and drink at my table." Aadi answered, "Indeed you harvest idle thoughts and uselessly burden my ears. Do not occupy me with this inane talk. As the saying goes, what is in the dish will come out in the ladle. Before long you will taste a choice cut of my sword and see how soon it will make you full to bursting with life! If you can escape with your life, you may host me yet and celebrate your existence. Deal me now the blow that you have." First, the two of them fought with maces, then Bahman caught hold of Aadi by his cummerbund and lifted him up to his knee[13] from the ground with mighty effort. Aadi showered powerful punches on his head, causing Bahman to lose his hold. Sounding the drums to announce the day's end, Bahman returned to his camp, unable to continue combat any further that day.

The next day, Bahman took Aadi Madi-Karib's six brothers captive. The fate of these champions falling prisoner to the enemy greatly grieved Amir Hamza. Amar Ayyar said to him, "If you should order me, I would go and secure the release of our warriors." Amir answered, "Nothing would gladden my heart more." Amar Ayyar then entered Bahman's camp in disguise. Bahman was quite overjoyed that night and ordered that the captive warriors from Hamza's camp be produced before him en masse. Then he asked Naushervan, "How do you recommend they be treated?" Naushervan said, "It would be best to put them to the sword. The more champions who are lost to Hamza's camp the better. To have them killed would best serve our purposes." Bakhtak said, "I recommend that they be hanged!" Zhopin said, "I say that they should be killed for their meat. You see how plump they are. They should be fed to the hunting dogs so that the animals may sink their fangs in their juicy flesh." Buzurjmehr commented, "The command given by a ruler is unalterable. Do what would be considered just in the judgment of brave men, and act as the demands of righteousness decree." Bahman next asked his sons and brothers, "What do you counsel and advise in this matter? Would it be just to take their lives?" They answered, "They should be decapitated and their heads displayed at the towers so that the enemy camp may find an example in their fate and terror may overwhelm their hearts." Bahman said to his sons, "I marvel at the depths of baseness to which your minds have sunk. It was Hamza who, when he had power over you, did you a signal favor. And now you advocate the murder of his companions? Do you not feel a single pang of shame, or does a sense of gratitude never make you pause and reconsider your thoughts?" Then Bahman conferred robes of honor on every captive man present there and released them all at once.

Amar Ayyar then revealed himself and said to Bahman, "I would like to offer you a thousand accolades for your wisdom and great plaudits for your sagacity. Your actions are becoming to a brave warrior like yourself. I had come here to secure the release of these men. If you had not set them free yourself, no one would have found it within their power to harm them even a little." Amar Ayyar then addressed Bakhtak, saying, "You were the one who counseled that Amir's commanders be hanged, and solicited other opinions favorable to yours as well. I will change my own name, O villain, if I do not see to it that your ass is pierced by the point of an impaling stake." Bakhtak trembled at these words, made several bows to Amar, and said, "I uttered those words only out of the consideration that my words do not offend Bahman; otherwise, I would have suggested exactly what Bahman himself did in the end. Indeed he acted most sagaciously by setting the men free." Before departing, Amar confiscated Bakhtak's headgear and said, after clouting him on the head, "It has been a long time since you sent me the tribute of your beard. Make sure to remit it without further delay to save me a trip to your pavilion and a second visit to your camp."

The commanders set free by Bahman returned to Amir Hamza and narrated their story to him. Amir Hamza praised Bahman and said, "I hope to God that he converts to the True Faith and is ennobled by the wealth of God's grace, for verily he is a noble champion."

The two armies again flooded the battlefield the next morning, and those valiant crocodiles readied themselves to ford the sea of war. Bahman entered the arena and called out, "O Hamza, why do you not show your face in the arena and display your bravery in combat, instead of sending your champions to fight me?" The moment Amir heard this challenge, he took the reins of Ashqar Devzad and rode out to answer his call. Bahman asked him to deal the first blow. Amir answered, "It is not the custom of the followers of the True God to take precedence in combat. Deal me the blow you are most proud of." Bahman was greatly pleased by Amir's reply and said, "O Hamza, I know you are a renowned warrior, famed for your courage and celebrated for your bravery, and you wish me to strike the first blow. It would be best if I tried to dislodge you from the ground by lifting you, and you do the same to me. The one who is the lesser of the two must obey the superior and surrender his arms to him." Amir happily consented to this proposition and said to him, "I would like you to try to lift me from the ground." Bahman caught hold of Amir's cummerbund and spent every last bit of energy he had in trying to lift him up, but he was unable to move him even a fraction of an inch.

Amir called out to Amar Ayyar in the language of *ayyars*, "Tell our companions to put cotton in their ears." Amar Ayyar immediately carried out his orders. Amir then let out a mighty cry of "God is Great!" Many men in Bahman's camp lost their hearing from the violent force of his bellow, and even the beasts of the forest retreated deep into the woods. If Bahman had not blocked his ears with his fingers, his eardrums would have burst, blood would have issued from his ears, and he would have gone deaf. Amir then caught hold of Bahman by his waistband and whirled him seven times around his head before tying him up and giving him to Amar Ayyar as a prisoner. Bahman's army was ready to attack, but Bahman signaled them to desist and kept them from assaulting Amir Hamza. Sounding the drums to announce the day's end, Hamza returned to his pavilion in all safety.

Amir sent for Bahman and offered him the jewel-encrusted chair of champions and, showing him much favor, said, "O Bahman! You have the choice to prove your manliness and honor your word, or revert on it. Say now that God has no partner and that the Faith of Ibrahim is the True Faith." Bahman said, "O Hamza, you well know that Naushervan and Zhopin approached me and sought my aid. I offered them support in the traditions of chivalry. Do me another great favor and forgive their offenses as well. For this kindness I will become your slave with all my heart and soul." Amir answered, "I will do so only on condition that they convert to the True Faith. If not, I will murder them with my own hands and they will never find reprieve from my sword, the slayer of infidels." Bahman replied, "If you should order it, I would go and prevail on them to submit to you and follow the path of the righteous. Then in one gathering all of them could convert to the True Faith and surrender their authority to you." Amir sent Bahman away after giving him a resplendent robe of honor. Bahman went and gave a whole account of events to Naushervan and Zhopin, and then said to them, "Since I was unable to overpower Hamza, I know for a fact that no one else in this world will triumph over him: Nobody will be able to subdue or overwhelm him."

Naushervan and Zhopin both admitted the truth of what Bahman said, and they accompanied him and other men of their court before Amir Hamza. Amir Hamza welcomed Naushervan, led him to his throne, and seated him there, treating him with great deference and respect. He offered Bahman a champion's throne and gave him high honor. Amir also offered separate thrones to Bakhtak and Zhopin and extended each man a rank and station according to his status. Bahman told Amir, "Order us, and say what you would like us to do now." Amir taught the Act of Faith to Naushervan, Bahman, Zhopin, and Bakhtak. Then he ordered his musicians to play festive tunes, and for a full two weeks he held celebrations in honor of Naushervan and Bahman.

Of Amir's Departure for Mecca, and of His Taking Prisoner Shaddad Abu-Amar Habashi, and of Shaddad's Converting to the True Faith

After these festivities were over, Aadi said to Amir, "There is very little animal fodder left in this region and the animals grow hungry and suffer from shortage of food. We must move our camp elsewhere." Amir said, "Very well! Move the advance camp toward Kaus Hisar!" Naushervan now said to Amir, "O Abul-Ala! Old age is upon me and I wish to retire to a peaceful nook where I can bide the rest of my borrowed existence reflecting on God. I wish to enthrone Qubad and make him emperor in my place." Amir yielded to him, saying, "Do as you please. I shall humbly obey your wishes in the matter." Then Naushervan enthroned Qubad and made him his heir, and departed for Ctesiphon along with Buzurjmehr, while Amir Hamza went toward Kaus Hisar and ordered his camp to move quarters there. Amir Hamza stayed in Kaus Hisar for a few days. He occupied himself with pursuits of the hunt during the day and indulged himself in revels at night. One day he was informed of the arrival of a messenger from Mecca bearing a missive for him. Amir sent for him and received Khvaja Abdul Muttalib's letter, which read:

> My dutiful son, ever since you have come of age no infidel has dared show his face for fear of you. But Shaddad Abu-Amar Habashi has sacked our city and intends to destroy Mecca. Pray arrive here speedily, or else no follower of the True Faith will be left alive here and none will escape his tyranny. It was my duty to communicate this news to you and I have fulfilled it.

Amir showed the letter to all the commanders of his army and then said to Bahman, "Until my return, I wish you to rule over my camp in my stead and carry out the duties of administration to the best of your abilities. Consider my companions and my sons as your own and treat them likewise. I shall depart on the campaign to Mecca and will triumph over the infidels with help from God Almighty. I shall soon return, as I will not be occupied there for many days, you may rest assured."

Bahman submitted respectfully, saying with folded arms, "It is not the place of a slave to occupy the seat of his master, and it would be a trespass for a man to ascend his lord's throne." Amir, however, prevailed on him to accept the trust. He left him in charge of his army and his sons, and instructed him in all the details of his duties and all the facts pertaining to his task. Afterward, Amir Hamza departed with Amar Ayyar for Mecca.

After passing all the stations of the journey, they came to Mecca, and Amir Hamza asked Amar, "What must we do now? What steps should we take to repel the foe?" Amar answered, "You must leave Ashqar Devzad in this wilderness to roam free, and proceed from here on foot." Amir said to Ashqar in the Jinni language, "Graze here without any fear or apprehension, and come to me when you hear my war cry."

Then Amir took Amar and they went on their way. When they approached the camp of the Ethiopians, Amar encountered an acrobat. They spoke together and Amar ingratiated himself into his graces with his loquacious tongue and by showing him all the signs of great endearment. Amar Ayyar said to Amir Hamza, "I am headed for the court of the king of Ethiopia to do my work. When I send for one Faulad Pehalwan, you must present yourself speedily and make no delay in appearing before me." After giving these instructions to Amir Hamza, Amar dressed himself as the master of a troupe of tumblers and took a procession to the entrance of the court of the king of Ethiopia, Shaddad Abu-Amar Habashi, and arrived at his door. Amar Ayyar said to the guards there, "Pray announce me and inform your king of my arrival. I hope to entertain the king and be rewarded by his munificence. I have come from a distant land, having heard the reputation of his court, and have brought many marvelous tricks to amuse him." The heralds announced the arrival of Amar Ayyar, and the king sent for him.

At the court, Amar displayed his many talents, which pleased King Shaddad. The king offered a reward to Amar, but he would not accept it. Instead, he went and stood respectfully before Shaddad, who said to Amar, "I offered you a reward, but you did not accept it. Tell me now what you wish to ask for." Amar declared with folded arms, "My uncle has a slave who has left his ancestral work and become a wrestler. He tor-

ments me night and day and rebukes and insults me. I wish you to warn
and chastise him so that he will refrain from his audacious ways and return to the path of obedience." Shaddad said, "Where is he? Send for him
and present him before me." Amar called out, "O Faulad Pehalwan! Present yourself!" Upon his call, Amir Hamza entered the court.

Shaddad was irked that Amir did not offer him any salutation or
greeting. Shaddad therefore said harshly, "O slave-born tumbler, why do
you torment your master and enroll your name in the ranks of ingrates?"
Amir answered, "I am no slave! But *you* must indeed be one, and ingratitude your middle name." Amar said to Shaddad, "See, my lord! He even
talks back to Your Honor! He is such a headstrong fool that even your
presence holds no fear for him." Shaddad ordered an executioner to sever
Amir Hamza's head. An Ethiopian executioner named Shamsheer-Zan
drew his sword and approached Amir to behead him, but Amir immediately lifted him over his head with one hand and began whirling him
around as if he were offering the executioner as his sacrifice.[14] Amir spun
him so hard and for so long that Shamsheer-Zan went limp and became
disoriented. While turning him over his head with one hand, Amir delivered him a mighty blow with the other, and Shamsheer-Zan sank to the
ground on his knees and his soul soon left his body.

Then Shaddad sent another executioner to do the job, and Amir dispatched him to Hell along the same road. One after another, Shaddad
sent forty Ethiopians to execute Amir, and he treated all of them to the
same fate and packed them all off to Hell. Then Shaddad ordered his
champion warriors to behead the slave, but none of them would step forward despite Shaddad's repeated commands. All of them kept away for
fear of Amir. So, Shaddad drew his own sword and charged Amir himself.
Shouting his war cry, Amir caught hold of Shaddad by his cummerbund,
whirled him overhead, and slammed him to the ground. Then, drawing
his dagger, Amir bore down upon him and declared, "Little did you know
that I am Hamza. Even if Rustam himself were to confront me, let alone
you, I would humiliate him the same way." Shaddad responded, "O Amir,
I took on this mission at the instigation of Naushervan. Indeed I was deceived by him into leading my army here. If you were to spare my life, I
would never return again or ever think of doing battle with you." Amir
said, "I will not let you go alive but will crush your head with my infidel-
smashing mace unless you convert to the True Faith." Shaddad was
forced to convert to the True Faith and submit to Amir's orders. Amir
then got up off the king's chest and embraced him and spared his life.

When the people of Mecca heard Amir's war cry, they gathered with Khvaja Abdul Muttalib to receive him. Amir rushed to throw himself at his father's feet. Then performing the ritual of walking around Khvaja Abdul Muttalib, he offered himself as his father's sacrifice. Khvaja Abdul Muttalib embraced his son and kissed his forehead and eyes and escorted him into Mecca. Everyone brought something to give away in sacrifice for Amir or to make as an offering to him. Amir Hamza conferred a robe of honor on the king of Ethiopia and ordered that repair work [?] be carried out in the city. Amir also bestowed a large sum of riches and rewards on all Meccans and relieved even the mendicants of their penury[?].

Shaddad went to Naushervan's court and told the guards to inform the emperor that Shaddad Abu-Amar Habashi was departing to his own land and had come to take his leave. Upon hearing this, Naushervan sent for him. Shaddad kissed the foot of his throne and said, "Your Honor caused me to be humiliated at Hamza's hands, and I suffered great distress at this." Having spoken, Shaddad took hold of Naushervan by his cummerbund and carried him out of his court. Observing that the hands of the royal slaves had moved to the hilts of their swords, Shaddad declared, "If anyone touches me, I will smash the emperor against the ground and he will die on the instant. Then the entire operation of the empire will be thrown into turmoil." Nobody interfered with Shaddad after this threat, and he took Naushervan prisoner to his land. There he constructed a cage and chained Naushervan's feet to its bars. Then he hung the cage in his court and put Naushervan on two rations of millet bread and water a day.

Having this harsh treatment meted out to him, Naushervan asked Shaddad, "What wrong did I ever do you to be recompensed in this manner? Have you no fear of God?" Shaddad answered, "If you had not sent for me and dispatched me to sack Mecca, I would never have been humiliated as I was by Hamza and led to compromise my dignity." Naushervan replied, "Indeed I am completely unaware of this scheme. It must have been Bakhtak who sent for you, and on whose account you suffered these calamities." Shaddad said, "If that is the case, send for Bakhtak and give him into my hands so that I may release you and imprison him instead in this cage." Naushervan fell silent, realizing that a helpless man's vexation gnaws only him, and he spoke not another word.

———

Now hear of Amir Hamza. After a few days' stay in Mecca, he sought leave of his father. Khvaja Abdul Muttalib said, "My dear son, I have now seen you after many years and my heart is not yet fully sated with the sight of you. If you stayed here another year, it would please me greatly." Upon that, Amir acquiesced to his father's wishes. Bakhtak, who had stayed behind with Bahman, had also heard that Khvaja Muttalib had not granted Hamza leave to depart Mecca, and Amir would be spending another year there. Bakhtak realized that the field had thus been left open to him and he should make use of the opportunity.

Bakhtak forged a letter from Naushervan addressed to Zhopin and Hurmuz. Giving it to a messenger, he instructed him to pretend that he had just arrived from Ctesiphon carrying Naushervan's missive. In that letter Bakhtak had written:

> Be it known to you that I sent Abu-Amar Habashi to Mecca to lay ruin to the city. The followers of the True Faith were slaughtered one and all, and the citizens of Mecca got retribution for their deeds. Shaddad took Hamza and Amar prisoner and brought them to his land, where he hanged them and put an end to their menace. You may slaughter the followers of the True Faith in Hamza's camp without the least worry, showing them no reprieve or mercy. Afterward, you may hand over Mehr-Nigar to Bahman's custody.

By chance, the messenger crossed paths with Zhopin, who had gone out for an excursion. The messenger handed him the missive, and upon reading it, Zhopin went straight to Bahman and showed him the letter. After perusing it, Bahman said to Zhopin, "This is nothing but a trick played by you. I know you well and I will never believe a word you say." Zhopin swore that while he could not vouch for the veracity of the report the letter had come to him through a royal messenger. In the end, Bahman believed the news of Hamza's death and assumed that Hamza had passed away. He said, "A thousand sighs, alas, that Hamza did not take me with him. He has left a gaping hole in my heart." Then Bahman said, "The will of God has prevailed. All that has happened came about by divine decree, and none may alter or influence it. Now Hamza's two sons and his grandson will have my allegiance and I will put myself at their service." Then he said to the messenger, "Tell me verily, what are the facts of the matter? I wish to know exactly what happened and how it came about."

The messenger had been instructed well by Bakhtak and had become versed in deceitful talk. He readily swore that Amir Hamza had been hanged before his eyes and that Bahman should believe this for a fact. Then Bakhtak said to Bahman, "To pledge your allegiance to someone of Hamza's caliber was perhaps acceptable at the time. However, a mighty champion and powerful lord like yourself must not demean himself by serving under mere boys. Moreover, Naushervan has expressed a desire to accept you as his son-in-law and conferred that high honor upon you. Would it be seemly to serve under boys when you can have the title of Naushervan's son-in-law?" Hearing talk of such an association with Naushervan, Bahman could not resist the temptation. He said to Bakhtak, "If you are counseling me to act on your advice, perhaps you should also tell me a way to do it." Bakhtak answered, "Keep it all a secret for now and do not speak a word of this matter to anyone until we have Mehr-Nigar secure in our hands, and our minds are at rest regarding her custody." Zhopin said, "Today when I present myself at the court, I will tell Hurmuz and King Qubad that the anniversary of my father's death will be commemorated tomorrow and it would be a signal honor for me to have Amir's sons attend the ceremony with their commanders." Bakhtak replied, "That would indeed be an appropriate course of action."

When Zhopin presented himself at the court that night, he made his request to Hurmuz, Qubad, and Amar bin Hamza who accepted his invitation, and the next day they arrived at Zhopin's house along with their commanders. Zhopin offered them food and wine, and when all of them were intoxicated, Zhopin rose and declared to Amar bin Hamza and Qubad, "In the same manner that Your Honors have augmented my honor by your presence, it would confer great honor on me if Princess Mehr-Nigar, too, would condescend to set foot here. I would be deemed worthy of greater respect by everyone because of this honor." Amir's sons sent a message to Princess Mehr-Nigar that it would not be beneath hear dignity to attend the gathering to confer honor on Zhopin.

Upon receiving this message, Princess Mehr-Nigar was conveyed to Zhopin's house to grant his request. As Mehr-Nigar sat there among the women, she overheard someone say, "For the moment the princess is the picture of happiness, but soon she will learn the news and hear what mischief has been afoot." At once, Mehr-Nigar dispatched an attendant to send for Qubad, and she said to him, "Arrange a conveyance for me without delay, and fetch me my palanquin. Some trouble seems under way and mischief is about to break loose." Qubad sent for the conveyance, as that seemed the safest course of action, and soon Mehr-Nigar departed for the fortress. Zhopin and Bahman were then told that Mehr-Nigar had left as soon as she had arrived. Both of them regretted the news and their hearts were cut to pieces by the saws of remorse and repentance. They rued the loss of the great fortune that had slipped from their hands. When Bakhtak learned of this, he comforted Bahman and said, "After losing her husband, she will not have too many avenues open to her. You will make her yours yet."

Following Bakhtak's instructions, Bahman wrung his hands remorsefully and said, "It is a shame that Naushervan's own son Prince Hurmuz must be passed over, and his grandson Qubad appointed heir to the throne—and someone undeserving of the honor should rule in Hurmuz's stead." Amar bin Hamza commented, "What is that to you, Bahman? Why do you wax so eloquent for a cause that is not your own?" Bahman answered, "I speak the truth when I say that this Arab lad is unworthy of the crown and throne, and has no right to rule this magnificent empire!"

When King Landhoor heard this speech, he grew irritated, and said to Bahman, "O Kohi![15] It is a shame that Amir Hamza put an unworthy wretch like yourself in charge of his affairs and office, and gave you a high rank. If he had kept you in your place, you would not have uttered these inauspicious words and made such lofty claims about yourself." Bahman now came into a rage and aimed his sword at Landhoor. But the Khusrau foiled it and answered with a powerful blow of his mace, which put Bahman's arm out of commission, as it inflicted a grievous injury on him. A sword fight broke out in the assembly and outdoors and many Arabs and several of Bahman's followers were injured. Bahman's men carried him away from that place and saved his life.

It came to pass that news of these events reached Bahman's sister, Noor Bano, who had fallen in love with Amar bin Hamza. When she learned that the infidels had imprisoned and injured the followers of the True Faith by dissimulation and deceit, and committed an injustice against them, she left her house and joined the fight, and made heaps of dead infidels on the battlefield with her shining sword. That bloodthirsty warrior killed a thousand men that day with her valiant blade. Homan went and said to her, "Have you taken leave of your senses? Go back to your quarters!" Noor Bano responded by cutting him up with her sword, and Homan fell in two pieces to the ground. When his younger brother saw Homan's riven corpse, he charged her with brandished sword. Noor Bano quickly sent him where she had dispatched his elder brother. After killing both of them, Noor Bano took the Arab commanders back to the fortress and ordered the moats to be filled up with water. The army of the infidels surrounded the fortress on all sides. When the wounds of the Arab commanders had healed, they climbed over the ramparts and did battle with the horde of infidels with great bravery and valor. The infidels then bivouacked beyond the fort's range.

One day the infidels stormed the fort. Qubad said to his mother, "The infidels have the upper hand in the battle. If I may have your permission, I would like to fight and kill them." Mehr-Nigar answered, "May my life become your sacrifice! You are a mere boy. How can I allow you to go into battle?" Qubad then said, "My father triumphed over mighty champions in his boyhood. I am of the same blood. If you do not give me your permission, I will kill myself before your eyes." Noor Bano said to Mehr-Nigar, "There is no harm in allowing Qubad to go to battle. Let him go, and grant him leave with a light heart. I shall accompany him and will be alert and ready to help and succor him. In all circumstances I will be there to assist him and will not allow him to fall into trouble." With a heavy heart, Mehr-Nigar gave Qubad permission to fight.

Qubad decorated himself with his arms and armor, and faced the infidels and challenged them, saying, "O infidels, he among you who desires death should face me and show the quality of his valor." Seeing Qubad in the arena, Bahman said to himself, *How fortunate that Qubad has come to seek combat and got permission from his mother to battle. I shall take him prisoner and keep him in my custody. Pangs of motherly love will rob Mehr-Nigar of her peace of mind, and she will be forced to come to me.* Bahman then faced Qubad and said, "O Arab lad, deal me your best blow!" Qubad answered, "My father has never dealt the first blow in combat, and I shall follow his tradition. I will not violate my father's rule. You should deal the first blow. If I survive it, I will return it and relieve your neck of the burden of your head." Bahman attacked Qubad with his mace, but the boy blocked the blow with his shield and answered with a sword thrust of such finesse that Bahman was grievously injured and barely escaped with his life. Amir's son chased him for a distance of four *kos,* all the while cutting down Bahman's men. Finally, seeing that the infidels had carried Bahman off as swiftly as the wind, the prince returned to his mother and gave her a full account of his battle. Mehr-Nigar offered a wealth of gold and jewels in sacrifice for her son, and gave many riches and goods to the invalids and the poor.

A few days later, Amar bin Hamza and Landhoor presented themselves before Mehr-Nigar and told her that Bahman bore no blame in the

736 • *The Adventures of Amir Hamza*

matter; that it was Bakhtak and Zhopin who were the root cause of the mischief, and that it was Bakhtak's wont to play such tricks. Amar bin Hamza then said, "What must we do now? What strategy should we employ? The infidels have besieged the castle and many of us are injured. There is nothing we can do in these circumstances, and therefore, we find our hearts gripped by trepidation." Qubad declared, "Open the fortress gate and array the army in the field." The commanders forthwith positioned their troops, the war drums were struck, and the sound of kettledrums rumbled in the air like claps of thunder.

Bahman entered the battle arena and called out, "O Arabs, why do you sacrifice your lives for an idle cause? Hamza died a long time ago. Hand Mehr-Nigar over to me and go your own way. Give up on your plans to battle with me, or else I will extract your brains from the skulls of each and every one of you, and put you all to death." Hearing Bahman's scurrilous words, Landhoor sought Amar bin Hamza's leave to fight. He answered, "I give you to God's care. Go into the field and put down the foe with your sword." Then Landhoor and Bahman fought with maces so forcefully that their healed wounds opened up again, and everyone who beheld this was confounded with wonder. They were still fighting when the sun covered its face with the veil of night and both camps sounded the drums of retreat to call back their warriors. The armies returned to their camps to rest and calm their frayed nerves.

In the morning they formed battle arrays again. However, the first soldier was yet to set foot in the arena when a dust cloud rose from the forest and the *ayyars* from both camps rushed there to gather intelligence. They brought back word that Furhad-Akka had come with a large force of intrepid warriors to help Zhopin, and his strength could be judged by the fact that he wielded a mace that weighed seven hundred *maunds*. Upon hearing this, Amir's son said, "We do not care in the least, for God will be our aid!" Then Zhopin received Furhad-Akka and brought him into his camp to brief him in detail about the history of the conflict.

Farhad bin Landhoor took leave of Amir's son to go to face Furhad-Akka. When Furhad-Akka asked him his name, Farhad replied, "My name is Farhad, and I am the son of Landhoor, the Khusrau of India, whose magnificent name and grandeur is known the whole world over." Furhad-Akka asked, "Where is your father?" Farhad answered, "He is with the rest of the army!" Furhad-Akka said, "Your father sent you to fight at a tender age and shamelessly kept himself away. That tells me that he is afraid of dying." Farhad exclaimed, "O wretch! Stop this vile talk! No one could face my father in the arena and walk away alive. Now deal me your blow!"

Irritated by his words, Furhad-Akka brought his seven-hundred-*maund* mace down on Farhad, who parried the blow and said, "I give you two more blows so that you may thus fulfill all your heart's desires. Then it will be my turn, and you will see how shining and sharp is my sword blade." Furhad-Akka struck two more blows, but Farhad did not yield an inch from his place and remained steadfast. After parrying those blows, he said, "Beware now, for I will strike you with my mace!" Farhad brought his mace down with such might that sparks flew from his weapon upon impact. Furhad-Akka parried his blow and replied, "Indeed you are the worthy son of a worthy father. Bravo a thousand times!" When the shining moon sallied forth on its excursion and the day hid its face again behind the shades of night, both camps sounded the call for the end of hostilities and the two armies returned to their camps.

The next morning a champion of the Sherwani tribe sought combat with Furhad-Akka. They fought until evening and proved their mettle in the battlefield. After skirmishing mightily, each of them returned to their camp at the end of the day.

———

Leaving the two armies engaged in battle, let us now hear an account of the Sahibqiran. One night in the realm of dreams, Amir saw that the infidels had conducted a night raid on the camp of the followers of the True Faith and that many of his commanders had been carried injured from the battlefield. He started from the dream and described it to Amar Ayyar, who said, "O Amir, you never have dreams that prove false. If you permit me, I will go investigate and find out what has come to pass." Amir gave Amar Ayyar leave to go and instructed him in the particulars of the camp and all of the delicacies of the situation.

Now hear of the battlefield. When Amar arrived there he found Furhad-Akka and Istaftanosh fighting each other. At his arrival, his camp rang with festive notes played by the music gallery. His army, which had lost confidence due to their smaller size, felt its spirits revive and each soldier took heart at the sight of Amar. Bahman said to Bakhtak, "You wretch! I thought you told us that Amar Ayyar and Hamza were both dead!" Bakhtak responded, "I know nothing of the matter. All I know is what Naushervan himself wrote in the letter and what I learned from his confirmation of the news." Bahman grabbed Bakhtak and hurled him toward Zhopin. As each man had life remaining to him, Bakhtak fell to the ground instead. Bahman felt great remorse at his past actions toward Hamza and lamented his shameful deeds.

After acquainting himself with all the facts, Amar Ayyar offered words of comfort to Qubad and Amar bin Hamza. He dressed the wounds of his champions with *noshidaru* and returned to Amir Hamza, traveling night and day without taking a break in his journey. When he reached Mecca, Amir asked him all the news. Then the Sahibqiran took leave of his father and prepared to go to his army's aid. He mounted Ashqar Devzad and, taking Amar along, departed for Kaus Hisar with a large entourage that included many of his friends.

Now hear an account of the battlefield. The two armies were arrayed in the field when a dust cloud sprang up billowing with great force from the direction of the forest. Scouts from both camps hastened there to gather the news and found out that a Turkic warrior named Sarkob had arrived with an intrepid and vast force to assist Naushervan's army. The infidels received Sarkob joyously and conducted him to their encampment, and his army set up camp in the same field. Sarkob asked, "Where is Hamza? Give me his particulars and identify him to me." Zhopin answered, "Hamza is not present, but his two sons are in the battlefield." Sarkob replied, "My army is all worn and tired today, but tomorrow I will see them on the battlefield. They will be taught a lesson they will never forget."

In the meanwhile, Furhad-Akka rode his steed into the battlefield and sought combat. Amar bin Hamza's son, Sa'ad, asked his father's permission to answer Furhad's call. Amar bin Hamza said to him, "Light of my eyes, you are not of age to go into battle. Do not think of the battleground and refrain from thoughts of fighting." His son replied, with arms folded across the chest in humility, "Uncle Qubad and I are of the same age, and there is no accomplishment to which he has a claim where I am lacking. I find it most shameful that while he participates in battle, I remain a mere spectator; and where he wins laurels as a warrior, I stand idle."

Amar bin Hamza was forced against his wishes to give Sa'ad leave to fight. Sa'ad started by reciting the name of God and then entered the arena to answer Furhad-Akka's call. Upon seeing him, the infidels said, "It is a strange nation where young boys take part in battles and face our champions without the least fear." Sarkob asked, "Who is this boy who has entered the arena?" Bahman answered, "He is Hamza's grandson, who is resolved upon combat with Furhad-Akka and has come to fight him."

Sarkob exclaimed, "How can a boy like him compete against Furhad-Akka?" Bahman answered, "Let us see! We will soon find out." While they were having this discussion, Sa'ad issued his challenge, crying, "O infidels! He among you who desires to drink from the goblet of doom should come forward and show me his worth." Furhad-Akka galloped forth and dealt Sa'ad a blow of his mace and declared, "There! I struck and laid him low!" Sa'ad emerged from the cloud of dust created by the blow and said, "You Gueber and black-faced liar! Do not wax so eloquent with false claims. Tell me who you struck and laid low, for I have descended into the arena as your Angel of Death and am still here before your eyes." Sa'ad then spurred on his horse and dealt Furhad-Akka a blow with his sword that severed his mace-wielding arm. It fell to the ground along with the mace. Furhad-Akka attempted to turn his back and escape to his army when Sa'ad spurred on his horse again and dealt him another blow, severing his other arm as well and dispatching that warrior to the Future State. Sa'ad's *ayyars* cut off Furhad-Akka's head with great alacrity, decapitating his filthy corpse. Festive notes were sounded in Amir Hamza's camp, while Naushervan's camp rang with cries of lamentation and the tongues there that had been wagging with tall claims suddenly fell silent. They were all shocked at witnessing a young boy killing a notable warrior like Furhad-Akka with supreme ease, without receiving the least cut or scratch himself. Sarkob said to Bahman, "Praiseworthy indeed are the parents who raised such a brave and strong son. His father has every reason to be proud of him." Then each camp sounded the drums of retreat and the armies returned to their resting places.

Hurmuz sat down for a meal with his commanders and champions. He indulged in all manner of pleasures, and meat and wine were sent for. Sarkob had too much wine and lost command of his reason. Seeing Bahman sitting beside Hurmuz, he called out, "O Kohi! How dare you seat yourself at a higher station than myself? The heady wine of pride has made you completely oblivious of all considerations of propriety." Bahman replied, "Have you gone mad that you say these harsh words to me? Have you no fear of my courage and might?" Sarkob rose from his place and threw a powerful punch at Bahman, who caught hold of Sarkob by his waist and, lifting him over his head, slammed him to the ground. Hurmuz interceded and settled the dispute between them by counseling both men, calling an end to their mischief, and dismissing the assembly.

In the morning, the warring armies had just arranged themselves in battle formation when a dust cloud rose from the ground in such abundance that it choked off even the wind. Ayyars from both camps rushed off to gather intelligence, and it was soon announced that Amar Ayyar and Amir Hamza were on their way there with a vast army. A wave of joy swept through Hamza's camp and their musicians sounded joyful notes. When he appeared before them, every commander and warrior kissed Amir Hamza's feet, and he embraced them in return. Amir's arrival brought much needed relief to his followers.

Amir Hamza rode Ashqar Devzad onto the battlefield and called out to Bahman, "O Kohi, what wrong did I ever do you and how did I injure you that you have avenged yourself on me in this way? If you really are a man of courage, come out and face me and prove how valiant you are!" Bahman said to Hurmuz, "I am unable even to look Hamza in the eye; I will not fight him. Verily, whoever has started this mischief has created a mountain of trouble. Now you are the master of your own fate. I will have nothing more to do with this business." Hurmuz answered, "Indeed it was not my doing but Bakhtak's!"

In the end, Sarkob went forward to encounter Amir and attacked him with his mace. Amir parried his blow and said to him, "O warrior, I shall give you two more chances so that you may exert yourself to the best of your ability and your heart may be requited of its yearnings." Sarkob attacked a second time and Amir Hamza again parried it. With great consternation, Sarkob struck mightily a third time, and a great spark was produced from the impact of the blow. Such a great amount of dust rose into the air that it covered both armies in a screen of darkness and no one was able to see a thing. Sarkob shouted his war cry and declared, "There! I have killed Hamza and returned clay to clay! He was a mere human being, after all. If I had landed such a blow on a mountain, it also would have become dust!"

But Amir spurred on his horse from out of the cloud of dust and declared, "O Gueber! Who is it you claim to have killed? Take guard now, for it is my turn to strike, and you will learn the true meaning of landing a blow! Even if you survive this, your entire existence will be called before your eyes and you will remain bereft of your senses until Judgment Day!" As Amir landed his mace on Sarkob's head, he exited his saddle and balanced himself on the horse's rump. The mace landed on Sarkob's horse's back, and the beast collapsed in the dust. When Sarkob tried to hamstring Amir's mount, the Sahibqiran deftly dismounted and stood face to face with Sarkob. After fighting with maces until midday, they drew swords and skirmished together for two hours. The glittering swords clashed and sparks flew without cease but neither received any injury by the hand of the other, and both remained ready to fight to the end.

Amir Hamza said, "O Sarkob, we have tried all the blows. The only test that now remains is for one of us to lift the other person from the ground. If you succeed, I will pledge allegiance to you and never fight you again. If I succeed, then you must pledge the same. If you consider yourself a warrior, you will not reject this proposal." Sarkob acquiesced happily to the proposition. He put his arms around Amir Hamza's waist and exerted himself so fully that his ankles sank into the ground and blood began to drip from his nostrils. Nevertheless, Amir did not budge in the least and his feet remained firmly planted on the ground. Thereafter, Amir caught hold of Sarkob by his waist and bellowed his war cry so lustily that it burst the eardrums of many infidels, and their blood froze in their veins from terror.

Sarkob thought that the Angel Israfil[16] had blown the Last Trumpet and the seventh heaven had crashed to the ground. He looked up toward the sky. Amir lifted him from the ground, and after whirling him around seven times over his head, slammed him to the ground. After securing Sarkob with a rope, Amir handed him to Amar Ayyar, much to the shame and ignominy of the adversary.

As darkness was falling, Amir Hamza ordered the call of retreat for the day and returned victorious and triumphant to the fort. The infidels also returned to their camp, crying and lamenting. From God's bounty the followers of the True Faith provided for a great revelry, and meat and wine were served. Amir sent for Sarkob and then asked him, "Tell me how I laid you low." Sarkob put his head at Amir's feet and replied, "O Amir, none on the face of the Earth would be able to defeat you. When apportioning power and might, He bestowed ninety-nine parts on you and distributed one part among the rest of all mankind. Instruct me in the tenets of the True Faith and let me be blessed by its wealth. I hereby renounce idols and idolatry." Amir instructed Sarkob in the Act of Faith and embraced him. He conferred a resplendent robe of honor on him and seated him on a gold throne. Amir gave him a high rank among those present, and then held revels for three days and three nights.

On the fourth day, Amir ordered the drums of war to be sounded and readied his camp to engage again in fighting the infidels. He arrayed his army in fourteen rows while the enemy forces also arranged themselves in battle formations. The preparations would remind one of the war between Sikander and Dara.[17] Again that day Amir Hamza entered the battlefield, and after making the cry of "God is Great!" challenged Bahman, shouting, "O Bahman, you returned evil for good. If you call yourself a man, come and face me and do not run away from the fight!" Bahman said to Hurmuz, "I will never face Hamza and be humiliated at his hands. Order the army and ready them to fall on Hamza as a body, and forbid them to turn back without killing him."

At a sign from Hurmuz, his entire army took rein. Amir drew his swords Samsam and Qumqam and confronted the infidels, plying the swords with both hands. For two hours Amir fought the whole army of the infidels by himself, showing his swordsmanship and proving his courage and mettle. Thousands of infidels died in the battle. Ashqar Devzad swam in a sea of gore, floating chest-deep in the blood of the infidels. At last Bahman said to Zhopin, "Amir is now growing exhausted from the fight. Foam flows from his mouth, and he is in a state of self-forgetfulness and is merely fighting reflexively. He has lost awareness of his body and is striking away in a state of semi-consciousness. His helmet has fallen from his head, and he has lost his self-possession. Amar Ayyar keeps hurling naphtha and fire at us and does not allow anyone to attack Hamza from behind. If you could separate Amar Ayyar from Hamza, I would be able to kill Hamza and behead him."

At Zhopin's command, seven hundred elephants were released on Amar, who began firing naphtha projectiles at them. Approaching Amir Hamza from behind, Bahman struck a blow to Amir's head with a two-handed sword that cut into Amir's skull to a depth of four digits. Immediately upon dealing the blow, Bahman ran away from Hamza exclaiming, "Friends, I put an end to Hamza's life! Indeed I won a great laurel today, and dealt him a blow with such deftness and skill that it carved his head down to his throat!"

When Amir's friends heard Bahman's remarks they became most grieved and were overtaken by anxiety. Amir realized that he had received a grievous wound, and he swam in and out of consciousness. He said to Ashqar in the Jinni language, "Take me from the arena and use any means to break the cordon." Amir clasped Ashqar's neck with both arms, and the horse carried him away. Ashqar made his way into the forest from the battlefield biting anyone who tried to bar his way and kicking the men who tried to approach him from behind. After galloping for several miles, the thirsty Ashqar spotted a river. He waded into the water to drink, and when he came out Amir Hamza fell from his back and the water ran red with his blood. Ashqar dragged Amir to the riverbank and saved him from drowning.

By chance, a shepherd named Siyah-Sher who had herded his goats to the riverbank to drink saw that the water had turned red. He saw an injured man lying near the riverbank and a horse lying beside him. It appeared that the horse was trying to pull the man up, and he dragged him with his teeth in an effort to get the man onto his back. However, the injured man was unconscious and could not regain his senses because of the grievous wound he had suffered. Upon witnessing this scene, Siyah-Sher reasoned that the injured man must be the king of some domain, for he bore a majestic mien and noble looks. Realizing that he must have been injured during a battle and his horse had brought him there to escape his enemies, Siyah-Sher decided that if he were to look after the man and comfort him, he would be rewarded richly. With that in mind, Siyah-Sher took much trouble to put Amir on the horse's back and secured him to the saddle with a rope. Then he took Amir to his house, in the hope that it would be advantageous for him to host him.

Siyah-Sher's mother asked him, "Who have you brought home, my son? Who is this man with you?" Siyah-Sher told the whole story to her, and after giving her an account of Amir's condition, said, "If he survives and becomes well, he will richly reward me; and if he dies, his horse and arms will become mine. In any event, keeping him here will be advantageous for us." Then he removed Amir's weapons and bandaged his wound. Ashqar watched Amir from his bedside without moving an inch and became enraged when Siyah-Sher tried to lead him outside. Frightened by the horse, Siyah-Sher gave up these attempts and desisted from even the thought of them.

Finally, seven days later, Amir opened his eyes and saw Ashqar and a stranger standing by his bedside. Amir said to Siyah-Sher, "Tell me who you are, what your name is, and the name of the person who owns this dwelling." He answered, "My name is Siyah-Sher and I am a shepherd. I look after my animals in the forest. I saw you lying near the riverside and felt pity for you and brought you home. When God makes you well I, too, hope to see happy days, find a worthy status, and have cause to derive some pleasure from my existence." Amir asked him to unsaddle the horse and said to Ashqar, "Go to the pastures nearby and graze there." Amir then said to Siyah-Sher, "Your hard work will not go unrewarded. Serving me will profit you greatly, and when I get well you will be rewarded well above your expectations. Have no worries in this regard: You will be happy that we crossed paths. Bring me one of your goats so that I may slaughter her according to God's law and you may make soup for me. Do not think that I ask her of you as a gift: I will recompense you for twice her value." Siyah-Sher let Amir slaughter a goat, and then he made soup of her and fed it to Amir. The next day he gave him soup of another goat and then again another the day after. On the fourth day he said to his mother, "This injured man has eaten up the soup of three goats in three days. Today is the fourth day. I ask your advice: Should I feed him another goat today or deny it to him and make some excuse?"

His mother went before Amir Hamza and asked, "Who are you, O stranger, and what is your name?" Amir answered, "My name is Sa'ad Shami and I am Hamza's cousin from his father's side. If you take care of me, I will reward you richly and will never forget your favor. Do me this kindness, and until I get well feed me the soup of a goat daily. For every goat that you serve me, I will give you ten goats and give you many other rewards besides." Upon hearing Amir Hamza's name, the old woman said, "May my life become your sacrifice. I shall serve you most willingly, and my flock of goats is at your disposal. It will be a pleasure and a joy for me to attend to you while you convalesce and are restored to health." From that day on, she fed Amir daily the soup of one goat and served him any other food that he desired.

———

Now hear the situation in Amir's camp: When Amar Ayyar did not find Amir Hamza on the battlefield, he searched for him among the martyrs and then continued his search beyond the battlefield, all careworn and anxious about his safety. He followed a trail of Amir's blood to the riverside and saw that its water had turned red. Amar Ayyar realized that Amir had been brought there by the horse, and that his blood had caused the water to turn red. After searching for him in all directions, Amar finally found Ashqar, who led Amar Ayyar to Siyah-Sher's dwelling and showed him where Amir Hamza was lodged. Amar Ayyar kissed Amir's feet, and upon inspecting his wound, expressed his grief and sorrow. Then Amar Ayyar prostrated himself before God and said a prayer of gratitude to Him for safeguarding Amir's life. Finally, Amar Ayyar said, "O Amir, let us return to the camp, where Mehr-Nigar and all the others have been reduced to tears in your absence and are anxious and grieved by your disappearance." Amir answered, "Khvaja, I would like you to bring them all here and conduct them into my presence."

Amar immediately returned to his camp and gave everyone the happy tidings of Amir's safety and well-being. Then he led Princess Mehr-Nigar and all of Amir's associates and relations, along with the whole camp to Amir's lodging. All of Amir's companions kissed his feet and Mehr-Nigar dropped her head upon Amir's neck and broke into tears, sobbing at his condition. Amir comforted every one of them and said, "This shepherd has tended to me in my need and provided me with every care and comfort in his house. Each one of you should reward him according to your means and give him all you can." All the commanders rewarded the shepherd accordingly and recompensed him for his services to Amir Hamza, who also asked Princess Mehr-Nigar to give a handsome reward of gold and jewels to the shepherd and his mother, and to confer on them robes of honor. In the end, the shepherd's abode was unable to hold all the riches and rewards he had received. Amir accounted for all the goats served to him in his sickness and gave ten goats in return for each goat he had eaten. Siyah-Sher received in return ten times everything that he had spent, in addition to the rewards. Then Amir said to him, "I declare you my brother before God!" The shepherd had become a rich man and, from that day on, began leading a life of luxury and comfort.

After Amir's wound had healed, he returned to his camp near the battlefield. He gathered his army for battle and the drums of war were sounded once again. The army of the infidels also arrayed for battle. Amir said to his companions, "Put a cordon around the enemy and attack them from all sides. Do not allow these weaklings to escape your hands with their lives." Amar bin Hamza cried out, "Bahman will answer to me alone!" Landhoor declared, "And Zhopin is my prey!" In short, their army fell upon the infidels like a lion attacking a flock of sheep. Within a few hours countless infidels were dispatched to Hell, for the swords of the brave had opened the doors of Hell for them. The infidels ran wherever they found a path of escape open to them, but the followers of the True Faith always frustrated their retreat. They kept up the slaughter and followed them the whole day until only a few men were left standing in the enemy army.

As Bahman escaped from Amar bin Hamza, he gave him chase on Siyah Qitas. After they had gone some distance, Bahman turned to confront him, thinking that Amar bin Hamza would be no match for him. Amar bin Hamza dealt him a full blow of the sword, which Bahman foiled although it killed his horse. Bahman then hamstrung Siyah Qitas, so Amar bin Hamza was forced to face him on foot, and he was certainly ready for combat. Amar bin Hamza changed his stance at lightning speed and dealt Bahman a blow that cut Bahman in two. His body fell to the ground severed; he had never found his chance to escape death. Amar bin Hamza beheaded Bahman's body and presented the head to Amir Hamza to show proof of his courage, and told Amir that Siyah Qitas had been hamstrung. Amir lamented the loss of Bahman and the horse and said, "It is not every day that one comes across a noble horse, nor a warrior of such mettle as Bahman. Indeed they are rarities in this world."

Later, Amir's commanders likewise piled up the heads of enemy commanders before him, and thousands of infidels lay beheaded. Amir ordered the drums of victory to be sounded, and he returned to his camp. The followers of the True Faith sounded joyous notes upon their victory over the infidels.

When Amir Hamza had received his wound at Bahman's hands, a *perizad* was passing above the battlefield who took the news of the incident and the details of Amir's injury and affliction to Aasman Peri. This greatly distressed Aasman Peri. She took Quraisha, her *perizads,* and Khvaja Abdur Rahman and departed from Qaf for Earth at the head of an intrepid army of *devs* and jinns. She was driven by a desire to set eyes on Amir and to provide him with relief and comfort, to fulfill her duty toward him.

Upon approaching the scene, she set up her camp two *kos* away and sent Khvaja Abdur Rahman to call on Amir. When Abdur Rahman appeared before him all of a sudden and kissed Amir Hamza's feet, Amir was greatly surprised to see him and wondered how he happened to be there, and who had given him the news. Amir asked him about Aasman Peri and Quraisha and inquired about the reason for his visit. Khvaja Abdur Rahman said, "The queen and your daughter, Quraisha, are camped two *kos* from here with an powerful army. A *perizad* brought us the news of your injury, and upon hearing it, the queen departed Qaf immediately. She had become disconsolate upon hearing the news, and has arrived here with great magnificence and grandeur."

Amir rode out with his commanders and warriors with great majesty to call on them. He embraced Aasman Peri and kissed Quraisha's forehead and seated her on his lap, showing her much affection. The *perizads* marveled at the grandeur of Amir's entourage and said among themselves, "It was on account of what he had left behind that Amir was so downcast in Qaf and wished to return to his world." They said to Amir, "We have now seen your friends and companions, but we are most desirous of seeing Princess Mehr-Nigar. We have fallen in love with her without even having seen her." Amir replied, "Just as you wish to see Princess Mehr-Nigar, my friends are desirous of beholding you with their own eyes. They are ever entreating and soliciting this of me, and therefore I request that you either appear to them without your invisible guise, or else line their eyes with the collyrium of Suleiman so that they may gain pleasure from the sight of you and their eyes may light up from your peerless beauty." The *perizads* replied, "O Amir! We fear that if we do this your companions may become bold and try to take liberties with us and allow evil thoughts to enter their hearts." Amir answered, "Nobody would dare even think of it. You may rest assured on that account, and not let any such anxieties burden you."

Thereupon the *perizads* lifted their veils of invisibility and presented their beauty to Amir's companions. When the warriors and champions of Amir's camp saw them, they were stunned and fell into a state of shock. When they regained their senses, they thanked Amir and said, "It is because of you that we who are made of clay were able to behold those made of fire. We could never have laid eyes on *peris* otherwise, as we do not have the wherewithal to set foot in Qaf." Amir retired to Mehr-Nigar's palace along with Aasman Peri, Quraisha, and the *perizads*, where they all derived joyous pleasure from one another's company.

Mehr-Nigar embraced Aasman Peri, kissed Quraisha's forehead and lips, and then received all the *peris*, hosting them in the finest traditions and attending to their every comfort. For three days and three nights Aasman Peri engaged in feasting with her companions and all affairs of the state were put in abeyance. On the fourth day Aasman Peri gave Mehr-Nigar the gifts she had brought for her from Qaf and returned to her abode.

After her departure, Amir asked his companions at court, "Do we know where the infidels have escaped to?" Amar Ayyar answered, "It is said that they have gone to Kashmir, where they have sought refuge with Jafar, the ruler of that land, who has pledged his support to them." Amar bin Hamza now spoke up, saying, "If I were ordered to do so, I would be only too glad to depart for Kashmir to annihilate the infidels. I would not leave a single one of them alive, God willing!" Amir Hamza said in reply, "Very well!" Then Amar bin Hamza took seven champion soldiers, including Aadi Madi-Karib, Farhad bin Landhoor, and Istaftanosh, along with their respective armies, and headed for Kashmir. When he entered the lands of Kashmir, the infidels hid themselves for fear in a fort. Amar bin Hamza surrounded the castle from all sides and laid siege to it.

One day, an onager[18] entered Amar bin Hamza's camp from the forest and injured many men with his teeth and hooves. When news of this reached Amar bin Hamza, he mounted his steed and gave chase to the animal in order to capture him alive. Upon reaching the side of a mountain, the wild ass quickly scampered up it. Amar bin Hamza followed but found no sign of the wild ass upon reaching the summit. He searched for him in the nearby bushes until evening but was unable to locate him or find any trace of him. Then Amar bin Hamza sat down to rest under a tree. He hunted and killed an animal, and roasted and made a meal of it. Afterward he lay down under the same tree and slept. When it was time for *fajar* prayers[19] the same onager again appeared and Amar bin Hamza again exerted himself in capturing him. When the sun rose and its rays fell on every inch of the mountain, the onager disappeared again. Amar searched for him again and was unable to find him as before. He was forced to depart empty-handed after failing in his search.

Along the way back to camp he came across a most captivating city whose citizens were paragons of beauty. When he inquired the name of the city, he was told that it was called Farkhar, the envy of the heavens, and the residence of Zhopin's sister Gul Chehra, whom the populace regarded as their mistress. It so happened that Gul Chehra caught sight of Amir's son from her balcony. She instantly fell madly in love and became hopelessly enamored of him. She sent one of her eunuchs to bring him to her by any means possible. The eunuch made obeisance before Amar bin Hamza and said, "The mistress of your slave is most desirous of meeting you and wishes to be granted an audience." Amar bin Hamza declined the invitation, flatly turning down her overture. After a while the eunuch returned to him with the same message and, kissing the ground before Amar bin Hamza, added with all humility and flattery, "Your Honor may step in for only a moment and leave immediately after showing her your face." Finally he convinced Amar bin Hamza and conducted him before Gul Chehra. She received him with great ceremony and fanfare and attended to him with great devotion.

Then she asked him, "What is your name and the name of the country whence you have come? And what has brought you to these parts?" He answered, "I am Amar bin Hamza. My father is renowned throughout the world." She said, "I have burned with love for you for a long time and bided my time thinking of you. I have cried from separation from you and have undergone a thousand hardships. Today God granted my desire and sent you to me when I least expected it." Afterward, Gul Chehra ordered food to be laid out, and they shared a meal.

Next, they had a round of drinks. Soon both she and Amar bin Hamza were intoxicated and Gul Chehra sought congress with him. Amar bin Hamza said to her, "I already have your sister in my harem. I will not couple with you and break God's law." She presented all manner of excuses to attain her goal. Finally, the prince was forced to reply, "My commanders are occupied with the siege of the fortress of Kashmir. I shall call upon them and ask their opinion in this matter. If they give their consent, I will take you to bed and take my pleasure of you." The shameless Gul Chehra immediately dispatched a messenger to send for Amar bin Hamza's commanders to tell them of the circumstances.

Now, an old man named Farkhar Sar-Shaban lived in that city and was held in reverence by all and sundry. When he heard that Hamza's son had arrived there, he sent for his two sons, Mehrdar Sar-Shaban and Dinar Sar-Shaban, and said to them, "You will find Hamza's son drinking wine with Zhopin's sister. Go and bring him captive to me. And if you are unable to take him alive, bring me his head. I wish you to display your true mettle in this endeavor." His sons headed for Gul Chehra's house carrying staffs. They accosted Amar bin Hamza and said, "You despicable thief, how dare you trespass on our land to hunt here and display your valor?" Amar bin Hamza did not answer them and held his peace. Then, one of them attacked Amar bin Hamza with his staff. Amar bin Hamza caught hold of it and pulled the staff toward him, which caused his adversary to fall flat on his face. He then dealt the intruder a blow with the same stick that flattened him to the ground and caused him to give up all thoughts of fighting. His brother charged him next, swinging his staff. He, too, met the same fate. When they returned to their senses they went back to their father and told him what had passed with them. Farkhar Sar-Shaban laughed at their story and said, "I have business with Hamza, not with his sons. But it seems unlikely now that I would be able to overpower him."

The next day Madi-Karib and the other commanders presented themselves before Amar bin Hamza in Farkhar. Gul Chehra received them with great honor and they found their time with her a delightful experience. She arranged a royal feast for them and told them of her passion for Amar bin Hamza, expressing her intentions to them. Afterward, Aadi said to Amar bin Hamza, "Why are you bent on killing this poor creature before her time? Who has ever heard of someone torturing a lover in this manner or setting up such difficulties in the path of desire's fulfillment?" Amar bin Hamza laughed at this speech and said, "How do you suppose I can commit an act that is forbidden and choose the proscribed path?" Madi-Karib replied, "You are the master of your actions. I only expressed my views after taking pity on this woman's incessant crying and longing."

In short, when Amar bin Hamza fell unconscious after drinking, Gul Chehra became overwhelmed with desire and embraced him amorously. Amar bin Hamza knitted his brows and said, "O shameless wretch, what is this unseemly act? What disgraceful enterprise have you decided upon in your heart? I will never be able to reciprocate your desires in this vile act!" With these words, he slapped her in warning. Gul Chehra was frustrated in her desire and said to herself, *He is in love with my sister, while I burn from the fire of his love and long to have congress with him. As the saying goes, what I cannot have another must not enjoy either! Let everything burn and go to blazes!* She drew her sword that same moment and beheaded Amar bin Hamza. Then realizing that Amar bin Hamza's commanders would kill her in retribution, she began shouting and screaming and raising an alarm, "Ah! Ah! Who was the enemy who killed Amir Hamza's son?"

Amar bin Hamza's companions came rushing inside, and upon seeing Amar bin Hamza lying dead, tore at their collars, threw dust on their heads, and gave themselves to ecstasies of sorrow. Aadi said, "It is neither a stranger nor an enemy who is responsible for killing Amar bin Hamza. It is all too likely that this shameless wretch was frustrated in her desire and killed him in her drunken rage. It is all her doing!" Aadi's companions agreed with his conclusion. They shackled that harlot and asked her, "Were you the one who killed him?" She answered, "I was overwhelmed by my passion and it forced me to commit this deed. Now punish me as you wish and kill me to avenge his death!" They said to one another, "It is proscribed for a man to raise his hand against a woman. How could we kill her even if we wanted to? It is an issue that is endlessly confounding and worrisome."

Meanwhile, Amir Hamza had a dream that his son was flailing in a sea of blood. He started from his sleep in fear and explained the dream to Amar Ayyar who immediately departed for Kashmir. When Amar Ayyar reached Kashmir, he discovered that Amir's son was in the city of Farkhar in the house of Zhopin's sister. Amar hastened to that woman's home, where Aadi and the others threw themselves at Amar's feet and told him everything. From there Amar Ayyar returned home beating his head and throwing dirt on it and said to Amir Hamza, "The prince lies injured in Farkhar at Zhopin's house, and he has sent for you urgently. Therefore yours truly has come here to take you to him!" Amir Hamza made preparations to leave and departed for Farkhar riding Ashqar Devzad. Amar thought it best to give Amir Hamza something to eat to fortify him against sudden shock and prevent him from going into ecstasies of sorrow upon learning the truth. Amar Ayyar said to him, "Let us rest a while in a garden and revive our spirits before we arrive at Gul Chehra's house." Upon his persuasion, Amir Hamza stopped in a garden where a flock of goats were grazing. Amar Ayyar slaughtered a goat and began roasting her, and Amir Hamza's mind was soon occupied fully in watching his proceedings.

When the shepherd of that flock saw smoke rising from the garden, he went to investigate and beheld two men roasting his master's goat. He rushed back to Farkhar Sar-Shaban, who was the owner of the garden and the herd that grazed there, and informed him that two men had entered the garden and were helping themselves to his property as if it were their own. Farkhar Sar-Shaban hastily entered the garden and saw the two men enjoying the roasted goat without a care in the world. He said to his sons, "Go and capture these two beastly men, and arrest them immediately!" His sons went and attacked Amir with their staffs. Amir wrenched their staffs from their hands without even getting up from his place and slammed the men to the ground so hard that they lost consciousness and became bereft of their senses.

Burning in the fires of rage, Farkhar Sar-Shaban thoughtlessly charged Amir carrying a seven-hundred-*maund* mace, shouting, "It seems that your death has driven you here, you beastly men, for you slaughtered and ate the goat belonging to your Angel of Death." With those words, he brought his mace down on Amir, who stopped the blow by catching hold of the weapon. Try as he might, Farkhar Sar-Shaban was unable to wrest it from Amir's hands and release it from his grip. Failing in his endeavor, he let go of his mace and, catching hold of Amir's cummerbund, began exerting himself to lift him. Amir then grabbed him and lifted Farkhar over his head still without even getting up from his place. He slammed the old man so forcefully on the ground that his body went limp from shock and he was unable to carry on fighting. He said to Amir Hamza, "O stranger, give me your name and tell me truthfully whence you have come." Amir Hamza said, "I am Hamza bin Abdul Muttalib and

I am the lord and commander of my armies." Farkhar Sar-Shaban said, "Indeed none other than Hamza could have forced me down and pressed my back to the ground."

Amir Hamza converted him to the True Faith and won his heart with his generosity and munificence. Amar Ayyar signaled to forbid Farkhar Sar-Shaban from speaking when he tried to bring up the subject of Amar bin Hamza's death. Amir sallied forth with Farkhar Sar-Shaban and his sons riding by his side. When Amir Hamza's companions caught sight of him, they broke into lamentations all over again. Amir asked, "What is the matter that the place is ringing with the cries of grief and lamentations?" Amar Ayyar answered, "Your son has died at the hands of Zhopin's sister." Amir said, "Take the deceased to his mother and bring that trollop there. Inform Naheed Maryam[20] that this harlot killed her son." Amar took Gul Chehra and gave her into the custody of Naheed Maryam, and said to the princess, "This woman killed your son, who was like a piece of your heart." Naheed Maryam let out the cry of "Ah! My son!" and died that instant, immediately surrendering her soul upon hearing of his death. Amir's grief was thus doubled, and he went into forty days of mourning for his son and sent his corpse, along with the captive Gul Chehra, to Kaus Hisar to Amar bin Hamza's wife, who avenged the death of her husband by killing her sister with her own hands.

Amir Hamza meanwhile declared, "I lost my son in this unlucky place. I must erase its existence from the face of the Earth and uproot it from its foundations." With these words, he brought down his mace and smashed the gates of the fortress of Farkhar and then entered to commence indiscriminate slaughter. Hurmuz escaped to Ctesiphon by a secret gate, but most of his companions died at Amir's hand and some converted to the True Faith. Finally, Amir turned on the Kashmiris and reckoned with them with his sword. Their ruler sought reprieve, and Amir pardoned him, sparing his life from his benevolent nature. Afterward, Amir headed for Kaus Hisar.

OF HURMUZ'S ARRIVAL IN CTESIPHON AND LEARNING OF NAUSHERVAN'S CAPTIVITY, AND OF HIS DEPARTURE TO SECURE HIS RELEASE

The narrator has said that when Hurmuz arrived in Ctesiphon after escaping from the fortress of Kashmir, he learned that Shaddad Abu-Amar Habashi had taken Naushervan prisoner and incarcerated him in his land. When Hurmuz asked Buzurjmehr's advice, he said, "It would be impossible to secure the emperor's release without Hamza agreeing to undertake the mission." Hurmuz said, "Why would Hamza agree to it? He has no reason to undertake these hardships at our bidding." Buzurjmehr replied, "If you were to ask your mother to write him a letter, Hamza would be forced to undertake the labor out of regard for her honor, and he would then certainly secure the emperor's release from that tyrant's clutches."

Hurmuz told his mother what Buzurjmehr had suggested and asked her, "What is your opinion in this matter? Is his counsel wise or misguided?" Empress Mehr-Angez responded by writing a letter to Hamza that read:

To my son and a part of my heart! A long time ago Naushervan was taken captive by Shaddad Abu-Amar Habashi, who inflicts a new torture on him every day. God alone knows what grudge he holds against Naushervan that he treats him in this manner. It is truly deplorable that in your lifetime someone should harm Naushervan and disgrace a magnificent emperor like him.

After reading her letter, Amir Hamza said, "Even though I have received nothing but harm from Naushervan's hands, I will continue to return his deeds with kindness. I shall secure his release. If he cannot desist from his evil acts toward me, should I desist from doing good? Even if he follows the course of injustice, I shall not stray from the path of integrity." Amir took Muqbil Vafadar with him and headed for Ethiopia, resolved on acquiescing to the request of Mehr-Angez against Amar Ayyar's advice.

When they arrived in Ethiopia, they dismounted in a garden near the walls of the city and left their horses to graze there, filling their time with anxious deliberations on how best to carry out their mission. That night, Amir said to Muqbil, "We should dress up as *ayyars* in order to break into Shaddad's palace and release Naushervan." Muqbil Vafadar replied, "We must follow any auspicious course of action that occurs to you, and use any means necessary to secure Naushervan's freedom." Amir put on his night livery and, using a rope ladder, scaled the walls of the fort. When they entered, they saw Shaddad Abu-Amar Habashi asleep on a throne surrounded by flagons of wine and salvers of meat and dried fruit, while Naushervan was trapped in a cage hanging near the throne. Amir Hamza was challenged by the palace guards, whom he swiftly killed, and then he partook of the wine, meat, and fruit laid out there. Next he wrote a note addressed to Shaddad Abu-Amar Habashi and left it near him: "I was here and have taken Naushervan, my mentor and my benevolent lord, from your prison after eating all the food lying here."

Then Amir took down Naushervan's cage and said to Muqbil, "You must remain on the alert and look sharp while I go in search of a fleet horse for Naushervan."

While Amir was gone, Shaddad Abu-Amar Habashi woke up and saw that Naushervan had disappeared with his cage and his guards lay murdered. He was astounded by the scene and wondered who might have been the culprit. Suddenly he caught sight of the note, and upon reading it, grew enraged.

Shaddad mustered a four-thousand-strong force and set out in search of Amir Hamza. They soon came upon a garden where they saw Naushervan sitting in his cage. When Shaddad asked Naushervan for Hamza's whereabouts, he replied, "I do not know where he is. I only know that he has gone in search of his horse." Shaddad released Naushervan and went to look for Amir Hamza. On the way he saw Muqbil coming toward him fearlessly on a horse. Shaddad called out, "Beware, O thief! You won't be able to slip away from my clutches now or escape with your life." Muqbil spurred on his horse and gave it free rein, but he and his horse were suddenly entangled in the nooses of seven hundred ropes that Shaddad's

troops threw to catch him. Taking Muqbil for Amir Hamza,[21] they secured him well, along with Ashqar Devzad. Muqbil said, "I am not
Hamza but Muqbil. If you do not believe me, I am willing to swear to the
veracity of my statement." Shaddad then said, "It seems that Hamza was
lost in the desert and died from thirst. The burning heat must have
claimed his life."

In the meantime, Shaddad returned to his abode and drank himself to
sleep. In the morning he set out for Kaus Hisar with Naushervan. Shaddad had decided that with Hamza dead he must kill Hamza's sons, and
then he could take Mehr-Nigar and ravish her as his reward. While
Shaddad was indulging in these vile thoughts, Amir Hamza had indeed
wandered into the desert and become lost. He suffered terribly from
loneliness, thirst, and the effects of the piercing sun. Wherever he
looked, he saw nothing but desolation. His eyes swept the horizon and
met neither shade nor water. That night Amar Ayyar saw Amir Hamza in
his dreams, wandering forlorn and distraught in a desert and looking bewildered and dizzy. The next morning he narrated the dream to his companions and said, "Remain on the alert and be ready for any eventuality.
I am off to recover some news of Amir Hamza and learn the state of his
well-being and safety." Then Amar Ayyar headed out. On his way, he saw
Shaddad's army and learned that Shaddad was headed for Kaus Hisar
with Naushervan, tempted by the prospect of acquiring Mehr-Nigar as
his reward. Amar also discovered that Amir Hamza had wandered into
the desert and become lost and his horse and his slave, Muqbil,[22] were in
the custody of Shaddad Abu-Amar Habashi.

Receiving these inauspicious tidings, Amar grew even more worried.
He hastened toward the desert, where he searched for Amir for seven
days and seven nights. On the eighth day, Amar finally found Amir
Hamza's weapons on the desert floor and saw signs that indicated that he
had been there. Amar searched the whole vicinity, calling out, "Hamza,
where are you? Answer me immediately if you are alive! I have come to
look for you here. In God's name, speak and forthwith inform me of your
state." Amar Ayyar's voice did indeed reach Amir Hamza, but he was unable to reply in an audible voice. He lay where he had fallen, staring at
the sky. Amar found him in the end, and saw that his eyes were bulging
out from thirst and his tongue was a veritable bed of thorns. Amir Hamza
was now unconscious from weakness, and Amar shed many tears at the
sight. He took out a goblet of sherbet from his *zambil* and dripped it
gently into Amir's mouth. After a while, Amir Hamza opened his eyes

and his senses were somewhat restored. Amir complained of thirst and Amar gave him another goblet of the sherbet to drink. After Amir had fully regained his faculties, he put on his accoutrements and returned to Ethiopia, where he found Muqbil and Ashqar tied up with ropes. At the sight of Amir Hamza, Ashqar broke his fetters.[23] Amir Hamza mounted him and made preparations to head into the city in the company of Amar and Muqbil.

The guards alerted Shaddad's son, Amar Habashi, of Amir Hamza's entry, and he intercepted Amir with a force of a thousand troops. Amir said to him, "O bastard! Why do you still show irreverence toward me and exhibit your recalcitrance when you well know that I once enslaved your father?" Amar Habashi remained deaf to Amir's words and attacked him with his sword. Amir Hamza wrested the sword from his hands and dealt him such a powerful blow that the knees of Shaddad's son gave out. Amar tied him up at Amir's orders, securing him in no time at all. Then Shaddad's son pleaded to Amir and said, "Do not put me in fetters! I am willing to pledge allegiance to you and would not dare defy you again!" Amir Hamza instructed him in the Act of Faith and he sincerely converted to the True Faith and became a believer in God and His prophets. Shaddad's son then conducted Amir into the fortress and held a feast for him there for three days. Amir stayed there as his guest and left for Kaus Hisar on the fourth day.

While Shaddad himself was on his way to Kaus Hisar with Naushervan, he sent a missive to Hurmuz that read: "I have killed Hamza and am bringing Naushervan to Kaus Hisar with me. You must arrive there with Zhopin and your army at the same time so that I can finish off the followers of the True Faith and lay claim to Mehr-Nigar and take her into my custody." Upon receiving that note, Hurmuz took Zhopin and departed with his entire army. Arriving at Kaus Hisar within a few days, he presented himself in Naushervan's service. Shaddad wasted no time in sounding the drums of war. He entered the arena astride his steed Shabrang, which was a matchless charger and a peerless mount whose horseshoes alone weighed one hundred and twenty *maunds*, and declared, "O Arabs! Hear that I am Shaddad Abu-Amar Habashi. I have killed Hamza and have Naushervan's permission to take Mehr-Nigar as mine. It is at the orders of the emperor that this army has arrived at your gates. Do not sacrifice your lives for an idle cause. You would do well to leave this place without injury to yourselves. If your death has started circling over your heads, however, you may choose to fight me." Landhoor moved forward and spurred on his horse to encounter Shaddad, who dealt him a blow of his mace. Landhoor parried this successfully and answered him with such a powerful blow of his mace that Shaddad's horse sank deep into the ground as if he had entered quicksand. Shaddad leapt from his saddle and the two exchanged mace blows. Neither had prevailed over his adversary or inflicted a grievous wound when Shaddad struck at Landhoor with his sword, and Landhoor received a deep cut. Despite his wound, however, Landhoor kept fighting until evening and did not withdraw from combat or waver even a little. Finally, Shaddad sounded the drums to announce the day's end, and the armies returned to their camps. The next day Landhoor's son, Farhad, fought with Shaddad and he, too, retired injured from the field. Shaddad injured many champions of the followers of the True Faith that day, and whoever confronted him was humiliated by his hand.

Farkhar Sar-Shaban saw that after injuring a few champions, Shaddad was bursting with conceited joy and thought nothing of any challenger. Farkhar rode into the arena wielding his lance. Shaddad asked him, "Who are you, O warrior? Give me your name and rank." Farkhar answered, "I am Farkhar Sar-Shaban and there is none who is my equal in bravery and courage. I am a citizen of Farkhar and the son of a renowned warrior. Now I ask you to deal me your blow!" Shaddad attacked with his mace, but Farkhar parried his blow and answered with a powerful strike of his seven-hundred-*maund* mace, which jolted men in both camps from the sound of the impact, and every soldier praised his might to the high heavens. If Shaddad had not foiled the blow, his bones would have been ground to a fine powder and not a single one of them in his body would have remained whole. The two warriors fought until evening, but neither was able to injure the other. Finally, Shaddad sounded the drums to announce the day's end, and both armies returned to their camps. The next day they skirmished anew and, frustrated by the encounter, Shaddad said to Farkhar Sar-Shaban, "You have skirmished with me to your heart's content. Now go and send someone else to fight me." Farkhar said, "Killing you is the only thing that will soothe my heart. I will not turn back without achieving my end." In the end, Shaddad turned tail and ran away, and Farkhar Sar-Shaban followed him all the way to his camp. The shades of the evening having fallen in the meanwhile, both armies returned to their resting places.

In the morning, Shaddad and Farkhar Sar-Shaban again stood facing each other and they battled together the whole day with swords. Toward evening, Farkhar Sar-Shaban found a chance to swipe Shaddad with his sword, severing Shaddad's arm. The injured man's eyes quickly became dark with pain. Before Farkhar Sar-Shaban could deal him another blow, Shaddad escaped and took refuge among the ranks of his soldiers. Farkhar returned triumphant to his camp and everyone was overjoyed at his victory. After that day, the battle was suspended.

About this time, an *ayyar* named Galeem said to Naushervan, "If you were to order me, I would behead every Arab commander and dispatch them all to the Future State." Naushervan answered, "I would like nothing better!" That same night Galeem wormed his way into the Arab camp and entered Qubad's pavilion. He found two *ayyars*, Zafar and Fatah, doing the rounds of vigil. However, Galeem escaped their notice and gained entry to Qubad's tent after pulling out one of its pegs. Finding Qubad asleep, he cut off his head and left.

But Amar's *ayyars* who were on duty outside did not let him get away. They frustrated his escape and arrested Galeem. A great hue and cry arose when Qubad's severed head was discovered in his possession. The Arab commanders came out of their tents and went together to Qubad's pavilion, where they found Qubad's headless corpse lying on the bed. An uproar and a pandemonium like the Judgment Day arose immediately and cries and lamentations were heard from every corner. Young and old alike were thrown into ecstasies of grief and sorrow by the prince's murder.

When Mehr-Nigar received the news, despair crushed her and raging grief burnt her heart to cinders. A mother who could have survived such sorrow would have been rare. In the morning, Galeem was cut to pieces in retribution. When Naushervan received the news of his grandson's murder, he went into mourning as well. For forty days both camps remained in the state of mourning and indulged in crying and lamentation. When the mourning period was over, both armies again stood facing each other and battled mightily. On that first day of renewed combat, Shaddad and Farkhar were locked in battle when a dust cloud rose from the direction of the forest and *ayyars* brought news that Amir Hamza and Amar had come at the head of a large army. Farkhar Sar-Shaban suspended fighting and went to receive Amir Hamza along with the other commanders of his camp. Shaddad used this opportunity to escape, deeming it inauspicious to stay on any longer. After meeting his friends and companions, Amir Hamza asked Farkhar Sar-Shaban, "Where is Shaddad? Why do I not hear him shouting his war cries today?" He answered, "I left him on the battlefield. It was in the arena that I last saw him today." Amir Hamza surveyed the whole battlefield but saw no trace of Shaddad and said, "It seems that he has run away upon hearing of my arrival!" Then Amir Hamza rode out in pursuit of him.

Shaddad had put a distance of many leagues between them by that time. Amir said to Ashqar in the Jinni language, "Take me to that tyrant without loss of time, my dear lad!" Ashqar took wing and closed the distance between them in just a moment. Shaddad realized that escape was impossible seeing Amir Hamza upon him. Darkness fell before his eyes and he saw his death circling over his head. Sighting a pagan temple nearby, he tried to enter its confines to save his life. But Amir Hamza put a noose around Shaddad's neck, gave the end of the rope to Landhoor, and said, "Pull it hard, O Khusrau!" Shaddad's soul flew straight to Hell when Landhoor pulled. The noose tightened about him and he gave up his soul; Landhoor's pull proved his death trap.

Amir Hamza conferred Shaddad's horse Shabrang on Landhoor, making a gift of that peerless steed to him. Landhoor said, "Indeed this horse is worthy of being your steed alone." In the meanwhile, Amar had arrived there, and he severed and raised Shaddad's head on a lance. Amir Hamza returned to his camp triumphant and victorious, leisurely exchanging pleasantries with his friends, for no one descended into the arena that day to fight him.

———

When Zhopin saw that the horizon was clear and Mehr-Nigar had been left alone, he decided it was an opportune time to overpower her and take her away with him. Entering Amir Hamza's pavilion with that plan, he killed the few guards who were standing at the door, gained admission to Mehr-Nigar's quarters, and entered her bedchamber. Mehr-Nigar fired a barrage of arrows at him and all of Zhopin's resolve seeped out of him through his wounds. Realizing that Mehr-Nigar must abhor him, Zhopin dealt her delicate body a blow of his sword and was about to strike again when Amir Hamza arrived on the scene. Zhopin was cornered and, finding escape impossible, he attacked Amir Hamza. Amir parried his blow and returned it as Zhopin was trying to escape. Amir's sword cut through his skull, his neck, and his spinal column, and Zhopin fell dead in his tracks.

Amir Hamza found Mehr-Nigar at death's door and he dispatched Amar to call Buzurjmehr there to witness her condition. While Amar was gone to fetch Buzurjmehr, Mehr-Nigar succumbed to her wounds and joined the company of the *houris* in heaven. Amir Hamza let out a cry of "Ahh!" and fell unconscious.

When Amir came to after an hour, he laughed and cried in turns maniacally, driving himself to the edge of his life. When Amar arrived with Buzurjmehr, he found Mehr-Nigar lifeless and Amir Hamza in a frenzy of grief. Amar was deeply troubled and said to Khvaja Buzurjmehr, "Sire, what is this that I see? Pray do something to dispel Amir's frenzy and return him to his senses!" Khvaja said, "O Amar! Amir Hamza will get well by himself on the twenty-first day from today and will become the master of his senses on his own. Do not have any worries in this regard."

Despite his frenzy, Amir Hamza prepared biers for Mehr-Nigar, Qubad, and Amar bin Hamza, and departed for Mecca in an entourage of his friends and companions. Amir came upon a pleasant field as they approached Mecca, where he ordered graves dug for his family members, and he buried these three there. He camped at that place for the night as he did not wish to enter the city yet. It is said that after twenty-one days had passed, Amar saw Prophet Ibrahim in his dream and drank a goblet of pure wine from his hand. Prophet Ibrahim said to Amir, "My son, it is against reason to reduce yourself to such a pitiable state for the sake of a woman. In your life you will find thousands like her. Many women will enter your service who would be far superior to Mehr-Nigar."

Amir Hamza awoke and opened his eyes and asked Amar Ayyar, "Where am I? What happened to me? Tell me truly, what has my condition been?" Amar Ayyar gave him a detailed account of all that had passed, and informed Amir as to his condition since the incident. Amir Hamza then told Amar and his friends what he had seen in the realm of dreams. His companions responded, "Sire, you are the progeny of Prophet Ibrahim. It is only proper that he should appear to counsel you in your dreams. Who else would do so, if he did not? Every parent feels his child's pain." Amir said, "In any event, I gave my word to Mehr-Nigar. To keep it, I shall become a devotee at her shrine and spend the last breaths of my life there. All of you may return home now, and do not bother me with anything anymore."

Amar Ayyar counseled him against following this course of action, but Amir Hamza spurned his advice. He took leave of everyone and, delegating the throne to his grandson Sa'ad bin Amar bin Hamza, he sent him toward Egypt. Amar Ayyar beseeched Amir Hamza, "O Amir! Do not send me away. Allow me to remain in your company." Amir answered, "Muqbil's presence will suffice me. I do not need another person's company. There is no need for you to stay here."

After everyone had left, Amir Hamza shaved his head, put on beggarly clothes, and spent his nights and days sweeping Mehr-Nigar's grave. Whenever sleep overcame him, he lay down at the foot of her grave.

Of the Arrival of Qaroon Akka bin Furhad-Akka and Kuliyat bin Galeem Ayyar, and of Their Taking Amir Hamza and Muqbil Vafadar Prisoner

The narrators of sweet discourse and the excellent stylists thus ride the galloping steed of the pen into the narrative's domain telling us that the news of Amir Hamza becoming a devotee at Mehr-Nigar's shrine spread far and wide. Seditious heads rose and recalcitrant souls stirred, and they all found the freedom to plan and plot Amir Hamza's murder. Thus it was that Qaroon Akka bin Furhad-Akka, who considered the might of Rustam an object of derision compared with his own, and who did not even fear demons much less human beings, resolved in his heart to kill Amir Hamza. He gathered a mighty army and started from his abode. On the way to Mecca he met Kuliyat, the son of Galeem Ayyar who had murdered Qubad, and asked him, "Where are you headed? And why are you putting yourself to the trouble of a journey?" He answered, "My father was killed by Hamza's companions. Upon receiving this news, I felt as if someone had chewed up my heart. I have heard that Hamza has now put down his weapons and become a devotee at the grave of Mehr-Nigar. I am headed there now and will either murder him or make him my prisoner. Qaroon Akka said to him, "I have set out with the same objective. It would be best if you joined me. The two of us will fulfill this mission together." Kuliyat agreed to this proposal and, traveling together, they arrived in the environs of Mecca in a few days.

Kuliyat said to Qaroon, "You should camp here. If Hamza sees you coming with a large army he will grow alert, and we will find it difficult to capture him. If you follow my counsel, it will not be too difficult to catch him." Qaroon Akka camped there while Kuliyat went to Mehr-Nigar's shrine dressed as a dervish. He saw Amir Hamza sitting at the graveside with his head bowed. When Kuliyat greeted him, Amir Hamza said, "Who are you and whence have you come? What is the purpose of your visit? Have you come here on your own, or has someone sent you?" Kuliyat answered, "I am a beggar and a traveler. I have come from the holy mosque in Jerusalem. It is my desire that the few days that I have remaining to my existence I should pass in your service, and spend my nights and days here." Amir said to him, "The presence of Muqbil is more than sufficient for my needs. I do not need anyone else. Indeed I have no desire to be attended to by another." Kuliyat responded, "I have no intention of leaving you. Now that I have arrived here, I won't go anywhere else." Amir Hamza could do little else but remain silent. After a while, Muqbil laid out the food and served what he had cooked. Amir invited Kuliyat to join them, and the three of them started eating. When Amir asked for water, Kuliyat poured some water that he had laced with a drug and served it to both Amir and Muqbil, without either of them becoming aware of his trick.

Then Kuliyat made himself scarce, and left them on the pretext of going to the toilet. He went straight to Qaroon Akka at his camp and said to him, "Mount your horse quickly and come with me without delay! I have administered a drug to Amir Hamza and Muqbil that will make them unconscious and render them senseless." Qaroon Akka soon arrived at Mehr-Nigar's shrine with Kuliyat and drew his sword to kill Amir Hamza. Seeing this, Muqbil rushed to defend Amir with his hand on the hilt of his sword but fell in a swoon to the ground. When he saw Qaroon Akka, Amir Hamza tried to rise, but he, too, fell to the ground in a faint and was unable to overpower Qaroon Akka, who bound him and Muqbil well with iron chains and fetters. He took them away to his camp, where he restored them to consciousness. Then, addressing harsh words at Amir Hamza, Qaroon Akka said, "O worthless Arab! How dare you have killed my father and the kings of the world and forcibly become Naushervan's son-in-law and ruled without any fear or trepidation? You will see now how I shall torture you to death and how ruthlessly I will kill you!" Amir declared, "You carrion-eating Gueber, indeed I killed with my relentless sword those kings of the world who fought me as well as those who did not convert to the True Faith after they had been overpowered. There is no chance that you will be able to kill me, for my death is in the hands of God Almighty, not in the hands of a carrion eater like yourself. There is no limit to your folly indeed!" The dastardly Qaroon Akka started whipping Amir Hamza, who called out, "O Gueber! Whip me only as hard as you yourself are able to withstand!" Qaroon Akka asked with great insolence, "Who is there in the whole world who can even touch me?" Then Qaroon Akka beat Amir Hamza again, and after sprinkling salt on his wounds, rolled him up in a fresh camel skin. He constructed a column one hundred and twenty yards high and attached bells to it at intervals, and hung Amir Hamza from the top. He made it his practice to whip Amir daily, sprinkle salt on him, wrap him up in freshly skinned hides, and hang him up from the pole of *uqabain* to avenge the death of his elders.

After some days had passed, he informed Naushervan of these circumstances. The emperor summoned his privy counselors and asked them, "What is your opinion in this matter? Shall I order Hamza's death or order his release?" All of them spoke with one voice, saying, "Now that even Mehr-Nigar is dead, you should not show any special consideration to Hamza out of the regard you had for the princess. In our opinion, it would be best for Your Honor to administer punishment to that Arab in person. You should humiliate him in the same manner in which he disgraced you." The faithless Naushervan accepted their counsel as judicious, and departed for Mecca with his army. He arrived at his destination within a few days and showed much favor to Qaroon Akka, who had Amir whipped in his presence every day and then had him rolled in a freshly skinned hide sprinkled with salt and hung from the column of *uqabain*. He disgraced and humiliated Amir and extended the hand of despotism toward the citizens of Mecca as well, inflicting a new tyranny on them each day.

A merchant conveyed the news of these events to Amar Ayyar who was at that time aboard a ship. Immediately upon receiving these tidings, Amar disembarked and headed for Mecca, greatly distressed and infuriated by the news. In Mecca, Khvaja Abdul Muttalib summoned Amir Hamza's old companions and commanders by dispatching letters to them, and they, too, expressed great surprise at the news. Khvaja Abdul Muttalib also sent a letter with Umayya Zamiri, Amar Ayyar's father, to the domicile of Aadi so that he could become appraised of the situation as well and come to Amir Hamza's aid.

It happened that Kuliyat Ayyar caught sight of Umayya Zamiri hastening on his way looking vigilant and alert, and reckoned that Umayya Zamiri's quick pace was not without cause. He guessed that something was the matter and decided that even if he was mistaken in his assumptions, he would still kill the old man to avenge the death of his father, and to please his heart with his enemy's murder. He arrested Umayya Zamiri and presented him before Naushervan, who bastinadoed him and demanded to know where he was headed and who had sent him on his mission. Trying to save his dear life and hoping to secure his release from those tyrants by telling the truth, Umayya Zamiri confessed the details of his mission and hastened to present the letters hidden in his shoes to Naushervan. After reading the letters, Naushervan had him killed and took the terrible consequences of the deed on his head. Bakhtak said to Kuliyat, "You know well that Umayya Zamiri is Amar Ayyar's father. You have been instrumental in having him killed, and the deed will bring about terrible consequences for you. It would bode well for you to watch out for him and guard yourself from his rage." Kuliyat answered, "I have taught scores of *ayyars* of his ilk; he will not be able to win over me with his trickery. I will make him drink the same potion that I gave his father, and dispatch him where his elder now lies. I only await his arrival! Just let him set foot here, and you will see!"

It so happened that Amar Ayyar arrived in Mecca the very next day and immediately learned the details of his father's murder. Kuliyat became informed of Amar's arrival and ordered his *ayyars* to arrest Amar upon sight and present him before him. Upon his orders everyone set out to catch Amar.

One day Kuliyat saw Amar walking alone outdoors and ran after him. They had gone for some distance in this manner with Kuliyat chasing Amar when Amar produced a flower steeped in a drug from his *zambil* and threw it to the ground. Kuliyat picked it up and smelled it. The moment he did so he fell unconscious, and Amar found his chance and cut off his enemy's head. At once, Amar went to the pole of *uqabain* and saw Amir Hamza and Muqbil Vafadar chained to it. When Amar offered his greetings, Muqbil returned the greeting and said, "O light of the Arab camp! Just because you were not here, both Amir Hamza and I were caught in this calamity and were rendered helpless and vulnerable." Amar told him, "Your worries are now over. I will release you and Amir from this trouble." Then Amar climbed the pole and removed Muqbil's fetters and stuck Kuliyat Ayyar's head on the pole of *uqabain*. He stuffed cotton in all the bells so that they did not ring.

Amir Hamza was delighted just to hear Amar's voice, and said to him, "Make sure that the bells do not move and their sound does not reach the ears of the enemy." Amar answered, "I have stuffed the mouths of the bells with cotton and they will not ring out." However, Amar had not noticed one bell that was placed above Amir Hamza's head. Since he had not stuffed it with cotton, when Amar tried to bring Amir down his head struck the bell and it rang loudly. The infidels rushed there from all corners and began shooting arrows at them. Amar jumped down from the column and disappeared.

When the infidels reached the column they saw Kuliyat Ayyar's head displayed there. They went to Qaroon Akka to give him the news of Kuliyat Ayyar's murder. When Bakhtak heard this as well, he said, "None but Amar Ayyar could have done this." Qaroon Akka said, "If you were to advise it, I would kill Hamza!" Bakhtak shook from terror at Qaroon Akka's words and said, "Until Amar is captured, you must drive such thoughts from your mind! You must truly fear Amar Ayyar. He will not spare you, Naushervan, or Buzurjmehr but will behead you one and all." Buzurjmehr said to this, "O perfidious man, what injury have I done Amar that he will harm me? He will kill only those who have done him wrong."

Now hear of Amar. He sent messages to Amir's champions and commanders that stated:

Amir Hamza was taken captive by Qaroon Akka a long time ago and was kept in a harsh confinement. It is incumbent upon you to put everything aside and rush here. Make no delay in hurrying to his rescue—if this letter finds you having your meal, you should think of arriving here first and washing your hands later.

Landhoor was heading home when he received Amar's message, and turned back in the middle of his journey. Amir Hamza's commanders started to arrive in Mecca daily and his champion warriors all began gathering there.

Qaroon Akka said to Naushervan, "Now that Amar has arrived he will surely gather an army, and then we will have even greater trouble on our hands. I am strongly of the opinion that Hamza should be killed, or else we should move to my city and not stay here any longer." Naushervan replied, "Killing Hamza is no longer an option, as it would not bode well for us at all. However, there is no harm in removing Hamza to your city." Qaroon Akka immediately departed with Hamza for his city, and after reaching his destination within a few days, began inflicting even greater pain and punishment on him. One day Amir Hamza again said to the accursed Qaroon Akka, "It is said that one should eat only as much as one can digest. Inflict on me only as much pain as you could yourself withstand." Qaroon Akka laughed at him and said, "Do you nurse hopes for release even now? Do you think you can avenge yourself on me and find me your prisoner someday?" With this, he hung Amir from a gate and said to his mace bearers, "Feed him one piece of barley bread and one cup of water daily, for the suffering of this Arab is my main pleasure and it is my desire that he should always remain engulfed in pain and suffering."

Now back to Amir's camp: Sa'ad bin Amar bin Hamza also arrived in Mecca, and champion soldiers, kings, and princes came there daily until the armies were established as before. The accursed Qaroon Akka trembled with terror to witness the magnificence and might of Amir Hamza's armies. He forgot all his vain airs and said to Naushervan, "Hamza's friends and companions have arrived in such strength that I am unable to confront them myself. I am forced to seek refuge in a fort." Qaroon Akka enclosed himself within the citadel and reinforced its ramparts and crenelations. Then he sat all alert and ready for action at his post.

Khvaja Amar Ayyar was on the lookout for a chance to break into this citadel, and one night he managed to sneak into the fortress disguised as a merchant. He made friends with a clothier there and convinced him that they had been friends of old, and he thus began a partnership in his shop. Amar did his best to seek out Amir Hamza but could not discover where he had been imprisoned.

It so happened that around this time Qaroon Akka's sister, Farzana, saw Prophet Ibrahim in her dreams. He instructed her in the Act of Faith and gave her these auspicious tidings: "O Farzana! You and Hamza will become a pair and the Creator will grant you an illustrious son from Hamza's seed. Go forth and secure his release. Exert yourself in this task now and do not make the least delay in this matter." Upon waking from the dream, Farzana immediately repaired to her brother's house and took Hamza back to her home after bribing and rewarding his guards. That night she tended and ministered to Amir Hamza with great devotion, and left nothing to chance in providing comfort to him. In the morning Qaroon Akka heard that Amir Hamza had disappeared. He sent his men in all directions to find some trace of him, but they returned empty-handed. Qaroon Akka said to his vizier, "If Hamza had returned to his camp, we would have heard the sound of festive music. Let us find where he is hiding through *ramal*." After making the calculations, the vizier began to laugh. When Qaroon Akka asked him the reason for his laughter and told him to give him the truth of the matter, he answered, "Hamza has been released by Farzana Bano, whose days now pass in joyfulness. She has been biding her time in the pleasure in Hamza's company." Qaroon Akka sent one of his female attendants to Farzana's house to find out who had released Hamza and if he was in Farzana's company or had already left her. She asked Farzana, "Was it you who released Hamza from the prison and invited great calamity on your head? The vizier calculated from *ramal* that Hamza was hiding with you."

Farzana came into a rage. She tore out her hair and wept, and then said, "It is a marvel that my honor should be considered so cheap that the vizier should accuse me of infidelity and overstep his office. Just because I did not agree to submit to his pleasure and fulfill his carnal desire, that vile man has maligned and dishonored me and accused me in this manner. When have I ever even seen Hamza? I have but one house. Whoever so wishes can take the trouble of searching for him here. I would certainly be to blame if he is found hiding with me." The slave girl returned to Qaroon Akka and narrated all that Farzana had said to her. In his rage Qaroon Akka put his vizier to the sword that very moment and killed that shameless mischief maker to avenge Farzana's name and honor. Then Qaroon Akka continued to search for Hamza as before.

Meanwhile Amir Hamza said to Farzana, "God knows whether or not Amar has found his way into the castle." Amir gave a detailed description of Amar to one of Farzana's clever slave girls, describing Amar's face and features to her, and said, "Go into the bazaar of the fort and find out if there is someone there who answers to this description. If you find him, call him here on behalf of your mistress and bring him along urgently." The slave girl at last came upon Amar's shop in the bazaar, and after inspecting him well, determined that he was the one whom Amir Hamza sought. She told Amar that her mistress required such and such kind of cloth, and he should bring it along if he desired to turn a tidy profit and find a fair price for his merchandise. Amar packed the cloth into a bundle and carried it tucked under his arm to Farzana Bano's palace, where he began to show it to her.

At the sound of Amar's voice, Amir Hamza emerged from the corner of the room. Amar prostrated himself before Amir and kissed his feet and broke into uncontrollable sobs upon beholding Amir Hamza's state. Amir Hamza embraced Amar and asked him, "What is the news from our camp, and what is the state of preparedness of our army?" Amar answered, "The forces are ready, and young and old alike await you." Amir said, "How can we get out of this fortress? Every man is our enemy here."

Amar answered, "Come with me and stay in my shop. We will find some way to escape." Amir replied, "In your shop there are no weapons, only cloth. It would be useless for me to go there with you. Without weapons I will not be able to overpower anyone. Take me to a blacksmith's instead." Amar took Amir to a blacksmith's shop, where Amir picked up a hammer and began pounding away at a piece of iron.

By chance, that very moment Qaroon Akka asked Bakhtak, "Find out from *ramal* where Hamza is hiding." Bakhtak made his *ramal* calculations and said, "You will find Hamza in the bazaar of the fort." The ill-starred Qaroon Akka went with Bakhtak and began searching the bazaar, inspecting all the shops and dwellings. By and by, Qaroon Akka arrived at the blacksmith's shop where Amir was sitting. Qaroon Akka let out a war cry and said, "O Hamza, how will you escape from me now? Tell me now, who can save your life from my hands?" Amir rose wielding a hammer and replied, "O infidel, do not make idle talk. You cannot harm me in the least. Attack me now and see!" Qaroon Akka drew his sword and attacked Amir, who snatched the sword from his hands and struck his malicious breast so powerfully with the hammer that Qaroon Akka fell flat on his back. Amir tied him up at once and imprisoned him. Bakhtak, meanwhile, made himself scarce from there. He went hastily before Naushervan, and after describing Qaroon Akka's capture, said to him, "We must make our exit by the back door of the fortress, or else we will be killed any moment. None will escape with their lives from Amir Hamza and Amar's hands." Both Naushervan and Bakhtak escaped through the back door.

Amir Hamza bellowed his war cry so mightily that the whole fortress shook and its denizens believed that the sky had burst and fallen on them. When the sound reached Amir Hamza's camp, everyone learned and became informed that Amir Hamza had been released from captivity. Young and old charged together and broke down the fortress gates. Their hearts' desires had been answered, and they began slaying and pillaging the infidel hordes. The blade came into action to slay the faithless. It is said that the riches taken by the armies of the True Faith that day were so vast that the soldiers could neither carry nor cart it all away. When the remaining dwellers of the fortress converted to the True Faith, they were given quarter and their lives were spared. Amir ascended the throne and sent for Qaroon Akka and said to him, "Tell me now, O Qaroon Akka, did I not say that you should inflict only as much pain on me as much you yourself could withstand? Tell me, what is your answer to that now? How must I punish you and avenge myself on you?" At this, Qaroon Akka began crying copious tears. Amir Hamza said to him, "If you convert to the True Faith I shall spare your life and will not put an end to your existence." Qaroon Akka, who deserved beheading, replied, "I shall never be able to do what you ask of me. Whether I lose my life or keep it, I shall not give up my forefathers' creed, and won't turn back from my faith." Amir Hamza gave him into Madi-Karib's power, and said, "Dispatch him to Hell by pounding him with the mace, for such is the just punishment for his deeds." Madi-Karib dealt Qaroon Akka such a powerful blow of his mace that every fiber in his body was pulverized. Amar severed his head and hung it upon the door of the castle and burned his body. Everyone occupied themselves with festivities, as their mission had been accomplished and their desires fulfilled.

———

Now hear of Naushervan. As he was making his escape toward Ctesiphon, he spotted a huge army whose camp occupied a large tract of land. He sent his *ayyars* to gather intelligence about the commander of that army, and to find out whence he had come and where he was headed. The *ayyars* brought news that the commanders of that army were two valiant and courageous brothers, Sar-Barahna Tapishi and Dewana Tapishi, who had come to assist Naushervan with their armies. Naushervan himself set up camp there and received the brothers with great favor and showed them much honor and told them his tale of woe from beginning to end. Bakhtak said of this change of events, "Now Hamza cannot escape alive. Such champion warriors were never before pitted against him."

Both brothers folded their arms with humility across their chests and said, "We are ready to sacrifice our lives in the emperor's service. We will remain obedient to you under all circumstances. Even if the entire horde of rebels from the Seven Climes should gather against you as a body, we will break open their heads and humiliate them utterly." The emperor was pleased to hear those words and conferred resplendent robes of honor on them, giving them many other gifts and rewards besides. He invited them to take wine in his company and ordered that choice foods be prepared for them.

———

Now for news of Amir Hamza. He wedded Farzana Bano at an auspicious moment and took his pleasure of her for forty nights and forty days, leisurely gratifying himself and fulfilling his heart's desires. On the forty-first day, Amir Hamza held court and asked everyone assembled, "Does anyone know what has passed with Naushervan?" Amar answered, "Two princes from the land of Tapish have brought a large army and joined Naushervan's side. They are waiting for you at the halfway mark from here to Ctesiphon." Amir Hamza said to Aadi, "Order our advance camp to head there without loss of time, and alert the army to make ready to join it." Aadi carried out the orders immediately. The next day Amir Hamza arrived near the enemy encampment and bivouacked opposite the army of the princes of Tapish, leaving just enough distance between the two camps to establish the battlefield, and struck the drums of war announcing his arrival. Amir made a battle formation of fourteen rows of men and the princes of Tapish also arrayed their army for battle.

First Sar-Barahna Tapishi rode into the battlefield, and after reciting martial songs, sought combat. Landhoor rode out on Shabrang and stood opposite him. Sar-Barahna Tapishi said, "O eunuch, tell me your name lest you die in anonymity." Landhoor answered, "You beast, my name is Landhoor bin Saadan. Who is there to rival me? Come, deal me a blow and see for yourself!" The prince landed a blow of his mace on Landhoor who took it on his shield and answered with a powerful strike of his seven-hundred-*maund* mace, which would have crushed a mountain to powder, but Sar-Barahna Tapishi remained unruffled. Until evening the two of them fought with their maces and skirmished together. Finally the drums were sounded to suspend combat, and both armies returned to their halting places. Amir asked Landhoor, "What is your estimation of Sar-Barahna Tapishi's prowess? Did you find him a worthy match?" Landhoor answered, "O Sahibqiran, I never saw even a *dev* of Qaf—let alone a human being on Earth—who could be said to be his equal. His strength is of a sort to confound the mind." Amir laughed and then said, "O Landhoor, his body is made of steel. Spear, sword, and mace will have no effect on it; he will not die by those weapons."

The next day Madi-Karib fought with Sar-Barahna, and the two of them skirmished together. Whenever Madi struck him with his mace, Sar-Barahna took it on his head without a single hair being harmed on his body. Madi-Karib tired of dealing blows, but Sar-Barahna remained unperturbed. Suddenly dust rose on the horizon from the direction of the forest and the *ayyars* from both camps brought news that Aljosh Barbari had come with forty thousand troops to aid Naushervan, many of his men being choice warriors and champions. Naushervan sent several of his kings to receive him, and when he finally arrived Naushervan saw that Aljosh Barbari was ninety yards tall, and he was a veritable hill of a man. Naushervan showed him honor and deference and told him all the details of his feud with Hamza and Amar Ayyar. After sounding the drums to suspend combat, Naushervan returned with him to his pavilion and arranged revels for him with wine, meat, music, and dancing, providing him with every comfort.

The next morning, Sar-Barahna Tapishi entered the arena and cried out with great vigor, "O Hamza, why do you not come out to fight me yourself? Why do you send common warriors to combat with me while you yourself bide your time in comfort and peace? Is this the proof of your courage? Is this how valiant men comport themselves?" Before Amir could go out to confront him, a dust cloud grew from the direction of the forest, and when the scissors of the wind cut it apart, everyone saw forty orange standards on the horizon. Amar said to Amir Hamza, "O Sahibqiran, it is the same Naqabdar Naranji-Posh who used to come to aid me in my hour of need and who often saved me from enemy hands!"

The Naqabdar soon arrived there and arrayed his army on one side and stationed his champions in battle positions. Addressing the infidel army, the Naqabdar declared, "Any Gueber whose claim on courage has made him vain must first fight me. Then he may fight the followers of the True Faith." Amir Hamza sent a message to the Naqabdar through Amar that his bravery, resolve, and chivalry were now plainly revealed to him, and ever since he had heard of his extraordinary qualities, he had hoped to meet him. Amir also said that he hoped the Naqabdar would witness his combat with this Gueber, as he had already challenged him and called him out by his name. Amir asked the Naqabdar not to depart when the fighting was suspended at the end of the day but to make sure to call on him. The Naqabdar acquiesced to Amir's wishes when Amar gave him this message.

Amir Hamza rode into the arena on Ashqar Devzad and said to Sar-Barahna Tapishi, "It is a waste of time to fight you with weapons. You and I must test our strength by trying to lift each other from the ground. If my feet rise from the ground I will submit to you, and if I lift your feet above the ground you must submit to me. Tell me now if this suggestion finds favor with you and satisfies you." Sar-Barahna agreed to it heartily and answered appropriately. Amir dismounted and Sar-Barahna joined him and began exerting himself to lift Amir Hamza by his waistband. He struggled at this until he sank knee-deep into the ground, but Amir did not budge. Sar-Barahna finally gave up in frustration, confessing his inability to lift Amir from the ground. Amar called out to his camp, "Beware, friends, any moment now Amir will make his war cry, the terror of which will cause scores of infidels to fall dead in an instant." All the infidels marveled at Amar's words and declared that the *ayyar* had spoken idly. They said Hamza was free to make all the war cries he wished, for all warriors made war cries and they never heard of any soldier falling dead from the sound of one.

Then Amir made his war cry. Most of the men in the infidel army fell into a faint, and many of them suffered burst eardrums. Thousands of men were deafened, and everyone marveled at the force and magnitude of Amir's war cry and their senses took leave of them. In short, Amir Hamza caught Sar-Barahna Tapishi by his waist and lifted him up above his head on his very first attempt. He whirled him over his head seven times and then threw him to the ground, tied him up, and gave him into Amar's custody.

Dewana Tapishi came charging at Hamza with drawn sword upon seeing his brother being taken prisoner in that manner. Amir Hamza caught his hand and kicked his horse out from under him, which made the animal retreat a full ten paces and caused Dewana Tapishi to fall to the ground. Before he could recover, Amir had tied him up also and given him to Amar's custody. With a heavy heart Naushervan announced the end of hostilities for the day and returned to his resting place. Both armies went back to their camps.

Naqabdar Naranji-Posh made a sign to his forces and ordered them to set up camp adjacent to Amir's and pitch their tents near the armies of the followers of the True Faith. Then the Naqabdar headed for Amir's pavilion and the two of them met and took delight in each other's company. Amir received the Naqabdar with great honor and respect, and showed him the many marvels of Qaf he had brought along. Then Amir expressed his gratitude to the Naqabdar for coming to Amar's assistance during his absence. Naqabdar Naranji-Posh said bashfully, "O Amir, do not make me melt away with shame and feel more embarrassed than I already feel. I have not done any deed so great that you should thank me. There was no service I rendered you which was praiseworthy. I feel mortified that such a long time has passed since your return from Qaf and you have faced countless trials and tribulations and experienced all manner of grief that I was unable to help you with."

From the softness of the Naqabdar's voice Amir reasoned that it was a woman. He caught the Naqabdar's hands and led her to another pavilion, saying, "I can bear the excitement no longer, nor can I tell you the secret reason for my acting in this wise. Please forgive my offense and do not hold me to blame." Amir Hamza lifted the Naqabdar's veil without delay and turned it over, uncovering cheeks that were the envy of the moon and a face that was as resplendent as the sun. Amir Hamza fell unconscious, overwhelmed by this woman's beauty. Amar's eyes were also blinded and filled by the radiance of the Naqabdar's aspect. However, Amar held himself together and sprinkled Amir Hamza's face with rose water and the essences of musk and orange blossom, and said to the Naqabdar, "Pray forgive me this license, but I request you in God's name to press your face against Amir's without delay so that when he inhales your perfume he is restored to his senses and receives comfort from the closeness of your body." With an embarrassed look Naranji-Posh, who had nursed the desire for such an opportunity for a long time and had lived in that hope, immediately pressed her face to Amir's and brought extreme joy to Amir Hamza by kissing and caressing him. Amir opened his eyes and Amar immediately brought wine, that notorious beautifier. They had had two goblets each when all their shame and embarrassment left them, and Amir seated the Naqabdar in his lap and inquired about her past.

The Naqabdar narrated her story thus: "My name is Naranj Peri. A long time ago I left Mount Qaf and made my dwelling on Koh-e Silan. My throne was flying in the air the day you were fighting Gustham, and I fell into a swoon after beholding your face, which was the very picture of the sun's resplendence. When my vizier's daughter, Nairanj Peri, saw that I had fainted, she carried me back to Koh-e Silan. When I returned to my senses, the desire to see you again made me return to the same place where I had first seen you. I took others with me, and had sent my *ayyar* to find news of you. I learned that the moment my vizier's daughter took me to my dwelling on Koh-e Silan, you had departed for Mount Qaf with Abdur Rahman Jinn. I cannot even begin to tell you what sorrows I suffered in separation from you and what hardships I underwent. I could do nothing else but pray for your safety and await your arrival, and pass my nights and days in these anxieties. When I learned that you had vouchsafed Mehr-Nigar to Amar's care, and her father Naushervan had decided to snatch her from you by force, I delegated some messenger *perizads* to inform me at once if an army ever threatened to overwhelm Amar's force. Thus it happened that whenever I heard that Amar was in danger of being overwhelmed in a battle, I would arrive for his assistance without delay. And by virtue of your prestige, I managed to defeat and rout the enemy and deliver Amar from the hands of the foe."

After hearing this speech, Amir Hamza kissed Naranj Peri's sugary lips and said, "My life, you slew the enemy with your relentless sword, and now you have put me to the sword of your chivalry and lofty conduct." He asked Amar Ayyar to read their nuptials, and he married Naranj Peri and spent the whole night in pleasure seeking, biding his time in giving and receiving pleasure.

In the morning, Amir bathed, changed, and held court. He ordered Sar-Barahna Tapishi and Dewana Tapishi to be brought before him. Then he told the brothers to approach his throne and asked them, "How did I overpower the two of you?" Both brothers replied with folded arms, "By the same tradition in which brave men defeat brave men. You showed courage like a valiant warrior. Now you are our master and we are your vassals." Amir instructed both of them in the Act of Faith, conferred Jamshedi robes of honor on them, and seated them on golden chairs by his side. He showed them much favor and offered comforting words to reassure them. Afterward Amir Hamza retired to the women's quarters and occupied himself in pleasure seeking with Naranj Peri.

One day the battle drums were sounded from the enemy camp, and Amir heard their thunder. He said, "Order the drums of war to be sounded from our side as well." Upon hearing the battle drums, mighty and intrepid warriors presented themselves into Amir's service, ready for battle. Amir headed for the battleground and formed his troops into fourteen rows. When Aljosh Barbari entered the arena seeking combat, Sarkob the Turk answered his challenge from Amir's camp. Aljosh leapt one hundred and seventy yards into the air from his saddle, and as he came tumbling down he kicked Sarkob and dealt him a blow of his staff so deftly that he fell to the ground writhing like a wounded snake and was about to faint from the violence of the blow. Aljosh regained his seat in the saddle, and when Sarkob tried to get to his feet and attack Aljosh with his mace, he kicked him as hard as he had before. Sarkob was unable to answer Aljosh's antics and laughter broke out in both camps. Young and old alike laughed loudly at this peculiar form of combat.

In the meanwhile a dust cloud formed on the horizon and the *ayyars* from both camps rushed off to gather news. They found out that four brothers, Samoom Aadi, Sina Aadi, Qubad Aadi, and Me'aad-Raz Aadi, had come from the Alburz to help Naushervan with four thousand fully equipped warriors of the Aadi tribe, and had brought a great many war supplies with them besides. Naushervan sent his commanders to greet them, and upon receiving the brothers, showed them much respect and honor.

An onager suddenly broke into the encampment for the followers of the True Faith and injured hundreds of men. Amir Hamza turned his attention toward the beast and gave him chase. The onager escaped and Amir Hamza followed in pursuit riding Ashqar Devzad. By late in the day the onager had traversed a great distance and Amir had crossed over the borders of another land. As soon as it was evening, the onager disappeared from his view, leaving Amir Hamza confounded and wondering where he had gone. When he was unable to find any trace of him, Amir hunted and roasted a wild animal, and after eating and drinking, he fell asleep under a tree.

When Amir Hamza awoke the next morning, he again caught sight of the onager and again gave him chase. The onager disappeared into a garden, and Amir followed him inside. He searched every corner of the garden, looking behind every bush and shrub, but the onager had vanished as if it had never existed. Amir sat down under a tree, but his heart was distressed by hunger and he was faint from weakness. He saw a herd of goats in a corner of the garden, and the sight offered him some hope. Amir slaughtered one of the goats and broke some branches from a tree to light a bonfire and roast the meat. The herdsman there saw a stranger roasting a goat in the garden. He ran to inform his master, Qunduz Sar-Shaban, about Amir Hamza. Upon receiving this news, Qunduz came to the garden swinging his seven-hundred-*maund* mace and attacked Amir with all his might. Amir picked him up and threw him into a pond. The thoroughly soaked Qunduz asked Amir with great surprise, "O stranger! Tell me truthfully who you are, for no one has ever been able to press my back to the ground, and I have never suffered a defeat. But you were able to throw me into the pond with tremendous ease and you humiliated me before my servants."

Amir Hamza answered, "My name is Sa'ad Shami, and I am Hamza's brother. I have been gifted with power from God and my body is as strong as steel." Qunduz fell at Hamza's feet, saying, "No one but Hamza himself could have exhibited such strength! None in this world has the ability to throw me down in this manner and ruin my name and reputation in just a moment. Indeed you are Hamza in person!" Amir reiterated that he was merely Hamza's brother. Qunduz replied, "I shall now spend my life at your feet and am resolved never to part company from you."

Amir said to him, "You may do so provided you convert to the True Faith and submit to the tenets of the righteous faith." Qunduz recited the Act of Faith sincerely then and there. He hosted Amir for a few days and showed him all manner of kindnesses and attended to him with great devotion. Amir asked him, "What land is it whose borders I have crossed?" Qunduz answered, "This is the land of Kharsana, which is the kingdom of Fatah Nosh. He has a daughter who is a paragon of beauty, and her face is so dazzling that it would be little wonder if the sun and the moon derived their brilliance from it. She holds her own in beauty; however, she will not accept anyone's suit. Kings and princes from every land have sought her hand, but she flatly refuses everyone's suit. Other than words of rejection, she has never uttered a single word. Amir said to him, "O Qunduz, take me to the city of that princess." Qunduz replied, "Very well, I am bound to your service and am ready to take you to her."

The next day Amir left with Qunduz for the princess's city. They had gone some ten *kos* when Qunduz said, "Let us dismount to eat and take some rest." They stopped and roasted two goats. Amir was unable to eat a whole goat by himself, but Qunduz ate his goat and then ate the leftover roast from Amir's share as well, leaving Amir marveling at his appetite. Then they traveled onward. After they had gone quite some distance, Qunduz said, "It is impossible for me to take another step for the pangs of my hunger." Amir wondered at Qunduz's speech and realized that Qunduz was a match for Aadi in his appetite. Amir said to Qunduz, "There is nothing here that I can offer you to eat, for it is difficult for me to arrange anything for you in this desolation. Let us go onward and we will surely find something."

Qunduz took a few steps and sat down and said, "My intestines are all in a tangle from the violence of my hunger." The power of his appetite again stupefied Amir and he wondered what he should do about it. Then he saw an encampment of merchants close by and went and met their leader, Karvan, and asked him if could have a little food. Now, Karvan was a noble and generous man. He answered, "Not just a little food, you can have as much food as you desire. Pray be our guest and eat to your heart's content." Amir returned to Qunduz and said, "Go have your fill," whereupon Qunduz helped himself until he was quite sated.

Amir asked Karvan, "Where is your caravan headed?" He answered, "We are headed for Kharsana, but we have heard that someone named Faulad, a rebel slave of the emperor of Greece, waylays caravans along this road. As we are bearing much merchandise and many goods, we are afraid of being looted by him and being left slaves." Amir said, "Since I am with you, you must not fear any thieves. Entertain no anxiety or fear." Karvan asked, "O young man, who are you, whence have you come, and where are you headed? Give me all your details and tell me where you are going." Amir answered, "My name is Sa'ad Shami, and I am Hamza's brother. An onager led me into this land and brought me this far. I heard the praise of the land of Kharsana and it ignited in me a desire to pay it a visit. Thus I was headed for Kharsana when I came upon you, and this is the whole and entire truth." Karvan's face lit up, and he said, "God be praised! You are the son of Abdul Muttalib who is my friend of old. Therefore, you are like a son to me. Consider all these goods yours. Have no worries about privation or indigence, and be satisfied on all counts. God willing, upon reaching Kharsana I will give you one fifth of the profit from this merchandise and will give you from my own share as well." Amir Hamza responded, "Since you have called me your son and assumed the title of father, and, moreover, since you have shown me all these kindnesses, it is idle to talk of rewards for my efforts. You should rest assured that even if Faulad's master, the emperor of Greece himself— much less Faulad—should desire to take away even a twig from your merchandise without your consent, I will cut off his hands and shake his empire at its foundations." Karvan was heartened by Amir Hamza's words and blessed him.

Qunduz said to Amir Hamza, "Why did you refuse when he himself offered to give you one fifth of the profits? Why must one reject riches when they are being offered? When God bestows on you from His Providence, why must you spurn it? When we reach the city, I will take my share as he promised and will not think twice about it." Amir Hamza said, "O Qunduz, how much wealth will you accumulate from that? Have no worries, you will soon find such great riches that you will not be able to store them or carry them away."

Amir camped that day with the merchants at their insistence and the next day he set off with them. The news of this convoy reached Faulad's ears and he was told that a group of merchants laden with goods and merchandise was heading for Kharsana, and appeared to be carrying gold and riches. Faulad surrounded the convoy and Qunduz confronted him. One of the thieves skirmished with him, and Qunduz dealt him a powerful blow of his mace that forced his brains out by way of his ears and broke his neck in just one strike. A great hue and cry rose among the thieves and Faulad himself confronted Qunduz and attacked him. Amir soon arrived and lifted Faulad clear off his saddle so that his feet left his stirrups. Then Amir kicked his horse, which retreated fifty paces, while Faulad remained in his hold. Amir spun Faulad overhead and slammed him to the ground. Faulad tried to get up and escape, but Qunduz dealt him a mace blow that made his head sink into the ground. Amir then said to Qunduz, "You must never commit such a deed again. If he had converted to the True Faith he would have become your friend. You must never kill an infidel without first hearing his reply to your invitation to convert to the True Faith."

In a few days they arrived in Kharsana and found lodgings at a caravanserai. Amir Hamza passed his time in great comfort and pleasure and the days of his existence were ruled by peace and bliss. Karvan brought the fifth part of his profit to Amir and offered it to him as his promised share, but Amir Hamza returned the largesse to him. Karvan insisted and pleaded with Amir Hamza to accept it, but he would not take a thing and gave away so much in charity from his own purse as well that all the mendicants of the city became men of means. Slowly the news traveled to King Fatah Nosh that a stranger who had newly arrived in the city was distributing wealth to its citizens with great generosity. Rabia Plas Posh, the king's daughter, also heard this news and said to herself, *The diviners often predicted that Hamza would arrive in this town someday and marry me. Perhaps the man in question is Hamza.* She said to her attendants, "Go and see who that man is who has surpassed Hatim in generosity, and is constantly crying, 'Come to me, O mendicants, and take what you need!' " When the female attendants went and saw Amir Hamza at the caravanserai, they said among themselves, "This young man greatly resembles the portrait our mistress keeps with her. Indeed it seems that he is the subject of that picture!" All of them went before the princess and said to her, "Congratulations, O Princess, the young man whose portrait you keep is present at the inn and distributing alms with great generosity. He has given out so much wealth and distributed so much in charity that every pauper has become wealthy and a veritable Qaroon in means." Plas Posh was delighted to hear this.

It so happened that Nasai, the son of the king of Farang, attacked Kharsana with a large army and began killing the populace and laying waste to the city. Fatah Nosh enclosed himself in the fortress with his populace when he received this intelligence. Slowly the noise of this attack reached Amir Hamza's ears. Amir asked the people of the city, "What is the reason for all the commotion? What is afoot that we hear this noise and rioting?" Those who were in the know told Amir, "The king of Farang had asked for the hand of Princess Rabia Plas Posh for Prince Nasai, and although King Fatah Nosh had no objection to the match himself, the princess turned down the proposal. It is for this reason that the prince has attacked the city and brought his army to sack it. He has already made hundreds of wealthy men destitute and ravaged several neighborhoods. Now he is assaulting the fortress."

Amir Hamza now said to Qunduz, "Have Ashqar saddled. Let us go and drive out the infidels!" Following Amir's orders, Qunduz saddled Ashqar Devzad and brought Amir's accoutrements to him and gave him all his weapons. Amir decorated himself with his arms and armor, mounted Ashqar Devzad, and prepared to go to battle. He took Qunduz with him and headed for the fortress gates, where he said to the city magistrate, "Open the gates so that I may inspect the cause of all the trouble." The magistrate answered, "You have seen what turmoil is brewing outside the walls. Now is not the time to step outside the city and seek any challenges." Amir entreated him repeatedly, but the magistrate refused to open the gates for him. Irritated, Qunduz landed his mace on the magistrate's head, inflicting a fatal blow that smashed his skull and made his brains flow out of his nose. Amir asked Qunduz, "You cruel man, why did you kill this weak mortal?" Qunduz replied, "For the reason that he did not open the gates!"

King Fatah Nosh learned that the stranger who distributed alms at the inn was heading out to fight the prince of Farang and demonstrate his courage and might. Fatah Nosh immediately rode out to meet Amir and said to him, "O dear friend, you are a stranger and all by yourself in this land. Why do you wish to fight the large enemy force alone and undertake such hardship? You are neither my slave to be duty bound to do so, nor have we ever met before, which might warrant this show of amity. Why do you wish to sacrifice your life for nothing and imperil yourself in this campaign? Yet if you are determined to carry out your plans, I would like to help you in every possible way. I wish to attach my forces to yours, although they are much fewer than the enemy's hordes and for that reason I enclosed myself in the fortress." Amir answered, "I have no need to take your army with me. You may go to the roof of the fortress and witness the spectacle there. When the foe is defeated and begins to retreat, you may come out of the fortress to raid them and take possession of the booty." Fatah Nosh was obliged to state, "If that is your desire then I am powerless. I will obey your wishes." Amir headed for the battlefield with

Qunduz, and the enemy troops were arrayed into position. Rabia Plas Posh also went to the roof of the fortress, and with unbraided hair she supplicated God, praying, "O Almighty God! Pray take this young man into your care, for he goes to do battle and takes on this hardship for the sake of strangers." Then she began surveying the battlefield with a spy-glass.

The Farangis thought that the two men coming out of the fortress had been sent to make a peace offering. As a precaution they sent a rider toward them to discover their intentions and ask them if they were carrying a message. The rider approached Amir and asked him, "Our leader demands to know your objectives, and has asked me to find out who has sent you." Qunduz answered, "Tell me, what are *your* intentions? If you call yourself a man, come and fight me here in the battlefield. Show me if you have any valor." The Farangi commented, "This ant has grown wings,[24] too?" The soldier attacked Qunduz with a sword, but Qunduz foiled his attack and dealt him a blow of his mace that made that Farangi sink into the ground along with his horse. Upon witnessing this, Prince Nasai ordered one of his champion warriors to go and take both men captive without delay. Qunduz sent that soldier to the same land where he had earlier dispatched the other trooper. In a short time, forty Farangi champion warriors lay dead at the hands of Qunduz.

The Farangis were terrified and said to one another, "These two men are not humans. They are from the race of jinns. Or perhaps they are a heavenly calamity sent to punish us. We will never find deliverance from their hands and will be packed off to the Land of Doom."

The king of Kharsana was greatly pleased by this scene and asked his vizier, "Who are these two men, whence have they come, and where are they headed? Give me the details of their origin." The vizier said, "A merchant caravan has arrived in the city and lodged at the caravanserai. Perhaps these two men have accompanied them." The king said, "Bring me the leader of the caravan so that I may meet him and find out the truth." When the leader of the caravan presented himself, the king asked him, "Tell me, who are these two men who are such excellent warriors?" The caravan leader narrated the whole incident of meeting the two men and said, "The one on horseback is Hamza's brother, and the one accompanying him on foot is his lieutenant. This is all I know of their particulars." The king said, "It is my conjecture that he is Hamza in person. Such bravery and courage, which have become a legend among all men, were bestowed on no other man. It is a shame that he arrived in my land so long ago and I never learned of his presence. Otherwise I would have hosted him and attended to his comforts. In any event, if we live there will be occasion for another meeting."

To cut a long story short, when all forty champion warriors sent to fight him had been killed by Qunduz, the standard-bearer of the Farangi army himself came to fight Qunduz, and drew close to challenge him. Qunduz also attacked him with his mace, but the man caught his weapon and tried to snatch it from his hands. Qunduz called out, "O brother Sa'ad Shami, come quickly to my aid, or else my mace will be snatched from me and I will be overpowered by this infidel!" Amir Hamza roared so mightily that it shook the entire expanse of the desert. The riders of the Farangi army fell from their horses into ditches, and their horses, finding their saddles empty, ran toward the forest. The arm of the standard-bearer of the Farangi army grew limp, and Qunduz exerted himself and snatched his mace from his grasp. The standard-bearer drew the sword from his scabbard and dealt a blow to Qunduz, but Amir Hamza threw his companion out of harm's way and struck the standard-bearer with his sword, severing his arm at the shoulder. A great commotion broke out in the Farangi army and Prince Nasai fled from the battlefield. Amir Hamza and Qunduz followed them for a distance of four *kos* and slaughtered thousands of Farangis, sparing none who came within the reach of their weapons.

Upon witnessing this excellent victory, Fatah Nosh emerged from the fortress with his army and looted the goods and riches of the Farangis with great abandon. Fatah Nosh said to his men, "No one may take a single item from this loot, for all of it is the property of Sa'ad Shami. Beware and make sure that no one touches or appropriates it." Rabia Plas Posh opened the gates of the treasury with a view to offering a sacrifice for Amir's life, and distributed a great many riches among the destitute. There was not one beggar in the whole city who did not become rich that day.

When Amir Hamza returned triumphant and victorious to the city, Fatah Nosh conducted him in an entourage to the fortress. His anxieties about the foe had been dispelled and he dismounted from his horse and kissed Amir Hamza's feet and put all the loot before him. Amir embraced him and said, "Distribute this wealth among your men, and dispense it to your army as their reward." Qunduz was shocked into silence upon hearing Amir's words. Fatah Nosh arranged a royal feast in Amir's honor and broke bread with him and joined him as his drinking fellow. Qunduz grew giddy with wine and picked a fight with one of Fatah Nosh's commanders, Yalan. Amir Hamza asked him to cease fighting and admonished him for conducting himself in that manner.

The revels continued for several days. One day Fatah Nosh took his vizier aside and said to him, "If Rabia is agreeable, no better match could be found for her than this man. Go and find out her intentions. If she gives her consent, I will put the proposal before this young man and offer her hand to him." The vizier broached the subject with Princess Rabia, who lowered her head and replied, "I shall obey the king's wishes in this matter. I will oblige myself to submit to his commands, whatever they may be."

Upon hearing Rabia's message, Fatah Nosh told Amir of his desire to make him his son-in-law. Amir Hamza agreed to his proposal with pleasure and enthusiasm, and the wedding preparations began immediately. Clairvoyants were sent for and asked to determine an auspicious time for holding the ceremony. On the day of the wedding, Amir remembered Amar and said, "It is a pity that Amar is not here today. Were he present, he would be gladdened by this event."

———

Now hear of Amar. The same day that Amir left the camp in pursuit of the onager, Amar had followed him. Amar had trekked past the same places that Amir had on his way to Kharsana. Amar kept following the course taken by Amir until he reached the garden of Qunduz. The shepherd there said to Amar, "We are not familiar with anyone called Amir or the Sahibqiran. However, someone called Sa'ad Shami, who is Hamza's brother, did indeed pass this way and stay here for a while. After staying for a few days he left for the city of Kharsana with our master." Amar realized that this man he spoke of was Amir Hamza. He left immediately and before long arrived in Kharsana.

God willed it so that Amar arrived at Fatah Nosh's doorstep two hours before the nuptials. He said to the guards, "Go and tell your king that my runaway slave, Sa'ad Shami, has sought refuge with him and hidden himself here. It is my desire that he be immediately arrested and brought as a prisoner to me, for any delays and dithering in this regard will mean grave consequences for you." The guards went and conveyed Amar's message to the king's court in Amar's same words.

Amir Hamza asked them, "Describe that man's shape and guise to me and tell me how he is dressed and what are his mien and manners." The guards replied, "He is some thirteen yards tall and sports a red broadcloth cap that rises a full five yards from his head. The two feathers attached to his cap move by themselves independent of the movement of the air, and he is dressed in a felt robe. A hamper hangs around his neck, a bow is secured to his body, two feathers and a few arrows without arrowheads or tail feathers are stuck at his waist. He is carrying a paper shield on his back and wields a staff weighing eighteen *maunds*. Over his felt robe he is wearing a flowing gown that is so long and loose that a lion cub could easily hide in its sleeve. One feels awestruck and dumb in his presence and finds it difficult to make reply." Upon hearing this description, Amir Hamza headed out of the court, and all those who heard the description marveled to the very limits of marveling.

Amar rushed forward and fell at Amir Hamza's feet, and Amir Hamza embraced him and showed him great kindness and favor. Then Amir Hamza led him by hand into King Fatah Nosh's court and introduced him to the king by describing Amar's trickery, his cunning, and his faithfulness. The king said, "Do tell me now who he is." Amir answered, "He is a clown from Naushervan's court." Amar said, "Clowns are indeed lords and kings. They are men of great honor and prestige. How could I be said to have attained their rank?" The whole assembly laughed at Amar's speech. When it was time to read the nuptials, Amir said to Amar, "Quickly go and fetch some *qadi*[25] to conduct the ceremony, but make sure he is a follower of the True Faith and a believer."

Amar left the court, changed his garb, and disguised himself as a holy man by sticking a two-yard-long flowing white beard on his face. Then he put on a loose shirt that was so large that a baby *simurgh* could be carried in its sleeve, tied a turban on his head that was closer to a dome in its dimensions, and arrived in the assembly limping and carrying a staff several yards long. All those present, including Amir Hamza and Fatah Nosh, received Amar with great deference. The entire assemblage said with one voice, "Indeed we never set eyes on such a saintly man in this city until today. God alone knows whence your holiness has arrived to make it possible for us to earn the distinction of attending to you." Amir Hamza seated him at a higher station on his right and asked him to conduct the *nikah* ceremony. Amar followed his wishes and read the sermon in such sweet and warbling tones that the eyes of everyone in the audience filled up with tears and the entire assembly fell into a trance.

The king put a thousand dirhams before Amar, who said, "I would never except such a meager offering, and will not take a farthing less than five thousand dirhams." Qunduz replied, "O mulla, if these thousand dirhams are of no use to you, then pray grant them to me. If they do not have any value for you, allow me to have them." Amar immediately stuffed the money into his shoe and disappeared after giving Qunduz a blow with his staff. Qunduz began complaining and wailing while muttering to himself, "No harm is done. Sooner or later I will meet this *qadi*. Then I will avenge myself on him and visit such terrible humiliation on him that he will remember it for all his living days." The king asked Amir Hamza, "Tell me, who was that man and where did he come from?" Amir answered, "He arrived from the Future State and God dispatched him here." Then Qunduz said, "God knows where that clown has disappeared who brought that accursed *qadi* here who struck me without justification and hit me so badly that my body aches still. If I do not find the *qadi*, I will settle scores with that clown and deal with him as he deserves." After a while Amar again entered the assembly and performed another one of his tricks. He put his foot over Qunduz's head and [?] danced in such a clownish manner that whoever saw him broke into uncontrollable laughter and marveled at his cunning and trickery. Fatah Nosh was greatly pleased by Amar's antics and said to his vizier, "I have never seen such a peerless man. Indeed he is a paragon of *ayyari* and is a past master of ruses and ploys."

Thereafter, rounds of goblets of colorful wines were served and the guests began dancing in a state of giddiness. Everyone became ecstatic from inebriation and all sorrow and grief sailed away from the shores of their hearts. The king richly rewarded Amar Ayyar and spread joy throughout the whole assembly with his liberality and munificence. The celebrations were held for seven days and seven nights. On the eighth day, Amir Hamza said to Amar Ayyar, "Return to the camp, and I will follow you in a few days. I will spend a little more time here enjoying myself." Amar returned to the camp and Amir retired to the palace to seek pleasure with Rabia Plas Posh. After some days the keeper of the palace presented himself before Amir and gave him the auspicious news that Rabia Plas Posh was with child. Amir said, "I will stay here until my son is born and will not make any plans to go anywhere else." Rabia Plas Posh replied, "O Sa'ad Shami, what you propose is also my heart's desire, for the days I have spent waiting for you were like days spent clad in rags. Now at last I have seen some happy moments and passed some days and nights of joy."

Of Amir's Departure for the Land of Fatah Nosh's Brother, Fatah Yar; of Amir Slaying a Dragon; and of the Birth of Prince Alam Shah Roomi

The narrators of sweet discourse and the scribes of legends thus relate that Fatah Nosh's younger brother, Fatah Yar, ruled a land neighboring Kharsana. He came to learn that Fatah Nosh had married Rabia to someone who was traveling through his land and had thus acted against the conventions of his tribe. Fatah Yar wrote a letter to his brother stating that he was desirous of meeting his son-in-law and requesting Fatah Nosh to send him to visit his land for a few days so that his people also might have the pleasure of meeting him.

Fatah Nosh showed the letter to Amir Hamza and told him of Fatah Yar's desire of meeting with him. Amir said, "There is no harm in this visit. I will go and take on the hardship of the journey for his sake." So, Amir Hamza departed for Fatah Yar's land the following day. When Amir arrived, Fatah Yar received him and conducted him into the city, showing him every token of honor and respect and seeing to his every comfort. He seated Amir on a golden throne and was conversing with him when all of a sudden a commotion was heard without. Amir asked Fatah Yar, "What is this noise and disturbance?" Fatah Yar answered, "A dragon lives near this city, and when he exhales, a flame darts from his mouth for a distance of seven *kos,* burning everything in its path. When the dragon inhales, everything for a distance of seven *kos* gets sucked into his open mouth. This city has lived with this scourge for many years, and all things animate and inanimate have been marked by his shadow. The dragon has just exhaled, causing all this commotion in the city and setting all creation to great ferment and turmoil."

Amir said, "It is a shame that Fatah Nosh never breathed a word about this dragon to me; otherwise I would have rid you of this scourge many days ago and crushed the dragon's head. In any event, I would like you to appoint someone to lead me to the dragon's lair, point it out to me from afar, and identify the dragon's abode to me." Fatah Yar said, "I shall accompany you myself." Amir saddled Ashqar and took Qunduz along, too, and headed out. Fatah Yar took his army along and rode out with Amir. Everyone wondered in their hearts how that man would kill the dragon and overpower such a monster. When Amir saw that the dragon was about to inhale, he dismounted and went toward him. As he approached the dragon, Amir drew his dagger, rushed at the monster, and, pressing his dagger to the dragon's scales cut through them all the way to his spine, killing the dragon. Such a huge amount of smoke billowed from the dragon's mouth that it became dark for many *kos* around, and the sky resembled a ball of smoke.

When the air finally dissipated the smoke cloud, Amir returned to Fatah Yar and said to him, "Praise be to God, that fiend has been killed." Fatah Yar went with his army and saw the dragon lying dead, heaped up like a small hillock. He kissed Amir Hamza's hands and arms, and thanked him for ridding him of that monster. The entire populace sang Amir Hamza's praise and everyone was happy and joyful.

After spending a few days with Fatah Yar, Amir Hamza returned to Kharsana, at which time Rabia Plas Posh's pregnancy came to an end. At an auspicious moment, an illustrious son was born to Amir and a long awaited star appeared in the heavens of his expectations. Amir Hamza named the boy Alam Shah Roomi. Fatah Nosh flung open the doors of his treasury and the destitute received from it whatever was appropriate to their need. When Amir's son was forty days old, Amir took his leave of Fatah Nosh and Rabia Plas Posh, and said, "When this boy comes of age, you must send him to the camp of Amir Hamza." Fatah Nosh put Amir under strict oath and said, "Tell me whether your name is Sa'ad Shami or Hamza." Amir answered, "Indeed I am Hamza himself." Fatah Nosh was greatly pleased by that and Qunduz was also beside himself with joy. He began telling everyone proudly, "Verily, none but Hamza had the wherewithal to overpower me. God be praised, I submitted only to Hamza. To have given myself to anyone else's service would have been disagreeable and repugnant to me." Rabia Plas Posh also offered thanks that she was the wife of Hamza, a legend of his time. In due course Amir Hamza departed for his camp with Qunduz.

Amir Hamza's camp, meanwhile, was engaged in daily warfare with Naushervan's forces. One day both armies had just arrayed themselves in battle formations when Amir arrived at his camp with Qunduz. His companions kissed his feet and told him of their campaign. Amir Hamza offered words of comfort to everyone and embraced them all, addressing each man by his name.

Then Amir sent Qunduz into the battlefield. Aljosh Barbari jumped from his horse, kicked Qunduz and dealt him a blow of the staff, and then regained his seat. Qunduz rolled in pain on the ground like a tumbler pigeon. When he regained composure, he again confronted Aljosh, who attacked him in the same manner once again. In short, Qunduz and Aljosh were engaged in combat until evening, when the drums were sounded to suspend combat for the day and both armies returned to their resting places.

The next day, Aljosh entered the battlefield and called out, "O Hamza, come out and display your bravery and courage, and face me yourself if you truly are a man. You have defeated many champions and now it is your turn to taste defeat at my hands." Amir Hamza spurred on Ashqar Devzad and rode out to skirmish. Aljosh attacked Amir Hamza twice, but Amir did not return the strikes and stood quietly watching. When Aljosh attacked him a third time and aimed to kick him, Amir caught his leg and spun him above his head. Aljosh grew limp and Amir slammed him to the ground and pinioned him, fastening his arms securely behind his back. Then Amir Hamza gave him to Amar's custody to be imprisoned. Amar said to Aljosh, "Get up on your feet and come with me." He answered, "Make me do it, if you have the power to do so. I would like to see how powerful you are." Amar took out his whip and gave Aljosh a few cuts with it. Before long he began trotting behind Amar, and everyone who witnessed the scene broke into fits of laughter. Amir Hamza sounded the drums to announce the day's end, returned joyfully to his camp, and retired to his pavilion.

That evening Amir had Aljosh appear in his court and asked him, "Tell me, what are your intentions now?" Aljosh answered, "What could be the intentions of one who has submitted? For as long as I live, I shall remain your slave." Amir Hamza converted him to the True Faith and seated him on a golden chair alongside him and raised him in honor and prestige before everyone. Amar put the hoop of slavery in Aljosh's ear and enrolled him in the ranks of Amir Hamza's slaves. Then at Amir's orders, Amar occupied himself with supervising the festivities and he delegated the attendants to different stations for the occasion.

The narrators tell that in the midst of the revelries that night, a palace attendant presented himself and gave news of the birth of a son to Amir Hamza by Naranj Peri. Amir ordered the musicians to play festive tunes and conferred gifts and rewards on everyone there according to their stations. He ordered a necklace weighing one *maund* and put it around his son's neck and named him Tauq-e Zarrin. Amir gave him into the care of nurses and mentors and assigned several people as his son's custodians and presented gifts to them.

Amir Hamza then rode with his companions into the battlefield. One of the warriors of the Aadi tribe who had come to aid Naushervan descended into the arena and sought combat by loudly challenging Amir Hamza's camp, whereupon Istaftanosh went to answer his challenge. At that time, a dust cloud rose from the direction of the forest. *Ayyars* from both camps exerted themselves to investigate it, and informed their respective armies of the arrival of the prince of Greece with a vast force he had brought to fight the champions of both armies. While the *ayyars* were making these reports, the Greek prince formed his battle arrays in between the two armies, and then rode his horse into the battlefield with great majesty and grandeur. He turned his face toward Naushervan's army and called out, "O Naushervan, send someone to fight me so that he may be acquainted with the mettle of the swords of brave men and may witness the courage and pluck of valiant men."

One of the Aadi warriors entered the arena and weighed his mace, aiming to bring it down on the head of the prince. The prince snatched the mace from his hands and, securing his hold on the Aadi's horse's saddle and martingale, lifted the horse along with its rider and slammed them both so hard on the ground that their bones were crushed. Shouts of "Bravo!" and "Well done!" rose from both camps at this show of might, and the tongues that had wagged before in making tall claims were silenced. The scribe of the *dastan* writes that in a matter of a few hours, well over a hundred Aadi warriors were killed by the prince. Naushervan's entire camp sank into disquiet and distress, and his fighters lost their hearts from fear. For two hours the prince challenged Naushervan's army, but none would come forward to answer his challenge nor did anyone dare to answer his call.

The prince was obliged to turn toward the camp of the followers of the True Faith, and he called out to them in a loud voice, "O Arabs, any man among you who dares to combat me should come forward and test his strength and display his martial arts." Farhad sought Amir Hamza's leave and led his elephant into the battlefield. The prince asked him, "O giant, give me your name so that you do not die an anonymous death and people do not grieve over an unmarked grave." Farhad answered, "My name is Farhad bin Landhoor, and my fighting style is unique among all men." The prince of Greece said, "Give me the blow you wish to deal." Farhad answered, "It is not our way to deal the first blow in battle. You deal the first blow, and if I survive it I will return it and you will then see my power and impact." The prince of Greece bellowed "In the name of God!" and struck a blow. Farhad foiled the blow by jumping back onto his elephant's rump. The mace landed on the elephant's head and its brains flew out of its ears. Farhad jumped from his elephant as it collapsed beneath him and died, departing forever from Farhad's service. Farhad tried to hamstring the horse of the prince of Greece, but the prince quickly jumped from the saddle and confronted Farhad on foot. Farhad seated himself on another elephant and readied for battle, and the prince mounted his horse again. Both of them fought with maces, and the prince observed that Farhad dealt the mace like a consummate fighter. He jumped from his horse again and picked Farhad up along with his elephant. Then making his war cry, the prince slammed Farhad and the elephant to the ground and said to him, "Go and send someone else to fight me, for now you are left with no strength to continue to combat with me." The scribes write that if Farhad had not quickly left his saddle, he would have been left with crushed bones like his elephant, and his skull would have cracked. Despite his alacrity, Farhad had suffered injuries and received grievous wounds.

Both camps again rang out with the cries of "Bravo!" and "Well done!" in witnessing the fight, and Amir Hamza said, "It was said of Rustam that he could lift his adversary along with his elephant and slam them both to the ground. I am now an eyewitness to this proof of the prince's strength myself." Those present there replied, "What has only reached us by way of tale about Rustam cannot hold precedence over what has been witnessed of the prince by the eyes. That was merely a tale and the account of an event. This has been for everyone to witness in reality."

Farhad now said to Amir Hamza, "He asked me to retire to my camp and send someone else to fight him." Amir Hamza signaled to Landhoor and ordered him to fight the prince. Landhoor rode on Shabrang against the prince of Greece. The prince spurred his own horse and came alongside Landhoor and linked his stirrups together with those of his adversary. Then he lifted Landhoor clear out of his saddle, raised him high above his head, and slammed him to the ground. Then he said to him, "Go and send someone else from your camp to fight me!"

Sa'ad bin Amar bin Hamza next answered his challenge. Each man caught hold of the other's cummerbund and exerted himself until his horse sank into the ground up to his knees. The prince of Greece left Sa'ad bin Amar bin Hamza and said to him, "Go and send me Hamza so that I can test his strength and see what he has to show for courage and valor." Sa'ad returned and conveyed his message to Amir Hamza, informing him of his claim and intentions. Landhoor said to Amir, "O Sahibqiran! I believe that this prince is your son, for his features and physiognomy reveal that." Amir responded, "If he were my son, he would not battle with my companions." Landhoor answered, "Amar bin Hamza also fought with you. This prince also might desire to test his strength against yours."

When Amir Hamza headed for the battlefield astride Ashqar Devzad, Bakhtak said to Naushervan, "I have not the least doubt that this prince is Hamza's own progeny. Often his sons show a similar temperament. Let us watch this bout, for it will be a historic one like the battle fought between Rustam and Sohrab."[26] Naushervan replied, "It would be little wonder if the prince turned out to be Hamza's son; we are witnessing a truly momentous event."

In the arena, Amir brought his steed next to the prince's mount. The prince secured a hold on Amir's cummerbund and Amir caught hold of the prince's belt. Father and son exerted themselves and, in the end, Amir Hamza bellowed his war cry and lifted the prince into the air. He was about to slam him to the ground when he heard a voice from the heavens and an angel brought him these auspicious tidings: "O Hamza, do not throw him down cruelly, for he is your own son." Upon hearing that voice, Amir Hamza put the prince down lightly on the ground and asked him, "What is your name?" He answered, "I am Alam Shah Roomi." He then kissed Amir Hamza's feet, and his father embraced him and kissed his face. They returned to Amir's camp and Hamza ordered festive music, most jubilant to have met the prince. He gave the prince the titles of Rustam-e Peel-Tan[27] and Sher-e Saf-Shikan.[28]

Amir then said to him, "You committed a grave wrong by humiliating my friends in the battlefield and fighting me." The prince answered, "Brother Amar bin Hamza was guilty of the same wrong that I committed. Your obedient servant was obliged to introduce himself thus." Amir Hamza introduced the prince to all his friends and companions and made the prince offer apologies to them. Considering that Alam Sher was Amir Hamza's dear son, everyone met the prince with great kindness, and for seven nights and seven days festivities were held to celebrate his arrival.

On the eighth day, the drums of war were sounded in the camp of the infidels. Amir ordered his camp to answer the call, and went into the field to array his forces in battle formations. One of the warriors of the Aadi tribe again came into the battlefield to seek combat. Rustam-e Peel-Tan took Amir's leave and went to answer his challenge. Alam Shah parried three strikes by the Aadi warrior and then dealt a sword blow that cut the man in two. The narrator says that Rustam-e Peel-Tan killed fifty enemy warriors that day and slew many notable commanders with his glittering sword. He then stayed on the battlefield for a full two hours, seeking combat and challenging the enemy, but none from the infidel camp emerged to answer his call. Alam Shah was then obliged to take to the reins and charge the enemy ranks.

Amir Hamza called out to his friends, "Rustam has charged the enemy ranks all by himself! Go to his aid and do not abandon him to fight alone." No sooner were the orders given than the commanders of Amir's camp fell on the enemy ranks like angry lions and made heaps of dead infidels with their swords. The remainder of the infidel warriors escaped with their tails between their legs. Rustam-e Peel-Tan chased them for a distance of four *kos* and returned triumphant and victorious. Amir's army took so much loot that day that they were unable to carry it all back to their resting places. They were obliged to use carts to take the goods and movable property to their camp. Alam Shah Roomi presented himself before Amir and kissed his feet. Amir embraced him and offered untold gold and riches in sacrifice for his life. Thereafter Amir occupied himself with celebrations, and all the regular functions of the court were suspended.

Meanwhile, Naushervan said to Bakhtak, "We were handed a resounding defeat and our army has been completely destroyed. All of our war equipment has been burned to cinders and the surviving army is terrified. What should we do now? Where should we go and what strategy can we employ?" Bakhtak answered, "The city of Khavar is nearby, and its ruler, Qeemaz Shah Khavari, is known for his bravery and generosity. The whole world rings with the renown of his courage and chivalry. If you were to take refuge with him and describe your troubles to him, he would consider it a matter of pride to show kindness to you, and would exert himself fully in obeying your commands." Thus Naushervan headed for the city of Khavar. When he approached there, messengers alerted Qeemaz Shah Khavari of his arrival and stated, "The Emperor of the Seven Climes, Naushervan, is arriving here to seek refuge with you from the tyranny and cruelty of Hamza, and is heading for your doorstep because of your reputation for beneficence." Qeemaz Shah rode out with great magnificence to receive Naushervan and conducted him into the city. Qeemaz Shah seated Naushervan on a throne and inquired of his welfare. After comforting and consoling him, Qeemaz Shah said, "If Hamza heads in this direction, he will receive the just deserts for his sins." Bakhtak said, "It was only because His Highness reposed such hope in your person that he came to seek shelter with you and took on all the hardships of the journey!"

Of Amir's Departure Toward the City of Khavar in Pursuit of Naushervan, and of His Converting Qeemaz Shah, the Ruler of Khavar, to the True Faith

The storytellers have it that after Amir had finished with the festivities, he asked Amar, "Do you have any news of Naushervan's whereabouts?" Amar answered, "It is said that he has gone to the city of Qeemaz Shah Khavari who has offered much comfort and consolation to him and received him with great kindness. He has promised Naushervan that if you were to head in that direction he would capture you and take you into his custody as a prisoner." Amir laughed at this and said, "Order our advance camp to head for the city of Khavar." The next day Amir departed for Khavar at the head of a sanguinary force. Nearing the city, Amir sent a missive to Qeemaz Shah that read:

> O Qeemaz Shah, know that Naushervan is my archenemy, and this time I am determined to punish him. Many times in the past [?] he sought my forgiveness for his trespasses and converted to the True Faith only to revert again to idol worship. There is no manner of chicanery and animosity that he has not shown me, and there is no form of torture that he has not used against me. Yet he has always tasted humiliation and met a miserable end and has always been trounced and vanquished by me. Now I hear that he has sought refuge with you, and that you have offered him your support. It is incumbent on you to send him and the ill-starred Bakhtak to me as prisoners immediately upon reading this letter. Otherwise, you will find your place in the coffin instead of on the throne, and you will be left with neither friend nor companion.

Amar carried Amir Hamza's letter to Qeemaz Shah's court and said to the gatekeeper, "Announce my arrival and do so with dispatch." The gatekeepers informed Qeemaz Shah that a messenger of great standing had arrived with Hamza's letter. Qeemaz Shah was holding court at the time and asked for Amar to be presented before him.

When Amar came into the court, Qeemaz Shah demanded to see the letter, to which Amar said, "First you must show deference to me and present an offering, then the letter will be given into your hands and what Amir Hamza has ordered will be carried out. Do you not know that this letter has come to you from a glorious personage? He is the Lord of the Chivalrous, the crown bestower to kings who wear his badge of slavery, the slayer of beastly fire-breathing dragons, the captor of ferocious lions, the Destroyer of *Tilisms,* the Slayer of the *Devs* of Qaf and Zulmat, the world-renowned champion warrior, the Lord of the Auspicious Planetary Conjunction of His Times, the Quake of Qaf, the Latter-day Suleiman, Abul-Ala, Amir Hamza bin Abdul Muttalib, the Lord of Arabia."

Qeemaz Shah could do little else than make an offering of gold and jewels, receive Amir Hamza's letter with deference, and raise it to his eyes as a token of respect. Despite all these elaborate rituals of tribute and reverence, when Amar gave the letter into Qeemaz Shah's hands and he read it, he tore it up immediately and said, "Hamza has written to tell me that if I do not produce Naushervan and Bakhtak as prisoners, I will receive a coffin for my throne. I neither pay vassalage to Hamza nor am I beholden to him in any way. Nor indeed do I have any awe for him that I would carry out his orders to arrest Naushervan and Bakhtak and send them to him." Amar answered, "O Qeemaz Shah, the Sahibqiran did not order me to do it, otherwise I would have ripped up your belly in the same way that you tore up that letter."

Qeemaz Shah turned to his slaves, who stood before him with folded arms, and said, "Catch this foul-mouthed messenger and do not allow him to escape!" The slaves surrounded Amar on all sides and put a cordon around him. Amar drew a steel dagger from his scabbard and released countless slaves from the misery of attending to Qeemaz Shah and burned the Garden of Life of many others with the lightning bolts of his sword blows. Then Amar slapped Qeemaz Shah, snatched his crown, and left after thoroughly humiliating him in this manner. Many ran to catch him, but Amar was not one to be caught and overpowered so easily. The wind could not touch the skirts of dust he kicked up in his wake and even the lightning marveled at his speed.

Bakhtak said to Qeemaz Shah, "Perhaps Your Honor is unfamiliar with this attendant of Hamza. He is such a monster that the eyes of heaven have never seen his equal. There has never been a more cunning master of subterfuge. Princes and kings tremble with terror at his name and ask for reprieve and mercy from him with every breath. You saw yourself how he escaped from this large crowd after committing an indelicate act." Qeemaz Shah answered, "Better late than never. You will see how I treat him and his master and quench my sword in his blood."

In short, Amar returned and gave an account of his visit to Amir Hamza. The next day Qeemaz Shah marched into the battlefield to the sound of war drums, and Amir arranged his army opposite him. First to arrive on the battlefield was Qeemaz Shah's sister, Khurshid Khavari, who was a master lance thrower and unsurpassed in martial arts. She considered all champion warriors equal to a mere mote before her might and believed none could match her in bravery and courage. She called out with great vanity and pride, "O champion warriors, come out and show me what you own in the name of valor. Fight me if you wish my lance to explore the insides of your chests."

One of the Sherwani warriors, Shermar, received Amir's leave to answer her challenge and entered the field wielding his lance. Khurshid Khavari lunged her horse forward and threw her lance at Shermar who escaped, but his horse received the blow and immediately collapsed under him. Khurshid Khavari threw a second lance and injured Shermar with a grievous wound. Amar Ayyar quickly carried him from the battlefield. In short, within an hour she had injured several champions from Amir's camp. Rustam-e Peel-Tan could not hold back his fury any longer, nor did he wish another man to fight her, so he took to the field and descended into the arena like lightning. Khurshid Khavari threw her lance at him and attacked him in the same way she had the others. The prince caught hold of her lance, and despite her exertions, she was unable to release it from his hands. The prince snatched the lance from her and removed the poison from its tip, and then dealt her a blow of its shaft that threw her from her horse. When the prince dismounted and tried to fasten her up, he discovered that this warrior was a woman. He carried her off on his horse in his lap, and produced her before Amir and everyone in the camp. Amir Hamza asked her, "O woman, who are you and what is your name? Tell me, what business do you have with battling in the arena?" She answered, "My name is Khurshid Khavari, and I am the sister of Qeemaz Shah." Amir ordered that she be conducted to the mother of Rustam-e Peel-Tan and given into her care. While Khurshid Khavari was being sent there, Rustam-e Peel-Tan fought Qeemaz Shah's brother and took him captive as well. Then he challenged the infidel army, saying, "O army of eunuchs, it suits you indeed to send women into the battlefield and watch the spectacle from afar. If you at all consider yourselves men, come into the battlefield and confront me yourselves." Qeemaz Shah's father, Nim-Tan Khavari, entered the arena and raised his hand to strike a blow and attack the prince with his mace. The prince caught hold of his hand as well as the mace, and punched him so hard on the neck that Nim-Tan Khavari fell unconscious from his horse onto the battlefield. The prince took him captive and gave him into Amar's custody. Qeemaz Shah's elder son, Homan Khavari, was likewise taken prisoner when he sought battle with the prince.

Qeemaz Shah said, "I have rarely seen anyone as powerful and stalwart as Hamza's son. He has been granted this strength as a gift from God. Within an hour he has taken several grand warriors prisoner and humiliated mighty champions. It seems that he must have entered the battlefield today at some very auspicious moment, which is why he overpowered everyone. One must not fight him today but instead avoid combat with him." With these words, Qeemaz Shah sounded the drums to announce the day's end and returned to his pavilion. Both armies went back to their resting places and took refuge from the hardships of the battlefield.

Amir embraced Rustam-e Peel-Tan and offered gold and jewels as a sacrifice of his life, and gave away even more in charity in gratitude for his safe return from the battlefield. That night, Amir Hamza sent for Homan and Nim-Tan Khavari and asked them, "Tell me, what are your intentions now? What is it that you desire?" They answered, "Until Qeemaz Shah presents himself to you and converts to the True Faith, we would like to be excused from making our intentions known." Amir Hamza gave both of them into the custody of Madi-Karib at his prison and occupied himself with festivities. Amir Hamza sent a message to Khurshid Khavari to inquire if she was willing and happy to accept Rustam-e Peel-Tan as her husband. She answered, "I would envy my own stars if I were granted such an illustrious husband and his company in which to enjoy life's pleasures." Amir Hamza engaged Rustam-e Peel-Tan and Khurshid Khavari in matrimony at an auspicious moment and then took part in the festivities.

For seven days and seven nights Rustam-e Peel-Tan remained in the palace, and on the eighth day he emerged to the sound of the drums of war and decorated himself with his arms and armor. Amir Hamza took to the battlefield and organized his army. Qeemaz Shah brought his horse into the arena and called out, "O Arab lad, come out and face me so that I can instruct you in the intricacies of combat. You are a complete ignoramus as far as the arts of war are concerned. Come now so that I may teach you the way to wage battle."

Rustam-e Peel-Tan spurred on his horse and when he came within reach Qeemaz Shah dealt him a blow with his eight-hundred-*maund* mace with all his might. The prince escaped the blow by stopping it with his shield, but his steed was injured. The prince dismounted and cut off the legs of Qeemaz Shah's horse. The two of them changed horses and resumed fighting. The prince dealt Qeemaz Shah such a powerful blow of his one-thousand-*maund* mace that if it had landed on a mountain it would have smashed it to dust. None could have escaped its impact alive. However Qeemaz Shah did not even turn a hair. He laughed and said, "O Hamza's son, is this all the power and might that you have brought to fight me? Is this the sum of your strength that makes you proud and vain? Go and send me your father so that he can fight me." The prince answered, "What harm have you inflicted on me that you desire combat with my father, and commit such vain words to your tongue? I am still safe and sound and standing before you as the adversary. If I am unable to overpower you, then you may inconvenience my father and make plans to fight him." Until noon the two of them fought with maces and then drew swords. When their swords grew blunt and serrated like saws, they wielded lances. They fought so mightily that their lances broke apart inch by inch, and their ferocity paralyzed their audience with terror.

Finally, Qeemaz Shah sounded the drums to announce the day's end, and the following day the armies again faced each other in the battleground and their swords saw action. Landhoor took Amir's leave and went to fight Qeemaz Shah. Qeemaz dealt him a blow of his mace that Landhoor parried with great effort and answered with his own mace. Qeemaz Shah said, "O Landhoor, indeed there is great disparity between legend and truth. I do not find you half as good as the tales report of your strength. I have not received a single wound from you that could discomfit me." Landhoor replied, "O Qeemaz, I struck this mace once on the tower of Ceylon and it was razed to its foundations. I cannot tell whether your body is made of steel or a similar material that you remain thus unharmed. Indeed it is a sight for me to marvel at."

Both warriors fought with such ferocity that the two armies constantly exclaimed "Bravo!" and "Well done!" With night falling, the trumpeters sounded the end of combat for the day. Both brave men returned to their pavilions and retired to their camps. Amir asked Alam Shah Roomi and Landhoor, "How did you find Qeemaz Shah?" They answered, "If there is anyone who can be said to have a claim to power and strength after you, it is Qeemaz Shah. Only God can safeguard one fighting him and provide refuge from his strikes."

The following day the two armies again faced each other in the battleground. A warrior had yet to enter the field from either side when a forty-yard-tall youth dressed in steel came forward from the direction of the forest and stood between the two armies. He turned his face toward the infidel army and roared like a lion, "O Naushervan, send one of your champions to fight me." Naushervan sent an Aadi warrior to combat with him. The rider lifted the Aadi warrior up and slammed him to the ground so fiercely that every bone in his body was crushed and he never rose to his feet again. A second Aadi warrior came into the field and suffered the same fate. Then nobody dared to confront and skirmish with the stranger. After waiting for an hour for someone from Naushervan's camp to challenge him, he turned toward the camp of the followers of the True Faith and called out, "O Arabs! The one among you who is courageous enough to fight should come out and win laurels in combat against me." Sarkob Turk took Amir Hamza's leave and confronted and faced this man in the arena. The youth also threw Sarkob on the ground and then allowed him to leave, saying to him, "Go and send me someone else to fight with me."

Amir Hamza asked Sarkob, "How did you find him in combat?" Sarkob answered, "O Amir, I can say nothing except that this youth is an unforeseen calamity. He has no match in valor, courage, and the arts of war." Qunduz Sar-Shaban next took Amir Hamza's leave and went to fight. That ferocious warrior caught Qunduz Sar-Shaban and separated him from his mount but left him unharmed and did not strike or injure him. The giant said, "Go back now and send me another man to fight." Qunduz returned and told Amir Hamza all he had undergone. Amir said to him, "From his face and features it seems to me that he is your son." Qunduz said, "If he is indeed my own blood, nothing will keep me from killing him and smashing his head with my mace for disgracing me in this manner before both camps and robbing me of my prestige."

Then Rustam-e Peel-Tan, Alam Shah Roomi, went into combat against that desert warrior. The youth caught hold of Rustam's cummerbund and exerted himself to the last iota of his strength to lift the prince, but he did not budge even slightly from his place. Rustam caught hold of the mysterious youth, bellowed his war cry, and lifted him clear out of the saddle several handspans into the air. Then Rustam put him lightly on the ground and asked, "Tell me truthfully who you are and what your name is and of which place are you a native." He answered: "My name is Shaban Taifi, and I am the son of Qunduz Sar-Shaban."

Rustam-e Peel-Tan brought him along and produced him into Amir Hamza's service. After he had made Shaban Taifi kiss Amir's feet, he explained his particulars. Amir Hamza embraced him and showed him much affection, and then sounded the drums to announce the day's end and returned to his pavilion. Amir Hamza gave Shaban Taifi the title of the Latter-day Hamza and seated him on the throne of his son Amar bin Hamza, augmenting his rank before the whole court. Celebrations were held for seven days and the destitute and needy were lavished with riches in Shaban Taifi's honor.

On the eighth day the two armies again faced each other in the battlefield and tested the might of their swords in the arena. Shaban Taifi fought Qeemaz Shah Khavari that day, but despite remaining engaged in combat the whole day neither was able to overpower the other. Each soldier returned to his pavilion at the end of the day. The next morning the battle arrays were formed again. Qeemaz Shah came out onto the field and challenged, "O Hamza, your warriors suffer defeat after defeat and still you feel no shame. Why do you not face me yourself instead of sending mere boys to fight me?" Amir Hamza rode Ashqar Devzad into the battlefield with a dexterity that dazzled and even blinded the eyes of his onlookers. Qeemaz Shah brought down his mace with all his strength, but Amir blocked it and then dealt a mace blow to Qeemaz Shah, who stopped it with his head. Although Qeemaz survived the blow, sweat streamed from every pore in his body and all four legs of his horse were broken from the impact. Qeemaz Shah jumped from his horse and tried to hamstring Ashqar Devzad, but Amir quickly left his saddle to face Qeemaz and block him. They fought until noon with maces and then they drew swords to continue the fight, but neither of them was able to achieve his end and secure victory over the other by any device.

Qeemaz Shah then praised Amir Hamza, who replied, "We have tried our weapons, and now only one thing remains." Qeemaz Shah asked, "What is it? Pray tell me." Amir replied, "I will catch hold of you by your waist and you should do the same and we will both try to raise each other from the ground. The one who loses must pay allegiance to the other and give himself unto the other's service for the rest of his life." Qeemaz Shah accepted the condition and said, "O Hamza, you have made a grave error in putting this condition to me. Indeed you have committed great folly and brought calamity on your head by making me this proposal." Thus speaking, Qeemaz Shah caught hold of Amir's cummerbund and exerted all his power and might to lift him, yet he was unable to raise Amir Hamza from the ground. He was utterly humiliated and, with all his pride evaporated, he said, "I have spent all the strength that I have. Now it is your turn. Catch hold of my waist and try your strength now!" Amir let out his war cry and lifted Qeemaz Shah above his head. After turning him seven times above his head, Amir threw him to the ground and pinioned him and gave him into Amar's custody.

Amir Hamza returned to his camp to the sound of festive music and ordered that all the Khavaris be sent for and brought before him. When Amar had done this, Amir Hamza said to Qeemaz Shah, "I won the wager and you are the loser. Therefore you must convert to the True Faith." He answered, "It is far more preferable for me to be killed than to convert to the True Faith. It is not the tradition of our forefathers to give up our ancestral faith." Amir was enraged and ordered Landhoor and Madi-Karib to kill him with their maces and dispatch the infidels to Hell. However, Qeemaz Shah remained unaffected by the mace blows showered on him by the two champions. Witnessing this, Amir Hamza became most sorrowful that a mighty warrior of Qeemaz's caliber should be lost to him for not obeying his commands. He said, "Give him into the custody of Madi-Karib." Qeemaz Shah asked, "How long will you keep me captive, and what will you achieve by imprisoning me?" Amir said, "I will not give up tormenting you. As long as you are alive, you will rot in prison."

At that moment Qeemaz Shah asked for water. Amir ordered sherbet made for him and had the Book of Ibrahim[29] recited over it. The moment Qeemaz Shah drank the sherbet, it melted his stony heart and he realized the truthfulness of the True Faith. He said to Amir, "Why do you not kill me?" Amir answered, "I am sorry for your plight, and I am rueful that a mighty warrior and a courageous and brave man like yourself should die in complete blindness to his own good." Then Qeemaz Shah laughed heartily and said, "O Hamza, I am now convinced that you are a great connoisseur of brave men and show mercy to the slaves of God. I am ready to submit to your every command since it would be against all wisdom to turn away from doing so. Tell me now, what is your pleasure?" Amir said, "That you should convert to the faith of Ibrahim." That very instant Qeemaz Shah ennobled himself with the True Faith, along with his father, brother, and son. Amir Hamza conferred robes of honor on all of them and, after conferring a Jamshedi robe of honor on Qeemaz Shah, seated him by his side on his throne and ordered revels to be arranged to celebrate the occasion.

When Naushervan heard the news, he said to Bakhtak, "To linger here any longer would be akin to cutting off our own path to safety. We will be taken prisoner before long and then we will not find release from their prison for the rest of our living days. We must depart for another refuge and escape from their clutches." Bakhtak answered, "The city of King Kayumars is not far from here. That sovereign is an accomplished spearsman and is so intrepid and stalwart that fear of him used to drive Qeemaz Shah to retreat into the mountains to save his life. We must go to him. If Hamza follows you there it will mean that his death has driven him there, and fate has dealt him the ultimate reverse."

Naushervan escaped with Bakhtak without loss of time. After a few days they arrived at their destination. Upon hearing of Naushervan's arrival, Kayumars Shah received him and conducted Naushervan to his court, where he seated him on his throne with great honor. He treated Naushervan with great munificence, and after hearing his account, said to him, "If Hamza comes here it will mean that his death has dispatched him here." Naushervan was greatly pleased by his words and began biding his time in waiting for Amir Hamza's arrival.

For the next few days Amir Hamza occupied himself with hunting in the domains of Qeemaz Shah and at night he busied himself in pleasure seeking. One day while his court was in session he asked Amar, "Where has Naushervan sought refuge now, and who has offered him his support?" Amar answered, "He has gone into the protection of the spearsman Kayumars Shah, who has shown him much favor and given him his word of honor and sworn on the allegiance he professed toward him that if you were to follow him there he would make you the prey of the crocodile of his spear." Amir smiled and said, "Order our advance camp to move toward his city. I will put him under my allegiance by the force of my sword and debase and disgrace him if he refuses to convert to the True Faith." Rustam-e Peel-Tan said, "Khurshid Khavari is with child. What are your wishes with regard to her?" Amir answered, "Send her to her mother [?]. You must depart with the advance camp." Rustam-e Peel-

Tan sent Khurshid Khavari to her home to be with her family and he marched with the advance camp.

The next day Amir marched toward Kayumars Shah's lands accompanied by his whole army. Qeemaz Shah accompanied him, along with his brothers and sons. The narrator states that when Amir set up camp at a distance of four *kos* from the city of Kayumars Shah, the *ayyars* rushed before the king with the news that Amir Hamza had arrived at the head of an intrepid army and was camped near his city, with each one of his champions bent on altercation and battle. Kayumars Shah said to Naushervan, "Pray order the drums of war to be beaten and array your army in the battlefield."

Amir Hamza received news that Kayumars Shah had descended into the arena and formed battle arrays. He decorated himself with his arms and armor and headed for the field with his army.

Kayumars Shah saw a dark and blinding dust cloud rise on the horizon. When the scissors of wind cut it asunder, Madi-Karib's insignia appeared on the horizon like the *Durfish Kaviani*.[30] Kayumars Shah beheld a tall, massively built mounted warrior whose face engendered awe and dread in the heart of the onlookers. Forty-five champions marched in a ring around his horse and fourteen thousand armored troops followed behind him, each one of whom resembled Rustam and Isfandiar in his bulk and stature. Kayumars asked Naushervan, "Is this the Amir whose courage is renowned all over the world?" Naushervan answered, "No, this man is the leader of the advance guard of Hamza's forces. He is called Aadi Madi-Karib and his reputation for brave deeds is known to all and sundry. The forty-five champions you see circled around him are his brothers."

Another warrior now came into Kayumars Shah's view riding an elephant with great majesty and grandeur and wielding a twelve-hundred-*maund* mace. One hundred and twenty parasols provided him shade and his mount was surrounded by seven hundred elephants. Kayumars Shah asked, "Is this Hamza?" Bakhtak replied, "Hamza's conveyance is still some distance away. The one you see before you is the Khusrau of India, King Landhoor bin Saadan, the sovereign of fourteen thousand islands and a warrior of great ferocity and valor."

Then two princes of Greece who were blood brothers rode past with great fanfare. Kayumars asked who they were, and Bakhtak answered, "They are the princes of Greece—just look at their dazzle and flourish. One of them is Istaftanosh and the other is called Istefunos." Two other warriors followed whom Bakhtak again identified as princes. The seven Zabuli brothers came into view next, riding with great fanfare. Kayumars Shah asked, "Who are they?" Bakhtak answered, "These seven brothers are princes of Aleppo." Shermar Sherwani went riding past then and Bakhtak told Kayumars that he was Naushervan's son-in-law and the prince of Sherwan, and he had a unique style and a manner all his own in battle. He was followed by Misqal Shah Misri; Rehan Shah; Pir Farkhari; Qunduz Sar-Shaban; Sarkob Turk, the prince of Turkistan; and the princes of Tapish, Sar-Barahna Tapishi and Dewana Tapishi. Afterward the ninety-yard-tall giant Aljosh Barbari and Sa'ad Zarrin-Tarkash, whose luminous aspect made the sun veil its face with shame, came forward with their respective armies. After identifying all of these warriors to Kayumars, Bakhtak said to him, "The one who rides behind them wearing a golden collar is Hamza's son, whose bravery cannot be described in words and whose praise is beyond the capability of speech."

In short, as the champions came forward in succession, Bakhtak called out their names to Kayumars Shah and informed him of their stations. When the thrones of Rustam-e Peel-Tan and Sa'ad bin Amar bin Hamza came into view, everyone gazed upon the two robust and beautiful warriors seated on them, whose beauty made the sun and the moon offer themselves to them in sacrifice. Several hundred parasols strung with all kinds of jewels shaded them, and several thousand mounted champions decorated with armor and cuirasses guarded their throne. When Kayumars Shah asked Bakhtak who they were, he replied, "Hamza's son Rustam-e Peel-Tan is seated on one throne and the other throne belongs to Sa'ad bin Amar bin Hamza, who is Hamza's grandson and the king of the armies of the True Faith."

Qeemaz Shah Khavari came next, and cries of "Keep off!" and "Stand back!" rose around him. The vast army that marched behind Qeemaz Shah blocked even the passage of the wind by its sheer numbers. Kayumars Shah asked, "Who is this man?" Bakhtak answered, "The first one who appears before your view is Qeemaz Shah Khavari, whose nature is anchored by courage and valor. The one behind him whose conveyance is surrounded by twelve thousand mounted slaves clad in golden robes and headgear who call out 'Keep off!' and 'Stand back!' and thus disperse men from their path, is the Prince of *Ayyars*, the Enslaver of Kings of the World, a trickster beyond compare in fraud and deceit and in conquering fortresses, Khvaja Amar bin Umayya Zamiri, the Lord of the *Ayyars* of

Hamza. Because of his supreme ability he is the leader and the prince of all commanders in the service of Hamza."

Then everyone took notice of the glaring dragon-shaped standard, which emitted a loud sound and instilled terror in the heart of every by-stander. Kayumars asked Bakhtak, "What was that sound?" Bakhtak replied, "It is the sound of Hamza's standard. It means that Hamza is about to emerge on the scene. He is the master of such grandeur that the whole of Mount Qaf shudders before it." Kayumars asked, "Who made that standard for him, and how did he come into such an excellent ensign?" Bakhtak answered, "It was made for him by Buzurjmehr. He was the one who gave this talismanic sign to Hamza." Kayumars said to Buzurjmehr, "Make me also such a standard and create for me a similar ensign." Buzurjmehr answered, "When you prevail over Hamza, I will make you such a standard and will carry out your wishes." While they were having that discussion, the dragon-shaped standard came into view and under its shade the sun of the universe—to wit, Hamza the Illustrious, appeared riding Ashqar Devzad. Fifty thousand Turkish, Nubian, Chinese, Tartar, Syrian, Greek, Egyptian, Balkhi, Bukhari, Indian, Arabian, Assamese, Aleppine, and Ethiopian slaves clad in golden robes and headpieces marched in a ring around his horse. Kayumars Shah said to Bakhtak, "I did not know that Hamza had such a magnificent entourage and such wide support." Others, who also saw Amir Hamza in his procession, praised him without reserve.

After Amir Hamza's army had arranged itself in battle formations, Kayumars came into the battlefield wielding a lance and called out loudly, "O nation of Arabs, he among you whose death flutters over his head must come out to face me in the arena and display his valor." Qeemaz Shah made a salutation to Amir Hamza and said, "If you were to order me, I would go to answer Kayumars Shah's challenge and bring him back a prisoner by virtue of your auspicious fortune." Amir replied, "Go forth. I give you into the custody and protection of God."

When Qeemaz Shah faced Kayumars, the latter said to him, "O eunuch, what is this humiliating and foolish deed you committed by allowing yourself to be reckoned among Hamza's slaves?" Qeemaz Shah answered, "There are many men better than I who have given themselves to Hamza's service and found worthy stations. It is only a matter of time before you, too, shall decorate your ear with a ring of allegiance to Hamza and drive these vain thoughts from your mind. Have no worries on this account." Kayumars took offense at these words and said, "There is no one who can enslave me or prevail over me. Deal me your blow now!" Qeemaz Shah said, "The True Faith does not allow its followers to start combat. Deal me first your best blow." Kayumars lunged his horse forward and dealt a blow to Qeemaz Shah with his lance. Qeemaz Shah did his best to foil the strike, but the point of the lance pierced Qeemaz Shah's foot, and since it was laced with a deadly poison, Qeemaz Shah returned to camp suffering from an unbearable burning pain. He fell unconscious immediately upon entering his pavilion. Amar put a bandage of *noshidaru* on his wound and went himself to face Kayumars Shah.

Seeing Amar's strange garb, Kayumars said, "O clown, has some madness seized you that you have come to face and fight me? It seems that the Angel of Death has herded you before me. You would have been better off presenting yourself at my court to amuse me and receive reward from my hands. The only reward you will find here will come as beating and pounding. You will lose your life for nothing." Amar answered, "If you return alive from this encounter I will make sure to present myself at your court to attend to your pleasure, and you will see my many tricks. I shall not disappoint you in them." Kayumars laughed and said, "Are you absolutely mad? Go and send another man to fight with me!" Amar replied, "What harm have you inflicted on me that you wish to fight another!" Then Kayumars became enraged and attacked Amar with his lance. Amar covered his face with a paper shield, charged, and dealt Kayumars Shah a blow on his head with his stick that thoroughly dazed Kayumars Shah. Amar immediately struck his hand as well, which was wielding the lance, causing Kayumars Shah to drop his weapon. Amar quickly grabbed it and took it into his possession, for it was encrusted with priceless jewels.

Kayumars said, "Give me back my lance! I will never again fight you or challenge you to battle." Amar answered, "It seems that you are not familiar with me. My good man, I deem myself the rightful owner of anything I find fallen on the ground." Kayumars pleaded with Amar in vain: Nothing that he said could change Amar's mind. In the meanwhile, the drums were sounded to announce the close of the day, and both armies returned to their camps. Amar presented the lance to Amir Hamza, who said, "Clean the poison from its tip and give it to Sa'ad Yemeni, who is a lance fighter and a spearsman beyond compare."

When night had fallen, an *ayyar* presented himself to Naushervan's service and said to him, "King Tassavuran has sent his daughter, who is unequaled in beauty and comeliness, to be given to you in marriage. Pray send for her and give permission for her to be brought into your presence." Naushervan was greatly pleased by these auspicious tidings and sent Buzurjmehr to bring her to him. Khvaja Buzurjmehr brought her into the camp and lodged her in the women's quarters, and her arrival afforded great pleasure to Naushervan.

The narrator states that this princess had once seen Hamza's portrait. She had become ardently enamored of him, and wished to sacrifice her life and soul at his feet. Some days after her arrival in Naushervan's camp, she found her chance and, dressed in night livery, she entered Amir Hamza's camp. She pulled out a peg from the back of Amir's tent and gained entry within. There she found Amir Hamza lost in sleep. She put a drug to his nostrils that made Amir sneeze and lose consciousness. She then made him into a bundle and retraced her steps, carrying Amir to a trench hidden from everyone's view. After diluting the effects of the drug in Amir's body, she disclosed her love for him and revealed to him the secret hidden in her heart. Amir asked her, "Who are you?" She answered, "I am Zar-Angez, the daughter of King Tassavuran, and none can compare with me in beauty. Now I am Naushervan's wife." Amir answered, "In the first place, Naushervan is my father-in-law, and in the second place, you have a husband. I would never inculpate myself in this manner with you. Such a deed is strictly proscribed in my religion and is considered a grave sin." Zar-Angez showered Amir with sweet words of love, but he paid her not the least attention and closed his ears to her words. When she saw that he refused her advances, she threatened him, saying, "O Hamza, I will kill you if you do not accept me!" Amir replied, "If that is written in my fate, then there is no help for it. But nothing that you do to harm me will have the least effect if it is not fated." They were still engaged in this exchange when the dawn arose. Zar-Angez left Amir imprisoned in the ditch and went back to her pavilion.

A great hue and cry rose in Amir's camp that morning. Seeing that he had disappeared from his tent, everyone began searching for him high and low. In due time news of this reached the camp of the infidels, and they, too, were surprised. Kayumars Shah boasted to Naushervan that Hamza had decamped for fear of his poison-tipped lance and escaped out of love for his own life. With these claims, he sounded the drums for combat and the two armies again faced each other in the arena. The camp of the followers of the True Faith sent Rustam-e Peel-Tan in place of Amir Hamza and formed their forces in battle arrays. Landhoor received permission from Rustam-e Peel-Tan to confront Kayumars Shah, who lunged his horse forward and aimed his lance at Landhoor's head. Landhoor flicked it away with his shield and cleverly foiled his attack. He then tried to attack Kayumars with his mace, but Kayumars turned his horse to attack Landhoor from the other side and injured him. Landhoor returned to his pavilion wounded and fell unconscious from the severe injury. Amar quickly bandaged him with *noshidaru* to provide him relief from his pain.

Landhoor's son Farhad confronted Kayumars Shah after seeing his father lying wounded and returned from the field wounded himself. Then Sarkob Turk fought Kayumars and was also injured in the combat. All those who fought Kayumars that day returned injured from the arena. As the shades of evening fell, the drums to announce the day's end were sounded in both camps and the armies went back to their resting places.

That strumpet visited Hamza again that night and told him that she was greatly distressed to see that three of his champions had been injured by Kayumars and that men who were the pride of his warriors had fared so ill at his hands. Amir said to her, "It is a shame that you have kept me a prisoner here. Set me free so that I may teach Kayumars the art of lance fighting and pour him the sherbet of death with my shining sword." That harlot answered him, "Not until I have achieved my end will I set you free. I shall never turn away from fulfilling my desire." Amir replied: "Whether or not you set me free, I shall never commit such a wrong as satisfying your carnal desire. I shall not act against the holy law and set foot on the path of sinfulness." In short, that night also ended in a stalemate, and that licentious woman left Amir as before to return to her pavilion.

In the morning Kayumars again entered the arena and bellowed loudly, "He whose death is nigh should face me and enter the arena!" This time, Sa'ad Yemeni took the prince's leave to face him. Kayumars charged at Sa'ad and raised his arm to strike him, but Sa'ad foiled his attack. After they had fought and exchanged thrusts of their spears, Kayumars found his chance and injured Sa'ad Yemeni. It was soon evening and the armies again retreated to their resting places.

That wanton woman returned to Amir, proclaiming her desire to Amir in the language of tears and crying with her head at his feet. It so happened that Amar Ayyar happened by that place in search of Amir and, hearing her words, confronted that whore, who immediately ran away at the sight of him. He asked Amir, "Who was she? If you order me, I will kill her and make her brains flow from her skull." Amir answered,

"Do not harm her. Let her go, for she is a woman. Spare her because that sinful creature is Naushervan's wife and he is very enamored of her." Amar tried to open Amir's bonds, but the Sahibqiran broke them all by himself. Amar asked him, "Why did you not try these two days to secure your release? Why could you not break these chains before?" Amir answered, "Everything is fated to happen at a particular time. It was God's will that a worthless woman should make me her prisoner." Amir exited the trench and offered his gratitude to God for his release. He sent for Ashqar and his arms and armor, and rode from there straight into the battlefield. Upon sighting him, his friends ordered festive music played, and their hearts were pacified.

Kayumars came into the arena and called out loudly, "O Arab, where did you run off to in fear of me?" Amir smiled, spurred on Ashqar to face him, and answered, "O braggart, deal me your blow!" Kayumars turned his horse and aimed his lance at Amir's head. Amir caught hold of his lance and gave it a powerful tug. Kayumars said, "O Hamza, indeed your fear of my lance is such that you have caught it with your hands. Verily, that was a most courageous act!" Amir smiled and said, "Why do you not snatch it back from my hands, then?" Kayumars tried with all his might but was unable to break Amir's grip on his lance. Then Amir pulled the lance away from his adversary with one tug, and after removing the poison from its tip, said, "O Kayumars! You are an absolute novice in the art of lance fighting. You have not the least notion how to fight with spears. You never learned the arts of a warrior, and now you must learn them from me." At this, Amir dealt Kayumars such a powerful blow with the shaft of his lance that Kayumars was stunned and darkness fell before his eyes. He fell from his horse and rolled on the ground like a slaughtered bird. Amir jumped from his horse and sat on his chest. After pinioning him and securing his limbs well, Amir gave him into Amar's custody.

When Naushervan saw what had happened, he said to Bakhtak, "Now Kayumars has been taken prisoner. We must worry for our own fates now and escape from the clutches of the foe." Bakhtak said, "Let us depart for Gilan, whose sovereign is King Gunjal. He also has a daughter whose beauty puts the *peris* to shame, and the eyes of Heaven fail to find anyone as beautiful as she. She has a masterful command of the arts of lancing, swordplay, mace fighting, and other arts of war, and none can take advantage of her in those disciplines. She is so valiant and powerful that she has overpowered many great warriors and has taught humility to renowned champions. Hamza stands nowhere in comparison to her power and martial prowess. In short, human speech is at a loss to sing her praise." Naushervan departed that very instant and, traveling night and day to pass all of the stations of the journey speedily, he arrived in Gilan, a city whose loveliness was the envy of all flower gardens. He wrote a missive to King Gunjal describing the hardships he had suffered at Hamza's hands and his own downtrodden condition, and seeking aid and succor from him. After reading this letter, King Gunjal came out to greet Naushervan and conducted him to his court offering him words of comfort and solace. He acted generously toward Naushervan and offered him every token of hospitality.

While Naushervan was awaiting Amir Hamza's arrival in Gilan with merry anticipation, Amir Hamza asked Kayumars, "What do you say now? What do you now intend to do?" He answered, "It is my intention to convert to the True Faith and remain in your service for the rest of my borrowed existence. I wish to remain your slave all my life." Amir ennobled Kayumars by converting him to the True Faith. Kayumars was released from his bonds and Amir conferred a robe of honor on him and offered him a golden seat alongside his throne. Amar put the ring of slavery in his ear and enrolled him among the ranks of Amir's slaves. After the meal was over, goblets of roseate wine were passed around and sweet-tongued singers warmed the assembly with their melodious tunes. Kayumars submitted to Hamza with folded arms and said, "I wish for you to set foot in my city to allow me to wait upon you and show you the wonders of my marvelous land." The next day Amir went to the court of Kayumars, who seated Amir on the throne and tended to Amir like a menial, with the folds of his robe tied around him, seeing to the pleasure of Amir's companions and performing every duty of a good host.

Of Amir's Departure for Gilan and Shah Gunjal's Converting to the True Faith, and of Amir's Marriage to Gili-Savar, the Daughter of King Gunjal

The narrator tells that Kayumars Shah's city had many pastures in its vicinity. The lure of the hunt kept Amir Hamza camped there for many days. He passed his days hunting and his nights in pleasure seeking, and his life there was an uninterrupted story of cheer and comfort. One day he asked Amar, "Have you had any news where Bakhtak has now led Naushervan?" Amar answered, "He is in Gilan with King Gunjal." Amir said, "We must also visit Gilan and see the sights that land has to offer." The advance camp left the same day for Gilan, and the next day Amir followed with his army. After some days, he arrived near Gilan and set up camp in its vicinity.

Spies brought intelligence of Amir's arrival to King Gunjal and gave him all the details of his army. Naushervan had the drums of war sounded that same day and the armies of Gilan and Mazandaran[31] descended to the arena while Amir arranged his forces in battle formations against the foe. A warrior had yet to come forward from either camp when a dust cloud rose from the direction of the forest. Both armies turned to see who would emerge from it, wondering to whose aid and assistance that large force had come. The moment the skirts of dust were torn apart, they all beheld a mounted warrior striding forth with a lance in his hand and with an appearance to strike awe in the hearts of his beholders. He arrived in the arena at a leisurely pace, and after sweeping both armies with his glance, sought combat with the army of the followers of the True Faith. Everyone marveled at his courage and valor, and Shermar Sherwani sought Amir Hamza's leave to combat against him.

With the very first lance strike the desert warrior dealt, he injured Shermar and threw him from his horse. Then he said to Shermar, "Noth-

ing will be served by killing you. Go and send me another man to fight."
Taz Turk from Amir Hamza's camp faced the rider next. The warrior
caught hold of his waist, threw Taz Turk to the ground, and said, "Go
and send another warrior to fight me." Kaus Sherwani next entered the
arena against the rider and suffered the same fate as Taz Turk. In the
meantime, the evening hours had crept over them and the combat was
soon ended for the day. Kaus Sherwani returned to his camp and the
rider turned back toward the forest. Amir Hamza and Amar followed him
to investigate the matter.

Hearing a sound behind him, the rider turned back and saw two men
following him on horseback with great vigilance. He speedily disappeared into a garden and Amir followed him. Amir found the garden
most pleasant and lavishly decorated. He dismounted and regarded the
scenery from a corner of the garden, and then watched the rider dismount near a pond. Mace bearers, attendants, and servants—all of them
women—rushed forward from all corners to receive the warrior, and
there was not a single man to be seen there. Amir said to Amar, "It appears that this rider is a woman." At that moment, the rider caught sight
of Amir and sent a eunuch to Amir Hamza and Amar to find out their
names, the reason for their presence in the garden, and what had led
them there. The eunuch asked Amir Hamza, "Who are you, and why
have you set foot here?" Amir replied, "My name is Hamza, and my companion is known as Khvaja Amar Ayyar, and indeed there is none who
can best him in cunning. But do tell me, O attendant, what is the name of
your princess?" The eunuch replied, "My princess is known as Gili-
Savar." At this, he rushed back to his mistress and told her the news, describing Amir Hamza's particulars to her.

The princess retired to the garden's summerhouse. She took off her
armor and exchanged her manly garb for a womanly costume. She came
forward to greet Amir Hamza and conducted him to the throne and
treated him with great respect and honor. After inviting Amir to share a
meal with her, she signaled fair cupbearers to come forth. She offered
Amir a crystal goblet filled with rose-colored wine and made him drunk.
She drank one herself as well, and after they had consumed a few cups of
wine, the princess herself became inebriated. She removed the veil from
her face and sat in Amir's lap, casting aside all modesty and shame.

When Amir's eyes beheld the gaze of that moonfaced beauty, her eyebrows shot out the arrows of her eyelashes and deeply pierced his heart.
He involuntarily yearned for marriage with her, and openly stated his

desire. As ardor and longing had already lodged themselves in her heart, she accepted Amir's proposal. Khvaja Amar Ayyar immediately tied them into the nuptial knot by reciting the wedding sermon and unifying the two hearts. Amir Hamza and Gili-Savar then retired to the bedchamber, where they took pleasure of each other and drank the nectar of nuptial delights.

News of the wedding reached King Gunjal, and he descended on them with four thousand troops and put a cordon around the garden. The princess said to Amir Hamza, "If you order it, I shall sever his head and dispatch him to the land of the hereafter." Amir answered, "He is your father, despite everything. You must never raise your hand to strike him. I will go to teach him a lesson for his arrogant ways." Amir then stepped out of the garden.

Upon seeing Amir, Gunjal said, "O Arab, did you consider my daughter to be like Naushervan's—someone you could marry by force? The same vanity has again possessed you. You shall see now how I punish you and take my revenge for your actions." King Gunjal drew his sword and rushed at Amir, who caught his arm and struck him with his bow, throwing the king from his horse. Amir drew his dagger and sat on his chest and said, "Say that God, who deserves honor and praise, is without a partner and the faith of Ibrahim is the True Faith." King Gunjal happily recited these words after Amir, who then set him free. Afterward, King Gunjal visited his daughter and related to her how he had converted to the True Faith. The news was broadcast abroad and young and old alike learned of all that had come to pass.

One night Amir was lying with Gili-Savar in the garden when Zar-Angez, who had kept Amir her prisoner for three days in the trench, came into the garden armed with her bow and quiver. Seeing Amir asleep holding Gili-Savar in his arms, Zar-Angez was beset by terrible pangs of jealousy. She said to herself, *Hamza spurned me and married Gili-Savar, inflicting a great wrong on me. Now is my chance to kill both of them and show them no mercy.* She was taking aim when Gili-Savar woke up and, seeing Zar-Angez standing nearby, rose from bed. Zar-Angez climbed down from the roof of the palace and by the time Gili-Savar came out to confront her, she had galloped away in fear. Gili-Savar followed her on horseback. After they emerged from the garden into the open field, that strumpet turned around and said, "I ran away from the garden in fear of Hamza, not because I was afraid of you. I have no fear of you and deem it absolutely unworthy of my status to feel any dread or anxiety because of you." She shot an arrow at Gili-Savar, who cut it in flight with her sword.

Gili-Savar then spurred on her horse, which flashed like lightning and came up to Zar-Angez. Joining her stirrups together, Gili-Savar dealt her a thrust of her sword that cut Zar-Angez in two; her body fell to the ground. Zar-Angez did not take another breath, but while she was still on Earth she had visions of the Future State.

Amir had witnessed everything from afar. When Gili-Savar killed Zar-Angez, he called out, "What have you done, O Gili-Savar! Naushervan will think that I killed her and will thus suffer terrible embarrassment and mortification." Gili-Savar answered, "What is done is done. There is no helping it, for we cannot ward off the decree of God!" Then Amir returned to the garden with Gili-Savar and rested there for the night.

In the morning Naushervan received news that Zar-Angez lay dead in the field, and her body was exposed in the open. He sent *ayyars* to bring back her corpse, and after expressing much sorrow, said, "It seems that this wanton woman went to see Hamza, who then killed her. A thousand pities and great shame that I should see the day when a woman would leave my side to be with another man without any regard for my name and honor. Now I cannot show my face to the world and will be covered with ignominy." He then said to his slaves, "I have had my fill of reigning over the empire. Now I wish to travel from one land to another and pass the remaining days of my life in this manner." They replied, "We shall obey your wishes and carry out what you order us. We shall do as you command us." Naushervan ordered his saddlebags filled with a great quantity of goods, gold, and jewels and, taking a thousand slaves with him, he left the city in the middle of the night and headed for Tartary. Whenever people asked him who he was, he identified himself as a merchant and held back his true identity.

The next morning Naushervan's camp was in an uproar over his disappearance. Some suggested that Amir Hamza had killed him, others said that Amar Ayyar had kidnapped him. Buzurjmehr said, "If Hamza killed the emperor or Amar kidnapped him, who took the thousand slaves? Naushervan must have departed in shame for the deeds of Zar-Angez." Prince Hurmuz sent his men to all corners of the empire to find him. At the advice of the courtiers and nobles he ascended the throne to look after the affairs of the empire and took over Naushervan's duties.

———

Now hear of Naushervan. He went on his way, bearing the hardships of the journey and telling everyone he met along the way that he was a merchant. It so happened that a bandit named Bahram heard from his spies that a merchant was on his way to Tartary amid great fanfare. He set out to intercept Naushervan with an army of several thousand bandits. Hearing that bandits were about, Naushervan set up camp at the station he had reached and prepared his defenses, but in the middle of the night Bahram conducted a raid on Naushervan's camp. Most of Naushervan's slaves were killed and all his goods and wealth were stolen. Bahram also took Naushervan prisoner, and upon reaching his den asked him, "O old man, tell me the truth. Who are you, whence have you come, and where are you headed?" Naushervan answered, "I am Naushervan bin Qubad, the fair and just king." Bahram said, "Why do you lie, you deceitful old man, and incriminate yourself with falsehoods? Where is the comparison between you and Naushervan? He is the Emperor of the Seven Climes who commands grandeur and majesty. What business would he have selling merchandise?" With these words, Bahram had Naushervan thrown out by the scruff of his neck, and robbed him of every last farthing. Naushervan put on the garb of beggars and crept along his way. It took him four days to complete what was one day's journey, and on the fourth day he finally arrived in Tartary.

Finding a stranger in their city, all the citizens there asked him, "O dervish, whence have you come?" Naushervan replied, "I am Naushervan bin Qubad. I became a merchant and set out for your land, but Bahram the bandit looted me on the way and left me completely destitute. As I was left with nothing, I thus became a beggar and continued on my way here." Everyone who heard this considered Naushervan a liar and rebuked him, calling him names. Slowly the news reached the king of Tartary that a fakir had newly arrived in his land claiming to be Naushervan bin Qubad. The king had him brought into his presence and asked Naushervan to tell him about himself. Naushervan again repeated what he had told everyone. The king did not believe him and ordered that the false dervish be sent away and driven out of his kingdom.

In short, Naushervan was driven away as an impostor and charlatan from every city and village he visited, whenever he gave people a true account of himself. In his travels, Naushervan finally arrived at the fire temple of Namrud. It was the custom of that place that any traveler who arrived there was given food for three days and on the fourth day he was sent on his way. If anyone wished to stay longer, he had to fetch wood from the forest for use in the fire temple and undertake this hardship by order of the man in charge of the place. Thus Naushervan received food for three days and on the fourth day he was told either to leave or, if he wished to continue receiving food and shelter there, to fetch wood from the forest.

Naushervan had never cut wood in his life; however, he was forced to comply due to the need to feed himself. He went into the forest to cut some wood and suffer that hardship, for he could do little else. The man in charge of the fire temple said, "This fakir has brought back very little wood, and therefore he deserves a like share of our food. As the amount of wood is small, so shall his portion be." That day Naushervan could not satisfy his hunger. When he went to the forest again the next day, he could not cut much wood at all and tried to steal some from other men's bundles. Someone caught sight of him stealing wood, and everyone there gave him a good beating and said to him, "O fakir, we did not know that you were also a thief! How dare you steal the wood we have cut and put it into your bundle?" Naushervan suffered a double misfortune in receiving the beating and having the wood he had cut himself taken from him. Naushervan returned with even less wood that day and, as a consequence, received even less food.

———

Now hear of Naushervan's camp. Hurmuz said to Buzurjmehr, "The emperor has not been found despite every effort we have made to locate him. Pray discover his whereabouts by *ramal* and inform us of his condition." Buzurjmehr answered, "I have already made the necessary calculations and learned that Naushervan is at the fire temple of Namrud and is suffering great hardships there. If no one goes there to aid him, he will die any day and will never again be seen alive by anyone." Hurmuz said, "O Khvaja, pray go and bring him back and carry out this mission for us." Buzurjmehr replied, "It will not serve our purpose if you or I go to bring him back. Not until Hamza goes to fetch him shall Naushervan ever return." Hurmuz said, "Why would Hamza ever go there to bring him back? Why would he take on this hardship for us?" Buzurjmehr replied, "If your mother were to write to him, Hamza would surely go and bring back Naushervan. He would certainly carry out her wishes, as he is not malicious nor is there an unkind bone in his body." Hurmuz then went and narrated the whole account to Mehr-Angez. The empress wrote a letter to Hamza that read:

O my dutiful son! It is true that the death of Mehr-Nigar has severed the ties of our relationship and our connection has been broken. It is also a fact that whenever he is counseled by Bakhtak, Naushervan has never done you a good turn, and at the provocation of mischief makers he always sought to inflict harm and injury on you. Yet, as God has gifted you with the qualities of courage, munificence, high-mindedness, and devotion, I am encouraged to request you to release Naushervan from his suffering and rescue him back from the fire temple of Namrud. Otherwise, he will come to his end, as he is unable to return on his own. This mission to release Naushervan from his plight would cause your name to be praised everywhere, and you would also earn divine blessing, as the emperor is caught in a terrible affliction and rendered completely helpless at the hands of his enemy.

Upon reading the letter, Amir Hamza sent Amar to Buzurjmehr to discover Naushervan's whereabouts and learn the directions in detail. Buzurjmehr said to him, "Tell Amir that Naushervan is languishing in the fire temple of Namrud. If you depart on foot without delay, you would arrive there in time. Otherwise, God alone knows how he will fare, and you would feel great sorrow as a consequence."

Of Amir's Departure for the Fire Temple of Namrud to Bring Back Naushervan, and of His Marrying Naushervan's Second Daughter upon Their Return

The narrator tells us that Amir cast off his royal garb and, wearing a sheet of cloth around his waist and putting on a habit of shreds and patches, set out for the fire temple of Namrud at an auspicious moment. Along the way, Amir learned that the bandit Bahram had looted Naushervan and ruthlessly plundered the mighty king. Amir arrived at Bahram's castle and made such an earsplitting war cry that the whole place shook from its foundations and anyone who heard it was beset with terror. Bahram rushed out of his castle in anxiety with a force of one thousand troops. Seeing Amir Hamza standing alone before him, he swung his mace and dealt him a blow. Amir parried his blow with the staff he was wielding and dealt Bahram a strike with the same staff, forcing him to fall flat on the ground. Amir climbed on his chest and said, "Proclaim that God Almighty is One and the faith of Ibrahim is the True Faith, or else I shall slaughter you with my knife and dispatch you to the next world!" Bahram replied, "First, tell me your name and all your details. Then I will act as I must and do as you ask me to do." Amir answered, "My name is Hamza." Upon hearing his name, Bahram sincerely converted to the True Faith by reciting the Act of Faith. Then he conducted Amir to his castle and feted him for several days and attended to his every comfort.

When Amir asked Bahram about Naushervan, he answered, "O Amir, I was indeed in the wrong about Naushervan. I plundered him thinking that he was a merchant. When he told me that he was Naushervan bin Qubad, I did not believe him and took for falsehoods everything that he told me. Considering him an impostor, I drove him away in humiliation and disgrace and left him completely helpless and destitute. I can only guess that he has gone toward Tartary."

Upon hearing this, Amir Hamza left for Tartary and Bahram the bandit accompanied him carrying a thousand dinars in his belt. In a few days they arrived in Tartary and began asking around about Naushervan by describing his appearance. The people told them that an old fakir had indeed arrived in their land who had proclaimed himself Naushervan bin Qubad. They told them that their ruler expelled him from the city as a liar, as he did not believe a word of his story, and it was not known to them where the man went afterward.

As Amir and Bahram were leaving the city, they crossed paths with two men. One of them was in the midst of saying to the other, "I never saw such a crazed fakir before. At his age and in his condition he makes such tall claims." The other said, "It would be little wonder if he speaks the truth. The revolutions of the heavens might have brought him to this pass and his misfortune shown him this day." Amir said to them, "Who are you, and where are you coming from? Tell us who you were speaking of." They answered, "We are artisans and are coming from the fire temple of Namrud. An old man arrived there from some place calling himself Naushervan bin Qubad and telling everyone stories about his eminent family and his ancestral empire. People refuse him charity thinking that he is a liar. It is only from fetching wood from the forest that he receives some sustenance from the fire temple. This is the manner in which he supports himself and such is his condition."

Upon hearing this account, Amir and Bahram headed for the fire temple. When they arrived there, the attendants brought food, and Amir shared the meal with Bahram. After they had eaten together, they sat down to watch those who entered and exited the place. In the evening, the woodcutters came back to the fire temple carrying their loads of wood. The attendants of the temple distributed one loaf of bread to each of them as per custom. After everyone else, Naushervan also arrived, carrying a few sticks of wood on his head. Seeing his small load, the attendants said, "O old man, your load never compares with what the others bring, and you cannot toil as much as others do. You cannot lay claim to a whole loaf of bread either, and will receive less than all the others." They gave Naushervan half a loaf of bread. Naushervan took the bread from the attendant without a word of protest, ate it in silence, and then lay down quietly in a corner. Amir Hamza's eyes welled up with tears upon seeing Naushervan, and he said, "Indeed God is the One who dispenses honor and disgrace at will! This is the same Naushervan from whose kitchen thousands of dishes have been served and thousands fed daily from his bounty."

In the meantime, the one in charge of the fire temple sent Amir a platter of sumptuous food. Amir said to Bahram, "Go without delay and call Naushervan to join us, but do not tell him anything about me nor call him by his name. Just say to him, 'Old man, come join us to share this food.' " Bahram addressed Naushervan as Amir Hamza had ordered him. Naushervan rushed to Amir Hamza, the lure of food causing him to hasten there. Amir greeted Naushervan with respect and, seeing his miserable condition, involuntarily broke into tears. Naushervan said, "O generous youth, why do you cry after showing mercy to me?" Amir answered, "Your face greatly resembles my father's. Therefore I lost my self-control and began crying." Amir seated Naushervan by his side and fed him with his own hands while weeping quietly to himself.

After Naushervan had eaten to his heart's content, he said to Amir, "Tell me, O youth, who you are, where you have come from, and what it was that drove you to this place." Amir answered, "I am a soldier, and I travel from land to land. I would like to know who you are and what your name is." Naushervan answered, "O youth, how would it serve you to learn my name? If I were to tell you the truth, you would show me violence and immediately drive me away." Amir said to him, "I swear that I will not censure or reproach you. Tell me the truth and have no anxieties about me. Rest assured that I will not cause you any grief." The old man then said, "I am Naushervan bin Qubad and fickle fate has shown me this day." Amir asked him, "Why did you dispense with your grandeur and prestige and renounce your empire and riches to take on these troubles? What made you leave your land?"

Naushervan answered, "The excesses of an Arab named Hamza made me renounce my empire and take to the road as a merchant, traveling through forests and facing these hardships. One day Bahram the bandit plundered all of my goods and left me absolutely destitute, and somehow I brought myself here. Indeed stratagem always plays second fiddle to fate." Amir Hamza asked him, "What injustices did Hamza commit against you? What grief did he cause you?" Naushervan replied, "He used to pay allegiance to me at first. Then he became enamored of my daughter and carried her away without my consent, leaving a hole in my heart. Considering it a great disgrace, I went out into the world to roam from one city to another." Amir said, "I have heard that Hamza did not have any designs on your throne, and that it was you yourself who was his enemy, always seeking some way to kill him. Now you prevaricate and tell a contrary tale." Naushervan answered, "O youth, indeed it is true that Hamza never sought my death or my throne. He never made attempts on my honor or my empire. It was Bakhtak, one of my viziers, who was a scoundrel and malefactor. It was that accursed fellow who sowed enmity between us, and on account of him the foundation of antagonism was laid between Hamza and me."

Amir Hamza now said, "Tell me, what would you give me and how would you reward me if I were to produce Hamza to you as a prisoner?" Naushervan's face lit up and he said, "O my illustrious son! Will my eyes ever see the day, by the grace of the gods Lat and Manat, that I will find that rebel in my power to dispense to him the punishment for his deeds?" Amir answered, "Rest assured on that account. I shall do you this service and produce Hamza to you a prisoner." Naushervan replied, "If you were to capture Hamza for me and do me this favor, O youth, I would give you my younger daughter, Mehr-Afroze, in marriage and live in your debt for the rest of my life."

Amir Hamza showed every kindness and favor to Naushervan and did not allow him to cut wood the next day. But he did not reveal his identity to him. He invited Naushervan to share food with him twice a day and gave him the seat of honor beside himself. Amir had been a guest there for three days and enjoyed every hospitality and comfort when, on the fourth day, the attendant of the fire temple said to Amir and Bahram, "According to our custom you have been our guests for three days. If you wish to stay here longer, you must bring us wood from the forest. Go with everyone to collect wood and, according to tradition, you will receive bread if you bring wood in a quantity comparable to the others." Amir went to the forest, along with Bahram and Naushervan, and stretched out under the shade of a tree using his staff for a pillow.

When the last few hours of daylight remained, Naushervan said to Amir, "O youth, how long will you sleep and waste your time? A little daylight remains yet. Let us go into the forest to cut wood so that we may earn some food." Amir said to him, "You should go to sleep yourself, for we will gather your share of wood and do the labor for you." After saying this, Amir closed his eyes, but Naushervan gathered wood from the area around them and stole some wood besides from the bundles made by other woodcutters. Amir Hamza saw his base act. He turned his eyes to the heavens and said these words by way of caution, "At Your decree, O God, the Emperors of the Seven Climes turn thieves! Indeed Your will brings about new marvels everywhere." With these words, Amir went to sleep. Around sunset Naushervan woke him up and said, "My son, you spent the whole day sleeping. Now all the woodcutters are returning with their loads of wood. When will you cut some and take it back? I was obliged to break some wood for myself." Amir said to him, "I forbade you from undertaking this hardship. Why did you then exert yourself for nothing?"

At last, Amir and Bahram got up and began pulling up dead trees by their roots. They broke them against the ground and made three large bundles of wood. The woodcutters could not believe their eyes and said to one another, "Are they human beings or *devs* who pull out such great trees from their roots and so lightly uproot these mountainous timbers?" Amir distributed the three loads between Naushervan, Bahram, and himself and headed toward the fire temple with the woodcutters. On the way, Amir regarded that Naushervan was staggering under his burden and was hardly able to carry it forward. Amir carried Naushervan and his bundle on his shoulders, relieving him from the ordeal. When they arrived near the fire temple, Amir put Naushervan down and piled up all the loads of wood. The attendants of the fire temple said, "Just these two men would suffice to supply wood for the fire temple. We will not need other woodcutters!" Then they sent delicious food for Amir and Bahram in great quantities. Amir had it in the company of Naushervan and Bahram, and each man sated himself and found relief.

That night Amir asked Naushervan, "Who undertakes the expenses of this fire temple, and where does the money come for its upkeep? From whose purse is the one in charge paid for the costs incurred in maintaining this place?" Naushervan answered, "My son, all these attendants are in fact my slaves and receive their stipend from my court." Amir asked, "Why do you not then reveal your identity to them?" Naushervan replied, "When I first arrived here, I gave them my name, but none of them believed it and did not even give me a place to take shelter. They manhandled me so badly besides that my whole body swelled up from the beating I received at their hands." Amir said, "If you swear to renounce fire worship and hold God as unique and alone, and consider the faith of Ibrahim the True Faith, I will kill these attendants and destroy the fire temple. I will settle you on the throne and make all of them show obedience to you." Naushervan swore to everything that Amir had asked. Amir threw one attendant into the fire, dispatched many others to Hell, and razed the fire temple to the ground along with the idols that surrounded it.

The fire worshippers were humiliated by Amir and sought quarter. Amir reprieved them and said, "O accursed men, do you not know that the hand of ill fate drove Naushervan the Emperor of the Seven Climes to this place? He was reduced to destitution by misfortune. You sent him out to cut wood and yet did not feed him well, mistreating your lord and master." All the men came forward and fell down at Naushervan's feet and said to him, "We hope to be forgiven, for we were completely unaware of the truth. For the sake of God, spare our offense and cleanse your heart of all rancor toward us." Naushervan forgave them and asked the one in charge of the temple for the keys to his treasure. He began dispensing it away in charity and made every beggar a man of means. Then Naushervan arranged to be surrounded by the royal paraphernalia and entered Tartary, deriving great confidence and courage from the support promised him by Amir Hamza.

When the king of Tartary came out of his palace to welcome his guests, Naushervan said to Amir, "There is no torture or wrong that this king has not inflicted on me. Kill him, and do not spare his life." The king of Tartary sought Amir's assistance to have his offense forgiven by Naushervan. He offered Amir many excuses and said, "I swear that I did not recognize His Majesty or realize that he was Naushervan in person. The reason I failed to identify him was that I had never before ennobled myself by setting eyes on His Majesty's face." Finally, at Amir Hamza's interceding and out of the regard in which he held the Sahibqiran, Naushervan forgave the offenses committed against him by the king of Tartary. The emperor said to Amir Hamza, "I am forgiving the king of Tartary in consideration of your appeal, but you must remember to capture Hamza and give him to my custody." Amir Hamza answered, "Your word is my command. I shall carry out your orders and presently arrange to have Hamza arrested."

Then Amir said to Naushervan, "Let us go into our camp all alone and see if anyone recognizes us and carries out our commands." Amir and Naushervan went to a baker, bought some bread, and sat down to eat it. Muqbil Vafadar happened to pass there, leading Ashqar to his water trough. The horse stopped in his tracks when he recognized Amir Hamza's smell. Amar also passed by there at that time, and saw Amir and Naushervan having a meal with a stranger, all three of them enjoying the repast. Amar greeted Amir Hamza and said, "Welcome back and happy return!" When Amar called out Amir's name, Naushervan finally recognized Amir and learned the identity of his companion.

Naushervan said to himself, *Hamza and I were together for so long, but I did not recognize him. There was no rebuke that I did not hurl at Hamza. He must harbor rancor against me to have maintained silence in the face of all I said to him.* With this in his mind, Naushervan got up and returned to his camp. The nobles of Naushervan's court were delighted to see him. Naushervan was seated on the throne, the music gallery was ordered to start playing festive music, and his courtiers and nobles made offerings to him.

Amir Hamza went into his own camp and met his companions, narrating all that had passed with him and apprising everyone of his adventures. The next day Amir said to Sa'ad bin Amar bin Hamza, "Tie my hands with rope and lead me before Naushervan so that I can fulfill my promise to him." Amar said, "I would not advise you to go before Naushervan in this manner, lest he harm you finding you in his power or threaten your safety." Amir answered, "I am willing to submit to my fate. I shall happily undergo all that I am dealt by fortune. As long as God's grace is with me, Naushervan can do me no harm." In the end, Sa'ad led Amir before Naushervan, who was dumbstruck by the spectacle and then asked, "What is all this? Why have you brought Amir a prisoner here?" Amir answered, "I promised you that I would bring Hamza to you as a prisoner. Therefore, I made myself be led before you so that I could keep my word. Now you must fulfill your part of the bargain and convert to the True Faith without hesitation."

At that moment Bakhtak rose from his station and whispered into Naushervan's ears, "This is an opportunity to kill Hamza easily and give him his due punishment without making any great effort. If this moment passes it will not return, and Hamza will not be prevailed over by another man." Naushervan gave Bakhtak no answer, but Amir Hamza deduced that Naushervan was not being truthful with him. Amir untied his own hands and said to Sa'ad, "Get hold of this accursed Bakhtak and whip him as much as his wickedness deserves." Sa'ad immediately carried out Amir's orders. Naushervan retired to his palace when he saw Bakhtak being whipped, and whoever tried to come to the aid of the ill-starred Bakhtak lost his life at Amir's hands. Finally, Amir returned to his camp. The following day he sent Amar to Naushervan's court with the message that he had fulfilled his promise and wished Naushervan to do the same, that is, to give Princess Mehr-Afroze to him in marriage as pledged. Amar went before Naushervan and delivered Amir's message to him.

At first Naushervan did not answer Amar and said to his courtiers and nobles, "I promised Hamza that I would give him Mehr-Afroze in marriage. What do you advise in this matter? Should I or should I not keep my word? What course of action would be to our advantage?" All of them replied with one voice, "After marrying just one of your daughters to Hamza, Your Highness suffered anxiety that has driven you from land to land. God alone knows what terrors would visit you after marrying a second daughter to him. We can only guess what humiliation and ignominy would befall you in its wake. Moreover, you must consider how the kings and princes of the world would receive the news: It would shock them no end." Naushervan answered, "Since I have given Hamza one of my daughters in marriage, I see no reason to make qualms about marrying a second daughter to him. None of this brings me disgrace. As far as I know, I could have no worthier son-in-law, as none can compare with Hamza in capability." With this, Naushervan said to Amar, "Go and tell Hamza to make preparations for the wedding." Then Naushervan ordered preparations for the marriage made at his palace, and arranged for all the necessities of the ceremony as befitted his status. The next day Amar recited the wedding sermon before Amir and Mehr-Afroze at an auspicious moment, and gave her in marriage to Amir, who retired with his bride to his court.

Bakhtak dispatched letters addressed to princes and kings everywhere in which he wrote: "O kings and princes of the world! It is a shame that while you still draw breath, a lowly Arab should wed two daughters of Naushervan to be titled the son-in-law of the Emperor of the Seven Climes and receive such riches from life. Not all is lost yet. If you have the courage—and I hope you muster it—you must advance and snatch Mehr-Afroze from the clutches of this Arab."

All the nobles of Naushervan's court consulted together and finally said to Hurmuz, "The emperor has lost his senses to dotage, but you are of lofty fortune and the master of your faculties. If you should so decide, Hamza would be killed speedily and receive just recompense for all his despicable deeds. Otherwise, the day is not far off when this empire will be completely lost to you." Hurmuz asked them, "What do you advise?" All of them said, "Advise the emperor to go to Mount Alburz to seek refuge with the king of Alburz. Even if a thousand Hamzas were to make an attempt on that king's life, they would die at the hands of his [?] warriors and would never prevail over the king of Alburz. If the emperor refuses to follow this advice, then you must send him toward Ctesiphon, ascend the throne yourself, and head for Mount Alburz to see what comes to pass there."

When Hurmuz put the proposal offered by the nobles before his father, Naushervan said, "You well know that I left no avenue unexplored to have Hamza killed, but none of our tactics harmed even a hair on his head. After all, there is such a thing as fate: I could not prevail against it and was helpless. As far as your proposal to head for Mount Alburz is concerned, I would like nothing better than if Hamza could be killed by this ploy and we could be rid of him. Order the advance camp to move toward Mount Alburz and tell everyone to make preparations to march." Naushervan's advance camp headed to Mount Alburz that very day, and the next day he followed and dispatched missives addressed to various sovereigns soliciting their aid.

Of Amir Hamza's Departure for
Mount Alburz

The narrator records that Amar Ayyar informed Amir Hamza that Bakhtak had incited Naushervan to head for Mount Alburz, and it was planned that if he followed Naushervan there, he would not return alive. Upon receiving this news, Amir Hamza smiled and said, "Order our advance camp to move to Mount Alburz as well." Amir Hamza passed that day and night making revels and started for his destination at daybreak. When they arrived at the foot of Mount Alburz, they saw Naushervan already camped there and his column-destroying champions ready to sacrifice their lives for him. Amir dismounted and bivouacked some distance from the enemy camp.

Warriors and champions poured in daily from all corners to aid Naushervan, and the arriving forces began making battle formations at their respective stations. When Bahram Chob-Gardaan and Aadi Chob-Gardaan—who were paragons of bravery and courage and unsurpassed in valor among the champions of the world—arrived with forty thousand troops to aid Naushervan, the emperor sounded the drums of war and led his army into the battlefield[?].

In the meantime, a rider came from the direction of the field and stood between the two camps, seeking combat with the infidels. Aadi Chob-Gardaan, who had planned to challenge Qeemaz Khavari, now faced the rider. He aimed his mace at the rider's head[?], but he received it on his shield and parried it. Then joining his stirrups together, the rider lifted Aadi Chob-Gardaan easily from his saddle, and after whirling him a few times overhead, slammed him so hard on the ground that every bone in his body was crushed to a fine powder. In just one blow he returned to dust,[32] earning the rider great renown in combat.

When Bahram saw his brother die in this manner, he attacked the rider, but soon shared the same fate, as the rider put him to death as well.[33] A rumble of fear rose among Naushervan's ranks and a wave of terror swept over their camp. None then dared to challenge the rider. All their courage sapped, they retreated to their tents.

When the rider saw that none came out to challenge him from the camp of the infidels, who had found some excuse to shun all thoughts of battle, he turned toward the camp of the followers of the True Faith and sought combat. Rustam-e Peel-Tan came forward and secured a hold on his waist. The rider caught hold of Rustam's belt and the two of them exerted themselves to lift each other. When their horses sank up to their knees into the ground and neither could prevail over the other, the rider said to Rustam, "Now you may send me Sa'ad Tauqi and return to your camp to relax and take some rest after this exertion." The rider tested his strength for two hours against Sa'ad Tauqi, and when their match of strength ended in a stalemate, the rider asked for Sa'ad bin Amar bin Hamza to come test his mettle against him. They, too, ended their combat as equals, and finally the rider asked for Amir Hamza himself.

When Amir came out to fight him, the rider grabbed him by his belt and tried to lift him up. Amir bellowed his war cry, shaking the whole expanse and stirring everyone's heart with dread and terror. Amir raised the rider above his head, spun him, and slammed him to the ground. As Amir sat on his chest to plunge his dagger into his neck to dispatch him to the Future State, the youth called out, "Do not kill me, for I am your grandson!" When Amir asked him the name of his father, he replied, "I am the son of Rustam-e Peel-Tan. My name is Qasim Khavari and valor has been gifted to me from God!" Amir lifted the boy up and embraced him and kissed his head and arms. Amir then sent for Rustam-e Peel-Tan and said to him, "O my son and light of my life, congratulations, for this is your son, your heart's delight and the light of my eyes!"

While they were having this exchange, a forty-yard-tall giant emerged from behind the ranks of the infidels on horseback and descended into the arena to challenge Homan Khavari, saying, "If you are indeed a man and a warrior, come face me and show me what claim you have to courage!" When Homan faced him in the arena, he lifted him up by his belt and then lightly set him down and said, "Go and send Qeemaz Shah Khavari to fight me so that he may test his mettle!" Then Qeemaz Shah began testing his strength with the giant until both of them were tired of the exercise. The giant let Qeemaz Shah go and said, "Return to your camp and send me Hamza to fight now. I would like to test the strength of his arm!"

Upon hearing this challenge, Amir entered the arena. The giant rushed forward and secured a hold on Amir's belt. Amir caught the giant by his belt, too, and the two began testing their might. When Amir was unable to overpower him, he let out his war cry. Then he lifted the giant above his head and said to him, "Tell me who you are or else I will slam you to the ground and turn your bones into powder, erasing your name from the register of the living." He answered, "My name is Qais Qeemaz Khavari, and I am the son of Qeemaz Shah Khavari, the illustrious king!" Amir slowly put him down and embraced him and showed him much affection. Then Amir sent for Qeemaz Shah and said to him, "May you have the pleasure of beholding your son!" Qeemaz Shah was greatly pleased by this news, and Amir sounded the drums to announce the day's end. He brought Qais Qeemaz Khavari back to his camp, where he ordered celebrations and organized an assembly of revelry and festivities.

The next day when the battle arrays were again formed, Aadi Chob-Gardaan came forward[34] from the ranks of the infidels and Farkhar Sar-Shaban came out from Amir Hamza's camp to meet him in combat. They fought until evening but neither of them could surmount his adversary and neither was overthrown or routed by his rival. The armies rested for the night and entered the arena again in the morning. Aadi Chob-Gardaan came into the battlefield, called out Amir Hamza's name, and challenged him to combat with much arrogance. Amir rode Ashqar into the battlefield with such might that clods of earth went flying wherever his hooves landed. Aadi Chob-Gardaan swung his wooden mace and aimed a blow at Amir's head. Amir Hamza caught hold of it and took it into his possession. Then Amir dealt his adversary a blow to his arm with his own mace, knocking him to the ground, where he rolled in ecstasies of pain. Amar tied him up and took him prisoner. Bahram Chob-Gardaan faced Amir[35] next in the arena. He, too, was taken prisoner, and Amir returned to his camp to clarions of victory.

In the evening Amir sent for Bahram Chob-Gardaan and Aadi Chob-Gardaan and said to them, "Tell me what you have decided and what it is that you wish to do." They answered, "We cannot have any other intention except to pay allegiance to you." Amir Hamza converted them to the True Faith and Amar put rings in their ears to enroll them among the ranks of Amir's slaves. Amir conferred robes of honor on them, broke bread with them, and seated them beside him with great honor and prestige. Cups of wine were soon passed around. Bahram Chob-Gardaan and Aadi Chob-Gardaan sent a message to their army ordering them to join the camp of the followers of the True Faith after making a night raid on Naushervan's camp so that they might earn divine blessings and earthly recompense.

The History of Prince Badiuz Zaman Being Born to Gili-Savar, the Daughter of King Gunjal; and of the Prince Being Put into a Chest and Dropped into the River; and of Quraisha, Daughter of Aasman Peri, Rearing the Prince at the Command of the Holy Khizr

The narrator records that when Amir Hamza departed for Mount Alburz, he sent Gili-Savar, who was with child, to King Gunjal, in effect leaving his family in trust with him. That ingrate Gunjal assembled all the servant girls and the midwife and ordered them to swear that when Gili-Savar was delivered of a boy, they would immediately bring him the child and make no delays. The attendants reasoned that since Gunjal was the grandfather, he must have foreseen something auspicious for the child, or else some clairvoyant must have alerted him to some fortunate or propitious hour. The moment the boy was born, they took him to Gunjal. That pitiless creature, who had converted to the True Faith for fear of losing his life, ordered the infant killed and commanded that the boy should be murdered on the instant. The infant's nanny took pity on the child's comely face and, disobeying the king's command, said to Gunjal, "If Your Honor should order it, I will inter the boy alive in the ground at just a word from you." He replied, "Very well, do so!" The nanny put the boy in a wooden chest instead and put this into the river, committing him to God's care.

It so happened that Aasman Peri and Quraisha were visiting the riverside that day. The chest came floating down the river and reached the bank near them. When they retrieved the chest from the river and opened it, they found inside an infant sucking his thumb, whose beauty was the envy of the sun and the moon. Love flooded their hearts at the sight of him, and when Aasman Peri regarded the shining mark on his forehead, she said, "This mark is the sign of the friends of God. He has been committed into the grace of God." At that moment the holy Khizr appeared before them and said to Aasman Peri, "This boy is Hamza's son. You should raise him in the best tradition, send him to Hamza when he comes of age, and name him Badiuz Zaman." With that, the holy Khizr disappeared, and Quraisha carried Badiuz Zaman to Qaf in her arms. They appointed *peris* as his wet nurses and raised him with great diligence and care.

When Badiuz Zaman reached the age of seven, Quraisha sent him to be trained in the arts of combat, and provided him with arms and armor once he had attained mastery in all arts of war. Whenever Quraisha went on a campaign, she took Badiuz Zaman along with her and introduced him to the realities of battle. When Badiuz Zaman reached his eleventh year, he asked Quraisha, "Who are my mother and father, and where are they? Tell me, what is the name of the city where they live?" Quraisha answered, "Both you and I are the children of the same father. He rules over the realm of men and his name is the Lord of the Auspicious Planetary Conjunction, the World Conqueror, the Quake of Qaf, the Latterday Suleiman, Abul-Ala, Amir Hamza bin Abdul Muttalib. However, I have no knowledge of your mother's name and identity, and know not who she was or where she lived." Then Quraisha told Badiuz Zaman how he was discovered in a chest floating in the river and provided him with all the details of the circumstances that had brought them together.

Badiuz Zaman said, "Pray do me the favor of sending me to my father." Aasman Peri and Quraisha provided many gifts of Qaf to accompany him and ordered the *peris* to conduct him safely to the camp of the followers of the True Faith near Mount Alburz, and to make sure he suffered no hardship on the journey. At parting, they told Badiuz Zaman the names of all his relatives and explained to him how all his brothers had challenged and fought with Amir Hamza at their first meeting, and that he, too, must continue the family tradition and give himself to his father's service only after performing this ritual.

In short, Badiuz Zaman took leave of Aasman Peri and arrived after a few days near Mount Alburz. He saw the two armies facing each other on the battlefield and the warriors wielding their swords. The *peris* gave Badiuz Zaman the particulars of both camps, showed him their resting places, and distinguished his father's camp from the camp of the infidels. Then they hid themselves from human view to witness what would transpire next.

Badiuz Zaman stood between both camps and called out facing the camp of the followers of the True Faith, "O Arabs, he among you who wishes to make a tryst with the Angel of Death should come forward to face me and show me what he possesses of courage and valor." Both camps marveled at Badiuz Zaman's comely youth, his fine garb, and his superior weapons, for they had never before set eyes on such a dazzling aspect or such attire and accoutrements. They wondered what land he belonged to and how he had come into all these trappings. In the meantime, Badiuz Zaman called out his challenge again, "O followers of the True Faith! I have sought combat all this time and none of you have come forward to meet me in the arena. None of you dares to fight me. If you fear for your lives so much, why did you come to the battlefield wearing arms and armor? Why do you not take to some corner dressed in a mantle, or retreat into some fox den if you fear death so?"

Upon hearing these words, Kayumars the spearsman took Amir Hamza's leave and went forward to fight Badiuz Zaman, spurring his horse on into the arena. Badiuz Zaman asked him to give his name, and Kayumars Shah answered, "I am Kayumars." When Badiuz Zaman asked him to strike the first blow, Kayumars replied, "My faith does not allow me to deal the first blow. You should take precedence and strike first. If I live, I shall answer it and deal the next blow." Badiuz Zaman reached out and lifted Kayumars Shah from his horse, and after spinning him over his head, put him down lightly on the ground and said to him, "Go and send me someone else to fight." Qeemaz Shah Khavari came to fight him next. Badiuz Zaman lifted him up similarly, whirled him over his head, and said, "Go and send someone else to fight me." Then Landhoor came forward, and after asking his name, Badiuz Zaman lifted him like a twig up into the air and slammed him to the ground, overpowering him like the others before him, and said, "Go back and send Hamza's sons to fight me. I have heard that they are peerless in might and are men of great courage and valor." Landhoor returned and said to Amir Hamza, "That youth wishes to fight your sons. I have never seen a warrior who fights the way he does."

Qasim Khavari sought Amir Hamza's permission to fight Badiuz Zaman. Amir said, "I give you into God's protection. Battle with him cautiously, for the fighting method of this youth makes me concerned. It seems difficult to overpower him, and none who have gone into combat with him have gained the slightest advantage over him."

Qasim went into the arena to face Badiuz Zaman, who immediately secured a hold on Qasim's cummerbund. Qasim took hold of his belt, and each of them attempted to lift the other. When their horses had sunk up to their knees in the earth, the soldiers dismounted and tried to force each other's hand. Finally, Badiuz Zaman lifted Qasim above his head, and after spinning him in the air, put him down on the ground. Qasim was overpowered just like the others before him, and Badiuz Zaman said to him, "Go and send me Rustam-e Peel-Tan. I am very eager to fight him. I would like to display my swordsmanship for him so that he may see my mastery of the art." Rustam now faced Badiuz Zaman, and after several hours of battling together, Badiuz Zaman prevailed over him, too. Then he said to Rustam, "Send me Sa'ad bin Amar bin Hamza!" He, too, went before Badiuz Zaman and was overpowered by him. Finally, Badiuz Zaman said to Sa'ad, "Go and send me your grandfather, Amir Hamza, so that I may find someone worthy to exert my strength against."

When Sa'ad conveyed this message to Amir Hamza, he descended into the arena and pitted himself against Badiuz Zaman, who raced his horse like lightning to reach the side of Amir and catch him by his cummerbund. Amir, meanwhile, secured a hold on Badiuz Zaman's belt. The two of them fought so mightily that their steeds were unnerved, and had they not dismounted, the animals would have broken their backs. When Amir was drenched in perspiration, he bellowed his war cry and tried to lift Badiuz Zaman from the ground and raise him above his head. However, Badiuz Zaman did not budge from his place. When Amir made his war cry a second time and made another attempt, he still achieved no results.

Bakhtak then said, "It would be little wonder if Hamza is defeated today by this youth and dies at his hands." The narrator has reported that Amir Hamza made several war cries that day and yet they did not perturb Badiuz Zaman in the slightest, and he did not seem the least bit affected by Amir's efforts. Finally, Amir Hamza came into a rage and drew both Samsam and Qumqam from his scabbards to deal blows to Badiuz Zaman and strike that youth with his lustrous swords. Then Quraisha appeared before him, stayed his hand, and informed him that Badiuz Zaman was his son and her brother. Amir was greatly surprised and wondered who had borne him such a son.

Then Quraisha narrated to him the whole incident of the wooden chest and told him everything that holy Khizr had said. Paternal love stirred in Amir Hamza's heart and he pressed Badiuz Zaman to his breast with joy. He called out to Amar, "Regard that this illustrious boy is my son! He is a piece of my heart and the light of my life. The Almighty God has sent him to strengthen my arm." Amir Hamza returned to his camp to the notes of festive music. He ordered forty days of celebrations and occupied himself with revelry and pleasure seeking, all the necessities for the festivities having been taken care of right away.

———

Now, the narrator states that Samandun Hazar-Dast Dev had escaped Qaf[36] for fear of Amir and taken refuge in Mount Alburz, considering that place a safe haven. When he received word of Amir Hamza's arrival, he used subterfuge to infiltrate Amir's camp one night after two watches had passed. As he entered the camp, he beheld the pavilion of Sa'ad bin Amar bin Hamza, and upon going inside, he found Sa'ad deep asleep. He made him unconscious and carried him away to his sanctuary. In the morning Amir Hamza received news that Sa'ad had disappeared from his tent. Amir was thrown into despair wondering who had kidnapped him and visited this suffering on him. He said to Amar, "We must consult Buzurjmehr to find out what has passed with Sa'ad, and inquire about the details."

Buzurjmehr said to Amar, "When Amir was slaying the *devs* of Qaf, a *dev* named Samandun went into exile and inhabited Mount Alburz for fear of him. When the expanse of Mount Alburz was thrown into a ferment by your battles, that *dev* went into Amir's camp. When he learned that it was the camp of Amir Hamza, he began searching for him. Unable to find him and accomplish his mission, he took Sa'ad away and imprisoned him in the castle across the river to cause grief to Amir. Only if Amir goes there alone will Sa'ad be found alive."

Upon receiving the news from Amar, Amir Hamza immediately took leave of his companions and waded across the river on Ashqar's back. He left Ashqar to graze and roam freely on the other shore and himself hunted and roasted a bird and satisfied his hunger at great leisure. That night Amir slept under a tree and in the morning he rode Ashqar to the place Buzurjmehr had described. When Amir arrived near the castle, the *devs* recognized him and alerted Samandun, rushing before him with the news that the Sahibqiran, the *dev* slayer, had arrived. Samandun left his castle with several thousand *devs* to face him.

When Amir saw Samandun, he said, "O accursed creature, why did you put me to the inconvenience of this journey with your deeds? You will not escape my hands alive and you will see what an example I make of you." Samandun ordered one of his *devs* who was held as a champion among them to arrest the human and speedily carry out his orders. Any *dev* who tried to capture Amir that day died at his hands. One after another seven wretched *devs* attempted to lay hands on Amir, and he dispatched them all to Hell. Then Samandun pleaded with the *devs* but none of them dared approach Amir Hamza. Upon that Samandun grew full of dread and hurled a several-hundred-*maund* rock at Amir, who foiled the attack and dealt Samandun a sword blow that severed all seven of his hands in one blow, causing the hearts of the *devs* to burst with fear at the scene. Samandun escaped from there, and he returned after a moment intact as before, and began fighting with Amir. And this same story repeated itself all that day until evening.

That night the *devs* retired to the castle and Amir fell asleep under a tree. The holy Khizr appeared to him in his dreams and said, "The Fountain of Life lies under the castle grounds. First, go and plug its source, and then fight the *dev.* Otherwise, you will keep fighting with him for the rest of your life and he will not be killed or laid low by your sword." Amir started from his dream and went to the castle that very moment and plugged the fountain that the holy Khizr had identified[37] with refuse and debris. After carrying out his instructions Amir returned to his post and went back to sleep as before.

In the morning Samandun emerged from the castle and arranged his army in battle formations in the field. As before, he hurled a thousand-*maund* stone at Amir's head. Amir foiled his attack and dealt the *dev* a sword blow that cut his neck in half and left it hanging from his torso. He turned tail and ran off, with Amir in pursuit. Amir saw that when the *dev* searched for the fountain and could not find it, he bashed his head against the ground and gave up his life. The *devs* who had accompanied him ran away pell-mell like rampaging camels. Amir cut off Samandun's head and hung it from his saddle straps, and then fed his vile corpse to the beasts of the desert. Amir next began searching for Sa'ad bin Amar bin Hamza. His quest finally led him to a chamber where he found Sa'ad lying unconscious, without any sense of his whereabouts or his condition. Amir recited the prayer of Ibrahim over some water and washed Sa'ad's face with it.

Sa'ad regained consciousness, and upon opening his eyes, saw his grandfather by his side. He felt great relief and expressed his gratitude to God. Amir led Sa'ad out of the castle and hunted an animal and roasted its meat for them. The next day Amir seated Sa'ad on Ashqar and headed for his camp. When they reached the river, Amir said to Sa'ad, "Remain in the saddle because you do not know how to swim." Amir himself crossed the river holding onto Ashqar's tail.

They arrived at their camp to witness a pitched battle being fought.

Amir Hamza threw the head of Samandun Hazar-Dast toward the camp of the infidels and called out, "This was the same *dev* who kidnapped my grandson. I went to kill him and have brought back his head. Indeed he received his deserved punishment at my hands." The infidels were stunned to see the *dev*'s head and marveled greatly at its size, realizing that a *dev* who had such a giant head could be no smaller in size than a mountain. They realized, too, that Hamza had surmounted and killed him with his mortal frame and reasoned that it would be impossible for them to fight one who could kill so mighty a *dev*.

They were yet discussing this when a dust cloud rose from the forest. *Ayyars* from both camps rushed there to learn whether it was an enemy or a friend who had arrived. They learned that Bakhya Shutarban and Malik Ashtar had arrived with intrepid warriors and a vast army to assist Naushervan.

Naushervan sent Hurmuz and other kings to receive them. When the two princes entered Naushervan's camp with their army, he derived untold comfort and reassurance from their presence. He conducted them into his court, showed them every mark of reverence, and conferred robes of honor on them, giving them preference over all his commanders. He arranged festivities in their honor and organized an assembly of revels for them.

THE *DASTAN* OF AJAL BIN ABDUL MUTTALIB, YOUNGER BROTHER OF AMIR HAMZA, LORD OF THE AUSPICIOUS PLANETARY CONJUNCTION

Narrators of sweet discourse relate that another son had been born to Khvaja Abdul Muttalib after Amir Hamza. Thus the oyster of nobility had revealed another pearl whom Khvaja named Ajal and occupied himself with raising him. Ajal had traversed twelve years of his life when Qalmaq Shah advanced on Mecca and stationed his army to do battle with its citizens, who could not defeat him in the battlefield and secluded themselves in their fortress, their small numbers making them fear for their safety. The news of their anxiety reached Ajal and he solicited Khvaja Abdul Muttalib for arms and a horse so that he could fight the infidel and slay every single man in his camp. Khvaja Abdul Muttalib laughed and replied, "Just consider your years and where you stand in your life, and then regard your ambition to fight a mighty commander like Qalmaq. I have eleven other sons, but it was only given to Hamza to fight with thousands of warriors and remain fearless before armies of hundreds of thousands of men." Ajal responded, "God is our savior. I am Hamza's brother after all." As Ajal's insistence to fight Qalmaq Shah kept growing, people said to Khvaja Abdul Muttalib, "Why do you hold Ajal back from fighting? Why do you not let him go to battle? Verily, the one who trusts in God has no worries or fears. We have learned that he is full of courage and exceedingly brave." Forced by everyone to give his consent, Abdul Muttalib provided Ajal with a horse and suitable weapons and recited the prayer for his safe return, giving his son into God's protection. Ajal put on the warrior's dress and decorated himself with the weapons. Then the brave boy exited the fort with great magnificence astride his horse with his companions walking alongside him. Qalmaq Shah saw a youth on horseback and some footmen coming toward him from the direction of the fortress and reasoned that he was headed there to plead for peace on behalf of the citizens of Mecca. Qalmaq dispatched a rider to meet them and find out what intention led the boy to approach their camp.

The rider went to Ajal and said, "O youth, what are your intentions? If you wish to sue for peace, come with me and I shall broker peace for you and also have you conferred with a robe of honor from the king." Ajal answered, "O infidel, whom do you wish me to plead for peace? Who would you have confer the robe of honor on me? Are you not aware that my name is Ajal, and I am Hamza's younger brother and Abdul Muttalib's son, the scion of an illustrious house and the Angel of Death of the infidels? If you call yourself a man, then strike me a blow." That infidel flew into a rage and struck Ajal with his sword. Ajal parried it easily with his shield. Then Ajal lifted him from his seat by his cummerbund and slammed him to the ground. Ajal's companions tied the infidel up and took him prisoner.

Qalmaq Shah ordered another one of his troops, "Go and capture this boy who has taken my soldier prisoner, and put your courage to the test!" That man attacked Ajal with his sword, and Ajal took him prisoner as well. In this way, Ajal took forty soldiers prisoner and, like an unrivaled champion warrior, captured everyone who confronted him. Beside himself with rage, Qalmaq Shah faced Ajal himself and aimed his mace at Ajal's head. Ajal foiled the blow and landed his own mace on Qalmaq Shah, the impact of which killed his horse instantly. Qalmaq Shah tried to hamstring Ajal's horse, but the youth quickly dismounted and, securing a hold on Qalmaq Shah's belt, raised him above his head. After spinning him around, he slammed him to the ground. Ajal climbed on his chest and pinioned Qalmaq Shah. Hearing of the incident, Qalmaq Shah's army prepared to charge Ajal with their full force, but Qalmaq Shah signaled to them to desist from it.

Ajal said to Qalmaq Shah, "Your life shall be spared if you convert to the True Faith. Otherwise, I will kill you immediately without the least fear of your army and warriors." Qalmaq Shah replied, "O Ajal, I will convert to the True Faith on the condition that you grant my wish of finding me service with Hamza." Ajal answered, "The thing that you wish for you would have received even without asking." Qalmaq Shah then converted to the True Faith and Ajal embraced him and took him to his father. Abdul Muttalib conferred robes of honor on both Ajal and Qalmaq Shah and made them gifts of a great many jewels. He arranged a feast in their honor, and showed much deference and respect to Qalmaq Shah.

The next day Ajal said to Khvaja Abdul Muttalib, "I wish to go and see my brother and tell him all my adventures." Abdul Muttalib gladly gave him leave and told him to make preparations to depart. After Ajal had journeyed for two days, he came across an army on the march. Ajal sent his *ayyars* to bring him news of them, and he was told that the army belonged to Karib Madi, Aadi's son by Gustham's daughter, and that Karib Madi was headed for Mount Alburz to meet his father, Aadi Madi-Karib. Ajal decided that he must introduce himself to Karib Madi. He went to embrace Karib and said to him, "I am headed for Mount Alburz to meet my brother, Hamza, and this is the reason I set out from my land. It was fortunate that the two of us crossed paths. Now the hardships of the journey will be less cumbersome, and we will reach our destination before we even know it." Karib Madi said to him, "If you wish me to be your riding companion, then I request that you camp here for a few days to relieve yourself of the stress of your journey while I make a pilgrimage to Mecca."

Ajal set camp there, and on the fourth day Karib Madi returned from his pilgrimage. The following day the two armies headed toward Mount Alburz together. Along the way, Ajal said to Karib Madi, "I have heard that whenever one of Hamza's sons first met him, he challenged him in the arena and tested his strength against Hamza's. We must test Hamza's strength at our first meeting and imitate this tradition." Karib Madi said, "Very well! Pray give the orders to set up camp here, as we are now four *kos* from Hamza's camp." Ajal said to him, "I will go there first by myself, and then you may follow me, but come alone and leave the army camped here."

In short, Ajal went on his way, and upon arriving at his destination, stood between both camps and called out, "Any of Hamza's sons who has a claim to courage should come out to face me!" Rustam-e Peel-Tan took Amir's leave and went to face the young man in the arena. Ajal rushed forward to secure hold of Rustam's belt, and Rustam caught hold of Ajal's waistcloth. The two pitted their strength against each other and both camps marveled at their test of prowess. Finally, Ajal said to Rustam, "I have tested your strength. Now send me another one of your brothers." Rustam returned from the arena and repeated Ajal's words to Amir, who sent the most excellent warrior and champion Badiuz Zaman to fight with him. As the two tested their strength, Badiuz Zaman was able to overpower Ajal. Then Ajal said, "O Badiuz Zaman, I have now tested your strength as well. May God augment it. Now go back and send me Hamza so that I may test my might against him as well and display my strength to him." Badiuz Zaman returned to camp and told Amir what Ajal had told him.

Amir Hamza strode out from the ranks astride Ashqar and faced Ajal. The two secured hold on each other's waistbands and began testing their might. Amir saw that he could not raise Ajal above his head, and that however much he tried, the brave warrior facing him would not yield. Finally, Amir let out his war cry and lifted Ajal up with a mighty effort. Then Amir asked him, "Tell me truthfully who you are and give me the name and station of your father and grandfather." Ajal replied, "I am your brother, and the son of Abdul Muttalib." Amir placed him lightly on the ground and embraced him, and his heart filled with fraternal love at the sight of his brother. Amir said to him, "Why did you have to arrive here in this manner? Had you informed me, I would have sent my army to receive you and would have brought you here myself. I would have conducted you here with much fanfare and magnificence."

While the brothers were having this discussion, Karib Madi entered the arena and stood there like a fierce lion. Amir asked Ajal, "Do you recognize this man?" Ajal professed his ignorance. Karib Madi dealt Amir such a powerful blow of his mace that sweat broke from every pore in his body and darkness fell before his eyes. Nevertheless, Amir withstood the blow and caught Karib by his waist. Amir kicked Karib's horse out from under him and lifted the boy into the air, while the horse flew back ten paces from the force of Amir's kick and its heart burst from the impact. Karib Madi said, "O Amir! Do not slam me on the ground, for I am your slave, the son of Madi-Karib." Amir put him lightly on the ground and embraced him. Then he called Aadi Madi-Karib and said to him, "Congratulations on your son!" He replied, "O Amir, he showed great irreverence toward you. Kill him and extract his brains from his skull." Amir replied, "I have forgiven him his trespasses and absolved him of them."

In the meantime, Qalmaq Shah arrived there with his army and made obeisance to Amir and showed him all tokens of reverence and submission. Amir returned to his pavilion with all three champions, conducting them there with displays of honor and distinction. He offered all of them golden thrones and ordered celebrations. Amir participated in the revels the whole night and in the morning he repaired to the battlefield upon hearing the drums of war.

The warrior Bakhya Shutarban came into the arena and challenged everyone in a loud voice, bellowing like a fierce lion, "O Arabs! He among you who longs for death should come out to face me, and I will dispatch him to the Future State in an instant." Shaban Taifi received permission from Amir to face him in the arena. Shaban Taifi said, "O Shutarban, why do you low and make these rutting noises?[38] Why commit idle words to your tongue? Come forward now and strike your blow!" Bakhya landed a mace blow on Shaban Taifi with all his might, but he did not even shed a hair and stood steadfast without moving an inch. Then Bakhya dealt him a second blow and a third, but Shaban Taifi parried both of them and answered with a mace blow to Bakhya's horse that ground its bones into a fine powder and left Bakhya without a mount. Shaban Taifi jumped from his horse and the two of them continued their fight on foot, battling with maces. In the evening both armies returned to their camps at the cessation of hostilities for the day.

In the morning Bakhya again entered the arena and both armies again heard his challenges and claims. Qais Qeemaz Khavari answered his challenge and the two of them fought with maces for half a day and then they grabbed each other's waistbands and tried to lift each other. Bakhya raised Qais with great effort above his head and slammed him down on the ground. As he attempted to climb on his chest to tie him up, Qais kicked Bakhya to the ground and rose to sit atop him. As he attempted to secure Bakhya's limbs, Bakhya put his feet together and kicked Qais so mightily that he was now thrown on the ground. In short, both champions fought in this manner the whole day, but neither of them could vanquish the other. That night the armies took rest, and the next day they made preparations for battle again and plied their swords.

Badiuz Zaman next went to fight Bakhya, who landed a seven-hundred-*maund* mace on him, striking the prince a mighty blow. Badiuz Zaman parried his strike and said to him, "I give you two more blows!" Bakhya landed the next two blows with all his might and put all his effort into them, but he failed to unnerve Badiuz Zaman even a little. Finally, Badiuz Zaman let out his war cry and lifted Bakhya up, raising him above his head with no effort. After spinning him overhead, he gave him into Amar's custody and Amar tied him up and imprisoned him in his tent.

When Malik Ashtar saw his uncle thus humiliated in the arena, he said to Naushervan, "Hamza's sons are truly mighty and brave. How easily did that youth capture my uncle!" Naushervan answered, "All of Hamza's progeny are cut from the same cloth." Malik Ashtar said, "Let the hostilities remain suspended for the day. I will fight him tomorrow so that none may get the chance to say that Malik Ashtar was unable to capture Hamza's son because he was tired from earlier combat." The drums announcing the day's end were struck in Naushervan's camp at his orders, and he returned to his pavilion.

Amir also retired to his court. There he distributed many riches in tribute to Badiuz Zaman and offered much in charity to the beggars and the destitute. Then Amir seated himself on the throne of the champions of the world, sent for Bakhya, and invited him to convert to the True Faith. Bakhya asked to be excused from committing himself without Malik Ashtar present there. Amir then gave him into the custody of Madi-Karib.

In the meantime, the presenter of petitions arrived and announced that a messenger had come from Kharsana carrying word from its people. Amir Hamza sent for him, whereupon the messenger appeared and presented Amir with a letter from Fatah Nosh, who had written: "Marzooq Farangi has attacked us and reduced our numbers to a miserable state. We have received untold losses at his hands and have been forced to seek refuge in the fort. Either come yourself to bring us aid, or else send Rustam-e Peel-Tan. Otherwise, you will lose the dominion of Kharsana and its people will lose their faith."

Amir read the letter to his companions and said, "I am headed to Kharsana to teach this rebel a lesson for his sedition. In my absence, pay your allegiance to Rustam-e Peel-Tan." Upon hearing this, Rustam-e Peel-Tan answered, "Pray order me to depart for Kharsana to punish that rebel and bring you his severed head." Amir said to him, "Very well! Take along fifty thousand troops and hasten there!" His son answered, "I have no need to take along an army. By your grace, I alone am enough to behead that infidel." Amir said, "The enemy is unnerved by the sight of a vast army. Therefore it is improper for you to go alone and attack such a powerful enemy without your army's support." Rustam-e Peel-Tan did not consent to take the army with him and took Amir's leave to travel alone, flying like wind toward Kharsana.

He arrived there within a few days, reaching his destination with courage and resolve. He beheld the armies of Farang besieging the fortress, resolved upon taking it by force. Rustam immediately made his war cry and sought combat. Marzooq Shah Farangi sent his elder son to fight Rustam. His name was Malia, and he was a fifty-yard-tall giant. When Malia asked Rustam who he was, he told him his name and pedigree. Malia drew his sword and attacked Rustam, who caught hold of his hand and wrested the sword from him. Then he dealt Malia a blow of his sword that cut through Malia's helmet and head, his breast and abdomen, and came out between his legs. Malia fell to the ground in two pieces. The scene caused a wave of terror to engulf the entire army of the infidels. Their warriors dreaded Rustam's mighty arm and none would come forward to challenge him. Then Rustam drew his sword and fell upon the army of the infidels just as a lion tears into a herd of goats. Anyone to whom he dealt a sword blow fell to the ground in two. Any rider his sword met fell from either side of his horse in pieces, and was instantly dispatched to the hereafter. A great unrest grew among the ranks of the Farangis and turmoil took over.

Marzooq saw that Malia's death had broken his army's spirits and robbed them of all courage. He went forward to challenge Rustam, but even that did not revive his army's spirits, and they retreated like a pack of foxes. Realizing that he would not be able to prevail over his adversary alone, Marzooq followed his retreating army with his companions. Rustam gave him chase for a distance of four *kos,* and with his sword he made heaps of dead infidels.

By that time Fatah Nosh had arrived at Rustam's aid with his army. He said to Rustam: "Now you have chased the enemy for four *kos* and inflicted grave losses on them. It would be against custom to follow them any farther. We do not wish to pursue them any longer." Rustam disagreed and said to him, "You should return to take care of the castle and strengthen its defenses lest the enemy, seeing the castle lying defenseless, should trick us and advance on it." While Fatah Nosh returned to his fortress and sent a complete account of the events to Amir Hamza, Rustam continued in his pursuit of the enemy.

In short, Rustam crossed into the frontiers of another land while chasing and killing the enemy. When it was night he fell asleep under a tree, and in the morning he woke up and hunted and roasted an animal for breakfast. Then he rode off again in pursuit of Marzooq Shah's fleeing army.

———

Now hear of Amir. The day Rustam departed for Kharsana, Nausher-van's daughter Mehr-Afroze was delivered of a son whom Amir named Mehr Shah. He ordered celebrations for forty nights and forty days and revels were held on a prodigous scale.

After the celebrations were over, Amir heard the drums of war from the enemy camp and ordered the Timbal of Sikander to be struck in reply. He ordered his camp to make preparations for battle and arrived in the arena with his forces. The hostilities had not yet begun when a messenger arrived with Fatah Nosh's letter. Amir read the letter and said to his friends, "Mark Rustam's childishness! He pursued Marzooq Shah all alone knowing full well that he had a large army at his command. He threw himself into this danger with open eyes. God alone knows what has passed with him. In any event, I must now go to his aid. All of you should pay your allegiance to Badiuz Zaman in my absence." Then Amir said to Amar, "I am taking five champion warriors with me. The rest of the army shall remain here under your command. I am leaving everything in your hands to arrange as you see fit. The entire camp will be under your rule, and troops and foot soldiers alike will all be answerable to you."

Amir took with him King Landhoor, Shaban Taifi, Karib Madi, Istaftanosh, and Qeemaz Khavari and headed toward Kharsana at great speed—making two and three days' journeys in a single day—and soon arrived at his destination. Fatah Nosh greeted Amir, conducted him into the fortress, and ordered festivities in his honor with all manner of dishes prepared for the occasion. Amir said to him, "I can barely swallow food, much less participate in festivities. God willing, I will join you in these celebrations on my way back. For I cannot rest easy until I have killed my enemy." The celebrations were canceled, and after resting there for the night, Amir headed in pursuit of Marzooq Shah's army.

Now hear of Marzooq Shah. When Rustam kept pursuing him for days, Marzooq reasoned that it was not Hamza but his son who had been following them because a retreating enemy was not followed for more than four *kos,* and wise and experienced commanders avoided such follies. Rustam had been following them, he decided, only on account of his inexperience, and with that realization, all fear and anxiety left him. He turned back to face Rustam and said, "O Arab lad, I had taken you for Hamza. Otherwise, I would never have turned away from an encounter with you, and would not have allowed myself to be inconvenienced and bothered on your account." Having said this, Marzooq Shah drew his sword and attacked the youth. Rustam parried his blow and struck Marzooq a blow that severed his hand. Marzooq pulled back his horse and called out to his army, "Kill him! Do not let him advance another step or escape from your hands!"

At his command, the whole army attacked Rustam, who took swords in both hands and fought back, piling up heaps of the slain. However, in the combat that ensued Rustam himself was wounded and his horse was killed. The infidels tried to take him prisoner, but no one could muster the courage to lay hands on him. Rustam finally climbed atop a rock and began shooting arrows at the infidels, each shot killing four and five infidels as it pierced their vile bodies.

Marzooq Shah Farangi kept shouting orders to his men to arrest Rustam and not allow him to escape. When Rustam's quiver was empty of arrows he grew anxious and raised his hands in supplication to God, praying, "O aid and assistance of the helpless! Now is a time when I need help and there is none beside You whom I can ask for assistance!" Rustam had not yet lowered his raised hands when Amir Hamza arrived there with warriors worthy of comparison with Sam. Seeing Rustam lying there wounded, Hamza and his companions fell upon the enemy host and attacked the ranks of the miscreants. Amir bellowed his war cry and proclaimed, "Let those who know fear and those who do not know learn that I am Hamza bin Abdul Muttalib, and my rage will only be quenched by your infidel blood!"

A great confusion took hold of the infidels after Amir Hamza's war cry. They lost their senses and could no longer distinguish one end of their swords from the other. Amir killed thousands of infidels, who drank the goblet of death from his hands. Marzooq Shah turned tail and escaped by shutting himself into his fortress. Amir Hamza approached Rustam, and after putting bandages of *noshidaru* on his wounds, turned his attention again to the foe.

Marzooq Shah realized that Hamza would not be deterred from taking the fortress. Once inside he would conduct wholesale carnage, and Marzooq's wife, children, and family would all be murdered, finding no reprieve at Hamza's hands. Marzooq left the fortress with his sons and grandsons holding their swords in their teeth. Presenting his wife and children to Amir, Marzooq fell down at Hamza's feet and asked for reprieve. Amir said to him, "If you convert, along with your sons and family, to the True Faith and give your daughter in marriage to Rustam, I will spare your life and the lives of your family, and forgive all you have done." Marzooq immediately converted to the True Faith with his sons and promised his daughter to Rustam in marriage.

Marzooq escorted Amir Hamza and his companions into the fortress and arranged a marriage assembly. Amir sent Landhoor to fetch Rustam and wedded him to Marzooq's daughter. While Amir's son retired to the nuptial bed to indulge in pleasure seeking, Amir and his companions busied themselves in revelry.

After some days, Amir returned to Kharsana with Marzooq and arranged a meeting to establish peace between Fatah Nosh and him. Amir remained Fatah Nosh's guest for a night and a day and enjoyed all pleasures and comforts. The next day Amir departed toward Mount Al-burz with Rustam, Marzooq, and the rest of his companions, and arrived there in the midst of the battle. The commanders of Amir's camp were delighted to see him return and all of them kissed his feet. Amir embraced them and apprised them of his adventures.

When he saw Amir Hamza had rejoined his camp, Malik Ashtar called out, "O Hamza, where did your fear of me drive you? Now your death has herded you back here, and you will taste the sweetmeat of doom from my hands." Amir answered him, "O warrior, champions do not indulge in idle boasting. Come, deal me the blow you take most pride in!" Malik Ashtar swung his mace and landed it on Amir with such force that sparks flew from the impact. But Amir withstood the attack and said to him, "I give you two more strikes. Then it shall be my turn!" Malik Ashtar attacked Amir with his mace twice, but Amir was not injured in the least. When it was Amir's turn to attack, he alerted Malik Ashtar and then landed such a mighty strike with Sam's eleven-hundred-*maund* mace that when Malik Ashtar received the blow on his shield, its impact broke the back of his steed and threw the warrior's senses into disarray. Malik Ashtar leapt from the saddle, whereupon Amir also dismounted his horse.

Malik Ashtar called out, "Bravo, O Hamza! All praise to your mighty arm! Indeed no man in this world is your equal. You are the prince of the champions of the world." Then Amir threw a second strike of his mace, which Malik Ashtar also withstood with great effort. The two of them fought with maces for several hours and then tossed them aside and drew swords. Finally, Malik Ashtar's sword broke, and he was left holding the hilt, which he threw at Amir. Amar rushed forward to pick it up. Malik Ashtar meanwhile shot an arrow at Amar, who received it on his paper shield. Then Amar leapt seventy-two yards into the air and, as he came tumbling down, dealt a blow to Malik Ashtar's neck that blinded his vision. A terror seized Malik Ashtar's heart, but he took hold of himself and fired a second arrow at Amar, who received that on his paper shield as well.

Malik Ashtar said to Amir, "O Hamza, you keep company with a veritable scourge, and his craftiness makes the mind numb with wonder. He is indeed a terror to reckon with!" Malik Ashtar then attacked Amir with his other sword, and Amir received the blow on his shield. Malik Ashtar's sword cut into it by four digits, but his weapon was nevertheless broken. Amar said to him, "O Malik, it is unseemly for you to stand there holding the hilt of your sword. Now your weapon is mine, and you must throw it to me." Malik Ashtar laughed and threw the hilt toward Amar Ayyar, who picked it up and cleaned it and put it into his *zambil*.

Malik Ashtar next weighed his lance in his hands and attacked Amir Hamza, who parried it. Catching hold of the lance, Amir gave it a tug to wrest it from Malik Ashtar's hand and thus disarmed his adversary. Amir removed the point from the lance and struck a powerful blow of the shaft to Malik Ashtar, which broke the weapon into pieces. Malik Ashtar took hold of himself and next tried to capture Amir with a lasso. Amir caught hold of the rope, and the two of them pulled it so hard that it broke. Amir said to Malik Ashtar, "We have tried our hand at all the arts of war to prevail over each other. Come, let us test our strength now by trying to lift each other. I will secure a hold on you at your waist, and you should do likewise. The one who is able to lift the other will be the victor. Then he may have the other's allegiance for life." Malik Ashtar willingly accepted Amir's terms and secured a hold on his waist while Amir did likewise. The two of them began testing their strength in this way, and both armies rang with the news that their champions' might would now be put to a final test.

When Malik did not budge from his place, Amir called out to him, "Beware, for I am now about to make my war cry!" Malik answered, "Boys fear your cries and wails and only men who have not seen the face of war would be terrified of them! My ears are not unfamiliar with war cries!" Then Amir bellowed "God is great!" and lifted Malik up above his head on the very first attempt. Amir raised him high into the air, and after spinning him about, slammed him so hard on the ground that Malik lost consciousness. Amar quickly bound his limbs with his rope. Then Malik said, "O Amir, it is not of any use to tie me up now. I shall remain your slave for life. For as long as I live, I will sincerely pay allegiance to you." Amir instructed him in the Act of Faith and embraced him and showed him much favor. At that very place Amar put the ring of slavery in Malik Ashtar's ear and enrolled him among the ranks of Amir's servants. Amir returned with Malik Ashtar to his pavilion to the sound of festive music and seated him on a golden throne. Amir sent for Bakhya Shutarban, who also converted to the True Faith without objection and wore the ring of slavery in his ear. Amir ordered him to be set free and provided him with a golden throne as well. After some time all of them sat down together to have a meal. Goblets of wine were passed in rounds and the dancers kept dancing the whole night. When it was morning, it was announced that Zhopin Faulad-Tan had arrived to aid Naushervan, and had a vast army at his command. Amir remained quiet upon hearing this news and continued with the festivities.

One day the presenter of petitions arrived at the court and announced that a man stood at Amir's door who claimed to be his father and beseeched that his arrival be announced to Amir without delay. Amir marveled at hearing this. He wondered who could have been his father other than Khvaja Abdul Muttalib, and as he thought about the matter, he felt both consternation and shame.

Then Qunduz spoke, saying, "O Amir, recall that we met a caravan of merchants on the way to Kharsana. Upon finding out that their leader was Khvaja Abdul Muttalib's friend, you addressed him as Father. It seems that this same man has been driven here by some need to see you." Amir said, "Go and see for yourself. If it is the same man, bring him to me without delay." When Qunduz left the court, he saw that it was indeed the same merchant and he led him into the court. Amir seated him next to himself with great respect and honor and showed him much favor. Amir asked after his welfare and then said, "Tell me, why is your face so wan? Is it an illness or some trouble that afflicts you?" The merchant answered, "I am troubled by the sickness called the fever of love, which has reduced me to this state. I do not know where to begin my story of woe." Amir said to him, "Pray give me a detailed account so that I may learn it and do all in my power to bring you redress."

The merchant took out a portrait, showed it to Amir, and said, "This is a portrait of the sister of Hardam, the sovereign of Baru. Their father said on his deathbed that the one who wishes to marry her must first prevail over Hardam in combat. Fate ordained that I should visit Baru and pass under her balcony. No sooner did our eyes meet than the demon of frenzy claimed me for his own. Her love made me oblivious to food and sleep, and I have lost my forbearance from my passion. I have been reduced to a most wretched state. I do not possess the power to vanquish Hardam in combat, and thus I have come to you so that I may win that treasure with your help. I keep the portrait of this moonfaced beauty with me, and whenever I am beset by the pangs of love, I look upon it for a while to bring a modicum of solace to my heart and relieve my humors of their terrible frenzy."

When Amir Hamza's commanders looked at the portrait, they all said, "The poor merchant is right to feel thus afflicted by his beloved. Indeed no one would be able to control the fluttering of his heart in such a case." Amir Hamza fed the merchant and sent him away after promising that he would unite him with his beloved[?].

The narrator states that, upon seeing the portrait of Hardam's sister, Sa'ad bin Amar bin Hamza fell head over heels in love with her. After two watches of the night had passed, he left the court and made preparations to depart on horseback for the land of Baru. Aurang and Gaurang were on vigil duty that night, and upon sighting Sa'ad, they said, "Where are you headed, O Prince?" Sa'ad answered, "If you wish to accompany me, come along without another word and do not let any apprehension or anxiety enter your heart. Do not ask me anything, and you will find out in due course where I am headed and with what intention." Both brothers accompanied Sa'ad, and within a few days they entered the frontiers of Baru. There they sighted a magnificent garden and were greatly taken with its grace and beauty. When they entered it and took a stroll, they saw a herd of goats grazing beside a pond and thus determined a means to feed themselves. Sa'ad said to his lieutenants, "Catch [?] four or five goats and roast them. Have no fear in this regard." Aurang and Gaurang carried out Sa'ad's orders, and before long the goats were roasted.

The shepherd of this garden was enraged at the sight of three men roasting and eating his goats with utmost abandon. He approached them and said, "O travelers, was it your doom that led you here? What idle desire has taken hold of you? Do you not know that these goats belong to Hardam, the Angel of Death?" Sa'ad answered, "Do not waste my time with your jabber. Go and tell Hardam that Hamza's grandson has arrived and sends for him. Then see what answer he gives you."

When the shepherd went and told this to Hardam, the king decorated himself with Prophet Daud's seven-piece suit of armor and headed for the garden wielding a mace in a state of raging frenzy. He went to where Sa'ad and his party were seated and said to them, "O youths, tell me who you are and whence have you come! Tell me truly what has brought you here." Sa'ad answered, "I am Sa'ad bin Amar bin Hamza, and I am the grandson of Amir Hamza. I have come here to arrest you. Take stock of my courage, for I have not brought along anyone except these two men." Hardam laughed heartily and said, "O Arab lad, there is a limit to idle talk. Do you not fear my vast army? Has Hamza never heard of my renown that he sent a minor like yourself to face me, carelessly appointing a single soul against a horde?" Sa'ad said to him, "First, you should answer my challenge. Then you may worry about challenging Hamza." As Hardam prepared for combat, Aurang and Gaurang said to Sa'ad, "Your Honor! We entered your service longing for the day when we might sacrifice our lives for you. Let him fight us first. Then he may fight you." Sa'ad tried to keep them from fighting Hardam, but death had marked those two champions for its own. Aurang faced Hardam and was put to death with just one blow. Gaurang fared no better in combat with Hardam, and also met his death at his hands. Sa'ad was greatly grieved by their deaths and confronted Hardam to avenge his companions. Hardam struck a blow with his mace, but Sa'ad parried it. Then Sa'ad stood back and fired a hail of arrows at Hardam that cut holes in his seven-piece suit of armor. Hardam then caught hold of Sa'ad's belt, lifted him up, slammed him to the ground, and said, "Go and send Hamza to fight me, for I have taken pity on you and I cannot bring myself to kill you with my hands."

Hardam returned to his castle and said to his sister, "Hamza's grandson came here with two companions. His companions died at my hands, but I let the prince go after overpowering him. I spared his life and asked him to send Hamza to fight with me." She replied, "You acted as the circumstances demanded!"

After Sa'ad exited the garden and traveled for some two *kos,* it occurred to him that he could not show his face to Amir Hamza and present himself before him. He reasoned that it would be better to go to some other land and hide his name and identity from everyone. Thus resolved, he headed for the forest. After journeying many *farsangs,* he came across a garden, and upon stepping inside, he found it a veritable template of Heaven. He left his horse to drink water from a rivulet that flowed there and sat down by a pool. After spreading out his saddle cloth and using his staff for a pillow, he was soon lost in reflections on his fate.

It so happened that Hardam's niece, who was the owner of that garden, arrived there with her face veiled to enjoy the sights and sounds of the place with some of her female attendants. Seeing a comely youth sitting by the pool, she approached Sa'ad and asked, "O youth, who are you and from where have you come? What was it that brought you to this place?" At the sight of her, Sa'ad quickly put on his arms and confronted her. Quick as lightning, she threw her lance at Sa'ad, who caught hold of it and sent her rolling on the ground with a sideways blow of its shaft. As Sa'ad sat on her chest to tie her up, his hand inadvertently touched her breasts and he immediately got up and removed the veil from her face. He beheld a fourteen-year-old girl whose beauty was the source from which the full moon imbibed its brilliance and shied from showing its face before her. Her beauty drove all thoughts of Hardam's sister from Sa'ad's mind and he was beside himself with joy upon beholding her.

He asked her: "O light of the world, who are you?" She answered, "I am Hardam's niece." Sa'ad said, "Hardam's sister is still unmarried. How were you born to her?" That beauty, who was the envy of the moon, replied, "She is my aunt!" Sa'ad said, "Since you have shown favor to my state, pray allow me to light my eyes with your splendorous beauty and make the desolation of my heart a flower garden at the sight of your charms." She answered, "I would be happy to attend to you for the rest of my life, but you must give me your true name and station in life and tell me the details of your pedigree." Sa'ad answered, "My name is Sa'ad bin Amar bin Hamza, and I am the grandson of Amir Hamza. The city of Mecca is our home and ancestral land." Then Sa'ad gave her a complete account of how he happened to be there and told her about his plans. That girl took Sa'ad to her home and happily gave herself to him in marriage, believing that she had found an inestimable treasure by fate's decree. The two of them passed their nights and days in pleasure seeking and derived all the joys of life from the delights of each other's bodies.

Now hear of Amir. He became most anxious upon hearing of Sa'ad's disappearance and dispatched his men in all directions to find some trace of him, but all of them returned empty-handed. Landhoor now said to Amir, "When the merchant was showing the portrait of his beloved, I noticed that Sa'ad seemed out of sorts. It would be little wonder if he departed for Baru with the intention of meeting that woman." In the meantime, news reached them that Aurang and Gaurang were also missing from the camp. Amir said, "Surely Sa'ad has left for Baru, and both Aurang and Gaurang have accompanied him." Amar Ayyar said, "I have been told that Hardam is an accomplished champion, and each warrior in his army is the very essence of valor. May the eye of injury turn its gaze upon Sa'ad's enemies."

Amir appointed Rustam-e Peel-Tan as the commander of the camp in his place and relinquished complete charge of his duties to him. Then Amir and Amar Ayyar headed for Baru. After some days they entered its frontiers and arrived at the same garden that Sa'ad had discovered. There they saw the corpses of Aurang and Gaurang lying on the ground. Amir said to Amar, "It is possible that Sa'ad was also killed." Amar answered, "If he had been killed, we would have found his corpse here also. I would not be surprised if Hardam has captured him alive and imprisoned him." Amir Hamza buried Aurang and Gaurang in that garden and wept many tears of grief at their fate.

They saw the very same herd of goats, and Amar slaughtered four of them and began roasting them. While they were leisurely having their meal, the shepherd, noticing four goats missing from his herd, happened upon the two men roasting and eating the animals without a care in the world. He rushed toward them and rebuked Amir, saying to him, "O soon-to-be corpse, was your death pulling at your skirts that you slaughtered and roasted these goats and took pleasure of another's property as your own? Some days ago Hamza's grandson arrived here with his two companions and he, too, roasted three of these goats. For this crime Hardam killed them without the least fear of consequence." Amir asked, "Was Hamza's grandson also killed or was he taken alive?" The shepherd replied, "While Hardam killed his companions, he spared the grandson's life in regard for Hamza, and did not shed his blood. It is not known where he went afterward." Amir prostrated himself before God to express his gratitude that Sa'ad was alive and had not been killed. He said to the shepherd, "Go and inform Hardam that Hamza has arrived. Send him to me so that I may convey something important to him."

The shepherd went to Hardam, who picked up his mace and headed for the garden that very instant. Upon seeing him arrive, Amir decorated himself with his arms and armor and mounted his steed. Hardam laughed and said, "O Hamza, ever since I first heard your name, I have nursed the desire to see you so that I could fight you and test your bravery and courage. Come now and strike your blow!" Amir answered, "Such is not our custom. You must strike the first blow, and then I will answer and return your blow."

Hardam swung his mace and aimed at Amir's head. As Amir blocked the blow with his own mace, the chain from Hardam's weapon wrapped around Amir's mace like a snake. Both of them began pulling, causing the links of Hardam's chain to snap open and making him lose his grip. Hardam threw the handle of his weapon at Amir, who intercepted it without harm. Hardam saw that Amir had foiled his strikes and he himself had been left empty-handed. He pulled a tree up from its roots and threw it at his adversary. Amir jumped aside and the tree broke into pieces where it fell. Hardam said, "Bravo, Hamza! Indeed the renown of your arm's strength is not exaggerated. I never saw a fighter more courageous than you. Pray remove the veil from your face and allow me to gaze on your consummate beauty, so that I may regard it with eyes of reverence and augment their light from its sight." Amir lifted up the veil from his luminous face and allowed his opponent to |behold his dazzling beauty. Hardam saw that the sun itself shied away from the brilliance of Amir's beauty—although his face showed signs of age and was the visage of a man who had drunk fully of experience and wisdom.

Hardam said to Amir, "It is evening now. I shall fight you again and enter into combat with you in the morning." Hardam returned to his home and sent some fattened goats and flagons of wine to the garden for Amir's repast. Amar Ayyar roasted the goats, and the two of them had their fill of meat and wine and lay down to rest in comfort and peace.

Hardam, meanwhile, praised Hamza to his sister and said, "Although he is advanced in years, one so endowed with might and gifted with beauty as he has never even been heard of, let alone seen. God has gifted him with excellence in all aspects." Hardam's sister was greatly pleased to hear his account.

The next day Hardam faced Amir for combat and challenged him with a mace. They fought until evening, when Hardam's mace broke under the strain of battle. He said to Amir, "I had two maces, and now both of them have been broken. I would like to suspend combat until a mace can be made for me." Amir answered, "Very well! I have no objections, but do tell me truthfully what became of my grandson." Hardam answered, "O Hamza, I let your grandson go unharmed when he mentioned your name, and did not commit any wrong against him. But I have no knowledge as to his whereabouts."

Then Hardam went back to his house and sent Hamza some fat-tailed sheep and flagons of wine for his meal. Later that day, Hardam narrated the whole account of Amir's manliness to his sister and said, "There could be no better match for you in this world." Then Hardam sent for the blacksmith and persuaded him to make him a nine-hundred-*maund* mace overnight, and to name his own price for the labor. By the time it was daylight, the mace was ready for Hardam. Having finished with his morning rituals, Hardam went into the garden and said to Amir, "I have already broken two of my maces and if this one is also broken by your own, I shall be in a great quandary. It would be so much better if you would simply put your mace aside. Indeed if you have a claim to bravery, you will assent to my request."

Amir granted Hardam's wish and agreed to receive the blows of Hardam's mace on his shield. This time, however, Hardam's mace made a deep impression in Hamza's skull after striking him powerfully. In consternation, Amir dealt Hardam a thrust of his sword, which cut through all seven pieces of Hardam's armor and injured him. Then Hardam drew a cold sigh and said, "I have spent my life in combat, but today is the first time that I have ever been wounded." Then the fight was suspended to allow both warriors to minister to their wounds. In a few days their wounds were healed and they renewed fighting.

As Hardam aimed his mace at Amir's old wound, Hamza rushed forward, caught him by his arms, and lifted him above his head after shouting his war cry. Then Amir spun him overhead and slammed him to the ground. Amir sat on Hardam's chest and asked him to convert to the True Faith, and bound him by oaths to do so. Hardam converted to the True Faith with a willing heart and showed every sign of obedience to Amir. He took Amir Hamza and Amar to his house, where he arranged a feast in their honor and said, "It was my father's dying wish that I should willingly give my sister in marriage to the man who prevailed over me in combat and pressed my back to the ground. Now that you have been victorious over me, pray marry my sister and take her as your wife." With Amir's permission, Amar recited the wedding sermon. Amir then retired to the palace to indulge in pleasure seeking with Hardam's sister.

Sa'ad bin Amar bin Hamza learned that Amir had arrived there and taken Hardam's sister as his wife. He armed himself and headed toward the city of Baru on horseback to meet Hardam. When he arrived at its gates and made his war cry, the sound of it reached Amir Hamza's ears. He said to Hardam, "Go and find out who has made this war cry and dared to issue a challenge." Hardam went armed with a mace and found a warrior standing at his door. Sa'ad dismounted and grabbed both of Hardam's arms and heaved him up from the ground. He spun him above his head, slammed him to the ground, and sat on his chest. Hardam said, "Give me your name, O brave one, and tell me who you are." Sa'ad answered, "I am Sa'ad bin Amar bin Hamza." Hardam said, "Get off my chest so that I may take you to meet your grandfather and offer you the pleasure of his company!" Sa'ad went along with Hardam, and upon beholding Amir, he rushed forward and fell at his grandfather's feet. Amir embraced his grandson and kissed his head and face, for the sight of the youth offered him great joy and solace.

Hardam said to Amir, "There is something that astonishes me no end. I lifted up your grandson, Sa'ad, with absolute ease the first time I encountered him, but today he lifted me up as a mighty champion might pick up an infant. Tell me what is the difference between that day and today, and how this marvel has come to pass." Amir replied, "Before, Sa'ad was afflicted with a corrosive love that disarrayed his senses, sapped his strength, and filled his heart with anxiety and apprehension. Now that he has recovered from it and has been restored to his natural strength, all those causes for anxiety and dread are completely dispelled from his humors." Amir made Sa'ad and Hardam embrace each other, and established friendship between them. Food was then ordered and all of them sat down together to eat. Moonfaced cupbearers as lovely as the sun arrived in the assembly carrying flagons of roseate wine, and sweet-lipped singers and fairy-shaped dancers began to entertain the assembly.

In the morning Amir said to Hardam, "I would now like to return to my camp. Tell me, what are your intentions and what do you wish to do?" He replied, "O Amir, I, Hardam, would not leave your side now even for an instant. For as long as I live, I shall remain every moment in your service." Amir then took his leave of Hardam's sister and headed back to his camp along with Hardam, Sa'ad, and Amar.

They arrived to find Marzooq Farangi locked in combat with Naushervan's commander, Zhopin Faulad-Tan, each man displaying his swordplay. Amir's commanders were delighted by his return and came forward to kiss his feet.

Meanwhile, Zhopin Faulad-Tan lifted Marzooq Farangi above his head and threw him to the ground, saying, "Go back, O Farangi, and send me someone else to fight, for killing you will win me no acclaim." Marzooq returned to his camp and described his plight to his friends. Malik Ashtar went to fight with Zhopin Faulad-Tan next. Zhopin dealt a powerful blow of his mace to Malik Ashtar, who broke into a sweat from the impact. Nonetheless, Malik Ashtar withstood the attack, and after gaining control of himself, answered with a mighty blow that left Zhopin Faulad-Tan stunned. The two champions fought with maces for several hours, and then drew their swords. Assaulting him with great courage, Zhopin Faulad-Tan was able to injure Malik Ashtar just as it was getting dark and he inflicted a grievous wound on him. The Trooper of the First

Heaven[39] interceded between them, and the two armies returned to their camps.

When the Emperor of the Fourth Heaven[40] ascended the throne of day to watch the spectacle of combat between champions, and his brilliance showed the aspect of Earth's expanse to advantage, both armies again arrived at the battlefield to test their strength against their adversaries.

Zhopin Faulad-Tan was challenged by Bakhya Shutarban, but Bakhya was felled from his horse by Zhopin's lance and Zhopin told him, "Go and send me another man to fight!" Then Bakhya returned to the ranks and Qunduz Sar-Shaban went out to fight Zhopin. Qunduz foiled Zhopin's strike and landed his mace on Zhopin, who warded off the blow and threw his rope at Qunduz, entangling him in its snare. Zhopin Faulad-Tan tightened the noose around his adversary's neck and pulled him from his horse.

Landhoor could not hold himself back at the sight of this and entered the arena. He fought Zhopin Faulad-Tan with his mace with such skill and excellence that both camps commended him with shouts of "Bravo!" and "Well done!" and every warrior praised his skill without reserve. When both armies returned to their camps in the evening, Bakhtak said to Naushervan, "I am certain that tomorrow we shall witness a fight between Zhopin Faulad-Tan and Badiuz Zaman, and the spectacle will amaze all the champions and warriors." Naushervan answered, "It would be little wonder if such a thing came to pass. I am myself convinced in my heart that it will." The night soon passed, and when it was morning, the two armies again flooded into the battlefield. Zhopin Faulad-Tan rode into the arena astride his horse with great confidence and sought combat.

From Amir Hamza's camp, Prince Badiuz Zaman led his horse into the arena to face Zhopin Faulad-Tan, who called out, "You dwarf! Tell me your name so that you do not die unsung, and your name is left for men to grieve over your fate." Badiuz Zaman answered, "I am Badiuz Zaman, son of Hamza. Now deal me the blow you wish to strike!" Zhopin Faulad-Tan swung his mace and brought it down on Prince Badiuz Zaman's head, causing blood to rush into all three hundred and sixty veins in his body and his every pore to break out with sweat. Amir's son remained steadfast, however, and said, "Deal me two more blows before I strike." Zhopin struck twice more, summoning all the force and might of his arm, and hammered Badiuz Zaman with consecutive blows of his mace. Badiuz Zaman parried both blows and then swung his mace powerfully at Zhopin, breaking his shield into shards. A veil of darkness dropped over Zhopin Faulad-Tan's vision from the impact, and everything disappeared from before his eyes. Both champions continued to fight for some hours in this manner with their maces. Then they drew their swords and fought mightily until their blades became worn and saw-toothed. They each tried capturing their opponent with ropes, and then both dismounted and began exerting themselves to lift each other from the ground. With great effort, Badiuz Zaman twice raised Zhopin Faulad-Tan from the ground up to knee level, but he could not lift him high enough to heave him above his shoulders. It was soon evening, and the drums to announce the day's end were sounded in both camps.

In the morning when the armies arrived in the arena, Zhopin Faulad-Tan entered the field issuing challenges to all the warriors in Hamza's camp. He called each man by his name, exclaiming, "The one who wishes to meet his death should face me. It will be impossible for him to escape with his life." Amir Hamza rode out on Ashqar from the center of the army and confronted Zhopin Faulad-Tan, who immediately caught hold of Amir by his belt. Amir secured a hold on his enemy's cummerbund and they pitted their strength against each other. When their steeds had sunk to their knees in the earth, the two brave men dismounted to wrestle. After trying countless locks on each other and breaking the other's holds, Amir Hamza made his war cry and lifted Zhopin Faulad-Tan and spun him above his head. He then slammed him to the ground and sat down on his chest. Amar Ayyar quickly secured his limbs with his rope and took him prisoner.

Amir returned to his camp to the notes of festive music and retired to the women's quarters. The commanders of Amir's camp gathered and said to Amar, "Zhopin Faulad-Tan has humiliated and disgraced all of us in the arena, and done irreparable harm to our reputations. If he lives, we will never be able to look him in the eye, and the whole world will call us pusillanimous weaklings. Were he somehow humiliated at our hands or killed, our sorrow would find an end." Amar answered, "Amir Hamza would never order the death of a warrior of Zhopin Faulad-Tan's caliber. Indeed he will value and favor him above all others, for one rarely comes across such a mighty champion. Those who put a value on valor never even dream of murdering brave men." When the commanders tempted Amar with money, he said to Hardam, "You should kill Zhopin Faulad-Tan with molten lead. If it grieves Hamza, I will be answerable to him, and will prevail on him to forgive the offense." Then Hardam poured molten lead into Zhopin Faulad-Tan's ear, which dissolved away his heart and liver. When Amir emerged from the women's quarters and sent for Zhopin Faulad-Tan, he was told that Hardam had fed him molten lead and killed him by deceit.

Amir expressed his displeasure with Hardam, who replied, "I did this at the behest of Amar Ayyar. It was at his bidding that I killed Zhopin with molten lead. I must not be blamed in this matter[?]." Amir was greatly upset with Amar and said to him, "What harm did you receive from Zhopin's hand that you arranged to have him killed?" Amar answered, "O Amir! That wretch (deserving a beheading) merited such a fate in order to keep all creatures of God safe from his hands." Amir replied, "My hands are tied. Had it been somebody else, instead of you, who had ordered this I swear by the God of Kaaba that I would have killed him." Amir Hamza gave Amar Ayyar seven lashes, and then said, "If you ever commit such an act again without my consent, I will make an example of you and punish you severely." Amar retorted, "If I do not lash you seventy times for this humiliation, I will consider myself a bastard not of my father's loins!"

With these words, Amar took himself straight to Naushervan and said to him, "O Emperor, I put myself to every hardship and pain in Hamza's service, and he rewarded me for it with seven lashes today for the sake of an infidel. He has humiliated me before all the commanders, forever leaving a mark on my heart. If Your Honor wishes to have my allegiance, I am willing to yield it to you. You would have my complete obedience." Naushervan was greatly pleased to hear this and said, "O Amar, your rightful place is in my heart." Naushervan conferred a robe of honor on Amar and ranked him in honor above all his courtiers. He granted Amar a chair in his court and bestowed much honor and prestige on him.

When Amir Hamza received these tidings, he was kept awake at night by fear, and he ordered his camp to maintain a state of great vigilance. Every night Amar made the rounds of Amir's camp with the intention of kidnapping him, but he quietly abandoned the plan each time he found Hamza awake. One night, however, Amir was unable to keep his eyes open, and he fell asleep. Finding Amir lost in slumber, Amar, who had been waiting for just such a chance, put a soporific drug in a tube and blew it into Amir's nose, rendering him unconscious. Then he tied up Amir with his rope and took him to the forest, where he tied him to a tree trunk in revenge for the lashes Amir had given him. Amar dispelled the effects of the drug, and when Amir came to he put his finger between his teeth in astonishment and marveled at his state and felt great shame.

Amar found a tree branch and hit Amir seventy times with it. Amir smiled and said, "You wily thief! I shall renounce my name if I do not shed your blood! Now I will not rest in peace until I murder you." At this, Amir broke his bonds, and Amar ran away from him like a wild camel. Amir then reached for his bow and arrow. Realizing that Amir's arrow never missed its mark, and that he would certainly die and not escape Hamza's clutches, Amar rushed toward Amir and said to him, "O Amir, forgive me my wrongs!" Amir responded, "I have sworn that I would draw blood from your body and punish you." Amar said, "If that is your wish, then I am standing before you: Cut my neck without hesitation and sever my head." To fulfill his promise, Amir took out his blade and cut Amar slightly to open a vein and draw a little blood from him. Then he returned to his camp, taking Amar along with him.

OF HAKIM MARZAK'S ENTRY INTO AMIR'S CAMP AT BAKHTAK'S BIDDING, AND OF HIS BLINDING AMIR HAMZA ALONG WITH HIS COMMANDERS

The narrator of the *dastan* tells that a man named Hakim Marzak was Bakhtak's bosom friend. He came to see Bakhtak one day and said, "If Naushervan were to order me, I would blind Hamza and all his companions, making them lose their sight by subterfuge." When Bakhtak communicated this to Naushervan, the emperor said, "A blind man needs aught but seeing eyes." He sent for Marzak and conferred a robe of honor on him, showing him much favor and showering him with gifts.

Marzak then went to Amar Ayyar and told him a tale of his pitiful helplessness and travails, and said, "If I could find a position in Amir's camp, I would earn my livelihood by administering medicine to the soldiers." Amar found an occasion to broach the subject with Amir Hamza, who said, "I have no objection to the proposal. If he were to earn his living by tending to the sick in the camp, God would bless me for this favor to my fellow humans." When Amar presented Hakim Marzak to Amir and praised his accomplishments to him, Hamza showed him great favor and said, "You are welcome to stay with the camp, attend to the sick men in their need, and administer physic to them." Thus Marzak found a position in Amir's camp.

It so happened that Amir Hamza came to experience a dimness of vision and a dullness of sight. He sent for Marzak and described the symptoms to him, and Marzak prepared a collyrium and lined Amir's eyes with it. Amir's symptoms went away and his eyes lit up as before. He used that collyrium more than once, and richly rewarded and praised Marzak for it. Upon learning the qualities of the collyrium, Amir Hamza's friends also lined their eyes with it, and everyone sought remedies from Marzak for their many symptoms. All those who were cured by Marzak's hand made offerings to him according to their station, and gave him what they could afford.

Marzak now mixed the collyrium with blinding agents. He went before Amir and said to him, "The collyrium I have prepared this time contains an ingredient that has made it greatly improved from the first preparation. Indeed it has now become a perfect remedy, and such are its properties that you will never need to line your eyes again after a single application, nor indeed will your eyes need it again." Then Amir, along with his friends, applied the collyrium to their eyes and lined them with it.

Marzak saw that his work there was done, and that they had all been blinded. He reckoned that if he stayed there any longer, Amir would have his eyes plucked from their sockets in punishment for his deeds. As he deemed it unwise to tarry there longer, he slipped out and sought a route of escape. He went before Naushervan and said, "I have blinded Hamza and all of his companions; they have lost their sight one and all." Naushervan asked him, "How are we to know that you tell the truth and have not laced your account with exaggeration?" He answered, "Strike the drums of war and you will soon have your proof. Their whole camp has been blinded, and none will answer the call." Naushervan immediately ordered the drums of war to be beaten.

Upon hearing the enemy's call to war, Amir and his companions sent for water to wash their faces. Then they realized that they could see nothing, and all of them were blind. Amir said, "Go and look for Marzak!" But Marzak was nowhere to be found. Amir said to his friends, "It is a terrible calamity that we cannot see and the enemy has struck the drums of war. If we do not go into the battlefield, they will advance on our camp in broad daylight and steal all we have, leaving us completely destitute. We must, at all costs, arrange our fighting ranks." With this, Amir went into the field and ordered his army into battle arrays.

Witnessing this, Naushervan said to Marzak, "If they were blind, they would not enter the arena and herd blind men into a battlefield." That villain answered, "Send someone to fight them and you will soon learn the truth." Naushervan sent one of the Aadi champions, who entered the arena and called out in a loud voice, "Have you become blind to my presence, O Arabs? I stand here seeking combat, and none of you enter the arena to display your bravery and courage." Hardam was vexed at his words. He led his horse into the arena to face him and, swinging his mace, landed a powerful blow on him, which killed the Aadi warrior and his horse instantly. One after another, Naushervan sent six Aadi warriors to fight Hardam, and all of them became the prey of the lion of his mace.

Then Naushervan ordered his army to surround Hardam, cut off his escape route, and then kill him. When Naushervan's army attacked Hardam, he struck them with his mace, killing hundreds of infidels. They could not withstand his blows and at last turned tail. From a safe distance, they began showering Hardam with arrows. Since Hardam was wearing Prophet Daud's seven-piece suit of armor, the arrows were ineffective and the barrage of the archers caused him no harm. Finally, Bakhtak said, "Friends, Hardam is wearing Daud's seven-piece suit of armor: The arrows cannot pierce his body. But if you aim at his foot, he will presently fall!" The archers followed Bakhtak's advice, whereupon Hardam called out to Amir Hamza, "O Amir, now I need your aid. Come quickly to rescue me from the hands of infidels!" Amir took Ashqar's reins and said to him in the Jinni language, "Right now I am completely blind. Lead me wherever you see the infidels so that I may rout them!" Amir plunged into the enemy ranks astride Ashqar and slew many of them, making heaps from the corpses of the faithless.

Naushervan said to his army, "All the men in the enemy ranks are blind. They will not remain standing for long and will soon tumble and fall over. Keep your spirits up, and seek out and kill every single one of them." At Naushervan's encouragement, his soldiers fought for some time but finally turned away. Amir returned to his pavilion in victory and triumph, and said to his companions, "It would not bode well for us to stay here until our sight is restored. We must head for some nearby city and seek treatment there for our blindness. Then we can worry about the enemy and prepare for the war with leisure." The champion Chob-Gardaan said, "Three days' journey from here is my city, Ardabil, which is well fortified. If Your Honor so wishes, you may retire there until you are fully restored to your strength." Amir answered him, "Very well! You may proceed with the advance camp and prepare the city's defenses. I shall follow you and bring the rest of the men along." Amir's camp marched for Ardabil that same day, and the entire army and the encampment was ordered to head there.

Thinking that they were blind, Naushervan gave them chase and ordered his army to pursue them. Amir had stayed behind with four warriors and he attacked the enemy ranks. That day Amir's sword saw more action and he killed more infidels than ever. Finally, the enemy forces turned tail and fled, and not a single infidel remained behind. Amir entered the city of Ardabil in triumph and victory and finally was relieved of all his anxieties and worries. He fortified the city gates and filled the moats with water, cutting off all avenues for the enemy to enter within. He sent reinforcements to the battlements and began supplicating God Almighty to restore the sight to his eyes. Naushervan arrived and attacked the fortress, but when the fortified army inflicted many casualties on his soldiers, he put a cordon around the castle and set up camp.

Of Hashim bin Hamza and Haris bin Sa'ad Entering Amir Hamza's Service, and of Amir's Eyes Being Cured with the Holy Khizr's Help

The narrator has said that a son was born to Amir Hamza by Hardam's sister, who named the child Hashim. A son was also born to Sa'ad bin Amar bin Hamza by Hardam's niece, and she named him Haris. The two boys, who were granduncle and grandnephew by relation, had now reached the age of nine, and they felt great love and affection for each other because they were of the same age. They went hunting together and took meals in each other's company. It was Hashim's custom that when he hunted a lion, he always roasted and ate his heart, for which reason he had become known as Hashim the Lion-Eater. When the news reached them that Amir was camped within the fort of Ardabil, the two boys headed there from Baru with a large army. They arrived there in a few days to find the infidels besieging the city and their standards hoisted everywhere.

Hashim and Haris drew their swords and, without the least fear or anxiety, attacked the encampment of the dastardly infidels like lions tearing into a flock of sheep. They showed such excellent swordsmanship and fought so bravely that the infidels lost their nerve. Thousands of infidels became the prey of the crocodile of their swords, and were flung by them into the embrace of the denizens of Hell. Finally, the enemy fled from the vicinity of the fortress and camped at a distance that was many bow shots away from it. The armies of the True Faith reasoned that they had been sent aid from the Future State. They opened the gates of the city and welcomed Hashim and Haris inside. Both of them kissed Amir's feet, informed him of their names and pedigrees, and narrated to him the whole account of their lives.

Amir Hamza now felt a strange and boundless joy that could not be described in words. He seated each of them on either knee and kissed them, and everyone scattered gold and jewels over their heads in sacrifice for them. Hashim submitted to Amir, saying, "This place is unsuitable, and our army will be put to inconvenience here. It would be better if you returned with us to Baru, where the armies can take rest and everyone can be comfortably accommodated." Amir ordered the timbal to be struck to announce their departure, and headed for Baru.

The army of the infidels followed them. When Amir entered the fortress of Baru with all his camp and entourage, the infidels laid siege to the place and set up camp.

Amir made tearful supplications night and day to God to restore his sight, and petitioned the Court of Heaven for a cure to his blindness. One day the holy Khizr appeared beside him and crushed a leaf and dropped a few drops of its liquid into Amir's eyes with his hands. Immediately, Amir's eyes lit up with vision and all the darkness and haze over them were cast away. Sight was restored to Amir's eyes and, ennobled by his meeting with the holy Khizr, Amir said, "I have been cured because of you, but all my friends are also crippled by blindness. They have been vulnerable and helpless since losing their sight, and a leader is rendered powerless without friends and companions." Then Khvaja Khizr gave Amir a few leaves and told him to squeeze their juice into his friends' eyes, explaining that the medicine would restore their sight and, by God's grace, they would all be cured of blindness. After instructing him, the holy Khizr disappeared. Amir squeezed the sap of these leaves into his friends' eyes, and it revived their vision. Their prayers were answered by the grace of the holy Khizr.

Amar Ayyar said to Amir, "It is plain that all this was the doing of Bakhtak, the wretch. I shall prepare a punishment for him, if you would so order, and avenge our suffering." Amir said, "He will receive his punishment in due time. It is not at all agreeable to me to cause grief to anyone." Amar remained quiet then and did not answer for fear of Amir Hamza, but he was furious with Bakhtak. Come evening, he dressed up as a cook and went to Bakhtak's pavilion and said to the guards, "Inform His Honor without delay that a cook has arrived at his doors from Greece who is a master of sweet and savory cuisine but is peerless in cooking the *hareesa*."[41] Bakhtak had him come to his pavilion, but feared lest the cook turn out to be Amar. Then he told himself that Amar had been blinded, and the person who had called on him must genuinely be a cook. Still, Bakhtak sent many wise *ayyars* to investigate the matter and find out whether or not Amar Ayyar was in Hamza's camp. The *ayyars* left Bakhtak's pavilion and decided after conferring together that if the cook was indeed Amar in disguise, he would hold a grudge against them for impeding him. Then he would avenge himself on them without fear of anyone, for such was Amar's reputation. Having come to that conclusion, they went back to the pavilion and, pretending to have returned from their mission, told Bakhtak that Amar Ayyar was with Hamza in his camp. Bakhtak was satisfied by this and ordered Amar to make the *hareesa*, and provided him with all the ingredients. Amar made such a delicious stew that Bakhtak licked the entire bowl and went before Naushervan to extol Amar's talents, praising the cook's culinary gifts to the high heavens and describing his wondrous cooking. Naushervan appointed Amar as the royal chef and gave him complete charge of his kitchen. Amar made new dishes every day and sent them to the royal table.

One night Amar put a three-*maund* pot on the fire and filled it with water but put no meat in it. In the middle of the night Amar drugged all the other cooks and entered Bakhtak's pavilion. He saw Bakhtak's eyes shut tight in sleep and heard his snores sounding loudly within. Amar blew several *mithcals* of a soporific powder into Bakhtak's nostrils, whereupon Bakhtak sneezed and was taken unconscious. Amar rolled him up in a sheet and carried him to the kitchen, where he threw him into the pot of boiling water. Once he was fully blanched, Amar buried his skin and skull in the ground and hid the hole cleverly. Then Amar made a fine *hareesa* from Bakhtak's flesh and laid out the dish for the king's meal. The king offered portions of the dish to many of his nobles and ate it praising Amar's handiwork.

It so happened that while Naushervan was being served, the soup ladle brought up one of Bakhtak's fingers, which bore a ring given him by the emperor. Seeing the finger, Naushervan stopped eating and asked one of the cooks, "Whose finger is this? What is it doing in our food and why did you cook it?" The cook said nothing, but recognized the ring as Bakhtak's. Naushervan said to his attendants, "Go and see what Bakhtak is doing and bring him before me." When the men went into Bakhtak's pavilion they found his bed empty, and no one could tell them what had become of him or what calamity had overtaken him. After conducting a search for him, they told the emperor that Bakhtak was missing from his pavilion. The emperor then realized that the *hareesa* had been made from

Bakhtak's flesh. He became sick and vomited until he was beside himself with illness and pain. Amar made himself scarce and fled to Hamza's camp.

In the meantime, Buzurjmehr arrived in the court. Naushervan said to him, "I have saved you a share of the *hareesa*. Have some and enjoy this delectable dish." Buzurjmehr made an excuse and said, "I have already had my meal. To eat after partaking one's meal causes indigestion and sluggishness." Then Naushervan said, "I understand why you do not eat and make excuses for not partaking of the *hareesa*. You must have learned about the matter by *ramal* but did not care to inform me, and did not share with me what you knew." Buzurjmehr answered, "It is against the custom of wise men to speak without being spoken to, let alone speak about a matter such as this." Buzurjmehr's words fully convinced Naushervan that he had known of the matter. In his anger, Naushervan ordered Buzurjmehr to be blinded, and his eyes were lined with indigo. Then Naushervan put Hurmuz on the throne in his place and went away to Ctesiphon.

———

Buzurjmehr now went before Amir Hamza and said to him, "My son, I have heard that the advent of the Last Prophet[42] (may God's peace and blessings be upon him) has been announced. Send me to Mecca so that I may take bliss in his sacred presence and receive divine blessing by kissing his feet." Amir sent Buzurjmehr to Mecca with a well-provisioned entourage, and gladly bid him adieu.

Khvaja Abdul Muttalib greeted Buzurjmehr warmly and received him in the finest traditions of hospitality, and took him to kiss the feet of the Last Prophet. When Buzurjmehr came before the luminous aspect of the Prophet, he picked up some dust from under his shoes and applied it to his eyes, whereupon his sight was immediately restored, and by the grace of this act his eyes filled with the light of divine knowledge as well. This miracle of the Holy Prophet became renowned in every corner of the world.

Now hear of Hurmuz. After Naushervan departed for Ctesiphon and left him in charge, he conferred a robe of ministerial rank on Siyavush bin Buzurjmehr and made him his first minister. He showed him much regard and honor and gave him a seat to the right of his throne. He also appointed Bakhtiarak bin Bakhtak—who surpassed his father in deceit and evildoing—as his minister and gave him a seat to the left of his throne. Within a few days Bakhtiarak wormed his way into Hurmuz's graces and became so firmly entrenched that Hurmuz never did anything without first consulting him, and it seemed as if Bakhtiarak himself were the real emperor.

One day Hurmuz said to Bakhtiarak, "O minister of sound advice, we must think of some way to have Hamza killed with all his sons, relatives, and friends so that my mind is put at ease on account of him." He replied, "The Bakhtaris are known to be cannibals. If we can solicit their aid, I have no doubt that your purposes will be served." Bakhtiarak then wrote a letter on behalf of Hurmuz addressed to Gaolangi, the king of Rakham, in which he complained of Hamza and wrote that the Arab had wreaked havoc in his empire and held its citizens in his power, and was now headed to destroy his kingdom and inflict the same fate on him[?].

When Gaolangi was apprised of the contents of the letter, he looked to his sons and said, "One of you should go and bring me Hamza as a captive, and show your courage in this enterprise." Answering this call, Gaolangi's son-in-law Marzaban Zardhasht rose and kissed the ground with reverence and declared, "The task will be mine." Gaolangi sent him off with thirty thousand soldiers riding lions. When Marzaban arrived at Baru, Hurmuz greeted him and brought him into his camp. He conferred a robe of honor on Marzaban and paid him all the duties of hospitality. Hurmuz ordered festive music to be played and all the necessities for revelry to be arranged in Marzaban's honor.

Meanwhile, Amir asked Amar, "Why is the enemy playing festive music today, with their timbals sounding like thunder?" Amar investigated the matter and replied, "Bakhtiarak sent a letter on behalf of Hurmuz soliciting aid from Gaolangi, the king of Rakham, who has sent his son-in-law Marzaban Zardhasht to aid Hurmuz. The infidels are celebrating his arrival in their camp." Amir Hamza smiled but said nothing, nor did he suffer any anxiety about the information Amar had given him.

In the morning the drums of war were struck in the infidel camp and their call reached the ears of all brave men. Amir headed for the arena and arranged his army in battle formations. Marzaban sent a lion rider into the arena, who faced the camp of the Arabs and declared, "He who wishes to have his soul extracted by my hands should come forward into the arena to display his courage, for I am his Angel of Death." Amir's commanders said to their leader, "Our horses will shy away from even the spoor of the lion, for they have never before seen this beast. It would be better for us to fight the lion riders on foot, and it would be a wiser strategy not to send riders to encounter these blackguards." Amir said,

"How will someone on foot prevail over a rider?" Hardam said, "O Amir, you well know that I always fight on foot. Pray order me to answer the lion rider's challenge and fight him." Amir said, "Go forth! I give you into the protection of God!"

When the lion rider attacked Hardam, he tangled the infidel's weapon in the chain of his mace and pulled it from his hands, taking possession of it with great speed. Then Hardam swung his mace and dealt a blow to the lion rider that crushed him and his mount into dust. Amar Ayyar rushed forward and cut off the lion's head and threw it before the horses so that they could smell it. Amir said to him, "What is this clownish trick, and what purpose will it serve?" Amar answered, "I am familiarizing the horses with this smell so that they no longer fear the lions and do not shy away and lose courage in battle." Amir laughed at Amar's reply.

In the meantime, a second lion rider had come out to fight Hardam and had been dispatched to his death to meet the first. In this manner, one after another, Hardam killed forty lion riders before the end of the day and sent them all to Hell with his bravery and courage. In the evening, both camps struck the drums to announce the day's end and returned to their resting places. Amir embraced Hardam and showered praise on him before everyone. In the morning Hardam again faced a lion rider in the arena, and he, too, died at Hardam's hands. Then no lion rider dared to enter the arena to challenge him.

Marzaban kept shouting orders at his men, but nobody paid him any heed. They made excuses and said, "Anyone who goes to fight that frenzied warrior does not return alive. We love our lives too much to challenge such a champion and die before our time." Marzaban was greatly embarrassed and mortified, and he faced Hardam himself, delivering him a mighty blow. As before, Hardam tried to pull the weapon from Marzaban's hands by winding the chain of his mace around it, but not only was he unable to do so, he began losing his grip on his own mace. Hardam immediately called out to Amir, "Hasten to my aid, O Amir, or else my mace will be snatched from my hands, and the enemy will overpower me!"

Amir spurred on Ashqar and, as he reached the combatants, he bellowed so loudly that Marzaban's limbs went numb and he looked up to the heavens to see if they were crashing down on him. Hardam pulled his mace from his adversary's hands, and Marzaban said to Amir, "Who are you, O warrior, to snatch my prey from my hands? For this transgression you will become my prey yourself!" Marzaban dealt a blow to Amir and said, "The Great Wall of Sikander[43] would have been razed by this blow. How could a small mortal such as you survive the blow and escape from my hands?" Amir said to him, "O wretch! Deal two more strikes and then you shall learn what a true mace blow feels like, and find out how brave men withstand the blows of champions."

Marzaban struck two more blows in succession, but Amir stood his ground and did not budge an inch. Then it was Amir's turn. He swung his mace and landed such a powerful blow on Marzaban that many in the infidel army were deafened by the sound of its impact, and every pore of Marzaban's body broke with sweat. Then Marzaban realized that Hamza was a mighty champion and as strong and powerful as a rutting elephant. He took stock of Amir's great strength and reasoned that it would be little wonder if he came to harm at his hands. He decided it was unwise to wager his sweet life for another's cause, and turned tail and fled with Amir Hamza in pursuit. As Amir's steed caught up with Marzaban's, Amir dealt him a powerful blow of his sword that broke Marzaban's arm and knocked his weapon from his hands. With his mouth spewing blood profusely and his arm severed, Marzaban went before Hurmuz and said to him, "O Prince, Hamza is both stronger and mightier than I and most courageous. I do not stand a chance against him in combat. If you wish to be delivered from his hands, you must depart to Qaza-va-Qadar[44] to seek refuge with Saryal bin Salasal, who is one hundred and forty yards tall, a great warrior, and a majestic and magnificent king. If you wish I could accompany you to his land and give him a complete account of your plight."

Hurmuz consulted the kings in his court and they said with one voice, "You must follow the course that results in Hamza's death, for we must seek revenge from him." Siyavush bin Buzurjmehr said, "I would not advise you to go there. If you do, you will face humiliation and embarrassment. I can assure you that it will cause you many worries and much anxiety." Bakhtiarak retorted, "Indeed he would say that, for one always tends to favor those of one's own faith." Siyavush kept his silence. The next day Hurmuz departed and headed with his army toward Qazava-Qadar, arriving at its frontiers after several days.

Now, Marzaban had already informed Saryal of Hurmuz's predicament. Saryal greeted Hurmuz and conducted him to his castle. That night, when they sat down to eat, Hurmuz saw a roasted boar lying before Saryal, who offered Hurmuz a piece of its meat with his own hand. When Hurmuz tried to refuse it on some pretext,[45] Marzaban whispered in his ear, "Saryal will take offense if you do not eat that piece of meat." Against his will Hurmuz put the meat in his mouth but immediately spat it out. Saryal took offense at this and said to his companions, "Go and feed yourselves on Hurmuz's men, for the gods Lat and Manat have sent you all these goats as their gift. Go and sink your teeth into their tender flesh!" Saryal's people fell upon Hurmuz's army and began capturing and eating them. Trapped in this terrible scrape, Hurmuz became fearful and helpless.

Hurmuz cursed Bakhtiarak and his advice a thousand times and, addressing Siyavush, said, "O Khvaja's son! Indeed I would have saved myself this disgrace and embarrassment had I followed your advice. I would not have landed myself and my army in this dreadful calamity. We must find a way to escape and use some strategy to flee from this place." Siyavush replied, "You will not be able to escape from here without Hamza's assistance. There is nothing I can do about it." Hurmuz said, "Why would Hamza come to my help at all? He is furious with me and would never set foot in this valley." Siyavush replied, "Since Hamza is a generous, munificent, and high-minded man, he will certainly rescue you if you ask him for help." Hurmuz said, "If you are of that mind, then go to him on my behalf and explain my plight to him." The next day Siyavush went before Amir Hamza and interceded for Hurmuz and sought his help. Amir said, "I would assist Hurmuz on the condition that he sincerely and truthfully convert to the True Faith and follow the writ of the Faith." Siyavush returned to tell Hurmuz what Amir Hamza had said to him.

Hurmuz went before Amir in the middle of the night and cried copious tears while narrating to him his tale of woe. Amir instructed him in the Act of Faith and comforted and consoled him. He seated Hurmuz on the throne and ordered a meal and shared it with him. Hurmuz said, "O Amir, show me this favor: Send me to Ctesiphon in safety." Amir answered, "You are free to go where you wish and do as you please, but do not fall away from the True Faith now, or else you will dearly regret it and repent your decision." With these words, Amir sent Hurmuz away.

Saryal was enraged by Hurmuz's departure. He immediately sounded the drums of war and went to the arena with his whole army to do battle. Amir also organized his army into fighting ranks. Catching sight of Amir Hamza, Saryal came forward on horseback and challenged his army, "O herd of sheep! The one among you who wishes to escape the knife should come forward so that I may eat him alive—bones, hide, and all." Ceylon's Black Lion, King Landhoor, took Amir's leave and confronted Saryal. Seeing his height and bulk, Saryal asked, "Are you Hamza?" Landhoor replied, "My name is Landhoor bin Saadan, and the whole world rings with the renown of my valor." Saryal struck Landhoor with his mace, but he withstood the blow with great effort and might, and did not allow it to unnerve him. Saryal said, "I have now learned that you are a mighty warrior. Come deal me a blow now!" Landhoor struck Saryal with his powerful mace. Saryal only laughed and said, "O Landhoor, look at your size and girth and then acknowledge the weakness of your arm! You have absolutely no strength."

The two fought with maces, but neither could injure his adversary. The armies retired after sunset to take rest at their appointed stations. The next day they formed battle arrays again. Qeemaz Shah came out to fight Saryal, and after foiling his attack, severed the feet of Saryal's mount. Qeemaz Shah also dismounted and wrestled with Saryal, who slammed him to the ground. Then Amir made his war cry and secured the release of Qeemaz Shah. Saryal mounted another horse and said to Amir, "O dwarf, why did you let my prey escape? You have made me suffer terribly because of this, and now it is only right that I make you my prey instead and take your life. Be quick and tell me your name and station so that you do not die unsung, and nobody regrets that you died without trace." Amir answered, "My name is Hamza bin Abdul Muttalib, and there is none high or low who is not familiar with my splendor and magnificence."

Saryal dealt a mace blow to Amir, who parried it with his shield and said, "O infidel! I give you two more blows and then it shall be my turn." Saryal delivered a second mace blow to Amir, who parried that, too. When Saryal struck a third time, Amir caught his mace by its handle and, putting his bow around Saryal's neck, pulled Saryal to the ground. Amar Ayyar caught Saryal with a rope and tied up his arms. Amir returned to his pavilion to the sound of the drums of victory, satisfied and contented on all accounts. He asked Saryal, "What are your intentions now?" He replied, "Enroll me among your slaves and admit me as a faithful servant in your court." Amir converted him to the True Faith and conferred a robe of honor upon him. Saryal was admitted among the ranks of the followers of the True Faith, and was given a golden throne above Landhoor's station for his seat. Amar put the ring of slavery in his ear and Saryal took Amir to his city, where he organized festivities in his honor.

After the festivities were over, Amir said to him, "O Saryal, take me to see the wonders of your land and teach me about the rarities of this place." Saryal replied, "Three days' journey from here is the Tilismat-e Jamshediya. Let us go visit it, and you shall enjoy its sights." Amir said to him, "If you have visited the *tilism,* describe it to me. Tell me who constructed it and give me its complete history." He answered, "When Jamshed was nearing his death, he emptied the city of its denizens [?] and installed wooden mace bearers and overseers at short intervals at its ramparts. Then he lay down in the grave he had constructed for himself. He enclosed himself there and severed himself from all worldly concerns. The other marvel is Jadu-e Jamshediya, also known as Damama-e Ilm. That, too, is a wondrous place. Sufaid Dev lives there,[46] whom everyone considers a man-eater." Amir said, "My terror drove that *dev* from Qaf. Now I learn that he has found a refuge here and has been hiding here ever since." Amir left his army behind and headed for Jadu-e Jamshediya with Amar and Saryal.

When he arrived there, Amir heard a dreadful voice that struck fear in the hearts of all who heard it. Amir asked, "Whose voice was that?" Saryal answered, "It is the voice of the *tilism.*" When they arrived at the gates and Amir tried to step inside to see its wonders, the soldiers standing guard attacked him with their swords. Amir leapt aside to dodge the blow. Saryal now said, "I have heard my grandfather say that all men in this city are made by *tilism.* A bird made by *tilism* lives inside the dome that you see before you. When it sees anyone, it cries out. If you were to kill the bird, you would learn all the secrets of this *tilism* and then you would come to no harm." When Amir studied the dome, he saw a bird chirping there with a melodious voice. Amir notched an arrow in his bow, took aim, and fired with such a steady hand that the arrow pierced the bird and it fell to the ground with a thud. The moment it fell down the *tilism* was broken. Amir opened the city gates, went inside, and saw the men who had attacked him lying on the ground with their weapons. Amir secured possession of the place. When he opened the city's treasury in Saryal's presence, he found it filled with hundreds of thousands of snakes and scorpions, and he closed and locked it as before.

Then Amir said to Saryal, "I have seen all the wonders of Jadu-e Jamshediya. Now tell me where Sufaid Dev is hiding and take me to his dwelling." Saryal took Amir into the Bayaban-e Akhzar and pointed to a well and said, "This is where Sufaid Dev lives." Amir said to Saryal, "Exert yourself a little and remove the stone from the mouth of the well." Saryal tried but was unable to move the stone. Then Amir kicked the stone, shattering it into pieces. Amir said to Saryal, "I am going to lower myself into the well. Keep alert and do not leave your post." Then Amir said to Ashqar Devzad in the Jinni language, "Beware not to move from here at all. Do not let anyone enter this place, and do not let any *dev* descend into the well."

Amir then lowered himself into the well with a rope, and once he reached the bottom he beheld a door covered by a stone slab. When Amir removed the slab, he saw Sufaid Dev sitting on a throne with a lowered head in a state of anxiety, wonderment, and surprise. Sufaid Dev asked one of his minions who had informed him of Amir's arrival there, "Did you see the Quake of Qaf with your own eyes and recognize him?" The *dev* answered, "The Quake of Qaf was riding a horse and two men were accompanying him on foot. As to the Quake of Qaf, I recognize and know him well." Sufaid Dev said, "In the eighteen years that that man lived in Qaf he destroyed the domicile of the *devs* and drowned hundreds of thousands in the sea of death. It was my fear of him that forced me to make my dwelling here, but he has arrived here as well like an unforeseen calamity. Regard his daring and courage that he entered even this well. It seems that the days of my life are at an end, for the signs of the diminishment of my power are becoming manifest."

Sufaid Dev had not yet finished his speech when Amir made his war cry. Sufaid Dev said, "O Quake of Qaf, I sent myself into exile for fear of you and left all my near and dear ones when I took myself to this corner. But you followed me here as well and have cornered me in this dark and narrow place. I shall do everything in my power to inflict on you a most painful death." At this, Sufaid Dev hurled a several-hundred-*maund* rock at Amir's head. Amir leapt to one side and the rock crashed to the ground. As Sufaid Dev bent to pick up another rock, Amir dealt him a blow of his sword from behind, carving through his skull and slicing his spine. Sufaid Dev fell on his face and cried, "Show me the kindness of dealing me another blow so that I may depart even sooner from this ephemeral world for the Permanent Land, and do not suffer the pain of my wounds any longer." Amir responded, "I know your race all too well. What you hope for will never come to pass." Sufaid Dev was thwarted, and he gave up his life by bashing his head against the ground. Most of the *devs* who had accompanied him were killed, while others fled and went their way. Still others asked for clemency, and Amir converted these *devs* to the True Faith and put them under his allegiance. Then he ordered them, "Return to Qaf and go to Quraisha and remain in her service."

Thereafter Amir emerged from the well carrying Sufaid Dev's head. He showed it to Saryal and hung it from his saddle straps, and thus vanquished those *devs*. Then Amir mounted his horse and departed. Some distance from there was a pasture where Amir occupied himself with hunting, putting all his anxieties and worries to rest.

Of Rustam, Qunduz Sar-Shaban, and Aljosh
Barbari Dying at the Hands of Ahriman
Sher-Gardaan, the Master of Bakhtar

The narrators relate that Rustam-e Peel-Tan noticed that a long period
of time had passed since Amir's departure and no news of him had been
received. He decided that Hamza's companions would be idling their
time to no purpose awaiting him there, and would do better to head for
Jamshediya and visit its *tilisms*. He appointed Saryal's sons as his guides and
headed from Qaza-va-Qadar with his army and arrived in the Tilismat-
e-Jamshediya after a few days. Finding it destroyed, he realized that
Amir must have razed it and headed onward after killing all the *devs*.
Then Rustam headed to the second land.

When he entered the place with all his forces and broke down the
dome, he saw Jamshed's body lying on a throne. He opened the treasury's
chambers and killed all the scorpions and snakes. Then he said to Saryal's
sons, "We should now head for Bakhtar and see its sights." They answered, "The king of Bakhtar is Ahriman Sher-Gardaan, a magnificent
and majestic lord. He is one hundred and twenty-five yards tall and his
people and soldiers are all cannibals. His entire kingdom is a picture of
God's wrath, and it would not bode well to head there, as no one has returned alive from his dominions."

Rustam said, "It seems to me that in power and might he is Saryal's
equal, which is the reason for his notoriety." They answered, "He is
mightier than Saryal and a thousand times more courageous. Whenever
he advanced on our kingdom, our father retreated into the mountains for
fear of him." Rustam asked them, "Where is Marzaban Zardhasht?" They
replied, "The day Amir Hamza routed Saryal, Marzaban fled to the lands
of Ahriman Sher-Gardaan and sought refuge there." Rustam now said to
his friends and brothers, "Amir has gone to kill Sufaid Dev. It is certain

that on his way back, he will visit Bakhtar to explore that land. If we advance now and vanquish Ahriman Sher-Gardaan before Amir's arrival, it will earn us great glory and we will be considered heroes and valiant champions." All of them replied in unison, "The wishes of our master are always supreme. We are your obedient slaves. We shall do as you order and never fail to submit to your commands."

Rustam departed that very instant and arrived on the outskirts of Bakhtar in a few days. Marzaban was already present in Ahriman's court and he informed his host of Rustam's arrival and alerted him of his advance. Ahriman laughed uproariously upon hearing these tidings. He took Marzaban, headed for Rustam's camp, and issued this challenge: "O herd of sheep! He among you who wishes to have his neck slit should come forward and face me!"

Qunduz Sar-Shaban took Rustam's leave to face Ahriman and was martyred at his hands. The cannibals swarmed over him, cut him up into small pieces, and ate him, bones and all. Aljosh Barbari in his turn attacked Ahriman with his dagger and landed a powerful blow that sank up to the hilt into Ahriman's body, but Ahriman did not feel a thing and no harm came to him. Ahriman tried to secure a hold of Aljosh Barbari to mangle him with his teeth, but Aljosh escaped with great effort and kept fighting. During the combat Ahriman finally prevailed over Aljosh Barbari and ate him alive.

When Rustam saw that two of his champions had been martyred he felt great consternation. He spurred on his horse and entered the arena to fight Ahriman himself. Ahriman dealt Rustam a blow of his mace, which he took on his shield. Rustam then answered with a sword blow that would have cut the cannibal in two and left him with no sign of life had it not missed its mark. Ahriman escaped the blow, jumped down from his horse, and caught Rustam's arms and pulled him till he ripped the skin from his abdomen. When Qasim Khavari saw that Rustam had been injured, he tore into the arena astride his horse, fearful that Rustam might die and his death would strike dread and terror into the hearts of his men. Qasim Khavari made his war cry and threw himself between Rustam and Ahriman, challenging the foe. The *ayyars* carried Rustam away to their camp.

Then Ahriman Sher-Gardaan asked Qasim, "Who was the man who was taken away, and who are you?" Qasim answered, "He was my father and Hamza's son." Ahriman said, "With Hamza there, why did he imperil his life and his father not help him?" Qasim answered, "Amir Hamza is not present in the camp, as he has gone to kill Sufaid Dev." Ahriman replied, "Since Hamza is not with you, it is useless for me to fight mere boys. It is not incumbent on me to fight you." At this, he retired to his dwelling.

While Ahriman headed off, Qasim returned to his camp with his whole army and found that Rustam had departed to meet his Maker from the wound Ahriman had inflicted on him. A terrible weeping and wailing rose from the camp of the followers of the True Faith, which burst even the heart of the pen that attempted to describe it. Those who heard the tragic news grew pale with grief. In the end, they performed Rustam's last rites and waited for Amir.

When Amir returned to Jamshediya from his hunting expedition, he saw signs that his army had camped there and said to Amar, "It seems certain from the signs that Rustam has been here, and after destroying the place, he headed for Bakhtar. May God ward off the eye of affliction from him and may I see him alive, for I suddenly feel a terrible anxiety and my heart is sinking." Amir Hamza then headed for Bakhtar himself. As he arrived in its environs, all his friends and sons came to him crying, bareheaded, and barefoot and fell at his feet. Upon hearing of the deaths of Rustam, Qunduz, and Aljosh, Amir dropped from his steed and rolled in the dust in ecstasies of grief, overtaken by terrible sorrow. When Amir's friends saw that he was beside himself with grief, they said to him, "O Amir, your friends and sons all grieve for Rustam, but you are suffering the most affliction and the hearts of those who behold your state bleed from pain. It would be better for you to head to the forest to divert yourself with hunting and the chase." They finally prevailed on Amir, and all of them headed for the forest.

It so happened that Marzaban Zardhasht was on his way to Rakham, after having taken his leave of Ahriman, when on the way he received news that Hamza was busy hunting with his friends and sons, and that the death of his son had wounded him deeply and made him oblivious to all concerns. Realizing that he would not find a better chance, Marzaban ordered a sorcerer to conjure him a horse from magic, complete with all the trappings. Then Marzaban stood the horse in a field and lay in wait with some companions on the path that led there. By chance, Sa'ad bin Amar bin Hamza happened to pass that way and was delighted to see the horse. He dismounted his steed and climbed into the saddle of the enchanted horse. Sa'ad gave the horse a cut with his whip and the horse took off like the wind. Sa'ad tried his best to rein him in, but the horse did not stop. Then Sa'ad drew his sword and beheaded the horse and both horse and rider fell to the ground. Marzaban rushed out and tied up Sa'ad and took him captive. Then he went on his way to Rakham.

Arriving before Gaolangi, he presented Sa'ad to him and said, "This is Hamza's grandson and the king of the followers of the True Faith. I overpowered him and brought him here a prisoner. Tell me if it was not a signal deed I accomplished." Sa'ad said, "O Gaolangi, since he states that he has overpowered me, order him to fight me before you. Everyone will find out who overpowers whom when we fight together. Then you may distinguish truth from falsehood." Gaolangi answered, "Yours is a fair request, and I would allow it!" He ordered Sa'ad's fetters removed and told everyone at court what was about to unfold before them.

Marzaban attacked Sa'ad with his mace, but he foiled the blow and, securing hold of Marzaban's arms, made his war cry and lifted him up over his shoulders. He raised him high above his head and slammed him to the floor. When Marzaban tried to rise to his feet, Gaolangi, who was a just man, killed him by dealing him a blow with his mace which forced his brains from his skull. Gaolangi heaped praises on Sa'ad, embraced him, sat him beside himself on his throne, and said, "My son, consider this place your home and do not give yourself over to any worries. I would gladly give you leave to depart, but I would like to detain you here, for Hamza will certainly head this way in search of you and take the trouble to come here to find you. I have long been desirous of meeting him. Because of your presence here my wish will be granted, and the sight of Hamza will afford me great delight." Seeing Gaolangi's loving and affectionate nature, Sa'ad willingly agreed to stay with him and was most grateful to him for his kindness.

Badiuz Zaman, meanwhile, was surprised to see Sa'ad's horse standing riderless and the enchanted horse lying dead nearby. The scene and Sa'ad's disappearance caused him untold worry. He had the surrounding area searched, but no trace of Sa'ad was discovered. Badiuz Zaman felt at a loss and said to his friends, "My friends, a great calamity has overtaken us with Sa'ad's disappearance. I am duty-bound to search for him. Amir is not yet fully recovered from mourning Rustam. If he hears of Sa'ad's disappearance, he will be reduced to an even worse plight, and his heart will bleed from excessive sorrow and grief. Let us go in search of Sa'ad and bring him back and not make a moment's delay in this undertaking. It stands to reason that it is all the doing of that villain, Marzaban. Surely it is he—the most accursed being in the world—who is behind it. But better late than never. God willing, he will receive the humiliation and disgrace he deserves from my hands."

Badiuz Zaman set out in search of Sa'ad. After many days he came upon a city and learned that its ruler was Taus Bakhtari, the son-in-law of Gaolangi. Badiuz Zaman said to his friends, "We must search for Sa'ad in this city. Perhaps Marzaban has brought him here and hidden him." Therefore, he wrote a letter to Taus Bakhtari that read:

O Taus Bakhtari, learn that I am Badiuz Zaman bin Hamza. Marzaban captured my nephew by deceit and I suspect that he has hidden him here. If he has given Sa'ad into your custody, I wish you to send him to me in safety without the least fear or apprehension. I also wish you to give Marzaban Zardhasht to my *ayyars* as a captive, or else I shall put out the light of your kingdom, and you will be disgraced and dishonored. I shall inflict such a terrible death on you that even the beasts would lament your fate. Finis.

Hardam Barui delivered Badiuz Zaman's missive to Taus and reported all the history of the incident to him. Upon receiving it, Taus Bakhtari tore up the letter, whereupon Hardam swung his mace and landed such a powerful blow on Taus that his throne became his coffin, and everyone who witnessed the scene was stunned. The infidels made a hue and cry and surrounded Hardam, who began swinging around his mace and killing them.

Learning of this development, Badiuz Zaman rushed to Hardam's aid with his companions and made the infidels the prey of the crocodile of his sword. After hundreds of them had been slaughtered, the remainder sought clemency, and Badiuz Zaman gave them reprieve and showed them mercy. He made a heap from the heads of the dead infidels and placed Taus Bakhtari's head at the top of the pile. Then he and his men traveled onward, and after two days they arrived in another city whose sovereign ruler was Gaolangi's other son-in-law. Badiuz Zaman wrote a similar missive to him and sent it by the agency of Hardam. This ruler also died at Hardam's hand for the excesses he took with Badiuz Zaman's missive. Badiuz Zaman ordered wholesale slaughter of the city's inhabitants and reprieved the few who survived, and then headed onward.

In a few days he arrived in Rakham and sent this same message to Gaolangi, having ordered Hardam to convey the message to Gaolangi in person and to tell him that if he refrained from obeying, he would die at

Badiuz Zaman's hands before his time. When Hardam arrived at the court, he saw Sa'ad and Gaolangi seated on the same throne. He beheld Gaolangi's height and stature with marveling eyes and figured that God must have created giants of this size to cause the heart to be seized by fear and dread. Seeing that Hardam was awed, Gaolangi said to him in a friendly tone, "Welcome, Hardam. Consider this your own house." Then, Gaolangi said to him, "Although Badiuz Zaman killed my sons-in-law, I refrained from murdering him out of the regard I feel for Hamza. Although I had the power to do it, I did not avenge myself."

Hardam was greatly embarrassed by Gaolangi's fine manners and was mortified to have to hand him such a communiqué considering how kindly Gaolangi had received him. But Hardam could not help it, as he had arrived there as a messenger, entrusted with delivering the missive. He handed the letter to Gaolangi and communicated the message in speech as well. After reading the letter, Gaolangi turned toward Sa'ad and said, "O Sa'ad, tell me if I have done you any wrong or submitted you to any torture for which your uncle has written me a letter that grieves my heart and causes me untold unease." Sa'ad answered, "He is unaware of all the kindnesses and favors that you have shown me as your guest. Had he known, he would never have sent you such a message." Gaolangi said, "What you say is indeed true."

He conferred a robe of honor on Hardam and said to him, "You may now leave. Pray convey my salutations to Badiuz Zaman and then inform him that it is true that Marzaban captured Sa'ad by deceit and brought him to me after overpowering him by fraud. For that, I killed him and dispatched him to join the denizens of Hell. I am keeping Sa'ad here as my guest until Hamza's arrival. I asked him to stay without any fear or anxiety, for I wish to invite Hamza here. You should also occupy yourself with hunting and the chase until Amir Hamza's arrival and you will receive provisions from my city in the meantime. If you chose to fight me instead, it would end in humiliation for you and would be a recipe for your destruction."

Upon hearing Gaolangi's message, Badiuz Zaman said, "The army should be given orders to march and array themselves in the arena for battle. I will take Sa'ad away from him in the flash of an eye and will hear no excuses from him." When Badiuz Zaman arrived at the fortress with his army, Gaolangi said to Sa'ad, "I have now learned that Badiuz Zaman is a rank idiot and no better than a beast. You may take a seat in the tower and witness as I go myself to chastise him and teach him a lesson for his vanity." After these words, Gaolangi rode out of the fort astride a bull.

All of Badiuz Zaman's companions tried to keep him from fighting with Gaolangi, but Badiuz Zaman would not listen to them. As he readied himself to ride into the arena, Landhoor caught the reins of his horse and said, "It was for just such a day that we warriors entered your service." Badiuz Zaman could not dissuade Landhoor and the Khusrau went and faced Gaolangi, who said, "O warrior, give me your particulars and tell me your name and station." Landhoor replied, "I am the Khusrau of India, King Landhoor bin Saadan. Although I am the king of eighteen thousand isles, I am nevertheless a slave to Hamza, and it is my obedience to him that earns me the esteem of all and sundry." Gaolangi said, "Your renown has indeed reached my ears. Come now and deal me your blow." Landhoor answered, "To take precedence in war is proscribed by Hamza's faith and his laws. You should strike first, and then I will answer and act according to my capability[?]."

When Landhoor withstood Gaolangi's blow, the king of Rakham praised him and said, "O Landhoor, truly you are a brave man. Until today nobody received my mace blow and remained standing. Go back to your pavilion to rest and send me another champion to face and fight me." Landhoor replied, "I cannot turn my back until you turn your back first." Gaolangi accepted his condition and left the arena. Then Landhoor went to his camp and narrated all that had passed.

Later, Gaolangi again entered the arena and issued his challenge, and this time Malik Ashtar faced him. When he tired of swinging his mace, Gaolangi asked for a fresh fighter. Then Sar-Barahna Tapishi rode to the field with great magnificence. Gaolangi said to him, "O warrior, ready the shield over your head for I shall now land my blow." Sar-Barahna Tapishi said, "I do not fear such strikes, for it is my wont to block them with my skull. Deal your blow freely." When Gaolangi swung his mace and landed the blow, Sar-Barahna Tapishi's head was pushed down into the cavity of his chest. Then Dewana Tapishi faced Gaolangi, who laid him low as well: Along with his steed, Gaolangi vanquished him. Gaolangi then dismounted his bull and carried both corpses before Badiuz Zaman and said to him, "O Prince, you had these two mighty warriors killed at my hands without reason, and you caused me to suffer grief and embarrassment before your father. However, what is past is past. Refrain from fighting me and do not think of making war against me. If you wish to have me killed, I have come before you unarmed. You should feel free to put me to death and behead me." Badiuz Zaman replied, "I am not some executioner who would first secure you before putting you to death. Nor am I a eunuch to act in this unchivalrous manner toward you. Go back and return here armed so that you can test my mettle."

Gaolangi was obliged to decorate himself with weapons, and mounted his bull to do combat. Presenting himself before the prince, he again expressed his reluctance, saying, "It is improper for you to fight in Hamza's absence, and these actions are unbecoming to the dignity of a prince. If you wish to fight me, you can fulfill all your desires when Hamza returns." Badiuz Zaman, however, could not be persuaded as he thought nothing of Gaolangi's might. At last, Gaolangi dealt the first blow with his mace. Badiuz Zaman withstood it and gave Gaolangi two strikes. After Gaolangi had dealt the prince more blows and Badiuz Zaman had withstood them all, Gaolangi praised him highly, commended his bravery and courage before everyone, and said, "His claim to fight me as an equal was justified."

Badiuz Zaman swung his mace and dealt such a mighty blow that Gaolangi's bull was killed from its impact—the poor beast gave up his life after just one blow, and sweat broke out from every pore on Gaolangi's body. Badiuz Zaman dismounted and fought on foot with Gaolangi with maces, swords, and the lance until evening, displaying his valor.

———

In the meantime, Amir Hamza received tidings that Marzaban had caught Sa'ad by deceit and that Badiuz Zaman had followed him to Rakham in search of him. Amir said to Amar, "Until I have finished my campaign against Ahriman Sher-Gardaan, I will not leave this place. However, I wish you to go with utmost haste to gather news of my sons and companions." Amar Ayyar set out like the wind and arrived in Rakham before long. There he witnessed Badiuz Zaman fighting with Gaolangi and the two of them clashing swords together. The commanders of the camp rushed forward to embrace Amar.

When he saw Amar's face, Gaolangi stopped the combat and tried to address Amar. But Amar jocularly said to him, "By the grace of God, you are too short, which is the reason I cannot hear you well. If I could sit beside your ear, I would be able to entertain you with my words." Amar leapt up and sat atop Gaolangi's arm and said, "I have long received news of your valor and have always been desirous of setting eyes on you and meeting you. But I am astonished that you deem it proper to fight Amir's sons during his absence and martyr his champions." Gaolangi replied, "I am blameless in this matter. I did not wish to commit an unjust act against Hamza, and I offered instead all manner of excuses and ruses to the prince and expressed my humility. Amir's whole camp is witness to my statement. Now that you are here, you must forbid the prince to fight so that I can show my face before Hamza and not have cause to feel ashamed."

Amar persuaded Badiuz Zaman to leave the arena, and then himself went with Gaolangi to his fortress. Amar sought leave to depart several times, but Gaolangi would not let him go. He kept Amar as his guest for the night and said to him, "I wish to see your *ayyari*, for people have praised your talents to me in glowing terms and told me of your wondrous qualities." Gaolangi sent for food and ate in the company of Amar and Sa'ad. After sharing the meat and drink, Gaolangi said to Amar, "You have many great qualities, but one blemish stains your character: You shave your beard and do not feel ashamed of this disgraceful act before men." Amar replied, "You would do well to pay me seven hundred dirhams as the tribute for your own beard, and tender the amount without delay, or else your beard will not remain on your good face for long and everyone will call you shameless like myself!" Gaolangi said, "I will consider you a man only if you are able to shave my beard. It would not make me angry if you could answer my challenge." Amar replied, "It is no difficult task to shave your whiskers. Very well, I shall do so this very night! You have now ample warning."

Gaolangi gave leave to the nobles to retire and sat alone on the throne drinking wine, so that he might pass the night in a state of wakefulness and not be tricked by Amar, who would try to carry out his threat and mark him with disgrace.

As for Amar, he saw Gaolangi sitting by himself drinking wine, and approached him in disguise and engaged him in conversation. While they were thus busy, Amar put a few *mithcals* of a drug in the king's wine flagon with great cunning. Gaolangi had consumed a few cups of the drugged wine when he suddenly fell unconscious from the throne. Amar quickly shaved one side of his face. Then he restored Gaolangi to consciousness, made him a respectful bow from afar, and asked him to look into the mirror. When Gaolangi did so, he saw half his face shaved and was deeply mortified. He praised Amar and said, "Indeed you are the Prince of the *Ayyars* of the World. Verily you are an *ayyar* without equal. I find your talent far exceeding your reputation and your trickery matchless. But now you must find some way to restore my beard to my face as before and ensure that none will hear a word of it, or else I will suffer great humiliation before my nobles and will be endlessly disgraced." Amar shaved off the remainder of Gaolangi's beard and took out a false beard from his *zambil*—in the exact shape of the king's real beard—and put it on Gaolangi's face and said, "This beard will stay on until you wash your face with warm water, and none will ever know it is false."

When Gaolangi looked in the mirror, he saw that his beard was just as before. In the morning Gaolangi put seven hundred *tomans* inside a robe of honor and conferred them on Amar during his court, and then gave him leave to depart. Amar went to Badiuz Zaman and instructed him not to fight Gaolangi until Amir's return, and to never let the thought even enter his head. Then Amar headed back to Amir Hamza.

After several days' journey Amar reached Amir's camp and gave him a detailed account of the entire situation. Amir was grieved to hear of the fate of Sar-Barahna Tapishi and Dewana Tapishi and lamented their deaths. The next morning Ahriman Sher-Gardaan struck the drums of war and went into the arena, making tall claims about his power and might. Amir formed his troops in battle arrays and confronted him. Ahriman landed a mace blow on Amir, but he withstood it and said, "Deal me two more strikes!" Ahriman was incensed and threw a powerful blow whose impact made Ashqar neigh in protest. After he had landed his third blow, Amir killed Ahriman's steed with the very first blow he dealt, releasing the horse into the pasture of doom. Then Amir dismounted Ashqar and faced his foe. They fought for a while with maces, and the earth shook at the impact of their weapons. Thereafter they fought with swords, then lances. They tried to snare each other with ropes, yet each man failed to catch his adversary. In the evening both armies returned to their camps. The following day Amir and Ahriman again fought until nightfall. Neither could defeat the other that day or the next. On the fourth day Amir made his war cry and lifted Ahriman above his head. He spun him around over his head and slammed him on the ground. Then he called to Amar, "Tie him up!" While Amar took Ahriman from the battlefield, Amir drew his sword and attacked the enemy ranks. Those who sought quarter found reprieve and a new lease on life, and the rest were cut down by his relentless sword.

Amir's companions said to Amar, "Amir would never kill Ahriman. You should kill him to avenge Rustam's blood." Amar immediately poured molten lead into Ahriman's ears, and dealt with him thus. That blackguard was dispatched to Hell, and all felt relief at his death. When

Amir returned and said to Amar, "Send for Ahriman and produce him before me," Amar answered, "He was made to pay for Rustam's blood with his life." Upon hearing those words, Amir fell silent.

The next day Amir Hamza said, "Dig a tunnel and blow up all the cannibals hiding in the fortress. Dispatch them all to Hell." A tunnel was dug and filled with gunpowder,[47] and Amar blew up the fort, carrying out Amir's command. All the cannibals were sent to burn in the Erebus of Hell, and everyone in Amir's camp was relieved of his fears and apprehensions. After securing victory in the campaign against Ahriman Sher-Gardaan, Amir marched out with his camp and arrived at Rakham within a few days.

Upon hearing of Amir Hamza's arrival, Gaolangi dressed Sa'ad in a robe of honor and sent him to Amir bearing gifts, and he also sent riches and provisions for Amir's companions, which afforded them great happiness and pleasure. Amir embraced Sa'ad and was greatly pleased to hear of the many kindnesses and favors Gaolangi had shown him.

In the morning Gaolangi struck the drums of war and entered the arena, where he arranged his troops. Amir decorated himself with his arms and went into the arena as well. Observing Amir's height and size, Gaolangi took him for a common warrior and said, "O warrior, I wish to fight Hamza, not you. To fight common warriors is not my wont. Go back and send me Hamza so that he can combat with me." Amir answered, "I am Hamza bin Abdul Muttalib." Gaolangi said, "O Amir, I thought that you would be as tall and mighty as myself. How have you vanquished thousands of powerful champions and made them submit to you? How did you lay low the tall and mighty *devs* of Qaf and bring them under your power?" Amir answered, "I may be weak of body but my Lord is all-powerful and before Him the Earth and the heavens are of no consequence. Come forward and strike your blow now, and give me proof of your manliness." Gaolangi said, "You should strike the first blow, as I wish to test your strength." Amir replied, "We, the followers of the True Faith, do not take precedence in the arena. It is against our way to attack first." Gaolangi delivered three blows to Amir in succession, which caused sweat to break out of every pore of Amir's body, but he held his ground manfully and did not vacillate in the least. Gaolangi marveled greatly at Amir's might, given how small of stature he was in comparison.

Amir landed his eleven-hundred-*maund* mace on Gaolangi, the impact of which killed Gaolangi's bull and rattled the king's nerves. Gaolangi tried to hamstring Ashqar, but Amir quickly dismounted and faced his adversary. Gaolangi struck him two blows of his sword, which cut through four inches of Amir's shield but also broke Gaolangi's weapon, as his sword broke at the hilt. Gaolangi threw away the hilt and secured hold of Amir's cummerbund. Amir took hold of Gaolangi's belt and the two tested their strength in this way until evening. Then Gaolangi said, "O Amir, the night is made for resting. Relax yourself and give me leave to go. What shall come to pass in the morning will come to pass." Amir replied, "I shall not turn back without a winner being decided in this fight." Food was sent for the warriors from their respective kitchens, and they sat down to eat together. After they had had a few goblets of wine, torches were lit and they continued testing their strength.

The narrator states that Amir and Gaolangi fought for twenty-one nights and days and remained at a stalemate. There was no strategem of war that they did not employ in their battle. Finally, on the twenty-second day, Amir Hamza said to Gaolangi, "We have exhausted all the maneuvers of our martial abilities. Now you should try to lift me from the ground, and I will try the same. The one who is lifted up must pay allegiance and submit to the other." Gaolangi happily consented, laughed, and replied, "O Amir, you made a grave mistake by setting this condition and you have duped yourself in making this wager. I easily pull out great and tall trees from their roots and lift them up like twigs. You certainly do not weigh more than those trees!" Amir replied, "Then there is no harm done. We shall presently test your claim and see who is humiliated."

Gaolangi exerted all his might and blood flowed from his fingers, nose, and ears. He grew near to fainting but was still unable to lift Amir up from the ground. Instead Amir sank up to his waist into the earth. Gaolangi said in a weakened voice, "O Amir, I have now completely exhausted all my strength." Amir replied, "Be on your guard now, for I am about to make my war cry." The king answered, "Cry all you wish! Make the surface of the earth tear open with your cries! I am not some little boy who will be frightened by it or feel any dread." Amir then let out his cry of "God is great!" which shook the ground for a distance of sixteen *kos*. Amir lifted Gaolangi up, and after spinning him around above his head, put him lightly on the ground, giving the lie to Gaolangi's tall claims.

Then Amir said to Amar, "Tie him up quickly, for he might find a chance to escape." Gaolangi said, "O Amir, why do you wish to secure me with ropes when I am tied up now by devotion to you?" Amir said, "If that is the case, then convert to the True Faith." Gaolangi sincerely recited the Act of Faith that very moment. Amir embraced him and told everyone the auspicious news of his conversion to the True Faith. Then Amir took him to his pavilion and introduced him to all the commanders and invited him to join him for a meal. Gaolangi took Amir, along with his sons and friends, to his own city, where they remained busy in celebrations for forty days.

Of Amir's Departure for Bakhtar, and of His Killing King Kakh Bakhtar

The narrator records that after the festivities were over, Amir asked Gaolangi, "Which other city lies beyond your own?" He answered, "It is the city of Bakhtar, which is ruled by King Kakh Bakhtar. It is a beautiful city, but Kakh Bakhtar is a cannibal who is one hundred and sixty yards tall and a wrestler without compare. He is peerless, too, in courage and might. Whenever he advances on my city, fear of him drives me to take refuge in the mountains with my sons. I thus save myself from his tyranny, for he is stronger than I am and as powerful as a rutting elephant. Besides, he is a magician himself and has sorcerers among his companions who are all past masters in their trade." Amir answered, "I am the mortal foe of sorcerers, cannibals, and infidels, and was born to crush their vanity into dust. Until I have annihilated them, I will find no rest; and my heart will have no peace until I have murdered them. According to Buzurjmehr, my title is the Disseminator of the Faith." Then Amir said to Gaolangi, "Farewell now, for I must take my leave." Gaolangi said, "O Amir, I will not separate myself from you now as long as I live. Why do you wish to leave me behind and inflict this pain on me?" Amir answered, "If it is your wish, then accompany me in God's name and erase the fear of separation from your heart." Gaolangi appointed his elder son, Rel Gaolangi, as his heir and, leaving all matters of the state in his hands, accompanied Amir Hamza in his travels.

After some time, they arrived within Bakhtar's borders, and after dismounting at a distance of four *kos* from the seat of the kingdom, Amir wrote a missive to Kakh Bakhtar that read: "O Kakh Bakhtar, present yourself before me and convert to the True Faith and pay allegiance to me. Otherwise, I will kill you with impunity and visit such a terrible fate upon you that the birds of the air and the beasts of the ground will lament your fortune."

When Amar Ayyar arrived at Kakh Bakhtar's court with the letter and the king was informed that a believer in God named Hamza had sent him a message, he ordered that the letter be brought and shown to him. Amar said to the king's attendants, "Tell him to show some sense. The communication that I have brought is not from some common person to be sent into his presence without the emissary." Kakh Bakhtar responded to this message, "Very well. Ask him to present himself and order him to enter."

Amar stepped inside and, as he handed the missive to Kakh Bakhtar, he marveled at God's handiwork in creating this giant of such great height and size. After reading just a few lines, Kakh Bakhtar's face turned crimson with rage and he ordered that the messenger be arrested. Amar put on his cap of invisibility and disappeared from the sight of those present. Before leaving the court, Amar removed the crown from Kakh Bakhtar's head by knocking it off his head. He put the diadem in his *zambil*, having secured it with great cunning. Amar then announced in a loud voice, "My hands are tied, as my master has not allowed it; otherwise, I would have punished you as you deserve, and avenged myself on you!"

Everyone present said with one voice, "We never saw anyone like that messenger. Was he an angel or a human being?" Kakh Bakhtar declared, "I shall exact retribution for that messenger's actions on his master in the arena, and shall kill Hamza at once." Amar returned to his camp and briefed Amir on what had passed at Kakh Bakhtar's court.

Amir passed the night drinking wine. When it was morning and Kakh Bakhtar took his place in the arena after striking the drums of war and leading his army into battle, Amir armed himself and went into the battlefield as well. Kakh Bakhtar said to Amir, "O weakling, I did not challenge you. Why did you come out to face me? It is Hamza whom I seek. Why do you wish to give your life for another?" Amir answered, "Hamza is my name." The king said, "How did you conquer the world with that weak body? Is it because you are a sorcerer?" Amir answered, "I hold magic and sorcerers to be accursed. My God is all-powerful and mighty, who returns me triumphant and victorious from battle and destroys and eradicates my enemy. Now deal me the blow you have!" Kakh Bakhtar swung his mace and struck Amir, who moved aside. The mace landed on the ground instead, causing a huge tract of land to sink upon impact and water to burst forth from the ground. All who witnessed the sight were terrorized. Kakh Bakhtar landed a second blow, and Amir foiled that also.

When he struck his mace a third time, Amir received it on his shield and sank to his knees in the ground from its force. Kakh Bakhtar exclaimed, "There, I have killed him and laid him low, and brought down a mighty champion!" Amir emerged from the dust and retorted, "You coward, who do you claim to have laid low and vanquished? I still stand against you as your adversary." With these words, Amir laid the king low with a thrust of his sword and transported him to Hell with just one strike. Kakh Bakhtar rolled on the ground like a slaughtered beast and died. His army fell upon Amir, who plied his sword with both hands against them. When only a few of them remained standing, they ran off and took refuge in the castle. Following Amir's orders, Amar blew up the castle by digging a tunnel underneath it and filling it up with gunpowder. The explosion turned them all to cinder in just an instant. All the cannibals became the fodder of the fires of doom and departed for the land of no return.

Thereafter, Amir headed for the city ruled by a giant named Ara'sh and arrived there in triumph from his campaign against Kakh Bakhtar. Ara'sh emerged from his fort upon hearing of Amir's arrival. Amir saw that he was a massively built giant who was one hundred and eighty yards tall. He hurled his mace at Amir, but Amir jumped aside and the blow landed on the ground, creating a crater with its impact. As Ara'sh reached to pick up his mace and strike him again a second time, Amir struck him with his sword while reciting "In the name of Allah!" Amir had cut Ara'sh in two, and the giant forthwith gave up his life. Upon witnessing that incident, Ara'sh's army took refuge in the fort and was rendered helpless and powerless. Amar blew up that fort as well with gunpowder after digging a tunnel underneath. Ara'sh's lands and dominions were all destroyed, and the cannibals were all killed and found quarters in Hell.

OF AMIR'S DEPARTURE FOR NESTAN, AND OF HIS KILLING KING SANG ANDAZ KHUNKHVAR NESTAN

The transcriber has recorded that after routing Ara'sh, Amir asked Gao-langi, "What other city lies ahead?" He answered, "It is called the city of Nestan and it is a magnificent metropolis. The name of its ruler is Sang Andaz Khunkhvar Nestan. He is the master of a brave and intrepid army and commands a vast force. He is one hundred and ninety yards tall and his eyes glow like burning ovens. The passage that leads to his city is so narrow that two men cannot pass through it walking shoulder to shoulder. Even the beasts of the air cannot gain entrance there[?]. The path is engulfed in flames that surround it on both sides and emit such profuse heat that they make even mountains melt away like wax."

Amir paid no heed to his remarks and headed for Nestan. When he arrived there, his army was unable to bear the violence of the temperature and its incendiary power, and his men began dying from excessive heat. Amir took out the rope given him by the holy Khizr and threw it across the fiery passage[?]. He asked his companions to advance holding its end and not let the least doubt enter their hearts. The narrator reports that nearly every man in Amir's army was burnt alive. Only one champion riding a camel and three hundred soldiers were able to ford that river of fire by holding the rope's end. The rest headed instead to the Land of Eternal Peace.

After much toil and trouble, when Amir arrived at the city, Sang Andaz Khunkhvar Nestan came out of the city with his army and brought his entire force to do battle. Amir saw that each of his soldiers had a bag full of stones tied to his neck. When they saw Amir, they started hurling them at him. Many of the three hundred men who had accompanied Amir this far were now stoned to death. Amir felt helpless finding himself in that unenviable plight. He drew his sword and assaulted the enemy ranks like a lion attacks a herd of goats. Amir plied his sword with both hands and started beheading his foes. Such a large number of Khunkhvar's warriors were killed that a veritable river of blood issued from the battlefield.

Everyone sang Amir's praises seeing the turn of events. In the end, Sang Andaz Khunkhvar Nestan came forward and dealt Amir a blow of his sword, which Amir parried. When the king reached for his mace, Amir leapt forward and dealt him a powerful blow of his sword, which severed both his legs at the thigh. The king's stumps of legs fell to the ground. Then Amir dealt him a second blow of his sword and dispatched him to Hell to enroll himself among its permanent denizens. The king's men who had shut themselves into the fortress were burned to cinders when it was torched.

Amir now announced, "I once heard from Buzurjmehr that I would leave Zulmat[48] with only seventy companions and would vanquish all my enemies. Now there are seventy-one men with me. It remains to be seen who is the one to die next and whose name will be erased from the register of the living." At this, Amir was stricken with grief.

Then Amir Hamza said to Gaolangi, "O friend, of the hundred thousand men who marched under me, a mere seventy-one remain. The rest died, causing me untold grief. Tell me which city comes next as we advance from here." Gaolangi replied, "A few days' journey from here lies the land of Ardabil, which is ruled by two brothers, Ardabil Peel-Dandan and Marzaban Peel-Dandan. Farther ahead lie the *tilisms* of Zardhasht Jadu, where you will find everything a marvel to behold."

Amir headed for Ardabil and arrived at his destination within a few days. Ardabil Peel-Dandan and Marzaban Peel-Dandan learned that the warrior named Hamza had entered their dominion and the Slayer of Infidels had crossed into their land from another. Both brothers led out their armies to do battle with him, arranged their troops, and began reciting martial songs. Amir armed himself and went into combat with them. Ardabil Peel-Dandan attacked Amir without loss of time and tried to mangle him with his teeth. Amir drew his sword and struck a blow that sent Ardabil's head flying away from his neck like a harvested ear of corn.

Seeing his brother dead, Marzaban Peel-Dandan rushed at Amir, who cooled his ardor with a single fatal blow and sent him to feed the fires of Hell. After putting their army to the sword, Amir headed onward and arrived at the *tilism* created by the sorcerer Zardhasht. There Amir saw an enclosure without an entrance. It contained a dome from which emanated music and the sound of singing, which carried far into the distance. Amir said to Gaolangi, "It seems that there are people within who sing and play this music that is so enticing and pleasant." Gaolangi answered, "There is no question of a human presence here. These *tilisms* are known to ring with such sounds, and such are the tricks that these enchantments play on the fancy." Amir said to him, "You are the tallest among us. Pray see what is going on inside and discover what is taking place." As Gaolangi looked over the wall of the enclosure, he cried out and jumped over to the other side as if he were unable to hold himself back. Amir then said to Landhoor, "Go and see what it is that caused Gaolangi to jump over to the other side." When Landhoor went and looked, he burst into uncontrollable laughter and jumped over as well. In short, anyone who looked in to investigate the matter was likewise caught in its trap, and none returned to make a report. In the end, only Amir and Amar were left standing there. Amar said, "If you were to order me, I would cover my face with a cloth and look inside to see what it is that makes everyone jump in without self-control." Amir replied, "Very well, but do so very carefully, lest you also end up the same as the rest of your companions and are caught in the same calamity." Amar said, "Never! I reason there is some beautiful woman inside the enclosure whose sight made our friends forgetful of themselves from love. I do not have amorous inclinations to become lovesick and forget myself in desire." Amar climbed the wall and, like his companions before him, burst into laughter and jumped over.

Amir Hamza was left alone and he began shedding tears and praying for his friends. He was near to giving up his life in grief for them when he was overtaken by sleep. In his dream he saw a throne descend from the heavens on which a holy man was seated. Amir greeted him and began crying, whereupon that holy man said, "Do not cry, my son. Kill the white bird sitting on the dome with an arrow and you will conquer the *tilism* and be released from this trouble." After the holy man had uttered these words, his throne rose into the heavens and disappeared from Amir's sight.

Amir woke up and saw that indeed a white bird was perched on the dome. When Amir shot an arrow at the bird, she fell to the ground. The same instant she fell, the *tilism* was broken. Amir's companions who had been caught in the enchantment returned to their senses and came out from under its spell. They fell down at Amir's feet, and he embraced

them and showered them with affection. Then Amir expressed his gratitude to the Almighty Lord—the God who dispenses both honor and disgrace. When Amir asked his companions their reason for jumping inside
the enclosure, all of them replied that they had beheld a holy and luminous face whose sight made them oblivious to everything, and the pleasure they derived from it made them jump inside. Amir said to them,
"Open the door of the dome so that we may see what is inside and discover its secret." Although everyone tried, the door of the dome did not
yield and none could force it open.

Finally, Amir broke down the door and went inside and saw a casket
hanging from the ceiling. When Amir brought it down, he saw the corpse
of Zardhasht the sorcerer laid carefully within, and it seemed that he had
just fallen asleep. Amir said, "There must be something else in the casket
with him as well. We must search it carefully and do so unhurriedly."
When Amar Ayyar searched it, he found a book on magic. Amir burnt the
sorcerer with the book, but Amar had first managed to remove several
pages from it. Those pages helped spread the magic in the world that has
continued to this day, and all those who practice it have their knowledge
from those pages.

In short, after Amir had torched Zardhasht's corpse along with the
book and was assured of their destruction, he reached the end of the
tilism and said to his friends, "This place is full of peril and we may lose
our lives here. We must not all sleep at once but take turns keeping
watch." Amir appointed Aadi to do the first shift of the watch, Malik
Ashtar to do the second, Landhoor the third, and himself the fourth and
final watch, and then he appointed the sleeping and waking hours for
everyone.

When Aadi sat down to do vigil duty, he saw a deer. Aadi hunted him
and started cleaning and cooking the meat. When the meat was ready, an
old crone appeared like an unforeseen calamity and began grinding her
teeth while looking at Aadi. He said to her, "O old woman, tell me who
you are, why you have arrived here and taken on the hardships of your
journey, and why you grind your teeth when you look at me. You must
truly tell me everything, or else I will punish you severely and murder
you instantly." The crone answered with great humility, "My son, I am
the wife of a merchant who was killed by a lion in the forest. Now I wander around without help or succor in great distress. Today is the fourth
day since I last had a morsel to eat. If you will give me some meat, I will
pray for your well-being and will be indebted to you forever." Aadi felt

pity for her and he reached out to serve her some meat from the pot. The old crone jumped up and slapped Aadi so hard that he fell unconscious to the ground. When he woke up after an hour and recovered from the shock, he found the pot empty. His watch having passed then, Aadi woke up Malik Ashtar and himself prepared to sleep.

Finding the pot empty, Malik Ashtar said, "O big-bellied fellow, you cooked the meat and ate it all by yourself. You did not invite us to share in it and left not even a little for us." Aadi answered, "I was hungry, therefore I ate it all. If you are hungry, you may as well hunt and eat something and not suffer the pangs of hunger." After some time, Malik Ashtar also saw a deer and hunted and cooked him. When the meat was ready, the same crone appeared before him and sought some meat after reciting to Malik Ashtar her tale of woe. He, too, took pity on her and tried to ladle some from the pot when that crone jumped forward and slapped him hard. While he lay unconscious on the ground, she ate up the meat and disappeared, having swallowed all the food that lay in the pot.

When Malik Ashtar came to his senses, it was Landhoor's turn to do vigil duty. Seeing the empty pot lying on the fire, he said, "Why, Malik Ashtar, you cooked and ate the meat but did not offer us even a small slice!" Malik Ashtar answered, "My friend, the meat was too little to satisfy my own hunger, let alone invite you to share it with me. The place abounds in animals and you may hunt and cook one for yourself. The deer here are particularly tasty and I hope you will enjoy your food."

Landhoor also hunted a deer and cooked the meat and the same crone slapped him unconscious and ate up all the meat and then disappeared after consuming everything in the pot. When Landhoor woke up and was restored to his senses, Aadi and Malik Ashtar said to him, "We, too, were treated in the same manner." Landhoor said to them, "If you had told me, I would have taken caution and not been deceived!" Aadi and Malik Ashtar said, "What is past is past. Now hold your tongue and do not say a word of it to anyone. Let us wake up Amir and see how he fares with the crone." Landhoor said, "I cannot bear to see Amir deceived or suffer any hardship." Aadi said, "Amir will never be fooled or deceived by her." After their conversation, they woke Amir up to do his round of watch duty.

Amir also hunted and began cooking. The crone had now become well accustomed to stealing the cooked meat. When it was ready, she appeared before Amir to sing her usual song and narrate her old story. Amir got a whiff of rotten meat from her mouth and said to himself, *This is a* tilism. *There is no knowing what new calamity awaits me in the guise of this crone. Indeed she must be a witch, and it would be justifiable to take caution.* Amir held his sword in one hand and began serving the meat with the other. When the crone tried to slap Amir, he dealt her a blow of his sword and severed her head. Immediately upon hitting the ground, the head rolled away. Amir pursued it and saw that the head had rolled into a well. Amir was standing at the edge of the well when his companions reached his side. Amir said, "Tie a rope to my shield so that I may lower myself into the well." Amar Ayyar said, "Why do you think I will allow you to do this while I am present? I will undertake the mission myself. You may stand at the edge of the well while I descend inside to bring you news of her." Amar Ayyar lowered himself into the well and beheld that the severed head lay on a golden platter before a fourteen-year-old beauty. The girl was crying and saying, "I told you not to go near Hamza, but you did not follow my advice and imperiled your life and put me in trouble as well."

Amar snared the girl with his rope and secured her with alacrity and cunning. He brought her out of the well and produced her before Amir, along with the head of the crone, and told him all that the beauty had said. Amir asked her, "Who are you, and who was that crone?" She replied, "I am Zardhasht's daughter, and the old woman was his mother." Amir asked her, "Are you alone or are there others besides you?" She answered, "I have two sisters who live in the *tilisms* with their armies. Upon hearing of our grandmother's murder, they will descend here and mourn her death and battle with you. They will do everything in their power to make life an unhappy prospect for you."

Amir Hamza gave her into Amar's custody and said to him, "Keep a strict watch on her and incarcerate her somewhere secure." They passed that night in peace, but the following morning sorcerers emerged from the well in waves and arranged themselves in battle formation. The armies were led by Zardhasht's daughters Gul-Rukh and Farrukh. They ordered their nanny, who was a renowned sorceress, to prepare her magic and to create a spell for them.

Amir sent for Zardhasht's daughter and asked her, "How do you think your sisters will fight me and stand their ground against me?" She answered, "Indeed, they do not have the wherewithal to fight with you by main force, but they will employ magic and prevail over you with its power. Then you will witness their machinations." Amir said to Amar, "Interrogate her yourself and ask her gently what that magic is and how it is created." Amar took her to his place and tried to extract the information from her by gentle persuasion and inveigling, but she would not reveal a thing. In the end, Amar tired of her and put her to death by smashing her skull until her brains flowed out of her cranium. Then he presented himself before Amir and said to him, "I tried all manner of persuasion, but she did not divulge a thing and never unveiled her secrets. Thus, I tired of her and killed her[?]." Amir said, "You killed her for no reason. Perhaps you could have extracted the secret and obtained the information from her by subterfuge." Amar answered, "O Amir, she was most cunning. I tried every trick I knew to extract the secret from her, but she always foiled me by one ruse or another. I killed her lest we should come to harm from her as well. As to obtaining information about the enemy, I shall bring it for you from her companions." Amar then headed for the sorcerers' camp without delay.

On the way Amar encountered a magician from the sorcerer's army who tried to capture and harm him. But Amar leapt up and sat atop his shoulders and killed the sorcerer by slitting open his neck. Then Amar dressed himself as the sorcerer and went into their camp to wait for an opportunity to break into their pavilion and fulfill his mission.

That night Amar went with several others to stand guard at the sorceress Farrukh's bed. A wizard arrived there in a state of great agitation and said to Farrukh, "Many days have passed since your nanny set out to prepare some magic against Hamza's camp. To date, we have seen no results. Nor do we know what became of her or if some peril overtook her." Farrukh answered, "The magic will be ready by evening the day after tomorrow. Then you will see what terrible destruction engulfs Hamza's camp. Not a soul will survive and none will find reprieve."

In the morning Amar returned with this information to Amir, who responded, "I wish we could find some way to turn the magic back on their own camp and use its destructive powers on their own forces." Amar replied, "That harridan is preparing her magic behind your encampment. It will be ready by tomorrow evening. I will go then to capture her and turn her magic against her own camp."

That day came to its culmination and the next day, late in the afternoon, Amar disguised himself as a wizard. Carrying a flagon of drugged wine, he went to the nanny and said, "Farrukh has sent me with the message that three days have passed since you started preparing your magic, and yet Hamza's camp shows no sign of its effects and are not the worse for it. She has also sent this flagon of wine for you." She answered, "The magic egg is now ready. It will show its marvels when the sun sets. Then everyone will see what terrors are let loose on Hamza's camp and how everyone is engulfed in calamity, and witness their end." She then put her mouth to the spout of the flagon and drank it all in big gulps, swallowing the wine in large swigs. As soon as the wine passed down her throat, she fell unconscious. Amar buried her alive in a hole and dispatched her to Hell. He took the magic egg and the bottle to Amir and said, "She has filled this egg and bottle with her magic, and now I am taking them to throw at Farrukh and Gul-Rukh's army and use it against their own camp." Amir said, "Make haste and do not tarry in carrying out your plan."

Amar went into the sorcerers' camp and destroyed all their pavilions and supplies by releasing the contents of the magic egg, burning everything to cinders in just the flash of an eye. Then Amar poured out the contents of the bottle. This caused such a heavy rainfall that the entire camp of Gul-Rukh and Farrukh sank underwater, all the goods and provisions left in their camp were destroyed, and not a single one of them survived.

Amir occupied himself with hunting in the environs for a few days. One day he said to Gaolangi, "Let me know if some other menace remains and give me news of any new scourge." He answered, "All the evil that had manifested itself from Bakhtar to Zulmat has been put down. Now you should head for Rakham and accompany me there so that you can rest a while." They set out for Rakham and arrived in that grand metropolis, where Gaolangi prepared festivities in Amir's honor on a most lavish scale and ordered his attendants and workers to provide all the apparatus for revelry.

When the festivities were over, they headed out of the city for hunting. Suddenly, Badiuz Zaman sighted a deer. He tried to make it his prey, but the deer galloped away with Badiuz Zaman in hot pursuit on horseback, and at last he took out his gun[49] to kill the animal. After running for some distance, the deer jumped into a pond. Badiuz Zaman followed him into the pond on horseback and Amir and his companions also rode into the water after them. The next moment, when they blinked their eyes they found themselves in a vast field surrounded by a strange forest. They searched for Badiuz Zaman in every direction but found no trace of him. Amir Hamza's eyes filled up with tears and he said to his companions with a voice full of sorrow and grief, "Finally, we are seventy. The seventy-first person was Badiuz Zaman, whom I was destined to lose. Alas, a new hole has been bored into my heart and grief now rends my breast." Amir's companions offered him words of consolation and said,

"O Amir, no man can fight fate. One cannot make an endeavor against the decree of God except to embrace silence. Fortitude and patience are the only cures for this wound." Amir uttered not a word then except to express his compliance and cheerful submission to God's will. He saw no recourse but to remain silent, and felt there was nothing he could do but suffer privately.

Of Amir's Departure for Mecca, and of His Attaining Martyrdom in the Victorious Service of Prophet Muhammad; and the Culmination of the *Dastan*

The master narrators thus tell this wondrous tale that after Amir had found a measure of fortitude and his restive heart had attained a modicum of peace, Gaolangi said to him, "You had mentioned that you would take me to kiss the feet of the Last Prophet of the Times and allow me an opportunity to regard his holy aspect. Thus we should head for Mecca!"

Amir, Gaolangi, and the rest of their companions now headed toward Mecca. As they passed Qaza-va-Qadar, Saryal greeted them and took Amir to his dwelling and satisfied all the duties of a host. After many days, Saryal's father departed from this world. Amir performed his last rites and, offering words of consolation to Saryal, seated him on the throne. Then they continued toward Mecca. After traveling for a few days, they arrived in its precincts. Gaolangi along with all the companions of Amir Hamza kissed the feet of the Holy Prophet and renewed their Faith and earned great glory in the world.

———

One day the Holy Prophet was present in the mosque when a desert Arab arrived with the news that infidels from Egypt, Greece, and Syria had banded together to advance on them with evil intent, and were bringing a vast army. The Holy Prophet first sent Amir Hamza with some men to Abu Qubais, then he headed there himself. When the infidels arrayed themselves, Amir gave Gaolangi leave to fight them. His challenge was answered by a massively built warrior from the infidel camp who made many great claims to his power and might upon entering the arena. Gaolangi lifted him above his head and spun him around for so long that he very nearly died from it; he was soon rendered completely powerless and helpless.

Gaolangi then slammed him to the ground, and the little life remaining to the infidel was flushed out of him. A second infidel warrior faced Gaolangi and fared the same. A few more infidels died at Gaolangi's hands, and then their companions were so terrified of him that none among them would come out to answer his challenge. Finally, the prince of India, Pur-Hindi, rode into the arena. He hurled his lance so powerfully at Gaolangi's chest that it exited from his back, causing him to give up his life to his Maker.

Amir suffered terrible grief at Gaolangi's death, and in his dismay he went and faced Pur-Hindi himself. Pur-Hindi said, "You dotard! Why do you volunteer your life? What idle thought stirs your fancy when even warriors in the prime of their youth avoid confronting me? But now that you are here, tell me who you are so that you do not die without anyone knowing your name and station and your corpse is not left exposed in the arena."

Amir answered, "O babbler, my name is Hamza bin Abdul Muttalib!" The prince said, "I had heard that Hamza had gone toward Bakhtar." Amir replied, "What you heard was right. I returned from Bakhtar not too long ago. Now deal me the blow you take pride in." Pur-Hindi aimed his lance at Amir, who caught hold of it at the handle and snatched it from his hands, rendering him defenseless. Amir threw the same lance at the prince's breast, and it shot through his heart and came out the other side of his body. Pur-Hindi fell from his horse and died that instant. Amir let out his war cry and fell upon his army, killing many an infidel and thousands of villains. Recognizing Amir, the infidels turned tail and fled en masse. The Holy Prophet returned triumphant and victorious to Mecca, and expressed his gratitude to God Almighty for his victory.

The narrator records that when Pur-Hindi's mother, a woman called Hinda, heard of his death, she gathered the kings and armies of India, Greece, Syria, China, Ethiopia, Zanzibar, and Turkistan, amassed a mighty army to avenge her son's death, and headed to Ctesiphon. She sought redress from Hurmuz, who then accompanied her with his army. When these armies approached Mecca, and the Holy Prophet received the news, he said, "My uncle Hamza is capable of routing these armies all by himself." As the Holy Prophet had not uttered the words "God willing" with his claim, the Almighty God was not pleased. When the Holy Prophet faced the infidels with Amir Hamza and his companions,

Hurmuz said to his men, "Do not fight these Arabs in single combat but fall upon them as a body and kill them at the same time. Otherwise, you will not defeat them." Hurmuz's entire force assaulted the followers of the True Faith as one, and Landhoor, Sa'ad bin Amar bin Hamza, and Aadi Madi-Karib—all Amir's dear companions—were martyred. Ali bin Abu Talib was showered by the infidels with arrows from all sides. One infidel threw a stone and broke a tooth of the Holy Prophet. Amar brought these tidings to Amir Hamza and communicated this heartrending news to his ears.

Amir put on his armor and mounted his steed and prepared to slaughter the infidels. While cutting through them, Amir Hamza drew near Hurmuz, who jumped from his throne and ran away. His army also stampeded off then, and none showed the wherewithal to put up a determined stand against Amir Hamza. He followed them for a distance of four *kos*, slaying infidel warriors along the way. Everywhere one looked the corpses of the infidels killed by Amir's lustrous sword lay piled in heaps. After killing them by the thousands, Amir returned to Mecca with the garlands of success adorning his neck.

Hinda had laid an ambush along Hamza's route to Mecca and was hiding with her army. She attacked him from behind and dealt a powerful thrust of her sword, which severed all four of Ashqar's legs. As Amir Hamza was taken by surprise, he fell to the ground when his steed collapsed. That accursed woman dealt a blow of her poison-laced sanguinary sword to Amir's immaculate head and decapitated him. She cut open his abdomen and plucked out and chewed up his heart, and then cut up his body into seventy pieces. Afterward, when her terrible folly became apparent to her, she feared the retribution Amir Hamza's daughter Quraisha would visit on her with the help of the *devs* and jinns of Qaf. That fear drove her to take refuge with the Holy Prophet. She shed bitter tears before him and repented her actions and converted to the True Faith.

The Holy Prophet said to her, "Take me to the corpse of my dear uncle so that I can see where that Lion of God lies." Hinda took him to see Amir Hamza's corpse and showed him to the place where he was martyred. The Holy Prophet gathered the pieces of Amir Hamza's body and said the funeral prayer separately for each part. It is said that Prophet Muhammad stood on his toes as he said the prayers. After the burial, people asked him why he had stood on his toes and Prophet Muhammad replied, "I stood in that manner because a great crowd of angels had inundated the prayer grounds and they all said the prayers seventy times for each part of his body." Thus the Holy Prophet informed everyone of Amir Hamza's holiness and lofty status.

When Prophet Muhammad turned back after burying Amir Hamza, Hinda presented herself before him. Prophet Muhammad turned his face away from her and showed her not the least favor. At that moment His Holiness received this divine message: "Dear friend! Hamza has indeed been martyred, but do look up to the heavens!" When His Holiness looked up, he saw Amir Hamza seated on a bejeweled throne in Heaven with *houris* and pages standing around him with folded arms. Then His Holiness smiled and said prayers of gratitude.

After several days, Quraisha arrived into the presence of the Holy Prophet with a huge army and asked for her father's murderer. The Holy Prophet showed Quraisha the lofty status attained by Amir Hamza and said, "O Quraisha, had your father not been martyred, he would not have found such a lofty station in Heaven, and God would not have promoted him to the rank of a holy personage. Thus you must obey my advice and shun all thoughts of revenge."

The narrator has said that that was the occasion when *Sura-e Jinn*[50] was revealed to the Holy Prophet and it comforted Quraisha's heart. Thus she was persuaded by the Holy Prophet to refrain from seeking revenge for her father's death. She did not speak another word about seeking vengeance but took her leave and departed for her land.

———

One tradition holds that it had displeased God that the Holy Prophet had not said the words "God willing" when stating that his uncle Hamza could rout the infidels alone and kill hundreds of thousands of them by himself, and that this was why Amir Hamza's body was cut into seventy pieces and the Holy Prophet lost a tooth in the battle.

Yet another tradition maintains that Prophet Muhammad's wife, Ayesha (peace be upon her soul), was darning and patching her clothes when the Holy Prophet entered her room and the lamp was accidentally extinguished, and the thread came out of her needle. As the Mother of the Faithful sat worrying in darkness, the Holy Prophet smiled and, in the light that emanated from his holy teeth, she was able to thread the needle. The tradition holds that the Almighty God was displeased when the Holy Prophet said, "Regard, O Ayesha, my teeth are so luminous that you were able to thread your needle in their light, and my teeth performed the work of a lamp." This tradition holds that the Holy Prophet's tooth was broken in the battle on account of this claim.

In the same battle, Prophet Muhammad's cousin, Ali bin Abu Talib, was wounded by an arrowhead that had lodged in his foot. The surgeon tried his best to remove the arrowhead but was unsuccessful. When Ali prostrated himself during prayers, the Holy Prophet said, "Draw out the arrowhead from Ali's foot so that he does not feel its pain." Then some champions removed the arrowhead with forceps, but Ali did not feel a thing. After he finished with his prayers, he noticed blood at his feet and asked, "Where has this blood come from, and when did I receive this wound?" His companions gave him a complete account, and then asked, "Your Honor, did you not know?" He answered, "By God, I did not know I was pierced by the arrow!"

. . .

May the beneficent God bless this translator[51] and transcriber as a sacrifice of Prophet Muhammad's (praise be unto him) martyred tooth and the wounded foot of Ali (may God have mercy on his soul); may He release him from dependence on everyone in this world and grant him His munificence by divine will; and may the truth and fiction of this tale be attributed to the inventors of the legend.

THE HISTORY OF THE LEGEND

LIST OF CHARACTERS, HISTORIC FIGURES, DEITIES, AND MYTHICAL BEINGS

SELECTED SOURCES

NOTES

THE HISTORY OF THE LEGEND

Musharraf Ali Farooqi

The *dastan* is an oral narrative genre, and the word itself means "tale" or "legend." The *dastan* of Amir Hamza has a rich folk history.

Storytellers brought the *dastans* to the Arabian peninsula via Persia as early as the seventh century C.E. It is related that a pagan named Nazr bin al-Haris of Mecca preferred Persian *dastans* to the message of Allah and turned men away from Prophet Muhammad's preaching. The Quran denounced him and others of his ilk, who preferred idle tales to life's realities.[1]

The hero of the *Dastan-e Amir Hamza* is based on Prophet Muhammad's uncle, Hamza bin Abdul Muttalib, who was renowned for his bravery. He was martyred in the battle of Uhad in 625 by a hired spearsman. But aside from the ancestral reference, there are no similarities between the Amir Hamza of this legend and the historic Hamza bin Abdul Muttalib.

The *dastan* relied heavily on familiar characters, icons, and legends to create scenes and situations. By using Amir Hamza's legend to describe the hero's bravery, using the names of idols and legendary villains of Islamic history to denote his enemies, using the rivalry between the Arab and Persian cultures to set up the conflict, using holy Khizr, the green-clad guide of legend, to be Amir Hamza's helper, and so forth, the story constantly evokes certain historical, cultural, and religious identifiers that allow it to narrate action without creating new histories and legends.

Like Amir Hamza, these characters, too, have no history beyond what is attributed to them by the story itself. The narrative discarded the real histories of the characters it chose, and sometimes even their legendary histories, and reassembled their legends.[2] To supernatural creatures such as jinns, which are part of the religious belief system, the story added *devs* and *peris*—creatures borrowed from the cultural belief system of folklore.[3]

But the name of Prophet Muhammad's brave uncle seemed to have stuck in people's imagination. Over time, folk legends continued to be grafted onto this legend. The seemingly contradictory claims about the origins of the story attest to this phenomenon.

According to one folk record, the *dastan* of Amir Hamza started as a commemorative account of the bravery and valor of the historic Hamza after his martyrdom, narrated by the women of Mecca. When Prophet Muhammad passed by the house of his uncle, he would stay awhile to hear these accounts of his bravery.[4]

Another source maintains that the legend was composed by the brother of the historic Hamza, Abbas bin Abdul Muttalib, who used to recite the legend of Hamza to Prophet Muhammad whenever the prophet grew nostalgic about the memory of his martyred uncle. According to the same source, two men compiled it into a book when Prophet Muhammad's followers were reviled in the time of the Umayyad dynasty (660–750). They composed this tale with help from historic and travelers' accounts as a rejoinder to the calumniators of Prophet Muhammad's companions and progeny. They recited it in the bazaars and in gatherings at coffee-sellers.[5]

Another legend has it that one of the caliphs of the Abbasid dynasty (750–1258) came down with delirium and remained incurable. Seven wise men—who were as wise as Aristotle himself—authored this *dastan*, and some of them were then deputed to read this story in the presence of the sick man night and day, until he was fully cured.[6]

Yet another tradition tells us that this story grew from the exploits of an early-ninth-century Persian adventurer named Hamza bin Abdullah, who belonged to the Kharjiite sect, which had rebelled against the Abbasid caliph Haroonur Rasheed—of *Arabian Nights* fame. Hamza bin Abdullah's legend, called the *Maghazi-e Hamza*, was supposed to be the origin of this story.[7]

The author of one of the Urdu versions of this *dastan*, Khalil Ali Khan Ashk, asserts that the tale was composed by "narrators of sweet speech" in the time of the Ghaznavid ruler Mahmud of Ghazna (971–1030).[8] Ghalib Lakhnavi, the original author of the present text, attests to Ashk's account, adding that the legend was composed because it described "all manner of humanity, and was an inspiration for plans of battle, capturing castles, and conquering countries."[9]

Other Indian narrators of Amir Hamza's legend give a different account. According to Ahmed Husain Qamar, one of the five authors of a longer version of *Dastan-e Amir Hamza*, this legend was first written by the Indian poet Amir Khusrau (1253–1325) in seven long manuscript volumes, and also by Emperor Akbar's poet laureate, Faizi (1547–1595).[10] Qamar also mentions that the Qajar king Nasiruddin Shah of Persia (1831–1896) sent for the seven books of Amir Hamza's legend from India and had them compiled at his court and published in two volumes in Persian.[11]

These are just a few of the more prominent names given as the sources of Amir Hamza's legend. What these seemingly contradictory accounts reveal is the legend's popularity over a long period of time, and the many sources from which it flowed down to the storytellers and their audiences.

If these accounts are accurate, the legend of Amir Hamza could have arrived on the Indian subcontinent around the tenth or eleventh century with Mahmud of Ghazna. However, the earliest known illustrated Indian manuscript of the legend dates from the late fifteenth century.[12]

It was the Quran itself that provided the first clue to the nature of the *dastan*, calling it "idle tales" aimed at escaping reality. Nearly a millennium later, the Mughal emperor Babur (1483–1530) condemned the *Hamzanama*, an early Persian version of the story. Discussing his chief justices, Babur wrote: "One was Mir Sar-e Barahna; he was from a village in Andijan and appears to have made claim to be a *sayyid*. He was a very agreeable companion, pleasant of temper and speech. His were the judgment and rulings that carried weight among men of letters and poets of Khurasan. He wasted his time by composing, in imitation of the story of Amir Hamza, a work that is one long, far-fetched lie, opposed to sense and nature."[13]

The phrase "one long, far-fetched lie, opposed to sense and nature" describes the development in this ideal. The "idle tale" has become even idler; it distorts reality, has a dynamic that does not follow the rules of cause and effect, and displays supernatural elements.

The Mughal emperor Akbar, disregarding his grandfather Babur's bias against the story, commissioned the celebrated illustration project of the *Hamzanama* around 1562–77. These miniatures reveal how contemporary reality was being woven into legends. We see anachronistic elements like firearms in these miniatures, as in this book. Other examples are seen in the details of clothes, jewelry, makeup, and cuisine in the story.

Amir Hamza's legend continued to spread in India. In the Indo-Muslim culture, the *dastan* literature played a vital role in the development of Urdu into a literary language. Four versions of *Dastan-e Amir Hamza* are known in Urdu. The longest version, printed between 1883 and 1917, combined many different traditions contributed by Urdu *dastan* narrators and comprised forty-six volumes and approximately forty-four thousand pages. It is considered the crown jewel of Urdu literature.

The true heroes of the *Dastan-e Amir Hamza* were the countless unknown and unsung *dastan-gos* (*dastan* narrators) whose imaginations made this legend grow and expand and leave a powerful imprint on world literature. Beside Urdu, it is known to exist in Arabic, Persian, Turkish, Sindhi, Malay, Javanese, Georgian, Balinese, Sudanese, Pashto, Bengali, and Hindi versions.

In nineteenth-century India, the popularity of *Dastan-e Amir Hamza* was widespread. *Dastan-gos* were employed at the regional courts and *dastan* narration was a greatly sought-after entertainment in public gatherings. Many *dastans* were also written and published during this period.

The tradition of *dastan* narration came to an end with the death of the last famous *dastan* narrator, Mir Baqir Ali, in 1928. The writing and publication of the *dastans* slowly ceased.

Over the next few decades, the vibrant Indo-Muslim civilization that had cultivated these legends underwent the catastrophic events of partition, and the communalization of the Indo-Muslim cultural heritage, which had begun as a project of the British colonial regime, was perpetuated for political gain by the new leadership of both India and Pakistan. Neither side was willing to commit to preserving the Indo-Muslim heritage. In this atmosphere, scholars, writers, and critics on both sides disregarded the *dastan* genre, and slowly the *dastan* literature was obliterated from the literary and cultural consciousness of the people of the subcontinent.

Recently, there has been reason for hope. The publication of the voluminous *dastan* study *Sahiri, Shahi, Sahibqirani* by Urdu's greatest living scholar, novelist, and critic, Shamsur Rahman Faruqi, was a landmark event in *dastan* scholarship. It bridged the huge gap in our knowledge of this genre and the many intricacies of this particular *dastan*. There is also a newfound interest in *dastan* narration. Mahmood Farooqi and Danish Husain in India are reviving *dastan* narration in a new format. Their performances have been great successes in both India and Pakistan, where new editions of the *dastan* are also being published. It suddenly seems possible that the *Dastan-e Amir Hamza* will soon reclaim its rightful place in the canon of Urdu literature.

NOTES

1. *The Holy Quran: English Translation of the Meanings and Commentary* (Medina: King Fahd Holy Quran Printing Complex, A.H. 1410), 31:6.

2. An example of this is the legend of the green-clad Khizr, who is traditionally considered a guide for the lost traveler. In the story, he was declared a prophet, shown to be the brother of Ilyas (Elias), and even had a mother, Asifa Ba-Safa. Moreover, he is shown killing the *devs* of Qaf to help Amir Hamza.

3. It should be pointed out that the concept of jinns itself was brought into the Islamic belief system from the Arab folklore tradition.

4. Haji Qissa-Khvan Hamdani, *Zubdat-ur Rumuz* (manuscript, c. 1613–14; Khda Bakhsh Library, Patna), 2.

5. *Kitab-e Rumuz-e Hamza* (Tehran: A.H. 1274–76 [1857–59]; British Museum Library), 2–3.

6. Ibid.

7. Suhail Bukhari, *Urdu Dastan: Tahqiqi va Tanqidi Mutaliah* (Islamabad: Muqtadira Qaumi Zaban, 1987); Suhail Bukhari, "Urdu Dastan Ka Fanni Tajziyah," *Nuqush* 105 (April–June 1966), 84–99.

8. Khalil Ali Khan Ashk, *Dastan-e Amir Hamza* (Lahore: Seth Adamji Publishers Bumbai Walay, n.d.), 2. Originally published 1801.

9. Mirza Aman Ali Khan Bahadur Ghalib Lakhnavi, *Tarjuma-e Dastan-e Sahibqiran Giti-sitan Aal-e Paighambar-e Aakhiruz Zaman Amir Hamza bin Abdul Muttalib bin Hashim bin Abdul Munaf* (Calcutta: Hakim Sahib Press, 1855), 2–3.

10. Ahmed Husain Qamar, *Tilism-e Hoshruba*, volume 6 (Kanpur: Naval Kishore Press, 1916), 924.

11. Ibid., 1373.

12. This manuscript is in the collection of Sitzung Preussicher Kulturbesitz, Tübingen, Germany. See Karl Khandalavala and Moti Chandra, *New Documents of Indian Painting: A Reappraisal* (Bombay: Board of Trustees of Prince of Wales Museum, 1969), 50–55.

13. Milo Cleveland Beach, *The Imperial Image: Paintings for the Mughal Court* (Washington, D.C.: Freer Gallery of Art, Smithsonian Institution, 1981), 58.

LIST OF CHARACTERS,
HISTORIC FIGURES, DEITIES,
AND MYTHICAL BEINGS

Names starting with honorifics such as *Amir* and *Malik* should be looked for under the proper name. For example, Malik Alqash can be found at Alqash. Among these honorifics are the following:

Amir: Title used for a commander or leader. In this book the title is used for the hero, Hamza.

Bibi: Title used for a respectable woman

Hakim: Title used for a wise man, or someone with a knowledge of medicine

Khusrau: Title used for a majestic king. In this book it is used for Landhoor bin Saadan.

Khvaja: Title used for a man of distinction, usually conferred on dignitaries

Malik: Title of royalty. Also a title conferred on viziers, as in the case of Malik Alqash.

Mehtar: Title conferred on a chief or commander

Also note that the loyalties of characters change often. Their affiliations as described here are not permanent.

AADAM: Adam. In the *dastan,* he is given the rank of a prophet.

AADI CHOB-GARDAAN: Warrior in Emperor Naushervan's service

AADI MADI-KARIB: Bandit who is defeated by Hamza and joins his cause. He is Hamza's foster brother and a voracious eater.

AADIYA BANO: Wet nurse of Amir Hamza, Muqbil Vafadar, and Amar Ayyar; mother of Aadi Madi-Karib

AASHOB (OR JAHANDAR QALANDAR): Brother of Bahlol; an orphan whom Amir rescues from a *dev* in Qaf

AASMAN PERI: Daughter of Emperor Shahpal bin Shahrukh of Qaf

AATISH: Commander of Emperor Naushervan's *ayyars*

ABA SAEED KHARQA-POSH: Acolyte of Amar Ayyar

ABDUL AZIZ: King of Egypt and father of Zehra Misri

ABDUL MUTTALIB: Chieftain of the Banu Hashim tribe of Arabia; father of Hamza

ABDUR RAHEEM JINN: Minister of Rashid Jinn

ABDUR RAHMAN JINN: Vizier of Emperor Shahpal bin Shahrukh of Qaf

ABU JAHAL: Literally, "father of folly." His real name was Amar bin Hashsham and he was one of Prophet Muhammad's sworn enemies in the city of Mecca.

ABU SAEED LANGARI: Acolyte of Amar Ayyar

ABU SUFYAN: Abu Sufyan bin al-Harith was one of Prophet Muhammad's cousins and foster brothers. He remained his enemy until his conversion to Islam late in life.

ABUL-ALA: *See* Hamza

AFRASIYAB: An ancient sovereign of Turan celebrated in Persian legends

AGHA BULBUL: Courtier and executioner in the service of Amir Hamza

AHRIMAN: A *dev* of Qaf. Father of Ifrit Dev. Not to be confused with Ahriman, the force of darkness in the Zoroastrian religion.

AHRIMAN SHER-GARDAAN: One of the kings of the lands of Bakhtar

AJAL: One of Hamza's eleven brothers; son of Abdul Muttalib

AJROOK KHWARZAMI: Commander who attacks the dominions of Landhoor bin Saadan

AKHZAR FILGOSH: Sassanid commander in Emperor Naushervan's service

AKVANA PERI: Associate of Aasman Peri

ALAF POSH: Chief of Emperor Naushervan's gardeners

ALAM SHAH ROOMI (OR ALAM SHER ROOMI, OR RUSTAM-E PEEL-TAN, OR SHER-E SAF-SHIKAN): Son of Amir Hamza by Rabia Plas Posh

ALAM SHER ROOMI: *See* Alam Shah Roomi

ALI (OR ALI BIN ABU TALIB): Islam's fourth caliph; Prophet Muhammad's cousin and son-in-law

ALI BIN ABU TALIB: *See* Ali

ALJOSH BARBARI: Ninety-yard-tall giant who is Emperor Naushervan's supporter

ALQAMAH SATOORDAST: Commander in Emperor Naushervan's service

ALQASH: Vizier of Qubad Kamran and maternal grandfather of Bakhtak

AMAR AYYAR: A trickster and companion of Hamza; son of Umayya Zamiri

AMAR BIL FATAH: Name given to Amar Ayyar by Buzurjmehr

AMAR BIN HAMZA: Amir Hamza's son by Naheed Maryam

AMAR HABASHI: Son of Shaddad Abu-Amar Habashi

ANIS SHAH: Ruler of Alania

ANTAR DEVDADI: Ruler of the Devdad fort

ANTAR FILGOSH: Commander in Emperor Naushervan's service

ANTAR TEGHZAN: Commander in Emperor Naushervan's service

AQIL KHAN: Vizier of Me'aad Shah Maghrebi

AQIQ: Commander in Amir Hamza's camp

AQLIMUN: Physician who treats Hamza when he is poisoned

ARA'SH: 180-yard-tall giant

ARBAB: Son of Antar Devdadi

ARDABIL PEEL-DANDAN: Co-ruler of Ardabil; brother of Marzaban Peel-Dandan

ARNAIS DEV: A confidant and mace-bearer of Prophet Suleiman; husband of Laneesa Peri and father of Ashqar Devzad

ARSHIVAN PERIZAD: Son of Landhoor and Rashida Peri

ARVANA: Hamza's *gao-sar* wife whom he marries in Qaf

ASAD ZARRIN-TARKASH: Nephew of Emperor Naushervan

ASHQAR DEVZAD: Hamza's favored mount. He is the son of Arnais Dev and Laneesa Peri, conceived when Arnais took the shape of a horse and coupled with Laneesa.

ASHTAR: Champion warrior in Emperor Naushervan's service

ASIF: Brother of Faridun Shah, the king of Greece

ASIF BIN BARKHIA: Minister of Prophet Suleiman

ASIFA BA-SAFA: Mother of prophets Khizr and Ilyas

ASRAR JADU: A *dev* from the Tilism-e Shehristan-e Zarrin

ATIQ: Commander in Amir Hamza's camp

AULAD BIN MARZABAN KAIKAUSI: Relative of Zhopin Kaus

AURANG: Prince of Lakhnauti; brother of Gaurang

AYASHAN MALIK: Warrior in Emperor Naushervan's service

AYESHA: Prophet Muhammad's wife

AYUB: Job

AZRA: Heroine of the romance *Wamiq and Azra;* the beloved of Wamiq

BABA SHIMLA: Name Amar invents for his teacher's turban

BABA ZUD-BURD: Amar Ayyar in disguise

BADI-UL-MULK: One of Amir Hamza's sons

BADIUZ ZAMAN: Amir Hamza's son by Gili-Savar, raised by Aasman Peri and Quraisha at Mount Qaf

BAHLOL (OR JAHANGIR QALANDAR): Brother of Aashob, an orphan whom Amir rescues from a *dev* in Qaf

BAHMAN JASAP: One of Emperor Naushervan's supporters

BAHMAN: Son of Salasal Shah

BAHMAN HAZAN: Emissary for Emperor Naushervan

BAHMAN SAKKAN: Emissary for Emperor Naushervan

BAHRAM: Bandit who robs Emperor Naushervan when he is in exile. Not to be confused with Bahram Gurd, the emperor of China.

BAHRAM CHOB-GARDAAN: Warrior in Emperor Naushervan's service

BAHRAM GUR: A legendary king of Persia known for his passion for the chase of the onager. Not to be confused with BAHRAM GURD.

BAHRAM GURD: Emperor of China and son of the grand emperor. He is not related to Mehr-Angez, the daughter of the Emperor of China, or her brothers Kebaba Chini and Qulaba Chini.

BAHZAD: Legendary Persian miniaturist (1450–1535 C.E.) who was the head of the royal ateliers in Herat and Tabriz during the late Timurid and early Safavid periods

BAKHT JAMAL: Buzurjmehr's father; teacher and friend of Alqash

BAKHTAK: Emperor Naushervan's vizier; son of Bakhtiar by Alqash's daughter, Saqar Ghar Bano

BAKHTIAR: Nubian slave of vizier Alqash; Bakhtak's father

BAKHTIARAK: Son of Bakhtak

BAKHYA SHUTARBAN: Champion warrior in Emperor Naushervan's service

BARKHIA: *See* Asif bin Barkhia

BASHEER: Khvaja Abdul Muttalib's slave; father of Muqbil Vafadar

BECHIN KAMRAN: Brother of Zhopin Kaus

BILQIS: The queen of Sheba

BURRAQ: Legendary winged horse on which Prophet Muhammad flew to visit the heavens

BUZURG UMMID: Son of Buzurjmehr

BUZURJMEHR: Son of Bakht Jamal; vizier of Emperor Qubad Kamran and Emperor Naushervan

CHAMBELI: Wet nurse whose name is invoked by cowards

CHAND: A farmer

CHHALAWA: According to popular belief, a *chhalawa* is a demon that appears in the shape of an infant and can travel at breathtaking speed.

DAJJAL: In Islamic mythology the name given to the Antichrist. According to popular belief, he will appear riding an ass.

DANYAL: Prophet Daniel

DARA: King Darius the Third of Persia (died 330 B.C.E.)

DARAB: Keeper of the fortress of Kurgistan; brother of Sohrab

DARAB AYYAR: An *ayyar* in the service of Sabir and Sabur

DARBAN JADU: A *dev* from the Tilism-e Shehristan-e Zarrin

DARYADIL: Buzurjmehr's son

DAUD: Prophet David

DEV: A demon or a giant

DEWANA TAPISHI: Commander in Emperor Naushervan's service; brother of Sar-Barahna Tapishi

DIL-AARAM: Slave girl of Emperor Qubad Kamran; a lute player

DIL-AAVEZ: Khvaja Arbab's daughter

DINAR SAR-SHABAN: Son of Farkhar Sar-Shaban

DURDANA PERI: Mother of Rehan Peri, wife of Junaid Shah Sabz-Posh

DUR-DUR POSH: Hamza's son by Rehan Peri

EUCLID: Greek mathematician (325–265 B.C.E.)

FAISAL: A goldwright

FARAMURZ: Son of Emperor Naushervan by Mehr-Angez

FARHAD: Hero of the romance *Shirin and Farhad;* the lover of Shirin

FARHAD BIN LANDHOOR: Son of Landhoor bin Saadan

FARIDUN: Persian king who ascended the throne after killing the tyrant Zahhak

FARIDUN SHAH: King of Greece

FARKHAR SAR-SHABAN: Old man from the city of Farkhar

FARRUKH: Daughter of Zardhasht Jadu the sorcerer

FARZANA BANO: Daughter of Furhad-Akka and sister of Qaroon Akka

FATAH AYYAR: An *ayyar* in the service of Amir Hamza

FATAH NOSH: King of Kharsana; brother of Fatah Yar and father of Rabia Plas Posh

FATAH YAR: Brother of Fatah Nosh

FATIMA: Prophet Muhammad's daughter; Ali bin Abu Talib's wife

FAULAD: Rebel slave of the emperor of Greece

FAULAD BIN GUSTHAM: Son of Gustham bin Ashk Zarrin Kafsh Sasani

FAULAD PEHLWAN: Alias used by Amir Hamza

FIROZ SHAH (OR FIROZ TURK): Turkish warrior who attacks Landhoor's dominions

FIROZ TURK: *See* Firoz Shah

FITNA BANO: Attendant of Princess Mehr-Nigar and daughter of Princess Mehr-Nigar's nanny; Amar Ayyar's beloved

FURHAD-AKKA: Warrior who battles Hamza

FUTUH NIM-TAN: King of *nim-tans*

GALEEM AYYAR: An *ayyar* in Emperor Naushervan's service

GALEEM-GOSH: Creatures with large ears that they wrap around their bodies

GALEN: Prominent ancient Greek physician

GAOLANGI: King of Rakham

GAO-PA: A race of cow-footed creatures

GAO-SAR: A race of cow-headed creatures

GARSHASP: Legendary Persian warrior

GAURANG: Prince of Lakhnauti; brother of Aurang

GHOL: Commonly translated as "ghoul," this is an imaginary demon that appears in different shapes and colors and devours men and animals.

GHUR-MUNHA: A race of horse-headed creatures

GILI-SAVAR: Daughter of King Gunjal; wife of Hamza

GOSH-FIL: A race of elephant-eared creatures

GUL CHEHRA: Sister of Zhopin Kaus

GUL-RUKH: Daughter of Zardhasht Jadu the sorcerer

GUNJAL: Sovereign of Gilan

GUSTHAM BIN ASHK ZARRIN KAFSH SASANI: Renowned Sassanid warrior and Amir Hamza's mortal enemy

HAAM: Ruler of Antabia

HAAM DEVDADI: Commander of the king of Devdad's *ayyars*

HADEES SHAH: Ruler of Aleppo

HAMAN: Vizier of Jamshed Shah

HAMAN SHAH: Keeper of a castle

HAMZA: Son of Abdul Muttalib and uncle of Prophet Muhammad. Given the title Amir Hamza, and also called Abul-Ala, the Sahibqiran, and the Quake of Qaf.

HARAS FIL-DANDAN: Warrior who comes to aid Malik Siraj and Ajrook Khwarzami against Landhoor

HARDAM: King of Baru whose niece marries Sa'ad bin Amar bin Hamza and whose sister is given to Amir Hamza in marriage

HARIS BIN SA'AD: Son of Sa'ad bin Amar bin Hamza by Hardam's niece

HARUT: Harut and Marut were angels who severely censured mankind before the throne of God. They were sent to Earth in human form to judge the temptations to which man is subject but they could not withstand them. They were seduced by women, and committed every kind of iniquity. For this they were suspended by their feet in a well in Babylon, where they are to remain in great torment until the Day of Judgment.

HARUT GURAZ-DANDAN: Commander in Emperor Naushervan's service; brother of Marut Guraz-Dandan

HASHSHAM BIN ALQAMAH KHAIBARI: Warrior from the city of Khaibar

HASHIM BIN HAMZA: Amir Hamza's son by Hardam's sister

HATIM: Arab chief of the Tay tribe known for his generosity and munificence, and the hero of the romance *The Adventures of Hatim-Tai*

HINDA: Mother of Pur-Hindi

HOMAN: Son of Bahman Jasap

HOMAN KHAVARI: Son of Qeemaz Shah Khavari

HUD: Prophet Heber

HUMA-E TAJDAR: Daughter of the king of Yemen; Sultan Bakht Maghrebi's beloved

HUMRAN ZARRIN KAMAR: Vassal of Emperor Naushervan and commander of a fortress

HURMUZ: Son of Emperor Naushervan by Mehr-Angez

HUSAIN: Grandson of Prophet Muhammad and son of Ali bin Abu Talib by Bibi Fatima

IBRAHIM: Prophet Abraham

IFRIT DEV: Villainous *dev* of Qaf, head of the rebels of Mount Qaf

ILYAS: Prophet Elias. According to one legend he saves the innocent from drowning. According to another, he is the brother of the holy Khizr and has drunk from the Fountain of Life and will live to see the Day of Judgment. Ilyas helps people on water while Khizr helps people on both land and water.

ILYAS: King encountered by Mehr-Nigar when she runs away after Amar's harsh treatment of her

INDAR: Also known as Indra. King of the gods and regent of the visible heavens in Indian mythology. The court of Indar is synonymous with a place of amusement and pleasure.

ISFANDIAR: Persian king

ISMAIL: Ishmael

ISRAFIL: According to Islamic belief, the Angel Israfil will usher in the Day of Judgment by blowing his trumpet.

ISTAFTANOSH: Prince of Greece; one of Hamza's commanders

ISTEFUNOS: Prince of Greece; brother of Istaftanosh

IZRAIL: The Angel of Death, according to Islamic legend

JAFAR: Ruler of Kashmir

JAHANDAR KABULI: Commander in Emperor Naushervan's service; Jahangir Kabuli's brother

JAHANDAR QALANDAR: Name given to Khvaja Aashob by Hamza

JAHANGIR KABULI: Commander in Emperor Naushervan's service; Jahandar Kabuli's brother

JAHANGIR QALANDAR: Name given to Khvaja Bahlol by Hamza

JAIPUR: Son of Shahpal, nephew of King Saadan Shah of Ceylon, and cousin of Landhoor

JAMASP: Buzurjmehr's maternal grandfather. According to legend he preached the Magian religion after the death of Zoroaster and wrote a book on alchemy called *Jamasp-nama.*

JAMSHED: Ancient king of Persia. The name is often attributed in legend to King Suleiman and Sikander, and is invoked in this book in connection with Emperor Naushervan's court to convey the grandeur and prestige of his empire.

JAMSHED SHAH: Master of the castle of Talva-Bahar

JAN: According to legend, the father of all jinns and *peris* who inhabited Earth before the creation of Aadam. They were later banished to Jinnistan, "the Land of the Jinns," for disobedience to the Supreme Being.

JIBRAIL: Angel Gabriel

JINN: Creatures made of fire. According to Islamic tradition, Iblis (Satan) was a jinn. *See* Jan.

JUNAID SHAH SABZ-POSH JINN (OR JUNAID SHAH SABZ-QABA): Elder brother of Emperor Shahpal bin Shahrukh of Qaf

KAIKAUS: King of Persia. His name is invoked to connote the grandeur and majesty of Emperor Naushervan's court.

KAI KHUSRAU: King Cyrus. His name is invoked to convey the grandeur and majesty of Emperor Naushervan's court.

KAKH BAKHTAR: Cannibal king of Bakhtar

KAUS SHERWANI: Champion warrior in Amir Hamza's service

KARIB MADI: Son of Aadi Madi-Karib by Gustham's daughter. This version of the *Dastan-e Amir Hamza* does not mention the marriage between Aadi Madi-Karib and Gustham's daughter.

KARGAS SASANI: An *ayyar* in the service of Hurmuz and Faramurz

KARVAN: Leader of a merchant caravan that Amir encounters on his way to Kharsana

KARVAN: Vizier of the king of Egypt

KATARA KABULI: Commander of Hurmuz's *ayyars;* nephew of Zhopin Kaus

KAYUMARS: Sovereign who offers refuge to Emperor Naushervan

KEBABA CHINI: Son of the emperor of China; brother of Mehr-Angez and Qulaba Chini

KHALIFA BULBUL: Mehr-Nigar's cook

KHALKHAL DEV: A *dev* of Qaf

KHARCHAL: Vicious *dev* who takes over the city of Simin in Qaf

KHARPAL: Vicious *dev* who takes over the city of Simin in Qaf

KHIZR: A holy personage of Islamic legend who led Sikander the Bicornous to the Fountain of Life. He guides lost travelers on land and water. In the *dastan* he is the brother of Prophet Ilyas (Elias) and is given the rank of a prophet.

KHURSHID KHAVARI: Sister of Qeemaz Shah Khavari

KHUSRAU: *See* Landhoor. In this book the title is used for Landhoor bin Saadan, unless accompanied by another name.

KOH BAKHT HINDI: Brother of Sarkash Hindi

KOH-PAIKAR: Sassanid warrior in Emperor Naushervan's service

KULIYAT: Son of Galeem Ayyar

LAHOOT SHAH: A jinn; master of the Castle of Zamarrud Hisar; father of Laneesa

LAILA: Heroine of the romance *Laila and Majnun;* the beloved of Qais (Majnun)

LANDHOOR BIN SAADAN: King of India; a descendent of Prophet Shis

LANEESA PERI: Daughter of Lahoot Shah and beloved of Arnais Dev. She bears Ashqar Devzad, Hamza's legendary steed.

LAT: Pre-Islamic goddess of the Arabs; condemned in the Quran (53:19)

MADAR SHAH: Saint who lived near Ajmer and was venerated by charlatans

MAGHLUB FIL-ZOR: Warrior who aids Malik Siraj and Ajrook Khwarzami against Landhoor

MAHMUD SIYAH-TAN: Amar Ayyar in disguise

MAIMOONA: She-elephant of Landhoor bin Saadan

MIAN FATTU: Water carrier whom Amar Ayyar kills and then impersonates to enter the castle of Devdad

MAJDAK: Officer of Emperor Naushervan's court

MAJNUN: *See* Qais

MALIA: Son of Marzooq Farangi, a fifty-yard-tall giant

MALIK: According to Islamic legend, the porter of Hell

MALOONA JADU: Mother of Ifrit Dev

MANAT: Pre-Islamic goddess of the Arabs; condemned in the Quran (53:20)

MANI: Persian painter and founder of the Manichean sect, celebrated for the beauty of his house

MANSOOR AYYAR: An *ayyar* in the employ of Salasal Shah

MANWA: Son of a grass cutter

MARUT: *See* Harut

MARUT GURAZ-DANDAN: Commander in Emperor Naushervan's service; brother of Harut Guraz-Dandan

MARZABAN PEEL-DANDAN: Co-ruler of Ardabil; brother of Ardabil Peel-Dandan

MARZABAN ZARDHASHT: Son-in-law of Gaolangi

MARZAK: Agent of Emperor Naushervan; Hakim who blinds Hamza and his companions

MARZOOQ FARANGI: Warrior who raids the land of Kharsana and is routed by Hamza

MAYMAR DEV: A *dev* who constructed most of the buildings in Qaf and ordered the imprisonment of Khvaja Aashob and Khvaja Bahlol

ME'AAD RAZ AADI: Warrior of the Aadi tribe

ME'AAD SHAH MAGHREBI: King who ordered Aadi Madi-Karib buried alive with his deceased wife

MEHD ZARRIN KAMAR: Ruler of Antaqia

MEHR-AFROZE: Emperor Naushervan's younger daughter and Mehr-Nigar's sister

MEHR-ANGEZ: Daughter of the emperor of China; Emperor Naushervan's wife and Mehr-Nigar's mother

MEHRDAR SAR-SHABAN: Son of Farkhar Sar-Shaban

MEHR-NIGAR: Daughter of Emperor Naushervan by Mehr-Angez

MEHR SHAH: Amir Hamza's son by Mehr-Afroze

MIR BHUCHRI: *See* PIR BHUCHRI

MISQAL SHAH: King of the castle of Tanj-e Maghreb

MISQAL SHAH MISRI: Companion of Amir Hamza. It is unclear if he is the same Misqal Shah who is the king of the castle of Tanj-e Maghreb.

MOHTRAM BANO: Qubad Kamran's cousin and wife; Emperor Naushervan's mother

MUHAMMAD BIN ABDULLAH BIN ABDUL MUTTALIB: The prophet of Islam

MUHLIL SAGSAR: One of the commanders who attacks the dominions of Landhoor bin Saadan

MULLA: Teacher of Amir Hamza, Muqbil Vafadar, and Amar Ayyar

MUNZIR SHAH YEMENI: King of Yemen

MUQBIL VAFADAR: Companion of Amir Hamza; son of Abdul Muttalib's slave Basheer and a faultless archer

MUSA: Prophet Moses

NAHEED MARYAM: Daughter of Faridun Shah; Amir Hamza's wife

NAIK RAI: Vizier of Malik Shuaib

NAIRANJ PERI: Daughter of Naranj Peri's vizier

NAMIAN: An *ayyar* in Amir Hamza's service

NAMRUD: Nimrod. The title of King Suriyus, who is said to have cast Prophet Ibrahim into a fire. In the *dastan* he is mentioned as a god of the fire worshippers.

NAQABDAR: Literally, "the veiled one"

NAQABDAR NARANJI-POSH: Veiled rider who comes to assist Amir Hamza's armies in times of need

NARANJ PERI: A *peri* of Qaf who appears as the Naqabdar Naranji-Posh

NARIMAN: Famous hero of Persia

NASAI: Son of the king of Farang

NASNAAS OF SULEIMAN: Beast that resembles human beings and can speak the Arabic language. It is said that the beast has only one leg, one eye, one arm, and one ear, and hops when walking.

NAUSHERVAN: Emperor of Persia; son of Qubad Kamran and father of Mehr-Nigar

NIHAL: Princess Mehr-Nigar's childhood attendant

NIM-TAN: An imaginary being that has half a face, one eye, one arm, and one foot. There are male and female *nim-tans:* The male has the right hand, foot, and so forth and the female the left. When united, the male and female resemble one human figure; when separated, they run with amazing speed on their single feet and are considered very dangerous.

NIM-TAN KHAVARI: Father of Qeemaz Shah Khavari

NOMAN: Son of King Munzir; shah of Yemen

NOOR BANO: Sister of Bahman and daughter of Salasal Shah

NUH: Prophet Noah

PAIK AYYAR: An *ayyar* in Emperor Naushervan's service

PALANG-SAR DEV: A *dev* of Qaf and a minion of Sufaid Dev

PERI: A female fairy

PERIZAD: A male *peri*. The term *perizad* is also used to describe any creature born of a *peri*.

PIRAN MAGHREBI: Sher Shah Qirwani's commander in chief

PIR BHUCHRI (OR MIR BHUCHRI): Saint venerated by the transvestites

PIR FARKHARI: Companion of Amir Hamza

PIR JALILAN: Name of a saint, or a place named after this saint. No other information is available.

PIR-UL-WALI: Title of the Indian saint Khvaja Moinuddin Hasan Chishti (1142–1238 C.E.), in whose name food offerings are made

PLATO: Greek philosopher (427–347 B.C.E.)

POTIPHAR: Ruler of Egypt to whom Yusuf (Joseph) was sold in slavery

PUR-HINDI: Indian prince

PYTHAGORAS: Greek philosopher (569–475 B.C.E.)

QAILUM: Sassanid warrior in Emperor Naushervan's service

QAIS: Hero of the romance *Laila and Majnun;* the lover of Laila. His patronymic was Majnun, "the frenzied one."

QAIS QEEMAZ KHAVARI: Son of Qeemaz Shah Khavari

QALMAQ SHAH: Warrior who advances on Mecca and is defeated by Ajal bin Abdul Muttalib

QAMAR CHEHRA PERI: Amir Hamza's *peri* wife; mother of Qamza-Zad

QAMZA-ZAD: Son of Amir Hamza by Qamar Chehra Peri

QARAN DEOBAND: Commander in Emperor Naushervan's service

QARAN FIL-GARDAN: Sassanid warrior in Emperor Naushervan's service

QAROON: King Croesus of Lydia (reigned 560–547 B.C.E.), whose name connotes wealth

QAROON AKKA: Son of Furhad-Akka

QASIM KHAVARI: Son of Alam Shah Roomi

QATRAN MAGHREBI: An *ayyar* in Sher Shah Qirwani's service

QAUS: A shepherd

QEEMAZ SHAH KHAVARI: Ruler of the city of Khavar

QUBAD: Woodcutter to whom Emperor Qubad gives away Dil-Aaram

QUBAD: Son of Amir Hamza by Mehr-Nigar

QUBAD AADI: Warrior of the Aadi tribe

QUBAD KAMRAN: Emperor of Persia and father of Naushervan

QUFUL NESTANI: Ruler of the fort of Nestan

QULABA CHINI: Son of the emperor of China; brother of Mehr-Angez

QUNDUZ SAR-SHABAN: Owner of a garden who becomes Amir Hamza's companion

QURAISHA: Daughter of Amir Hamza by Aasman Peri

RA'AD DEV: Two-headed *dev* Amir Hamza encounters in Qaf

RA'AD SHATIR DEV: Nephew of Ifrit Dev and lord of the castles of Siyah Boom and Sufaid Boom

RABIA PLAS POSH: Daughter of King Fatah Nosh, the sovereign of Kharsana

RAE-BEL: Wet nurse whose name is invoked by cowards

RAHDAR DEV: First *dev* of Qaf killed by Amir Hamza

RAHMAN: Father of Vizier Haman

RAM: A Hindu god

RASHID JINN: King of the lands of Abyaz Min Muzafat, a dominion of Qaf

RASHIDA PERI: Daughter of Rashid Jinn

RAUF JINN: Minister of Junaid Shah Sabz-Posh Jinn

REHAN PERI: Daughter of Junaid Shah Sabz-Posh Jinn

REL GAOLANGI: Son of Gaolangi

RIZWAN: According to Islamic legend, the porter of Heaven

RIZWAN PERIZAD: One of the attendants of Aasman Peri

RUKH: Giant bird that is the enemy of King Tulu Gao-Pa

RUSTAM: Legendary Persian warrior and son of Zal

RUSTAM-E PEEL-TAN: *See* Alam Shah Roomi

SA'AD BIN AMAR BIN HAMZA: Son of Amar bin Hamza and grandson of Amir Hamza

SA'AD SHAMI: Alias used by Amir Hamza

SA'AD TAUQI: Warrior in Amir Hamza's service

SA'AD YEMENI: Amir Hamza's companion

SA'AD ZARRIN-TARKASH: Nephew of Emperor Naushervan

SA'AD ZULMATI: Amar Ayyar disguised as a bearded forty-yard-tall giant

SAADAN SHAH: King of Ceylon; father of Landhoor

SAALIM: A holy man and descendent of Prophet Nuh

SAAM: Ruler of Antakia

SABIR: Son of Shahpal Hindi and brother of Sabur

SABIR NAMADPOSH AYYAR: An *ayyar* in Emperor Naushervan's service

SABIT SHAH: One of two masters of the castle of Rahtas Gadh; *see* Tahmuras Shah

SABUR: Son of Shahpal Hindi and brother of Sabir

SAEED BAZARGAN: Khvaja Abdur Rahman Jinn in disguise; the master of a ship Amir sees being loaded in Qaf

SAHIB-E HAL ATA: According to *dastan* scholar Shamsur Rahman Faruqi, this is from the phrase *"sahib-e hal ata"* and is a name signifying Ali bin Abu Talib. Chapter 76 of the Quran, the *Dahr,* or *Insan,* begins with this phrase. It means "has there not passed, or been?" Verse 8 of this chapter speaks of people who go hungry themselves while feeding others. Some interpreters of the Quran say that this verse refers to Ali bin Abu Talib, and it is therefore presumed that the whole chapter is about Ali bin Abu Talib in some way. Since the chapter starts with *"hal ata,"* Ali bin Abu Talib is occasionally described as the *sahib*, or the *tajdar* of *"hal ata."*

SAHIBQIRAN: Title for the Lord of the Auspicious Planetary Conjunction; given to those born under the conjunction of Jupiter and Venus. These planets were thought to be benevolent, and their conjunction was considered most fortunate. This epithet is also applied to a monarch who has ruled for forty years. In this book, the title is used exclusively for Amir Hamza.

SALASAL PERIZAD: Companion of Emperor Shahpal bin Shahrukh of Qaf, and messenger of Aasman Peri

SALASAL SHAH: Master of the fort of Salasal Hisar

SALEEM KOHI: Father of Susan Peri

SALEH: Prophet sent to the tribe of Samud. Some associate him with the biblical Shelah.

SALIM SHAIRAN: Queen of the land of Zulmat in Qaf

SAM BIN NARIMAN: Legendary Persian warrior; father of Zal and grandfather of Rustam

SAMAN SEEMA PERI: One of Amir Hamza's *peri* wives from Qaf

SAMANDAR KHAN: An expert in pyrotechnics; brother of Zaad Khan

SAMANDUN HAZAR-DAST DEV: A *dev* whom Amir Hamza fights in Qaf

SAMAWA AYYAR: An *ayyar* in Emperor Naushervan's service

SAMERI: Magician who was the contemporary of Prophet Musa. According to Islamic legend, he conjured a calf that had the power of speech.

SAMOOM AADI: Warrior of the Aadi tribe

SAMRAT GAO-SAR: King of the *gao-sars*; his daughter, Arvana, marries Hamza

SANG ANDAZ KHUNKHVAR NESTAN: King of Nestan, 190-yard-tall giant

SAQAR GHAR BANO: Mother of Bakhtak

SAQRA-E BARAHMAN: Chief of Sufaid Dev's minions

SAR-BARAHNA TAPISHI: Commander in Emperor Naushervan's service; brother of Dewana Tapishi

SARHANG MISRI: Chief of the *ayyars* of the king of Egypt

SARKASH HINDI: Ruler of Sindh; brother of Koh Bakht Hindi

SARKOB TURK: Warrior in Amir Hamza's service

SARYAL BIN SALASAL: Forty-yard-tall giant; the king of Qaza-va-Qadar

SAUDAI QALANDAR: Alias used by Amar Ayyar

SAYYAD: An *ayyar* in the service of Sabit Shah

SEHBA JADU: Chief sorceress of the Tilism-e Anjabal where Rashida Peri and Arshivan are imprisoned

SEH-CHASHMI DEV: Creator of the Tilism-e Anjabal

SHABAN TAIFI: Son of Qunduz Sar-Shaban, titled Hamza-e Sani, "the Latter-day Hamza," by Amir Hamza

SHABRANG: Horse of Shaddad Abu-Amar Habashi

SHADDAD: Cruel monarch who arrogated divine power to himself. He was the founder of the legendary Gardens of Irum. Reviled in the Quran (89:6–8).

SHADDAD ABU-AMAR HABASHI: King of Ethiopia

SHAHPAL: Brother of King Saadan Shah of Ceylon; Jaipur's father and Landhoor's uncle. Not to be confused with Shahpal Hindi.

SHAHPAL BIN KARBAL BIN TAVEEL ZULMATI: An alias used by Amar Ayyar

SHAHPAL BIN SHAHRUKH: A jinn; emperor of Qaf and father of Aasman Peri

SHAHPAL HINDI: Father of Sabir and Sabur; not to be confused with King Shahpal, who is Landhoor's uncle

SHAMIM: Vizier of Sabit Shah

SHAMSHEER-ZAN: Executioner in the court of Shaddad Abu-Amar Habashi

SHANKAVAH: Nubian who tyrannizes Faridun Shah's lands and is killed by Landhoor

SHARARA JADU: Mother of Ra'ad, the two-headed *dev*

SHATIR: Commander in the service of Prince Hurmuz

SIIER SHAH QIRWANI: Sovereign of Qirwan

SHERMAR: Sherwani warrior in the service of Amir Hamza

SHIDAI QALANDAR: Alias used by Amar Ayyar

SHIRIN: Heroine of the romance *Shirin and Farhad*; Farhad's beloved

SHIRIN: Ruler of the city of women

SHIS: Prophet Seth

SHIS YEMENI: Amir Hamza's commander and camp guard

MIAN SHORA: Musician associated with the court of Asaf-ul-Dawla in Avadh who developed and refined the *tappa* style of singing

SHUAIB: Ruler of Mando

SIKANDER: Name often used for both Alexander of Macedon and the prince Sikander Zulqarnain (Alexander the Bicornous)

SIKANDER ZULQARNAIN: *See* Sikander

SIKANDER ZULMATI: Emperor of Zulmat

SIMURGH: Giant bird whom Hamza befriends in Qaf

SIMURGH'S FEMALE: Holy guardian of the women of the city of Shirin

SINA AADI: Warrior of the Aadi tribe

SIRAJ: Commander who attacks Landhoor's lands

SIYAH QITAS: Horse of Prophet Ishaq (Isaac); given to Amir Hamza by Angel Jibrail

SIYAH SHER: Shepherd who looks after Hamza when he is wounded in battle

SIYAVUSH (OR SIYAVUSH BIN BUZURJMEHR): Buzurjmehr's son

SOHRAB: Legendary Persian warrior; son of Rustam

SOHRAB: Brother of Darab, keeper of the fortress of Kurgistan

SUFAID DEV: Commander of Samandun Hazar-Dast Dev

SUHAIL: A goldsmith

SUHAIL YEMENI: Commander of the king of Yemen who becomes Amir Hamza's companion

SULEIMAN: King Solomon. According to the Islamic tradition, he had power over men, jinns, and beasts.

SULTAN BAKHT MAGHREBI: Prince of Maghreb

SULTAN BIN ZAL SHAMAMA JADU: Fictitious name adopted by one of Naqabdar Naranji-Posh's *ayyars* in imitating the king of Turkistan

SUSAN PERI (OR SUSAN JADU): Daughter of Saleem Kohi and guardian of Maloona Jadu's *tilism*

TAAN-SEN: Court musician of the Mughal emperor Akbar

TAHMURAS DEOBAND: King of Persia. According to legend, he enslaved a demon and made him his mount. He was therefore titled *deoband,* "the demon rider."

TAHMURAS SHAH: One of two masters of the castle of Rahtas Gadh. *See* Sabit Shah

TAIFUS BIN MAYUS BIN SARBUS BIN TAQ BIN TAMTARAQ BAZARGAN: An alias used by Amar Ayyar when disguised as a merchant

TARAR KHOOBAN: Attendant of Princess Mehr-Nigar; Muqbil Vafadar's beloved

TASMA-PA: A race of beings that have leathery thongs for legs

TASSAVURAN: A king; father of Zar-Angez

TAUQ BIN HEYRAN: Robber and bandit who renounces banditry and becomes Amir Hamza's companion

TAUQ-E ZARRIN: Son of Amir Hamza by Naranj Peri

TAUS BAKHTARI: One of the rulers of the lands of Bakhtar

TAZ TURK: Champion warrior in Amir Hamza's service

TOMIAN: An *ayyar* in Amir Hamza's service

TULU GAO-PA: King of the *gao-pas*

UMAYYA ZAMIRI: A cameleer; father of Amar Ayyar

WAILUM: Sassanid warrior in Emperor Naushervan's service

WAMIQ: Hero of the romance *Wamiq and Azra;* lover of Azra

WAQ: Talking tree whose fruit is shaped like human heads

YALAN: Commander in the service of Fatah Nosh

YAQUB: Jacob

YEZID: The second caliph of the Umayyad dynasty; ruled from C.E. 680–683. Prophet Muhammad's grandson Husain and his family were put to death at Karbala on Yezid's orders. An archetypal villain.

YUSUF: Joseph

ZAAD KHAN: An expert in pyrotechnics; brother of Samandar Khan

ZAFAR: An *ayyar* in the service of Amir Hamza

ZAIGHAM: Commander for Malik Shuaib

ZAL: Persian hero who was the father of Rustam and the son of Sam

ZAR-ANGEZ: Daughter of King Tassavuran; wife of Emperor Naushervan

ZARAQ JADU: A *dev* who encounters Amir in Tilism-e Shehristan-e Zarrin

ZARDHASHT JADU: Sorcerer and author of a book on magic

ZEHRA MISRI: Daughter of the king of Egypt

ZHOPIN FAULAD-TAN: Warrior in Emperor Naushervan's service

ZHOPIN KAUS (OR ZHOPIN ZABULI): Warrior in Emperor Naushervan's service

ZHOPIN ZABULI: *See* Zhopin Kaus

ZULAIKHA: Potiphar's wife

ZURA ZARAH-POSH: Commander in Emperor Naushervan's service

SELECTED SOURCES

ENGLISH

Burton, Sir Richard Francis. *The Book of the Sword*. (New York: Dover, 1987).

Egerton of Tatton, Lord. *Indian and Oriental Armour* (London: Arms and Armour Press, Lionel Leventhal Ltd., 1968).

Fallon, S. W. *English-Urdu Dictionary* (Rpt., Lahore: Urdu Science Board, 1993).

Faridany-Akhavan, Zahra. "The Problems of the Mughal Manuscript of the Hamza-Nama 1562–77: A Reconstruction." Ph.D. dissertation, Harvard University, 1989.

Hosain, Shaikh Sajjad. *The Amir Hamza: An Oriental Novel*. Part I (Calcutta: Sarat Chandra Bysack & Co, 1892).

Khoneli, Mose. *Amir Darejian—A Cycle of Medieval Georgian Tales Traditionally Ascribed to Mose Khoneli*. Translated by R. G. Stevenson (Oxford: Oxford University Press, 1958).

Lyons, M. C. *The Arabian Epic: Heroic and Oral Story-Telling*. Vols. I–III (New York: Cambridge University Press, 2005).

Pant, G. N. *Indian Arms and Armour*, Vol. I, *Pre- and Protohistoric Weapons and Archery* (New Delhi: Department of Arms and Armour, National Museum, Army Educational Stores, 1978). Vol. II, *Swords and Daggers*, 1980.

Platts, John T. *A Dictionary of Urdu, Classical Hindi and English* (Rpt., Lahore: Sang-e Meel, 1994).

Pritchett, Frances W. *The Romance Tradition in Urdu: Adventures from the Dastan of Amir Hamzah* (New York: Columbia University Press, 1991).

Seyller, John. *The Adventures of Hamza: Painting and Story-Telling in Mughal India* (Washington, D.C., and London: Freer Gallery of Art; Arthur M. Sackler Gallery, Smithsonian Institution, in association with Azimuth Editions, 2002).

Steingass, F. *A Comprehensive Persian-English Dictionary* (New York: Routledge & Kegan Paul, in association with Iran University Press, 1995).

al-Thalibi, Abu Mansur Abd al-Malik bin Muhammad bin Ismail. *Lataif al-Ma'arif* (The Book of Curious and Entertaining Information). Translated and with introduction and notes by Clifford Edmund Bosworth (Edinburgh: Edinburgh University Press, 1968).

Walker, Warren S., ed. *A Turkish Folktale: The Art of Behçet Mahir* (New York and London: Garland Publishing, Inc., 1996).

URDU

Bilgrami, Abdullah Husain. *Dastan-e Amir Hamza Sahibqiran* (Lucknow, India: Naval Kishore Press, 1871).

Dehlvi, Syed Ahmed. *Farhang-e Asifya,* Vols. I–II (Rpt., Lahore, Pakistan: Urdu Science Board, 1995).

Faruqi, Shamsur Rahman. *Sahiri, Shahi, Sahibqirani: Dastan-e Amir Hamza ka Mutalaa.* Vol. I, *Nazari Mubahis* (New Delhi: National Council for the Promotion of Urdu Language, 1999). Vol. II, *Amali Mubahis* (New Delhi: National Council for the Promotion of Urdu Language, 2006). Vol. III, *Jahan-e Hamza* (New Delhi: National Council for the Promotion of Urdu Language, 2006).

Jah, Syed Muhammad Husain. *Tilism-e Hoshruba.* Vols. I–IV (Lucknow, India: Naval Kishore Press, 1883–90; rpt., Lahore, Pakistan: Sang-e Meel Publications, n.d.). Vol. V, Part I (Lucknow, India: Husaini Press, 1890; rpt., Patna, India: Khuda Bakhsh Library, 2000).

Jain, Gyan Chand. *Urdu ki Nasri Dastanen* (Lucknow, India: Uttar Pradesh Urdu Academy, 1987).

Kakorvi, Noor-ul Hasan Nayyar. *Noor-ul Lughat.* Vols. I–II (Rpt., Lahore, Pakistan: Sang-e Meel Publications, 1983).

Lakhnavi, Mirza Aman Ali Khan Bahadur Ghalib. *Tarjuma-e Dastan-e Sahibqiran Giti-sitan Aal-e Paighambar-e Aakhiruz Zaman Amir Hamza bin Abdul-Muttalib bin Hashim bin Abdul Munaf* (Calcutta: Hakim Sahib Press, 1855).

Majeed, Khvaja Abdul. *Jama-ul Lughat.* Vols. I–II (Rpt., Lahore, Pakistan: Urdu Science Board, 1999).

Qamar, Ahmad Husain. *Tilism-e Hoshruba.* Vols. V–VII (Lucknow, India: Naval Kishore Press, 1890–93; rpt., Lahore, Pakistan: Sang-e Meel Publications, n.d.).

PERSIAN

Hamdani, Haji Qissa-Khvan. *Zubdatur Rumuz* (MS, c. 1613–14; Khuda Bakhsh Library, Patna).

Kitab-e Rumuz-e Hamza (Tehran: A.H. 1274–76 [1857–59]; British Museum Library).

Mirza Muhammad Khan 'malik-ul kuttab.' *Kitab-e Dastan-e Amir Hamza Sahibqiran* (Bombay: Matba-e Sapehr-e Matla, A.H. 1327 [1909]).

Shiar, Jafar, ed. *Qissa-e Hamza.* 2 vols. (Tehran: University of Tehran Press, A.H. 1347 [1968–69]).

GERMAN

Egger, Gerhart. *Der Hamza Roman: Eine Mughal-Handschrift Asunder Zeit Akbar des Großen* (Vienna: Österreich Museum für angewandte Kunst, 1969).

Glück, Heinrich. *Die Indischen Miniaturen des Hamza-e Romanes im Österreichischen Museum für Kunst und Industrie in Wien und in anderen Sammlungen* (Zurich: Amalthea-Verlag, 1925).

Hamza-nama: Vollständige Wiedergabe der bekannten Blätter der Handschrift aus den Beständen aller erreichbaren Sammlungen. Codices selecti phototypice impressi, Vol. 52 (Graz: Akademische Druck- und Verlagsanstalt, 1974).

FRENCH

"Les artistes de la court d'Akbar et les illustrations de Dastan i Amir Hamzae." In *Arts Asiatiques.* Vol. II, fase 1–2 (1995).

DUTCH

Van Ronkel, Ph. S. *De Roman van Amir Hamza* (Lieden: E. J. Brill, 1895).

NOTES

BOOK ONE

1. *Ctesiphon: (Mada'in)* the collective name of seven cities that flourished in the reign of Naushervan in the seventh century C.E.
2. *henna from the palm:* The words used in the Urdu text are *duzd-e henna*, literally, "the thief of henna." It is a term used to describe the white parts of the hand that escape the application of henna.
3. *viziers:* ministers.
4. *abecedarians:* ones who are learning the alphabet; absolute beginners.
5. ramal, jafar: *Ramal* is an occult science of the Islamic world resembling geomancy, used to ascertain the present and predict future events; *jafar* is another occult science of the Islamic world used for divination.
6. *Khvaja:* a man of distinction. A title conferred on dignitaries.
7. hikmat: a high degree of wisdom. Also a lesser-known school of philosophy.
8. *Malik:* title of royalty. Also conferred on viziers, as in the case of Malik Alqash.
9. This verse is by Mir Hasan Ahmed Sabir Bilgrami, pen name Sabir, a lesser-known Urdu poet of India.
10. kalma: an act of faith consisting of the affirmation of the existence of one God and the prophethood of Muhammad.
11. Verse is by Muslih-ud-Din Mushrif bin Abdullah (ca. 1184–1283/1291 C.E.), pen name Saadi.
12. Verse is by Shaikh Imam Bakhsh (1776–1838), pen name Nasikh, a renowned Urdu poet.
13. Verse is by Nasikh.
14. Verse is by Mir Hasan, an Urdu poet. Unclear whether he is Mir Hasan Ahmed Sabir Bilgrami or another poet.
15. maunds: A *maund* is a measurement of weight equivalent to a little more than 82 pounds, or 38.25 kilograms.
16. *Tabrizi* maund: a measure of weight equivalent to 3 kilograms.
17. Verse is by Nasikh.

18. Verse is by Sabir.
19. *howdahs:* seats fitted on elephants' backs.
20. *Banarasi:* embroidered cloth made in the city of Banaras (present-day Varanasi).
21. *ostlers:* those who take care of horses.
22. *Chaugoshia:* a horse of a Turkic breed.
23. *Mujannas:* a cross between the Arabian and the Turkish horse.
24. *martingales:* devices for steadying horses' heads or checking their upward movement.
25. *surcingles:* belts or bands that pass around the bodies of horses.
26. mashru: Muslim men are forbidden to pray in clothes made of pure silk according to sharia. *Mashru* (from *sharia*) is a kind of cloth blending silk and cotton. Men clothed in a garment made of this cloth are permitted to pray.
27. *panniers:* packs consisting of two bags for carriage by pack animals.
28. *galloon:* a narrow ornamental fabric for trimming or finishing cloth.
29. *Khorasani*...bahbudi: The Khorasani has a flat back or base. A curved, bulging line carries the angle of resistance, giving the section a biconvex form. *Isfahani* is an Indian steel sword made in Isfahan by the damascene process; *Qazvini* is a sword with fine workmanship made at Qazvin by the damascene process; *Portuguese* (also *Farangi*) refers to a cut-and-thrust straight-bladed sword introduced by the Portuguese in India in the sixteenth century C.E.; *Gujarati* is another name for the *Alamani* sword; *Alamani* is a sword shaped like the old German hussar saber, and was probably introduced by Hyder Ali's German soldiers; *Maghrebi* refers to a sword made by the damascene process; *Janubi* is a curved sword that tapers toward its point and is single-edged at the hilt and double-edged at the tip; *Egyptian* refers to a short sword used in close combat; *Farrukh-Begi* is a kind of sword; *Tirah* refers to a sword made in the town of Tirah; *Sirohi* is a densely tempered curved-blade sword made in the village of Sirohi in Rajasthan; *kaj-bhuj* is a combination ax and dagger; *chhuri* is a knife with a slight curve to the blade; *qarauli* is a kind of dagger with a single, instead of a double, curve; *peshqabz* is a one-edged dagger with a thick, straight back to the blade and a straight handle without a guard; *bichhawa* is an Indian dagger with a double-curved, double-edged blade named for its resemblance to a scorpion's tail; *baank,* which literally means "a curvature," or "a bend," is a dagger with a sickle-shaped blade and a straight handle used by Marathas (a race of warriors); *katar* is a knife with a short, leaf-shaped pointed blade. Sometimes the poniard and stiletto daggers are referred to as *katar; dashnah* is also called *"khapwah"* in Hindi, which means "the finisher; the dealer of the coup de grâce"; the name is derived from *khapna,* meaning "to fill up" or "to complete"; *qama* is a heavy, two-edged knife of very hard waved steel that is deeply grooved and slightly ornamented with gold and usually fitted with a horn handle; *bahbudi* means "well-being" and refers to a dagger. It may be so named since it is carried as a protective weapon.
30. chanaboot: a kind of cloth.

31. gulbadan: a kind of silken cloth.
32. jamdani... tanzeb: *Jamdani* is a kind of muslin; *kamdani* refers to a pattern of small flowers worked on muslin or net with gold or silver thread; *mahmoodi* is a fine variety of muslin; *chandeli* was a very fine variety of cotton cloth worn in the Indian courts, the best quality of which sold for its weight in silver; *shabnam* refers to a fine variety of linen, and also a very fine muslin; *chaqan* is a method of making flowers on muslin or other cloth; *tar-shumar* is a kind of needlework in which fine cloth is run through with gold or silver thread; *tar-andaam* refers to a fine variety of cloth; *neno* is ornamented muslin; *nen-sukh* is a thick variety of jaconet muslin; *tanzeb* is a fine cotton cloth that is a little thicker than muslin.
33. jamawar: chintz sheets or shawls adorned with flower patterns.
34. kaleecha: a closely sewn, resplendent garment.
35. laals: the male birds of the species *Fringilla amandava*.
36. sina-baz: a kind of bird.
37. phirki: a variety of the Indian marigold.
38. juhi... farang: *Juhi* is the jasmine flower *Jasminum auriculatum*; *ra'e-bel* is the species of jasmine *Jasminum sambac*; *ketki* (same as *keora*) is the flower *Pandanus odoratissimus*; *farang* is the flower *Vinca rosea*, commonly known as the periwinkle.
39. gul-e Abbasi ... and chiraghan: *Gul-e Abbasi* (same as *dupehriya*) is the flower Marvel of Peru; *chiraghan* is another kind of flower.
40. chapni: a kind of flower.
41. maulsari: the flower *Mimusops elengi*.
42. *(peace be upon the Holy Prophet!):* This injunction is used on occasions when the storyteller is overwhelmed by the praiseworthiness of a situation or scene.
43. maang-tikas: ornaments worn by women along the parting of their hair.
44. *Jamshedi robe of honor:* a royal gift consisting of eleven pieces of cloth; usually conferred on viziers as a mark of honor.
45. *hakim:* a wise man; also someone who has knowledge of medicine; a healer.
46. *God forbid ... harm:* The term *enemies* is substituted for a person's name from the superstition that just mentioning the name of a person in the context of a calamity would bring the calamity down on his head. Thus if person A is unwell, his friends would ask, "Are the enemies of A unwell?"
47. Verse is by Nasikh.
48. *Mount of Wisdom:* A pun is intended here in Urdu as well. The word used is *khar-e hukma. Khar* means "ass" as well as "great." So the literal translation of the term would be "ass of the wise men" and "wisest of the wise," both of which are conveyed in the term *Mount of Wisdom.*
49. *seven treasures of Shaddad:* In classical literature, not seven treasures but seven gates of Shaddad's city Irum are mentioned. It was the emperor Khusrau who was known to have seven treasures. In the *dastan* tradition these references are typically mixed up.
50. Verse is by Saadi.
51. Verse is by Saadi.

52. fateha: invoking of blessings upon a deceased relative by reading the opening chapter of the Quran (*Sura Fateha,* The Exordium), and distributing alms and food. See also notes 82 and 189.

53. chehlum: the fortieth day after an Indian Muslim's death, after which the bereavement is officially over. In this case the forty days of mourning commenced from the day Khvaja Bakht Jamal was buried. *Chehlum* was an Indian Muslim tradition and was unknown in pre-Islamic times, during which this *dastan* is supposedly based.

54. *houri-faced:* as beautiful as a *houri* of Heaven.

55. *ossifrage:* also known as osprey. A large harmless hawk that is dark brown above and pure white below.

56. *tercelets:* male falcons (one-third smaller than the females).

57. *stannels:* a kind of kestrel.

58. *Fountain of Life:* also Spring of Life or Water of Life. According to Islamic legend, a subterranean body of water that can revive the dead and make those who drink of it immortal.

59. buzi: no translation available.

60. Shirazi, kavak: no translations available.

61. paseen, ghora-roz: no translations available.

62. *Seven Climes: (Haft Aqlim)* an approach used by classical Islamic geographers to divide the Earth into the Greek system of zones or climes.

63. bhands...kalanots: *Bhand* is a name given to any jester, buffoon, actor, mime, mimic, or strolling player; *bhagat* is a Hindu artist who dances or performs for entertainment; *kathak* is a singer, bard, or dancing boy; *kashmiri* here means a dancing boy; *qawwal* is a singer-musician; *dharis* are singers among the retinue of nobility who walk before their entourages chanting praises; *kalanot* is a class of singers or musicians.

64. *astrolabe:* an instrument for observing the positions of celestial bodies. In old times the armillary sphere was used.

65. ayyars: tricksters or spies. In the *dastan* the word *ayyar* is mostly used with Amar's name. Amar is an *ayyar,* a most cunning fellow unmatched in slyness. While his resourcefulness derives in part from divine gifts, his slyness and craftiness are native.

66. *the prince Naushervan:* The name *Naushervan* is constructed from the composition of the two words *nosh,* meaning "drinking," and *ravan,* meaning "flowing," used in the context of the water spring.

67. *Prince of the Heavens:* allusion to the king, who, being God's vice-regent, has dominion over all creation under the divine authority.

68. *dulcimer:* a type of stringed instrument, harp, or psaltery played by hand without making use of any plectrum or bow.

69. *Seven Concentric Circles:* Classical Islamic geographers divided the Earth into the Persian system of seven concentric circles with the western Iranian region of Iraq as the cynosure, where the Sassanid Empire had its capital.

70. delivered woman: The word in the Urdu text is *zaccha,* meaning a woman who has recently given birth. She retains the status of *zaccha* until the forti-

eth day after her delivery, after which her confinement ends and she is permitted to step out of the house. It is considered an auspicious moment because it signifies the woman's safe deliverance from all postpartum ailments.

71. Shab-e Baraat: the fourteenth night of the Islamic calendar month *Sha'ban,* which is considered holy by Muslims. Here the term is used with *riayat-e lafzi* to also connote "the night of the wedding procession," *shab* meaning "night" and *baraat* "wedding procession."

72. *chain:* a chain hung outside his court by Emperor Naushervan, which allowed petitioners a direct and personal audience with him.

73. *Kaaba:* the holy shrine in Mecca toward which all Muslims turn when saying their prayers.

74. *Mount Qaf: (Koh Qaf)* according to Islamic legend, the huge mountain in the middle of which the Earth is sunk, as a night light is placed in a cup. It binds the horizon on all sides. Its foundation is the emerald *Sakhrat,* the reflection of which gives the azure hue to the sky.

75. *collyrium of Suleiman: (Surma-e Suleimani)* according to legend, a powder that makes one able to see the hidden treasures of the Earth. The collyrium of Suleiman in the *dastan,* however, makes one see jinns, *devs, peris,* etc., who otherwise remain invisible to the human eye.

76. *carbuncles:* any of several red precious stones such as the ruby.

77. *lost Yusuf:* A parallel is drawn between Yaqub (Jacob) being reunited with his son Yusuf (Joseph) and Khvaja Abdul Muttalib with his son Hamza.

78. *Throne of Kaikaus:* The name of the mighty Persian emperor Kaikaus is invoked here to suggest the grandeur of Emperor Naushervan's court and his throne. See also notes 115 and 126.

79. *Bismillah:* (literal meaning, "in the name of Allah") the festivities observed among Muslims on a child's first commencing studies.

80. *aleph is upright:* a play on words, alluding to the straight vertical form of the letter aleph.

81. *its numeric value is one:* arrangement of the Arabic alphabet called *abjad,* according to the numeral value of the letters from one to a thousand. According to this scheme, aleph, the first letter of the alphabet, has a numeric value of one.

82. fateha: a prayer read on an offering. Generally the first chapter of the Quran, *Sura Fateha,* also known as the Exordium, is read on offerings. See also notes 52 and 189.

83. *benison:* the divine recompense for a good deed.

84. *Shimla:* a turban.

85. peras: sweetmeats made of curds.

86. *"You are so fluent... this language."* This is one of those untranslatable passages with a simultaneous play on sound and words. *Ra* is an inseparable particle added to Persian nouns, generally serving to denote the accusative and dative. The mulla addresses Amar accusingly as *Aray Amar!* (O Amar!). Amar tells his teacher that he is becoming abusive and that he would also retort by uttering *laam kaaf* (i.e., abusive speech), the initials of *laanat* "curse" and *karahat* "abomination."

87. tola: a traditional Indian unit of mass, now standardized as 11.66 grams.
88. *burqa:* a robelike veil for the whole body, which also covers the head, supplied with an opening for the eyes.
89. khagina: a dish similar to an omelet but containing more spices, and sometimes mince as well.
90. shir-maals: kind of bread made of flour kneaded with milk and sugar.
91. nihari: a kind of meat curry or mulligatawny traditionally prepared for breakfast.
92. Verse is by Nasikh.
93. *five vices:* The five defects in a horse as described in the sharia are: *hashri,* a stallion who is violent and impetuous with the mare; *sitara-peshani,* having a star on the forehead; *kamari,* a horse weak in the loins; *shab-kur,* having night blindness, or suffering from a disease known as *rataundhia;* and *kuhan-lang,* being unable to budge from its spot.
94. *sharia:* the code of social life modeled on the teachings and traditions of the Prophet Muhammad.
95. Sahib-e Hal Ata: This phrase signifies Ali, the fourth caliph of Islam. Chapter 76 of the Quran, called *Dahr,* or *Insan,* begins with this phrase. It means "has there not passed, or been?" Verse 8 of this sura, or chapter, speaks of people who themselves go hungry but feed others. Some interpreters of the Quran say that this verse refers to Ali, and it is presumed that the whole sura is about Ali in some way. Since the sura starts with *hal ata,* Ali is occasionally described as the *sahib,* or the *tajdar,* of *hal ata.* For this information I am indebted to Shamsur Rahman Faruqi.
96. *Second of the Five Holies:* The Five Holies are usually listed as: Muhammad, first; Fatima, second; Ali, third; Hasan, fourth; and Husain, fifth. However, in this instance, Ali is listed as the second.
97. *a seven-year-old boy:* The *dastan* follows the classical tradition of heroes acquiring prodigious strength at a very young age.
98. *Erebus of Hell:* the darkest region of Hell.
99. *thousands... lying murdered:* The exaggeration in numbers is sometimes used in the *dastan* to emphasize some aspect of the scene—in this case, the sheer havoc caused by Hamza and his companions.
100. *amir:* a commander or leader. In this book this title is used for Hamza, the hero of the story.
101. Verse is by Nasikh.
102. In this instance Abdullah Bilgrami, one of the authors of the book, is incorporating his own poetry into the narrative as its narrator. In the *dastan* tradition such licenses are an accepted practice.
103. vasokht *style:* a form of Urdu poetry, conventionally defined as one in which the lover asserts his pride and self-regard. However, the verses in question do not strictly adhere to this definition.
104. bid for a Yusuf: an allusion to the time when Joseph of Canaan was acquired by Potiphar's wife, Zulaikha, as a slave and all the tribulations that she underwent on account of her passion for him.

105. To angels: an allusion to the fallen angels Harut and Marut. Having severely censured mankind before the throne of God, Harut and Marut were sent down to Earth in human form to judge the temptations to which man is subjected. They could not withstand them. They were seduced by women and committed every kind of iniquity, for which they were suspended by their feet in a well in Babylon, where they are to remain in great torment until the Day of Judgment.

106. *horse-shinty: (chogan)* an eastern game of which polo is the modern form.

107. rajaz *meter:* a meter of Arabic poetry in which poems detailing deeds of valor are composed.

108. *Khatti spear:* a spear made at Khatt in Arabia.

109. *Hashimi blood:* an allusion to Amir Hamza's noble bloodline. See also notes 14 (Book Two) and 21 (Book Three).

110. Verse is by Saadi.

111. Verse is by Khaqani, a Persian poet (ca. 1120–1190 C.E.).

112. *we seek God's refuge from such wickedness!:* This exclamation is part of the narrator's speech. While narrating the conversation between Hashsham and his counselors, the narrator, who is a Muslim, seeks God's protection from the vile prospect of razing the Kaaba, or the House of God, which is held in supreme esteem by Muslims.

113. *winding-sheet:* the piece of cloth in which Muslims are wrapped for burial.

114. *ringdove perched on a cypress branch:* The poets traditionally considered the ringdove a lover of the cypress tree. The event suggests the image of a lover (ringdove) coming to his beloved (cypress tree) in distress. It is also significant that the ringdove as a citizen in Naushervan's land has come to seek redress at the emperor's court.

115. *court of Jamshed:* An ancient king of Persia, Jamshed (often confused in legends with Alexander and King Solomon) is invoked here to suggest the grandeur of Emperor Naushervan's court. See also notes 78 and 126.

116. *Abul-Ala:* This is one of the titles used by Amir Hamza.

117. *Maghrebi wrestling:* The Greek style of wrestling is most likely intended by this reference.

118. *Mehtar:* a commander.

119. tomans: old Persian coins.

120. *tent of the prophet Danyal:* A tent on which magic had no effect.

121. aafat-band: The term *aafat-band* could perhaps be interpreted as a crotch-guard that protects one's private parts by securing them against perils (*aafat* means "peril" or "scourge"; *band* means "a guard" or "a protection.")

122. *aigrette and fillet:* An aigrette is a spray of feathers or gems often worn in a headdress. A fillet is a narrow strip of ornamental material for a headdress.

123. *theriaca:* an antidote for poison.

124. hava-mohra: some kind of conch shell.

125. *six high-key notes … improvisation:* The translations of these musical terms are at best approximate. (For the original, see Abdullah Bilgrami, *Dastan-e Amir Hamza,* 1871, p. 110, line 8.)

126. *Throne of Kai-Khusrau:* The name of the mighty Persian emperor Kai Khus-
    rau (King Cyrus) is invoked here to suggest the grandeur of Emperor
    Naushervan's court and his throne. See also notes 78 and 115.

127. *Turan:* the ancient Iranian name for Central Asia, literally meaning "the
    land of the Tur." According to legend, the nomadic tribes who inhabited
    these lands were ruled by Tur, who was the emperor Faridun's elder son.

128. *Rustam's Throne:* The most celebrated champion of the Persian court occu-
    pies the traditional seat of Rustam, the ancient warrior and hero of the
    Shahnamah. This seat has been given to Gustham bin Ashk Zarrin Kafsh in
    view of his might and valor. It is this chair that Hamza occupies in
    Gustham's absence when Naushervan offers him a seat of his choice in his
    court.

129. farsangs: ancient Persian units of distance, which usually corresponded to
    approximately 5.6 kilometers.

130. *auxiliaries:* The word used in the text is *tilanga,* a term specifically used for a
    foot soldier enrolled in the British Indian army and based in the town of
    Tilangana. Later this term became the generic name for all foot soldiers in
    the British Indian army.

131. do-tara: a stringed instrument with two wires. Here and on p. 157, Amar is
    seen playing the *do-tara* when the instrument will be bestowed upon him
    much later. See the Translator's Preface for explanation of these apparent
    inconsistencies. See also note 192.

132. ragay: a kind of armor worn on the thighs.

133. *pipe of seven joints:* a reed pipe of seven segments that Amar uses as a wind
    instrument and as a device for blowing drugs into people's noses to render
    them unconscious.

134. Verse is by Sabir.

135. momiyai: the name of a medicinal substance found in the mountains and
    considered curative for cuts and wounds. Some people mistakenly believe
    that it is made from human blood.

136. Verse is by Nasikh.

137. Verse is by Nasikh.

138. ambarcha: a neck ornament that has a cavity for storing amber.

139. Verse is by Nasikh.

140. *spikenard:* The spikenard plant is often compared to the locks of a mistress
    in the Persian poetic tradition, just as the rose is compared to the beloved's
    face.

141. *katan:* a variety of linen that is so fine that some people say it is rent by ex-
    posure to moonlight. Therefore, it is represented in the Persian and Urdu
    poetic traditions as being enamored of the moon.

142. *missi-tinged:* Missi is a powder, chiefly composed of yellow myrobalan, gall-
    nut, iron filings, vitriol, and other ingredients, that women used for color-
    ing their teeth.

143. Verse is by Nawab Bahadur Zaki, a lesser-known Urdu poet of India.

144. Chahal-kunji: a prayer in which the Arabic letter *kaaf* occurs forty times. In

this instance, the prayer was engraved or written on a bowl so that any liquid poured into that bowl would become consecrated upon coming into contact with it.

145. Ayat al-Kursi: a passage in the Quran that is believed to ward off calamity when recited by or read over a person.

146. Naad-e Ali: a prayer beginning with the words *naad-e Ali,* which is engraved on silver or on stones and hung as charms around the necks of children.

147. Verse is by Shapur, a Persian poet.

148. *Harut and Marut:* See note 105.

149. *The knife...citron:* an allusion to an episode in the Quran (12:31). When Potiphar's wife, Zulaikha, heard the gossips say that she desired her page, Yusuf (Joseph), she prepared a banquet for them and gave each woman a knife and a citron, and asked Yusuf to appear before them. When he came out the women were so struck by his beauty that they cut their hands instead of the citrons.

150. *sarapa:* a grouping of verses in which a poet elaborately details the corporeal beauty of his female beloved.

151. *Musa's miraculous White Hand: (Yad-e Baiza)* one of the miracles performed by Musa (Moses). He put his hand under his armpit, and when he took it out it shone with great resplendence.

152. *The partridge...gait:* The partridge dove is famous in Persian and Urdu poetry for the beauty of its gait.

153. *chhalawa:* According to popular belief, the *chhalawa* is a demon that appears in the shape of an infant and can travel at breathtaking pace. Here the allusion is made facetiously.

154. Verse is by Hafiz, a celebrated Persian poet (ca. 1320–1390 C.E.).

155. *Sahibqiran:* Lord of the Auspicious Planetary Conjunction. Someone born under the conjunction of Jupiter and Venus was given this title. Jupiter and Venus were thought to be benevolent planets, and their conjunction was considered most fortunate. This epithet is also applied to a monarch who has ruled for forty years. In this book the title is used exclusively for Amir Hamza.

156. Verse is by Dost Ali Khalil, a lesser-known Urdu poet of India.

157. Verse is by Nasikh.

158. Verse is by Nasikh.

159. Verse is by Sehr (pen name), a lesser-known Urdu poet of India.

160. Verse is by Nasikh.

161. *simurgh:* a legendary bird.

162. *moon's partridge dove:* See note 152.

163. Verse is by Nasikh.

164. Verse is by Nasikh.

165. Verse (*ghazal*) is by Aman Ali Khan Ghalib Lakhnavi, whose 1855 version of the *dastan* was the basis of Abdullah Bilgrami's emended *Dastan-e Amir Hamza.* This *ghazal* is found on p. 148 of the Bilgrami version and pp. 94–95 of Ghalib Lakhnavi's version.

166. Verse is by Nasikh.

167. *a bezel for the signet of love:* illegible text (Abdullah Bilgrami, *Dastan-e Amir Hamza,* 1871, p. 148, last line).

168. *the mighty Suleiman:* The poverty and weakness of the ant is proverbial. The allusion is to the legendary encounter between the mighty King Suleiman and the King of the Ants.

169. *Venus-like:* According to legend, the woman the angels Harut and Marut fell in love with was named Zehra (Venus). There is a play on words here with *zehra* and *zehra-shumail* (meaning "those of Venus-like charms").

170. *Moon of Canaan: (Mah-e Kan'an)* the title for Yusuf, whose beauty is proverbial.

171. Verse is by Mir Hasan Khan Abad, a lesser-known Urdu poet of India.

172. *seven adornments: (Har-haft)* the seven traditional cosmetic treatments used by women were privet, woad, rouge, ceruse, antimony, gold leaf, and civet.

173. *like Khizr approaching... without:* allusion to the fulfillment of a desire even before it is uttered. Khizr traditionally plays the role of a guide for lost travelers.

174. Verse is by Sabir.

175. Verse is by Nasikh.

176. chor mahtabs: a kind of torch that creates a silvery luminance when lit.

177. Verse is by Sabir.

178. Verse is by the celebrated Urdu poet Asadullah Khan Ghalib (1796–1869 C.E.), pen name Ghalib.

179. *Khusrau:* a title used for a majestic king. In this book it is used for Landhoor bin Saadan, unless accompanied by another name.

180. gilauris: a large preparations of the areca nut seasoned with spices and *chunam* and enveloped in leaves of the betel palm.

181. purdah: the area called *zenana,* segregated for the use of women where only their close blood relatives are allowed to enter. The area segregated for the use of men is called the *mardana.*

182. *Shah Mohra:* a precious stone, said to be found in a serpent's mouth or a dragon's head, that is reputed to have curative properties.

183. *salve of Daud: (Marham-e Daudi)* a legendary ointment that is known for its miraculous healing properties.

184. Shab-e Yalda: the longest night of winter.

185. *the Deluge:* the deluge of Noah.

186. *Skipper of the Vessel of Oneness:* an allusion to God's unified nature.

187. *minim:* the smallest or least possible part or particle.

188. *boars: (mendha)* the swells of the tide. Here the word is used in its literal meaning.

189. *"over which fateha has been said":* to cause blessings to be invoked upon a dead relative. This is done by having the opening chapter of the Quran, the *Sura Fateha* or the Exordium, read over the deceased for forty days after his death, and by distributing alms and food. See also notes 52 and 82.

190. dev-jama: a garment of animal skin with the hairy part outside. Also refers to a lion's skin in which the warriors clothed themselves.

191. zambil: Amar's *zambil* is perhaps based on *Zambil-e Suleiman,* a wallet or leather bag in Suleiman's possession which produced anything he wished for. (It was also called *Amban-e Suleiman.*) In the Turkish version told by Behçet Mahir we find that Amar's pouch was made from the skin of the sheep that Prophet Ibrahim had sacrificed to Allah instead of his son. Thus that sheepskin had been waiting there for Amar since the time of Prophet Ibrahim.

192. do-tara: See note 131.

193. *"You shall run ... tire":* It is interesting to note that earlier Khizr also gave the same miracle to Amar. In the Turkish version of Behçet Mahir, Amar could run as fast as the wind because he did not have any kneecaps. Also in this version, Izrail, the Angel of Death, was unable to catch him and take his soul because Amar ran faster than Izrail could fly. When Izrail asked Allah's advice, the Almighty God told him to place a golden pickax and a silver shovel in a newly dug grave and to catch Amar when his greed for the gold and silver lured him there. Izrail acted on Allah's advice and successfully captured Amar's soul.

194. lezam: an exercise aid, traditionally used in India, built in the shape of a bow with an iron chain instead of a string.

195. mithcals: measures of weight.

196. *Eid:* The day to celebrate the end of fasting commemorated by Muslims at the end of the month of Ramazan of the Islamic calendar.

197. *perfume of good fortune: (Itr-e suhag)* a perfume rubbed on both the bride and the bridegroom, thought to bring good luck to newlyweds. In this instance it symbolizes the fighter's preparedness to embrace the bride of martyrdom in battle.

198. *"an offering of a banner":* an offering made by erecting a small flag bearing the saint's name at his mausoleum.

199. *Pir Jalilan:* the name of a saint or a place named after him.

200. *Pir Bhuchri's halva:* an offering of halva made to Pir Bhuchri, the priest of transvestites, on the occasion of the admission of a novice to his society. According to popular legend, anyone who eats the halva yields himself to joining their ranks.

201. *syce:* a groom or a stable keeper.

202. sitar: a stringed musical instrument.

203. augi: an ornamental edging sewn on finely crafted country shoes, which was a specialty of Delhi.

204. *twelve musical modes ... improvisation:* As stated in note 125, the translation of musical terms is at best approximate (Abdullah Bilgrami, *Dastan-e Amir Hamza,* 1871, p. 206, lines 13–14).

205. *Sikander's rampart: (Sadd-e Sikander)* according to legend, a rampart built by Alexander the Bicornous to hold back Gog and Magog.

206. Koh-e Besutoon: the great mountain through which Farhad, the legendary lover of Shirin, had to cut a channel as a precondition for winning his beloved.

207. *Bardwani:* of or pertaining to Bardwan, a city in Bengal.

208. raga: one of the traditional patterns of Indian music.

209. *perfumed goat leather: (adim)* a beautiful tanned leather from Yemen.

210. *the day of Eid ... the night of Shab-e Baraat:* See notes 71 and 196.

211. gao-dida: a leavened bread made in the shape of an ox's eye.

212. qorma: a kind of curry made with meat.

213. pulao: a rice dish made with meat and aromatic spices.

214. *Iraq:* This is not the modern-day Iraq. Both Mesopotamia and a region of western Iran were called Iraq in ancient times.

215. *old woman of Ctesiphon:* According to legend, an old woman who lived near Naushervan's palace whose cooking wafted smoke into the emperor's palace. Naushervan offered to give her another place to live but she refused, and he did not use coercion to have her moved despite his discomfort due to the smoke.

216. Verse is by Mir Hasan.

217. *Gueber:* a derogatory term used for Zoroastrians.

218. noshidaru: a confection that is supposed to be a sovereign antidote against all kinds of maladies.

219. "mandwa, kodon": *Mandwa* is a variety of low-quality grain or grain-bearing grass found in alluvial lands. It is the common name for *Eleusine coracana, Cynosurus coracanus,* and *Panicum frumentaceum. Kodon* is a kind of hard grain, and is the common name for *Paspalum scrobiculatum, Paspalum kora,* and *Panicum milliaceum.*

220. *chain of justice:* See note 72.

221. *"Your Honor ... I will not pay":* a conversation conducted in an Indian regional dialect (Abdullah Bilgrami, *Dastan-e Amir Hamza,* 1871, p. 235, lines 8–13, 15–16, 21–23).

222. mashas: traditional units of weight used in India, approximately equivalent to one gram.

223. *Greek fire:* an incendiary composition used by the Byzantine Greeks in warfare that burst into flame on wetting.

224. *King of the Four Climes:* an allusion to the sun, which shines on the four corners of the globe.

225. maiyoon: a ceremony of Indian Muslims in which a few days before the wedding the bride is sent into seclusion and no man is allowed to approach her, so her thoughts may become focused on her bridegroom.

226. *One hundred and seventy-five gods:* The *dastan* mixes social and cultural references, which explains the presence of Brahmins in a Zoroastrian funeral procession.

227. *squib:* a firecracker in which the powder burns with a fizz.

228. *cypress chandelier:* a light fixture made in the shape of the cypress tree and used at assemblies and gatherings.

229. *Anno Hegirae ... Anno Domini: Anno Hegirae* is used to indicate the time from the first year of the Muslim calendar (622 C.E.); *Anno Domini* is used to indicate the time from the birth of Jesus of Nazareth.

BOOK TWO

1. *circling seven times around...sacrifice for Amir's:* a ritual practiced in India whereby one would circle seven times around a loved one, to attract all the ills and misfortunes affecting the loved one on oneself, to the extent of pledging one's own life to ward off death from the other.

2. *rubbed with oil:* the ceremony of *tel charhana* or *tel pan karna.* This ritual calls for the head, shoulders, hands, and feet of both the bride and the bridegroom to be anointed with oil and turmeric paste.

3. *henna was applied... hands:* The *henna-bandi* is a ceremony that Muslims from the Indian subcontinent hold a day before a wedding, in which women from the bridegroom's household visit the bride's house with salvers of henna, which are decorated with four burning candles.

4. sarod *and the* arghanun: A *sarod* is a stringed musical instrument similar to the lute. The *arghanun* is a musical instrument whose invention is attributed to Plato. It has multiple pipes, which play when a key is pressed.

5. *Musa himself... no effect on him:* an allusion to the prophet Musa (Moses) trying to preach the True Faith to the pharaoh without success. The allusion is employed in connection with the king of Egypt, who like the pharaoh ruled over the land of Egypt.

6. *incarcerated Yusuf:* an allusion to the incarceration of Yusuf (Joseph) in a well by his brothers.

7. *avis of Buzurjmehr's reason flew away:* In the Indo-Persian literary tradition, reason is likened to an avis or bird. The avis of reason is said to have flown away from someone who is so utterly confounded by an event that he is rendered helpless and sees no remedy to his predicament. Compare note 9.

8. *pole of* uqubain: *(chob-e uqabain)* a kind of torture to which Hamza is subjected. This episode is described in Book Four.

9. *avis of Naushervan's soul:* In the Indo-Persian literary tradition the soul is likened to an avis or bird. When the corporeal self dies the soul flies away. A state of extreme fear or agitation is said to cause the soul to begin fluttering inside the cage of the corporeal self. In this instance, however, Amar Ayyar makes a wordplay on the allegory by threatening to pluck the avis of Naushervan's soul. Compare note 7.

10. *recounted by Amar Ayyar:* Amar Ayyar intrudes here as a narrative voice. In the *dastan* tradition, it is not an unusual practice for a character to be quoted as a narrator of an event.

11. *The westbound bird:* an allusion to the sun, for its movement from east to west in the sky.

12. asr *prayers:* the third set of prayers said by Muslims daily, occurring in late afternoon or early evening.

13. maghreb *prayers:* the fourth set of prayers said by Muslims daily, occurring after sunset.

14. *House of Hashim:* the ancestral line of Prophet Muhammad and Amir Hamza,

which is traced from Hamza's grandfather, Hashim. See also note 109, Book One.

15. shahi: a coin of indeterminate value.

16. paratha: a flatbread panfried in butter or oil.

17. *Yezid:* The son of Muawiyah, who claimed the mantle of caliph and at whose orders Muhammad's grandson Husain and his family were put to death at Karbala.

18. *It is related . . . to chastise him:* The writer must have consulted other texts and known other traditions of the *dastan* of Amir Hamza. Here he mentions one of them.

19. *Farkhar:* a city known for the beauty of its inhabitants.

20. *Potentate of the First Heaven:* an allusion to the moon. In Islamic mythology the skies were divided into regions named first heaven, et cetera.

21. *who loses his betel satchel:* Probably from some obscure betting ritual among men in which the loser surrenders the pouch in which he carries his betel nuts.

22. *salve of Suleiman:* The invention of this salve is attributed to Prophet Suleiman (Solomon); it is supposed to have miraculous healing properties. See also note 183, Book One.

23. dastan: an epic, romance, adventure, or story. It is an oral narrative form.

24. *Kashani velvet:* a kind of fine velvet produced in Kashan, in the province of Isfahan, Iran.

25. zuhr *prayers:* the second set of prayers said by Muslims daily, occurring in the afternoon.

26. *catechu, and kohl:* Catechu is an astringent. It is the extract of *Acacia catechu*, produced by boiling the wood in water and evaporating the resulting brew; kohl is a dark gray ore of lead usually used to outline the eyes.

27. shabchiragh: a ruby reputed to glow like a lamp in the dark of night.

28. char-kovay: a kind of exotic bird.

29. chaha: a species of quail that appears in summer.

30. chanaks: a species of quail that appears in summer.

31. *Samsam, Qumqam, Aqrab-e Suleimani, and Zul-Hajam:* names of legendary swords that belonged to Prophet Suleiman.

32. *buried Khvaja Nihal alive:* Khvaja Nihal dies here, but the text shows him alive again in Book Three.

33. *the forty saints:* According to popular belief of Muslims of the Indian subcontinent, the forty unknown saints in their continued presence are the reason the world is not destroyed by the wrath of God.

34. *"a mere fakir":* A fakir is a mendicant. The term is also used for someone who has renounced the world.

35. *palanquin:* a conveyance for the transport of one person that consists of an enclosed litter with four projecting poles, which allow it to be carried on the shoulders of bearers.

36. *"make a living!":* The grass cutter's speech is in a regional Indian dialect.

37. *Maghrebi language:* possibly a reference to one of the many African languages.

38. *Naqabdar:* literally, "the veiled one."

39. ubtan: a cosmetic for the protection, nourishment, and beautification of the skin.

40. *crocodile of the soul-extracting sword:* The narrator has used a mixed metaphor here, likening the sword's function to the crocodile, which kills, and the Angel of Death, who extracts souls.

41. *accursed as her name:* Maloona is from *malaoon,* meaning "damned."

42. *Kamru's magic:* refers to the arts of the district of Kamrup, which was situated between Bengal and Khota, famed for its magicians.

43. tilism: The word as used here means an enchantment or an enchanted region. It also refers to a device or a combination of devices that have magical attributes.

44. *Daughters of the Deceased: (banat a'n-na'sh)* the constellations Ursa Major and Ursa Minor, the Greater and Lesser Bear, which consist of seven stars, four of which are thought to resemble a *na'sh,* or corpse, and the remaining three to be the *banat,* or daughters, walking in front of it.

45. *Koh-e Besutoon:* In the earlier instance, the term was used to describe the great mountain through which Farhad, the legendary lover of Shirin, had to cut a channel as a condition to winning his beloved. In this case, it is a fixture of Qaf. See note 206 (Book One).

46. *a perfumed orange at Amir's breast:* Derived from the Persian term *turanj zadan,* this refers to a Persian marriage custom in which the bride and the bridegroom, upon entering the latter's house, throw an orange, generally made of gold, back and forth to each other.

47. *the Peacock Throne:* a relic from Mughal India, used in the *dastan* as a furnishing for the Court of Suleiman.

48. zangala: some type of weapon; no definition or translation is available.

49. *gave up the ghost with just one cry:* This is the first time we see Sufaid Dev being killed. However, because of multiple *dastan* traditions intervening in the text, he appears alive on two subsequent occasions, and is killed each time. See note 12 (Book Three) and note 46 (Book Four).

50. *the crocodile of death:* a metaphor for death on the battlefield, a bloody death.

51. *Court of Indar:* In Indian mythology Indar is the king of the gods and the regent of the visible heavens. The Court of Indar connotes a place of amusement and pleasure.

52. *"ass of the Dajjal":* According to popular belief, Dajjal, the equivalent of the Antichrist in Arab mythology, will appear riding an ass.

53. "Ishq-Allah": a salutation, meaning "love of God," of the sect of fakirs called *Azad* or *Be-Nawa.* The traditional reply to this salutation is *"Madad-Allah,"* which means "succor of God." See also note 55.

54. *cowries' worth:* Cowry shells were used as the smallest units of currency in the Indian subcontinent until the early twentieth century.

55. *Azad fakir:* An *Azad* is a straight mark from the top of the nose to the forehead made by a cast of fakirs called the *Azads* or the *Be-Nawa,* who act freely and seldom observe the proscriptions of the sharia law. The mark symbolizes the oneness of God. See also note 53.

56. seli: a string made of hair, dark thread, or silk and worn by dervishes.

57. *Shidai Qalandar:* a dervish who is loyal in his love.

58. *Saudai Qalandar:* a dervish who is disloyal in his love.

59. *shamed the empyrean:* In ancient cosmology, the empyrean is the highest heaven, described as a sphere of fire or light.

60. *Tooba:* a tree that grows in Paradise. It is alluded to in the Quran (13: 29).

61. *snake stick:* the folk name of the wood *Staphylea emodit,* whose spotted bark resembles a snakeskin. It is believed that by touching it a prisoner could become free of his fetters. It is also known to keep away snakes. Known as *nag-daun* in the Indian subcontinent.

62. *Badi-ul-Mulk:* Badi-ul-Mulk never appears in this story. See A Note on the Text.

BOOK THREE

1. *with unbraided hair:* Loosened, unbraided hair is a gesture of humility and submission that the supplicant employs while soliciting divine help.

2. *Lake Kausar:* according to the Quran, the name of a lake in Paradise.

3. *cavesson:* a noseband made of metal or other hard material, usually used to lead camels.

4. *Zandan-e Suleimani:* a prison built by Prophet Suleiman.

5. *signet of Suleiman:* also known as the Seal of Suleiman. The signet worn by Prophet Suleiman. It is said that because this ring had the Most Great Name inscribed on it the jinns obeyed the prophet.

6. *"fated to eat and drink":* According to popular Islamic belief, every drop of water and every morsel of food is marked with the name of the person who will receive it.

7. *color of Mars:* Red is the color most often associated with the planet Mars. As Mars is also the God of War, wearing red clothes signifies the sanguinary mood of the wearer.

8. *a giant crane:* the species of gigantic crane *Ardea argala,* known as "the bone swallower."

9. nanbai: a baker of breads who used a traditional oven dug in the ground.

10. *The Seven Enchanted Seas of Suleiman:* The names or descriptions of two of these seas are not given in the book. Others are the magnetic sea and the seas of clay, mercury, blood, and fire.

11. *Some transcribers . . . a false tradition:* Here two versions of the event are mentioned as described by the *dastan* narrators of the time: In one Hamza divorces Aasman Peri and in the other he does not. It is not specified in this passage which one is chosen by the author of this narrative. We find out later that it was the one in which Hamza divorced Aasman Peri. See note 16 below.

12. *He killed him . . . draw another breath:* In this passage Sufaid Dev dies at Landhoor's hands, but in Book Four we discover he is alive; he is ultimately killed by Amir Hamza. See note 49 (Book Two).

13. *these lines composed by this narrator:* This is a case in which the author of the book recites verses of his own composition to explain what a character in the *dastan* said. Such intervention of the present reality in a narrative supposedly describing an event from the distant past was part of the oral narrative tradition of the *dastan.* Compare note 165, Book One.

14. *Khvaja Nihal:* See note 32, Book Two. Earlier, Amar was shown to have killed Khvaja Nihal. In this passage we see Khvaja Nihal alive. This disparity exists, perhaps, because of the various, often conflicting, narrative traditions of the *Dastan-e Amir Hamza* used by the author to compose his own version. See also A Note on the Text.

15. *Amir touched his earlobes:* a gesture used in South Asia to express shock or revulsion to a proposition or action proscribed by the religious or social code of conduct.

16. *Because Amir had divorced:* See note 11 above. In this passage we finally learn which tradition the narrator chose to build his story. See also A Note on the Text.

17. *The stories of these princes ... will be narrated in their turn:* These stories are not given in this book. The author alludes here to the oral narrative of the Bala-Bakhtar episode in the *Dastan-e Amir Hamza.* In 1892, the Naval Kishore Press published a version of the *Bala-Bakhtar* written by Tasadduq Husain as the fifth volume of the 46-volume *Dastan-e Amir Hamza.* See note 62 (Book Two).

18. *Shish-Mahal:* Mughal architectural term for a room decorated with mirror mosaics. The term can also be described as "glass palace."

19. *the eternal decree of the Divine Essence:* This refers to one Islamic belief which holds that all events that have occurred or will occur are predestined and recorded in the divine essence since eternity.

20. *gave up his life and fell dead:* In this passage Samandun Hazar-Dast Dev dies, but in Book Four we discover he is alive and is ultimately killed by Amir Hamza in similar circumstances.

21. *"his Hashimi vein":* Amir Hamza had a prominent vein on his forehead that was a feature of his Hashimi ancestry. See also note 109 to Book One.

22. *as wise as his name:* The word *aqil* means "prudent and wise."

23. *"O qalandar!":* The word *qalandar* is used for a dervish or mendicant.

BOOK FOUR

1. *the cymbal of Afrasiyab ... the fife of Jamshed:* The names of musical instruments of legendary kings are invoked here to describe the powerful call to arms sounded in Amir Hamza's camp.

2. *cloth saddles: (char-jama)* a kind of saddle made of cloth that lacks a pommel.

3. *Almighty Victor:* an allusion to God.

4. *"tabla or sarangi":* A tabla is an Indian musical instrument. It is a small drum or pair of drums tuned to different pitches and played with the hands. A *sarangi* is an Indian musical instrument that has a violin-like sound.

5. *Emperor of the Fourth Heaven:* an allusion to the sun.

6. *Angel of Death:* an allusion to the presence of death on the eve of the battle.

7. *Extractor of Souls:* an allusion to the angel Izrail, who, according to Islamic belief, is assigned the task of extracting human souls from their bodies at the time of their death.

8. *pavilion of Jamshed:* The name of Jamshed, an ancient king of Persia, is often confused in legend with that of Prophet Suleiman. In this instance, the Pavilion of Jamshed is interchangeable with the Pavilion of Suleiman. See also note 9.

9. *Pavilion of Suleiman...Char-Bazar of Bilqis:* These are enchanted pavilions and tents, according to the *dastan*. They have more than one story, multiple chambers, and interconnecting passages or spaces.

10. *the Chapter of Light:* the twenty-fourth chapter of the Quran.

11. banat *and the* aarsi-mushaf: *Banat* is an Indian custom, also known as *baan*, in which the bride and the bridegroom are bathed three to eleven times before the wedding. *Aarsi-mushaf* is a wedding ceremony of South Asian Muslims in which the *aarsi* (mirror) is put between the bride and the bridegroom with the *mushaf* (Quran) open at the 112th sura, *Al-Ikhlas*. The bride keeps her eyes closed until her companions persuade the bridegroom to avow himself a slave of the bride.

12. *a precious pearl:* an allusion to the act of conception. Earlier in this passage the same imagery was used to describe the act of coition.

13. *lifted him up to his knee:* In the heroic literature from the *dastan* tradition, lifting an adversary above one's head is the ultimate test of strength. The one deemed the most powerful is he who cannot be lifted up from the ground at all. The inability to lift one's adversary above one's shoulder or waist is a sign of physical weakness.

14. *the executioner as his sacrifice:* The gesture of making a circle in the air above one's head while holding alms signifies that one is offering those alms as a sacrifice for one's well-being. This passage alludes to this gesture except that it is an executioner who is caught in Amir Hamza's hands.

15. *Kohi:* also Kohistani. A denizen of Kohistan.

16. *Israfil:* According to Islamic belief, Angel Israfil will usher in the Day of Judgment by blowing on his trumpet.

17. *the war between Sikander and Dara:* an allusion to the encounter between King Darius III of Persia and Alexander of Macedon.

18. *onager:* a wild ass.

19. Fajar *prayers:* the first set of prayers said by Muslims in the morning.

20. *Naheed Maryam:* The *dastan* mistakenly has "Mehr-Nigar" here.

21. *Taking Muqbil for Amir Hamza:* In the *dastan* tradition Muqbil and Amir Hamza share a likeness of features.

22. *his horse and his slave, Muqbil:* Muqbil Vafadar's father, Basheer, was the slave of Hamza's father. By that relationship Muqbil is Hamza's slave. However, this fact is rarely mentioned in the *dastan* and Muqbil is treated as a distinguished companion of Amir Hamza.

23. *Ashqar broke his fetters:* Ashqar Devzad breaks his fetters by himself when aid arrives. Throughout the *dastan,* the champions of Amir Hamza's camp similarly are able to set themselves free when their friends arrive at their imprisonment to save them.

24. *"ant has grown wings":* It is a South Asian folk belief that an ant grows wings when its death approaches.

25. qadi: in Muslim culture, the person who reads the wedding sermon and solemnizes the nuptials.

26. *"the battle fought between Rustam and Sohrab":* an allusion to the fight between the legendary Persian champion Rustam and his son Sohrab in which Sohrab is killed, as his identity was not known to Rustam.

27. *Rustam-e Peel-Tan:* literally, "elephant-bodied Rustam." It should be noted that the word *peel-tan* connotes great physical strength and is a title reserved only for the greatest of champions. The title does not signify that the person is of an elephantine size.

28. *Sher-e Saf-Shikan:* the Rank-Destroying Lion.

29. *Book of Ibrahim:* the Holy Book that Prophet Ibrahim received from God.

30. Durfish Kaviani: the legendary standard of Kava, the smith of Isfahan, who defeated the usurper Zahhak and established Faridun on the throne of Persia.

31. *Mazandaran:* name of a region near Gilan.

32. *he returned to dust:* The death of Aadi Chob-Gardaan is announced here, but he is shown alive subsequently. See also note 34.

33. *put him to death as well:* The death of Bahram Chob-Gardaan is announced here, but he is shown alive subsequently. See also note 35.

34. *Aadi Chob-Gardaan came forward:* See note 32.

35. *Bahram Chob-Gardaan faced Amir:* See note 33.

36. *Samandun Hazar-Dast Dev had escaped Qaf:* In Book Three, Amir Hamza is shown to have killed Samandun Hazar-Dast Dev. Here the narrator recounts another tradition, according to which Samandun Hazar-Dast Dev escaped Qaf and the deadly encounter with Hamza. However, the manner in which Samandun Hazar-Dast Dev is subsequently killed in this passage is similar to the one in which he is killed in Book Three. See also note 20, Book Three.

37. *holy Khizr had identified:* In this passage it is Hamza who plugs the Fountain of Life. In Book Three, however, it was Khizr who stopped it, which resulted in Samandun Hazar-Dast Dev's death. See also note 36 above and note 20, Book Three.

38. *"O Shutarban . . . these rutting noises":* This is a play on Shutarban's name. *Shurtarban* means "camel driver."

39. *Trooper of the First Heaven:* an allusion to the moon. Compare note 20, Book Two.

40. *Emperor of the Fourth Heaven:* an allusion to the sun.

41. hareesa: a kind of stew made of crushed wheat boiled to a thick consistency, to which is added meat, butter, cinnamon, and aromatic herbs.

42. *the Last Prophet:* This is a reference to Muhammad bin Abdullah bin Abdul Muttalib, the Prophet of Islam (ca. 570–632 C.E.).

43. *Great Wall of Sikander:* according to legend, the wall built by Sikander the Bicornous to keep Gog and Magog from raiding population centers.

44. *Qaza-va-Qadar:* In this instance the term *Qaza-va-Qadar* is a geographical location. It should not be confused with the Islamic concept of predestination also described by this term.

45. *When Hurmuz ... on some pretext:* Some Zoroastrians interpret their religion as advocating the avoidance of pork and beef, and it is perhaps on account of this that Hurmuz avoids eating pork on this occasion.

46. *Sufaid Dev lives there:* In an earlier passage in Book Three, Sufaid Dev was killed at Landhoor's hands. See note 49 (Book Two) and note 12 (Book Three).

47. *filled with gunpowder:* The use of gunpowder in the times described by the *dastan* seems anachronistic. It should be noted that the *dastan* genre did not observe verisimilitude too strictly. The incorporation of contemporary reality in artistic creations was evident in the Indian visual arts of the time as well. Several illustrations of the *Hamzanama* (another name for the *Dastan-e Amir Hamza*) commissioned by the Mughal emperor Akbar in the mid-sixteenth century also depicted characters wielding and firing firearms.

48. *"I would leave Zulmat":* The reference to Zulmat (literally, "the Land of Darkness") is also found in the *Iskander-Nama* ("The Romance of Alexander"). However, in the *dastan,* Zulmat is often depicted as a land populated by sorcerers and magicians.

49. *he took out his gun:* See note 47.

50. Sura-e Jinn: the seventy-second chapter of the Quran, which mentions the jinns.

51. *this translator:* This is a reference to Ghalib Lakhnavi, the author of this version of the *Dastan-e Amir Hamza,* who called his work a translation. See also A Note on the Text.

About the Translator

MUSHARRAF ALI FAROOQI is an author and translator. He
has translated works by the contemporary Urdu poet Afzal
Ahmed Syed and is currently working on the Urdu Project
(www.urduproject.com), an online resource for the study of
the Urdu language and literature.

A NOTE ON THE TYPE

The text of this Modern Library edition
was set in a digitized version of Janson, a typeface that
dates from about 1690 and was cut by Nicholas Kis,
a Hungarian working in Amsterdam. The original matrices have
survived and are held by the Stempel foundry in Germany.
Hermann Zapf redesigned some of the weights and sizes for
Stempel, basing his revisions on the original design.

Modern Library is online at
www.modernlibrary.com

MODERN LIBRARY ONLINE IS YOUR GUIDE TO CLASSIC LITERATURE ON THE WEB

THE MODERN LIBRARY E-NEWSLETTER

Our free e-mail newsletter is sent to subscribers, and features sample chapters, interviews with and essays by our authors, upcoming books, special promotions, announcements, and news. To subscribe to the Modern Library e-newsletter, visit **www.modernlibrary.com**

THE MODERN LIBRARY WEBSITE

Check out the Modern Library website at
www.modernlibrary.com for:

- The Modern Library e-newsletter
- A list of our current and upcoming titles and series
- Reading Group Guides and exclusive author spotlights
- Special features with information on the classics and other paperback series
- Excerpts from new releases and other titles
- A list of our e-books and information on where to buy them
- The Modern Library Editorial Board's 100 Best Novels and 100 Best Nonfiction Books of the Twentieth Century written in the English language
- News and announcements

Questions? E-mail us at **modernlibrary@randomhouse.com**.
For questions about examination or desk copies, please visit the Random House Academic Resources site at
www.randomhouse.com/academic.